'Set in post-independence India, the novel follows for eighteen months or so four linked families in Calcutta, the province of Purva Pradesh and its capital Brahmpur, and the cities—Delhi, Kanpur, Lucknow—trawled by the heroine's mother in her search for a "suitable boy"... But the greatness of the novel, its unassailable truthfulness, owes less to research than to imagination, an instinctive knowledge of the human heart—with all its varieties of kindness and cruelty... As with all the best books, one feels only dismay when the pages on the right of the tome start thinning out.'

—*The Observer*

A Suitable Boy

By the same author

FICTION

The Golden Gate: A Novel in Verse
An Equal Music

POETRY

Mappings
The Humble Administrator's Garden
All You Who Sleep Tonight
Three Chinese Poets (*translations*)
Beastly Tales from Here and There (*fables*)
Arion and the Dolphin (*libretto*)
The Rivered Earth (*libretti and essays*)
Summer Requiem

MEMOIR

Two Lives

NON-FICTION

From Heaven Lake: Travels through Sinkiang and Tibet

A Suitable Boy

{ VOLUME ONE }

VIKRAM SETH

SPEAKING TIGER

SPEAKING TIGER BOOKS LLP
125A, Ground Floor, Shahpur Jat,
New Delhi–110002, India

First published by Penguin India 1993
This edition published by Speaking Tiger Books 2023

ISBN: 978-93-5447-487-3

10 9 8 7 6 5 4 3 2 1

Printed at Chaman Enterprises, New Delhi

The author would personally like to thank Jaishree Ram Mohan and her enthusiastic young team at Penguin India for proofreading A Suitable Boy *in 2013, and Ajith Kumar for typesetting it.*

To
Papa and Mama
and
the memory of Amma

A WORD OF THANKS

To these I owe a debt past telling:
My several muses, harsh and kind;
My folks, who stood my sulks and yelling,
And (in the long run) did not mind;
Dead legislators, whose orations
I've filched to mix my own potations;
Indeed, all those whose brains I've pressed,
Unmerciful, because obsessed;
My own dumb soul, which on a pittance
Survived to weave this fictive spell;
And, gentle reader, you as well,
The fountainhead of all remittance.
Buy me before good sense insists
You'll strain your purse and sprain your wrists.

CONTENTS (Volume One)

ACKNOWLEDGEMENTS

The author and publishers would like to thank the following for permission to quote copyright material:

The Ministry of Human Resources Development, Govt of India for extracts from *Letters to Chief Ministers*, Vol. 2, 1950–1952 by Jawaharlal Nehru, general editor G. Parthasarathi (Jawaharlal Nehru Memorial Fund, distributed by Oxford University Press, 1986)

HarperCollins Publishers Ltd for extracts from *The Koran Interpreted* by A.J. Arberry (George Allen & Unwin Ltd; and Oxford University Press, 1964)

Oxford University Press for an extract from *The Select Nonsense of Sukumar Ray* translated by Sukanta Chaudhuri (Oxford University Press, 1987)

Faber & Faber for an extract from the poem 'Law, Say the Gardeners' published in *W.H. Auden: Collected Poems* edited by Edward Mendelson (Faber & Faber)

Penguin Books Ltd for extracts from *Selected Poems* by Rabindranath Tagore, translated by William Radice (Penguin Books, 1985)

Bantam Books Inc. for extracts from *The Bhagavad-Gita* translated by Barbara Stoler Miller (Bantam Books, 1986)

The Sahitya Akademi for extracts from *Mir Anis* by Ali Jawad Zaidi published in the series 'Makers of Indian Literature' (Sahitya Akademi, 1986)

The Gita Press, Gorakhpur, for extracts from *Sri Ramacharitamanasa* translated into English (Gita Press, 1968)

While every effort has been made to trace copyright holders and obtain permission, this has not been possible in all cases; any omissions brought to our attention will be remedied in future editions.

MEHRAS

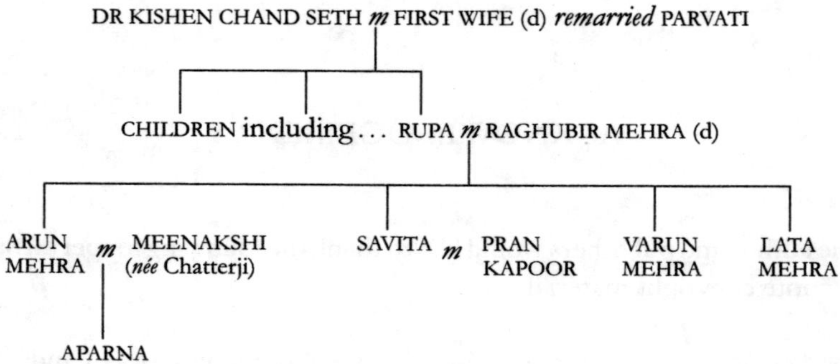

KAPOORS

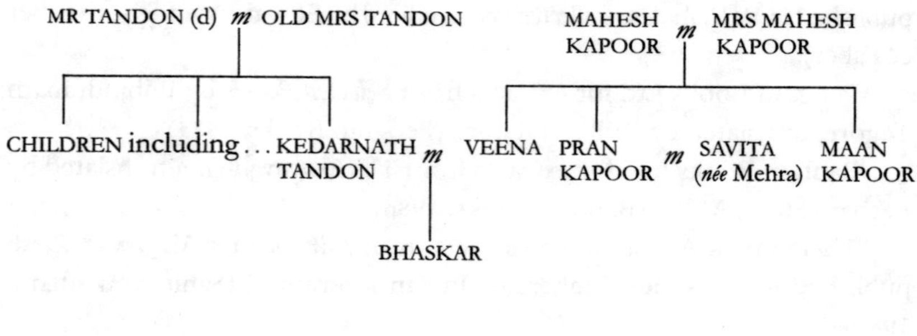

KHANS

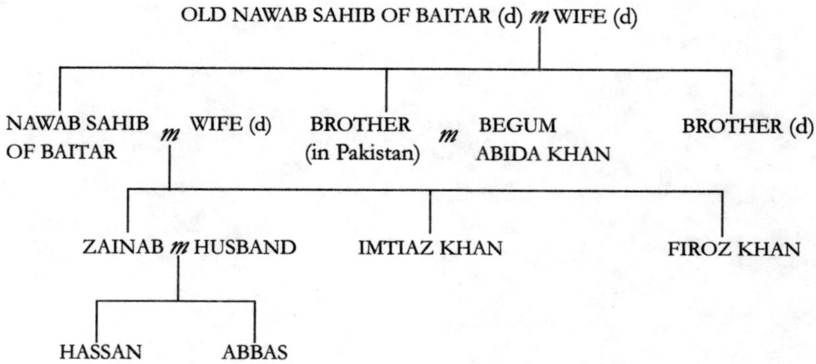

CHATTERJIS

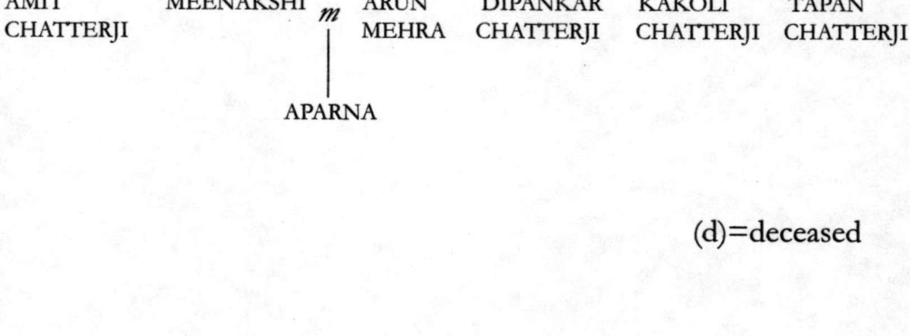

(d)=deceased

The superfluous, that very necessary thing. . . .

VOLTAIRE

The secret of being a bore is to say everything.

VOLTAIRE

Part One

1.1

'You too will marry a boy I choose,' said Mrs Rupa Mehra firmly to her younger daughter.

Lata avoided the maternal imperative by looking around the great lamp-lit garden of Prem Nivas. The wedding guests were gathered on the lawn. 'Hmm,' she said. This annoyed her mother further.

'I know what your hmms mean, young lady, and I can tell you I will not stand for hmms in this matter. I do know what is best. I am doing it all for you. Do you think it is easy for me, trying to arrange things for all four of my children without His help?' Her nose began to redden at the thought of her husband, who would, she felt certain, be partaking of their present joy from somewhere benevolently above. Mrs Rupa Mehra believed, of course, in reincarnation, but at moments of exceptional sentiment, she imagined that the late Raghubir Mehra still inhabited the form in which she had known him when he was alive: the robust, cheerful form of his early forties before overwork had brought about his heart attack at the height of the Second World War. Eight years ago, eight years, thought Mrs Rupa Mehra miserably.

'Now, now, Ma, you can't cry on Savita's wedding day,' said Lata, putting her arm gently but not very concernedly around her mother's shoulder.

'If He had been here, I could have worn the tissue-patola sari I wore for my own wedding,' sighed Mrs Rupa Mehra. 'But it is too rich for a widow to wear.'

'Ma!' said Lata, a little exasperated at the emotional capital her mother insisted on making out of every possible circumstance. 'People are looking at you. They want to congratulate you, and they'll think it very odd if they see you crying in this way.'

Several guests were indeed doing namaste to Mrs Rupa Mehra and smiling at her; the cream of Brahmpur society, she was pleased to note.

'Let them see me!' said Mrs Rupa Mehra defiantly, dabbing at her eyes hastily with a handkerchief perfumed with 4711 Eau de Cologne. 'They will only think it is because of my happiness at Savita's wedding. Everything I do is for you, and no one appreciates me. I have chosen such a good boy for Savita, and all everyone does is complain.'

Lata reflected that of the four brothers and sisters, the only one who hadn't complained of the match had been the sweet-tempered, fair-complexioned, beautiful Savita herself.

'He is a little thin, Ma,' said Lata a bit thoughtlessly. This was putting it mildly. Pran Kapoor, soon to be her brother-in-law, was lank, dark, gangly, and asthmatic.

'Thin? What is thin? Everyone is trying to become thin these days. Even I have had to fast the whole day and it is not good for my diabetes. And if Savita is not complaining, everyone should be happy with him. Arun and Varun are always complaining: why didn't they choose a boy for their sister then? Pran is a good, decent, cultured khatri boy.'

There was no denying that Pran, at thirty, was a good boy, a decent boy, and belonged to the right caste. And, indeed, Lata did like Pran. Oddly enough, she knew him better than her sister did—or, at least, had seen him for longer than her sister had. Lata was studying English at Brahmpur University, and Pran Kapoor was a popular lecturer there. Lata had attended his class on the Elizabethans, while Savita, the bride, had met him for only an hour, and that too in her mother's company.

'And Savita will fatten him up,' added Mrs Rupa Mehra. 'Why are you trying to annoy me when I am so happy? And Pran and Savita will be happy, you will see. They will be happy,' she continued emphatically. 'Thank you, thank you,' she now beamed at those who were coming up to greet her. 'It is so wonderful—the boy of my dreams, and such a good family. The Minister Sahib has been very kind to us. And Savita is so happy. Please eat something, please eat: they have made such delicious gulab-jamuns, but owing to my diabetes I cannot eat them even after the ceremonies. I am not even allowed gajak, which is so difficult to resist in winter. But please eat, please eat. I must go in to check what is happening: the time that the pandits have given is coming up, and there is no sign of either bride or groom!' She looked at Lata, frowning. Her younger daughter was going to prove more difficult than her elder, she decided.

'Don't forget what I told you,' she said in an admonitory voice.

'Hmm,' said Lata. 'Ma, your handkerchief's sticking out of your blouse.'

'Oh!' said Mrs Rupa Mehra, worriedly tucking it in. 'And tell Arun to please take his duties seriously. He is just standing there in a corner talking to that Meenakshi and his silly friend from Calcutta. He should see that everyone is drinking and eating properly and having a gala time.'

'That Meenakshi' was Arun's glamorous wife and her own disrespectful daughter-in-law. In four years of marriage Meenakshi's only worthwhile act, in Mrs Rupa Mehra's eyes, had been to give birth to her beloved granddaughter, Aparna, who even now had found her way to her grandmother's brown silk sari and was tugging at it for attention. Mrs Rupa Mehra was delighted. She gave her a kiss and told her:

'Aparna, you must stay with your Mummy or with Lata Bua, otherwise you will get lost. And then where would we be?'

'Can't I come with you?' asked Aparna, who, at three, naturally had views and preferences of her own.

'Sweetheart, I wish you could,' said Mrs Rupa Mehra, 'but I have to make sure that your Savita Bua is ready to be married. She is so late already.' And Mrs Rupa Mehra looked once again at the little gold watch that had been her husband's first gift to her and which had not missed a beat for two and a half decades.

'I want to see Savita Bua!' said Aparna, holding her ground.

Mrs Rupa Mehra looked a little harassed and nodded vaguely at Aparna.

Lata picked Aparna up. 'When Savita Bua comes out, we'll go over there together, shall we, and I'll hold you up like this, and we'll both get a good view. Meanwhile, should we go and see if we can get some ice-cream? I feel like some too.'

Aparna approved of this, as of most of Lata's suggestions. It was never too cold for ice-cream. They walked towards the buffet table together, three-year-old and nineteen-year-old hand in hand. A few rose petals wafted down on them from somewhere.

'What is good enough for your sister is good enough for you,' said Mrs Rupa Mehra to Lata as a parting shot.

'We can't both marry Pran,' said Lata, laughing.

1.2

The other chief host of the wedding was the groom's father, Mr Mahesh Kapoor, who was the Minister of Revenue of the state of Purva Pradesh. It was in fact in his large, C-shaped, cream-coloured, two-storey family house, Prem Nivas, situated in the quietest, greenest residential area of the ancient, and—for the most part—over-populated city of Brahmpur, that the wedding was taking place.

This was so unusual that the whole of Brahmpur had been buzzing about it for days. Mrs Rupa Mehra's father, who was supposed to be the host, had taken sudden umbrage a fortnight before the wedding, had locked up his house, and had disappeared. Mrs Rupa Mehra had been distraught. The Minister Sahib had stepped in ('Your honour is our honour'), and had insisted on putting on the wedding himself. As for the ensuing gossip, he ignored it.

There was no question of Mrs Rupa Mehra helping to pay for the wedding. The Minister Sahib would not hear of it. Nor had he at any time asked for any dowry. He was an old friend and bridge partner of Mrs Rupa Mehra's father and he had liked what he had seen of her daughter Savita (though he could never remember the girl's name). He was sympathetic to economic hardship, for he too had tasted it. During the several years he had spent in British jails during the struggle for Independence, there had been no one to run his farm or his cloth business. As a result very little income had come in, and his wife and family had struggled along with great difficulty.

Those unhappy times, however, were only a memory for the able, impatient, and powerful Minister. It was the early winter of 1950, and India had been free for over three years. But freedom for the country did not mean freedom for his younger son, Maan, who even now was being told by his father:

'What is good enough for your brother is good enough for you.'

'Yes, Baoji,' said Maan, smiling.

Mr Mahesh Kapoor frowned. His younger son, while succeeding to his own habit of fine dress, had not succeeded to his obsession with hard work. Nor did he appear to have any ambition to speak of.

'It is no use being a good-looking young wastrel forever,' said his father. 'And marriage will force you to settle down and take things seriously. I have written to the Banaras people, and I expect a favourable answer any day.'

Marriage was the last thing on Maan's mind; he had caught a friend's eye in the crowd and was waving at him. Hundreds of small coloured lights strung through the hedge came on all at once, and the silk saris and jewellery of the women glimmered and glinted even more brightly. The high, reedy shehnai music burst into a pattern of speed and brilliance. Maan was entranced. He noticed Lata making her way through the guests. Quite an attractive girl, Savita's sister, he thought. Not very tall and not very fair, but attractive, with an oval face, a shy light in her dark eyes and an affectionate manner towards the child she was leading by the hand.

'Yes, Baoji,' said Maan obediently.

'What did I say?' demanded his father.

'About marriage, Baoji,' said Maan.

'What about marriage?'

Maan was nonplussed.

'Don't you listen?' demanded Mahesh Kapoor, wanting to twist Maan's ear. 'You are as bad as the clerks in the Revenue Department. You were not paying attention, you were waving at Firoz.'

Maan looked a little shamefaced. He knew what his father thought of him. But he had been enjoying himself until a couple of minutes ago, and it was just like Baoji to come and puncture his light spirits.

'So that's all fixed up,' continued his father. 'Don't tell me later that I didn't warn you. And don't get that weak-willed woman, your mother, to change her mind and come telling me that you aren't yet ready to take on the responsibilities of a man.'

'No, Baoji,' said Maan, getting the drift of things and looking a trifle glum.

'We chose well for Veena, we have chosen well for Pran, and you are not to complain about our choice of a bride for you.'

Maan said nothing. He was wondering how to repair the puncture. He had a bottle of Scotch upstairs in his room, and perhaps he and Firoz could escape for a few minutes before the ceremony—or even during it—for refreshment.

His father paused to smile brusquely at a few well-wishers, then turned to Maan again.

'I don't want to have to waste any more time with you today. God knows I have enough to do as it is. What has happened to Pran and that girl, what's her name? It's getting late. They were supposed to come out from opposite ends of the house and meet here for the jaymala five minutes ago.'

'Savita,' prompted Maan.

'Yes, yes,' said his father impatiently. 'Savita. Your superstitious mother will start panicking if they miss the correct configuration of the stars. Go and calm her down. Go! Do some good.'

And Mahesh Kapoor went back to his own duties as a host. He frowned impatiently at one of the officiating priests, who smiled weakly back. He narrowly avoided being butted in the stomach and knocked over by three children, offspring of his rural relatives, who were careering joyfully around the garden as if it were a field of stubble. And he greeted, before he had walked ten steps, a professor of literature (who could be useful for Pran's career); two influential members of the state legislature from the Congress Party (who might well agree to back him in his perennial power struggle with the Home Minister); a judge, the very last Englishman to remain on the bench of the Brahmpur High Court after Independence; and his old friend the Nawab Sahib of Baitar, one of the largest landowners in the state.

1.3

Lata, who had heard a part of Maan's conversation with his father, could not help smiling to herself as she walked past.

'I see you're enjoying yourself,' said Maan to her in English.

His conversation with his father had been in Hindi, hers with her mother in English. Maan spoke both well.

Lata was struck shy, as she sometimes was with strangers, especially those who smiled as boldly as Maan. Let him do the smiling for both of us, she thought.

'Yes,' she said simply, her eyes resting on his face for just a second. Aparna tugged at her hand.

'Well, now, we're almost family,' said Maan, perhaps sensing her awkwardness. 'A few minutes more, and the ceremonies will start.'

'Yes,' agreed Lata, looking up at him again more confidently. She paused and frowned. 'My mother's concerned that they won't start on time.'

'So is my father,' said Maan.

Lata began smiling again, but when Maan asked her why she shook her head.

'Well,' said Maan, flicking a rose petal off his beautiful tight white achkan, 'you're not laughing at me, are you?'

'I'm not laughing at all,' said Lata.

'Smiling, I meant.'

'No, not at you,' said Lata. 'At myself.'

'That's very mysterious,' said Maan. His good-natured face melted into an expression of exaggerated perplexity.

'It'll have to remain so, I'm afraid,' said Lata, almost laughing now. 'Aparna here wants her ice-cream, and I must supply it.'

'Try the pistachio ice-cream,' suggested Maan. His eyes followed her pink sari for a few seconds. Good-looking girl—in a way, he thought again. Pink's the wrong colour for her complexion, though. She should be dressed in deep green or dark blue . . . like that woman there. His attention veered to a new object of contemplation.

A few seconds later Lata bumped into her best friend, Malati, a medical student who shared her room at the student hostel. Malati was very outgoing and never lost her tongue with strangers. Strangers, however, blinking into her lovely green eyes, sometimes lost their tongues with her.

'Who was that Cad you were talking to?' she asked Lata eagerly.

This wasn't as bad as it sounded. A good-looking young man, in the slang of Brahmpur University girls, was a Cad. The term derived from Cadbury's chocolate.

'Oh, that's just Maan, he's Pran's younger brother.'

'Really! But he's so good-looking and Pran's so, well, not ugly, but, you know, dark, and nothing special.'

'Maybe he's a dark Cad,' suggested Lata. 'Bitter but sustaining.'

Malati considered this.

'And,' continued Lata, 'as my aunts have reminded me five times in the last hour, I'm not all that fair either, and will therefore find it impossible to get a suitable husband.'

'How can you put up with them, Lata?' asked Malati, who had been brought up, fatherless and brotherless, in a circle of very supportive women.

'Oh, I like most of them,' said Lata. 'And if it wasn't for this sort of speculation it wouldn't be much of a wedding for them. Once they see the bride and groom together, they'll have an even better time. Beauty and the Beast.'

'Well, he's looked rather beast-like whenever I've seen him on the university campus,' said Malati. 'Like a dark giraffe.'

'Don't be mean,' said Lata, laughing. 'Anyway, Pran's very popular as a lecturer,' she continued. 'And I like him. And you're going to have to visit me at his house once I leave the hostel and start living there. And since he'll be my brother-in-law you'll have to like him too. Promise me you will.'

'I won't,' said Malati firmly. 'He's taking you away from me.'

'He's doing nothing of the sort, Malati,' said Lata. 'My mother, with her fine sense of household economy, is dumping me on him.'

'Well, I don't see why you should obey your mother. Tell her you can't bear to be parted from me.'

'I always obey my mother,' said Lata. 'And besides, who will pay my hostel fees if she doesn't? And it will be very nice for me to live with Savita for a while. I refuse to lose you. You really must visit us—you must keep visiting us. If you don't, I'll know how much value to put on your friendship.'

Malati looked unhappy for a second or two, then recovered. 'Who's this?' she asked. Aparna was looking at her in a severe and uncompromising manner.

'My niece, Aparna,' said Lata. 'Say hello to Malati Aunty, Aparna.'

'Hello,' said Aparna, who had reached the end of her patience. 'Can I have a pistachio ice-cream, please?'

'Yes, kuchuk, of course, I'm sorry,' said Lata. 'Come, let's all go together and get some.'

1.4

Lata soon lost Malati to a clutch of college friends, but before she and Aparna could get much further, they were captured by Aparna's parents.

'So there you are, you precious little runaway,' said the resplendent Meenakshi, implanting a kiss on her daughter's forehead. 'Isn't she precious, Arun? Now where have you been, you precious truant?'

'I went to find Daadi,' began Aparna. 'And then I found her, but she had to go into the house because of Savita Bua, but I couldn't go with her, and then Lata Bua took me to have ice-cream, but we couldn't because—'

But Meenakshi had lost interest and had turned to Lata.

'That pink doesn't really suit you, Luts,' said Meenakshi. 'It lacks a certain—a certain—'

'Je ne sais quoi?' prompted a suave friend of her husband's, who was standing nearby.

'Thank you,' said Meenakshi, with such withering charm that the young fellow glided away for a while and pretended to stare at the stars.

'No, pink's just not right for you, Luts,' reaffirmed Meenakshi, stretching her long, tawny neck like a relaxed cat and appraising her sister-in-law.

She herself was wearing a green-and-gold sari of Banaras silk, with a green choli that exposed more of her midriff than Brahmpur society was normally privileged or prepared to see.

'Oh,' said Lata, suddenly self-conscious. She knew she didn't have much dress sense, and imagined she looked rather drab standing next to this bird of paradise.

'Who was that fellow you were talking to?' demanded her brother Arun, who, unlike his wife, had noticed Lata talking to Maan. Arun was twenty-five, a tall, fair, intelligent, pleasant-looking bully who kept his siblings in place by pummelling their egos. He was fond of reminding them that after their father's death, he was 'in a manner of speaking', in loco parentis to them.

'That was Maan, Pran's brother.'

'Ah.' The word spoke volumes of disapproval.

Arun and Meenakshi had arrived just this morning by overnight train from Calcutta, where Arun worked as one of the few Indian executives in the prestigious and largely white firm of Bentsen & Pryce. He had had neither the time nor the desire to acquaint himself with the Kapoor family—or clan, as he called it—with whom his mother had contrived a match for his sister. He cast his eyes balefully around. Typical of their type to overdo everything, he thought, looking at the coloured lights in the hedge. The crassness of the state politicians, white-capped and effusive, and of Mahesh Kapoor's contingent of rustic relatives excited his finely tuned disdain. And the fact that neither the brigadier from the Brahmpur Cantonment nor the Brahmpur representatives of companies like Burmah Shell, Imperial Tobacco, and Caltex were represented in the crowd of invitees blinded his eyes to the presence of the larger part of the professional elite of Brahmpur.

'A bit of a bounder, I'd say,' said Arun, who had noticed Maan's eyes casually following Lata before he had turned them elsewhere.

Lata smiled, and her meek brother Varun, who was a nervous shadow to Arun and Meenakshi, smiled too in a kind of stifled complicity. Varun was studying—or trying to study—mathematics at Calcutta University, and he lived with Arun and Meenakshi in their small ground-floor flat. He was thin, unsure of himself, sweet-natured and shifty-eyed; and he was Lata's favourite. Though he was a year older than her, she felt protective of him. Varun was terrified, in different ways, of both Arun and Meenakshi, and in some ways even of the precocious Aparna. His enjoyment of mathematics was mainly limited to the calculation of odds and handicaps on the racing form. In winter, as Varun's excitement rose with the racing season, so did his elder brother's ire. Arun was fond of calling him a bounder as well.

And what would you know about bounding, Arun Bhai? thought Lata to herself. Aloud she said: 'He seemed quite nice.'

'An aunty we met called him a Cad,' contributed Aparna.

'Did she, precious?' said Meenakshi, interested. 'Do point him out to me, Arun.' But Maan was now nowhere to be seen.

'I blame myself to some extent,' said Arun in a voice which implied nothing of the sort; Arun was not capable of blaming himself for anything. 'I really should have done something,' he continued. 'If I hadn't been so tied up with work, I might have prevented this whole fiasco. But once Ma got it into her head that this Kapoor chap was suitable, it was impossible to dissuade her. It's impossible to talk reason with Ma; she just turns on the waterworks.'

What had also helped deflect Arun's suspicions had been the fact that Dr Pran Kapoor taught English. And yet, to Arun's chagrin, there was hardly an English face in this whole provincial crowd.

How fearfully dowdy! said Meenakshi wearily to herself, encapsulating her husband's thoughts. 'And how utterly unlike Calcutta. Precious, you have smut on your nose,' she added to Aparna, half looking around to tell an imaginary ayah to wipe it off with a handkerchief.

'I'm enjoying it here,' Varun ventured, seeing Lata look hurt. He knew that she liked Brahmpur, though it was clearly no metropolis.

'You be quiet,' snapped Arun brutally. His judgement was being challenged by his subordinate, and he would have none of it.

Varun struggled with himself; he glared, then looked down.

'Don't talk about what you don't understand,' added Arun, putting the boot in.

Varun glowered silently.

'Did you hear me?'

'Yes,' said Varun.

'Yes, what?'

'Yes, Arun Bhai,' muttered Varun.

This pulverization was standard fare for Varun, and Lata was not surprised by the exchange. But she felt very bad for him, and indignant at Arun. She could not understand either the pleasure or the purpose of it. She decided she would speak to Varun as soon after the wedding as possible to try to help him withstand—at least internally—such assaults upon his spirit. Even if I'm not very good at withstanding them myself, Lata thought.

'Well, Arun Bhai,' she said innocently, 'I suppose it's too late. We're all one big happy family now, and we'll have to put up with each other as well as we can.'

The phrase, however, was not innocent. 'One big happy family' was an ironically used Chatterji phrase. Meenakshi Mehra had been a Chatterji before she and Arun had met at a cocktail party, fallen in torrid, rapturous and elegant love, and got married within a month, to the shock of both families. Whether or not Mr Justice Chatterji of the Calcutta High Court and his wife were happy to welcome the non-Bengali Arun as the first appendage to their ring of five children (plus Cuddles the dog), and whether or not Mrs Rupa Mehra had been delighted at the thought of her firstborn, the apple of her eye, marrying outside the khatri caste (and to a spoilt supersophisticate like Meenakshi at that), Arun certainly valued the Chatterji connection greatly. The Chatterjis had wealth and position and a grand Calcutta house where they threw enormous (but tasteful) parties. And even if the big happy family, especially Meenakshi's brothers and sisters, sometimes bothered him with their endless, unchokable wit and improvised rhyming couplets, he accepted it precisely because it appeared to him to be undeniably urbane. It was a far cry from this provincial capital, this Kapoor crowd and these garish light-in-the-hedge celebrations—with pomegranate juice in lieu of alcohol!

'What precisely do you mean by that?' demanded Arun of Lata. 'Do you think that if Daddy had been alive we would have married into this sort of a family?'

Arun hardly seemed to care that they might be overheard. Lata flushed. But the brutal point was well made. Had Raghubir Mehra not died in his forties but continued his meteoric rise in the Railway Service, he would—when the British left Indian government service in droves in 1947—certainly have become a member of the Railway Board. His excellence and experience might even have made him Chairman. The family would not have had to struggle, as it had had to for years and was still forced to, on Mrs Rupa Mehra's depleted savings, the kindness of friends and, lately, her elder son's salary. She would not have had to sell most of her jewellery and even their small house in Darjeeling to give her children the schooling which she felt that, above everything else, they must have. Beneath her pervasive sentimentality—and her attachment to the seemingly secure physical objects that reminded her of her beloved husband—lay a sense of sacrifice and a sense of values that determinedly melted them down into the insecure, intangible benefits of an excellent English-medium boarding school education. And so Arun and Varun had continued to go to St George's School, and Savita and Lata had not been withdrawn from St Sophia's Convent.

The Kapoors might be all very well for Brahmpur society, thought Arun, but if Daddy had been alive, a constellation of brilliant matches would have been strewn at the feet of the Mehras. At least he, for one, had overcome their circumstances and done well in the way of in-laws. What possible comparison could there be between Pran's brother, that ogling fellow whom Lata had just been talking to—who ran, of all things, a cloth shop in Banaras, from what Arun had heard—and, say, Meenakshi's elder brother, who had been to Oxford, was supposed to be studying law at Lincoln's Inn, and was, in addition, a published poet?

Arun's speculations were brought down to earth by his daughter, who threatened to scream if she didn't get her ice-cream. She knew from experience that screaming (or even the threat of it) worked wonders with her parents. And, after all, they sometimes screamed at each other, and often at the servants.

Lata looked guilty. 'It's my fault, darling,' she said to Aparna. 'Let's go at once before we get caught up in something else. But you mustn't cry or yell, promise me that. It won't work with me.'

Aparna, who knew it wouldn't, was silent.

But just at that moment the bridegroom emerged from one side of the house, dressed all in white, his dark, rather nervous face veiled with hanging strings of white flowers; everyone crowded forward towards the door from which the bride would emerge; and Aparna, lifted into her Lata Bua's arms, was forced to defer once again both treat and threat.

1.5

It was a little untraditional, Lata couldn't help thinking, that Pran hadn't ridden up to the gate on a white horse with a little nephew sitting in front of him and with the groom's party in tow to claim his bride; but then Prem Nivas was the groom's house after all. And no doubt if he had followed the convention, Arun would have found further cause for mockery. As it was, Lata found it difficult to imagine the lecturer on Elizabethan Drama under that veil of tuberoses. He was now placing a garland of dark red, heavily fragrant roses around her sister Savita's neck—and Savita was doing the same to him. She looked lovely in her red-and-gold wedding sari, and quite subdued; Lata thought she might even have been crying. Her head was covered, and she looked down at the ground as her mother had doubtless instructed her to do. It was not proper, even when she was putting the garland round his neck, that she should look full in the face of the man with whom she was to live her life.

The welcoming ceremony completed, bride and groom moved together to the middle of the garden, where a small platform, decorated with more white flowers and open to the auspicious stars, had been erected. Here the priests, one from each family, and Mrs Rupa Mehra and the parents of the groom sat around the small fire that would be the witness of their vows.

Mrs Rupa Mehra's brother, whom the family very rarely met, had earlier in the day taken charge of the bangle ceremony. Arun was annoyed that he had not been allowed to take charge of anything. He had suggested to his mother, after the crisis brought on by his grandfather's inexplicable actions, that they should move the wedding to Calcutta. But it was too late for that, and she would not hear of it.

Now that the exchange of garlands was over, the crowd paid no great attention to the actual wedding rites. These would go on for the better part of an hour while the guests milled and chattered round the lawns of Prem Nivas. They laughed; they shook hands or folded them to their foreheads; they coalesced into little knots, the men here, the women there; they warmed themselves at the charcoal-filled clay stoves placed strategically around the garden while their frosted, gossip-laden breath rose into the air; they admired the multicoloured lights; they smiled for the photographer as he murmured 'Steady, please!' in English; they breathed deeply the scent of flowers and perfume and cooked spices; they exchanged births and deaths and politics and scandal under the brightly coloured cloth canopy at the back of the garden beneath which long tables of food had been laid out; they sat down exhaustedly on chairs with their plates full and tucked in inexhaustibly. Servants, some in white livery, some in khaki, brought around fruit juice and tea and coffee and snacks to those who were standing in the garden: samosas, kachauris, laddus, gulab-jamuns, barfis and gajak and ice-cream were consumed and replenished along with puris and six kinds of vegetables. Friends who had not met each other for months fell upon each other with loud cries, relatives who met only at weddings and funerals embraced tearfully and exchanged the latest news of third cousins thrice removed. Lata's aunt from Kanpur, horrified by the complexion of the groom, was talking to an aunt from Lucknow about 'Rupa's black grandchildren', as if they already existed. They made much of Aparna, who was obviously going to be Rupa's last fair grandchild, and praised her even when she spooned pistachio ice-cream down the front of her pale yellow cashmere sweater. The barbaric children from rustic Rudhia ran around yelling as if they were playing pitthu on the farm. And though the plaintive, festive music of the shehnai had now ceased, a happy babble of convivial voices rose to the skies and quite drowned out the irrelevant chant of the ceremonies.

Lata, however, stood close by and watched with an attentive mixture of fascination and dismay. The two bare-chested priests, one very fat and one fairly thin, both apparently immune to the cold, were locked in mildly insistent competition as to who knew a more elaborate form of the service. So, while the stars stayed their courses in order to keep the auspicious time in abeyance, the Sanskrit wound interminably on. Even the groom's parents were asked by the fat priest to repeat something after him. Mahesh Kapoor's eyebrows were quivering; he was about to blow his rather short fuse.

Lata tried to imagine what Savita was thinking. How could she have agreed to get married without knowing this man? Kind-hearted and accommodating though she was, she did have views of her own. Lata loved her deeply and admired her generous, even temper; the evenness was certainly a contrast to her own erratic swings of mood. Savita was free from any vanity about her fresh and lovely looks; but didn't she rebel against the fact that Pran would fail the most lenient test of glamour? Did Savita really accept that Mother knew best? It was difficult to speak to Savita, or sometimes even to guess what she was thinking. Since Lata had gone to college, it was Malati rather than her sister who had become her confidante. And Malati, she knew, would never have agreed to be married off in this summary manner by all the mothers in the world conjoined.

In a few minutes Savita would relinquish even her name to Pran. She would no longer be a Mehra, like the rest of them, but a Kapoor. Arun, thank God, had never had to do that. Lata tried 'Savita Kapoor' on her tongue, and did not like it at all.

The smoke from the fire—or possibly the pollen from the flowers—was beginning to bother Pran, and he coughed a little, covering his mouth with his hand. His mother said something to him in a low voice. Savita too looked up at him very quickly, with a glance, Lata thought, of gentle concern. Savita, it was true, would have been concerned about anyone who was suffering from anything; but there was a special tenderness here that irritated and confused Lata. Savita had only met this man for an hour! And now he was returning her affectionate look. It was too much.

Lata forgot that she had been defending Pran to Malati just a short while ago, and began to discover things to irritate herself with.

'Prem Nivas' for a start: the abode of love. An idiotic name, thought Lata crossly, for this house of arranged marriages. And a needlessly grandiloquent one: as if it were the centre of the universe and felt obliged to make a philosophical statement about it. And the scene, looked at objectively, was absurd: seven living people, none of them stupid, sitting around a fire intoning a dead language that only three of them understood. And yet, Lata thought, her mind wandering from one thing to another, perhaps this little fire was indeed the centre of the universe. For here it burned, in the middle of this fragrant garden, itself in the heart of Pasand Bagh, the pleasantest locality of Brahmpur, which was the capital of the state of Purva Pradesh, which lay in the centre of the Gangetic plains, which was itself the heartland of India . . . and so on through the galaxies to the outer limits of perception and knowledge. The thought did not seem in the least trite to Lata; it helped her control her irritation at, indeed resentment of, Pran.

'Speak up! Speak up! If your mother had mumbled like you, we would never have got married.'

Mahesh Kapoor had turned impatiently towards his dumpy little wife, who became even more tongue-tied as a result.

Pran turned and smiled encouragingly at his mother, and quickly rose again in Lata's estimation.

Mahesh Kapoor frowned, but held his peace for a few minutes, after which he burst out, this time to the family priest:

'Is this mumbo jumbo going to go on forever?'

The priest said something soothing in Sanskrit, as if blessing Mahesh Kapoor, who felt obliged to lapse into an irked silence. He was irritated for several reasons, one of which was the distinct and unwelcome sight of his arch political rival, the Home Minister, deep in conversation with the large and venerable Chief Minister S.S. Sharma. What could they be plotting? he thought. My stupid wife insisted on inviting Agarwal because our daughters are friends, even though she knew it would sour things for me. And now the Chief Minister is talking to him as if no one else exists. And in my garden!

His other major irritation was directed at Mrs Rupa Mehra. Mahesh Kapoor, once he had taken over the arrangements, had set his heart on inviting a beautiful and renowned singer of ghazals to perform at Prem Nivas, as was the tradition whenever anyone in his family got married. But Mrs Rupa Mehra, though she was not even paying for the wedding, had put her foot down. She could not have 'that sort of person' singing love-lyrics at the wedding of her daughter. 'That sort of person' meant both a Muslim and a courtesan.

Mahesh Kapoor muffed his responses, and the priest repeated them gently.

'Yes, yes, go on, go on,' said Mahesh Kapoor. He glowered at the fire.

But now Savita was being given away by her mother with a handful of rose petals, and all three women were in tears.

Really! thought Mahesh Kapoor. They'll douse the flames. He looked in exasperation at the main culprit, whose sobs were the most obstreperous.

But Mrs Rupa Mehra was not even bothering to tuck her handkerchief back into her blouse. Her eyes were red and her nose and cheeks were flushed with weeping. She was thinking back to her own wedding. The scent of 4711 Eau de Cologne brought back unbearably happy memories of her late husband. Then she thought downwards one generation to her beloved Savita who would soon be walking around this fire with Pran to begin her own married life. May it be a longer one than mine, prayed Mrs Rupa Mehra. May she wear this very sari to her own daughter's wedding.

She also thought upwards a generation to her father, and this brought on a fresh gush of tears. What the septuagenarian radiologist Dr Kishen Chand Seth had taken offence at, no one knew: probably something said or done by his friend Mahesh Kapoor, but quite possibly by his own daughter; no one could tell for sure. Apart from repudiating his duties as a host, he had chosen not even to attend his granddaughter's wedding, and had gone furiously off to Delhi 'for a conference of cardiologists', as he claimed. He had taken with him the insufferable Parvati, his thirty-five-year-old second wife, who was ten years younger than Mrs Rupa Mehra herself.

It was also possible, though this did not cross his daughter's mind, that Dr Kishen Chand Seth would have gone mad at the wedding had he attended it, and had in fact fled from that specific eventuality. Short and trim though he had always been, he was enormously fond of food; but owing to a digestive disorder combined with diabetes his diet was now confined to boiled eggs, weak tea, lemon squash, and arrowroot biscuits.

I don't care who stares at me, I have plenty of reasons to cry, said Mrs Rupa Mehra to herself defiantly. I am so happy and heartbroken today.

But her heartbreak lasted only a few minutes more. The groom and bride walked around the fire seven times, Savita keeping her head meekly down, her eyelashes wet with tears; and Pran and she were man and wife.

After a few concluding words by the priests, everyone rose. The newly-weds were escorted to a flower-shrouded bench near a sweet-smelling, rough-leafed harsingar tree in white-and-orange bloom; and congratulations fell on them and their parents and all the Mehras and Kapoors present as copiously as those delicate flowers fall to the ground at dawn.

Mrs Rupa Mehra's joy was unconfined. She gobbled the congratulations down like forbidden gulab-jamuns. She looked a little speculatively at her younger daughter, who appeared to be laughing at her from a distance. Or was she laughing at her sister? Well, she would find out soon enough what the happy tears of matrimony were all about!

Pran's much-shouted-at mother, subdued yet happy, after blessing her son and daughter-in-law, and failing to see her younger son Maan anywhere, had gone over to her daughter Veena. Veena embraced her; Mrs Mahesh Kapoor, temporarily overcome, said nothing, but sobbed and smiled simultaneously. The dreaded Home Minister and his daughter Priya joined them for a few minutes, and in return for their congratulations, Mrs Mahesh Kapoor had a few kind words to say to each of them. Priya, who was married and virtually immured by her in-laws in a house in the old, cramped part of Brahmpur, said, rather wistfully, that the garden looked beautiful. And it was true, thought Mrs Mahesh Kapoor with quiet pride: the garden was indeed looking beautiful. The grass was rich, the gardenias were creamy and fragrant, and a few chrysanthemums and roses were already in bloom. And though she could take no credit for the sudden, prolific blossoming of the harsingar tree, that was surely the grace of the gods whose prized and contested possession, in mythical times, it used to be.

1.6

Her lord and master the Minister of Revenue was meanwhile accepting congratulations from the Chief Minister of Purva Pradesh, Shri S.S. Sharma. Sharmaji was rather a hulking man with a perceptible limp and an unconscious and slight vibration of the head, which was exacerbated when, as now, he had had a long day. He ran the state with a mixture of guile, charisma and benevolence. Delhi was far away and rarely interested in his legislative and administrative fief. Though he was uncommunicative about his discussion with his Home Minister, he was nevertheless in good spirits.

Noticing the rowdy kids from Rudhia, he said in his slightly nasal voice to Mahesh Kapoor:

'So you're cultivating a rural constituency for the coming elections?'

Mahesh Kapoor smiled. Ever since 1937 he had stood from the same urban constituency in the heart of Old Brahmpur—a constituency that included much of Misri Mandi, the home of the shoe trade of the city. Despite his farm and his knowledge of rural affairs—he was the prime mover of a bill to abolish large and unproductive landholdings in the state—it was unimaginable that he would desert his electoral home and choose to contest from a rural constituency. By way of answer, he indicated his garments; the handsome black achkan he was wearing, the tight off-white pyjamas, and the brilliantly embroidered white jutis with their up-turned toes would present an incongruous picture in a rice field.

'Why, nothing is impossible in politics,' said Sharmaji slowly. 'After your Zamindari Abolition Bill goes through, you will become a hero throughout the countryside. If you chose, you could become Chief Minister. Why not?' said Sharmaji generously and warily. He looked around, and his eye fell on the Nawab Sahib of Baitar, who was stroking his beard and looking around perplexedly. 'Of course, you might lose a friend or two in the process,' he added.

Mahesh Kapoor, who had followed his glance without turning his head, said quietly: 'There are zamindars and zamindars. Not all of them tie their friendship to their land. The Nawab Sahib knows that I am acting out of principle.' He paused, and continued: 'Some of my own relatives in Rudhia stand to lose their land.'

The Chief Minister nodded at the sermon, then rubbed his hands, which were cold. 'Well, he is a good man,' he said indulgently. 'And so was his father,' he added.

Mahesh Kapoor was silent. The one thing Sharmaji could not be called was rash; and yet here was a rash statement if ever there was one. It was well known that the Nawab Sahib's father, the late Nawab Sahib of Baitar, had been an active member of the Muslim League; and though he had not lived to see the birth of Pakistan, that above all was what he had dedicated his life to.

The tall, grey-bearded Nawab Sahib, noticing four eyes on him, gravely raised his cupped hand to his forehead in polite salutation, then tilted his head sideways with a quiet smile, as if to congratulate his old friend.

'You haven't seen Firoz and Imtiaz anywhere, have you?' he asked Mahesh Kapoor, after walking slowly over.

'No, no—but I haven't seen my son either, so I assume. . . .'

The Nawab Sahib raised his hands slightly, palms forward, in a gesture of helplessness.

After a while he said: 'So Pran is married, and Maan is next. I would imagine you will find him a little less tractable.'

'Well, tractable or not, there are some people in Banaras I have been talking to,' said Mahesh Kapoor in a determined tone. 'Maan has met the father. He's also in the cloth business. We're making inquiries. Let's see. And what about your twins? A joint wedding to two sisters?'

'Let's see, let's see,' said the Nawab Sahib, thinking rather sadly about his wife, buried these many years; 'Inshallah, all of them will settle down soon enough.'

1.7

'To the law,' said Maan, raising his third glass of Scotch to Firoz, who was sitting on his bed with a glass of his own. Imtiaz was lounging in a stuffed chair and examining the bottle.

'Thank you,' said Firoz. 'But not to new laws, I hope.'

'Oh, don't worry, don't worry, my father's bill will never pass,' said Maan. 'And even if it does, you'll be much richer than me. Look at me,' he added, gloomily. 'I have to work for a living.'

Since Firoz was a lawyer and his brother a doctor, it was not as if they fitted the popular mould of the idle sons of aristocracy.

'And soon,' went on Maan, 'if my father has his way, I'll have to work on behalf of two people. And later for more. Oh God!'

'What—your father isn't getting you married off, is he?' asked Firoz, halfway between a smile and a frown.

'Well, the buffer zone disappeared tonight,' said Maan disconsolately. 'Have another.'

'No, no thanks, I still have plenty,' said Firoz. Firoz enjoyed his drink, but with a slightly guilty feeling; his father would approve even less than Maan's. 'So when's the happy hour?' he added uncertainly.

'God knows. It's at the inquiry stage,' said Maan.

'At the first reading,' Imtiaz added.

For some reason, this delighted Maan. 'At the first reading!' he repeated. 'Well, let's hope it never gets to the third reading! And, even if it does, that the President withholds his assent!'

He laughed and took a couple of long swigs. 'And what about your marriage?' he demanded of Firoz.

Firoz looked a little evasively around the room. It was as bare and functional as most of the rooms in Prem Nivas—which looked as if they expected the imminent arrival of a herd of constituents. 'My marriage!' he said with a laugh.

Maan nodded vigorously.

'Change the subject,' said Firoz.

'Why, if you were to go into the garden instead of drinking here in seclusion—'

'It's hardly seclusion.'

'Don't interrupt,' said Maan, throwing an arm around him. 'If you were to go down into the garden, a good-looking, elegant fellow like you, you would be surrounded within seconds by eligible young beauties. And ineligible ones too. They'd cling to you like bees to a lotus. Curly locks, curly locks, will you be mine?'

Firoz flushed. 'You've got the metaphor slightly wrong,' he said. 'Men are bees, women lotuses.'

Maan quoted a couplet from an Urdu ghazal to the effect that the hunter could turn into the hunted, and Imtiaz laughed.

'Shut up, both of you,' said Firoz, attempting to appear more annoyed than he was; he had had enough of this sort of nonsense. 'I'm going down. Abba will be wondering where on earth we've got to. And so will your father. And besides, we ought to find out if your brother is formally married yet—and whether you really do now have a beautiful sister-in-law to scold you and curb your excesses.'

'All right, all right, we'll all go down,' said Maan genially. 'Maybe some of the bees will cling to us too. And if we get stung to the heart, Doctor Sahib here can cure us. Can't you, Imtiaz? All you would have to do would be to apply a rose petal to the wound, isn't that so?'

'As long as there are no contraindications,' said Imtiaz seriously.

'No contraindications,' said Maan, laughing as he led the way down the stairs.

'You may laugh,' said Imtiaz. 'But some people are allergic even to rose petals. Talking of which, you have one sticking to your cap.'

'Do I?' asked Maan. 'These things float down from nowhere.'

'So they do,' said Firoz, who was walking down just behind him. He gently brushed it away.

1.8

Because the Nawab Sahib had been looking somewhat lost without his sons, Mahesh Kapoor's daughter Veena had drawn him into her family circle. She asked him about his eldest child, his daughter Zainab, who was a childhood friend of hers but who, after her marriage, had disappeared into the world of purdah. The old man talked about her rather guardedly, but about her two children with transparent delight. His grandchildren were the only two beings in the world who had the right to interrupt him when he was studying in his library. But now the great yellow ancestral mansion of Baitar House, just a few minutes' walk from Prem Nivas, was somewhat run down, and the library too had suffered. 'Silverfish, you know,' said the Nawab Sahib. 'And I need help with cataloguing. It's a gigantic task, and in some ways not very heartening. Some of the early editions of Ghalib can't be traced now; and some valuable manuscripts by our own poet Mast. My brother never made a list of what he took with him to Pakistan. . . .'

At the word Pakistan, Veena's mother-in-law, withered old Mrs Tandon, flinched. Three years ago, her whole family had had to flee the blood and flames and unforgettable terror of Lahore. They had been wealthy, 'propertied' people, but almost everything they had owned was lost, and they had been lucky to escape with their lives. Her son Kedarnath, Veena's husband, still had scars on his hands from an attack by rioters on his refugee convoy. Several of their friends had been butchered.

The young, old Mrs Tandon thought bitterly, are very resilient: her grandchild Bhaskar had of course only been six at the time; but even Veena and Kedarnath had not let those events embitter their lives. They had returned here to Veena's hometown, and Kedarnath had set himself up in a small way in—of all polluting, carcass-tainted things—the shoe trade. For old Mrs Tandon, the descent from a decent prosperity could not have been more painful. She had been willing to tolerate talking to the Nawab Sahib though he was a Muslim, but when he mentioned comings and goings from Pakistan, it was too much for her imagination. She felt ill. The pleasant chatter of the garden in Brahmpur was amplified into the cries of the blood-mad mobs on the streets of Lahore, the lights into fire. Daily, sometimes hourly, in her imagination she returned to what she still thought of as her city and her home. It had been beautiful before it had become so suddenly hideous; it had appeared completely secure so shortly before it was lost forever.

The Nawab Sahib did not notice that anything was the matter, but Veena did, and quickly changed the subject even at the cost of appearing rude. 'Where's Bhaskar?' she asked her husband.

'I don't know. I think I saw him near the food, the little frog,' said Kedarnath.

'I wish you wouldn't call him that,' said Veena. 'He is your son. It's not auspicious. . . .'

'It's not my name for him, it's Maan's,' said Kedarnath with a smile. He enjoyed being mildly henpecked. 'But I'll call him whatever you want me to.'

Veena led her mother-in-law away. And to distract the old lady she did in fact get involved in looking for her son. Finally they found Bhaskar. He was not eating anything but simply standing under the great multicoloured cloth canopy that covered the food tables, gazing upwards with pleased and abstract wonderment at the elaborate geometrical patterns—red rhombuses, green trapeziums, yellow squares and blue triangles—from which it had been stitched together.

1.9

The crowds had thinned; the guests, some chewing paan, were departing at the gate; a heap of gifts had grown by the side of the bench where Pran and Savita had been sitting. Finally only they and a few members of the family were left—and the yawning servants who would put away the more valuable furniture for the night, or pack the gifts in a trunk under the watchful eye of Mrs Rupa Mehra.

The bride and groom were lost in their thoughts. They avoided looking at each other now. They would spend the night in a carefully prepared room in Prem Nivas, and leave for a week's honeymoon in Simla tomorrow.

Lata tried to imagine the nuptial room. Presumably it would be fragrant with tuberoses; that, at least, was Malati's confident opinion. I'll always associate tuberoses with Pran, Lata thought. It was not at all pleasant to follow her imagination further. That Savita would be sleeping with Pran tonight did not bear thinking of. It did not strike her as being at all romantic. Perhaps they would be too exhausted, she thought optimistically.

'What are you thinking of, Lata?' asked her mother.

'Oh, nothing, Ma,' said Lata automatically.

'You turned up your nose. I saw it.'

Lata blushed.

'I don't think I ever want to get married,' she said emphatically.

Mrs Rupa Mehra was too wearied by the wedding, too exhausted by emotion, too softened by Sanskrit, too cumbered with congratulations, too overwrought, in short, to do anything but stare at Lata for ten seconds. What on earth had got into the girl? What was good enough for her mother and her mother's mother and her mother's mother's mother should be good enough for her. Lata, though, had always been a difficult one, with a strange will of her own, quiet but unpredictable—like that time in St Sophia's when she had wanted to become a nun! But Mrs Rupa Mehra too had a will, and she was determined to have her own way, even if she was under no illusions as to Lata's pliability.

And yet, Lata was named after that most pliable thing, a vine, which was trained to cling: first to her family, then to her husband. Indeed, when she was a baby, Lata's fingers had had a strong and coiling grasp which even now came back with a sweet vividness to her mother. Suddenly Mrs Rupa Mehra burst out with the inspired remark:

'Lata, you are a vine, you must cling to your husband!'

It was not a success.

'Cling?' said Lata. 'Cling?' The word was pronounced with such quiet scorn that her mother could not help bursting into tears. How terrible it was to have an ungrateful daughter. And how unpredictable a baby could be.

Now that the tears were running down her cheeks, Mrs Rupa Mehra transferred them fluidly from one daughter to the other. She clasped Savita to her bosom and wept loudly. 'You must write to me, Savita darling,' she said. 'You must write to me every day from Simla. Pran, you are like my own son now, you must be responsible and see to it. Soon I will be all alone in Calcutta—all alone.'

This was of course quite untrue. Arun and Varun and Meenakshi and Aparna would all be crowded together with her in Arun's little flat in Sunny Park. But Mrs Rupa Mehra was one who believed with unformulated but absolute conviction in the paramountcy of subjective over objective truth.

1.10

The tonga clip-clopped along the road, and the tonga-wallah sang out:

'A heart was shattered into bits—and one fell here, and one fell there. . . .'

Varun started to hum along, then sang louder, then suddenly stopped.

'Oh, don't stop,' said Malati, nudging Lata gently. 'You have a nice voice. Like a bulbul.'

'In a china-china-shop,' she whispered to Lata.

'Heh, heh, heh.' Varun's laugh was nervous. Realizing that it sounded weak, he tried to make it slightly sinister. But it didn't work. He felt miserable. And Malati, with her green eyes and sarcasm—for it had to be sarcasm—wasn't helping.

The tonga was quite crowded: Varun was sitting with young Bhaskar in the front, next to the tonga-wallah; and back to back with them sat Lata and Malati—both dressed in salwaar-kameez—and Aparna in her ice-cream-stained sweater and a frock. It was a sunny winter morning.

The white-turbaned old tonga-wallah enjoyed driving furiously through this part of town with its broad, relatively uncrowded streets—unlike the cramped madness of Old Brahmpur. He started talking to his horse, urging him on.

Malati now began to sing the words of the popular film song herself. She hadn't meant to discourage Varun. It was pleasant to think of shattered hearts on a cloudless morning.

Varun didn't join in. But after a while he took his life in his hands and said, turning around:

'You have a—a wonderful voice.'

It was true. Malati loved music, and studied classical singing under Ustad Majeed Khan, one of the finest singers in north India. She had even got Lata interested in Indian classical music during the time they had lived together in the student hostel. As a result, Lata often found herself humming some tune or other in one of her favourite raags.

Malati did not disclaim Varun's compliment.

'Do you think so?' she said, turning around to look deeply into his eyes. 'You are very sweet to say so.'

Varun blushed to the depths of his soul and was speechless for a few minutes. But as they passed the Brahmpur Racecourse, he gripped the tonga-wallah's arm and cried:

'Stop!'

'What's the matter?' asked Lata.

'Oh—nothing—nothing—if we're in a hurry, let's go on. Yes, let's go on.'

'Of course we're not, Varun Bhai,' she said. 'We're only going to the zoo. Let's stop if you want.'

After they had got down, Varun, almost uncontrollably excited, wandered to the white palings and stared through.

'It's the only anticlockwise racecourse in India other than Lucknow,' he breathed, almost to himself, awestruck. 'They say it's based on the Derby,' he added to young Bhaskar, who happened to be standing next to him.

'But what's the difference?' asked Bhaskar. 'The distance is the same, isn't it, whether you run clockwise or anticlockwise?'

Varun paid no attention to Bhaskar's question. He had started walking slowly, dreamily, by himself, anticlockwise along the fence. He was almost pawing the earth.

Lata caught up with him: 'Varun Bhai?' she said.

'Er—yes? Yes?'

'About yesterday evening.'

'Yesterday evening?' Varun dragged himself back to the two-legged world. 'What happened?'

'Our sister got married.'

'Ah. Oh. Yes, yes, I know. Savita,' he added, hoping to imply alertness by specificity.

'Well,' said Lata, 'don't let yourself be bullied by Arun Bhai. Just don't.' She stopped smiling, and looked at him as a shadow crossed his face. 'I really hate it, Varun Bhai, I really hate seeing him bully you. I don't mean that you should cheek him or answer back or anything, just that you shouldn't let it hurt you the way that—well, that I can see it does.'

'No, no—' he said, uncertainly.

'Just because he's a few years older doesn't make him your father and teacher and sergeant major all rolled into one.'

Varun nodded unhappily. He was too well aware that while he lived in his elder brother's house he was subject to his elder brother's will.

'Anyway, I think you should be more confident,' continued Lata. 'Arun Bhai tries to crush everyone around him like a steamroller, and it's up to us to remove our egos from his path. I have a hard enough time, and I'm not even in Calcutta. I just thought I'd say so now, because at the house I'll hardly get the chance to talk to you alone. And tomorrow you'll be gone.'

Lata spoke from experience, as Varun well knew. Arun, when angry, hardly cared what he said. When Lata had taken it into her head to become a nun—a foolish, adolescent notion, but her own—Arun, exasperated with the lack of success of his bludgeoning attempts at dissuasion, had said: 'All right, go ahead, become a nun, ruin your life, no one would have married you anyway, you look just like the Bible—flat in front and flat at the back.' Lata thanked God that she wasn't studying at Calcutta University; for most of the year at least, she was outside the range of Arun's blunderbuss. Even though those words were no longer true, the memory of them still stung.

'I wish you were in Calcutta,' said Varun.

'Surely you must have some friends—' said Lata.

'Well, in the evening Arun Bhai and Meenakshi Bhabhi are often out and I have to mind Aparna,' said Varun, smiling weakly. 'Not that I mind,' he added.

'Varun, this won't do,' said Lata. She placed her hand firmly on his slouching shoulder and said: 'I want you to go out with your friends—with people you really like and who like you—for at least two evenings a week. Pretend you have to attend a coaching session or something.' Lata didn't care for deception, and she didn't know whether Varun would be any good at it, but she didn't want things to continue as they were. She was worried about Varun. He had looked even more jittery at the wedding than when she had seen him a few months previously.

A train hooted suddenly from alarmingly close, and the tonga horse shied.

'How amazing,' said Varun to himself, all thoughts of everything else obliterated.

He patted the horse when they got back into the tonga.

'How far is the station from here?' he asked the tonga-wallah.

'Oh, it's just over there,' said the tonga-wallah, indicating vaguely the built-up area beyond the well-laid-out gardens of the racecourse. 'Not far from the zoo.'

I wonder if it gives the local horses an advantage, Varun said to himself. Would the others tend to bolt? What difference would it make to the odds?

1.11

When they got to the zoo, Bhaskar and Aparna joined forces and asked to ride on the children's railway, which, Bhaskar noted, also went around anticlockwise. Lata and Malati wanted a walk after the tonga ride, but they were overruled. All five of them sat in a small, post-box-red compartment, squashed together and facing each other this time, while the little green steam engine puffed along on its one-foot-wide track. Varun sat opposite Malati, their knees almost touching. Malati enjoyed the fun of this, but Varun was so disconcerted that he looked desperately around at the giraffes, and even stared attentively at the crowds of schoolchildren, some of whom were licking huge bobbins of pink spun candy. Aparna's eyes began to shine with anticipation.

Since Bhaskar was nine, and Aparna a third of his age, they did not have much to say to each other. They attached themselves to their most-favoured adults. Aparna, brought up by her socialite parents with alternating indulgence and irritation, found Lata reassuringly certain in her affection. In Lata's company she behaved in a less brat-like manner. Bhaskar and Varun got on famously once Bhaskar succeeded in getting him to concentrate. They discussed mathematics, with special reference to racing odds.

They saw the elephant, the camel, the emu, the common bat, the brown pelican, the red fox, and all the big cats. They even saw a smaller one, the black-spotted leopard-cat, as he paced frenziedly across the floor of his cage.

But the best stop of all was the reptile house. Both children were eager to see the snake pit, which was full of fairly sluggish pythons, and the glass cases with their deadly vipers and kraits and cobras. And also, of course, the cold, corrugated crocodiles on to whose backs some schoolchildren and visiting villagers were throwing coins—while others, as the white, serrated mouths opened lazily far below, leaned over the railings and pointed and squealed and shuddered. Luckily Varun had a taste for the sinister, and took the kids inside. Lata and Malati refused to go in.

'I see enough horrifying things as a medical student,' said Malati.

'I wish you wouldn't tease Varun,' said Lata after a while.

'Oh, I wasn't teasing him,' said Malati. 'Just listening to him attentively. It's good for him.' She laughed.

'Mm—you make him nervous.'

'You're very protective of your elder brother.'

'He's not—oh, I see—yes, my younger elder brother. Well, since I don't have a younger brother, I suppose I've given him the part. But seriously, Malati, I am worried about him. And so is my mother. We don't know what he's going to do when he graduates in a few months. He hasn't shown much aptitude for anything. And Arun bullies him fearfully. I wish some nice girl would take him in charge.'

'And I'm not the one? I must say, he has a certain feeble charm. Heh, heh!' Malati imitated Varun's laugh.

'Don't be facetious, Malati. I don't know about Varun, but my mother would have a fit,' said Lata.

This was certainly true. Even though it was an impossible proposition geographically, the very thought of it would have given Mrs Rupa Mehra nightmares. Malati Trivedi, apart from being one of a small handful of girls among the almost five hundred boys at the Prince of Wales Medical College, was notorious for her outspoken views, her participation in the activities of the Socialist Party, and her love affairs—though not with any of those five hundred boys, whom, by and large, she treated with contempt.

'Your mother likes me, I can tell,' said Malati.

'That's beside the point,' said Lata. 'And actually, I'm quite amazed that she does. She usually judges things by influences. I would have thought you're a bad influence on me.'

But this was not entirely true, even from Mrs Rupa Mehra's viewpoint. Malati had certainly given Lata more confidence than she had had when she had emerged wet-feathered from St Sophia's. And Malati had succeeded in getting Lata to enjoy Indian classical music, which (unlike ghazals) Mrs Rupa Mehra approved of. That they should have become room-mates at all was because the government medical college (usually referred to by its royal title) had no provision for housing its small contingent of women and had persuaded the university to accommodate them in its hostels.

Malati was charming, dressed conservatively but attractively, and could talk to Mrs Rupa Mehra about everything from religious fasts to cooking to genealogy, matters that her own westernized children showed very little interest in. She was also fair, an enormous plus in Mrs Rupa Mehra's subconscious calculus. Mrs Rupa Mehra was convinced that Malati Trivedi, with her dangerously attractive greenish eyes, must have Kashmiri or Sindhi blood in her. So far, however, she had not discovered any.

Though they did not often talk about it, the bond of paternal loss also tied Lata and Malati together.

Malati had lost her adored father, a surgeon from Agra, when she was eight. He had been a successful and handsome man with a wide acquaintance and a varied history of work: he had been attached to the army for a while and had gone to Afghanistan; he had taught in Lucknow at the medical college; he had also been in private practice. At the time of his death, although he had not been very good at saving money, he had owned a fair amount of property—largely in the form of houses. Every five years or so he would uproot himself and move to another town in U.P.—Meerut, Bareilly, Lucknow, Agra. Wherever he lived he built a new house, but without disposing of the old ones. When he died, Malati's mother went into what seemed like an irreversible depression, and remained in that state for two years.

Then she pulled herself together. She had a large family to take care of, and it was essential that she think of things in a practical way. She was a very simple, idealistic, upright woman, and she was concerned more with what was right than with what was convenient or approved of or monetarily beneficial. It was in that light that she was determined to bring up her family.

And what a family!—almost all girls. The eldest was a proper tomboy, sixteen years old when her father died, and already married to a rural landlord's son; she lived about twenty miles away from Agra in a huge house with twenty servants, lichi orchards, and endless fields, but even after her marriage she joined her sisters in Agra for months at a time. This daughter had been followed by two sons, but they had both died in childhood, one aged five, the other three. The boys had been followed by Malati herself, who was eight years younger than her sister. She also grew up as a sort of boy—though not by any means like the tomboy her sister was—for a variety of reasons connected with her infancy: the direct gaze in her unusual eyes, her boyish look, the fact that the boys' clothes were at hand, the sadness that her parents had experienced at the death of their two sons. After Malati came three girls, one after another; then another boy; and then her father died.

Malati had therefore been brought up almost entirely among women; even her little brother had been like a little sister; he had been too young to be treated as anything different. (After a while, perhaps out of perplexity, he had gone the way of his brothers.) The girls grew up in an atmosphere where men came to be seen as exploitative and threatening; many of the men Malati came into contact with were precisely that. No one could touch the memory of her father. Malati was determined to become a doctor like him, and never allowed his instruments to rust. She intended one day to use them.

Who were these men? One was the cousin who did them out of many of the things that her father had collected and used, but which were lying in storage after his death. Malati's mother had cleared out what she had seen as inessentials from their life. It was not necessary now to have two kitchens, one European and one Indian. The china and fine cutlery for western food was put away, together with a great deal of furniture, in a garage. The cousin came, got the keys from the grieving widow, told her he would manage matters, and cleaned out whatever had been stored. Malati's mother never saw a rupee of the proceeds. 'Well,' she had said philosophically, 'at least my sins have lessened.'

Another was the servant who acted as an intermediary for the sale of the houses. He would contact property agents or other prospective buyers in the towns where the houses were located, and make deals with them. He had something of a reputation as a cheat.

Yet another was her father's younger brother, who still lived in the Lucknow house, with his wife downstairs and a dancing girl upstairs. He would happily have cheated them, if he had been able to, over the sale of that house. He needed money to spend on the dancing girl.

Then there was the young—well, twenty-six-year-old—but rather sleazy college teacher who had lived downstairs in a rented room when Malati was fifteen or so. Malati's mother wanted her to learn English, and had no compunction, no matter what the neighbours said (and they said a great deal, not much of it charitable) about sending Malati to learn from him—though he was a bachelor. Perhaps in this case the neighbours were right. He very soon fell madly in love with Malati, and requested her mother for permission to marry her. When Malati was asked by her mother for her views on the matter, she was amazed and shocked, and refused point-blank.

At the medical college in Brahmpur, and before that, when she had studied Intermediate Science in Agra, Malati had had a lot to put up with: teasing, gossip, the pulling of the light chunni around her neck, and remarks such as 'She wants to be a boy.' This was very far from the truth. The remarks were unbearable and only diminished when, provoked by one boy beyond endurance, she had slapped his face hard in front of his friends.

Men fell for her at a rapid rate, but she saw them as beneath her attention. It was not as if she truly hated men; most of the time she didn't. It was just that her standards were too high. No one came near the image she and her sisters had of their father, and most men struck her as being immature. Besides, marriage was a distraction for someone who had set her sights upon the career of medicine, and she was not enormously concerned if she never got married.

She overfilled the unforgiving minute. As a girl of twelve or thirteen, she had been a loner, even in her crowded family. She loved reading, and people knew better than to talk to her when she had a book in her hands. When this happened, her mother did not insist that she help with cooking and housework. 'Malati's reading,' was enough for people to avoid the room where she lay or sat crouched, for she would pounce angrily on anyone who dared disturb her. Sometimes she would actually hide from people, seeking out a corner where no one would be likely to find her. They got the message soon enough. As the years passed, she guided the education of her younger sisters. Her elder sister, the tomboy, guided them all—or, rather, bossed them around—in other matters.

Malati's mother was remarkable in that she wished her daughters to be independent. She wanted them, apart from their schooling at a Hindi-medium school, to learn music and dancing and languages (and especially to be good at English); and if this meant that they had to go to someone's house to learn what was needed, they would go—regardless of what people said. If a tutor had to be called to the house of the six women, he would be called. Young men would look up in fascination at the first floor of the house, as they heard five girls singing along undemurely together. If the girls wanted ice-cream as a special treat, they would be allowed to go to the shop by themselves and eat it. When neighbours objected to the shamelessness of letting young girls go around by themselves in Agra, they were allowed occasionally to go to the shop after dark instead—which, presumably, was worse, though less detectable. Malati's mother made it clear to the girls that she would give them the best education possible, but that they would have to find their own husbands.

Soon after she came to Brahmpur, Malati fell in love with a married musician, who was a socialist. She remained involved with the Socialist Party even when their affair ended. Then she had another rather unhappy love affair. At the moment she was unattached.

Though full of energy most of the time, Malati would fall ill every few months or so, and her mother would come down from Agra to Brahmpur to cure her of the evil eye, an influence that lay outside the province of western medicine. Because Malati had such remarkable eyes herself, she was a special target of the evil eye.

A dirty, grey, pink-legged crane surveyed Malati and Lata with its small, intense red eyes; then a grey film blinked sideways across each eyeball, and it walked carefully away.

'Let's surprise the kids by buying some of that spun candy for them,' said Lata as a vendor went past. 'I wonder what's keeping them. What's the matter, Malati? What are you thinking of?'

'Love,' said Malati.

'Oh, love, what a boring subject,' said Lata. 'I'll never fall in love. I know you do from time to time. But—' She lapsed into silence, thinking once again, with some distaste, of Savita and Pran, who had left for Simla. Presumably they would return from the hills deeply in love. It was intolerable.

'Well, sex then.'

'Oh please, Malati,' said Lata looking around quickly. 'I'm not interested in that either,' she added, blushing.

'Well, marriage then. I'm wondering whom you'll get married to. Your mother will get you married off within a year, I'm sure of it. And like an obedient little mouse, you'll obey her.'

'Quite right,' said Lata.

This rather annoyed Malati, who bent down and plucked three narcissi growing immediately in front of a sign that read, *Do not pluck the flowers.* One she kept, and two she handed to Lata, who felt very awkward holding such illegally gotten gains. Then Malati bought five sticks of flossy pink candy, handed four to Lata to hold with her two narcissi, and began to eat the fifth.

Lata started to laugh.

'And what will happen then to your plan to teach in a small school for poor children?' demanded Malati.

'Look, here they come,' said Lata.

Aparna was looking petrified and holding Varun's hand tightly. For a few minutes they all ate their candy, walking towards the exit. At the turnstile a ragged urchin looked longingly at them, and Lata quickly gave him a small coin. He had been on the point of begging, but hadn't yet done so, and looked astonished.

One of her narcissi went into the horse's mane. The tonga-wallah again began to sing of his shattered heart. This time they all joined in. Passers-by turned their heads as the tonga trotted past.

The crocodiles had had a liberating effect on Varun. But when they got back to Pran's house on the university campus, where Arun and Meenakshi and Mrs Rupa Mehra were staying, he had to face the consequences of returning an hour late. Aparna's mother and grandmother were looking anxious.

'You damn irresponsible fool,' said Arun, dressing him down in front of everyone. 'You, as the man, are in charge, and if you say twelve thirty, it had better be twelve thirty, especially since you have my daughter with you. And my sister. I don't want to hear any excuses. You damned idiot.' He was furious. 'And you—' he added to Lata, 'you should have known better than to let him lose track of the time. You know what he's like.'

Varun bowed his head and looked shiftily at his feet. He was thinking how satisfying it would be to feed his elder brother, head first, to the largest of the crocodiles.

1.12

One of the reasons why Lata was studying in Brahmpur was because this was where her grandfather, Dr Kishen Chand Seth, lived. He had promised his daughter Rupa when Lata first came to study here that he would take very good care of her. But this had never happened. Dr Kishen Chand Seth was far too preoccupied either with bridge at the Subzipore Club or feuds with the likes of the Minister of Revenue or passion for his young wife Parvati to be capable of fulfilling any guardian-like role towards Lata. Since it was from his grandfather that Arun had inherited his atrocious temper, perhaps this was, all in all, not a bad thing. At any rate, Lata did not mind living in the university dormitory. Far better for her studies, she thought, than under the wing of her irascible Nana.

Just after Raghubir Mehra had died, Mrs Rupa Mehra and her family had gone to live with her father, who at that stage had not yet remarried. Given her straitened finances, this seemed to be the only thing to do; she also thought that he might be lonely, and hoped to help him with his household affairs. The experiment had lasted a few months, and had been a disaster. Dr Kishen Chand Seth was an impossible man to live with. Tiny though he was, he was a force to reckon with not only at the medical college, from which he had retired as Principal, but in Brahmpur at large: everyone was scared of him and obeyed him tremblingly. He expected his home life to run on similar lines. He overrode Rupa Mehra's writ with respect to her own children. He left home suddenly for weeks on end without leaving money or instructions for the staff. Finally, he accused his daughter, whose good looks had survived her widowhood, of making eyes at his colleagues when he invited them home—a shocking accusation for the heartbroken though sociable Rupa. The teenaged Arun had threatened to beat up his grandfather. There had been tears and yells and Dr Kishen Chand Seth had pounded the floor with his stick. Then Mrs Rupa Mehra had left, weeping and determined, with her brood of four, and had sought refuge with sympathetic friends in Darjeeling.

Reconciliation had been effected a year later in a renewed bout of weeping. Since then things had jolted along. The marriage with Parvati (which had shocked not just his family but Brahmpur at large because of the disparity of age), Lata's enrolment at Brahmpur University, Savita's engagement (which Dr Kishen Chand Seth had helped arrange), Savita's wedding (which he had almost wrecked and from which he had wilfully absented himself): all these were landmarks along an extremely bumpy road. But family was family, and, as Mrs Rupa Mehra continually told herself, one had to take the rough with the smooth.

Several months had now passed since Savita's wedding. Winter had gone and the pythons in the zoo had emerged from hibernation. Roses had replaced narcissi, and had been replaced in their turn by the purple-wreath creeper, whose five-bladed flowers helicoptered gently to the ground in the hot breeze. The broad, silty-brown Ganga, flowing due east past the ugly chimneys of the tannery and the marble edifice of the Barsaat Mahal, past Old Brahmpur with its crowded bazaars and alleys, temples and mosques, past the bathing ghats and the cremation ghat and the Brahmpur Fort, past the whitewashed pillars of the Subzipore Club and the spacious estate of the university, had shrunken with the summer, but boats and steamers still plied busily up and down its length, as did trains along the parallel railway line that bounded Brahmpur to the south.

Lata had left the hostel and had gone to live with Savita and Pran, who had descended from Simla to the plains very much in love. Malati visited Lata often, and had grown to like the lanky Pran, of whom she had formed such an unfavourable first impression. Lata too liked his decent, affectionate ways, and was not too upset to learn that Savita was pregnant. Mrs Rupa Mehra wrote long letters to her daughters from Arun's flat in Calcutta, and complained repeatedly that no one replied to her letters either soon enough or often enough.

Though she did not mention this in any of her letters for fear of enraging her daughter, Mrs Rupa Mehra had tried—without success—to find a match for Lata in Calcutta. Perhaps she had not made enough effort, she told herself: she was, after all, still recovering from the excitement and exertion of Savita's wedding. But now at last she was going back to

Brahmpur for a three-month stint at what she had begun to call her second home: her daughter's home, not her father's. As the train puffed along towards Brahmpur, the propitious city which had yielded her one son-in-law already, Mrs Rupa Mehra promised herself that she would make another attempt. Within a day or two of her arrival she would go to her father for advice.

1.13

In the event, it was not necessary to go to Dr Kishen Chand Seth for advice. He drove to the university the next day in a fury and arrived at Pran Kapoor's house.

It was three in the afternoon, and hot. Pran was at the department. Lata was attending a lecture on the Metaphysical Poets. Savita had gone shopping. Mansoor, the young servant, tried to soothe Dr Kishen Chand Seth by offering him tea, coffee or fresh lime juice. All this was brushed brusquely aside.

'Is anyone at home? Where is everyone?' asked Dr Kishen Chand Seth in a rage. His short, compressed and very jowly appearance made him look a little like a fierce and wrinkled Tibetan watchdog. (Mrs Rupa Mehra's good looks had been the gift of her mother.) He carried a carved Kashmiri cane which he used more for emphasis than for support. Mansoor hurried inside.

'Burri Memsahib?' he called, knocking at the door of Mrs Rupa Mehra's room.

'What? . . . Who?'

'Burri Memsahib, your father is here.'

'Oh. Oh.' Mrs Rupa Mehra, who had been enjoying an afternoon nap, woke into a nightmare. 'Tell him I will be with him immediately, and offer him some tea.'

'Yes, Memsahib.'

Mansoor entered the drawing room. Dr Seth was staring at an ashtray.

'Well? Are you dumb as well as half-witted?' asked Dr Kishen Chand Seth.

'She's just coming, Sahib.'

'Who's just coming? Fool!'

'Burri Memsahib, Sahib. She was resting.'

That Rupa, his mere chit of a daughter, could ever somehow have been elevated into not just a Memsahib but a Burri Memsahib puzzled and annoyed Dr Seth.

Mansoor said, 'Will you have some tea, Sahib? Or coffee?'

'Just now you offered me nimbu pani.'

'Yes, Sahib.'

'A glass of nimbu pani.'

'Yes, Sahib. At once.' Mansoor made to go.

'And oh—'

'Yes, Sahib?'

'Are there any arrowroot biscuits in this house?'

'I think so, Sahib.'

Mansoor went into the back garden to pluck a couple of limes, then returned to the kitchen to squeeze them into juice.

Dr Kishen Chand Seth picked up a day-old *Statesman* in preference to that day's *Brahmpur Chronicle*, and sat down to read in an armchair. Everyone was half-witted in this house.

Mrs Rupa Mehra dressed hurriedly in a black-and-white cotton sari and emerged from her room. She entered the drawing room, and began to apologize.

'Oh, stop it, stop it, stop all this nonsense,' said Dr Kishen Chand Seth impatiently in Hindi.

'Yes, Baoji.'

'After waiting for a week I decided to visit you. What kind of daughter are you?'

'A week?' said Mrs Rupa Mehra palely.

'Yes, yes, a week. You heard me, Burri Memsahib.'

Mrs Rupa Mehra didn't know which was worse, her father's anger or his sarcasm.

'But I only arrived from Calcutta yesterday.'

Her father seemed ready to explode at this patent fiction when Mansoor came in with the nimbu pani and a plate of arrowroot biscuits. He noticed the expression on Dr Seth's face and stood hesitantly by the door.

'Yes, yes, put it down here, what are you waiting for?'

Mansoor set the tray down on a small glass-topped table and turned to leave. Dr Seth took a sip and bellowed in fury—

'Scoundrel!'

Mansoor turned, trembling. He was only sixteen, and was standing in for his father, who had taken a short leave. None of his teachers during his five years at a village school had inspired in him such erratic terror as Burri Memsahib's crazy father.

'You rogue—do you want to poison me?'

'No, Sahib.'

'What have you given me?'

'Nimbu pani, Sahib.'

Dr Seth, jowls shaking, looked closely at Mansoor. Was he trying to cheek him?

'Of course it's nimbu pani. Did you think I thought it was whisky?'

'Sahib.' Mansoor was nonplussed.

'What have you put in it?'

'Sugar, Sahib.'

'You buffoon! I have my nimbu pani made with salt, not sugar,' roared Dr Kishen Chand Seth. 'Sugar is poison for me. I have diabetes, like your Burri Memsahib. How many times have I told you that?'

Mansoor was tempted to reply, 'Never,' but thought better of it. Usually Dr Seth had tea, and he brought the milk and sugar separately.

Dr Kishen Chand Seth rapped his stick on the floor. 'Go. Why are you staring at me like an owl?'

'Yes, Sahib. I'll make another glass.'

'Leave it. No. Yes—make another glass.'

'With salt, Sahib.' Mansoor ventured to smile. He had quite a nice smile.

'What are you laughing at like a donkey?' asked Dr Seth. 'With salt, of course.'

'Yes, Sahib.'

'And, idiot—'

'Yes, Sahib?'

'With pepper too.'

'Yes, Sahib.'

Dr Kishen Chand Seth veered around towards his daughter. She wilted before him.

'What kind of daughter do I have?' he asked rhetorically. Rupa Mehra waited for the answer, and it was not long in coming. 'Ungrateful!' Her father bit into an arrowroot biscuit for emphasis. 'Soggy!' he added in disgust.

Mrs Rupa Mehra knew better than to protest.

Dr Kishen Chand Seth went on:

'You have been back from Calcutta for a week and you haven't visited me once. Is it me you hate so much or your stepmother?'

Since her stepmother, Parvati, was considerably younger than herself, Mrs Rupa Mehra found it very difficult to think of her other than as her father's nurse and, later, mistress. Though fastidious, Mrs Rupa Mehra did not entirely resent Parvati. Her father had been lonely for three decades after her mother had died. Parvati was good to him and (she supposed) good for him. Anyway, thought Mrs Rupa Mehra, this is the way things happen in the world. It is best to be on good terms with everyone.

'But I only arrived here yesterday,' she said. She had told him so a minute ago, but he evidently did not believe her.

'Hunh!' said Dr Seth dismissively.

'By the Brahmpur Mail.'

'You wrote in your letter that you would be coming last week.'

'But I couldn't get reservations, Baoji, so I decided to stay in Calcutta another week.' This was true, but the pleasure of spending time with her three-year-old granddaughter Aparna had also been a factor in her delay.

'Have you heard of telegrams?'

'I thought of sending you one, Baoji, but I didn't think it was so important. Then, the expense. . . .'

'Ever since you became a Mehra you have become completely evasive.'

This was an unkind cut, and could not fail to wound. Mrs Rupa Mehra bowed her head.

'Here. Have a biscuit,' said her father in a conciliatory manner.

Mrs Rupa Mehra shook her head.

'Eat, fool!' said her father with rough affection. 'Or are you still keeping those brainless fasts that are so bad for your health?'

'It is Ekadashi today.' Mrs Rupa Mehra fasted on the eleventh day of each lunar fortnight in memory of her husband.

'I don't care if it's ten Ekadashis,' said her father with some heat. 'Ever since you came under the influence of the Mehras you have become as religious as your ill-fated mother. There have been too many mismatched marriages in this family.'

The combination of these two sentences, loosely coupled in several possible wounding interpretations, was too much for Mrs Rupa Mehra. Her nose began to redden. Her husband's family was no more religious than it was evasive. Raghubir's brothers and sisters had taken her to their heart in a manner both affecting and comforting to a sixteen-year-old bride, and still, eight years after her husband's death, she visited as many of them as possible in the course of what her children called her Annual Trans-India

Rail-Pilgrimage. If she was growing to be 'as religious as her mother' (which she was not—at least not yet), the operative influence was probably the obvious one: that of her mother, who had died in the post-First-World-War influenza epidemic, when Rupa was very young. A faded image now came before her eyes: the soft spirit of Dr Kishen Chand Seth's first wife could not have been more distant from his own freethinking, allopathic soul. His comment about mismatched marriages injured the memory of two loved ghosts, and was possibly even intended as an insult to the asthmatic Pran.

'Oh don't be so sensitive!' said Dr Kishen Chand Seth brutally. Most women, he had decided, spent two-thirds of their time weeping and whimpering. What good did they think it did? As an afterthought he added, 'You should get Lata married off soon.'

Mrs Rupa Mehra's head jerked up. 'Oh? Do you think so?' she said. Her father seemed even more full of surprises than usual.

'Yes. She must be nearly twenty. Far too late. Parvati got married when she was in her thirties, and see what she got. A suitable boy must be found for Lata.'

'Yes, yes, I was just thinking the same,' said Mrs Rupa Mehra. 'But I don't know what Lata will say.'

Dr Kishen Chand Seth frowned at this irrelevance.

'And where will I find a suitable boy?' she continued. 'We were lucky with Savita.'

'Lucky—nothing! I made the introduction. Is she pregnant? No one tells me anything,' said Dr Kishen Chand Seth.

'Yes, Baoji.'

Dr Seth paused to interpret the yes. Then he said: 'It's about time. I hope I get a great-grandson this time.' He paused again. 'How is she?'

'Well, a bit of morning sickness,' began Mrs Rupa Mehra.

'No, idiot, I mean my great-granddaughter, Arun's child,' said Dr Kishen Chand Seth impatiently.

'Oh, Aparna? She's very sweet. She's grown very attached to me,' said Mrs Rupa Mehra happily. 'Arun and Meenakshi send their love.'

This seemed to satisfy Dr Seth for the moment, and he bit his arrowroot biscuit carefully. 'Soft,' he complained. 'Soft.'

Things had to be just so for her father, Mrs Rupa Mehra knew. When she was a child she had not been allowed to drink water with her meals. Each morsel had to be chewed twenty-four times to aid digestion. For a man so particular about, indeed so fond of, his food, it was sad to see him reduced to biscuits and boiled eggs.

'I'll see what I can do for Lata,' her father went on. 'There's a young radiologist at the Prince of Wales. I can't remember his name. If we had thought about it earlier and used our imaginations we could have captured Pran's younger brother and had a double wedding. But now they say he's got engaged to that Banaras girl. Perhaps that is just as well,' he added, remembering that he was supposed to be feuding with the Minister.

'But you can't go now, Baoji. Everyone will be back soon,' protested Mrs Rupa Mehra.

'Can't? Can't? Where is everyone when I want them?' retorted Dr Kishen Chand Seth. He clicked his tongue impatiently. 'Don't forget your stepmother's birthday next week,' he added as he walked to the door.

Mrs Rupa Mehra looked wistfully and worriedly from the doorway at her father's back. On the way to his car he paused by a bed of red and yellow cannas in Pran's front garden, and she noticed him get more and more agitated. Bureaucratic flowers (among which he also classified marigolds, bougainvillaea and petunias) infuriated him. He had banned them at the Prince of Wales Medical College as long as he had wielded supreme power there; now they were making a comeback. With one swipe of his Kashmiri walking stick he lopped off the head of a yellow canna. As his daughter tremblingly watched, he got into his ancient grey Buick. This noble machine, a Raja among the rabble of Austins and Morrises that plied the Indian roads, was still slightly dented from the time when, ten years ago, Arun (on a visit during his vacation from St George's) had taken it for a catastrophic joyride. Arun was the only one in the family who could defy his grandfather and get away with it, indeed was loved the more for it. As Dr Kishen Chand Seth drove off, he told himself that this had been a satisfying visit. It had given him something to think about, something to plan.

Mrs Rupa Mehra took a few moments to recover from her father's bracing company. Suddenly realizing how hungry she was, she began to think of her sunset meal. She could not break her fast with grain, so young Mansoor was dispatched to the market to buy some raw bananas to make into cutlets. As he went through the kitchen to get the bicycle key and the shopping bag, he passed by the counter, and noticed the rejected glass of nimbu pani: cool, sour, inviting.

He swiftly gulped it down.

1.14

Everyone who knew Mrs Rupa Mehra knew how much she loved roses and, particularly, pictures of roses, and therefore most of the birthday cards she received featured roses of various colours and sizes, and various degrees of copiousness and blatancy. This afternoon, sitting with her reading glasses on at the desk in the room she shared with Lata, she was going through old cards for a practical purpose, although the project threatened to overwhelm her with its resonances of ancient sentiment. Red roses, yellow roses, even a blue rose here and there combined themselves with ribbons, pictures of kittens and one of a guilty-looking puppy. Apples and grapes and roses in a basket; sheep in a field with a foreground of roses; roses in a misty pewter mug with a bowl of strawberries resting nearby; violet-flushed roses graced with unrose-like, unserrated leaves and mild, even inviting, green thorns: birthday cards from family, friends and assorted well-wishers all over India, and even some from abroad—everything reminded her of everything, as her elder son was apt to remark.

Mrs Rupa Mehra glanced in a cursory manner over her piles of old New Year cards before returning to the birthday roses. She took out a small pair of scissors from the recesses of her great black handbag, and tried to decide which card she would have to sacrifice. It was very rarely that Mrs Rupa Mehra bought a card for anyone, no matter how close or dear the person was. The habit of necessary thrift had sunk deep into her mind, but eight years of the deprivation of small luxuries could not reduce for her the sanctity of the birthday greeting. She could not afford cards, so she made them. In fact she enjoyed the creative challenge of making them. Scraps of cardboard, shreds of ribbon, lengths of coloured paper, little silver stars and adhesive golden numerals lay in a variegated trove at the bottom of the largest of her three suitcases, and these were now pressed into service. The scissors poised, descended. Three silver stars were parted from their fellows, and pasted (with the help of borrowed glue—this was the only constituent Mrs Rupa Mehra did not, for fear of leakage, carry with her) on to three corners of the front of the folded blank white piece of cardboard. The fourth corner, the northwest corner, could contain two golden numerals indicating the age of the recipient.

But now Mrs Rupa Mehra paused—for surely the age of the recipient would be an ambivalent detail in the present case. Her stepmother, as she could never cease to remember, was fully ten years younger than she was, and the accusing '35', even—or perhaps especially—in gold, could be seen—would be seen—as implying an unacceptable disparity, possibly even an unacceptable motivation. The golden numerals were put aside, and a fourth silver star joined its fellows in a pattern of innocuous symmetry.

Postponing the decision of illustration, Mrs Rupa Mehra now looked for assistance in building up a rhyming text for her card. The rose-and-pewter card contained the following lines:

May the gladness you have scattered
    Along life's shining way
And the little deeds of kindness
    That are yours from day to day
And the happiness you've showered
    On others all life through
Return to swell your blessings
    In this birthday hour for you.

This would not do for Parvati, Mrs Rupa Mehra decided. She turned to the card illustrated with grapes and apples.

'Tis a day for hugs and kisses,
    For cakes and candles too,
A day for all who love you
    To renew their love anew,
A day for sweet reflection
    Along life's shining way,
And a day for all to tell you:
    Have the wonderfullest day.

This showed promise but there was something wrong with the fourth line, Mrs Rupa Mehra instinctively felt. Also, she would have to alter 'hugs and kisses' to 'special greetings'; Parvati might very well deserve hugs and kisses but Mrs Rupa Mehra was incapable of giving them to her.

Who had sent her this card? Queenie and Pussy Kapadia, two unmarried sisters in their forties whom she had not met for years. Unmarried! The very word was like a knell. Mrs Rupa Mehra paused in her thoughts for a moment, and moved resolutely on.

The puppy yapped an unrhymed and therefore unusable text—a mere

'Happy Birthday and Many Happy Returns'—but the sheep bleated in rhymes identical to but sentiment marginally distinct from the others:

> It's not a standard greeting
> For just one joyful day
> But a wish that's meant to cover
> Life's bright and shining way—
> To wish you all the special things
> That mean the most to you
> So that this year and every year
> Your fondest dreams come true.

Yes! Life's shining way, a concept dear to Mrs Rupa Mehra, was here polished to an even finer lustre. Nor did the lines commit her to any deep protestation of affection for her father's second wife. At the same time the greeting was not accusably distant. She got out her black-and-gold Mont Blanc fountain pen, Raghubir's present to her when Arun was born—twenty-five years old and still going strong, she reflected with a sad smile—and began to write.

Mrs Rupa Mehra's handwriting was very small and well formed, and this presented her in the present instance with a problem. She had chosen too large a size of card in proportion to her affection, but the silver stars had been stuck and it was too late to change that parameter. She now wished to fill as much space as possible with the rhymed message so that she would not have to inscribe more than a few words in her own right to supplement the verse. The first three couplets were therefore laid out—with as much white space in between as would not appear too obvious—on the left-hand side; an ellipsis of seven dots spoored across the page in a semblance of suspense; and the concluding couplet was allowed to crash down with thunderous blandness on the right.

'To Dear Parvati—a very happy birthday, much love, Rupa,' wrote Mrs Rupa Mehra with a dutiful expression. Then, repenting, she added 'est' to the 'Dear'. It looked a little cramped now, but only a careful eye would perceive it as an afterthought.

Now came the heartbreaking part: not the mere transcription of a stanza but the actual sacrifice of an old card. Which of the roses would have to be transplanted? After some thought, Mrs Rupa Mehra decided that she could not bear to part with any of them. The dog, then? He looked mournful, even guilty—besides, the picture of a dog, however appealing his appearance, was open to misinterpretation. The sheep perhaps—yes, they would do. They were fluffy and unemotional. She did not mind parting with them. Mrs Rupa Mehra was a vegetarian, whereas both her father and Parvati were avid meat-eaters. The roses in the foreground of the old card were preserved for future use, and the three sheared sheep were driven carefully towards new pastures.

Before she sealed the envelope Mrs Rupa Mehra got out a small writing pad, and wrote a few lines to her father:

Dearest Baoji,

Words cannot express how much happiness it gave me to see you yesterday. Pran and Savita and Lata were very disappointed. They did not get the chance to be there, but such is life. About the radiologist, or any other prospect for Lata, please pursue enquiries. A good khatri boy would be best of course, but after Arun's marriage I am capable of considering others. Fair or dark, as you know, one cannot be choosy. I have recovered from my journey and remain, with much affection,

Your everloving daughter,
Rupa

The house was quiet. She asked Mansoor for a cup of tea, and decided to write a letter to Arun. She unfolded a green inland letter form, dated it carefully in her minute and lucid script, and began.

My darling Arun,

I hope you are feeling much better and the pain in your back as well as the toothache is much less. I was very sad and upset in Calcutta as we did not have much time to spend at the station together due to the traffic on Strand and Howrah Bridge and you having to leave before the train left because Meenakshi wanted you home early. You don't know how very much you are in my thoughts—much more than words can say. I thought maybe the preparations for the party could have been postponed by ten minutes but it was not to be. Meenakshi knows best. Anyway whatever it all was the net result was that we didn't have long at the station and tears rolled down my cheeks due to disappointment. My dear Varun also had to go back because he came in your car to see me off. Such is life one doesn't often get the things one wants. Now I only pray for you to get well soon and keep good health wherever you are and have no more trouble with your back so that you can play golf again which you are so fond of. If it be God's will we will meet again very soon. I love you lots and wish you all the happiness and success you well deserve. Your Daddy would have been so proud to see you in Bentsen and Pryce, and now with wife and child. Love and kisses to darling Aparna.

The journey passed peacefully and as planned, but I must admit I could not resist having some mihidana at Burdwan. If you had been there you would have scolded me, but I could not resist my sweet tooth. The ladies in my Ladies' Reserve compartment were very friendly and we played rummy and three-two-five and had a good chat. One of the ladies knew the Miss Pal we used to visit in Darjeeling, the one who was engaged to the army captain but he died in the War. I had the set of cards that Varun gave me for my last birthday in my bag, and they helped to while away the journey. Whenever I travel I remember our saloon days with your Daddy. Please give him my love and tell him to study hard in the good traditions of his father.

Savita is looking very well, and Pran is a first-class husband except for his asthma and most caring. I think that he is having some difficulty with his department but he does not like to talk about it. Your grandfather visited yesterday and could have given him some medical advice but unfortunately only I was at home. By the way it is the birthday of your step-grandmother next week, and maybe you should send her a card. Better late than sorry.

I am suffering some pain in my foot but that is expected. Monsoons will be here in two three months and then my joints will play up. Unfortunately Pran cannot afford a car on his lecturer's salary and the transport situation is not good. I take a bus or tonga to go here and there and sometimes I walk. As you know, the Ganges is not far from the house and Lata also goes walking quite a lot, she seems to enjoy it. It is quite safe as far as the dhobi-ghat near the university, though there is a bit of a monkey menace.

Has Meenakshi had Daddy's gold medals set yet? I like the idea of a neck-pendant for one and the lid of a little cardamom-container for the other. That way you can read what is written on both sides of the medal.

Now Arun mine, do not be cross with me for what I am saying, but I have been thinking a lot about Lata lately, and I think you should build up her confidence which she is lacking despite her brilliant record of studies. She is quite afraid of your comments, sometimes even I am afraid of them. I know you do not mean to be harsh, but she is a sensitive girl and now that she is of marriageable age she is super-sensitive. I am going to write to Mr. Gaur's daughter Kalpana in Delhi—she knows everyone, and may help us find a suitable match for Lata. Also I think it is time for you to help in the matter. I could see how busy you were with work, so I mentioned it very rarely when I was in Calcutta but it was always on my mind. Another covenanted boy from a good family, does not have to be khatri, would be a dream come true. Now that the college year is almost over Lata will have time. I may have many faults but I think I am a loving mother, and I long to see all my children well settled.

Soon it will be April and I am afraid I will again be very depressed and lonely at heart because that month will bring back memories of your father's illness and death as if they happened only the other day and it is eight long years that have gone by and so much has happened under the bridge in this period. I know there are thousands who have had and are having much more to suffer but to every human being one's own sufferings seem the most and I am still very much human and have not risen very much above the usual feelings of sorrow and disappointments. I am trying very hard though believe me to rise above all this, and (D.V.) I will.

Here the inland letter form ended, and Mrs Rupa Mehra began to fill in—transversely—the space left blank near the head of the letter:

Anyway space is short so my darling Arun I will end now. Do not worry at all about me, my blood sugar level is OK I am sure, Pran is making me go for a test at the university clinic tomorrow morning, and I have been careful about my diet except for one glass of very sweet nimbu pani when I arrived tired after my journey.

Here she went on to write on the non-adhesive flap:

After I have written to Kalpana I will play a game of patience with

Varun's cards. Lots and lots of love to you and to Varun and a big hug and lots of kisses to my little sweetheart Aparna, and of course to Meenakshi also.

Yours everloving,
Ma

Fearing that her pen might run out during the course of her next letter, Mrs Rupa Mehra opened her handbag and took out an already opened bottle of ink—Parker's Quink Royal Washable Blue—effectively separated from the other contents of the handbag by several layers of rags and cellophane. A bottle of glue she habitually carried had once leaked from its slit rubber cap with disastrous consequences, and glue had thenceforth been banished from her handbag, but ink had so far caused her only minor problems.

Mrs Rupa Mehra took out another inland letter form, then decided that this would be a false economy in the present case, and began writing on a well-husbanded pad of cream-coloured cambric bond:

Dearest Kalpana,

You have always been like a daughter to me so I will speak from the heart. You know how worried I have been about Lata this last year or so. As you know, since your Uncle Raghubir died I have had a hard time in many ways, and your father—who was so close to Uncle during his lifetime—has been as good to me after his sad demise. Whenever I come to Delhi which is sadly not often of late I feel happy when I am with you, despite the jackals that bark all night behind your house, and since your dear mother passed away I have felt like a mother to you.

Now the time has come to get Lata well settled, and I must look all out for a suitable boy. Arun should shoulder some responsibility in the matter but you know how it is, he is so occupied with work and family. Varun is too young to help and is quite unsteady also. You my dear Kalpana are a few years older to Lata and I hope you can suggest some suitable names among your old college friends or others in Delhi. Maybe in October in the Divali holidays—or in December in the Christmas-New Year holidays—Lata and I can come to Delhi to look into things? I only mention this to mention it. Do please say what you think?

How is your dear father? I am writing from Brahmpur where I am staying with Savita and Pran. All is well but the heat is already very delapidating and I am dreading April-May-June. I wish you could have come to their wedding but what with Pimmy's appendix operation I can understand. I was worried to know she had not been well. I hope it is all resolved now. I am in good health and my blood sugar is fine. I have taken your advice and had new glasses made and can read and write without strain.

Please write soonest to this address. I will be here throughout March and April, maybe even in May till Lata's results for this year are out.

With fondest love,
Yours ever,
Ma (Mrs. Rupa Mehra)

P.S. Lata sometimes comes up with the idea that she will not get married. I hope you will cure her of such theories. I know how you feel about early marriage after what happened with your engagement, but in a different way I also feel that 'tis better to have loved and lost etc. Not that love is always an unmixed blessing.
P.S. Divali would be better than New Year for us to come to Delhi, because it fits in better with my annual travel plans, but whichever time you say is fine.

Lovingly, Ma

Mrs Rupa Mehra looked over her letter (and her signature—she insisted on all young people calling her Ma), folded it neatly in four, and sealed it in a matching envelope. She fished out a stamp from her bag, licked it thoughtfully, stuck it on the envelope, and wrote Kalpana's address (from memory) as well as Pran's address on the back. Then she closed her eyes and sat perfectly still for a few minutes. It was a warm afternoon. After a while she took out the pack of playing cards from her bag. When Mansoor came in to take away the tea and to do the accounts, he found she had dozed off over a game of patience.

1.15

The Imperial Book Depot was one of the two best bookshops in town, and was located on Nabiganj, the fashionable street that was the last bulwark of modernity before the labyrinthine alleys and ancient, cluttered neighbourhoods of Old Brahmpur. Though it was a couple of miles away from the university proper it had a greater following among students and teachers than the University and Allied Bookshop, which was just a few minutes away from campus. The Imperial Book Depot was run by two brothers, Yashwant and Balwant, both almost illiterate in English, but both (despite their prosperous roundness) so energetic and entrepreneurial that it apparently made no difference. They had the best stock in town, and were extremely helpful to their customers. If a book was not available in the shop, they asked the customer himself to write down its name on the appropriate order form.

Twice a week an impoverished university student was paid to sort new arrivals on to the designated shelves. And since the bookshop prided itself on its academic as well as general stock, the proprietors unashamedly collared university teachers who wandered in to browse, sat them down with a cup of tea and a couple of publishers' lists, and made them tick off titles that they thought the bookshop should consider ordering. These teachers were happy to ensure that books they needed for their courses would be readily available to their students. Many of them resented the University and Allied Bookshop for its entrenched, lethargic, unresponsive and high-handed ways.

After classes, Lata and Malati, both dressed casually in their usual salwaar-kameez, went to Nabiganj to wander around and have a cup of coffee at the Blue Danube coffee house. This activity, known to university students as 'ganjing', they could afford to indulge in about once a week. As they passed the Imperial Book Depot, they were drawn magnetically in. Each wandered off to her favourite shelves and subjects. Malati headed straight for the novels, Lata went for poetry. On the way, however, she paused by the science shelves, not because she understood much science, but, rather, because she did not. Whenever she opened a scientific book and saw whole paragraphs of incomprehensible words and symbols, she felt a sense of wonder at the great territories of learning that lay beyond her—the sum of so many noble and purposive attempts to make objective sense of the world. She enjoyed the feeling; it suited her serious moods;

and this afternoon she was feeling serious. She picked up a random book and read a random paragraph:

> It follows from De Moivre's formula that $z^n = r^n$ (cos n + i sin n). Thus, if we allow complex number z to describe a circle of radius r about the origin, z^n will describe n complete times a circle of radius r^n as z describes its circle once. We also recall that r, the modulus of z, written $|z|$, gives the distance of z from O, and that if $z'=x'+iy'$, then $|z-z'|$ is the distance between z and z′. With these preliminaries we may proceed to the proof of the theorem.

What exactly it was that pleased her in these sentences she did not know, but they conveyed weight, comfort, inevitability. Her mind strayed to Varun and his mathematical studies. She hoped that her brief words to him the day after the wedding had done him some good. She should have written to him more often to bolster his courage, but with exams coming up she had very little time for anything. It was at the insistence of Malati—who was even busier than she was—that she had gone ganjing at all.

She read the paragraph again, looking serious. 'We also recall' and 'with these preliminaries' drew her into a compact with the author of these verities and mysteries. The words were assured, and therefore reassuring: things were what they were even in this uncertain world, and she could proceed from there.

She smiled to herself now not aware of her surroundings. Still holding the book, she looked up. And this was how a young man, who had been standing not far from her, was included, unintentionally, in her smile. He was pleasantly startled, and smiled back at her. Lata frowned at him and looked down at the page again. But she could not concentrate on it, and after a few moments, replaced it on the shelf before making her way to Poetry.

Lata, whatever she thought of love itself, liked love poetry. 'Maud' was one of her favourite poems. She began to flip through a volume of Tennyson.

The tall young man, who had (Lata noticed) slightly wavy black hair and very good, rather aquiline, looks, seemed to be as interested in poetry as in mathematics, because a few minutes later Lata was aware that he had shifted his attention to the poetry shelves, and was glancing through the anthologies. Lata felt that his eyes were on her from time to time. This annoyed her and she did not look up. When, despite herself, she did, she noticed him innocently immersed in his reading. She could not resist glancing at the cover of his book. It was a Penguin: *Contemporary Verse.* He now looked up, and the tables were turned. Before she could glance down again, he said: 'It's unusual for someone to be interested in both poetry and mathematics.'

'Is that so?' said Lata severely.

'Courant and Robbins—it's an excellent work.'

'Oh?' said Lata. Then, realizing that the young man was referring to the mathematics book she had picked randomly off the shelf, she said, 'Is it?' by way of closure.

But the young man was eager to continue the conversation.

'My father says so,' he went on. 'Not as a text but as a broad introduction to various, well, facets of the subject. He teaches maths at the university.'

Lata looked around to see if Malati was listening. But Malati was intent on her browsing in the front of the shop. Nor was anyone else eavesdropping; the shop was not busy at this time of year—or this time of day.

'Actually, I'm not interested in mathematics,' said Lata with an air of finality. The young man looked a little downcast before he rallied and confided, genially: 'You know, nor am I. I'm a history student myself.'

Lata was amazed at his determination and, looking straight at him, said, 'I must go now. My friend is waiting for me.' Even as she was saying this, however, she could not help noticing how sensitive, even vulnerable, this wavy-haired young man looked. This appeared to contradict his determined, bold behaviour in speaking to an unknown, unintroduced, girl in a bookshop.

'I'm sorry, I suppose I've been disturbing you?' he apologized, as if reading her thoughts.

'No,' said Lata. She was about to go to the front of the shop when he added quickly, with a nervous smile, 'In that case, may I ask you your name?'

'Lata,' said Lata shortly, though she didn't see the logic of 'in that case'.

'Aren't you going to ask me mine?' asked the young man, his smile broadening amiably.

'No,' said Lata, quite kindly, and rejoined Malati, who had a couple of paperback novels in her hand.

'Who's he?' whispered Malati conspiratorially.

'Just someone,' said Lata, glancing back a bit anxiously. 'I don't know. He just came up to me and began a conversation. Hurry up. Let's go. I'm feeling hungry. And thirsty. It's hot in here.'

The man at the counter was looking at Lata and Malati with the energetic friendliness he showered on regular customers. The little finger of his left hand was searching for wax in the crevices of his ear. He shook his head with reproving benevolence and said in Hindi to Malati:

'Exams are coming up, Malatiji, and you are still buying novels? Twelve annas plus one rupee four annas makes two rupees altogether. I should not allow this. You are like daughters to me.'

'Balwantji, you would go out of business if we did not read your novels. We are sacrificing our examination results at the altar of your prosperity,' said Malati.

'I'm not,' said Lata. The young man must have disappeared behind a bookshelf, because she couldn't see him anywhere.

'Good girl, good girl,' said Balwant, possibly referring to both of them.

'Actually, we were going to get some coffee and came into your shop unplanned,' said Malati, 'so I didn't bring—' She left the sentence unfinished and flung a winning smile at Balwant.

'No, no, that is not necessary—you can give it later,' said Balwant. He and his brother extended terms of easy credit to many students. When asked whether this wasn't bad for business, they would reply that they had never lost money trusting anyone who bought books. And, certainly, they were doing very well for themselves. They reminded Lata of the priests of a well-endowed temple. The reverence with which the brothers treated their books supported the analogy.

'Since you suddenly feel famished, we are going straight to the Blue Danube,' said Malati decisively once they were outside the shop. 'And there you will tell me exactly what happened between that Cad and you.'

'Nothing,' said Lata.

'Hah!' said Malati in affectionate scorn. 'So what did you two talk about?'

'Nothing,' said Lata. 'Seriously, Malati, he just came up and started talking nonsense, and I said nothing in reply. Or monosyllables. Don't add chillies to boiled potatoes.'

They continued to stroll down Nabiganj.

'Quite tall,' said Malati, a couple of minutes later.

Lata said nothing.

'Not exactly dark,' said Malati.

Lata did not think this was worth responding to either. 'Dark', as she understood it, referred in novels to hair, not skin.

'But very handsome,' persisted Malati.

Lata made a wry face at her friend, but she was, to her own surprise, quite enjoying her description.

'What's his name?' continued Malati.

'I don't know,' said Lata, looking at herself in the glass front of a shoe shop.

Malati was astonished at Lata's ineptness. 'You talked to him for fifteen minutes and you don't know his name?'

'We did not talk for fifteen minutes,' said Lata. 'And I hardly talked at all. If you're so keen on him, why don't you go back to the Imperial Book Depot and ask him his name? Like you, he has no compunctions about talking to anyone.'

'So you don't like him?'

Lata was silent. Then she said, 'No, I don't. I've no reason to like him.'

'It's not all that easy for men to talk to us, you know,' said Malati. 'We shouldn't be so hard on them.'

'Malati defending the weaker sex!' said Lata. 'I never thought I'd see the day.'

'Don't change the subject,' said Malati. 'He didn't seem the brazen type. I know. Trust my five-hundredfold experience.'

Lata flushed. 'It seemed pretty easy for him to talk to me,' she said. 'As if I was the sort of girl who . . .'

'Who what?'

'Who can be talked to,' ended Lata uncertainly. Visions of her mother's disapproval floated across her mind. She made an effort to push these away.

'Well,' said Malati, a little more quietly than usual as they entered the Blue Danube, 'he really does have nice looks.'

They sat down.

'Nice hair,' continued Malati, surveying the menu.

'Let's order,' said Lata. Malati appeared to be in love with the word 'nice'. They ordered coffee and pastries.

'Nice eyes,' said Malati, five minutes later, laughing now at Lata's studied unresponsiveness.

Lata remembered the young man's temporary nervousness when she had looked straight at him.

'Yes,' she agreed. 'But so what? I have nice eyes too, and one pair is enough.'

1.16

While his mother-in-law was playing patience and his sister-in-law was fending off Malati's leading questions, Dr Pran Kapoor, that first-class husband and son-in-law, was battling with the departmental problems he was reticent about burdening his family with.

Pran, though a calm man by and large, and a kind man, regarded the head of the English Department, Professor Mishra, with a loathing that made him almost ill. Professor O.P. Mishra was a huge, pale, oily hulk, political and manipulative to the very depths of his being. The four members of the syllabus committee of the English Department were seated this afternoon around an oval table in the staff room. It was an unusually warm day. The single window was open (to the view of a dusty laburnum tree), but there was no breeze; everyone looked uncomfortable, but Professor Mishra was sweating in profuse drops that gathered on his forehead, wet his thin eyebrows, and trickled down the sides of his large nose. His lips were sweetly pursed and he was saying in his genial, high-pitched voice, 'Dr Kapoor, your point is well taken, but I think that we will need a little convincing.'

The point was the inclusion of James Joyce on the syllabus for the paper on Modern British Literature. Pran Kapoor had been pressing this on the syllabus committee for two terms—ever since he had been appointed a member—and at last the committee had decided to agree whether to consider it.

Why, Pran wondered, did he dislike Professor Mishra so intensely? Although Pran had been appointed to his lecturership five years ago under the headship of his predecessor, Professor Mishra, as a senior member of the department, must have had a say in hiring him. When he first came to the department, Professor Mishra had gone out of his way to be gracious to him, even inviting him to tea at his house. Mrs Mishra was a small, busy, worried woman, and Pran had liked her. But despite Professor Mishra's open-armed avuncularity, his Falstaffian bulk and charm, Pran detected something dangerous: his wife and two young sons were, so it seemed to him, afraid of their father.

Pran had never been able to understand why people loved power, but he accepted it as a fact of life. His own father, for instance, was greatly attracted by it: his enjoyment in its exercise went beyond the pleasure of being able to realize his ideological principles. Mahesh Kapoor enjoyed being Revenue Minister, and he would probably be happy to become either Chief Minister of Purva Pradesh or a Minister in Prime Minister Nehru's Cabinet in Delhi. The headaches, the overwork, the responsibility, the lack of control over one's own time, the complete absence of opportunity to contemplate the world from a calm vantage point: these mattered little to him. Perhaps it was true to say that Mahesh Kapoor had contemplated the world sufficiently long from the calm vantage point of his cell in a prison in British India, and now required what he had in fact acquired: an intensely active role in running things. It was almost as if father and son had exchanged between themselves the second and third stages of the accepted Hindu scheme of life: the father was entangled in the world, the son longed to separate himself into a life of philosophical detachment.

Pran, however, whether he liked it or not, was what the scriptures would call a householder. He enjoyed Savita's company, he basked in her warmth and care and beauty, he looked forward to the birth of their child. He was determined not to depend on his father for financial support, although the small salary of a department lecturer—200 rupees per month—was barely enough to subsist on—'to subside on', as he told himself in moments of cynicism. But he had applied for a readership that had recently fallen open in the department; the salary attached to that post was less pitiful, and it would be a step up in terms of the academic hierarchy. Pran did not care about titular prestige, but he realized that designations helped one's designs. He wanted to see certain things done, and being a reader would help him do them. He believed that he deserved the job, but he had also learned that merit was only one criterion among several.

His experience of the recurrent asthmatic illness that had afflicted him since childhood had made him calm. Excitement disturbed his breathing, and caused him pain and incapacitation, and he had therefore almost dispensed with excitability. This was the simple logic of it, but the path itself had been difficult. He had studied patience, and by slow practice he had become patient. But Professor O.P. Mishra had got under his skin in a way Pran had not been able to envisage.

'Professor Mishra,' said Pran, 'I am pleased that the committee has decided to consider this proposal, and I am delighted that it has been placed second on the agenda today and has at last come up for discussion. My main argument is quite simple. You have read my note on the subject'—he nodded around the table to Dr Gupta and Dr Narayanan—'and you will, I am sure, appreciate that there is nothing radical in my suggestion.' He looked down at the pale blue type of the cyclostyled sheets before him. 'As you can see, we have twenty-one writers whose works we consider it essential for our B.A. students to read in order for them to obtain a proper understanding of Modern British Literature. But there is no Joyce. And, I might add, no Lawrence. These two writers—'

'Wouldn't it be better,' interrupted Professor Mishra, wiping an eyelash away from the corner of his eye, 'wouldn't it be better if we were to concentrate on Joyce for the moment? We will take up Lawrence at our session next month—before we adjourn for the summer vacation.'

'The two matters are interlinked, surely,' said Pran, looking around the table for support. Dr Narayanan was about to say something when Professor Mishra pointed out:

'But not on this agenda, Dr Kapoor, not on this agenda.' He smiled at Pran sweetly, and his eyes twinkled. He then placed his huge white hands, palms down, on the table and said, 'But what were you saying when I so rudely interrupted?'

Pran looked at the large white hands emanating from the grand pulp of Professor Mishra's round body, and thought, I may look thin and fit, but I am not, and this man, for all his slug-like pallor and bulk, has a great deal of stamina. If I am to get agreement on this measure I must remain calm and collected.

He smiled around the table, and said: 'Joyce is a great writer. This is now universally acknowledged. He is, for instance, the subject of increasing academic study in America. I do think he should be on our syllabus too.'

'Dr Kapoor,' the high voice responded, 'each point in the universe must make up its own mind on the question of acknowledgement before acknowledgement can be considered to be universal. We in India pride ourselves on our Independence—an Independence won at great expense by the best men of several generations, a fact I need not emphasize to the illustrious son of an even more illustrious father. We should hesitate before we blindly allow the American dissertation mill to order our priorities. What do you say, Dr Narayanan?'

Dr Narayanan, who was a Romantic Revivalist, seemed to look deep into his soul for a few seconds. 'That is a good point,' he said judiciously, shaking his head sideways for emphasis.

'If we do not keep pace with our companions,' continued Professor Mishra, 'perhaps it is because we hear a different drummer. Let us step to the music that we hear, we in India. To quote an American,' he added.

Pran looked down at the table and said quietly: 'I say Joyce is a great writer because I believe he is a great writer, not because of what the Americans say.' He remembered his first introduction to Joyce: a friend had lent him *Ulysses* a month before his Ph.D. oral examination at Allahabad University and he had, as a result, ignored his own subject to the point where he had jeopardized his academic career.

Dr Narayanan looked at him and came out suddenly in unexpected support. '"The Dead",' said Dr Narayanan. 'A fine story. I read it twice.'

Pran looked at him gratefully.

Professor Mishra looked at Dr Narayanan's small, bald head almost approvingly. 'Very good, very good,' he said, as if applauding a small child. 'But'—and his voice assumed a cutting edge—'there is more to Joyce than "The Dead". There is the unreadable *Ulysses.* There is the worse than unreadable *Finnegans Wake.* This kind of writing is unhealthy for our students. It encourages them, as it were, in sloppy and ungrammatical writing. And what about the ending of *Ulysses*? There are young and impressionable women whom in our courses it is our responsibility to introduce to the higher things of life, Dr Kapoor—your charming sister-in-law for example. Would you put a book like *Ulysses* into her hands?' Professor Mishra smiled benignly.

'Yes,' said Pran simply.

Dr Narayanan looked interested. Dr Gupta, who was mainly interested in Anglo-Saxon and Middle English, looked at his nails.

'It is heartening to come across a young man—a young lecturer'—Professor Mishra looked over at the rank-conscious reader, Dr Gupta—'who is so, shall I say, so, well, direct in his opinions and so willing to share them with his colleagues, however senior they may be. It is heartening. We may disagree of course; but India is a democracy and we can speak our minds. . . .' He stopped for a few seconds, and stared out of the window at the dusty laburnum. 'A democracy. Yes. But even democracies are faced with hard choices. There can be only one head of department, for example. And when a post falls open, of all the deserving candidates only one can be selected. We are already hard-pressed to teach twenty-one writers in the time we allot to this paper. If Joyce goes in, what comes out?'

'Flecker,' said Pran without a moment's hesitation.

Professor Mishra laughed indulgently. 'Ah, Dr Kapoor, Dr Kapoor . . .' he intoned,

'Pass not beneath, O Caravan, or pass not singing. Have you heard
That silence where the birds are dead yet something pipeth like a bird?

James Elroy Flecker, James Elroy Flecker.' That seemed to settle it in his mind.

Pran's face became completely impassive. Does he believe this? he thought. Does he really believe what he is implying? Aloud he said, 'If Fletcher—Flecker—is indispensable, I suggest we include Joyce as our twenty-second writer. I would be pleased to put it to the committee for a vote.' Surely, thought Pran, the ignominy of being known to have turned Joyce down (as opposed to merely having deferred the decision indefinitely) would be something that the committee would not be willing to face.

'Ah, Dr Kapoor, you are angry. Do not get angry. You want to pin us down,' said Professor Mishra playfully. He turned his palms up on the table to display his own helplessness. 'But we did not agree to decide the matter at this meeting, only to decide whether to decide it.'

This was too much for Pran in his present mood, though he knew it was true.

'Please do not misunderstand me, Professor Mishra,' he said, 'but that line of argument may be taken by those of us not well versed in the finer forms of parliamentary byplay to be a species of quibbling.'

'A species of quibbling . . . a species of quibbling.' Professor Mishra appeared delighted by the phrase, while both his colleagues looked appalled at Pran's insubordination. (This is like playing bridge with two dummies, thought Pran.) Professor Mishra continued: 'I will now order coffee, and we will collect ourselves and approach the issues calmly, as it were.'

Dr Narayanan perked up at the prospect of coffee. Professor Mishra clapped his hands, and a lean peon in a threadbare green uniform came in.

'Is coffee ready?' asked Professor Mishra in Hindi.

'Yes, Sahib.'

'Good.' Professor Mishra indicated that it should be served.

The peon brought in a tray with a coffee pot, a small jug of hot milk, a bowl of sugar, and four cups. Professor Mishra indicated that he should serve the others first. The peon did so in the usual manner. Then Professor Mishra was offered coffee. As Professor Mishra poured coffee into his cup, the peon moved the tray deferentially backwards. Professor Mishra made to set down the coffee pot, and the peon moved the tray forward. Professor Mishra picked up the milk jug and began to add milk to his coffee, and the peon moved the tray backwards. And so on for each of three spoons of sugar. It was like a comic ballet. It would have been merely ridiculous, thought Pran, this display of the naked gradient of power and obsequiousness between the department head and the department peon, if it had only been some other department at some other university. But it was the English Department of Brahmpur University—and it was through this man that Pran had to apply to the selection committee for the readership he both wanted and needed.

This same man whom in my first term I considered jovial, bluff, expansive, charming, why have I transformed him in my mind into such a caricature of a villain? thought Pran looking into his cup. Does he loathe me? No, that is his strength: he doesn't. He just wants his own way. In effective politics hatred is just not useful. For him all this is like a game of chess—on a slightly vibrating board. He is fifty-eight—he has two more years until he retires. How will I be able to put up with him for so long? A sudden murderous impulse seized Pran, whom murderous impulses never seized, and he realized his hands were trembling slightly. And all this over Joyce, he said to himself. At least I haven't had a bronchial attack. He looked down at the pad on which he, as the junior member of the committee, was taking the minutes of the meeting. It read simply:

> Present: Professor O.P. Mishra (head); Dr R.B. Gupta;
> Dr T.R. Narayanan; Dr P. Kapoor.
> 1. The Minutes of the last meeting were read and approved.

We have got nowhere, and we will get nowhere, he thought.

A few well-known lines from Tagore came into his head in Tagore's own English translation:

> Where the clear stream of reason has not lost its way into the
> dreary desert sand of dead habit;
> Where the mind is led forward by Thee into ever-widening
> thought and action—
> Into that heaven of freedom, my Father, let my country awake.

At least his own mortal father had given him principles, thought Pran, even if he had given him almost no time or company when he was younger. His mind wandered back home, to the small whitewashed house, to Savita, her sister, her mother—the family that he had taken into his heart and that had taken him into theirs; and then to the Ganges flowing close by the house. (When he thought in English, it was the Ganges, rather than the Ganga, to him.) He followed it first downstream to Patna and Calcutta, then upstream past Banaras till it divided at Allahabad; there he chose the Yamuna and followed it to Delhi. Are things as closed-minded in the capital? he asked himself. As mad, as mean, as silly, as rigid? How will I be able to live in Brahmpur all my life? And Mishra will doubtless give me an excellent report just to see the back of me.

1.17

But now Dr Gupta was laughing at a remark of Dr Narayanan's, and Professor Mishra was saying, 'Consensus—consensus is the goal, the civilized goal—how can we vote when we might be divided two votes against two? There were five Pandavas, they could have voted if they chose, but even they did everything by consensus. They even took a wife by consensus, ha, ha, ha! And Dr Varma is indisposed as usual, so we are only four.'

Pran looked at the twinkling eyes, the great nose, the sweetly pursed lips with reluctant admiration. University statutes required that the syllabus committee, like departmental committees of any kind, should consist of an odd number of members. But Professor Mishra, as head of the department, appointed the members of each committee within his purview in such a way as always to include someone who for reasons of health or research was likely to be indisposed or absent. With an even number of members present, committees were more reluctant than ever to bring things to the climax of a vote. And the head, with his control over the agenda and the pacing of a meeting, could in the circumstances gather even more effective power into his hands.

'I think we have, as it were, expended enough time on item two,' said Professor Mishra. 'Shall we go on to chiasmus and anacoluthia?' He was referring to a proposal, put forward by himself, that they eliminate too detailed a study of traditional figures of speech for the paper in Literary Theory and Criticism. 'And then we have the question of symmetrical auxiliaries proposed by the junior member of the committee. Though this will, of course, depend upon other departments agreeing to our proposals.

And finally, since the shades of night are falling,' continued Professor Mishra, 'I think we should, without prejudice to items five, six, and seven, wind up the meeting. We can take up those items next month.'

But Pran was unwilling to be dissuaded from pressing on with the unresolved question of Joyce. 'I think we have now collected ourselves,' he said, 'and can approach the issue under discussion quite calmly. If I were willing to accept that *Ulysses* might be a bit, well, difficult for B.A. students, would the committee agree to include *Dubliners* on the syllabus as a first step? Dr Gupta, what do you think?'

Dr Gupta looked up at the slowly circulating fan. His ability to get speakers on Old and Middle English invited to the departmental seminar depended upon Professor Mishra's goodwill: outside speakers entailed incidental expenses, and funds had to be approved by the head of the department. Dr Gupta knew as well as anyone what 'as a first step' implied. He looked up at Pran and said, 'I would be willing—'

But he was swiftly interrupted in his sentence, whatever that might have been. 'We are forgetting,' Professor Mishra cut in, 'something that even I, I must admit, did not bear in mind earlier in this discussion. I mean that, by tradition, the Modern British Literature paper does not include writers who were living at the time of the Second World War.' This was news to Pran, who must have looked astonished, because Professor Mishra felt compelled to explain: 'This is not altogether a matter for surprise. We need the distance of time objectively to appraise the stature of modern writers, to include them in our canon, as it were. Do remind me, Dr Kapoor . . . when did Joyce die?'

'1941,' said Pran sharply. It was clear that the great white whale had known this all along.

'Well, there you are . . .' said Professor Mishra helplessly. His finger moved down the agenda.

'Eliot, of course, is still alive,' said Pran quietly, looking at the list of prescribed authors.

The head of the department looked as if he had been slapped across the face. He opened his mouth slightly, then pursed his lips together. The jolly twinkle appeared again in his eyes. 'But Eliot, Eliot, surely—we have objective criteria enough in his case—why, even Dr Leavis—'

Professor Mishra clearly responded to a different drummer from the Americans, reflected Pran. Aloud he said, 'Dr Leavis, as we know, greatly approves of Lawrence too. . . .'

'We have agreed to discuss Lawrence next time,' Professor Mishra expostulated.

Pran gazed out of the window. It was getting dark and the leaves of the laburnum now looked cool, not dusty. He went on, not looking at Professor Mishra: '. . . and, besides, Joyce has a better claim as a British writer in Modern British Literature than Eliot. So if we—'

'That, my young friend, if I may say so,' cut in Professor Mishra, 'could be considered a species of quibbling.' He was recovering quickly from his shock. In a minute he would be quoting Prufrock.

What is it about Eliot, thought Pran irrelevantly, his mind wandering from the subject at hand, that makes him such a sacred cow for us Indian intellectuals? Aloud he said: 'Let us hope that T.S. Eliot has many more years of life, of productive life. I am glad that, unlike Joyce, he did not die in 1941. But we are now living in 1951, which implies that the pre-war rule you mentioned, even if it is a tradition, could not be a very ancient one. If we can't do away with it, why not update it? Surely its purpose is that we should revere the dead above the living—or, to be less sceptical, appraise the dead before the living. Eliot, who is alive, has been granted a waiver. I propose we grant Joyce one. A friendly compromise.' Pran paused, then added: 'As it were.' He smiled. 'Dr Narayanan, are you for "The Dead"?'

'Yes, well, I think so,' said Dr Narayanan with the faintest of responding smiles, before Professor Mishra could interrupt.

'Dr Gupta?' asked Pran.

Dr Gupta could not look Professor Mishra in the eye.

'I agree with Dr Narayanan,' said Professor Gupta.

There was silence for a few seconds. Pran thought, I can't believe it. I've won. I've won. I can't believe it.

And indeed, it seemed that he had. Everyone knew that the approval of the Academic Council of the university was usually a formality once the syllabus committee of a department had decided matters.

As if nothing in the least untoward had occurred, the head of the department gathered together the reins of the meeting. The great soft hands scuttled across the cyclostyled sheets. 'The next item . . .' said Professor Mishra with a smile, then paused and began again: 'but before we go on to the next item, I should say that I personally have always greatly admired James Joyce as a writer. I am delighted, needless to say—'

A couple of lines of poetry came terrifyingly unbidden to Pran's mind:

Pale hands I loved beside the Shalimar,
Where are you now? Who lies beneath your spell?

and he burst into a fit of sudden laughter, incomprehensible even to himself, which went on for twenty seconds and ended in a spasm of coughing. He bent his head and tears streamed down his cheeks. Professor Mishra rewarded him with a look of unfeigned fury and hatred.

'Sorry, sorry,' muttered Pran as he recovered. Dr Gupta was thumping him vigorously on the back, which was not helpful. 'Please continue—I was overcome—it sometimes happens. . . .' But to offer any further explanation was impossible.

The meeting was resumed and the next two points discussed quickly. There was no real disagreement. It was dark now; the meeting was adjourned. As Pran left the room Professor Mishra put a friendly arm around his shoulder. 'My dear boy, that was a fine performance.' Pran shuddered at the memory. 'You are clearly a man of great integrity, intellectual and otherwise.' Oh, oh, what is he up to now? thought Pran. Professor Mishra continued: 'The Proctor has been badgering me since last Tuesday to submit a member of my department—it's our turn, you know—to join the student welfare committee of the university. . . .' Oh no, thought Pran, there goes one day every week. '. . . and I have decided to volunteer you.' I didn't know the verb was transitive, thought Pran. In the darkness—they were now walking across the campus—it was difficult for Professor Mishra entirely to disguise the active dislike in his high voice. Pran could almost see the pursed lips, the specious twinkle. He was silent, and that, to the head of the English Department, implied acceptance.

'I realize you are busy, my dear Dr Kapoor, what with your extra tutorials, the Debating Society, the Colloquium, putting on plays and so on. . . .' said Professor Mishra. 'The sort of thing that makes one deservedly popular with students. But you are comparatively new here, my dear fellow—five years is not a long time from the perspective of an old fogey like me—and you must allow me to give you a word of advice. Cut down on your unacademic activities. Don't tire yourself out unnecessarily. Don't take things so seriously. What were those wonderful lines of Yeats?

She bid me take life easy as the leaves grown on the tree,
But I being young and foolish with her did not agree.

I'm sure your charming wife would endorse that. Don't drive yourself so hard—your health depends on it. And your future, I dare say. . . . In some ways you are your own worst enemy.'

But I am only my metaphorical enemy, thought Pran. And obstinacy on my part has earned me the actual enmity of the formidable Professor Mishra. But was Professor Mishra more dangerous or less dangerous to him—in this matter of the readership, for instance, now that Pran had won his hatred?

What was Professor Mishra thinking, wondered Pran. He imagined his thoughts went something like this: I should never have got this uppity young lecturer on to the syllabus committee. It's too late, however, to regret all that. But at least his presence here has kept him from working mischief in, say, the admissions committee; there he could have brought up all kinds of objections to students I wanted to bring in if they weren't selected entirely on the basis of merit. As for the university's selection committee for the readership in English, I must rig this somehow before I allow it to meet—

But Pran got no further clues to the inner working of that mysterious intelligence. For at this point the paths of the two colleagues diverged and, with expressions of great mutual respect, they parted from each other.

1.18

Meenakshi, Arun's wife, was feeling utterly bored, so she decided to have her daughter Aparna brought to her. Aparna was looking even more pretty than usual: round and fair and black-haired with gorgeous eyes, as sharp as those of her mother. Meenakshi pressed the electric buzzer twice (the signal for the child's ayah) and looked at the book in her lap. It was Thomas Mann's *Buddenbrooks*, and it was unutterably dull. She didn't know how she was going to get through another five pages of it. Arun, delighted though he normally was with her, had the irksome habit of throwing an improving book her way now and then, and Meenakshi felt his suggestions were more in the way of subtle commands. 'A wonderful book. . . .' Arun would say some evening, laughing, in the company of the oddly flippant crowd they mixed with, a crowd that Meenakshi felt convinced could not possibly be more interested than she was in *Buddenbrooks* or any other such clotted Germanic construct. '. . . I have been reading this marvellous book by Mann, and I'm now getting Meenakshi involved in it.' Some of the others, especially the languid Billy Irani, would look from Arun to Meenakshi in momentary wonderment, and the topic would pass to office matters or the social world or racing or dancing or golf or the Calcutta Club or complaints about 'these bloody politicians' or 'these brainless bureaucrats', and Thomas Mann would be quite forgotten. But Meenakshi would now feel obliged to read enough of the book to convey an acquaintance with its contents, and it seemed to make Arun happy to see her do so.

How wonderful Arun was, thought Meenakshi, and how pleasant it was to live in this nice flat in Sunny Park, not far from her father's house on Ballygunge Circular Road, and why did they have to have all these furious tiffs? Arun was incredibly hotheaded and jealous, and she had only to look languidly at the languid Billy for Arun to start smouldering somewhere deep inside. It might be wonderful to have a smouldering husband in bed later, Meenakshi reflected, but such advantages did not come unadulterated. Sometimes Arun would go off into a smouldering sulk, and was quite spoilt for love-making. Billy Irani had a girlfriend, Shireen, but that made no difference to Arun, who suspected Meenakshi (quite correctly) of harbouring a casual lust for his friend. Shireen for her part occasionally sighed amidst her cocktails and announced that Billy was incorrigible.

When the ayah arrived in answer to the bell, Meenakshi said, 'Baby lao!' in a kind of pidgin Hindi. The aged ayah, most of whose reactions were slow, turned creakingly to fulfil her mistress's behest. Aparna was fetched. She had been having her afternoon nap, and yawned as she was brought in to her mother. Her small fists were rubbing her eyes.

'Mummy!' said Aparna in English. 'I'm sleepy, and Miriam woke me up.' Miriam, the ayah, upon hearing her name spoken, although she could understand no English, grinned at the child with toothless goodwill.

'I know, precious baby doll,' said Meenakshi, 'but Mummy had to see you, she was so bored. Come and give—yes—and now on the other side.'

Aparna was wearing a mauve dress of flouncy fluffy stuff and was looking, thought her mother, inexcusably enchanting. Meenakshi's eyes went to her dressing-table mirror and she noticed with a surge of joy what a wonderful mother-and-child pair they made. 'You are looking *so* lovely,' she informed Aparna, 'that I think I will have a whole line of little girls . . . Aparna, and Bibeka, and Charulata, and—'

Here she was cut off by Aparna's glare. 'If another baby comes into this house,' announced Aparna, 'I will throw it straight into the waste-paper basket.'

'Oh,' said Meenakshi, more than a little startled. Aparna, living among so many opinionated personalities, had quite early developed a powerful vocabulary. But three-year-olds were not supposed to express themselves so lucidly, and in conditional sentences at that. Meenakshi looked at Aparna and sighed.

'You are *so* scrumptious,' she told Aparna. 'Now have your milk.' To the ayah she said, 'Dudh lao. Ek dum!' And Miriam creaked off to get a glass of milk for the little girl.

For some reason the ayah's slow-moving back irritated Meenakshi and she thought: We really ought to replace the T.C. She's quite needlessly senile. This was her and Arun's private abbreviation for the ayah and Meenakshi laughed with pleasure as she remembered the occasion over the breakfast table when Arun had turned from the *Statesman* crossword to say, 'Oh, do get the toothless crone out of the room. She quite puts me off my omelette.' Miriam had been the T.C. ever since. Living with Arun was full of sudden delightful moments like that, thought Meenakshi. If only it could all be that way.

But the trouble was that she also had to run the house, and she hated it. The elder daughter of Mr Justice Chatterji had always had everything done for her—and she was now discovering how trying it could be to handle things on her own. Managing the staff (ayah, servant-cum-cook, part-time sweeper, part-time gardener; Arun supervised the driver, who was on the company payroll); doing the accounts; buying those items that one simply couldn't trust the servant or the ayah to buy; and making sure that everything fitted within the budget. This last she found especially difficult. She had been brought up in some luxury, and though she had insisted (against her parents' advice) on the romantic adventure of standing after marriage entirely on their own four feet, she had found it impossible to curb her taste for certain items (foreign soap, foreign butter and so on) that were intrinsic to the fabric of a civilized life. She was very conscious of the fact that Arun helped support everyone in his own family and often commented to him about the fact.

'Well,' Arun had said just recently, 'now that Savita's married, that's one less, you'll agree, darling.' Meenakshi had sighed, replying in a couplet:

'Marry one—and what's my fate?
Every Mehra on my plate.'

Arun had frowned. He had been reminded once again of the fact that Meenakshi's elder brother was a poet. It was from long familiarity—almost obsession—with rhyme that most of the younger Chatterjis had learned to improvise couplets, sometimes of surpassing puerility.

The ayah brought the milk and left. Meenakshi turned her lovely eyes back to *Buddenbrooks* while Aparna sat on the bed drinking her milk. With a sound of impatience Meenakshi threw Thomas Mann on to the bed and followed him there, closed her eyes and went off to sleep. She was awakened with a shock twenty minutes later by Aparna, who was pinching her breast.

'Don't be horrid, Aparna precious. Mummy's trying to sleep,' said Meenakshi.

'Don't sleep,' said Aparna. 'I want to play.' Unlike other children of her age, Aparna never used her name in the Caesarean third person, though her mother did.

'Darling sweetheart, Mummy is tired, she's been reading a book and she doesn't want to play. Not now, anyway. Later, when Daddy comes home, you can play with him. Or you can play with Uncle Varun when he returns from college. What have you done with your glass?'

'When will Daddy come home?'

'I'd say in about an hour,' replied Meenakshi.

'I'd say in about an hour,' said Aparna speculatively, as if she liked the phrase. 'I want a necklace too,' she added, and tugged at her mother's gold chain.

Meenakshi gave her daughter a hug. 'And you shall have one,' she said, and dismissed the subject. 'Now go to Miriam.'

'No.'

'Then stay here if you want. But do be quiet, darling.'

Aparna was quiet for a while. She looked at *Buddenbrooks*, at her empty glass, at her sleeping mother, at the quilt, at the mirror, at the ceiling. Then she said, 'Mummy?' tentatively. There was no response.

'Mummy?' Aparna attempted a few notches louder.

'Mmm?'

'MUMMY!' yelled Aparna at the top of her lungs.

Meenakshi sat bolt upright and shook Aparna. 'Do you want me to spank you?' she asked.

'No,' replied Aparna definitively.

'Then what is it? Why are you shouting? What were you going to say?'

'Have you had a hard day, darling?' asked Aparna, hoping to arouse a response to her imitative charm.

'Yes,' said Meenakshi shortly. 'Now darling, pick up that glass and go to Miriam at once.'

'Shall I comb your hair?'

'No.'

Aparna got down reluctantly from the bed and made her way to the door. She toyed with the idea of saying, 'I'll tell Daddy!' though what she could have complained about was left unformulated. Her mother meanwhile was once again sleeping sweetly, her lips slightly parted, her long black hair spread across the pillow. It was so hot in the afternoon, and everything tilted her towards a long and languorous sleep. Her breasts rose and fell gently, and she dreamed about Arun, who was handsome and dashing and covenanted, and who would be coming home in an hour. And after a while she began to dream about Billy Irani, whom they would be meeting later that evening.

When Arun arrived, he left his briefcase in the drawing room, walked into the bedroom, and closed the door. Seeing Meenakshi asleep, he paced up and down for a while, then took off his coat and tie, and lay down beside her without disturbing her sleep. But after a while his hand moved to her forehead and then down her face to her breasts. Meenakshi opened her eyes and said, 'Oh.' She was momentarily bewildered. After a while she asked, 'What's the time?'

'Five thirty. I came home early just as I promised—and I found you asleep.'

'I couldn't sleep earlier, darling. Aparna woke me up every few minutes.'

'What's the programme for the evening?'

'Dinner and dancing with Billy and Shireen.'

'Oh yes, of course.' After a pause Arun continued: 'To tell you the truth, darling, I'm rather tired. I wonder whether we shouldn't simply call it off tonight?'

'Oh, you'll revive quickly enough after you've had a drink,' said Meenakshi brightly. 'And a glance or two from Shireen,' she added.

'I suppose you're right, dear.' Arun reached out for her. He had had a little trouble with his back a month ago, but had quite recovered.

'Naughty boy,' said Meenakshi, and pushed his hand away. After a while she added, 'The T.C. has been cheating us on the Ostermilk.'

'Ah? Has she?' said Arun indifferently, then swerved off to a subject that interested him—'I discovered today that we were being overcharged sixty thousand on the new paper project by one of our local businessmen. We've asked him to revise his estimates, of course, but it does rather shock one. . . . No sense of business ethics—or personal ethics either. He was in the office the other day, and he assured me that he was making us a special offer because of what he called our long-standing relationship. Now I find, after talking to Jock Mackay, that that's the line he took with them as well—but charged them sixty thousand less than us.'

'What will you do?' Meenakshi asked dutifully. She had switched off a few sentences ago.

Arun talked on for five minutes or so, while Meenakshi's mind wandered. When he stopped and looked at her questioningly, she said, yawning a little from residual sleepiness:

'How has your boss reacted to all this?'

'Difficult to say. With Basil Cox it's difficult to say anything, even when he's delighted. In this case I think he's as annoyed by the possible delay as pleased by the definite saving.' Arun unburdened himself for another five minutes while Meenakshi began to buff her nails.

The bedroom door had been bolted against interruption, but when Aparna saw her father's briefcase she knew that he had returned and insisted upon being admitted. Arun opened the door and gave her a hug, and for the next hour or so they did a jigsaw featuring a giraffe, which Aparna had seen in a toyshop a week after being taken to the Brahmpur Zoo. They had done the jigsaw several times before, but Aparna had not yet tired of it. Nor had Arun. He adored his daughter and occasionally felt it was a pity that he and Meenakshi went out almost every evening. But one simply couldn't let one's life come to a standstill because one had a child. What, after all, were ayahs for? What, for that matter, were younger brothers for?

'Mummy has promised me a necklace,' said Aparna.

'Has she, darling?' said Arun. 'How does she imagine she's going to buy it? We can't afford it at the moment.'

Aparna looked so disappointed at this latest intelligence that Arun and Meenakshi turned to each other with transferred adoration.

'But she will,' said Aparna, quietly and determinedly. 'Now I want to do a jigsaw.'

'But we've just done one,' protested Arun.

'I want to do another.'

'You handle her, Meenakshi,' said Arun.

'You handle her, darling,' said Meenakshi. 'I must get ready. And please clear the bedroom floor.'

So for a while Arun and Aparna, banished to the drawing room this time, lay on the carpet putting together a jigsaw of the Victoria Memorial while Meenakshi bathed and dressed and perfumed and ornamented herself.

Varun returned from college, slid past Arun into his tiny box of a room, and sat down with his books. But he seemed nervous, and could not settle down to studying. When Arun went to get ready, Aparna was transferred to him; and the rest of Varun's evening was spent at home trying to keep her amused.

The long-necked Meenakshi turned numerous heads when their party of four entered Firpo's for dinner. Arun told Shireen she was looking gorgeous and Billy looked with soulful languor at Meenakshi and said that she looked divine, and things went wonderfully well and were followed by some pleasantly titillating dancing at the 300 Club. Meenakshi and Arun were not really able to afford all this—Billy Irani had independent means—but it seemed intolerable that they, for whom this kind of life was so obviously intended, should be deprived of it by a mere lack of funds. Meenakshi could not help noticing, through dinner and beyond, the lovely little gold danglers that Shireen was wearing, and that hung so becomingly from her little velvety ears.

It was a warm evening. In the car on the way back home Arun said to Meenakshi, 'Give me your hand, darling,' and Meenakshi, placing one red nail-polished fingertip on the back of his hand, said, 'Here!' Arun thought that this was delightfully elegant and flirtatious. But Meenakshi had her mind on something else.

Later, when Arun had gone to bed, Meenakshi unlocked her jewellery case (the Chatterjis did not believe in giving their daughter great quantities of jewellery but she had been given quite enough for her likely requirements) and took out the two gold medals so precious to Mrs Rupa Mehra's heart. She had given these to Meenakshi at the time of her wedding as a gift to the bride of her elder son. This she felt was the appropriate thing to do; she had nothing else to give, and she felt that her husband would have approved. On the back of the medals was engraved: 'Thomasson Engineering College Roorkee. Raghubir Mehra. Civil Engg. First. 1916' and 'Physics. First. 1916' respectively. Two lions crouched sternly on pedestals on each medal. Meenakshi looked at the medals, then balanced them in her hands, then held the cool and precious discs to her cheeks. She wondered how much they weighed. She thought of the gold chain she had promised Aparna and the gold drops she had virtually promised herself. She had examined them quite carefully as they hung from Shireen's little ears. The danglers were shaped like tiny pears.

When Arun rather impatiently called her to bed, she murmured, 'Just coming.' But it was a minute or two before she joined him. 'What are you thinking of, darling?' he asked her. 'You look dangerously preoccupied.' But Meenakshi instinctively realized that to mention what had passed through her head—what she planned to do with those dowdy medals—would not be a good idea, and she avoided the subject by nibbling at the lobe of his left ear.

1.19

The next morning at ten o'clock Meenakshi phoned her younger sister Kakoli.

'Kuku, a friend of mine from the Shady Ladies—my club, you know—wants to find out where she can get some gold melted down discreetly. Do you know of a good jeweller?'

'Well, Satram Das or Lilaram, I suppose,' yawned Kuku, barely awake.

'No, I am not talking of Park Street jewellers—or any jewellers of that kind,' said Meenakshi with a sigh. 'I want to go somewhere where they don't know me.'

'*You* want to go somewhere?'

There was a short silence at the other end. 'Well, you may as well know,' said Meenakshi: 'I've set my heart on a pair of earrings—they look adorable—just like tiny little pears—and I want to melt down those fat ugly medals that Arun's mother gave me for my wedding.'

'Oh, don't do that,' said Kakoli in a kind of alarmed warble.

'Kuku, I want your advice about the place, not about the decision.'

'Well, you could go to Sarkar's. No—try Jauhri's on Rashbehari Avenue. Does Arun know?'

'The medals were given to me,' said Meenakshi. 'If Arun wants to melt his golf clubs down to make a back brace I won't object.'

When she got to the jeweller's, she was astonished to meet opposition there as well.

'Madam,' said Mr Jauhri in Bengali, looking at the medals won by her father-in-law, 'these are beautiful medals.' His fingers, blunt and dark, slightly incongruous for someone who held and supervised work of such fineness and beauty, touched the embossed lions lovingly, and circled around the smooth, unmilled edges.

Meenakshi stroked the side of her neck with the long, red-polished nail of the middle finger of her right hand.

'Yes,' she said indifferently.

'Madam, if I might advise you, why not order these earrings and this chain and pay for them separately? There is really no need to melt down these medals.' A well-dressed and evidently wealthy lady would presumably not find any difficulty in this suggestion.

Meenakshi looked at the jeweller with cool surprise. 'Now that I know the approximate weight of the medals, I propose to melt down one, not both,' she said. Somewhat annoyed by his impertinence—these shopkeepers sometimes got above themselves—she went on: 'I came here to get a job done; I would normally have gone to my regular jewellers. How long do you think it will take?'

Mr Jauhri did not dispute the issue further. 'It will take two weeks,' he said.

'That's rather a long time.'

'Well, you know how it is, Madam. Artisans of the requisite skill are scarce, and we have many orders.'

'But it is March. The wedding season is virtually over.'

'Nevertheless, Madam.'

'Well, I suppose that will have to do,' Meenakshi said. She picked up one medal—it happened to be the Physics one—and popped it back in her purse. The jeweller looked somewhat regretfully at the Engineering Medal lying on a small velvet square on his table. He had not dared to ask whose it was, but when Meenakshi took a receipt for the medal after it had been weighed exactly on his scales, he had deduced from her name that it must have been awarded to her father-in-law. He was not to know that Meenakshi had never known her father-in-law and felt no particular closeness to him.

As Meenakshi turned to leave, he said, 'Madam, if you happen to change your mind . . .'

Meenakshi turned to him, and snapped: 'Mr Jauhri, if I wish for your advice I will ask for it. I came to you specifically because you were recommended to me.'

'Quite right, Madam, quite right. Of course it is entirely up to you. In two weeks then.' Mr Jauhri frowned sadly at the medal before summoning his master artisan.

Two weeks later, Arun discovered through a casual conversational slip what Meenakshi had done. He was livid.

Meenakshi sighed. 'It's pointless talking to you when you are as cross as this,' she said. 'You behave quite heartlessly. Come, Aparna darling, Daddy's angry with us, let's go into the other room.'

A few days later Arun wrote—or, rather, scrawled—a letter to his mother:

Dear Ma,

Sorry not written to you earlier in response to your letter re Lata. Yes, by all means, will look for someone. But don't be sanguine, the covenanted are almost twice-born and get dowry offers in the tens of thousands, even lakhs. Still, situation not entirely hopeless. Will try, but I suggest Lata come to Calcutta in the summer. Will effect introductions &c. But she must cooperate. Varun lackadaisical, studies hard only when I take a hand. Shows no interest in girls, only the fourfooted as usual, and dreadful songs. Aparna in fine fettle, asks after her Daadi continually so rest assured she misses you. Daddy's Engg. Medal melted down for ear-drops and chain by M, but I've placed injunction on Physics, not to worry. All else well, back OK, Chatterjis much the same, will write at length when time.

Love and xxx from all,
Arun

This brief note, written in Arun's illegible telegraphese (the upright lines of the letters tilting at angles of thirty degrees randomly to left or right), landed like a grenade in Brahmpur by the second post one afternoon. When Mrs Rupa Mehra read it, she burst into tears without even (as Arun might have been tempted to remark had he been there) the customary preliminary of a reddening nose. In fact, not to make cynical light of the matter, she was deeply upset, and for every obvious reason.

The horror of the melted medal, the callousness of her daughter-in-law, her disregard of every tender feeling as evidenced by this shallow act of vanity upset Mrs Rupa Mehra more than anything had in years, more even than Arun's marriage to Meenakshi in the first place. She saw before her very eyes her husband's golden name being physically melted away in a crucible. Mrs Rupa Mehra had loved and admired her husband almost to excess, and the thought that one of the few things that tied his presence to the earth was now maliciously—for what was such wounding indifference but a kind of malice—and irretrievably lost made her weep tears of bitterness, anger and frustration. He had been a brilliant student at the Roorkee College and his memories of his student days had been happy ones. He had hardly studied, yet had done extremely well. He had been liked by both his fellow-students and his teachers. The only subject he had been weak in had been Drawing. In that he had barely scraped through. Mrs Rupa Mehra remembered his little sketches in the children's autograph books and felt that the examiners had been ignorant and unjust.

Collecting herself after a while and dabbing her forehead with eau de cologne, she went out into the garden. It was a warm day, but a breeze was blowing from the river. Savita was sleeping, and all the others were out. She looked over at the unswept path past the bed of cannas. The young sweeper-woman was talking to the gardener in the shade of a mulberry tree. I must speak to her about this, thought Mrs Rupa Mehra absently.

Mansoor's father, the far shrewder Mateen, came out on to the verandah with the account book. Mrs Rupa Mehra was in no mood for the accounts, but felt it was her duty to do them. Wearily she returned to the verandah, got her spectacles out of her black bag and looked at the book.

The sweeper-woman took up a broom and started sweeping up the dust, dried leaves, twigs, and fallen flowers from the path. Mrs Rupa Mehra glanced unseeingly at the open page of the account book.

'Should I come back later?' asked Mateen.

'No, I'll do them now. Wait a minute.' She got out a blue pencil and looked at the lists of purchases. Doing the accounts had become much more of a strain since Mateen's return from his village. Quite apart from his odd variant of the Hindi script, Mateen was more experienced than his son at cooking the books.

'What is this?' asked Mrs Rupa Mehra. 'Another four-seer tin of ghee? Do you think we are millionaires? When did we order our last tin?'

'Must be two months ago, Burri Memsahib.'

'When you were away loafing in the village, didn't Mansoor buy a tin?'

'He may have, Burri Memsahib. I don't know; I didn't see it.'

Mrs Rupa Mehra started riffling back through the pages of the account book until she came upon the entry in Mansoor's more legible hand. 'He bought one a month ago. Almost twenty rupees. What happened to it? We're not a family of twelve to go through a tin at such a rate.'

'I've just returned, myself,' Mateen ventured, with a glance at the sweeper-woman.

'You'd buy us a sixteen-seer tin of ghee a week if given half the chance,' said Mrs Rupa Mehra. 'Find out what happened to the rest of it.'

'It goes in puris and parathas and on the daal—and Memsahib likes Sahib to put some ghee every day on his chapatis and rice—' began Mateen.

'Yes, yes,' Mrs Rupa Mehra interrupted. 'I can work out how much should go into all that. I want to find out what happened to the rest of it. We don't keep open house—nor has this become the shop of a sweetseller.'

'Yes, Burri Memsahib.'

'Though young Mansoor seems to treat it like one.'

Mateen said nothing, but frowned, as if in disapproval.

'He eats the sweets and drinks the nimbu pani that is kept aside for guests,' continued Mrs Rupa Mehra.

'I'll speak to him, Burri Memsahib.'

'I'm not sure about the sweets,' said Mrs Rupa Mehra scrupulously. 'He is a self-willed boy. And you—you never bring my tea regularly. Why does no one take care of me in this house? When I am at Arun Sahib's house in Calcutta his servant brings me tea all the time. No one even asks here. If I had my own house, it would have been different.'

Mateen, understanding that the accounts session was over, went to get Mrs Rupa Mehra her tea. About fifteen minutes later, Savita, who had emerged from her afternoon nap looking groggily beautiful, came on to the verandah to find her mother rereading Arun's letter in tears, and saying, 'Ear-drops! He even calls them ear-drops!' When Savita found out what the matter was she felt a rush of sympathy towards her mother and indignation towards Meenakshi.

'How could she have done that?' she asked. Savita's fierce defensiveness towards those whom she loved was masked by her gentle nature. She was independent-spirited but in such a low key that only those who knew her very well got any sense that her life and desires were not entirely determined by the easy drift of circumstance. She held her mother close and said, 'I am amazed at Meenakshi. I will make sure that nothing happens to the other medal. Daddy's memory is worth a great deal more than her small-minded whims. Don't cry, Ma. I'll send a letter off immediately. Or if you want we can write one together.'

'No, no.' Mrs Rupa Mehra looked down sadly at her empty cup.

When Lata returned and heard the news, she too was shocked. She had been her father's darling and had loved looking at his academic medals; indeed she had been very unhappy when they had been given to Meenakshi. What could they mean to her, Lata had wondered, compared to what they would mean to his daughters? She was now most unpleasantly being proved right. She was angry too with Arun who, she felt, had permitted this sorry business by his consent or indulgence and who now made light of the event in his fatuously casual letter. His brutal little attempts to shock or tease his mother made Lata fume. As to his suggestion that she go to Calcutta and cooperate in his introductions—Lata decided that that would be the last thing in the world she would do.

Pran returned late from his first meeting of the student welfare committee to a household that was clearly not itself, but he was too exhausted to inquire immediately what the matter was. He sat in his favourite chair—a rocking chair requisitioned from Prem Nivas—and read for a few minutes. After a while he asked Savita if she wanted to go for a walk, and during the course of it he was briefed on the crisis. He asked Savita whether he could look over the letter she had written to Meenakshi. It was not that he lacked faith in his wife's judgement—quite the contrary. But he hoped that he, not being a Mehra and therefore less taut with a sense of injury, might be of help in preventing irretrievable words from exacerbating irretrievable acts. Family quarrels, whether over property or sentiment, were bitter things; their prevention was almost a public duty.

Savita was happy to show him the letter. Pran looked it over, nodding from time to time. 'This is fine,' he said rather gravely, as if approving a student's essay. 'Diplomatic but deadly! Soft steel,' he added in a different tone. He looked at his wife with an expression of amused curiosity. 'Well, I'll see it goes off tomorrow.'

Malati came over later. Lata filled her in about the medal. Malati described some experiments that they had been required to perform at the medical college, and Mrs Rupa Mehra was sufficiently disgusted to be distracted—at least for a while.

Savita noticed for the first time over dinner that Malati had a crush on her husband. It was evident in the way the girl looked at him over the soup and avoided looking at him over the main course. Savita was not at all annoyed. She assumed that but to know Pran was to love him; Malati's affection was both natural and harmless. Pran, it was clear, was unaware of this; he was talking about the play that he had put on for Annual Day the previous year: *Julius Caesar*—a typical university choice (Pran was saying) since so few parents wanted their daughters to act on stage . . . but, on the other hand, the themes of violence, patriotism and a change of regime had given it a freshness in the present historical context that it would not otherwise have had.

The obtuseness of intelligent men, thought Savita with a smile, is half of what makes them lovable. She closed her eyes for a second to say a prayer for his health and her own and that of her unborn child.

Part Two

2.1

On the morning of Holi, Maan woke up smiling. He drank not just one but several glasses of thandai laced with bhang and was soon as high as a kite. He felt the ceiling floating down towards him—or was it he who was floating up towards it? As if in a mist he saw his friends Firoz and Imtiaz together with the Nawab Sahib arrive at Prem Nivas to greet the family. He went forward to wish them a happy Holi. But all he could manage was a continuous stream of laughter. They smeared his face with colour and he went on laughing. They sat him down in a corner and he continued laughing until the tears rolled down his cheeks. The ceiling had now floated away entirely, and it was the walls that were pulsing in and out in an immensely puzzling way. Suddenly he got up and put his arms around Firoz and Imtiaz and made for the door, pushing them along with him.

'Where are we going?' asked Firoz.

'To Pran's,' Maan replied. 'I have to play Holi with my sister-in-law.' He grabbed a couple of packets of coloured powder and put them in the pocket of his kurta.

'You'd better not drive your father's car in this state,' Firoz said.

'Oh, we'll take a tonga, a tonga,' Maan said, waving his arms around, and then embracing Firoz. 'But first drink some thandai. It's got an amazing kick.'

They were lucky. There weren't many tongas out this morning, but one trotted up just as they got on to Cornwallis Road. The horse was nervous as he passed the crowds of stained and shouting merrymakers on the way to the university. They paid the tonga-wallah double his regular fare and smeared his forehead pink and that of his horse green for good measure. When Pran saw them dismounting he went up and welcomed them into the garden. Just outside the door on the verandah of the house was a large bathtub filled with pink colour and several foot-long copper syringes. Pran's kurta and pyjama were soaked and his face and hair smeared with yellow and pink powder.

'Where's my bhabhi?' shouted Maan.

'I'm not coming out—' said Savita from inside.

'That's fine,' shouted Maan, 'we'll come in.'

'Oh no you won't,' said Savita. 'Not unless you've brought me a sari.'

'You'll get your sari, what I want now is my pound of flesh,' Maan said.

'Very funny,' said Savita. 'You can play Holi as much as you like with my husband, but promise me you'll only put a bit of colour on me.'

'Yes, yes, I promise! Just a smidgeon, no more, of powder—and then a bit on your pretty little sister's face—and I'll be satisfied—until next year.'

Savita opened the door cautiously. She was wearing an old and faded salwaar-kameez and looked lovely: laughing and cautious, half-poised for flight.

Maan held the packet of pink powder in his left hand. He now smeared a bit on his sister-in-law's forehead. She reached into the packet to do the same to him.

'—and a little bit on each cheek—' Maan continued as he smeared more powder on her face.

'Good, that's fine,' said Savita. 'Very good. Happy Holi!'

'—and a little bit here—' said Maan, rubbing more on her neck and shoulders and back, holding her firmly and fondling her a bit as she struggled to get away.

'You're a real ruffian, I'll never trust you again,' said Savita. 'Please let me go, please stop it, no, Maan, please—not in my condition. . . .'

'So I'm a ruffian, am I?' said Maan, reaching for a mug and dipping it in the tub.

'No, no, no—' said Savita. 'I didn't mean it. Pran, please help me,' said Savita, half laughing and half crying. Mrs Rupa Mehra was peeping in alarm through the window. 'No wet colour, Maan, please—' cried Savita, her voice rising to a scream.

But despite all her pleading Maan poured three or four mugs of cold pink water over her head, and rubbed the moist powder on to her kameez over her breasts, laughing all the while.

Lata was looking out of the window too, amazed by Maan's bold, licentious attack—the licence presumably being provided by the day. She could almost feel Maan's hands on her and then the cold shock of the water. To her surprise, and to that of her mother, who was standing next to her, she gave a gasp and a shiver. But nothing would induce her to go outside, where Maan was continuing his polychrome pleasures.

'Stop—' cried Savita, outraged. 'What kind of cowards are you? Why don't you help me? He's had bhang, I can see it—just look at his eyes—'

Firoz and Pran managed to distract Maan by squirting several syringes full of coloured water at him, and he fled into the garden. He was not very steady on his feet as it was, and he stumbled and fell into the bed of yellow cannas. He raised his head among the flowers long enough to sing the single line: 'Oh revellers, it's Holi in the land of Braj!' and sat down again, disappearing from view. A minute later, like a cuckoo clock, he got up to repeat the same line and sat down once more. Savita, bent on revenge, filled a small brass pot with coloured water and came down the steps into the garden. She made her way stealthily to the bed of cannas. Just at that moment Maan got up once again to sing. As his head appeared above the cannas he saw Savita and the lota of water. But it was too late. Savita, fierce and determined, threw the entire contents on his face and chest. Looking at Maan's astonished expression she began to giggle. But Maan had sat down once again and was now crying, 'Bhabhi doesn't love me, my bhabhi doesn't love me.'

'Of course, I don't,' said Savita. 'Why should I?'

Tears rolled down Maan's cheeks and he was inconsolable. When Firoz tried to get him on to his feet he clung to him. 'You're my only real friend,' he wept. 'Where are the sweets?'

Now that Maan had neutralized himself, Lata ventured out and played a little mild Holi with Pran, Firoz and Savita. Mrs Rupa Mehra got smeared with a bit of colour too.

But all the while Lata kept wondering what it would have felt like to be rubbed and smeared by the cheerful Maan in such a public and intimate way. And this was a man who was engaged! She had never seen anyone behave even remotely like Maan—and Pran was very far from furious. A strange family, the Kapoors, she thought.

Meanwhile Imtiaz, like Maan, had got fairly stoned on the bhang in his thandai and was sitting on the steps, smiling at the world and murmuring repeatedly to himself a word that sounded like 'myocardial'. Sometimes he murmured it, sometimes he sang it, at other times it seemed to be a question both profound and unanswerable. Occasionally he would touch the small mole on his cheek in a thoughtful manner.

A group of about twenty students—multicoloured and almost unrecognizable—appeared along the road. There were even a few girls in the group—and one of them was the now purple-skinned (but still green-eyed) Malati. They had induced Professor Mishra to join them; he lived just a few houses away. His whale-like bulk was unmistakable, and besides, he had very little colour on him.

'What an honour, what an honour,' said Pran, 'but I should have come to your house, Sir, not you to mine.'

'Oh, I don't stand on ceremony in such matters,' said Professor Mishra, pursing his lips and twinkling his eyes. 'Now, do tell me, where is the charming Mrs Kapoor?'

'Hello, Professor Mishra, how nice of you to have come to play Holi with us,' Savita said, advancing with a little powder in her hand. 'Welcome, all of you. Hello, Malati, we were wondering what had happened to you. It's almost noon. Welcome, welcome—'

A little colour was applied to the Professor's broad forehead as he bent downwards.

But Maan, who had been leaning, downcast, on Firoz's shoulder, now dropped a canna he had been toying with and advanced with an open-hearted smile towards Professor Mishra. 'So you are the notorious Professor Mishra,' he said in delighted welcome. 'How wonderful to meet so infamous a man.' He embraced him warmly. 'Tell me, are you really an Enemy of the People?' he asked encouragingly. 'What a remarkable face, what a mobile expression!' he murmured in awed appreciation as Professor Mishra's jaw dropped.

'Maan,' said Pran, startled.

'So nefarious!' said Maan, in wholehearted approval.

Professor Mishra stared at him.

'My brother calls you Moby-Dick, the great white whale,' continued Maan in a friendly way. 'Now I see why. Come for a swim,' he invited Professor Mishra generously, indicating the tub full of pink water.

'No, no, I don't think—' began Professor Mishra weakly.

'Imtiaz, give me a hand,' said Maan.

'Myocardial,' said Imtiaz to indicate his willingness. They lifted Professor Mishra by the shoulders and led him physically to the tub.

'No, no, I'll get pneumonia!' cried Professor Mishra in anger and bewilderment.

'Stop it, Maan!' said Pran sharply.

'What do you say, Doctor Sahib?' Maan asked Imtiaz.

'No contraindications,' said Imtiaz, and the two pushed the unprepared professor into the tub. He splashed around, wet to the bone, submerged in pinkness, wild with rage and confusion. Maan looked on, helpless with happy laughter, while Imtiaz grinned beneficently. Pran sat down on a step with his head in his hands. Everyone else looked on horrified.

When Professor Mishra got out of the tub he stood on the verandah for a second, trembling with wetness and emotion. Then he looked around the company like a bull at bay, and walked dripping down the steps and out of the garden. Pran was too taken aback even to apologize. With indignant dignity the great pink figure made its way out of the gate and disappeared along the road.

Maan looked around at the assembled company for approval. Savita avoided looking at him, and everyone else was quiet and subdued, and Maan felt that for some reason he was in the doghouse again.

2.2

Dressed in a fresh, clean kurta-pyjama after a long bath, happy under the influence of bhang and a warm afternoon, Maan had gone to sleep back in Prem Nivas. He dreamed an unusual dream: he was about to catch a train to Banaras to meet his fiancée. He realized that if he did not catch this train he would be imprisoned, but under what charge he did not know. A large body of policemen, from the Inspector-General of Purva Pradesh down to a dozen constables, had formed a cordon around him, and he, together with a number of mud-spattered villagers and about twenty festively dressed women students, was being herded into a compartment. But he had left something behind and was pleading for permission to go and get it. No one was listening to him and he was becoming more and more vehement and upset. And he was falling at the feet of the policemen and the ticket examiner and pleading that he be allowed to go out: he had left something somewhere else, perhaps at home, perhaps on another platform, and it was imperative that he be allowed to go and get it. But now the whistle was blowing and he had been forced on to the train. Some of the women were laughing at him as he got more and more desperate. 'Please let me out,' he kept insisting, but the train had left the station and was picking up speed. He looked up and saw a small red-and-white sign: *To Stop Train Pull Chain. Penalty for Improper Use Rupees 50*. He leapt on to a berth. The villagers tried to stop him as they saw what he was about to do, but he struggled against them and grabbed hold of the chain and pulled it down with all his might. But it had no effect. The train kept gathering speed, and now the women were laughing even more openly at him. 'I've left something there,' he kept repeating, pointing in the general direction from which they had come, as if somehow the train would listen to his explanation and consent to stop. He took out his wallet and begged the ticket examiner: 'Here is fifty rupees. Just stop the train. I beg you—turn it back. I don't mind going to jail.' But the man kept examining everyone else's ticket and shrugging off Maan as if he was a harmless madman.

Maan woke up, sweating, and was relieved to return to the familiar objects of his room in Prem Nivas—the stuffed chair and the overhead fan and the red rug and the five or six paperback thrillers.

Quickly dismissing the dream from his mind, he went to wash his face. But as he looked at his startled expression in the mirror a picture of the women in the dream came vividly back to him. Why were they laughing at me? he asked himself. Was the laughter unkind . . .? It was just a dream, he went on, reassuringly. But though he kept splashing water on his face, he could not get the notion out of his head that there was an explanation, and that it lay just beyond his reach. He closed his eyes to recapture something of the dream once more, but it was all extremely vague now, and only his unease, the sense that he had left something behind, remained. The faces of the women, the villagers, the ticket collector, the policemen, had all been washed away. What could I have left behind? he wondered. Why were they laughing at me?

From somewhere in the house he could hear his father calling sharply: 'Maan, Maan—are you awake? The guests will start arriving for the concert in half an hour.' He did not answer and looked at himself in the mirror. Not a bad face, he thought: lively, fresh, strong-featured, but balding slightly at the temples—which struck him as being a bit unfair, considering that he was only twenty-five. A few minutes later a servant was sent to inform him that his father wished to see him in the courtyard. Maan asked the servant if his sister Veena had arrived yet, and heard that she and her family had come and gone. Veena had in fact come to his room but, finding him asleep, had not let her son Bhaskar disturb him.

Maan frowned, yawned, and went to the clothes' cupboard. He wasn't interested in guests and concerts and he wanted to go to sleep again, dreamlessly this time. That was how he usually spent the evening of Holi when he was in Banaras—sleeping off his bhang.

Downstairs the guests had started coming in. They were most of them dressed in new clothes and, apart from a little red under the nails and in the hair, were not outwardly coloured by the morning's revels. But they were all in excellent humour, and smiling, not just from the effect of the bhang. Mahesh Kapoor's Holi concerts were an annual ritual, and had been going on at Prem Nivas for as long as anyone could remember. His father and grandfather had hosted them as well, and the only years that anyone could remember that they had not been held were when their host had been in jail.

Saeeda Bai Firozabadi was the singer tonight, as she had been for the last two years. She lived not far from Prem Nivas, came from a family of singers and courtesans, and had a fine, rich, and powerfully emotional voice. She was a woman of about thirty-five, but her fame as a singer had already spread outwards from Brahmpur and nowadays she was called for recitals as far away as Bombay and Calcutta. Many of Mahesh Kapoor's guests this evening had come not so much to enjoy their host's—or, more accurately, their unobtrusive hostess's—excellent hospitality as to listen to Saeeda Bai. Maan, who had spent his previous two Holis in Banaras, knew of her fame but had not heard her sing.

Rugs and white sheets were spread over the semi-circular courtyard, which was bounded by whitewashed rooms and open corridors along the curve, and was open to the garden on the straight side. There was no stage, no microphone, no visible separation of the singer's area from the audience. There were no chairs, just pillows and bolsters to lean on, and a few potted plants around the edge of the sitting area. The first few guests were standing around sipping fruit juice or thandai and nibbling kababs or nuts or traditional Holi sweets. Mahesh Kapoor stood greeting his guests as they came into the courtyard, but he was waiting for Maan to come down to relieve him so that he could spend a little time talking to some of his guests instead of merely exchanging perfunctory pleasantries with all of them. If he doesn't come down in five minutes, said Mahesh Kapoor to himself, I'll go upstairs and shake him awake myself. He may as well be in Banaras for all his usefulness. Where is the boy? The car's already been sent for Saeeda Bai.

2.3

The car had in fact been sent for Saeeda Bai and her musicians more than half an hour ago, and Mahesh Kapoor was just beginning to be concerned.

Most of the audience had by now sat down, but some were still standing around and talking. Saeeda Bai was known on occasion to have committed to sing somewhere and then simply gone off on an impulse somewhere else—perhaps to visit an old or a new flame, or to see a relative, or even to sing to a small circle of friends. She behaved very much to suit her own inclinations. This policy, or rather tendency, could have done her a great deal of harm professionally if her voice and her manner had not been as captivating as they were. There was even a mystery to her irresponsibility if seen in a certain light. This light had begun to dim for Mahesh Kapoor, however, when he heard a buzz of muted exclamation from the door: Saeeda Bai and her three accompanists had finally arrived.

She looked stunning. If she had not sung a word all evening but had kept smiling at familiar faces and looking appreciatively around the room, pausing whenever she saw a handsome man or a good-looking (if modern) woman, that would have been enough for most of the men present. But very shortly she made her way to the open side of the courtyard—the part bordering the garden—and sat down near her harmonium, which a servant of the house had carried from the car. She moved the pallu of her silk sari further forward over her head: it tended to slip down, and one of her most charming gestures—to be repeated throughout the evening—was to adjust her sari to ensure that her head was not left uncovered. The musicians—a tabla player, a sarangi player, and a man who strummed the tanpura—sat down and started tuning their instruments as she pressed down a black key with a heavily ringed right hand, gently forcing air through the bellows with an equally bejewelled left. The tabla player used a small silver hammer to tauten the leather straps on his right-hand drum, the sarangi player adjusted his tuning pegs and bowed a few phrases on the strings. The audience adjusted itself and found places for new arrivals. Several boys, some as young as six, sat down near their fathers or uncles. There was an air of pleasant expectancy. Shallow bowls filled with rose and jasmine petals were passed around: those who, like Imtiaz, were still somewhat high on bhang, lingered delightedly over their enhanced fragrance.

Upstairs on the balcony two of the (less modern) women looked down through the slits in a cane screen and discussed Saeeda Bai's dress, ornament, face, manner, antecedents and voice.

'Nice sari, but nothing special. She always wears Banarasi silk. Red tonight. Last year it was green. Stop and go.'

'Look at that zari work in the sari.'

'Very flashy, very flashy—but I suppose all that is necessary in her profession, poor thing.'

'I wouldn't say "poor thing". Look at her jewels. That heavy gold necklace with the enamel work—'

'It comes down a bit too low for my taste—'

'—well, anyway, they say it was given to her by the Sitagarh people!'

'Oh.'

'And many of those rings too, I should think. She's quite a favourite of the Nawab of Sitagarh. They say he's quite a lover of music.'

'And of music-makers?'

'Naturally. Now she's greeting Maheshji and his son Maan. He looks very pleased with himself. Is that the Governor he's—'

'Yes, yes, all these Congress-wallahs are the same. They talk about simplicity and plain living, and then they invite this kind of person to the house to entertain their friends.'

'Well, she's not a dancer or anything like that.'

'No, but you can't deny what she is!'

'But your husband has come as well.'

'My husband!'

The two ladies—one the wife of an ear, nose and throat specialist, one the wife of an important middleman in the shoe trade—looked at each other in exasperated resignation at the ways of men.

'She's exchanging greetings with the Governor now. Look at him grinning. What a fat little man—but they say he's very capable.'

'Aré, what does a Governor have to do except snip a few ribbons here and there and enjoy the luxuries of Government House? Can you hear what she's saying?'

'No.'

'Every time she shakes her head the diamond on her nose-pin flashes. It's like the headlight of a car.'

'A car that has seen many passengers in its time.'

'What time? She's only thirty-five. She's guaranteed for many more miles. And all those rings. No wonder she loves doing adaab to anyone she sees.'

'Diamonds and sapphires mainly, though I can't see clearly from here. What a large diamond that is on her right hand—'

'No, that's a white something—I was going to say a white sapphire, but it isn't that—I was told it was even more expensive than a diamond, but I can't remember what they call it.'

'Why does she need to wear all those bright glass bangles among the gold ones. They look a bit cheap!'

'Well, she's not called Firozabadi for nothing. Even if her forefathers—her foremothers—don't come from Firozabad, at least her glass bangles do. Oh-hoh, look at the eyes she's making at the young men!'

'Shameless.'

'That poor young man doesn't know where to look.'

'Who is he?'

'Dr Durrani's younger son, Hashim. He's just eighteen.'

'Hmm. . . .'

'Very good-looking. Look at him blush.'

'Blush! All these Muslim boys might look innocent, but they are lascivious in their hearts, let me tell you. When we used to live in Karachi—'

But at this point Saeeda Bai Firozabadi, having exchanged salutations with various members of the audience, having spoken to her musicians in a low tone, having placed a paan in the corner of her right cheek, and having coughed twice to clear her throat, began to sing.

2.4

Only a few words had emerged from that lovely throat when the 'wah! wahs!' and other appreciative comments of the audience elicited an acknowledging smile from Saeeda Bai. Lovely she certainly was, and yet in what did her loveliness lie? Most of the men there would have been hard-pressed to explain it; the women sitting above might have been more perceptive. She was no more than pleasing-looking, but she had all the airs of the distinguished courtesan—the small marks of favour, the tilt of the head, the flash of the nose-pin, a delightful mixture of directness and circuitousness in her attentions to those whom she was attracted by, a knowledge of Urdu poetry, especially of the ghazal, that was by no means viewed as shallow even in an audience of cognoscenti. But more than all this, and more than her clothes and jewels and even her exceptional natural talent and musical training, was a touch of heartache in her voice. Where it had come from, no one knew for sure, though rumours about her past were common enough in Brahmpur. Even the women could not say that this sadness was a device. She seemed somehow to be both bold and vulnerable, and it was this combination that was irresistible.

It being Holi, she began her recital with a few Holi songs. Saeeda Bai Firozabadi was Muslim, but sang these happy descriptions of young Krishna playing Holi with the milkmaids of his foster-father's village with such charm and energy that one would have had to be convinced that she saw the scene before her own eyes. The little boys in the audience looked at her wonderingly. Even Savita, whose first Holi this was at her parents-in-law's house, and who had come more out of duty than from the expectation of pleasure, began to enjoy herself.

Mrs Rupa Mehra, torn between the need to protect her younger daughter and the inappropriateness of one of her generation, particularly a widow, forming a part of the downstairs audience, had (with a strict admonition to Pran to keep an eye on Lata) disappeared upstairs. She was looking through a gap in the cane screen and saying to Mrs Mahesh Kapoor, 'In my time, no women would have been allowed in the courtyard for such an evening.' It was a little unfair of Mrs Rupa Mehra to make such an objection known to her quiet, much-put-upon hostess, who had in fact spoken about this very matter to her husband, and had been impatiently overruled by him on the grounds that the times were changing.

People came in and out of the courtyard during the recital, and, as Saeeda Bai's eye caught a movement somewhere in the audience, she acknowledged the new guest with a gesture of her hand that broke the line of her self-accompaniment on the harmonium. But the mournful bowed strings of the sarangi were more than a sufficient shadow to her voice, and she often turned to the player with a look of appreciation for some particularly fine imitation or improvisation. Most of her attention, however, was devoted to young Hashim Durrani, who sat in the front row and blushed beetroot whenever she broke off singing to make some pointed remark or address some casual couplet towards him. Saeeda Bai was notorious for choosing a single person in the audience early in the evening and addressing all her songs to that one person—he would become for her the cruel one, the slayer, the hunter, the executioner and so on—the anchor, in fact, for her ghazals.

Saeeda Bai enjoyed most of all singing the ghazals of Mir and Ghalib, but she also had a taste for Vali Dakkani—and for Mast, whose poetry was not particularly distinguished, but who was a great local favourite because he had spent much of his unhappy life in Brahmpur, reciting many of his ghazals for the first time in the Barsaat Mahal for the culture-stricken Nawab of Brahmpur before his incompetent, bankrupt, and heirless kingdom was annexed by the British. So her first ghazal was one of Mast's, and no sooner had the first phrase been sung than the enraptured audience burst into a roar of appreciation.

'I do not stoop, yet find my collar torn . . .' she began, and half-closed her eyes.

> 'I do not stoop, yet find my collar torn.
> The thorns were here, beneath my feet, not there.'

'Ah,' said Mr Justice Maheshwari helplessly, his head vibrating in ecstasy on his plump neck. Saeeda Bai continued:

> 'Can I be blameless when no voice will blame
> The hunter who has caught me in this snare?'

Here Saeeda Bai shot a half-melting, half-accusing look at the poor eighteen-year-old. He looked down immediately, and one of his friends nudged him and repeated delightedly, 'Can you be blameless?' which embarrassed him yet further.

Lata looked at the young fellow with sympathy, and at Saeeda Bai with fascination. How can she do this? she thought, admiring and slightly horrified—she's just moulding their feelings like putty, and all those men can do is grin and groan! And Maan's the worst of the lot! Lata liked more serious classical music as a rule. But now she—like her sister—found herself enjoying the ghazal too, and also—though it was strange to her—the transformed, romantic atmosphere of Prem Nivas. She was glad her mother was upstairs.

Meanwhile, Saeeda Bai, extending an arm to the guests, sang on:

> 'The pious people shun the tavern door—
> But I need courage to outstare their stare.'

'Wah! wah!' cried Imtiaz loudly from the back. Saeeda Bai graced him with a dazzling smile, then frowned as if startled. However, gathering herself together, she continued:

> 'After a wakeful night outside that lane,
> The breeze of morning stirs the scented air.

> Interpretation's Gate is closed and barred
> But I go through and neither know nor care.'

'And neither know nor care,' was sung simultaneously by twenty voices.

Saeeda Bai rewarded their enthusiasm with a tilt of her head. But the unorthodoxy of this couplet was outdone by that of the next:

> 'I kneel within the Kaaba of my heart
> And to my idol raise my face in prayer.'

The audience sighed and groaned; her voice almost broke at the word 'prayer'; one would have had to be an unfeeling idol oneself to have disapproved.

> 'Though blinded by the sun I see, O Mast,
> The moonlight of the face, the clouds of hair.'

Maan was so affected by Saeeda Bai's recitation of this final couplet that he raised his arms helplessly towards her. Saeeda Bai coughed to clear her throat, and looked at him enigmatically. Maan felt hot and shivery all over, and was speechless for a while, but drummed a tabla beat on the head of one of his rustic nephews, aged seven.

'What will you listen to next, Maheshji?' Saeeda Bai asked his father. 'What a grand audience you always provide in your house. And so knowledgeable that I sometimes feel myself redundant. I need only sing two words and you gentlemen complete the rest of the ghazal.'

There were cries of 'No, no!', 'What are you saying?' and 'We are your mere shadows, Saeeda Begum!'

'I know that it is not because of my voice but through your grace—and that of the one above—' she added, 'that I am here tonight. I see your son is as appreciative of my poor efforts as you have been for many years. Such things must run in the blood. Your father, may he rest in peace, was full of kindness to my mother. And now I am the recipient of your graciousness.'

'Who has graced whom?' responded Mahesh Kapoor gallantly.

Lata looked at him in some surprise. Maan caught her eye and winked—and Lata could not help smiling back. Now that he was a relative, she felt much easier with him. Her mind flashed back to his behaviour this morning, and again a smile curled up at the corners of her mouth. Lata would never be able to hear Professor Mishra lecturing again without seeing him emerge from the tub as wet and pink and helpless as a baby.

'But some young men are so silent,' Saeeda Bai continued, 'that they might as well themselves be idols in temples. Perhaps they have opened their veins so often that they have no blood left. Hanh?' She laughed delightfully.

> 'Why should my heart not be tied to him?' she quoted—
> 'Today he is dressed in colourful clothes.'

Young Hashim looked down guiltily at his blue, embroidered kurta. But Saeeda Bai continued unmercifully:

> 'How can I praise his fine taste in dress?
> In appearance he is like a prince.'

Since much Urdu poetry, like much Persian and Arabic poetry before it, had been addressed by poets to young men, Saeeda Bai found it mischievously easy to find such references to male dress and demeanour as would make it clear whom she was aiming her shafts at. Hashim might blush and burn and bite his lower lip but her quiver was not likely to run out of couplets. She looked at him and recited:

> 'Your red lips are full of nectar.
> How rightly you have been named Amrit Lal!'

Hashim's friends were by now convulsed with laughter. But perhaps Saeeda Bai realized that he could not take much more amorous baiting for the moment, and she graciously permitted him a little respite. By now the audience felt bold enough to make its own suggestions, and after Saeeda Bai had indulged her taste for one of the more abstruse and referential ghazals of Ghalib—a strongly intellectual taste for so sensuous a singer—someone in the audience suggested one of his simpler favourites, 'Where have those meetings and those partings gone?'

Saeeda Bai assented by turning to the sarangi and tabla players and murmuring a few words. The sarangi began to play an introduction to the slow, melancholy, nostalgic ghazal, written by Ghalib not in his old age but when he was not much older than the singer herself. But Saeeda Bai invested each of its questioning couplets with such bitterness and sweetness that even the hearts of the oldest in the audience were moved. When they joined in at the end of a familiar sentimental line it was as if they were asking a question of themselves rather than displaying their knowledge to their neighbours. And this attentiveness brought forth a yet deeper response from the singer, so that even the difficult last couplet, where Ghalib reverts to his metaphysical abstractions, climaxed rather than ebbed away from the ghazal as a whole.

After this wonderful rendition, the audience was eating out of the palm of Saeeda Bai's hand. Those who had planned to leave at the latest by eleven o'clock found themselves unable to tear themselves away, and soon it was past midnight.

Maan's little nephew had gone off to sleep in his lap, as had many of the other young boys, and they had been taken off to bed by the servants. Maan himself, who had been in love often enough in the past and was therefore prone to a sort of cheerful nostalgia, was overwhelmed by Saeeda Bai's last ghazal, and popped a thoughtful cashew nut into his mouth. What could he do?—he felt he was falling irresistibly in love with her. Saeeda Bai had now reverted to her playfulness with Hashim, and Maan felt a little jab of jealousy as she tried to get a response out of the boy. When

> 'The tulip and the rose, how do they compare with you?
> They are no more than incomplete metaphors'

produced no result beyond a restless shifting in his place, she attempted the bolder couplet:

> 'Your beauty was that which once bewitched the world—
> Even after the first down came on your cheeks it was a wonder.'

This found its mark. There were two puns here, one mild and one not so mild: 'world' and 'wonder' were the same word—aalam—and 'the first down' could possibly be taken as meaning 'a letter'. Hashim, who had a very light down on his face, tried his best to act as if 'khat' simply meant letter, but it cost him a great deal of discomfiture. He looked around at his father for support in his suffering—his own friends were less than no help, having long ago decided to join in teasing him—but the absent-minded Dr Durrani was half-asleep somewhere at the back. One of his friends rubbed his palm gently along Hashim's cheek and sighed strickenly. Blushing,

Hashim got up to leave the courtyard and take a walk in the garden. He was only half on his feet when Saeeda Bai fired a barrel of Ghalib at him:

> 'At the mere mention of my name in the gathering she got up to go. . . .'

Hashim, almost in tears, did adaab to Saeeda Bai, and walked out of the courtyard. Lata, her eyes shining with quiet excitement, felt rather sorry for him; but soon she too had to leave with her mother and Savita and Pran.

2.5

Maan, on the other hand, did not feel at all sorry for his lily-livered rival. He came forward, and with a nod to the left and the right, and a respectful salutation to the singer, seated himself in Hashim's place. Saeeda Bai, happy to have a prepossessing if not quite so sprig-like a volunteer as her source of inspiration for the rest of the evening, smiled at him and said:

> 'By no means forsake constancy, O heart,
> For love without constancy has weak foundations.'

To which Maan replied instantly and stoutly:

> 'Wherever Dagh has sat down he has sat down.
> Others may quit your assembly, not he!'

This met with laughter from the audience, but Saeeda Bai decided to have the last word by repaying him in his own poet:

> 'Dagh is ogling and peeping once more.
> He will trip up and get ensnared somewhere.'

At this just response the audience burst into spontaneous applause. Maan was as delighted as anyone that Saeeda Bai Firozabadi had trumped his ace or, as she would have put it, tenned his nine. She was laughing as hard as anyone, and so were her accompanists, the fat tabla player and his lean counterpart on the sarangi. After a while, Saeeda Bai raised her hand for silence and said, 'I hope that half that applause was intended for my witty young friend here.'

Maan replied with playful contrition: 'Ah, Saeeda Begum, I had the temerity to banter with you but—all my arrangements were in vain.'

The audience laughed again, and Saeeda Bai Firozabadi rewarded this quotation from Mir with a lovely rendition of the appropriate ghazal:

'All my arrangements were in vain, no drug could cure my malady.
It was an ailment of my heart that made a final end of me.

My term of youth I passed in tears, in age I closed my eyes at last;
That is: I lay awake long nights till dawn and sleep came finally.'

Maan looked at her, bewitched, entranced and enraptured. What would it be like to lie awake long nights till dawn, listening to her voice in his ear?

'We who were helpless were accused of independent thought and deed.
They did whatever they desired, and us they smeared with calumny.

Here in this world of darkness and of light this is my only part:
To somehow pass from day to night and night to day in misery.

Why do you ask what has become of Mir's religion, his Islam?
Wearing the brahmin's mark he haunts the temples of idolatry.'

The night continued with alternating banter and music. It was very late now; the audience of a hundred had thinned to a dozen. But Saeeda Bai was now so deep in the flow of music that those who remained, remained spellbound. They moved forward into a more intimate group. Maan did not know whether he was held there more by his ears or by his eyes. From time to time Saeeda Bai paused in her singing and talked to the surviving faithful. She dismissed the sarangi and tanpura players. Finally she even dismissed her tabla player, who could hardly keep his eyes open. Her voice and the harmonium were all that were left, and they provided enchantment enough. It was near dawn when she herself yawned and rose.

Maan looked at her with half-longing, half-laughing eyes. 'I'll arrange for the car,' he said.

'I'll walk in the garden till then,' said Saeeda Bai. 'This is the most beautiful time of night. Just have this'—she indicated the harmonium—'and the other things—sent back to my place tomorrow morning. Well, then,' she continued to the five or six people left in the courtyard:

> 'Now Mir takes his leave from the temple of idols—
> We shall meet again . . .'

Maan completed the couplet: '. . . if it be God's will.'

He looked at her for an acknowledging nod, but she had turned towards the garden already.

Saeeda Bai Firozabadi, suddenly weary 'of all this' (but what was 'all this'?) strolled for a minute or two through the garden of Prem Nivas. She touched the glossy leaves of a pomelo tree. The harsingar was no longer in bloom, but a jacaranda flower dropped downwards in the darkness. She looked up and smiled to herself a little sadly. Everything was quiet: not even a watchman, not even a dog. A few favourite lines from a minor poet, Minai, came to her mind, and she recited, rather than sang, them aloud:

> 'The meeting has dispersed; the moths
>   Bid farewell to the candlelight.
> Departure's hour is on the sky.
>   Only a few stars mark the night. . . .'

She coughed a little—for the night had got chilly all of a sudden—wrapped her light shawl more closely around her, and waited for someone to escort her to her own house, also in Pasand Bagh, no more than a few minutes away.

2.6

The day after Saeeda Bai sang at Prem Nivas was Sunday. The light-hearted spirit of Holi was still in the air. Maan could not get her out of his mind.

He wandered about in a daze. He arranged for her harmonium to be sent on to her house early in the afternoon, and was tempted to get into the car himself. But that was hardly the time to visit Saeeda Bai—who had, anyway, given him no indication that she would be pleased to see him again.

Maan had nothing as such to do. That was part of his problem. In Banaras there was business of a kind to keep him busy; in Brahmpur he had always felt himself to be at a loose end. He didn't really mind, though. Reading was not something he enjoyed much, but he did like wandering around with friends. Perhaps he should visit Firoz, he thought.

Then, thinking of the ghazals of Mast, he jumped into a tonga, and told the tonga-wallah to take him to the Barsaat Mahal. It had been years since Maan had been there, and the thought of seeing it appealed to him today.

The tonga passed through the green residential 'colonies' of the eastern part of Brahmpur, and came to Nabiganj, the commercial street that marked the end of spaciousness and the start of clutter and confusion. Old Brahmpur lay beyond it, and, almost at the western end of the old town, on the Ganga itself, stood the beautiful grounds and the still more beautiful marble structure of the Barsaat Mahal.

Nabiganj was the fashionable shopping street where the quality of Brahmpur were to be seen strolling up and down of an evening. At the moment, in the heat of the afternoon, there were not many shoppers about, and only a few cars and tongas and bicycles. The signs of Nabiganj were painted in English, and the prices matched the signs. Bookshops like the Imperial Book Depot, well-stocked general stores such as Dowling & Snapp (now under Indian management), fine tailors such as Magourian's where Firoz had all his clothes (from suits to achkans) made, the Praha shoe shop, an elegant jeweller's, restaurants and coffee houses such as the Red Fox, Chez Yasmeen, and the Blue Danube, and two cinema halls—Manorma Talkies (which showed Hindi films) and the Rialto (which leaned towards Hollywood and Ealing): each of these places had played some minor or major role in one or another of Maan's romances. But today, as the tonga trotted through the broad street, Maan paid them no attention. The tonga turned off on to a smaller road, and almost immediately on to a yet smaller one, and they were now in a different world.

There was just enough room for the tonga to get through among the bullock-carts, rickshaws, cycles and pedestrians who thronged both the road and the pavement—which they shared with barbers plying their trade out of doors, fortune tellers, flimsy tea-stalls, vegetable-stands, monkey-trainers, ear-cleaners, pickpockets, stray cattle, the odd sleepy policeman sauntering along in faded khaki, sweat-soaked men carrying impossible loads of copper, steel rods, glass or scrap paper on their backs as they yelled 'Look out! Look out!' in voices that somehow pierced through the din, shops of brassware and cloth (the owners attempting with shouts and gestures to entice uncertain shoppers in), the small carved stone entrance of the Tinny Tots (English Medium) School which opened out on to the courtyard of the reconverted haveli of a bankrupt aristocrat, and beggars—young and old, aggressive and meek, leprous, maimed or blinded—who would quietly invade Nabiganj as evening fell, attempting to avoid the police as they worked the queues in front of the cinema halls. Crows cawed, small boys in rags rushed around on errands (one balancing six small dirty glasses of tea on a cheap tin tray as he weaved through the crowd), monkeys chattered in and bounded about a great shivering-leafed pipal tree and tried to raid unwary customers as they left the well-guarded fruit-stand, women shuffled along in anonymous burqas or bright saris, with or without their menfolk, a few students from the university lounging around a chaat-stand shouted at each other from a foot away either out of habit or in order to be heard, mangy dogs snapped and were kicked, skeletal cats mewed and were stoned, and flies settled everywhere: on heaps of foetid, rotting rubbish, on the uncovered sweets at the sweetseller's in whose huge curved pans of ghee sizzled delicious jalebis, on the faces of the sari-clad but not the burqa-clad women, and on the horse's nostrils as he shook his blinkered head and tried to forge his way through Old Brahmpur in the direction of the Barsaat Mahal.

Maan's thoughts were suddenly interrupted by the sight of Firoz standing by a pavement stall. He halted the tonga at once and got down.

'Firoz, you'll have a long life—I was just thinking about you. Well, half an hour ago!'

Firoz said that he was just wandering about, and had decided to buy a walking stick.

'For yourself or for your father?'

'For myself.'

'A man who has to buy himself a walking stick in his twenties might not have such a long life after all,' said Maan.

Firoz, after leaning at various angles on various sticks, decided upon one and, without haggling about the price, bought it.

'And you, what are you doing here? Paying a visit to Tarbuz ka Bazaar?' he asked.

'Don't be disgusting,' said Maan cheerfully. Tarbuz ka Bazaar was the street of singing girls and prostitutes.

'Oh, but I forgot,' said Firoz slyly: 'Why should you consort with mere melons when you can taste the peaches of Samarkand?'

Maan frowned.

'What further news of Saeeda Bai?' continued Firoz, who, from the back of the audience, had enjoyed the previous night. Though he had left by midnight, he had sensed that, Maan's engagement notwithstanding, romance was once again entering his friend's life. More, perhaps, than anyone else, he knew and understood Maan.

'What do you expect?' asked Maan, a little glumly. 'Things will happen the way they will. She didn't even allow me to escort her back.'

This was quite unlike Maan, thought Firoz, who had very rarely seen his friend depressed. 'So where are you going?' he asked him.

'To the Barsaat Mahal.'

'To end it all?' inquired Firoz tenderly. The parapet of the Barsaat Mahal faced the Ganga and was the venue of a number of romantic suicides every year.

'Yes, yes, to end it all,' said Maan impatiently. 'Now tell me, Firoz, what do you advise?'

Firoz laughed. 'Say that again. I can't believe it,' he said. 'Maan Kapoor, beau of Brahmpur, at whose feet young women of good families, heedless of reputation, hasten to fling themselves like bees on a lotus, seeks the advice of the steely and stainless Firoz on how to proceed in a matter of the heart. You're not asking for my legal advice, are you?'

'If you're going to act like that—' began Maan, disgruntled. Suddenly a thought struck him. 'Firoz, why is Saeeda Bai called Firozabadi? I thought she came from these parts.'

Firoz replied: 'Well, her people did in fact originally come from Firozabad. But that's all history. In fact her mother Mohsina Bai settled in Tarbuz ka Bazaar, and Saeeda Bai was brought up in this part of the city.' He pointed his stick towards the disreputable quarter. 'But naturally Saeeda Bai herself, now that she's made good and lives in Pasand Bagh—and breathes the same air as you and I—doesn't like people to talk about her local origins.'

Maan mused over this for a few moments. 'How do you know so much about her?' he asked, puzzled.

'Oh, I don't know,' said Firoz, waving away a fly. 'This sort of information just floats around in the air.' Not reacting to Maan's look of astonishment, he went on, 'But I must be off. My father wants me to meet someone boring who's coming to tea.' Firoz leapt into Maan's tonga. 'It's too crowded to ride a tonga through Old Brahmpur; you're better off on foot,' he told Maan, and drove off.

Maan wandered along, mulling—but not for long—over what Firoz had said. He hummed a bit of the ghazal that had embedded itself in his mind, stopped to buy a paan (he preferred the spicier, darker green leaves of the desi paan to the paler Banarasi), manoeuvred his way across the road through a crowd of cycles, rickshaws, pushcarts, men and cattle, and found himself in Misri Mandi, near a small vegetable-stall, close to where his sister Veena lived.

Feeling guilty for having been asleep when she came to Prem Nivas the previous afternoon, Maan decided impulsively to visit her—and his brother-in-law Kedarnath and nephew Bhaskar. Maan was very fond of Bhaskar and liked throwing arithmetical problems at him like a ball to a performing seal.

As he entered the residential areas of Misri Mandi, the alleys became narrower and cooler and somewhat quieter, though there were still plenty of people getting about from place to place and others just lounging around or playing chess on the ledge near the Radhakrishna Temple, whose walls were still bright with the stains of Holi colours. The strip of bright sunlight above his head was now thin and unoppressive, and there were fewer flies. After turning into a still narrower alley, just three feet across, and avoiding a urinating cow, he arrived at his sister's house.

It was a very narrow house: three storeys and a flat rooftop, with about a room and a half on each storey and a central grating in the middle of the stairwell that allowed light from the sky all the way through to the bottom. Maan entered through the unlocked door and saw old Mrs Tandon, Veena's mother-in-law, cooking something in a pan. Old Mrs Tandon disapproved of Veena's taste for music, and it was because of her that the family had had to come back the previous evening without listening to Saeeda Bai. She always gave Maan the shivers; and so, after a perfunctory greeting, he went up the stairs, and soon found Veena and Kedarnath on the roof—playing chaupar in the shade of a trellis and evidently deep in an argument.

2.7

Veena was a few years older than Maan, and she took after her mother in shape—she was short and a bit dumpy. When Maan appeared on the roof, her voice had been raised, and her plump, cheerful face was frowning, but when she saw Maan she beamed at him. Then she remembered something and frowned again.

'So you've come to apologize. Good! And not a moment too soon. We were all very annoyed with you yesterday. What kind of brother are you, sleeping for hours on end when you know that we're bound to visit Prem Nivas?'

'But I thought you'd stay for the singing—' said Maan.

'Yes, yes,' said Veena nodding her head. 'I'm quite sure you thought of all that when you dozed off. It had nothing to do with bhang, for instance. And it simply slipped your mind that we had to get Kedarnath's mother home before the music began. At least Pran came early and met us at Prem Nivas, with Savita and his mother-in-law and Lata—'

'Oh, Pran, Pran, Pran—' said Maan in exasperation. 'He's always the hero and I'm always the villain.'

'That's not true, don't dramatize things,' said Veena, thinking of Maan as a small boy trying to shoot pigeons with a catapult in the garden and claiming to be an archer in the Mahabharata. 'It's just that you have no sense of responsibility.'

'Anyway, what were you quarrelling about when I came up the stairs? And where's Bhaskar?' asked Maan, thinking of his father's recent remarks and trying to change the subject.

'He's out with his friends flying kites. Yes, he was annoyed as well. He wanted to wake you up. You'll have to have dinner with us today to make up.'

'Oh—uh—' said Maan undecidedly, wondering whether he might not risk visiting Saeeda Bai's house in the evening. He coughed. 'But what were you quarrelling about?'

'We weren't quarrelling,' said the mild Kedarnath, smiling at Maan. He was in his thirties, but already greying. A worried optimist, he, unlike Maan, had—if anything—too strong a sense of his responsibilities, and the difficulties of starting from scratch in Brahmpur after Partition had aged him prematurely. When he was not on the road somewhere in south India drumming up orders, he was working till late at night in his shop in Misri Mandi. It was in the evenings that business was conducted there, when middlemen like him bought baskets of shoes from the shoemakers. His afternoons, though, were fairly free.

'No, not quarrelling, not quarrelling at all. Just arguing about chaupar, that's all,' said Veena hastily, throwing the cowrie-shells down once more, counting her tally, and moving her pieces forward on the cross-shaped cloth board.

'Yes, yes, I'm quite sure,' said Maan.

He sat down on the rug and looked around at the flowerpots filled with leafy plants, which Mrs Mahesh Kapoor had contributed to her daughter's roof garden. Veena's saris were hanging up to dry on one side of the roof, and there were bright splashes of Holi colour all over the terrace. Beyond the roof a jumble of rooftops, minarets, towers and temple-tops stretched out as far as the railway station in 'New' Brahmpur. A few paper kites, pink, green and yellow, like the colours of Holi, fought each other in the cloudless sky.

'Don't you want something to drink?' asked Veena quickly. 'I'll get you some sherbet—or will you have tea? I'm afraid we don't have any thandai,' she added gratuitously.

'No, thank you. . . . But you can answer my question. What was the debate about?' demanded Maan. 'Let me guess. Kedarnath wants to keep a second wife, and he naturally wants your consent.'

'Don't be stupid,' said Veena, a little sharply. 'I want a second child and I naturally want his consent. Oh!' she exclaimed, realizing her indiscretion and looking at her husband. 'I didn't mean to—anyway, he's my brother—we can ask his advice, surely.'

'But you don't want my mother's advice in the matter, do you?' countered Kedarnath.

'Well, it's too late now,' said Maan genially. 'What do you want a second child for? Isn't Bhaskar enough?'

'We can't afford a second child,' said Kedarnath, with his eyes closed—a habit that Veena still found bothersome. 'Not at the moment, at any rate. My business is—well, you know how it is. And now there's the possibility of a shoemakers' strike.' He opened his eyes. 'And Bhaskar is so bright that we want to send him to the very best schools. And they don't come cheap.'

'Yes, we wish he was stupid, but unfortunately—'

'Veena is being witty as usual,' said Kedarnath. 'Just two days before Holi she reminded me that it was difficult to make ends meet, what with the rent and the rise in food prices and everything. And the cost of her music lessons and my mother's medicines and Bhaskar's special maths books and my cigarettes. Then she said that we had to count the rupees, and now she's saying that we should have another child because every grain of rice it will eat has already been marked with its name. The logic of women! She was born into a family of three children, so she thinks that having three children is a law of nature. Can you imagine how we'll survive if they're all as bright as Bhaskar?'

Kedarnath, who was usually quite henpecked, was putting up a good fight.

'Only the first child is bright as a rule,' said Veena. 'I guarantee that my next two will be as stupid as Pran and Maan.' She resumed her sewing.

Kedarnath smiled, picked up the speckled cowries in his scarred palm, and threw them on to the board. Normally he was a very polite man and would have given Maan his full attention, but chaupar was chaupar, and it was almost impossible to stop playing once the game had begun. It was even more addictive than chess. Dinners grew cold in Misri Mandi, guests left, creditors threw tantrums, but the chaupar players pleaded for just one more game. Old Mrs Tandon had once thrown the cloth board and the sinful shells into a disused well in a neighbouring lane, but, despite the family finances, another set had been procured, and the truant couple now played on the roof, even though it was hotter there. In this way they avoided Kedarnath's mother, whose gastric and arthritic problems made climbing stairs difficult. In Lahore, both because of the horizontal geography of the house and because of her role as the confident matriarch of a wealthy and unscattered family, she had exercised tight, even tyrannical, control. Her world had collapsed with the trauma of Partition.

Their conversation was interrupted by a scream of outrage from a neighbouring rooftop. A large, middle-aged woman in a scarlet cotton sari was shouting down from her roof at an invisible adversary:

'They want to suck my blood, it's clear! Neither can I lie down anywhere nor can I sit anywhere in peace. The sound of the thumping of balls is driving me mad. . . . Of course what takes place on the roof can be heard downstairs! You wretched kahars, you useless washers of dishes, can't you keep your children under control?'

Noticing Veena and Kedarnath on their roof, she walked over the connecting rooftops, clambering through a low gap in the far wall. With her piercing voice, wild teeth and large, spreading, sagging breasts, she made a powerful impression on Maan.

After Veena had introduced them, the woman said with a fierce smile: 'Oh, so this is the one who isn't getting married.'

'He's the one,' admitted Veena. She didn't tempt fate by mentioning Maan's tentative engagement to the girl from Banaras.

'But didn't you tell me you'd introduced him to that girl—what's her name, remind me—the one who came here from Allahabad to visit her brother?'

Maan said: 'Amazing how it is with some people. You write "A" and they read "Z".'

'Well, it's quite natural,' said the woman in a predatory manner. 'A young man, a young woman. . . .'

'She was very pretty,' Veena said. 'With eyes like a deer.'

'But she doesn't have her brother's nose—luckily,' added the woman.

'No—it's much finer. And it even quivers a bit like a deer's.'

Kedarnath, despairing of his game of chaupar, got up to go downstairs. He couldn't stand visits from this over-friendly neighbour. Ever since her husband had got a telephone installed in their house, she had become even more self-confident and strident.

'What shall I call you?' Maan asked the woman.

'Bhabhi. Just bhabhi,' said Veena.

'So—how did you like her?' asked the woman.

'Fine,' said Maan.

'Fine?' said the woman, pouncing delightedly on the word.

'I meant, fine that I should call you bhabhi.'

'He's very cunning,' said Veena.

'I'm no less so,' asserted her neighbour. 'You should come here, meet people, meet nice women,' she told Maan. 'What is the charm of living in the colonies? I tell you, when I visit Pasand Bagh or Civil Lines my brain goes dead in four hours. When I return to the lanes of our neighbourhood it starts whirring again. People here care for each other; if someone falls ill the whole neighbourhood asks about them. But it may be difficult to fix you up. You should get a slightly taller girl than average—'

'I'm not concerned about all that,' said Maan, laughing. 'A short one is fine by me.'

'So you don't mind whether she's tall or short, dark or fair, thin or fat, ugly or beautiful?'

'Z for A again,' said Maan, glancing in the direction of her roof. 'By the way, I like your method of drying your blouses.'

The woman gave a short hoot of laughter, which might have been self-deprecatory if it hadn't been so loud. She looked back at the rack-like arrangement of steel on the top of her water tank.

'There's no other place on my roof,' she said. 'You've got lines all over on your side. . . . You know,' continued the woman, off on a tangent, 'marriage is strange. I read in *Star-Gazer* that a girl from Madras, well married, with two children, saw *Hulchul* five times—five times!—and got completely besotted with Daleep Kumar—to the extent that she went off her head. She went down to Bombay, clearly not knowing what she was doing, because she didn't even have his address. Then she found it with the help of one of these filmi fan magazines, took a taxi there, and confronted him with all kinds of mad, obsessed remarks. Eventually he gave her a hundred rupees to help her get back, and threw her out. But she returned.'

'Daleep Kumar!' said Veena, frowning. 'I don't think much of his acting. I think he must have made it all up for publicity.'

'Oh no, no! Have you seen him in *Deedar*? He is amazing! And *Star-Gazer* says he's such a nice man—he would never go after publicity. You must tell Kedarnath to beware of Madrasi women, he spends so much time there, they're very fierce. . . . I hear that they don't even wash their silk saris gently, they just go dhup! dhup! dhup! like washerwomen under the tap—Oh! my milk!' cried the woman in sudden alarm. 'I must go—I hope it hasn't—my husband—' And she rushed off like a great red apparition across the rooftops.

Maan burst out laughing.

'Now I'm off as well,' he said. 'I've had enough of life outside the colonies. My brain's whirring too much.'

'You can't go,' said Veena sternly and sweetly. 'You've just come. They said you played Holi the whole morning with Pran and his professor and Savita and Lata, so you can certainly spend this afternoon with us. And Bhaskar will be very annoyed if he misses you again. You should have seen him yesterday. He looked like a black imp.'

'Will he be at the shop this evening?' asked Maan, coughing a bit.

'Yes. I suppose so. Thinking about the patterns of the shoeboxes. Strange boy,' said Veena.

'Then I'll visit him on my way back.'

'On your way back from where?' asked Veena. 'And aren't you coming for dinner?'

'I'll try—I promise,' said Maan.

'What's wrong with your throat?' asked Veena. 'You've been up till late, haven't you? How late, I wonder? Or is it just from getting soaked at Holi? I'll give you some dushanda to cure it.'

'No—that vile stuff! Take it yourself as a preventative,' exclaimed Maan.

'So—how was the singing? And the singer?' asked Veena.

Maan shrugged so indifferently that Veena got worried.

'Be careful, Maan,' she warned him.

Maan knew his sister too well to try to protest his innocence. Besides, Veena would soon enough hear about his public flirting.

'It's not her that you're going to visit?' asked Veena sharply.

'No—heaven forbid,' said Maan.

'Yes, heaven forbid. So where are you going?'

'To the Barsaat Mahal,' said Maan. 'Come along with me! You remember we used to go there for picnics as children? Come. All you're doing is playing chaupar.'

'So that's how you think I fill my days, do you? Let me tell you, I work almost as hard as Ammaji. Which reminds me, I saw yesterday that they'd chopped the top of the neem tree down, the one you used to climb to get to the upstairs window. It makes a difference to Prem Nivas.'

'Yes, she was very angry,' said Maan, thinking of his mother. 'The Public Works Department were just supposed to trim it to get rid of the vulture's roost, but they hired a contractor who chopped down as much wood as possible and made off with it. But you know Ammaji. All she said was, "What you have done is really not right."'

'If Baoji had been in the least concerned about these matters, he'd have done to that man what he did to that tree,' said Veena. 'There's so little greenery in this part of town that you really learn to appreciate it when you see it. When my friend Priya came to Pran's wedding, the garden was looking so beautiful that she said to me: "I feel as if I've been let out of a cage." She doesn't even have a roof garden, poor thing. And they hardly ever let her out of the house. "Come in the palanquin, leave on the bier": that's the way it is with the daughters-in-law in that house.' Veena looked darkly over the rooftops towards her friend's house in the next neighbourhood. A thought struck her. 'Did Baoji talk to anyone about Pran's job yesterday evening? Doesn't the Governor have something to do with these appointments? In his capacity as Chancellor of the university?'

'If he did I didn't hear him,' said Maan.

'Hmm,' said Veena, not very pleased. 'If I know Baoji, he probably thought about it, and then pushed the thought aside as being unworthy of him. Even we had to wait in line for our turn to get that pitiful compensation for the loss of our business in Lahore. And that too when Ammaji was working day and night in the refugee camps. I sometimes think he cares for nothing but politics. Priya says her father's equally bad. All right, eight o'clock. I'll make your favourite alu paratha.'

'You can bully Kedarnath, but not me,' said Maan with a smile.

'All right, go, go!' said Veena, tossing her head. 'You'd think we were still in Lahore from the amount we get to see you.'

Maan made a propitiatory sound, a tongue-click followed by a half-sigh.

'With all his sales trips, I sometimes feel I have a quarter of a husband,' continued Veena. 'And an eighth of a brother each.' She rolled up the chaupar board. 'When are you returning to Banaras to do an honest day's work?'

'Ah, Banaras,' said Maan with a smile, as if Veena had suggested Saturn. And Veena left it at that.

2.8

It was evening by the time Maan got to the Barsaat Mahal, and the grounds were not crowded. He walked through the arched entrance in the boundary wall, and passed through the outer grounds, a sort of park which was for the most part covered with dry grass and bushes. A few antelope browsed under a large neem tree, bounding lazily away as he approached.

The inner wall was lower, the arched entranceway less imposing, more delicate. Verses from the Quran in black stone and bold geometrical patterns in coloured stone were embedded in its marble facade. Like the outer wall, the inner wall ran along three sides of a rectangle. The fourth side was common to both: a sheer drop from a stone platform—protected only by a balustrade—to the waters of the Ganga below.

Between the inner entrance and the river was the celebrated garden and the small but exquisite palace. The garden itself was a triumph as much of geometry as of horticulture. It was unlikely in fact that the flowers with which it was now planted—other than jasmine and the dark-red, deep-scented Indian rose—were the same as those for which it had been planned more than two centuries ago. What few flowers remained now looked exhausted from the daily heat. But the well-tended, well-watered lawns, the great, shady neem trees dispersed symmetrically about the grounds, and the narrow sandstone strips that divided the flower beds and lawns into octagons and squares provided an island of calm in a troubled and crowded town. Most beautiful of all was the small, perfectly shaped pleasure-palace of the Nawabs of Brahmpur, set in the exact centre of the inner gardens, a filigreed jewel box of white marble, its spirit compounded equally of extravagant dissipation and architectural restraint.

In the days of the Nawabs, peacocks used to roam the grounds, and their raucous voices would on occasion compete with the musical entertainments laid on for those reclining and declining rulers: a performance by dancing girls, a more serious performance of khyaal by a court musician, a poetry competition, a new ghazal by the poet Mast.

The thought of Mast brought the wonder of the previous evening back into Maan's mind. The clear lines of the ghazal, the soft lines of Saeeda Bai's face, her banter, which now seemed to Maan to be both lively and tender, the way she would pull her sari over her head as it threatened to slip off, the special attentions she had granted Maan, all these came back to him as he wandered up and down along the parapet with thoughts very far from suicide. The river breeze was pleasant, and Maan began to feel encouraged by events. He had been wondering whether to stop by Saeeda Bai's house in the evening, and he felt suddenly optimistic.

The great red sky covered the burnished Ganga like an inflamed bowl. On the far shore the sands stretched endlessly away.

As he looked at the river he was struck by a remark he had heard from the mother of his fiancée. She, pious woman, was convinced that on the festival of Ganga Dussehra the obedient river would begin to rise again and would cover on that particular day one of the steps along the ghats of her native Banaras. Maan began to think about his fiancée and her family and became depressed about his engagement, as he usually did when he gave it any thought. His father had arranged it, as he had threatened to do; Maan, taking the path of least resistance, had gone along with it; and now it was an ominous fact of life. He would sooner or later have to get married to her. Maan felt no affection for her—they had hardly met each other except in the company of their families—and he did not really want to think about her. He was much happier thinking about Samia, who was now in Pakistan with her family but who wanted to return to Brahmpur just to visit Maan, or Sarla, the daughter of the former Inspector-General of Police, or any of his other earlier passions. A later flame, however brightly it burned, did not douse an earlier one in Maan's heart. He continued to feel sudden throbs of warmth and goodwill at the thought of almost any of them.

2.9

It was dark by the time Maan walked back into the crowded town, uncertain once again about whether he should try his luck at Saeeda Bai's. He was in Misri Mandi in a few minutes. It was a Sunday, but not a holiday here. The shoe market was full of bustle, light and noise: Kedarnath Tandon's shop was open, as were all the other shops in the arcade—known as the Brahmpur Shoe Mart—that was located just off the main street. The so-called basket-wallahs ran hastily from shop to shop with baskets on their heads, offering their wares to the wholesalers: shoes that they and their families had made during the day and that they would have to sell in order to buy food as well as leather and other materials for their next day's work. These shoemakers, mainly members of the 'untouchable' jatav caste or a few lower-caste Muslims, a large number of whom had remained in Brahmpur after Partition, were gaunt and poorly clad, and many of them looked desperate. The shops were elevated three feet or so above street level to enable them to place their baskets at the edge of the cloth-covered floor for examination by a possible buyer. Kedarnath, for instance, might take a pair of shoes out of a basket submitted for his inspection. If he rejected the basket, the seller would have to run to the next wholesaler—or to one in another arcade. Or Kedarnath might offer a lower price, which the shoemaker might or might not accept. Or Kedarnath might husband his funds by offering the shoemaker the same price but less cash, making up the remainder with a credit note or 'chit' that would be accepted by a discount agent or a seller of raw materials. Even after the shoes were sold, the material for the next day remained to be bought, and the basket-wallahs were virtually forced to sell to someone not too late in the evening, even on unfavourable terms.

Maan did not understand the system, the large turnover of which depended on an effective network of credit in which chits were everything and banks played almost no role. Not that he wanted to understand it; the cloth business in Banaras was dependent on different financial structures. He had merely dropped in for a social chat, a cup of tea, and a chance to meet his nephew. Bhaskar, who was dressed in a white kurta-pyjama like his father, was sitting barefoot on the white cloth spread out on the floor of the shop. Kedarnath would occasionally turn to him and ask him to calculate something—sometimes to keep the boy entertained, sometimes because he was of real help. Bhaskar found the shop very exciting—what with the pleasure of working out discount rates or postal rates for distant orders, and the intriguing geometrical and arithmetical relationships of the stacked shoeboxes. He would delay going to bed as long as possible in order to remain with his father, and Veena sometimes had to send word more than once that he should come home.

'How's the frog?' asked Maan, holding Bhaskar's nose. 'Is he awake? He's looking very neat today.'

'You should have seen him yesterday morning,' said Kedarnath. 'You could only see his eyes.'

Bhaskar's face lit up. 'What have you brought me?' he asked Maan. 'You were the one who was sleeping. You have to pay me a forfeit.'

'Son—' began his father reprovingly.

'Nothing,' said Maan gravely, releasing his nose and clapping his hand over his mouth. 'But tell me—what do you want? Quickly!'

Bhaskar furrowed his forehead in thought.

Two men walked past, talking about the impending strike by the basket-wallahs. A radio blared. A policeman shouted. The shop boy brought in two glasses of tea from the market and, after blowing on the surface for a minute, Maan began drinking.

'Is everything going well?' he asked Kedarnath. 'We didn't get much chance to talk this afternoon.'

Kedarnath shrugged, then nodded.

'Everything's fine. But you look preoccupied.'

'Preoccupied? Me? Oh, no, no—' Maan protested. 'But what's this I hear about the basket-wallahs threatening to go on strike?'

'Well—' said Kedarnath.

He could imagine the havoc that the threatened strike would spell, and didn't want to get on to the subject. He passed his hand through his greying hair in an anxious gesture and closed his eyes.

'I'm still thinking,' said Bhaskar.

'That's a good habit,' said Maan. 'Well, tell me your decision next time—or send me a postcard.'

'All right,' said Bhaskar, with the faintest of smiles.

'Bye, now.'

'Bye, Maan Maama . . . oh, did you know that if you have a triangle like this, and if you draw squares on the sides like this, and then add up these two squares you get that square,' Bhaskar gesticulated. 'Every time,' he added.

'Yes, I do know that.' Smug frog, thought Maan.

Bhaskar looked disappointed, then cheered up. 'Shall I tell you why?' he asked Maan.

'Not today. I have to go. Do you want a goodbye sum?'

Bhaskar was tempted to say, 'Not today,' but changed his mind. 'Yes,' he said.

'What is 256 times 512?' asked Maan, who had worked this out beforehand.

'That's too easy,' said Bhaskar. 'Ask me another one.'

'Well, what's the answer, then?'

'One lakh, thirty-one thousand and seventy-two.'

'Hmm. What's 400 times 400?'

Bhaskar turned away, hurt.

'All right, all right,' said Maan. 'What's 789 times 987?'

'Seven lakhs, seventy-eight thousand, seven hundred and forty-three,' said Bhaskar after a pause of a few seconds.

'I'll take your word for it,' said Maan. The thought had suddenly entered his mind that perhaps he had better not risk his luck with Saeeda Bai, who was so notoriously temperamental.

'Aren't you going to check?' asked Bhaskar.

'No, genius, I have to be off.' He tousled his nephew's hair, gave his brother-in-law a nod, and walked out on to the main street of Misri Mandi. There he hailed a tonga to go back home.

On the way he changed his mind yet again and went straight to Saeeda Bai's instead.

The khaki-turbaned watchman at the entrance appraised him for a moment and told him that Saeeda Bai was not in. Maan thought of writing her a note, but was faced with a problem. Which language should he write it in? Saeeda Bai would certainly not be able to read English and would almost certainly not be able to read Hindi, and Maan could not write Urdu. He tipped the watchman a rupee and said, 'Please inform her that I came to pay my respects.'

The watchman raised his right hand to his turban in a salute, and said: 'And Sahib's name?'

Maan was about to give his name when he thought of something better.

'Tell her that I am one who lives in love,' he said. This was an atrocious pun on Prem Nivas.

The watchman nodded impassively.

Maan looked at the small, two-storeyed, rose-coloured house. Some lights were on inside, but that might not mean anything. With a sinking heart and a sense of deep frustration he turned away and walked in the general direction of home. But then he did what he usually did when he was feeling low or at a loose end—he sought out the company of friends. He told the tonga-wallah to take him to the house of the Nawab Sahib of Baitar. Upon finding that Firoz and Imtiaz were out till late, he decided to pay a visit to Pran. Pran hadn't been pleased about the ducking of the whale, and Maan felt he should smooth his ruffled feathers. His brother struck him as being a decent fellow, but a man of tepid, unboisterous affections. Maan thought cheerfully that Pran just did not have it in him to be as love-struck and miserable as he was.

2.10

Returning later to the sadly ill-maintained mansion of Baitar House, Maan chatted till late with Firoz and Imtiaz, and then stayed overnight.

Imtiaz went out very early on a call, yawning and cursing his profession.

Firoz had some urgent work with a client, went into the section of his father's vast library that served as his chambers, remained closeted in there for a couple of hours, and emerged whistling in time for a late breakfast.

Maan, who had deferred having breakfast until Firoz could eat with him, was still sitting in his guest bedroom, looking over the *Brahmpur Chronicle*, and yawning. He had a slight hangover.

An ancient retainer of the Nawab Sahib's family appeared before him and, after making his obeisance and salutation, announced that the younger Sahib—Chhoté Sahib—would be coming for breakfast immediately, and would Maan Sahib be pleased to go downstairs? All this was pronounced in stately and measured Urdu.

Maan nodded. After about half a minute he noticed that the old servant was still standing a little distance away and gazing expectantly at him. Maan looked at him quizzically.

'Any other command?' asked the servant, who—Maan noticed—looked at least seventy years old, but quite spry. He would have to be fit, thought Maan, in order to negotiate the stairs of the Nawab Sahib's house several times a day. Maan wondered why he had never seen him before.

'No,' said Maan. 'You can go. I'll be down shortly.' Then, as the old man raised his cupped palm to his forehead in polite salutation and turned to leave, Maan said, 'Er, wait. . . .'

The old man turned around and waited to hear what Maan had to say.

'You must have been with the Nawab Sahib for many years,' said Maan.

'Yes, Huzoor, that I have. I am an old servitor of the family. Most of my life I have worked at Baitar Fort, but now in my old age it has pleased him to bring me here.'

Maan smiled to see how unselfconsciously and with what quiet pride the old man referred to himself in the very words—'purana khidmatgar'—that Maan had used mentally to classify him.

Seeing Maan silent, the old man went on. 'I entered service when I was, I think, ten years old. I came from the Nawab Sahib's village of Raipur on the Baitar Estate. In those days I would get a rupee a month, and it was more than sufficient for my needs. This war, Huzoor, has raised the price of things so much that with many times such a salary people find the going difficult. And now with Partition—and all its troubles, and with the Nawab Sahib's brother going to Pakistan and all these laws threatening the property—things are uncertain, very'—he paused to find another word, but in the end merely repeated himself—'very uncertain.'

Maan shook his head in the hope of clearing it and said, 'Is there any aspirin available here?'

The old man looked pleased that he could be of some use, and said, 'Yes, I believe so, Huzoor. I will go and get some for you.'

'Excellent,' said Maan. 'No, don't get it for me,' he added, having second thoughts about making the old man exert himself. 'Just leave a couple of tablets near my plate when I come downstairs for breakfast. Oh, by the way,' he went on, as he visualized the two small tablets at the side of his plate, 'why is Firoz called Chhoté Sahib, when he and Imtiaz were born at the same time?'

The old man looked out of the window at the spreading magnolia tree which had been planted a few days after the twins had been born. He coughed for a second, and said, 'Chhoté Sahib, that is Firoz Sahib, was born seven minutes after Burré Sahib.'

'Ah,' said Maan.

'That is why he looks more delicate, less robust, than Burré Sahib.'

Maan was silent, pondering this physiological theory.

'He has his mother's fine features,' said the old man, then stopped, as if he had transgressed some limit of explanation.

Maan recalled that the Begum Sahiba—the Nawab of Baitar's wife and the mother of his daughter and twin sons—had maintained strict purdah throughout her life. He wondered how a male servant could have known what she looked like, but could sense the old man's embarrassment and did not ask. Possibly a photograph, much more likely discussion among the servants, he thought.

'Or so they say,' added the old man. Then he paused, and said, 'She was a very good woman, rest her soul. She was good to us all. She had a strong will.'

Maan was intrigued by the old man's hesitant but eager incursions into the history of the family to which he had given his life. But he was—despite his headache—quite hungry now, and decided that this was not the time to talk. So he said, 'Tell Chhoté Sahib I will be down in, well, in seven minutes.'

If the old man was puzzled by Maan's unusual sense of timing, he did not show it. He nodded and was about to go.

'What do they call you?' asked Maan.

'Ghulam Rusool, Huzoor,' said the old servant.

Maan nodded and he left.

2.11

'Did you sleep well?' asked Firoz, smiling at Maan.

'Very. But you rose early.'

'Not earlier than usual. I like to get a great deal of work done before breakfast. If it hadn't been a client, it would have been my briefs. It seems to me that you don't work at all.'

Maan looked at the two little pills lying on his quarter-plate, but said nothing, so Firoz went on.

'Now, I don't know anything about cloth—' began Firoz.

Maan groaned. 'Is this a serious conversation?' he asked.

'Yes, of course,' said Firoz, laughing. 'I've been up at least two hours.'

'Well, I have a hangover,' said Maan. 'Have a heart.'

'I do,' said Firoz, reddening a bit. 'I can assure you.' He looked at the clock on the wall. 'But I'm due at the Riding Club. One day I'm going to teach you polo, you know, Maan, all your protests notwithstanding.' He got up and walked towards the corridor.

'Oh, good,' said Maan, more cheerfully. 'That's more in my line.'

An omelette came. It was lukewarm, having had to traverse the vast distance between the kitchens and the breakfast room in Baitar House. Maan looked at it for a while, then gingerly bit a slice of unbuttered toast. His hunger had disappeared again. He swallowed the aspirins.

Firoz, meanwhile, had just got to the front door when he noticed his father's private secretary, Murtaza Ali, arguing with a young man at the entrance. The young man wanted to meet the Nawab Sahib. Murtaza Ali, who was not much older, was trying, in his sympathetic, troubled way, to prevent him from doing so. The young man was not dressed very well—his kurta was of homespun white cotton—but his Urdu was cultured in both accent and expression. He was saying:

'But he told me to come at this time, and here I am.'

The intensity of expression on his lean features made Firoz pause.

'What seems to be the matter?' asked Firoz.

Murtaza Ali turned and said: 'Chhoté Sahib, it appears that this man wants to meet your father in connection with a job in the library. He says he has an appointment.'

'Do you know anything about this?' Firoz asked Murtaza Ali.

'I'm afraid not, Chhoté Sahib.'

The young man said: 'I have come from some distance and with some difficulty. The Nawab Sahib told me expressly that I should be here at ten o'clock to meet him.'

Firoz, in a not unkindly tone, said: 'Are you sure he meant today?'

'Yes, quite sure.'

'If my father had said he was to be disturbed, he would have left word,' said Firoz. 'The problem is that once my father is in the library, well, he's in a different world. You will, I am afraid, have to wait till he comes out. Or could you perhaps come back later?'

A strong emotion began to work at the corners of the young man's mouth. Clearly he needed the income from the job, but equally clearly he had a sense of pride. 'I am not prepared to run around like this,' he said clearly but quietly.

Firoz was surprised. This definiteness, it appeared to him, bordered on incivility. He had not said, for example: 'The Nawabzada will appreciate that it is difficult for me . . .' or any such ameliorative phrase. Simply: 'I am not prepared. . . .'

'Well, that is up to you,' said Firoz, easily. 'Now, forgive me, I have to be somewhere very soon.' He frowned slightly as he got into the car.

2.12

The previous evening, when Maan had stopped by, Saeeda Bai had been entertaining an old but gross client of hers: the Raja of Marh, a small princely state in Madhya Bharat. The Raja was in Brahmpur for a few days, partly to supervise the management of some of his Brahmpur lands, and partly to help in the construction of a new temple to Shiva on the land he owned near the Alamgiri Mosque in Old Brahmpur. The Raja was familiar with Brahmpur from his student days twenty years ago; he had frequented Mohsina Bai's establishment when she was still living with her daughter Saeeda in the infamous alley of Tarbuz ka Bazaar.

Throughout Saeeda Bai's childhood she and her mother had shared the upper floor of a house with three other courtesans, the oldest of whom, by virtue of the fact that she owned the place, had acted for years as their madam. Saeeda Bai's mother did not like this arrangement, and as her daughter's fame and attractiveness grew she was able to assert their independence. When Saeeda Bai was seventeen or so, she came to the attention of the Maharaja of a large state in Rajasthan, and later the Nawab of Sitagarh; and from then on there had been no looking back.

In time, Saeeda Bai had been able to afford her present house in Pasand Bagh, and had gone to live there with her mother and young sister. The three women, separated by gaps of about twenty and fifteen years respectively, were all attractive, each in her own way. If the mother had the strength and brightness of brass, Saeeda Bai had the tarnishable brilliance of silver, and young, soft-hearted Tasneem, named after a spring in Paradise, protected by both mother and sister from the profession of their ancestors, had the lively elusiveness of mercury.

Mohsina Bai had died two years ago. This had been a terrible blow for Saeeda Bai, who sometimes still visited the graveyard and lay weeping, stretched out on her mother's grave. Saeeda Bai and Tasneem now lived alone in the house in Pasand Bagh with two women servants: a maid and a cook. At night the calm watchman guarded the gate. Tonight Saeeda Bai was not expecting to entertain visitors; she was sitting with her tabla player and sarangi player, and amusing herself with gossip and music.

Saeeda Bai's accompanists were a study in contrast. Both were about twenty-five, and both were devoted and skilled musicians. Both were fond of each other, and deeply attached—by economics and affection—to Saeeda Bai. But beyond that the resemblance ended. Ishaq Khan, who bowed his sarangi with such ease and harmoniousness, almost self-effacement, was a slightly sardonic bachelor. Motu Chand, so nicknamed because of his plumpness, was a contented man, already a father of four. He looked a bit like a bulldog with his large eyes and snuffling mouth, and was benignly torpid except when frenziedly drumming his tabla.

They were discussing Ustad Majeed Khan, one of the most famous classical singers of India, a notoriously aloof man who lived in the old city, not far from where Saeeda Bai had grown up.

'But what I don't understand, Saeeda Begum,' said Motu Chand, leaning awkwardly backwards because of his paunch, 'is why he should be so critical of us small people. There he sits with his head above the clouds, like Lord Shiva on Kailash. Why should he open his third eye to burn us up?'

'There is no accounting for the moods of the great,' said Ishaq Khan. He touched his sarangi with his left hand and went on, 'Now look at this sarangi—it's a noble instrument—yet the noble Majeed Khan hates it. He never allows it to accompany him.'

Saeeda Bai nodded; Motu Chand made reassuring sounds. 'It is the loveliest of all instruments,' he said.

'You kafir,' said Ishaq Khan, smiling twistedly at his friend. 'How can you pretend to like this instrument? What is it made of?'

'Well, wood of course,' said Motu Chand, now leaning forward with an effort.

'Look at the little wrestler,' laughed Saeeda Bai. 'We must feed him some laddus.' She called out for her maid, and sent her to get some sweets.

Ishaq continued to wind the coils of his argument around the struggling Motu Chand.

'Wood!' he cried. 'And what else?'

'Oh, well, you know, Khan Sahib—strings and so on,' said Motu Chand, defeated as to Ishaq's intention.

'And what are these strings made of?' continued Ishaq Khan relentlessly.

'Ah!' said Motu Chand, getting a glimpse of his meaning. Ishaq was not a bad fellow, but he appeared to get a cruel pleasure from worsting Motu Chand in an argument.

'Gut,' said Ishaq. 'These strings are made of gut. As you well know. And the front of a sarangi is made of skin. The hide of a dead animal. Now what would your brahmins of Brahmpur say if they were forced to touch it? Would they not be polluted by it?'

Motu Chand looked downcast, then rallied. 'Anyway, I'm not a brahmin, you know . . .' he began.

'Don't tease him,' said Saeeda Bai to Ishaq Khan.

'I love the fat kafir too much to want to tease him,' said Ishaq Khan.

This was not true. Since Motu Chand was of an alarmingly equable bent of mind, what Ishaq Khan liked more than anything else was to upset his balance. But this time Motu Chand reacted in an irksomely philosophical manner.

'Khan Sahib is very kind,' he said. 'But sometimes even the ignorant have wisdom, and he would be the first to acknowledge this. Now for me the sarangi is not what it is made of but what it makes—these divine sounds. In the hands of an artist even this gut and this skin can be made to sing.' His face wreathed with a contented, almost Sufi, smile. 'After all, what are we all but gut and skin? And yet'—his forehead creased with concentration—'in the hands of one who—the One. . . .'

But the maid now came in with the sweets and Motu Chand's theological meanderings halted. His plump and agile fingers quickly reached for a laddu as round as himself and popped it whole into his mouth.

After a while Saeeda Bai said, 'But we were not discussing the One above'—she pointed upwards—'but the One to the West.' She pointed in the direction of Old Brahmpur.

'They are the same,' said Ishaq Khan. 'We pray both westwards and upwards. I am sure Ustad Majeed Khan would not take it amiss if we were mistakenly to turn to him in prayer one evening. And why not?' he ended ambiguously. 'When we pray to such lofty art, we are praying to God himself.' He looked at Motu Chand for approval, but Motu appeared to be either sulking or concentrating on his laddu.

The maid re-entered and announced: 'There is some trouble at the gate.'

Saeeda Bai looked more interested than alarmed.

'What sort of trouble, Bibbo?' she asked.

The maid looked at her cheekily and said, 'It seems that a young man is quarrelling with the watchman.'

'Shameless thing, wipe that expression off your face,' said Saeeda Bai. 'Hmm,' she went on, 'what does he look like?'

'How would I know, Begum Sahiba?' protested the maid.

'Don't be troublesome, Bibbo. Does he look respectable?'

'Yes,' admitted the maid. 'But the streetlights were not bright enough for me to see anything more.'

'Call the watchman,' said Saeeda Bai. 'There's only us here,' she added, as the maid looked hesitant.

'But the young man?' asked the maid.

'If he's as respectable as you say, Bibbo, he'll remain outside.'

'Yes, Begum Sahiba,' said the maid and went to do her bidding.

'Who do you think it could be?' mused Saeeda Bai aloud, and was silent for a minute.

The watchman entered the house, left his spear at the front entrance, and climbed heavily up the stairs to the gallery. He stood at the doorway of the room where they were sitting, and saluted. With his khaki turban, khaki uniform, thick boots and bushy moustache, he was completely out of place in that femininely furnished room. But he did not seem at all ill at ease.

'Who is this man and what does he want?' asked Saeeda Bai.

'He wants to come in and speak with you,' said the watchman phlegmatically.

'Yes, yes, I thought as much—but what is his name?'

'He won't say, Begum Sahiba. Nor will he take no for an answer. Yesterday too he came, and told me to give you a message, but it was so impertinent, I decided not to.'

Saeeda Bai's eyes flashed. 'You decided not to?' she asked.

'The Raja Sahib was here,' said the watchman calmly.

'Hmmh. And the message?'

'That he is one who lives in love,' said the watchman impassively.

He had used a different word for love and had thus lost the pun on Prem Nivas.

'One who lives in love? What can he mean?' remarked Saeeda Bai to Motu and Ishaq. The two looked at each other, Ishaq Khan with a slight smirk of disdain.

'This world is populated by donkeys,' said Saeeda Bai, but whom she was referring to was unclear. 'Why didn't he leave a note? So those were his exact words? Neither very idiomatic nor very witty.'

The watchman searched his memory and came out with a closer approximation to the actual words Maan had used the previous evening. At any rate, 'prem' and 'nivas' both figured in his sentence.

All three musicians solved the riddle immediately.

'Ah!' said Saeeda Bai, amused. 'I think I have an admirer. What do you say? Shall we let him in? Why not?'

Neither of the others demurred—as, indeed, how could they? The watchman was told to let the young man in. And Bibbo was told to tell Tasneem to stay in her room.

2.13

Maan, who was fretting by the gate, could hardly believe his good fortune at being so speedily admitted. He felt a surge of gratitude towards the watchman and pressed a rupee into his hand. The watchman left him at the door of the house, and the maid pointed him up to the room.

As Maan's footsteps were heard in the gallery outside Saeeda Bai's room, she called out, 'Come in, come in, Dagh Sahib. Sit down and illumine our gathering.'

Maan stood outside the door for a second, and looked at Saeeda Bai. He was smiling with pleasure, and Saeeda Bai could not help smiling back at him. He was dressed simply and immaculately in a well-starched white kurta-pyjama. The fine chikan embroidery on his kurta complemented the embroidery on his fine white cotton cap. His shoes—slip-on jutis of soft leather, pointed at the toe—were also white.

'How did you come?' asked Saeeda Bai.

'I walked.'

'These are fine clothes to risk in the dust.'

Maan said simply, 'It is just a few minutes away.'

'Please—sit down.'

Maan sat cross-legged on the white-sheeted floor.

Saeeda Bai began to busy herself making paan. Maan looked at her wonderingly.

'I came yesterday too, but was less fortunate.'

'I know, I know,' said Saeeda Bai. 'My fool of a watchman turned you away. What can I say? We are not all blessed with the faculty of discrimination. . . .'

'But I'm here today,' said Maan, rather obviously.

'Wherever Dagh has sat down, he has sat down?' asked Saeeda Bai, with a smile. Her head was bent, and she was spreading a little white dab of lime on the paan leaves.

'He may not quit your assembly at all this time,' said Maan.

Since she was not looking directly at him, he could look at her without embarrassment. She had covered her head with her sari before he had come in. But the soft, smooth skin of her neck and shoulders was exposed, and Maan found the tilt of her neck as she bent over her task indescribably charming.

Having made a pair of paans she impaled them on a little silver toothpick with tassels, and offered them to him. He took them and put them in his mouth, pleasantly surprised at the taste of coconut, which was an ingredient Saeeda Bai was fond of adding to her paan.

'I see you are wearing your own style of Gandhi cap,' said Saeeda Bai, after popping a couple of paans into her mouth. She did not offer any to Ishaq Khan or Motu Chand, but then they seemed to have virtually melted into the background.

Maan touched the side of his embroidered white cap nervously, unsure of himself.

'No, no, Dagh Sahib, don't trouble yourself. This isn't a church, you know.' Saeeda Bai looked at him and said, 'I was reminded of other white caps one sees floating around in Brahmpur. The heads that wear them have grown taller recently.'

'I am afraid you are going to accuse me of the accident of my birth,' said Maan.

'No, no,' said Saeeda Bai. 'Your father has been an old patron of the arts. It is the other Congress-wallahs I was thinking of.'

'Perhaps I should wear a cap of a different colour the next time I come,' said Maan.

Saeeda Bai raised an eyebrow.

'Assuming I am ushered into your presence,' Maan added humbly.

Saeeda Bai thought to herself: What a well-brought-up young man. She indicated to Motu Chand that he should bring the tablas and harmonium that were lying in the corner of the room.

To Maan she said, 'And now what does Hazrat Dagh command us to sing?'

'Why, anything,' said Maan, throwing banter to the winds.

'Not a ghazal, I hope,' said Saeeda Bai, pressing down a key on the harmonium to help the tabla and sarangi tune up.

'No?' asked Maan, disappointed.

'Ghazals are for open gatherings or the intimacy of lovers,' said Saeeda Bai. 'I'll sing what my family is best known for and what my Ustad best taught me.'

She began a thumri in Raag Pilu, 'Why then are you not speaking to me?' and Maan's face brightened up. As she sang he floated off into a state of intoxication. The sight of her face, the sound of her voice, and the scent of her perfume were intertwined in his happiness.

After two or three thumris and a dadra, Saeeda Bai indicated that she was tired, and that Maan should leave.

He left reluctantly, showing, however, more good humour than reluctance. Downstairs, the watchman found a five-rupee note pressed into his hand.

Out on the street Maan trod on air.

She will sing a ghazal for me sometime, he promised himself. She will, she certainly will.

2.14

It was Sunday morning. The sky was bright and clear. The weekly bird market near the Barsaat Mahal was in full swing. Thousands of birds—mynas, partridges, pigeons, parakeets—fighting birds, eating birds, racing birds, talking birds—sat or fluttered in iron or cane cages in little stalls from which rowdy hawkers cried out the excellence and cheapness of their wares. The pavement had been taken over by the bird market, and buyers or passers-by like Ishaq had to walk on the road surface, bumping against rickshaws and bicycles and the occasional tonga.

There was even a pavement stall with books about birds. Ishaq picked up a flimsy, blunt-typed paperback about owls and spells, and looked idly through to see what uses this unlucky bird could be put to. It appeared to be a book of Hindu black magic, *The Tantra of Owls*, though it was printed in Urdu. He read:

> *Sovereign Remedy to Obtain Employment*
> Take the tail-feathers of an owl and a crow, and burn them together in a fire made from mango wood until they form ash. Place this ash on your forehead like a caste-mark when you go to seek employment, and you will most certainly obtain it.

He frowned and read on:

> *Method of Keeping a Woman in Your Power*
> If you want to keep a woman in your control, and wish to prevent her from coming under the influence of anyone else, then use the technique described below:
>
> Take the blood of an owl, the blood of a jungle fowl and the

> blood of a bat in equal proportions, and after smearing the mixture on your penis have intercourse with the woman. Then she will never desire another man.

Ishaq felt almost sick. These Hindus! he thought. On an impulse he bought the book, deciding that it was an excellent means of provoking his friend Motu Chand.

'I have one on vultures as well,' said the bookseller helpfully.

'No, this is all I want,' said Ishaq, and walked on.

He stopped at a stall where a large number of tiny, almost formless grey-green balls of stubbly flesh lay imprisoned in a hooped cage.

'Ah!' he said.

His look of interest had an immediate effect on the white-capped stall-keeper, who appraised him, glancing at the book in his hand.

'These are not ordinary parakeets, Huzoor, these are hill parakeets, Alexandrine parakeets as the English sahibs say.'

The English had left more than three years ago, but Ishaq let it pass.

'I know, I know,' he said.

'I can tell an expert when I see one,' said the stall-keeper in a most friendly manner. 'Now, why not have this one? Only two rupees—and it will sing like an angel.'

'A male angel or a female angel?' said Ishaq severely.

The stall-keeper suddenly became obsequious.

'Oh, you must forgive me, you must forgive me. People here are so ignorant, one can hardly bear to part with one's most promising birds, but for one who knows parakeets I will do anything, anything. Have this one, Huzoor.' And he picked out one with a larger head, a male.

Ishaq held it for a few seconds, then placed it back in the cage. The man shook his head, then said:

'Now for a true fancier, what can I provide that is better than this? Is it a bird from Rudhia District that you want? Or from the foothills in Horshana? They talk better than mynas.'

Ishaq simply said, 'Let's see something worth seeing.'

The man went to the back of the shop and opened a cage in which three little half-fledged birds sat huddled together. Ishaq looked at them silently, then asked to see one of them.

He smiled, thinking of parakeets he had known. His aunt was very fond of them, and had one who was still alive at the age of seventeen. 'This one,' he said to the man. 'And you know by now that I will not be fooled about the price either.'

They haggled for a while. Until the money changed hands the stall-keeper seemed a bit resentful. Then, as Ishaq was about to leave—with his purchase nestled in his handkerchief—the stall-keeper said in an anxious voice, 'Tell me how he is doing when you come by next time.'

'What do they call you?' asked Ishaq.

'Muhammad Ismail, Huzoor. And how are you addressed?'

'Ishaq Khan.'

'Then we are brothers!' beamed the stall-keeper. 'You must always get your birds from my shop.'

'Yes, yes,' agreed Ishaq, and walked hurriedly away. This was a good bird he had got, and would delight the heart of young Tasneem.

2.15

Ishaq went home, had lunch, and fed the bird a little flour mixed with water. Later, carrying the parakeet in his handkerchief, he made his way to Saeeda Bai's house. From time to time he looked at it in appreciation, imagining what an excellent and intelligent bird it potentially was. He was in high spirits. A good Alexandrine parakeet was his favourite kind of parrot. As he walked towards Nabiganj he almost bumped into a hand-cart.

He arrived at Saeeda Bai's house at about four and told Tasneem that he had brought something for her. She was to try and guess what it was.

'Don't tease me, Ishaq Bhai,' she said, fixing her beautiful large eyes on his face. 'Please tell me what it is.'

Ishaq looked at her and thought that 'gazelle-like' really did suit Tasneem. Delicate-featured, tall and slender, she did not greatly resemble her elder sister. Her eyes were liquid and her expression tender. She was lively, but always seemed to be on the point of taking flight.

'Why do you insist on calling me Bhai?' he asked.

'Because you are virtually my brother,' said Tasneem. 'I need one, too. And your bringing me this gift proves it. Now please don't keep me in suspense. Is it something to wear?'

'Oh no—that would be superfluous to your beauty,' said Ishaq, smiling.

'Please don't talk that way,' said Tasneem, frowning. 'Apa might hear you, and then there will be trouble.'

'Well, here it is. . . .' And Ishaq took out what looked like a soft ball of fluffy material wrapped in a handkerchief.

'A ball of wool! You want me to knit you a pair of socks. Well, I won't. I have better things to do.'

'Like what?' said Ishaq.

'Like . . .' began Tasneem, then was silent. She glanced uncomfortably at a long mirror on the wall. What did she do? Cut vegetables to help the cook, talk to her sister, read novels, gossip with the maid, think about life. But before she could meditate too deeply on the subject, the ball moved, and her eyes lit up with pleasure.

'So you see—' said Ishaq, 'it's a mouse.'

'It is not—' said Tasneem with contempt. 'It's a bird. I'm not a child, you know.'

'And I'm not exactly your brother, you know,' said Ishaq. He unwrapped the parakeet and they looked at it together. Then he placed it on a table near a red lacquer vase. The stubbly ball of flesh looked quite disgusting.

'How lovely,' said Tasneem.

'I selected him this morning,' said Ishaq. 'It took me hours, but I wanted to have one that would be just right for you.'

Tasneem gazed at the bird, then stretched out her hand and touched it. Despite its stubble it was very soft. Its colour was very slightly green, as its feathers had only just begun to emerge.

'A parakeet?'

'Yes, but not a regular one. He's a hill parakeet. He'll talk as well as a myna.'

When Mohsina Bai died, her highly talkative myna had quickly followed her. Tasneem had been even lonelier without the bird, but she was glad that Ishaq had not got her another myna but something quite different. That was doubly considerate of him.

'What is he called?'

Ishaq laughed. 'Why do you want to call him anything? Just "tota" will do. He's not a warhorse that he should be called Ruksh or Bucephalas.'

Both of them were standing and looking at the baby parakeet. At the same moment each stretched out a hand to touch him. Tasneem swiftly drew her hand back.

'You go ahead,' said Ishaq. 'I've had him all day.'

'Has he eaten anything?'

'A bit of flour mixed with water,' said Ishaq.

'How do they get such tiny birds?' asked Tasneem.

Their eyes were level, and Ishaq, looking at her head, covered with a yellow scarf, found himself speaking without paying any attention to his words.

'Oh, they're taken from their nests when they're very young—if you don't get them young they don't learn to speak—and you should get a male one—he'll develop a lovely rose-and-black ring around his neck—and males are more intelligent. The best talkers come from the foothills, you know. There were three of them in the stall from the same nest, and I had to think quite hard before I decided—'

'You mean, he's separated from his brothers and sisters?' Tasneem broke in.

'But of course,' said Ishaq. 'He had to be. If you get a pair of them, they don't learn to imitate anything we say.'

'How cruel,' said Tasneem. Her eyes grew moist.

'But he had already been taken from his nest when I bought him,' said Ishaq, upset that he had caused her pain. 'You can't put them back or they'll be rejected by their parents.' He put his hand on hers—she didn't draw back at once—and said: 'Now it's up to you to give him a good life. Put him in a nest of cloth in the cage in which your mother's myna used to be kept. And for the first few days feed him a little parched gram flour moistened with water or a little daal soaked overnight. If he doesn't like that cage, I'll get him another one.'

Tasneem withdrew her hand gently from under Ishaq's. Poor parakeet, loved and unfree! He could change one cage for another. And she would change these four walls for a different four. Her sister, fifteen years her senior, and experienced in the ways of the world, would arrange all that soon enough. And then—

'Sometimes I wish I could fly. . . .' She stopped, embarrassed.

Ishaq looked at her seriously. 'It is a good thing we can't, Tasneem—or can you imagine the confusion? The police have a hard enough time controlling traffic in Chowk—but if we could fly as well as walk it would be a hundred times worse.'

Tasneem tried not to smile.

'But it would be worse still if birds, like us, could only walk,' continued Ishaq. 'Imagine them strolling up and down Nabiganj with their walking sticks in the evenings.'

Now she was laughing. Ishaq too started laughing, and the two of them, delighted by the picture they had conjured up, felt the tears rolling down their cheeks. Ishaq wiped his away with his hand, Tasneem hers with her yellow dupatta. Their laughter sounded through the house.

The baby parakeet sat quite still on the tabletop near the red lacquer vase; his translucent gullet worked up and down.

Saeeda Bai, roused from her afternoon nap, came into the room, and in a surprised voice, with something of a stern edge, said: 'Ishaq—what's all this? Is one not to be permitted to rest even in the afternoon?' Then her eyes alighted on the baby parakeet, and she clicked her tongue in irritation.

'No—no more birds in this house. That miserable myna of my mother's caused me enough trouble.' She paused, then added: 'One singer is enough in any establishment. Get rid of it.'

2.16

No one spoke. After a while Saeeda Bai broke the silence. 'Ishaq, you are here early,' she said.

Ishaq looked guilty. Tasneem looked down with half a sob. The parakeet made a feeble attempt to move. Saeeda Bai, looking from one to the other, suddenly said:

'Where is your sarangi anyway?'

Ishaq realized he had not even brought it. He flushed.

'I forgot. I was thinking of the parakeet.'

'Well?'

'Of course I'll go and get it immediately.'

'The Raja of Marh has sent word he will be coming this evening.'

'I'm just going,' said Ishaq. Then he added, looking at Tasneem, 'Shall I take the parakeet?'

'No, no—' said Saeeda Bai, 'why should you want to take it? Just get your sarangi. And don't be all day about it.'

Ishaq left hurriedly.

Tasneem, who had been close to tears, looked gratefully at her sister. Saeeda Bai, however, was far away. The business of the bird had woken her up from a haunting and peculiar dream involving the death of her mother and her own earlier life—and when Ishaq left, its atmosphere of dread and even guilt had surged back over her.

Tasneem, noticing her sister suddenly sad, held her hand.

'What's the matter, Apa?' she asked, using the term of endearment and respect she always used for her elder sister.

Saeeda Bai began to sob, and hugged Tasneem to her, kissing her forehead and cheeks.

'You are the only thing I care for in the world,' she said. 'May God keep you happy. . . .'

Tasneem hugged her and said, 'Why, Apa, why are you crying? Why are you so overwrought? Is it Ammi-jaan's grave you are thinking of?'

'Yes, yes,' said Saeeda Bai quickly, and turned away. 'Now go inside, get the cage lying in Ammi-jaan's old room. Polish it and bring it here. And soak some daal—some chané ki daal—for him to eat later.'

Tasneem went in towards the kitchen. Saeeda Bai sat down, looking a bit dazed. Then she held the small parakeet in her hands to keep him warm. She was sitting like this when the maidservant came in to announce that someone had arrived from the Nawab Sahib's place, and was waiting outside.

Saeeda Bai pulled herself together and dried her eyes. 'Let him in,' she said.

But when Firoz walked in, handsome and smiling, gripping his elegant walking stick lightly in his right hand, she gave a startled gasp.

'You?'

'Yes,' said Firoz. 'I've brought an envelope from my father.'

'You've come late. . . . I mean, he usually sends someone in the morning,' murmured Saeeda Bai, trying to still the confusion in her mind. 'Please sit down, please sit down.'

Until now the Nawab Sahib had sent a servant with the monthly envelope. For the last two months, Saeeda Bai remembered it had been just a couple of days after her period. And this month too, of course. . . .

Her thoughts were interrupted by Firoz, who said: 'I happened to bump into my father's private secretary, who was coming—'

'Yes, yes.' Saeeda Bai looked upset. Firoz wondered why his appearance should have distressed her so much. That many years ago there must have been something between the Nawab Sahib and Saeeda Bai's mother—and that his father continued to send a little something each month to support the family—surely there was nothing in this to cause her such agitation. Then he realized that she must have been upset even before his arrival by something quite different.

I have come at a bad time, he thought, and decided to go.

Tasneem walked in with the copper birdcage and, seeing him, suddenly stopped.

They looked at each other. For Tasneem, Firoz was just another handsome admirer of her sister's—but startlingly so. She lowered her eyes quickly, then looked at him again.

She stood there with her yellow dupatta, the birdcage in her right hand, her mouth slightly open in astonishment—perhaps at his astonishment. Firoz was staring at her, transfixed.

'Have we met before?' he asked gently, his heart beating fast.

Tasneem was about to reply when Saeeda Bai said, 'Whenever my sister goes out of the house she goes in purdah. And this is the first time that the Nawabzada has graced my poor lodgings with his presence. So it is not possible that you could have met. Tasneem, put the cage down, and go back to your Arabic exercises. I have not got you a new teacher for nothing.'

'But . . .' began Tasneem.

'Go back to your room at once. I will take care of the bird. Have you soaked the daal yet?'

'I . . .'

'Go and do so immediately. Do you want the bird to starve?'

When the bewildered Tasneem had left, Firoz tried to orient his thoughts. His mouth was dry. He felt strangely disturbed. Surely, he felt, even if we have not met on this mortal plane, we have met in some former life. The thought, counter to the religion he nominally adhered to, affected him the more powerfully for all that. The girl with the birdcage had in a few short moments made the most profound and unsettling impression on him.

After abridged pleasantries with Saeeda Bai, who seemed to be paying as little attention to his words as he to hers, he walked slowly out of the door.

Saeeda Bai sat perfectly still on the sofa for a few minutes. Her hands still cradled the little parakeet gently. He appeared to have gone off to sleep. She wrapped him up warmly in a piece of cloth and set him down near the red vase again. From outside she heard the call to evening prayer, and she covered her head.

All over India, all over the world, as the sun or the shadow of darkness moves from east to west, the call to prayer moves with it, and people kneel down in a wave to pray to God. Five waves each day—one for each namaaz—ripple across the globe from longitude to longitude. The component elements change direction, like iron filings near a magnet—towards the house of God in Mecca. Saeeda Bai got up to go to an inner room where she performed the ritual ablution and began her prayers:

In the Name of God, the Merciful, the Compassionate

Praise belongs to God, the Lord of all Being,
the All-Merciful, the All-Compassionate,
  the Master of the Day of Doom.
Thee only we serve; to Thee alone we pray for succour.
  Guide us in the straight path,
the path of those whom Thou hast blessed,
  not those against whom Thou art wrathful,
  nor of those who are astray.

But through this, and through her subsequent kneelings and prostrations, one terrifying line from the Holy Book recurred again and again to her mind:

And God alone knows what you keep secret
  and what you publish.

2.17

Saeeda Bai's pretty young maidservant, Bibbo, sensing her mistress was distressed, thought she would try to cheer her up by talking of the Raja of Marh, who was to visit that evening. With his tiger hunts and mountain fastnesses, his reputation as temple-builder and tyrant, and his strange tastes in sex, the Raja was not the ideal subject for comic relief. He had come to lay the foundation of the Shiva temple, his latest venture, in the centre of the old town. The temple was to stand cheek by jowl with the grand mosque constructed by order of the Emperor Aurangzeb two and a half centuries ago on the ruins of an earlier temple to Shiva. If the Raja of Marh had had his way, the foundation of his temple would have stood on the rubble of the mosque itself.

Given this background, it was interesting that the Raja of Marh had once been so utterly besotted with Saeeda Bai that he had some years ago proposed to marry her even though there was no question of her renouncing her beliefs as a Muslim. The thought of being his wife made Saeeda Bai so uneasy that she set impossible conditions upon him. Any possible heirs of the Raja's present wife were to be dispossessed, and Saeeda Bai's eldest son by him—assuming she had any—was to inherit Marh. Saeeda Bai made this demand of the Raja despite the fact that the Rani of Marh and the Dowager Rani of Marh had both treated her with kindness when she had been summoned to the state to perform at the wedding of the Raja's sister; she liked the Ranis, and knew that there was no possibility of her conditions being accepted. But the Raja thought with his crotch rather than his brain. He accepted these demands, and Saeeda Bai, trapped, had to fall seriously ill and be told by compliant doctors that to move her away from the city to a princely hill state would very likely kill her.

The Raja, whose looks resembled those of a huge water buffalo, pawed the earth dangerously for a while. He suspected duplicity and fell into a drunken and—literally—bloodshot rage; probably the main factor that prevented his hiring someone to get rid of Saeeda Bai was the knowledge that the British, if they discovered the truth, would probably depose him—as they had other Rajas, and even Maharajas, for similar scandals and killings.

Not a great deal of this was known to the maidservant Bibbo, who was, however, keyed into the gossip that the Raja had some years previously proposed to her mistress. Saeeda Bai was talking to Tasneem's bird—rather prematurely, considering how tiny it was, but Saeeda Bai felt that this was how birds learned best—when Bibbo appeared.

'Are any special arrangements to be made for the Raja Sahib?' she asked.

'Why? No, of course not,' said Saeeda Bai.

'Perhaps I should get a garland of marigolds—'

'Are you crazy, Bibbo?'

'—for him to eat.'

Saeeda Bai smiled.

Bibbo went on: 'Will we have to move to Marh, Rani Sahiba?'

'Oh do be quiet,' said Saeeda Bai.

'But to rule a state—'

'No one really rules their states now; Delhi does,' said Saeeda Bai. 'And listen, Bibbo, it would not be the crown I would have to marry but the buffalo underneath. Now go—you are ruining the education of this parakeet.'

The maidservant turned to leave.

'Oh, yes, and get me a little sugar, and see if the daal that you soaked earlier is soft yet. It probably isn't.'

Saeeda Bai continued to talk to the parakeet, who was sitting on a little nest of clean rags in the middle of the brass cage that had once held Mohsina Bai's myna.

'Now, Miya Mitthu,' said Saeeda Bai rather sadly to the parakeet, 'you had better learn good and auspicious things at an early age, or you'll be ruined for life, like that foul-mouthed myna. As they say, if you don't learn your alif-be-pe-te clearly, you'll never amount to a calligrapher. What do you have to say for yourself? Do you want to learn?'

The small, unfeathered ball of flesh was in no position to answer, and didn't.

'Now look at me,' said Saeeda Bai. 'I still feel young, though I admit I am naturally not as young as you. I am waiting to spend the evening with this disgustingly ugly man who is fifty-five years old, who picks his nose and belches, and who is going to be drunk even before he gets here. Then he'll want me to sing romantic songs to him. Everyone feels that I am the epitome of romance, Miya Mitthu, but what about my feelings? How can I feel anything for these ancient animals, whose skin hangs from their jaws—like that of the old cattle straying around Chowk?'

The parakeet opened his mouth.

'Miya Mitthu,' said Saeeda Bai.

The parakeet rocked a little from side to side. His big head looked unsteady.

'Miya Mitthu,' repeated Saeeda Bai, trying to imprint the syllables on his mind.

The parakeet closed his mouth.

'What I really want tonight is not to entertain but to be entertained. By someone young and handsome,' she added.

Saeeda Bai smiled at the thought of Maan.

'What do you think of him, Miya Mitthu?' continued Saeeda Bai. 'Oh, I'm sorry, you haven't yet met Dagh Sahib, you have just brought your presence here today. And you must be hungry, that's why you are refusing to talk to me—you can't sing bhajans on an empty stomach. I'm sorry the service is so slow in this establishment, but Bibbo is a very scatterbrained girl.'

But soon Bibbo came in and the parakeet was fed.

The old cook had decided that a little daal should be boiled and then cooled, rather than merely soaked, for the bird. Now she too came to look at him.

Ishaq Khan came in with his sarangi, looking a little shamefaced.

Motu Chand came in and admired the parakeet.

Tasneem put down the novel she was reading, and came in to say 'Miya Mitthu' and 'Mitthu Miya' several times to the parakeet, delighting Ishaq with each iteration. At least she loved his bird.

And in due course the Raja of Marh was announced.

2.18

His Highness the Raja of Marh was less drunk on arrival than he usually was, but rapidly remedied the situation. He had brought along a bottle of Black Dog, his favourite whisky. This immediately reminded Saeeda Bai of one of his more unpleasant characteristics, the fact that he would get incredibly excited when he saw dogs copulating. In Marh, when Saeeda Bai had visited, he had twice got dogs to mount a bitch in heat. This was the prelude to his flinging his own gross body on Saeeda Bai.

This took place a couple of years before Independence; despite Saeeda Bai's revulsion she had not been able immediately to escape from Marh, where the crass Raja, restrained only by a succession of disgusted but tactful British Residents, held ultimate sway. Afterwards, she was too frightened of the sluggish and brutal man and his hired ruffians to cut off relations completely with him. She could only hope that his visits to Brahmpur would become less frequent with time.

The Raja had degenerated from his student days in Brahmpur, when he had given the impression of being tolerably presentable. His son, who had been protected from his father's way of life by the Rani and Dowager Rani, was now himself a student at Brahmpur University; no doubt he too, upon returning to feudal Marh as an adult, would shake off the maternal influence and grow to be as tamasic as his father: ignorant, brutal, slothful, and rank.

The father ignored the son during his stay in town and visited a series of courtesans and prostitutes. Today, once again, it was Saeeda Bai's turn. He arrived adorned with diamond ear-tops and a ruby in his silk turban, and smelling strongly of attar of musk. He placed a small silken pouch containing five hundred rupees on a table near the door of the upstairs room where Saeeda Bai entertained. The Raja then stretched out against a long white bolster on the white-sheeted floor, and looked around for glasses. They were lying on the low table where the tablas and harmonium stood. The Black Dog was opened and the whisky poured into two glasses. The musicians remained downstairs.

'How long it has been since these eyes last saw you—' said Saeeda Bai, sipping her whisky and restraining a grimace at its strong taste.

The Raja was too involved with his drink to think of answering.

'You have become as difficult to sight as the moon at Id.'

The Raja grunted at the pleasantry. After he had downed a few whiskies, he became more affable, and told her how beautiful she was looking—before pushing her thickly towards the door that led into the bedroom.

After half an hour, they came out, and the musicians were summoned. Saeeda Bai was looking slightly sick.

He made her sing the same set of ghazals he always did; she sang them with the same break in her voice at the same heartrending phrases—something she had learned to do without difficulty. She nursed her glass of whisky. The Raja had finished a third of his bottle by now, and his eyes were becoming red. From time to time he shouted, 'wah! wah!' in indiscriminate praise, or belched or snorted or gaped or scratched his crotch.

2.19

While the ghazals were proceeding upstairs, Maan was walking towards the house. From the street he could not make out the sound of singing. He told the watchman he was there to see Saeeda Bai, but the stolid man told him that she was indisposed.

'Oh,' said Maan, his voice filled with concern. 'Let me go in—I'll see how she is—perhaps I can fetch a doctor.'

'Begum Sahiba is not admitting anyone today.'

'But I have something for her with me here,' said Maan. He had a large book in his left hand. He reached into his pocket with his right and extracted his wallet. 'Would you see she gets it?'

'Yes, Huzoor,' said the watchman, accepting a five-rupee note.

'Well, then—' said Maan and, with a disappointed look at the rose-coloured house beyond the small green gate, walked slowly away.

The watchman carried the book a couple of minutes later to the front door and gave it to Bibbo.

'What—for me?' said Bibbo flirtatiously.

The watchman looked at her with such a lack of expression it was almost an expression in itself.

'No. And tell Begum Sahiba it was from that young man who came the other day.'

'The one who got you into such trouble with Begum Sahiba?'

'I was not in trouble.'

And the watchman walked back to the gate.

Bibbo giggled and closed the door. She looked at the book for a few minutes. It was very handsome and—apart from print—contained pictures of languid men and women in various romantic settings. One particular picture took her fancy. A woman in a black robe was kneeling by a grave. Her eyes were closed. There were stars in the sky behind a high wall in the background. In the foreground was a short, gnarled, leafless tree, its roots entwined among large stones. Bibbo stood wondering for a few moments. Then, without thinking about the Raja of Marh, she closed the book to take it up to Saeeda Bai.

Like a spark on a slow fuse, the book now moved from the gate to the front door, across the hall, up the stairs and along the gallery to the open doorway of the room where Saeeda Bai was entertaining the Raja. When she saw him, Bibbo stopped abruptly and tried to retreat along the gallery. But Saeeda Bai had spotted her. She broke off the ghazal she was singing.

'Bibbo, what's the matter? Come in.'

'Nothing, Saeeda Begum. I'll come back later.'

'What's the matter with the girl? First she interrupts, then it's "Nothing, Saeeda Begum, I'll come back later!" What's that in your hands?'

'Nothing, Begum Sahiba.'

'Let's have a look at that nothing,' said Saeeda Bai.

Bibbo entered with a frightened salaam, and handed the book to her. On the brown cover in gold letters it said in Urdu: *The Poetical Works of Ghalib. An Album of Pictures by Chughtai.*

It was clearly no ordinary collected poems of Ghalib. Saeeda Bai could not resist opening it. She turned the pages. The book contained a few words of introduction and an essay by the artist Chughtai, the entire collected Urdu poems of the great Ghalib, a group of plates of the most beautiful paintings in the Persian style (each illustrating a line or two of Ghalib's poetry), and some text in English. This English text was probably a foreword when seen from the other side, thought Saeeda Bai, who was still amused by the fact that books in English opened at the wrong end.

So delighted was she by the gift that she placed it on the harmonium and began to leaf through the illustrations. 'Who sent it?' she asked, when she noticed that there was no inscription. In her pleasure she had forgotten the presence of the Raja, who was simmering with anger and jealousy.

Bibbo, with a quick glance around the room for inspiration, said, 'It came with the watchman.'

She had sensed the Raja's dangerous rage, and did not wish her mistress to display the involuntary joy she might if her admirer's name were mentioned directly. Besides, the Raja would not be tenderly disposed towards the sender of the book; and Bibbo, though mischievous, did not wish Maan ill. Far from it, in fact.

Meanwhile, Saeeda Bai, her head down, was looking at a picture of an old woman, a young woman and a boy praying before a window towards a new moon at sunset. 'Yes, yes—' she said '—but who sent it?' She looked up and frowned.

Bibbo, now under duress, tried to name Maan as elliptically as possible. Hoping that the Raja would not notice, she pointed to a spot on the white-sheeted floor where he had spilt some of his whisky. Aloud she said, 'I don't know. No name was left. May I go?'

'Yes, yes—what a fool—' said her mistress, impatient with Bibbo's enigmatic behaviour.

But the Raja of Marh had had enough of this insolent interruption. With an ugly snort he moved forward to snatch the book from Saeeda Bai's hands. If she had not moved it swiftly away at the last moment he would have ripped it from her grasp.

Now, breathing heavily, he said: 'Who is he? How much is his life worth? What is his name? Is this exhibition to be part of my entertainment?'

'No—no—' said Saeeda Bai, 'please forgive the silly girl. It is impossible to teach etiquette and discrimination to these unsophisticated things.' Then, to mollify him, she added: 'But look at this picture—how lovely it is—their hands raised in prayer—the sunset, the white dome and minaret of the mosque—'

It was the wrong word to use. With a guttural grunt of rage, the Raja of Marh ripped out the page she was showing him. Saeeda Bai stared at him, petrified.

'Play!' he roared at Motu and Ishaq. And to Saeeda Bai he said, moving his face forward in threat: 'Sing! Finish the ghazal—No! begin it again. Remember who has reserved you for the evening.'

Saeeda Bai replaced the ragged page in the book, closed it, and set it by the harmonium. Then, closing her eyes, she began again to sing the words of love. Her voice was trembling and there was no life to the lines. Indeed, she was not even thinking of them. Beneath her tears she was in a white rage. If she had had the freedom to, she would have lashed out against the Raja—flung her whisky at his bulging red eyes, slashed his face, thrown him out on to the street. But she knew that, for all her worldly wisdom, she was utterly powerless. To avoid these thoughts her mind strayed to Bibbo's gestures.

Whisky? Liquor? Floor? Sheet? she wondered to herself.

Then suddenly she realized what Bibbo had tried to say to her. It was the word for stain—'dagh'.

With a song now in her heart, not only on her lips, Saeeda Bai opened her eyes and smiled, looking at the whisky stain. As of a black dog pissing! she thought. I must give that quick-thinking girl a gift.

She thought of Maan, one man—the only man, in fact—whom she both liked and felt she could have almost complete control over. Perhaps she had not treated him well enough—perhaps she had been too cavalier with his infatuation.

The ghazal she was singing bloomed into life. Ishaq Khan was startled and could not understand it. Even Motu Chand was puzzled.

It certainly also had charms to soothe the savage breast. The Raja of Marh's head sank gently on to his chest, and in a while he began snoring.

2.20

The next evening, when Maan asked the watchman about Saeeda Bai's health, he was told that she had left instructions that he was to be sent up. This was wonderful, considering that he had neither left word nor sent a note to say that he would be coming.

As he walked up the stairs at the end of the hall he paused to admire himself in the mirror, and greeted himself with a sotto voce 'Adaab arz, Dagh Sahib', raising his cupped hand to his forehead in happy salutation. He was dressed as smartly as ever in a starched and immaculate kurta-pyjama; he wore the same white cap that had drawn a comment from Saeeda Bai.

When he got to the upstairs gallery that fringed the hall below, he stopped. There was no sound of music or talk. Saeeda Bai would probably be alone. He was filled with a pleased expectation; his heart began beating hard.

She must have heard his footsteps: she had put down the slim novel she had been reading—at least it appeared to be a novel from the illustration on the cover—and had stood up to greet him.

As he entered the doorway she said, 'Dagh Sahib, Dagh Sahib, you did not need to do that.'

Maan looked at her—she appeared a little tired. She was wearing the same red silk sari that she had worn in Prem Nivas. He smiled and said: 'Every object strives for its proper place. A book seeks to be near its truest admirer. Just as this helpless moth seeks to be near the candle that infatuates him.'

'But, Maan Sahib, books are chosen with care and treated with love,' said Saeeda Bai, addressing him tenderly by his own name for—was it?—the first time, and entirely disregarding his conventionally gallant remark. 'You must have had this book in your library for many years. You should not have parted with it.'

Maan had in fact had the book on his bookshelf, but in Banaras. He had remembered it for some reason, had thought immediately of Saeeda Bai, and after some search had obtained a perfect second-hand copy from a bookseller in Chowk. But in the pleasure of hearing himself so gently addressed, all he now said was, 'The Urdu, even of those poems that I know by heart, is wasted on me. I cannot read the script. Did you like it?'

'Yes,' said Saeeda Bai very quietly. 'Everyone gives me jewels and other glittering things, but nothing has caught my eyes or my heart like your gift. But why are we standing? Please sit down.'

Maan sat down. There was the same slight fragrance that he had noticed before in this room. But today attar of roses was slightly interfused with attar of musk, a combination which made the robust Maan almost weak with longing.

'Will you have some whisky, Dagh Sahib?' asked Saeeda Bai. 'I am sorry that this is the only kind we have got,' she added, indicating the half-empty bottle of Black Dog.

'But this is excellent whisky, Saeeda Begum,' said Maan.

'We've had it for some time,' she said, handing him the glass.

Maan sat silent for a while, leaning against a long cylindrical bolster and sipping his Scotch. Then he said, 'I've often wondered about the couplets that inspired Chughtai's paintings, but have never got around to asking someone who knows Urdu to read them to me. For instance, there is one picture that has always intrigued me. I can describe it even without opening the book. It shows a watery landscape in orange and brown, with a tree, a withered tree, rising out from the water. And somewhere in the middle of the water floats a lotus on which a small, smoky oil lamp is resting. Do you know the one I'm talking about? I think it's somewhere at the beginning of the book. On the page of tissue that covers it is the single word "Life!" That's all there is in English, and it is very mysterious—because there is a whole couplet underneath in Urdu. Perhaps you could tell me how it reads?'

Saeeda Bai fetched the book. She sat down on Maan's left, and as he turned the pages of his magnificent gift, she prayed that he would not come upon the torn page that she had carefully patched together. The English titles were oddly succinct. After flipping past 'Around the Beloved', 'The Brimming Cup', and 'The Wasted Vigil', Maan came to 'Life!'

'This is the one,' he said, as they re-examined the mysterious painting. 'Ghalib has plenty of couplets dealing with lamps. I wonder which one this is.'

Saeeda Bai turned back to the covering sheet of tissue, and as she did their hands touched for a moment. With a slight intake of breath, Saeeda Bai looked down at the Urdu couplet, then read it out:

> 'The horse of time is galloping fast: let us see where he halts.
> Neither is the hand on the reins nor the foot in the stirrup.'

Maan burst out laughing. 'Well,' he said, 'that should teach me how dangerous it is to come to conclusions based on shaky assumptions.'

They went through a couple of other couplets, and then Saeeda Bai said: 'When I looked through the poems this morning, I wondered what the few pages in English at the end of the book were all about.'

The beginning of the book from my point of view, thought Maan, still smiling. Aloud, he said: 'I suppose it's a translation of the Urdu pages at the other end—but why don't we make sure?'

'Certainly,' said Saeeda Bai. 'But to do so you will have to change places with me and sit on my left. Then you can read a sentence in English and I can read its translation in Urdu. It will be like having a private tutor,' she added, a slight smile forming on her lips.

The very nearness of Saeeda Bai in these last few minutes, delightful as it had been, now created a small problem for Maan. Before he got up to change places with her he had to make a slight adjustment to his clothing in order not to let her see how aroused he was. But when he sat down again it seemed to him that Saeeda Bai was more amused than ever. She's a real sitam-zareef, he thought to himself—a tyrant with a smile.

'So, Ustad Sahib, let's begin our lesson,' she said, raising an eyebrow.

'Well,' said Maan, not looking at her, but acutely conscious of her closeness. 'The first item is an introduction by a certain James Cousins to Chughtai's illustrations.'

'Oh,' said Saeeda Bai, 'the first item from the Urdu side is an explanation by the artist himself of what he hoped to do by having this book printed.'

'And,' continued Maan, 'my second item is a foreword by the poet Iqbal to the book as a whole.'

'And mine,' said Saeeda Bai, 'is a long essay, again by Chughtai himself, on various matters, including his views on art.'

'Look at this,' said Maan, suddenly involved in what he was reading. 'I'd forgotten what a pompous foreword Iqbal wrote. All he seems to talk about is his own books, not the one that he's introducing. "In this book of mine I said this, in that book of mine I said that"—and only a few patronizing remarks about Chughtai and how young he is—'

He stopped indignantly.

'Dagh Sahib,' said Saeeda Bai, 'you're getting heated all right.'

They looked at each other, Maan thrown a little off balance by her directness. It seemed to him that she was trying to refrain from laughing outright. 'Perhaps I should cool you down with a melancholy ghazal,' continued Saeeda Bai.

'Yes, why don't you try?' said Maan, remembering what she had once said about ghazals. 'Let's see what effect it has on me.'

'Let me summon my musicians,' said Saeeda Bai.

'No,' said Maan, placing his hand on hers. 'Just you and the harmonium, that'll be enough.'

'At least the tabla player?'

'I'll keep the beat with my heart,' said Maan.

With a slight inclination of the head—a gesture that made Maan's heart almost skip a beat—Saeeda Bai acquiesced. 'Would you be capable of standing up and getting it for me?' she asked slyly.

'Hmm,' said Maan, but remained seated.

'And I also see that your glass is empty,' added Saeeda Bai.

Refusing this time to be embarrassed by anything, Maan got up. He fetched her the harmonium and himself another drink. Saeeda Bai hummed for a few seconds and said, 'Yes, I know which one will do.' She began to sing the enigmatic lines:

> 'No grain of dust in the garden is wasted.
> Even the path is like a lamp to the tulip's stain.'

At the word 'dagh' Saeeda Bai shot Maan a quick and amused glance. The next couplet was fairly uneventful. But it was followed by:

> 'The rose laughs at the activities of the nightingale—
> What they call love is a defect of the mind.'

Maan, who knew these lines well, must have shown a very transparent dismay; for as soon as Saeeda Bai looked at him, she threw back her head and laughed with pleasure. The sight of her soft white throat exposed, her sudden, slightly husky laughter, and the piquancy of not knowing whether she was laughing with or at him made Maan completely forget himself. Before he knew it and despite the hindrance of the harmonium, he had leaned over and kissed her on the neck, and before she knew it she was responding.

'Not now, not now, Dagh Sahib,' she said, a little out of breath.

'Now—now—' said Maan.

'Then we'd better go to the other room,' said Saeeda Bai. 'You are getting into the habit of interrupting my ghazals.'

'When else have I interrupted your ghazals?' asked Maan as she led him to her bedroom.

'I'll tell you some other time,' said Saeeda Bai.

Part Three

3.1

Sunday breakfast at Pran's house was usually a bit later than during the week. The *Brahmpur Chronicle* had arrived and Pran had his nose fixed in the Sunday Supplement. Savita sat to one side eating her toast and buttering Pran's. Mrs Rupa Mehra came into the room and asked, in a worried tone, 'Have you seen Lata anywhere?'

Pran shook his head behind his newspaper.

'No, Ma,' said Savita.

'I hope she's all right,' said Mrs Rupa Mehra anxiously. She looked around and said to Mateen: 'Where's the spice powder? I am always forgotten when you lay the table.'

'Why wouldn't she be all right, Ma?' said Pran. 'This is Brahmpur, not Calcutta.'

'Calcutta's very safe,' said Mrs Rupa Mehra, defending the city of her only grandchild. 'It may be a big city, but the people are very good. It's quite safe for a girl to walk about at any time.'

'Ma, you're just homesick for Arun,' said Savita. 'Everyone knows who your favourite child is.'

'I don't have favourites,' said Mrs Rupa Mehra.

The phone rang. 'I'll take it,' said Pran casually. 'It's probably something to do with tonight's debating contest. Why do I consent to organize all these wretched activities?'

'For the looks of adoration in your students' eyes,' said Savita.

Pran picked up the phone. The other two continued with their breakfast. A sharp, exclamatory tone in Pran's voice, however, told Savita that it was something serious. Pran looked shocked, and glanced worriedly at Mrs Rupa Mehra.

'Ma—' said Pran, but could say nothing further.

'It's about Lata,' said Mrs Rupa Mehra, reading his face. 'She's had an accident.'

'No—' said Pran.

'Thank God.'

'She's eloped—' said Pran.

'Oh my God,' said Mrs Rupa Mehra.

'With whom?' asked Savita, transfixed, still holding a piece of toast in her hand.

'—with Maan,' said Pran, shaking his head slowly back and forth in disbelief. 'How—' he went on, but was temporarily unable to speak.

'Oh my God,' said Savita and her mother almost simultaneously.

For a few seconds there was stunned silence.

'He phoned my father from the railway station,' continued Pran, shaking his head. 'Why didn't he talk it over with me? I don't see any objection to the match as such, except for Maan's previous engagement—'

'No objection—' whispered Mrs Rupa Mehra in astonishment. Her nose had gone red and two tears had started helplessly down her cheeks. Her hands were clasped together as if in prayer.

'Your brother—' began Savita indignantly, 'may think he is the cat's whiskers, but how you can think that we—'

'Oh my poor daughter, oh my poor daughter,' wept Mrs Rupa Mehra.

The door opened, and Lata walked in.

'Yes, Ma?' said Lata. 'Were you calling me?' She looked at the dramatic tableau in surprise, and went over to comfort her mother. 'Now what's the matter?' she asked, looking around the table. 'Not the other medal, I hope.'

'Say it isn't true, say it isn't true,' cried Mrs Rupa Mehra. 'How could you think of doing this? And with Maan! How can you break my heart like this?' A thought suddenly occurred to her. 'But—it can't be true. The railway station?'

'I haven't been to any station,' said Lata. 'What's going on, Ma? Pran told me you were going to have a long session by yourselves about plans and prospects for me'—she frowned a little—'and that it would only embarrass me to be here. He told me to come back late for breakfast. What have I done that has upset you all so much?'

Savita looked at Pran in angry astonishment; now, to her outrage, he simply yawned.

'Those who aren't conscious of the date,' said Pran, tapping the head of the paper, 'must take the consequences.'

It was the 1st of April.

Mrs Rupa Mehra had stopped weeping but was still bewildered. Savita looked at her husband and her sister in severe reproof and said, 'Ma, this is Pran and Lata's idea of an April Fool joke.'

'Not mine,' said Lata, beginning to understand what had happened in her absence. She began to laugh. Then she sat down and looked at the others. 'Really, Pran,' said Savita. She turned to her sister: 'It's not so funny, Lata.'

'Yes,' said Mrs Rupa Mehra. 'And at exam time—it will disturb your studies—and all this time and money will have gone down the drain. Don't laugh.'

'Cheer up, cheer up, everyone. Lata is still unmarried. God's in his Heaven,' Pran said unrepentantly, and hid behind his newspaper again. He too was laughing, but silently to himself. Savita and Mrs Rupa Mehra looked daggers at the *Brahmpur Chronicle.*

A sudden thought struck Savita. 'I could have had a miscarriage,' she said.

'Oh, no,' said Pran unconcernedly. 'You're robust. I'm the frail one. Besides, this was done entirely for your benefit: to liven up your Sunday morning. You're always complaining about how dull Sunday is.'

'Well, I prefer boredom to this. Aren't you at least going to apologize to us?'

'Of course,' said Pran readily. Though he was not very happy with himself for having brought his mother-in-law to tears, he was delighted at the way the trick had come off. And Lata at least had enjoyed it. 'Sorry, Ma. Sorry, darling.'

'I should hope so. Say sorry to Lata too,' Savita said.

'Sorry, Lata,' said Pran, laughing. 'You must be hungry. Why don't you order your egg?'

'Though actually,' continued Pran, undoing most of the goodwill he had salvaged, 'I don't see why I should apologize. I don't enjoy these April fooleries. It's because I've married into a westernized family that I decided, well, Pran, you have to keep your end up or they'll think you are a peasant, and you'll never be able to face Arun Mehra again.'

'You can stop making snide remarks about my brother,' said Savita. 'You've been doing so ever since the wedding. Yours is equally vulnerable. More so, in fact.'

Pran considered this for a moment. People had begun talking about Maan.

'Come on, darling, forgive me,' he said with a little more genuine contrition in his voice. 'What do I have to do to make up?'

'Take us to see a film,' Savita said immediately. 'I want to see a Hindi film today—just to emphasize how westernized I am.' Savita enjoyed Hindi movies (the more sentimental the better); she also knew that Pran, for the most part, detested them.

'A Hindi film?' said Pran. 'I thought the strange tastes of expecting mothers extended only to food and drink.'

'All right, that's fixed then,' said Savita. 'Which one should we see?'

'Sorry,' said Pran, 'impossible. There's that debate this evening.'

'A matinee then,' said Savita, flicking the butter off the end of her toast in a decisive manner.

'Oh, all right, all right, I suppose I've brought this upon myself,' said Pran. He turned to the appropriate page in the newspaper. 'How about this? *Sangraam.* At the Odeon. "Acclaimed by all—a greatest movie marvel. For adults only." Ashok Kumar's acting in it—he makes Ma's heart beat faster.'

'You're teasing me,' Mrs Rupa Mehra said, somewhat appeased. 'But I do like his acting. Still, somehow, you know all these adult movies, I feel—'

'All right,' said Pran. 'Next one. No—there's no afternoon show for that. Um, um, here's something that looks interesting. *Kalé Badal.* An epic of love and romance. Meena, Shyam, Gulab, Jeewan, et cetera, et cetera, even Baby Tabassum! Just right for you in your present condition,' he added to Savita.

'No,' said Savita. 'I don't like any of the actors.'

'This family is very particular,' Pran said. 'First they want a film, then they reject all the options.'

'Keep reading,' said Savita, rather sternly.

'Yes, Memsahib,' said Pran. 'Well, then we have *Hulchul.* Great Gala Opening. Nargis—'

'I like her,' said Mrs Rupa Mehra. 'She has such expressive features—'

'Daleep Kumar—'

'Ah!' said Mrs Rupa Mehra.

'Restrain yourself, Ma,' said Pran. '—Sitara, Yaqub, K.N. Singh and Jeewan. "Great in story. Great in stars. Great in music. In 30 years of Indian films no picture like this." Well?'

'Where's it showing?'

'At the Majestic. "Renovated, luxuriously furnished and fitted with fresh air circulating device for cool comfort."'

'That sounds right in every way,' said Mrs Rupa Mehra with careful optimism, as if she were discussing a prospective match for Lata.

'But wait!' said Pran. 'Here's an ad that's so big I missed it: it's for *Deedar.* Showing in the, let's see, in the equally well-appointed Manorma Talkies which also has a fresh air circulating device. Here's what it says: "It's a star-studded! Playing for 5th week. Punched with Lusty Songs & Romance To Warm Your Cockles. Nargis, Ashok Kumar—"'

He paused for the expected exclamation from his mother-in-law.

'You are always teasing me, Pran,' said Mrs Rupa Mehra happily, all her tears forgotten.

'"—Nimmi, Daleep Kumar—" (amazing luck, Ma) "—Yaqub, Baby Tabassum—" (we've hit the jackpot) "—Musical-Miracle songs which are sung in every street of the city. Acclaimed, Applauded, Admired by All. The only Picture for Families. A Storm of Movie. A Rainfall of Melody. Filmkar's *Deedar*! Star-studded Gem amongst Pictures! No Greater Picture will come your Way for So Many Years." Well, what do you say?'

He looked around him at three wondering faces. 'Thunderstruck!' said Pran approvingly. 'Twice in one morning.'

3.2

That afternoon the four of them went to warm their cockles at Manorma Talkies. They bought the best tickets in the balcony section, high above the hoi polloi, and a bar of Cadbury's chocolate of which Lata and Savita ate the major portion. Mrs Rupa Mehra was allowed one square despite her diabetes and Pran wanted no more than one. Pran and Lata were almost dry-eyed, Savita sniffed, and Mrs Rupa Mehra sobbed broken-heartedly. The film was indeed very sad, and the songs were sad too, and it was not clear whether it was the piteous fate of the blind singer or the tenderness of the love story that had most affected her. An entirely good time would have been had by all had it not been for a man a row or two behind them who, every time the blind Daleep Kumar appeared on the screen, burst into a horrific frenzy of weeping and once or twice even knocked his stick on the floor to indicate perhaps an outraged protest against Fate or the director. Eventually Pran could bear it no longer, turned around and exclaimed: 'Sir, do you think you could refrain from knocking that—'

He stopped suddenly as he saw that the culprit was Mrs Rupa Mehra's father. 'Oh, my God,' he said to Savita, 'it's your grandfather! I'm so sorry, Sir! Please don't mind what I said, Sir. Ma is here as well, Sir, I mean Mrs Rupa Mehra. Terribly sorry. And Savita and Lata are here too. We do hope you will meet us after the film is over.'

By this time Pran himself was being shushed by others in the audience, and he turned back to the screen, shaking his head. The others were equally horror-struck. All this had no apparent effect on the emotions of Dr Kishen Chand Seth, who wept with as much clamour and energy through the last half hour of the movie as before.

'How was it we didn't meet during the interval?' Pran asked himself. 'And didn't he notice us either? We were sitting in front of him.' What Pran could not know was that Dr Kishen Chand Seth was impervious to any extraneous visual or auditory stimulus once he was involved in a film. As for the matter of the interval, that was—and was to remain—a mystery, especially since Dr Kishen Chand Seth and his wife Parvati had come together.

When the movie was over and they had been extruded out of the hall like the rest of the crowd, everyone met in the lobby. Dr Kishen Chand Seth was still streaming copious tears, the others were dabbing at their eyes with handkerchiefs.

Parvati and Mrs Rupa Mehra made a couple of brave but hopeless attempts to pretend liking for each other. Parvati was a strong, bony, rather hard-boiled woman of thirty-five. She had brown, sun-hardened skin, and an attitude towards the world that seemed to be an extension of her attitude to her more enfeebled patients: it was as if she had suddenly decided she was not going to empty anyone's bedpans any more. She was wearing a georgette sari with what looked like pink pine cones printed all over it. Her lipstick, however, was not pink but orange.

Mrs Rupa Mehta, shrinking from this impressive vision, tried to explain why she had not been able to visit Parvati for her birthday.

'How nice to meet you here, though,' she added.

'Yes, isn't it?' said Parvati. 'I was saying to Kishy just the other day . . .'

But the rest of the sentence was lost on Mrs Rupa Mehra, who had never heard her seventy-year-old father referred to in terms of such odious triviality. 'My husband' was bad enough; but 'Kishy'? She looked at him, but he seemed still to be locked in a globe of celluloid.

Dr Kishen Chand Seth emerged from this sentimental aura in a minute or two. 'We must go home,' he announced.

'Please come over to our place for tea, and then go back,' suggested Pran.

'No, no, impossible, impossible today. Some other time. Yes. Tell your father we expect him for bridge tomorrow evening. At seven thirty sharp. Surgeon's time, not politician's.'

'Oh,' said Pran, smiling now, 'I'd be glad to. I'm glad your misunderstanding has been sorted out.'

Dr Kishen Chand Seth realized with a start that of course it hadn't. Under the filmy mist that had engulfed him—for in *Deedar* good friends had spoken bitter words to each other—he had forgotten about his falling out with Mahesh Kapoor. He looked at Pran with annoyance. Parvati came to a sudden decision.

'Yes, it's been sorted out in my husband's mind. Please tell him we look forward to seeing him.' She looked at Dr Seth for confirmation; he gave a disgusted grunt, but thought it best to let things be. Suddenly his attention shifted.

'When?' he demanded, indicating Savita's stomach with the handle of his cane.

'August or September, that's what we've been told,' said Pran, rather vaguely, as if afraid that Dr Kishen Chand Seth might decide to take over things again.

Dr Kishen Chand Seth turned to Lata. 'Why aren't you married yet? Don't you like my radiologist?' he asked her.

Lata looked at him and tried to hide her amazement. Her cheeks burned.

'You haven't introduced her to the radiologist yet,' Mrs Rupa Mehra interposed quickly. 'And now it is almost time for her exams.'

'What radiologist?' asked Lata. 'It's still the 1st of April. Is that it?'

'Yes, the radiologist. Call me tomorrow,' said Dr Kishen Chand Seth to his daughter. 'Remind me, Parvati. Now we must go. I must see this film again next week. So sad,' he added approvingly.

On the way to his grey Buick Dr Kishen Chand Seth noticed a wrongly parked car. He yelled at the policeman on duty at the busy intersection. The policeman, who recognized the terrifying Dr Seth, as did most of the forces of order and disorder in Brahmpur, left the traffic to fend for itself, came over promptly, and took down the number of the car. A beggar limped alongside and asked for a couple of pice. Dr Kishen Chand Seth looked at him in fury and gave him a brutal whack on the leg with his stick. He and Parvati got into the car and the policeman cleared the traffic for them.

3.3

'No talking, please,' said the invigilator.

'I was just borrowing a ruler, Sir.'

'If you have to do that, do it through me.'

'Yes, Sir.'

The boy sat down and applied himself once more to the question paper in front of him.

A fly buzzed against the windowpane of the examination hall. Outside the window the red crown of a gulmohur tree could be seen below the stone steps. The fans whirled slowly around. Row after row of heads, row after row of hands, drop after drop of ink, words and yet more words. Someone got up to have a drink of water from the earthenware pitcher near the exit. Someone leaned back against his chair and sighed.

Lata had stopped writing about half an hour ago, and had been staring at her paper sightlessly since. She was trembling. She could not think of the questions at all. She was breathing deeply and the sweat stood out on her forehead. Neither of the girls on either side of her noticed. Who were they? She didn't recognize them from the English lectures.

What do these questions mean? she asked herself. And how was I managing to answer them just a little while ago? Do Shakespeare's tragic heroes deserve their fates? Does anyone deserve her fate? She looked around again. What is the matter with me, I who am so good at taking exams? I don't have a headache, I don't have a period, what is my excuse? What will Ma say—

An image of her bedroom in Pran's house came to her mind. In it she saw her mother's three suitcases, filled with most of what she owned in the world. Standard appendages of her Annual Rail-Pilgrimage, they lay in a corner, with her large handbag resting like a self-confident black swan upon them. Nearby lay a small square dark-green copy of the Bhagavad Gita and a glass that contained her false teeth. She had worn them ever since a car accident ten years ago.

What would my father have thought? wondered Lata—with his brilliant record—his gold medals—how can I fail him like this? It was in April that he died. Gulmohurs were in bloom then too. . . . I must concentrate. I must concentrate. Something has happened to me and I must not panic. I must relax and things will be all right again.

She fell into a reverie once more. The fly buzzed in a steady drone.

'No humming. Please be silent.'

Lata realized with a start that it was she who had been humming softly to herself and that both her neighbours were now looking at her: one appeared puzzled, the other annoyed. She bent her head towards her answer book. The pale blue lines stretched out without any potential meaning across the blank page.

'If at first you don't succeed—' she heard her mother's voice say.

She quickly turned back to a previous question she had already answered, but what she had written made no sense to her.

'The disappearance of Julius Caesar from his own play as early as Act III would seem to imply . . .'

Lata rested her head on her hands.

'Are you feeling all right?'

She raised her head and looked at the troubled face of a young lecturer from the Philosophy Department who happened to be on invigilation duty that day.

'Yes.'

'You're quite sure?' he murmured.

Lata nodded.

She picked up her pen and began to write something in her answer book. A few minutes passed, and the invigilator announced: 'Half an hour left.'

Lata realized that at least an hour of her three-hour paper had vanished into nothingness. She had answered only two questions so far. Activated by sudden alarm, she began to write answers to the two remaining questions—she chose them virtually at random—in a rapid, panic-stricken scrawl, smearing her fingers with ink, smudging the answer book, hardly conscious of what she was writing. The buzzing of the fly seemed to her to have entered her brain. Her normally attractive handwriting now looked worse than Arun's, and this thought almost made her seize up again.

'Five minutes left.'

Lata continued to write, hardly aware of what it was she was writing.

'Pens down, please.'

Lata's hand continued to move across the page.

'No more writing, please. Time's up.'

Lata put her pen down and buried her head in her hands.

'Bring your papers to the front of the hall. Please make sure that your roll numbers are correctly inscribed on the front and that your supplementary booklets, if you have any, are arranged in the right order. No talking, please, until you have left the hall.'

Lata handed in her booklet. On the way out she rested her right wrist for a few seconds against the cool earthenware pitcher.

She did not know what had come over her.

3.4

Lata stood outside the hall for a minute. Sunlight poured on to the stone steps. The edge of her middle finger was smeared with dark-blue ink, and she looked at it, frowning. She was close to tears.

Other English students stood on the steps and chatted. A post-mortem of the paper was being held, and it was dominated by an optimistic and chubby girl who was ticking off on her fingers the various points she had answered correctly.

'This is one paper I know I have done really well,' she said. 'Especially the *King Lear* question. I think that the answer was "Yes".' Others were looking excited or depressed. Everyone agreed that several of the questions were far harder than they had needed to be. A knot of history students stood not far away, discussing their paper, which had been held simultaneously in the same building. One of them was the young man who had brought himself to Lata's attention in the Imperial Book Depot, and he was looking a little worried. He had spent a great deal of time these last few months in extracurricular activities—particularly cricket—and this had taken its toll upon his performance.

Lata walked to a bench beneath the gulmohur tree, and sat down to collect herself. When she got home for lunch she would be pestered with a hundred questions about how well she had done. She looked down at the red flowers that lay scattered at her feet. In her head she could still hear the buzzing of the fly.

The young man, though he had been talking to his classmates, had noticed her walking down the steps. When she sat down on the far bench under the tree, he decided to have a word with her. He told his friends that he had to go home for lunch—that his father would be waiting for him—and hurried along the path past the gulmohur. As he came to the bench, he uttered an exclamation of surprise and stopped.

'Hello,' he said.

Lata raised her head and recognized him. She flushed with embarrassment that he should see her in her present visible distress.

'I suppose you don't remember me?' he said.

'I do,' said Lata, surprised that he should continue to talk to her despite her obvious wish that he should walk on. She said nothing further, nor did he for a few seconds.

'We met at the bookshop,' he said.

'Yes,' said Lata. Then, quickly, she added: 'Please, just let me be. I don't feel like talking to anyone.'

'It's the exam, isn't it?'

'Yes.'

'Don't worry,' he said. 'You'll have forgotten all about it in five years.'

Lata became indignant. She did not care for his glib philosophy. Who on earth did he think he was? Why didn't he just buzz off—like that wretched fly?

'I say that,' he continued, 'because a student of my father's once tried to kill himself after he had done badly in his final exams. It's a good thing he didn't succeed, because when the results came out he found he'd got a first.'

'How can you think you've done badly in mathematics when you've done well?' asked Lata, interested despite herself. 'Your answers are either right or wrong. I can understand it in history or English, but . . .'

'Well, that's an encouraging thought,' said the young man, pleased that she had remembered something about him. 'Both of us have probably done less badly than we think.'

'So you've done badly too?' asked Lata.

'Yes,' he said, simply.

Lata found it hard to believe him, as he didn't appear distressed in the least.

There was silence for a few moments. Some of the young man's friends passed by the bench but very tactfully forbore from greeting him. He knew, however, that this would not prevent them from taxing him later about the beginnings of a grand passion.

'But look, don't worry . . .' he went on. 'One paper in six is bound to be difficult. Do you want a dry handkerchief?'

'No, thank you.' She glared at him, then looked away.

'When I was standing there, feeling low,' he said, pointing to the top of the steps, 'I noticed you here looking even worse, and that cheered me up. May I sit down?'

'Please don't,' said Lata. Then, realizing how rude her words had sounded, she said, 'No, do. But I have to be off. I hope you've done better than you think.'

'I hope you'll feel better than you do,' said the young man, sitting down. 'Has it helped to talk to me?'

'No,' said Lata. 'Not at all.'

'Oh,' said the young man, a bit disconcerted. 'Anyway, remember,' he went on, 'there are more important things in the world than exams.' He stretched backwards on the bench, and looked up at the reddish-orange flowers.

'Like what?' asked Lata.

'Like friendship,' he said, a little severely.

'Really?' said Lata, smiling a little now despite herself.

'Really,' he said. 'Talking to you has certainly cheered me up.' But he continued to look stern.

Lata stood up and started to walk away from the bench.

'You don't have any objection to my walking along with you for a bit?' he said, getting up himself.

'I can't very well stop you,' said Lata. 'India is a free country now.'

'All right. I'll sit on this bench and think of you,' he said melodramatically, sitting down again. 'And of that attractive and mysterious ink stain near your nose. It's been some days since Holi.'

Lata made a sound of impatience and walked away. The young man's eyes were following her, and she was aware of it. She rubbed her stained middle finger with her thumb to control her awkwardness. She was annoyed with him and with herself, and unsettled by her unexpected enjoyment of his unexpected company. But these thoughts did have the effect of replacing her anxiety—indeed, panic—about how badly she'd done in the paper on Drama with the wish to look at a mirror at once.

3.5

Later that afternoon, Lata and Malati and a couple of their friends—all girls, of course—were taking a walk together to the jacaranda grove where they liked to sit and study. The jacaranda grove by tradition was open only to girls. Malati was carrying an incongruously fat medical textbook.

It was a hot day. The two wandered hand in hand among the jacaranda trees. A few soft mauve flowers drifted down to earth. When they were out of earshot of the others, Malati said, with quiet amusement:

'What is on your mind?'

When Lata looked at her quizzically, Malati continued, undeterred: 'No, no, it's no use looking at me like that, I know that something is bothering you. In fact I know what it is that's bothering you. I have my sources of information.'

Lata responded: 'I know what you're going to say, and it's not true.'

Malati looked at her friend and said: 'All that Christian training at St Sophia's has had a bad influence on you, Lata. It's made you into a terrible liar. No, I don't mean that exactly. What I mean is that when you do lie, you do it terribly.'

'All right, then, what were you going to say?' said Lata.

'I've forgotten now,' said Malati.

'Please,' said Lata, 'I didn't get up from my books for this. Don't be mean, don't be elliptical, and don't tease me. It's bad enough as it is.'

'Why?' said Malati. 'Are you in love already? It's high time, spring is over.'

'Of course not,' said Lata indignantly. 'Are you mad?'

'No,' said Malati.

'Then why do you have to ask such astonishing questions?'

'I heard about the way he walked familiarly up to you while you were sitting on the bench after the exam,' said Malati, 'so I assumed that you must have been meeting off and on since the Imperial Book Depot.' From her informant's description Malati had assumed that it had been the same fellow. And she was pleased she was right.

Lata looked at her friend with more exasperation than affection. News travels much too fast, she thought, and Malati listens in on every line.

'We have not been meeting either off or on,' she said. 'I don't know where you get your information from, Malati. I wish you would talk about music or the news or something sensible. Even your socialism. This is only the second time we've met, and I don't even know his name. Here, give me your textbook, and let's sit down. If I read a paragraph or two of something I don't understand, I'll be all right.'

'You don't even know his name?' said Malati, now looking at Lata as if she was the one who was mad. 'Poor fellow! Does he know yours?'

'I think I told him at the bookshop. Yes, I did. And then he asked me if I was going to ask him his—and I said no.'

'And you wish you hadn't,' said Malati, watching her face closely.

Lata was silent. She sat down and leaned against a jacaranda.

'And I suppose he would like to have told you,' said Malati, sitting down as well.

'I suppose he would,' said Lata laughing.

'Poor boiled potatoes,' said Malati.

'Boiled—what?'

'You know—"Don't put chillies on boiled potatoes."' Malati imitated Lata.

Lata blushed.

'You do like him, don't you?' said Malati. 'If you lie, I'd know it.'

Lata did not respond immediately. She had been able to face her mother with reasonable calmness at lunch, despite the strange, trance-like event of the Drama paper. Then she said:

'He could see that I was upset after the paper. I don't think it was easy for him to come up and talk to me when I had, well, in a way rebuffed him at the bookshop.'

'Oh, I don't know,' said Malati casually. 'Boys are such louts. He could very well have done it for the challenge. They're always daring each other to do idiotic things—for instance, storming the Women's Hostel at Holi. They think they are such heroes.'

'He is not a lout,' said Lata, bridling. 'And as for heroism, I think it does take at least a little courage to do something when you know that your head can be bitten off as a result. You said something to the same effect in the Blue Danube.'

'Not courage, boldness,' said Malati, who was thoroughly enjoying her friend's reactions. 'Boys aren't in love, they're just bold. When the four of us were walking to the grove just now, I noticed a couple of boys on bicycles following us in a pathetic sort of way. Neither really wanted to brave an encounter with us, but neither could say so. So it was quite a relief to them when we entered the grove and the question became moot.'

Lata was silent. She lay down on the grass and stared up at the sky through the jacaranda branches. She was thinking of the smear on her nose, which she had washed off before lunch.

'Sometimes they'll come up to you together,' continued Malati, 'and grin more at each other than at you. At other times they're so afraid that their friends will come up with a better "line" than they themselves can think of that they'll actually take their life in their hands and come up to you alone. And what are their lines? Nine times out of ten it is "May I borrow your notes?"—perhaps tempered with a lukewarm, feeble-minded "Namaste". What, incidentally, was the introductory line of the Potato Man?'

Lata kicked Malati.

'Sorry—I meant the apple of your heart.'

'What did he say?' said Lata, almost to herself. When she tried to recall exactly how the conversation had begun, she realized that, although it had taken place just a few hours ago, it had already grown hazy in her mind. What remained, however, was the memory that her initial nervousness at the young man's presence had ended in a sense of confused warmth: at least someone, if only a good-looking stranger, had understood that she had been bewildered and upset, and had cared enough to do something to lift her spirits.

3.6

A couple of days later there was a music recital in the Bharatendu Auditorium, one of the two largest auditoriums in town. One of the performers was Ustad Majeed Khan.

Lata and Malati both managed to get tickets. So did Hema, a tall, thin, and high-spirited friend of theirs who lived with innumerable cousins—boys and girls—in a house not far from Nabiganj. They were all under the care of a strict elder member of the family who was referred to by everyone as 'Tauji'. Hema's Tauji had quite a job on his hands, as he was not only responsible for the well-being and reputation of the girls of the family but also had to make sure that the boys did not get into the countless kinds of mischief that boys are prone to. He had often cursed his luck that he was the sole representative in a university town of a large and far-flung family. He had on occasion threatened to send everyone straight back home when they had caused him more trouble than he could bear. But his wife, 'Taiji' to everyone, though she herself had been brought up with almost no liberty or latitude, felt it was a great pity that her nieces and grandnieces should be similarly constrained. She managed to obtain for the girls what they could not obtain by a more direct approach.

This evening Hema and her cousins had thus succeeded in reserving the use of Tauji's large maroon Packard, and went around town collecting their friends for the concert. No sooner was Tauji out of sight than they had entirely forgotten his outraged parting comment: 'Flowers? Flowers in your hair? Rushing off in exam time—and listening to all this pleasure-music! Everyone will think you are completely dissolute—you will never get married.'

Eleven girls, including Lata and Malati, emerged from the Packard at Bharatendu Auditorium. Strangely enough, their saris were not crushed, though perhaps they looked slightly dishevelled. They stood outside the auditorium rearranging their own and each other's hair, chattering excitedly. Then in a busy shimmer of colour they streamed inside. There was no place for all of them to sit together, so they broke up into twos and threes, and sat down, rapt but no less voluble. A few fans whirled round overhead, but it had been a hot day, and the auditorium was stuffy. Lata and her friends started fanning themselves with their programmes, and waited for the recital to begin.

The first half consisted of a disappointingly indifferent sitar recital by a well-known musician. At the interval, Lata and Malati were standing by the staircase in the lobby when the Potato Man walked towards them.

Malati saw him first, nudged Lata's attention in his direction, and said: 'Meeting number three. I'm going to make myself scarce.'

'Malati, please stay here,' said Lata in sudden desperation, but Malati had disappeared with the admonition: 'Don't be a mouse. Be a tigress.'

The young man approached her with fairly assured steps.

'Is it all right to interrupt you?' he said, not very loudly.

Lata could not make out what he was saying in the noise of the crowded lobby, and indicated as much.

This was taken by the young man as permission to approach. He came closer, smiled at her, and said:

'I wondered if it was all right to interrupt you.'

'To interrupt me?' said Lata. 'But I was doing nothing.' Her heart was beating fast.

'I meant, to interrupt your thoughts.'

'I wasn't having any,' said Lata, trying to control a sudden overload of them. She thought of Malati's comment about her being a poor liar and felt the blood rush to her cheeks.

'Quite stuffy in there,' said the young man. 'Here too, of course.'

Lata nodded. I'm not a mouse or a tigress, she thought, I'm a hedgehog.

'Lovely music,' he said.

'Yes,' agreed Lata, though she hadn't thought so. His presence so close to her was making her tingle. Besides, she was embarrassed about being seen with a young man. She knew that if she looked around she would see someone she recognized looking at her. But having been unkind to him twice already she was determined not to rebuff him again. Holding up her side of the conversation, however, was difficult when she was feeling so distracted. Since it was hard for her to meet his eye, she looked down instead.

The young man was saying: '. . . though, of course, I don't often go there. How about you?'

Lata, nonplussed, because she had either not heard or not registered what went before, did not reply.

'You're very quiet,' he said.

'I'm always very quiet,' said Lata. 'It balances out.'

'No, you aren't,' said the young man with a faint smile. 'You and your friends were chattering like a flock of jungle babblers when you came in—and some of you continued to chatter while the sitar player was tuning up.'

'Do you think,' Lata said, looking up a little sharply, 'that men don't chatter and babble as much as women?'

'I do,' said the young man airily, happy that she was talking at last. 'It's a fact of nature. Shall I tell you a folk tale about Akbar and Birbal? It's very relevant to this subject.'

'I don't know,' said Lata. 'Once I've heard it I'll tell you if you should have told it.'

'Well, maybe at our next meeting?'

Lata took this remark quite coolly.

'I suppose there will be one,' she said. 'We seem to keep meeting by chance.'

'Does it have to be by chance?' asked the young man. 'When I talked about you and your friends, the fact is that I had eyes mostly for you. The moment I saw you enter, I thought how lovely you looked—in a simple green sari with just a white rose in your hair.'

The word 'mostly' bothered Lata, but the rest was music. She smiled.

He smiled back, and suddenly became very specific.

'There's a meeting of the Brahmpur Literary Society at five o'clock on Friday evening at old Mr Nowrojee's house—20 Hastings Road. It should be interesting—and it's open to anyone who feels like coming. With the university vacations coming up, they seem to want to welcome outsiders to make up the numbers.'

The university vacations, thought Lata. Perhaps we won't see each other again after all. The thought saddened her.

'Oh, I know what I wanted to ask you,' she said.

'Yes?' asked the young man, looking puzzled. 'Go ahead.'

'What's your name?' asked Lata.

The young man's face broke into a happy grin. 'Ah!' he said, 'I thought you would never ask. I'm Kabir, but very recently my friends have started calling me Galahad.'

'Why?' asked Lata, surprised.

'Because they think that I spend my time rescuing damsels in distress.'

'I was not in such distress that I needed rescuing,' said Lata.

Kabir laughed. 'I know you weren't, you know you weren't, but my friends are such idiots,' he said.

'So are mine,' said Lata disloyally. Malati had, after all, left her in the lurch.

'Why don't we exchange last names as well?' said the young man, pursuing his advantage.

Some instinct of self-preservation made Lata pause. She liked him, and she very much hoped she would meet him again—but he might ask her for her address next. Images of Mrs Rupa Mehra's interrogations came to mind.

'No, let's not,' said Lata. Then, feeling her abruptness and the hurt she might have caused him, she quickly blurted out the first thing she could think of. 'Do you have any brothers and sisters?'

'Yes, a younger brother.'

'No sisters?' Lata smiled, though she did not quite know why.

'I had a younger sister till last year.'

'Oh—I am so sorry,' said Lata in dismay. 'How terrible that must have been for you—and for your parents.'

'Well, for my father,' said Kabir quietly. 'But it looks as if Ustad Majeed Khan has begun. Maybe we should go in?'

Lata, moved by a rush of sympathy and even tenderness, hardly heard him; but as he walked towards the door, so did she. Inside the hall the maestro had begun his slow and magnificent rendition of Raag Shri. They separated, resumed their previous places, and sat down to listen.

3.7

Normally Lata would have been transfixed by Ustad Majeed Khan's music. Malati, sitting next to her, was. But her encounter with Kabir had set her mind wandering in so many different directions, often simultaneously, that she might as well have been listening to silence. She felt suddenly light-hearted and started smiling to herself at the thought of the rose in her hair. A minute later, remembering the last part of their conversation, she rebuked herself for being so unfeeling. She tried to make sense of what he had meant by saying—and so quietly at that—'Well, for my father.' Was it that his mother had already died? That would place him and Lata in a curiously symmetrical position. Or was his mother so estranged from the family that she was unconscious of or not much distressed by the loss of her daughter? Why am I thinking such impossible thoughts? Lata wondered. Indeed, when Kabir had said, 'I had a younger sister till last year,' did that have to imply the conclusion to which Lata had automatically jumped? But, poor fellow, he had grown so tense and subdued by the last few words that had passed between them that he had himself suggested that they return to the hall.

Malati was kind enough and smart enough neither to glance at her nor to nudge her. And soon Lata too sank into the music and lost herself in it.

3.8

The next time Lata saw Kabir, he was looking the very opposite of tense and subdued. She was walking across the campus with a book and a file under her arm when she saw him and another student, both wearing cricket clothes, sauntering along the path that led to the sports fields. Kabir was casually swinging a bat as he walked and the two of them appeared to be engaged in relaxed and occasional conversation. Lata was too far behind them to make out anything of what they were saying. Suddenly Kabir leaned his head back and burst out laughing. He looked so handsome in the morning sunlight and his laughter was so open-hearted and free from tension that Lata, who had been about to turn towards the library, found herself continuing to follow him. She was astonished by this, but didn't rebuke herself. Well, why shouldn't I? she thought. Since he's approached me three times already, I don't see why I shouldn't follow him for once. But I thought the cricket season was over. I didn't know there was a match on in the middle of exams.

As it happened, Kabir and his friend were off for a bit of practice at the nets. It was his way of taking a break from studies. The far end of the sports fields, where the practice nets had been set up, was close to a small stand of bamboos. Lata sat down in the shade and—herself unobserved—watched the two take turns with bat and ball. She did not know the first thing about cricket—even Pran's enthusiasm had not affected her at all—but she was drowsily entranced by the sight of Kabir, dressed completely in white, shirt unbuttoned at the collar, capless and with ruffled hair, running in to bowl—or standing at the crease wielding his bat with what seemed like easy skill. Kabir was an inch or two under six feet, slim and athletic, with a 'fair to wheatish' complexion, an aquiline nose, and black, wavy hair. Lata did not know how long she sat there, but it must have been for more than half an hour. The sound of bat on ball, the rustle of a slight breeze in the bamboo, the twittering of a few sparrows, the calls of a couple of mynas, and, above all, the sound of the young men's easy laughter and indistinct conversation all combined to make her almost oblivious of herself. It was quite a while before she came to.

I'm behaving like a fascinated gopi, she thought. Soon, instead of feeling jealous of Krishna's flute I'll start envying Kabir's bat! She smiled at the thought, then got up, brushed a few dried leaves from her salwaar-kameez, and—still unnoticed—walked back the way she had come.

'You have to find out who he is,' she told Malati that afternoon, plucking a leaf and absent-mindedly running it up and down her arm.

'Who?' said Malati. She was delighted.

Lata made a sound of exasperation.

'Well, I could have told you something about him,' said Malati, 'if you'd allowed me to after the concert.'

'Like what?' said Lata expectantly.

'Well, here are two facts to begin with,' said Malati tantalizingly. 'His name is Kabir, and he plays cricket.'

'But I know that already,' protested Lata. 'And that's about all I do know. Don't you know anything else?'

'No,' said Malati. She toyed with the idea of inventing a streak of criminality in his family, but decided that that was too cruel.

'But you said "to begin with". That means you must have something else.'

'No,' said Malati. 'The second half of the concert began just as I was about to ask my informant a few more questions.'

'I'm sure you can find out everything about him if you put your mind to it.' Lata's faith in her friend was touching.

Malati doubted it. She had a wide circle of acquaintance. But it was nearly the end of term and she didn't know where to begin inquiries. Some students—those whose exams were over—had already left Brahmpur; these included her informant at the concert. She herself would be leaving in a couple of days to go back to Agra for a while.

'The Trivedi Detective Agency needs a clue or two to start with,' she said. 'And time is short. You've got to think back over your conversations. Isn't there anything else you know about him that could help me?'

Lata thought for a while but came up with a blank. 'Nothing,' she said.

'Oh, wait—his father teaches maths.'

'At Brahmpur University?' asked Malati.

'I don't know,' said Lata. 'And another thing: I think he's fond of literature. He wanted me to come to the Lit Soc meeting tomorrow.'

'Then why don't you go there and ask him about himself,' said Malati, who believed in the Approach Audacious. 'Whether he brushes his teeth with Kolynos, for instance. "There's magic in a Kolynos smile."'

'I can't,' said Lata, so forcefully that Malati was a little taken aback.

'Surely you're not falling for him!' she said. 'You don't know the first thing about him—his family, or even his full name.'

'I feel I know more important things about him than the first thing,' said Lata.

'Yes, yes,' said Malati, 'like the whiteness of his teeth and the blackness of his hair. "She floated on a magical cloud high in the sky, sensing his strong presence around her with every fibre of her being. He was her whole universe. He was the be-all and end-all and catch-all and hold-all of her existence." I know the feeling.'

'If you're going to talk nonsense—' said Lata, feeling the warmth rise to her face.

'No, no, no, no, no,' said Malati, still laughing. 'I'll find out whatever I can.'

Several thoughts went through her mind: cricket reports in the university magazine? The Mathematics Department? The Registrar's Office?

Aloud she said, 'Leave Boiled Potatoes to me. I'll smother him with chillies and present him to you on a platter. Anyway, Lata, from your face, no one would know you still had a paper left. Being in love is good for you. You must do it more often.'

'Yes, I will,' said Lata. 'When you become a doctor, prescribe it to all your patients.'

3.9

Lata arrived at 20 Hastings Road at five o'clock the next day. She had finished her last paper that morning. She was convinced she had not done well in it, but when she started to feel upset, she thought of Kabir and instantly cheered up. Now she looked around for him among the group of about fifteen men and women who were sitting in old Mr Nowrojee's drawing room—the room in which the weekly meetings of the Brahmpur Literary Society had been held from as far back as anyone could remember. But either Kabir had not yet arrived or else he had changed his mind about coming.

The room was full of stuffed chairs with flowery prints and overstuffed cushions with flowery prints.

Mr Nowrojee, a thin, short and gentle man, with an immaculate white goatee beard and an immaculate light-grey suit, presided over the occasion. Noticing that Lata was a new face, he introduced himself and made her feel welcome. The others, who were sitting or standing in small groups, paid no attention to her. Feeling awkward at first, she walked over to a window and gazed out towards a small, well-tended garden with a sundial in the middle. She was looking forward so much to seeing him that she vehemently pushed aside the thought that he might not turn up.

'Good afternoon, Kabir.'

'Good afternoon, Mr Nowrojee.'

Lata turned around at the mention of Kabir's name and the sound of his low, pleasant voice, and gave him such a happy smile that he put his hand to his forehead and staggered back a few steps.

Lata did not know what to make of his buffoonery, which luckily no one else had noticed. Mr Nowrojee was now seated at the oblong table at the end of the room and was coughing mildly for attention. Lata and Kabir sat down on an empty sofa near the wall farthest from the table. Before they could say anything to each other, a middle-aged man with a plump, bright-eyed, cheerful face handed them each a sheaf of carbon copies which appeared to be covered with poetry.

'Makhijani,' he said mysteriously as he passed.

Mr Nowrojee took a sip of water from one of the three glasses in front of him. 'Fellow-members of the Brahmpur Literary Society—and friends,' he said in a voice that barely carried to where Lata and Kabir were sitting, 'we have gathered here for the 1,698th meeting of our society. I now declare the meeting open.'

He looked wistfully out of the window, and rubbed his glasses with a handkerchief. Then he continued: 'I remember when Edmund Blunden addressed us. He said—and I remember his words to this very day—he said—'

Mr Nowrojee stopped, coughed, and looked down at the sheet of paper in front of him. His skin itself appeared to be as thin as paper.

He went on: '1,698th meeting. Poetry recitation of their own poetry by members of the society. Copies, I see, have been handed out. Next week Professor O.P. Mishra of the English Department will present to us a paper on the subject: "Eliot: Whither?"'

Lata, who enjoyed Professor Mishra's lectures despite the pinkness with which he was now invested in her mind, looked interested, though the title was a bit mystifying.

'Three poets will be reading from their own work today,' continued Mr Nowrojee, 'following which I hope you will join us for tea. I am sorry to see that my young friend Mr Sorabjee has not been able to make the time to come,' he added in tones of gentle rebuke.

Mr Sorabjee, fifty-seven years old, and—like Mr Nowrojee himself—a Parsi, was the Proctor of Brahmpur University. He rarely missed a meeting of the literary societies of either the university or the town. But he always managed to avoid meetings where members read out their own literary efforts.

Mr Nowrojee smiled indecisively. 'The poets reading today are Dr Vikas Makhijani, Mrs Supriya Joshi—'

'Shrimati Supriya Joshi,' said a booming female voice. The broad-bosomed Mrs Joshi had stood up to make the correction.

'Er, yes, our, er, talented poetess Shrimati Supriya Joshi—and, of course, myself, Mr R.P. Nowrojee. As I am already seated at the table I will avail myself of the chairman's prerogative of reading my own poems first—by way of an aperitif to the more substantial fare that is to follow. Bon appétit.' He allowed himself a sad, rather wintry, chuckle before clearing his throat and taking another sip of water.

'The first poem that I would like to read is entitled "Haunting Passion",' said Mr Nowrojee primly. And he read the following poem:

> I'm haunted by a tender passion,
>   The ghost of which will never die.
> The leaves of autumn have grown ashen:
> I'm haunted by a tender passion.
> And spring-time too, in its own fashion,
>   Burns me with love's sweet song—so I—
> I'm haunted by a tender passion,
>   The ghost of which will never die.

As Mr Nowrojee completed his poem, he seemed to be manfully holding back his tears. He looked out towards the garden, towards the sundial, and, pulling himself together, said:

'That is a triolet. Now I will read you a ballade. It is called "Buried Flames".'

After he had read this and three other poems in a similar vein with diminishing vigour, he stopped, spent of all emotion. He then got up like one who has completed an infinitely distant and exhausting journey, and sat down on a stuffed chair not far from the speaker's table.

In the brief interval between him and the next reader Kabir looked inquiringly at Lata and she looked quizzically back at him. They were both trying to control their laughter, and looking at each other was not helping them do this.

Luckily, the happy, plump-faced man who had handed them the poems that he planned to read now rushed forward energetically to the speaker's table and, before sitting down, said the single word:

'Makhijani.'

After he had announced his name, he looked even more delighted than before. He riffled through his sheaf of papers with an expression of intense and pleasurable concentration, then smiled at Mr Nowrojee, who shrank in his chair like a sparrow cowering in a niche before a gale. Mr Nowrojee had tried at one stage to dissuade Dr Makhijani from reading, but had met with such good-natured outrage that he had had to give in. But having read a copy of the poems earlier in the day, he could not help wishing that the banquet had ended with the aperitif.

'A Hymn to Mother India,' said Dr Makhijani sententiously, then beamed at his audience. He leaned forward with the concentration of a burly blacksmith and read his poem through, including the stanza numbers, which he hammered out like horseshoes.

1. Who a child has not seen drinking milk
   At bright breasts of Mother, rags she wears or silks?
   Love of mild Mother like rain-racked gift of cloud.
   In poet's words, Mother to thee I bow.

2. What poor gift when doctor patient treats.
   Hearts he hears but so much his heart bleats?
   Where is doctor that can cure my pains?
   Why suffers Mother? Where to base the blame?

3. Her raiments rain-drenched with May or Monsoon,
   Like Savitri sweet she wins from Yama her sons,
   Cheating death with millions of population,
   Leading to chaste and virtuous nation.

4. From shore of Kanyakumari to Kashmir,
   From tiger of Assam to rampant beast of Gir,
   Freedom's dawn now bathing, laving her face,
   Tremble of jetty locks is Ganga's grace.

5. How to describe bondage of Mother pure
   By pervert punies chained through shackles of law?
   British cut-throat, Indian smiling and slave:
   Such shame will not dispense till a sweating grave.

While reading the above stanza, Dr Makhijani became highly agitated, but he was restored to equanimity by the next one:

6. Let me recall history of heroes proud,
   Mother-milk fed their breasts, who did not bow.
   Fought they fiercely, carrying worlds of weight,
   Establishing firm foundation of Indian state.

Nodding at the nervous Mr Nowrojee, Dr Makhijani now lauded his namesake, one of the fathers of the Indian freedom movement:

7. Dadabhai Naoroji entered Parliament,
   As MP from Finsbury, grace was heaven-sent.
   But he forgot not Mother's plumpy breasts:
   Dreams were of India, living in the West.

Lata and Kabir looked at each other in mingled delight and horror.

8. B.G. Tilak from Maharashtra hailed.
   'Swaraj my birthright is' he ever wailed.
   But cruel captors sent him to the sweltry jail
   In Forts of Mandalay, a six-year sail.

9. Shame of the Mother bold Bengal reviled.
   Terrorist pistol in hand of the Kali child.

Draupadi's sari twirling off and off—
White Duryodhanas laugh to scorn and scoff.

Dr Makhijani's voice trembled with belligerence at these vivid lines. Several stanzas later he descended on figures of the immediate past and present:

26. Mahatma came to us like summer 'andhi',
Sweeping the dungs and dirt, was M.K. Gandhi.
Murder has mayhemed peace beyond understanding.
Respect and sorrow leave me soiled and standing.

At this point Dr Makhijani stood up as a mark of veneration, and remained standing for the final three stanzas:

27. Then when the British left after all,
We had as PM our own Jawahar Lal.
Like rosy shimmers to the throne he came,
And gave to our India a glorious name.

28. Muslim, Hindu, Sikh, Christian, revere him.
Parsis, Jains, Buddhists also endear him.
Cynosure of eyes, he stalks with regal mien
Breathing spirit of a splendid scene.

29. We are all masters, each a Raja or Rani.
No slave, or high or low, says Makhijani.
Liberty equality fraternity justice as in Constitution.
In homage of Mother we will find all solutions.

In the tradition of Urdu or Hindi poetry, the bard had imbedded his own name in the last stanza. He now sat down, wiping the sweat from his forehead, and beaming.

Kabir had been scribbling a note. He passed it on to Lata; their hands touched accidentally. Though she was in pain with her attempt to suppress her laughter, she felt a shock of excitement at his touch. It was he who, after a few seconds, moved his hand away, and she saw what he had written:

Prompt escape from 20 Hastings Road
Is my desire, although prized poets' abode.

Desert not friendship. Renegade with me
From raptured realm of Mr Nowrojee.

It was not quite up to Dr Makhijani's efforts, but it got its point across. Lata and Kabir, as if at a signal, got up quickly and, before they could be intercepted by a cheated Dr Makhijani, got to the front door.

Out on the sober street they laughed delightedly for a few minutes, quoting back at each other bits of Dr Makhijani's patriotic hymn. When the laughter had died down, Kabir said to her:

'How about a coffee? We could go to the Blue Danube.'

Lata, worried that she might meet someone she knew and already thinking of Mrs Rupa Mehra, said, 'No, I really can't. I have to go back home. To my Mother,' she added mischievously.

Kabir could not take his eyes off her.

'But your exams are over,' he said. 'You should be celebrating. It's I who have two papers left.'

'I wish I could. But meeting you here has been a pretty bold step for me.'

'Well, won't we at least meet here again next week? For "Eliot: Whither?"' Kabir made an airy gesture, rather like a foppish courtier, and Lata smiled.

'But are you going to be in Brahmpur next Friday?' she asked. 'The holidays . . .'

'Oh yes,' said Kabir. 'I live here.'

He was unwilling to say goodbye, but did so at last.

'See you next Friday then—or before,' he said, getting on to his bike. 'Are you sure I can't drop you anywhere—on my bicycle made for two? Smudged or unsmudged, you do look beautiful.'

Lata looked around, blushing.

'No, I'm sure. Goodbye,' she said. 'And—well—thank you.'

3.10

When Lata got home she avoided her mother and sister and went straight to the bedroom. She lay on the bed and stared at the ceiling just as, a few days before, she had lain on the grass and stared at the sky through the jacaranda branches. The accidental touch of his hand as he had passed her the note was what she most wanted to recall.

Later, during dinner, the phone rang. Lata, sitting closest to the telephone, went to pick up the receiver.

'Hello?' said Lata.

'Hello—Lata?' said Malati.

'Yes,' said Lata happily.

'I've found out a couple of things. I'm going away tonight for a fortnight, so I thought I'd better tell you at once. Are you by yourself?' Malati added cautiously.

'No,' said Lata.

'Will you be by yourself within the next half hour or so?'

'No, I don't think so,' said Lata.

'It isn't good news, Lata,' said Malati, seriously. 'You had better drop him.'

Lata said nothing.

'Are you still there?' asked Malati, concerned.

'Yes,' said Lata, glancing at the other three seated around the dining table. 'Go on.'

'Well, he's on the university cricket team,' said Malati, reluctant to break the ultimate bad news to her friend. 'There's a photograph of the team in the university magazine.'

'Yes?' said Lata, puzzled. 'But what—'

'Lata,' said Malati, unable to beat about the bush any further. 'His surname is Durrani.'

So what? thought Lata. What does that make him? Is he a Sindhi or something? Like—well—Chetwani or Advani—or . . . or Makhijani?

'He's a Muslim,' said Malati, cutting into her thoughts. 'Are you still there?'

Lata was staring straight ahead. Savita put down her knife and fork, and looked anxiously at her sister.

Malati continued: 'You haven't a chance. Your family will be dead set against him. Forget him. Put it down to experience. And always find out the last name of anyone with an ambiguous first name. . . . Why don't you say something? Are you listening?'

'Yes,' said Lata, her heart in turmoil.

She had a hundred questions, and more than ever she needed her friend's advice and sympathy and help. She said, slowly and evenly, 'I'd better go now. We're in the middle of dinner.'

Malati said, 'It didn't occur to me—it just didn't occur to me—but didn't it occur to you either? With a name like that—though all the Kabirs I know are Hindu—Kabir Bhandare, Kabir Sondhi—'

'It didn't occur to me,' said Lata. 'Thanks, Malu,' she added, using the form of Malati's name she sometimes used out of affection. 'Thank you for—well—'

'I'm so sorry. Poor Lata.'

'No. See you when you return.'

'Read a P.G. Wodehouse or two,' said Malati by way of parting advice. 'Bye.'

'Bye,' said Lata and put down the receiver carefully.

She returned to the table but she could not eat. Mrs Rupa Mehra immediately tried to find out what the matter was. Savita decided not to say anything at all for the moment. Pran looked on, puzzled.

'It's nothing,' Lata said, looking at her mother's anxious face.

After dinner, she went to the bedroom. She couldn't bear to talk with the family or listen to the late news on the radio. She lay face down on her bed and burst into tears—as quietly as she could—repeating his name with love and with angry reproach.

3.11

It did not need Malati to tell her that it was impossible. Lata knew it well enough herself. She knew her mother and the deep pain and horror she would suffer if she heard that her daughter had been seeing a Muslim boy.

Any boy was worrisome enough, but this was too shameful, too painful, to believe. Lata could hear Mrs Rupa Mehra's voice: 'What did I do in my past life that I have deserved this?' And she could see her mother's tears as she faced the horror of her beloved daughter being given over to the nameless 'them'. Her old age would be embittered and she would be past consoling.

Lata lay on the bed. It was getting light. Her mother had gone through two chapters of the Gita that she recited every day at dawn. The Gita asked for detachment, tranquil wisdom, indifference to the fruits of action. This was a lesson that Mrs Rupa Mehra would never learn, could never learn. The lesson did not suit her temperament, even if its recitation did. The day she learned to be detached and indifferent and tranquil she would cease to be herself.

Lata knew that her mother was worried about her. But perhaps she attributed Lata's undisguisable misery over the next few days to anxiety about the results of the exams.

If only Malati were here, Lata said to herself.

If only she had not met him in the first place. If only their hands had not touched. If only.

If only I could stop acting like a fool! Lata said to herself. Malati always insisted that it was boys who behaved like morons when they were in love, sighing in their hostel rooms and wallowing in the Shelley-like treacle of ghazals. It was going to be a week before she met Kabir again. If she had known how to get in touch with him before then, she would have been even more torn with indecision.

She thought of yesterday's laughter outside Mr Nowrojee's house and angry tears came to her eyes again. She went to Pran's bookshelf and picked up the first P.G. Wodehouse she saw: *Pigs Have Wings*. Malati, though flippant, both meant and prescribed well.

'Are you all right?' asked Savita.

'Yes,' said Lata. 'Did it kick last night?'

'I don't think so. At least I didn't wake up.'

'Men should have to bear them,' said Lata, apropos of nothing. 'I'm going for a walk by the river.' She assumed, correctly, that Savita was in no state to join her down the steep path that led from the campus to the sands.

She changed her slippers for sandals, which made walking easier. As she descended the clayey slope, almost a mud cliff, to the shore of the Ganga, she noticed a troupe of monkeys cavorting in a couple of banyan trees—two trees that had fused into one through the intertwining of their branches. A small orange-smeared statue of a god was jammed between the central trunks. The monkeys were usually pleased to see her—she brought them fruits and nuts whenever she remembered to. Today she had forgotten, and they made clear their displeasure. A couple of the smaller ones pulled at her elbow in request, while one of the larger ones, a fierce male, bared his teeth in annoyance—but from a distance.

She needed to be distracted. She suddenly felt very gentle towards the animal world—which seemed to her, probably incorrectly, to be a simpler place than the world of humans. Though she was halfway down the cliff, she walked back up again, went to the kitchen, and got a paper bag full of peanuts and another filled with three large musammis for the monkeys. She knew they did not like them as much as oranges, but in the summer only the thicker-skinned green sweet-limes were available.

They were, however, entirely delighted. Even before she said 'Aa! Aa!'—something she had once heard an old sadhu say to entice them—the monkeys noticed the paper bags. They gathered around, grabbing, grasping, pleading, clambering up the trees and down the trees in excitement, even hanging down from the branches and suspended roots and stretching their arms. The little ones squeaked, the big ones growled. One brute, possibly the one who had bared his teeth at her earlier, stored some of the peanuts in his cheek pouches while he tried to grab more. Lata scattered a few, but fed them mainly by hand. She even ate a couple of peanuts herself. The two smallest monkeys, as before, grabbed—and even stroked—her elbow for attention. When she kept her hands closed to tease them, they opened them quite gently, not with their teeth but with their fingers.

When she tried to peel the musammis, the biggest monkeys would have none of it. She usually succeeded in a democratic distribution, but this time all three musammis were grabbed by fairly large monkeys. One went a little farther down the slope, and sat on a large root to eat it: he half peeled it, then ate it from the inside. Another, less particular, ate his skin and all.

Lata, laughing, finally swung what was left of the bag of peanuts around her head, and it flew off into the tree; it was caught in a high branch, but then came free, fell a little more, and got caught on a branch again. A great red-bottomed monkey climbed towards it, turning around at intervals to threaten one or two others who were climbing up the other root-branches that hung down from the main body of the banyan tree. He grabbed the whole packet and climbed higher to enjoy his monopoly. But the mouth of the bag suddenly came open and the nuts scattered all around. Seeing this, a thin baby monkey leapt in its excitement from one branch to another, lost its hold, banged its head against the trunk, and dropped down to the ground. It ran off squeaking.

Instead of going down to the river as she had planned, Lata now sat down on the exposed root where the monkey had just been eating his musammi, and tried to address herself to the book in her hands. It did not succeed in diverting her thoughts. She got up, climbed the path up the slope again, then walked to the library.

She looked through the last season's issues of the university magazine, reading through with intense interest what she had never so much as glanced at before: the cricket reports and the names beneath the team photographs. The writer of the reports, who signed himself 'S.K.', had a style of lively formality. He wrote, for example, not about Akhilesh and Kabir but about Mr Mittal and Mr Durrani and their excellent seventh-wicket stand.

It appeared that Kabir was a good bowler and a fair batsman. Though he was usually placed low in the batting order, he had saved a number of matches by remaining unflappable in the face of considerable odds. And he must have been an incredibly swift runner, because he had sometimes run three runs, and on one occasion, had actually run four. In the words of S.K.:

> This reporter has never seen anything like it. It is true that the outfield was not merely sluggish but torpid with the morning's rain. It is undeniable that the mid-wicket boundary at our opponents' field is more than ordinarily distant. It is irrefutable that there was confusion in the ranks of their fielders, and that one of them actually slipped and fell in pursuit of the ball. But what will be remembered are not these detracting circumstances. What will be remembered by Brahmpurians in time to come is the quicksilver crossing of two human bullets ricocheting from crease to crease and back again with a velocity appropriate more to the track than the pitch, and unusual even there. Mr Durrani and Mr Mittal ran four runs where no four was, on a ball that did not even cross the boundary; and that they were home and dry with more than a yard to spare attests to the fact that theirs was no flamboyant or unseasoned risk.

Lata read and relived matches that had been layered over by the pressure of recency even for the participants themselves, and the more she read the more she felt herself in love with Kabir—both as she knew him and as he was revealed to her by the judicious eye of S.K.

Mr Durrani, she thought, this should have been a different world.

If, as Kabir said, he lived in the town, it was more than likely that it was at Brahmpur University that his father taught. Lata, with a flair for research that she did not know she possessed, now looked up the fat volume of the Brahmpur University Calendar, and found what she was seeking under 'Faculty of Arts: Department of Mathematics'. Dr Durrani was not the head of his department, but the three magic letters after his name that indicated that he was a Fellow of the Royal Society outgloried twenty 'Professors'.

And Mrs Durrani? Lata said the two words aloud, appraising them. What of her? And of Kabir's brother and the sister he had had 'until last year'? Over the last few days her mind had time and again recurred to these elusive beings and those few elusive comments. But even if she had thought about them in the course of the happy conversation outside Mr Nowrojee's—and she hadn't—she could not have brought herself to ask him about them at the time. Now, of course, it was too late. If she did not want to lose her own family, she would have to shade herself from the bright beam of sudden sunlight that had strayed into her life.

Outside the library she tried to take stock of things. She realized that she could not now attend next Friday's meeting of the Brahmpur Literary Society.

'Lata: Whither?' she said to herself, laughed for a second or two, and found herself in tears.

Don't! she thought. You might attract another Galahad. This made her laugh once again. But it was a laughter that swept nothing away and unsettled her still further.

3.12

Kabir confronted her next Saturday morning not far from her house. She had gone out for a walk. He was on his bicycle, leaning against a tree. He looked rather like a horseman. His face was grim. When she saw him her heart went into her mouth.

It was not possible to avoid him. He had clearly been waiting for her. She put on a brave front.

'Hello, Kabir.'

'Hello. I thought you'd never come out of your house.'

'How did you find out where I live?'

'I instituted inquiries,' he said unsmilingly.

'Whom did you ask?' said Lata, feeling a little guilty for the inquiries she herself had 'instituted'.

'That doesn't matter,' said Kabir with a shake of his head.

Lata looked at him in distress. 'Are your exams over?' she asked, her tone betraying a touch of tenderness.

'Yes. Yesterday.' He didn't elaborate.

Lata stared at his bicycle unhappily. She wanted to say to him: 'Why didn't you tell me? Why didn't you tell me about yourself as soon as we exchanged words in the bookshop, so that I could have made sure I didn't feel anything for you?' But how often had they in fact met, and were they in any sense of the word intimate enough for such a direct, almost despairing, question? Did he feel what she felt for him? He liked her, she knew. But how much more could be added to that?

He pre-empted any possible question of hers by saying:

'Why didn't you come yesterday?'

'I couldn't,' she said helplessly.

'Don't twist the end of your dupatta, you'll crumple it.'

'Oh, sorry.' Lata looked at her hands in surprise.

'I waited for you. I went early. I sat through the whole lecture. I even chomped through Mrs Nowrojee's rock-hard little cakes. I had built up a good appetite by then.'

'Oh—I didn't know there was a Mrs Nowrojee,' said Lata, seizing upon the remark. 'I wondered about the inspiration for his poem, what was it called—"Haunted Passion"? Can you imagine her reaction to that? What does she look like?'

'Lata—' said Kabir with some pain, 'you're going to ask me next if Professor Mishra's lecture was any good. It was, but I didn't care. Mrs Nowrojee is fat and fair, but I couldn't care less. Why didn't you come?'

'I couldn't,' said Lata quietly. It would be better all around, she reflected, if she could summon up some anger to deal with his questions. All she could summon up was dismay.

'Then come and have some coffee with me now at the university coffee house.'

'I can't,' she said. He shook his head wonderingly. 'I really can't,' she repeated. 'Please let me go.'

'I'm not stopping you,' he said.

Lata looked at him and sighed: 'We can't stand here.'

Kabir refused to be affected by all these can'ts and couldn'ts.

'Well, let's stand somewhere else, then. Let's go for a walk in Curzon Park.'

'Oh no,' said Lata. Half the world walked in Curzon Park.

'Where then?'

They walked to the banyan trees on the slope leading down to the sands by the river. Kabir chained his bike to a tree at the top of the path. The monkeys were nowhere to be seen. Through the scarcely moving leaves of the gnarled trees they looked out at the Ganga. The wide brown river glinted in the sunlight. Neither said anything. Lata sat down on the upraised root, and Kabir followed.

'How beautiful it is here,' she said.

Kabir nodded. There was a bitterness about his mouth. If he had spoken, it would have been reflected in his voice.

Though Malati had warned her sternly off him, Lata just wanted to be with him for some time. She felt that if he were now to get up and go, she would try to dissuade him. Even if they were not talking, even in his present mood, she wanted to sit here with him.

Kabir was looking out over the river. With sudden eagerness, as if he had forgotten his grimness of a moment ago, he said: 'Let's go boating.'

Lata thought of Windermere, the lake near the High Court where they sometimes had department parties. Friends hired boats there and went out boating together. On Saturdays it was full of married couples and their children.

'Everyone goes to Windermere,' Lata said. 'Someone will recognize us.'

'I didn't mean Windermere. I meant up the Ganges. It always amazes me that people go sailing or boating on that foolish lake when they have the greatest river in the world at their doorstep. We'll go up the Ganges to the Barsaat Mahal. It's a wonderful sight by night. We'll get a boatman to keep the boat still in midstream, and you'll see it reflected by moonlight.' He turned to her.

Lata could not bear to look at him.

Kabir could not understand why she was so aloof and depressed. Nor could he understand why he had so suddenly fallen out of favour.

'Why are you so distant? Is it something to do with me?' he asked. 'Have I said something?'

Lata shook her head.

'Have I done something then?'

For some reason the thought of him running that impossible four runs came to her mind. She shook her head again.

'You'll forget about all this in five years,' she said.

'What sort of answer is that?' said Kabir, alarmed.

'It's what you said to me once.'

'Did I?' Kabir was surprised.

'Yes, on the bench, when you were rescuing me. I really can't come with you, Kabir, I really can't,' said Lata with sudden vehemence. 'You should know better than to ask me to come boating with you at midnight.' Ah, here was that blessed anger.

Kabir was about to respond in kind, but stopped himself. He paused, then said with surprising quietness:

'I won't tell you that I live from our one meeting to the next. You probably know that. It doesn't have to be by moonlight. Dawn is fine. If you're concerned about other people, don't worry. No one will see us; no one we're likely to know goes out in a boat at dawn. Bring a friend along. Bring ten friends along if you like. I just wanted to show you the Barsaat Mahal reflected in the water. If your mood has nothing to do with me, you must come.'

'Dawn—' said Lata, thinking aloud. 'There's no harm in dawn.'

'Harm?' Kabir looked at her incredulously. 'Don't you trust me?'

Lata said nothing. Kabir went on:

'Don't you care for me at all?'

She was silent.

'Listen,' said Kabir, 'if anyone asks you, it was just an educational trip. By daylight. With a friend, or as many friends as you wish to bring. I'll tell you the history of the Barsaat Mahal. The Nawab Sahib of Baitar has given me access to his library, and I've found out quite a few surprising facts about the place. You'll be the students. I'll be the guide: "a young history student, I can't remember his name now—he came with us and pointed out the spots of historical interest—provided quite a passable commentary—really quite a nice chap."'

Lata smiled ruefully.

Feeling that he had almost broken through some unseen defence, Kabir said:

'I'll see you and your friends here at this very spot on Monday morning at six sharp. Wear a sweater; there'll be a river breeze.' He burst into Makhijanian doggerel:

> 'Oh Miss Lata, meet me here
> Far from banks of Windermere.
> On the Ganga we will skim—
> Many hers and single him.'

Lata laughed.

'Say you'll come with me,' said Kabir.

'All right,' said Lata, shaking her head, not—as it appeared to Kabir—in partial denial of her own decision but in partial regret at her own weakness.

3.13

Lata did not want ten friends to accompany her, and even if she had she would not have been able to round up half that number. One was enough. Malati unfortunately had left Brahmpur. Lata decided to go over to Hema's place to persuade her to come. Hema was very excited at the prospect, and readily agreed. It sounded romantic and conspiratorial. 'I'll keep it a secret,' she said, but made the mistake of confiding it on pain of lifelong enmity to one of her innumerable cousins, who confided it to another cousin on similarly strict terms. Within a day it had come to Taiji's ears. Taiji, normally lenient, saw grave dangers in this enterprise. She did not know—nor for that matter did Hema—that Kabir was Muslim. But going out with any boy in a boat at six in the morning: even she baulked here. She told Hema she would not be allowed to go out. Hema sulked but succumbed, and phoned Lata on Sunday evening. Lata went to bed in great anxiety, but, having made up her mind, did not sleep badly.

She could not let Kabir down again. She pictured him standing in the banyan grove, cold and anxious, without even the granitic sustenance of Mrs Nowrojee's little cakes, waiting for her as the minutes passed and she did not come. At a quarter to six the next morning she got out of bed, dressed quickly, pulled on a baggy grey sweater that had once belonged to her father, told her mother she was going for a long walk in the university grounds, and went to meet Kabir at the appointed place.

He was waiting for her. It was light, and the whole grove was filled with the sound of waking birds.

'You're looking very unusual in that sweater,' he said approvingly.

'You look just the same as ever,' she said, also approvingly. 'Have you been waiting long?'

He shook his head.

She told him about the confusion with Hema.

'I hope you're not going to call it off because you don't have a chaperone,' he said.

'No,' said Lata. She felt as bold as Malati. She had not had much time to think about things this morning, and did not want to either. Despite her evening's anxiety, her oval face looked fresh and attractive, and her lively eyes were no longer sleepy.

They got down to the river and walked along the sand for a while until they came to some stone steps. A few washermen were standing in the water, beating clothes against the steps. On a small path going up the slope at this point stood a few bored little donkeys overburdened with bundles of clothes. A washerman's dog barked at them in uncertain, staccato yaps.

'Are you sure we'll get a boat?' said Lata.

'Oh, yes, there's always someone. I've done this often enough.'

A small, sharp pulse of pain went through Lata, though Kabir had meant merely that he enjoyed going out on the Ganga at dawn.

'Ah, there's one,' he said. A boatman was scouting up and down with his boat in midstream. It was April, so the river was low and the current sluggish. Kabir cupped his hands and shouted:

'Aré, mallah!'

The boatman, however, made no attempt to row towards them.

'What's the matter?' he yelled in Hindi that had a strong Brahmpuri accent; he gave the verb 'hai' an unusual emphasis.

'Can you take us to a point where we can see the Barsaat Mahal and its reflection?' said Kabir.

'Sure!'

'How much?'

'Two rupees.' He was now approaching the shore in his old flat-bottomed boat.

Kabir got annoyed. 'Aren't you ashamed to ask so much?' he said angrily.

'It's what everyone charges, Sahib.'

'I'm not some outsider that you can cheat me,' said Kabir.

'Oh,' said Lata, 'please don't quarrel over nothing—'

She stopped short; presumably Kabir would insist on paying, and he, like her, probably did not have much money.

Kabir went on angrily, shouting to be heard over the sound of the clothes hitting the steps of the ghat:

'We come empty-handed into this world and go out empty-handed. Do you have to lie so early in the morning? Will you take this money with you when you go?'

The boatman, presumably intrigued at being so philosophically addressed, said:

'Sahib, come down. Whatever you think is appropriate I will accept.' He guided Kabir towards a spot a couple of hundred yards away where the boat could come close to the shore. By the time Lata and Kabir had reached the spot, he had gone up the river.

'He's gone away,' said Lata. 'Perhaps we'll find another one.'

Kabir shook his head. He said:

'We've spoken. He'll return.'

The boatman, after rowing upstream and to the far shore, got something from the bank, and rowed back.

'Do you swim?' he asked them.

'I do,' said Kabir, and turned towards Lata.

'No,' said Lata, 'I don't.'

Kabir looked surprised.

'I never learned,' explained Lata. 'Darjeeling and Mussourie.'

'I trust your rowing,' said Kabir to the boatman, a brown, bristle-faced man dressed in a shirt and lungi with a woollen bundi to cover his chest. 'If there's an accident, you handle yourself, I'll handle her.'

'Right,' said the boatman.

'Now, how much?'

'Well, whatever you—'

'No,' said Kabir, 'let's fix a price. I've never dealt with boatmen any other way.'

'All right,' said the boatman, 'what do you think is right?'

'One rupee four annas.'

'Fine.'

Kabir stepped on board, then stretched his hand out for Lata. With an assured grip he pulled her on to the boat. She looked flushed and happy. For an unnecessary second he did not release her hand. Then, sensing she was about to pull away, he let her go.

There was still a slight mist on the river. Kabir and Lata sat facing the boatman as he pulled on the oars. They were more than two hundred yards from the dhobi-ghat, but the sound of the beating of clothes, though faint, was still audible. The details of the bank disappeared in the mist.

'Ah,' said Kabir. 'It's wonderful to be here on the river surrounded by mist—and it's rare at this time of year. It reminds me of the holiday we once spent in Simla. All the problems of the world slipped away. It was as if we were a different family altogether.'

'Do you go to a hill station every summer?' asked Lata. Though she had been schooled at St Sophia's in Mussourie, there was no question now of being able to afford to take a house in the hills whenever they chose.

'Oh yes,' said Kabir. 'My father insists on it. We usually go to a different hill station every year—Almora, Nainital, Ranikhet, Mussourie, Simla, even Darjeeling. He says that the fresh air "opens up his assumptions", whatever that means. Once, when he came down from the hills, he said that like Zarathustra he had gained enough mathematical insight on the mountainside in six weeks to last a lifetime. But of course, we went up to the hills the next year as usual.'

'And you?' asked Lata. 'What about you?'

'What about me?' said Kabir. He seemed troubled by some memory.

'Do you like it in the hills? Will you be going this year as usual?'

'I don't know about this year,' said Kabir. 'I do like it up there. It's like swimming.'

'Swimming?' asked Lata, trailing a hand in the water.

A thought suddenly struck Kabir. He said to the boatman: 'How much do you charge local people to take them all the way up to the Barsaat Mahal from near the dhobi-ghat?'

'Four annas a head,' said the boatman.

'Well then,' said Kabir, 'we should be paying you a rupee—at the most—considering that half your journey is downstream. And I'm paying you a rupee and four annas. So it's not unfair.'

'I'm not complaining,' said the boatman, surprised.

The mist had cleared, and now before them on the bank of the river stood the grand grey edifice of the Brahmpur Fort, with a broad reach of sand stretching out in front of it. Near it, and leading down to the sands, was a huge earthen ramp, and above it a great pipal tree, its leaves shimmering in the morning breeze.

'What did you mean by "swimming"?' asked Lata.

'Oh yes,' said Kabir. 'What I meant was that you're in a completely different element. All your movements are different—and, as a result, all your thoughts. When I went tobogganing in Gulmarg once, I remember thinking that I didn't really exist. All that existed was the clean, pure air, the high snows, this rush of swift movement. The flat, drab plains bring you back to yourself. Except, perhaps, well, like now on the river.'

'Like music?' said Lata.

The question was addressed as much to herself as to Kabir.

'Mmm, yes, I think so, in a way,' Kabir mused. 'No, not really,' he decided.

He had been thinking of a change of spirit brought about by a change of physical activity.

'But,' said Lata, following her own thoughts, 'music really does do that to me. Simply strumming the tanpura, even if I don't sing a single note, puts me into a trance. Sometimes I do it for fifteen minutes before I come back to myself. When things get to be too much for me, it's the first thing I turn to. And when I think that I only took up singing under Malati's influence last year I realize how lucky I've been. Do you know that my mother is so unmusical that when I was a child and she would sing lullabies to me, I would beg her to stop and let my ayah sing them instead?'

Kabir was smiling. He put his arm around her shoulder and, instead of protesting, she let it remain. It seemed to be in the right place.

'Why aren't you saying anything?' she said.

'I was just hoping that you'd go on talking. It's unusual to hear you talking about yourself. I sometimes think I don't know the first thing about you. Who is this Malati, for instance?'

'The first thing?' said Lata, recalling a shred of conversation she'd had with Malati. 'Even after all the inquiries you've instituted?'

'Yes,' said Kabir. 'Tell me about yourself.'

'That's not much use as a request. Be more specific. Where should I begin?'

'Oh, anywhere. Begin at the beginning, go on until you reach the end and then stop.'

'Well,' said Lata, 'it's before breakfast, so you'll have to hear at least six impossible things.'

'Good,' said Kabir, laughing.

'Except that my life probably doesn't contain six impossible things. It's quite humdrum.'

'Begin with the family,' said Kabir.

Lata began to talk about her family—her much-beloved father, who seemed even now to cast a protective aura over her, not least significantly in the shape of a grey sweater; her mother, with her Gita, waterworks, and affectionate volubility; Arun and Meenakshi and Aparna and Varun in Calcutta; and of course Savita and Pran and the baby-to-be. She talked freely, even moving a little closer to Kabir. Strangely enough, for one who was sometimes so unsure of herself, she did not at all doubt his affection.

The Fort and the sands had gone past, as had the cremation ghat and a glimpse of the temples of Old Brahmpur and the minarets of the Alamgiri Mosque. Now as they came round a gentle bend in the river they saw before them the delicate white structure of the Barsaat Mahal, at first from an angle, and then, gradually, full face.

The water was not clear, but it was quite calm and its surface was like murky glass. The boatman moved into mid-stream as he rowed. Then he settled the boat dead centre—in line with the vertical axis of symmetry of the Barsaat Mahal—and plunged the long pole that he had earlier fetched from the opposite bank deep into the middle of the river. It hit the bottom, and the boat was still.

'Now sit and watch for five minutes,' said the boatman. 'This is a sight you will never forget in your lives.'

Indeed it was, and neither of them was to forget it. The Barsaat Mahal, site of statesmanship and intrigue, love and dissolute enjoyment, glory and slow decay, was transfigured into something of abstract and final beauty. Above its sheer river wall it rose, its reflection in the water almost perfect, almost unrippled. They were in a stretch of the river where even the sounds of the old town were dim. For a few minutes they said nothing at all.

3.14

After a little while, without as such being told to, the boatman pulled his pole out of the mud at the bottom of the river. He continued to row upstream, past the Barsaat Mahal. The river narrowed slightly because of a spit of sand jutting almost into mid-stream from the opposite bank. The chimneys of a shoe factory, a tannery and a flour mill came into view. Kabir stretched and yawned, releasing Lata's shoulder.

'Now I'll turn around and we'll drift past it,' said the boatman.

Kabir nodded.

'This is where the easy part begins for me,' said the boatman, turning the boat around. 'It's good it's not too hot yet.' Steering with an occasional stroke of the oar, he let the boat drift downstream on the current.

'Lots of suicides from that place there,' he commented cheerfully, pointing at the sheer drop from the Barsaat Mahal to the water. 'There was one last week. The hotter the weather, the crazier people get. Crazy people, crazy people.' He gestured along the shore. Clearly, in his mind, the perpetually land-bound could never be quite sane.

As they passed the Barsaat Mahal again, Kabir took a small booklet entitled *Diamond Guide to Brahmpur* out of his pocket. He read out the following to Lata:

> Although Fatima Jaan was only third wife of Nawab Khushwaqt still it was to her that he made the nobile edifice of Barsaat Mahal. Her feminine grace, dignity of heart and wit proved so powerful that Nawab Khushwaqt's all affections were soon transferred to his new bride, their Impassionate love made them inseparatable companions both in the palaces as well as in the court. To her he built Barsaat Mahal, miracle of marble filligral work, for their life and pleasures.
>
> Once she also accompanied him in the campaign. At that time she gave birth to a weakly son and unfortunately, due to some disorder in the system, she looked despairingly at her lord. At this, the Nawab was shocked too much. His heart was sank with grief and face grew much too pale. . . . Alas! On the day of 23 April, 1735, Fatima Jaan closed her eyes at a shortage of 33 before her broken-hearted lover.

'But is all this true?' said Lata laughing.

'Every word,' said Kabir. 'Trust your historian.' He went on:

> Nawab Khushwaqt was so much grieved that his mind was upset, he was even prepared to die which he, of course, could not do. For a long time he could not forget her though all possible efforts were made. On each Friday he went on foot to the grave of his best-loved and himself read fatiha on final resting spot of her bones.

'Please,' said Lata, 'please stop. You'll ruin the Barsaat Mahal for me.' But Kabir read mercilessly on:

> After her death the palace became sordid and sad. No longer did the tanks full of golden and silvery fish afford sportive amusements to the Nawab. He became lustrious and debauching. He built now a dark room where refractory members of harem were hanged and their bodies were swept away in the river. This left a blot on his personality. During those days these punishments were usual without distinction of sexes. There was no law except the Nawab's orders and the punishments were drastic and furious.
>
> The fountains played still with frangrant water and an unceasing water rolled on the floors. The palace was not less than a heaven where beauty and charms were scattered freely. But after expiry of the One of his life what to him mattered the innumerable blooming

ladies? He breathed his last on the 14 January gazzing steadfastly at a picture of F. Jaan.

'Which year did he die in?' asked Lata.

'I believe the *Diamond Guide to Brahmpur* is silent on this subject, but I can supply the date myself. It was 1766. Nor does it tell us why it was called the Barsaat Mahal in the first place.'

'Why was it?' asked Lata. 'Because an unceasing water rolled freely?' she speculated.

'Actually it has to do with the poet Mast,' said Kabir. 'It used to be called the Fatima Mahal. Mast, during one of his recitations there, made a poetic analogy between Khushwaqt's unceasing tears and the monsoon rains. The ghazal containing that particular couplet became popular.'

'Ah,' said Lata, and closed her eyes.

'Also,' continued Kabir, 'the Nawab's successors—including his weakly son—used to be found more often in the pleasure grounds of the Fatima Mahal during the monsoons than at any other time. Most things stopped during the rains except pleasure. And so its popular name changed.'

'And what was that other story you were about to tell me about Akbar and Birbal?' asked Lata.

'About Akbar and Birbal?' asked Kabir.

'Not today; at the concert.'

'Oh,' said Kabir. 'Did I? But there are so many stories. Which one was I referring to? I mean, what was the context?'

How is it, thought Lata, that he doesn't remember these remarks of his that I remember so well?

'I think it was about me and my friends reminding you of jungle babblers.'

'Oh, yes.' Kabir's face lit up at the memory. 'This is how it goes. Akbar was bored with things, so he asked his court to tell him something truly astonishing—but not something that they had merely heard about, something that they themselves had seen. The most astonishing story would win a prize. All his courtiers and ministers came up with different and astonishing facts—all the usual ones. One said that he had seen an elephant trumpeting in terror before an ant. Another said that he had seen a ship flying in the sky. Another that he had met a Sheikh who could see treasure buried in the earth. Another that he had seen a buffalo with three heads. And so on and so forth. When it came to Birbal's turn, he didn't say anything. Finally, he admitted that he had seen something unusual while riding to court that day: about fifty women sitting under a tree together, absolutely silent. And everyone immediately agreed that Birbal should get the prize.' Kabir threw back his head and laughed.

Lata was not pleased by the story, and was about to tell him so when she thought of Mrs Rupa Mehra, who found it impossible to remain silent for even a couple of minutes in grief, joy, sickness or health, in a railway carriage or at a concert or indeed anywhere at all.

'Why do you always remind me of my mother?' asked Lata.

'Do I?' said Kabir. 'I didn't mean to.' And he put his arm around her again.

He became silent; his thoughts had wandered off to his own family. Lata too was silent; she still could not work out what had caused her to panic in the exam, and it had returned to perplex her.

The shoreline of Brahmpur again drifted past but now there was more activity at the water's edge. The boatman had chosen to keep closer to the shore. They could hear more clearly the oars of other boats; bathers splashing, clearing their throats, coughing and blowing their noses; crows cawing; verses from the scriptures being chanted over a loudspeaker; and beyond the sands the sound of temple bells and conches.

The river flowed due east at this point, and the risen sun was reflected in its surface far beyond the university. A marigold garland floated in the water. Pyres were burning at the cremation ghat. From the Fort came the shouted commands of parade. As they drifted downstream they once more heard the ceaseless sounds of the washermen and the occasional braying of their donkeys.

The boat reached the steps. Kabir offered the boatman two rupees.

He nobly refused it.

'We came to an understanding beforehand. Next time you'll look out for me,' he said.

When the boat stopped moving Lata felt a pang of regret. She thought of what Kabir had said about swimming or tobogganing—about the ease conferred by a new element, a different physical motion. The movement of the boat, their feeling of freedom and distance from the world would soon, she felt, disperse. But when Kabir helped her ashore, she did not pull away, and they walked hand in hand along the edge of the river towards the banyan grove and the minor shrine. They did not say much.

It was more difficult to climb up the path than to walk down it in her slippers, but he helped pull her up. He might be gentle, she thought, but he is certainly strong. It struck her as amazing that they had hardly talked about the university, their exams, cricket, teachers, plans, the world immediately above the cliffs. She blessed the qualms of Hema's Taiji.

They sat on the twisted root of the twin banyan trees. Lata was at a loss as to what to say. She heard herself saying:

'Kabir, are you interested in politics?'

He looked at her in amazement at the unexpected question, then simply said, 'No,' and kissed her.

Her heart turned over completely. She responded to his kiss—without thinking anything out—but with a sense of amazement at herself—that she could be so reckless and happy.

When the kiss was over, Lata suddenly began thinking again, and more furiously than ever.

'I love you,' said Kabir.

When she was silent, he said:

'Well, aren't you going to say anything?'

'Oh, I love you too,' said Lata, stating a fact that was completely obvious to her and therefore should have been obvious to him. 'But it's pointless to say so, so take it back.'

Kabir started. But before he could say anything, Lata said:

'Kabir, why didn't you tell me your last name?'

'It's Durrani.'

'I know.' Hearing him say it so casually brought all the cares of the world back on her head.

'You know?' Kabir was surprised. 'But I remember that at the concert you refused to exchange last names with me.'

Lata smiled; his memory was quite selective. Then she grew serious again.

'You're Muslim,' she said quietly.

'Yes, yes, but why is all this so important to you? Is that why you've been so strange and distant sometimes?' There was a humorous light in his eyes.

'Important?' It was Lata's turn to be amazed. 'It's all-important. Don't you know what it means in my family?' Was he deliberately refusing to see difficulties, she wondered, or did he truly believe that it made no difference?

Kabir held her hand and said, 'You love me. And I love you. That's all that matters.'

Lata persisted: 'Doesn't your father care?'

'No. Unlike many Muslim families, I suppose we were sheltered during

Partition—and before. He hardly thinks of anything except his parameters and perimeters. And an equation is the same whether it's written in red or green ink. I don't see why we have to talk about this.'

Lata tied her grey sweater around her waist, and they walked to the top of the path. They agreed to meet again in three days at the same place at the same time. Kabir was going to be occupied for a couple of days doing some work for his father. He unchained his bike and—looking quickly around—kissed her again. When he was about to cycle off, she said to him:

'Have you kissed anyone else?'

'What was that?' He looked amused.

She was looking at his face; she didn't repeat the question.

'Do you mean ever?' he asked. 'No. I don't think so. Not seriously.'

And he rode off.

3.15

Later that day, Mrs Rupa Mehra was sitting with her daughters, embroidering a tiny handkerchief with a rose for the baby. White was a sexually neutral colour, but white-on-white was too drab for Mrs Rupa Mehra's tastes, and so she decided on yellow. After her beloved granddaughter Aparna, she wanted—and had predicted—a grandson. She would have embroidered the handkerchief in blue, except that this would certainly have invited Fate to change the sex of the child in the womb.

Rafi Ahmad Kidwai, the Union Minister of Communications, had just announced that postal charges were to be raised. Since replying to her abundant correspondence was what occupied at least a third of Mrs Rupa Mehra's time, this had hit her hard. Rafi Sahib was the most secular-minded, least communally impassioned man possible, but he happened to be Muslim. Mrs Rupa Mehra felt like hitting out, and he presented a direct target. She said:

'Nehru indulges them too much, he only talks to Azad and Kidwai, does he think he's the Prime Minister of Pakistan? Then see what they do.'

Lata and Savita usually let their mother have her say, but today Lata protested:

'Ma, I don't agree at all. He's the Prime Minister of India, not just of the Hindus. What's the harm if he has two Muslim Ministers in his Cabinet?'

'You have too many educated ideas,' said Mrs Rupa Mehra, who normally revered education.

Mrs Rupa Mehra may have also been upset because the older women were making no headway in persuading Mahesh Kapoor to agree to a recitation of the Ramcharitmanas in Prem Nivas on the occasion of Ramnavami. The troubles of the Shiva Temple in Chowk weighed upon Mahesh Kapoor's mind, and many of the largest landlords that his Zamindari Abolition Bill would dispossess were Muslim. He felt that he should at least stay clear of exacerbating the situation.

'I know about all these Muslims,' said Mrs Rupa Mehra darkly, almost to herself. At that moment she did not think of Uncle Shafi and Talat Khala, old friends of the family.

Lata looked at her indignantly but said nothing. Savita looked at Lata, but said nothing either.

'Don't make big-big eyes at me,' said Mrs Rupa Mehra fiercely to her younger daughter. 'I know facts. You don't know them like I do. You have no experience of life.'

Lata said, 'I'm going to study.' She got up from Pran's rocking chair, where she had been sitting.

Mrs Rupa Mehra was in a belligerent mood. 'Why?' she demanded. 'Why must you study? Your exams are over. Will you be studying for the next year? All work and no play makes Jack a dull boy. Sit and talk to me. Or go for a walk. It will be good for your complexion.'

'I went for a walk this morning,' said Lata. 'I'm always going for walks.'

'You are a very stubborn girl,' said Mrs Rupa Mehra.

Yes, thought Lata, and, with the faintest shadow of a smile on her face, went to her room.

Savita had observed this little flare-up, and felt that the provocation was too small, too impersonal, to upset Lata in the ordinary course of things. Clearly, something was weighing on her heart. The phone call from Malati which had had such an acute effect on her also came to Savita's mind. The two and two which she put together did not quite make four, but the pair of swan-like digits sitting side by side were still quite disquieting. She was worried for her sister. Lata seemed to be in a volatile state of excitement these days, but did not appear to wish to confide in anyone. Nor was Malati, her friend and confidante, in town. Savita waited for an opportunity to talk to Lata alone, which was not easy. And when she did, she seized it at once.

Lata was lying on the bed, her face cupped in her hands, reading. She had finished *Pigs Have Wings* and had gone on to *Galahad at Blandings*. She thought that the title was appropriate now that she and Kabir were in love. These three days of separation would be like a month, and she would have to distract herself with as much Wodehouse as possible.

Lata was not overjoyed to be disturbed, even by her sister.

'May I sit down here on the bed?' asked Savita.

Lata nodded, and Savita sat down.

'What's that you're reading?' asked Savita.

Lata held up the cover for quick inspection, then went back to her reading.

'I've been feeling a bit low today,' said Savita.

'Oh.' Lata sat up promptly and looked at her sister. 'Are you having your period or something?'

Savita started laughing. 'When you're expecting you don't have periods.' She looked at Lata in surprise. 'Didn't you know that?' It seemed to Savita that she herself had known this elementary fact for a long time, but perhaps that wasn't so.

'No,' said Lata. Since her conversations with the informative Malati were quite wide-ranging, it was surprising that this had never come up. But it struck her as entirely right that Savita should not have to cope with two physical problems at the same time. 'What's the matter, then?'

'Oh, nothing, I don't know what it is. I just feel this way sometimes—lately, quite a lot. Maybe it's Pran's health.' She put her arm gently on Lata's.

Savita was not a moody person, and Lata knew it. She looked at her sister affectionately, and said: 'Do you love Pran?' This suddenly seemed very important.

'Of course I do,' said Savita, surprised.

'Why "of course", Didi?'

'I don't know,' said Savita. 'I love him. I feel better when he's here. I feel worried about him. And sometimes I feel worried about his baby.'

'Oh, he'll be all right,' said Lata, 'judging from his kicking.'

She lay down again, and tried to go back to her book. But she couldn't concentrate even on Wodehouse. After a pause, she said:

'Do you like being pregnant?'

'Yes,' said Savita with a smile.

'Do you like being married?'

'Yes,' said Savita, her smile widening.

'To a man who was chosen for you—whom you didn't really know before your marriage?'

'Don't talk like that about Pran, it's as if you were talking about a stranger,' said Savita, taken aback. 'You're funny sometimes, Lata. Don't you love him too?'

'Yes,' said Lata, frowning at this non sequitur, 'but I don't have to be close to him in the same way. What I can't understand is how—well, it was other people who decided he was suitable for you—but if you didn't find him attractive—'

She was thinking that Pran was not good-looking, and she did not believe that his goodness was a substitute for—what?—a spark.

'Why are you asking me all these questions?' asked Savita, stroking her sister's hair.

'Well, I might have to face a problem like that some day.'

'Are you in love, Lata?'

The head beneath Savita's hand jerked up very slightly and then pretended it hadn't. Savita had her answer, and in half an hour she had most of the details about Kabir and Lata and their various meetings. Lata was so relieved to talk to someone who loved her and understood her that she poured out all her hopes and visions of bliss. Savita saw at once how impossible these were, but let Lata talk on. She felt increasingly sad as Lata grew more elated.

'But what should I do?' said Lata.

'Do?' repeated Savita. The answer that came to her mind was that Lata should give Kabir up immediately before their infatuation went any further, but she knew better than to say so to Lata, who could be very contrary.

'Should I tell Ma?' said Lata.

'No!' said Savita. 'No. Don't tell Ma, whatever you do.' She could imagine her mother's shock and pain.

'Please don't tell anyone either, Didi. Anyone,' said Lata.

'I can't keep any secrets from Pran,' said Savita.

'Please keep this one,' said Lata. 'Rumours get around so easily. You're my *sister*. You've known this man for less than a year.' As soon as the words were out of her mouth, Lata felt bad about the way she had referred to Pran, whom she now adored. She should have phrased it better.

Savita nodded, a little unhappily.

Although she hated the atmosphere of conspiracy that her question might generate, Savita felt that she had to help her sister, even guard her in some way.

'Shouldn't I meet Kabir?' she asked.

'I'll ask him,' said Lata. She felt sure that Kabir would not have any reservations about meeting anyone who was basically sympathetic, but she did not think he would enjoy it particularly. Nor did she want him to meet anyone from her family for some time yet. She sensed that everything would become troubled and confused, and that the carefree spirit of their boat ride would quickly disappear.

'Please be careful, Lata,' said Savita. 'He may be very good-looking and from a good family, but—'

She left the second half of her sentence unfinished, and later Lata tried to fit various endings to it.

3.16

Early that evening, when the heat of the day had somewhat died down, Savita went to visit her mother-in-law, whom she had grown to be very fond of. It had been almost a week since they had seen each other. Mrs Mahesh Kapoor was out in the garden, and rushed over to Savita when she saw the tonga arrive. She was pleased to see her, but concerned that she should be jolting about in a tonga when she was pregnant. She questioned Savita about her own health and Pran's; complained that he came over very rarely; inquired after Mrs Rupa Mehra, who was due to come over to Prem Nivas the next day; and asked Savita whether either of her brothers was by any chance in town. Savita, slightly puzzled by this last question, said that they weren't. Mrs Mahesh Kapoor and she then wandered into the garden.

The garden was looking a bit dry, despite the fact that it had been watered a couple of days previously; but a gulmohur tree was in bloom: its petals were almost scarlet, rather than the usual red-orange. Everything, Savita thought, appeared more intense in the garden at Prem Nivas. It was almost as if the plants understood that their mistress, though she would not overtly complain about a weak performance, would not be happy with less than their best.

The head gardener Gajraj and Mrs Mahesh Kapoor had been at loggerheads for a few days now. They were agreed upon what cuttings to propagate, which varieties to select for seed collection, which shrubs to prune, and when to transplant the small chrysanthemum plants to larger pots. But ever since the ground had begun to be prepared for the sowing of new lawns, an apparently irreconcilable difference had emerged.

This year, as an experiment, Mrs Mahesh Kapoor proposed that a part of the lawn be left unlevelled before sowing. This had struck the mali as being eccentric in the extreme, and utterly at variance with Mrs Mahesh Kapoor's usual instructions. He complained that it would be impossible to water the lawn properly, that mowing it would be difficult, that muddy puddles would form in the monsoons and the winter rains, that the garden would be infested with pond herons feeding on water beetles and other insects, and that the Flower Show Judges' Committee would see the lack of evenness as a sign of lack of balance—aesthetically speaking, of course.

Mrs Mahesh Kapoor had replied that she had only proposed an unevenness for the side lawn, not the front lawn; that the unevenness that she proposed was slight; that he could water the higher parts with a hose; that the small proportion of the mowing that proved difficult for the grand, blunt lawnmower dragged by the Public Works Department's placid white bullock could be done with a small foreign-made lawnmower that she would borrow from a friend; that the Flower Show Judges' Committee might look at the garden for an hour in February but that it gave her pleasure all the year round; that level had nothing to do with balance; and, finally, that it was precisely because of the puddles and the pond herons that she had proposed the experiment.

One day in late December, a couple of months after Savita's wedding, when the honey-scented harsingar had still been in blossom, when the roses were in their first full flush, when the sweet alyssum and sweet william had begun to bloom, when those beds of feathery-leafed larkspur that the partridges had not gobbled down almost to the root were doing their best to recover in front of the tall ranks of equally feathery-leafed but untempting cosmos, there had been a tremendous, almost torrential rainstorm. It had been gloomy, gusty and cold, and there had been no sun for two days, but the garden had been full of birds: pond herons, partridges, mynas, small puffed-up grey babblers in their chattering groups of seven, hoopoes and parakeets in a combination that reminded her of the colours of the Congress flag, a pair of red-wattled lapwings, and a couple of vultures, flying with huge twigs in their mouth to the neem tree. Despite their heroism in the Ramayana, Mrs Mahesh Kapoor had never been able to reconcile herself to vultures. But what had truly delighted her had been the three plump, dowdy pond herons, each standing near a separate small pool, almost entirely motionless as they gazed at the water, taking a careful minute over every step they made, and thoroughly content with the squelchiness of their environment. But the pools on the level lawn had quickly dried up when the sun had emerged. Mrs Mahesh Kapoor wanted to offer the hospitality of her lawn to a few more pond herons this year, and she did not want to leave matters to chance.

All this she explained to her daughter-in-law, gasping a little as she spoke because of her allergy to neem blossoms. Savita reflected that Mrs Mahesh Kapoor looked a bit like a pond heron herself. Drab, earthy-brown, dumpy unlike the rest of the species, inelegant, hunched-up but alert, and endlessly patient, she was capable of suddenly flashing a brilliant white wing as she rose up in flight.

Savita was amused by her analogy, and began to smile. But Mrs Mahesh Kapoor, though she smiled in response, did not attempt to find out what Savita was so happy about.

How unlike Ma she is, thought Savita to herself as the two continued to walk around the garden. She could see resemblances between Mrs Mahesh Kapoor and Pran, and an obvious physical resemblance between her and the more animated Veena. But how she could have produced such a son as Maan was still to Savita a matter of amusement and amazement.

3.17

The next morning Mrs Rupa Mehra, old Mrs Tandon and Mrs Mahesh Kapoor met in Prem Nivas for a chat. It was fitting that the kind and gentle Mrs Mahesh Kapoor should have acted as host. She was the samdhin—the 'co-mother-in-law'—of both of the others, the link in the chain. Besides, she was the only one whose own husband was still living, the only one who was still mistress in her own house.

Mrs Rupa Mehra loved company of any kind, and this kind was ideal. First they had tea, and matthri with a mango pickle that Mrs Mahesh Kapoor had herself prepared. It was declared delicious all round. The recipe of the pickle was analysed and compared with that of seven or eight other kinds of mango pickle. As for the matthri, Mrs Rupa Mehra said:

'It is just as it should be: crisp and flaky, but it holds together very well.'

'I can't have much because of my digestion,' said old Mrs Tandon, helping herself to another.

'What can one do when one gets old—' said Mrs Rupa Mehra with fellow-feeling. She was only in her mid-forties but liked to imagine herself old in older company; and indeed, having been widowed for several years, she felt that she had partaken of at least part of the experience of old age.

The entire conversation proceeded in Hindi with the occasional English word. Mrs Mahesh Kapoor, for instance, when referring to her husband, often called him 'Minister Sahib'. Sometimes, in Hindi, she even called him 'Pran's father'. To refer to him by name would have been unthinkable. Even 'my husband' was unacceptable to her, but 'my this' was all right.

They compared the prices of vegetables with what they had been at the same time the previous year. Minister Sahib cared more for the clauses of his bill than for his food, but he sometimes got very annoyed when there was too much or too little salt—or the food was too highly spiced. He was particularly fond of karela, the bitterest of all vegetables—and the more bitter the better.

Mrs Rupa Mehra felt very close to old Mrs Tandon. For someone who believed that everyone in a railway carriage existed mainly to be absorbed into a network of acquaintance, a samdhin's samdhin was virtually a sister. They were both widowed, and both had problematical daughters-in-law.

Mrs Rupa Mehra complained about Meenakshi; she had already told them some weeks ago about the medal that had been so heartlessly melted down. But, naturally, old Mrs Tandon could not complain about Veena and her fondness for irreligious music in front of Mrs Mahesh Kapoor.

Grandchildren were also discussed: Bhaskar and Aparna and Savita's unborn baby each made an appearance.

Then the conversation moved into a different mode.

'Can't we do something about Ramnavami? Won't Minister Sahib change his mind?' asked old Mrs Tandon, probably the most insistently pious of the three.

'Uff! What can I say, he's so stubborn,' said Mrs Mahesh Kapoor. 'And nowadays he is under so much pressure that he gets impatient at every little thing I say. I get pains these days, but I hardly worry about them, I'm worrying about him so much.' She smiled. 'I'll tell you frankly,' she continued in her quiet voice, 'I'm afraid to say anything to him. I told him, all right, if you don't want the whole Ramcharitmanas to be recited, at least let us get a priest to recite some part of it, maybe just the Sundar Kanda, and all he said was, "You women will burn down this town. Do what you like!" and stalked out of the room.'

Mrs Rupa Mehra and old Mrs Tandon made sympathetic noises.

'Later he was striding up and down the garden in the heat, which is good neither for him nor for the plants. I said to him, we could get Maan's future parents-in-law from Banaras to enjoy it with us. They are also fond of recitations. That will help cement the ties. Maan is getting so'—she searched for the proper word—'so out of control these days. . . .' She trailed off, distressed.

Rumours of Maan and Saeeda Bai were by now rife in Brahmpur.

'What did he say?' asked Mrs Rupa Mehra, rapt.

'He just waved me away, saying, "All these plots and plans!"'

Old Mrs Tandon shook her head and said:

'When Zaidi's son passed the civil service exam, his wife arranged a reading of the whole Quran in her house: thirty women came, and they each read a—what do they call it? paara; yes, paara.' The word seemed to displease her.

'Really?' said Mrs Rupa Mehra, struck by the injustice of it. 'Should I speak to Minister Sahib?' She had a vague sense that this would help.

'No, no, no—' said Mrs Mahesh Kapoor, worried at the thought of these two powerful wills colliding. 'He will only say this and that. Once when I touched upon the subject he even said: "If you must have it, go to your great friend the Home Minister—he will certainly support this kind of mischief." I was too frightened to say anything after that.'

They all bewailed the general decline of true piety.

Old Mrs Tandon said: 'Nowadays, everyone goes in for big functions in the temples—chanting and bhajans and recitations and discourses and puja—but they don't have proper ceremonies in the home.'

'True,' said the other two.

Old Mrs Tandon continued: 'At least in our neighbourhood we will have our own Ramlila in six months' time. Bhaskar is too young to be one of the main characters, but he can certainly be a monkey-warrior.'

'Lata used to be very fond of monkeys,' reflected Mrs Rupa Mehra vaguely.

Old Mrs Tandon and Mrs Mahesh Kapoor exchanged glances.

Mrs Rupa Mehra snapped out of her vagueness and looked at the others. 'Why—is something the matter?' she asked.

'Before you came we were just talking—you know, just like that,' said old Mrs Tandon soothingly.

'Is it about Lata?' said Mrs Rupa Mehra, reading her tone as accurately as she had read her glance.

The two ladies looked at each other and nodded seriously.

'Tell me, tell me quick,' said Mrs Rupa Mehra, thoroughly alarmed.

'You see, it is like this,' said Mrs Mahesh Kapoor gently, 'please look after your daughter, because someone saw her walking with a boy on the bank of the Ganga near the dhobi-ghat yesterday morning.'

'What boy?'

'That I don't know. But they were walking hand in hand.'

'Who saw them?'

'What should I hide from you?' said Mrs Mahesh Kapoor sympathetically. 'It was Avtar Bhai's brother-in-law. He recognized Lata but he didn't recognize the boy. I told him it must have been one of your sons, but I know from Savita that they are in Calcutta.'

Mrs Rupa Mehra's nose started to redden with unhappiness and shame. Two tears rolled down her cheeks, and she reached into her capacious handbag for an embroidered handkerchief.

'Yesterday morning?' she said in a trembling voice.

She tried to remember where Lata had said she'd gone. This was what happened when you trusted your children, when you let them roam around, taking walks everywhere. Nowhere was safe.

'That's what he said,' said Mrs Mahesh Kapoor gently. 'Have some tea. Don't get too alarmed. All these girls see these modern love films and it has an effect on them, but Lata is a good girl. Only talk to her.'

But Mrs Rupa Mehra was very alarmed, gulped down her tea, even sweetening it with sugar by mistake, and went home as soon as she politely could.

3.18

Mrs Rupa Mehra came breathlessly through the door.

She had been crying in the tonga. The tonga-wallah, concerned that such a decently dressed lady should be weeping so openly, had tried to keep up a monologue in order to pretend that he hadn't noticed, but she had now gone through not only her embroidered handkerchief but her reserve handkerchief as well.

'Oh my daughter!' she said, 'oh, my daughter.'

Savita said, 'Yes, Ma?' She was shocked to see her mother's tear-streaked face.

'Not you,' said Mrs Rupa Mehra. 'Where is that shameless Lata?'

Savita sensed that their mother had discovered something. But what? And how much? She moved instinctively towards her to calm her down.

'Ma, sit down, calm down, have some tea,' said Savita, guiding Mrs Rupa Mehra, who seemed quite distracted, to her favourite armchair.

'Tea! Tea! More and more tea!' said Mrs Rupa Mehra in resistant misery.

Savita went and told Mateen to get some tea for the two of them.

'Where is she? What will become of us all? Who will marry her now?'

'Ma, don't over-dramatize things,' said Savita soothingly. 'It will blow over.'

Mrs Rupa Mehra sat up abruptly. 'So you knew! You knew! And you didn't tell me. And I had to learn this from strangers.' This new betrayal engendered a new bout of sobbing. Savita squeezed her mother's shoulders, and offered her another handkerchief. After a few minutes of this, Savita said:

'Don't cry, Ma, don't cry. What did you hear?'

'Oh, my poor Lata—is he from a good family? I had a sense something was going on. Oh God! What would her father have said if he had been alive? Oh, my daughter.'

'Ma, his father teaches mathematics at the university. He's a decent boy. And Lata's a sensible girl.'

Mateen brought the tea in, registered the scene with deferential interest, and went back towards the kitchen.

Lata walked in a few seconds later. She had taken a book to the banyan grove, where she had sat down undisturbed for a while, lost in Wodehouse and her own enchanted thoughts. Two more days, one more day, and she would see Kabir again.

She was unprepared for the scene before her, and stopped in the doorway.

'Where have you been, young lady?' demanded Mrs Rupa Mehra, her voice quivering with anger.

'For a walk,' faltered Lata.

'Walk? Walk?' Mrs Rupa Mehra's voice rose to a crescendo. 'I'll give you walk.'

Lata's mouth flew open, and she looked at Savita. Savita shook both her head and her right hand slightly, as if to say that it was not she who had given her away.

'Who is he?' demanded Mrs Rupa Mehra. 'Come here. Come here at once.'

Lata looked at Savita. Savita nodded.

'Just a friend,' said Lata, approaching her mother.

'Just a friend! A friend! And friends are for holding hands with? Is this what I brought you up for? All of you—and is this—'

'Ma, sit down,' said Savita, for Mrs Rupa Mehra had half risen out of her chair.

'Who told you?' asked Lata. 'Hema's Taiji?'

'Hema's Taiji? Hema's Taiji? Is she in this too?' exclaimed Mrs Rupa Mehra with new indignation. 'She lets those girls run around all over the place with flowers in their hair in the evening. Who told me? The wretched girl asks me who told me. No one told me. It's the talk of the town, everyone knows about it. Everyone thought you were a good girl with a good reputation—and now it is too late. Too late,' she sobbed.

'Ma, you always say Malati is such a nice girl,' said Lata by way of self-defence. 'And she has friends like that—you know that—everyone knows that.'

'Be quiet! Don't answer me back! I'll give you two tight slaps. Roaming around shamelessly near the dhobi-ghat and having a gala time.'

'But Malati—'

'Malati! Malati! I'm talking about you, not about Malati. Studying medicine and cutting up frogs—' Mrs Rupa Mehra's voice rose once more. 'Do you want to be like her? And lying to your mother. I'll never let you go for a walk again. You'll stay in this house, do you hear? Do you hear?' Mrs Rupa Mehra had stood up.

'Yes, Ma,' said Lata, remembering with a twinge of shame that she had had to lie to her mother in order to meet Kabir. The enchantment was being torn apart; she felt alarmed and miserable.

'What's his name?'

'Kabir,' said Lata, growing pale.

'Kabir what?'

Lata stood still and didn't answer. A tear rolled down her cheek.

Mrs Rupa Mehra was in no mood for sympathy. What were all these ridiculous tears? She caught hold of Lata's ear and twisted it. Lata gasped.

'He has a name, doesn't he? What is he—Kabir Lal, Kabir Mehra—or what? Are you waiting for the tea to get cold? Or have you forgotten?'

Lata closed her eyes.

'Kabir Durrani,' she said, and waited for the house to come tumbling down.

The three deadly syllables had their effect. Mrs Rupa Mehra clutched at her heart, opened her mouth in silent horror, looked unseeingly around the room, and sat down.

Savita rushed to her immediately. Her own heart was beating far too fast.

One last faint possibility struck Mrs Rupa Mehra. 'Is he a Parsi?' she asked weakly, almost pleadingly. The thought was odious but not so calamitously horrifying. But a look at Savita's face told her the truth.

'A Muslim!' said Mrs Rupa Mehra more to herself now than to anyone else. 'What did I do in my past life that I have brought this upon my beloved daughter?'

Savita was standing near her and held her hand. Mrs Rupa Mehra's hand was inert as she stared in front of her. Suddenly she became aware of the gentle curve of Savita's stomach, and fresh horrors came to her mind.

She stood up again. 'Never, never, never—' she said.

By now Lata, having conjured up the image of Kabir in her mind, had gained a little strength. She opened her eyes. Her tears had stopped and there was a defiant set to her mouth.

'Never, never, absolutely not—dirty, violent, cruel, lecherous—'

'Like Talat Khala?' demanded Lata. 'Like Uncle Shafi? Like the Nawab Sahib of Baitar? Like Firoz and Imtiaz?'

'Do you want to marry him?' cried Mrs Rupa Mehra in a fury.

'Yes!' said Lata, carried away, and angrier by the second.

'He'll marry you—and next year he'll say "Talaq talaq talaq" and you'll be out on the streets. You obstinate, stupid girl! You should drown yourself in a handful of water for sheer shame.'

'I *will* marry him,' said Lata, unilaterally.

'I'll lock you up. Like when you said you wanted to become a nun.'

Savita tried to intercede.

'You go to your room!' said Mrs Rupa Mehra. 'This isn't good for you.' She pointed her finger, and Savita, not used to being ordered about in her own home, meekly complied.

'I wish I had become a nun,' said Lata. 'I remember Daddy used to tell us we should follow our own hearts.'

'Still answering back?' said Mrs Rupa Mehra, infuriated by the mention of Daddy. 'I'll give you two tight slaps.'

She slapped her daughter hard, twice, and instantly burst into tears.

3.19

Mrs Rupa Mehra was not more prejudiced against Muslims than most upper-caste Hindu women of her age and background. As Lata had inopportunely pointed out, she even had friends who were Muslims, though almost all of them were not orthodox at all. The Nawab Sahib was, perhaps, quite orthodox, but then he was, for Mrs Rupa Mehra, more a social acquaintance than a friend.

The more Mrs Rupa Mehra thought, the more agitated she became. Even marrying a non-khatri Hindu was bad enough. But this was unspeakable. It was one thing to mix socially with Muslims, entirely another to dream of polluting one's blood and sacrificing one's daughter.

Whom could she turn to in her hour of darkness? When Pran came home for lunch and heard the story, he suggested mildly that they meet the boy. Mrs Rupa Mehra threw another fit. It was utterly out of the question. Pran then decided to stay out of things and to let them die down. He had not been hurt when he realized that Savita had kept her sister's confidence from him, and Savita loved him still more for that. She tried to calm her mother down, console Lata, and keep them in separate rooms—at least during the day.

Lata looked around the bedroom and wondered what she was doing in this house with her mother when her heart was entirely elsewhere, anywhere but here—a boat, a cricket field, a concert, a banyan grove, a cottage in the hills, Blandings Castle, anywhere, anywhere, so long as she was with Kabir. No matter what happened, she would meet him as planned, tomorrow. She told herself again and again that the path of true love never did run smooth.

Mrs Rupa Mehra wrote a letter on an inland form to Arun in Calcutta. Her tears fell on the letter and blotched the ink. She added: 'P.S. My tears have fallen on this letter, but what to do? My heart is broken and only God will show a way out. But His will be done.' Because the postage had just gone up she had to stick an extra stamp on the prepaid form.

In much bitterness of spirit, she went to see her father. It would be a humiliating visit. She would have to brave his temper in order to get his advice. Her father may have married a crass woman half his age, but that was a heaven-made match compared to what Lata was threatened with.

As expected, Dr Kishen Chand Seth rebuked Mrs Rupa Mehra roundly in front of the dreadful Parvati and told her what a useless mother she was.

But then, he added, everyone seemed to be brainless these days. Just last week he had told a patient whom he had seen at the hospital: 'You are a stupid man. In ten to fifteen days you will be dead. Throw away money if you want to on an operation, it'll only kill you quicker.' The stupid patient had been quite upset. It was clear that no one knew how to take or to give advice these days. And no one knew how to discipline their children; that was where all the trouble in the world sprang from.

'Look at Mahesh Kapoor!' he added with satisfaction.

Mrs Rupa Mehra nodded.

'And you are worse.'

Mrs Rupa Mehra sobbed.

'You spoiled the eldest'—he chuckled at the memory of Arun's jaunt in his car—'and now you have spoiled the youngest, and you have only yourself to blame. And you come to me for advice when it is too late.'

His daughter said nothing.

'And your beloved Chatterjis are just the same,' he added with relish. 'I hear from Calcutta circles that they have no control over their children. None.' This thought gave him an idea.

Mrs Rupa Mehra was now satisfactorily in tears, so he gave her some advice and told her to put it into effect immediately.

Mrs Rupa Mehra went home, got out some money, and went straight to the Brahmpur Junction Railway Station. She bought two tickets for Calcutta by the next evening's train.

Instead of posting her letter to Arun, she sent him a telegram.

Savita tried to dissuade her mother but to no effect. 'At least wait till the beginning of May when the exam results come out,' she said. 'Lata will be needlessly worried about them.'

Mrs Rupa Mehra told Savita that exam results meant nothing if a girl's character was ruined, and that they could be transmitted by mail. She knew what Lata was worried about all right. She then turned the emotional tables on Savita by saying that any scenes between Lata and herself should take place elsewhere, not within earshot of Savita. Savita was pregnant and should stay calm. 'Calm, that's the word,' repeated Mrs Rupa Mehra forcefully.

As for Lata, she said nothing to her mother, simply remaining tight-lipped when she was told to pack her things for the journey. 'We are going to Calcutta tomorrow evening by the 6.22 train—and that is that. Don't you dare say anything,' said Mrs Rupa Mehra.

Lata did not say anything. She refused to show any emotion to her mother. She packed carefully. She even ate something for dinner. The image of Kabir kept her company.

After dinner she sat on the roof, thinking. When she came to bed, she did not say goodnight to Mrs Rupa Mehra, who was lying sleeplessly in the next bed. Mrs Rupa Mehra was heartbroken, but Lata was not feeling very charitable. She went to sleep quite soon, and dreamed, among other things, of a washerman's donkey with the face of Dr Makhijani, chewing up Mrs Rupa Mehra's black handbag and all her little silver stars.

3.20

She awoke, rested. It was still dark. She had agreed to meet Kabir at six. She went to the bathroom, locked it from the inside, then slipped out from the back into the garden. She did not dare to take a sweater with her, as this would have made her mother suspicious. Anyway, it was not too cold.

But she was trembling. She walked down towards the mud cliffs, then down the path. Kabir was waiting for her, sitting on their root in the banyan grove. He got up when he heard her coming. His hair was ruffled, and he looked sleepy. He even yawned while she walked up towards him. In the dawn light his face looked even more handsome than when he had thrown his head back and laughed near the cricket field.

She seemed to him to be very tense and excited, but not unhappy. They kissed. Then Kabir said:

'Good morning.'

'Good morning.'

'Did you sleep well?'

'Very well, thank you,' said Lata. 'I dreamed of a donkey.'

'Oh, not of me?'

'No.'

'I can't remember what I dreamed of,' said Kabir, 'but I didn't have a restful night.'

'I love sleeping,' said Lata. 'I can sleep for nine or ten hours a day.'

'Ah . . . aren't you cold? Why don't you wear this?' Kabir made to take off his sweater.

'I've been longing to see you again,' said Lata.

'Lata?' said Kabir. 'What's happened to upset you?' Her eyes were unusually bright.

'Nothing,' said Lata, fighting back her tears. 'I don't know when I'll see you again.'

'What's happened?'

'I'm going to Calcutta tonight. My mother's found out about us. When she heard your name she threw a fit—I told you what my family was like.'

Kabir sat down on the root and said, 'Oh no.'

Lata sat down too. 'Do you still love me?' she said after a while.

'Still?' Kabir laughed bitterly. 'What is the matter with you?'

'You remember what you said the last time: that we loved each other and that that was all that mattered?'

'Yes,' said Kabir. 'It is.'

'Let's go away—'

'Away,' said Kabir sadly. 'Where?'

'Anywhere—to the hills—anywhere, really.'

'And leave everything?'

'Everything. I don't care. I've even packed some things.'

This hint of practicality made him smile instead of alarming him. He said, 'Lata, we don't have a chance if we go away. Let's wait and see how things work out. We'll make them work out.'

'I thought you lived from our one meeting to the next.'

Kabir put an arm around her.

'I do. But we can't decide everything. I don't want to disillusion you, but—'

'You are, you are disillusioning me. How long will we have to wait?'

'Two years, I think. First I have to finish my degree. After that I'm going to apply to get into Cambridge—or maybe take the exam for the Indian Foreign Service—'

'Ah—' It was a low cry of almost physical pain.

He stopped, realizing how selfish he must have sounded.

'I'll be married off in two years,' said Lata, covering her face in her hands. 'You're not a girl. You don't understand. My mother might not even let me come back to Brahmpur—'

Two lines from one of their meetings came to her mind:

> Desert not friendship. Renegade with me
> From raptured realm of Mr Nowrojee.

She got up. She made no attempt to hide her tears. 'I'm going,' she said.

'Please don't, Lata. Please listen,' said Kabir. 'When will we be able to speak to each other again? If we don't talk now—'

Lata was walking quickly up the path, trying to escape from his company now.

'Lata, be reasonable.'

She had reached the flat top of the path. Kabir walked behind her. She seemed so walled off from him that he didn't touch her. He sensed that she would have brushed him off, maybe with another painful remark.

Halfway to the house was a shrubbery of the most fragrant kamini, some bushes of which had grown as tall as trees. The air was thick with their scent, the branches full of small white blossoms against dark-green leaves, the ground covered with petals. As they passed below, he tousled the leaves gently, and a shower of fragrant petals fell on her hair. If she even noticed this, she gave no indication of it.

They walked on, unspeaking. Then Lata turned around.

'That's my sister's husband there in a dressing gown. They've been looking for me. Go back. No one's seen us yet.'

'Yes; Dr Kapoor. I know. I'll—I'll talk to him. I'll convince them—'

'You can't run four runs every day,' said Lata.

Kabir stopped dead in his tracks, a look of puzzlement rather than pain on his face. Lata walked on without looking back.

She never wanted to see him again.

At the house, Mrs Rupa Mehra was having hysterics. Pran was grim. Savita had been crying. Lata refused to answer any questions.

Mrs Rupa Mehra and Lata left for Calcutta that evening. Mrs Rupa Mehra kept up a litany of how shameful and inconsiderate Lata was; how she was forcing her mother to leave Brahmpur before Ramnavami; how she had been the cause of unnecessary disruption and expense.

Receiving no response, she finally gave up. For once, she hardly talked to the other passengers.

Lata kept quiet. She looked out of the train window till it became completely dark. She felt heartbroken and humiliated. She was sick of her mother, and of Kabir, and of the mess that was life.

Part Four

4.1

While Lata was falling in love with Kabir, a quite different set of events was taking place in Old Brahmpur, which, however, were to prove not irrelevant to her story. These events involved Pran's sister, Veena, and her family.

Veena Tandon entered her house in Misri Mandi, to be greeted by her son Bhaskar with a kiss, which she happily accepted despite the fact that he had a cold. He then rushed back to the small sofa where he had been sitting—his father on one side and his father's guest on the other—and continued his explanation of the powers of ten.

Kedarnath Tandon looked at his son indulgently but, happy in the consciousness of Bhaskar's genius, did not pay much attention to what he was saying. His father's guest, Haresh Khanna, who had been introduced to Kedarnath by a mutual acquaintance in the shoe business, would have been happier talking about the leather and footwear trade of Brahmpur, but felt it best to indulge his host's son—especially as Bhaskar, carried away by his enthusiasm, would have been very disappointed to lose his indoor audience on a day when he had not been allowed to go out kite-flying. He tried to concentrate on what Bhaskar was saying.

'Well, you see, Haresh Chacha, it's like this. First you have ten, that's just ten, that is, ten to the first power. Then you have a hundred, which is ten times ten, which makes it ten to the second power. Then you have a thousand, which is ten to the third power. Then you have ten thousand, which is ten to the fourth power—but this is where the problem begins, don't you see? We don't have a special word for that—and we really should. Ten times that is ten to the fifth power, which is a lakh. Then we have ten to the sixth power, which is a million, ten to the seventh power which is a crore, and then we come to another power for which we don't have a word—which is ten to the eighth. We should have a word for that as well. Then ten to the ninth power is a billion, and then comes ten to the tenth. Now it's amazing that we don't have a word in either English or Hindi for a number that is as important as ten to the tenth. Don't you agree with me, Haresh Chacha?' he continued, his bright eyes fixed on Haresh's face.

'But you know,' said Haresh, pulling something out of his recent memory for the enthusiastic Bhaskar, 'I think there is a special word for ten thousand. The Chinese tanners of Calcutta, with whom we have some dealings, once told me that they used the number ten-thousand as a standard unit of counting. What they call it I can't remember, but just as we use a lakh as a natural measuring point, they use ten-thousand.'

Bhaskar was electrified. 'But Haresh Chacha, you must find that number for me,' he said. 'You must find out what they call it. I have to know,' he said, his eyes burning with mystical fire, and his small frog-like features taking on an astonishing radiance.

'All right,' said Haresh. 'I'll tell you what. When I go back to Kanpur, I'll make inquiries, and as soon as I find out what that number is, I'll send you a letter. Who knows, perhaps they even have a number for ten to the eighth.'

'Do you really think so?' breathed Bhaskar wonderingly. His pleasure was akin to that of a stamp collector who finds the two missing values in an incomplete series suddenly supplied to him by a total stranger. 'When are you going back to Kanpur?'

Veena, who had just come in bearing cups of tea, rebuked Bhaskar for his inhospitable comment, and asked Haresh how many spoonfuls of sugar he took.

Haresh could not help noticing that when he had seen her a few minutes earlier her head had been uncovered, but now, after returning from the kitchen, she had covered it with her sari. He guessed correctly that it was at her mother-in-law's behest that she had done so. Although Veena was a little older than him, and quite plump, he could not help thinking how animated her features were. The slight touches of anxiety about her eyes only added to her liveliness of character.

Veena, for her part, could not help noticing that her husband's guest was a good-looking young man. Haresh was short, well built without being stocky, fair in complexion, with a squarish rather than an oval face. His eyes were not large, but they had a directness of gaze which she believed was a key to straightforwardness of character. Silk shirt and agate cufflinks, she observed to herself.

'Now, Bhaskar, go and talk to your grandmother,' said Veena. 'Papa's friend wants to talk to him about important matters.'

Bhaskar looked at the two men in inquiring appeal. His father, though he had closed his eyes, sensed that Bhaskar was waiting for his word.

'Yes. Do as your mother says,' said Kedarnath. Haresh said nothing, but smiled. Bhaskar went off, rather annoyed at being excluded.

'Don't mind him, he's never annoyed for long,' said Veena apologetically. 'He doesn't like being left out of things that interest him. When we play chaupar together—Kedarnath and I—we have to make sure Bhaskar isn't in the house, otherwise he insists on playing and beats both of us. Very bothersome.'

'I can imagine it would be,' said Haresh.

'The trouble is that he has no one to talk to about his maths, and sometimes he becomes very withdrawn. His teachers at school are less proud of him than worried about him. Sometimes it seems he deliberately does badly in maths—if a question annoys him, for instance. Once, when he was very young, I remember Maan—that's my brother—asked him for the answer to 17 minus 6. When he got 11, Maan asked him to subtract 6 again. When he got 5, Maan asked him to subtract 6 yet again. And Bhaskar actually began to cry! "No, no," he said, "Maan Maama is playing a trick on me. Stop him!" And he wouldn't speak to him for a week.'

'Well, for a day or two at least,' said Kedarnath. 'But that was before he learned about negative numbers. Once he did, he insisted on taking bigger things away from smaller things the whole day long. I suppose, the way things are going with my work, he'll get plenty of practice in that line.'

'By the way,' said Veena to her husband anxiously, 'I think you should go out this afternoon. Bajaj came this morning and, when he didn't find you in, he said he would drop by at about three.'

From her expression and his, Haresh guessed that Bajaj might be a creditor.

'Once the strike's over, things will improve,' said Kedarnath a bit apologetically to Haresh. 'I'm a little over-extended at present.'

'The trouble is,' said Veena, 'that there's so much mistrust. And the local leaders make it much worse. Because my father's so busy with his department and the legislature, Kedarnath tries to help him by keeping in touch with his constituency. So when there's trouble of some kind, people often come to him. But this time, when Kedarnath tried to mediate, although—I know I shouldn't be saying this and he doesn't like me to, but it's quite true—although he's quite well-liked and respected by people on both sides, the shoemakers' leaders have undermined all his efforts—just because he's a trader.'

'Well, that's not quite it,' said Kedarnath, but decided to defer his explanation until he and Haresh were alone. He had closed his eyes again. Haresh looked a little concerned.

'Don't worry,' said Veena to Haresh. 'He's not asleep or bored or even praying before lunch.' Her husband opened his eyes quickly. 'He does it all the time,' she explained. 'Even at our wedding—but it was less obvious behind those strings of flowers.'

She got up to see if the rice was ready. After the men had been served and had eaten, old Mrs Tandon came in for a short while to exchange a few words. Upon hearing that Haresh Khanna was originally from Delhi she asked him whether he belonged to the Khannas of Neel Darvaza or those who lived in Lakkhi Kothi. When Haresh said he was from Neel Darvaza, she told him she had visited it once as a girl.

Haresh described a few changes, recounted a few personal anecdotes, praised the simple but tasty vegetarian food that the two women had prepared, and was a hit with the old lady.

'My son has to travel a lot,' she confided to Haresh, 'and no one feeds him properly on the way. Even here, if it wasn't for me—'

'Quite right,' said Veena, attempting to take the wind out of her sails. 'It is so important for a man to be treated as a child. In matters of food, of course. Kedarnath—I mean Bhaskar's father'—she corrected herself as her mother-in-law shot a look at her—'simply loves the food his mother prepares. It's a pity men don't like being sung to sleep with lullabies.'

Haresh's eyes twinkled and almost disappeared between his eyelids, but he kept his lips steady.

'I wonder if Bhaskar will continue to like the food I prepare,' continued Veena. 'Probably not. When he gets married—'

Kedarnath held up his hand. 'Really,' he said, in mild reproof.

Haresh noticed that Kedarnath's palm was badly scarred.

'Now what have I done?' asked Veena innocently, but she changed the subject. Her husband had a decency which rather frightened her, and she didn't want to be judged badly by him.

'You know, I blame myself for Bhaskar's obsession with mathematics,' she continued. 'I named him Bhaskar after the sun. Then, when he was a year old, someone told me that one of our ancient mathematicians was called Bhaskar, and now our Bhaskar can't live without his mathematics. Names are terribly important. My father wasn't in town when I was born, and my mother named me Veena, thinking it would please him because he's so fond of music. But as a result I've become obsessed with music, and

I can't live without it either.'

'Really?' said Haresh. 'And do you play the veena?'

'No,' laughed Veena, her eyes shining. 'I sing. I sing. I can't live without singing.'

Old Mrs Tandon got up and left the room.

After a while, with a shrug, Veena followed her.

4.2

When the men were left alone, Haresh—who had been sent to Brahmpur for a few days to purchase some materials by his employers, the Cawnpore Leather & Footwear Company—turned to Kedarnath and said: 'Well, I've been around the markets during the last couple of days and have got some idea of what goes on there, or at least what is supposed to go on there. But despite all this running around, I don't think I've been able to make complete sense of it. Especially your system of credit—what with all these chits and promissory notes and so on. And why have the small manufacturers—who make shoes in their own homes—gone on strike? Surely it must cause them terrible hardship. And it must be very bad for traders like yourself who buy directly from them.'

'Well,' said Kedarnath, passing his hand through his slightly greyed hair, 'about the chit system—it confused me too at the beginning. As I mentioned, we were forced out of Lahore at the time of Partition and even then I was not exactly in the footwear trade. I did happen to go through Agra and Kanpur on the way here and you're quite right, Kanpur has nothing like the system that we have here. But have you been to Agra?'

'Yes,' said Haresh. 'I have. But that was before I entered the industry.'

'Well, Agra has a system somewhat similar to ours.' And Kedarnath outlined it roughly.

Because they were perennially short of cash, the traders paid the shoemakers partly with post-dated chits. The shoemakers could only get cash to buy raw materials by discounting these chits elsewhere. They had felt for years that the traders had been squeezing a kind of unwarranted credit out of them. Finally, when the traders, as a body, had tried to winch up the proportion of chit to cash, the shoemakers had struck.

'And of course, you're right,' Kedarnath added, 'the strike hurts everyone—they could starve and we could be ruined.'

'I suppose the shoemakers would claim,' said Haresh, with a meditative air, 'that as a result of the chit system they are the ones who are financing your expansion.'

There was no tone of accusation in Haresh's voice, simply the curiosity of a pragmatic man trying to get facts and attitudes straight. Kedarnath responded to his interest and went on:

'That's indeed what they claim,' he agreed. 'But it is also their own expansion, the expansion of the whole market, that they are financing,' he said. 'And, besides, it is only a portion of their payment that is made by post-dated chits. Most of it is still made by cash. I'm afraid that everyone has begun to see matters in black and white, with the traders usually being the ones who are painted black. It's a good thing that the Home Minister, L.N. Agarwal, comes from a trading community. He's the MLA for a part of this area, and he does at least see our side of the matter. My wife's father doesn't get along well with him at all politically—or even personally, really—but, as I tell Veena when she's in a mood to listen, Agarwal understands the ways of business better than her father does.'

'Well, do you think that you could take me around Misri Mandi in the afternoon?' asked Haresh. 'I'll get a more informed perspective that way.'

It was interesting, thought Haresh, that the two powerful—and rival—Ministers should represent contiguous constituencies.

Kedarnath was in two minds as to whether to agree, and Haresh must have seen this in his face. Kedarnath had been impressed by Haresh's technical knowledge of shoe manufacture, and by his enterprising spirit, and was thinking of proposing a business connection. Perhaps, he thought, the Cawnpore Leather & Footwear Company would be interested in buying shoes directly from him. After all, it sometimes happened that companies like CLFC received small orders from shoe stores, perhaps for 5,000 pairs of a particular kind of shoe, and it was not worth their while to retool their own plant to fulfil such orders. In such a case, if Kedarnath could ensure that he got shoes from local Brahmpur shoemakers that fulfilled CLFC's quality requirements, and shipped them to Kanpur, it might work out well both for him and for Haresh's employers.

However, these were disturbed days, everyone was under great financial pressure, and the impression that Haresh might obtain of the reliability or efficiency of the shoe trade in Brahmpur would not be a favourable one.

But Haresh's small kindness to his son and his respectful attitude to his mother tilted the balance. 'All right, we'll go,' he said. 'But the market will really only open later, towards the evening—even at the level to which the strike has reduced it. The Brahmpur Shoe Mart, where I have my stall, opens at six. But I have a suggestion in the meanwhile. I'll take you to see a few places where shoes are actually made. It'll be a change for you from the conditions of manufacture that you've seen in England—or at your Kanpur factory.'

Haresh agreed readily.

As they walked downstairs, with the afternoon sunlight falling on them from above through the layers of grating, Haresh thought how similar in design this house was to his foster-father's house in Neel Darvaza—though of course, much smaller.

At the corner of the alley, where it opened out into a slightly broader and more crowded lane, there was a paan stand. They stopped. 'Plain or sweet?' asked Kedarnath.

'Plain, with tobacco.'

For the next five minutes, as they walked along together, Haresh did not say anything because he kept the paan in his mouth without swallowing it. He would spit it out later into an opening in the small drain that ran along the side of the alley. But for the moment, under the pleasant intoxication of the tobacco, amid the bustle all around him, the shouts and chatter and the sound of bicycle-bells, cow-bells, and bells from the Radhakrishna Temple, he was again reminded of the alley near his foster-father's house in Old Delhi where he had been brought up after his parents died.

As for Kedarnath, though he had got a plain paan for himself, he did not speak much either. He would be taking this silk-shirted young man to one of the poorest parts of the city, where the jatav shoemakers lived and worked in conditions of wretched squalor, and he wondered how he would react. He thought of his own sudden fall from wealth in Lahore to the virtual destitution of 1947; the hard-won security he had obtained for Veena and Bhaskar over the last few years; the problems of the present strike and the dangers it would mean for them. That there was some special spark of genius in his son he believed with utter conviction. He dreamed of sending him to a school like Doon, and perhaps later even to Oxford or Cambridge. But times were hard, and whether Bhaskar would obtain the special education he deserved, whether Veena could keep up with the music she craved, whether they could even continue to afford their modest rent, were questions that troubled and aged him.

But these are the hostages of love, he said to himself, and it is meaningless to ask myself whether I would exchange a head of unworried hair for my wife and child.

4.3

They emerged on to a yet broader alley, and then on to a hot, dusty street not far from the high ground of the Chowk. One of the two great landmarks of this crowded area was a huge, pink three-storey building. This was the kotwali or city police station, the largest in Purva Pradesh. The other landmark, a hundred yards away, was the beautiful and austere Alamgiri Mosque, ordered by the Emperor Aurangzeb to be built in the heart of the city upon the ruins of a great temple.

Late Mughal and British records attest to a series of Hindu-Muslim riots around this spot. It is not clear what exactly incurred the wrath of the emperor. He was the least tolerant of the great emperors of his dynasty, true, but the area around Brahmpur had been spared his worst excesses. The reimposition of the poll-tax on unbelievers, a tax rescinded by his great-grandfather Akbar, affected the citizens of Brahmpur as it did those throughout the empire. But the razing of temples usually required some extraordinary impetus, such as the indication that it was being used as a centre for armed or political resistance. Apologists for Aurangzeb were apt to claim that he had a worse reputation for intolerance than he deserved and that he was as harsh with Shias as he was with Hindus. But for the more orthodox Hindu citizenry of Brahmpur, the previous 250 years of history had not dimmed their loathing for a man who had dared to destroy one of the holiest temples of the great destroyer Shiva himself.

The great Shiva-linga of the inner sanctum of the temple was rumoured to have been preserved by the priests of the so-called Chandrachur Temple on the night before it was reduced to rubble. They sank it not in a deep well as was often the case in those days, but in the shallows and sands near the cremation ground by the Ganga. How the huge stone object was carried there is not known. Apparently the knowledge of its location was secretly maintained and passed on for more than ten generations from head-priest to head-priest in hereditary succession. Of all the common images of Hindu worship it was probably the sacred phallus, the Shiva-linga, which was most despised by the orthodox theologians of Islam. Where they could destroy it, they did so with a particular sense of righteous disgust. While there was any chance that the Muslim peril might resurface, the priests did not act upon their family knowledge. But after Independence and the Partition of Pakistan and India, the priest of the long-since-destroyed Chandrachur Temple—who lived in poverty in a shack near the cremation ghat—felt that it was safe to emerge and identify himself. He tried to get his temple rebuilt and the Shiva-linga excavated and reinstalled. At first the Archaeological Survey had refused to believe the particulars he gave of the location of the linga. The rumour of its preservation was unsupported by other records. And even if it were true, the Ganga had changed course, the sands and shallows had shifted, and the unwritten verses or mantras describing its location could themselves have grown inaccurate through repeated transmission. It is also possible that officers of the Archaeological Survey were aware or had been apprised of the possible effects of unearthing the linga and had decided that for the sake of public peace it was safer horizontal under the sand than vertical in a sanctum. At any rate, the priest obtained no help from them.

As they passed below the red walls of the mosque, Haresh, not being a native of Brahmpur, asked why black flags were hanging at the outer gates. Kedarnath replied in an indifferent voice that they had come up just the previous week when the ground had been broken for a temple in the neighbouring plot of land. For one who had lost his house, his land and his livelihood in Lahore, he did not appear to be embittered against Muslims so much as exhausted by religious zealots in general. His mother was very upset at his evenhandedness.

'Some local pujari located a Shiva-linga in the Ganga,' said Kedarnath. 'It is supposed to have come from the Chandrachur Temple, the great Shiva temple that they say Aurangzeb destroyed. The pillars of the mosque do have bits of Hindu carving, so it must have been made out of some ruined temple, God knows how long ago. Mind your step!'

Haresh narrowly avoided stepping into some dog-shit. He was wearing a rather smart pair of maroon brogues, and was very glad to have been warned.

'Anyway,' continued Kedarnath, smiling at Haresh's agility, 'the Raja of Marh has title to the house that stands—stood, rather—beyond the western wall of the mosque. He has had it broken down and is building a temple there. A new Chandrachur Temple. He's a real lunatic. Since he can't destroy the mosque and build on the original site, he's decided to build to the immediate west and install the linga in the sanctum there. For him it's a great joke to think that the Muslims will be bowing down in the direction of his Shiva-linga five times a day.'

Noticing an unoccupied cycle rickshaw, Kedarnath hailed it, and they got in. 'To Ravidaspur,' he said, and then continued: 'You know, for a supposedly gentle, spiritual people, we seem to delight in rubbing other people's noses in dog-shit, don't you think? Certainly I cannot understand people like the Raja of Marh. He imagines himself to be a new Ganesh whose divine mission in life is to lead the armies of Shiva to victory over the demons. And yet he's besotted with half the Muslim courtesans of the city. When he laid the foundation stone of the temple two people died. Not that this meant anything to him, he's probably had twenty times that number murdered in his own time in his own state. Anyway, one of the two was a Muslim and that's when the mullahs put the black flags up on the gate of the mosque. And if you look carefully, you'll see that there are even some smaller ones on the minarets.'

Haresh turned back to look, but suddenly the cycle rickshaw, which had been gathering speed downhill, collided with a slowly moving car, and they came to a sudden halt. The car had been crawling along the crowded road, and there was no damage to anyone, but a couple of the bicycle's spokes had got bent. The rickshaw-wallah, who looked thin and unassertive, jumped off the cycle, glanced quickly at his front wheel, and banged aggressively on the window of the car.

'Give me money! Phataphat! Immediately!' he yelled.

The liveried driver and the passengers, who were two middle-aged women, looked surprised at this sudden demand. The driver half-recovered, and put his head out of the window

'Why?' he shouted. 'You were coming down the slope without control. We weren't even moving. If you want to commit suicide do I have to pay for your funeral?'

'Money! Quickly! Three spokes—three rupees!' said the rickshaw-wallah, as brusquely as a highwayman.

The driver turned his face away. The rickshaw-wallah grew angrier:

'You daughter-fucker! I don't have all day. If you don't pay for my damages, I'll give your car some of its own.'

The driver would probably have responded with some insults in kind, but since he was with his employers, who were getting nervous, he remained tight-lipped.

Another rickshaw-wallah passed, and shouted in encouragement: 'That's right, brother, don't be afraid.' By now about twenty people had gathered round to watch the sport.

'Oh, pay him and let's go on,' said one of the ladies at the back. 'It's too hot to argue.'

'Three rupees!' repeated the rickshaw-wallah.

Haresh was about to leap out of the rickshaw to put an end to this extortion when the driver of the car suddenly flung an eight-anna coin at the rickshaw-wallah. 'Take this—and fuck off!' the driver said, stung to rage by his helplessness.

When the car had gone and the crowd had cleared, the rickshaw-wallah started singing with delight. He bent down and straightened the two bent spokes in twenty seconds, and they were on their way again.

4.4

'I've only been a couple of times to Jagat Ram's place, so I'll have to make inquiries once we get to Ravidaspur,' said Kedarnath.

'Jagat Ram?' asked Haresh, still thinking of the incident of the spokes and angry with the rickshaw-wallah.

'The shoemaker whose workshop we're going to see. He's a shoemaker, a jatav. He was originally one of those basket-wallahs I told you about who bring their shoes to Misri Mandi to sell to any trader who'll buy them.'

'And now?'

'Now he has his own workshop. He's reliable, unlike most of these shoemakers who, once they have a bit of money in their pockets, don't care about deadlines or promises. And he's skilled. And he doesn't drink—not much. I began by giving him a small order for a few dozen pairs, and he did a good job. Soon I was ordering from him regularly. Now he's able to hire two or three people in addition to his own family. It's helped both him and me. And perhaps you might want to see if the quality of his work comes up to the standard that your people at CLFC need. If so . . .' Kedarnath left the rest of the sentence in the air.

Haresh nodded, and gave him a comforting smile. After a pause, Haresh said, 'It's hot now that we're out of the alleys. And it smells worse than a tannery. Where are we now? In Ravidaspur?'

'Not yet. That's on the other side of the railway line. It doesn't smell quite so bad there. Yes, there's an area here where they prepare the leather, but it isn't a proper tannery like the one on the Ganga—'

'Perhaps we should get down and see it,' said Haresh with interest.

'But there's nothing to see,' protested Kedarnath, covering his nose.

'Have you been here before?' asked Haresh.

'No!'

Haresh laughed. 'Stop here!' he shouted at the rickshaw-wallah. Over Kedarnath's protests, he got him to dismount, and the two of them entered the warren of stinking paths and low huts, led by their noses towards the tanning pits.

The dirt paths stopped suddenly at a large open area surrounded by shacks and pockmarked by circular pits which had been dug into the ground and lined with hardened clay. A fearsome stench rose from the entire zone. Haresh felt sick; Kedarnath almost vomited with disgust. The sun shone harshly down, and the heat made the stench worse still. Some of the pits were filled with a white liquid, others with a brown tannic brew. Dark, scrawny men dressed only in lungis stood to one side of the pits, scraping off fat and hair from a pile of hides. One of them stood in a pit and seemed to be wrestling with a large hide. A pig was drinking at a ditch filled with stagnant black water. Two children with filthy matted hair were playing in the dust near the pits. When they saw the strangers they stopped abruptly and stared at them.

'If you had wanted to see the whole process from the beginning I could have taken you to see the ground where dead buffaloes are stripped and left to the vultures,' said Kedarnath wryly. 'It's near the unfinished bypass.'

Haresh, slightly regretful for having forced his companion into accompanying him here, shook his head. He looked at the nearest shack, which was empty except for a rudimentary fleshing machine. Haresh went up and examined it. In the next shack was an ancient splitting machine and a wattle pit. Three young men were rubbing a black paste on to a buffalo hide lying on the ground. Next to them was a white pile of salted sheepskins. When they saw the strangers they stopped working and looked at them.

No one said a word, neither the children, nor the three young men, nor the two strangers.

Eventually Kedarnath broke the silence. 'Bhai,' he said, addressing one of the three young men. 'We have just come to see how the leather is prepared. Would you show us around?'

The man looked at him closely, and then stared at Haresh, taking in his off-white silk shirt, his brogues, his briefcase, his businesslike air.

'Where are you from?' he asked Kedarnath.

'We're from the town. We're on our way to Ravidaspur. There's a local man there whom I work with.'

Ravidaspur was almost entirely a shoemaker's neighbourhood. But if Kedarnath imagined that by implying that another leatherworker was a colleague of his he would win acceptance here among the tanners, he was mistaken. Even among the leatherworkers or chamars, there was a hierarchy. The shoemakers—like the man they were going to visit—looked down upon the flayers and tanners. In turn, those who were looked down upon expressed their dislike of the shoemakers.

'That is a neighbourhood we do not like to go to,' said one of the young men shortly.

'Where does the paste come from?' asked Haresh, after a pause.

'From Brahmpur,' said the young man, refusing to be specific.

There was another long silence.

Then an old man appeared with his hands wet and dripping with some dark sticky liquid. He stood at the entrance of the shack and observed them.

'You! This wattle water—pani!' he said in English before lapsing into crude Hindi again. His voice was cracked, and he was drunk. He picked up a piece of rough, red-dyed leather from the ground and said, 'This is better than cherry leather from Japan! Have you heard of Japan? I had a fight with them, and I made them fail. Patent leather from China? I can match them all. I am sixty years old and I have a full knowledge of all pastes, all masalas, all techniques.'

Kedarnath began to get worried, and tried to move out of the shack. The old man barred his way by stretching his hands out sideways in a servile gesture of aggression. 'You cannot see the pits. You are a spy from the CID, from the police, from the bank—' He held his ears in a gesture of shame, then lapsed into English: 'No, no, no, bilkul no!'

By now the stench and the tension had made Kedarnath somewhat desperate. His face was drawn, he was sweating with anxiety as much as heat. 'Let us go, we have to get to Ravidaspur,' he said.

The old man moved towards him and held out his stained and dripping hand: 'Money!' he said. 'Fees! To drink—otherwise you cannot see the pits. You go to Ravidaspur. We don't like the jatavs, we are not like them, they eat the meat of buffaloes. Chhhi!' He spat out a syllable of disgust. 'We only eat goats and sheep.'

Kedarnath shrank back. Haresh began to get annoyed.

The old man sensed that he had got under his skin. This gave him a perverse sense of encouragement. Mercenary, suspicious and boastful by turn, he now led them towards the pits. 'We get no money from the government,' he whispered. 'We need money, each family, for buying materials, chemicals. The government gives us too little money. You are my Hindu brother,' he said mockingly. 'Bring me a bottle—I will give you samples of the best dyes, the best liquor, the best medicine!' He laughed at his joke. 'Look!' He pointed at a reddish liquid in a pit.

One of the young men, a short man who was blind in one eye, said, 'They stop us from moving raw materials, stop us from getting chemicals. We have to have supporting documents and registration. We are harassed in transit. You tell your government department to exempt us from duty and give us money. Look at our children. Look—' He gestured towards a child who was defecating on a rubbish heap.

To Kedarnath the whole slum was unbearably vile. He said in a low voice: 'We are not from a government department.'

The young man suddenly got annoyed. His lips tightened and he said: 'Where are you from then?' The eyelid over his blind eye began to twitch. 'Where are you from? Why have you come here? What do you want from this place?'

Kedarnath could tell that Haresh was about to flare up. He sensed that Haresh was abrupt and quite fearless, but believed that it was pointless being fearless when there was something to fear. He knew how things could suddenly explode from acrimony into violence. He put one arm around Haresh's shoulder and led him back between the pits. The ground oozed, and the lower part of Haresh's brogues was splattered with black filth.

The young man followed them, and at one point it seemed that he was about to lay his hands on Kedarnath. 'I'll recognize you,' he said. 'You don't come back. You want to make money from our blood. There is more money in leather than in silver and gold—or you wouldn't come to this stinking place.'

'No—no—' said the drunken old man aggressively, 'bilkul no!'

Kedarnath and Haresh re-entered the neighbouring lanes; the stench was hardly better. Just at the opening of a lane, at the periphery of the open, pit-riddled ground, Haresh noticed a large red stone, flat on the top. On it a boy of about seventeen had laid a piece of sheepskin, largely cleaned of wool and fat. With a fleshing knife he was removing the remaining pieces of flesh off the skin. He was utterly intent upon what he was doing. The skins piled up nearby were cleaner than they could have been if they had been fleshed by a machine. Despite what had happened before, Haresh was fascinated. Normally he would have stopped to ask a few questions, but Kedarnath hurried him on.

The tanners had left them. Haresh and Kedarnath, dust-covered and sweating, made their way back through the dirt paths. When they got to their rickshaw on the street they gratefully breathed in the air that had seemed at first unbearably foul. And indeed, compared to what they had taken in for the last half hour, it was the breath of paradise.

4.5

After waiting in the heat for fifteen minutes for a late, long and very slow goods train to pass a level crossing, they finally got to Ravidaspur. It was somewhat less crowded in the lanes of this outlying neighbourhood than in the old heart of Brahmpur where Kedarnath lived, but far more insanitary, with sluggish sewage trickling along and across the lanes. Picking their way between flea-ridden dogs, grunting filth-spattered pigs and various unpleasant static objects, and crossing an open sewer on a rickety wooden bridge, they found their way to Jagat Ram's small, rectangular, windowless brick-and-mud workshop. At night after the work was cleared away, this was where his six children slept; he and his wife usually slept in a brick-walled room with a corrugated iron roof which he had built on top of the flat roof of the workshop.

Several men and two young boys were working inside by the sunlight entering through the doorway and a couple of dim, bare electric bulbs. They were dressed in lungis for the most part, except for one man, who was dressed in kurta-pyjama, and Jagat Ram himself, who wore a shirt and trousers. They were sitting cross-legged on the ground in front of low platforms—square in shape and made of grey stone—on which their materials were placed. They were intent on their work—cutting, skiving, pasting, folding, trimming or hammering—and their heads were bent down, but from time to time one or the other would make a comment—about work or personal gossip or politics or the world in general—and this would lead to a little ripple of conversation among the sounds of hammers, knives, and the single pedal-operated Singer sewing machine.

When he saw Kedarnath and Haresh, Jagat Ram looked mystified. He touched his moustache in an unconscious gesture. He had expected other visitors.

'Welcome,' he said calmly. 'Come in. What brings you here? I've told you that the strike won't come in the way of fulfilling your order,' he added, anticipating a possible reason for Kedarnath's presence.

A little girl of about five, Jagat Ram's daughter, sat on the step. Now she began singing 'Lovely walé aa gayé! Lovely walé aa gayé!' and clapped her hands.

It was Kedarnath's turn to look surprised—and not entirely pleased. Her father, a little disconcerted, corrected her: 'These are not the people from Lovely, Meera—now go and tell your mother we need some tea.'

He turned to Kedarnath and said, 'Actually, I was expecting the people from Lovely.' He did not feel the need to volunteer any further information.

Kedarnath nodded. The Lovely Shoe Shop, one of the more recent shops to appear just off Nabiganj, had a good selection of women's shoes. Normally the man who ran the shop would have got the Bombay middlemen to supply him, as Bombay was where most women's shoes in the country were produced. Now he was obviously looking close to home for his supplies, and tapping a source that Kedarnath would have been happier tapping—or at least mediating—himself.

Dismissing the subject from his mind for the moment, he said, 'This is Mr Haresh Khanna, who is originally from Delhi, but is working for CLFC in Kanpur. He has studied footwear manufacture in England. And, well, I have brought him here to show him what work our Brahmpur shoemakers are capable of, even with their simple tools.'

Jagat Ram nodded, quite pleased.

There was a small wooden stool near the entrance of the workshop, and Jagat Ram asked Kedarnath to sit down. Kedarnath in turn invited Haresh to sit, but Haresh courteously declined. He sat down instead on one of the small stone platforms at which no one was working. The artisans stiffened, looking at him in displeasure and astonishment. Their reaction was so palpable that Haresh quickly got up again. Clearly he had done something wrong and, being a direct man, he turned to Jagat Ram and said, 'What's the matter? Can't one sit on those?'

Jagat Ram had reacted with similar resentment when Haresh had sat down, but the straightforwardness of Haresh's query—and his obvious lack of intention to offend anyone—caused him to respond mildly.

'A workman calls his work-platform his rozi or "employment"; he does not sit on it,' he said quietly. He did not mention that each man kept his rozi immaculately polished, and even said a brief prayer to it before beginning his day's work. To his son he said, 'Get up—let Haresh Sahib sit down.'

A boy of fifteen got up from the chair near the sewing machine, and despite Haresh's protests that he did not want to interrupt anyone's work he was made to sit down. Jagat Ram's youngest son, who was seven, came in with three cups of tea.

The cups were thick and small, chipped here and there on their white surface, but clean. There was a little talk of this and that, of the strike in Misri Mandi, of the claim by a newspaper that the smoke from the tannery and the Praha Shoe Factory were damaging the Barsaat Mahal, of the new municipal market-tax, of various local personalities.

After a while, Haresh became impatient, as he tended to do when he was sitting idle. He got up to look around the workshop and find out what everyone was doing. A batch of women's sandals was being made; they looked quite attractive with their green and black plaited leather straps.

Haresh was indeed surprised at the skill of the workmen. With rudimentary tools—chisel and knife and awl and hammer and foot-operated sewing machine—they were producing shoes that were not far below the quality of those made by the machines of CLFC. He told them what he thought of their skill and the quality of their product, given the limitations under which they worked; and they warmed to him.

One of the bolder workmen—Jagat Ram's younger brother, a friendly, round-faced man—asked to see Haresh's shoes, the maroon brogues that he was wearing. Haresh took them off, mentioning that they were not very clean. In fact they were by now completely splattered and caked with mud. They were passed around for general admiration and examination.

Jagat Ram read out the letters painstakingly and spelt 'Saxone'. 'Saksena from England,' he explained with some pride.

'I can see that you make men's shoes as well,' said Haresh. He had noticed a large clump of wooden lasts for men hanging grape-like from the ceiling in a dark corner of the room.

'Of course,' said Jagat Ram's brother with a jovial grin. 'But there's more profit in what few others can do. It's much better for us to make women's shoes—'

'Not necessarily,' said Haresh, whipping out—to everyone's, including Kedarnath's, surprise—a set of paper patterns from his briefcase. 'Now, Jagat Ram, tell me, are your workmen skilled enough to give me a shoe—also a brogue—based on these patterns?'

'Yes,' said Jagat Ram, almost without thinking.

'Don't say yes so quickly,' said Haresh, though he was pleased by the ready and confident response. He too enjoyed taking up challenges as much as he enjoyed throwing them down.

Jagat Ram was looking at the patterns—they were for a size 7 winged brogue—with great interest. Just by looking at the flat pieces of thin cardboard that made up the patterns—the fine punched design, the shape of the toe, the vamp, the quarters—the whole shoe came to vivid, three-dimensional shape before his eyes.

'Who is making these shoes?' he asked, his forehead creased with curiosity. 'They are somewhat different from the brogues you are wearing.'

'We are, at CLFC. And if you do a good job, you may be too—for us.'

Jagat Ram, though clearly very surprised and interested by Haresh's statement, did not say anything for a while in response, but continued to examine the patterns.

Pleased with the dramatic effect of his sudden production of the patterns, Haresh said: 'Keep them. Look over them today. I can see that those lasts hanging there are non-standard, so I'll send you a pair of size 7 standard lasts tomorrow. I've brought a couple of pairs to Brahmpur. Now then, apart from the lasts, what will you need? Let's say, three square feet of leather, calf leather—let's make that maroon as well—'

'And lining leather,' said Jagat Ram.

'Right; suppose we say natural cow, also three square feet—I'll get that from town.'

'And leather for the sole and insole?' asked Jagat Ram.

'No, that's readily available and not very expensive. You can manage that. I'll give you twenty rupees to cover costs and time—and you can get the material for the heels yourself. I've brought a few counters and toe-puffs of decent quality—they are always a problem—and some thread; but they're at the house where I'm staying.'

Kedarnath, though his eyes were closed, raised his eyebrows in admiration at this enterprising fellow who had had the foresight to think of all these details before he left on a brief out-of-town trip intended mainly for purchasing materials. He was, however, concerned that Jagat Ram might be taken over by Haresh and that he himself might be cut out. The mention of the Lovely Shoe Shop came back to worry him as well.

'Now, if I came over tomorrow morning with these things,' Haresh was saying, 'when could you let me have the shoes?'

'I think I could have them ready in five days,' said Jagat Ram.

Haresh shook his head impatiently.

'I can't stay in town for five days just for a pair of shoes. How about three?'

'I'll have to leave them on the lasts for at least seventy-two hours,' said Jagat Ram. 'If you want me to make a pair of shoes which retain their shape, you know that that is a minimum.'

Now that both of them were standing up, he towered over Haresh. But Haresh, who had always treated his shortness with the irritation that befitted an inconvenient but psychologically insignificant fact, was not in the least overpowered. Besides, he was the one ordering the shoes.

'Four.'

'Well, if you send the leather to me tonight, so that we can start with the cutting first thing tomorrow morning—'

'Done,' said Haresh. 'Four days. I'll come over personally tomorrow with the other components to see how you're getting on. Now we'd better go.'

'One more thing strikes me, Haresh Sahib,' said Jagat Ram, as they were leaving. 'Ideally I'd like to have a sample of the shoe that you want me to reproduce.'

'Yes,' said Kedarnath with a smile. 'Why aren't you wearing a pair of brogues manufactured by your own company—instead of these English shoes? Take them off immediately, and I'll have you carried back to the rickshaw.'

'I'm afraid my feet have got used to these,' said Haresh, returning the smile, though he knew as well as anyone that it was more his heart than his feet. He loved good clothes and he loved good shoes, and he felt bad that CLFC products did not achieve the international standards of quality that, both by instinct and by training, he so greatly admired.

'Well, I'll try to get you a sample pair of those,' he continued, pointing at the paper patterns in Jagat Ram's hands, 'by one means or another.'

He had given a pair of CLFC winged brogues as a present to the old college friend whom he was staying with. Now he would have to borrow his own gift back for a few days. But he had no compunction about doing that. When it came to work, he never felt awkward in the least about anything. In fact, Haresh was not given to feeling awkward in general.

As they walked back to the waiting rickshaw, Haresh felt very pleased with the way things were going. Brahmpur had got off to a sleepy start, but was proving to be very interesting, indeed, unpredictable.

He got out a small card from his pocket and noted down in English:

Action Points—

1. Misri Mandi—see trading.
2. Purchase leather.
3. Send leather to Jagat Ram.
4. Dinner at Sunil's; recover brogues from him.
5. Tmro: Jagat Ram/Ravidaspur.
6. Telegram—late return to Cawnpore.

Having made his list, he scanned it through, and realized that it would be difficult to send the leather to Jagat Ram, because no one would be able to find his place, especially at night. He toyed with the idea of getting the rickshaw-wallah to see where Jagat Ram lived and hiring him to take the leather to him later. Then he had a better idea. He walked back to the workshop and told Jagat Ram to send someone to Kedarnath Tandon's shop in the Brahmpur Shoe Mart in Misri Mandi at nine o'clock sharp that night. The leather would be waiting for him there. He had only to pick it up and to begin work at first light the next day.

4.6

It was ten o'clock, and Haresh and the other young men sitting and standing around Sunil Patwardhan's room near the university were happily intoxicated on a mixture of alcohol and high spirits.

Sunil Patwardhan was a mathematics lecturer at Brahmpur University. He had been a friend of Haresh's at St Stephen's College in Delhi; after that, what with Haresh going to England for his footwear course, they had been out of touch for years, and had heard about each other only through mutual friends. Although he was a mathematician, Sunil had had a reputation at St Stephen's for being one of the lads. He was big and quite plump, but filled as he was with sluggish energy and lazy wit and Urdu ghazals and Shakespearian quotations, many women found him attractive. He also enjoyed drinking, and had tried during his college days to get Haresh to drink—without success, because Haresh used to be a teetotaller then.

Sunil Patwardhan had believed as a student that to get one true mathematical insight a fortnight was enough by way of work; for the rest of the time he paid no attention to his studies, and did excellently. Now that he was teaching students he found it hard to impose an academic discipline on them that he himself had no faith in.

He was delighted to see Haresh again after several years. Haresh, true to form, had not informed him that he would be coming to Brahmpur on work but had landed on his doorstep two or three days earlier, had left his luggage in the drawing room, had talked for half an hour, and had then rushed off somewhere, saying something incomprehensible about the purchase of micro-sheets and leatherboard.

'Here, these are for you,' he had added in parting, depositing a cardboard shoebox on the drawing room table.

Sunil had opened it and been delighted. Haresh had said:

'I know you never wear anything except brogues.'

'But how did you remember my size?'

Haresh laughed and said, 'People's feet are like cars to me. I just remember their size—don't ask me how I do it. And your feet are like Rolls-Royces.'

Sunil remembered the time when he and a couple of friends had challenged Haresh—who was being his usual irritatingly overconfident self—to identify from a distance each of the fifty or so cars parked outside the college on the occasion of an official function. Haresh had got every one of them right. Considering his almost perfect memory for objects, it was odd that he had emerged from his English B.A. Honours course with a third, and had messed up his Poetry paper with innumerable misquotations.

God knows, thought Sunil, how he's wandered into the shoe trade, but it probably suits him. It would have been a tragedy for the world and for him if he had become an academic like me. What is amazing is that he should ever have chosen English as a subject in the first place.

'Good! Now that you're here, we'll have a party,' Sunil had said. 'It'll be like old times. I'll get a couple of old Stephanians who are in Brahmpur to join the more lively of my academic colleagues. But if you want soft drinks you'll have to bring your own.'

Haresh had promised to try to come, 'work permitting'. Sunil had threatened him with excommunication if he didn't.

Now he was here, but talking endlessly and enthusiastically about his day's efforts.

'Oh stop it, Haresh, don't tell us about chamars and micro-sheets,' said

Sunil. 'We're not interested in all that. What happened to that Sikh girl you used to chase in your headier days?'

'It wasn't a sardarni, it was the inimitable Kalpana Gaur,' said a young historian. He tilted his head to the left as wistfully as he could in exaggerated imitation of Kalpana Gaur's adoring gaze at Haresh from the other side of the room during lectures on Byron. Kalpana had been one of the few women students at St Stephen's.

'Uh—' said Sunil with dismissive authority. 'You don't know the true facts of the matter. Kalpana Gaur was chasing him, and he was chasing the sardarni. He used to serenade her outside the walls of her family's house and send her letters through go-betweens. The Sikh family couldn't bear the thought of their beloved daughter getting married to a Lala. If you want further details—'

'He's intoxicated with his own voice,' said Haresh.

'So I am,' said Sunil. 'But you—you misdirected yours. You should have wooed not the girl but the mother and the grandmother.'

'Thanks,' said Haresh.

'So do you still keep in touch with her? What was her name—'

Haresh did not oblige with any information. He was in no mood to tell these affable idiots that he was still very much in love with her after all these years—and that, together with his toe-puffs and counters, he kept a silver framed photograph of her in his suitcase.

'Take those shoes off,' he said to Sunil. 'I want them back.'

'You swine!' said Sunil. 'Just because I happened to mention the holiest of holies. . . .'

'You donkey,' replied Haresh. 'I'm not going to eat them—I'll give them back to you in a few days.'

'What are you going to do with them?'

'You'd be bored if I told you. Come on, take them off.'

'What, now?'

'Yes, why not? A few drinks later I'll have forgotten and you'll have gone off to sleep with them on.'

'Oh, all right!' said Sunil obligingly and took off his shoes.

'That's better,' said Haresh. 'It's brought you an inch closer to my height. What glorious socks,' he added, as Sunil's bright red cotton tartan socks came more fully into view.

'Wah! wah!' There were cries of approval from all sides.

'What beautiful ankles,' continued Haresh. 'Let's have a performance!'

'Light the chandeliers,' cried someone.

'Bring out the emerald goblets.'

'Sprinkle the attar of roses.'

'Lay a white sheet on the floor and charge an entrance fee!'

The young historian, in the affected tones of an official announcer, informed the audience: 'The famous courtesan Sunil Patwardhan will now perform for us her exquisite rendering of the kathak dance. Lord Krishna is dancing with the milkmaids. "Come," he says to the gopis, "come to me. What is there to fear?"'

'Tha-tha-thai-thai!' said a drunken physicist, imitating the sound of the dance steps.

'Not courtesan, you lout, artiste!'

'Artiste!' said the historian, prolonging the last vowel.

'Come on, Sunil—we're waiting.'

And Sunil, obliging fellow that he was, danced a few clumpish steps of quasi-kathak while his friends rolled around with laughter. He simpered coyly as he twirled his chubby bulk about the room, knocking a book down here and spilling someone's drink there. He then became completely engrossed in what he was doing, and followed his rendition of Krishna and the gopis—in which he played both parts—with an impromptu scene representing the Vice-Chancellor of Brahmpur University (a notorious and indiscriminate womanizer) oilily greeting the poet Sarojini Naidu when she came as the chief guest at the Annual Day ceremonies. Some of his friends, helpless with laughter, begged him to stop, and others, equally helpless, begged him to dance forever.

4.7

Into this scene walked a tall, white-haired gentleman, Dr Durrani. He was mildly surprised to see what was going on inside. Sunil froze in mid-dance, indeed in mid-stance—but then went forward to greet his unexpected guest.

Dr Durrani was not as surprised as he should have been; a mathematical problem was occupying the larger part of his cerebrum. He had decided to walk over and discuss it with his young colleague. In fact it had been Sunil who had given him the impetus for his idea in the first place.

'Er, I, have I, er, chosen a bad time—er—?' he asked in his maddeningly slow voice.

'Well, no—not, er, exactly—' said Sunil. He liked Dr Durrani and was somewhat in awe of him. Dr Durrani was one of the two Fellows of the Royal Society that Brahmpur University could boast of, the other being Professor Ramaswami, the well-known physicist.

Dr Durrani did not even notice that Sunil was imitating his manner of speech; Sunil himself was still in an imitative mode after his kathak performance, and only noticed it himself after he had done it.

'Er, well, Patwardhan, er, I do feel that, perhaps, I am, er, impinging?' continued Dr Durrani. He had a strong square face, with a handsome white moustache, but scrunched up his eyes for punctuation every time he said 'er'. This syllable also caused his eyebrows and the lower part of the skin on his forehead to move up and down.

'No, no, Dr Durrani, of course not. Please do join us.' Sunil led Dr Durrani to the centre of the room, planning to introduce him to the other guests. Dr Durrani and Sunil Patwardhan were a study in physical contrast despite the fact that they were both rather tall.

'Well, if you are, er, certain, you know, that I'm not going to, er, er, be in the way. You see,' went on Dr Durrani more fluently but just as slowly, 'what has been troubling me for the last day or so is this question of what you might call, er, super-operations. I—well, I—you see, I, um, thought that on the basis of all that, we could come up with several quite surprising series: you see, er—'

Such was the force of Dr Durrani's innocent involvement in his magical world, and so uncensorious was he about the indecorous high jinks of his juniors, that they did not seem greatly put out by the fact that he had intruded on their evening.

'Now you see, Patwardhan,'—Dr Durrani treated the whole world on terms of gentle distance—'it isn't just a question of 1, 3, 6, 10, 15—which would be a, er, trivial series based on the, er, primary combinative operation—or even 1, 2, 6, 24, 120—which would be based on the secondary combinative operation. It could go much, er, much further. The tertiary combinative operation would result in 1, 2, 9, 262144, and then 5 to the power of 262144. And of course that only, er, takes us to the fifth term in the, er, third such operation. Where will the, er, where will the steepness end?' He looked both excited and distressed.

'Ah,' said Sunil, his whisky-rich mind not quite on the problem.

'But of course what I am saying is, er, quite obvious. I didn't mean to, er, er, trouble you with that. But I did think that I, er,'—he looked around the room, his eye alighting on a cuckoo clock on the wall—'that I would, well, pick your brains on something that might be quite, er, quite unintuitive. Now take 1, 4, 216, 72576 and so on. Does that surprise you?'

'Well—' said Sunil.

'Ah!' said Dr Durrani, 'I thought not.' He looked approvingly at his younger colleague, whose brains he often picked in this manner. 'Well, well, well! Now shall I tell you what the impetus, the, er, catalyst, for all this, was?'

'Oh, please do,' said Sunil.

'It was a, er, a remark—a very, er, perceptive remark of yours.'

'Ah!'

'You said, apropos the Pergolesi Lemma, "The concept will form a tree." It was a, er, a brilliant comment—I never thought of it in those terms before.'

'Oh—' said Sunil.

Haresh winked at him, but Sunil frowned. Making deliberate fun of Dr Durrani was lese-majesty in his eyes.

'And indeed,' went on Dr Durrani generously, 'though I was, er, blind to it at the time'—he scrunched up his deep-set eyes almost into nothingness by way of unconscious illustration—'it, well, it does form a tree. An unprunable one.'

He saw in his mind's eye a huge, proliferating, and—worst of all—uncontrollable banyan tree spreading over a flat landscape, and continued, with increasing distress and excitement: 'Because whatever, er, method of super-operating is chosen—that is, type 1 or type 2—it cannot, er, it cannot definitely be applied at each, er, at each stage. To choose a particular, well, clumping of types may, may . . . er, yes, it may indeed prune the branches but it will be too, er, arbitrary. The alternative will not yield a, er, consistent algorithm. So this, er, question arose in my, er, mind: how can one generalize it as one moves to higher operations?' Dr Durrani, who tended to stoop slightly, now straightened up. Clearly, action was required in the face of these terrible uncertainties.

'What conclusion did you come to?' said Sunil, tottering a bit.

'Oh, but that is just it. I didn't. Of course, er, super-operation n+1 has to act vis-à-vis super-operation n as n acts to n–1. That goes without saying. What troubles me is, er, the question of iteration. Does the same sub-operation, the same, er, sub-super-operation, if I might call it that'—he smiled at the thought of his terminology—'does it, er—would it—'

The sentence was left unfinished as Professor Durrani looked around the room, pleasingly mystified.

'Do join us for dinner, Dr Durrani,' said Sunil. 'It's open house. And may I offer you something to drink?'

'Oh, no, no, er, no,' said Dr Durrani kindly. 'You young people go ahead. Don't mind me.'

Haresh, suddenly thinking of Bhaskar, approached Dr Durrani and said, 'Excuse me, Sir, but I wonder if I might force a very bright young man on to your attention. I think he would very much enjoy meeting you—and I hope you would enjoy meeting him.'

Dr Durrani looked inquiringly at Haresh but did not say anything. What did young people have to do with anything? he wondered. (Or people, for that matter.)

'He was talking of the powers of ten the other day,' said Haresh, 'and he regretted that neither in English nor in Hindi is there a word for ten to the power of four or ten to the power of eight.'

'Yes, er, well, it is a great pity,' said Dr Durrani with some feeling. 'Of course, in the accounts of Al-Biruni one finds. . . .'

'He seemed to feel that something should be done about it.'

'How old is this young man?' said Dr Durrani, quite interested.

'Nine.'

Dr Durrani stooped once more in order to put himself on talking terms with Haresh. 'Ah,' he said. 'Well, er, er, send him along. You know where I, er, live,' he added, and turned to go.

Since neither Haresh nor Dr Durrani had ever seen each other before, this was unlikely. But Haresh thanked him, very pleased to be able to put two like minds into contact with each other. He did not feel uncomfortable that he might be encroaching on the time and energies of the great man. In fact the thought did not even occur to him.

4.8

Pran, who dropped in a bit later, was not an old Stephanian. He had been invited by Sunil as a friend and colleague. He missed seeing Dr Durrani, with whom he had a nodding acquaintance, and missed hearing about Bhaskar. In common with almost everyone in the family, he was a little in awe of his nephew, who seemed in certain respects just like any other child—fond of flying kites, fond of playing truant from school, and affectionate most of all towards his grandmothers.

'Why have you come so late?' asked Sunil a little belligerently. 'And why is Savita not here? We were trusting her to leaven our cloddish company. Or is she walking ten paces behind you? No—I don't see her anywhere. Did she think she'd cramp our style?'

'I'll answer the two questions worth answering,' said Pran. 'One—Savita decided she was feeling too tired; she begs you to excuse her. Two—I'm late because I've had dinner before coming. I know how things run in your house. Dinner isn't served until midnight—if you remember to serve it at all—and even then it's inedible. We usually have to get kababs at some wayside stall to fill ourselves up on the way home. You should get married yourself, you know, Sunil—then your household wouldn't run so haphazardly. Besides, there would be someone to darn those atrocious socks. Anyway, why don't you have your shoes on?'

Sunil sighed. 'That's because Haresh decided he needed two pairs of shoes for himself. "My need is greater than thine." There they are in the corner, and I know I'll never see them again. Oh, but you two haven't met,' said Sunil, talking now in Hindi. 'Haresh Khanna—Pran Kapoor. Both of you have studied English literature, and I've never met anyone who knows more about it than the one, or less about it than the other.'

The two men shook hands.

'Well,' said Pran with a smile. 'Why do you need two pairs of shoes?'

'This fellow delights in creating mysteries,' said Haresh, 'but there's a simple explanation. I'm using it as a sample to have another pair made.'

'For yourself?'

'Oh, no. I work with CLFC and I'm in Brahmpur for a few days on work.'

Haresh assumed that the abbreviations he often used were entirely familiar to everyone else.

'CLFC?' asked Pran.

'Cawnpore Leather & Footwear Company.'

'Oh. So you work in the shoe trade,' said Pran. 'That's a far cry from English literature.'

'All I am living by is with the awl,' said Haresh lightly, and offered no more by way of explanation and misquotation.

'My brother-in-law works in the shoe trade as well,' said Pran. 'Perhaps you've met him. He's a trader in the Brahmpur Shoe Mart.'

'I may have,' said Haresh, 'though because of the strike not all the traders have their stalls open. What's his name?'

'Kedarnath Tandon.'

'Kedarnath Tandon! But of course I know him. He's been showing me around all sorts of places—' Haresh was very pleased. 'In fact, it's because of him in a way that Sunil has lost his shoes. So you're his sala—sorry, I mean Veena's brother. Are you the older one or the younger one?'

Sunil Patwardhan had loomed back into the conversation. 'The elder,' he said. 'The younger one—Maan—was invited too, but his evenings nowadays are otherwise occupied.'

'Well, tell me,' said Pran, turning determinedly towards Sunil, 'is there some special occasion for this party? It's not your birthday, is it?'

'No it's not. And you're not very good at changing the subject. But I'll let you wriggle out of this one because I have a question for you, Dr Kapoor. One of my best students has been suffering because of you. Why were you so harsh—you and your disciplinary committee—what do they call it? student welfare committee?—with the boys who indulged in a little high spirits over Holi?'

'A little high spirits?' exclaimed Pran. 'Those girls looked like they had been dyed in red and blue ink. It's lucky they didn't catch pneumonia. And really, there was a lot of, you know, unnecessary rubbing of colour here and there.'

'But throwing the boys out of their hostels and threatening them with expulsion?'

'Do you call that harsh?' said Pran.

'Of course. At the time that they're preparing for their final exams?'

'They certainly weren't preparing for their exams on Holi when they decided—it seems that a few of them had even taken bhang—to storm the Women's Hostel and lock up the warden in the common room.'

'Oh, that steel-hearted bitch!' said Sunil dismissively, then burst out laughing at the image of the women's warden locked up, banging perhaps on the carom board in frustration. The warden was a draconian if rather good-looking woman who kept her charges on a strict leash, wore lots of make-up, and glared at any of the girls who did the same.

'Come on, Sunil, she's quite attractive—I think you have a soft spot for her yourself.'

Sunil snorted at the ridiculous idea.

'I bet she asked for them to be expelled immediately. Or rusticated. Or electrocuted. Like those Russian spies in America the other day. The trouble is that no one remembers their own student days once they are on the other side.'

'What would you have done in her place?' asked Pran. 'Or in our place for that matter? The girls' parents would have been up in arms if we had taken no action. And, quite apart from the question of such repercussions, I don't think the punishment was unfair. A couple of members of the committee wanted them expelled.'

'Who? The Proctor?'

'Well—a couple of members,' said Pran.

'Come on, come on, don't be secretive, you're among friends—' said Sunil, putting a broad arm around Pran's gangly shoulders.

'No, really, Sunil, I've said too much already.'

'You, of course, voted for leniency.'

Pran rebutted the friendly sarcasm seriously. 'As it happens, yes, I did suggest leniency. Besides, I know how things can get out of hand. I thought of what happened when Maan decided to play Holi with Moby-Dick.' The incident with Professor Mishra was by now notorious throughout the university.

'Oh, yes,' said the physicist who had wandered over, 'what's happened to your readership?'

Pran sucked in his breath slowly. 'Nothing,' he said.

'But it's been months that the post has been lying open.'

'I know,' said Pran. 'It's even been advertised, but they don't seem to want to set a date for the selection committee to meet.'

'It's not right. I'll talk to someone at the *Brahmpur Chronicle*,' said the young physicist.

'Yes, yes,' said Sunil enthusiastically. 'It has come to our knowledge that despite the chronic understaffing in the English Department of our renowned university and the availability of a more than suitable local candidate for the post of reader which has been lying unfilled now for an unconscionable length of time—'

'Please—' said Pran, not at all calmly. 'Just let things take their natural course. Don't get the papers involved in all this.'

Sunil looked meditative for a while, as if he was working something out. 'All right, all right, have a drink!' he said suddenly. 'Why don't you have a drink in your hand?'

'First he grills me for half an hour without offering me a drink, then he asks me why I don't have one. I'll have whisky—with water,' said Pran, in a less agitated tone.

As the evening went on, the talk of the party turned to news in the town, to India's consistently poor performance in international cricket ('I doubt we will ever win a Test match,' said Pran with confident pessimism), to politics in Purva Pradesh and the world at large, and to the peculiarities of various teachers, both at Brahmpur University and—for the Stephanians—at St Stephen's in Delhi. To the mystification of the non-Stephanians, they participated in chorus with a querulous: 'In my class I will say one thing: you may not understand, you may not want to understand, but you will understand!'

Dinner was served, and it was just as rudimentary as Pran had predicted. Sunil, for all his good-natured bullying of his friends, was himself bullied by an old servant whose affection for his master (whom he had served since Sunil was a child) was only equalled by his unwillingness to do any work.

Over dinner there was a discussion—somewhat incoherent because some of the participants were either belligerent or erratic with whisky—about the economy and the political situation. Making complete sense of it was difficult, but a part of it went like this:

'Look, the only reason why Nehru became PM was because he was Gandhi's favourite. Everyone knows that. All he knows how to do is to make those bloody long speeches that never go anywhere. He never seems to take a stand on anything. Just think. Even in the Congress Party, where Tandon and his cronies are pushing him to the wall, what does he do? He just goes along with it, and we have to—'

'But what can he do? He's not a dictator.'

'Do you mind not interrupting? I mean to say, may I make my point? After that you can say whatever you want for as long as you want. So what does Nehru do? I mean to say, what does he do? He sends a message to some society that he's been asked to address and he says, "We often feel a sense of darkness." Darkness—who cares about his darkness or what's going on inside his head? He may have a handsome head and that red rose may look pretty in his buttonhole, but what we need is someone with a stout heart, not a sensitive one. It's his duty as Prime Minister to give a lead to the country, and he's just not got the strength of character to do it.'

'Well—'

'Well, what?'

'You just try to run a country. Try to feed the people, for a start. Keep the Hindus from slaughtering the Muslims—'

'Or vice versa.'

'All right, or vice versa. And try to abolish the zamindars' estates when they fight you every inch of the way.'

'He isn't doing that as PM—land revenue isn't a Central subject—it's a state subject. Nehru will make his vague speeches, but you ask Pran who's the real brains behind our Zamindari Abolition Bill.'

'Yes,' admitted Pran, 'it's my father. At any rate, my mother says he works terribly late and sometimes comes back home from the Secretariat after midnight, dog-tired, then reads through the night to prepare for the next day's arguments in the Assembly.' He laughed shortly and shook his head. 'My mother's worried because he's ruining his health. Two hundred clauses, two hundred ulcers, she thinks. And now that the Zamindari Act in Bihar has been declared unconstitutional, everyone's in a panic. As if there's not enough to panic about anyway, what with the trouble in Chowk.'

'What trouble in Chowk?' asked someone, thinking Pran was referring to something that might have happened that day.

'The Raja of Marh and his damned Shiva Temple,' said Haresh promptly. Though he was the only one from out of town, he had just been filled in on the facts by Kedarnath, and had made them his own.

'Don't call it a damned Shiva Temple,' said the historian.

'It is a damned Shiva Temple, it's caused enough deaths already.'

'You're a Hindu, and you call it a damned temple—you should look at yourself in the mirror. The British have left, in case you need reminding, so don't put on their airs. Damned temple, damned natives—'

'Oh God! I'll have another drink after all,' said Haresh to Sunil.

As the discussion rose and subsided over dinner and afterwards, and people formed themselves into small knots or tied themselves into worse ones, Pran drew Sunil aside and inquired casually, 'Is that fellow Haresh married or engaged or anything?'

'Anything.'

'What?' said Pran, frowning.

'He's not married or engaged,' said Sunil, 'but he's certainly "anything".'

'Sunil, don't talk in riddles. It's midnight.'

'This is what comes of turning up late for my party. Before you came we were talking at length about him and that sardarni, Simran Kaur, whom he's still infatuated with. Now why didn't I remember her name an hour ago? There was a couplet about him at college:

Chased by Gaur and chasing Kaur;
Chaste before but chaste no more!

I can't vouch for the facts of the second line. But, anyway, it was clear from his face today that he's still in love with her. And I can't blame him. I met her once and she was a real beauty.'

Sunil Patwardhan recited a couplet in Urdu about the black monsoon clouds of her hair.

'Well, well, well,' said Pran.

'But why do you want to know?'

'Nothing,' shrugged Pran. 'I think he's a man who knows his own mind, and I was curious.'

A little later the guests started taking their leave. Sunil suggested that they all visit Old Brahmpur 'to see if anything's going on'.

'Tonight at the midnight hour,' he intoned in a sing-song, Nehruvian voice, 'while the world sleeps, Brahmpur will awake to life and freedom.'

As Sunil saw his guests to the door he suddenly became depressed. 'Good night,' he said gently; then in a more melancholy tone: 'Good night, ladies, good night, sweet ladies, good night, good night.' And a little later, as he closed the door, more to himself than anyone else, he mumbled, in the liltingly incomplete cadence with which Nehru ended his Hindi speeches: 'Brothers and sisters—Jai Hind!'

But Pran walked home in high spirits. He had enjoyed the party, had enjoyed getting away both from work and—he had to admit it—the family circle of wife, mother-in-law, and sister-in-law.

What a pity, he thought, that Haresh was already spoken for. Despite his misquotations, Pran had liked him, and wondered if he might be a possible 'prospect' for Lata. Pran was concerned about her. Ever since she had received a phone call at dinner a few days ago, she had not been herself. But it had become difficult to talk even to Savita about her sister. Sometimes, thought Pran, I feel they all see me as an interloper—a mere meddler among Mehras.

4.9

Haresh, with an effort, woke up early despite a heavy head, and took a rickshaw to Ravidaspur. He had with him the lasts, the other materials he had promised, and Sunil's shoes. People in rags were moving about the lanes among the thatched mud huts. A boy was dragging a piece of wood with a string and another boy was trying to hit it with a stick. As he walked across the unstable bridge, he noticed that a thick, whitish vapour lay over the black water of the open sewer, where people were performing their morning ablutions. How can they live like this? he thought to himself.

A couple of electric wires hung casually from poles or were tangled among the branches of a dusty tree. A few houses tapped illegally into this meagre source by slinging a wire over the main line. From the dark interiors of the other huts came the flicker of makeshift lamps: tins filled with kerosene, whose smoke filled the huts. It was easy for a child or a dog or a calf to knock these over, and fires sometimes started this way, spreading from hut to hut and burning everything hidden in the thatch for safe-keeping, including the precious ration-cards. Haresh shook his head at the waste of it all.

He got to the workshop and found Jagat Ram sitting on the step by himself, watched only by his small daughter. But to Haresh's annoyance he found that what he was working on was not the brogues but a wooden toy: a cat, it appeared. He was whittling away at it with great concentration, and looked surprised to see Haresh. He set the unfinished cat down on the step and stood up.

'You've come early,' he said.

'I have,' said Haresh brusquely. 'And I find you are working on something else. I am making every effort on my part to supply you with materials as quickly as possible, but I have no intention of working with someone who is unreliable.'

Jagat Ram touched his moustache. His eyes took on a dull glow, and his speech became staccato:

'What I mean to say—' he began, '—have you even asked? What I mean to say is—do you think I am not a man of my word?'

He stood up, went inside, and fetched the pieces he had cut according to the patterns Haresh had given him from the handsome maroon leather that he had fetched the previous night. While Haresh was examining them, he said:

'I haven't punched them with the brogue design yet—but I thought I'd do the cutting myself, not leave it to my cutter. I've been up since dawn.'

'Good, good,' said Haresh, nodding his head and in a kinder tone. 'Let's see the piece of leather I left for you.'

Jagat Ram rather reluctantly took it out from one of the brick shelves embedded in the wall of the small room. Quite a lot of it was still unused. Haresh examined it carefully, and handed it back. Jagat Ram looked relieved. He moved his hand to his greying moustache and rubbed it meditatively, saying nothing.

'Excellent,' said Haresh with generous enthusiasm. Jagat Ram's cutting had been both surprisingly swift and extremely economical of the leather. In fact, he appeared to have an intuitive spatial mastery that was very rare even among trained shoemakers of many years' standing. It had been hinted at yesterday in his comments when he had constructed the shoe in his mind's eye after just a brief glance at the components of the pattern.

'Where's your daughter disappeared to?'

Jagat Ram permitted himself a slight smile. 'She was late for school,' he said.

'Did the people from the Lovely Shoe Shop turn up yesterday?' asked Haresh.

'Well, yes and no,' said Jagat Ram and did not elaborate further.

Since Haresh had no direct interest in the Lovely people, he did not press the question. He thought that perhaps Jagat Ram did not want to talk about one of Kedarnath's competitors in front of Kedarnath's friend.

'Well,' said Haresh. 'Here is all the other stuff you need.' He opened his briefcase and took out the thread and the components, the lasts and the shoes. As Jagat Ram turned the lasts around appreciatively in his hands, Haresh continued: 'I will see you three days from today at two o'clock in the afternoon, and I will expect the brogues to be ready by then. I have bought my ticket for the six-thirty train back to Kanpur that evening. If the shoes are well made, I expect I will be able to get you an order. If they are not, I'm not going to delay my journey back.'

'I will hope to work directly with you if things work out,' said Jagat Ram.

Haresh shook his head. 'I met you through Kedarnath and I'll deal with you through Kedarnath,' he replied.

Jagat Ram nodded a little grimly, and saw Haresh to the door. There seemed to be no getting away from these bloodsucking middlemen. First the Muslims, now these Punjabis who had taken their place. Kedarnath, however, had given him his first break, and was not such a bad man—as such things went. Perhaps he was merely blood-sipping.

'Good,' said Haresh. 'Excellent. Well, I have a lot of things to do. I must be off.'

And he walked off with his usual high energy through the dirty paths of Ravidaspur. Today he was wearing ordinary black Oxfords. In an open but filthy space near a little white shrine he saw a group of small boys gambling with a tattered pack of cards—one of them was Jagat Ram's youngest son—and he clicked his tongue, not so much from moral disapproval as from a feeling of annoyance that this should be the state of things. Illiteracy, poverty, indiscipline, dirt! It wasn't as if people here didn't have potential. If he had his way and was given funds and labour, he would have this neighbourhood on its feet in six months. Sanitation, drinking water, electricity, paving, civic sense—it was simply a question of making sensible decisions and having the requisite facilities to implement them. Haresh was as keen on 'requisite facilities' as he was on his 'To Do' list. He was impatient with himself if anything was lacking in the former or undone in the latter. He also believed in 'following things through'.

Oh yes; Kedarnath's son, what's his name now, Bhaskar! he said to himself. I should have got Dr Durrani's address from Sunil last night. He frowned at his own lack of foresight.

But after lunch he collected Bhaskar anyway and took a tonga to Sunil's. Dr Durrani looked as if he had walked to Sunil's house, reflected Haresh, so he couldn't live all that far away.

Bhaskar accompanied Haresh in silence, and Haresh, for his own part, was happy not to say anything other than where they were going.

Sunil's faithful, lazy servant pointed out Dr Durrani's house, which was a few doors away. Haresh paid off the tonga, and walked over with Bhaskar.

4.10

A tall, good-looking fellow in cricket whites opened the door.

'We've come to see Dr Durrani,' said Haresh. 'Do you think he might be free?'

'I'll just see what my father is doing,' said the young man in a low, pleasant, slightly rough-edged voice. 'Please come in.'

A minute or two later he emerged and said, 'My father will be out in a minute. He asked me who you were, and I realized I hadn't asked. I'm sorry, I should introduce myself first. My name's Kabir.'

Haresh, impressed by the young man's looks and manner, held out his hand, smiled in a clipped sort of way, and introduced himself. 'And this is

Bhaskar, a friend's son.'

The young man seemed a bit troubled about something, but did his best to make conversation.

'Hello, Bhaskar,' said Kabir. 'How old are you?'

'Nine,' said Bhaskar, not objecting to this least original of questions. He was pondering what all this was about.

After a while Kabir said, 'I wonder what's keeping my father,' and went back in.

When Dr Durrani finally came into the drawing room, he was quite surprised to see his visitors. Noticing Bhaskar, he asked Haresh:

'Have you come to see one of my, er, sons?'

Bhaskar's eyes lit up at this unusual adult behaviour. He liked Dr Durrani's strong, square face, and in particular the balance and symmetry of his magnificent white moustache. Haresh, who had stood up, said:

'No indeed, Dr Durrani, it's you we've come to see. I don't know if you remember me—we met at Sunil's party. . . .'

'Sunil?' said Dr Durrani, his eyes scrunched up in utter perplexity, his eyebrows working up and down. 'Sunil . . . Sunil . . .' He seemed to be weighing something up with great seriousness, and coming closer and closer to a conclusion. 'Patwardhan,' he said, with the air of having arrived at a considerable insight. He appraised this new premise from several angles in silence.

Haresh decided to speed up the process. He said, rather briskly:

'Dr Durrani, you said that we could drop in to see you. This is my young friend Bhaskar, whom I told you about. I think his interest in mathematics is remarkable, and I felt he should meet you.'

Dr Durrani looked quite pleased, and asked Bhaskar what two plus two was.

Haresh was taken aback, but Bhaskar—though he normally rejected considerably more complex sums as unworthy of his attention—was not, apparently, insulted. In a very tentative voice he replied:

'Four?'

Dr Durrani was silent. He appeared to be mulling over this answer. Haresh began to feel ill at ease.

'Well, yes, you can, er, leave him here for a while,' said Dr Durrani.

'Shall I come back to pick him up at four o'clock?' asked Haresh.

'More or less,' said Dr Durrani.

When he and Bhaskar were left alone, both of them were silent. After a while, Bhaskar said:

'Was that the right answer?'

'More or less,' said Dr Durrani. 'You see,' he said, picking up a musammi from a bowl on the dining table, 'it's rather, er, it's rather like the question of the, er, sum of the angles in a—in a triangle. What have they, er, taught you that is?'

'180 degrees,' said Bhaskar.

'Well, more or less,' said Dr Durrani. 'On the, er, surface of it, at least. But on the surface of this, er, musammi, for instance—'

For a while he gazed at the green citrus, following a mysterious train of thought. Once it had served his purpose, he looked at it wonderingly, as if he could not figure out what it was doing in his hand. He peeled it with some difficulty because of its thick skin and began to eat it.

'Would you, er, like some?' he asked Bhaskar matter-of-factly.

'Yes, please,' said Bhaskar, and held out both hands for a segment, as if he were receiving a sanctified offering from a temple.

An hour later, when Haresh returned, he got the sense that he was an unwelcome interruption. They were now both sitting at the dining table, on which were lying—among other things—several musammis, several peels of musammis, a large number of toothpicks in various configurations, an inverted ashtray, some strips of newspaper stuck together in odd-looking twisted loops, and a purple kite. The remaining surface of the dining room table was covered with equations in yellow chalk.

Before Bhaskar left with Haresh, he took with him the loops of newspaper, the purple kite, and exactly sixteen toothpicks. Neither Dr Durrani nor Bhaskar thanked each other for the time they had spent together. In the tonga back to Misri Mandi, Haresh could not resist asking Bhaskar:

'Did you understand all those equations?'

'No,' said Bhaskar. It was clear from the tone of his answer, however, that he did not think this mattered.

Though Bhaskar did not say anything when he got home, his mother could tell from one glance at his face that he had had a wonderfully stimulating time. She took his various objects off him and told him to wash his gummy hands. Then, almost with tears in her eyes, she thanked Haresh.

'It's so kind of you to have taken this trouble, Haresh Bhai. I can tell what this has meant to him,' Veena said.

'Well,' said Haresh with a smile, 'that's more than I can.'

4.11

Meanwhile, the brogues were sitting on their lasts in Jagat Ram's workshop. Two days passed. On the appointed day at two o'clock, Haresh came to collect the shoes and the lasts. Jagat Ram's little daughter recognized him, and clapped her hands at his arrival. She was entertaining herself with a song, and since he was there, she entertained him too. The song went as follows:

Ram Ram Shah,	Ram Ram Shah,
Alu ka rasa,	Gravy made from spuds,
Mendaki ki chatni—	Chutney made from female frog—
Aa gaya nasha!	Drink it, and you're drunk!

Haresh looked the shoes over with a practised eye. They were well made. The uppers had been stitched excellently, though on the simple sewing machine in front of him. The lasting had been carefully done—there were no bubbles or wrinkles. The finishing was fine, down to the coloration of the leather of the punched brogue. He was well pleased. He had been strict in his demands, but now he gave Jagat Ram one and a half times as much as he had promised him by way of payment.

'You will be hearing from me,' he promised.

'Well, Haresh Sahib, I certainly hope so,' said Jagat Ram. 'You're really leaving today? A pity.'

'Yes, I'm afraid so.'

'And you stayed on just for this?'

'Yes, I would have left in two days instead of four otherwise.'

'Well, I hope they like this pair at CLFC.'

With that they parted. Haresh did a few chores, made a few small purchases, went back to Sunil's, returned his brogues, packed, said goodbye, and took a tonga to the station to catch the evening train to Kanpur. On the way he stopped at Kedarnath's to thank him.

'I hope I can be of some help to you,' said Haresh, shaking his hand warmly.

'You already have, Veena tells me.'

'I meant, by way of business.'

'I certainly hope so,' said Kedarnath, 'and, well, if I can help you in any way—'

They shook hands.

'Tell me—' said Haresh suddenly. 'I have been meaning to ask you this for several days now—how did you get all those scars on the inside of your hands? They don't look as if they've been caught in a machine—they'd be scarred on both sides if they had.'

Kedarnath was silent for a few seconds, as if adjusting to a change of thought. 'I got those during Partition,' he said. He paused and continued, 'At the time that we were forced to flee from Lahore, I got a place in a convoy of army trucks and we got into the first truck—my younger brother and I. Nothing, I thought, could be safer. But, well, it was a Baluchi regiment. They stopped just before the Ravi Bridge, and Muslim ruffians came from behind the timber yards there and started butchering us with their spears. My younger brother has marks on his back and I have these on my palms and my wrist—I tried to hold on to the blade of the spear. . . . I was in hospital for a month.'

Haresh's face betrayed his shock. Kedarnath continued, closing his eyes, but in a calm voice:

'Twenty or thirty people were slaughtered in two minutes—someone's father, someone's daughter. . . . By the greatest of luck a Gurkha regiment was coming from the other side and they began to fire. And, well, the looters fled, and I'm here to tell you the story.'

'Where was the family?' asked Haresh. 'In the other trucks?'

'No—I'd sent them on by train a little earlier. Bhaskar was only six at the time. Not that the trains were safe either, as you know.'

'I don't know if I should have asked these questions,' said Haresh, feeling atypically embarrassed.

'No, no—that's all right. We were fortunate, as these things go. The Muslim trader who used to own my shop here in Brahmpur—well. . . . Strange, though—after all that happened there, I still miss Lahore,' said Kedarnath. 'But you'd better hurry or you'll miss your train.'

Brahmpur Junction was as crowded and noisy and smelly as ever: hissing clouds of steam, the whistles of incoming trains, hawkers' shouts, the stench of fish, the buzz of flies, the scurrying babble of passengers. Haresh felt tired. Though it was past six o'clock it was still very warm. He touched an agate cufflink and wondered at its coolness.

Glancing at the crowd, he noticed a young woman in a light-blue cotton sari standing near her mother. The English teacher whom he had met at Sunil's party was seeing them off on the down train to Calcutta. The mother's back was turned towards Haresh, so he could not get a proper glimpse of her. The daughter's face was striking. It was not classically beautiful—it did not catch at his heart as did the photograph he kept with him—but it had a quality of such attractive intensity that Haresh stopped for a second. The young woman seemed to be determinedly fighting back some sadness that went beyond the normal sadness of parting at a railway platform. Haresh thought of pausing for a little to reintroduce himself to the young lecturer, but something in the girl's expression of inwardness, almost despair, stopped him from doing so. Besides, his train was leaving soon, his coolie was already quite far ahead of him, and Haresh, not being tall, was concerned that he might lose him in the crowd.

Part Five

5.1

Some riots are caused, some bring themselves into being. The problems at Misri Mandi were not expected to reach a point of violence. A few days after Haresh left, however, the heart of Misri Mandi—including the area around Kedarnath's shop, was full of armed police.

The previous evening there had been a fight inside a cheap drinking place along the unpaved road that led towards the tannery from Old Brahmpur. The strike meant less money but more time for everyone, so the kalari's joint was about as crowded as usual. The place was mainly frequented by jatavs, but not exclusively so. Drink equalized the drinkers, and they didn't care who was sitting at the plain wooden table next to them. They drank, laughed, cried, then tottered and staggered out, sometimes singing, sometimes cursing. They swore undying friendship, they divulged confidences, they imagined insults. The assistant of a trader in Misri Mandi was in a foul mood because he was having a hard time with his father-in-law. He was drinking alone and working himself into a generalized state of aggressiveness. He overheard a comment from behind him about the sharp practice of his employer, and his hands clenched into a fist. Knocking his bench over as he twisted around to see who was speaking, he fell on to the floor.

The three men at the table behind him laughed. They were jatavs who had dealt with him before. It was he who used to take the shoes from their baskets when they scurried desperately in the evening to Misri Mandi—his employer the trader did not like to touch shoes because he felt they would pollute him. The jatavs knew that the breakdown of the trade in Misri Mandi had particularly hurt those traders who had over-extended themselves on the chit system. That it had hurt themselves still more, they also knew—but for them it was not a case of the mighty being brought to their knees. Here, however, literally in front of them, it was.

The locally distilled cheap alcohol had gone to their heads, and they did not have the money to buy the pakoras and other snacks that could have settled it. They laughed uncontrollably.

'He's wrestling with the air,' jeered one.

'I bet he'd rather be doing another kind of wrestling,' sneered another.

'But would he be any good at it? They say that's why he has trouble at home—'

'What a reject,' taunted the first man, waving him away with the airy gesture of a trader rejecting a basket on the basis of a single faulty pair.

Their speech was slurred, their eyes contemptuous. The man who had fallen lunged at them, and they set upon him. A couple of people, including the kalari, tried to make peace, but most gathered around to enjoy the fun and shout drunken encouragement. The four rolled around on the floor, fighting.

It ended with the man who had started the fight being beaten unconscious, and all of the others being injured. One was bleeding from the eye and screaming in pain.

That night, when he lost the sight of his eye, an ominous crowd of jatavs gathered at the Govind Shoe Mart, where the trader had his stall. They found the stall closed. The crowd began to shout slogans, then threatened to burn the stall down. One of the other traders tried to reason with the crowd, and they set upon him. A couple of policemen, sensing the crowd's mood, ran to the local police station for reinforcements. Ten policemen now emerged, armed with short stout bamboo lathis, and they began to beat people up indiscriminately. The crowd scattered.

Surprisingly soon, every relevant authority knew about the matter: from the Superintendent of Police of the district to the Inspector-General of Purva Pradesh, from the Home Secretary to the Home Minister. Everyone received different facts and interpretations, and had different suggestions for action or inaction.

The Chief Minister was out of town. In his absence—and because law and order lay in his domain—the Home Minister ran things. Mahesh Kapoor, though Revenue Minister, and not therefore directly concerned, heard about the unrest because part of Misri Mandi lay in his constituency. He hurried to the spot and talked with the Superintendent of Police and the District Magistrate. The SP and the DM believed that things would blow over if neither side was provoked. However, the Home Minister, L.N. Agarwal, part of whose constituency also lay in Misri Mandi, did not think it necessary to go to the spot. He received a number of phone calls at home and decided that something by way of a salutary example needed to be provided.

These jatavs had disrupted the trade of the city long enough with their frivolous complaints and their mischievous strike. They had doubtless been stirred up by union leaders. Now they were threatening to block the entrance of the Govind Shoe Mart at the point where it joined the main road of Misri Mandi. Many traders there were already in financial straits. The threatened picketing would finish them off. L.N. Agarwal himself came from a shopkeeping family and some of the traders were good friends of his. Others supplied him with election funds. He had received three desperate calls from them. It was a time not for talk but for action. It was not merely a question of law, but of order, the order of society itself. Surely this is what the Iron Man of India, the late Sardar Patel, would have felt in his place.

But what would he have done had he been here? As if in a dream, the Home Minister conjured up the domed and severe head of his political mentor, dead these four months. He sat in thought for a while. Then he told his personal assistant to get him the District Magistrate on the phone.

The District Magistrate, who was in his mid-thirties, was directly in charge of the civil administration of Brahmpur District and, together with the SP—as the Superintendent of Police was referred to by everyone—maintained law and order.

The PA tried to get through, then said: 'Sorry, Sir, DM is out on the site. He is trying to conciliate—'

'Give me the phone,' said the Home Minister in a calm voice. The PA nervously handed him the receiver.

'Who? . . . Where? . . . I am Agarwal speaking, that's who . . . yes, direct instructions . . . I don't care. Get Dayal at once. . . . Yes, ten minutes . . . call me back. . . . The SP is there, that is enough surely, is it a cinema show?'

He put down the phone and grasped the grey curls that curved like a horseshoe around his otherwise bald head.

After a while he made as if to pick up the receiver again, then decided against it, and turned his attention to a file.

Ten minutes later the young District Magistrate, Krishan Dayal, was on the phone. The Home Minister told him to guard the entrance of the Govind Shoe Mart. He was to disperse any pickets forthwith, if necessary by reading out Section 144 of the Criminal Procedure Code—and then firing if the crowd did not disperse.

The line was unclear but the message disturbingly clear. Krishan Dayal said in a strong voice, but one which was fraught with concern: 'Sir, with respect, may I suggest an alternative course of action? We are talking with the leaders of the crowd—'

'So there are leaders, are there, it is not spontaneous?'

'Sir, it is spontaneous, but there are leaders.'

L.N. Agarwal reflected that it was puppies of the ilk of Krishan Dayal who used to lock him up in British jails. He said, calmly:

'Are you being witty, Mr Dayal?'

'No, Sir, I—'

'You have your instructions. This is an emergency. I have discussed things with the Chief Secretary by phone. I understand that the crowd is some three hundred strong. I want the SP to get the police stationed everywhere along the main road of Misri Mandi and to guard all entrances—Govind Shoe Mart, Brahmpur Shoe Mart and so on—you just do the needful.'

There was a pause. The Home Minister was about to put down the phone when the DM said:

'Sir, we may not be able to spare such a large number of police at short notice. A number of policemen are stationed at the site of the Shiva Temple in case of trouble. Things are very tense, Sir. The Revenue Minister thinks that on Friday—'

'Are they there at the moment? I did not notice them this morning,' said L.N. Agarwal in a relaxed but steely tone.

'No, Sir, but they are in the main police station in the Chowk area, so it is sufficiently close to the temple site. It is best to keep them there for a true emergency.' Krishan Dayal had been in the army during the war, but he was rattled by the Home Minister's calm air of almost dismissive interrogation and command.

'God will take care of the Shiva Temple. I am in close touch with many members of the committee, do you think I do not know the circumstances?' He had been irked by Dayal's reference to 'a true emergency' as much as by his mention of Mahesh Kapoor, his rival and—as abrasive chance would have it—the MLA from the constituency contiguous to his own.

'Yes, Sir,' said Krishan Dayal, his face reddening—which luckily the Home Minister could not see. 'And may I know how long the police are to remain there?'

'Until further notice,' said the Home Minister and put down the phone to pre-empt further backchat. He did not like the way these so-called civil servants answered back to those above them in the chain of command—who were besides, twenty years older than them. It was necessary to have an administrative service, no doubt, but it was equally necessary that it should learn that it no longer ruled this country.

5.2

On Friday at the midday prayer the hereditary Imam of the Alamgiri Mosque gave his sermon. He was a short, plump man with short breath, but this did not stem his jerky crescendos of oratory. If anything, his breathlessness gave the impression that he was choked with emotion. The construction of the Shiva Temple was going ahead. The Imam's appeals to everyone from the Governor down had fallen on deaf ears. A legal case contesting the Raja of Marh's title to the land contiguous to the mosque had been instituted and was at present going through the lowest court. A stay order on the construction of the temple, however, could not be immediately obtained—indeed, perhaps could not be obtained at all. Meanwhile the dung-heap was growing before the Imam's agonized eyes.

His congregation was tense already. It was with dismay that many Muslims in Brahmpur had, over the months, seen the foundations of the temple rising in the plot to the west of their mosque. Now, after the first part of the prayers, the Imam gave his audience the most stirring and inflammatory speech he had given in years, very far removed from his ordinary sermon on personal morality or cleanliness or alms or piety. His grief and frustration as much as their own bitter anxiety called for something stronger. Their religion was in danger. The barbarians were at the gates. They prayed, these infidels, to their pictures and stones and perpetuated themselves in ignorance and sin. Let them do what they wanted to in their dens of filth. But God could see what was happening now. They had brought their beastliness near the very precincts of the mosque itself. The land that the kafirs sought to build on—why sought? were at this very moment building on—was disputed land—disputed in God's eyes and in man's eyes—but not in the eyes of animals who spent their time blowing conches and worshipping parts of the body whose very names it was shameful to mention. Did the people of the faith gathered here in God's presence know how it was planned to consecrate this Shiva-linga? Naked ash-smeared savages would dance before it—naked! These were the shameless, like the people of Sodom, who mocked at the power of the All-Merciful.

> . . . God guides not the people
> of the unbelievers.
> Those—God has set a seal on their
> hearts, and their hearing, and their eyes,
> and those—they are the heedless ones;
> Without a doubt, in the world to come they
> will be the losers.

They worshipped their hundreds of idols that they claimed were divine—idols with four heads and five heads and the heads of elephants—and now the infidels who held power in the land wanted Muslims, when they turned their faces westwards in prayer to the Kaaba, to face these same idols and these same obscene objects with their heads bowed. 'But,' continued the Imam, 'we who have lived through hard and bitter times and have suffered for our faith and paid for our faith in blood need only remember the fate of the idolaters:

> And they set up compeers to God, that
> they might lead astray from His way.
> Say: "Take your joy! Your homecoming
> shall be—the Fire!"'

A slow, attentive, shocked expectation filled the silence that followed.

'But even now,' cried the Imam in renewed frenzy, half-gasping for air, 'even as I speak—they could be hatching their designs to prevent our evening devotion by blowing their conches to drown out the call to prayer. Ignorant they may be, but they are full of guile. They are already getting rid of Muslims in the police force so that the community of God will be left defenceless. Then they can attack and enslave us. Now it is too clear to us that we are living not in a land of protection but a land of enmity. We have appealed for justice, and have been kicked down at the very doors where we have gone pleading. The Home Minister himself supports this temple committee—and its guiding spirit is the debauched buffalo of Marh! Let it not happen that our holy places are to be polluted by the proximity of filth—let it not happen—but what can save us now that we are left defenceless before the sword of our enemies in the land of the Hindus, what can save us but our own efforts, our own'—here he struggled for breath and emphasis again—'our own direct action—to protect ourselves. And not just ourselves, not just our families but these few feet of paved earth that have been given to us for centuries, where we have unrolled our mats and raised our hands in tears to the All-Powerful, which are worn smooth by the devotions of our ancestors and ourselves and—if God so wills—will so be by our descendants also. But have no fear, God does so will, have no fear, God will be with you:

> Hast thou not seen how thy Lord did with Ad,
> Iram of the pillars,
> the like of which was never created in the land,
> and Thamood, who hollowed the rocks in the valley,
> and Pharaoh, he of the tent-pegs,
> who all were insolent in the land
> and worked much corruption therein?
> Thy Lord unloosed on them a scourge of chastisement;
> surely thy Lord is ever on the watch.

O God, help those who help the religion of the Prophet Muhammad, peace be upon Him. May we also do the same. Make those weak, who weaken the religion of Muhammad. Praise be to God, the Lord of all Being.'

The plump Imam descended from the pulpit, and led the people in more prayer.

That evening there was a riot.

5.3

Because of the instructions of the Home Minister, the greater part of the police was stationed at sensitive points in Misri Mandi. There were only about fifteen policemen left in the main police station in Chowk by evening. As the call for prayer from the Alamgiri Mosque trembled across the evening sky, by some unfortunate chance or possibly intentional provocation, the sound of a conch was heard interrupting it several times. Normally such a thing might have been angrily shrugged off, but not today.

No one knew how the men who were gathering in the narrow alleys of the Muslim neighbourhood that lay on one side of Chowk became a mob. One moment they were walking individually or in small groups through the alleys towards the mosque for evening prayer, then they had coalesced into larger clusters, excitedly discussing the ominous signals they had heard. After the midday sermon most were in no mood to listen to any voice of moderation. A couple of the more eager members of the Alamgiri Masjid Hifaazat Committee made a few crowd-rousing remarks, a few local hotheads and toughs stirred themselves and those around them into a state of rage, the crowd increased in size as the alleys joined into larger alleys, its density and speed and sense of indistinct determination increased, and it was no longer a collection but a thing—wounded and enraged, and wanting nothing less than to wound and enrage. There were cries of 'Allah-u-Akbar' which could be heard all the way to the police station. A few of those who joined the crowd had sticks in their hands. One or two even had knives. Now it was not the mosque that they were headed for but the partly constructed temple just next to it. It was from here that the blasphemy had originated, it was this that must be destroyed.

Since the Superintendent of Police of the district was occupied in Misri Mandi, the young District Magistrate, Krishan Dayal, had himself gone to the tall pink edifice of the main police station about an hour earlier to ensure that things would remain stable in the Chowk area. He feared the increased tension that Friday often brought. When he heard about the Imam's sermon, he asked the kotwal—as the Deputy Superintendent of Police for the City was called—what he planned to do to protect the area.

The kotwal of Brahmpur, however, was a lazy man who wanted nothing better than to be left alone to take his bribes in peace.

'There will be no trouble, Sir, believe me,' he assured the District Magistrate. 'Agarwal Sahib himself has phoned me. Now he tells me I am to go to Misri Mandi to join the SP—so I must be off, Sir, with your leave, of course.' And he bustled off in a preoccupied sort of way, taking two other lower officers with him, and leaving the kotwali virtually in the charge of a head constable. 'I will just be sending the Inspector back,' he said in a reassuring manner. 'You should not stay, Sir,' he added ingratiatingly. 'It is late. This is a peaceful time. After the previous troubles at the mosque we have defused the situation, I am glad to say.'

Krishan Dayal, left with a force of about twelve constables, thought he would wait until the Inspector returned before he decided whether to go home. His wife was used to him coming back at odd hours, and would wait for him; it was not necessary to phone her. He did not actually expect a riot; he merely felt that tension was running high and that it was not worth taking a chance. He believed that the Home Minister had his priorities wrong where Chowk and Misri Mandi were concerned; but then the Home Minister was arguably the most powerful man in the state next to the Chief Minister, and he himself was just a DM.

He was sitting and waiting in this unworried but uneasy frame of mind when he heard what was to be recalled by several policemen at the subsequent inquiry—the inquiry by a senior officer that is required to be held after every magisterial order to fire. First he heard the coinciding sounds of the conch and the muezzin's call to prayer. This worried him mildly, but the reports he had had of the Imam's speech had not included his prescient reference to a conch. Then, after a while, came the distant murmur of shouting voices interspersed by high cries. Even before he could make out the individual syllables, he could tell what was being shouted by the direction from which it came and the general shape and fervour of the sound. He sent a policeman to the top of the police station—it was three storeys high—to judge where the mob now was. The mob itself would be invisible—hidden as it was by the intervening houses of the labyrinthine alleys—but the direction of the heads of the spectators from the rooftops would give its position away. As the cries of 'Allah-u-Akbar! Allah-u-Akbar!' came closer, the DM urgently told the small force of twelve constables to stand with him in a line—rifles at the ready—before the foundations and rudimentary walls of the site of the Shiva Temple. The thought flashed through his mind that despite his training in the army he had not learned to think tactically in a terrain of urban lawlessness. Was there nothing better he could do than to perform this mad sacrificial duty of standing against a wall and facing overwhelming odds?

The constables under his effective command were Muslims and Rajputs, mainly Muslims. The police force before Partition was very largely composed of Muslims as the result of the sound imperialist policy of divide and rule: it helped the British that the predominantly Hindu Congress-wallahs should be beaten up by predominantly Muslim policemen. Even after the exodus to Pakistan in 1947 there were large numbers of Muslims in the force. They would not be happy to fire upon other Muslims.

Krishan Dayal believed in general that although it was not always necessary to give effect to maximum force, it was necessary to give the impression that you were prepared to do so. In a strong voice he told the policemen that they were to fire when he gave the order. He himself stood there, pistol in hand. But he felt more vulnerable than ever before in his life. He told himself that a good officer, together with a force on which he could absolutely rely, could almost always carry the day, but he had reservations about the 'absolutely'; and the 'almost' worried him. Once the mob, still a few alleys away, came round the final bend, broke into a charge, and made straight for the temple, the patently, pathetically ineffective police force would be overwhelmed. A couple of men had just come running to tell him that there were perhaps a thousand men in the mob, that they were well armed, and that—judging by their speed—they would be upon them in two or three minutes.

Now that he knew he might be dead in a few minutes—dead if he fired, dead if he did not—the young DM gave his wife a brief thought, then his parents, and finally an old schoolmaster of his who had once confiscated a blue toy pistol that he had brought to class. His wandering thoughts were brought back to earth by the head constable who was addressing him urgently.

'Sahib!'

'Yes—yes?'

'Sahib—you are determined to shoot if necessary?' The head constable was a Muslim; it must have struck him as strange that he was about to die shooting Muslims in the course of defending a half-built Hindu temple that was an affront to the very mosque in which he himself often prayed.

'What do you think?' Krishan Dayal said in a voice that made things quite clear. 'Do I need to repeat my orders?'

'Sahib, if you take my advice—' said the head constable quickly, 'we should not stand here where we will be overpowered. We should stand in wait for them just before they turn the last bend before the temple—and just as they turn the bend we should charge and fire simultaneously. They won't know how many we are, and they won't know what's hit them. There's a ninety-nine per cent chance they will disperse.'

The astonished DM said to the head constable: 'You should have my job.'

He turned to the others, who appeared petrified. He immediately ordered them to run with him towards the bend. They stationed themselves on either side of the alley, about twenty feet from the bend itself. The mob was less than a minute away. He could hear it screaming and yelling; he could feel the vibration of the ground as hundreds of feet rushed forward.

At the last moment he gave the signal. The thirteen men roared and charged and fired.

The wild and dangerous mob, hundreds strong, faced with this sudden terror, halted, staggered, turned and fled. It was uncanny. Within thirty seconds it had melted away. Two bodies were left in the street: one young man had been shot through the neck and was dying or dead; the other, an old man with a white beard, had fallen and been crushed by the retreating mob. He was badly, perhaps fatally, injured. Slippers and sticks were scattered here and there. There was blood in several places in the alley, so it was apparent that there had been other injuries, possibly deaths. Friends or members of their families had probably dragged the bodies back into the doorways of neighbouring houses. No one wanted to be brought to the attention of the police.

The DM looked around at his men. A couple of them were trembling, most of them were jubilant. None of them was injured. He caught the head constable's eye. Both of them started laughing with relief, then stopped. A couple of women were wailing in nearby houses. Otherwise, everything was peaceful or, rather, still.

5.4

The next day L.N. Agarwal visited his only child, his married daughter Priya. He did so because he liked visiting her and her husband, and also to escape from the panic-stricken MLAs of his faction who were desperately worried about the aftermath of the firing in Chowk, and were making his life miserable with their misery.

L.N. Agarwal's daughter lived in Old Brahmpur in the Shahi Darvaza area, not far from Misri Mandi where her childhood friend Veena Tandon lived. Priya lived in a joint family which included her husband's brothers and their wives and children. Her husband was Ram Vilas Goyal, a lawyer with a practice concentrated mainly in the District Court—though he did appear in the High Court from time to time. He worked mainly on civil, not criminal cases. He was a placid, good-natured, bland-featured man, sparing with his words, and with only a mild interest in politics. Law and a little business on the side was enough for him; that and a calm family background and the peaceful ratchet of routine, which he expected Priya to provide. His colleagues respected him for his scrupulous honesty and his slow but clear-headed legal abilities. And his father-in-law the Home Minister enjoyed talking to him: he maintained confidences, refrained from giving advice, and had no passion for politics.

Priya Goyal for her part was a fiery spirit. Every morning, winter or summer, she paced fiercely along the roof. It was a long roof, since it covered three contiguous narrow houses, connected lengthways at each of the three storeys. In effect the whole operated as one large house, and was treated as such by the family and the neighbours. It was known locally as the Rai Bahadur's house because Ram Vilas Goyal's grandfather (still alive at eighty-eight), who had been given that title by the British, had bought and restructured the property half a century ago.

On the ground floor were a number of storerooms and the servants' quarters. On the floor above lived Ram Vilas's ancient grandfather, the Rai Bahadur; his father and stepmother; and his sister. The common kitchen was also located on this floor as was the puja room (which the unpious, even impious, Priya rarely visited). On the top floor were the rooms, respectively, of the families of the three brothers; Ram Vilas was the middle brother and he occupied the two rooms of the top floor of the middle 'house'. Above this was the roof with its washing lines and water tanks.

When she paced up and down the roof, Priya Goyal would picture herself as a panther in a cage. She would look longingly towards the small house just a few minutes' walk away—and just visible through the jungle of intervening roofs—in which her childhood friend Veena Tandon lived. Veena, she knew, was not well off any longer, but she was free to do as she pleased: to go to the market, to walk around by herself, to go for music lessons. In Priya's own household there was no question of that. For a daughter-in-law from the house of the Rai Bahadur to be seen in the market would have been disgraceful. That she was thirty-two years old with a girl of ten and a boy of eight was irrelevant. Ram Vilas, ever placid, would have none of it. It was simply not his way; more importantly, it would cause pain to his father and stepmother and grandfather and elder brother—and Ram Vilas sincerely believed in maintaining the decencies of a joint family.

Priya hated living in a joint family. She had never done so until she came to live with the Goyals of Shahi Darvaza. This was because her father, Lakshmi Narayan Agarwal, had been the only son to survive to adulthood, and he in his turn had only had the one daughter. When his wife died, he had been stricken, and had taken the Gandhian vow of sexual abstinence. He was a man of spartan habits. Although Home Minister, he lived in two rooms in a hostel for Members of the Legislative Assembly.

'The first years of married life are the hardest—they require the most adjustment,' Priya had been told; but she felt that in some ways it was getting more and more intolerable as time went on. Unlike Veena, she had no proper paternal—and more importantly, maternal—home to run away to with her children for at least a month a year—the prerogative of all married women. Even her grandparents (with whom she had spent the time when her father was in jail) were now dead. Her father loved her dearly as his only child; it was his love that had in a sense spoiled her for the constrained life of the Goyal joint family, for it had imbued her with a spirit of independence; and now, living in austerity as he did, he could not himself provide her with any refuge.

If her husband had not been so kind, she felt she would have gone mad. He did not understand her but he was understanding. He tried to make things easier for her in small ways, and he never once raised his voice. Also, she liked the ancient Rai Bahadur, her grandfather-in-law. There was a spark to him. The rest of the family and particularly the women—her mother-in-law, her husband's sister, and her husband's elder brother's wife—had done their best to make her miserable as a young bride, and she could not stand them. But she had to pretend she did, every day, all the time—except when she paced up and down on the roof—where she was not even permitted to have a garden, on the grounds that it would attract monkeys. Ram Vilas's stepmother had even tried to dissuade her from her daily to-ing and fro-ing ('Just think, Priya, how will it look to the neighbours?'), but for once Priya had refused to go along. The sisters-in-law above whose heads she paced at dawn reported her to their mother-in-law. But perhaps the old witch sensed that she had driven Priya to the limit, and did not phrase her complaint in a direct manner again. Anything indirect on the matter Priya chose not to understand.

L.N. Agarwal came dressed as always in an immaculately starched (but not fancy) kurta, dhoti and Congress cap. Below the white cap could be seen his curve of curly grey hair but not the baldness it enclosed. Whenever he ventured out to Shahi Darvaza he kept his cane handy to scare away the monkeys that frequented, some would say dominated, the neighbourhood. He dismissed his rickshaw near the local market, and turned off the main road into a tiny side-lane which opened out into a small square. In the middle of the square was a large pipal tree. One entire side of the square was the Rai Bahadur's house.

The door below the stairs was kept closed because of the monkeys, and he rapped on it with his cane. A couple of faces appeared at the enclosed wrought-iron balconies of the floors above. His daughter's face lit up when she saw him; she quickly coiled her loose black hair into a bun and came downstairs to open the door. Her father embraced her and they went upstairs again.

'And where has Vakil Sahib disappeared?' he asked in Hindi.

He liked to refer to his son-in-law as the lawyer, although the appellation was equally appropriate to Ram Vilas's father and grandfather.

'He was here a minute ago,' replied Priya, and got up to search for him.

'Don't bother yet,' said her father in a warm, relaxed voice. 'First give me some tea.'

For a few minutes the Home Minister enjoyed home comforts: well-made tea (not the useless stuff he got at the MLA hostel); sweets and kachauris made by the women of his daughter's house—maybe by his daughter herself; some minutes with his grandson and granddaughter, who preferred, however, to play with their friends on the heat of the roof or below in the square (his granddaughter was good at street cricket); and a few words with his daughter, whom he saw rarely enough and missed a great deal.

He had no compunction, as some fathers-in-law had, about accepting food, drink and hospitality at his son-in-law's house. He talked with Priya about his health and his grandchildren and their schooling and character; about how Vakil Sahib was working far too hard, a little about Priya's mother in passing, at the mention of whom a sadness came into both their eyes, and about the antics of the old servants of the Goyal household.

As they talked, other people passed the open door of the room, saw them, and came in. They included Ram Vilas's father, rather a helpless character who was terrorized by his second wife. Soon the whole Goyal clan had dropped by—except for the Rai Bahadur, who did not like climbing stairs.

'But where is Vakil Sahib?' repeated L.N. Agarwal.

'Oh,' said someone, 'he's downstairs talking with the Rai Bahadur. He knows you are in the house and he will come up as soon as he is released.'

'Why don't I go down and pay my respects to the Rai Bahadur now?' said L.N. Agarwal, and got up.

Downstairs, grandfather and grandson were talking in the large room that the Rai Bahadur had reserved as his own—mainly because he was attached to the beautiful peacock tiles that decorated the fireplace. L.N. Agarwal, being of the middle generation, paid his respects and had respects paid to him.

'Of course you'll have tea?' said the Rai Bahadur.

'I've had some upstairs.'

'Since when have Leaders of the People placed a limit on their tea-consumption?' asked the Rai Bahadur in a creaky and lucid voice. The word he used was 'Neta-log', which had about the same level of mock deference as 'Vakil Sahib'.

'Now, tell me,' he continued, 'what is all this killing you've been doing in Chowk?'

It was not meant the way it sounded, it was merely the old Rai Bahadur's style of speech, but L.N. Agarwal could have done without direct examination. He would probably get enough of that on the floor of the House on Monday. What he would have preferred was a quiet chat with his placid son-in-law, an unloading of his troubled mind.

'Nothing, nothing, it will all blow over,' he said.

'I heard that twenty Muslims were killed,' said the old Rai Bahadur philosophically.

'No, not that many,' said L.N. Agarwal. 'A few. Matters are well in hand.' He paused, ruminating on the fact that he had misjudged the situation. 'This is a hard town to manage,' he continued. 'If it isn't one thing it's another. We are an ill-disciplined people. The lathi and the gun are the only things that will teach us discipline.'

'In British days law and order was not such a problem,' said the creaky voice.

The Home Minister did not rise to the Rai Bahadur's bait. In fact, he was not sure that the remark was not delivered innocently.

'Still, there it is,' he responded.

'Mahesh Kapoor's daughter was here the other day,' ventured the Rai Bahadur.

Surely this could not be an innocent comment. Or was it? Perhaps the Rai Bahadur was merely following a train of thought.

'Yes, she is a good girl,' said L.N. Agarwal. He rubbed his perimeter of hair in a thoughtful way. Then, after a pause, he added calmly: 'I can handle the town; it is not the tension that disturbs me. Ten Misri Mandis and twenty Chowks are nothing. It is the politics, the politicians—'

The Rai Bahadur allowed himself a smile. This too was somewhat creaky, as if the separate plates of his aged face were gradually reconfiguring themselves with difficulty.

L.N. Agarwal shook his head, then went on. 'Until two this morning the MLAs were gathering around me like chicks around their mother. They were in a state of panic. The Chief Minister goes out of town for a few days and see what happens in his absence! What will Sharmaji say when he comes back? What capital will Mahesh Kapoor's faction make out of all this? In Misri Mandi they will emphasize the lot of the jatavs, in Chowk that of the Muslims. What will the effect of all this be on the jatav vote and the Muslim vote? The General Elections are just a few months away. Will these vote banks swing away from the Congress? If so, in what numbers? One or two gentlemen have even asked if there is the danger of further conflagration—though usually this is the least of their concerns.'

'And what do you tell them when they come running to you?' asked the Rai Bahadur. His daughter-in-law—the arch-witch in Priya's demonology—had just brought in the tea. The top of her head was covered with her sari. She poured the tea, gave them a sharp look, exchanged a couple of words, and went out.

The thread of the conversation had been lost, but the Rai Bahadur, perhaps remembering the cross-examinations for which he had been famous in his prime, drew it gently back again.

'Oh, nothing,' said L.N. Agarwal quite calmly. 'I just tell them whatever is necessary to stop them from keeping me awake.'

'Nothing?'

'No, nothing much. Just that things will blow over; that what's done is done; that a little discipline never did a neighbourhood any harm; that the General Elections are still far enough away. That sort of thing.' L.N. Agarwal sipped his tea before continuing: 'The fact of the matter is that the country has far more important things to think about. Food is the main one. Bihar is virtually starving. And if we have a bad monsoon, we will be too. Mere Muslims threatening us from inside the country or across the border we can deal with. If Nehru were not so soft-hearted we would have dealt with them properly a few years ago. And now these jatavs, these'—his expression conveyed distaste at the words—'these scheduled caste people are becoming a problem once again. But let's see, let's see. . . .'

Ram Vilas Goyal had sat silent through the whole exchange. Once he frowned slightly, once he nodded.

That is what I like about my son-in-law, reflected L.N. Agarwal. He's not dumb, but he doesn't speak. He decided yet again that he had made the right match for his daughter. Priya could provoke, and he would simply not allow himself to be provoked.

5.5

Meanwhile, upstairs, Priya was talking to Veena, who had come to pay her a visit. But it was more than a social visit, it was an emergency. Veena was very distressed. She had come home and found Kedarnath not merely with his eyes closed but with his head in his hands. This was far worse than his general state of optimistic anxiety. He had not wanted to talk about it, but she had eventually discovered that he was in very grave financial trouble. With the pickets and the stationing of the police in Chowk, the wholesale shoe market had finally ground from a slowdown to a complete halt. Every day now his chits were coming due, and he just did not have the cash to pay them. Those who owed him money, particularly two large stores in Bombay, had deferred paying him for past supplies because they thought he could not ensure future supplies. The supplies he got from people like Jagat Ram, who made shoes to order, were not enough. To fulfil the orders that buyers around the country had placed with him, he needed the shoes of the basket-wallahs, and they did not dare come to Misri Mandi these days.

But the immediate problem was how to pay for the chits that were coming due. He had no one to go to; all his associates were themselves short of cash. Going to his father-in-law was for him out of the question. He was at his wits' end. He would try once more to talk to his creditors—the moneylenders who held his chits and their commission agents who came to him for payment when they were due. He would try to persuade them that it would do no one any good to drive him and others like him to the wall in a credit squeeze. This situation would surely not last long. He was not insolvent, just illiquid. But even as he spoke he knew what their answer would be. He knew that money, unlike labour, owed no allegiance to a particular trade, and could flow out of shoes and into, say, cold storage facilities without retraining or compunction or doubt. It only asked two questions: 'What interest?' and 'What risk?'

Veena had not come to Priya for financial help, but to ask her how best to sell the jewellery she had got from her mother upon her marriage—and to weep on her shoulder. She had brought the jewellery with her. Only a little had remained from the traumatic days after the family's flight from Lahore. Every piece meant so much to her that she started crying when she thought of losing it. She had only two requests—that her husband not find out until the jewellery had actually been sold; and that for a few weeks at least her father and mother should not know.

They talked quickly, because there was no privacy in the house, and at any moment anyone could walk into Priya's room.

'My father's here,' Priya said. 'Downstairs, talking politics.'

'We will always be friends, no matter what,' said Veena suddenly, and started crying again.

Priya hugged her friend, told her to have courage, and suggested a brisk walk on the roof.

'What, in this heat, are you mad?' asked Veena.

'Why not? It's either heatstroke or interruption by my mother-in-law—and I know which I'd prefer.'

'I'm scared of your monkeys,' said Veena as a second line of defence. 'First they fight on the roof of the daal factory, then they leap over on to your roof. Shahi Darvaza should be renamed Hanuman Dwar.'

'You're not scared of anything. I don't believe you,' said Priya. 'In fact, I envy you. You can walk over by yourself any time. Look at me. And look at these bars on the balcony. The monkeys can't come in, and I can't go out.'

'Ah,' said Veena, 'you shouldn't envy me.'

They were silent for a while.

'How is Bhaskar?' asked Priya.

Veena's plump face lit up in a smile, rather a sad one. 'He's very well—as well as your pair, anyway. He insisted on coming along. At the moment they are all playing cricket in the square downstairs. The pipal tree doesn't seem to bother them. . . . I wish for your sake, Priya, that you had a brother or sister,' Veena added suddenly, thinking of her own childhood.

The two friends went to the balcony and looked down through the wrought-iron grille. Their three children, together with two others, were playing cricket in the small square. Priya's ten-year-old daughter was by far the best of them. She was a fair bowler and a fine batsman. She usually managed to avoid the pipal tree, which gave the others endless trouble.

'Why don't you stay for lunch?' asked Priya.

'I can't,' said Veena, thinking of Kedarnath and her mother-in-law, who would be expecting her. 'Tomorrow perhaps.'

'Tomorrow then.'

Veena left the bag of jewellery with Priya, who locked it up in a steel almirah. As she stood by the cupboard Veena said: 'You're putting on weight.'

'I've always been fat,' said Priya, 'and because I do nothing but sit here all day like a caged bird, I've grown fatter'.

'You're not fat and you never have been,' said her friend. 'And since when have you stopped pacing on the roof?'

'I haven't,' said Priya, 'but one day I'm going to throw myself off it.'

'Now if you talk like that I'm going to leave at once,' said Veena and made to go.

'No, don't go. Seeing you has cheered me up,' said Priya. 'I hope you have lots of bad fortune. Then you'll come running to me all the time. If it hadn't been for Partition you'd never have come back to Brahmpur.'

Veena laughed.

'Come on, let's go to the roof,' continued Priya. 'I really can't talk freely to you here. People are always coming in and listening from the balcony. I hate it here, I'm so unhappy, if I don't tell you I'll burst.' She laughed, and pulled Veena to her feet. 'I'll tell Bablu to get us something cold to prevent heatstroke.'

Bablu was the weird fifty-year-old servant who had come to the family as a child and had grown more eccentric with each passing year. Lately he had taken to eating everyone's medicines.

When they got to the roof, they sat in the shade of the water tank and started laughing like schoolgirls.

'We should live next to each other,' said Priya, shaking out her jet black hair, which she had washed and oiled that morning. 'Then, even if I throw myself off my roof, I'll fall on to yours.'

'It would be awful if we lived next to each other,' said Veena, laughing. 'The witch and the scarecrow would get together every afternoon and complain about their daughters-in-law. "O, she's bewitched my son, they play chaupar on the roof all the time, she'll make him as dark as soot. And she sings on the roof so shamelessly to the whole neighbourhood. And she deliberately prepares rich food so that I fill up with gas. One day I'll explode and she'll dance over my bones."'

Priya giggled. 'No,' she said, 'it'll be fine. The two kitchens will face each other, and the vegetables can join us in complaining about our oppression. "O friend Potato, the khatri scarecrow is boiling me. Tell everyone I died miserably. Farewell, farewell, never forget me." "O friend Pumpkin, the bania witch has spared me for only another two days. I'll weep for you but I won't be able to attend your chautha. Forgive me, forgive me."'

Veena's laughter bubbled out again. 'Actually, I feel quite sorry for my scarecrow,' she said. 'She had a hard time during Partition. But she was quite horrible to me even in Lahore, even after Bhaskar was born. When she sees I'm not miserable she becomes even more miserable. When we become mothers-in-law, Priya, we'll feed our daughters-in-law ghee and sugar every day.'

'I certainly don't feel sorry for my witch,' said Priya disgustedly. 'And I shall certainly bully my daughter-in-law from morning till night until I've completely crushed her spirit. Women look much more beautiful when they're unhappy, don't you think?' She shook her thick black hair from side to side and glared at the stairs. 'This is a vile house,' she added. 'I'd much rather be a monkey and fight on the roof of the daal factory than a daughter-in-law in the Rai Bahadur's house. I'd run to the market and steal bananas. I'd fight the dogs, I'd snap at the bats. I'd go to Tarbuz ka Bazaar and pinch the bottoms of all the pretty prostitutes. I'd . . . do you know what the monkeys did here the other day?'

'No,' said Veena. 'Tell me.'

'I was just going to. Bablu, who is getting crazier by the minute, placed the Rai Bahadur's alarm clocks on the ledge. Well, the next thing we saw was three monkeys in the pipal tree, examining them, saying, "Mmmmmmm", "Mmmmmmmm", in a high-pitched voice, as if to say, "Well? We have your clocks. What now?" The witch went out. We didn't have the little packets of wheat which we usually bribe them with, so she took some musammis and bananas and carrots and tried to tempt them down, saying, "Here, here, come, beautiful ones, come, come, I swear by Hanuman I'll give you lovely things to eat. . . ." And they came down all right, one by one they came down, very cautiously, each with a clock tucked beneath his arm. Then they began to eat the food, first with one hand, like this—then, putting the clocks down, with both hands. Well—no sooner were all three clocks on the ground than the witch took a stick which she had hidden behind her back and threatened their lives with it—using such filthy language that I was forced to admire her. The carrot and the stick, don't they say in English? So the story has a happy ending. But the monkeys of Shahi Darvaza are very smart. They know what they can hold up to ransom, and what they can't.'

Bablu had come up the stairs, gripping with four dirty fingers of one hand four glasses of cold nimbu pani filled almost to the brim. 'Here!' he said, setting them down. 'Drink! If you sit in the sun like this, you'll catch pneumonia.' Then he disappeared.

'The same as ever?' asked Veena.

'The same, but even more so,' said Priya. 'Nothing changes. The only comforting constant here is that Vakil Sahib snores as loudly as ever.

Sometimes at night when the bed vibrates, I think he'll disappear, and all that will be left for me to weep over will be his snore. But I can't tell you some of the things that go on in this house,' she added darkly. 'You're lucky you don't have much money. What people will do for money, Veena, I can't tell you. And what does it go into? Not into education or art or music or literature—no, it all goes into jewellery. And the women of the house have to wear ten tons of it on their necks at every wedding. And you should see them all sizing each other up. Oh, Veena—' she said, suddenly realizing her insensitivity, 'I have a habit of blabbering. Tell me to be quiet.'

'No, no, I'm enjoying it,' said Veena. 'But tell me, when the jeweller comes to your house next time will you be able to get an estimate? For the small pieces—and, well, especially for my navratan? Will you be able to get a few minutes with him alone so that your mother-in-law doesn't come to know? If I had to go to a jeweller myself I'd certainly be cheated. But you know all about these things.'

Priya nodded. 'I'll try,' she said. The navratan was a lovely piece; she had last seen it round Veena's neck at Pran and Savita's wedding. It consisted of an arc of nine square gold compartments, each the setting of a different precious stone, with delicate enamel work at the sides and even on the back, where it could not be seen. Topaz, white sapphire, emerald, blue sapphire, ruby, diamond, pearl, cat's eye and coral: instead of looking cluttered and disordered, the heavy necklace had a wonderful combination of traditional solidity and charm. For Veena it had more than that: of all her mother's gifts it was the one she loved most.

'I think our fathers are mad to dislike each other so much,' said Priya out of the blue. 'Who cares who the next Chief Minister of Purva Pradesh will be?'

Veena nodded as she sipped her nimbu pani.

'What news of Maan?' asked Priya.

They gossiped on: Maan and Saeeda Bai; the Nawab Sahib's daughter and whether her situation in purdah was worse than Priya's; Savita's pregnancy; even, at second-hand, Mrs Rupa Mehra, and how she was trying to corrupt her samdhins by teaching them rummy.

They had forgotten about the world. But suddenly Bablu's large head and rounded shoulders appeared at the top of the stairs. 'Oh my God,' said Priya with a start. 'My duties in the kitchen—since I've been talking to you, they've gone straight out of my head. My mother-in-law must have finished her stupid rigmarole of cooking her own food in a wet dhoti after her bath, and she's yelling for me. I've got to run. She does it for purity, so she says—though she doesn't mind that we have cockroaches the size of buffaloes running around all over the house, and rats that bite off your hair at night if you don't wash the oil off. Oh, do stay for lunch, Veena, I never get to see you!'

'I really can't,' said Veena. 'The Sleeper likes his food just so. And so does the Snorer, I'm sure.'

'Oh, he's not so particular,' said Priya, frowning. 'He puts up with all my nonsense. But I can't go out, I can't go out, I can't go out anywhere except for weddings and the odd trip to the temple or a religious fair and you know what I think of those. If he wasn't so good, I would go completely mad. Wife-beating is something of a common sport in our neighbourhood, you aren't considered much of a man if you don't slap your wife around a couple of times, but Ram Vilas wouldn't even beat a drum at Dussehra. And he's so respectful to the witch it makes me sick, though she's only his stepmother. They say he's so nice to witnesses that they tell him the truth—even though they're in court! Well, if you can't stay, you must come tomorrow. Promise me again.'

Veena promised, and the two friends went down to the room on the top floor. Priya's daughter and son were sitting on the bed, and they informed Veena that Bhaskar had gone back home.

'What? By himself?' said Veena anxiously.

'He's nine years old, and it's five minutes away,' said the boy.

'Shh!' said Priya. 'Speak properly to your elders.'

'I'd better go at once,' said Veena.

On the way down, Veena met L.N. Agarwal coming up. The stairs were narrow and steep. She pressed herself against the wall and said namaste. He acknowledged the greeting with a 'Jeeti raho, beti', and went up.

But though he had addressed her as 'daughter', Veena felt that he had been reminded the instant he saw her of the ministerial rival whose daughter she really was.

5.6

'Is the Government aware that the Brahmpur Police made a lathi charge on the members of the jatav community last week when they demonstrated in front of the Govind Shoe Mart?'

The Minister for Home Affairs, Shri L.N. Agarwal, got to his feet. 'There was no lathi charge,' he replied.

'Mild lathi charge, if you like. Is the Government aware of the incident I am referring to?'

The Home Minister looked across the well of the great circular chamber, and stated calmly:

'There was no lathi charge in the usual sense. The police were forced to use light canes, one inch thick, when the unruly crowd had stoned and manhandled several members of the public and one policeman, and when it was apparent that the safety of the Govind Shoe Mart, and of the public, and of the policemen themselves was seriously threatened.'

He stared at his interrogator, Ram Dhan, a short, dark, pockmarked man in his forties, who asked his questions—in standard Hindi but with a strong Brahmpuri accent—with his arms folded across his chest.

'Is it a fact,' continued the questioner, 'that on the same evening, the police beat up a large number of jatavs who were peacefully attempting to picket the Brahmpur Shoe Mart nearby?' Shri Ram Dhan was an Independent MLA from the scheduled castes, and he stressed the word 'jatavs'. A kind of indignant murmur rose from all around the House. The Speaker called for order, and the Home Minister stood up again.

'It is not a fact,' he stated, keeping his voice level. 'The police, being hard pressed by an angry mob, defended themselves and, in the course of this action, three people were injured. As for the honourable member's innuendo that the police singled out members of a particular caste from the mob or were especially severe because the mob consisted largely of members of that caste, I would advise him to be more just to the police. Let me assure him that the action would have been no different had the mob been constituted differently.'

Limpet-like, however, Shri Ram Dhan continued: 'Is it a fact that the honourable Home Minister was in constant touch with the local authorities of Brahmpur, in particular the District Magistrate and the Superintendent of Police?'

'Yes.' L.N. Agarwal looked upwards, having delivered himself of this single syllable and as if seeking patience, towards the great dome of white frosted glass through which the late morning light poured down on the Legislative Assembly.

'Was the specific sanction of the Home Minister taken by the district authorities before making the lathi charge on the unarmed mob? If so, when? If not, why not?'

The Home Minister sighed with exasperation rather than weariness as he stood up again: 'May I reiterate that I do not accept the use of the words "lathi charge" in this context. Nor was the mob unarmed, since they used stones. However, I am glad that the honourable member admits that it was a mob that the police were facing. Indeed, from the fact that he uses the word in a printed, starred question, it is clear that he knew this before today.'

'Would the honourable Minister kindly answer the question put to him?' said Ram Dhan heatedly, opening his arms and clenching his fists.

'I should have thought the answer was obvious,' said L.N. Agarwal. He paused, then continued, as if reciting: 'The developing situation on the ground is sometimes such that it is often tactically impossible to foresee what will happen, and a certain flexibility must be left to the local authorities.'

But Ram Dhan clung on. 'If as the honourable Minister admits, no such specific sanction was taken, was the honourable Home Minister informed of the proposed action of the police? Did he or the Chief Minister give their tacit approval?'

Once again the Home Minister rose. He glanced at a point in the dead centre of the dark-green carpet that covered the well. 'The action was not premeditated. It had to be taken forthwith in order to meet a grave situation which had suddenly developed. It did not admit of any previous reference to Government.'

A member shouted: 'And what about the Chief Minister?'

The Speaker of the House, a learned but not normally very assertive man who was dressed in a kurta and dhoti, looked down from his high platform below the seal of Purva Pradesh—a great pipal tree—and said: 'These short-order starred questions are addressed specifically to the honourable Home Minister, and his answers must be taken to be sufficient.'

Several voices now rose. One, dominating the others, boomed out: 'Since the honourable Chief Minister is present in the House after his travels in other parts, perhaps he would care to oblige us with an answer even though he is not compelled by the Standing Orders to do so? I believe the House would appreciate it.'

The Chief Minister, Shri S.S. Sharma, stood up without his stick, leaned with his left hand on his dark wooden desk and looked to his left and right. He was positioned along the curve of the central well, almost exactly between L.N. Agarwal and Mahesh Kapoor. He addressed the Speaker in his nasal, rather paternal, voice, nodding his head gently as he did so: 'I have no objection to speaking, Mr Speaker, but I have nothing to add. The action taken—call it by what name the honourable members will—was taken under the aegis of the responsible Cabinet Minister.' There was a pause, during which it was not clear what the Chief Minister was going to add, if anything. 'Whom I naturally support,' he said.

He had not even sat down when the inexorable Ram Dhan came back into the fray. 'I am much obliged to the honourable Chief Minister,' he said, 'but I would like to seek a clarification. By saying that he supports the Home Minister, does the Chief Minister mean to imply that he approves of the policy of the district authorities?'

Before the Chief Minister could reply, the Home Minister quickly rose again to say: 'I hope that we have made ourselves clear on this point. It was not a case of prior approval. An inquiry was held immediately after the incident. The District Magistrate went into the matter fully and found that the very minimum force which was absolutely unavoidable was used. The Government regret that such an occasion should have arisen, but are satisfied that the finding of the District Magistrate is correct. It was accepted by practically all concerned that the authorities faced a serious situation with tact and due restraint.'

A member of the Socialist Party stood up. 'Is it true,' he asked, 'that it was on the prodding of members of the bania trading community to which he belongs that the honourable Home Minister'—angry murmurs rose from the Government benches—'let me finish—that the Minister subsequently posted troops—I mean police—throughout the length and breadth of Misri Mandi?'

'I disallow that question,' said the Speaker.

'Well,' continued the member, 'would the honourable Minister kindly inform us on whose advice he decided on the placing of this threatening body of police?'

The Home Minister grasped the curve of hair under his cap and said: 'Government made its own decision, bearing the totality of the situation in mind. And in the event it has proved to be effective. There is peace at last in Misri Mandi.'

A babble of indignant shouts, earnest chatter and ostentatious laughter arose on all sides. There were shouts of 'What peace?' 'Shame!' 'Who is the DM to judge the matter?' 'What about the mosque?' and so on.

'Order! Order!' cried the Speaker, looking flustered as another member rose to his feet and said:

'Will the Government consider the advisability of creating machineries other than the interested district authorities for making inquiries in such cases?'

'I do not allow this question,' said the Speaker, shaking his head like a sparrow. 'Under Standing Orders questions making suggestions for action are not permissible and I am not prepared to allow them during Question Time.'

It was the end of the Home Minister's grilling on the Misri Mandi incident. Though there had been only five questions on the printed sheet, the supplementary questions had given the exchange the character almost of a cross-examination. The intervention of the Chief Minister had been more disturbing than reassuring to L.N. Agarwal. Was S.S. Sharma, in his wily, indirect way, trying to palm off full responsibility for the action on to his second-in-command? L.N. Agarwal sat down, sweating slightly, but he knew that he would have to be on his feet immediately again. And, though he prided himself on maintaining his calm in difficult circumstances, he did not relish what he would now have to face.

5.7

Begum Abida Khan slowly stood up. She was dressed in a dark blue, almost black, sari, and her pale and furious face riveted the house even before she began to speak. She was the wife of the Nawab of Baitar's younger brother, and one of the leaders of the Democratic Party, the party that sought to protect the interests of the landowners in the face of the impending passage of the Zamindari Abolition Bill. Although a Shia, she had the reputation of being an aggressive protector of the rights of all Muslims in the new, truncated Independent India. Her husband, like his father, had been a member of the Muslim League before Independence and had left for Pakistan shortly afterwards. Despite the powerful persuasion and reproach of many relatives, she, however, had chosen not to go. 'I'll be useless there, sitting and gossiping. Here in Brahmpur at least I know where I am and what I can do,' she had said. And this morning she knew exactly what she wanted to do. Looking straight at the man whom she considered to be one of the less savoury manifestations of humankind, she began her questioning from her list of starred questions.

'Is the honourable Minister for Home Affairs aware that at least five people were killed by the police in the firing near Chowk last Friday?'

The Home Minister, who at the best of times could not stand the Begum, replied: 'Indeed, I was not.'

It was somewhat obstructive of him not to elaborate, but he did not feel like being forthcoming before this pale harridan.

Begum Abida Khan veered from her script. 'Will the honourable Minister inform us exactly what he is aware of?' she inquired acidly.

'I disallow that question,' murmured the Speaker.

'What would the honourable Minister say was the death toll in the firing in Chowk?' demanded Begum Abida Khan.

'One,' said L.N. Agarwal.

Begum Abida Khan's voice was incredulous: 'One?' she cried. 'One?'

'One,' replied the Home Minister, holding up the index finger of his right hand, as if to an idiot child who had difficulty with numbers or hearing or both.

Begum Abida Khan cried out angrily: 'If I may inform the honourable Minister, it was at least five, and I have good proof of this fact. Here are copies of the death certificates of four of the deceased. Indeed, it is likely that two more men will shortly—'

'I rise on a point of order, Sir,' said L.N. Agarwal, ignoring her and addressing the Speaker directly. 'I understand that Question Time is used for getting information from and not for giving information to Ministers.'

Begum Abida Khan's voice continued regardless: '—two more men will shortly be receiving such certificates of honour thanks to the henchmen of the honourable Minister. I would like to table these death certificates—these copies of death certificates.'

'I am afraid that that is not possible under the Standing Orders. . . .' protested the Speaker.

Begum Abida Khan waved the documents around, and raised her voice higher: 'The newspapers have copies of them, why is the House not entitled to see them? When the blood of innocent men, of mere boys, is being callously shed—'

'The honourable member will not use Question Time to make speeches,' said the Speaker, and banged his gavel.

Begum Abida Khan suddenly pulled herself together, and once again addressed L.N. Agarwal.

'Will the honourable Minister kindly inform the House on what basis he came to the total figure of one?'

'The report was furnished by the District Magistrate, who was present at the time of the event.'

'By "present" you mean that he ordered the mowing down of these unfortunate people, is that not so?'

L.N. Agarwal paused before answering:

'The District Magistrate is a seasoned officer, who took whatever steps he considered the situation required. As the honourable member is aware, an inquiry under a more senior officer will shortly be made, as it is in all cases of an order to fire; and I suggest to her that we wait until such time as the report is published before we give vent to speculation.'

'Speculation?' burst out Begum Abida Khan. 'Speculation? Do you call this speculation? You should be—the honourable Minister'—she emphasized the word maananiya or honourable—'the honourable Minister should be ashamed of himself. I have seen the corpses of two men with these very eyes. I am not speculating. If it were the blood of his own co-religionists that was flowing in the streets, the honourable Minister would not "wait until such time". We know of the overt and tacit support he gives that foul organization the Linga Rakshak Samiti, set up expressly to destroy the sanctity of our mosque—'

The House was getting increasingly excited under her oratory, inappropriate though it may have been. L.N. Agarwal was grasping his curve of grey hair with his right hand, tense as a claw, and—having cast his calm demeanour to the winds—was glaring at her at every scornful 'honourable'. The frail-looking Speaker made another attempt to stem the flow:

'The honourable member may perhaps need reminding that according to my Question List, she has three starred questions remaining.'

'I thank you, Sir,' said Begum Abida Khan. 'I shall come to them. In fact I shall ask the next one immediately. It is very germane to the subject. Will the honourable Minister of Home Affairs inform us whether prior to the firings in Chowk a warning to disperse was read out under Section 144 of the Criminal Procedure Code? If so, when? If not, why not?'

Brutally and angrily L.N. Agarwal replied:

'It was not. It could not have been. There was no time to do so. If people start riots for religious reasons and attempt to destroy temples they must accept the consequences. Or mosques, of course, for that matter—'

But now Begum Abida Khan was almost shouting. 'Riot? Riot? How does the honourable Minister come to the conclusion that that was the intention of the crowd? It was the time of evening prayer. They were proceeding to the mosque—'

'From all reports, it was obvious. They were rushing forward violently, shouting with their accustomed zealotry, and brandishing weapons,' said the Home Minister.

There was uproar.

A member of the Socialist Party cried: 'Was the honourable Minister present?'

A member of the Congress Party said: 'He can't be everywhere.'

'But this was brutal,' shouted someone else. 'They fired at point-blank range.'

'Honourable members are reminded that the Minister is to answer his own questions,' cried the Speaker.

'I thank you, Sir—' began the Home Minister. But to his utter amazement and, indeed, horror, a Muslim member of the Congress Party, Abdus Salaam, who happened also to be Parliamentary Secretary to the Revenue Minister, now rose to ask: 'How could such a grave step—an order to fire—have been taken without either giving due warning to disperse or attempting to ascertain the intention of the crowd?'

That Abdus Salaam should have risen to his feet shocked the House. In a sense it was not clear where he was addressing the question—he was looking at an indeterminate point somewhere to the right of the great seal of Purva Pradesh above the Speaker's chair. He seemed, in fact, to be thinking aloud. He was a scholarly young man, known particularly for his excellent understanding of land tenure law, and was one of the chief architects of the Purva Pradesh Zamindari Abolition Bill. That he should make common cause with a leader of the Democratic Party—the party of the zamindars—on this issue, stunned members of all parties. Mahesh Kapoor himself was surprised at this intervention by his Parliamentary Secretary and turned around with a frown, not entirely pleased. The Chief Minister scowled. L.N. Agarwal was gripped with outrage and humiliation. Several members of the House were on their feet, waving their order papers, and no one, not even the Speaker, could be clearly heard. It was becoming a free-for-all.

When, after repeated thumps of the Speaker's gavel, a semblance of order was restored, the Home Minister, though still in shock, rose to ask:

'May I know, Sir, whether a Parliamentary Secretary to a Minister is authorized to put questions to Government?'

Abdus Salaam, looking around in bewilderment, amazed by the furore he had unwittingly caused, said: 'I withdraw.'

But now there were cries of: 'No, no!' 'How can you do that?' and 'If you won't ask it, I will.'

The Speaker sighed.

'As far as procedure is concerned, every member is at liberty to put questions,' he ruled.

'Why then?' asked a member angrily. 'Why was it done? Will the honourable Minister answer or not?'

'I did not catch the question,' said L.N. Agarwal. 'I believe it has been withdrawn.'

'I am asking, like the other member, why no one found out what the crowd wanted? How did the DM know it was violent?' repeated the member.

'There should be an adjournment motion on this,' cried another.

'The Speaker already has such a notice with him,' said a third.

Over all this rose the piercing voice of Begum Abida Khan: 'It was as brutal as the violence of Partition. A youth was killed who was not even part of the demonstration. Would the honourable Minister for Home Affairs care to explain how this happened?' She sat down and glared.

'Demonstration?' said L.N. Agarwal with an air of forensic triumph.

'Crowd, rather—' said the battling Begum, leaping up again and slipping out of his coils. 'You are not going to deny, surely, that it was the time of prayer? The demonstration—the demonstration of gross inhumanity, for that is what it was—was on the part of the police. Now will the honourable Minister not take refuge in semantics and deal with the facts.'

When he saw the wretched woman get up again, the Home Minister felt a stab of hatred in his heart. She was a thorn in his flesh and had insulted and humiliated him before the House and he now decided that, come what may, he was going to get back at her and her house—the family of the Nawab Sahib of Baitar. They were all fanatics, these Muslims, who appeared not to realize they were here in this country on sufferance. A calm dose of well-applied law would do them good.

'I can only answer one question at a time,' L.N. Agarwal said in a dangerous growl.

'The supplementary questions of the honourable member who asked the starred questions will take precedence,' said the Speaker.

Begum Abida Khan smiled grimly.

The Home Minister said: 'We must wait till the report is published.

Government is not aware that an innocent youth was fired upon, let alone injured or killed.'

Now Abdus Salaam stood up again. From around the House outraged cries rose: 'Sit down, sit down.' 'Shame!' 'Why are you attacking your own side?'

'Why should he sit down?' 'What have you got to hide?' 'You are a Congress member—you should know better.'

But so unprecedented was the situation that even those who opposed his intervention were curious.

When the cries had died down to a sort of volatile muttering, Abdus Salaam, still looking rather puzzled, asked: 'What I have been wondering about during the course of this discussion is, well, why was a deterrent police force—well, maybe just an adequate police force—not maintained at the site of the temple? Then there would have been no need to fire in this panicky manner.'

The Home Minister drew in his breath. Everyone is looking at me, he thought. I must control my expression.

'Is this supplementary question addressed to the honourable Minister?' asked the Speaker.

'Yes, it is, Sir,' said Abdus Salaam, suddenly determined. 'I will not withdraw this question. Would the honourable Minister inform us why there was not a sufficient and deterrent police force maintained either at the kotwali or at the site of the temple itself? Why were there only a dozen men left to maintain law and order in this grievously disturbed area, especially after the contents of the Friday sermon at the Alamgiri Mosque became known to the authorities?'

This was the question that L.N. Agarwal had been dreading, and he was appalled and enraged that it had been asked by an MLA from his own party, and a Parliamentary Secretary at that. He felt defenceless. Was this a plot by Mahesh Kapoor to undermine him? He looked at the Chief Minister, who was waiting for his response with an unreadable expression. L.N. Agarwal suddenly realized that he had been on his feet for a long time, and wanted very badly to urinate. And he wanted to get out of here as quickly as possible. He began to take refuge in the kind of stonewalling that the Chief Minister himself often used, but to much shabbier effect than that master of parliamentary evasion. By now, however, he hardly cared. He was convinced that this was indeed a plot by Muslims and so-called secular Hindus to attack him—and that his own party had been infected with treason.

Looking with calm hatred first at Abdus Salaam, then at Begum Abida Khan, he said: 'I can merely reiterate—wait for the report.'

A member asked: 'Why were so many police diverted to Misri Mandi for a totally unnecessary show of force when they were really needed in Chowk?'

'Wait for the report,' said the Home Minister, glaring around the House, as if challenging the members to goad him further.

Begum Abida Khan stood up. 'Has the Government taken any action against the District Magistrate responsible for this unprovoked firing?' she demanded.

'The question does not arise.'

'If the much-anticipated report shows that the firing was uncalled for and irregular, does Government plan to take any steps in this regard?'

'That will be seen in due course. I should think it might.'

'What steps does Government intend to take?'

'Proper and adequate steps.'

'Has Government taken any such steps in similar situations in the past?'

'It has.'

'What are those steps that have been taken?'

'Such steps as were considered reasonable and proper.'

Begum Abida Khan looked at him as she would at a snake, wounded but still evading the final blow by twisting its head from side to side. Well, she was not done with him yet.

'Will the honourable Minister name the wards or neighbourhoods in which restrictions have now been placed with regard to the possession of cold steel? Have these restrictions been placed as a result of the recent firing? If so, why were they not placed earlier?'

The Home Minister looked at the pipal tree in the great seal, and said: 'Government presumes that the honourable member means by the phrase "cold steel" objects such as swords, daggers, axes, and similar weapons.'

'Household knives have also been wrested by the police from housewives,' said Begum Abida Khan in more of a jeer than a statement. 'Well, what are the neighbourhoods?'

'Chowk, Hazrat Mahal, and Captainganj,' said L.N. Agarwal.

'Not Misri Mandi?'

'No.'

'Although that was the site of the heaviest police presence?' persisted Begum Abida Khan.

'Police had to be shifted in large numbers to the real trouble spots—' began L.N. Agarwal.

He stopped abruptly, realizing too late how he had exposed himself by what he had started to say.

'So the honourable Minister admits—' began Begum Abida Khan, her eyes gleaming triumphantly.

'The Government admits nothing. The report will detail everything,' said the Home Minister, appalled by the confession she had elicited from him.

Begum Abida Khan smiled contemptuously, and decided that the reactionary, trigger-happy, anti-Muslim bully had just condemned himself out of his own mouth sufficiently for much further skewering to be productive. She let her questions taper away.

'Why were these restrictions on cold steel imposed?'

'In order to prevent crimes and incidents of violence.'

'Incidents?'

'Such as riots by inflamed mobs,' he cried out in weary rage.

'How long will these restrictions continue?' asked Begum Abida Khan, almost laughing.

'Till they are withdrawn.'

'And when does the Government propose to withdraw these restrictions?'

'As soon as the situation permits.'

Begum Abida Khan gently sat down.

There followed a notice for adjournment of the House in order to discuss the issue of the firing, but the Speaker disposed of this quickly enough. Adjournment motions were only granted in the most exceptional cases of crisis or emergency, where discussion could brook no delay; to grant them or not was in the Speaker's absolute discretion. The subject of the police firing, even had it been such a subject—which, to his mind, it was not—had been sufficiently aired already. The questions of that remarkable, almost unreinable woman had virtually become a debate.

The Speaker went on to the next items on the day's business: first, the announcement of bills passed by the state legislature that had received the assent of the Governor of the state or the President of India; next, the most important matter on the agenda for the entire session: the continuing debate on the Zamindari Abolition Bill.

But L.N. Agarwal did not stay to listen to discussions on the bill. As soon as the notice for an adjournment motion had been rejected by the Speaker, he fled—not directly across the well to the exit but along an aisle to the perimeter gallery, and then along the dark, wood-panelled wall. His tension and animus were palpable in the way he walked. He was unconsciously crushing his order papers in his hand. Several members tried to talk to him, to sympathize with him. He brushed them off. He walked unseeingly to the exit, and made straight for the bathroom.

5.8

L.N. Agarwal undid the drawstring of his pyjamas and stood at the urinal. But he was so angry that he was unable to urinate for a while.

He stared at the long, white-tiled wall and saw in it an image of the packed chamber, the taunting face of Begum Abida Khan, the furrowed academic expression of Abdus Salaam, Mahesh Kapoor's uninterpretable frown, the patient but condescending look on the face of the Chief Minister as he had fumbled pathetically through the poisonous swamp of Question Time.

There was no one in the lavatory except a couple of sweepers, and they were talking to each other. A few words of their conversation broke in upon L.N. Agarwal's fury. They were complaining about the difficulties of obtaining grain even at the government ration shops. They talked casually, not paying any attention to the powerful Home Minister and very little attention to their own work. As they continued to talk, a feeling of unreality descended upon L.N. Agarwal. He was taken out of his own world, his own passions, ambitions, hatreds and ideals into a realization of the continuing and urgent lives of people other than himself. He even felt a little ashamed of himself.

The sweepers were now discussing a movie that one of them had seen. It happened to be *Deedar.*

'But it was Daleep Kumar's role—oh—it brought tears to my eyes—he always has that quiet smile on his lips even when singing the saddest songs—such a good-natured man—blind himself, and yet giving pleasure to the whole world—'

He began humming one of the hit songs from the movie—'Do not forget the days of childhood. . . .'

The second man, who had not seen the movie yet, joined in the song—which, ever since the film had been released, was on almost everyone's lips.

He now said: 'Nargis looked so beautiful on the poster I thought I would see the movie last night, but my wife takes my money from me as soon as I get my pay.'

The first man laughed. 'If she let you keep the money, all she would see of it would be empty envelopes and empty bottles.'

The second man continued wistfully, trying to conjure up the divine images of his heroine. 'So, tell me, what was she like? How did she act? What a contrast—that cheap dancing girl Nimmi or Pimmi or whatever her name is—and Nargis—so high-class, so delicate.'

The first man grunted. 'Give me Nimmi any day, I'd rather live with her than with Nargis—Nargis is too thin, too full of herself. Anyway, what's the difference in class between them? She was also one of those.'

The second man looked shocked. 'Nargis?'

'Yes, yes, your Nargis. How do you think she got her first chance in the movies?' And he laughed and began to hum to himself again. The other man was silent and began to scrub the floor once more.

L.N. Agarwal's thoughts, as he listened to the sweepers talking, turned from Nargis to another 'one of those'—Saeeda Bai—and to the now commonplace gossip about her relationship with Mahesh Kapoor's son. Good! he thought. Mahesh Kapoor may starch his delicately embroidered kurtas into rigidity, but his son lies at the feet of prostitutes.

Though less possessed by rage, he had once again entered his own familiar world of politics and rivalry. He walked along the curved corridor that led to his room. He knew, however, that as soon as he entered his office, he would be set upon by his anxious supporters. What little calm he had achieved in the last few minutes would be destroyed.

'No—I'll go to the library instead,' he muttered to himself.

Upstairs, in the cool, quiet precincts of the library of the Legislative Assembly, he sat down, took off his cap, and rested his chin on his hands. A couple of other MLAs were sitting and reading at the long wooden tables. They looked up, greeted him, and continued with their work. L.N. Agarwal closed his eyes and tried to make his mind blank. He needed to establish his equanimity again before he faced the legislators below. But the image that came before him was not the blank nothingness he sought, but the spurious blankness of the urinal wall. His thoughts turned to the virulent Begum Abida Khan once more, and once more he had to fight down his rage and humiliation. How little there was in common between this shameless, exhibitionistic woman who smoked in private and screeched in public, who had not even followed her husband when he had left for Pakistan but had immodestly and spouselessly remained in Purva Pradesh to make trouble—and his own late wife, Priya's mother, who had sweetened his life through her years of selfless care and love.

I wonder if some part of Baitar House could be construed as evacuee property now that that woman's husband is living in Pakistan, thought L.N. Agarwal. A word to the Custodian, an order to the police, and let's see what I am able to do.

After ten minutes of thought, he got up, nodded at the two MLAs, and went downstairs to his room.

A few MLAs were already sitting in his room when he arrived, and several more gathered in the next few minutes as they came to know that he was holding court. Imperturbable, even smiling slightly to himself, L.N. Agarwal now held forth as he was accustomed to doing. He calmed down his agitated followers, he placed matters in perspective, he mapped out strategy. To one of the MLAs, who had commiserated with his leader because the twin misfortunes of Misri Mandi and Chowk had fallen simultaneously upon him, L.N. Agarwal replied:

'You are a case in point that a good man will not make a good politician. Just think—if you had to do a number of outrageous things, would you want the public to forget them or remember them?'

Clearly the answer was intended to be 'Forget them,' and this was the MLA's response.

'As quickly as possible?' asked L.N. Agarwal.

'As quickly as possible, Minister Sahib.'

'Then the answer,' said L.N. Agarwal, 'if you have a number of outrageous things to do is to do them simultaneously. People will scatter their complaints, not concentrate them. When the dust settles, at least two or three out of five battles will be yours. And the public has a short memory. As for the firing in Chowk, and those dead rioters, it will all be stale news in a week.'

The MLA looked doubtful, but nodded in agreement.

'A lesson here and there,' went on L.N. Agarwal, 'never did anyone any harm. Either you rule, or you don't. The British knew that they had to make an example sometimes—that's why they blew the mutineers from cannons in 1857. Anyway, people are always dying—and I would prefer death by a bullet to death by starvation.'

Needless to say, this was not a choice that faced him. But he was in a philosophical mood.

'Our problems are very simple, you know. In fact, they all boil down to two things: lack of food and lack of morality. And the policies of our rulers in Delhi—what shall I say?—don't help much either.'

'Now that Sardar Patel is dead, no one can control Panditji,' remarked one young but very conservative MLA.

'Even before Patel died who would Nehru listen to?' said L.N. Agarwal dismissively. 'Except, of course, his great Muslim friend—Maulana Azad.'

He clutched his arc of grey hair, then turned to his personal assistant. 'Get me the Custodian on the phone.'

'Custodian—of Enemy Property, Sir?' asked the PA.

Very calmly and slowly and looking him full in the face, the Home Minister said to his rather scatterbrained PA: 'There is no war on. Use what intelligence God has given you. I would like to talk to the Custodian of Evacuee Property. I will talk to him in fifteen minutes.'

After a while he continued: 'Look at our situation today. We beg America for food, we have to buy whatever we can get from China and Russia, there's virtual famine in our neighbouring state. Last year landless labourers were selling themselves for five rupees each. And instead of giving the farmers and the traders a free hand so that they can produce more and store things better and distribute them efficiently, Delhi forces us to impose price controls and government godowns and rationing and every populist and unthought-out measure possible. It isn't just their hearts that are soft, it is their brains as well.'

'Panditji means well,' said someone.

'Means well—means well—' sighed L.N. Agarwal. 'He meant well when he gave away Pakistan. He meant well when he gave away half of Kashmir. If it hadn't been for Patel, we wouldn't even have the country that we do. Jawaharlal Nehru has built up his entire career by meaning well. Gandhiji loved him because he meant well. And the poor, stupid people love him because he means well. God save us from people who mean well. And these well-meaning letters he writes every month to the Chief Ministers. Why does he bother to write them? The Chief Ministers are not delighted to read them.' He shook his head, and continued: 'Do you know what they contain? Long homilies about Korea and the dismissal of General MacArthur. What is General MacArthur to us?—yet so noble and sensitive is our Prime Minister that he considers all the ills of the world to be his own. He means well about Nepal and Egypt and God knows what else, and expects us to mean well too. He doesn't have the least idea of administration but he talks about the kind of food committees we should set up. Nor does he understand our society and our scriptures, yet he wants to overturn our family life and our family morals through his wonderful Hindu Code Bill. . . .'

L.N. Agarwal would have gone on with his own homily for quite a while if his PA had not said, 'Sir, the Custodian is on the line.'

'All right then,' said L.N. Agarwal, with a slight wave of his hand, which the others knew was a signal to withdraw. 'I'll see you all in the canteen.'

Left alone, the Home Minister talked for ten minutes to the Custodian of Evacuee Property. The discussion was precise and cold. For another few minutes the Home Minister sat at his desk, wondering if he had left any aspect of the matter ambiguous or vulnerable. He came to the conclusion that he had not.

He then got up, and walked rather wearily to the Assembly canteen. In the old days his wife used to send him a tiffin-carrier containing his simple food prepared exactly the way he liked it. Now he was at the mercy of indifferent cooks and their institutional cooking. There was a limit even to asceticism.

As he walked along the curved corridor he was reminded of the presence of the central chamber that the corridors circumscribed—the huge, domed chamber whose height and majestic elegance made almost trivial the frenetic and partisan proceedings below. But his insight did not succeed, except momentarily, in detaching his mind from this morning's events and the bitterness that they had aroused in him, nor did it make him regret in the least what he had been planning and preparing a few minutes ago.

5.9

Though it had been less than five minutes since he had sent off the peon to fetch his Parliamentary Secretary, Mahesh Kapoor was waiting in the Legal Remembrancer's Office with great impatience. He was alone, as he had sent the regular occupants of the office scurrying about to get various papers and law-books.

'Ah, Huzoor has brought his presence to the Secretariat at last!' he said when he saw Abdus Salaam.

Abdus Salaam did a respectful—or was it ironical?—adaab, and asked what he could do.

'I'll come to that in a moment. The question is what you've done already.'

'Already?' Abdus Salaam was nonplussed.

'This morning. On the floor of the House. Making a kabab out of our honourable Home Minister.'

'I only asked—'

'I know what you only asked, Salaam,' said his Minister with a smile. 'I'm asking you why you asked it.'

'I was wondering why the police—'

'My good fool,' said Mahesh Kapoor fondly, 'don't you realize that Lakshmi Narayan Agarwal thinks I put you up to it?'

'You?'

'Yes, me!' Mahesh Kapoor was in good humour, thinking of this morning's proceedings and his rival's extreme discomfiture. 'It's exactly the kind of thing he would do—so he imagines the same of me. Tell me'—he went on—'did he go to the canteen for lunch?'

'Oh, yes.'

'And was the Chief Minister there? What did he have to say?'

'No, Sharma Sahib was not there.'

The image of S.S. Sharma eating lunch seated traditionally on the floor at home, his upper body bare except for his sacred thread, passed before Mahesh Kapoor's eyes.

'No, I suppose not,' he said with some regret. 'So, how did he appear?'

'You mean Agarwal Sahib? Quite well, I think. Quite composed.'

'Uff! You are a useless informant,' said Mahesh Kapoor impatiently. 'Anyway, I've been thinking a little about this. You had better mind what you say or you'll make things difficult for both Agarwal and myself. At least restrain yourself until the Zamindari Bill has passed. Everyone needs everyone's cooperation on that.'

'All right, Minister Sahib.'

'Speaking of which, why have these people not returned yet?' asked Mahesh Kapoor, looking around the Legal Remembrancer's Office. 'I sent them out an hour ago.' This was not quite true. 'Everyone is always late and no one values time in this country. That's our main problem. . . . Yes, what is it? Come in, come in,' he continued, hearing a light knock at the door.

It was a peon with his lunch, which he usually ate quite late.

Opening his tiffin-carrier, Mahesh Kapoor spared half a moment's thought for his wife, who, despite her own ailments, took such pains on his behalf. April in Brahmpur was almost unbearable for her because of her allergy to neem blossoms, and the problem had become increasingly acute over the years. Sometimes, when the neem trees were in flower, she was reduced to a breathlessness that superficially resembled Pran's asthma.

She was also very upset these days by her younger son's affair with Saeeda Bai. So far, Mahesh Kapoor himself had not taken the matter as seriously as he would have had he realized the extent of Maan's infatuation. He was far too busy with matters that affected the lives of millions to have much time to go into the more irksome regions of his own family life. Maan would have to be brought to heel sooner or later, he thought, but for the moment he had other work to attend to.

'Have some of this: I suppose I've dragged you away from your lunch,' said Mahesh Kapoor to his Parliamentary Secretary.

'No, thank you, Minister Sahib, I'd finished when you sent for me. So do you think that everything is going well with the bill?'

'Yes, basically—at least on the floor, wouldn't you say? Now that it has come back from the Legislative Council with only a few minor changes, it shouldn't be difficult to get it repassed in its amended form by the Legislative Assembly. Of course, nothing is certain.' Mahesh Kapoor looked into his tiffin-carrier. After a while he went on: 'Ah, good, cauliflower pickle. . . . What really concerns me is what is going to happen to the bill later, assuming that it passes.'

'Well, legal challenges should not be much of a problem,' said Abdus Salaam. 'It's been well drafted, and I think it should pass muster.'

'You think so, do you, Salaam? What did you think about the Bihar Zamindari Act being struck down by the Patna High Court?' demanded Mahesh Kapoor.

'I think people are more worried than they need to be, Minister Sahib. As you know, the Brahmpur High Court does not have to follow the Patna High Court. It is only bound by the judgements of the Supreme Court in Delhi.'

'That may be true in theory,' said Mahesh Kapoor, frowning. 'In practice, previous judgements set psychological precedents. We have got to find a way, even at this late stage in the passage of the bill, of amending it so that it will be less vulnerable to legal challenge—especially on this question of equal protection.'

There was a pause for a while. The Minister had high regard for his scholarly young colleague, but did not hold out much hope that he would come up with something brilliant at short notice. But he respected his experience in this particular area and knew that his brains were the best that he could pick.

'Something occurred to me a few days ago,' said Abdus Salaam after a minute. 'Let me think about it further, Minister Sahib. I might have a helpful idea or two.'

The Revenue Minister looked at his Parliamentary Secretary with what might almost have been an amused expression, and said:

'Give me a draft of your ideas by tonight.'

'By tonight?' Abdus Salaam looked astonished.

'Yes,' said Mahesh Kapoor. 'The bill is going through its second reading. If anything is to be done, it must be done now.'

'Well,' said Abdus Salaam with a dazed look on his face, 'I had better go off to the library at once.' At the door he turned around and said, 'Perhaps you could ask the Legal Remembrancer to send me a couple of people from his drafting cell later this afternoon. But won't you need me on the floor this afternoon while the bill is being discussed?'

'No, this is far more important,' replied the Minister, getting up to wash his hands. 'Besides, I think you've caused enough mischief for one day on the floor of the House.'

As he washed his hands, Mahesh Kapoor thought about his old friend, the Nawab of Baitar. He would be one of those most deeply affected by the passage of the Zamindari Abolition Bill. His lands around Baitar in Rudhia District, from which he probably derived two-thirds of his income, would, if the act went into effect, be vested in the state of Purva Pradesh. He would not receive much compensation. The tenants would have the right to purchase the land they tilled, and until they did so their rents would go not into the coffers of the Nawab Sahib but directly into those of the Revenue Department of the State Government. Mahesh Kapoor believed, however, that he was doing the right thing. Although his was an urban constituency, he had lived on his own farm in Rudhia District long enough to see the immiserating effects of the zamindari system on the countryside all around him. With his own eyes he had seen the lack of productivity and the consequent hunger, the absence of investment in land improvement, the worst forms of feudal arrogance and subservience, the arbitrary oppression of the weak and the miserable by the agents and musclemen of the typical landlord. If the lifestyle of a few good men like the Nawab Sahib had to be sacrificed for the greater good of millions of tenant farmers, it was a cost that had to be borne.

Having washed his hands, Mahesh Kapoor dried them carefully, left a note for the Legal Remembrancer, and walked over to the Legislative Building.

5.10

The ancestral Baitar House, where the Nawab Sahib and his sons lived, was one of the most handsome buildings in Brahmpur. A long, pale yellow facade, dark-green shutters, colonnades, high ceilings, tall mirrors, immensely heavy dark furniture, chandeliers, oil portraits of previous aristocratic denizens and framed photographs along the corridors commemorating the visits of various high British officials: most visitors to the huge house, surveying their surroundings, succumbed to a kind of gloomy awe—reinforced in recent days by the dusty and uncared-for appearance of those large sections of the mansion the former occupants of which had left for Pakistan.

Begum Abida Khan too used to live here once with her husband, the Nawab Sahib's younger brother. She spent years chafing in the women's quarters before she persuaded him to allow her more reasonable and direct access to the outside world. There she had proved to be more effective than him in social and political causes. With the coming of Partition, her husband—a firm supporter of that Partition—had realized how vulnerable his position was in Brahmpur and decided to leave. He went to Karachi at first. Then—partly because he was uncertain of the effect his settling in Pakistan might have on his Indian property and the fortunes of his wife, and partly because he was restless, and partly because he was religious—he went on to Iraq on a visit to the various holy shrines of the Shias, and decided to live there for a few years. Three years had passed since he had last returned to India, and no one knew what he planned to do. He and Abida were childless, so perhaps it did not greatly matter.

The entire question of property rights was unsettled. Baitar was not—like Marh—a princely state subject to primogeniture but a large zamindari estate whose territory lay squarely within British India and was subject to the Muslim personal law of inheritance. Division of the property upon death or dissolution of the family was possible, but for generations now there had been no effective division, and almost everyone had continued to live in the same rambling house in Brahmpur or at Baitar Fort in the countryside, if not amicably, at least not litigiously. And owing to the constant bustle, the visiting, the festivals, the celebrations, in both the men's and the women's quarters it had had a grand atmosphere of energy and life.

With Partition things had changed. The house was no longer the great community it had been. It had become, in many ways, lonely. Uncles and cousins had dispersed to Karachi or Lahore. Of the three brothers, one had died, one had gone away, and only that gentle widower, the Nawab Sahib, remained. He spent more and more of his time in his library reading Persian poetry or Roman history or whatever he felt inclined to on any particular day. He left most of the management of his country estate in Baitar—the source of most of his income—to his munshi. That crafty half-steward, half-clerk did not encourage him to spend much time going over his own zamindari affairs. For matters not related to his estate, the Nawab Sahib kept a private secretary.

With the death of his wife and his own increasing years the Nawab Sahib had become less sociable, more aware of the approach of death. He wanted to spend more time with his sons, but they were now in their twenties, and inclined to treat their father with affectionate distance. Firoz's law, Imtiaz's medicine, their own circle of young friends, their love affairs (of which he heard little) all drew them outside the orbit of Baitar House. And his dear daughter Zainab visited only rarely—once every few months—whenever her husband allowed her and the Nawab Sahib's two grandsons to come to Brahmpur.

Sometimes he even missed the lightning-like presence of Abida, a woman of whose immodesty and forwardness the Nawab Sahib instinctively disapproved. Begum Abida Khan, MLA, had refused to abide by the strictures of the zenana quarters and the constraints of a mansion, and was now living in a small house closer to the Legislative Assembly. She believed in being aggressive and if necessary immodest in fighting for causes she considered just or useful, and she looked upon the Nawab Sahib as utterly ineffectual. Indeed, she did not have a very high opinion of her own husband who had, as she thought, 'fled' Brahmpur at Partition in a state of panic and was now crawling around the Middle East in a state of religious dotage. Because her niece Zainab—of whom she was fond—was visiting, she did pay a visit to Baitar House, but the purdah she was expected to maintain irked her, and so did the inevitable criticism of her style of life that she faced from the old women of the zenana.

But who were these old women after all?—the repository of tradition and old affection and family history. Only two old aunts of the Nawab Sahib, and the widow of his other brother—no one else remained of that whole busy zenana. The only children in Baitar House were the two who were visiting, the six- and three-year-old grandchildren of the Nawab Sahib. They loved visiting Baitar House and Brahmpur because they found the huge old house exciting, because they could see mongooses sliding under the doors of locked and deserted rooms, because much was made of them by everyone from Firoz Mamu and Imtiaz Mamu to the 'old servitors' and the cooks. And because their mother seemed much happier here than at home.

*

The Nawab Sahib did not at all like to be disturbed when he was reading, but he made more than an exception for his grandsons. Hassan and Abbas were given a free run of the house. No matter what mood he was in, they lifted it; and even when he was sunk in the impersonal comfort of history, he was happy to be brought back to the present world, as long as it was personally through them. Like the rest of the house, the library too was running to seed. The magnificent collection, built up by his father and incorporating additions by the three brothers—each with his different tastes—was housed in an equally magnificent alcoved and high-windowed room. The Nawab Sahib, wearing a freshly starched kurta-pyjama—with a few small squarish holes in the kurta which looked a bit like moth-holes (but what moth would bite quite so squarely?)—was seated this morning at a round table in one of the alcoves, reading *The Marginal Notes of Lord Macaulay* selected by his nephew G.O. Trevelyan.

Macaulay's comments on Shakespeare, Plato and Cicero were as trenchant as they were discriminating, and the editor clearly believed that the marginalia of his distinguished uncle were well worth publishing. His own remarks were openly admiring: 'Even for Cicero's poetry Macaulay had enough respect to distinguish carefully between the bad and the less bad,' was one sentence that drew a mild smile from the Nawab Sahib.

But what, after all, thought the Nawab Sahib, is worth doing, and what is not? For people like me at least things are in decline, and I do not feel it worth my while consuming the rest of my life fighting politicians or tenants or silverfish or my son-in-law or Abida to preserve and maintain worlds that I find exhausting to preserve or maintain. Each of us lives in a small domain and returns to nothing. I suppose if I had a distinguished uncle I might spend a year or two collating and printing his marginal notes.

And he fell to musing about how Baitar House would eventually fall into ruin with the abolition of zamindari and the exhaustion of funds from the estate. Already it was becoming difficult, according to his munshi, to extract the standard rent from the tenants. They pleaded hard times, but underneath the pleas was the sense that the political equations of ownership and dependence were inexorably shifting. Among those who were most vocal against the Nawab Sahib were some whom he had treated with exceptional leniency, even generosity, in the past, and who found this difficult to forgive.

What would survive him? It occurred to him that although he had dabbled in Urdu poetry much of his life, he had never written a single poem, a single couplet, that would be remembered. Those who do not live in Brahmpur decry the poetry of Mast, he thought, but they can complete in their sleep many of the ghazals he has written. It struck him, with a start, that there had never been a truly scholarly edition of the poems of Mast, and he began to stare at the motes in the beam of sunlight that fell on his table.

Perhaps, he said to himself, this is the labour that I am best fitted for at this stage of things. At any rate, it is probably what I would most enjoy.

He read on, savouring the insight with which Macaulay unsparingly analysed the character of Cicero, a man taken over by the aristocracy into which he had been adopted, two-faced, eaten up by vanity and hatred, yet undoubtedly 'great'. The Nawab Sahib, who thought much of death these days, was startled by Macaulay's remark: 'I really think that he met with little more than his deserts from the Triumvirs.'

Despite the fact that the book had been dusted with a white preservative powder, a silverfish crawled out of the spine and scuttled across the band of sunlight on the round table. The Nawab Sahib looked at it for an instant, and wondered what had happened to the young man who had sounded so enthusiastic about taking charge of his library. He had said he would come over to Baitar House but that had been the last that the Nawab Sahib had heard of him—and it must have been at least a month ago. He shut the book and shook it, opened it again on a random page, and continued reading as if the new paragraph had led directly on from the previous one:

> The document which he most admired in the whole collection of the correspondence was Caesar's answer to Cicero's message of gratitude for the humanity which the conqueror had displayed towards those political adversaries who had fallen into his power at the surrender of Corfinium. It contained (so Macaulay used to say) the finest sentence ever written:
>
> 'I triumph and rejoice that my action should have obtained your approval; nor am I disturbed when I hear it said that those whom I have sent off alive and free will again bear arms against me; for there is nothing which I so much covet as that I should be like myself, and they like themselves.'

The Nawab Sahib read the sentence several times. He had once hired a Latin tutor but had not got very far. Now he attempted to fit the resonant phrases of the English to what must have been the still more resonant phrases of the original. He sat in a reverie for a good ten minutes meditating on the content and manner of the sentence, and would have continued to do so had he not felt a tug at the leg of his pyjamas.

5.11

It was his younger grandson, Abbas, who was tugging at him with both hands. The Nawab Sahib had not seen him come in, and looked at him with pleased surprise. A little behind Abbas stood his six-year-old brother Hassan. And behind Hassan stood the old servant, Ghulam Rusool.

The servant announced that lunch was waiting for the Nawab Sahib and his daughter in the small room adjoining the zenana quarters. He also apologized for allowing Hassan and Abbas into the library when the Nawab Sahib was reading. 'But Sahib, they insisted, and would not listen to reason.'

The Nawab Sahib nodded his approval and turned happily from Macaulay and Cicero to Hassan and Abbas.

'Are we eating on the floor or at the table today, Nana-jaan?' asked Hassan.

'It's just us—so we'll eat inside—on the rug,' replied his grandfather.

'Oh, good,' said Hassan, who got nervous when his feet were not on the ground.

'What's in that room, Nana-jaan?' asked three-year-old Abbas as they walked down a corridor past a room with a huge brass lock.

'Mongooses, of course,' said his elder brother knowledgeably.

'No, I mean inside the room,' Abbas insisted.

'I think we store some carpets in there,' said the Nawab Sahib. Turning to Ghulam Rusool, he asked: 'What do we store in there?'

'Sahib, they say it has been two years since that room was locked. It is all on a list with Murtaza Ali. I will ask him and inform you.'

'Oh no, that's not necessary,' said the Nawab Sahib stroking his beard and trying to recall—for, to his surprise, it had slipped his mind—who used to use that particular room. 'As long as it's on a list,' he said.

'Tell us a ghost story, Nana-jaan,' said Hassan, tugging at his grandfather's right hand.

'Yes, yes,' said Abbas, who readily agreed with most of his elder brother's suggestions, even when he did not understand what was being suggested. 'Tell us a ghost story.'

'No, no,' said the Nawab Sahib. 'All the ghost stories I know are very frightening and if I tell you one you'll be so frightened you won't be able to eat your lunch.'

'We won't be frightened,' said Hassan.

'Not frightened,' said Abbas.

They reached the small room where lunch was awaiting them. The Nawab Sahib smiled to see his daughter, and washed his and his grandsons' hands in a small washbasin with cool water from a nearby jug, and sat them down, each in front of a small thali into which food had already been served.

'Do you know what your two sons are demanding of me?' asked the Nawab Sahib.

Zainab turned to her children and scolded them.

'I told you not to disturb your Nana-jaan in the library, but the moment my back is turned you do what you like. Now what have you been asking for?'

'Nothing,' said Hassan, rather sullenly.

'Nothing,' repeated Abbas, sweetly.

Zainab looked at her father with affection and thought of the days when she used to cling on to his hands and make her own importunate demands, often using his indulgence to get around her mother's firmness. He was sitting on the rug in front of his silver thali with the same erect bearing that she remembered from her earliest childhood, but the thinness of the flesh on his cheekbones and the small square moth-holes on his immaculately starched kurta filled her with a sudden tenderness. It had been ten years since her mother had died—her own children only knew of her through photographs and stories—and those ten years of widowerhood had aged her father as twenty years would have done in the ordinary course of time.

'What are they asking for, Abba-jaan?' said Zainab with a smile.

'They want a ghost story,' said the Nawab Sahib. 'Just like you used to.'

'But I never asked for a ghost story at lunch,' said Zainab.

To her children she said, 'No ghost stories. Abbas, stop playing with your food. If you're very good maybe you'll get a story at night before you go to sleep.'

'No, now! Now—' said Hassan.

'Hassan,' said his mother warningly.

'Now! Now!' Hassan began crying and shouting.

The Nawab Sahib was quite distressed at his grandchildren's insubordination towards their mother, and told them not to speak in this way. Good children, he made it clear, didn't.

'I hope they listen to their father at least,' he said in mild rebuke.

To his horror he saw a tear roll down his daughter's cheek. He put his arm around her shoulder, and said, 'Is everything all right? Is everything all right there?'

It was the instinctive thing to say, but he realized as soon as he had said it that he should perhaps have waited until his grandchildren had finished their lunch and he was left alone with his daughter. He had heard indirectly that all was not well with his daughter's marriage.

'Yes, Abba-jaan. It's just that I think I'm a little tired.'

He kept his arm around her till her tears had ceased. The children looked bewildered. However, some of their favourite food had been prepared and they soon forgot about their mother's tears. Indeed, she too became involved in feeding them, especially the younger one, who was having trouble tearing the naan. Even the Nawab Sahib, looking at the picture the three of them made together, felt a little rush of painful happiness. Zainab was small, like her mother had been, and many of the gestures of affection or reproof that she made reminded him of those that his wife used to make when trying to get Firoz and Imtiaz to eat their food.

As if in response to his thoughts, Firoz now entered the room. Zainab and the children were delighted to see him.

'Firoz Mamu, Firoz Mamu!' said the children. 'Why didn't you have lunch with us?'

Firoz looked impatient and troubled. He placed his hand on Hassan's head.

'Abba-jaan, your munshi has arrived from Baitar. He wants to talk to you,' he said.

'Oh,' said the Nawab Sahib, not happy about this demand on his time when he would rather have been talking to his daughter.

'He wants you to come to the estate today. There is some crisis or other brewing.'

'What manner of crisis?' asked the Nawab Sahib. He did not relish the thought of a three-hour drive in a jeep in the April sun.

'You'd better speak to him,' said Firoz. 'You know how I feel about your munshi. If you think that I should come with you to Baitar, or go instead of you, that's all right. I don't have anything on this afternoon. Oh yes, I do have a meeting with a client, but his case isn't due to come up for a while, so I can postpone it.'

The Nawab Sahib got up with a sigh and washed his hands.

When he got to the anteroom where the munshi was waiting, he asked him brusquely what the matter was. Apparently, there were two problems, both brewing simultaneously. The main one was the perennial difficulty of realizing land-rent from the peasants. The Nawab Sahib did not like the strong-arm methods that the munshi was inclined to employ: the use of local toughs to deal with defaulters. As a result, collections had diminished, and the munshi now felt that the Nawab Sahib's personal presence at Baitar Fort for a day or two and a private talk with a couple of local politicians would help matters considerably. Normally, the sly munshi would have been unwilling to involve his master in the stewardship of his own estate, but this was an exception. He had even brought along a small local landlord to confirm that matters were troubled and required the Nawab Sahib's presence in the area immediately, not only on his own behalf but also because it would help the other landlords.

After a brief discussion (the other problem involved trouble at the local madrasa or school), the Nawab Sahib said: 'I have some things to do this afternoon. But I'll talk matters over with my son. Please wait here.'

Firoz said that on the whole he felt his father should go, if only to make sure that the munshi was not robbing him blind. He would come along as well and look at the accounts. They might well have to spend a night or two in Baitar, and he did not want his father to be by himself. As for Zainab, whom the Nawab Sahib was reluctant to leave 'alone in the house' as he put it, she was matter-of-fact about his departure, though sorry to see him go.

'But Abba-jaan, you'll be back tomorrow or the day after and I'm here for another week. Anyway, isn't Imtiaz due to return tomorrow? And please don't worry about me, I've lived in this house most of my life.' She smiled. 'Just because I'm now a married woman doesn't mean that I am less capable of taking care of myself. I'll spend my time gossiping in the zenana, and I'll even take over your duty of telling the children a ghost story.'

Though somewhat apprehensive—about what exactly he would not have been able to say—the Nawab Sahib acquiesced in what was obviously sound advice and, taking affectionate leave of his daughter and only forbearing from kissing his grandchildren because they were having an afternoon nap, left Brahmpur for Baitar within the hour.

5.12

Evening came. Baitar House wore a deserted look. Half the house was unoccupied anyway, and servants no longer moved through the rooms at dusk, lighting candles or lamps or turning on electric lights. On this particular evening even the rooms of the Nawab Sahib and his sons and the occasionally occupied guest room were unlit, and from the road it would almost have seemed that no one lived there any longer. The only activity, conversation, bustle, movement took place in the zenana quarters, which did not face the road.

It was not yet dark. The children were asleep. It had been less difficult than Zainab had thought to distract them from the fact that their grandfather was not there to tell them the promised ghost story. Both of them were tired out from their previous day's journey to Brahmpur, although they had insisted the previous night on remaining awake till ten.

Zainab would have liked to settle down with a book, but decided to spend the evening talking to her aunt and great-aunts. These women, whom she had known from childhood, had spent their entire lives since the age of fifteen in purdah—either in their father's or in their husband's house. So had Zainab, although she considered herself, by virtue of her education, to have a wider sense of the world. The constraints of the zenana, the women's world that had driven Abida Khan almost crazy—the narrow circle of conversation, the religiosity, the halter on boldness or unorthodoxy of any kind—were seen by these women in an entirely different light. Their world was not busy with great concerns of state, but was essentially a human one. Food, festivals, family relations, objects of use and beauty, these—mainly for good but sometimes for ill—formed the basis, though not the entirety, of their interests. It was not as if they were ignorant of the great world outside. It was rather that the world was seen more heavily filtered through the interests of family and friends than it would be for a sojourner with more direct experience. The clues they received were more indirect, needing more sensitive interpretation; and so were those they gave out. For Zainab—who saw elegance, subtlety, etiquette and family culture as qualities to be prized in their own right—the world of the zenana was a complete world, even if a constrained one. She did not believe that because her aunts had met no men other than those of the family since they were young, and had been to very few rooms other than their own, they were as a result lacking in perspicacity about the world or understanding of human nature. She liked them, she enjoyed talking to them, and she knew what enjoyment they obtained from her occasional visits. But she was reluctant to sit and gossip with them on this particular visit to her father's house only because they would almost certainly touch upon matters that would hurt her. Any mention of her husband would remind her once again of the infidelities that she had only recently come to know of, and that caused her such startling anguish. She would have to pretend to her aunts that all was well with her, and even indulge in light banter about the intimacies of her family life.

They had been sitting and talking for only a few minutes when two panic-stricken young maidservants rushed into the room and, without making even the usual salutation, gasped out:

'The police—the police are here.'

They then burst into tears and became so incoherent that it was impossible to get any sense out of them.

Zainab managed to calm one of them down a little, and asked her what the police were doing.

'They have come to take over the house,' said the girl with a fresh bout of sobbing.

Everyone looked aghast at the wretched girl, who was wiping her eyes with her sleeve.

'Hai, hai!' cried an aunt in pitiable distress, and began weeping. 'What will we do? There is no one in the house.'

Zainab, though shocked at the sudden turn of events, thought of what her mother would have done if there had been no one—that is, no men—in the house.

After she had partially recovered from the shock, she shot a few quick questions at the maidservant:

'Where are they—the police? Are they actually in the house? What are the servants doing? And where is Murtaza Ali? Why do they want to take over the house? Munni, sit up and don't sob. I can't make any sense out of what you are saying.' She shook and consoled the girl alternately.

All that Zainab could ascertain was that young Murtaza Ali, her father's personal secretary, was standing at the far end of the lawn in front of Baitar House desperately trying to dissuade the police from carrying out their orders. The maidservant was particularly terrified because the group of policemen was headed by a Sikh officer.

'Munni, listen,' said Zainab. 'I want to talk to Murtaza.'

'But—'

'Now go and tell Ghulam Rusool or some other manservant to tell Murtaza Ali that I want to talk to him immediately.'

Her aunts stared at her, appalled.

'And, yes, take this note to Rusool to give to the Inspector or whoever it is who is in charge of the police. Make sure that it gets to him.'

Zainab wrote a short note in English as follows:

> Dear Inspector Sahib,
>
> My father, the Nawab of Baitar, is not at home, and since no legitimate action should be taken without intimating him first, I must ask you not to proceed further in this matter. I would like to speak to Mr Murtaza Ali, my father's personal secretary, immediately, and request you to make him available. I would also ask you to note that this is the hour of evening prayer, and that any incursion into our ancestral house at a time when the occupants are at prayer will be deeply injurious to all people of good faith.
>
> Sincerely,
> Zainab Khan

Munni took the note and left the room, still snivelling but no longer panic-stricken. Zainab avoided her aunts' glances, and told the other girl, who had calmed down a little as well, to make sure that Hassan and Abbas had not been woken up by the commotion.

5.13

When the Deputy Superintendent of Police who was in charge of the contingent that had come to take over Baitar House read the note, he flushed red, shrugged his shoulders, had a few words with the Nawab Sahib's private secretary, and—quickly glancing at his watch—said:

'All right, then, half an hour.'

His duty was clear and there was no getting around it, but he believed in firmness rather than brutality, and half an hour's delay was acceptable.

Zainab had got the two young maidservants to open the doorway that led from the zenana to the mardana, and to stretch a sheet across it. Then, despite the unbelieving 'toba's' and other pious exclamations of her aunts, she told Munni to tell a manservant to tell Murtaza Ali to stand on the other side of it. The young man, crimson-faced with embarrassment and shame, stood close by the door which he had never imagined he would ever even approach in his lifetime.

'Murtaza Sahib, I must apologize for your embarrassment—and my own,' said Zainab softly in elegant and unornate Urdu. 'I know you are a modest man and I understand your qualms. Please forgive me. I too feel I have been driven to this recourse. But this is an emergency, and I know that it will not be taken amiss.'

She unconsciously used the first person plural rather than the singular that she was used to. Both were colloquially acceptable, but since the plural was invariant with respect to gender, it defused to some small extent the tension across the geographical line that lay between the mardana and zenana quarters, the breach of which had so shocked her aunts. Besides, there was implicit in the plural a mild sense of command, and this helped set a tone that enabled the exchange not merely of embarrassment—which was unavoidable—but of information as well.

In equally cultured but slightly ornate Urdu young Murtaza Ali replied: 'There is nothing to forgive, believe me, Begum Sahiba. I am only sorry that I was fated to be the messenger of such news.'

'Then let me ask you to tell me as briefly as you can what has happened. What are the police doing here in my father's house? And is it true that they wish to take over this house? On what grounds?'

'Begum Sahiba, I don't know where to begin. They are here, and they intend to take over this house as soon as they can. They were going to enter immediately but the DSP read your note and granted us half an hour's grace. He has an order from the Custodian of Evacuee Property and the Home Minister to take possession of all parts of the house that are not inhabited, in view of the fact that most of the former residents have now established residence in Pakistan.'

'Does this include entering the zenana?' said Zainab as calmly as she could.

'I do not know what it includes, Begum Sahiba. He said "all unoccupied portions".'

'How does he know that so much of the house is unoccupied?' asked Zainab.

'I am afraid, Begum Sahiba, that it is obvious. Partly, of course, it is common knowledge. I tried to persuade him that people were living here, but he pointed to the dark windows. Even the Nawab Sahib is not here at the moment. Nor the Nawabzadas.'

Zainab was silent for a moment. Then she said, 'Murtaza Sahib, I am not going to give up in half an hour what has belonged to our family for generations. We must try to contact Abida Chachi immediately. Her property too is at stake. And Kapoor Sahib, the Revenue Minister, who is an old friend of the family. You will have to do this, as there is no telephone in the zenana.'

'I will do so at once. I pray that I will get through.'

'I am afraid that you will have to forgo your regular prayers this evening,' said Zainab with a smile that could be heard in her voice.

'I fear I will have to,' replied Murtaza Ali, surprised that he too could smile at such an unhappy moment. 'Perhaps I should go now and try to get through to the Revenue Minister.'

'Send the car for him—no, wait—' said Zainab. 'It may be needed. Make sure it is standing by.'

She thought for a minute. Murtaza Ali felt the seconds ticking away.

'Who has the keys to the house?' asked Zainab. 'I mean to the empty rooms?'

'The zenana keys are with—'

'No, those rooms can't be seen from the road—they aren't important—I mean the mardana rooms.'

'I have some of them, some of them are with Ghulam Rusool, and some, I believe, have been taken by the Nawab Sahib to Baitar with him.'

'Now this is what you must do,' said Zainab quietly. 'We have very little time. Get all the menservants and the maidservants in this house to bring candles, torches, lamps, any kind of flame that we have in the house, and to light up a little of every room in this house that faces the road—you understand—even if it means entering rooms that you normally need permission to enter, and even if it means breaking a lock or a door here or there.'

It was a measure of Murtaza Ali's mind that he did not expostulate, but simply accepted the good—if desperate—sense of this measure.

'It must look from the road that the house is inhabited, even if the DSP has reason to believe it is not. He must be given an excuse to withdraw if he is inclined to, even if we do not actually make him believe it.'

'Yes, Begum Sahiba.' Murtaza was filled with admiration for this woman with the gentle voice whom he had never seen—nor ever would.

'I know this house like the back of my hand,' continued Zainab. 'I was born here, unlike my aunts. Even though now I am confined to this section, I am familiar with the other section from my childhood, and I know it has not changed much in structure. We are very short of time, and I plan to help personally in lighting the rooms. I know my father will understand, and it does not matter much to me if no one else does.'

'I beg you, Begum Sahiba,' said her father's private secretary, pain and dismay audible in his voice, 'I beg you do not do so. Arrange things in the zenana and get as many lamps and so on ready as you can so that they can be passed on to us on this side. But please stay where you are. I will see that everything is performed as you command. Now I must go, and I will send word within fifteen minutes about how things are going. God keep your family and this house in his protection.' With this he took his leave.

Zainab kept Munni with her, and told the other girl to help fetch and light the lamps, and take them across to the other side of the house. She then went back to her room and looked at Hassan and Abbas, who were still sleeping. It is your history, your inheritance, your world too that I am protecting, she thought, passing a hand through the younger one's hair. Hassan, usually so sullen, was smiling, and he had his arms wrapped around his younger brother. Her aunts were praying aloud in the next room.

Zainab closed her eyes, said the fatiha, and sat down exhausted. Then she remembered something her father had once said to her, reflected on its importance for a few seconds, and began to draft another letter.

She told Munni to wake up the boys and quickly dress them in their formal best—a small white kurta for Abbas, and a white angarkha for his elder brother. On their heads they were to wear white embroidered caps.

When, fifteen minutes later, Zainab had not heard from Murtaza Ali, she sent for him. On his arrival she asked him:

'Is it done?'

'Yes, Begum Sahiba, it is. The house looks as if it is lit. There is some light visible from every outside window.'

'And Kapoor Sahib?'

'I am afraid that I have not been able to get him on the phone, though Mrs Mahesh Kapoor has sent for him. He may be working late somewhere in the Secretariat. But no one is picking up the phone in his office.'

'Abida Chachi?'

'Her telephone appears to be out of order, and I have only just written her a note. Forgive me. I have been remiss.'

'Murtaza Sahib, you have already done far more than seemed possible to me. Now listen to this letter, and tell me how it can be improved.'

Very swiftly they went through the brief draft of the letter. It was in English, only seven or eight lines long. Murtaza Ali asked for a couple of explanations, and made a couple of suggestions; Zainab incorporated them and made a fair copy.

'Now, Hassan and Abbas,' she said to her sons, their eyes still full of sleep and wonderment at this unexpected game, 'you are to go with Murtaza Sahib and do everything he tells you to do. Your Nana-jaan will be very pleased with you when he comes back, and so will I. And so will Imtiaz Mamu and Firoz Mamu.' She gave each of them a kiss, and sent them to the other side of the screen, where Murtaza Ali took charge of them.

'They should be the ones to give him the letter,' said Zainab. 'Take the car, tell the Inspector—I mean the DSP—where you are going, and go at once. I do not know how to thank you for your help. If you had not been here we would certainly have been lost already.'

'I cannot repay your father's kindness, Begum Sahiba,' said Murtaza Ali. 'I will make sure that your sons come back within the hour.'

He walked down the corridor with a boy clutching each hand. He was too full of trepidation to say anything at first to either, but after he had walked for a minute towards the far end of the lawn where the police were standing, he said to the boys:

'Hassan, Abbas, do adaab to the DSP Sahib.'

'Adaab arz, DSP Sahib,' said Hassan in salutation.

Abbas looked up at his brother and repeated his words, except that his came out as 'Dipsy Sahib'.

'The Nawab Sahib's grandsons,' explained the private secretary.

The Deputy Superintendent of Police smiled warily.

'I am sorry,' he said to Murtaza Ali. 'My time is up and so is yours. The house may look as if it is lived in, but our information tells us otherwise, and we will have to investigate. We must do our duty. The Home Minister himself has instructed us.'

'I quite understand, DSP Sahib,' said Murtaza Ali. 'But may I beg you for a little more time? These two boys are carrying a letter which must be delivered before any action can be taken.'

The DSP shook his head. He held up his hand to indicate that enough was enough, and said: 'Agarwalji has told me personally that he will not entertain any petitions in this respect and that we are not to brook any delay. I am sorry. The decision can always be challenged or appealed later.'

'This letter is for the Chief Minister.'

The policeman stiffened slightly.

'What does this mean?' he said in a voice that was both irritated and bewildered. 'What does the letter say? What do you hope to achieve by this?'

Murtaza Ali said gravely:

'I cannot be expected to know the contents of a private and urgent letter between the daughter of the Nawab Sahib of Baitar and the Chief Minister of Purva Pradesh. Clearly it touches on this matter of the house, but about what it says it would be impertinent of me to speculate. The car, however, is ready, and I must escort these little messengers to Sharmaji's house before they lose their own. DSP Sahib, I hope you will wait for my return before you do anything sudden.'

The DSP, foiled for the moment, said nothing. He knew he would have to wait.

Murtaza Ali took his leave, gathered his charges and drove off in the Nawab Sahib's car.

Fifty yards outside the gates of Baitar House, however, the car came to a sudden halt and could not be restarted. Murtaza Ali told the driver to wait, walked back to the house with Abbas, deposited him with a servant, got out his bicycle and returned. He then propped a surprisingly unprotesting Hassan in front of him, and cycled off with him into the night.

5.14

When they got to the Chief Minister's house fifteen minutes later, they were immediately admitted to his office, where he was working late.

After the usual salutations, they were asked to sit down. Murtaza Ali was sweating—he had been bicycling as fast as he could, considering the safety of his cargo. But Hassan looked cool and crisp in his fine white angarkha, if a little sleepy.

'Now to what do I owe this pleasure?'

The Chief Minister looked from the six-year-old boy to the Nawab Sahib's thirty-year-old secretary while nodding his head slightly from side to side as he sometimes did when tired.

Murtaza Ali had never met the Chief Minister in person. Since he had no idea how best to approach the matter, he simply said: 'Chief Minister Sahib, this letter will tell you everything.'

The Chief Minister looked over the letter only once, but slowly. Then in an angry and determined voice, nasal but with the unmistakable ring of authority, he said:

'Get me Agarwal on the phone!'

While the call was being connected, the Chief Minister ticked off Murtaza Ali for having brought the 'poor boy' with him so long past his bedtime. But it had clearly had an effect on his feelings. He would probably have had harsher things to say, reflected Murtaza Ali, if I had brought Abbas along as well.

When the call came through, the Chief Minister had a few words with the Home Minister. There was no mistaking the annoyance in his voice.

'Agarwal, what does this Baitar House business mean?' asked the Chief Minister.

After a minute he said: 'No, I am not interested in all that. I have a good understanding of what the Custodian's job is. I cannot have this sort of thing going on under my nose. Call it off at once.'

A few seconds later he said, even more exasperatedly:

'No. It will not be sorted out in the morning. Tell the police to leave immediately. If you have to, put my signature on it.' He was about to put down the receiver when he added: 'And call me in half an hour.'

After the Chief Minister had put the phone down, he glanced at Zainab's letter again. Then he turned to Hassan and said, shaking his head a little:

'Go home now, things will be all right.'

5.15

Begum Abida Khan (*Democratic Party*): I do not understand what the honourable member is saying. Is he claiming that we should take the government's word on this as on other matters? Does the honourable member not know what happened just the other day in this city—in Baitar House to be precise—where on the orders of this government, a gang of policemen, armed to the teeth, would have set upon the helpless members of an unprotected zenana—and, if it had not been for the grace of God—

The Hon'ble the Speaker: The honourable member is reminded that this is not germane to the Zamindari Bill that is being discussed. I must remind her of the rules of debate and ask her to refrain from introducing extraneous matter into her speeches.

Begum Abida Khan: I am deeply grateful to the honourable Speaker. This House has its own rules, but God too judges us from above and if I may say so without disrespect to this House, God too has His own rules and we will see which prevails. How can zamindars expect justice from this government in the countryside where redress is so distant when even in this city, in the sight of this honourable House, the honour of other honourable houses is being ravished?

The Hon'ble the Speaker: I will not remind the honourable member again. If there are further digressions in this vein I will ask her to resume her seat.

Begum Abida Khan: The honourable Speaker has been very indulgent with me, and I have no intention of troubling this House further with my feeble voice. But I will say that the entire conduct, the entire manner in which this bill has been created, amended, passed by the Upper House, brought down to this Lower House and amended drastically yet again by the government itself shows a lack of faith and a lack of responsibility, even integrity, with respect to its proclaimed original intent, and the people of this state will not forgive the government for this. They have used their brute majority to force through amendments which are patently mala fide. What we saw when the bill—as amended by the Legislative Council—was undergoing its second reading in this Legislative Assembly was something so shocking that even I—who have lived through many shocking events in my life—was appalled. It had been agreed that compensation was to be paid to landlords. Since they are going to be deprived of their ancestral means of livelihood, that is the least that we can expect in justice. But the amount that is being paid is a pittance—half of which we are expected, indeed enjoined, to accept in government bonds of uncertain date!

A member: You need not accept it. The treasury will be happy to keep it warm for you.

Begum Abida Khan: And even that bond-weakened pittance is on a graduated scale so that the larger landlords—many of whom have establishments on which hundreds of people depend—managers, relatives, retainers, musicians—

A member: Wrestlers, bullies, courtesans, wastrels—

Begum Abida Khan: —will not be paid in proportion to the land that is rightfully theirs. What will these poor people do? Where will they go? The Government does not care. It thinks that this bill will be popular with the people and it has an eye on the General Elections that will be taking place in just a few months. That is the truth of the matter. That is the real truth and I do not accept any denials from the Minister of Revenue or his Parliamentary Secretary or the Chief Minister or anyone. They were afraid that the High Court of Brahmpur would strike down their graduated scale of payment. So what did they do at a late stage of the proceedings yesterday—at the very end of the second reading? Something that was so deceitful, so shameful, yet so transparent, that even a child would be able to see through it. They split up the compensation into two parts—a non-graduated so-called compensation—and a graduated so-called Rehabilitation Grant for zamindars—and passed an amendment late in the day to validate this new scheme of payment. Do they really think the court will accept that the compensation is 'equal treatment' for all—when by mere jugglery the Revenue Minister and his Parliamentary Secretary have transferred three-quarters of the compensation money into another category with a long and pious name—a category where there is blatantly unequal treatment of the larger landlords? You may be assured that we will fight this injustice while there is breath in our bodies—

A member: Or voice in our lungs.

The Hon'ble the Speaker: I would request members not to interrupt needlessly the speeches of other members.

Begum Abida Khan: But what is the use of my raising my voice for justice in a House where all we meet with is mockery and boorishness? We are called degenerates and wastrels but it is the sons of Ministers, believe me, who are the true proficients of dissipation. The class of people who preserved the culture, the music, the etiquette of this province is to be dispossessed, is to be driven through the lanes to beg its bread. But we will bear our vicissitudes with the dignity that is the inheritance of the aristocracy. This chamber may rubber-stamp this bill. The Upper Chamber may give it another cursory reading and rubber-stamp it. The President may sign it blindly. But the courts will vindicate us. As in our fellow-state of Bihar, this pernicious legislation will be struck down. And we will fight for justice, yes, before the bench and in the press and at the hustings—as long as there is breath in our bodies—and, yes, as long as there is voice in our lungs.

Shri Devakinandan Rai (Socialist Party): It has been very enlightening to be lectured to by the honourable member. I must confess that I see no likelihood of her begging for her bread through the lanes of Brahmpur. Perhaps for cake, but I doubt that too. If I had my way she would not beg for her bread, but she and those of her class would certainly have to work for it. This is what simple justice requires, and this is what is required also for the economic health of this province. I, and the members of the Socialist Party, agree with the honourable member who has just spoken that this bill is an election gimmick by the Congress Party and the government. But our belief is based on the grounds that this is a toothless bill, ineffectual and compromised. It does not go anywhere near what is needed for a thorough overhaul of agricultural relations in this province.

Compensation for the landlords! What? Compensation for the blood that they have already sucked from the limbs of a helpless and oppressed peasantry? Or compensation for their God-given right—I notice that the honourable member is in the habit of invoking God whenever His assistance is required to strengthen her weak arguments—their God-given right to continue to gorge themselves and their useless train of unemployed relations on the ghee of this state when the poor farmer, the poor tenant, the poor landless labourer, the poor worker can hardly afford half a sip of milk for his hungry children? Why is the treasury being depleted? Why are we writing ourselves and our children into debt with these promised bonds when this idle and vicious class of zamindars and taluqdars and landlords of all kinds should be summarily dispossessed—without any thought of compensation—of the lands that they are sitting on and have been sitting on for generations for the sole reason that they betrayed their country at the time of the Mutiny and were richly rewarded for their treason by the British? Is it just, Sir—is it reasonable that they should be awarded this compensation? The money that this government in its culpable so-called generosity is pouring into the laps of these hereditary oppressors should go into roads and schools, into housing for the landless and land reclamation, into clinics and agricultural research centres, not into the luxurious expenditure which is all that the aristocracy is accustomed to or capable of.

Mirza Amanat Hussain Khan (Democratic Party): I rise to a point of order, Sir. Is the honourable member to be permitted to wander off the subject and take up the time of the House with irrelevancies?

The Hon'ble the Speaker: I think he is not irrelevant. He is speaking on the general question of the relations between the tenants, the zamindars, and the government. That question is more or less before us and any remark which the honourable member now offers on that point is not irrelevant. You may like it or not, I may like it or not, but it is not out of order.

Shri Devakinandan Rai: I thank you, Sir. There stands the naked peasant in the hot sun, and here we sit in our cool debating rooms and discuss points of order and definitions of relevancy and make laws that leave him no better than before, that deprive him of hope, that take the part of the capitalist, oppressing, exploiting class. Why must the peasant pay for the land that is his by right, by right of effort, by right of pain, by right of nature, by right, if you will, of God? The only reason why we expect the peasant to pay this huge and unseemly purchase price to the treasury is in order to finance the landlord's exorbitant compensation. End the compensation, and there will be no need for a purchase price. Refuse to accept the notion of a purchase price, and any compensation becomes financially impossible. I have been arguing this point since the inception of the bill two years ago, and throughout the second reading last week. But at this stage of the proceedings what can I do? It is too late. What can I do but say to the treasury benches: you have set up an unholy alliance with the landlords and you are attempting to break the spirit of our people. But we will see what happens when the people realize how they have been cheated. The General Elections will throw out this cowardly and compromised government and replace it with a government worthy of the name: one that springs from the people, that works for the people and gives no support to its class enemies.

5.16

The Nawab Sahib had entered the House during the earlier part of this last speech. He was sitting in the Visitors' Gallery, although, had he wished to, he would have been welcome in the Governor's Gallery. He had returned from Baitar the previous day in response to an urgent message from Brahmpur. He was shocked and embittered by what had happened and horrified that his daughter had had to face such a situation virtually on her own. His concern for her had been so much more patent than his pride in what she had done that Zainab had not been able to help smiling. For a long time he had hugged her and his two grandchildren with tears running down his cheeks. Hassan had been puzzled, but little Abbas had accepted this as a natural state of affairs and had enjoyed it all—he could tell that his grandfather was not at all unhappy to see them. Firoz had been white with anger, and it had taken all of Imtiaz's good humour when he arrived late that afternoon, to calm the family down.

The Nawab Sahib was almost as angry with his hornet of a sister-in-law as with L.N. Agarwal. He knew that it was she who had brought this visitation upon their heads. Then, when the worst was over, she had made light of the police action and was almost cavalier in her assumption that Zainab would have handled things with such tactical courage. As for L.N. Agarwal, the Nawab Sahib looked down on to the floor of the House, and saw him talking very civilly with the Revenue Minister, who had wandered over to his desk and was conferring with him on some point, probably floor management with respect to the impending and critical vote later this afternoon.

The Nawab Sahib had not had the opportunity to talk to his friend Mahesh Kapoor since his return, nor to convey his heartfelt thanks to the Chief Minister. He thought that he would do so after today's session in the Assembly was over. But another reason why he was present in the House today was that he realized—as did many others, for the press and public galleries were all crowded—that it was a historic occasion. For him, and for those like him, the impending vote was one that would—unless halted by the courts—spell a swift and precipitous decline.

Well, he thought fatalistically, it has to happen sooner or later. He was under no illusions that his class was a particularly meritorious one. Those who constituted it included not only a small number of decent men but also a large number of brutes and an even larger number of idiots. He remembered a petition that the Zamindars' Association had submitted to the Governor twelve years ago: a good third of the signatories had used their thumb-prints.

Perhaps if Pakistan had not come into existence, the landowners would have been able to parlay their way into self-preservation: in a united but unstable India each power bloc might have been able to use its critical strength to maintain the status quo. The princely states, too, could have wielded their weight, and men such as the Raja of Marh might well have remained Rajas in fact as well as in name. The ifs and buts of history, thought the Nawab Sahib, form an insubstantial if intoxicating diet.

Since the annexation of Brahmpur by the British in the early 1850s the Nawabs of Baitar and other courtiers of the erstwhile royal house of Brahmpur had not even had the psychological satisfaction of serving the state, a satisfaction claimed by many aristocracies widely separated in space and time. The British had been happy to let the zamindars collect the revenue from land-rent (and were content in practice to allow them whatever they obtained in excess of the agreed British share) but for the administration of the state they had trusted no one but civil servants of their own race, selected in, partially trained in, and imported from England—or, later, brown equivalents so close in education and ethos as made no appreciable difference.

And indeed, apart from racial mistrust, there was, the Nawab Sahib was compelled to admit, the question of competence. Most zamindars—himself alas, perhaps included—could hardly administer even their own estates and were fleeced by their munshis and moneylenders. For most of the landlords the primary question of management was not indeed how to increase their income but how to spend it. Very few invested it in industry or urban property. Some, certainly, had spent it on music and books and the fine arts. Others, like the present Prime Minister of Pakistan, Liaquat Ali Khan, who had been a good friend of the Nawab Sahib's father, had spent it to build up influence in politics. But for the most part the princes and landlords had squandered their money on high living of one kind or another: on hunting or wine or women or opium. A couple of images flashed irresistibly and unwelcomely across his mind. One ruler had such a passion for dogs that his entire life revolved around them: he dreamed, slept, woke, imagined, fantasized about dogs; everything he could do was done to their greater glory. Another was an opium addict who was only content when a few women were thrown into his lap; even then, he was not always roused to action; sometimes he just snored on.

The Nawab of Baitar's thoughts continued to oscillate between the debate on the floor of the Assembly and his own meditations. At one point there was a brief intervention by L.N. Agarwal, who made a few amusing comments—at which even Mahesh Kapoor laughed. The Nawab Sahib stared at the bald head ringed with a horseshoe of grey hair and wondered at the thoughts that must be seething under that layer of flesh and bone. How could a man like this deliberately, indeed happily, cause so much misery to him and to those he held so dear? What satisfaction could it have given him that the relatives of someone who had worsted him in a debate would be dispossessed of the home in which they had spent the greater part of their lives?

It was now about half-past four, and there was less than half an hour before the division of votes. The final speeches were continuing and the Nawab Sahib listened with a somewhat wry expression as his sister-in-law circumscribed the institution of zamindari with a luminous purple halo.

Begum Abida Khan: For more than an hour we have been listening to speech after speech from the government benches, filled with the most odious self-congratulation. I did not think that I would wish to speak again, but I must do so now. I would have thought that it would be more appropriate to let those people speak whose death and burial you wish to preside over—I mean the zamindars, whom you wish to deprive of justice and redress and the means of livelihood. The same record has been going on and on for an hour—if it is not the Minister of Revenue it is some pawn of his who has been trained to sing the same song: His Master's Voice. I may tell you that the music is not very pleasant: it is monotonous without being soothing. It is not the voice of reason or reasonableness but the voice of majority power and self-righteousness. But it is pointless to speak further on this.

I pity this government that has lost its way and is trying to find a path out of the swamp of its own policies. They have no foresight, and they cannot, they dare not, keep their eyes on the future. It is said that we should 'Beware of the day that is to come', and in the same way I say to this Congress government: 'Beware of the time that you are about to bring upon yourself and upon this country.' It is three years since we obtained Independence but look at the poor of the land: they have neither food to eat nor clothes to wear nor shelter to protect themselves from the sky. You promised Paradise and green gardens under which rivers flow, and gulled the people into believing that the cause of their pitiable condition was zamindari. Well, zamindari will go, but when your promises of these green gardens prove to be false, let us see then what the people say about you and do to you. You are dispossessing eight lakh people, and openly inviting communism. The people will soon find out who you are.

What are you doing that we did not do? You are not giving them the land, you are renting it out just as we did. But what do you care about them? We lived for generations together, we were like their fathers and grandfathers, they loved us and we loved them, we knew their temperament and they knew ours. They were happy with whatever we gave them, and we were happy with whatever they gave us. You have come between us and destroyed what was hallowed by the bonds of ancient emotion. And the crimes and oppressions you blame on us, what proof do these poor people have that you will be any better than you claim we are? They will have to go to the venal clerk and the gluttonous Sub-Divisional Officer, and they will be sucked dry. We were never like that. You have separated the nail from the flesh, and you are happy with the result. . . .

As for compensation, I have said enough already. But is this decency, is this a just provision—that you should go to someone's shop and tell him: 'Give me this and this at such and such a price' and if he doesn't agree to sell it, you take it anyway? And then when he pleads with you at least to give him what you promised him, to turn around and then say, 'Here is one rupee now, and the rest you will get in instalments over twenty-five years'?

You may call us all kinds of names and invent all manner of miseries for us—but the fact is that it is we zamindars who made this province what it is—who made it strong, who gave it its special flavour. In every field of life we have made our contribution, a contribution that will long outlive us, and that you cannot wipe away. The universities, the colleges, the traditions of classical music, the schools, the very culture of this place were established by us. When foreigners and those from other states in our country come to this province what do they see—what do they admire? The Barsaat Mahal, the Shahi Darvaza, the Imambaras, the gardens and the mansions that have come down to you from us. These things that are fragrant to the world you say are filled with the scent of exploitation, of rotting corpses. Are you not ashamed when you speak in this vein? When you curse and rob those who created this splendour and this beauty? When you do not give them enough compensation even to whitewash the buildings that are the heritage of this city and this state? This is the worst form of meanness, this is the grasping attitude of the village shopkeeper, the bania who smiles and smiles and grasps without any mercy—

The Hon'ble the Minister for Home Affairs (Shri L.N. Agarwal): I hope that the honourable member is not casting imputations upon my community. This is getting to be common sport in this House.

Begum Abida Khan: You understand very well what I am saying, you who are a master at twisting words and manipulating the law. But I will not waste my time arguing with you. Today you have made common cause with the Minister of Revenue in the shameful exploitation of a scapegoat class, but tomorrow will show you what such friendships of convenience are worth—and when you look around for friends everyone will have turned their face away from you. Then you will remember this day and what I have said, and you and your government will come to wish that you had behaved with greater justice and humanity.

There followed an extremely long-winded speech by a socialist member; and then the Chief Minister S.S. Sharma talked for about five minutes, thanking various people for their role in shaping this legislation—particularly Mahesh Kapoor, the Minister of Revenue, and Abdus Salaam, his Parliamentary Secretary. He advised the landowners to live in amity with their erstwhile tenants when the divestiture of their property took place. They should live together like brothers, he stated mildly and nasally. It was an opportunity for the landlords to show their goodness of heart. They should think of the teachings of Gandhiji and devote their lives to the service of their fellowmen. Finally Mahesh Kapoor, the chief architect of the bill, got the chance to round off the debate in the House. But time was too short for him to say more than a few words:

The Hon'ble the Minister of Revenue (Shri Mahesh Kapoor): Mr Speaker, I had hoped that my friend from the socialist benches, who talked so movingly of equality and a classless society and took the Government to task for producing an impotent and unjust bill, would be a just man himself and would confer some equality on me. It is the end of the last day. If he had taken a little less time for his speech I would have had a little more. As it is I now have barely two minutes to speak. He claimed that my bill was a measure created with the intention merely of preventing revolution—a revolution that he believes to be desirable. If that is so, I would be interested to see which way he and his party vote in a couple of minutes. After the honourable Chief Minister's words of thanks and advice—advice which I sincerely hope will be taken by the landlords—I have nothing to add except a few further words of thanks—to my colleagues in this section of the

House and, yes, in that section too, who have made the passage of this bill possible, and to the officers of the Revenue Department and the Printing Department and the Law Department, in particular the drafting cell and the Office of the Legal Remembrancer. I thank them all for their months and years of assistance and advice, and I hope that I speak for the people of Purva Pradesh when I say that my thanks are not merely personal.

The Hon'ble the Speaker: The question before the House is that the Purva Pradesh Zamindari Abolition Bill of original date 1948 as passed by the Legislative Assembly, amended by the Legislative Council and further amended by the Legislative Assembly, be passed.

The motion was put and the House passed the bill by a large majority, consisting mainly of the Congress Party, whose numbers dominated the House. The Socialist Party had to vote, however reluctantly, in favour of the bill on the grounds that half a loaf was better than none, and despite the fact that it somewhat assuaged the hunger that would have allowed them to flourish. Had they voted against it they would never have lived it down. The Democratic Party voted against it unanimously, also as expected. The smaller parties and Independents voted predominantly for the bill.

Begum Abida Khan: With the permission of the Speaker I would like a minute's time to say something.

The Hon'ble the Speaker: I will give you a minute's time.

Begum Abida Khan: I would like to say on behalf of myself and the Democratic Party that the advice given by the pious and honourable Chief Minister to the zamindars—that they should maintain good relations with their tenants—is very valuable advice, and I thank him for it. But we would have maintained such excellent relations anyway regardless of his excellent advice, and regardless of the passage of this bill—this bill which will force so many people into poverty and unemployment, which will utterly destroy the economy and culture of this province, and which will at the same time grant not the least benefit to those who—

The Hon'ble the Minister of Revenue (Shri Mahesh Kapoor): Mr Speaker, what sort of occasion is this for speech-making?

The Hon'ble the Speaker: I gave her permission merely to make a short statement. I would request the honourable member—

Begum Abida Khan: As a result of its unjust passage by a brute majority we are left at this time with no other constitutional means of expressing our displeasure and sense of injustice other than to walk out of this House, which is a constitutional recourse, and I therefore call upon the members of my party to stage a walkout to protest the passage of this bill.

The members of the Democratic Party walked out of the Assembly. There were a few hisses and cries of 'Shame!' but for the most part the Assembly was silent. It was the end of the day, so the gesture was symbolic rather than effective. After a few moments, the Speaker adjourned the House until eleven o'clock the next morning. Mahesh Kapoor gathered his papers together, looked up at the huge, frosted dome, sighed, then allowed his gaze to wander around the slowly emptying chamber. He looked across at the gallery and his eye caught that of the Nawab Sahib. They nodded at each other in a gesture of greeting that was almost entirely friendly, though the discomfort of the situation—not quite an irony—was lost on neither of them. Neither of them wished to talk to the other just yet, and each of them understood this. So Mahesh Kapoor continued to put his papers in order, and the Nawab Sahib, stroking his beard in thought, walked out of the gallery to look for the Chief Minister.

Part Six

6.1

Arriving at the Haridas College of Music, Ustad Majeed Khan nodded absently to a couple of other music teachers, grimaced with distaste at two female kathak dancers who were carrying their jangling anklets into a nearby practice room on the ground floor, and arrived at the closed door of his room. Outside the room, in casual disarray, lay three sets of chappals and one pair of shoes. Ustad Majeed Khan, realizing that this meant that he was forty-five minutes late, sighed a half-irritated and half-exhausted 'Ya Allah', took off his own Peshawari chappals, and entered the room.

The room that he entered was a plain, rectangular, high-ceilinged box with not very much natural light. What few rays came in from outside were provided by a small skylight high on the far wall. On the wall to the left as he entered was a long cupboard with a rack where a number of tanpuras were resting. On the floor was a pale blue unpatterned cotton rug; this had been quite difficult to obtain, as most of the rugs available on the market had floral or other designs of one kind or another. But he had insisted on having a plain rug so that he would not be distracted in his music, and the authorities had very surprisingly agreed to find him one. On the rug facing him sat a short, fat young man whom he had never seen; the man stood up as soon as he entered. Facing away from him were seated a young man and two young women. They turned when the door opened and, as soon as they saw it was him, got up respectfully to greet him. One of the women—it was Malati Trivedi—even bent down to touch his feet. Ustad Majeed Khan was not displeased. As she got up he said reprovingly to her:

'So you've decided to make a reappearance, have you? Now that the university is closed I suppose I can expect to see my classes fill up again. Everyone talks about their devotion to music but during examination time they disappear like rabbits into their burrows.'

The Ustad then turned to the stranger. This was Motu Chand, the plump tabla player who as a rule accompanied Saeeda Bai. Ustad Majeed Khan, surprised to see someone whom he did not immediately recognize in place of his regular tabla player, looked at him sternly and said, 'Yes?'

Motu Chand, smiling benignly, said, 'Excuse me, Ustad Sahib, for my presumption. Your regular tabla player, my wife's sister's husband's friend, is not well and he asked me if I would stand in for him today.'

'Do you have a name?'

'Well, they call me Motu Chand, but actually—'

'Hmmh!' said Ustad Majeed Khan, picked up his tanpura from the rack, sat down and began to tune it. His students sat down as well, but Motu Chand continued standing.

'Oh-hoh, sit down,' said Ustad Majeed Khan irritably, not deigning to look at Motu Chand.

As he was tuning his tanpura, Ustad Majeed Khan looked up, wondering to which of the three students he would give the first fifteen-minute slot. Strictly speaking, it belonged to the boy, but because a bright ray from the skylight happened to fall on Malati's cheerful face Ustad Majeed Khan decided on a whim to ask her to begin. She got up, fetched one of the smaller tanpuras, and began to tune it. Motu Chand adjusted the pitch of his tabla accordingly.

'Now which raag was I teaching you—Bhairava?' asked Ustad Majeed Khan.

'No, Ustad Sahib, Ramkali,' said Malati, gently strumming the tanpura which she had laid flat on the rug in front of her.

'Hmmm!' said Ustad Majeed Khan. He began to sing a few slow phrases of the raag and Malati repeated the phrases after him. The other students listened intently. From the low notes of the raag the Ustad moved to its upper reaches and then, with an indication to Motu Chand to begin playing the tabla in a rhythmic cycle of sixteen beats, he began to sing the composition that Malati had been learning. Although Malati did her best to concentrate, she was distracted by the entrance of two more students—both girls—who paid their respects to Ustad Majeed Khan before sitting down.

Clearly the Ustad was in a good mood once again; at one point he stopped singing to comment: 'So, you really want to become a doctor?' Turning away from Malati, he added ironically, 'With a voice like hers she will cause more heartache than even she will be able to cure, but if she wants to be a good musician she cannot give it second place in her life.' Then, turning back to Malati he said, 'Music requires as much concentration as surgery. You can't disappear for a month in the middle of an operation and take it up at will.'

'Yes, Ustad Sahib,' said Malati Trivedi with the suspicion of a smile.

'A woman as a doctor!' said Ustad Majeed Khan, musing. 'All right, all right, let us continue—which part of the composition were we at?'

His question was interrupted by a prolonged series of thumps from the room above. The bharatnatyam dancers had begun their practice. Unlike the kathak dancers whom the Ustad had glared at in the hall, they did not wear anklets for their practice session. But what they lost in tinkling distraction they more than compensated for in the vigour with which they pounded their heels and soles on the floor directly above. Ustad Majeed Khan's brows blackened and he abruptly terminated the lesson he was giving Malati.

The next student was the boy. He had a good voice and had put in a lot of work between lessons, but for some reason Ustad Majeed Khan treated him rather abruptly. Perhaps he was still upset by the bharatnatyam which sounded sporadically from above. The boy left as soon as his lesson was over.

Meanwhile, Veena Tandon entered, sat down, and began to listen. She looked troubled. She sat next to Malati, whom she knew both as a fellow-student of music and as a friend of Lata's. Motu Chand, who was facing them while playing, thought that they made an interesting contrast: Malati with her fair, fine features, brownish hair, and slightly amused green eyes, and Veena with her darker, plumper features, black hair, and dark eyes, animated but anxious.

After the boy came the turn of a cheerful but shy middle-aged Bengali woman, whose accent Ustad Majeed Khan enjoyed mimicking. She would normally come in the evenings, and at present he was teaching her Raag Malkauns. This she would sometimes call 'Malkosh' to the amusement of the Ustad.

'So you've come in the morning today,' said Ustad Majeed Khan. 'How can I teach you Malkosh in the morning?'

'My husband says I should come in the morning,' said the Bengali lady.

'So you are willing to sacrifice your art for your marriage?' asked the Ustad.

'Not entirely,' said the Bengali lady, keeping her eyes down. She had three children, and was bringing them up well, but was still incurably shy, especially when criticized by her Ustad.

'What do you mean, not entirely?'

'Well,' said the lady, 'my husband would prefer me to sing not classical music but Rabindrasangeet.'

'Hmmh!' said Ustad Majeed Khan. That the sickly-sweet so-called music of Rabindranath Tagore's songs should be more attractive to any man's ears than the beauty of classical khyaal clearly marked such a man as a buffoon. To the shy Bengali woman, the Ustad said in a tone of lenient contempt: 'So I expect he'll be asking you to sing him a "gojol" next.'

At his cruel mispronunciation the Bengali lady retreated entirely into a flustered silence, but Malati and Veena glanced at each other with amusement.

Ustad Majeed Khan, apropos of his earlier lesson, said: 'The boy has a good voice and he works hard, but he sings as if he were in church. It must be his earlier training in western music. It's a good tradition in its own way,' he went on tolerantly. Then, after a pause, he continued, 'But you can't unlearn it. The voice vibrates too much in the wrong kind of way. Hmm.' He turned to the Bengali woman: 'Tune the tanpura down to the "ma"; I may as well teach you your "Malkosh". One should not leave a raag half-taught even if it is the wrong time of day to sing it. But then I suppose one can set yogurt in the morning and eat it at night.'

Despite her nervousness, the Bengali lady acquitted herself well. The Ustad let her improvise a little on her own, and even said an encouraging 'May you live long!' a couple of times. If the truth be told, music mattered more to the Bengali lady than her husband and her three well-brought-up sons, but it was impossible, given the constraints of her life, for her to give it priority. The Ustad was pleased with her and gave her a longer lesson than usual. When it was over, she sat quietly to one side to listen to what was to follow.

What followed was Veena Tandon's lesson. She was to sing Raag Bhairava, for which the tanpura had to be retuned to 'pa'. But so distracted was she by various worries about her husband and her son that she began to strum it immediately.

'What raag are you studying?' said Ustad Majeed Khan, slightly puzzled. 'Isn't it Bhairava?'

'Yes, Guruji,' said Veena, somewhat perplexed herself.

'Guruji?' said Ustad Majeed Khan in a voice that would have been indignant if it had not been so astonished. Veena was one of his favourite pupils, and he could not imagine what had got into her.

'Ustad Sahib,' Veena corrected herself. She too was surprised that in addressing her Muslim teacher she had used the title of respect due to a Hindu one.

Ustad Majeed Khan continued: 'And if you are singing Bhairava, don't you think it would be a good idea to retune the tanpura?'

'Oh,' said Veena, looking down in surprise at the tanpura, as if it were somehow to blame for her own absence of mind.

After she had retuned it, the Ustad sang a few phrases of a slow alaap for her to imitate, but her performance was so unsatisfactory that at one point he said sharply to her: 'Listen. Listen first. Listen first, then sing. Listening is fifteen annas in the rupee. Reproducing it is one anna—it's the work of a parrot. Are you worried about something?' Veena did not think it right to speak of her anxieties before her teacher, and Ustad Majeed Khan continued: 'Why don't you strum the tanpura so that I can hear it? You should eat almonds for breakfast—that will increase your strength. All right, let's go on to the composition—"Jaago Mohan Pyaare",' he added impatiently.

Motu Chand started the rhythmic cycle on the tabla and they began to sing. The words of the well-known composition lent stability to Veena's unsteady thoughts and the increasing confidence and liveliness of her singing pleased Ustad Majeed Khan. After a while first Malati, and then the Bengali woman got up to leave. The word 'gojol' flashed through the Ustad's mind and it dawned upon him where he had heard of Motu Chand before. Wasn't he the tabla player who accompanied the ghazals of Saeeda Bai, that desecrater of the holy shrine of music, the courtesan who served the notorious Raja of Marh? One thought led to another; he turned abruptly towards Veena and said, 'If your father, the Minister, is bent upon destroying our livelihood, at least he can protect our religion.'

Veena stopped singing and looked at him in bewildered silence. She realized that 'livelihood' referred to the patronage of the great rural landlords whose lands the Zamindari Abolition Bill was attempting to snatch away. But what the Ustad Sahib meant by a threat to his religion, she could not comprehend at all.

'Tell him that,' continued Ustad Majeed Khan.

'I will, Ustad Sahib,' said Veena in a subdued voice.

'The Congress-wallahs will finish Nehru and Maulana Azad and Rafi Sahib off. And our worthy Chief Minister and Home Minister will sooner or later suppress your father as well. But while he has some political life, he can do something to help those of us who depend on the likes of him for protection. Once they start singing their bhajans from the temple while we are at prayer, it can only end badly.'

Veena realized that Ustad Majeed Khan was referring to the Shiva Temple being constructed in Chowk, only a couple of lanes away from Ustad Majeed Khan's house.

After humming to himself for a few seconds the Ustad paused, cleared his throat and said, almost to himself: 'It is becoming unlivable in our area. Apart from Marh's madness, there is the whole insane business of Misri Mandi. It's amazing,' he went on, 'the whole place is on strike, no one ever works, and all they do is yell slogans and threats at each other. The small shoemakers starve and scream, the traders tighten their belts and bluster, and there are no shoes in the stores, no employment in the whole Mandi. Everyone's interests are harmed, yet no one will compromise. And this is Man whom God has made out of a clot of blood, and to whom he has given reason and discrimination.'

The Ustad finished his comment with a dismissive wave of his hand, a wave that implied that everything he had ever thought about human nature had been confirmed.

Seeing Veena look even more upset, an expression of concern passed over Majeed Khan's face. 'Why am I telling you this?' he said, almost in self-reproach. 'Your husband knows all this better than I do. So that's why you are distracted—of course, of course.'

Veena, moved though she was by this expression of sympathy from the normally unsympathetic Ustad, was silent, and continued to strum the tanpura. They resumed where they had left off, but it must have been obvious that her mind was not on the composition or the rhythmic patterns—the 'taans'—which followed. At one point, the Ustad said to her: 'You're singing the word "ga", "ga", "ga", but is that really the note "ga" you are singing? I think you have too much on your mind. You should leave such things with your shoes outside this room when you come in.'

He began to sing a complex series of taans, and Motu Chand, carried away by the pleasure of the music, started to improvise a pleasant filigree of rhythmic accompaniment on the tabla. The Ustad abruptly stopped.

He turned to Motu Chand with sarcastic deference. 'Please go on, Guruji,' he said.

The tabla player smiled embarrassedly.

'No, do go on, we were enjoying your solo,' continued Ustad Majeed Khan.

Motu Chand's smile became unhappier still.

'Do you know how to play a simple theka—the plain unornamented rhythmic cycle? Or are you in too high a circle of Paradise for that?'

Motu Chand looked pleadingly at Ustad Majeed Khan and said, 'It was the beauty of your singing that carried me away, Ustad Sahib. But I won't let it happen again.'

Ustad Majeed Khan looked sharply at him, but he had intended no impertinence.

After her lesson was over, Veena got up to leave. Normally she stayed as long as she could, but this was not possible today. Bhaskar had a fever and wanted her attention; Kedarnath needed cheering up; and her mother-in-law had just that morning made a hurtful comment on the amount of time she spent at the Haridas College of Music.

The Ustad glanced at his watch. There was still an hour before the noon prayer. He thought of the call to prayer which he heard every morning first from his local mosque and then at slightly staggered intervals from other mosques across the city. What he particularly liked in the morning call to prayer was the twice-repeated line that did not appear in the azaan later in the day: 'Prayer is better than sleep.'

Music too was prayer to him, and some mornings he would be up long before dawn to sing Lalit or some other early morning raag. Then the first words of the azaan, 'Allah-u-Akbar'—God is Great—would vibrate across the rooftops in the cool air and his ears would lie in wait for the sentence that admonished those who attempted to sleep on. When he heard it, he would smile. It was one of the pleasures of his day.

If the new Shiva Temple was built, the sound of the muezzin's early cry would be challenged by that of the conch. The thought was unbearable. Surely something must be done to prevent it. Surely the powerful Minister Mahesh Kapoor—who was taunted by some in his party for being, like the Prime Minister Jawaharlal Nehru, almost an honorary Muslim—could do something about it. The Ustad began meditatively to hum the words of the composition that he had just been teaching the Minister's daughter—'Jaago Mohan Pyaare'. Humming it, he forgot himself. He forgot the room he was in and the students still waiting for their lessons. It was very far from his mind that the words were addressed to the dark god Krishna, asking him to wake up with the arrival of morning, or that Bhairava—the name of the raag he was singing—was an epithet of the great god Shiva himself.

6.2

Ishaq Khan, Saeeda Bai's sarangi player, had been trying for several days to help his sister's husband—who was also a sarangi player—to get transferred from All India Radio Lucknow, where he was a 'staff artist', to All India Radio Brahmpur.

This morning too, Ishaq Khan had gone down to the AIR offices and tried his luck by talking to an assistant producer of music, but to no avail. It was a bitter business for the young man to realize that he could not even get to state his case properly to the Station Director. He did, however, state his case vociferously to a couple of musician friends he met there. The sun was warm, and they sat under a large and shady neem tree on the lawn outside the buildings. They looked at the cannas and talked of this and that. One of them had a radio—which he had ingeniously connected up to a socket inside the main building—and they switched it on to the only station they could receive clearly, which was their own.

The unmistakable voice of Ustad Majeed Khan singing Raag Miya-ki-Todi filled their ears. He had just begun singing and was accompanied only by the tabla and his own tanpura.

It was glorious music: grand, stately, sad, full of a deep sense of calm. They stopped gossiping and listened. Even an orange-crested hoopoe stopped pecking around the flower bed for a minute.

As always with Ustad Majeed Khan, the clean unfolding of the raag occurred through a very slow rhythmic section rather than a rhythmless alaap. After about fifteen minutes he turned to a faster composition in the raag, and then, far, far too soon, Raag Todi was over, and a children's programme was on the air.

Ishaq Khan turned off the radio and sat still, deep more in trance than in thought.

After a while they got up and went to the AIR staff canteen. Ishaq Khan's friends, like his brother-in-law, were staff artists, with fixed hours and assured salaries. Ishaq Khan, who had only accompanied other musicians a few times on the air, fell into the category of 'casual artist'.

The small canteen was crowded with musicians, writers of programmes, administrators, and waiters. A couple of peons lounged against the wall. The entire scene was messy, noisy and cosy. The canteen was famous for its strong tea and delicious samosas. A board facing the entrance proclaimed that no credit would be given; but as the musicians were perennially short of cash, it always was.

Every table except one was crowded. Ustad Majeed Khan sat alone at the head of the table by the far wall, musing and stirring his tea. Perhaps out of deference to him, because he was considered something better than even an A-grade artist, no one presumed to sit near him. For all the apparent camaraderie and democracy of the canteen, there were distinctions. B-grade artists for instance would not normally sit with those of superior classifications such as B-plus or A—unless, of course, they happened to be their disciples—and would usually defer to them even in speech.

Ishaq Khan looked around the room and, seeing five empty chairs ranged down the oblong length of Ustad Majeed Khan's table, moved towards it. His two friends followed a little hesitantly.

As they approached, a few people from another table got up, perhaps because they were performing next on the air. But Ishaq Khan chose to ignore this, and walked up to Ustad Majeed Khan's table. 'May we?' he asked politely. As the great musician was lost in some other world, Ishaq and his friends sat down at the three chairs at the opposite end. There were still two empty chairs, one on either side of Majeed Khan. He did not seem to register the presence of the new arrivals, and was now drinking his tea with both hands on the cup, though the weather was warm.

Ishaq sat at the other end facing Majeed Khan, and looked at that noble and arrogant face, softened as it appeared to be by some transient memory or thought rather than by the permanent impress of late middle age.

So profound had the effect of his brief performance of Raag Todi been on Ishaq that he wanted desperately to convey his appreciation. Ustad Majeed Khan was not a tall man, but seated either on the stage in his long black achkan—so tightly buttoned at the neck that one would have thought it would constrict his voice—or even at a table drinking tea, he conveyed, through his upright, rigid stance, a commanding presence; indeed, even an illusion of height. At the moment he seemed almost unapproachable.

If only he would say something to me, thought Ishaq, I would tell him what I felt about his performance. He must know we are sitting here. And he used to know my father. There were many things that the younger man did not like about the elder, but the music he and his friends had just listened to placed them in their trivial perspective.

They ordered their tea. The service in the canteen, despite the fact that it was part of a government organization, was prompt. The three friends began to talk among themselves. Ustad Majeed Khan continued to sip his tea in silence and abstraction.

Ishaq was quite popular in spite of his slightly sarcastic nature, and had a number of good friends. He was always willing to take the errands and burdens of others upon himself. After his father's death he and his sister had had to support their three young brothers. This was one reason why it was important that his sister's family move from Lucknow to Brahmpur.

One of Ishaq's two friends, a tabla player, now made the suggestion that Ishaq's brother-in-law change places with another sarangi player, Rafiq, who was keen to move to Lucknow.

'But Rafiq is a B-plus artist. What's your brother-in-law's grade?' asked Ishaq's other friend.

'B.'

'The Station Director won't want to lose a B-plus for a B. Still, you can try.'

Ishaq picked up his cup, wincing slightly as he did so, and sipped his tea.

'Unless he can upgrade himself,' continued his friend. 'I agree, it's a silly system, to grade someone in Delhi on the basis of a single tape of a performance, but that's the system we have.'

'Well,' said Ishaq, remembering his father who, in the last years of his life, had made it to A, 'it's not a bad system. It's impartial—and ensures a certain level of competence.'

'Competence!' It was Ustad Majeed Khan speaking. The three friends looked at him in amazement. The word was spoken with a contempt that seemed to come from the deepest level of his being. 'Mere pleasing competence is not worth having.'

Ishaq looked at Ustad Majeed Khan, deeply disquieted. The memory of his father made him bold enough to speak.

'Khan Sahib, for someone like you, competence is not even a question. But for the rest of us. . . .' His voice trailed off.

Ustad Majeed Khan, displeased at being even mildly contradicted, sat tight-lipped and silent. He seemed to be collecting his thoughts. After a while he spoke.

'You should not have a problem,' he said. 'For a sarangi-wallah no great musicianship is required. You don't need to be a master of a style. Whatever style the soloist has, you simply follow it. In musical terms it's actually a distraction.' He continued in an indifferent voice: 'If you want my help I'll speak to the Station Director. He knows I'm impartial—I don't need or use sarangi-wallahs. Rafiq or your sister's husband—it hardly matters who is where.'

Ishaq's face had gone white. Without thinking of what he was doing or where he was, he looked straight at Majeed Khan and said in a bitter and cutting voice:

'I have no objection to being called a mere sarangi-wallah rather than a sarangiya by a great man. I consider myself blessed that he has deigned to notice me. But these are matters about which Khan Sahib has personal knowledge. Perhaps he can elaborate on the uselessness of the instrument.'

It was no secret that Ustad Majeed Khan himself came from a family of hereditary sarangi players. His artistic strivings as a vocalist were bound up painfully with another endeavour: the attempt to dissociate himself from the demeaning sarangi tradition and its historical connection with courtesans and prostitutes—and to associate himself and his son and daughter with the so-called 'kalawant' families of higher-caste musicians.

But the taint of the sarangi was too strong, and no kalawant family wanted to marry into Majeed Khan's. This was one of the searing disappointments of his life. Another was that his music would end with himself, for he had never found a disciple whom he considered worthy of his art. His own son had the voice and musicianship of a frog. As for his daughter, she was musical all right, but the last thing that Ustad Majeed Khan wanted for her was that she should develop her voice and become a singer.

Ustad Majeed Khan cleared his throat but said nothing.

The thought of the great artist's treason, the contempt with which Majeed Khan, despite his own undoubted gifts, had treated the tradition that had given him birth continued to enrage Ishaq.

'Why does Khan Sahib not favour us with a response?' he went on, oblivious to his friends' attempts to restrain him. 'There are subjects, no matter how distanced he is today, on which Khan Sahib can illuminate our understanding. Who else has the background? We have heard of Khan Sahib's illustrious father and grandfather.'

'Ishaq, I knew your father, and I knew your grandfather. They were men who understood the meaning of respect and discrimination.'

'They looked at the worn grooves on their fingernails without feeling dishonoured,' retorted Ishaq.

The people at the neighbouring tables had stopped talking, and were listening to the exchange between the younger and the older man. That Ishaq, baited himself, was now doing the baiting, attempting to hurt and humiliate Ustad Majeed Khan, was painful and obvious. The scene was horrible, but everyone seemed to be frozen into immobility.

Ustad Majeed Khan said slowly and passionlessly: 'But they, believe me, would have felt dishonoured if they had been alive to see their son flirting with the sister of an employer, whose body his bow helps sell.'

He looked at his watch and got up. He had another performance in ten minutes. Almost to himself and with the utmost simplicity and sincerity, he said, 'Music is not a cheap spectacle—not the entertainment of the brothel. It is like prayer.'

Before Ishaq could respond he had started walking towards the door. Ishaq got up and almost lunged towards him. He was gripped by an uncontrollable spasm of pain and fury, and his two friends had to force him bodily down into his chair. Other people joined in, for Ishaq was well liked, and had to be prevented from doing further damage.

'Ishaq Bhai, enough's been said.'

'Listen, Ishaq, one must swallow it—whatever our elders say, however bitter.'

'Don't ruin yourself. Think of your brothers. If he talks to the Director Sahib. . . .'

'Ishaq Bhai, how many times have I told you to guard your tongue!'

'Listen, you must apologize to him immediately.'

But Ishaq was almost incoherent:

'Never—never—I'll never apologize—on my father's grave—to that—to think, that such a man who insults the memory of his elders and mine—everyone creeps on all fours before him—yes, Khan Sahib, you can have a twenty-five-minute slot—yes, yes, Khan Sahib, you decide which raag you will sing—O God! If Miya Tansen were alive he would have cried to hear him sing his raag today—that God should have given him this gift—'

'Enough, enough, Ishaq. . . .' said an old sitar player. Ishaq turned towards him with tears of hurt and anger:

'Would you marry your son to his daughter? Or your daughter to his son? Who is he that God is in his pocket?—he talks like a mullah about prayer and devotion—this man who spent half his youth in Tarbuz ka Bazaar—'

People began to turn away in pity and discomfort from Ishaq. Several of Ishaq's well-wishers left the canteen to try and pacify the insulted maestro, who was about to agitate the airwaves in his own great agitation.

'Khan Sahib, the boy didn't know what he was saying.'

Ustad Majeed Khan, who was almost at the door of the studio, said nothing.

'Khan Sahib, elders have always treated their youngers like children, with tolerance. You must not take what he said seriously. None of it is true.'

Ustad Majeed Khan looked at the interceder and said: 'If a dog pisses on my achkan, do I become a tree?'

The sitar player shook his head and said, 'I know it was the worst time he could have chosen—when you were about to perform, Ustad Sahib. . . .'

But Ustad Majeed Khan went on to sing a Hindol of calm and surpassing beauty.

6.3

It had been some days since Saeeda Bai had saved Maan from suicide, as he put it. Of course it was extremely unlikely—and his friend Firoz had told him so when he had complained to him of his lovelorn miseries—that that happy-go-lucky young man would have made any attempt even to cut himself while shaving in order to prove his passion for her. But Maan knew that Saeeda Bai, though hard-headed, was—at least to him—tender-hearted; and although he knew she did not believe that he was in any danger from himself if she refused to make love to him, he also knew that she would take it as more than a merely flattering figure of speech. Everything is in the saying, and Maan, while saying that he could not go on in this harsh world without her, had been as soulful as it was possible for him to be. For a while all his past loves vanished from his heart. The dozen or more 'girls of good family' from Brahmpur whom he had been in love with and who in general had loved him in return, ceased to exist. Saeeda Bai—for that moment at least—became everything for him.

And after they had made love, she became more than everything for him. Like that other source of domestic strife, Saeeda Bai too made hungry where most she satisfied. Part of it was simply the delicious skill with which she made love. But even more than that it was her nakhra, the art of pretended hurt or disaffection that she had learned from her mother and other courtesans in the early days in Tarbuz ka Bazaar. Saeeda Bai practised this with such curious restraint that it became infinitely more believable. One tear, one remark that implied—perhaps, only perhaps implied—that something he had said or done had caused her injury—and Maan's heart would go out to her. No matter what the cost to himself, he would protect her from the cruel, censorious world. For minutes at a time he would lean over her shoulder and kiss her neck, glancing every few moments at her face in the hope of seeing her mood lift. And when it did, and he saw that same bright, sad smile that had so captivated him when she sang at Holi at Prem Nivas, he would be seized by a frenzy of sexual desire. Saeeda Bai seemed to know this, and graced him with a smile only when she herself was in the mood to satisfy him.

She had framed one of the paintings from the album of Ghalib's poems that Maan had given her. Although she had, as far as was possible, repaired the page that the Raja of Marh had ripped out of the volume, she had not dared to display that particular illustration for fear of exciting his further fury. What she had framed was 'A Persian Idyll', which showed a young woman dressed in pale orange, sitting near an arched doorway on a very pale orange rug, holding in her slender fingers a musical instrument resembling a sitar, and looking out of the archway into a mysterious garden. The woman's features were sharp and delicate, unlike Saeeda Bai's very attractive but unclassical, perhaps not even beautiful, face. And the instrument that the woman was holding—unlike Saeeda Bai's strong and responsive harmonium—was so finely tapered in the stylized illustration that it would have been entirely impossible to play it.

Maan did not care that the book might be considered damaged by having the painting thus plundered from its pages. He could not have been happier at this sign of Saeeda Bai's attachment to his gift. He lay in her bedroom and stared at the painting and was filled with a happiness as mysterious as the garden through the archway. Whether glowing with the immediate memory of her embraces or chewing contentedly at the delicate coconut-flavoured paan that she had just offered to him at the end of a small ornamented silver pin, it seemed to him that he himself had been led by her and her music and her affection into a paradisal garden, most insubstantial and yet most real.

'How unimaginable it is,' said Maan out loud rather dreamily, 'that our parents also must have—just like us—'

This remark struck Saeeda Bai as being in somewhat poor taste. She did not at all wish her imagination to be transported to the domestic love-making of Mahesh Kapoor—or anyone else for that matter. She did not know who her own father was: her mother, Mohsina Bai, had claimed not to know. Besides, domesticity and its standard concerns were not objects of fond contemplation for her. She had been accused by Brahmpur gossip of destroying several settled marriages by casting her lurid nets around hapless men. She said a little sharply to Maan:

'It is good to live in a household like I do where one does not have to imagine such things.'

Maan looked a little chastened. Saeeda Bai, who was quite fond of him by now and knew that he usually blurted out the first thing that came into his head, tried to cheer him up by saying:

'But Dagh Sahib looks distressed. Would he have been happier to have been immaculately conceived?'

'I think so,' said Maan. 'I sometimes think I would be happier without a father.'

'Oh?' said Saeeda Bai, who had clearly not been expecting this.

'Oh, yes,' said Maan. 'I often feel that whatever I do my father looks upon with contempt. When I opened the cloth business in Banaras, Baoji told me it would be a complete failure. Now that I have made a go of it, he is taking the line that I should sit there every day of every month of every year of my life. Why should I?'

Saeeda Bai did not say anything.

'And why should I marry?' continued Maan, spreading his arms wide on the bed and touching Saeeda Bai's cheek with his left hand. 'Why? Why? Why? Why? Why?'

'Because your father can get me to sing at your wedding,' said Saeeda Bai with a smile. 'And at the birth of your children. And at their mundan ceremony. And at their marriages, of course.' She was silent for a few seconds. 'But I won't be alive to do that,' she went on. 'In fact I sometimes wonder what you see in an old woman like me.'

Maan became very indignant. He raised his voice and said, 'Why do you say things like that? Do you do it just to get me annoyed? No one ever meant much to me until I met you. That girl in Banaras whom I met twice under heavy escort is less than nothing to me—and everyone thinks I must marry her just because my father and mother say so.'

Saeeda Bai turned towards him and buried her face in his arm. 'But you must get married,' she said. 'You cannot cause your parents so much pain.'

'I don't find her at all attractive,' said Maan angrily.

'That will merely take time,' advised Saeeda Bai.

'And I won't be able to visit you after I'm married,' said Maan.

'Oh?' said Saeeda Bai in such a way that the question, rather than leading to a reply, implied the closure of the conversation.

6.4

After a while they got up and moved to the other room. Saeeda Bai called for the parakeet, of whom she had become fond. Ishaq Khan brought in the cage, and a discussion ensued about when he would learn to speak. Saeeda Bai seemed to think that a couple of months would be sufficient, but Ishaq was doubtful. 'My grandfather had a parakeet who didn't speak for a whole year—and then wouldn't stop talking for the rest of his life,' he said.

'I've never heard anything like that,' said Saeeda Bai dismissively. 'Anyway, why are you holding that cage in such a funny way?'

'Oh, it's nothing really,' said Ishaq, setting the cage down on a table and rubbing his right wrist. 'Just a pain in my wrist.'

In fact it was very painful and had become worse during the previous few weeks.

'You seem to play well enough,' said Saeeda Bai, not very sympathetically.

'Saeeda Begum, what would I do if I didn't play?'

'Oh, I don't know,' said Saeeda Bai, tickling the little parakeet's beak. 'There's probably nothing the matter with your hand. You don't have plans to go off for a wedding in the family, do you? Or to leave town until your famous explosion at the radio station is forgotten?'

If Ishaq was injured by this painful reference or these unjust suspicions, he did not show it. Saeeda Bai told him to fetch Motu Chand, and the three of them soon began to make music for Maan's pleasure. Ishaq bit his lower lip from time to time as his bow moved across the strings, but he said nothing.

Saeeda Bai sat on a Persian rug with her harmonium in front of her. Her head was covered with her sari, and she stroked the double string of pearls hanging around her neck with a finger of her left hand. Then, humming to herself, and moving her left hand on to the bellows of the harmonium, she began to play a few notes of Raag Pilu. After a little while, and as if undecided about her mood and the kind of song she wished to sing, she modulated to a few other raags.

'What would you like to hear?' she asked Maan gently.

She had used a more intimate 'you' than she had ever used so far—'tum' instead of 'aap'. Maan looked at her, smiling.

'Well?' said Saeeda Bai, after a minute had gone by.

'Well, Saeeda Begum?' said Maan.

'What do you want to hear?' Again she used tum instead of aap and sent Maan's world into a happy spin. A couplet he'd heard somewhere came to his mind:

> Among the lovers the Saki thus drew distinction's line,
> Handing the wine-cups one by one: 'For you, Sir'; 'Yours'; and 'Thine'.

'Oh, anything,' said Maan. 'Anything at all. Whatever you feel is in your heart.'

Maan had still not plucked up the courage to use 'tum' or plain 'Saeeda' with Saeeda Bai, except when he was making love, when he hardly knew what he said. Perhaps, he thought, she just used it absent-mindedly with me and will be offended if I reciprocate.

But Saeeda Bai was inclined to take offence at something else.

'I'm giving you the choice of music and you are returning the problem to me,' she said. 'There are twenty different things in my heart. Can't you hear me changing from raag to raag?' Then, turning away from Maan, she said: 'So, Motu, what is to be sung?'

'Whatever you wish, Saeeda Begum,' said Motu Chand happily.

'You blockhead, I'm giving you an opportunity that most of my audiences would kill themselves to receive and all you do is smile back at me like a weak-brained baby, and say, "Whatever you wish, Saeeda Begum." What ghazal? Quickly. Or do you want to hear a thumri instead of a ghazal?'

'A ghazal will be best, Saeeda Bai,' said Motu Chand, and suggested 'It's just a heart, not brick and stone' by Ghalib.

At the end of the ghazal Saeeda Bai turned to Maan and said: 'You must write a dedication in your book.'

'What, in English?' asked Maan.

'It amazes me,' said Saeeda Bai, 'to see the great poet Dagh illiterate in his own language. We must do something about it.'

'I'll learn Urdu!' said Maan enthusiastically.

Motu Chand and Ishaq Khan exchanged glances. Clearly they thought that Maan was quite far gone in his fascination with Saeeda Bai.

Saeeda Bai laughed. She asked Maan teasingly, 'Will you really?' Then she asked Ishaq to call the maidservant.

For some reason Saeeda Bai was annoyed with Bibbo today. Bibbo seemed to know this, but to be unaffected by it. She came in grinning, and this reignited Saeeda Bai's annoyance.

'You're smiling just to annoy me,' she said impatiently. 'And you forgot to tell the cook that the parakeet's daal was not soft enough yesterday—do you think he has the jaws of a tiger? Stop grinning, you silly girl, and tell me—what time is Abdur Rasheed coming to give Tasneem her Arabic lesson?'

Saeeda Bai felt safe enough with Maan to mention Tasneem's name in his presence.

Bibbo assumed a satisfactorily apologetic expression and said:

'But he's here already, as you know, Saeeda Bai.'

'As I know? As I know?' said Saeeda Bai with renewed impatience. 'I don't know anything. And nor do you,' she added. 'Tell him to come up at once.'

A few minutes later Bibbo was back, but alone.

'Well?' said Saeeda Bai.

'He won't come,' said Bibbo.

'He won't come? Does he know who pays him to give tuition to Tasneem? Does he think his honour will be unsafe if he comes upstairs to this room? Or is it just that he is giving himself airs because he is a university student?'

'I don't know, Begum Sahiba,' said Bibbo.

'Then go, girl, and ask him why. It's his income I want to increase, not my own.'

Five minutes later Bibbo returned with a very broad grin on her face and said, 'He was very angry when I interrupted him again. He was teaching Tasneem a complicated passage in the Quran Sharif and told me that the divine word would have to take precedence over his earthly income. But he will come when the lesson is over.'

'Actually, I'm not sure I want to learn Urdu,' said Maan, who was beginning to regret his sudden enthusiasm. He didn't really want to be saddled with a lot of hard work. And he hadn't expected the conversation to take such a practical turn so suddenly. He was always making resolutions such as, 'I must learn polo' (to Firoz, who enjoyed introducing his friends to the tastes and joys of his own Nawabi lifestyle), or 'I must settle down' (to Veena, who was the only one in the family who was capable of ticking him off to some effect), or even 'I will not give swimming lessons to whales' (which Pran considered ill-judged levity). But he made these resolutions safe in the knowledge that their implementation was very far away.

By now, however, the young Arabic teacher was standing outside the door, quite hesitantly and a little disapprovingly. He did adaab to the whole company, and waited to hear what was required of him.

'Rasheed, can you teach my young friend here Urdu?' asked Saeeda Bai, coming straight to the point.

The young man nodded a little reluctantly.

'The understanding will be the same as with Tasneem,' said Saeeda Bai, who believed in getting practical matters sorted out quickly.

'That will be fine,' said Rasheed. He spoke in a somewhat clipped manner, as if he were still slightly piqued by the earlier interruptions to his Arabic lesson. 'And the name of the gentleman?'

'Oh yes, I'm sorry,' said Saeeda Bai. 'This is Dagh Sahib, whom the world so far knows only by the name of Maan Kapoor. He is the son of Mahesh Kapoor, the Minister. And his elder brother Pran teaches at the university, where you study.'

The young man was frowning with a sort of inward concentration. Then, fixing his sharp eyes on Maan he said, 'It will be an honour to teach the son of Mahesh Kapoor. I am afraid I am a little late already for my next tuition. I hope that when I come tomorrow we can fix up a suitable time for our lesson. When do you tend to be free?'

'Oh, he tends to be free all the time,' said Saeeda Bai with a tender smile. 'Time is not a problem with Dagh Sahib.'

6.5

One night, exhausted from marking examination papers, Pran was sleeping soundly when he was awakened with a jolt. He had been kicked. His wife had her arms around him, but she was sleeping soundly still.

'Savita, Savita—the baby kicked me!' said Pran excitedly, shaking his wife's shoulder.

Savita opened a reluctant eye, felt Pran's lanky and comforting body near her, and smiled in the dark, before sinking back to sleep.

'Are you awake?' asked Pran.

'Uh,' said Savita. 'Mm.'

'But it really did!' said Pran, unhappy with her lack of response.

'What did?' said Savita sleepily.

'The baby.'

'What baby?'

'Our baby.'

'Our baby did what?'

'It kicked me.'

Savita sat up carefully, kissed Pran's forehead, rather as if he were a baby himself, and gave him a hug. 'It couldn't have. You're dreaming. Go back to sleep. And I'll also go back to sleep. And so will the baby.'

'It did,' said Pran, a little indignantly.

'It couldn't have,' said Savita, lying down again. 'I'd have felt it.'

'Well it did, that's all. You probably don't feel its kicks any more. And you sleep very soundly. But it kicked me through your belly, it definitely did, and it woke me up.' He was very insistent.

'Oh, all right,' said Savita. 'Have it your way. I think he must have known that you were having bad dreams, all about chiasmus and Anna—whatever her name is.'

'Anacoluthia.'

'Yes, and I was having good dreams and he didn't want to disturb me.'

'Excellent baby,' said Pran.

'Our baby,' said Savita. Pran got another hug.

They were silent for a while. Then, as Pran was drifting off to sleep, Savita said:

'He seems to have a lot of energy.'

'Oh?' said Pran, half asleep.

Savita, now wide awake with her thoughts, was in no mood to cut off this conversation.

'Do you think he will turn out to be like Maan?' she asked.

'He?'

'I sense he's a boy,' said Savita in a resolved sort of way.

'In what sense like Maan?' asked Pran, suddenly remembering that his mother had asked him to talk to his brother about the direction of his life—and especially about Saeeda Bai, whom his mother referred to only as 'woh'—that woman.

'Handsome—and a flirt?'

'Maybe,' said Pran, his mind on other matters.

'Or an intellectual like his father?'

'Oh, why not?' said Pran, drawn back in. 'He could do worse. But without his asthma, I hope.'

'Or do you think he'll have the temper of my grandfather?'

'No, I don't think it was an angry sort of kick. Just informative. "Here I am; it's two in the morning, and all's well." Or perhaps he was, as you say, interrupting a nightmare.'

'Maybe he'll be like Arun—very dashing and sophisticated.'

'Sorry, Savita,' said Pran. 'If he turns out to be like your brother, I'll disown him. But he'll have disowned us long before that. In fact, if he's like Arun, he's probably thinking at this very moment: "Awful service in this room; I must speak to the manager so that I can get my nutrients on time. And they should adjust the temperature of the amniotic fluid in this indoor swimming pool, as they do in five-star wombs. But what can you expect in India? Nothing works at all in this damned country. What the natives need is a good solid dose of discipline." Perhaps that's why he kicked me.'

Savita laughed. 'You don't know Arun well enough,' was her response.

Pran merely grunted.

'Anyway, he might take after the women in this family,' Savita went on. 'He might turn out to be like your mother or mine.' The thought pleased her.

Pran frowned, but this latest flight of Savita's fancy was too taxing at two in the morning. 'Do you want me to get you something to drink?' he asked her.

'No, mm, yes, a glass of water.'

Pran sat up, coughed a little, turned towards the bedside table, switched on the bedside lamp, and poured out a glass of cool water from the thermos flask.

'Here, darling,' he said, looking at her with slightly rueful affection. How beautiful she looked now, and how wonderful it would be to make love with her.

'You don't sound too good, Pran,' said Savita.

Pran smiled, and passed his hand across her forehead. 'I'm fine.'

'I worry about you.'

'I don't,' Pran lied.

'You don't get enough fresh air, and you use your lungs too much. I wish you were a writer, not a lecturer.' Savita drank the water slowly, savouring its coolness in the warm night.

'Thanks,' said Pran. 'But you don't get enough exercise either. You should walk around a bit, even during your pregnancy.'

'I know,' said Savita, yawning now. 'I've been reading the book my mother gave me.'

'All right, goodnight, darling. Give me the glass.'

He switched off the light and lay in the dark, his eyes still open. I never expected to be as happy as this, he told himself. I'm asking myself if I'm happy, and it hasn't made me cease to be so. But how long will this last? It isn't just me but my wife and child who are saddled with my useless lungs. I must take care of myself. I must take care of myself. I must not overwork. And I must get to sleep quickly.

And in five minutes he was in fact asleep again.

6.6

The next morning a letter from Calcutta arrived in the post. It was written in Mrs Rupa Mehra's inimitable small handwriting, and went as follows:

Dearest Savita and Pran,

I have just a little while ago received your dear letter and it is needless to say how delighted I am to get it. I was not expecting a letter from you Pran as I know you are working very hard and could hardly get any time to write letters so the pleasure of receiving it is even greater.

I am sure inspite of difficulties Pran dearest your dreams in the department will come true. You must have patience, it is a lesson I have learned in life. One must work hard and everything else is not in one's hands. I am blessed that my sweetheart Savita has such a good husband, only he must take care of his health.

By now the baby must be kicking even more and tears come into my eyes that I cannot be there with you my Savita to share the joy. I remember when you were kicking it was so gentle a kick and Daddy bless him was there and put his hand on my stomach and could not even feel it. Now my darlingest S, you are yourself to be a mother. You are so much in my thoughts. Sometimes Arun says to me you only care for Lata and Savita but it is not true, I care for all four of my children boys or girls and take an interest in all they do. Varun is so troubled this year in his maths studies that I am very worried for him.

Aparna is a sweetheart and so fond of her grandmother. I am often left with her in the evenings. Arun and Meenakshi go out and socialise, it is important for his job I know—and I am happy to play with her. Sometimes I read. Varun comes back very late from college, in the past he used to entertain her and that was good because children should not spend all their time with their ayahs, it can be bad for their upbringing. So now it has fallen to me and Aparna has grown so attached to me. Yesterday she said to her mother who had dressed up to go out to dinner: 'You can go, I don't care; if Daadi stays here I don't care two hoots.' Those were her exact words and I was so proud of her that at three years she could say so much. I am teaching her not to call me 'Grandma' but 'Daadi' but Meenakshi thinks if she does not learn correct English now when will she learn?

Meenakshi sometimes I find has moods, and then she stares at me and then Savita dearest I feel that I am not wanted in the house. I want to stare back but sometimes I start crying. I can't help it at all. Then Arun says to me, 'Ma, don't start the waterworks, you are always making a fuss over nothing.' So I try not to cry, but when I think about your Daddy's gold medal the tears are there.

Lata is nowadays spending a lot of time with Meenakshi's family. Meenakshi's father Mr Justice Chatterji thinks highly of Lata I think, and Meenakshi's sister Kakoli is also fond of her. Then there are the three boys Amit and Dipankar and Tapan Chatterji, who all seem more and more strange to me. Amit says Lata should learn Bengali, it is the only truly civilised language in India. He himself as you know writes his books in English so why does he say that only Bengali is civilised and Hindi is not? I don't know, but the Chatterjis are an unusual family. They have a piano but the father wears a dhoti quite a lot in the evenings. Kakoli sings Rabindrasangeet and also western music, but her voice is not to my taste and she has a modern reputation in Calcutta. Sometimes I wonder how my Arun got married into such a family but all is for the best as I have my Aparna.

Lata I fear was very angry and hurt with me when we first came to Calcutta and also worried about her exam results and not like herself at all. You must telegram the results as soon as they come, no matter whether good or bad. It was that boy K of course and nothing else whom she met in Brahmpur and he was clearly a bad influence. Sometimes she made a bitter remark to me and sometimes only gave minimum answers to my questions, but can you imagine if I had let things go on in that way? I had no help or sympathy from Arun at all in this but now I have told him to introduce Lata to his covenanted and other friends and let us see. If only I could find a husband like Pran for my Lata, I would die contented. If Daddy had seen you Pran, he would have known that his Savita was in good hands.

One day I was so hurt that I said to Lata, it was all very well to have non-cooperation in Gandhiji's time against the British, but I am your own mother, and it is very stubborn of you that you are doing this. Doing what? she said—and it was so indifferent that I felt my heart had broken. My dearest Savita, I pray, if you have a daughter—although actually it is time for a grandson in the family—then she will not ever be so cold to you. But at other times, she forgets she is angry with me—and then she is quite affectionate until she remembers.

May God Almighty keep you well and happy to carry out all your plans. And soon in the Monsoon I will see you, D.V.

Lots and lots of love to both of you from me, Arun, Varun, Lata, Aparna and Meenakshi and a big hug and kiss as well. Don't worry about me, my blood sugar is all right.

From your everloving Ma

P.S. Please give my love to Maan, Veena, Kedarnath and also Bhaskar and Kedarnath's mother and your own parents Pran (I hope the neem blossoms are less troublesome now)—and my father and Parvati—and of course to the Baby Expected. Also give my salaams to Mansoor and Mateen and the other servants. It is so hot in Calcutta but it must be worse in Brahmpur and in your condition Savita you must remain very cool and not go out in the sun or take unnecessary exercise. You must get plenty of rest. When in doubt about what to do, you must remember to do nothing. After the birth you will be busy enough, believe me, my dearest Savita, and you must conserve your strength.

6.7

The reference to neem blossoms reminded Pran that he had not visited his mother in several days. Mrs Mahesh Kapoor had been even more badly affected this year by the pollen of the neem trees than she usually was. Some days she could hardly breathe. Even her husband, who treated all allergies as if they were wilfully inflicted by the victims upon themselves, was forced to take some notice of his wife. As for Pran, who knew from experience what it felt like to struggle for breath, he thought of his mother with a feeling of sad helplessness—and with some anger towards his father who insisted that she remain in town in order to manage the household.

'Where should she go where there are no neem trees?' Mahesh Kapoor had said. 'Abroad?'

'Well, Baoji, perhaps to the south somewhere—or to the hills.'

'Don't be unrealistic. Who will take care of her there? Or do you think I should give up my work?'

There was no obvious answer to this. Mahesh Kapoor had always been dismissive of other people's illnesses and bodily pain, and had disappeared from town whenever his wife had been about to give birth. He could not stand 'the mess and the fuss and so on'.

Lately, Mrs Mahesh Kapoor had been much exercised by one issue which seemed to aggravate her condition. This was Maan's involvement with Saeeda Bai, and his loitering around in Brahmpur when he had work and other obligations in Banaras. When his fiancée's family sent an indirect inquiry through a relative about fixing a date for the marriage, Mrs Mahesh Kapoor had begged Pran to speak to him. Pran had told her that he had very little control over his younger brother. 'He only listens to Veena,' he had said, 'and even then he goes and does exactly as he pleases.' But his mother had looked so unhappy that he had agreed to talk to Maan. He had, however, put it off now for several days.

Right, said Pran to himself. I'll talk to him today. And it'll be a good opportunity to visit Prem Nivas.

It was already too hot to walk, so they went by tonga. Savita sat smiling silently and—Pran thought—quite mysteriously. In fact she was merely pleased to be visiting her mother-in-law, whom she liked, and with whom she enjoyed discussing neem trees and vultures and lawns and lilies.

When they got to Prem Nivas they found that Maan was still asleep. Leaving Savita with Mrs Mahesh Kapoor, who looked a little better than before, Pran went off to wake his brother up. Maan was lying in his room with his face buried in his pillow. A ceiling fan was going round and round, but the room was still quite warm.

'Get up! Get up!' said Pran.

'Oh!' said Maan, trying to ward off the light of day.

'Get up! I have to talk to you.'

'What? Oh! Why? All right, let me wash my face.'

Maan got up, shook his head several times, examined his face in the mirror quite carefully, did a respectful adaab to himself when his brother was not watching and, after splashing some water upon himself, came back and lay down flat on the bed once more—but on his back.

'Who's told you to speak to me?' said Maan. Then, remembering what he had been dreaming about, he said, regretfully: 'I was having the most wonderful dream. I was walking near the Barsaat Mahal with a young woman—not so young really, but her face was unlined still—'

Pran started smiling. Maan looked a little hurt.

'Aren't you interested?' he asked.

'No.'

'Well, why have you come, Bhai Sahib? Why don't you sit down on the bed—it's much more comfortable. Oh yes,' he said, remembering: 'you've come to speak to me. Who has put you up to it?'

'Does someone have to have put me up to it?'

'Yes. You never proffer brotherly advice as a rule, and I can tell from your face that I am in for some proffering. All right, all right, go ahead. It's about Saeeda Bai, I suppose.'

'You're absolutely right.'

'Well, what's there to say?' said Maan, with a sort of happy hangdog look. 'I'm terribly in love with her. But I don't know if she cares for me at all.'

'Oh, you idiot,' said Pran affectionately.

'Don't make fun of me. I can't bear it. I'm feeling very low,' said Maan, gradually convincing himself of his romantic depression. 'But no one believes me. Even Firoz says—'

'And he's quite right. You're feeling nothing of the kind. Now tell me, do you really think that that kind of person is capable of loving?'

'Oh?' asked Maan. 'Why not?'

He thought back to the last evening that he had spent in Saeeda Bai's arms, and began to feel fuzzily amorous once more.

'Because it's her job not to,' replied Pran. 'If she fell in love with you it wouldn't be at all good for her work—or her reputation! So she won't. She's too hard-headed. Anyone with one good eye can see that, and I've seen her for three Holis in succession.'

'You just don't know her, Pran,' said his brother ardently.

This was the second time in a few hours that someone had told Pran that he just didn't understand someone else, and he reacted impatiently.

'Now listen, Maan, you're making a complete fool of yourself. Women like that are brought up to pretend they're in love with gullible men—to make their hearts light and their purses even lighter. You know that Saeeda Bai is notorious for this sort of thing.'

Maan just turned over on to his stomach and pressed his face into the pillow.

Pran found it very difficult to be righteous with his idiot of a brother. Well, I've done my duty, he thought. If I say anything further it'll have just the opposite reaction to what Ammaji wants.

He tousled his brother's hair and said: 'Maan—are you in difficulties with money?'

Maan's voice, slightly muffled by the pillow, said: 'Well, it isn't easy, you know. I'm not a client or anything, but I can't just go empty-handed. So, well, I've given her a few gifts. You know.'

Pran was silent. He did not know. Then he said: 'You haven't eaten into the money you came to Brahmpur to do business with, have you, Maan? You know how Baoji would react if he came to know of that.'

'No,' said Maan, frowning. He had turned around again, and was looking up at the fan. 'Baoji, you know, said something sharp to me a few days ago—but I'm sure he doesn't really mind at all about Saeeda Bai. After all, he's had quite a lively youth himself—and, besides, he's invited her several times to sing at Prem Nivas.'

Pran said nothing. He was quite certain that his father was very displeased.

Maan went on: 'And just a few days ago I asked him for money—"for this and for that"—and he gave me quite a generous amount.'

Pran reflected that whenever his father was occupied with a piece of legislation or some other project, he hated being disturbed, and almost paid people off so as to be able to get on with his own work.

'So you see,' said Maan, 'there isn't a problem at all.' Having made the problem disappear, he went on: 'But where is my lovely bhabhi? I'd much rather be scolded by her.'

'She's downstairs.'

'Is she angry with me too?'

'I'm not exactly angry with you, Maan,' said Pran. 'All right, get ready and come down. She's looking forward to seeing you.'

'What's happening about your job?' asked Maan.

Pran made a gesture with his right hand which was the equivalent of a shrug.

'Oh, yes, and is Professor Mishra still furious with you?'

Pran frowned. 'He's not the sort of man who forgets little acts of kindness such as yours. Do you know, if you had been a student and did what you did at Holi, I might, as a member of the student welfare committee, have had to recommend your expulsion.'

'Your students sound a very lively lot,' said Maan approvingly.

After a while he added, with a happy smile on his face:

'Do you know that she calls me Dagh Sahib?'

'Oh, really?' said Pran. 'Very charming. I'll see you downstairs in a few minutes.'

6.8

One evening after a longish day in the High Court, Firoz was on his way to the cantonment for some polo and a ride when he noticed his father's secretary, Murtaza Ali, bicycling down the road with a white envelope in his hand. Firoz halted the car and called out, and Murtaza Ali stopped.

'Where are you off to?' asked Firoz.

'Oh, nowhere, just within Pasand Bagh.'

'Who's that envelope for?'

'Saeeda Bai Firozabadi,' said Murtaza Ali rather reluctantly.

'Well, that's on my way. I'll drop it off.' Firoz looked at his watch. 'It shouldn't make me late.'

He reached out of the window to take the packet, but Murtaza Ali held back.

'It isn't any trouble at all, Chhoté Sahib,' he said, smiling. 'I must not palm off my duties on others. You are looking very well turned out in those new jodhpurs.'

'It's not a duty for me. Here—' And Firoz reached out once again for the packet. He reflected that it would provide him with the ostensibly innocent means to see that lovely girl Tasneem once more.

'I'm sorry, Chhoté Sahib, the Nawab Sahib was quite explicit that I deliver it.'

'That makes no sense to me,' said Firoz, now speaking in a somewhat patrician manner. 'I delivered the packet before—you let me take it to save you trouble when it was on my way—and I am capable of taking it again.'

'Chhoté Sahib, it is such a small matter, please let it be.'

'Now, good fellow, let me have the packet.'

'I cannot.'

'Cannot?' Firoz's voice became commandingly aloof.

'You see, Chhoté Sahib, the last time I did, the Nawab Sahib was extremely annoyed. He told me very firmly that this was never to happen again. I must ask your forgiveness for my rudeness, but your father was so vehement that I dare not risk his displeasure again.'

'I see.' Firoz was perplexed. He could not understand his father's inordinate annoyance about this harmless matter. He had been looking forward to his game, but now his mood was spoilt. Why was his father behaving in this excessively puritanical way? He knew that it was not the done thing to socialize with singing girls, but what harm was there in simply delivering a letter? But perhaps that was not the problem at all.

'Let me get this clear,' he went on after a moment's thought. 'Was my father displeased that you had not delivered the packet or that I had delivered it?'

'That I could not say, Chhoté Sahib. I wish I understood it myself.' Murtaza Ali continued to stand politely beside his bicycle, holding the envelope firmly in one hand, as if he feared that Firoz might, on a sudden impulse, snatch it away from him after all.

'All right,' said Firoz and, with a curt nod at Murtaza Ali, drove on towards the cantonment.

It was a slightly cloudy day. Though it was only early evening, it was comparatively cool. On both sides of Kitchener Road stood tall gulmohur trees in full orange bloom. The peculiar scent of the flowers, not sweet as such but as evocative as that of geraniums, was heavy in the air, and the light, fan-shaped petals were strewn across the road. Firoz decided to talk to his father when he got back to Baitar House, and this resolution helped him put the incident out of his mind.

He recalled his first glimpse of Tasneem and remembered the sudden and disturbing attraction he had felt for her—a sense that he had seen her before, somewhere 'if not in this life then in some earlier one'. But after a while, as he came closer to the polo grounds and smelt the familiar scent of horse dung and passed by the familiar buildings and waved to the familiar people, the game reasserted itself and Tasneem too faded into the background.

Firoz had promised to teach Maan a bit of polo this evening, and now he looked around for him at the club. In fact it would be more accurate to say that he had compelled a reluctant Maan to learn a little about the game.

'It's the best game in the world,' he had told him. 'You'll be an addict soon enough. And you have too much time on your hands.' Firoz had gripped Maan's hands in his own and had said: 'They're going soft from too much pampering.'

But Maan was nowhere to be seen at this moment, and Firoz glanced a little impatiently at his watch and at the lessening light.

6.9

A few minutes later, Maan came riding up towards him, doffed his riding cap in a cheerful gesture of greeting, and dismounted.

'Where were you?' asked Firoz. 'They're quite strict here about timing, and if we don't get to the wooden horse within ten minutes of the time for which we've reserved it, well, someone else will take it. Anyway, how did you manage to persuade them to allow you to ride one of their horses without being accompanied by a member?'

'Oh, I don't know,' said Maan. 'I just walked over and talked to one of the grooms for a few minutes, and he saddled up this bay for me.'

Firoz reflected that he should not have been too surprised: his friend had the knack of winging it in all kinds of unlikely situations through sheer insouciance. The groom must have taken it for granted that Maan was a fully-fledged member of the club.

With Maan uncomfortably astride the wooden horse, Firoz began his education. The light bamboo polo stick was put in Maan's right hand, and he was asked to point and swing it a few times for good measure.

'But this is no fun at all,' said Maan, after about five minutes.

'Nothing is fun in the first five minutes,' replied Firoz calmly. 'No, don't hold the stick that way—keep your arm straight—no, completely straight—that's right—yes, now swing it—just a half swing—good!—your arm should act like an extension of the stick itself.'

'I can think of one thing at least that's fun in the first five minutes,' said Maan with a slightly idiotic grin, heaving the stick around and losing his balance slightly.

Firoz surveyed Maan's posture coolly. 'I'm talking about anything requiring skill and practice,' he said.

'That requires a lot of skill and practice,' said Maan.

'Don't be flippant,' said Firoz, who took his polo seriously. 'Now just stay exactly as you are, and look at me. Notice that the line between my shoulders runs parallel to the spine of the horse. Aim for that position.'

Maan tried, but found it even more uncomfortable. 'Do you really think that everything that requires skill is painful at the beginning?' he asked. 'My Urdu teacher appears to take exactly the same view.' He rested the polo stick between his legs and wiped his forehead with the back of his right hand.

'Come now, Maan,' said Firoz, 'you can't say you're tired after just five minutes of this. I'm going to try you out with the ball now.'

'I am rather tired, actually,' said Maan. 'My wrist's hurting a little. And my elbow, and my shoulder.'

Firoz flashed him an encouraging smile and placed the ball on the ground. Maan swung his stick towards it and missed it entirely. He tried again and missed again.

'You know,' said Maan, 'I'm not at all in the mood for this. I'd rather be somewhere else.'

Firoz, ignoring him, said: 'Don't look at anything, just at the ball—just at the ball—nothing else—not at me—not at where the ball is going to go—not even at a distant image of Saeeda Bai.'

This last comment, instead of making Maan lose his swing entirely, actually resulted in a small impact as the mallet skimmed the top of the ball.

'Things aren't going all that well with Saeeda Bai, you know, Firoz,' said Maan. 'She got very annoyed with me yesterday, and I don't know what it was I did.'

'What brought it on?' said Firoz, not very sympathetically.

'Well, her sister came in while we were talking and said something about the parrot looking as if he was exhausted. Well, it's a parakeet actually, but that's a sort of parrot, isn't it? So I smiled at her and mentioned our Urdu teacher and said that the two of us had something in common. Meaning, of course, that Tasneem and I did. And Saeeda Bai just flared up. She just flared up. It was half an hour before she would talk to me affectionately again.' Maan looked as abstracted as it was possible for him to look.

'Hmm,' said Firoz, thinking of how sharp Saeeda Bai had been with Tasneem when he had visited the house to deliver the envelope.

'It almost seemed as if she was jealous,' Maan went on after a pause and a few more shots. 'But why would someone as amazingly beautiful as her need to be jealous of anyone else? Especially her sister.'

Firoz reflected that he would never have used the words 'amazingly beautiful' of Saeeda Bai. It was her sister who had amazed him with her beauty. He could well imagine that Saeeda Bai might envy her freshness and youth.

'Well,' he said to Maan, a smile playing on his own fresh and handsome features, 'I wouldn't take it as a bad sign at all. I don't see why you're depressed about it. You should know by now that women are like that.'

'So you think jealousy is a healthy sign?' demanded Maan, who was quite prone to jealousy himself. 'But there must be something to feel jealous about, don't you think? Have you ever seen the younger sister? How could she even compare with Saeeda Bai?'

Firoz said nothing for a while, then made the brief comment: 'Yes, I've seen her. She's a pretty girl.' He didn't volunteer anything else.

But Maan, while hitting the ball ineffectually across the top, had his mind on Saeeda Bai again. 'I sometimes think she cares more for that parakeet than for me,' he said, frowning. 'She's never angry with him. I can't go on like this—I'm exhausted.'

The last sentence referred not to his heart but to his arm. Maan was expending a great deal of energy playing his shots, and Firoz appeared to enjoy seeing him huff and puff a little.

'How did your arm feel when you made that last shot?' he asked.

'It got quite a jolt,' said Maan. 'How long do you want me to go on?'

'Oh, till I feel you've had enough,' said Firoz. 'It's quite encouraging—you are making all the standard beginner's mistakes. What you just did was to top the ball. Don't do that—aim at a point at the bottom of the ball, and it'll rise very nicely. If you aim at the top, all the strength of the impact will be absorbed by the ground. The ball won't go far and, besides, you'll find as you did just now that your arm gets a sharp little shock.'

'I say, Firoz,' said Maan, 'how did you and Imtiaz learn Urdu? Wasn't it very difficult? I'm finding it impossible—all those dots and squiggles.'

'We had an old maulvi who came to the house especially to teach us,' said Firoz. 'My mother was very keen that we learn Persian and Arabic as well, but Zainab was the only one who got very far with those.'

'How is Zainab?' asked Maan. He reflected that though he had been a favourite of hers in childhood, he had not seen her for many years now—ever since she had disappeared into the world of purdah. She was six years older than him and he had adored her. In fact she had once saved his life in a swimming accident when he was six. I doubt I'll ever see her again, he thought to himself. How awful—and how strange.

'Don't use force, use strength—' said Firoz. 'Or hasn't your instructress taught you that?'

Maan aimed a gentle swipe at Firoz with his stick.

By now there were only about ten minutes of daylight left, and Firoz could see that Maan was not happy sitting on a merely wooden horse. 'Well, one last shot,' he said.

Maan pointed at the ball, made a light half-swing, and with one smooth, full, circular motion of his arm and wrist, hit the ball squarely in the centre. Pokk! The ball made a wonderful wooden sound, and flew up in a fine low parabola, passing over the net at the top of the pit.

Both Firoz and Maan were astonished.

'Good shot!' said Maan, very pleased with himself.

'Yes,' said Firoz. 'Good shot. Beginner's luck. Tomorrow we'll see if you can do that consistently. But now I'm going to get you to ride a real polo pony for a few minutes, and see if you can control the reins with the left hand alone.'

'Perhaps tomorrow,' said Maan. His shoulders were stiff and his back felt twisted, and he had had more than enough of polo. 'How about a ride instead?'

'I can see that, like your Urdu teacher, I'll have to teach you discipline before I teach you your subject,' said Firoz. 'Riding with one hand isn't hard at all. It's no more difficult than learning riding in the first place—or learning your alif-be-pe-te. If you try it now, you'll be in a better position tomorrow.'

'But I'm not very keen to try it today,' protested Maan. 'It's dark anyway, and I won't enjoy myself. Oh, all right, whatever you say, Firoz. You're the boss.'

He dismounted and put his arm around his friend's shoulder, and they walked towards the stables.

'The trouble with my Urdu teacher,' continued Maan, apropos of nothing immediate, 'is that he only wants to teach me the finer points of calligraphy and pronunciation, and I only want to learn how to read love poetry.'

'That's the trouble with the *teacher*, is it?' asked Firoz, holding his friend's polo stick to prevent retaliation. He was feeling cheerful again. Maan's company almost invariably did that to him.

'Well, don't you think I should have a say in the matter?' asked Maan.

'Perhaps,' said Firoz. 'If I thought you knew what was good for you.'

6.10

After he got home, Firoz decided to have a word with his father. He was far less annoyed than he had been immediately after his exchange with Murtaza Ali, but just as puzzled as before. He had a suspicion that his father's private secretary was misinterpreting, or at least exaggerating, his father's words. What could his father have meant by issuing such a curious instruction? Did it apply to Imtiaz as well? If so, why was his father being so protective of them? What did he think his sons would be likely to go and do? Perhaps, Firoz felt, he should reassure him.

When he did not find his father in his room, he assumed that he had gone into the zenana to talk to Zainab, and decided not to follow him. It was just as well that he did not do so, because the Nawab Sahib was talking to her about a matter so personal that the presence of anyone else, even a beloved brother, would have put an abrupt end to the conversation.

Zainab, who had shown such courage when Baitar House was under siege by the police, was now sitting near her father and sobbing quietly with misery. The Nawab Sahib had his arm around her and there was an expression of great bitterness on his face.

'Yes,' he was saying softly, 'I have heard rumours that he goes out. But one should not take everything everyone says as true.'

Zainab said nothing for a while, then, covering her face with her hands, she said: 'Abba-jaan, I know it is true.'

The Nawab Sahib stroked her hair gently, thinking back to the days when Zainab was four years old and would come and sit on his lap whenever something troubled her. It was unbearably bitter to him that his son-in-law had, by his infidelities, injured her so deeply. He looked back at his own marriage, at the practical and gentle woman whom for many years he had hardly known, and who, late in their marriage and long after the birth of their three children, had entirely won his heart. All he said to Zainab was:

'Be patient like your mother. He will come around one day.'

Zainab did not look up, but she wondered that her father had invoked her mother's memory. After a while, her father added, almost as if he were speaking to himself:

'I came to realize her worth very late in life. God rest her soul.'

For many years now, the Nawab Sahib had visited his wife's grave as often as possible to read the fatiha over it. And indeed the old Begum Sahiba had been a most remarkable woman. She had put up with what she knew of the Nawab's own unsettled youth, had run much of the estate efficiently from behind the walls of her seclusion, had endured his later phases of piety (not as excessive, fortunately, as that of his younger brother), and had brought up her children and helped bring up her nephews and nieces with discipline and culture. Her influence on the zenana had been both diffuse and powerful. She had read; and, despite that, she had thought.

In fact, it was probably the books that she lent her sister-in-law Abida that had first planted a few scattered seeds of rebellion in that restless, chafing heart. Though Zainab's mother had no thoughts of leaving the zenana herself, it was only her presence that had made it bearable for Abida. When she died, Abida compelled her husband—and his elder brother the Nawab Sahib—by reason, cajolery, and threats of suicide (which she fully intended to carry out, and which they could see she did) to let her escape from what had become to her an intolerable bondage. Abida, the firebrand of the legislature, had little respect for the Nawab Sahib, whom she saw as weak and feckless, and who (again, as she saw it) had killed all desire in his wife ever to emerge from purdah. But she had great affection for his children: for Zainab, because her temperament was like her mother's; for Imtiaz, because his laughter and many of his expressions resembled hers; and for Firoz, whose long head and clear and handsome looks bore the imprint of his mother's face.

Hassan and Abbas were now brought in by the maidservant and Zainab kissed them a tearful goodnight.

Hassan, looking slightly sullen, said to his mother: 'Who's been making you cry, Ammi-jaan?'

His mother, smiling, hugged him to her and said, 'No one, sweetheart. No one.'

Hassan then demanded from his grandfather the ghost story that he had promised to tell them some nights earlier. The Nawab Sahib complied. As he was narrating his exciting and fairly bloodthirsty tale to the evident delight of the two boys, even the three-year-old, he reflected over the many ghost stories attached to this very house that he had been told in childhood by his own servants and family. The house and all its memories had been threatened with dissolution just a few nights ago. No one had been able to prevent the attack and it was a mere matter of grace or chance or fate that it had been saved. We are each of us alone, thought the Nawab Sahib; blessedly, we rarely realize this.

His old friend Mahesh Kapoor came to his mind and it struck him that in times of trouble it sometimes happened that even those who wanted to help were unable to. They might be tied down themselves for one reason or another; or else circumstances of expediency or some greater need could have kept them less involuntarily away.

6.11

Mahesh Kapoor too had been thinking of his old friend, and with a sense of guilt. He had not received the emergency message from Baitar House on the night that L.N. Agarwal had sent the police to take possession of it. The peon whom Mrs Mahesh Kapoor had sent to find him had not been able to do so.

Unlike rural land (now threatened by the prospect of the abolition of zamindari), urban land and buildings were under no threat of appropriation at all—except if they fell into the hands of the Custodian of Evacuee Property. Mahesh Kapoor had not thought it at all likely that Baitar House, one of the great houses of Brahmpur—indeed, one of the landmarks of the city—could be at risk. The Nawab Sahib continued to live there, his sister-in-law Begum Abida Khan was a powerful voice in the Assembly, and the grounds and gardens in the front of the house were well taken care of, even if many—or most—of the rooms inside were now empty and unused. He regretted that he had been too preoccupied to advise his friend to provide each room with at least the semblance of occupancy. And he felt very bad that he had not been able to intercede with the Chief Minister in order to help on the night of the crisis.

As it had turned out, Zainab's intercession had achieved all that Mahesh Kapoor could have hoped to. S.S. Sharma's heart had been touched, and his indignation against the Home Minister had been unfeigned.

The letter that Zainab had written to him had mentioned a circumstance that the Nawab Sahib had told her about some years previously; it had stuck in her memory. S.S. Sharma—the ex-Premier of the Protected Provinces (as the Chief Minister of Purva Pradesh was called before Independence)—had been held virtually incommunicado in a British prison during the Quit India Movement of 1942, and could do as little for his family as they could for him. At this time the Nawab Sahib's father had come to know that Sharma's wife was ill and had come to her help. It was a simple matter of a doctor, medicines and a visit or two, but in those days not many, whether they believed in British rule or not, wished to be seen associating with the families of subversives. Sharma had in fact been Premier when the P.P. Land Tenancy Act of 1938 had been passed—an act that the Nawab Sahib's father had considered, correctly, to be the thin end of the wedge of more far-reaching land reform. Nonetheless, simple humanity and even a sense of admiration for his enemy had inspired this crucial assistance. Sharma had been deeply grateful for the kindness that his family had received in their hour of need, and when Hassan, the six-year-old great-grandchild of the man who had helped him then, had come to him with a letter requesting his help and protection, he had been very moved.

Mahesh Kapoor knew nothing of these circumstances, for neither party had wanted them known, and he had been astonished to hear of the Chief Minister's swift and unambiguous response. It made him feel even more strongly how ineffectual he himself had been. And when, after the passage of the Zamindari Bill in the Assembly, he had caught the Nawab Sahib's eye, something had held him back from going up to his friend—in order to commiserate, explain and apologize. Was it shame about his inaction—or simply the obvious immediate discomfort at the fact that the bill that he had just successfully steered through the House would, though there was no animus in it, injure the Nawab Sahib's interests as surely as the police action of the Home Minister?

Now still more time had passed, and the matter continued to prey on his mind. I must visit Baitar House this evening, said Mahesh Kapoor to himself. I cannot keep putting it off.

6.12

But meanwhile, this morning, there was work that needed to be done. A large number of people both from his constituency in Old Brahmpur and from elsewhere had gathered on the verandahs of Prem Nivas. Some of them were even milling around in the courtyard and wandering out into the garden. Mahesh Kapoor's personal secretary and personal assistants were doing what they could to control the crowd and regulate the flow of visitors into the small office that the Minister of Revenue maintained at home.

Mahesh Kapoor sat at a table in the corner of the office. The two narrow benches that ran along the walls were occupied by a variety of people: farmers, traders, minor politicians, suppliants of one kind or another. An old man, a teacher, sat on the chair that faced Mahesh Kapoor across the table. He was younger, but looked older than the Minister. He had been worn out by a lifetime of care. He was an old freedom fighter, who had spent many years in jail under the British, and had seen his family reduced to poverty. He had obtained a B.A. in 1921, and with a qualification like that in those days he might well have gone on to retire at the very highest levels of Government. But in the later twenties he had left everything to follow Gandhiji, and this idealistic impulse had cost him dearly. When he was in jail, his wife, with no one to support her, had died of tuberculosis, and his children, reduced to eating other people's scraps, had suffered nearly fatal starvation. With the coming of Independence he had hoped that his sacrifice would result in an order of things closer to the ideals he had fought for, but he had been bitterly disappointed. He saw the corruption that had begun to eat into the rationing system and the system of government contracts with a rapacity that surpassed anything he had known under the British. The police too had become more overt in their extortions. What was worse was that the local politicians, the members of the local Congress Committees, were often hand in glove with the corrupt petty officials. But when the old man had gone to the Chief Minister, S.S. Sharma, on behalf of the people of his neighbourhood, to ask him to take action against specific politicians, that great figure had merely smiled tiredly and said to him:

'Masterji, your work, that of the teacher, is a sacred occupation. Politics is like the coal trade. How can you blame people if their hands and faces become a little black?'

The old man was now talking to Mahesh Kapoor, trying to persuade him that the Congress Party had become as shamefully vested in its interests and as shamefully oppressive in its rule as the British had ever been.

'What you, of all people, are doing in this party, Kapoor Sahib, I don't know,' he said in Hindi that had more of an Allahabad than a Brahmpur accent. 'You should have left it long ago.'

The old man knew that everyone in the room could hear what he was saying but he did not care. Mahesh Kapoor looked at him directly and said:

'Masterji, the times of Gandhiji have gone. I have seen him at his zenith, and I have seen him lose his hold so completely that he was not able to prevent the Partition of this country. He, however, was wise enough to see that his power and his inspiration were not absolute. He once said that it was not he but the situation that held the magic.'

The old man said nothing for a few seconds. Then, his mouth working slightly at the edges, he said: 'Minister Sahib, what are you saying to me?'

The change in his mode of address was not lost on Mahesh Kapoor, and he felt slightly ashamed at his own evasion. 'Masterji,' he went on, 'I may have suffered in the old days, but I have not suffered as you have. It is not that I am not disenchanted with what I see around me. I just fear that I will be of less use outside the party than in it.'

The old man, half to himself, said: 'Gandhiji was right when he foresaw what would happen if the Congress Party continued after Independence as the party of Government. That is why he said that it should be disbanded and its members should dedicate themselves to social work.'

Mahesh Kapoor did not mince his words in response. He simply said: 'If all of us had done that, there would have been anarchy in the country. It was the duty of those of us who had had some experience in the provincial governments in the late thirties to at least keep the administration going. You are right when you describe what is going on all around us. But if people like you, Masterji, and I were to wash our hands of this coal trade, you can imagine what kind of people would take over. Previously politics was not profitable. You languished in jail, your children starved. Now politics is profitable, and naturally the kind of people who are interested in making money are keen to join the game. If we move out, they move in. It is as simple as that. Look at all these people milling around,' he went on in a voice that did not carry beyond the old man's ears, embracing in a broad gesture of his hands the room, the verandahs and the lawn, 'I can't tell you how many of them are begging me to get them Congress Party tickets for the coming elections. And I know as well as you do that in the times of the British, they would have run a hundred miles before accepting such a mark of favour!'

'I was not suggesting that you move out of politics, Kapoor Sahib,' said the old man; 'just that you help to form another party. Everyone knows that Pandit Nehru often feels that Congress is not the right place for him. Everyone knows how unhappy he is about Tandonji becoming the Congress President through questionable means. Everyone knows that Panditji has almost lost his grip on his own party. Everyone knows that he respects you, and I believe that it is your duty to go to Delhi and help persuade him to leave. With Pandit Nehru and the less self-satisfied parts of Congress splitting off, the new party they form will have a good chance of winning the next elections. I believe that; indeed, if I did not believe that I would be in despair.'

Mahesh Kapoor nodded his head, then said: 'I will think deeply about what you have said, Masterji. I would not like to deceive you into thinking that I have not considered such matters before. But there is a logic to events, and a method to timing, and I will ask you to leave it at that.'

The old man nodded his head, got up, and walked away with an expression of undisguised disappointment on his face.

6.13

A number of other people, some individually, some in pairs, some in groups, and some in what could only be called throngs, spoke to Mahesh Kapoor during the morning and early afternoon. Cups of tea came from the kitchen and went back empty. Lunchtime came and went, and the Minister Sahib remained energetic though unfed. Mrs Mahesh Kapoor sent word to him through a servant; he waved him impatiently away. She would never have dreamed of eating before her husband did, but her main concern was not that she was hungry but that he needed food and did not know it.

Mahesh Kapoor gave as patient an audience as he could to the people who were channelled his way. There were ticket-seekers and favour-seekers of all kinds, politicos of various shades of honesty and opinion, advisers, gossipmongers, agents, assistants, lobbyists, MLAs and other colleagues and associates, local businessmen clad in nothing but a dhoti (yet worth lakhs of rupees) who were looking for a contract or information or simply to be able to tell people that they had been received by the Revenue Minister, good people, bad people, happy people, unhappy people (more of the latter), people who had just come to pay their respects because they were in town, people who had come to gape in open-mouthed awe and who took in nothing of what he was saying, people who wanted to pull him to the right, people who wanted to push him further towards the left, Congressmen, socialists, communists, Hindu revivalists, old members of the Muslim League who wanted admission into Congress, the indignant members of a deputation from Rudhia who were complaining about some decision made by the local Sub-Divisional Officer. As a Governor once wrote about his experience of popularly elected provincial governments in the late 1930s: 'nothing was too petty, too local, too palpably groundless' not to justify small local leaders appealing to politicians over the head of the district administration.

Mahesh Kapoor listened, explained, conciliated, tied matters together, disentangled others, wrote notes, issued instructions, spoke loudly, spoke softly, examined copies of sections of the new electoral rolls that were being revised for the coming General Elections, got angry and was extremely sharp with someone, smiled wryly at someone else, yawned at a third, stood up as a renowned lawyer came in, and asked that tea be served to him in more elegant china.

At nine o'clock he was explaining what he understood about the provisions of the Hindu Code Bill to farmers who were worried and resentful that their sons' right to their land would be shared by their daughters (and therefore their sons-in-law) under the laws of intestate succession under consideration by Parliament in Delhi.

At ten o'clock he was saying to an old colleague and lawyer: 'As for that bastard, do you think that he can get his way with me? He came into my office with a wad of money, trying to get me to soften a provision of the Zamindari Bill, and I was tempted to have him arrested—title or no title. He might have ruled Marh once, but he had better learn that other men rule Purva Pradesh. Of course I know that he and his kind will challenge the bill in court. Do you think we are not going to be ready ourselves? That is why I wanted to consult you.'

At eleven o'clock he was saying: 'The basic problem for me personally is not the temple or the mosque. The basic problem is how the two religions will get on with each other in Brahmpur. Maulvi Sahib, you know my views on this. I've lived here most of my life. Naturally there is mistrust: the question is how to overcome it. You know how it is. The rank and file of Congress opposes old Muslim Leaguers who wish to join Congress. Well, this is only to be expected. But Congress has had a long tradition of Hindu-Muslim collaboration, and, believe me, it is the obvious party to join. And as far as tickets are concerned, I am giving you my word that there will be fair representation for Muslims. You won't regret that we have no reserved seats or separate electorates. Yes, the nationalist Muslims, who have been with our party throughout their careers, will receive preference in this matter, but if I have anything to do with it there will be some room for others as well.'

At noon he was saying: 'Damodarji, that's a very handsome ring you have on your finger. How much is it worth? Twelve hundred rupees? No, no, I'm pleased to see you, but as you can see'—he pointed to the papers piled on his desk with one hand and gestured towards the crowds with the other—'I have much less time to talk to my old friends than I would wish. . . .'

At one o'clock he was saying: 'Are you telling me that the lathi charge was necessary? Have you seen how these people live? And you have the gall to tell me that there should be some threat of further punitive action? Go and talk to the Home Minister, you'll find a more sympathetic audience. I am sorry—you can see how many people are waiting—'

At two o'clock he was saying: 'I suppose I have a little influence. I'll see what I can do. Tell the boy to come around to see me next week. Obviously, a lot will depend upon his exam results. No, no, don't thank me—and certainly don't thank me in advance.'

At three o'clock he was saying quietly: 'Look, Agarwal has about a hundred MLAs in his hand. I have about eighty. The rest are uncommitted, and will go wherever they sense victory. But I'm not going to think of mounting a challenge to Sharmaji. It's only if Panditji calls him to join the Central Cabinet in Delhi that the question of the leadership will come up. Still, I agree that there's no harm in keeping the issue alive—one has to remain in the public eye.'

At a quarter past three, Mrs Mahesh Kapoor came in, reproved the PAs gently, and pleaded with her husband to come and have lunch and lie down for a while. She herself was clearly still suffering from the residual neem blossoms, and her allergy was causing her to gasp a little. Mahesh Kapoor did not snap at her as he often did. He acquiesced and retired. People drifted away reluctantly and very gradually, and after a while Prem Nivas once more reverted from a political stage, clinic, and fairground to a private home.

After Mahesh Kapoor had eaten, he lay down for a short nap, and Mrs Mahesh Kapoor finally ate lunch herself.

6.14

After lunch, Mahesh Kapoor asked his wife to read him some passages from the *Proceedings of the P.P. Legislative Council* that dealt with the debate on the Zamindari Bill when it had first gone to the Upper House from the Assembly. Since it was about to go there again with its new encrustation of amendments, he wanted to regain his sense of the possible obstacles it might face in that chamber.

Mahesh Kapoor himself found it very difficult to read the Purva Pradesh legislative debates of the last few years. Some members took peculiar pride these days in couching their speeches in a heavily Sanskritized Hindi which no one in his right mind could understand. That, however, was not the main problem. The real difficulty was that Mahesh Kapoor was not very familiar with the Hindi—or Devanagari—script. He had been brought up at a time when boys were taught to read and write the Urdu—or Arabic—script. In the 1930s the *Proceedings of the Protected Provinces Legislative Assembly* were printed speech by speech in English, Urdu, and Hindi—depending on the language that the speaker wrote or spoke. His own speeches were printed in Urdu, for instance, and so were the speeches of a good many others. The English speeches he could of course read without difficulty. But he tended to skip the Hindi ones, as they made him struggle. Now, after Independence, the *Proceedings* were printed entirely in the official language of the state, which was Hindi; Urdu speeches too were printed in the Hindi script, and English could only be spoken—and that too extremely rarely—with the express permission of the Speaker of the House. This was why Mahesh Kapoor often asked his wife to read the debates out to him. She had been taught—like many women at the time—to read and write under the influence of the Hindu revivalist organization, the Arya Samaj, and the script that she had been taught was, naturally enough, the script of the ancient Sanskrit texts—and the modern Hindi language.

Perhaps there was also an element of vanity or prudence in having his wife, rather than his personal assistants, read him these debates. The Minister did not wish the world at large to know that he could not read Hindi. As it happened, his PAs knew that he could not, but they were fairly discreet, and the word did not get around.

Mrs Mahesh Kapoor read in a rather monotonous voice, a bit as if she were chanting the scriptures. The pallu of her sari covered her head and a part of her face, and she did not look directly at her husband. Her breath was a little short these days, so she had to pause from time to time, and Mahesh Kapoor would become quite impatient. 'Yes, yes, go on, go on!' he would say whenever there was a longish pause, and she, patient woman that she was, would do so without complaint.

From time to time—usually between one debate and another, or as she reached for a different volume—she would mention something entirely outside the political sphere that had been on her mind. Since her husband was always busy, this was one of the few opportunities she got to talk to him. One such matter was that Mahesh Kapoor had not met his old friend and bridge partner Dr Kishen Chand Seth for some time.

'Yes, yes, I know,' said her husband impatiently. 'Go on, go on, yes, from page 303.' Mrs Mahesh Kapoor, having tested the water and found it too warm, was quiet for a while.

At the second opening she saw, she mentioned that she would like to have the Ramcharitmanas recited in the house some day soon. It would be good for the house and family in general: for Pran's job and health, for Maan, for Veena and Kedarnath and Bhaskar, for Savita's forthcoming baby. The ideal time, the nine nights leading up to and including the birthday of Rama, had gone by, and both her samdhins had been disappointed that she had not been able to persuade her husband to allow the recitation. At that time she could understand that he had been preoccupied with a number of things, but surely now—

She was interrupted abruptly. Mahesh Kapoor, pointing his finger at the volume of debates, exclaimed: 'Oh, fortunate one—' (fortunate to have married him, that is) '—first recite the scriptures that I've asked you to recite.'

'But you promised that—'

'Enough of this. You three mothers-in-law can plot as much as you like, but I can't allow it in Prem Nivas. I have a secular image—and in a town like this where everyone is beating the drum of religion, I am not going to join in with the shehnai. Anyway, I don't believe in this chanting and hypocrisy—and all this fasting by saffron-clad heroes who want to ban cow slaughter and revive the Somnath Temple and the Shiva Temple and God knows what else.'

'The President of India himself will be going to Somnath to help inaugurate the new temple there—'

'Let the President of India do what he likes,' said Mahesh Kapoor sharply. 'Rajendra Babu does not have to win an election or face the Assembly. I do.'

Mrs Mahesh Kapoor waited for the next hiatus in the debates before venturing: 'I know that the nine nights of Ramnavami have gone, but the nine nights of Dussehra are still to come. If you think that in October—'

In her eagerness to convince her husband, she had begun to gasp a little.

'Calm down, calm down,' said Mahesh Kapoor, relenting slightly. 'We'll see all about that in due course.'

Even if the door was not exactly ajar, it had not been slammed shut, reflected Mrs Mahesh Kapoor. She retired from this subject with a sense that something, however slight, had been gained. She believed—though she would not have voiced the belief—that her husband was quite wrong-headed in divesting himself of the religious rites and ceremonies that gave meaning to life and donning the drab robes of his new religion of secularism.

At the next pause Mrs Mahesh Kapoor murmured tentatively: 'I have had a letter.'

Mahesh Kapoor clicked his tongue impatiently, dragged once again from his own thoughts down into the trivial vortices of domesticity. 'All right, all right, what is it that you want to talk about? Who is this letter from? What disaster am I in for?' He was used to the fact that his wife led these piecemeal conversations step by step and subject by subject from the most innocuous to the most troubling.

'It is from the Banaras people,' said Mrs Mahesh Kapoor.

'Hmmh!' said Mahesh Kapoor.

'They send their best wishes to everyone,' said Mrs Mahesh Kapoor.

'Yes, yes, yes! Get to the point. They realize no doubt that our son is too good for their daughter and want to call the whole thing off.'

Sometimes wisdom lies in not taking an ironical remark as ironical. Mrs Mahesh Kapoor said: 'No, quite the opposite. They want to fix the date as quickly as possible—and I don't know what to reply. If you read between the lines it seems that they even have some idea about—well, about "that". Why else would they be so concerned?'

'Uff-oh!' said Mahesh Kapoor impatiently. 'Do I have to hear about this from everyone? In the Assembly canteen, in my own office, everywhere I hear about Maan and his idiocy! This morning two or three people brought it up. Is there nothing more important in the world to talk about?'

But Mrs Mahesh Kapoor persevered.

'It is very important for our family,' she said. 'How can we hold our heads up in front of people if this goes on? And it is not good for Maan either to spend all his time and money like this. He was supposed to come here on business, and he has done nothing in that line. Please speak to him.'

'You speak to him,' said Mahesh Kapoor brutally. 'You have spoilt him all his life.'

Mrs Mahesh Kapoor was silent, but a tear trickled down her cheek. Then she rallied and said: 'Is it good for your public image either? A son who does nothing but spend his time with that kind of person? The rest of the time he lies down on his bed and stares up at the fan. He should do something else, something serious. I don't have the heart to say anything to him. After all, what can a mother say?'

'All right, all right, all right,' said Mahesh Kapoor, and closed his eyes.

He reflected that the cloth business in Banaras was, under the care of a competent assistant, doing better in Maan's absence than it had been doing when he was there. What then was to be done with Maan?

At about eight o'clock that evening he was about to get into the car to visit Baitar House when he told the driver to wait. Then he sent a servant to see if Maan was in the house. When the servant told him that he was sleeping, Mahesh Kapoor said:

'Wake up the good-for-nothing fellow, and tell him to dress and come down at once. We are going to visit the Nawab Sahib of Baitar.'

Maan came down looking none too happy. Earlier in the day he had been exercising hard on the wooden horse, and now he was looking forward to visiting Saeeda Bai and exercising his wit, among other things.

'Baoji?' he said inquiringly.

'Get into the car. We're going to Baitar House.'

'Do you want me to come along?' asked Maan.

'Yes.'

'All right, then.' Maan got into the car. There was, he realized, no way to avoid being kidnapped.

'I am assuming you have nothing better to do,' said his father.

'No. . . . Not really.'

'Then you should get used to adult company again,' said his father sternly.

As it happened, he also enjoyed Maan's cheerfulness, and thought it would be good to take him along for moral support when he went to apologize to his old friend the Nawab Sahib. But Maan was less than cheerful at the moment. He was thinking of Saeeda Bai. She would be expecting him and he would not even be able to send her a message to say that he could not come.

6.15

As they entered the grounds of Baitar House, however, he cheered up a little at the thought that he might meet Firoz. At polo practice Firoz had not mentioned that he would be going out for dinner.

They were asked to sit in the lobby for a few minutes. The old servant said that the Nawab Sahib was in the library, and that he would be informed of the Minister's arrival. After ten minutes or so, Mahesh Kapoor got up from the old leather sofa and started walking up and down. He was tired of twiddling his thumbs and staring at photographs of white men with dead tigers at their feet.

A few minutes more, and his patience was at an end. He told Maan to come with him, and walked through the high-ceilinged rooms and somewhat ill-lit corridors towards the library. Ghulam Rusool made a few ineffectual attempts at dissuasion, but to no effect. Murtaza Ali, who was hanging around near the library, was brushed aside as well. The Minister of Revenue with his son in tow strode up to the library door and flung it open.

Brilliant light blinded him for a moment. Not only the mellower reading lights but the great chandelier in the middle of the library had been lit. And at the large round table below—with papers spread out around them and even a couple of buff leather-bound law-books lying open before them—sat three other sets of fathers and sons: The Nawab Sahib of Baitar and Firoz; the Raja and Rajkumar of Marh; and two Bony Bespectacled Bannerji Barristers (as that famous family of lawyers was known in Brahmpur).

It would be difficult to say who was most embarrassed by this sudden intrusion.

The crass Marh snarled: 'Speak of the Devil.'

Firoz, though he found the situation uncomfortable, was pleased to see Maan and went up to him immediately to shake his hand. Maan put his left arm around his friend's shoulder and said: 'Don't shake my right hand—you've crippled it already.'

The Rajkumar of Marh, who was interested in young men more than in the jargon of the Zamindari Bill, looked at the handsome pair with a little more than approval.

The elder Bannerji ('P.N.') glanced quickly at his son ('S.N.') as if to say, I told you we should have had the conference in our chambers.

The Nawab Sahib felt that he had been caught red-handed, plotting against Mahesh Kapoor's bill with a man whom he would normally have shunned.

And Mahesh Kapoor realized instantly that he was the least welcome intruder imaginable at this working conference—for it was he who was the enemy, the expropriator, the government, the fount of injustice, the other side.

It was, however, Mahesh Kapoor who broke the ice among the elder circle by going up to the Nawab Sahib and taking his hand. He did not say anything, but slowly nodded his head. No words of sympathy or apology were needed. The Nawab Sahib knew immediately that his friend would have done anything in his power to help him when Baitar House was under siege—but that he had been ignorant of the crisis.

The Raja of Marh broke the silence with a laugh:

'So you have come to spy on us! We are flattered. No mere minion but the Minister himself.'

Mahesh Kapoor said:

'Since I was not blinded by the vision of your gold number plates outside, I could hardly have known you were here. Presumably, you came by rickshaw.'

'I will have to count my number plates before I leave,' continued the Raja of Marh.

'If you need any help, let me send my son with you. He can count till two,' said Mahesh Kapoor.

The Raja of Marh had become red in the face. 'Was this planned?' he demanded of the Nawab Sahib. He was thinking that this could well be a plot by the Muslims and their sympathizers to humiliate him.

The Nawab Sahib found his voice. 'No, Your Highness, it was not. And I apologize to all of you, especially to you, Mr Bannerji—I should not have insisted that we meet here.'

Since common interest in the impending litigation had thrown him together with the Raja of Marh anyway, the Nawab Sahib had hoped that by inviting the Raja to his own house he might get the chance to talk to him a little about the Shiva Temple in Chowk—or at least to create the possibility of a later talk. The communal situation among the Hindus and Muslims in Brahmpur was so troubling that the Nawab had swallowed his gorge and a little of his pride in order to help sort things out. The move had now backfired.

The elder of the Bony Bespectacleds, appalled by what had gone before, now said in a rather finicky voice: 'Well, I think we have already discussed the main lines of the matter, and can adjourn for the moment. I will inform my father by letter of what has been said by all sides, and I hope I can persuade him to appear for us in this matter if and when it is necessary.'

He was referring to the great G.N. Bannerji, a lawyer of legendary fame, acumen, and rapacity. If, as was now almost inevitable, the amended bill went through in the Upper House, obtained the President of India's signature, and became law, it would certainly be challenged in the Brahmpur High Court. If G.N. Bannerji could be persuaded to appear on behalf of the landlords, it would considerably improve their chances of having the act declared unconstitutional, and therefore null and void.

The Bannerjis took their leave. The younger Bannerji, though no older than Firoz, had a flourishing practice already. He was intelligent, worked hard, had cases shovelled his way by his family's old clients, and thought of Firoz as rather too languid for life at the Bar. Firoz admired his intelligence but thought him a prig, a little along the lines of his finicky father. His grandfather, the great G.N. Bannerji, however, was not a prig. Though he was in his seventies, he was as energetic erect on his feet in court as erect off his feet in bed. The huge, some would say unscrupulous, fees he insisted on before he accepted a case went to support a scattered harem of women; but he still succeeded in living beyond his means.

The Rajkumar of Marh was a basically decent and not bad-looking but somewhat weak young man who was bullied by his father. Firoz loathed the crude, Muslim-baiting Raja: 'black as coal with his diamond buttons and ear-tops'. His sense of family honour made him keep his distance from the Rajkumar as well. Not so Maan, who was inclined to like people unless they made themselves unlikable. The Rajkumar, quite attracted by Maan, and discovering that he was at a loose end these days, suggested a few things that they could do together, and Maan agreed to meet him later in the week.

Meanwhile the Raja of Marh, the Nawab Sahib, and Mahesh Kapoor were standing by the table in the full light of the chandelier. Mahesh Kapoor's eyes fell on the papers spread out on the table, but then, remembering the Raja's earlier jeer, he quickly turned his gaze away.

'No, no, be our guest, Minister Sahib,' sneered the Raja of Marh. 'Read away. And in exchange, tell me when exactly you plan to vest the ownership of our lands in your own pocket.'

'My own pocket?'

A silverfish scurried across the table. The Raja crushed it with his thumb.

'I meant, of course, the Revenue Department of the great state of Purva Pradesh.'

'In due course.'

'Now you are talking like your dear friend Agarwal in the Assembly.'

Mahesh Kapoor did not respond. The Nawab Sahib said: 'Should we move into the drawing room?'

The Raja of Marh made no attempt to move. He said, almost equally to the Nawab Sahib and the Minister of Revenue: 'I asked you that question merely from altruistic motives. I am supporting the other zamindars simply because I do not care for the attitude of the government—or political insects like you. I myself have nothing to lose. My lands are protected from your laws.'

'Oh?' said Mahesh Kapoor. 'One law for men and another for monkeys?'

'If you still call yourself a Hindu,' said the Raja of Marh, 'you may recall that it was the army of monkeys that defeated the army of demons.'

'And what miracle do you expect this time?' Mahesh Kapoor could not resist asking.

'Article 362 of the Constitution,' said the Raja of Marh, gleefully spitting out a number larger than two. 'These are our private lands, Minister Sahib, our own private lands, and by the covenants of merger that we rulers made when we agreed to join your India, the law cannot loot them and the courts cannot touch them.'

It was well known that the Raja of Marh had gone drunk and babbling to the dour Home Minister of India, Sardar Patel, to sign the Instrument of Accession by which he made over his state to the Indian Union, and had even smudged his signature with his tears—thus creating a unique historical document.

'We will see,' said Mahesh Kapoor. 'We will see. No doubt G.N. Bannerji will defend Your Highness in the future as ably as he has defended your lowness in the past.'

Whatever story lay behind this taunt, it had a signal effect.

The Raja of Marh made a sudden, growling, vicious lunge towards Mahesh Kapoor. Luckily he stumbled over a chair, and fell towards his left on to the table. Winded, he raised his face from among the law-books and scattered papers. But a page of a law-book had got torn.

For a second, staring at the torn page, the Raja of Marh looked dazed, as if he was uncertain where he was. Firoz, taking advantage of his disorientation, quickly went up to him, and with an assured arm led him towards the drawing room. It was all over in a few seconds. The Rajkumar followed his father.

The Nawab Sahib looked towards Mahesh Kapoor, and raised one hand slightly, as if to say, 'Let things be.' Mahesh Kapoor said, 'I am sorry, very sorry'; but both he and his friend knew that he was referring less to the immediate incident than to his delay in coming to Baitar House.

After a while, he said to his son: 'Come, Maan, let's go.' On the way out, they noticed the Raja's long black Lancia with its solid gold ingot-like licence plates stamped 'MARH 1' lurking in the drive.

In the car back to Prem Nivas, each was lost in his own thoughts. Mahesh Kapoor was thinking that, despite his explosive timing, he was glad that he had not waited still longer to reassure his friend. He could sense how affected the Nawab Sahib had been when he had taken his hand.

Mahesh Kapoor expected that the Nawab Sahib would call him up the next day to apologize for what had happened, but not offer any substantial explanations. The whole business was very uncomfortable: there was a strange, unresolved air to events. And it was disturbing that a coalition—however volatile—of former enemies was coming into being out of self-interest or self-preservation against his long-nurtured legislation. He would very much have liked to know what legal weaknesses, if any, the lawyers had found in his bill.

Maan was thinking how glad he was that he had met his friend again. He had told Firoz that he would probably be stuck with his father the whole evening, and Firoz had promised to send a message to Saeeda Bai—and if necessary to take it there personally—to inform her that Dagh Sahib had been detained.

6.16

'No; be careful; think.'

The voice was slightly mocking, but not without concern. It appeared to care that the task should be done well—that the neatly lined page should not become a record of shame and shapelessness. In a way, it appeared to care about what happened to Maan as well. Maan frowned, then wrote the character 'meem' again. It looked to him like a curved spermatozoon.

'Your mind isn't on the tip of your nib,' said Rasheed. 'If you want to make use of my time—and I am here at your service—why not concentrate on what you're doing?'

'Yes, yes, all right, all right,' said Maan shortly, sounding for a second remarkably like his father. He tried again. The Urdu alphabet, he felt, was difficult, multiform, fussy, elusive, unlike either the solid Hindi or the solid English script.

'I can't do this. It looks beautiful on the printed page, but to write it—'

'Try again. Don't be impatient.' Rasheed took the bamboo pen from his hand, dipped it in the inkwell, and wrote a perfect, dark-blue 'meem'. He then wrote another below it: the letters were identical, as two letters rarely are.

'What does it matter, anyway?' asked Maan, looking up from the sloping desk at which he was sitting, cross-legged, on the floor. 'I want to read Urdu and to write it, not to practise calligraphy. Do I have to do this?' He reflected that he was asking for permission as he used to when he was a child. Rasheed was no older than he was, but had taken complete control of him in his role as a teacher.

'Well, you have put yourself in my hands, and I don't want you to start on shaky foundations. So what would you like to read now?' Rasheed inquired with a slight smile, hoping that Maan's answer would not be the predictable one once more.

'Ghazals,' said Maan unhesitatingly. 'Mir, Ghalib, Dagh. . . .'

'Yes, well—' Rasheed said nothing for a while. There was tension in his eyes at the thought of having to teach ghazals to Maan shortly before going over passages of the Holy Book with Tasneem.

'So what do you say?' said Maan. 'Why don't we start today?'

'That would be like teaching a baby to run the marathon,' Rasheed responded after a few seconds, having found an analogy ridiculous enough to suit his dismay. 'Eventually, of course, you will be able to. But for now, just try that meem again.'

Maan put the pen down and stood up. He knew that Saeeda Bai was paying Rasheed, and he sensed that Rasheed needed the money. He had nothing against his teacher; in a way he liked his conscientiousness. But he rebelled against his attempt to impose a new infancy on him. What Rasheed was pointing out to him was the first step on an endless and intolerably tedious road; at this rate it would be years before he would be able to read even those ghazals that he knew by heart. And decades before he could pen the love letters he yearned to write. Yet Saeeda Bai had made a compulsory half-hour lesson a day with Rasheed 'the little bitter foretaste' that would whet his appetite for her company.

The whole thing was so cruelly erratic, however, thought Maan. Sometimes she would see him, sometimes not, just as it suited her. He had no sense of what to expect, and it ruined his concentration. And so here he had to sit in a cool room on the ground floor of his beloved's house with his back hunched over a pad with sixty aliphs and forty zaals and twenty misshapen meems, while occasionally a few magical notes from the harmonium, a phrase from the sarangi, a strain of a thumri floated down the inner balcony and filtered through the door to frustrate both his lesson and him.

Maan never enjoyed being entirely by himself at the best of times, but these evenings, when his lesson was over, if word came through Bibbo or Ishaq that Saeeda Bai preferred to be alone, he felt crazy with unhappiness and frustration. Then, if Firoz and Imtiaz were not at home, and if family life appeared, as it usually did, unbearably bland and tense and pointless, Maan would fall in with his latest acquaintances, the Rajkumar of Marh and his set, and lose his sorrows and his money in gambling and drink.

'Look, if you aren't in the mood for a lesson today. . . .' Rasheed's voice was kinder than Maan had expected, though there was rather a sharp expression on his wolf-like face.

'No, no, that's fine. Let's go on. It's just a question of self-control.' Maan sat down again.

'Indeed it is,' said Rasheed, reverting to his former tone of voice. Self-control, it struck him, was what Maan needed even more than perfect meems. 'Why have you got yourself trapped in a place like this?' he wanted to ask Maan. 'Isn't it pathetic that you should be sacrificing your dignity for a person of Saeeda Begum's profession?'

Perhaps all this was present in his three crisp words. At any rate, Maan suddenly felt like confiding in him.

'You see, it's like this—' began Maan. 'I have a weak will, and when I fall into bad company—' He stopped. What on earth was he saying? And how would Rasheed know what he was talking about? And why, even if he did, should he care?

But Rasheed appeared to understand. 'When I was younger,' he said, 'I—who now consider myself truly sober—would spend my time beating people up. My grandfather used to do so in our village, and he was a well-respected man, so I thought that beating people up was what made people look up to him. There were about five or six of us, and we would egg each other on. We'd just go up to some schoolfellow, who might be wandering innocently along, and slap him hard across the face. What I would never have dared to do alone, I did without any hesitation in company. But, well, I don't any more. I've learned to follow another voice, to be alone and to understand things—maybe to be alone and to be misunderstood.'

To Maan this sounded like the advice of a good angel; or perhaps a risen one. In his imagination's eye he saw the Rajkumar and Rasheed struggling for his soul. One was coaxing him towards hell with five poker cards, one beating him towards paradise with a quill. He botched another meem before asking:

'And is your grandfather still alive?'

'Oh yes,' said Rasheed, frowning. 'He sits on a cot in the shade and reads the Quran Sharif all day, and chases the village children away when they disturb him. And soon he will try to chase the officers of the law away too, because he doesn't like your father's plans.'

'So you're zamindars?' Maan was surprised.

Rasheed thought this over before saying: 'My grandfather was, before he divided his wealth among his sons. And so is my father and so is my, well, my uncle. As for myself—' He paused, appeared to look over Maan's page, then continued, without finishing his previous sentence, 'Well, who am I to set myself up in judgement in these matters? They are very happy, naturally, to keep things as they are. But I have lived in the village almost all my life, and I have seen the whole system. I know how it works. The zamindars—and my family is not so extraordinary as to be an exception to this—the zamindars do nothing but make their living from the misery of others; and they try to force their sons into the same ugly mould as themselves.' Here Rasheed paused, and the area around the corners of his mouth tightened. 'If their sons want to do anything else, they make life miserable for them too,' he continued. 'They talk a great deal about family honour, but they have no sense of honour except to gratify the promises of pleasure they have made to themselves.'

He was silent for a second, as if hesitating; then went on:

'Some of the most respected of landlords do not even keep their word, they are so petty. You might find this hard to believe but I was virtually offered a job here in Brahmpur as the curator of the library of one such great man, but when I got to the grand house I was told—well, anyway, all this is irrelevant. The main fact is that the system of landlords isn't good for the villagers, it isn't good for the countryside as a whole, it isn't good for the country, and until it goes. . . .' The sentence remained unfinished. Rasheed was pressing his fingertips to his forehead, as if he was in pain.

This was a far cry from meem, but Maan listened with sympathy to the young tutor, who appeared to speak out of some terrible pressure, not merely of circumstances. Only a few minutes earlier he had been counselling care, concentration, and moderation for Maan.

There was a knock on the door, and Rasheed quickly straightened up. Ishaq Khan and Motu Chand entered.

'Our apologies, Kapoor Sahib.'

'No, no, you're quite right to enter,' said Maan. 'The time for my lesson is over, and I'm depriving Begum Sahiba's sister of her Arabic.' He got up. 'Well, I'll see you tomorrow, and my meems will be matchless,' he promised Rasheed impetuously. 'Well?' he nodded genially at the musicians, 'Is it life or death?'

But from Motu Chand's downcast looks he anticipated Ishaq Khan's words.

'Kapoor Sahib, I fear that this evening—I mean the Begum Sahiba asked me to inform you. . . .'

'Yes, yes,' said Maan, angry and hurt. 'Good. My deep respects to the Begum Sahiba. Till tomorrow, then.'

'It is just that she is indisposed.' Ishaq disliked lying and was bad at it.

'Yes,' said Maan, who would have been very much more concerned if he had believed in her indisposition. 'I trust that she will recover rapidly.' At the door he turned and added: 'If I thought it would do any good, I would prescribe her a string of meems, one to be taken every hour and several before she retires.'

Motu Chand looked at Ishaq for a clue, but Ishaq's face reflected his own perplexity.

'It's no more than she has prescribed for me,' said Maan. 'And, as you can see, I am flourishing as a result. My soul, at any rate, has avoided indisposition as successfully as she has been avoiding me.'

6.17

Rasheed was just picking up his books when Ishaq Khan, who was still standing by the door, blurted out:

'And Tasneem is indisposed as well.'

Motu Chand glanced at his friend. Rasheed's back was towards them, but it had stiffened. He had heard Ishaq Khan's excuse to Maan; it had not increased his respect for the sarangi player that he had acted in this demeaning manner as an emissary for Saeeda Bai. Was he now acting as an emissary for Tasneem as well?

'What gives you that understanding?' he asked, turning around slowly.

Ishaq Khan coloured at the patent disbelief in the teacher's voice.

'Well, whatever state she is in now, she will be indisposed after her lesson with you,' he replied challengingly. And, indeed, it was true. Tasneem was often in tears after her lessons with Rasheed.

'She has a tendency to tears,' said Rasheed, sounding more harsh than he intended. 'But she is not unintelligent and is making good progress. If there are any problems with my teaching, her guardian can inform me in person—or in writing.'

'Can't you be a little less rigorous with her, Master Sahib?' said Ishaq hotly. 'She is a delicate girl. She is not training to become a mullah, you know. Or a haafiz.'

And yet, tears or no tears, reflected Ishaq painfully, Tasneem was spending so much of her spare time on Arabic these days that she had very little left for anyone else. Her lessons appeared to have redirected her even from romantic novels. Did he really wish her young teacher to start behaving gently towards her?

Rasheed had gathered up his papers and books. He now spoke almost to himself. 'I am no more rigorous with her than I am with'—he had been about to say 'myself'—'with anyone else. One's emotions are largely a matter of self-control. Nothing is painless,' he added a little bitterly.

Ishaq's eyes flashed. Motu Chand placed a restraining hand on his shoulder.

'And anyway,' continued Rasheed, 'Tasneem has a tendency to indolence.'

'She appears to have lots of tendencies, Master Sahib.'

Rasheed frowned. 'And this is exacerbated by that half-witted parakeet which she keeps interrupting her work to feed or indulge. It is no pleasure to hear fragments of the Book of God being mangled in the beak of a blasphemous bird.'

Ishaq was too dumbstruck to say anything. Rasheed walked past him and out of the room.

'What made you provoke him like that, Ishaq Bhai?' said Motu Chand after a few seconds.

'Provoke him? Why, he provoked me. His last remark—'

'He couldn't have known that you had given her the parakeet.'

'Why, everyone knows.'

'He probably doesn't. He doesn't interest himself in that kind of thing, our upright Rasheed. What got into you? Why are you provoking everyone these days?'

The reference to Ustad Majeed Khan was not lost on Ishaq, but the subject was one he could hardly bear to think of. He said:

'So that owl book provoked you, did it? Have you tried any of its recipes? How many women has it lured into your power, Motu? And what does your wife have to say about your newfound prowess?'

'You know what I mean,' said Motu Chand, undeflected. 'Listen, Ishaq, there's nothing to be gained by putting people's backs up. Just now—'

'It's these wretched hands of mine,' cried Ishaq, holding them up and looking at them as if he hated them. 'These wretched hands. For the last hour upstairs it has been torture.'

'But you were playing so well—'

'What will happen to me? To my younger brothers? I can't get employment on the basis of my brilliant wit. And even my brother-in-law won't be able to come to Brahmpur to help us now. How can I show my face at the radio station, let alone ask for a transfer for him?'

'It's bound to get better, Ishaq Bhai. Don't distress yourself like this. I'll help you—'

This was of course impossible. Motu Chand had four small children.

Even music means agony to me now, said Ishaq Khan to himself, shaking his head. Even music. I cannot bear to hear it even when I am not on duty. This hand follows the tune by itself, and it seizes up with pain. If my father had been alive, what would he have said if he had heard me speaking like this?

6.18

'The Begum Sahiba was very explicit,' said the watchman. 'She is not seeing anyone this evening.'

'Why?' demanded Maan. 'Why?'

'I do not know,' said the watchman.

'Please find out,' said Maan, slipping a two-rupee note into the man's hand.

The watchman took the note and said: 'She is not well.'

'But you knew that before,' said Maan, a bit aggrieved. 'That means I must go and see her. She will be wanting to see me.'

'No,' said the watchman, standing before the gate. 'She will not be wanting to see you.'

This struck Maan as distinctly unfriendly. 'Now look,' he said, 'you have to let me in.' He tried to shoulder his way past the watchman, but the watchman resisted, and there was a scuffle.

Voices were heard from inside, and Bibbo emerged. When she saw what was happening, her hand flew to her mouth. Then she gasped out: 'Phool Singh—stop it! Dagh Sahib, please—please—what will Begum Sahiba say?'

This thought brought Maan to his senses, and he brushed down his kurta, looking rather shamefaced. Neither he nor the watchman was injured. The watchman continued to look entirely matter-of-fact about the whole incident.

'Bibbo, is she very ill?' asked Maan in vicarious pain.

'Ill?' said Bibbo. 'Who's ill?'

'Saeeda Bai, of course.'

'She's not in the least ill,' said Bibbo, laughing. Then, as she caught the watchman's eye, she added: 'At least not until half an hour ago, when she had a sharp pain around her heart. She can't see you—or anyone.'

'Who's with her?' demanded Maan.

'No one, that is, well, as I've just said—no one.'

'Someone is with her,' said Maan fiercely, with a sharp stab of jealousy.

'Dagh Sahib,' said Bibbo, not without sympathy, 'it is not like you to be like this.'

'Like what?' said Maan.

'Jealous. Begum Sahiba has her old admirers—she cannot cast them off. This house depends on their generosity.'

'Is she angry with me?' asked Maan.

'Angry? Why?' asked Bibbo blankly.

'Because I didn't come that day as I had promised,' said Maan. 'I tried—I just couldn't get away.'

'I don't think she was angry with you,' said Bibbo. 'But she was certainly angry with your messenger.'

'With Firoz?' said Maan, astonished.

'Yes, with the Nawabzada.'

'Did he deliver a note?' asked Maan. He reflected with a little envy that Firoz, who could read and write Urdu, could thereby communicate in writing with Saeeda Bai.

'I think so,' said Bibbo, a little vaguely.

'And why was she angry?' asked Maan.

'I don't know,' said Bibbo with a light laugh. 'I must go in now.' And she left Maan standing on the pavement looking very agitated.

Saeeda Bai had in fact been greatly displeased to see Firoz, and was annoyed at Maan for having sent him. Yet, when she received Maan's message that he could not come on the appointed evening, she could not help feeling disappointed and sad. And this fact too annoyed her. She could not afford to get emotionally attached to this light-hearted, light-headed, and probably light-footed young man. She had a profession to keep up, and he was definitely in the nature of a distraction, however pleasant. And so she began to realize that it might be a good thing if he stayed away for a while. Since she was entertaining a patron this evening, she had instructed the watchman to keep everyone else—and particularly Maan—away.

When Bibbo later reported to her what had happened, Saeeda Bai's reaction was irritation at what she saw as Maan's interference in her professional life: he had no claim on her time or what she did with it. But later still, talking to the parakeet, she said, 'Dagh Sahib, Dagh Sahib' quite a number of times, her expression ranging from sexual passion to flirtatiousness to tenderness to indifference to irritation to anger. The parakeet was receiving a more elaborate education in the ways of the world than most of his fellows.

*

Maan had wandered off, wondering what to do with his time, incapable of getting Saeeda Bai out of his mind, but craving some, any, activity that could distract him at least for a moment. He remembered that he'd said he would drop by to see the Rajkumar of Marh, and so he made his way to the lodgings not far from the university that the Rajkumar had taken with six or seven other students, four of whom were still in Brahmpur at the beginning of the summer vacation. These students—two the scions of other petty princedoms, and one the son of a large zamindar—were not short of money. Most of them got a couple of hundred rupees a month to spend as they liked. This would have been just about equal to Pran's entire salary, and these students looked upon their unwealthy lecturers with easy contempt.

The Rajkumar and his friends ate together, played cards together, and shared each other's company a good deal. Each of them spent fifteen rupees a month on mess fees (they had their own cook) and another twenty rupees a month on what they called 'girl fees'. These went to support a very beautiful nineteen-year-old dancing girl who lived with her mother on a street not far from the university. Rupvati would entertain the friends quite often, and one of them would stay behind afterwards. This way each of them got a turn once every two weeks by rotation. On the other nights, Rupvati was free to entertain any of them or to take a night off, but the understanding was that she would have no other clients. The mother would greet the boys very affectionately; she was very pleased to see them, and often told them that she did not know what she and her daughter would have done if it hadn't been for their kindness.

Within half an hour of meeting the Rajkumar of Marh and drinking a fair amount of whisky, Maan had spilt out all his troubles on his shoulder. The Rajkumar mentioned Rupvati, and suggested that they visit her. Maan cheered up slightly at this and, taking the bottle with them, they began to walk in the direction of her house. But the Rajkumar suddenly remembered that this was one of her nights off and that they would not be entirely welcome there.

'I know what we'll do. We'll visit Tarbuz ka Bazaar instead,' said the Rajkumar, hailing a tonga and pulling Maan on to it. Maan was in no mood to resist this suggestion.

But when the Rajkumar, who had placed a friendly hand on his thigh, moved it significantly upwards, he shook it away with a laugh.

The Rajkumar did not take this rejection at all amiss, and in a couple of minutes, with the bottle passing between them, they were talking as easily as before.

'This is a great risk for me,' said the Rajkumar, 'but because of our great friendship I am doing it.'

Maan began to laugh. 'Don't do it again,' he said. 'I feel ticklish.'

Now it was the Rajkumar's turn to laugh. 'I don't mean that,' he said. 'I mean that taking you to Tarbuz ka Bazaar is a risk for me.'

'Oh, how?' said Maan.

'Because "any student who is seen in an undesirable place shall be liable to immediate expulsion".'

The Rajkumar was quoting from the curious and detailed rules of conduct promulgated for the students of Brahmpur University. This particular rule sounded so vague and yet at the same time so delightfully draconian that the Rajkumar and his friends had learned it by heart and used to chant it in chorus to the lilt of the Gayatri Mantra whenever they went out to gamble or drink or whore.

6.19

They soon got to Old Brahmpur, and wound through the narrow streets towards Tarbuz ka Bazaar. Maan was beginning to have second thoughts.

'Why not some other night—?' he began.

'Oh, they serve very good biryani there,' said the Rajkumar.

'Where?'

'At Tahmina Bai's. I've been there once or twice when it's been a non-Rupvati day.'

Maan's head sank on his chest and he went off to sleep. When they got to Tarbuz ka Bazaar, the Rajkumar woke him up.

'From here we'll have to walk.'

'Not far?'

'No—not far. Tahmina Bai's place is just around the corner.'

They dismounted, paid the tonga-wallah, and walked hand in hand into a side alley. The Rajkumar then walked up a flight of narrow and steep stairs, pulling a tipsy Maan behind him.

But when they got to the top of the stairs they heard a confused noise, and when they had walked a few steps along the corridor they were faced with a curious scene.

The plump, pretty, dreamy-eyed Tahmina Bai was giggling in delight as an opium-eyed, vacant-faced, red-tongued, barrel-bodied, middle-aged man—an income tax clerk—was beating on the tabla and singing an obscene song in a thin voice. Two scruffy lower division clerks were lounging around, one of them with his head in her lap. They were trying to sing along.

The Rajkumar and Maan were about to beat a retreat, when the madam of the establishment saw them and bustled quickly towards them along the corridor. She knew who the Rajkumar was, and hastened to reassure him that the others would be cleared out in a couple of minutes.

The two loitered around a paan shop for a few minutes, then went back upstairs. Tahmina Bai, alone, and with a beatific smile on her face, was ready to entertain them.

First she sang a thumri, then—realizing that time was getting on—she fell into a sulk.

'Oh, do sing,' said the Rajkumar, prodding Maan to placate Tahmina Bai as well.

'Ye-es—' said Maan.

'No, I won't, you don't appreciate my voice.' She looked downwards and pouted.

'Well,' said the Rajkumar, 'at least grace us with some poetry.'

This sent Tahmina Bai into gales of laughter. Her pretty little jowls shook, and she snorted with delight. The Rajkumar was mystified. After another swig from his bottle, he looked at her in wonderment.

'Oh, it's too—ah, ah—grace us with some—hah, hah—poetry!'

Tahmina Bai was no longer in a sulk but in an ungovernable fit of laughter. She squealed and squealed and held her sides and gasped, the tears running down her face.

When she was finally capable of speech, she told them a joke.

'The poet Akbar Allahabadi was in Banaras when he was lured by some friends into a street just like ours. He had drunk quite a lot—just like you—so he leaned against a wall to urinate. And then—what happened?—a courtesan, leaning out from a window above, recognized him from one of his poetry recitals and—and she said—' Tahmina Bai giggled, then started laughing again, shaking from side to side. 'She said—Akbar Sahib is gracing us with his poetry!' Tahmina Bai began to laugh uncontrollably once more, and to Maan's fuddled amazement he found himself joining in.

But Tahmina Bai had not finished her joke, and went on:

'So when he heard her, the poet made this remark on the spur of the moment:

> "Alas—what poor poetry can Akbar write
> When the pen is in his hand and the inkpot upstairs?"'

This was followed by squeals and snorts of laughter. Then Tahmina Bai told Maan that she herself had something to show him in the other room, and led him in, while the Rajkumar took another couple of swigs.

After a few minutes she emerged, with Maan looking bedraggled and disgusted. But Tahmina Bai was pouting sweetly. She said to the Rajkumar: 'Now, I have something to show you.'

'No, no,' said the Rajkumar. 'I've already—no, I'm not in the mood—come, Maan, let's go.'

Tahmina Bai looked affronted, and said: 'Both of you are—are—very similar! What do you need me for?'

The Rajkumar had got up. He put an arm around Maan and they

struggled towards the door. As they walked into the corridor they heard her say:

'At least have some biryani before you leave. It will be ready in a few minutes—'

Hearing no response from them, Tahmina Bai let fly:

'It might give you strength. Neither of you could grace me with your poetry!'

She began to laugh and shake, and her laughter followed them all the way down the stairs into the street.

6.20

Even though he had not done anything as such with her, Maan was feeling so remorseful about having visited such a low singing girl as Tahmina Bai that he wanted to go to Saeeda Bai's again immediately and beg her forgiveness. The Rajkumar persuaded him to go home instead. He took him to the gate of Prem Nivas and left him there.

Mrs Mahesh Kapoor was awake. When she saw Maan so drunk and unsteady she was very unhappy. Though she did not say anything to him, she was afraid for him. If his father had seen him in his present state he would have had a fit.

Maan, guided to his room, fell on his bed and went off to sleep.

The next day, contrite, he visited Saeeda Bai, and she was glad to see him. They spent the evening together. But she told him that she would be occupied for the next two days, and that he should not take it amiss.

Maan took it greatly amiss. He suffered from acute jealousy and thwarted desire, and wondered what he had done wrong. Even if he could have seen Saeeda Bai every evening, his days would merely have trickled by drop by drop. Now not only the days but the nights as well stretched interminably ahead of him, black and empty.

He practised a bit of polo with Firoz, but Firoz was busy during the days and sometimes even during the evenings with law or other work. Unlike the young Bespectacled Bannerji, Firoz did not treat time spent playing polo or deciding on a proper walking stick as wasted; he considered these activities proper to the son of a Nawab. Compared to Maan, however, Firoz was an addict to his profession.

Maan tried to follow suit—to do a bit of purchasing and to seek a few orders for the cloth business in Banaras—but found it too irksome to pursue. He paid a visit or two to his brother Pran and his sister Veena, but the very domesticity and purposefulness of their lives was a rebuke to his own. Veena told him off roundly, asking him what kind of an example he thought he was setting for young Bhaskar, and old Mrs Tandon looked at him even more suspiciously and disapprovingly than before. Kedarnath, however, patted Maan on the shoulder, as if to compensate for his mother's coldness.

Having exhausted all his other possibilities, Maan began to hang around the Rajkumar of Marh's set and (though he did not visit Tarbuz ka Bazaar again) drank and gambled away much of the money that had been reserved for the business. The gambling—usually flush, but sometimes even poker, for which there was a recent craze among the more self-consciously dissolute students in Brahmpur—took place mainly in the students' rooms, but sometimes in informal gambling dens in private houses here and there in the city. Their drink was invariably Scotch. Maan thought of Saeeda Bai all the time, and declined a visit even to the beautiful Rupvati. For this he was chaffed by all his new companions, who told him that he might lose his abilities permanently for lack of exercise.

One day Maan, separated from his companions, was walking up and down Nabiganj in a lovesick haze when he bumped into an old flame of his. She was now married, but retained a great affection for Maan. Maan too continued to like her a great deal. Her husband—who had the unlikely nickname of Pigeon—asked Maan if he would join them for coffee at the Red Fox. But Maan, who would normally have accepted the invitation with alacrity, looked away unhappily and said that he had to be going.

'Why is your old admirer behaving so strangely?' said her husband to her with a smile.

'I don't know,' she said, mystified.

'Surely he's not fallen out of love with you.'

'That's possible—but unlikely. Maan Kapoor doesn't fall out of love with anyone as a rule.'

They let it go at that, and went into the Red Fox.

6.21

Maan was not the only target of old Mrs Tandon's suspicions. Of late, the old lady, who kept tabs on everything, began to notice that Veena had not been wearing certain items of her jewellery: that though she continued to wear her in-laws' pieces, she had ceased to wear those that came from her parents. One day she reported this matter to her son.

Kedarnath paid no attention.

His mother kept at him, until eventually he agreed to ask Veena to put on her navratan.

Veena flushed. 'I've lent it to Priya, who wants to copy the design,' she said. 'She saw me wear it at Pran's wedding and liked it.'

But Veena looked so unhappy with her lie that the truth soon came out. Kedarnath discovered that running the household cost far more than she had told him it did; he, domestically impractical and often absent, had simply not noticed. She had hoped that by asking him for less household money she would reduce the financial pressure on his business. But now he realized that she had taken steps to pawn or sell her jewellery.

Kedarnath also learned that Bhaskar's school fees and books were already being supplied out of Mrs Mahesh Kapoor's monthly household money, some of which she diverted to her daughter.

'We can't have that,' said Kedarnath. 'Your father helped us enough three years ago.'

'Why not?' demanded Veena. 'Bhaskar's Nani is surely allowed to give him those, why not? It's not as if she's supplying us our rations.'

'There's something out of tune with my Veena today,' said Kedarnath, smiling a bit sadly.

Veena was not mollified.

'You never tell me anything,' she burst out, 'and then I find you with your head in your hands, and your eyes closed for minutes on end. What am I to think? And you are always away. Sometimes when you're away I cry to myself all night long; it would have been better to have a drunkard as a husband, as long as he slept here every night.'

'Now calm down. Where are these jewels?'

'Priya has them. She said she'd get me an estimate.'

'They haven't yet been sold then?'

'No.'

'Go and get them back.'

'No.'

'Go and get them back, Veena. How can you gamble with your mother's navratan?'

'How can you play chaupar with Bhaskar's future?'

Kedarnath closed his eyes for a few seconds.

'You understand nothing about business,' he said.

'I understand enough to know that you can't keep "over-extending" yourself.'

'Over-extension is just over-extension. All great fortunes are based on debt.'

'Well we, I know, will never be greatly fortunate again,' burst out Veena passionately. 'This isn't Lahore. Why can't we guard what little we have?'

Kedarnath was silent for a while. Then he said:

'Get the jewellery back. It's all right, it really is. Haresh's arrangement with the brogues is about to come through any day, and our long-term problems will be solved.'

Veena looked at her husband very dubiously.

'Everything good is always about to happen, and everything bad always happens.'

'Now that's not true. At least in the short term something good has happened to me. The shops in Bombay have paid up at last. I promise you that that is true. I know I'm a bad liar, so I don't even attempt it. Now get the navratan back.'

'Show me the money first!'

Kedarnath burst out laughing. Veena burst into tears.

'Where's Bhaskar?' he asked, after she had sobbed for a bit and subsided into silence.

'At Dr Durrani's.'

'Good. I hope he stays there a couple of hours more. Let's play a game of chaupar, you and I.'

Veena dabbed at her eyes with her handkerchief.

'It's too hot on the roof. Your mother won't want her beloved son to turn black as ink.'

'Well, we'll play in this room, then,' said Kedarnath with decision.

*

Veena got the jewellery back late that afternoon. Priya was not able to give her an estimate; with the witch hanging around the gossipy jeweller every minute of his previous visit, she had decided to subjugate urgency to discretion.

Veena looked at the navratan, gazing reminiscently at each stone in turn.

Early the same evening, Kedarnath went over with it to his father-in-law, and asked him to keep it in his custody at Prem Nivas.

'What on earth for?' asked Mahesh Kapoor. 'Why are you bothering me with these trinkets?'

'Baoji, it belongs to Veena, and I want to make sure she keeps it. If it's in my house, she might suddenly be struck with noble fancies and pawn it.'

'Pawn it?'

'Pawn it or sell it.'

'What madness. What's been going on? Have all my children taken leave of their senses?'

After a brief account of the navratan incident, Mahesh Kapoor said:

'And how is your business now that the strike is finally over?'

'I can't say it's going well—but it hasn't collapsed yet.'

'Kedarnath, run my farm instead.'

'No, but thank you, Baoji. I should be getting back now. The market must have opened already.' A further thought struck him. 'And besides, Baoji, who would mind your constituency if I decided to leave Misri Mandi?'

'True. All right. Fine. It's good that you have to go back because I have to deal with these files before tomorrow morning,' said Mahesh Kapoor inhospitably. 'I'll be working all night. Put it down here somewhere.'

'What—on the files, Baoji?' There was nowhere else on the table to place the navratan.

'Where else then—around my neck? Yes, yes, on that pink one: "Orders of the State Government on the Assessment Proposals". Don't look so anxious, Kedarnath, it won't disappear again. I'll see that Veena's mother puts the stupid thing away somewhere.'

6.22

Later that night in the house where the Rajkumar and his friends lived, Maan lost more than two hundred rupees gambling on flush. He usually held on to his cards far too long before packing them in or asking for a show. The predictability of his optimism was fatal to his chances. Besides, he was entirely un-poker-faced, and his fellow-players had a shrewd idea of how good his cards were from the instant he picked them up. He lost ten rupees or more on hand after hand—and when he held three kings, all he won was four rupees.

The more he drank, the more he lost, and vice versa.

Every time he got a queen—or begum—in his hand, he thought with a pang of the Begum Sahiba whom he was allowed to see so rarely these days. He could sense that even when he was with her, despite their mutual excitement and affection, she was finding him less amusing as he became more intense.

After he had got completely cleaned out, he muttered in a slurred voice that he had to be off.

'Spend the night here if you wish—go home in the morning,' suggested the Rajkumar.

'No, no—' said Maan, and left.

He wandered over to Saeeda Bai's, reciting some poetry on the way and singing from time to time.

It was past midnight. The watchman, seeing the state he was in, asked him to go home. Maan started singing, appealing over his head to Saeeda Bai:

'It's just a heart, not brick and stone, why should it then not fill
with pain?
Yes, I will weep a thousand times, why should you torture me in vain?'

'Kapoor Sahib, you will wake up everyone on the street,' said the watchman matter-of-factly. He bore Maan no grudge for the scuffle they had had the other night.

Bibbo came out and chided Maan gently. 'Kindly go home, Dagh Sahib. This is a respectable house. Begum Sahiba asked who was singing, and when I told her, she was most annoyed. I believe she is fond of you, Dagh Sahib, but she will not see you tonight, and she has asked me to tell you that she will never see you in this state. Please forgive my impertinence, I am only repeating her words.'

'It's just a heart, not brick and stone,' sang Maan.

'Come, Sahib,' said the watchman calmly and led Maan gently but firmly down the street in the direction of Prem Nivas.

'Here, this is for you—you're a good man—' said Maan, reaching into his kurta pockets. He turned them inside out, but there was no money in them.

'Take my tip on account,' he suggested.

'Yes, Sahib,' said the watchman, and turned back to the rose-coloured house.

6.23

Drunk, broke, and far from happy, Maan tottered back to Prem Nivas. To his surprise and rather unfocused distress, his mother was waiting up for him again. When she saw him, tears rolled down her cheeks. She was already overwrought because of the business with the navratan.

'Maan, my dear son, what has come over you? What has she done to my boy? Do you know what people are saying about you? Even the Banaras people know by now.'

'What Banaras people?' Maan inquired, his curiosity aroused.

'What Banaras people, he asks,' said Mrs Mahesh Kapoor, and began to cry even more intensely. There was a strong smell of whisky on her son's breath.

Maan put his arm protectively around her shoulder, and told her to go to sleep. She told him to go up to his room by the garden stairs to avoid disturbing his father, who was working late in his office.

But Maan, who had not taken in this last instruction, went humming off to bed by the main stairs.

'Who's that? Who's that? Is it Maan?' came his father's angry voice.

'Yes, Baoji,' said Maan, and continued to walk up the stairs.

'Did you hear me?' called his father in a voice that reverberated across half of Prem Nivas.

'Yes, Baoji,' Maan stopped.

'Then come down here at once.'

'Yes, Baoji.' Maan stumbled down the stairs and into his father's office. He sat down on the chair across the small table at which his father was sitting. There was no one in the office besides the two of them and a couple of lizards that kept scurrying across the ceiling throughout their conversation.

'Stand up. Did I tell you to sit down?'

Maan tried to stand up, but failed. Then he tried again, and leaned across the table towards his father. His eyes were glazed. The papers on the table and the glass of water near his father's hand seemed to frighten him.

Mahesh Kapoor stood up, his mouth set in a tight line, his eyes stern. He had a file in his right hand, which he slowly transferred to his left. He was about to slap Maan hard across the face when Mrs Mahesh Kapoor rushed in and said:

'Don't—don't—don't do that—'

Her voice and eyes pleaded with her husband, and he relented. Maan, meanwhile, closed his eyes and collapsed back into the chair. He began to drift off to sleep.

His father, enraged, came around the table, and started shaking him as if he wanted to jolt every bone in his body.

'Baoji!' said Maan, awoken by the sensation, and began to laugh.

His father raised his right arm again, and with the back of his hand slapped his twenty-five-year-old son across the face. Maan gasped, stared at his father, and raised his hand to touch his cheek.

Mrs Mahesh Kapoor sat down on one of the benches that ran along the wall. She was crying.

'Now you listen, Maan, unless you want another of those—listen to me,' said his father, even more furious now that his wife was crying because of something he had done. 'I don't care how much of this you remember tomorrow morning but I am not going to wait until you are sober. Do you understand?' He raised his voice and repeated, 'Do you understand?'

Maan nodded his head, suppressing his first instinct, which was to close his eyes again. He was so sleepy that he could only hear a few words drifting in and out of his consciousness. Somewhere, it seemed to him, there was a sort of tingling pain. But whose?

'Have you seen yourself? Can you imagine how you look? Your hair wild, your eyes glazed, your pockets hanging out, a whisky stain all the way down your kurta—'

Maan shook his head, then let it droop gently on his chest. All he wanted to do was to cut off what was going on outside his head: this angry face, this shouting, this tingling.

He yawned.

Mahesh Kapoor picked up the glass and threw the water on Maan's face. Some of it fell on his own papers but he didn't even look down at them. Maan coughed and choked and sat up with a start. His mother covered her eyes with her hands and sobbed.

'What did you do with the money? What did you do with it?' asked Mahesh Kapoor.

'What money?' asked Maan, watching the water drip down the front of his kurta, one channel taking the route of his whisky stain.

'The business money.'

Maan shrugged, and frowned in concentration.

'And the spending money I gave you?' continued his father threateningly.

Maan frowned in deeper concentration, and shrugged again.

'What did you do with it? I'll tell you what you did with it—you spent it on that whore.' Mahesh Kapoor would never have referred to Saeeda Bai in such terms if he had not been driven beyond the limit of restraint.

Mrs Mahesh Kapoor put her hands to her ears. Her husband snorted. She was behaving, he thought impatiently, like all three of Gandhiji's monkeys rolled into one. She would be clapping her hands over her mouth next.

Maan looked at his father, thought for a second, then said, 'No. I only brought her small presents. She never asked for anything more. . . .' He was wondering to himself where the money could have gone.

'Then you must have drunk and gambled it away,' said his father in disgust.

Ah yes, that was it, recalled Maan, relieved. Aloud he said, in a pleased tone, as if an intractable problem had, after long endeavour, suddenly been solved:

'Yes, that is it, Baoji. Drunk—gambled—gone.' Then the implications of this last word struck him, and he looked shamefaced.

'Shameless—shameless—you are behaving worse than a depraved zamindar, and I will not have it,' cried Mahesh Kapoor. He thumped the pink file in front of him. 'I will not have it, and I will not have you here any longer. Get out of town, get out of Brahmpur. Get out at once. I will not have you here. You are ruining your mother's peace of mind, and your own life, and my political career, and our family reputation. I give you money, and what do you do with it?—you gamble with it or spend it on whores or on whisky. Is debauchery your only skill? I never thought I would be ashamed of a son of mine. If you want to see someone with real hardships look at your brother-in-law—he never asks for money for his business, let alone "for this and for that". And what of your fiancée? We find a suitable girl from a good family, we arrange a good match for you—and then you chase after Saeeda Bai, whose life and history are an open book.'

'But I love her,' said Maan.

'Love?' cried his father, his incredulity mixed with rage. 'Go to bed at once. This is your last night in this house. I want you out by tomorrow. Get out! Go to Banaras or wherever you choose, but get out of Brahmpur. Out!'

Mrs Mahesh Kapoor begged her husband to rescind this drastic command, but to no avail. Maan looked at the two geckos on the ceiling as they scurried about to and fro. Then—suddenly—he got up with great resolution and without assistance, and said:

'All right. Goodnight! Goodnight! Goodnight! I'll go! I'll leave this house tomorrow.'

And he went off to bed without help, even remembering to take his shoes off before he fell off to sleep.

6.24

The next morning he woke up with a dreadful headache, which, however, cleared up miraculously in a couple of hours. He remembered that his father and he had exchanged words, and waited till the Minister of Revenue had gone to the Assembly before he went to ask his mother what it was they had said to each other. Mrs Mahesh Kapoor was at her wits' end: her husband had been so incensed last night that he hadn't slept for hours. Nor had he been able to work, and this had incensed him further. Any suggestion of reconciliation from her had been met with an almost incoherently angry rebuke from him. She realized that he was quite serious, that Maan would have to leave. Hugging her son to her she said:

'Go back to Banaras, work hard, behave responsibly, win back your father's heart.'

None of these four clauses appealed particularly to Maan, but he assured his mother that he would not cause trouble at Prem Nivas any longer. He ordered a servant to pack his things. He decided that he would go and stay with Firoz; or, failing that, with Pran; or, failing that, with the Rajkumar and his friends; or, failing that, somewhere else in Brahmpur. He would not leave this beautiful city or forgo the chance to meet the woman he loved because his disapproving, desiccated father told him so.

'Shall I get your father's PA to arrange your ticket to Banaras?' asked Mrs Mahesh Kapoor.

'No. If I need to, I'll do that at the station.'

After shaving and bathing he donned a crisp white kurta-pyjama and made his way a little shamefacedly towards Saeeda Bai's house. If he had been as drunk as his mother seemed to think he had been, he supposed that he must have been equally so outside Saeeda Bai's gate, where he had a vague sense of having gone.

He arrived at Saeeda Bai's house. He was admitted. Apparently, he was expected.

On the way up the stairs, he glanced at himself in the mirror. Unlike before, he now looked at himself quite critically. A white, embroidered cap covered his head; he took it off and surveyed his prematurely balding temples before putting it on again, thinking ruefully that perhaps it was his baldness that Saeeda Bai did not like. But what can I do about it? he thought.

When she heard his step on the corridor, Saeeda Bai called out in a welcoming voice, 'Come in, come in, Dagh Sahib. Your footsteps sound regular today. Let us hope that your heart is beating as regularly.'

Saeeda Bai had slept over the question of Maan and had concluded that something had to be done. Though she had to admit to herself that he was good for her, he was getting to be too demanding of her time and energy, too obsessively attached, for her to handle easily.

When Maan told her about his scene with his father, and that he had been thrown out of the house, she was very upset. Prem Nivas, where she sang regularly at Holi and had once sung at Dussehra, had become a regular fixture of her annual calendar. She had to consider the question of her income. Equally importantly, she did not want her young friend to remain in trouble with his father. 'Where do you plan to go?' she asked him.

'Why, nowhere!' exclaimed Maan. 'My father has delusions of grandeur. He thinks that because he can strip a million landlords of their inheritance, he can equally easily order his son about. I am going to stay in Brahmpur—with friends.' A sudden thought struck him. 'Why not here?' he asked.

'Toba, toba!' cried Saeeda Bai, putting her hands to her shocked ears.

'Why should I be separated from you? From the town where you live?' He leaned towards her and began to embrace her. 'And your cook makes such delicious shami kababs,' he added.

Saeeda Bai might have been pleased by Maan's ardour, but she was thinking hard. 'I know,' she said, disengaging herself. 'I know what you must do.'

'Mmh,' said Maan, attempting to engage himself again.

'Do sit still and listen, Dagh Sahib,' said Saeeda Bai in a coquettish voice. 'You want to be close to me, to understand me, don't you?'

'Yes, yes, of course.'

'Why, Dagh Sahib?'

'Why?' asked Maan incredulously.

'Why?' persisted Saeeda Bai.

'Because I love you.'

'What is love—this ill-natured thing that makes enemies even of friends?'

This was too much for Maan, who was in no mood to get involved in abstract speculations. A sudden, horrible thought struck him: 'Do *you* want me to go as well?'

Saeeda Bai was silent, then she tugged her sari, which had slipped down slightly, back over her head. Her kohl-blackened eyes seemed to look into Maan's very soul.

'Dagh Sahib, Dagh Sahib!' she rebuked him.

Maan was instantly repentant, and hung his head. 'I just feared that you might want to test our love by distance,' he said.

'That would cause me as much pain as you,' she told him sadly. 'But what I was thinking was quite different.'

She was silent, then played a few notes on the harmonium and said:

'Your Urdu teacher, Rasheed, is leaving for his village in a few days. He will be gone for a month. I don't know how to arrange for an Arabic teacher for Tasneem or an Urdu teacher for you in his absence. And I feel that in order to understand me truly, to appreciate my art, to resonate to my passion, you must learn my language, the language of the poetry I recite, the ghazals I sing, the very thoughts I think.'

'Yes, yes,' whispered Maan, enraptured.

'So you must go to the village with your Urdu teacher for a while—for a month.'

'What?' cried Maan, who felt that another glass of water had been flung in his face.

Saeeda Bai was apparently so upset by her own solution to the problem—it was the obvious solution, she murmured, biting her lower lip sadly, but she did not know how she could bear being separated from him, etc.—that in a few minutes it was Maan who was consoling her rather than she him. It was the only way out of the problem, he assured her: even if he had nowhere to live in the village, he would sleep in the open, he would speak—think—write—the language of her soul, he would send her letters written in the Urdu of an angel. Even his father would be proud of him.

'You have made me see that there is no other way,' said Saeeda Bai at length, letting herself be convinced gradually.

Maan noticed that the parakeet, who was in the room with them, was giving him a cynical look. He frowned.

'When is Rasheed leaving?'

'Tomorrow.'

Maan went pale. 'But that only leaves tonight!' he cried, his heart sinking. His courage failed him. 'No—I can't go—I can't leave you.'

'Dagh Sahib, if you are faithless to your own logic, how can I believe you will be faithful to me?'

'Then I must spend this evening here. It will be our last night together in a—in a month.'

A month? Even as he said the word, his mind rebelled at the thought. He refused to accept it.

'It will not work this evening,' said Saeeda Bai in a practical tone, thinking of her commitments.

'Then I won't go,' cried Maan. 'I can't. How can I? Anyway, we haven't consulted Rasheed.'

'Rasheed will be honoured to give you hospitality. He respects your father very much—no doubt because of his skill as a woodcutter—and, of course, he respects you very much—no doubt because of your skill as a calligrapher.'

'I must see you tonight,' insisted Maan. 'I must. What woodcutter?' he added, frowning.

Saeeda Bai sighed. 'It is very difficult to cut down a banyan tree, Dagh Sahib, especially one that has been rooted so long in the soil of this province. But I can hear your father's impatient axe on the last of its trunks. Soon it will be torn from the earth. The snakes will be driven from its roots and the termites burned with its rotten wood. But what will happen to the birds and monkeys who sang or chattered in its branches? Tell me that, Dagh Sahib. This is how things stand with us today.' Then, seeing Maan look crestfallen, she added, with another sigh: 'Come at one o'clock in the morning. I will tell your friend the watchman to make the Shahenshah's entry a triumphal one.'

Maan felt that she might be laughing at him. But the thought of seeing her tonight cheered him up instantly, even if he knew she was merely sweetening a bitter pill.

'Of course, I can't promise anything,' Saeeda Bai went on. 'If he tells you I am asleep, you must not make a scene or wake up the neighbourhood.'

It was Maan's turn to sigh:

> 'If Mir so loudly goes on weeping,
> How can his neighbour go on sleeping?'

But, as it happened, everything worked out well. Abdur Rasheed agreed to house Maan in his village and to continue to teach him Urdu. Mahesh

Kapoor, who had been afraid that Maan might attempt to defy him by staying in Brahmpur, was not altogether displeased that he would not be going to Banaras, for he knew what Maan did not—that the cloth business was doing pretty well without him. Mrs Mahesh Kapoor (though she would miss him) was glad that he would be in the charge of a strict and sober teacher and away from 'that'. Maan did at least receive the ecstatic sop of a last passionate night with Saeeda Bai. And Saeeda Bai heaved a sigh of relief tinged only slightly with regret when morning came.

A few hours later a glum Maan, fretting and exasperated at being so neatly pincered by his father and his beloved, together with Rasheed, who was conscious for the moment only of the pleasure of getting out of congested Brahmpur into the openness of the countryside, were on board a narrow-gauge train that swung in a painfully slow and halting arc towards Rudhia District and Rasheed's home village.

6.25

Tasneem did not realize till Rasheed had gone how much she had enjoyed her Arabic lessons. Everything else she did was related to the household, and opened no windows on to a larger world. But her serious young teacher, with his insistence on the importance of grammar and his refusal to compromise with her tendency to take flight when faced with difficulties, had made her aware that she had within herself an ability for application that she had not known. She admired him, too, because he was making his own way in the world without support from his family. And when he refused to answer her sister's summons because he was explaining a passage from the Quran to her, she had greatly approved of his sense of principle.

All this admiration was silent. Rasheed had never once indicated that he was interested in her in any way other than as a teacher. Their hands had never touched accidentally over a book. That this should not have happened over a span of weeks spoke of deliberateness on his part, for in the ordinary innocent course of things it was bound to have occurred by chance, even if they had instantly drawn back afterwards.

Now he would be out of Brahmpur for a month, and Tasneem found herself feeling sad, far sadder than the loss of Arabic lessons would have accounted for. Ishaq Khan, sensing her mood, and the cause for it as well, tried to cheer her up.

'Listen, Tasneem.'

'Yes, Ishaq Bhai?' Tasneem replied, a little listlessly.

'Why do you insist on that "Bhai"?' said Ishaq.

Tasneem was silent.

'All right, call me brother if you wish—just get out of that tearful mood.'

'I can't,' said Tasneem. 'I'm feeling sad.'

'Poor Tasneem. He'll be back,' said Ishaq, trying not to sound anything but sympathetic.

'I wasn't thinking of him,' said Tasneem quickly. 'I was thinking that I'll have nothing useful to do now except read novels and cut vegetables. Nothing useful to learn—'

'Well, you could teach, even if not learn,' said Ishaq Khan, attempting to sound bright.

'Teach?'

'Teach Miya Mitthu how to speak. The first few months of life are very important in the education of a parakeet.'

Tasneem brightened up for a second. Then she said: 'Apa has appropriated my parakeet. The cage is always in her room, seldom in mine.' She sighed. 'It seems,' she added under her breath, 'that everything of mine becomes hers.'

'I'll get it,' said Ishaq Khan gallantly.

'Oh, you mustn't,' said Tasneem. 'Your hands—'

'Oh, I'm not as crippled as all that.'

'But it must be bad. Whenever I see you practising, I can see how painful it is from your face.'

'What if it is?' said Ishaq Khan. 'I have to play and I have to practise.'

'Why don't you show it to a doctor?'

'It'll go away.'

'Still—there's no harm in having it seen.'

'All right,' said Ishaq with a smile. 'I will, because you've asked me to.'

Sometimes when Ishaq accompanied Saeeda Bai these days it was all he could do not to cry out in pain. This trouble in his wrists had grown worse. What was strange was that it now affected both his wrists, despite the fact that his two hands—the right on the bow and the left on the strings—performed very different functions.

Since his livelihood and that of the younger brothers whom he supported depended on his hands, he was extremely anxious. As for the transfer of his brother-in-law: Ishaq had not dared to try to get an interview with the Station Director—who would certainly have heard about what had happened in the canteen and who would have been very unfavourably disposed towards him, especially if the great Ustad himself had made it a point to express his displeasure.

Ishaq Khan remembered his father saying to him, 'Practise at least four hours every day. Clerks push their pens in offices for longer than that, and you cannot insult your art by offering less.' Ishaq's father would sometimes—in the middle of a conversation—take Ishaq's left hand and look at it carefully; if the string-abraded grooves in the fingernails showed signs of recent wear, he would say, 'Good.' Otherwise he would merely continue with the conversation, not visibly but palpably disappointed. Of late, because of the sometimes unbearable pain in the tendons of his wrists, Ishaq Khan had been unable to practise for more than an hour or two a day. But the moment the pain let up he increased the regimen.

Sometimes it was difficult to concentrate on other matters. Lifting a cage, stirring his tea, opening a door, every action reminded him of his hands. He could turn to no one for help. If he told Saeeda Bai how painful it had become to accompany her, especially in fast passages, would he be able to blame her if she looked for someone else?

'It is not sensible to practise so much. You should rest—and use some balm,' murmured Tasneem.

'Do you think I don't want to rest—do you think it's easier for me to practise—'

'But you must use proper medicine: it is very unwise not to,' said Tasneem.

'Go and get some for me, then—' said Ishaq Khan with sudden and uncharacteristic sharpness. 'Everyone sympathizes, everyone advises, no one helps. Go—go—'

He stopped dead, and covered his eyes with his right hand. He did not want to open them.

He imagined Tasneem's startled face, her deer-like eyes starting with tears. If pain has made me so selfish, he thought, I will have to rest and restore myself, even if it means risking my work.

Aloud, after he had collected himself, he said: 'Tasneem, you will have to help me. Talk to your sister and tell her what I can't.' He sighed. 'I'll speak to her later. I cannot find other work in my present state. She will have to keep me on even if I cannot play for a while.'

Tasneem said, 'Yes.' Her voice betrayed that she was, as he had thought, crying silently.

'Please don't take what I said badly,' continued Ishaq. 'I'm not myself. I will rest.' He shook his head from side to side.

Tasneem put her hand on his shoulder. He became very still, and remained so even when she took it away.

'I'll talk to Apa,' she said. 'Should I go now?'

'Yes. No, stay here for a while.'

'What do you want to talk about?' said Tasneem.

'I don't want to talk,' said Ishaq. After a pause he looked up and saw her face. It was tear-stained.

He looked down again, then said: 'May I use that pen?'

Tasneem handed him the wooden pen with its broad split bamboo nib that Rasheed made her use for her calligraphy. The letters it wrote were large, almost childishly so; the dots above the letters came out like little rhombuses.

Ishaq Khan thought for a minute while she watched him. Then, drawing to himself a large sheet of lined paper—which she used for her exercises—he wrote a few lines with some effort, and handed them to her wordlessly even before the ink was dry:

> Dear hands, that cause me so much pain,
> When can I gain your use again?
>
> When can we once again be friends?
> Forgive me, and I'll make amends.
>
> Never again will I enforce
> My fiat, disciplined and coarse
>
> Without consulting both of you
> On any work we need to do,
>
> Nor cause you seizure or distress
> But win your trust through gentleness.

He looked at her while her lovely, liquid eyes moved from right to left, noticing with a kind of painful pleasure the flush that came to her face as they rested on the final couplet.

6.26

When Tasneem entered her sister's bedroom, she found her sitting in front of the mirror applying kajal to her eyelids.

Most people have an expression that they reserve exclusively for looking at themselves in the mirror. Some pout, others arch their eyebrows, still others look superciliously down their noses at themselves. Saeeda Bai had a whole range of mirror faces. Just as her comments to her parakeet ran the gamut of emotions from passion to annoyance, so too did these expressions. When Tasneem entered, she was moving her head slowly from side to side with a dreamy air. It would have been difficult to guess that her thick black hair had just revealed a single white one, and that she was looking around for others.

A silver paan container was resting among the vials and phials on her dressing table and Saeeda Bai was eating a couple of paans laced with the fragrant, semi-solid tobacco known as kimam. When Tasneem appeared in the mirror and their eyes met, the first thought that struck Saeeda Bai was that she, Saeeda, was getting old and that in five years she would be forty. Her expression changed to one of melancholy, and she turned back to her own face in the mirror, looking at herself in the iris, first of one eye, then of the other. Then, recalling the guest whom she had invited to the house in the evening, she smiled at herself in affectionate welcome.

'What's the matter, Tasneem, tell me,' she said—somewhat indistinctly, because of the paan.

'Apa,' said Tasneem nervously, 'it's about Ishaq.'

'Has he been teasing you?' said Saeeda Bai a little sharply, misinterpreting Tasneem's nervousness. 'I'll speak to him. Send him here.'

'No, no, Apa, it's this,' said Tasneem, and handed her sister Ishaq's poem.

After reading it through Saeeda Bai set it down, and started toying with the only lipstick on the dressing table. She never used lipstick, as her lips had a natural redness which was enhanced by paan, but it had been given to her a long time ago by the guest who would be coming this evening, and to whom she was, in a mild sort of way, sentimentally attached.

'What do you think, Apa?' said Tasneem. 'Say something.'

'It's well expressed and badly written,' said Saeeda Bai, 'but what does it mean? He's not going on about his hands, is he?'

'They are giving him a lot of pain,' said Tasneem, 'and he's afraid that if he speaks to you, you'll ask him to leave.'

Saeeda Bai, remembering with a smile how she had got Maan to leave, was silent. She was about to apply a drop of perfume to her wrist when Bibbo came in with a great bustle.

'Oh-hoh, what is it now?' said Saeeda Bai. 'Go out, you wretched girl, can't I have a moment of peace? Have you fed the parakeet?'

'Yes, Begum Sahiba,' said Bibbo impertinently. 'But what shall I tell the cook to feed you and your guest this evening?'

Saeeda Bai addressed Bibbo's reflection in the mirror sternly:

'Wretched girl, you will never amount to anything—even after having stayed here so long you have not acquired the slightest sense of etiquette or discrimination.'

Bibbo looked unconvincingly penitent. Saeeda Bai went on: 'Find out what is growing in the kitchen garden and come back after five minutes.'

When Bibbo had disappeared, Saeeda Bai said to Tasneem:

'So he's sent you to speak to me, has he?'

'No,' said Tasneem. 'I came myself. I thought he needed help.'

'You're sure he hasn't been misbehaving?'

Tasneem shook her head.

'Maybe he can write a ghazal or two for me to sing,' said Saeeda Bai after a pause. 'I'll have to put him to some sort of work. Provisionally, at least.' She applied a drop of perfume. 'I suppose his hand works well enough to allow him to write?'

'Yes,' said Tasneem happily.

'Then let's leave it at that,' said Saeeda Bai.

But in her mind she was thinking about a permanent replacement. She knew she couldn't support Ishaq endlessly—or till some indefinite time when his hands decided to behave.

'Thank you, Apa,' said Tasneem, smiling.

'Don't thank me,' said Saeeda Bai crossly. 'I am used to taking all the world's troubles on to my own head. Now I'll have to find a sarangi player till your Ishaq Bhai is capable of wrestling with his sarangi again, and I also have to find someone to teach you Arabic—'

'Oh, no, no,' said Tasneem quickly, 'you needn't do that.'

'I needn't do that?' said Saeeda Bai, turning around to face not Tasneem's image but Tasneem herself. 'I thought you enjoyed your Arabic lessons.'

Bibbo had bounced back into the room again. Saeeda Bai looked at her impatiently and cried, 'Yes, yes, Bibbo? What is it? I told you to come back after five minutes.'

'But I've found out what's ripe in the back garden,' said Bibbo enthusiastically.

'All right, all right,' said Saeeda Bai, defeated. 'What is there apart from ladies' fingers? Has the karela begun?'

'Yes, Begum Sahiba, and there is even a pumpkin.'

'Well, then, tell the cook to make kababs as usual—shami kababs—and some vegetable of her choice—and let her make mutton with karela as well.'

Tasneem made a slight grimace, which was not lost on Saeeda Bai.

'If you find the karela too bitter, you don't have to eat it,' she said in an impatient voice. 'No one is forcing you. I work my heart out to keep you in comfort, and you don't appreciate it. And oh yes,' she said, turning to Bibbo again, 'let's have some phirni afterwards.'

'But there's so little sugar left from our ration,' cried Bibbo.

'Get it on the black market,' said Saeeda Bai. 'Bilgrami Sahib is very fond of phirni.'

Then she dismissed both Tasneem and Bibbo, and continued with her toilette in peace.

The guest whom she was expecting that evening was an old friend. He was a doctor, a general practitioner about ten years older than her, good-looking and cultivated. He was unmarried, and had proposed to her a number of times. Though at one stage he had been a client, he was now a friend. She felt no passion for him, but was grateful that he was always there when she needed him. She had not seen him for about three months now, and that was why she had invited him over this evening. He was bound to propose to her again, and this would cheer her up. Her refusal, being equally inevitable, would not upset him unduly.

She looked around the room, and her eyes fell on the framed picture of the woman looking out through an archway into a mysterious garden.

By now, she thought, Dagh Sahib will have reached his destination. I did not really want to send him off, but I did. He did not really want to go, but he did. Well, it is all for the best.

Dagh Sahib, however, would not have agreed with this assessment.

6.27

Ishaq Khan waited for Ustad Majeed Khan not far from his house. When he came out, carrying a small string bag in his hand, walking gravely along,

Ishaq followed him at a distance. He turned towards Tarbuz ka Bazaar, past the road leading to the mosque, then into the comparatively open area of the local vegetable market. He moved from stall to stall to see if there was something that interested him. It was good to see tomatoes still plentiful and at a tolerable price so late in the season. Besides, they made the market look more cheerful. It was a pity that the season for spinach was almost over; it was one of his favourite vegetables. And carrots, cauliflowers, cabbages, all were virtually gone till next winter. Even those few that were available were dry, dingy, and dear, and had none of the flavour of their peak.

It was with thoughts such as these that the maestro was occupied that morning when he heard a voice say, respectfully:

'Adaab arz, Ustad Sahib.'

Ustad Majeed Khan turned to see Ishaq. A single glance at the young man was sufficient to remove the ease of his meditations and to remind him of the insults that he had had to face in the canteen. His face grew dark with the memory; he picked up two or three tomatoes from the stall, and asked their price.

'I have a request to make of you.' It was Ishaq Khan again.

'Yes?' The contempt in the great musician's voice was unmistakable. As he recalled, it was after he had offered his help to the young man in some footling matter that the whole exchange had occurred.

'I also have an apology to make.'

'Please do not waste my time.'

'I have followed you here from your house. I need your help. I am in trouble. I need work to support myself and my younger brothers, and I cannot get it. After that day, All India Radio has not called me even once to perform.'

The maestro shrugged his shoulders.

'I beg of you, Ustad Sahib, whatever you think of me, do not ruin my family. You knew my father and grandfather. Excuse any mistake that I may have made for their sakes.'

'That you may have made?'

'That I have made. I do not know what came over me.'

'I am not ruining you. Go in peace.'

'Ustad Sahib, since that day I have had no work, and my sister's husband has heard nothing about his transfer from Lucknow. I dare not approach the Director.'

'But you dare approach me. You follow me from my house—'

'Only to get the chance to speak to you. You might understand—as a fellow-musician.' The Ustad winced. 'And of late my hands have been giving me trouble. I showed them to a doctor, but—'

'I had heard,' said the maestro dryly, but did not mention where.

'My employer has made it clear to me that I cannot be supported for my own sake much longer.'

'Your employer!' The great singer was about to walk on in disgust when he added: 'Go and thank God for that. Throw yourself on His mercy.'

'I am throwing myself on yours,' said Ishaq Khan desperately.

'I have said nothing for or against you to the Station Director. What happened that morning I shall put down to an aberration in your brain. If your work has fallen off, that is not my doing. In any case, with your hands, what do you propose to do? You are very proud of your long hours of practice. My advice to you is to practise less.'

This had been Tasneem's advice as well. Ishaq Khan nodded miserably. There was no hope, and since his pride had already suffered through his desperation, he felt that he could lose nothing by completing the apology he had begun and that he had come to believe he should make.

'On another matter,' he said, 'if I may presume on your further indulgence—I have been wishing for a long time to apologize for what I know is not forgivable. That morning, Ustad Sahib, the reason why I made so bold as to sit at your table in the canteen was because I had heard your Todi just a little earlier.'

The maestro, who had been examining the vegetables, turned towards him slightly.

'I had been sitting beneath the neem tree outside with those friends of mine. One of them had a radio. We were entranced, at least I was. I thought I would find some way of saying so to you. But then things went wrong, and other thoughts took over.'

He could not say any more by way of apology without, he felt, bringing in other matters—such as the memory of his own father, which he felt that the Ustad had demeaned.

Ustad Majeed Khan nodded his head almost imperceptibly by way of acknowledgement. He looked at the young man's hands, noticing the worn groove in the fingernail, and for a second he also found himself wondering why he did not have a bag to carry his vegetables home in.

'So—you liked my Todi,' he said.

'Yours—or God's,' said Ishaq Khan. 'I felt that the great Tansen himself would have listened rapt to that rendering of his raag. But since then I have never been able to listen to you.'

The maestro frowned, but did not deign to ask Ishaq what he meant by that last remark.

'I will be practising Todi this morning,' said Ustad Majeed Khan. 'Follow me after this.'

Ishaq's face expressed complete disbelief; it was as if heaven had fallen into his hands. He forgot his hands, his pride, the financial desperation that had forced him to speak to Ustad Majeed Khan. He merely listened as if in a dream to the Ustad's further conversation with the vegetable seller:

'How much are these?'

'Two and a half annas per pao,' replied the vegetable seller.

'Beyond Subzipur you can get them for one and a half annas.'

'Bhai Sahib, these are not the prices of Subzipur but of Chowk.'

'Very high, these prices of yours.'

'Oh, we had a child last year—since then my prices have gone up.' The vegetable seller, seated calmly on the ground on a bit of jute matting, looked up at the Ustad.

Ustad Majeed Khan did not smile at the vendor's quips. 'Two annas per pao—that's it.'

'I have to earn my meals from you, Sir, not from the charity of a gurudwara.'

'All right—all right—' And Ustad Majeed Khan threw him a couple of coins.

After buying a bit of ginger and some chillies, the Ustad decided to get a few tindas.

'Mind that you give me small ones.'

'Yes, yes, that's what I'm doing.'

'And these tomatoes—they are soft.'

'Soft, Sir?'

'Yes, look—' The Ustad took them off the scales. 'Weigh these ones instead.' He rummaged around among the selection.

'They wouldn't have gone soft in a week—but whatever you say, Sir.'

'Weigh them properly,' growled the Ustad. 'If you keep putting weights on one pan, I can keep putting tomatoes on the other. My pan should sink in the balance.'

Suddenly, the Ustad's attention was caught by a couple of cauliflowers which looked comparatively fresh, not like the stunted outriders of the season. But when the vegetable seller named the price, he was appalled.

'Don't you fear God?'

'For you, Sir, I have quoted a special price.'

'What do you mean, for me? It's what you charge everyone, you rogue, I am certain. Special price—'

'Ah, but these cauliflowers are special—you don't require oil to fry them.'

Ishaq smiled slightly, but Ustad Majeed Khan simply said to the local wit: 'Huh! Give me this one.'

Ishaq said: 'Let me carry them, Ustad Sahib.'

Ustad Majeed Khan gave Ishaq the bag of vegetables to carry, forgetful of his hands. On the way home he did not say anything. Ishaq walked along quietly.

At his door, Ustad Majeed Khan said in a loud voice: 'There is someone with me.' There was a sound of flustered female voices and then of people leaving the front room. They entered. The tanpura was in a corner. Ustad Majeed Khan told Ishaq to put the vegetables down and to wait for him. Ishaq remained standing, but looked about him. The room was full of cheap knick-knacks and tasteless furniture. There could not have been a greater contrast to Saeeda Bai's immaculate outer chamber.

Ustad Majeed Khan came back in, having washed his face and hands. He told Ishaq to sit down, and tuned the tanpura for a while. Finally, satisfied, he started to practise in Raag Todi.

There was no tabla player, and Ustad Majeed Khan began to sense his way around the raag in a freer, less rhythmic but more intense manner than Ishaq Khan had ever heard from him before. He always began his public performances not with a free alaap such as this but with a very slow composition in a long rhythmic cycle which allowed him a liberty that was almost, but not quite, comparable. The flavour of these few minutes was so startlingly different from those other great performances that Ishaq was enraptured. He closed his eyes, and the room ceased to exist; and then, after a while, himself; and finally even the singer.

He did not know how long he had been sitting there when he heard Ustad Majeed Khan saying:

'Now, you strum it.'

He opened his eyes. The maestro, sitting bolt upright, indicated the tanpura that was lying before him.

Ishaq's hands did not cause him any pain as he turned it towards himself and began to strum the four wires, tuned perfectly to the open and hypnotic combination of tonic and dominant. He assumed that the maestro was going to continue his practice.

'Now, sing this after me.' And the Ustad sang a phrase.

Ishaq Khan was literally dumbstruck.

'What is taking you so long?' asked the Ustad sternly, in the tone known so well to his students at the Haridas College of Music.

Ishaq Khan sang the phrase.

The Ustad continued to offer him phrases, at first brief, and then increasingly long and complex. Ishaq repeated them to the best of his ability, at first with unmusical hesitancy but after a while entirely forgetting himself in the surge and ebb of the music.

'Sarangi-wallahs are good at copying,' said the Ustad thoughtfully. 'But there is something in you that goes beyond that.'

So astonished was Ishaq that his hands stopped strumming the tanpura.

The Ustad was silent for a while. The only sound in the room was the ticking of a cheap clock. Ustad Majeed Khan looked at it, as if conscious for the first time of its presence, then turned his gaze towards Ishaq.

It struck him that possibly, but only just possibly, he may have found in Ishaq that disciple whom he had looked for now for years—someone to whom he could pass on his art, someone who, unlike his own frog-voiced son, loved music with a passion, who had a grounding in performance, whose voice was not displeasing, whose sense of pitch and ornament was exceptional, and who had that additional element of indefinable expressivity, even when he copied his own phrases, which was the soul of music. But originality in composition—did he possess that—or at least the germ of such originality? Only time would tell—months, perhaps years, of time.

'Come again tomorrow, but at seven in the morning,' said the Ustad, dismissing him. Ishaq Khan nodded slowly, then stood up to leave.

Part Seven

7.1

Lata saw the envelope on the salver. Arun's servant had brought the mail in just before breakfast and laid it on the dining table. As soon as she saw the letter she took in her breath sharply. She even glanced around the dining room. No one else had yet entered. Breakfast was an erratic meal in this household.

Lata knew Kabir's handwriting from the note that he had scribbled to her during the meeting of the Brahmpur Literary Society. She had not expected him to write to her, and could not think how he had obtained her address in Calcutta. She had not wanted him to write. She did not want to hear from him or about him. Now that she looked back she saw that she had been happy before she had met him: anxious about her exams perhaps, worried about a few small differences she may have had with her mother or a friend, troubled about this constant talk of finding a suitable boy for her, but not miserable as she had been during this so-called holiday so suddenly enforced by her mother.

There was a paperknife on the salver. Lata picked it up, then stood undecided. Her mother might come in at any moment, and—as she usually did—ask Lata whom the letter was from and what it said. She put the knife down and picked the letter up.

Arun entered. He was wearing a red-and-black striped tie over his starched white shirt, and was carrying his jacket in one hand and holding the *Statesman* in the other. He draped the jacket across the back of his chair, folded the newspaper to give him convenient access to the crossword, greeted Lata affectionately, and riffled through the post.

Lata wandered into the small drawing room that adjoined the dining room, got out a large volume on Egyptian mythology that no one ever read, and inserted her envelope in it. Then she returned to the dining room and sat down, humming to herself in Raag Todi. Arun frowned. Lata stopped. The servant brought her a fried egg.

Arun began whistling 'Three Coins in a Fountain' to himself. He had already solved several clues of the crossword puzzle while in the bathroom, and he filled in a few more at the breakfast table. Now he opened some of his mail, glanced through it and said:

'When is that damned fool going to bring me my bloody egg? I shall be late.'

He reached out for a piece of toast, and buttered it.

Varun entered. He was wearing the torn kurta-pyjama that he had obviously been sleeping in. 'Good morning. Good morning,' he said. He sounded uncertain, almost guilty. Then he sat down. When Hanif, the servant-cum-cook, came in with Arun's egg, he ordered his own. He first asked for an omelette, then decided on a scrambled egg. Meanwhile he took a piece of toast from the rack and buttered it.

'You might think of using the butter knife,' growled Arun from the head of the table.

Varun had extracted butter from the butter dish with his own knife to butter his toast. He accepted the rebuke in silence.

'Did you hear me?'

'Yes, Arun Bhai.'

'Then you would do well to acknowledge my remark with a word or at the very least a nod.'

'Yes.'

'There is a purpose to table manners, you know.'

Varun grimaced. Lata glanced sympathetically in his direction.

'Not everyone enjoys seeing the butter encrusted with crumbs from your toast.'

'All right, all right,' said Varun, driven to impatience. It was a feeble protest, and it was dealt with promptly.

Arun put down his knife and fork, looked at him, and waited.

'All right, Arun Bhai,' said Varun meekly.

He had been undecided as to whether to have marmalade or honey, but now decided on marmalade, since negotiating with the honey spoon was bound to bring reproof down on his head. As he spread the marmalade, he looked across at Lata, and they exchanged smiles. Lata's was a half-smile, very typical of her these days. Varun's was rather a twisted smile, as if he was not sure whether to be happy or despairing. It was the kind of smile that drove his elder brother mad and convinced him that Varun was a hopeless case. Varun had just got a Second in his mathematics B.A., and when he told his family the result, it was with exactly this kind of smile.

Soon after the term was over, instead of getting a job and contributing to expenses, Varun had, to Arun's annoyance, fallen ill. He was still somewhat weak, and started at loud sounds. Arun told himself that he really had to have a frank talk with his younger brother in the next week or so about how the world did not owe one a living, and about what Daddy would have said had he been alive.

Meenakshi came in with Aparna.

'Where's Daadi?' asked Aparna, looking around the table for Mrs Rupa Mehra.

'Grandma will be coming in a moment, Aparna precious,' said Meenakshi. 'She's probably reciting the Vedas,' she added vaguely.

Mrs Rupa Mehra, who recited a chapter or two from the Gita very early each morning, was in fact dressing.

As she came in, she beamed around the table. But when she noticed Aparna's golden chain, which Meenakshi in an unthinking moment had put around her neck, the smile died on her lips. Meenakshi was blithely unaware of anything being the matter, but Aparna asked a few minutes later:

'Why are you looking so sad, Daadi?'

Mrs Rupa Mehra finished chewing a bite of fried tomatoes on toast and said: 'I'm not sad, darling.'

'Are you angry with me, Daadi?' said Aparna.

'No, sweetheart, not with you.'

'Then with who?'

'With myself, perhaps,' said Mrs Rupa Mehra. She did not look at the medal-melter, but glanced across at Lata, who was gazing out of the window at the small garden. Lata was more than usually quiet this morning, and Mrs Rupa Mehra told herself that she had to get the silly girl to snap out of this mood. Well, tomorrow there was a party at the Chatterjis', and, like it or not, Lata would have to go.

A car horn sounded loudly outside, and Varun flinched.

'I should fire that bloody driver,' said Arun. Then he laughed and added: 'But he certainly makes me aware when it's time to leave for the office. Bye, darling.' He swallowed a gulp of coffee and kissed Meenakshi. 'I'll send the car back in half an hour. Bye, Ugly.' He kissed Aparna and rubbed his cheek against hers. 'Bye, Ma. Bye, everyone. Don't forget, Basil Cox will be coming for dinner.'

Carrying his jacket over one arm and his briefcase in the other, he walked, rather, strode out to the little sky-blue Austin outside. It was never clear until the last moment whether Arun would take the newspaper with him to the office; it was part of the general uncertainty of living with him, just as were his sudden switches from anger to affection to urbanity. Today, to everyone's relief, he let the newspaper remain.

Normally Varun and Lata would both have made a grab for it, and today Varun was disappointed when Lata did not. The atmosphere had lightened since Arun's departure. Aparna now became the focus of attention. Her mother fed her incompetently, then called for the Toothless Crone to handle her. Varun read bits of the news to her, and she listened with a careful pretence at comprehension and interest.

All Lata could think of was when and where, in this household of two and a half bedrooms and no privacy to speak of, she would find time and space to read her letter. She was thankful that she had been able to take possession of what (though Mrs Rupa Mehra would have disputed this) belonged to her alone. But as she looked out of the window towards the small, brilliantly green lawn with its white tracery of spider lilies, she thought of its possible contents with a mixture of longing and foreboding.

7.2

Meanwhile there was work to be done in preparation for the evening's dinner. Basil Cox, who would be coming over with his wife Patricia, was Arun's department head at Bentsen & Pryce. Hanif was dispatched to Jaggubazaar to get two chickens, a fish, and vegetables, while Meenakshi—accompanied by Lata and Mrs Rupa Mehra—went off to New Market in the car, which had just returned from Arun's office.

Meenakshi bought her fortnightly stores—her white flour, her jam and Chivers Marmalade and Lyle's Golden Syrup and Anchor Butter and tea and coffee and cheese and clean sugar ('Not this dirty ration stuff')—from Baboralley, a couple of loaves of bread from a shop in Middleton Row ('The bread one gets from the market is so awful, Luts'), some salami from a cold store in Free School Street ('The salami from Keventers is dreadfully bland, I've decided never to go there again'), and half a dozen bottles of Beck's beer from Shaw Brothers. Lata tagged along everywhere, though Mrs Rupa Mehra refused to enter either the cold store or the liquor shop. She was astonished by Meenakshi's extravagance, and by the whimsical nature of some of her purchases ('Oh, Arun is bound to like that, yes, I'll take two,' said Meenakshi whenever the shopkeeper suggested something that he thought Madam would appreciate). All the purchases went into a large basket which a ragged little boy carried on his head and finally took to the car. Whenever she was accosted by beggars, Meenakshi looked straight through them.

Lata wanted to visit a bookshop on Park Street, and spent about fifteen minutes there while Meenakshi chafed impatiently. When she found that Lata hadn't in fact bought anything, she thought it very peculiar. Mrs Rupa Mehra was content to browse timelessly.

Upon their return home, Meenakshi found Hanif in a flap. He was not sure about the exact proportions for the soufflé, and as for the hilsa, Meenakshi would have to instruct him about the kind of fire it needed to be smoked on. Aparna too was sulking because of her mother's absence. She now threatened to throw a tantrum. This was too much for Meenakshi, who was getting late for the canasta which she played with her ladies' club—the Shady Ladies—once a week, and which (Basil Cox or no Basil Cox) she could not possibly miss. She got into a flap herself and shouted at Aparna and the Toothless Crone and the cook. Varun locked himself in his small room and covered his head with a pillow.

'You should not get into a temper for nothing,' said Mrs Rupa Mehra unhelpfully.

Meenakshi turned towards her in exasperation. 'That's a big help, Ma,' she said. 'What do you expect me to do? Miss my canasta?'

'No, no, you will not miss your canasta,' said Mrs Rupa Mehra. 'That I am not asking you to do, Meenakshi, but you must not shout at Aparna like that. It is not good for her.' Hearing this, Aparna edged towards her grandmother's chair.

Meenakshi made an impatient sound.

The impossibility of her position suddenly came home to her. This cook was a real incompetent. Arun would be terribly, terribly angry with her if anything went wrong this evening. It was so important for his job too—and what could she do? Cut out the smoked hilsa? At least this idiot Hanif could handle the roast chicken. But he was a temperamental fellow, and had been known even to misfry an egg. Meenakshi looked around the room in wild distress.

'Ask your mother if you can borrow her Mugh cook,' said Lata with sudden inspiration.

Meenakshi gazed at Lata in wonder. 'What an Einstein you are, Luts!' she said, and immediately telephoned her mother. Mrs Chatterji rallied to her daughter's aid. She had two cooks, one for Bengali and one for western food. The Bengali cook was told that he would have to prepare dinner in the Chatterji household that evening, and the Mugh cook, who came from Chittagong and excelled in European food, was dispatched to Sunny Park within the half hour. Meanwhile, Meenakshi had gone off for her canasta lunch with the Shady Ladies and had almost forgotten the tribulations of existence.

She returned in the middle of the afternoon to find a rebellion on her hands. The gramophone was blaring and the chickens were cackling in alarm. The Mugh cook told her as snootily as he could that he was not accustomed to being farmed out in this manner, that he was not used to working in such a small kitchen, that her cook-cum-bearer had behaved insolently towards him, that the fish and chickens that had been bought were none too fresh, and that he needed a certain kind of lemon extract for the soufflé which she had not had the foresight to provide. Hanif for his part was glaring resentfully, and was on the verge of giving notice. He was holding a squawking chicken out in front of him and saying: 'Feel, feel its breast—Memsahib—this is a young and fresh chicken. Why should I work below this man? Who is he to boss me around in my own kitchen? He keeps saying, "I am Mr Justice Chatterji's cook. I am Mr Justice Chatterji's cook."'

'No, no, I trust you, I don't need to—' cried Meenakshi, shuddering fastidiously and drawing back her red-polished fingernails as her cook pushed the chicken's feathers aside and offered its breast for her to assay.

Mrs Rupa Mehra, while not displeased at Meenakshi's discomfiture, did not want to jeopardize this dinner for the boss of her darling son. She was good at making peace between refractory servants, and she now did so. Harmony was restored, and she went into the drawing room to play a game of patience.

Varun had put on the gramophone about half an hour earlier and was playing the same scratchy 78-rpm record again and again: the Hindi film song 'Two intoxicating eyes', a song that no one, not even the sentimental Mrs Rupa Mehra, could tolerate after its fifth repetition. Varun had been singing the words to himself moodily and dreamily before Meenakshi returned. In her presence Varun stopped singing, but he continued to rewind the gramophone every few minutes and hum the song softly to himself by way of accompaniment. As he put away the spent needles one by one in the little compartment that fitted into the side of the machine, he reflected gloomily on his own fleeting life and personal uselessness.

Lata took the book on Egyptian mythology down from the shelf, and was about to go into the garden with it when her mother said:

'Where are you going?'

'To sit in the garden, Ma.'

'But it's so hot, Lata.'

'I know, Ma, but I can't read with this music going on.'

'I'll tell him to turn it off. All this sun is bad for your complexion. Varun, turn it off.' She had to repeat her request a few times before Varun heard what she was saying.

Lata took the book into the bedroom.

'Lata, sit with me, darling,' said Mrs Rupa Mehra.

'Ma, please let me be,' said Lata.

'You have been ignoring me for days,' said Mrs Rupa Mehra. 'Even when I told you your results, your kiss was half-hearted.'

'Ma, I have not been ignoring you,' said Lata.

'You have, you can't deny it. I feel it—here.' Mrs Rupa Mehra pointed to the region of her heart.

'All right, Ma, I have been ignoring you. Now please let me read.'

'What's that you're reading? Let me see the book.'

Lata replaced it on the shelf, and said: 'All right, Ma, I won't read it, I'll talk to you. Happy?'

'What do you want to talk about, darling?' asked Mrs Rupa Mehra sympathetically.

'I don't want to talk. You want to talk,' Lata pointed out.

'Read your silly book!' cried Mrs Rupa Mehra in a sudden temper. 'I have to do everything in this house, and no one cares for me. Everything goes wrong and I have to make peace. I have slaved for you all my life, and you don't care if I live or die. Only when I'm burned on the pyre will you realize my worth.' The tears started rolling down her cheeks and she placed a black nine on a red ten.

Normally Lata would have made some dutiful attempt to console her mother, but she was so frustrated and annoyed by her sudden emotional sleight of hand that she did nothing. After a while, she took the book down from the shelf again, and walked into the garden.

'It will rain,' said Mrs Rupa Mehra, 'and the book will get spoiled. You have no sense of the value of money.'

Good, thought Lata violently. I hope the book and everything in it—and I too—get washed away.

7.3

The small green garden was empty. The part-time mali had gone. An intelligent-looking crow cawed from a banana tree. The delicate spider lilies were in bloom. Lata sat down on the slatted green wooden bench in the shade of a tall flame-of-the-forest tree. Everything was rain-washed and clean, unlike in Brahmpur where each leaf had looked dusty and each blade of grass parched.

Lata looked at the envelope with its firm handwriting and Brahmpur postmark. Her name was followed immediately by the address; it was not 'care of' anybody.

She pulled out a hairpin and opened the envelope. The letter was only a page long. She had expected Kabir's letter to be effusive and apologetic. It was not exactly that.

After the address and date it went:

Dearest Lata,

Why should I repeat that I love you? I don't see why you should disbelieve me. I don't disbelieve you. Please tell me what the matter is. I don't want things to end in this way between us.

I can't think about anything except you, but I am annoyed that I should have to say so. I couldn't and I can't run off with you to some earthly paradise, but how could you have expected me to? Suppose I had agreed to your crazy plan. I know that you would then have discovered twenty reasons why it was impossible to carry it out. But perhaps I should have agreed anyway. Perhaps you would have felt reassured because I would have proved how much I cared for you. Well, I don't care for you so much that I'm willing to abdicate my intelligence. I don't even care for myself that much. I'm not made that way, and I do think ahead a bit.

Darling Lata, you are so brilliant, why don't you see things in perspective? I love you. You really owe me an apology.

Anyway, congratulations on your exam results. You must be very pleased—but I am not very surprised. You must not spend your time sitting on benches and crying in future. Who knows who might want to rescue you. Perhaps whenever you're tempted to do so, you can think of me returning to the pavilion and crying every time I fail to make a century.

Two days ago I hired a boat and went up the Ganges to the Barsaat Mahal. But, like Nawab Khushwaqt, I was so much grieved that my mind was upset, and the place was sordid and sad. For a long time I could not forget you though all possible efforts were made. I felt a strong kinship with him even though my tears did not fall fast and furious into the frangrant waters.

My father, though he is fairly absent-minded, can see that there is something the matter with me. Yesterday he said, 'It's not your results, so what is it, Kabir? I believe it must be a girl or something.' I too believe it must be a girl or something.

Well, now that you have my address why don't you write to me? I have been unhappy since you left and unable to concentrate on anything. I knew you couldn't write to me even if you wanted to because you didn't have my address. Well, now you do. So please do write. Otherwise I'll know what to think. And the next time I go to Mr Nowrojee's place I will have to read out some stricken verses of my own.

With all my love, my darling Lata,
Yours,
Kabir

7.4

For a long while Lata sat in a kind of reverie. She did not at first reread the letter. She felt a great many emotions, but they pulled her in conflicting directions. Under ordinary circumstances the pressure of her feelings might have caused her to shed a few unselfconscious tears, but there were a couple of remarks in the letter which made that impossible. Her first sense was that she had been cheated, cheated out of something that she had expected. There was no apology in the letter for the pain that he must have known he had caused her. There were declarations of love, but they were not as fervent or untinged with irony as she had thought they would be. Perhaps she had given Kabir no opportunity to explain himself at their last meeting, but now that he was writing to her, he could have explained himself better. He had not addressed anything seriously, and Lata had above all wanted him to be serious. For her it had been a matter of life and death.

Nor had he given her much—or any—news of himself, and Lata longed for it. She wanted to know everything about him—including how well he had done in his exams. From his father's remark it was probable that he had not done badly, but that was not the only interpretation of his remark. It might simply have meant that with the results out, even if he had merely passed, one area of uncertainty had been closed as a possible explanation for his downcast—or perhaps merely unsettled—mood. And how had he obtained her address? Surely not from Pran and Savita? From Malati perhaps? But as far as she knew Kabir did not even know Malati.

He did not want to take any responsibility for her feelings, that was clear. If anything it was she who—according to him—should be the one to apologize. In one sentence he praised her intelligence, in another he treated her like a dunce. Lata got the sense that he was trying to jolly her along without making any commitment to her beyond 'love'. And what was love?

Even more than their kisses, she remembered the morning when she had followed him to the cricket field and watched him practising in the nets. She had been in a trance, she had been entranced. He had leaned his head back and burst out laughing at something. His shirt had been open at the collar; there had been a faint breeze in the bamboos; a couple of mynas were quarrelling; it had been warm.

She read through the letter once again. Despite his injunction to her that she should not sit crying on benches, tears gathered in her eyes. Having finished the letter, she began, hardly conscious of what she was doing, to read a paragraph of the book on Egyptian mythology. But the words formed no pattern in her mind.

She was startled by Varun's voice, a couple of yards away.

'You'd better go in, Lata, Ma is getting anxious.'

Lata controlled herself and nodded.

'What's the matter?' he asked, noticing that she was—or had been—in tears. 'Have you been quarrelling with her?'

Lata shook her head.

Varun, glancing down at the book, saw the letter, and immediately understood who it was from.

'I'll kill him,' said Varun with timorous ferocity.

'There's nothing to kill,' said Lata, more angrily than sadly. 'Just don't tell Ma, please, Varun Bhai. It would drive both of us crazy.'

7.5

When Arun came back from work that day, he was in excellent spirits. He had had a productive day, and he sensed that the evening was going to go off well. Meenakshi, her domestic crisis resolved, was no longer running around nervously; indeed, so elegantly collected was she that Arun could never have guessed she had been in the least distraught. After kissing him on the cheek and giving him the benefit of her tinkly laugh, she went in to change. Aparna was delighted to see her father and bestowed a few kisses on him too but was unable to convince him to do a jigsaw puzzle with her.

Arun thought that Lata looked a bit sulky, but then that was par for the course with Lata these days. Ma, well, Ma, there was no accounting for her moods. She looked impatient, probably because her tea had not come on time. Varun was his usual scruffy, shifty self. Why, Arun asked himself, did his brother have so little spine and initiative and why did he always dress in tattered kurta-pyjamas that looked as if they had been slept in? 'Turn off that bloody noise,' he shouted as he entered the drawing room and received the full power of 'Two intoxicating eyes'.

Varun, cowed down though he was by Arun and his bullying sophistication, occasionally raised his head, usually to have it brutally slashed off. It took time for another head to grow, but today it happened to have done so. Varun did turn off the gramophone, but his resentment smouldered. Having been subject to his brother's authority since boyhood, he hated it—and, in fact, all authority. He had once, in a fit of anti-imperialism and xenophobia, scrawled 'Pig' on two Bibles at St George's School, and had been soundly thrashed for it by the white headmaster. Arun too had bawled him out after that incident, using every possible hurtful reference to his pathetic childhood and past felonies, and Varun had duly flinched. But even while flinching before his well-built elder brother's attack, and expecting to be slapped by him at any moment, Varun thought to himself: All he knows how to do is to suck up to the British and crawl in their tracks. Pig! Pig! He must have looked his thoughts, for he did get the slap he expected.

Arun used to listen to Churchill's speeches on the radio during the War and murmur, as he had heard the English murmur, 'Good old Winnie!' Churchill loathed Indians and made no secret of it, and spoke with contempt of Gandhi, a far greater man than he could ever aspire to be; and Varun regarded Churchill with a visceral hatred.

'And change out of those crumpled pyjamas. Basil Cox will be coming within an hour and I don't want him to think I run a third-class dharamshala.'

'I'll change into cleaner ones,' said Varun sullenly.

'You will not,' said Arun. 'You will change into proper clothes.'

'Proper clothes!' mumbled Varun softly in a mocking tone.

'What did you say?' asked Arun slowly and threateningly.

'Nothing,' said Varun with a scowl.

'Please don't fight like this. It isn't good for my nerves,' said Mrs Rupa Mehra.

'Ma, you keep out of this,' said Arun, bluntly. He pointed in the direction of Varun's small bedroom—more a storeroom than a bedroom. 'Now get out and change.'

'I planned to anyway,' said Varun, edging out of the door.

'Bloody fool,' said Arun to himself. Then, affectionately, he turned to Lata: 'So, what's the matter, why are you looking so down in the mouth?'

Lata smiled. 'I'm fine, Arun Bhai,' she said. 'I think I'll go and get ready as well.'

Arun went in to change too. About fifteen minutes before Basil Cox and his wife were due to arrive, he came out to find everyone except Varun dressed and ready. Meenakshi emerged from the kitchen where she had been doing some last-minute supervising. The table had been laid for seven with the best glassware and crockery and cutlery, the flower arrangement was perfect, the hors d'oeuvre had been tasted and found to be fine, the whisky and sherry and campari and so forth had been taken out of the cabinet, and Aparna had been put to bed.

'Where is he now?' demanded Arun of the three women.

'He hasn't come out. He must be in his room,' said Mrs Rupa Mehra. 'I do wish you wouldn't shout at him.'

'He should learn how to behave in a civilized household. This isn't some dhoti-wallah's establishment. Proper clothes indeed!'

Varun emerged a few minutes later. He was wearing a clean kurta-pyjama, not torn exactly, but with a button missing. He had shaved in a rudimentary sort of way after his bath. He reckoned he looked presentable.

Arun did not reckon so. His face reddened. Varun noticed it reddening, and—though he was scared—he was quite pleased as well.

For a second Arun was so furious he could hardly speak. Then he exploded.

'You bloody idiot!' he roared. 'Do you want to embarrass us all?'

Varun looked at him shiftily. 'What's embarrassing about Indian clothes?' he asked. 'Can't I wear what I want to? Ma and Lata and Bhabhiji wear saris, not dresses. Or do I have to keep imitating the whiteys even in my own house? I don't think it's a good idea.'

'I don't care what you bloody well think. In my house you will do as I tell you. Now you change into shirt and tie—or—or—'

'Or else what, Arun Bhai?' said Varun, cheeking his brother and enjoying his rage. 'You won't give me dinner with your Colin Box? Actually, I'd much rather have dinner with my own friends anyway than bow and scrape before this box-wallah and his box-walli.'

'Meenakshi, tell Hanif to remove one place,' said Arun.

Meenakshi looked undecided.

'Did you hear me?' asked Arun in a dangerous voice.

Meenakshi got up to do his bidding.

'Now get out,' shouted Arun. 'Go and have dinner with your Shamshu-drinking friends. And don't let me see you anywhere near this house for the rest of the evening. And let me tell you here and now that I won't put up with this sort of thing from you at all. If you live in this house, you bloody well abide by its rules.'

Varun looked uncertainly towards his mother for support.

'Darling, please do what he says. You look so much nicer in a shirt and trousers. Besides, that button is missing. These foreigners don't understand. He's Arun's boss, we must make a good impression.'

'He, for one, is incapable of making a good impression, no matter what he wears or does.' Arun put the boot in. 'I don't want him putting Basil Cox's back up, and he's perfectly capable of doing so. Now, Ma, will you stop these waterworks? See—you've upset everyone, you blithering fool,' said Arun, turning on Varun again.

But Varun had slipped out already.

7.6

Although Arun was feeling more venomous than calm, he smiled a brave, morale-building smile and even put his arm around his mother's shoulder. Meenakshi reflected that the seating around the oval table looked a little more symmetrical now, though there would be an even greater imbalance between men and women. Still, it was not as if any other guests had been invited. It was just the Coxes and the family.

Basil Cox and his wife arrived punctually, and Meenakshi made small talk, interspersing comments about the weather ('so sultry, so unbearably close it's been these last few days, but then, this *is* Calcutta—') with her chiming laugh. She asked for a sherry and sipped it with a distant look in her eyes. The cigarettes were passed around; she lit up, and so did Arun and Basil Cox.

Basil Cox was in his late thirties, pink, shrewd, sound, and bespectacled. Patricia Cox was a small, dull sort of woman, a great contrast to the glamorous Meenakshi. She did not smoke. She drank quite rapidly however, and with a sort of desperation. She did not find Calcutta company interesting, and if there was anything she disliked more than large parties it was small ones, where she felt trapped into compulsory sociability.

Lata had a small sherry. Mrs Rupa Mehra had a nimbu pani.

Hanif, looking very smart in his starched white uniform, offered around the tray of hors d'oeuvre: bits of salami and cheese and asparagus on small squares of bread. If the guests had not so obviously been sahibs—office guests—he might have allowed his disgruntlement with the turn of affairs in his kitchen to be more apparent. As it was, he was at his obliging best.

Arun had begun to hold forth with his usual savoir faire and charm on various subjects: recent plays in London, books that had just appeared and were considered to be significant, the Persian oil crisis, the Korean conflict. The Reds were being pushed back, and not a moment too soon, in Arun's opinion, though of course the Americans, idiots that they were, would probably not make use of their tactical advantage. But then again, with this as with other matters, what could one do?

This Arun—affable, genial, engaging and knowledgeable, even (at times) diffident—was a very different creature from the domestic tyrant and bully of half an hour ago. Basil Cox was charmed. Arun was good at his work, but Cox had not imagined that he was so widely read, indeed better read than most Englishmen of his acquaintance.

Patricia Cox talked to Meenakshi about her little pear-shaped earrings. 'Very pretty,' she commented. 'Where did you get them made?'

Meenakshi told her and promised to take her to the shop. She cast a glance in Mrs Rupa Mehra's direction, but noticed to her relief that she was listening, rapt, to Arun and Basil Cox. In her bedroom earlier this evening, Meenakshi had paused for a second before putting them on—but then she had said to herself: Well, sooner or later Ma will have to get used to the facts of life. I can't always tread softly around her feelings.

Dinner passed smoothly. It was a full four-course meal: soup, smoked hilsa, roast chicken, lemon soufflé. Basil Cox tried to bring Lata and Mrs Rupa Mehra into the conversation, but they tended to speak only when spoken to. Lata's mind was far away. She was brought back with a start when she heard Meenakshi describing how the hilsa was smoked.

'It's a wonderful old recipe that's been in our family for ages,' said Meenakshi. 'It's smoked in a basket over a coal fire after it's been carefully deboned, and hilsa is absolute hell to debone.'

'It's delicious, my dear,' said Basil Cox.

'Of course, the real secret,' continued Meenakshi knowledgeably—though she had only discovered this afternoon how it was done, and that too because the Mugh cook had insisted on the correct ingredients being supplied to him—'the real secret is in the fire. We throw puffed rice on it and crude brown sugar or jaggery—what we in this country call "gur"—' (She rhymed it with 'fur'.)

As she prattled on and on Lata looked at her wonderingly.

'Of course, every girl in the family learns these things at an early age.'

For the first time Patricia Cox looked less than completely bored.

But by the time the soufflé came around, she had lapsed into passivity.

After dinner, coffee and liqueur, Arun brought out the cigars. He and Basil Cox talked a little about work. Arun would not have brought up the subject of the office, but Basil, having made up his mind that Arun was a thorough gentleman, wanted his opinion on a colleague. 'Between us, you know, and strictly between us, I've rather begun to doubt his soundness,' he said. Arun passed his finger around the rim of his liqueur glass, sighed a little, and confirmed his boss's opinion, adding a reason or two of his own.

'Mmm, well, yes, it's interesting that you should think so too,' said Basil Cox.

Arun stared contentedly and contemplatively into the grey and comforting haze around them.

Suddenly the untuneful and slurred notes of 'Two intoxicating eyes' were followed by the fumbling of the key in the front door. Varun, fortified by Shamshu, the cheap but effective Chinese spirit that he and his friends could just about afford, had returned to the fold.

Arun started as if at Banquo's ghost. He got up, fully intending to hustle

Varun out of the house before he entered the drawing room. But he was too late.

Varun, tilting a little, and in an exceptional display of confidence, greeted everyone. The fumes of Shamshu filled the room. He kissed Mrs Rupa Mehra. She drew back. He trembled a little when he saw Meenakshi, who was looking even more dazzlingly beautiful now that she was so horror-struck. He greeted the guests.

'Hello, Mr Box, Mrs Box—er, Mrs Box, Mr Box,' he corrected himself. He bowed, and fumbled with the buttonhole that corresponded to the missing button. The drawstring of his pyjamas hung out below his kurta.

'I don't believe we've met before,' said Basil Cox, looking troubled.

'Oh,' said Arun, his fair face beet red with fury and embarrassment. 'This is, actually, this is—well, my brother Varun. He's a little, er—will you excuse me a minute?' He guided Varun with mildly suppressed violence towards the door, then towards his room. 'Not one word!' he hissed, looking with fury straight into Varun's puzzled eyes. 'Not one word, or I'll strangle you with my bare hands.'

He locked Varun's door from the outside.

He was his charming self by the time he returned to the drawing room.

'Well, as I was saying, he's a little—er, well, uncontrollable at times. I'm sure you understand. Black sheep and all that. Perfectly all right, not violent or anything, but—'

'It looked as if he'd been on a binge,' said Patricia Cox, suddenly livening up.

'Sent to try us, I'm afraid,' continued Arun. 'My father's early death and so on. Every family has one. Has his quirks: insists on wearing those ridiculous clothes.'

'Very strong, whatever it was. I can still smell it,' said Patricia. 'Unusual too. Is it a kind of whisky? I'd like to try it. Do you know what it is?'

'I'm afraid it's what's known as Shamshu.'

'Shamshu?' said Mrs Cox with the liveliest interest, trying the word out on her tongue three or four times. 'Shamshu. Do you know what that is, Basil?' She looked alive again. All her mousiness had disappeared.

'I don't believe I do, my dear,' said her husband.

'I believe it's made from rice,' said Arun. 'It's a Chinese concoction of some kind.'

'Would Shaw Brothers carry it?' asked Patricia Cox.

'I rather doubt it. It ought to be available in Chinatown,' said Arun.

In fact Varun and his friends did get it from Chinatown, from a hole-in-the-wall sort of place at eight annas a glass.

'It must be powerful stuff, whatever it is. Smoked hilsa and Shamshu—how marvellous to learn two entirely different things at dinner. One never does, you know,' Patricia confided. 'Usually, I'm bored as a fish.'

Bored as a fish? thought Arun. But by now Varun had started singing to himself inside his room.

'What a very interesting young man,' continued Patricia Cox. 'And he's your brother, you say. What is he singing? Why didn't he join us for dinner? We must have all of you around sometime soon. Mustn't we, darling?' Basil Cox looked very severely doubtful. Patricia Cox decided to take this for assent. 'I haven't had so much fun since I was at RADA. And do bring a bottle of Shamshu.'

Heaven forbid, thought Basil Cox.

Heaven forbid, thought Arun.

7.7

The guests were about to arrive at Mr Justice Chatterji's house in Ballygunge. This was one of the three or four grand parties that he took it upon himself to give at short notice during the course of the year. There was a peculiar mixture of guests for two reasons. First, because of Mr Justice Chatterji himself, whose net of friendship and acquaintance was very varied. (He was an absent-minded man, who picked up friends here and there.) Secondly, because any party of this kind was invariably treated by the whole Chatterji family as an opportunity to invite all their own friends as well. Mrs Chatterji invited some of hers, and so did their children; only Tapan, who had returned for his school holidays, was considered too young to tag on his own list of invitees to a party where there would be drinking.

Mr Justice Chatterji was not an orderly man, but he had produced five children in strict alternation of sex: Amit, Meenakshi (who was married to Arun Mehra), Dipankar, Kakoli, and Tapan. None of them worked, but each had an occupation. Amit wrote poetry, Meenakshi played canasta, Dipankar sought the Meaning of Life, Kakoli kept the telephone busy, and Tapan, who was only twelve or thirteen, and by far the youngest, went to the prestigious boarding school, Jheel.

Amit, the poet, had studied Jurisprudence at Oxford, but having got his degree, had not completed, to his father's exasperation, what should have been easy enough for him to complete: his studies for the Bar at Lincoln's Inn, his father's old Inn. He had eaten most of his dinners and had even passed a paper or two, but had then lost interest in the law. Instead, on the strength of a couple of university prizes for poetry, some short fiction published here and there in literary magazines, and a book of poetry which had won him a prize in England (and therefore adulation in Calcutta), he was sitting pretty in his father's house and doing nothing that counted as real work.

At the moment he was talking to his two sisters and to Lata.

'How many do we expect?' asked Amit.

'I don't know,' said Kakoli. 'Fifty?'

Amit looked amused. 'Fifty would just about cover half your friends, Kuku. I'd say one hundred and fifty.'

'I can't abide these large parties,' said Meenakshi in high excitement.

'No, nor can I,' said Kakoli, glancing at herself in the tall mirror in the hall.

'I suppose the guest list consists entirely of those invited by Ma and Tapan and myself,' said Amit, naming the three least sociable members of the family.

'Vereeeee funneeeee,' said (or, rather, sang) Kakoli, whose name implied the songbird that she was.

'You should go up to your room, Amit,' said Meenakshi, 'and settle down on a sofa with Jane Austen. We'll tell you when dinner is served. Or better still, we'll send it up to you. That way you can avoid all your admirers.'

'He's very peculiar,' said Kakoli to Lata. 'Jane Austen is the only woman in his life.'

'But half the bhadralok in Calcutta want him as a match for their daughters,' added Meenakshi. 'They believe he has brains.'

Kakoli recited:

'Amit Chatterji, what a catch!
Is a highly suitable match.'

Meenakshi added:

'Why he has not married yet?
Always playing hard to get.'

Kakoli continued:

> 'Famous poet, so they say.
> "Besh" decent in every way.'

She giggled.

Lata said to Amit: 'Why do you let them get away with this?'

'You mean with their doggerel?' said Amit.

'I mean with teasing you,' said Lata.

'Oh, I don't mind. It runs off my back like duck's water,' said Amit.

Lata looked surprised, but Kakoli said, 'He's doing a Biswas on you.'

'A Biswas?'

'Biswas Babu, my father's old clerk. He still comes around a couple of times a week to help with this and that, and gives us advice on life. He advised Meenakshi against marrying your brother,' said Kakoli.

In fact the opposition to Meenakshi's sudden affair and marriage had been wider and deeper. Meenakshi's parents had not particularly cared for the fact that she had married outside the community. Arun Mehra was neither a Brahmo, nor of Brahmin stock, nor even a Bengali. He came from a family that was struggling financially. To give the Chatterjis credit, this last fact did not matter very much to them, though they themselves had been more than affluent for generations. They were only (with respect to this objection) concerned that their daughter might not be able to afford the comforts of life that she had grown up with. But again, they had not swamped their married daughter with gifts. Even though Mr Justice Chatterji did not have an instinctive rapport with his son-in-law, he did not think that that would be fair.

'What does Biswas Babu have to do with duck's water?' asked Lata, who found Meenakshi's family amusing but confusing.

'Oh—that's just one of his expressions. I don't think it's very kind of Amit not to explain family references to outsiders.'

'She's not an outsider,' said Amit. 'Or she shouldn't be. Actually, we are all very fond of Biswas Babu, and he is very fond of us. He was my grandfather's clerk originally.'

'But he won't be Amit's—to his heart-deep regret,' said Meenakshi. 'In fact, Biswas Babu is even more upset than our father that Amit has deserted the Bar.'

'I can still practise if I choose to,' said Amit. 'A university degree is enough in Calcutta.'

'Ah, but you won't be admitted to the Bar Library.'

'Who cares?' said Amit. 'Actually, I'd be happy editing a small journal and writing a few good poems and a novel or two and passing gently into senility and posterity. May I offer you a drink? A sherry?'

'I'll have a sherry,' said Kakoli.

'Not you, Kuku, you can help yourself. I was offering Lata a drink.'

'Ouch,' said Kakoli. She looked at Lata's pale blue cotton sari with its fine chikan embroidery, and said: 'Do you know, Lata—pink is what would really suit you.'

Lata said: 'I'd better not have anything as dangerous as a sherry. Could I have some—oh, why not? A small sherry, please.'

Amit went to the bar with a smile and said: 'Do you think I might have two glasses of sherry?'

'Dry, medium or sweet, Sir?' asked Tapan.

Tapan was the baby of the family, whom everyone loved and fussed over, and who was even allowed an occasional sip of sherry himself. This evening he was helping at the bar.

'One sweet and one dry, please,' said Amit. 'Where's Dipankar?' he asked Tapan.

'I think he's in his room, Dada,' said Tapan. 'Shall I call him down?'

'No, no, you help with the bar,' said Amit, patting his brother on the shoulder. 'You're doing a fine job. I'll just see what he's up to.'

Dipankar, their middle brother, was a dreamer. He had studied economics, but spent most of his time reading about the poet and patriot Sri Aurobindo, whose flaccid mystical verse he was (to Amit's disgust) at present deeply engrossed in. Dipankar was indecisive by nature. Amit knew that it would be best simply to bring him downstairs himself. Left to his own devices, Dipankar treated every decision like a spiritual crisis. Whether to have one spoon of sugar in his tea or two, whether to come down now or fifteen minutes later, whether to enjoy the good life of Ballygunge or to take up Sri Aurobindo's path of renunciation, all these decisions caused him endless agony. A succession of strong women passed through his life and made most of his decisions for him, before they became impatient with his vacillation ('Is she really the one for me?') and moved on. His views moulded themselves to theirs while they lasted, then began to float freely again.

Dipankar was fond of making remarks such as, 'It is all the Void,' at breakfast, thus casting a mystical aura over the scrambled eggs.

Amit went up to Dipankar's room, and found him sitting on a prayer mat at the harmonium, untunefully singing a song by Rabindranath Tagore.

'You had better come down soon,' Amit said in Bengali. 'The guests have begun to arrive.'

'Just coming, just coming,' said Dipankar. 'I'll just finish this song, and then I'll . . . I'll come down. I will.'

'I'll wait,' said Amit.

'You can go down, Dada. Don't trouble yourself. Please.'

'It's no trouble,' said Amit. After Dipankar had finished his song, unembarrassed by its tunelessness—for all pitches, no doubt, stood equal before the Void—Amit escorted him down the teak-balustraded marble stairs.

7.8

'Where's Cuddles?' asked Amit when they were halfway down.

'Oh,' said Dipankar vaguely, 'I don't know.'

'He might bite someone.'

'Yes,' agreed Dipankar, not greatly troubled by the thought.

Cuddles was not a hospitable dog. He had been with the Chatterji family for more than ten years, during which time he had bitten Biswas Babu, several schoolchildren (friends who had come to play), a number of lawyers (who had visited Mr Justice Chatterji's chambers for conferences during his years as a barrister), a middle-level executive, a doctor on a house call, and the standard mixture of postmen and electricians.

Cuddles' most recent victim had been the man who had come to the door to take the decennial census.

The only creature Cuddles treated with respect was Mr Justice Chatterji's father's cat Pillow, who lived in the next house, and who was so fierce that he was taken for walks on a leash.

'You should have tied him up,' said Amit.

Dipankar frowned. His thoughts were with Sri Aurobindo. 'I think I have,' he said.

'We'd better make sure,' said Amit. 'Just in case.'

It was good that they did. Cuddles rarely growled to identify his position, and Dipankar could not remember where—if at all—he had put him. He might still be ranging the garden in order to savage any guests who wandered on to the verandah.

They found Cuddles in the bedroom which had been set aside for people to leave their bags and other apparatus in. He was crouched quietly near a bedside table, watching them with shiny little black eyes. He was a small black dog, with some white on his chest and on his paws. When they had bought him the Chatterjis had been told he was an apso, but he had turned out to be a mutt with a large proportion of Tibetan terrier.

In order to avoid trouble at the party, he had been fastened by a leash to a bedpost. Dipankar could not recall having done this, so it might have been someone else. He and Amit approached Cuddles. Cuddles normally loved the family, but today he was jittery.

Cuddles surveyed them closely without growling, and when he judged that the moment was ripe, he flew intently and viciously through the air towards them until the sudden restraint of the leash jerked him back. He strained against it, but could not get into biting range. All the Chatterjis knew how to step back rapidly when instinct told them Cuddles was on the attack. But perhaps the guests would not react so swiftly.

'I think we should move him out of this room,' said Amit. Strictly speaking, Cuddles was Dipankar's dog, and thus his responsibility, but he now in effect belonged to all of them—or, rather, was, accepted as one of them, like the sixth point of a regular hexagon.

'He seems quite happy here,' said Dipankar. 'He's a living being too. Naturally he gets nervous with all this coming and going in the house.'

'Take it from me,' said Amit, 'he's going to bite someone.'

'Hmm. . . . Should I put a notice on the door: Beware of Dog?' asked Dipankar.

'No. I think you should get him out of here. Lock him up in your room.'

'I can't do that,' said Dipankar. 'He hates being upstairs when everyone else is downstairs. He is a sort of lapdog, after all.'

Amit reflected that Cuddles was the most psychotic lapdog he had known. He too blamed his temperament on the constant stream of visitors to the house. Kakoli's friends of late had flooded the Chatterji mansion. Now, as it happened, Kakoli herself entered the room with a friend.

'Ah, there you are, Dada, we were wondering what had happened to you. Have you met Neera? Neera, these are my berruthers Amit and Dipankar. Oh yes, put it down on the bed,' said Kakoli. 'It'll be quite safe here. And the bathroom's through there.' Cuddles prepared for a lunge. 'Watch out for the dog—he's harmless but sometimes he has moods. We have moods, don't we, Cuddlu? Poor Cuddlu, left all alone in the bedroom.

> Darling Cuddles, what to do
> When the house is such a zoo!'

sang Kakoli, then disappeared.

'We'd better take him upstairs,' said Amit. 'Come on.'

Dipankar consented. Cuddles growled. They calmed him down and took him up. Then Dipankar played a few soothing chords on the harmonium to reassure him, and they returned downstairs.

Many of the guests had arrived by now, and the party was in full swing. In the grand drawing room with its grand piano and grander chandelier milled scores of guests in full summer evening finery, the women fluttering and flattering and sizing each other up, the men engaging themselves in more self-important chatter. British and Indian, Bengali and non-Bengali, old and middle-aged and young, saris shimmering and necklaces glimmering, crisp Shantipuri dhotis edged with a fine line of gold and hand-creased to perfection, kurtas of raw off-white silk with gold buttons, chiffon saris of various pastel hues, white cotton saris with red borders, Dhakai saris with a white background and a pattern in the weave—or (still more elegant) a grey background with a white design, white dinner jackets with black trousers and black bow ties and black patent leather Derbys or Oxfords (each bearing a little reflected chandelier), long dresses of flowery-printed fine poplin chintz and finely polka-dotted white cotton organdy, even an off-the-shoulder silk dress or two in the lightest and most summery of silks: brilliant were the clothes, and glittering the people who filled them.

Arun, who considered it too hot for a jacket, was wearing a stylish cummerbund instead—a maroon monochrome sash with a shimmering pattern through the weave—and a matching bow tie. He was talking rather gravely to Jock Mackay, a cheerful bachelor in his mid-forties who was one of the directors of the managing agency of McKibbin & Ross.

Meenakshi was dressed in a striking orange French chiffon sari and an electric-blue backless choli tied on around her neck and waist with narrow cloth bands. Her midriff was gloriously exposed, around her long and fragrant neck was clasped a Jaipur enamel choker in blue and orange with matching bracelets on her arms, her already considerable height was enhanced by stiletto heels and a tall bun, large earrings dangled deliciously below her chin, the orange tika on her forehead was as huge as her eyes, and most striking and ornamental of all was her devastating smile.

She advanced towards Amit, exuding a fragrance of Shocking Schiaparelli.

But before Amit could greet her, he was accosted by a middle-aged, accusing-looking woman with large, popping eyes whom he did not recognize. She said to him:

'I loved your last book but I can't say I understood it.' She waited for a response.

'Oh—well, thank you,' said Amit.

'Surely that's not all you're going to say?' said the woman, disappointed. 'I thought poets were more articulate. I'm an old friend of your mother's though we haven't met for many years,' she added, irrelevantly. 'We go back to Shantiniketan.'

'Ah, I see,' said Amit. Although he did not much care for this woman, he did not move away. He felt he ought to say something.

'Well, I'm not so much of a poet now. I'm writing a novel,' he said.

'But that's no excuse at all,' said the woman. Then she added: 'Tell me, what is it about? Or is that a trade secret of the famous Amit Chatterji?'

'No, no, not really,' said Amit, who hated to talk about his current work. 'It's about a moneylender at the time of the Bengal Famine. As you know, my mother's family comes from East Bengal—'

'How wonderful that you should want to write about your own country,' said the woman. 'Especially after winning all those prizes abroad. Tell me, are you in India a lot?'

Amit noticed that both his sisters were standing near him now and listening in.

'Oh yes, well, now that I've returned I am here most of the time. I'm, well, in and out—'

'In and out,' repeated the woman wonderingly.

'Back and forth,' said Meenakshi helpfully.

'Off and on,' said Kakoli, who was incapable of restraint.

The woman frowned.

'To and fro,' said Meenakshi.

'Here and there,' said Kakoli.

She and Meenakshi started giggling. Then they waved to someone at the far side of the huge room, and instantly disappeared.

Amit smiled apologetically. But the woman was looking at him angrily. Were the young Chatterjis trying to make fun of her?

She said to Amit: 'I am quite sick of reading about you.'

Amit said mildly: 'Mmm. Yes.'

'And of hearing about you.'

'If I weren't me,' said Amit, 'I would be pretty sick of hearing about myself.' The woman frowned. Then, recovering, she said: 'I think my drink's finished.'

She noticed her husband hovering nearby, and handed him her empty glass, which was stained with crimson lipstick around the rim. 'But tell me, how do you write?'

'Do you mean—' began Amit.

'I mean, is it inspiration? Or is it hard work?'

'Well,' said Amit, 'without inspiration one can't—'

'I knew, I just knew it was inspiration. But without being married, how did you write that poem about the young bride?'

She sounded disapproving.

Amit looked thoughtful, and said: 'I just—'

'And tell me,' continued the woman, 'does it take you long to think of a book? I'm dying to read your new book.'

'So am I,' said Amit.

'I have some good ideas for books,' said the woman. 'When I was in Shantiniketan, the influence of Gurudeb on me was very deep . . . you know—our own Rabindranath. . . .'

Amit said, 'Ah.'

'It could not take you long, I know . . . but the writing itself must be so difficult. I could never be a writer. I don't have the gift. It is a gift from God.'

'Yes, it seems to come—'

'I once wrote poetry,' said the woman. 'In English, like you. Though I have an aunt who writes Bengali poetry. She was a true disciple of Robi Babu. Does your poetry rhyme?'

'Yes.'

'Mine didn't. It was modern. I was young, in Darjeeling. I wrote about nature, not about love. I hadn't met Mihir then. My husband, you know. Later I typed them. I showed them to Mihir. Once I spent a night in a hospital bitten by mosquitoes. And a poem came out suddenly. But he said, "It doesn't rhyme."'

She looked disapprovingly at her husband, who was hovering around like a cup-bearer with her refilled glass.

'Your husband said that?' said Amit.

'Yes. Then I never had the urge again. I don't know why.'

'You've killed a poet,' said Amit to her husband, who seemed a good enough fellow.

'Come,' he continued to Lata, who had been listening to the last part of the conversation, 'I'll introduce you to a few people, as I promised. Excuse me for a minute.'

Amit had made no such promise, but it enabled him to get away.

7.9

'Well, whom do you want to meet?' said Amit to Lata.

'No one,' said Lata.

'No one?' asked Amit. He looked amused.

'Anyone. How about that woman there with the red-and-white cotton sari?'

'The one with the short grey hair—who looks as if she's laying down the law to Dipankar and my grandfather?'

'Yes.'

'That's Ila Chattopadhyay. Dr Ila Chattopadhyay. She's related to us. She has strong and immediate opinions. You'll like her.'

Though Lata was unsure about the value of strong and immediate opinions, she liked the look of the woman. Dr Ila Chattopadhyay was shaking her finger at Dipankar and saying something to him with great and apparently affectionate vigour. Her sari was rather crushed.

'May we interrupt?' asked Amit.

'Of course you may, Amit, don't be stupid,' said Dr Ila Chattopadhyay.

'This is Lata, Arun's sister.'

'Good,' said Dr Ila Chattopadhyay, appraising her in a second. 'I'm sure she's nicer than her bumptious brother. I was telling Dipankar that economics is a pointless subject. He would have done far better to study mathematics. Don't you agree?'

'Of course,' said Amit.

'Now that you're back in India you must stay here permanently, Amit. Your country needs you—and I don't say that lightly.'

'Of course,' said Amit.

Dr Ila Chattopadhyay said to Lata: 'I never pay any attention to Amit, he always agrees with me.'

'Ila Kaki never pays any attention to anyone,' said Amit.

'No. And do you know why? It's because of your grandfather.'

'Because of me?' asked the old man.

'Yes,' said Dr Ila Chattopadhyay. 'Many years ago you told me that until you were forty you were very concerned about what people thought of you. Then you decided to be concerned about what you thought of other people instead.'

'Did I say that?' said old Mr Chatterji, surprised.

'Yes, indeed, whether you remember it or not. I too used to make myself miserable bothering about other people's opinions, so I decided to adopt your philosophy immediately, even though I wasn't forty then—or even thirty. Do you really not remember that remark of yours? I was trying to decide whether to give up my career, and was under a lot of pressure from my husband's family to do so. My talk with you made all the difference.'

'Well,' said old Mr Chatterji, 'I remember some things but not other things these days. But I'm very glad my remark made such a, such a, well, profound impression on you. Do you know, the other day I forgot the name of my last cat but one. I tried to recall it, but it didn't come to me.'

'Biplob,' said Amit.

'Yes, of course, and it did come back to me eventually. I had named him that because I was a friend of Subhas Bose—well, let me say I knew the family. . . . Of course, in my position as a judge, a name like that would have to be, er—'

Amit waited while the old man searched for the right word, then helped him out.

'Ironic?'

'No, I wasn't looking for that word, Amit, I was—well, "ironic" will do. Of course, those were different times, mm, mm. Do you know, I can't even draw a map of India now. It seems so unimaginable. And the law too is changing every day. One keeps reading about writ petitions being brought up before the High Courts. Well, in my day we were content with regular suits. But I'm an old man, things must move ahead, and I must fall back. Now girls like Ila, and young people like you'—he gesticulated towards Amit and Lata—'must carry things forward.'

'I'm hardly a girl,' said Dr Ila Chattopadhyay. 'My own daughter is twenty-five now.'

'For me, dear Ila, you will always be a girl,' said old Mr Chatterji.

Dr Ila Chattopadhyay made an impatient sound. 'Anyway, my students don't treat me like a girl. The other day I was discussing a chapter in one of my old books with a junior colleague of mine, a very serious young man, and he said, "Madam, far be it for me, not only as your junior but also as one who is appreciative of the situation of the book in the context of its time and the fact that you have not many years remaining, to suggest that—" I was quite charmed. Remarks like that rejuvenate me.'

'What book was that?' asked Lata.

'It was a book about Donne,' said Dr Ila Chattopadhyay. '*Metaphysical Causality*. It's a very stupid book.'

'Oh, so you teach English!' said Lata, surprised. 'I thought you were a doctor—I mean, a medical doctor.'

'What on earth have you been telling her?' said Dr Ila Chattopadhyay to Amit.

'Nothing. I didn't really get the chance to introduce you properly. You were telling Dipankar so forcefully that he should have dropped economics that I didn't dare to interrupt.'

'So I was. And so he should have. But where has he got to?'

Amit scanned the room cursorily, and noticed Dipankar standing with Kakoli and her babble-rabble. Dipankar, despite his mystical and religious tendencies, was fond of even foolish young women.

'Shall I deliver him back to you?' asked Amit.

'Oh, no,' said Dr Ila Chattopadhyay, 'arguing with him only upsets me, it's like battling a blancmange . . . all his mushy ideas about the spiritual roots of India and the genius of Bengal. Well, if he were a true Bengali, he'd change his name back to Chattopadhyay—and so would you all, instead of continuing to cater to the feeble tongues and brains of the British. . . . Where are you studying?'

Lata, still a little shaken by Dr Ila Chattopadhyay's emphatic energy, said: 'Brahmpur.'

'Oh, Brahmpur,' said Dr Ila Chattopadhyay. 'An impossible place. I once was—no, no, I won't say it, it's too cruel, and you're a nice girl.'

'Oh, do go on, Ila Kaki,' said Amit. 'I adore cruelty, and I'm sure Lata can take anything you have to say.'

'Well, Brahmpur!' said Dr Ila Chattopadhyay, needing no second bidding. 'Brahmpur! I had to go there for a day about ten years ago to attend some conference or other in the English Department, and I'd heard so much about Brahmpur and the Barsaat Mahal and so on that I stayed on for a couple of extra days. It made me almost ill. All that courtly culture with its Yes Huzoor and No Huzoor and nothing robust about it at all. "How are you?" "Oh, well, I'm alive." I just couldn't stand it. "Yes, I'll have two florets of rice, and one drop of daal. . . ." All that subtlety and etiquette and bowing and scraping and ghazals and kathak. Kathak! When I saw those fat women twirling around like tops, I wanted to say to them, "Run! Run! don't dance, run!"'

'It's a good thing you didn't, Ila Kaki, you'd have been strangled.'

'Well, at least it would have meant an end to my suffering. The next evening I had to undergo some more of your Brahmpuri culture. We had to go and listen to one of those ghazal singers. Dreadful, dreadful, I'll never forget it! One of those soulful women, Saeeda something, whom you couldn't see for her jewellery—it was like staring into the sun. Wild horses wouldn't drag me there again . . . and all those brainless men in that silly northern dress, the pyjama, looking as if they'd just got out of bed, rolling about in ecstasy—or agony—groaning "wah! wah!" to the most abjectly self-pitying insipid verse—or so it seemed to me when my friends translated it. . . . Do you like that sort of music?'

'Well, I do like classical music,' began Lata tentatively, waiting for Dr Ila Chattopadhyay to pronounce that she was completely misguided. 'Ustad Majeed Khan's performances of raags like Darbari, for instance. . . .'

Amit, without waiting for Lata to finish her sentence, stepped swiftly in to draw Dr Ila Chattopadhyay's fire.

'So do I, so do I,' he said. 'I've always felt that the performance of a raag resembles a novel—or at least the kind of novel I'm attempting to write. You know,' he continued, extemporizing as he went along, 'first you take one note and explore it for a while, then another to discover its possibilities, then perhaps you get to the dominant, and pause for a bit, and it's only gradually that the phrases begin to form and the tabla joins in with the beat . . . and then the more brilliant improvisations and diversions begin, with the main theme returning from time to time, and finally it all speeds up, and the excitement increases to a climax.'

Dr Ila Chattopadhyay was looking at him in astonishment. 'What utter nonsense,' she said to Amit. 'You're getting to be as fluffy as Dipankar. Don't pay any attention to him, Lata,' continued the author of *Metaphysical Causality*. 'He's just a writer, he knows nothing at all about literature. Nonsense always makes me hungry, I must get some food at once. At least the family serves dinner at a sensible hour. "Two florets of rice" indeed!' And, shaking her grey locks emphatically, she made for the buffet table.

Amit offered to bring some food on a plate to his grandfather, and the old man acquiesced. He sat down in a comfortable armchair, and Amit and Lata went towards the buffet. On the way, a pretty young woman detached herself from Kakoli's giggling, gossiping group, and came up to Amit.

'Don't you remember me?' she asked. 'We met at the Sarkars'.'

Amit, trying to work out when and at which Sarkars' they might have met, frowned and smiled simultaneously.

The girl looked at him reproachfully. 'We had a long conversation,' she said.

'Ah.'

'About Bankim Babu's attitude towards the British, and how it affected the form as opposed to the content of his writing.'

Amit thought: Oh God! Aloud he said: 'Yes . . . yes. . . .'

Lata, though she felt sorry for both Amit and the girl, could not help smiling. She was glad she had come to the party after all.

The girl persisted: 'Don't you remember?'

Amit suddenly became voluble. 'I am so forgetful—' he said; '—and forgettable,' he added quickly, 'that I sometimes wonder if I ever existed. Nothing I've ever done seems to have happened. . . .'

The girl nodded. 'I know just what you mean,' she said. But she soon wandered away a little sadly.

Amit frowned.

Lata, who could tell that he was feeling bad for having made the girl feel bad, said:

'Your responsibilities don't end with having written your books, it seems.'

'What?' said Amit, as if noticing her for the first time. 'Oh yes, oh yes, that's certainly true. Here, Lata. Have a plate.'

7.10

Although Amit was not too conscientious about his general duties as a host, he tried to make sure that Lata at least was not left stranded during the evening. Varun (who might otherwise have kept her company) had not come to the party; he preferred his Shamshu friends. Meenakshi (who was fond of Lata and normally would have escorted her around) was talking to her parents during a brief respite in their hostly duties, describing the events in the kitchen yesterday afternoon with the Mugh cook and in the drawing room yesterday evening with the Coxes. She had had the Coxes invited this evening as well because she thought it might be good for Arun.

'But she's a drab little thing,' said Meenakshi. 'Her clothes look as if they've been bought off the hook.'

'She didn't look all that drab when she introduced herself,' said her father.

Meenakshi looked around the room casually and started slightly. Patricia Cox was wearing a beautiful green silk dress with a pearl necklace. Her gold-brown hair was short and, under the light of the chandelier, curiously radiant. This was not the mousy Patricia Cox of yesterday. Meenakshi's expression was not ecstatic.

'I hope things are well with you, Meenakshi,' said Mrs Chatterji, reverting for a moment to Bengali.

'Wonderfully well, Mago,' replied Meenakshi in English. 'I'm so much in love.'

This brought an anxious frown to Mrs Chatterji's face.

'We're so worried about Kakoli,' she said.

'We?' said Mr Justice Chatterji. 'Well, I suppose that's right.'

'Your father doesn't take things seriously enough. First it was that boy at Calcutta University, the, you know, the—'

'The commie,' said Mr Justice Chatterji benevolently.

'Then it was the boy with the deformed hand and the strange sense of humour, what was his name?'

'Tapan.'

'Yes, what an unfortunate coincidence.' Mrs Chatterji glanced at the bar where her own Tapan was still on duty. Poor baby. She must tell him to go to bed soon. Had he had time to snatch a bite to eat?

'And now?' asked Meenakshi, looking over at the corner where Kakoli and her friends were nattering and chattering away.

'Now,' said her mother, 'it's a foreigner. Well, I may as well tell you, it's that German fellow there.'

'He's very good-looking,' said Meenakshi, who noticed important things first. 'Why hasn't Kakoli told me?'

'She's quite secretive these days,' said her mother.

'On the contrary, she's very open,' said Mr Justice Chatterji.

'It's the same thing,' said Mrs Chatterji. 'We hear about so many friends and special friends that we never really know who the real one is. If indeed there is one at all.'

'Well, dear,' said Mr Justice Chatterji to his wife, 'you worried about the commie and that came to nothing, and about the boy with the hand, and that came to nothing. So why worry? Look at Arun's mother there, she's always smiling, she never worries about anything.'

'Baba,' said Meenakshi, 'that's simply not true, she's the biggest worrier of all. She worries about everything—no matter how trivial.'

'Is that so?' said her father with interest.

'Anyway,' continued Meenakshi, 'how do you know that there is any romantic interest between them?'

'He keeps inviting her to all these diplomatic functions,' said her mother. 'He's a Second Secretary at the German Consulate General. He even pretends to like Rabindrasangeet. It's too much.'

'Darling, you're not being quite fair,' said Mr Justice Chatterji. 'Kakoli too has suddenly evinced an interest in playing the piano parts of Schubert songs. If we're lucky, we may even hear an impromptu recital tonight.'

'She says he has a lovely baritone voice, and it makes her swoon. She will completely ruin her reputation,' said Mrs Chatterji.

'What's his name?' asked Meenakshi.

'Hans,' said Mrs Chatterji.

'Just Hans?'

'Hans something. Really, Meenakshi, it's too upsetting. If he's not serious, it'll break her heart. And if she marries him she'll leave India and we'll never see her again.'

'Hans Sieber,' said her father. 'Incidentally, if you introduce yourself as Mrs Mehra rather than as Miss Chatterji, he is liable to seize your hand and kiss it. I think his family was originally Austrian. Courtesy is something of a disease there.'

'Really?' breathed Meenakshi, intrigued.

'Really. Even Ila was charmed. But it didn't work with your mother; she considers him a sort of pallid Ravana come to spirit her daughter away to distant wilds.'

The analogy was not apt, but Mr Justice Chatterji, off the bench, relaxed considerably the logical rigour he was renowned for.

'So you think he might kiss my hand?'

'Not might, will. But that's nothing to what he did with mine.'

'What did he do, Baba?' Meenakshi fixed her huge eyes on her father.

'He nearly crushed it to pulp.' Her father opened his right hand and looked at it for a few seconds.

'Why did he do that?' asked Meenakshi, laughing in her tinkling way.

'I think he wanted to be reassuring,' said her father. 'And your husband was similarly reassured a few minutes later. At any rate, I noticed him open his mouth slightly when he was receiving his handshake.'

'Oh, poor Arun,' said Meenakshi with unconcern.

She looked across at Hans, who was gazing adoringly at Kakoli surrounded by her circle of jabberers. Then, to her mother's considerable distress, she repeated:

'He's very good-looking. Tall too. What's wrong with him? Aren't we Brahmos supposed to be very open-minded? Why shouldn't we marry Kuku off to a foreigner? It would be rather chic.'

'Yes, why not?' said her father. 'His limbs appear to be intact.'

Mrs Chatterji said: 'I wish you could dissuade your sister from acting rashly. I should never have let her learn that brutal language from that awful Miss Hebel.'

Meenakshi said: 'I don't think anything we say to one another has much effect. Didn't you want Kuku to dissuade me from marrying Arun a few years ago?'

'Oh, that was quite different,' said Mrs Chatterji. 'And besides, we're used to Arun now,' she continued unconvincingly. 'We're all one big happy family now.'

The conversation was interrupted by Mr Kohli, a very round teacher of physics who was fond of his drink, and was trying to avoid bumping into his reproving wife on his way to the bar. 'Hello, judge,' he said. 'What do you think of the verdict in the Bandel Road case?'

'Ah, well, as you know, I can't comment on it,' said Mr Justice Chatterji. 'It might turn up in my court on appeal. And really, I haven't been following it closely either, though everyone else I know appears to have been.'

Mrs Chatterji had no such compunctions, however. All the newspapers had carried long reports about the progress of the case and everyone had an opinion about it. 'It really is shocking,' she said. 'I can't see how a mere magistrate has the right—'

'A Sessions Judge, my dear,' interjected Mr Justice Chatterji.

'Yes, well, I don't see how he can possibly have the right to overturn the verdict of a jury. Is that justice? Twelve good men and true, don't they say? How dare he set himself up above them?'

'Nine, dear. It's nine in Calcutta. As for their goodness and truth—'

'Yes, well. And to call the verdict perverse—isn't that what he said—?'

'Perverse, unreasonable, manifestly wrong and against the weight of the evidence,' recited the bald-headed Mr Kohli with a relish he usually reserved for his whisky. His small mouth was half open, a little like that of a meditative fish.

'Perverse, unreasonably wrong and so on, well, does he have a right to do that? It is so—so undemocratic somehow,' continued Mrs Chatterji, 'and, like it or not, we live in democratic times. And democracy is half our trouble. And that's why we have all these disorders and all this bloodshed, and then we have jury trials—why we still have them in Calcutta when everyone else in India has got rid of them I really don't know—and someone bribes or intimidates the jury, and they bring in these impossible verdicts. If it weren't for courageous judges who set these verdicts aside, where would we be? Don't you agree, dear?' Mrs Chatterji sounded indignant.

Mr Justice Chatterji said, 'Yes, dear, of course. Well there you are, Mr Kohli; now you know what I think. But your glass is empty.'

Mr Kohli, bewildered, said, 'Yes, I think I'll get another.' He looked quickly around to make sure the coast was clear.

'And please tell Tapan he should go to bed at once,' said Mrs Chatterji. 'Unless he hasn't eaten. If he hasn't eaten, he shouldn't go to bed at once. He should eat first.'

'Do you know, Meenakshi,' said Mr Justice Chatterji, 'that your mother and I were arguing with each other so convincingly one day last week that the next day by breakfast we had convinced ourselves of each other's points of view and argued just as fiercely as before?'

'What were you arguing about?' said Meenakshi. 'I miss our breakfast parliaments.'

'I can't remember,' said Mr Justice Chatterji. 'Can you? Wasn't it something to do with Biswas Babu?'

'It was something to do with Cuddles,' said Mrs Chatterji.

'Was it? I'm not sure it was. I thought it was—well, anyway, Meenakshi, you must come for breakfast one day soon. Sunny Park is almost walking distance from the house.'

'I know,' said Meenakshi. 'But it's so difficult to get away in the morning. Arun is very particular about things being just so, and Aparna is always so taxing and tedious before eleven. Mago, your cook really saved my life yesterday. Now I think I'll go and say hello to Hans. And who's that young man who's glowering at Hans and Kakoli? He's not even wearing a bow tie.'

Indeed, the young man was virtually naked: dressed merely in a standard white shirt and white trousers with a regular striped tie. He was a college student.

'I don't know, dear,' said Mrs Chatterji.

'Another mushroom?' asked Meenakshi.

Mr Justice Chatterji, who had first coined the phrase when Kakoli's friends started springing up in profusion, nodded. 'I'm sure he is,' he said.

Halfway across the room, Meenakshi bumped into Amit, and repeated the question.

'He introduced himself to me as Krishnan,' said Amit. 'Kakoli knows him very well, it seems.'

'Oh,' said Meenakshi. 'What does he do?'

'I don't know. He's one of her close friends, he says.'

'One of her closest friends?'

'Oh no,' said Amit. 'He couldn't be one of her closest friends. She knows the names of those.'

'Well, I'm going to meet Kuku's Kraut,' said Meenakshi with decision. 'Where's Luts? She was with you a few minutes ago.'

'I don't know. Somewhere there.' Amit pointed in the direction of the piano, to a dense and voluble section of the crowd. 'By the way, watch your hands when watching Hans.'

'Yes, I know,' said Meenakshi. 'Daddy warned me too. But it's a safe moment. He's eating. Surely he won't set down his plate to seize my hand?'

'You can never tell,' said Amit darkly.

'Too delicious,' said Meenakshi.

7.11

Meanwhile Lata, who was in the thickest part of the party, felt as if she was swimming in a sea of language. She was quite amazed by the glitter and glory of it all. Sometimes a half-comprehensible English wave would rise, sometimes an incomprehensible Bengali one. Like magpies cackling over baubles—or discovering occasional gems and imagining them to be baubles—the excited guests chattered on. Despite the fact that they were shovelling in a great deal of food, everyone managed to shovel out a great many words.

'Oh, no, no, Dipankar . . . you don't understand—the fundamental construct of Indian civilization is the Square—the four stages of life, the four purposes of life—love, wealth, duty, and final liberation—even the four arms of our ancient symbol, the swastika, so sadly abused of late . . . yes, it is the square and the square alone that is the fundamental construct of our spirituality . . . you will only understand this when you are an old lady like me. . . .'

'She keeps two cooks, that is the reason, no other. Truly—but you must try the luchis. No, no, you must have everything in the right order . . . that is the secret of Bengali food. . . .'

'*Such* a good speaker at the Ramakrishna Mission the other day; quite a young man but *so* spiritual . . . Creativity in an Age of Crisis . . . you really *must* go next week: he will be talking about the Quest for Peace and Harmony. . . .'

'Everyone said that if I went down to the Sundarbans I'd see scores of tigers. I didn't even see a mosquito. Water, water everywhere—and nothing else at all. People are such dreadful liars.'

'They should be expelled—stiff exam or no stiff exam, is that a reason for snatching papers in the examination hall? These are commerce students of Calcutta University, mind you. What will happen to the economic order without discipline? If Sir Asutosh were alive today what would he say? Is this what Independence means?'

'Montoo is looking so sweet. But Poltoo and Loltoo are looking a little under par. Ever since their father's illness, of course. They say it is—that it is, you know . . . well, liver . . . from too much drink.'

'Oh, no, no, no, Dipankar—the elemental paradigm—I would never have said construct—of our ancient civilization is of course the Trinity . . . I don't mean the Christian trinity, of course; all that seems so crude somehow—but the Trinity as Process and Aspect—Creation and Preservation and Destruction—yes, the Trinity, that is the elemental paradigm of our civilization, and no other. . . .'

'Ridiculous nonsense, of course. So I called the union leaders in and I read them the riot act. Naturally it took a little straight talk for them to come into line again. Well, I won't say there wasn't a payment to one or two of the most recalcitrant of them, but all that is handled by Personnel.'

'That's not Je Reviens—that's Quelques Fleurs—all the difference in the world. Not that my husband would know the difference. He can't even recognize Chanel!'

'Then I said to Robi Babu: "You are like a God to us, please give me a name for my child," and he consented. That is the reason why she is called Hemangini. . . . Actually, the name was not to my liking, but what could I do?'

'If the mullahs want war, they can have one. Our trade with East Pakistan has virtually come to a halt. Well, one happy side effect is that the price of mangoes has come down! The Maldah growers had a huge crop this year, and they don't know what to do with them. . . . Of course it's a transport problem too, just like the Bengal Famine.'

'Oh, no, no, no, Dipankar, you haven't got it at all—the primeval texture of Indian philosophy is that of Duality . . . yes, Duality. . . . The warp and weft of our ancient garment, the sari itself—a single length of cloth which yet swathes our Indian womanhood—the warp and weft of the universe itself, the tension between Being and Non-Being—yes, indubitably it is Duality alone that reigns over us here in our ancient land.'

'I felt like crying when I read the poem. They must be so proud of him. So proud.'

'Hello, Arun, where's Meenakshi?'

Lata turned around and saw Arun's rather displeased expression. It was his friend Billy Irani. This was the third time someone had spoken to him with the sole intention of finding out where his wife was. He looked around the room for her orange sari, and spied her near the Kakoli crowd.

'There she is, Billy, near Kuku's nest. If you want to meet her, I'll walk over with you and detach her,' he said.

Lata wondered for a second what her friend Malati would have made of all this. She attached herself to Arun as if to a life raft, and floated across to where Kakoli was standing. Somehow or other Mrs Rupa Mehra, as well as an old Marwari gentleman clad in a dhoti, had infiltrated the crowd of bright young things.

The old gentleman, unconscious of the gilded youth surrounding him, was saying, rather fussily, to Hans:

'Ever since the year 1933 I have been drinking the juice of bitter gourds. You know bitter gourd? It is our famous Indian vegetable, called karela. It looks like this'—he gesticulated elongatedly—'and it is green, and ribbed.'

Hans looked mystified. His informant continued:

'Every week my servant takes a seer of bitter gourd, and from the skin only, mark you, he will make juice. Each seer will yield one jam jar of juice.' His eyes squinted in concentration. 'What they do with the rest I do not care.'

He made a dismissive gesture.

'Yes?' said Hans politely. 'That makes me so interested.'

Kakoli had begun to giggle. Mrs Rupa Mehra was looking deeply interested. Arun caught Meenakshi's eye and frowned. Bloody Marwari, he was thinking. Trust them to make a fool of themselves in front of foreigners.

Sweetly oblivious of Arun's disapproval, the gourd-proponent continued: 'Then every morning for my breakfast he will give me one sherry glass or liqueur glass—so much—of this juice. Every day since 1933. And I have no sugar problems. I can eat sweetmeats without anxiety. My dermatology is also very good, and all bowel movements are very satisfactory.'

As if to prove the point he bit into a gulab-jamun which was dripping with syrup.

Mrs Rupa Mehra, fascinated, said: 'Only the skin?' If this was true, diabetes need no longer interpose itself between her palate and her desires.

'Yes,' said the man fastidiously. 'Only the skin, like I have said. The rest is a superfluity. Beauty of bitter gourd is only skin-deep.'

7.12

'Enjoying yourself?' Jock Mackay asked Basil Cox as they wandered out on to the verandah.

'Well, yes, rather,' said Basil Cox, resting his whisky precariously on the white cast-iron railing. He felt light-headed, almost as if he wanted to balance on the railings himself. The fragrance of gardenias wafted across the lawn.

'First time I've seen you at the Chatterjis. Patricia's looking ravishing.'

'Thanks . . . she is, isn't she? I can never predict when she's going to have a good time. Do you know, when I had to come out to India, she was most unwilling. She even, well. . . .'

Basil, moving his thumb gently across his lower lip, looked out into the garden, where a few mellow golden globes lit up the underside of a huge laburnum tree covered with grape-like clusters of yellow flowers. There appeared to be a hut of sorts under the tree.

'But you're enjoying it here, are you?'

'I suppose so. . . . Puzzling sort of place, though. . . . Of course, I've been here less than a year.'

'What do you mean?'

'Well, what's that bird for instance that was singing a moment ago—pu-puuuuuu-pu! pu-puuuuu-pu! higher and higher. It certainly isn't a cuckoo and I rather wish it was. Disconcerting. And I find all these lakhs and crores and annas and pice quite confusing still. I have to recalculate things in my head. I suppose I'll get used to it all with time.' From the expression on Basil Cox's face it didn't look likely. Twelve pence to the shilling and twenty shillings to the pound was infinitely more logical than four pice to the anna and sixteen annas to the rupee.

'Well, it is a cuckoo, as a matter of fact,' said Jock Mackay, 'it's the hawk cuckoo—or brainfever bird . . . didn't you know that? It's hard to believe, but I've got so used to it that I miss it when I'm back home on leave. The song of the birds I don't mind at all, what I can't abide is the dreadful music Indian singers make . . . awful wailing stuff. . . . But do you know the question that disconcerted me most of all when I first came here twenty years ago and saw all these beautiful, elegantly dressed women?' Jock Mackay cheerfully and confidingly jerked his head towards the drawing room. 'How do you fuck in a sari?'

Basil Cox made a sudden movement, and his drink fell over into a flower bed. Jock Mackay looked faintly amused.

'Well,' said Basil Cox, rather annoyed, 'did you find out?'

'Everyone makes his own discoveries sooner or later,' said Jock Mackay in an enigmatic manner. 'But it's a charming country on the whole,' he continued expansively. 'By the end of the Raj they were so busy slitting each other's throats that they left ours unslit. Lucky.' He sipped his drink.

'Well, there doesn't seem to be any resentment—quite the opposite, if anything,' said Basil Cox after a while, looking over into the flower bed. 'But I wonder what people like the Chatterjis really think of us. . . . After all, we're still quite a presence in Calcutta. We still run things here—commercially speaking, of course.'

'Oh, I shouldn't worry if I were you. What people think or don't think is never very interesting,' said Jock Mackay. 'Horses, now, I often wonder what they're thinking. . . .'

'Well, I had dinner with their son-in-law the other day—yesterday, as a matter of fact—Arun Mehra, he works with us—oh, of course, you know Arun—and suddenly his brother tumbles in, drunk as a lord and singing away—and reeking of some fearsome Shimsham fire-water—well, I'd never in a hundred years have guessed that Arun had a brother like that. And dressed in crumpled pyjamas!'

'No, it is puzzling,' agreed Jock Mackay. 'I knew an old ICS chap, Indian, but pukka enough, who, when he retired, renounced everything, became a sadhu and was never heard of again. And he was a married man with a couple of grown-up children.'

'Really?'

'Really. But a charming people, I'd say: face-flattering, back-biting, name-dropping, all-knowing, self-praising, law-mongering, power-worshipping, road-hogging, spittle-hawking. . . . There were a few more items to my litany once, but I've forgotten them.'

'You sound as if you hate the place,' said Basil Cox.

'Quite the contrary,' said Jock Mackay. 'I wouldn't be surprised if I decided to retire here. But should we go back in? I see you've lost your drink.'

7.13

'Don't think of anything serious before you are thirty,' young Tapan was being advised by the round Mr Kohli, who had managed to free himself of his wife for a few minutes. He had his glass in his hand, and looked like a large, worried, almost disconsolate teddy bear in a slow hurry; his huge dome—a phrenological marvel—glistened as he leaned over the bar; he half closed his heavily lidded eyes and half opened his small mouth after he had delivered himself of one of his bon mots.

'Now, Baby Sahib,' said the old servant Bahadur firmly to Tapan, 'Memsahib says you must go to bed at once.'

Tapan began laughing.

'Tell Ma I'll go to bed when I'm thirty,' he said, dismissing Bahadur.

'People are stuck at seventeen, you know,' continued Mr Kohli. 'That's where they imagine themselves ever afterwards—always seventeen, and always happy. Not that they're happy when they're actually seventeen. But you have some years to go still. How old are you?'

'Thirteen—almost.'

'Good—stay there, that's my advice,' suggested Mr Kohli.

'Are you serious?' said Tapan, suddenly looking more than a little unhappy. 'You mean things don't get any better?'

'Oh, don't take anything I say seriously,' said Mr Kohli. He paused for a sip. 'On the other hand,' he added, 'take everything I say more seriously than what other adults say.'

'Go to bed at once, Tapan,' said Mrs Chatterji, coming up to them. 'What's this you've been saying to Bahadur? You won't be allowed to stay up late if you behave like this. Now pour Mr Kohli a drink, and then go to bed at once.'

7.14

'Oh, no, no, no, Dipankar,' said the Grande Dame of Culture, slowly shaking her ancient and benevolent head from side to side in pitying condescension as she held him with her dully glittering eye, 'that's not it at all, not Duality, I could never have said Duality, Dipankar, oh dear me, no—the intrinsic essence of our being here in India is a Oneness, yes, a Oneness of Being, an ecumenical assimilation of all that pours into this great subcontinent of ours.' She gestured around the drawing room tolerantly, maternally. 'It is Unity that governs our souls, here in our ancient land.'

Dipankar nodded furiously, blinked rapidly, and gulped his Scotch down, while Kakoli winked at him. That's what she liked about Dipankar, thought Kakoli: he was the only serious younger Chatterji, and because he was such a gentle, accommodating soul, he made the ideal captive listener for any purveyors of pabulum who happened to stray into the irreverent household. And everyone in the family could go to him when they wanted unflippant advice.

'Dipankar,' said Kakoli, 'Hemangini wants to talk to you, she's pining away without you, and she has to leave in ten minutes.'

'Yes, Kuku, thanks,' said Dipankar unhappily, and blinking a little more than usual as a result. 'Try to keep her here as long as you can . . . we were just having this interesting discussion. . . . Why don't you join us, Kuku?' he added desperately. 'It's all about how Unity is the intrinsic essence of our being. . . .'

'Oh, no, no, no, no, Dipankar,' said the Grande Dame, correcting him a trifle sadly, but still patiently: 'Not Unity, not Unity, but Zero, Nullity itself is the guiding principle of our existence. I could never have used the term intrinsic essence—for what is an essence if it is not intrinsic? India is the land of the Zero, for it was from the horizons of our soil that it rose like a vast sun to spread its light on the world of knowledge.' She surveyed a gulab-jamun for a few seconds. 'It is the Zero, Dipankar, represented by the Mandala, the circle, the circular nature of Time itself, that is the guiding principle of our civilization. All this'—she waved her arm around the drawing room once more, taking in, in one slow plump sweep the piano, the bookcases, the flowers in their huge cut-glass vases, the cigarettes smouldering at the edges of ashtrays, two plates of gulab-jamuns, the glittering guests, and Dipankar himself—'all this is Non-Being. It is the Non-ness of things, Dipankar, that you must accept, for in Nothing lies the secret of Everything.'

7.15

The Chatterji parliament (including Kakoli, who normally found it difficult to wake up before ten) was assembled for breakfast the next day.

All signs of the party had been cleared away. Cuddles had been unleashed upon the world. He had bounded around the garden in delight, and had disturbed Dipankar's meditations in the small hut that he had made for himself in a corner of the garden. He had also dug up a few plants in the vegetable garden that Dipankar took so much interest in. Dipankar took all this calmly. Cuddles had probably buried something there, and after the trauma of last night merely wanted to reassure himself that the world and the objects in it were as they used to be.

Kakoli had left instructions that she was to be woken up at seven. She had to make a phone call to Hans after he came back from his morning ride. How he managed to wake up at five—like Dipankar—and do all these vigorous things on a horse she did not know. But she felt that he must have great strength of will.

Kakoli was deeply attached to the telephone, and monopolized it shamelessly—as she did the car. Often she would burble on for forty-five minutes on end and her father sometimes found it impossible to get through to his house from the High Court or the Calcutta Club. There were fewer than ten thousand telephones in the whole of Calcutta, so a second phone would have been an unimaginable luxury. Ever since Kakoli had had an extension installed in her room, however, the unimaginable had begun to appear to him almost reasonable.

Since it had been a late night, the old servant Bahadur, who usually performed the difficult task of waking the unwilling Kuku and placating her with milk, had been told to sleep late. Amit had therefore taken on the duty of waking his sister.

He knocked gently on her door. There was no response. He opened the door. Light was streaming through the window on to Kakoli's bed. She was sleeping diagonally across the bed with her arm thrown across her eyes. Her pretty, round face was covered with dried Lacto Calamine, which, like papaya pulp, she used to improve her complexion.

Amit said, 'Kuku, wake up. It's seven o'clock.'

Kakoli continued to sleep soundly.

'Wake up, Kuku.'

Kakoli stirred slightly, then said what sounded like 'choo-moo'. It was a sound of complaint.

After about five minutes of trying to get her to wake up, first by gentle words and then by a gentle shake or two of the shoulders, and being rewarded with nothing but 'choo-moo', Amit threw a pillow rather ungently over her head.

Kakoli bestirred herself enough to say: 'Take a lesson from Bahadur. Wake people up nicely.'

Amit said, 'I don't have the practice. He has probably had to stand around your bed ten thousand times murmuring, "Kuku Baby, wake up; wake up, Baby Memsahib," for twenty minutes while you do your "choo-moo".'

'Ungh,' said Kakoli.

'Open your eyes at least,' said Amit. 'Otherwise you'll just roll over and go back to sleep.' After a pause he added, 'Kuku Baby.'

'Ungh,' said Kakoli irritably. She opened both her eyes a fraction, however.

'Do you want your teddy bear? Your telephone? A glass of milk?' said Amit.

'Milk.'

'How many glasses?'

'A glass of milk.'

'All right.'

Amit went off to fetch her a glass of milk.

When he returned he found that she was sitting on the bed, with the telephone receiver in one hand and Cuddles tucked under the other arm. She was treating Cuddles to a stream of Chatterji chatter.

'Oh you beastie,' she was saying: 'oh you beastly beastie—oh you ghastly, beastly beastie.' She stroked his head with the telephone receiver. 'Oh you vastly ghastly mostly beastly beastie.' She paid no attention to Amit.

'Do shut up, Kuku, and take your milk,' said Amit irritably. 'I have other things to do than wait on you, you know.'

This remark struck Kakoli with novel force. She was well practised in the art of being helpless when there were helpful people around.

'Or do you want me to drink it for you as well?' added Amit gratuitously.

'Go bite Amit,' Kakoli instructed Cuddles. Cuddles did not comply.

'Shall I set it down here, Madam?'

'Yes, do.' Kakoli ignored the sarcasm.

'Will that be all, Madam?'

'Yes.'

'Yes what?'

'Yes, thank you.'

'I was going to ask for a good-morning kiss, but that Lacto Calamine looks so disgusting I think I'll defer it.'

Kakoli surveyed Amit severely. 'You are a horrible, insensitive person,' she informed him. 'I don't know why women swoooooon over your poetry.'

'That's because my poetry is so sensitive,' said Amit.

'I pity the girl who marries you. I reeeeeally pity her.'

'And I pity the man who marries you. I reeeeeeally pity him. By the way, was that my future brother-in-law you were going to call? The nutcracker?'

'The nutcracker?'

Amit held out his right hand as if shaking it with an invisible man. Slowly his mouth opened in shock and agony.

'Do go away, Amit, you've spoilt my mood completely,' said Kakoli.

'What there was to spoil,' said Amit.

'When I say anything about the women you're interested in you get very peeved.'

'Like who? Jane Austen?'

'May I make my phone call in peace and privacy?'

'Yes, yes, Kuku Baby,' said Amit, succeeding in being both sarcastic and placatory, 'I'm just going, I'm just going. See you at breakfast.'

7.16

The Chatterji family at breakfast presented a scene of cordial conflict. It was an intelligent family where everyone thought of everyone else as an idiot. Some people thought the Chatterjis obnoxious because they appeared to enjoy each other's company even more than the company of others. But if they had dropped by at the Chatterjis' for breakfast and seen them bickering, they would probably have disliked them less.

Mr Justice Chatterji sat at the head of the table. Though small in size, short-sighted, and fairly absent-minded, he was a man of some dignity. He inspired respect in court and a sort of obedience even in his eccentric family. He didn't like to talk more than was necessary.

'Anyone who likes mixed fruit jam is a lunatic,' said Amit.

'Are you calling me a lunatic?' asked Kakoli.

'No, of course not, Kuku, I'm working from general principles. Please pass me the butter.'

'You can reach for it yourself,' said Kuku.

'Now, now, Kuku,' murmured Mrs Chatterji.

'I can't,' protested Amit. 'My hand's been crushed.'

Tapan laughed. Kakoli gave him a black look, then began to look glum in preparation for a request.

'I need the car today, Baba,' said Kuku after a few seconds. 'I have to go out. I need it for the whole day.'

'But Baba,' said Tapan, 'I'm spending the day with Pankaj.'

'I really must go to Hamilton's this morning to get the silver inkstand back,' said Mrs Chatterji.

Mr Justice Chatterji raised his eyebrows. 'Amit?' he asked.

'No bid,' said Amit.

Dipankar, who also declined transport, wondered aloud why Kuku was looking so wistful. Kuku frowned.

Amit and Tapan promptly began an antiphonal chant.

'We look before and after, and pine for what is—'

'NOT!'

'Our sincerest laughter with some pain is—'

'FROT!'

'Our sweetest songs are those that tell of saddest—'

'THOT!' cried Tapan jubilantly, for he hero-worshipped Amit.

'Don't worry, darling,' said Mrs Chatterji comfortingly; 'everything will come out all right in the end.'

'You don't have any idea what I was thinking of,' countered Kakoli.

'You mean who,' said Tapan.

'You be quiet, you amoeba,' said Kakoli.

'He seemed a nice enough chap,' ventured Dipankar.

'Oh no, he's just a glamdip,' countered Amit.

'Glamdip? Glamdip? Have I missed something?' asked their father.

Mrs Chatterji looked equally mystified. 'Yes, what is a glamdip, darling?' she asked Amit.

'A glamorous diplomat,' replied Amit. 'Very vacant, very charming. The kind of person whom Meenakshi used to sigh after. And talking of which, one of them is coming around to visit me this morning. He wants to ask me about culture and literature.'

'Really, Amit?' asked Mrs Chatterji eagerly. 'Who?'

'Some South American ambassador—from Peru or Chile or somewhere,' said Amit, 'with an interest in the arts. I got a phone call from Delhi a week or two ago, and we fixed it up. Or was it Bolivia? He wanted to meet an author on his visit to Calcutta. I doubt he's read anything by me.'

Mrs Chatterji looked flustered. 'But then I must make sure that everything is in order—' she said. 'And you told Biswas Babu you'd see him this morning.'

'So I did, so I did,' agreed Amit. 'And so I will.'

'He is not just a glamdip,' said Kakoli suddenly. 'You've hardly met him.'

'No, he is a good boy for our Kuku,' said Tapan. 'He is so shinsheer.'

This was one of Biswas Babu's adjectives of high praise. Kuku felt that Tapan should have his ears boxed.

'I like Hans,' said Dipankar. 'He was very polite to the man who told him to drink the juice of bitter gourds. He does have a good heart.'

'O my darling, don't be heartless.
Hold my hand. Let us be partless,'

murmured Amit.

'But don't hold it too hard,' laughed Tapan.

'Stop it!' cried Kuku. 'You are all being utterly horrible.'

'He is good wedding-bell material for our Kuku,' continued Tapan, tempting retribution.

'Wedding bell? Or bedding well?' asked Amit. Tapan grinned delightedly.

'Now, that's enough, Amit,' said Mr Justice Chatterji before his wife could intervene. 'No bloodshed at breakfast. Let's talk about something else.'

'Yes,' agreed Kuku. 'Like the way Amit was mooning over Lata last night.'

'Over Lata?' said Amit, genuinely astonished.

'Over Lata?' repeated Kuku, imitating him.

'Really, Kuku, love has destroyed your brain,' said Amit. 'I didn't notice I was spending any time with her at all.'

'No, I'm sure you didn't.'

'She's just a nice girl, that's all,' said Amit. 'If Meenakshi hadn't been so busy gossiping and Arun making contacts I wouldn't have assumed any responsibility for her at all.'

'So we needn't invite her over unnecessarily while she's in Calcutta,' murmured Kuku.

Mrs Chatterji said nothing, but had begun to look anxious.

'I'll invite whoever I like over,' said Amit. 'You, Kuku, invited fifty-odd people to the party last night.'

'Fifty odd people,' Tapan couldn't resist saying.

Kuku turned on him severely.

'Little boys shouldn't interrupt adult conversations,' she said.

Tapan, from the safety of the other side of the table, made a face at her. Once Kuku had actually got so incensed she had chased him around the table, but usually she was sluggish till noon.

'Yes,' Amit frowned. 'Some of them were very odd, Kuku. Who is that fellow Krishnan? Dark chap, south Indian, I imagine. He was glaring at you and your Second Secretary very resentfully.'

'Oh, he's just a friend,' said Kuku, spreading her butter with more than usual concentration. 'I suppose he's annoyed with me.'

Amit could not resist delivering a Kakoli-couplet:

> 'What is Krishnan in the end?
> Just a mushroom, just a friend.'

Tapan continued:

> 'Always eating dosa-iddly,
> Drinking beer and going piddly!'

'Tapan!' gasped his mother.

Amit, Meenakshi and Kuku, it appeared, had completely corrupted her baby with their stupid rhyming.

Mr Justice Chatterji put down his toast. 'That's enough from you, Tapan,' he said.

'But Baba, I was only joking,' protested Tapan, thinking it unfair that he should have been singled out. Just because I'm the youngest, he thought. And it was a pretty good couplet too.

'A joke's a joke, but enough's enough,' said his father. 'And you too, Amit. You'd have a better claim to criticizing others if you did something useful yourself.'

'Yes, that's right,' added Kuku happily, seeing the tables turning. 'Do some serious work, Dada. Act like a useful member of society before you criticize others.'

'What's wrong with writing poems and novels?' asked Amit. 'Or has passion made you illiterate as well?'

'It's all right as an amusement, Amit,' said Mr Justice Chatterji. 'But it's not a living. And what's wrong with the law?'

'Well, it's like going back to school,' said Amit.

'I don't quite see how you come to that conclusion,' said his father dryly.

'Well,' said Amit, 'you have to be properly dressed—that's like school uniform. And instead of saying "Sir" you say "My Lord"—which is just as bad—until you're raised to the bench and people say it to you instead. And you get holidays, and you get good chits and bad chits just like Tapan does: I mean judgements in your favour and against you.'

'Well,' said Justice Chatterji, not entirely pleased by the analogy, 'it was good enough for your grandfather and for me.'

'But Amit has a special gift,' broke in Mrs Chatterji. 'Aren't you proud of him?'

'He can practise his special gifts in his spare time,' said her husband.

'Is that what they said to Rabindranath Tagore?' asked Amit.

'I'm sure you'll admit there's a difference between you and Tagore,' said his father, looking at his eldest son in surprise.

'I'll admit there's a difference, Baba,' said Amit. 'But what's the relevance of the difference to the point I'm making?'

But at the mention of Tagore, Mrs Chatterji had entered a mode of righteous reverence.

'Amit, Amit,' she cried, 'how can you think of Gurudeb like that?'

'Mago, I didn't say—' began Amit.

Mrs Chatterji broke in. 'Amit, Robi Babu is like a saint. We in Bengal owe everything to him. When I was in Shantiniketan, I remember he once said to me—'

But now Kakoli joined forces with Amit.

'Please, Mago, really—we've heard enough about Shantiniketan and how idyllic it is. I know that if I had to live there I'd commit suicide every day.'

'His voice is like a cry in the wilderness,' continued her mother, hardly hearing her.

'I'd hardly say so, Ma,' said Amit. 'We idolize him more than the English do Shakespeare.'

'And with good reason,' said Mrs Chatterji. 'His songs come to our lips—his poems come to our hearts—'

'Actually,' said Kakoli, '*Abol Tabol* is the only good book in the whole of Bengali literature.

The Griffonling from birth
Is indisposed to mirth.
To laugh or grin he counts a sin
And shudders, "Not on earth."

Oh, yes, and I like *The Sketches of Hutom the Owl*. And when I take up literature, I shall write my own: *The Sketches of Cuddles the Dog*.'

'Kuku, you are a really shameless girl,' cried Mrs Chatterji, incensed. 'Please stop her from saying these things.'

'It's just an opinion, dear,' said Mr Justice Chatterji, 'I can't stop her from holding opinions.'

'But about Gurudeb, whose songs she sings—about Robi Babu—'

Kakoli, who had been force-fed, almost from birth, with Rabindrasangeet, now warbled out to the tune of a truncated 'Shonkochero bihvalata nijere apoman':

'Robi Babu, R. Tagore, O, he's such a bore!
Robi Babu, R. Tagore, O, he's such a bore!
O, he's su-uch a bore.
Such a, such a bore.
Such a, such a bore,
O, he's such a, O, he's such a, O, he's such a bore.
Robi Babu, R. Tagore, O, he's such a bore!'

'Stop! Stop it at once! Kakoli, do you hear me?' cried Mrs Chatterji, appalled. 'Stop it! How dare you! You stupid, shameless, shallow girl.'

'Really, Ma,' continued Kakoli, 'reading him is like trying to swim breaststroke through treacle. You should hear Ila Chattopadhyay on your

Robi Babu. Flowers and moonlight and nuptial beds. . . .'

'Ma,' said Dipankar, 'why do you let them get to you? You should take the best in the words and mould them to your own spirit. That way, you can attain stillness.'

Mrs Chatterji was unsoothed. Stillness was very far from her.

'May I get up? I've finished my breakfast,' said Tapan.

'Of course, Tapan,' said his father, 'I'll see about the car.'

'Ila Chattopadhyay is a very ignorant girl, I've always thought so,' burst out Mrs Chatterji. 'As for her books—I think that the more people write, the less they think. And she was dressed in a completely crushed sari last night.'

'She's hardly a girl any more, dear,' said her husband. 'She's quite an elderly woman—must be at least fifty-five.'

Mrs Chatterji glanced with annoyance at her husband. Fifty-five was hardly elderly.

'And one should heed her opinions,' added Amit. 'She's quite hard-headed. She was advising Dipankar yesterday that there was no future in economics. She appeared to know.'

'She always appears to know,' said Mrs Chatterji. 'Anyway, she's from your father's side of the family,' she added irrelevantly. 'And if she doesn't appreciate Gurudeb she must have a heart of stone.'

'You can't blame her,' said Amit. 'After a life so full of tragedy anyone would become hard.'

'What tragedy?' asked Mrs Chatterji.

'Well, when she was four,' said Amit, 'her mother slapped her—it was quite traumatic—and then things went on in that vein. When she was twelve she came second in an exam. . . . It hardens you.'

'Where did you get such mad children?' Mrs Chatterji asked her husband.

'I don't know,' he replied.

'If you had spent more time with them instead of going to the club every day, they wouldn't have turned out this way,' said Mrs Chatterji in a rare rebuke; but she was overwrought.

The phone rang.

'Ten to one it's for Kuku,' said Amit.

'It's not.'

'I suppose you can tell from the kind of ring, hunh, Kuku?'

'It's for Kuku,' cried Tapan from the door.

'Oh. Who's it from?' asked Kuku, and poked her tongue out at Amit.

'Krishnan.'

'Tell him I can't come to the phone. I'll call back later,' said Kuku.

'Shall I tell him you're having a bath? Or sleeping? Or out in the car? Or all three?' Tapan grinned.

'Please, Tapan,' said Kuku, 'be a sweet boy and make some excuse. Yes, say I've gone out.'

Mrs Chatterji was shocked into exclaiming: 'But, Kuku, that's a barefaced lie.'

'I know, Ma,' said Kuku, 'but he's so tedious, what can I do?'

'Yes, what can one do when one has a hundred best friends?' muttered Amit, looking mournful.

'Just because nobody loves you—' cried Kuku, stung to fierceness.

'Lots of people love me,' said Amit, 'don't you, Dipankar?'

'Yes, Dada,' said Dipankar, who thought it best to be simply factual.

'And all my fans love me,' added Amit.

'That's because they don't know you,' said Kakoli.

'I won't contest that point,' said Amit; 'and, talking of unseen fans, I'd better get ready for His Excellency. Excuse me.'

Amit got up to go, and so did Dipankar; and Mr Justice Chatterji settled the use of the car between the two main claimants, while keeping Tapan's interests in mind as well.

7.17

About fifteen minutes after the Ambassador was due to arrive at the house for their one-hour talk, Amit was informed by telephone that he would be 'a little late'. That would be fine, said Amit.

About half an hour after he was due to arrive, Amit was told that he might be a little later still. This annoyed him somewhat, as he could have done some writing in the meantime. 'Has the Ambassador arrived in Calcutta?' he asked the man on the phone. 'Oh, yes,' said the voice. 'He arrived yesterday afternoon. He is just running a little late. But he left for your house ten minutes ago. He should be there in the next five minutes.'

Since Biswas Babu was due to arrive soon and Amit did not want to keep the family's old clerk waiting, he was irritated. But he swallowed his irritation, and muttered something polite.

Fifteen minutes later, Señor Bernardo Lopez arrived at the door in a great black car. He came with a lively young woman whose first name was

Anna-Maria. He was extremely apologetic and full of cultural goodwill; she on the other hand was brisk and energetic and extracted a pocketbook from her handbag the moment they sat down.

During the flow of his ponderous and gentle words, all slowly weighed, deliberated and qualified before they could be expressed, the Ambassador looked everywhere but at Amit: he looked at his teacup, at his own flexed or drumming fingers, at Anna-Maria (to whom he nodded reassuringly), and at a globe in a corner of the room. From time to time he would smile. He pronounced 'very' with a 'b'.

Caressing his pointed bald head nervously and gravely, and conscious of the fact that he was an inexcusable forty-five minutes late, he attempted to come straight to the point:

'Well, Mr Chatterji, Mr Amit Chatterji, if I may make so bold, I am often called upon in my official duties, as you know, being Ambassador and so on, which I have been for about a year now—unfortunately, with us it is not permanent, or indeed definite; there is an element of, I might even say, or it would perhaps not be unfair to say (yes, that is better put, if I might be allowed to praise myself for a locution in another language) that there is an element of arbitrariness in it, in our stay in a particular place, I mean; unlike you writers who . . . but anyway, what I meant was that I would like to put to you one question directly, which is to say, forgive me, but as you know I have arrived here forty-five minutes in tardiness and have taken up forty-five minutes of your good time (of your good self, as I notice some say here), partly because I set out very tardily (I came here directly from a friend's home here in this remarkable city, to which I hope you will come sometime when you are more at leisure—or to Delhi needlessly—by which I mean rather, needless to say, to our own home—though you must of course tell me if I am imposing myself on you) but I asked my secretary to inform you of that (I hope he did, yes?), but partly because our driver led us to Hazra Road, a, I understand, very natural mistake, because the streets are almost parallel and close to each other, where we met a gentleman who was kind enough to redirect us to this beautiful house—I speak as an appreciator of not just the architecture but the way you have preserved its atmosphere, its perhaps ingenuity, no, ingenuousness, even virginity—but as I said I am (to come to the point) late, and indeed forty-five, well, what I must now ask you as I have asked others in the course of my official duties, although this is by no means an official duty but one entirely of pleasure (though I indeed do have something to ask of you, or rather, ask you about), I have to ask you as I ask other officials who have schedules to keep, not that you are official, but, well, a busy man: do you have any appointment after this hour that you have allotted me, or can we perhaps exceed . . . yes? Do I make myself clear?'

Amit, terrified that he might have to face more of this, said hastily: 'Alas, Your Excellency will forgive me, but I have a pressing engagement in fifteen minutes, no, forgive me, five minutes now, with an old colleague of my father's.'

'Tomorrow then?' asked Anna-Maria.

'No, alas, I am going to Palashnagar tomorrow,' said Amit, naming the fictitious town in which his novel was set. He reflected that this was no more than the truth.

'A pity, a pity,' said Bernardo Lopez. 'But we still have five minutes, so let me ask simply this, a long puzzlement to me: What is all this about "being" and birds and boats and the river of life—that we find in Indian poetry, the great Tagore unexcluded? But let me say in qualification that by "we" I mean merely we of the West, if the South may be subsumed in the West, and by "find" I mean that which is as if to say that Columbus found America which we know needed no finding, for there were those there for whom "finding" would be more insulting than superfluous, and of course by Indian poetry, I mean such poetry as has been made accessible to us, which is to say, such as has been traduced by translation. In that light, can you enlighten me? Us?'

'I will try,' said Amit.

'You see?' said Bernardo Lopez with mild triumph to Anna-Maria, who had put down her notebook. 'The unanswerables are not unanswerable in the lands of the East. Felix qui potuit rerum cognoscere causas, and when it is true of a whole nation, it makes one marvel the more. Truly when I came here one year ago I had a sense—'

But Bahadur now entered, and informed Amit that Biswas Babu was waiting for him in his father's study.

'Forgive me, Your Excellency,' said Amit, getting up, 'it appears as though my father's colleague has arrived. But I shall give earnest thought to what you have said. And I am deeply honoured and grateful.'

'And I, young man, though young here is merely to say that the earth has gone around the sun less often since your inception, er, conception, than mine (and is that to say anything at all?), I too will bear in mind the result of this confabulation, and consider it "in vacant or in pensive mood", as the Poet of the Lake has chosen to express it. Its intensity, the urgings I have felt during this brief interview, which have led me upwards from nescience to science—yet is that in truth an upward movement? Will time even tell us that? Does time tell us anything at all?—such I will cherish.'

'Yes, we are indebted,' said Anna-Maria, picking up her notebook.

As the great black car spirited them away, no longer running behind time, Amit stood on the porch step waving slowly.

Though the fluffy white cat Pillow, led on a leash by his grandfather's servant, crossed his field of vision, Amit did not follow it with his eyes, as he normally did.

He had a headache, and was in no mood to talk to anyone. But Biswas Babu had come specially to see him, probably to make him see sense and take up the law again, and Amit felt that his father's old clerk, whom everyone treated with great affection and respect, should not be required to sit and cool his heels longer than necessary—or rather, shake his knees, which was a habit with him.

7.18

What made matters slightly uncomfortable was that though Amit's Bengali was fine and Biswas Babu's spoken English was not, he had insisted—ever since Amit had returned from England 'laden with laurels' as he put it—on speaking to him almost exclusively in English. For the others, this privilege was only occasional; Amit had always been Biswas Babu's favourite, and he deserved a special effort.

Though it was summer, Biswas Babu was dressed in a coat and dhoti. He had an umbrella with him and a black bag. Bahadur had given him a cup of tea, which he was stirring thoughtfully while looking around at the room in which he had worked for so many years—both for Amit's father and for his grandfather. When Amit entered, he stood up.

After respectful greetings to Biswas Babu, Amit sat down at his father's large mahogany desk. Biswas Babu was sitting on the other side of it. After the usual questions about how everyone was doing and whether either could perform any service for the other, the conversation petered out.

Biswas Babu then helped himself to a small amount of snuff. He placed a bit in each nostril and sniffed. There was clearly something weighing on his mind but he was reluctant to bring it up.

'Now, Biswas Babu, I have an idea of what has brought you here,' said Amit.

'You have?' said Biswas Babu, startled, and looking rather guilty.

'But I have to tell you that I don't think that even your advocacy is going to work.'

'No?' said Biswas Babu, leaning forward. His knees started vibrating rapidly in and out.

'You see, Biswas Babu, I know you feel I have let the family down.'

'Yes?' said Biswas Babu.

'You see, my grandfather went in for it, and my father, but I haven't. And you probably think it is very peculiar. I know you are disappointed in me.'

'It is not peculiar, it is just late. But you are probably making hail while the sun shines, and sowing oats. That is why I have come.'

'Sowing oats?' Amit was puzzled.

'But Meenakshi has rolled the ball, now you must follow it.'

It suddenly struck Amit that Biswas Babu was talking not about the law but about marriage. He began to laugh.

'So it is about this, Biswas Babu, that you have come to talk to me?' he said. 'And you are speaking to me about the matter, not to my father.'

'I also spoke to your father. But that was one year ago, and where is the progress?'

Amit, despite his headache, was smiling.

Biswas Babu was not offended. He told Amit:

'Man without life companion is either god or beast. Now you can decide where to place yourself. Unless you are above such thoughts. . . .'

Amit confessed that he wasn't.

Very few were, said Biswas Babu. Perhaps only people like Dipankar, with his spiritual leanings, were able to renounce such yearnings. That made it all the more imperative that Amit should continue the family line.

'Don't believe it, Biswas Babu,' said Amit. 'It is all Scotch and sannyaas with Dipankar.'

But Biswas Babu was not to be distracted from his purpose. 'I was thinking about you three days ago,' he said. 'You are so old—twenty-nine or more—and are still issueless. How can you give joy to your parents? You owe to them. Even Mrs Biswas agrees. They are so proud of your achievement.'

'But Meenakshi has given them Aparna.'

Obviously a non-Chatterji like Aparna, and a girl at that, did not count for much in Biswas Babu's eyes. He shook his head and pursed his lips in disagreement.

'In my heart-deep opinion—' he began, and stopped, so that Amit could encourage him to continue.

'What do you advise me to do, Biswas Babu?' asked Amit obligingly. 'When my parents were keen that I should meet that girl Shormishtha, you made your objections known to my father, and he passed them on to me.'

'Sorry to say, she had tinted reputation,' said Biswas Babu, frowning at the corner of the desk. This conversation was proving more difficult than he had imagined it would. 'I did not want trouble for you. Inquiries were necessary.'

'And so you made them.'

'Yes, Amit Babu. Now maybe about law you know best. But I know about early life and youth. It is hard to restrain, and then there is danger.'

'I am not sure I understand.'

After a pause Biswas Babu went on. He seemed a little embarrassed, but the consciousness of his duty as an adviser to the family kept him going.

'Of course it is dangerous business but any lady who cohabits with more than one man increases risks. It is but natural,' he added.

Amit did not know what to say, as he had not got Biswas Babu's drift.

'Indeed, any lady who has the opportunity to go to second man will know no limits,' Biswas Babu remarked gravely, even sadly, as if admonishing Amit in a muted way.

'In fact,' he ruminated, 'though not admitted in our Hindu society, lady is more excited than man as a rule, I will have to say. That is why there should not be too much difference. So that lady can cool down with man.'

Amit looked startled.

'I mean,' continued Biswas Babu, 'difference in age of course. That way they are commenstruate. Otherwise of course an older man is cool in later years when his wife is in the prime of lusty life and there is scope for mischief.'

'Mischief,' echoed Amit. Biswas Babu had never talked in this vein to him before.

'Of course,' thought Biswas Babu aloud, glancing in a melancholy way at the rows of law-books around him, 'that is not true in all cases. But you must not leave it till you are more than thirty. Do you have headache?' he asked, concerned, for Amit looked as if he was in pain.

'A slight headache,' said Amit. 'Nothing serious.'

'An arranged marriage with a sober girl, that is the solution. And I will also think about a helpmeet for Dipankar.'

They were both quiet for a minute. Amit broke the silence.

'Nowadays people say that you should choose your own life partner, Biswas Babu. Certainly, poets like myself say that.'

'What people think, what people say, and what people do are two different things,' said Biswas Babu. 'Now I and Mrs Biswas are happily married for thirty-four years. Where is the harm in an arrangement like that? Nobody asked me. One day my father said it is fixed.'

'But if I find someone myself—'

Biswas Babu was willing to compromise. 'Good. But then there should be inquiries also. She should be a sober girl from—'

'—from a good family?' prompted Amit.

'From a good family.'

'Well educated?'

'Well educated. Saraswati gives better blessings in long run than Lakshmi.'

'Well, now I have heard the whole case, I will reserve judgement.'

'Do not reserve it too long, Amit Babu,' said Biswas Babu with an anxious, almost paternal, smile. 'Sooner or later you will have to cut Gordon's knot.'

'And tie it?'

'Tie it?'

'Tie the knot, I mean,' said Amit.

'Surely you must then also tie the knot,' said Biswas Babu.

7.19

Later that evening, in the same room, Mr Justice Chatterji, who was wearing a dhoti-kurta rather than his black tie of the previous evening, said to his two elder sons:

'Well, Amit—Dipankar—I've called you here because I have something to say to both of you. I've decided to speak to you alone, because your mother gets emotional about things, and that doesn't really help. It's about financial matters, our family investments and property and so on. I've continued to handle these affairs so far, for more than thirty years in fact, but it puts a heavy burden on me in addition to all my other work, and the time has come for one or the other of you to take over the running of that side of things. . . . Now wait, wait'—Mr Justice Chatterji held up a hand—'let me finish, then both of you will have the chance to speak. The one thing I will not change is my decision to hand things over. My burden of work—and this is true of all my brother judges—has increased very considerably over the last year, and, well, I am not getting any younger. At first I was simply going to tell you, Amit, to manage things. You are the eldest and it is, strictly speaking, your duty. But your mother and I have discussed the whole issue at length, and we have taken your literary interests into account, and we now agree that it does not have to be you. You have studied law—whether or not you are practising it—and Dipankar, you have a degree in economics. There are no better qualifications for managing the family properties—now, wait a second, Dipankar, I have not finished—and both of you are intelligent. So what we have decided is this. If you, Dipankar, put your degree in economics to some use instead of concentrating on the—well, the spiritual side of things, well and good. If not, I am afraid, Amit, that the job will fall to you.'

'But, Baba—' protested Dipankar, blinking in distress, 'economics is the worst possible qualification for running anything. It's the most useless, impractical subject in the world.'

'Dipankar,' said his father, not very pleased, 'you have studied it for several years now, and you must have learned something—certainly more than I did as a student—about how economic affairs are handled. Even without your training I have—in earlier days with Biswas Babu's help, and now largely without it—somehow managed to deal with our affairs. Even if, as you claim, a degree in economics doesn't help, I do not believe it can actually be a hindrance. And it is new to my ears to hear you claim that impractical things are useless.'

Dipankar said nothing. Nor did Amit.

'Well, Amit?' asked Mr Justice Chatterji.

'What should I say, Baba?' said Amit. 'I don't want you to have to keep on doing this work. I suppose I hadn't realized quite how time-consuming it must be. But, well, my literary interests aren't just interests, they are my vocation—my obsession, almost. If it was a question of my own share of the property, I would just sell it all, put the money in a bank, and live off the interest—or, if that wasn't enough, I'd let it run down while I kept working at my novels and my poems. But, well, that isn't the case. We can't jeopardize everyone's future—Tapan's, Kuku's, Ma's, to some extent

Meenakshi's as well. I suppose I'm glad that there's at least the possibility that I might not have to do it—that is, if Dipankar—'

'Why don't we both do a bit, Dada?' asked Dipankar, turning towards Amit.

Their father shook his head. 'That would only cause confusion and difficulties within the family. One or the other.'

Both of them looked subdued. Mr Justice Chatterji turned to Dipankar and continued: 'Now I know that you have your heart set on going to the Pul Mela, and, for all I know, after you have submerged yourself in the Ganga a few times, it might help you decide things one way or another. At any rate, I am willing to wait for a few more months, say, till the end of this year, for you to mull over matters and make up your mind. My view of it is that you should get a job in a firm—in a bank, preferably; then all of this would probably fall comfortably into the kind of work you'll be doing anyway. But, as Amit will tell you, my views of things are not always sound—and, whether sound or not, are not always acceptable. But, well, if you don't agree, then, Amit, it will have to be you. Your novel will take at least another year or two to complete, and I cannot wait that long. You will have to work on your literary activities on the side.'

Neither brother looked at the other.

'Do you think I am being unjust?' asked Mr Justice Chatterji in Bengali, with a smile.

'No, of course not, Baba,' said Amit, trying to smile, but only succeeding in looking deeply troubled.

7.20

Arun Mehra arrived at his office in Dalhousie Square not long after 9.30. The sky was black with clouds and the rain was coming down in sheets. The rain swept across the vast facade of the Writers' Building, and added its direct contribution to the huge tank in the middle of the square.

'Bloody monsoon.'

He got out of the car, leaving his briefcase inside and protecting himself with the *Statesman*. His peon, who had been standing in the porch of the building, started when he saw his master's little blue car. It had been raining so hard that he had not seen it until it had almost stopped. Agitated, he opened the umbrella and rushed out to protect the sahib. He was a second or two late.

'Bloody idiot.'

The peon, though several inches shorter than Arun Mehra, contrived to hold the umbrella over the sacred head as Arun sauntered into the building. He got into the lift, and nodded in a preoccupied manner at the lift-boy.

The peon rushed back to the car to get his master's briefcase, and climbed the stairs to the second floor of the large building.

The head office of the managing agency, Bentsen & Pryce, more popularly known as Bentsen Pryce, occupied the entire second floor.

From these surroundings, officials of the company controlled their share of the trade and commerce of India. Though Calcutta was not what it had been before 1912—the capital of the Government of India—it was, nearly four decades later and nearly four years after Independence, indisputably the commercial capital still. More than half the exports of the country flowed down the silty Hooghly to the Bay of Bengal. The Calcutta-based managing agencies such as Bentsen Pryce managed the bulk of the foreign trade of India; they controlled, besides, a large share of the production of the goods that were processed or manufactured in the hinterland of Calcutta, and the services, such as insurance, that went into ensuring their smooth movement down the channels of commerce.

The managing agencies typically owned controlling interests in the actual manufacturing companies that operated the factories, and supervised them all from the Calcutta head office. Almost without exception these agencies were still owned by the British, and almost without exception the executive officers of the managing agencies near Dalhousie Square—the commercial heart of Calcutta—were white. Final control lay with the directors in the London office and the shareholders in England—but they were usually content to leave things to the Calcutta head office so long as the profits kept flowing in.

The web was wide and the work both interesting and substantial. Bentsen Pryce itself was involved in the following areas, as one of its advertisements stated:

> Abrasives, Air Conditioning, Belting, Brushes, Building, Cement, Chemicals and Pigments, Coal, Coal Mining Machinery, Copper & Brass, Cutch & Katha, Disinfectants, Drugs & Medicines, Drums and Containers, Engineering, Handling Materials, Industrial

> Heating, Insurance, Jute Mills, Lead Pipes, Linen Thread, Loose Leaf Equipment, Oils inc. Linseed Oil Products, Paints, Paper, Rope, Ropeway Construction, Ropeways, Shipping, Spraying Equipment, Tea, Timber, Vertical Turbine Pumps, Wire Rope.

The young men who came out from England in their twenties, most of them from Oxford or Cambridge, fell easily into the pattern of command that was a tradition at Bentsen Pryce, Andrew Yule, Bird & Company, or any of a number of similar firms that considered themselves (and were considered by others to be) the pinnacle of the Calcutta—and therefore Indian—business establishment. They were covenanted assistants, bound by covenant or rolling contract to the company. At Bentsen Pryce, until a few years ago, there had been no place for Indians in the company's European Covenanted Service. Indians were slotted into the Indian Covenanted Service, where the levels of both responsibility and remuneration were far lower.

Around the time of Independence, under pressure from the government and as a concession to the changing times, a few Indians had been grudgingly allowed to enter the cool sanctum of the inner offices of Bentsen Pryce. As a result, by 1951 five of the eighty executives in the firm (though so far none of the department heads, let alone directors) were what could be called brown-whites.

All of them were extraordinarily conscious of their exceptional position, and none more so than Arun Mehra. If ever there was a man enraptured by England and the English it was he. And here he was, hobnobbing with them on terms of tolerable familiarity.

The British knew how to run things, reflected Arun Mehra. They worked hard and they played hard. They believed in command, and so did he. They assumed that if you couldn't command at twenty-five, you didn't have it in you. Their fresh-faced young men came out to India even earlier; it was hard to restrain them from commanding at twenty-one. What was wrong with this country was a lack of initiative. All that Indians wanted was a safe job.

Bloody pen-pushers, the whole lot of them, Arun said to himself as he surveyed the sweltering clerical section on his way to the air-conditioned executive offices beyond.

He was in a bad mood not only because of the foul weather but because he had solved only about a third of the *Statesman* crossword puzzle, and James Pettigrew, a friend of his from another firm, with whom he exchanged clues and solutions by phone most mornings, would probably have solved most of them by now. Arun Mehra enjoyed explaining things, and did not like having things explained to him. He enjoyed giving the impression to others that he knew whatever was worth knowing, and he had virtually succeeded in giving himself the same impression.

7.21

The morning mail was sorted out by Arun's department head Basil Cox with the help of a couple of his principal lieutenants. This morning about ten letters had been marked out to Arun. One of them was from the Persian Fine Teas Company, and he looked it over with particular interest.

'Would you take down a letter, Miss Christie?' he said to his secretary, an exceptionally discreet and cheerful young Anglo-Indian woman, who had grown accustomed to his moods. Miss Christie had at first been resentful of the fact that she had been allocated to an Indian rather than a British executive, but Arun had charmed and patronized her into accepting his authority.

'Yes, Mr Mehra, I'm ready.'

'The usual heading. Dear Mr Poorzahedy, We have received your description of the contents of the shipment of tea—take down the particulars from the letter, Miss Christie—to Teheran—sorry, make that Khurramshahr and Teheran—that you wish us to insure from auction in Calcutta to arrival by customs bond to consignee in Teheran. Our rates, as before, are five annas per hundred rupees for the standard policy, including SR&CC as well as TPND. The shipment is valued at six lakhs, thirty-nine thousand, nine hundred and seventy rupees, and the premium payable will be—would you work that out, Miss Christie?—thank you—yours sincerely, and so on. . . . Wasn't there a claim from them about a month ago?'

'I think so, Mr Mehra.'

'Hmm.' Arun pointed his hands together under his chin, then said: 'I think I'll have a word with the burra babu.'

Rather than call the head clerk of the department into his office, he decided to pay him a visit. The burra babu had served in the insurance department of Bentsen Pryce for twenty-five years and there was nothing about the nuts and bolts of the department that he did not know. He was something like a regimental sergeant major, and everything at the lower levels passed through his hands. The European executives never dealt with anyone but him.

When Arun wandered over to his desk, the burra babu was looking over a sheaf of cheques and duplicates of letters, and telling his underlings what to do. 'Tridib, you handle this one,' he was saying; 'Sarat, you make out this invoice.' It was a muggy day, and the ceiling fans were rustling the high piles of paper on the clerks' desks.

Seeing Arun, the burra babu stood up. 'Sir,' he said.

'Do sit down,' said Arun casually. 'Tell me, what has been happening lately with Persian Fine Teas? On the claims side, I mean.'

'Binoy, tell the claims clerk to come here with the claims ledger.'

After Arun, who was dressed in his suit, as was appropriate to (and unavoidable for) one of his position, had spent a sweaty but enlightening twenty minutes with the clerks and ledgers, he returned to the chilled sanctum of his office and told Miss Christie to hold off typing the letter he had dictated.

'Anyway, it's Friday,' he said. 'It can wait, if necessary, till Monday. I won't be taking calls for the next fifteen minutes or so. Oh yes, and I won't be in this afternoon either. I have a lunch appointment at the Calcutta Club and then I have to visit that damned jute factory at Puttigurh with Mr Cox and Mr Swindon.'

Mr Swindon was from the jute department, and they were going to visit a factory that another company wished to insure against fire. Arun could not see the sense of visiting a particular jute factory, when the insurance for all such factories was clearly based on a standard tariff that depended upon very little other than the process of manufacture used. But Swindon had apparently told Basil Cox that it was important to look over the plant, and Basil had asked Arun to accompany him.

'All a waste of time if you ask me,' said Arun. Friday afternoon by tradition at Bentsen Pryce usually meant a long, leisurely meal at the club followed by a round of golf and possibly a token appearance at the office around closing time. The week's work was effectively over by Thursday afternoon. But, upon reflection, Arun thought it possible that by asking him to help with a matter of Fire Insurance when his normal duties fell under Marine Insurance, Basil Cox was attempting to groom him for wider responsibilities. In fact, now that he considered it, a number of matters of General Insurance had also been marked out to him lately. All this could only mean that the powers above approved of him and his work.

Cheered by this thought, he knocked at Basil Cox's door.

'Come in. Yes, Arun?' Basil Cox gestured to a chair, and, taking his hand off the mouthpiece of the phone, continued: 'Well, that's excellent. Lunch then, and—yes, we'll both look forward to seeing you ride. Bye.'

He turned to Arun and said: 'I do apologize, dear boy, for nibbling away at your Friday afternoon. But I wonder if I can make up for it by inviting you and Meenakshi to the races at Tolly tomorrow as our guests.'

'We'd be delighted,' said Arun.

'I was talking to Jock Mackay. It appears he's riding in one of the races. It might be rather fun to see him. Of course, if the weather keeps up, they'll be swimming their horses round the track.'

Arun permitted himself a chuckle.

'I didn't know he'd be riding tomorrow. Did you?' said Basil Cox.

'No, I can't say I did. But he rides often enough,' said Arun. He reflected that Varun, the racing fiend, would have known not only that Jock Mackay was riding, but in which race he would be riding, on what horse, with what handicap and at what probable odds. Varun and his Shamshu friends usually bought a provisional or kutcha racing form the moment it appeared on the streets on Wednesday, and from then until Saturday afternoon would think about and discuss little else.

'And now?' Basil Cox prompted Arun.

'It's about the tariffs for Persian Fine Teas. They want us to insure another shipment.'

'Yes. I marked that letter out to you. Purely routine, isn't it?'

'I'm not so sure.'

Basil Cox stroked his lower lip with his thumb and waited for Arun to go on.

'I don't think our claims experience with them is so good,' said Arun.

'Well, that's easily checked.'

'I've already done so.'

'I see.'

'Claims are a hundred and fifty-two per cent of premiums if you take the last three years. Not a happy situation.'

'No, no, indeed,' said Basil Cox, considering. 'Not a happy situation. What do they usually claim for? Pilferage, I seem to recall. Or is it rainwater damage? And didn't they have a claim for taint once? Leather in the same hold as tea or something like that.'

'Rainwater damage was another company. And taint we disallowed after getting a report from Lloyds, our claims settlement agents on the spot. Their surveyors said that taint was minimal, even though the Persians appear to judge their tea more by fragrance than by flavour. It's pilferage that has really harmed them. Or, rather, us. Skilful pilferage at the customs warehouse in Khurramshahr. It's a bad port, and for all we know the customs authorities may be in on it.'

'Well, what is the premium at present? Five annas?'

'Yes.'

'Put it up to eight annas.'

'I'm not sure that would work,' said Arun. 'I could call upon their agent in Calcutta and do that. But I don't think he'd take kindly to it. He once mentioned that even our five-anna rate was barely competitive with what Commercial Union was willing to insure them for. We would very likely lose them.'

'Well, do you have anything else to suggest?' said Basil Cox with a rather tired smile. From experience he knew that Arun very likely did have something else to suggest.

'As it happens, I do,' said Arun.

'Ah,' said Basil Cox, pretending surprise.

'We could write to Lloyds and ask them what steps had been taken to prevent or reduce pilferage from the customs warehouse.'

Basil Cox was rather disappointed but did not say so.

'I see. Well, thank you, Arun.'

But Arun had not finished.

'And we could offer to reduce the premium.'

'Reduce it, did you say?' Basil Cox raised both eyebrows.

'Yes. Just remove the Theft, Pilferage and Non-Delivery clause. They can have everything else: the standard policy of fire, storm, leakage, piracy, forced jettison and so on, plus Strike, Riot and Civil Commotion, rainwater damage, even taint, whatever they want. All on very favourable terms. But no TPND. That they can insure with someone else. They obviously have very little incentive to protect their cargo if we fork out their claims every time someone decides to drink their tea for them.'

Basil Cox smiled. 'It's an idea. Let me think about it. We'll talk about it in the car this afternoon on the way to Puttigurh.'

'There's one other matter, Basil.'

'Could it wait till the afternoon too?'

'Actually, one of our friends from Rajasthan is coming to see me in an hour and it has to do with him. I should have brought it up earlier, but I thought it could wait. I didn't know he was so eager to have a quick response.'

This was a stock euphemism for a Marwari businessman. The grasping, enterprising, canny, energetic and above all ungentlemanly traits of that community were intensely distasteful to the leisured and gentlemanly sahibs of the managing agencies. The managing agency might borrow a great deal of money from a certain kind of Marwari businessman, but the chairman would not dream of inviting him to his club, even if it were one to which Indians were admitted.

But in this case it was the Marwari businessman who wanted Bentsen Pryce to finance him. His suggestion, in brief, was this: his house wanted to expand into a new line of operations, but he wanted Bentsen Pryce to invest in this expansion. In return, he would give them whatever insurance business arose from the new operations.

Arun, swallowing his own instinctive distaste for the community, and reminding himself that business was business, put the matter to Basil Cox as objectively as he could. He forbore from mentioning that this was no more than what one British firm did for another in the regular way of business. He knew that his boss was not unaware of that fact.

Basil Cox did not ask him for his advice. He looked at a point beyond Arun's right shoulder for a disconcertingly long time, then said:

'I don't like it—it smells a bit Marwari to me.'

By his tone he implied that it was a species of sharp practice. Arun was about to speak when he added:

'No. It's definitely not for us. And Finance, I know, would not like it at all. Let's leave it at that. So I'll see you at two thirty?'

'Right,' said Arun.

When he got back to his room, he wondered how he would put things to his visitor, and what reasons he could adduce to defend the decision. But he did not need to. Mr Jhunjhunwala took the decision surprisingly well. When Arun told him that his company couldn't go ahead with the proposal, Mr Jhunjhunwala did not ask him to explain himself. He merely nodded, then said in Hindi—implying an awful complicity, it seemed to Arun, a complicity of one Indian with another—'You know, that's the trouble with Bentsen Pryce: they won't take something on unless there's a bit of a smell of the English in it.'

7.22

After Mr Jhunjhunwala had gone, Arun phoned Meenakshi to say that he would be back from work fairly late that evening, but that they should still plan to go for cocktails at the Finlays' at about seven thirty. He then answered a couple of other letters, and finally settled back to his crossword.

But before he could solve more than two or three more clues, the phone rang. It was James Pettigrew.

'Well, Arun, how many?'

'Not many, I'm afraid. I've just begun to look at it.'

This was an outright lie. Apart from straining every brain cell he could while sitting on the toilet, Arun had frowned at the crossword over breakfast and even scribbled the letters of possible anagrams underneath the clues while being driven to work. Since his handwriting was illegible, even to himself, this usually didn't help him much.

'I won't ask you if you got "that confounded pane in the neck".'

'Thanks,' said Arun. 'I'm glad you give me credit for an IQ of at least eighty.'

'And "Johnson's rose"?'

'Yes.'

'How about "Knife a gentleman buys in Paris"?'

'No—but since you're obviously eager to tell me, why don't you put both of us out of our agony?'

'Machete.'

'Machete?'

'Machete.'

'I'm afraid I don't quite see how—'

'Ah, Arun, you'll have to learn French some day,' said James Pettigrew infuriatingly.

'Well, what didn't you get?' asked Arun with ill-masked irritation.

'Very little, as it happens,' said the obnoxious James.

'So you've solved it all, have you?' said Arun.

'Well, not exactly, not exactly. There are a couple that are still troubling me a little.'

'Oh, just a couple?'

'Well, perhaps a couple of couples.'

'For example?'

'"Musician who sounds rapacious", five letters, third letter T, fifth letter R.'

'Luter,' said Arun promptly.

'Aaah, that's got to be right. But I always thought the right word was lutanist or perhaps lutist.'

'Does the L give you any help in the other direction?'

'Er . . . let's see . . . yes, it does. That must be "Belfry". Thank you.'

'Don't mention it,' said Arun. 'As it happens, I had a linguistic advantage with that one.'

'How so?' said James.

'The word "loot" comes from Hindi.'

'So it does, so it does,' said James Pettigrew. 'Anyway,' he continued, 'it seems that I've won the Ashes three to two, and you owe me lunch sometime next week.'

He was referring to their weekly crossword stakes that ran from Monday to Friday. Arun grunted his admission of defeat.

*

While this conversation, devoted largely to the peculiarities of words, and not entirely pleasing to Arun Mehra, was taking place, another telephone conversation, also dealing with the peculiarities of words, was taking place, which, had he been aware of it, would have pleased Arun Mehra even less.

Meenakshi: Hello.

Billy Irani: Hello!

Meenakshi: You sound different. Is there anyone in the office with you?

Billy: No. But I wish you wouldn't call me at the office.

Meenakshi: It's so difficult for me to call at other times. But everyone happens to be out this morning. How are you?

Billy: I'm in fine, er, fettle.

Meenakshi: That makes you sound like a sort of stallion.

Billy: Are you sure you're not thinking of fetlock?

Meenakshi: Silly Billy! Of course not. Fetlock is the hair somewhere. It's what you catch a horse by, I think. I think it's the part of the mane at the base of the neck. Hair equals lock.

Billy: Well then, tell me, how can you sprain a fetlock or break one? You keep hearing of a horse having to be shot because it's broken a fetlock. By the way, are you going to the races tomorrow at Tolly?

Meenakshi: Yes, as it happens. Arun just called me from the office. Basil Cox has invited us. So will I see you there?

Billy: I'm not sure I'm going tomorrow. But we're all meeting this evening aren't we, for cocktails at the Finlays'—and then dinner and dancing somewhere?

Meenakshi: But I won't get a chance to say a word to you—what with Shireen guarding you like an emerald egg, and Arun—and my sister-in-law.

Billy: Your sister-in-law?

Meenakshi: She's quite nice; she needs to be brought out a bit, though. I thought we'd throw her in with Bish, and see how they get along.

Billy: And did you call me an emerald egg?

Meenakshi: Yes. You are rather like an emerald egg. And that brings me to the point. Arun is going to be out in Puttigurh or somewhere until seven o'clock or so. What are you doing this afternoon? I know it's Friday, so don't say you're working.

Billy: Actually, I have lunch first, then a game of golf.

Meenakshi: What? In this weather? You'll be swept out to sea. So let's meet—for tea and so on.

Billy: Well—I'm not sure all this is such a good idea.

Meenakshi: Let's go to the zoo. It'll be pouring with rain so we won't meet the usual good citizen. We'll meet a horse—or a zebra and we'll ask him if he's sprained his hair or his neck. I'm so funny, aren't I?

Billy: Yes, hilarious. Well, I'll meet you at four thirty. At the Fairlawn Hotel. For tea.

Meenakshi: For tea and so on.

Billy [rather reluctantly]: And so on. Yes.

Meenakshi: At three o'clock.

Billy: Four o'clock.

Meenakshi: Four o'clock. Four o'clock. Perhaps you were thinking of forelock when you said fetlock.

Billy: Perhaps I was.

Meenakshi: Or foreskin.

Billy: I wouldn't grab a horse by that.

Meenakshi: Silly Billy! But what is a fetlock then?

Billy: Look up a dictionary—and tell me this afternoon. Or show me.

Meenakshi: Naughty.

Billy [with a sigh]: You're far naughtier than I am, Meenakshi. I don't think this is at all a good idea.

Meenakshi: Four o'clock then. I'll take a taxi. Bye.

Billy: Bye.

Meenakshi: I don't love you a bit.

Billy: Thank God.

7.23

When Meenakshi returned from her assignation with Billy, it was half-past six, and she was smiling contentedly. She was so pleasant to Mrs Rupa Mehra that it quite unsettled her, and she asked Meenakshi if something was the matter. Meenakshi assured her that nothing at all was the matter.

Lata couldn't decide what to wear for the evening. She entered the drawing room carrying a light-pink cotton sari, a part of which she had draped over her shoulder. 'What do you think of this, Ma?' she said.

'Very nice, darling,' said Mrs Rupa Mehra, and fanned a fly away from Aparna's sleeping head.

'What nonsense, Ma, it's absolutely awful,' said Meenakshi.

'It is not at all awful,' said Mrs Rupa Mehra defensively. 'Pink was your father-in-law's favourite colour.'

'Pink?' Meenakshi started laughing. 'He liked wearing pink?'

'On me. When I wore it!' Mrs Rupa Mehra was angry. Meenakshi had changed from nice to nasty in an instant. 'If you don't have any respect for me, at least have respect for my husband. You have no sense of proportion. Going off gallivanting to New Market and leaving Aparna for the servants to take care of.'

'Now, Ma, I'm sure pink looked lovely on you,' said Meenakshi in a conciliatory manner. 'But it's absolutely the wrong thing for Luts's complexion. And for Calcutta, and for the evening, and for this kind of society. And cotton just won't do. I'll see what Luts has and help her choose something that will make her look her best. We'd better hurry, Arun will be home at any moment, and then we won't have time for anything. Come on, Luts.'

And Lata was taken in hand. She was finally dressed in one of Meenakshi's deep-blue chiffon saris which happened to go with one of her own blue blouses. (She had to tuck the sari in considerably more than

Meenakshi, since she was a few inches shorter.) A peacock brooch of light blue, dark blue and green enamel, also belonging to Meenakshi, pinned her sari to her blouse. Lata had never worn a brooch in her life, and had to be scolded by Meenakshi into it.

Meenakshi next overruled the tight bun into which Lata usually coiled her hair. 'That style looks simply too prim, Luts,' said her mentor. 'It really isn't flattering to you. You have to leave it open.'

'No, I can't do that,' protested Lata. 'It just isn't proper. Ma would have a fit.'

'Proper!' exclaimed Meenakshi. 'Well, let's at least soften up the front of it so that you don't look so schoolmarmish.'

Finally, Meenakshi marched Lata off to the dressing table in her bedroom, and put the final touches to her face with a bit of mascara. 'This will make your eyelashes look longer,' she said.

Lata fluttered her eyelashes experimentally. 'Do you think they'll fall like flies?' she asked Meenakshi, laughing.

'Yes, Luts,' said Meenakshi. 'And you must keep smiling. Your eyes really do look appealing now.'

And when she looked at herself in the mirror, Lata had to admit they did.

'Now what perfume would suit you?' said Meenakshi aloud to herself. 'Worth seems about right for you.'

But before she could come to a final decision, the doorbell rang impatiently. Arun was back from Puttigurh. Everyone hopped around and danced attendance on him for the next few minutes.

When he was ready, he became frustrated that Meenakshi was taking so long. When she did finally emerge, Mrs Rupa Mehra stared at her in outrage. She was wearing a sleeveless, low-cut, magenta blouse in open-back choli style, with a bottle-green sari of exquisitely fine chiffon.

'You can't wear that!' gasped Mrs Rupa Mehra, making what in the Mehra family were known as big-big eyes. Her glance veered from Meenakshi's cleavage to her midriff to her entirely exposed arms. 'You can't, you—you can't. It is even worse than last night at your parents' house.'

'Of course I can, Maloos dear, don't be so old-fashioned.'

'Well? Are you finally ready?' asked Arun, looking pointedly at his watch.

'Not quite, darling. Would you close the clasp on my choker for me?' And Meenakshi with a slow, sensuous gesture passed her hand across her neck just below her thick gold choker.

Her mother-in-law averted her eyes.

'Why do you allow her to wear this?' she asked her son. 'Can't she wear a decent blouse like other Indian girls?'

'Ma, I'm sorry, we're getting late,' said Arun.

'One can't tango in a dowdy choli,' said Meenakshi. 'Come, Luts.'

Lata gave her mother a kiss. 'Don't worry, Ma, I'll be fine.'

'Tango?' said Mrs Rupa Mehra in alarm. 'What is tango?'

'Bye, Ma,' said Meenakshi. 'Tango. A dance. We're going to the Golden Slipper. Nothing to worry about. There's just a large crowd and a band and dancing.'

'Abandoned dancing!' Mrs Rupa Mehra could hardly believe her ears.

But before she could think of anything to say the little sky-blue Austin had started off on the first leg of the night's revels.

7.24

Cocktails at the Finlays' was a hubbub of chatter. Everyone stood around talking about the 'monsoonish' weather, which had struck earlier than usual this year. Opinion was divided as to whether today's tremendous rains were monsoonal or pre-monsoonal. Golf had been quite impossible this afternoon, and though the races at Tollygunge were very rarely cancelled owing to the weather (after all, it was known as the Monsoon Racing Season to distinguish it from the winter one), if the rains were as heavy tomorrow as they had been today, the ground might be complete slush and the going too difficult for the horses. English county cricket too played a large part in the conversation, and Lata heard more than she might have wished to about Denis Compton's brilliant batting and his left-arm spinners, and how superbly he was doing as captain of Middlesex. She nodded in agreement wherever necessary, her mind on a different cricketer.

About a third of the crowd was Indian: executives of managing agencies like Arun, with a smattering of civil servants, lawyers, doctors and army officers. Unlike in Brahmpur, which she had just been visiting in her thoughts, in this stratum of Calcutta society—even more obviously than at the Chatterjis'—men and women mixed freely and unselfconsciously. The hawk-nosed hostess, Mrs Finlay, was very kind to her and introduced her to a couple of people when she noticed her standing by herself. But Lata felt ill at ease. Meenakshi, on the other hand, was in her element, and her laughter could be heard from time to time tinkling above the general mash of sociable noise.

Arun and Meenakshi were both floating a few inches above the ground by the time they and Lata drove over from Alipore to Firpo's. The rain had stopped a couple of hours earlier. They drove by the Victoria Memorial, where the ice-cream and jhaal-muri sellers provisioned the couples and families who had come out for a stroll in the comparative cool of the evening. Chowringhee was uncrowded. Even at night the broad and spacious frontage of the street presented an impressive appearance. To the left a few late trams plied along the edge of the Maidan.

At the entrance to Firpo's, they met Bishwanath Bhaduri: a dark, tall young man of about Arun's age with a square-set jaw and hair combed neatly back. He bent at the waist when introduced to Lata, and told her that he was Bish, and that he was charmed.

They waited for Billy Irani and Shireen Framjee for a few minutes. 'I told them we were leaving the party,' said Arun. 'Why the hell haven't they appeared?'

Perhaps responding to his importunity, they appeared within seconds, and after they had been introduced to Lata—there had been no time for Arun and Meenakshi to make the necessary introductions at the Finlays' once they had got caught up in small talk—they all went up together to the restaurant, and were shown to the table they had reserved.

Lata found the food at Firpo's delicious and the talk of Bishwanath Bhaduri glitteringly insipid. He mentioned that he had happened to be in Brahmpur at the time of her sister Savita's wedding, to which he had gone with Arun. 'A lovely bride—one felt like snatching her away from the altar oneself. But of course not as lovely as her younger sister,' he added suavely.

Lata stared at him incredulously for a second or two, then looked at the rolls, imagining them into pellets.

'I suppose the shehnai should have been playing "Here Comes the Bride",' she could not resist saying as she looked up again.

'What? Er, hum, yes?' said Bish, nonplussed. Then he added, glancing at a neighbouring table, that what he liked about Firpo's was that you could see 'the world and their wife' here.

Lata reflected that her remark had clearly run off his back like duck's water. And at the thought of that phrase, she began to smile.

Bishwanath Bhaduri, for his part, found Lata puzzling but attractive. At least she looked at him while she talked. Most Calcutta girls in his set spent half their time looking around to see who else was at Firpo's.

Arun had decided that Bish would be a good possibility for Lata, and had told her that he was an 'up-and-coming young fellow'.

Now Bish was telling Lata about his passage to England:

'One feels discontented and searches about for one's soul. . . . One feels homesick at Aden and buys one's postcards at Port Said. . . . One does a certain sort of job and gets used to it. . . . Back in Calcutta one sometimes imagines that Chowringhee is Piccadilly. . . . Of course, sometimes when one is on tour, one misses one's connections. . . . One stops at a railway station and finds nothing behind it—and spends the night with the coolies snoring on the platform. . . .' He picked up the menu again. 'I wonder whether I should have something sweet . . . one's Bengali tooth, you know. . . .'

Lata began to wish that he were up-and-going.

Bish had begun to discuss some matter in his department in which he had acquitted himself particularly well.

'. . . and of course, not that one wants to take personal credit for it, but the upshot of it all was that one secured the contract, and one has been handling the business ever since. Naturally'—and here he smiled smoothly at Lata—'there was considerable disquiet among one's competitors. They couldn't imagine how one had swung it.'

'Oh?' said Lata, frowning as she tackled her peach melba. 'Was there? Was the disquiet considerable?'

Bishwanath Bhaduri shot her a quick glance of—not dislike exactly but, well, disquiet.

Shireen wanted to dance at the 300 Club, but was overruled, and they all went to the Golden Slipper in Free School Street instead, where it was livelier if less exclusive. The bright young things sometimes believed in slumming it.

Bish, perhaps sensing that Lata had not taken to him, made an excuse and disappeared after dinner.

'See you anon,' were his parting words.

Billy Irani had been remarkably quiet throughout the evening, and he did not appear to want to dance at all—not even foxtrots and waltzes. Arun made Lata dance a waltz with him despite her protests that she did not know how to dance at all. 'Nonsense,' said Arun affectionately. 'You do, you just don't know it.' He was right; she quickly got the hang of it, and enjoyed it too.

Shireen forced Billy on to his feet. Later, when the orchestra struck up an intimate number, Meenakshi requisitioned him. When they returned to the table Billy was blushing furiously.

'Look at him blush,' said Meenakshi delightedly. 'I think he likes holding me close. He was pressing me so close to his broad chest with his strong, golf-playing arms that I could feel his heart thump.'

'I was not,' said Billy indignantly.

'I wish you would,' said Meenakshi with a sigh. 'I nurture a secret lust for you, you know, Billy.'

Shireen laughed. Billy glared fiercely at Meenakshi and blushed even more furiously.

'That's enough nonsense,' said Arun. 'Don't embarrass my friend—or my younger sister.'

'Oh, I'm not embarrassed, Arun Bhai,' said Lata, though she was amazed all right by the tenor of the conversation.

But what amazed Lata most of all was the tango. At about one thirty in the morning, by which time the two couples were fairly high, Meenakshi sent a note to the band leader, and five minutes later he struck up a tango. Since very few people knew how to tango, the couples on the floor stood around looking a little perplexed. But Meenakshi went straight up to a man dressed in a dinner jacket who was sitting with some friends at a table across the room—and enchanted him on to the floor. She did not know him but she recognized him as a wonderful dancer whom she had once seen in action before. His friends prodded him on as well. Everyone cleared the floor for them, and without even any initial discomfiture, they paced and twirled and froze together in swift, jerky, stylized movements with such erotic control and abandon that very soon the entire nightclub was cheering them on. Lata felt her own heart beating faster. She was fascinated by Meenakshi's brazenness and dazzled by the play of light on the gold choker round her neck. Clearly Meenakshi was right; one couldn't tango in a dowdy choli.

They stumbled out of the nightclub at two thirty, and Arun shouted: 'Let's go—let's go to Falta! The waterworks—a picnic—I'm hungry—kababs at Nizam's.'

'It's getting rather late, Arun,' said Billy. 'Perhaps we should call it a night. I'll drop Shireen and—'

'No nonsense—I'm master of ceremonies,' insisted Arun. 'You get into my car. We'll all go—no, into the back—I'll sit with this pretty girl in the front—no, no, no, Saturday tomorrow—and we'll all go now—at once—

we'll all go and have breakfast at the airport—airport picnic—all to the airport for breakfast—bloody car won't start—oh, wrong key.'

Off zoomed the little car through the streets, with Arun at the shaky helm, Shireen sitting with him in front, and Billy squashed between the two other women at the back. Lata must have appeared very nervous, because Billy patted her hand kindly once. A little later, she noticed that Billy's other hand was interlocked with Meenakshi's. She was surprised, but—after the torrid tango—not suspicious; she assumed that that was how things were done when one went for a drive in this kind of society. But she hoped for the sake of their common safety that the same sort of thing was not going on in the front seat.

Although there was no broad and direct road to the airport, even the narrower streets of North Calcutta were deserted at this hour, and driving was not intrinsically difficult. Arun roared along, blowing his horn loudly from time to time. But suddenly a child rushed out from behind a cart straight into their path. Arun swerved wildly, narrowly missed hitting it, and came to a halt before a lamp post.

Luckily neither child nor car was damaged. The child disappeared as suddenly as it had appeared.

Arun got out of the car in a black fury and started shouting into the night. There was a piece of smouldering rope hanging from the lamp post for people to light their biris with, and Arun started pulling it as if it were a bell-rope. 'Get up—get up—all of you—all of you bastards—' he shouted at the entire neighbourhood.

'Arun—Arun—please don't,' said Meenakshi.

'Bloody idiots—can't control their children—at three in the bloody morning—'

A few destitute people, sleeping in their rags on the narrow pavement next to a pile of rubbish, stirred themselves.

'Do shut up, Arun,' said Billy Irani. 'You'll cause trouble.'

'You trying to take charge, Billy?—No good—good fellow, but not much there—' He turned his attention to the unseen enemy, the breeding, stupid masses. 'Get up—you bastards—can't you hear me?' He followed this up with a few other Hindi swear words, since he could not speak Bengali.

Meenakshi knew that if she said anything, Arun would snap at her.

'Arun Bhai,' said Lata as calmly as she could. 'I'm very sleepy, and Ma will be worried about us. Let's go home now.'

'Home? Yes, let's go home.' Arun, startled by this excellent suggestion, smiled at his brilliant sister.

Billy was about to suggest that he drive, then thought better of it.

When he and Shireen were dropped off near his car, he was in a thoughtful mood, though he said nothing except to wish everyone goodnight.

Mrs Rupa Mehra was sitting up late for them. She was so relieved to hear the car drive up that when they came in she could not at first speak.

'Why are you up at this hour, Ma?' said Meenakshi, yawning.

'I will get no sleep tonight at all thanks to your selfishness,' said Mrs Rupa Mehra. 'Soon it will be time to get up.'

'Ma, you know we always come back late when we go dancing,' said Meenakshi. Arun had meanwhile gone into the bedroom, and Varun too, who had been woken up at two by his alarmed mother and forced to sit up with her, had seized the opportunity and slunk away to bed.

'Yes, you can behave as irresponsibly as you like when you are gallivanting around by yourselves,' said Mrs Rupa Mehra. 'But not when you have my daughter with you. Are you all right, darling?' she asked Lata.

'Yes, Ma, I had a good time,' said Lata, yawning as well. She remembered the tango and began to smile.

Mrs Rupa Mehra looked doubtful. 'You must tell me everything you did. What you ate, what you saw, whom you met, what you did.'

'Yes, Ma. Tomorrow,' said Lata with another yawn.

'All right,' conceded Mrs Rupa Mehra.

7.25

Lata woke up almost at noon the next day with a headache that did not improve when she had to give a recitation of the previous night's events. Both Aparna and Mrs Rupa Mehra wanted to know about the tango. After she had absorbed the details of the dance, the scarily precocious Aparna wanted reassurance, for some reason, on one particular point:

'So Mummy tangoed and everyone clapped?'

'Yes, sweetheart.'

'Daddy also?'

'Oh yes. Daddy clapped too.'

'Will you teach me to tango?'

'I don't know how to tango,' said Lata. 'But if I did, I would.'

'Does Uncle Varun know how to tango?'

Lata tried to visualize Varun's terror if Meenakshi had tried to prise him away from a table on to the dance floor. 'I doubt it,' she said. 'Where is Varun anyway?' she asked her mother.

'He went out,' said Mrs Rupa Mehra shortly. 'Sajid and Jason turned up, and they disappeared.'

Lata had only met these two Shamshu friends once. Sajid had a cigarette that hung down, literally hung down, with no apparent means of support, from the left side of his lower lip. What he did for a living she did not know. Jason frowned toughly when speaking to her. He was an Anglo-Indian, and had been in the Calcutta police before he had been thrown out a few months earlier for sleeping with another Sub-Inspector's wife. Varun knew both of them from St George's. Arun shuddered to think that his own alma mater could have produced such seedy characters.

'Isn't Varun studying at all for the IAS?' asked Lata. The other day Varun had been talking about sitting for the civil service exams later in the year.

'No,' said Mrs Rupa Mehra with a sigh. 'And there's nothing I can do. He does not listen to his mother any more. When I say anything to him, he just agrees with me and then goes off with his friends an hour later.'

'Perhaps he's not cut out for the administrative service,' suggested Lata.

But her mother would have none of that.

'Studying is a good discipline,' she said. 'It needs application. Your father used to say that it does not matter what you study. As long as you study hard, it improves the mind.'

By that criterion, the late Raghubir Mehra should have been proud of his younger son. Varun, Sajid and Jason were at that moment standing in the two-rupee enclosure at the Tollygunge racetrack, cheek by jowl with what Arun would have considered the riff-raff of the solar system, studying with intense concentration the pukka or final version of the racing form for the afternoon's six races. They were hoping that they would thereby improve, if not their mind, at least their economic situation.

Normally they would not have invested the six annas that it cost to buy a pukka racing form, and would—with the help of the handicap list and information about cancellations—have simply pencilled in changes on the provisional form that they had bought on Wednesday. But Sajid had lost it.

A thin, warm rain was falling all over Calcutta, and the Tollygunge racecourse was slushy. The discontented horses being walked around the paddock were being eyed keenly from all sides through the drizzle. The Tolly had gymkhana racing, not turf racing, unlike the Royal Calcutta Turf Club, whose monsoon season began more than a month later. This meant that professional jockeys were not compulsory, and there were plenty of gentleman-jockeys and even one or two ladies who rode in the races. Since the riders were sometimes quite heavy, the handicap on the horses too started at a heavier level.

'Heart's Story has 11 stones 6 pounds on her,' said Jason glumly. 'I would have bet on her, but—'

'So what?' said Sajid. 'She's used to Jock Mackay, and he can outride anyone on this track. He'll use up a good part of that 11 stones odd, and that's live weight, not lead pellets. It makes a difference.'

'It makes no difference. Weight is weight,' said Jason. His attention was caught by a strikingly attractive European woman of middle age, who was talking to Jock Mackay in low tones.

'My God—that's Mrs DiPiero!' said Varun, in a voice half fascinated, half terrified. 'She's dangerous!' he added with admiration.

Mrs DiPiero was a merry widow who usually did well at the races by gleaning tips from knowledgeable sources, in particular from Jock Mackay, who was reputed to be her lover. She often bet a few thousand rupees on a single race.

'Quick! Follow her!' said Jason, though the direction of his intentions only became clear when she went to the bookies and he turned his attention from her figure to the chalk markings on the blackboards which the bookies were rapidly rubbing out and re-marking. She was placing her bets in such a low voice that they could not hear her. But the bookies' notations told their own tale. They were changing their odds in the wake of her heavy betting. Heart's Story had come down from 7-to-1 to 6-to-1.

'That's it!' said Sajid languorously. 'I'm betting on that one.'

'Don't be too hasty,' said Jason. 'Obviously he'd praise his own horse.'

'But not at the cost of her displeasure. He must know it's undervalued at the odds.'

'Mmm,' intervened Varun. 'One thing worries me.'

'What?' said Sajid and Jason simultaneously. Varun's interventions were usually to the point in racing matters. He was a true but cautious addict.

'It's the rain. The heavily handicapped horses suffer the most when the ground is so wet. And 11 stones 6 pounds is about the heaviest handicap you can get. I think they penalized that mare because her rider held her back three weeks ago on the finishing straight.'

Sajid disagreed. His cigarette bobbed up and down as he spoke. 'It's a short race,' he said. 'Handicap doesn't matter all that much in a short race. I'm going to bet on her anyway. You two can do as you please.'

'What do you say, Varun?' said Jason, undecided.

'Yes. OK.'

They went to buy their tickets from the tote rather than the bookies, since a couple of two-rupee tickets each was all they could afford. Besides, the bookies' odds on Heart's Story had now come down to 5-to-1.

They returned to their enclosure and stared out at the rainy course in a state of uncontainable excitement.

It was a short race, only five furlongs of a mile. The starting point, on the other side of the course, was invisible because of the rain and the distance, especially from their lowly position, so far below the members' enclosure. But the thundering sound of the horses' hooves and their indistinct, swift movement through the blurred wall of rain had them shouting and screaming. Varun was almost foaming at the mouth with excitement and yelling: 'Heart's Story! Come on, Heart's Story!' at the top of his lungs. At the end all he could manage was:

'Heart! Heart! Heart! Heart!'

He was grasping Sajid's shoulder in an ecstasy of uncertainty.

The horses emerged round the bend for the final straight. Their colours and the colours of their riders became more distinct—and it became clear that the green-and-red colours of Jock Mackay on the bay were to the fore, closely followed by Anne Hodge on Outrageous Fortune. She made a valiant effort to spur him on for a last effort. Exhausted by the churned earth around his ankles—his fetlocks perhaps—he gave up the struggle when it seemed certain that he would succeed: just twenty yards from the finishing line.

Heart's Story had won by a length and a half.

There were groans of disappointment and screams of delight all around them. The three friends went wild with excitement. Their winnings swelled in their imaginations to vast proportions. They might have won as much as fifteen rupees each! A bottle of Scotch—why even think of Shamshu?—was only fourteen rupees.

Joy!

All they had to do now was to wait for the white cone to go up, and to collect their winnings.

A red cone went up with the white.

Despair.

There had been an objection. 'Number seven has objected to Number two crossing,' said someone nearby.

'How can they tell in all that rain?'

'Of course they can tell.'

'He'd never do it to her. These are gentlemen.'

'Anne Hodge wouldn't lie about something like that.'

'This Jock chap is very unscrupulous. He'll do anything to win.'

'These things can happen by mistake as well.'

'By mistake!'

The suspense was unbearable. Three minutes passed. Varun was gasping with emotion and stress, and Sajid's cigarette was quivering. Jason was trying to look tough and unconcerned, and failing dismally. When the red cone slowly went down, confirming the result of the race, they embraced each other as if they were long-lost brothers, and went off immediately to collect their earnings—and to place their bets on the next race.

'Hello! Varun isn't it?' She pronounced it Vay-roon.

Varun swung around and stared at Patricia Cox, dressed elegantly in an airy white cotton dress and carrying a white umbrella which doubled as a parasol. She was not looking mousy at all, but rather cat-like in fact. She too had just won on Heart's Story.

Varun's hair was wild, his face red; the racing form in his hands was crushed; his shirt was wet with rain and sweat. Jason and Sajid were flanking him. They had just received their winnings and were jumping up and down.

Miraculously, however, Sajid's cigarette had not been dislodged, and was hanging down from his lip as supportlessly as ever.

'Heh, heh,' laughed Varun nervously, looking this way and that.

'How delightful to meet you again,' said Patricia Cox with unmistakable pleasure.

'Erh, eh, heh, heh,' said Varun. 'Hum. Er.' He couldn't remember her name. Box? He looked undecided.

'Patricia Cox,' said Patricia Cox helpfully. 'We met that evening at your house after dinner. But I suppose you've forgotten.'

'No, er, no, heh, heh!' laughed Varun weakly, looking for escape.

'And I suppose these are your Shamshu friends,' she continued with approval.

Jason and Sajid, who had been looking on astonished, now gaped at

Patricia Cox, then turned questioningly and a little threateningly towards Varun.

'Heh, heh,' bleated Varun pathetically.

'Do you have any recommendations for the next race?' asked Patricia Cox. 'Your brother's here as our guest. Would you like to—'

'No—no—I have to go—' Varun found his voice at last, and almost fled from the hall without even laying a bet on the next race.

When Patricia Cox returned to the members' enclosure she said brightly to Arun: 'You didn't tell me your brother would be here. We didn't know he was keen on the races. We would have invited him too.'

Arun stiffened. 'Here? Oh yes, here. Yes, sometimes. Of course. Rain's let up.'

'I'm afraid he doesn't like me much,' continued Patricia Cox sadly.

'He's probably afraid of you,' said Meenakshi perceptively.

'Of me?' Patricia Cox found this difficult to believe.

During the next race, Arun found it impossible to concentrate on the track. While everyone else around him was (with some restraint) cheering on the horses, his eyes, as if of their own accord, strayed downwards. Beyond the path from the paddock to the track was the exclusive (and exclusively European) Tollygunge Club where, now that the rain had stopped, a few members were having tea on the lawn and watching the races at leisure. And here, where Arun was sitting as a guest of the Coxes, was the balancing social pinnacle of the members' enclosure.

But in between the two, in the two-rupee enclosure, stood Arun's brother, sandwiched between his two disreputable companions, and so caught up in the excitement of the next race that he had forgotten his traumatic meeting of a few minutes ago and was jumping up and down, red in the face and screaming words that were unintelligible from this distance but were almost certainly the name of the horse on which he had laid, if not his bet, his heart. He looked almost, but not quite, unrecognizable.

Arun's nostrils quivered slightly and after a few seconds he looked away. He told himself that he had better start being his brother's keeper—for that beast, once out of its cage, could do no end of damage to the equilibrium of the universe.

7.26

Mrs Rupa Mehra and Lata were continuing their conversation. From Varun and the IAS they had moved on to Savita and the baby. Though not yet a reality, in Mrs Rupa Mehra's mind the baby was already a professor or a judge. Needless to say, it was a boy.

'I have had no news from my daughter for a week. I am very upset with her,' said Mrs Rupa Mehra. When she was with Lata, Mrs Rupa Mehra referred to Savita as 'my daughter', and vice versa.

'She's fine, Ma,' said Lata reassuringly. 'Or you would certainly have heard.'

'And to be expecting in this heat!' said Mrs Rupa Mehra, implying that Savita should have timed it better. 'You were also born in the monsoon,' she told Lata. 'You were a very difficult birth,' she added, and her eyes glistened with emotion.

Lata had heard about her own difficult birth a hundred times before. Sometimes when her mother was angry with her she flung this fact at her accusingly. At other times, when she was feeling especially fond of her, she mentioned it as a reminder of how precious to her Lata had always been. Lata had also heard a number of times about the tenacious grip she had as a baby.

'And poor Pran. I hear it has not yet rained in Brahmpur,' continued Mrs Rupa Mehra.

'It has, Ma, a little.'

'Not proper rain—just a droplet or two here and there. It is still so dusty, and terrible for his asthma.'

Lata said: 'Ma, you shouldn't worry about him. Savita keeps a careful eye on him, and so does his mother.' She knew, however, that it was no use. Mrs Rupa Mehra thrived on worrying. One of the marvellous by-products of Savita's marriage was a whole new family to worry about.

'But his mother herself is not well,' said Mrs Rupa Mehra triumphantly. 'And, talking of which, I have been feeling like visiting my homoeopath.'

If Arun had been present, he would have told his mother that all homoeopaths were charlatans. Lata merely said:

'But do those little white pills do you any good, Ma? I think it's all faith healing.'

'What is wrong with faith?' asked Mrs Rupa Mehra. 'In your generation no one believes in anything.'

Lata did not defend her generation.

'Except in having a good time and staying out till four in the morning,' added Mrs Rupa Mehra.

Lata, to her own surprise, laughed.

'What is it?' her mother demanded. 'Why are you laughing? You weren't laughing two days ago.'

'Nothing, Ma, I was just laughing, that's all. Can't I laugh once in a while?' She had stopped laughing, though, having suddenly thought of Kabir.

Mrs Rupa Mehra ignored the general point, and homed in on the particular.

'But you were laughing for some reason. There must be a reason. You can tell your mother.'

'Ma, I'm not a baby, I'm allowed to have my own thoughts.'

'For me, you will always be my baby.'

'Even when I'm sixty?'

Mrs Rupa Mehra looked at her daughter in surprise. Although she had just visualized Savita's unborn child as a judge, she had never visualized Lata as a woman of sixty. She attempted to now, but the thought was too daunting. Luckily, another intervened.

'God will have taken me away long before then,' she sighed. 'And it is only when I am dead and gone and you see my empty chair that you will appreciate me. Now you are hiding everything from me, as if you don't trust me.'

Lata reflected, painfully, that she did not in fact trust her mother to understand much of what she felt. She thought of Kabir's letter, which she had transferred from the book on Egyptian mythology to a writing pad at the bottom of her suitcase. Where had he got her address from? How often did he think of her? She thought again of the flippant tone of his letter and felt a rush of anger.

Perhaps it wasn't really flippant, though, she said to herself. And perhaps he had been right in suggesting that she hadn't given him much of a chance to explain himself. She thought of their last meeting—it seemed very long ago—and of her own behaviour: it had bordered on the hysterical. But for her it had been her whole life and for him probably no more than a pleasant early-morning outing. He clearly had not expected the intensity of her outburst. Perhaps, Lata admitted, perhaps he could not have been expected to expect it.

As it was, her heart ached for him. It was him and not her brother whom she had, in her imagination, been dancing with last night. And she had dreamed about him in her sleep this morning, strangely enough reciting his letter to her in a declamation contest for which she was one of the judges.

'So why were you laughing?' said Mrs Rupa Mehra.

Lata said: 'I was thinking about Bishwanath Bhaduri and his ridiculous comments last night at Firpo's.'

'But he is covenanted,' her mother pointed out.

'He told me I was more beautiful than Savita, and that my hair was like a river.'

'You are quite pretty when you put your mind to it, darling,' said her mother reassuringly. 'But your hair was in a bun, wasn't it?'

Lata nodded and yawned. It was past noon. Except when studying for her exams, she rarely felt so sleepy so late in the day. Meenakshi was the one who usually yawned—yawned with decided elegance whenever it suited the occasion.

'Where's Varun?' Lata asked. 'I was supposed to look through the *Gazette* with him—it's got details about the IAS exams. Do you think he's gone to the races too?'

'You are always saying things to upset me, Lata,' exclaimed Mrs Rupa Mehra with sudden indignation. 'I have so many troubles, and then you say things like this. Races. No one cares about my troubles, they are always thinking about their own.'

'What troubles, Ma?' said Lata unsympathetically. 'You are well taken care of, and everyone who knows you loves you.'

Mrs Rupa Mehra looked at Lata sternly. Savita would never have asked such a brutal question. In fact, it was more in the nature of a comment or even judgement than a question. Sometimes, she said to herself, I don't understand Lata at all.

'I have plenty of troubles,' said Mrs Rupa Mehra in a decided manner. 'You know them as well as I do. Look at Meenakshi and how she handles the child. And Varun and his studies—what will happen to him—smoking and drinking and gambling and all that? And you don't get married—isn't that a trouble? And Savita, expecting. And Pran with his illness. And Pran's brother: doing all those things and people talking about it all over Brahmpur. And Meenakshi's sister—people are talking about her also. Do you think I don't have to listen to these things from people? Just yesterday Purobi Ray was gossiping about Kuku. So these are my troubles, and now you've upset me even more. And I am a widow with diabetes,' she added, almost as an afterthought. 'Isn't that a trouble?'

Lata admitted that the last would count as a true trouble.

'And Arun shouts, which is very bad for my blood pressure. And today Hanif has taken a day off so I am expected to do everything myself, even make tea.'

'I'll make it for you, Ma,' said Lata. 'Would you like some now?'

'No, darling, you're yawning, you go and rest,' said Mrs Rupa Mehra, suddenly accommodating. By offering to make tea, Lata had as good as made it for her.

'I don't want to rest, Ma,' said Lata.

'Then why are you yawning, darling?'

'Probably because I've slept too much. Would you like some tea?'

'Not if it's too much trouble.'

Lata went to the kitchen. She had been brought up by her mother 'not to give trouble but to take trouble'. After her father's death, they had lived for a number of years in the house—and therefore in a sense on the charity, however graciously bestowed—of friends, so it was natural that Mrs Rupa Mehra should have been concerned about giving trouble either directly or because of her children. A great deal in the personality of all four children could be traced to these years. The sense of uncertainty and the consciousness of obligation to others outside the family had had its effect on them. Savita had been affected least of all, it seemed; but then with Savita one sometimes got the impression that her kindness and gentleness had come to her as a baby, and that no circumstances of mere environment could have greatly altered them.

'Was Savita sunny even as a baby?' asked Lata a few minutes later when she returned with the tea. Lata knew the answer to her question not only because it was part of Mehra folklore but because there were plenty of photographs to attest to Savita's sunniness: baby pictures of her wolfing down quarter-boiled eggs with a beatific grin, or smiling in her infant sleep. But she asked it anyway, perhaps in order to put her mother in a better mood.

'Yes, very sunny,' said Mrs Rupa Mehra. 'But, darling, you have forgotten my saccharine.'

7.27

A little later Amit and Dipankar dropped by in the Chatterji car, a large white Humber. They could tell that Lata and her mother were slightly surprised to see them.

'Where's Meenakshi?' asked Dipankar, looking around slowly. 'Nice spider lilies outside.'

'She's gone with Arun to the races,' said Mrs Rupa Mehra. 'They are determined to catch pneumonia. We were just having a cup of tea. Lata will make another pot.'

'No, really, it isn't necessary,' said Amit.

'That's all right,' said Lata with a smile. 'The water's hot.'

'How like Meenakshi,' said Amit, a bit irked and a bit amused. 'And she said it would be fine to drop by this afternoon. I suppose we'd better be going. Dipankar has some work in the library of the Asiatic Society.'

'You can't do that,' said Mrs Rupa Mehra hospitably. 'Not without having tea.'

'But didn't she even tell you we'd be coming?'

'No one ever tells me anything,' said Mrs Rupa Mehra automatically.

> 'Setting off without a brolly,
> Meenee-haha goes to Tolly,'

remarked Amit.

Mrs Rupa Mehra frowned. She always found it difficult to hold a coherent conversation with any of the younger Chatterjis.

Dipankar, having looked around once more, asked: 'Where's Varun?' He liked talking to Varun. Even when Varun was bored, he was too nervous to object, and Dipankar construed his silence as interest. Certainly he was a better listener than anyone in Dipankar's own family, who became impatient when he talked about the Skein of Nothingness or the Cessation of Desire. When he had talked about the latter subject at the breakfast table, Kakoli had listed his girlfriends seriatim and stated that she saw no marked Deceleration, let alone Cessation, in his own life so far. Kuku did not see things in the abstract, thought Dipankar. She was still trapped on the plane of contingent actuality.

'Varun's gone out too,' said Lata, returning with the tea. 'Should I tell him to phone you when he returns?'

'If we are to meet, we will meet,' said Dipankar thoughtfully. He then walked into the garden, though it was still drizzling and his shoes would get muddy.

Meenakshi's brothers! thought Mrs Rupa Mehra.

Since Amit was sitting in silence, and Mrs Rupa Mehra abhorred silence, she asked after Tapan.

'Oh, he's very well,' said Amit. 'We've just dropped him and Cuddles at a friend's place. They have a lot of dogs, and Cuddles, oddly enough, gets along with them.'

'Oddly enough' was right, thought Mrs Rupa Mehra. Cuddles had flown through the air on their first meeting and tried to bite her. Luckily, he had been tied to the leg of the piano, and had remained just out of range. Meanwhile Kakoli had continued to play her Chopin without missing a beat. 'Don't mind him,' she had said, 'he means well.' Truly a mad family, reflected Mrs Rupa Mehra.

'And dear Kakoli?' she asked.

'She's singing Schubert with Hans. Or rather, she's playing, he's singing.'

Mrs Rupa Mehra looked stern. This must be the boy whom Purobi Ray had mentioned in connection with Kakoli. Most unsuitable.

'At home, of course,' she said.

'No, at Hans's place. He came to fetch her. A good thing too, otherwise Kuku would have beaten us to the car.'

'Who is with them?' asked Mrs Rupa Mehra.

'The spirit of Schubert,' replied Amit casually.

'For Kuku's sake you *must* be careful,' said Mrs Rupa Mehra, startled as much by his tone as by what he had said. She simply could not understand the Chatterjis' attitude to the risks their sister was running. 'Why can't they sing in Ballygunge?'

'Well, for a start, there's often a conflict between the harmonium and the piano. And I can't write in that din.'

'My husband wrote his railway inspection reports with four children shouting all around him,' said Mrs Rupa Mehra.

'Ma, that's not the same thing at all,' said Lata. 'Amit's a poet. Poetry's different.'

Amit shot her a grateful glance, even though he wondered whether the novel he was engaged on—or even poetry—was different from inspection reports to quite the extent that she imagined.

Dipankar came in from the garden, fairly wet. He did, however, wipe his feet on the mat before he entered. He was reciting, indeed, chanting, a passage from Sri Aurobindo's mystic poem 'Savitri':

> 'Calm heavens of imperishable Light,
> Illumined continents of violet peace,
> Oceans and rivers of the mirth of God
> And griefless countries under purple suns. . . .'

He turned towards them. 'Oh, the tea,' he said, and fell to wondering how much sugar he ought to have.

Amit turned to Lata. 'Did you understand that?' he asked.

Dipankar fixed a look of gentle condescension upon his elder brother. 'Amit Da is a cynic,' he said, 'and believes in Life and Matter. But what about the psychical entity behind the vital and physical mentality?'

'What about it?' said Amit.

'You mean you don't believe in the Supramental?' asked Dipankar, beginning to blink. It was as if Amit had questioned the existence of Saturday—which, as a matter of fact, he was capable of doing.

'I don't know if I believe in it or not,' said Amit. 'I don't know what it is. But it's all right—no, don't—don't tell me.'

'It's the plane on which the Divine meets the individual soul and transforms the individual to a "gnostic being",' explained Dipankar with mild disdain.

'How interesting,' said Mrs Rupa Mehra, who from time to time wondered about the Divine. She began to feel quite positive about Dipankar. Of all the Chatterji children he appeared to be the most serious-minded. He blinked a lot, which was disconcerting, but Mrs Rupa Mehra was willing to make allowances.

'Yes,' said Dipankar, stirring a third spoon of sugar into his tea. 'It is below Brahma and sat-chit-ananda, but acts like a conduit or conductor.'

'Is it sweet enough?' asked Mrs Rupa Mehra with concern.

'I think so,' said Dipankar with an air of appraisal.

Having found a listener, Dipankar now expanded into several channels that interested him. His interests in mysticism were wide-ranging, and included Tantra and the worship of the Mother-Goddess besides the more conceptual 'synthetic' philosophy he had just been expounding. Soon he and Mrs Rupa Mehra were chatting happily about the great seers Ramakrishna and Vivekananda. Half an hour later it was Unity, Duality, and the Trinity, on which Dipankar had recently had a crash course. Mrs Rupa Mehra was trying her best to keep up with Dipankar's free flow of ideas.

'It all comes to a climax in the Pul Mela at Brahmpur,' said Dipankar. 'That is when the astral conjunctions are most powerful. On the night of the full moon of the month of Jeth the gravitational pull of the moon will act with full force upon all our chakras. I don't believe in all the legends, but one can't deny science. I will be going this year, and we can immerse ourselves in the Ganga together. I have already booked my ticket.'

Mrs Rupa Mehra looked doubtful. Then she said:

'That is a good idea. Let us see how things turn out.'

She had just recalled with relief that she would not be in Brahmpur at the time.

7.28

Amit, meanwhile, was talking to Lata about Kakoli. He was telling Lata about her latest beau, the German nutcracker. Kuku had even got him to paint a diplomatically unsuitable Reichsadler above her bathtub. The tub itself had been painted inside and out with turtles, fish, crabs and other watery creatures by Kuku's more artistic friends. Kuku loved the sea, especially at the delta of the Ganga, the Sundarbans. And fish and crabs reminded her of delicious Bengali dishes, and enhanced the wallowing luxuriousness of her bath.

'And your parents didn't object?' asked Lata, recalling the stateliness of the Chatterji mansion.

'My parents may mind,' said Amit, 'but Kuku can twist my father around her little finger. She's his favourite. I think even my mother is jealous of the way he indulges her. A few days ago there was talk of letting her have a telephone of her own rather than just an extension.'

Two telephones in one home seemed utterly extravagant to Lata. She asked why they were necessary, and Amit told her about Kakoli's umbilical linkage to the telephone. He even imitated her characteristic greetings for her A-level, B-level and C-level friends. 'But the phone holds such magic for her that she will readily desert an A-level friend who's taken the trouble to visit her in order to talk to a C-level friend for twenty minutes if he happens to be on the line.'

'I suppose she's very sociable. I've never seen her alone,' said Lata.

'She is,' said Amit.

'Does she mean to be?'

'What do you mean?'

'Is it of her own volition?'

'That's a difficult question,' said Amit.

'Well,' said Lata, picturing the good-humouredly giggling Kakoli surrounded by a large crowd at the party, 'she's very nice, and attractive, and lively. I'm not surprised people like her.'

'Mmm,' said Amit. 'She doesn't call people on the phone herself and ignores messages that come when she's out of the house, so she doesn't show a lot of volition as such. And yet she's always on the phone. They always call back.'

'So she's, well, passively volitional.' Lata looked rather surprised at her own phrase.

'Well, passively volitional—in a lively way,' said Amit, thinking this was an odd way to describe Kuku.

'My mother's getting along well with your brother,' said Lata, with a glance towards them.

'Looks like it,' said Amit with a smile.

'And what sort of music does she like?' asked Lata. 'I mean Kuku.'

Amit thought for a second. 'Despairing music,' he said.

Lata waited for him to elaborate, but he didn't. Instead he said, 'And what kind of music do you like?'

'I?' said Lata.

'You,' said Amit.

'Oh, all sorts. I told you I liked Indian classical music. And don't tell your Ila Kaki, but the one time I went to a ghazal concert, I enjoyed it. And you?'

'All sorts as well.'

'Does Kuku have any reason for liking despairing music?' asked Lata.

'Well, I'm sure she's suffered her share of heartbreak,' said Amit rather callously. 'But she wouldn't have found Hans if someone else hadn't broken her heart.'

Lata looked curiously at Amit, perhaps almost sternly. 'I can hardly believe you're a poet,' she said.

'No. Nor can I,' said Amit. 'Have you read anything by me?'

'No,' said Lata. 'I was sure there'd be a copy of your book in this house, but—'

'And are you fond of poetry?'

'Very fond.'

There was a pause. Then Amit said:

'What have you seen of Calcutta so far?'

'Victoria Memorial and Howrah Bridge.'

'That's all?'

'That's all.'

It was Amit's turn to look stern.

'And what are you doing this afternoon?' he asked.

'Nothing,' said Lata, surprised.

'Good. I'll show you a few places of poetic interest. We've got the car, which is good. And there are a couple of umbrellas in the car—so we won't get wet when we walk around the cemetery.'

But even though it was 'just Amit', as Lata pointed out, whom she would be going out with, Mrs Rupa Mehra unreasonably insisted on someone accompanying them. Amit for Mrs Rupa Mehra was merely Meenakshi's brother—and not a risk in any sense of the word. But, well, he was a young man, and for form's sake it was important that someone be with them, so that they would not be seen alone together. On the other hand, Mrs Rupa Mehra was prepared to be fairly flexible as to who the chaperon could be. She herself was certainly not going to walk around with them in the rain. But Dipankar would do.

'I can't go with you, Dada,' said Dipankar. 'I have to go to the library.'

'Well, I'll phone Tapan at his friend's place and see what he has to say,' said Amit.

Tapan agreed on the condition that Cuddles could accompany them—on a leash of course.

Since Cuddles was nominally Dipankar's dog, his sanction was required as well. This he readily gave.

And so, on a warm, rainy Saturday afternoon, Amit, Lata, Dipankar (who would go with them as far as the Asiatic Society), Tapan and Cuddles went for a drive and a walk with the acquiescence of Mrs Rupa Mehra, who was relieved that Lata was at last behaving more like her normal self again.

7.29

When the mass of the British left India at Independence, they left behind them a great number of pianos, and one of them, a large, black, tropicalized

Steinway, stood in the drawing room of Hans Sieber's apartment in Queens Mansions. Kakoli was seated at it and Hans was standing behind her, singing from the same score that she was playing from, and feeling extremely happy although the songs that he was singing were extremely gloomy.

Hans adored Schubert. They were singing through *Winterreise*, a snowbound song cycle of rejection and dejection that ends in madness. Outside, the warm Calcutta rain came down in sheets. It flooded the streets, gurgled down the inadequate drainage system, poured into the Hooghly, and finally flowed down into the Indian Ocean. In an earlier incarnation it could well have been the soft German snow that had whirled around the memory-haunted traveller, and in a later one it might well become part of the icy brook into whose surface he had carved his initials and those of his faithless beloved. Or possibly even his hot tears that threatened to melt all the snow of winter.

Kakoli had not at first been ecstatic about Schubert, her tastes running more to Chopin, whom she played with heavy rubato and gloom. But now that she was accompanying Hans's singing she had grown to like Schubert more and more.

The same was true about her feeling for Hans, whose excessive courtliness had at first amused her, then irked her, and now reassured her. Hans, for his part, was as smitten by Kuku as any of her mushrooms had ever been. But he felt that she took him lightly, only returning one in three of his calls. If he had known of her even poorer rate of return with other friends, he would have realized how highly she valued him.

Of the twenty-four lieder in the song cycle they had now arrived at the last song but one, 'The Mock Suns'. Hans was singing this cheerfully and briskly. Kuku was dragging the pace on the piano. It was a tussle of interpretation.

'No, no, Hans,' said Kakoli when he leaned over and turned the page to the final song. 'You sang that too fast.'

'Too fast?' said Hans. 'I felt the accompaniment was not very brisk. You wanted to go slower, yes? "Ach, meine Sonnen seid ihr nicht!"' He dragged it out. 'So?'

'Yes.'

'Well, he is mad, Kakoli, you know.' The real reason why Hans had sung the song so energetically was Kuku's perfect presence.

'*Almost* mad,' said Kuku. 'In the next song he goes quite mad. You can sing that as fast as you like.'

'But that last song must be very slow,' said Hans. 'Like this—' And he played out what he meant with his right hand in the treble reaches of the piano. His hand touched Kuku's for a second at the end of the first line. 'There, you see, Kakoli, he is resigned to his fate.'

'So he's suddenly stopped being mad?' said Kakoli. What nonsense, she thought.

'Maybe he is mad and resigned to his fate. Mixed.'

Kuku tried it, and shook her head. 'I'd go to sleep,' she said.

'So now, Kakoli, you think "The Mock Suns" must be slow and "The Organ-grinder" must be fast.'

'Exactly.' Kakoli liked it when Hans spoke her name; he pronounced the three syllables with equal weight. Very rarely did he call her Kuku.

'And I think "The Mock Suns" must be fast and "The Organ-grinder" must be slow,' continued Hans.

'Yes,' said Kuku. How dreadfully incompatible we are, she thought. And everything should be perfect—just perfect. If it wasn't perfect it was awful.

'So each of us thinks that one song must be fast and one slow,' said Hans with triumphant logic. This seemed to prove to him that, given an adjustment or two, he and Kakoli were unusually compatible.

Kuku looked at Hans's square and handsome face, which was glowing with pleasure. 'You see,' said Hans, 'most times I hear it, people sing both slow.'

'Both slow?' said Kuku. 'That would never do.'

'No, never do,' said Hans. 'Shall we take it again from there with slower tempo, like you suggest?'

'Yes,' said Kakoli. 'But what on earth does it mean? Or in the sky? The song, I mean.'

'There are three suns,' explained Hans, 'and two go and then one is left.'

'Hans,' said Kakoli. 'I think you are very lovable. And your subtraction is accurate. But you haven't added to my understanding.'

Hans blushed. 'I think the two suns are the girl and her mother, and he himself is the third.'

Kakoli stared at him. 'Her mother?' she said incredulously. Perhaps Hans had too stodgy a soul after all.

Hans looked doubtful. 'Maybe not,' he admitted. 'But who else?' He reflected that the mother had appeared somewhere in the song cycle, though much earlier.

'I don't understand it at all. It's a mystery,' said Kakoli. 'But it's certainly not the mother.' She sensed that a major crisis was brewing. This was almost as bad as Hans's dislike of Bengali food.

'Yes?' said Hans. 'A mystery?'

'Anyway, Hans, you sing very well,' said Kuku. 'I like it when you sing about heartbreak. It sounds very professional. We must do this again next week.'

Hans blushed once more, and offered Kakoli a drink. Although he was expert at kissing the hands of married women, he had not kissed Kakoli yet. He did not think she would approve of it; but he was wrong.

7.30

When they got to the Park Street Cemetery, Amit and Lata got out of the car. Dipankar decided he'd wait in the car with Tapan, since they were only going to be a few minutes and, besides, there were only two umbrellas.

They walked through a wrought-iron gate. The cemetery was laid out in a grid with narrow avenues between clusters of tombs. A few soggy palm trees stood here and there in clumps, and the cawing of crows interspersed with thunder and the noise of rain. It was a melancholy place. Founded in 1767, it had filled up quickly with the European dead. Young and old alike—mostly victims of the feverish climate—lay buried here, compacted under great slabs and pyramids, mausolea and cenotaphs, urns and columns, all decayed and greyed now by ten generations of Calcutta heat and rain. So densely packed were the tombs that it was in places difficult to walk between them. Rich, rain-fed grass grew between the graves, and the rain poured down ceaselessly over it all. Compared to Brahmpur or Banaras, Allahabad or Agra, Lucknow or Delhi, Calcutta could hardly be considered to have a history, but the climate had bestowed on its comparative recency a desolate and unromantic sense of slow ruin.

'Why have you brought me here?' asked Lata.

'Do you know Landor?'

'Landor? No.'

'You've never heard of Walter Savage Landor?' asked Amit, disappointed.

'Oh yes. Walter Savage Landor. Of course. "Rose Aylmer, whom these watchful eyes".'

'Wakeful. Well, she lies buried here. As does Thackeray's father and one of Dickens's sons, and the original for Byron's *Don Juan*,' said Amit, with a proper Calcuttan pride.

'Really?' said Lata. 'Here? Here in Calcutta?' It was as if she had suddenly heard that Hamlet was the Prince of Delhi. 'Ah, what avails the sceptred race!'

'Ah, what the form divine!' continued Amit.

'What every virtue, every grace!' cried Lata with sudden enthusiasm.

'Rose Aylmer, all were thine.'

A roll of thunder punctuated the two stanzas.

'Rose Aylmer, whom these watchful eyes—' continued Lata.

'Wakeful.'

'Sorry, wakeful. Rose Aylmer, whom these wakeful eyes—'

'May weep, but never see,' said Amit, brandishing his umbrella.

'A night of memories and sighs.'

'I consecrate to thee.'

Amit paused. 'Ah, lovely poem, lovely poem,' he said, looking delightedly at Lata. He paused again, then said: 'Actually, it's "A night of memories and of sighs".'

'Isn't that what I said?' asked Lata, thinking of nights—or parts of nights—that she herself had recently spent in a similar fashion.

'No. You left out the second "of".'

'A night of memories and sighs. Of memories and of sighs. I see what you mean. But does it make such a difference?'

'Yes, it makes a difference. Not all the difference in the world but, well, a difference. A mere "of"; conventionally permitted to rhyme with "love". But she is in her grave, and oh, the difference to him.'

They walked on. Walking two abreast was not possible, and their umbrellas complicated matters among the cluttered monuments. Not that her tomb was so far away—it was at the first intersection—but Amit had chosen a circuitous route. It was a small tomb capped by a conical pillar with swirling lines; Landor's poem was inscribed on a plaque on one side beneath her name and age and a few lines of pedestrian pentameter:

> What was her fate? Long, long before her hour,
> Death called her tender soul by break of bliss
> From the first blossoms, from the buds of joy;
> Those few our noxious fate unblasted leaves
> In this inclement clime of human life.

Lata looked at the tomb and then at Amit, who appeared to be deep in thought. She thought to herself: he has a comfortable sort of face.

'So she was twenty when she died?' said Lata.

'Yes. Just about your age. They met in the Swansea Circulating Library. And then her parents took her out to India. Poor Landor. Noble Savage. Go, lovely Rose.'

'What did she die of? The sorrow of parting?'

'A surfeit of pineapples.'

Lata looked shocked.

'I can see you don't believe me, but oh, 'tis true, 'tis true,' said Amit. 'We'd better go back,' he continued. 'They will not wait for us—and who can wonder? You're drenched.'

'And so are you.'

'Her tomb,' continued Amit, 'looks like an upside-down ice-cream cone.'

Lata said nothing. She was rather annoyed with Amit.

After Dipankar had been dropped off at the Asiatic Society, Amit asked the driver to take them down Chowringhee to the Presidency Hospital. As they passed the Victoria Memorial he said:

'So the Victoria Memorial and Howrah Bridge is all you know and all you need to know of Calcutta?'

'Not all I need to know,' said Lata. 'All I happen to know. And Firpo's and The Golden Slipper. And the New Market.'

Tapan greeted this news with a Kakoli-couplet:

> 'Cuddles, Cuddles, gentle dog,
> Go and bite Sir Stuart Hogg.'

Lata looked mystified. Since neither Tapan nor Amit explained the reference, she went on: 'But Arun has said we'll go for a picnic to the Botanical Gardens.'

'Under the spreading banyan tree,' said Amit.

'It's the biggest in the world,' said Tapan, with a Calcutta chauvinism equal to his brother's.

'And will you go there in the rains?' said Amit.

'Well, if not now, then at Christmas.'

'So you'll be back at Christmas?' asked Amit, pleased.

'I think so,' said Lata.

'Good, good,' said Amit. 'There are lots of concerts of Indian classical music in winter. And Calcutta is very pleasant. I'll show you around. I'll dispel your ignorance. I'll expand your mind. I'll teach you Bangla!'

Lata laughed. 'I'll look forward to it,' she said.

Cuddles gave a blood-curdling growl.

'What's the matter with you now?' asked Tapan. 'Will you hold this for a second?' he asked Lata, handing her the leash.

Cuddles subsided into silence.

Tapan bent down and looked carefully at Cuddles' ear.

'He hasn't had his walk yet,' said Tapan. 'And I haven't had my milkshake.'

'You're right,' said Amit. 'Well, the rain's let up. Let's just look at the second great poetic relic and then we'll go out on to the Maidan and the two of you can get as muddy as you like. And on the way back we'll stop at Keventers.' He continued, turning to Lata: 'I was thinking of taking you to Rabindranath Tagore's house in North Calcutta, but it's quite far and a bit slushy and it can wait for another day. But you haven't told me if there's anything particular that you'd like to see.'

'I'd like to see the university area some day,' said Lata. 'College Street and all that. But nothing else really. Are you sure you can spare the time?'

'Yes,' said Amit. 'And here we are. It was in that small building there that Sir Ronald Ross discovered what caused malaria.' He pointed to a plaque affixed to the gate. 'And he wrote a poem to celebrate it.'

Everyone got down this time, though Tapan and Cuddles took no interest in the plaque. Lata read it through with a great deal of curiosity. She was not used to the comprehensible writings of scientists, and did not know what to expect.

This day relenting God
Hath placed within my hand
A wondrous thing; and God
Be praised. At his command,

Seeking his secret deeds
With tears and toiling breath,
I find thy cunning seeds
O million-murdering death.

I know this little thing
A myriad men will save.
O death where is thy sting?
Thy victory, O grave?

Lata read it a second time. 'What do you think of it?' asked Amit.

'Not much,' said Lata.

'Really? Why?'

'I'm not sure,' said Lata. 'I just don't. "Tears and toiling", "million-murdering"—it's too alliterative. And why should "God" be allowed to rhyme with "God"? Do you like it?'

'Well, yes, in a way,' said Amit. 'I do like it. But equally I can't defend that feeling. Perhaps I find it moving that a Surgeon-Major should write so fervently and with such religious force about something he'd done. I like the quaint chiasmus at the end. Ah, I've just created a pentameter,' he said, pleased.

Lata was frowning slightly, still looking at the plaque, and Amit could see she was not convinced.

'You're quite severe in your judgement,' he said with a smile. 'I wonder what you'd say about my poems.'

'Maybe some day I'll read them,' said Lata. 'I can't imagine the kind of poetry you write. You seem so cheerful and cynical.'

'I'm certainly cynical,' said Amit.

'Do you ever recite your poetry?'

'Almost never,' said Amit.

'Don't people ask you to?'

'Yes, all the time,' said Amit. 'Have you listened to poets reading their work? It's usually awful.'

Lata thought back to the Brahmpur Literary Society and smiled broadly. Then she thought again of Kabir. She felt confused and sad.

Amit saw the swift change of expression on her face. He hesitated for a few seconds, wanting to ask her what had brought it about, but before he could do so she asked, pointing to the plaque:

'How did he discover it?'

'Oh,' said Amit, 'he sent his servant to get some mosquitoes, then got the mosquitoes to bite him—his servant, that is—and when he got malaria soon afterwards, Ross realized that it was mosquitoes that caused it. O million-murdering death.'

'Almost a million and one,' said Lata.

'Yes, I see what you mean. But people have always treated their servants strangely. Landor of the memories and sighs once threw his cook out of a window.'

'I'm not sure I like Calcutta poets,' said Lata.

7.31

After the Maidan and the milkshake, Amit asked Lata if she had time for a cup of tea at his house before returning home. Lata said she did. She liked the fertile turmoil of that house, the piano, the books, the verandah, the large garden. When Amit asked that tea for two be sent up to his room, the servant Bahadur, who took a proprietorial interest in Amit, asked him if there was someone else to drink it with him.

'Oh no,' said Amit, 'I'm going to drink both cups myself.'

'You mustn't mind him,' said Amit later, when Bahadur had looked at Lata appraisingly as he set the tea tray down. 'He thinks that I plan to marry everyone I have tea with. One or two?'

'Two please,' said Lata. She continued mischievously, since the question was riskless: 'And do you?'

'Oh, not so far,' said Amit. 'But he doesn't believe it. Our servants haven't given up trying to run our lives. Bahadur has seen me staring at the moon at odd hours, and wants to cure me by getting me married within the year. Dipankar has been dreaming of surrounding his hut with papaya and banana plants, and the mali has been lecturing him about herbaceous borders. The Mugh cook almost gave notice because Tapan, when he came back from boarding school, insisted on eating lamb chops and mango ice-cream for breakfast for a whole week.'

'And Kuku?'

'Kuku drives the driver cuckoo.'

'What a crazy family you are,' said Lata.

'On the contrary,' said Amit. 'We're a hotbed of sanity.'

7.32

When Lata returned home towards evening Mrs Rupa Mehra did not ask her for a detailed account of where she had been and what she had seen. She was too distressed to do so. Arun and Varun had had a grand flare-up, and the smell of combustion was still thick in the air.

Varun had returned to the house with his winnings in his pocket. He was not drunk yet, but it was clear where his windfall was going to go. Arun had told him he was irresponsible; he should contribute the winnings to the family kitty and never go to the racetrack again. He was wasting his life, and didn't know the meaning of sacrifice and hard work. Varun, who knew that Arun had been at the races himself, had told him what he could do with his advice. Arun, purple-faced, had ordered him to get out of the house. Mrs Rupa Mehra had wept and pleaded and acted as an exacerbating intermediary. Meenakshi had said she couldn't live in such a noisy family and had threatened to go back to Ballygunge. She was glad, she said, that it was Hanif's day off. Aparna had started bawling. Even her ayah had not been able to pacify her.

Aparna's bawling had calmed everyone down, perhaps even made them feel a little ashamed. Now Meenakshi and Arun had just left for a party, and Varun was sitting in his small half-room, muttering to himself.

'I wish Savita was here,' said Mrs Rupa Mehra. 'Only she can control Arun when he is in one of his moods.'

'It's good she isn't here, Ma,' said Lata. 'Anyway, Varun's the one I'm more worried about. I'm going to see how he is.' It seemed to her that her advice to him in Brahmpur had been futile.

When she knocked at his door and entered, she found him sprawled on the bed with the *Gazette of India* lying open in front of him.

'I've decided to improve myself,' Varun said in a nervous manner, looking this way and that. 'I'm going through the rules for the IAS exams. They're to be held this September, and I haven't even begun studying. Arun Bhai thinks I'm irresponsible, and he's right. I'm terribly irresponsible. I'm wasting my life. Daddy would have been ashamed of me. Look at me, Luts, just look at me. What am I?' He was growing more and more agitated. 'I'm a bloody fool,' he concluded, with the Arun-like condemnation pronounced in an Arun-like tone of dismissal. 'Bloody fool!' he repeated for good measure. 'Don't you think so too?' he asked Lata hopefully.

'Shall I make you some tea?' asked Lata, wondering why he, in the manner of Meenakshi, had called her 'Luts'. Varun was far too easily led.

Varun looked gloomily at the Pay Scales, the lists of Optional and Compulsory Papers, the Standard and Syllabus of the Examinations, even the List of Scheduled Castes.

'Yes. If you think that's best,' he said at last.

When Lata came back with the tea, she found him plunged into renewed despair. He had just read the paragraph on the Viva Voce:

> The candidate will be interviewed by a Board who will have before them a record of his / her career. He / she will be asked questions on

> matters of general interest. The object of the interview is to assess his / her suitability for the Service for which he / she is entered, and in framing their assessment the Board will attach particular importance to his / her intelligence and alertness, his / her vigour and strength of character and his / her potential qualities of leadership.

'Read this!' said Varun. 'Just read this.' Lata picked up the *Gazette* and began to read it with interest.

'I don't have a chance,' continued Varun. 'I have such a poor personality. I don't make a good impression on anyone. I don't make an impression at all. And the interview counts for 400 marks. No. I may as well accept it. I'm not fit for the civil service. They want people with qualities of leadership—not fifth-class bloody fools like me.'

'Here, have some tea, Varun Bhai,' said Lata.

Varun accepted with tears in his eyes. 'But what else can I do?' he asked her. 'I can't teach, I can't join a managing agency, all the Indian business firms are family run, I don't have the guts to set up in business on my own—or to get the money to do so. And Arun shouts at me all the time. I've been reading *How to Win Friends and Influence People*,' he confided. 'To improve my personality.'

'Is it working?' asked Lata.

'I don't know,' said Varun. 'I can't even judge that.'

'Varun Bhai, why didn't you listen to what I told you that day at the zoo?' asked Lata.

'I did. I'm going out with my friends now. And see where that has led me!' said Varun.

There was a pause. They sipped tea silently together in the little room. Then Lata, who had been scanning the *Gazette*, sat up with sudden indignation. 'Listen to this,' she said. '"For the Indian Administrative Service and the Indian Police Service the Government of India may not select a woman candidate who is married and might require a woman to resign from the service in the event of her marrying subsequently."'

'Oh,' said Varun, who was not sure what was wrong with that. Jason was, or had been, a policeman, and Varun wondered whether any woman, married or not, should be permitted to do his kind of brutal work.

'And it gets worse,' continued Lata. '"For the Indian Foreign Service a woman candidate is eligible only if she is unmarried or a widow without encumbrances. If such a candidate is selected, she will be appointed on the express condition that she might be called upon to resign the service on marriage or remarriage."'

'Without encumbrances?' said Varun.

'That means children, I suppose. Presumably you can be a widower with encumbrances and handle both your family life and your work. But not if you're a widow. . . . I'm sorry, I've taken over the *Gazette*.'

'Oh, no, no, you read it. I've suddenly remembered I must go out. I promised.'

'Promised whom?' said Lata. 'Sajid and Jason?'

'No, not exactly,' said Varun shiftily. 'Anyway, a promise is a promise and never should be broken.' He laughed weakly; he was quoting one of his mother's adages. 'But I'll tell them that I can't see them any more. I'm too busy studying. Will you talk to Ma for a little while?'

'While you slip out?' said Lata. 'No fears.'

'Please, Luts, what can I say to her? She's bound to ask me where I'm going.'

'Tell her you're going to get disgustingly drunk on Shamshu.'

'It won't be Shamshu today,' said Varun, cheering up.

After he had left, Lata went to her room with the *Gazette*. Kabir had said that he wanted to sit for the IFS exams after he had got his degree. She had no doubt that if he got to that stage, he would do well in the interview. He certainly had leadership qualities and vigour. She could imagine what a good impression he would make on the Board. She could picture his alertness, his open smile, the ready way in which he would admit to not knowing something.

She looked through the rules, wondering which optional subjects he might select. One was described simply as: 'World History. 1789 to 1939.'

Once more she wondered whether she should reply to his letter, and once more she wondered what she could possibly say. She looked idly down the list of optionals till her eye fell on an item a few lines further on. At first it puzzled her, then it made her laugh, and finally it helped somewhat to restore her equilibrium. It read as follows:

> Philosophy. The subject covers the history and the theory of Ethics, Eastern and Western, and includes moral standards and their application, the problems of moral order and progress of Society and the State, and theories of punishment. It includes also the history of Western Philosophy and should be studied with special reference

to the problems of space, time and causality, evolution and value and the nature of God.

'Child's play,' said Lata to herself, and decided to go and talk to her mother, who was sitting alone in the next room. All of a sudden she began to feel quite light-headed.

7.33

My sweet Rat, my sweetest sweetest Rat,

I dreamed of you all last night. I woke up twice and each time it was from a dream of you. I don't know why you insist on coming into my mind so often, and inflicting memories and sighs on me. I was determined after our last meeting not to think of you, and your letter annoys me still. How can you write so coolly when you know what you mean to me and what I thought I meant to you?

I was in a room—at first it was a dark room with no way out. After a while a window appeared, and I saw a sundial through it. Then, somehow, the room was lit, and there was furniture in it—and before I knew it, it was the room at 20 Hastings Road, complete with Mr Nowrojee and Shrimati Supriya Joshi and Dr Makhijani, but, strangely enough, there was no door anywhere, so I assumed that they must have climbed in through the window. And how had I come in myself? Anyway, before I could puzzle all this out, a door did appear just where it should have been, and someone knocked at it—casually, but impatiently. I knew it was you—though I've never heard you knock on a door, in fact we've only met out of doors except that once—and, yes, also at Ustad Majeed Khan's concert. I was convinced it was you, and my heart started beating so fast I could hardly bear it, I was looking forward to seeing you so much. Then it turned out to be someone else, and I breathed a sigh of relief.

Dearest Kabir, I am not going to mail this letter, so you needn't worry about my becoming passionately fond of you and disturbing all your plans for the Indian Foreign Service and Cambridge and the rest of it. If you think I was unreasonable, well, perhaps I was, but I've never been in love before and it is certainly an unreasonable feeling too—and one that I never want to feel again for you or for anyone.

I read your letter sitting among spider-lilies, but all I could think about was gulmohur flowers at my feet, and your telling me that I'd forget about all my troubles in five years. Oh, yes, and shaking kamini flowers out of my hair and crying.

The second dream—well, why don't I tell you, since it won't reach your eyes anyway. We were lying together by ourselves on a boat far away from both shores, and you were kissing me, and—oh, it was absolute bliss. Then later you got up and said, 'I've got to go now and swim four lengths; if I do, our team will win the match, and if I don't it won't,' and you left me alone in the boat. My heart sank, but you were quite determined to leave. Luckily the boat didn't sink, and I rowed it alone to the shore. I think I have finally got rid of you. At least I hope I have. I have decided to remain a spinster without encumbrances, and to devote my time to thinking about space, time and causality, evolution and value and the nature of God.

So Godspeed, sweet prince, sweet Rat-prince, and may you emerge near the dhobi-ghat, safe but bedraggled, and do brilliantly in life.

With all my love too, my darling Kabir,
Lata.

Lata folded the letter into an envelope, and wrote Kabir's name on it. Then, instead of writing his address, she wrote his name here and there on the envelope a few more times for good measure. Then she drew a stamp on the corner of the envelope ('Waste not, want not') and marked it 'Postage Due'. Finally, she tore the whole thing into tiny pieces and began crying.

If I achieve nothing else in life, thought Lata, I shall at least have turned into one of the World's Great Neurotics.

7.34

Amit asked Lata to lunch and tea the next day at the Chatterjis.

'I thought I'd ask you over so that you could see us Brahmos at our clannish best,' he said. 'Ila Chattopadhyay, whom you met the other day, will be there, as will an aunt and uncle on my mother's side and all their brood. And of course now you're part of the clan by marriage.'

So the next day at Amit's house they sat down to a traditional Bengali meal, unlike the party fare of the previous week. Amit assumed that Lata had eaten this sort of food before. But when she saw a small helping of karela and rice—and nothing else—in front of her, she appeared so surprised that he had to tell her that there were other courses coming.

It was odd, thought Amit, that she shouldn't have known. Before Arun and Meenakshi had got married, though he himself had been in England, he knew that the Mehras had been invited once or twice to the Chatterjis'. But perhaps it hadn't been to this sort of meal.

Lunch had begun a little late. They had waited for Dr Ila Chattopadhyay, but had eventually decided to eat because the children were hungry. Amit's uncle Mr Ganguly was an extremely taciturn man whose energies went entirely into eating. His jowls worked vigorously, swiftly, almost twice a second, and only occasionally pausing, while his mild, bland, bovine eyes looked at his hosts and fellow-guests who were doing the talking. His wife was a fat, highly emotional woman who wore a great deal of sindoor in her hair and had a very large bindi of equally brilliant red in the middle of her forehead. She was a shocking gossip and in between extracting fine fishbones from her large paan-stained mouth she impaled the reputations of all her neighbours and any of her relatives who were not present. Embezzlement, drunkenness, gangsterism, incest: whatever could be stated was stated and whatever could not be was implied. Mrs Chatterji was shocked, pretended to be even more shocked than she was, and enjoyed her company greatly. The only thing that worried her was what Mrs Ganguly would say about their family—especially about Kuku—once she had left the house.

For Kuku was behaving as freely as she always did, encouraged by Tapan and Amit. Soon Dr Ila Chattopadhyay turned up ('I am such a stupid woman, I always forget lunch timings. Am I late? Stupid question. Hello. Hello. Hello. Oh, you again? Lalita? Lata? I never remember names') and things became even more boisterous.

Bahadur announced that there was a phone call for Kakoli.

'Tell whoever it is that Kuku will take it after lunch,' said her father.

'Oh, Baba!' Kuku turned a liquid gaze on her father.

'Who is it?' Mr Justice Chatterji asked Bahadur.

'That German Sahib.'

Mrs Ganguly's intelligent, pig-like eyes darted from face to face.

'Oh, Baba, it's Hans. I must go.' The 'Hans' was pleadingly elongated.

Mr Justice Chatterji nodded slightly, and Kuku leapt up and ran to the phone.

When Kakoli returned to the table, everyone except the children turned towards her. The children were consuming large quantities of tomato chutney, and their mother was not even reproving them, so keen was she to hear what Kuku was going to say.

But Kuku had turned from love to food. 'Oh, gulab-jamun,' she said, imitating Biswas Babu, 'and the chumchum! And mishti doi. Oh—the bhery mhemory makesh my shallybhery juishes to phlow.'

'Kuku.' Mr Justice Chatterji was seriously displeased.

'Sorry, Baba. Sorry. Sorry. Let me join in the gossip. What were you talking about in my absence?'

'Have a sandesh, Kuku,' said her mother.

'So, Dipankar,' said Dr Ila Chattopadhyay. 'Have you changed your subject yet?'

'I can't, Ila Kaki,' said Dipankar.

'Why not? The sooner you make the move the better. There isn't a single decent human being I know who is an economist. Why can't you change?'

'Because I've already graduated.'

'Oh!' Dr Ila Chattopadhyay appeared temporarily floored. 'And what are you going to do with yourself?'

'I'll decide in a week or two. I'll think things out when I'm at the Pul Mela. It'll be a time for appraising myself in the spiritual and intellectual context.'

Dr Ila Chattopadhyay, breaking a sandesh in half, said: 'Really, Lata, have you ever heard such unconvincing prevarication? I've never understood what "the spiritual context" means. Spiritual matters are an utter waste of time. I'd rather spend my time listening to the kind of gossip your aunt purveys and that your mother pretends to suffer through than go to something like the Pul Mela. Isn't it very dirty?' She turned to Dipankar. 'All those millions of pilgrims crowded along a strip of sand just under the Brahmpur Fort? And doing—doing everything there.'

'I don't know,' said Dipankar. 'I've never been. But it's supposed to be well organized. They even have a District Magistrate allocated especially for the great Pul Mela every sixth year. This year's a sixth year, so bathing is especially auspicious.'

'The Ganges is an absolutely filthy river,' said Dr Ila Chattopadhyay. 'I hope you don't propose to bathe in it. . . . Oh, do stop blinking, Dipankar, it ruins my concentration.'

'If I bathe,' said Dipankar, 'I'll wash away not only my own sins but those of six generations above me. That might even include you, Ila Kaki.'

'God forbid,' said Dr Ila Chattopadhyay.

Turning to Lata, Dipankar said: 'You should come too, Lata. After all, you're from Brahmpur.'

'I'm not really from Brahmpur,' said Lata, with a glance at Dr Ila Chattopadhyay.

'Where are you from, then?' asked Dipankar.

'Nowhere now,' said Lata.

'Anyway,' continued Dipankar earnestly, 'I think I've convinced your mother to come.'

'I doubt it,' said Lata, smiling at the thought of Mrs Rupa Mehra and Dipankar guiding each other through the Pul Mela crowds and the labyrinths of time and causality. 'She won't be in Brahmpur at the time. But where will you live in Brahmpur?'

'On the sands—I'll find a place in someone's tent,' said Dipankar optimistically.

'Don't you know anyone in Brahmpur?'

'No. Well, Savita, of course. And there's an old Mr Maitra who's related to us somehow, whom I met once as a child.'

'You must look up Savita and her husband when you get there,' said Lata. 'I'll write and tell Pran you'll be coming. You can always stay with them if the sand runs out. And it's useful anyway to have an address and phone number in a strange town.'

'Thank you,' said Dipankar. 'Oh, there's a lecture at the Ramakrishna Mission tonight on Popular Religion and its Philosophical Dimensions. Why don't you come? It's bound to cover the Pul Mela.'

'Really, Dipankar, you are more of an idiot than I thought,' said Dr Ila Chattopadhyay to her nephew. 'Why am I wasting my time on you? Don't you waste your time on him either,' she advised Lata. 'I'm going to talk to Amit. Where is he?'

Amit was in the garden. He had been forced by the children to show them the frog spawn in the lily pond.

7.35

The hall was almost full. There must have been about two hundred people, though Lata noticed that there were only about five women. The lecture, which was in English, started on time, at seven o'clock. Professor Dutta-Ray (who had a bad cough) introduced the speaker, informing the audience of the young luminary's biography and credentials, and continuing for a few minutes to speculate about what he would say.

The young speaker stood up. He did not look at all like someone who had been, as the professor had stated, a sadhu for five years. He had a round, anxious face. He was wearing a well-starched kurta and dhoti, and there were two pens in the pocket of his kurta. He did not speak about Popular Religion and its Philosophical Dimensions, though he did mention the Pul Mela once, elliptically, as 'this great concourse that will be assembling on the banks of the Ganga to lave itself in the light of the full moon'. For the most part he treated the patient audience to a speech of exceptional banality. He soared and veered over a vast terrain, and assumed that his droppings would make an intelligible pattern.

Every few sentences, he stretched his arms out in a gentle, all-inclusive gesture as if he were a bird spreading its wings.

Dipankar looked rapt, Amit bored, Lata perplexed.

The speaker was now in full flight: 'Humanity must be made incarnate in the present . . . shatter the horizons of the mind . . . the challenge is interior . . . birth is a remarkable thing . . . the bird feels the vast quivering of the leaf . . . a certain relation of sacrality can be maintained between the popular and the philosophical . . . an open-ended mind through which life can flow, through which one can hear the birdsong, the impulse of space-time.'

Finally, an hour down the line, he came to the Great Question:

'Can humanity even tell where a newer inspiration will emerge? Can we penetrate those great darknesses within ourselves where symbols are born? I say that our rites, call them popular if you will, do penetrate this darkness. The alternative is the death of the mind, and not "re-death" or punarmrityu, which is the first reference to "rebirth" in our scriptures, but ultimate death, the death of ignorance. Let me then emphasize to you all'—he stretched his arms out towards the audience—'that, let objectors say what they will, it is only by preserving the ancient forms of sacrality, however perverse, however superstitious they may seem to the philosophical eye, that we can maintain our elementality, our ethos, our evolution, our very essence.' He sat down.

'Our eggshells,' said Amit to Lata.

The audience applauded guardedly.

But now the venerable Professor Dutta-Ray, who had introduced the speaker so paternally at first, got up and, shooting glances of undisguised hostility at him, proceeded to demolish what he saw as the theories he had just propounded. (It was clear that the Professor saw himself as one of the 'objectors' referred to in the speech.) But were there any theories in the speech at all? There was certainly a tenor, but it was difficult to demolish a tenor. At any rate, the Professor tried to, his voice, mild at first, rising to this hoarse-throated battle cry:

'Let us not deceive ourselves! For whilst it may often be the case that the theses are intrinsically plausible, they are by the same token impossible to substantiate or refute with more than illustrative evidence; indeed, it is in practice difficult to know whether they come into the orbit of reference of the key question, which, although it may well shed light on the tendency, can scarcely tell us whether an answer can be couched convincingly in terms of what might broadly be called its evolving patterns; in this perspective, then, though admittedly the theory may appear—to the ignorant eye—well founded, it is not compelling as an analysis of the basic difficulty, which traces to considerations we must descry elsewhere; to be quite specific, its failure to explain must make it seem irrelevant even if it does not, as it were, actually refute it; but to stipulate this is to remove the underpinnings of the entire analytical framework, and the most pertinent and cogent argument must be abandoned.'

He looked with triumph and malice at the speaker before continuing: 'As a broad generalization, one might tentatively hazard a guess therefore, that, all other things being equal, one should not make particular generalizations when general particularizations are equally available—and available to far less idle effect.'

Dipankar was looking shocked, Amit bored, Lata puzzled.

Several people in the audience wanted to ask questions, but Amit had had enough. Lata was willingly, and Dipankar unwillingly, drawn out of the hall. She was feeling slightly dizzy, and not only because of the rarefied abstractions she had just breathed. It had been hot and stuffy inside.

For a minute or two none of them spoke. Lata, who had noticed Amit's boredom, expected him to show his annoyance, and Dipankar to expostulate. Instead, Amit merely said:

'When faced with something like that, if I am caught short without paper and pencil, I amuse myself by taking any word that the speaker has used—like "bird" or "cloth" or "central" or "blue"—and try to imagine different varieties of them.'

'Even words like "central"?' asked Lata, amused by the idea.

'Even those,' said Amit. 'Most words are fertile.'

He felt in his pocket for an anna, and bought a small, fragrant garland of fresh white bela flowers from a vendor. 'Here,' he said, giving it to Lata.

Lata, very pleased, said 'Thank you,' and after inhaling its fragrance with a delighted smile, put it unselfconsciously in her hair.

There was something so pleasing, natural and unpretentious about her gesture that Amit found himself thinking: She may be more intelligent than my sisters, but I'm glad she's not as sophisticated. She's the nicest girl I've met for a long time.

Lata for her part was thinking how much she liked Meenakshi's family. They brought her out of herself and her stupid, self-created misery. In their company it was possible to enjoy, after a fashion, even such a lecture as she had just sat through.

7.36

Mr Justice Chatterji was sitting in his study. In front of him lay a half-completed judgement. On his desk stood a black-and-white photograph of his parents, and another of himself, his wife, and their five children that had been taken many years ago by a fashionable Calcutta studio. Kakoli, wilful child, had insisted on including her teddy bear; Tapan had been too small at the time to have had an articulate will at all.

The case involved the confirmation of the death sentence on six members of a gang of dacoits. Such cases caused Mr Justice Chatterji a great deal of pain. He did not like criminal work at all, and looked forward to being reallocated civil work, which was both more intellectually stimulating and less distressing. There was no question that these six men had been found guilty according to law and that the sentence of the Sessions Judge was not unreasonable or perverse. And so Mr Justice Chatterji knew that he would not set it aside. Not all of them may have intended specifically to cause the death of the men they were robbing but, under the Indian Penal Code, in a case of dacoity-cum-murder each criminal was severally liable for the act.

This was not a case for the Supreme Court. The High Court at Calcutta was the last effective court of appeal. He would sign the judgement, and so would his brother judge, and that, for these men, would be the end. One morning a few weeks down the line, they would be hanged in Alipore Jail.

Mr Justice Chatterji looked at the photograph of his family for a minute or two, and then around his room. Three of the walls were lined with the buff-coloured half-calf or deep-blue bindings of law-books: the *Indian Law Reports*, the *All India Reporter*, the *Income Tax Reports*, the *All England Law Reports*, *Halsbury's Laws*, a few textbooks and books on general jurisprudence, the *Constitution of India* (just over a year old) and the various codes and statutes with their commentaries. Though the Judges' Library at the High Court now provided him with any books he might need, he still continued to subscribe to the journals he had always subscribed to. He did not wish to cut off the series, partly because he liked on occasion to write his judgements at home, partly because he continued to hope that Amit would follow in his footsteps—just as he had followed in his own father's footsteps, down to choosing for himself and later for his son the same Inn to qualify from.

It was not absence of mind that had made Mr Justice Chatterji evade his duties as a host this afternoon, nor the fat gossip, nor the noise made by her children, of whom he was in fact quite fond. It was the gossip's husband, Mr Ganguly, who had suddenly—after a prolonged silence throughout lunch—begun on the verandah to talk about his favourite great man—Hitler: six years dead but still revered by him like a god. In his monotonous voice, chewing his thoughts like cud, he had begun the kind of monologue that Mr Justice Chatterji had heard from him twice before: how even Napoleon (another great Bengali hero) did not come up to Hitlerian standards, how Hitler had helped Netaji Subhas Chandra Bose when he wanted to fight the dreadful British, how atavistic and admirable a force the Indo-Germanic bond was, and how terrible it was that the Germans and the British would within a month be officially terminating the state of war that had existed between them since 1939. (Mr Justice Chatterji thought that it was high time, but did not say so; he refused to get drawn into what was essentially a soliloquy.)

Now that Kakoli's 'German Sahib' had been mentioned over lunch, this man had expressed his gratification at the possibility that the 'Indo-Germanic bond' might become manifest even in his own family. Mr Justice Chatterji had listened for a while with amiable disgust; he had then made a polite excuse, got up, and not returned.

Mr Justice Chatterji had nothing against Hans. He liked what little he had seen of him. Hans was handsome and well dressed and in every sense presentable, and he behaved with amusing if aggressive politeness. Kakoli liked him a great deal. In time he would probably even learn not to mangle people's hands. What Justice Chatterji could not abide, however, was the syndrome just exemplified by his wife's relative—a combination that was by no means uncommon in Bengal: the mad deification of the patriot Subhas Bose who had fled to Germany and Japan and later established the Indian National Army to fight the British; the eulogization of Hitler and Fascism and violence; the denigration of all things British or tainted with 'pseudo-British liberalism'; and resentment bordering on contempt for the sly milksop Gandhi who had dispossessed Bose of the presidentship of the Congress Party which he had won by election many years before. Netaji Subhas Chandra Bose was a Bengali, and Mr Justice Chatterji was certainly as proud of being a Bengali as of being an Indian, but he—like his father, 'old Mr Chatterji'—was profoundly grateful that the likes of Subhas Bose had never succeeded in ruling the country. His father had much preferred Subhas Bose's quieter and equally patriotic brother Sarat, also a lawyer, whom he had known and, after a fashion, admired.

If this fellow wasn't related to my wife, he would be the last person I'd ruin my Sunday afternoon with, thought Mr Justice Chatterji. Families contain far too great a range of temperament—and, unlike acquaintances, they can't be dropped. And we'll continue to be related till one of us drops dead.

Such thoughts on death, such overviews of life were more appropriate to his father, who was nearly eighty, than to himself, thought Mr Justice Chatterji. But the older man seemed so content with his cat and his leisured reading of Sanskrit classics (literary, not religious ones) that he hardly seemed to think of mortality or the passage of time. His wife had died after they had been married ten years, and he had very rarely mentioned her after that. Did he think about her any more often these days? 'I like reading those old plays,' he had said to his son a few days ago. 'King, princess, maidservant—whatever they thought then is still true now. Birth, awareness, love, ambition, hate, death, all the same. All the same.'

With a start Mr Justice Chatterji realized that he himself did not think very often of his wife. They had met at one of those—what were they called, those special festivals for young people held by the Brahmo Samaj, where teenagers and so on could get to meet?—Jubok Juboti Dibosh. His father had approved of her, and they had got married. They got on well; the house ran well; the children, eccentric though they were, were not bad as children went. He spent the earlier part of his evenings at the club. She very rarely complained about this; in fact, he suspected that she did not mind having the early evening to herself and the children.

She was there in his life, and had been there for thirty years. He would doubtless miss her if she wasn't. But he spent more time thinking about his children—especially Amit and Kakoli, both of whom worried him—than about her. And this was probably true of her as well. Their conversations, including the recent one that had resulted in his ultimatum to Amit and Dipankar, were largely child-bound: 'Kuku's on the phone the whole time, and I never know who she's speaking with. And now she's taken to going out at odd hours, and evading my questions.' 'Oh, let her be. She knows what she's doing.' 'Well, you know what happened to the Lahiri girl.' And so it would start. His wife was on the committee of a school for the poor and was involved in other social causes dear to women, but most of her aspirations centred on her children's welfare. That they should be married and well settled was what, above all, she desired.

She had been greatly upset at first by Meenakshi's marriage to Arun Mehra. Predictably enough, once Aparna was born she had come around. But Mr Justice Chatterji himself, though he had behaved with grace and decency in the matter, had felt increasingly rather than decreasingly uneasy about the marriage. For a start, there was Arun's mother, who was, in his mind, a peculiar woman—overly sentimental and liable to make much of nothing. (He had thought that she was not a worrier, but Meenakshi had filled him in with her version of the matter of the medals.) And there was Meenakshi, who sometimes displayed glints of a cold selfishness that even as a father he could not completely blind himself to; he missed her, but their breakfast parliaments, when she lived at home, had been more seriously acrimonious than they now were.

Finally, there was Arun himself. Mr Justice Chatterji respected his drive and his intelligence, but not much else. He seemed to him to be a needlessly aggressive man and a rank snob. They met at the Calcutta Club from time to time, but never found anything much to say. Each moved in his separate cluster at the club, clusters suited to their difference of age and profession. Arun's crowd struck him as gratuitously boisterous, slightly unbefitting the palms and the panelling. But perhaps this was just the intolerance of age, thought Mr Justice Chatterji. The times were changing beneath him, and he was reacting exactly as everyone—king, princess, maidservant—had reacted to the same situation.

But who would have thought that things would have changed as much and as swiftly as they had. Less than ten years ago Hitler had England by the throat, Japan had bombed Pearl Harbour, Gandhi was fasting in jail while Churchill was inquiring impatiently why he was not yet dead, and Tagore had just died. Amit was involved in student politics and in danger of being jailed by the British. Tapan was three and had almost died of nephritis. But in the High Court things were going well. His work as a barrister became increasingly interesting as he grappled with cases based on the War Profits Act and the Excess Income Act. His acuity was undiminished and Biswas Babu's excellent filing system kept his absent-mindedness in check.

In the first year after Independence he had been offered judgeship, something that had delighted his father and his clerk even more than himself. Though Biswas Babu knew that he himself would have to find a new position, his pride in the family and his sense of the lineal fitness of things had made him relish the fact that his employer would now be followed around, as his father before him had been, by a turbaned servitor in red, white and gold livery. What he had regretted was that Amit Babu was not immediately ready to step into his father's practice; but surely, he had thought, that would not be more than a couple of years away.

7.37

The bench that Mr Justice Chatterji had joined, however, was very different from the one he had imagined—even a few years earlier—that he might be appointed to. He got up from his large mahogany desk and went to the shelf that held the more recent volumes of the *All India Reporter* in their bindings of buff, red, black and gold. He took down two volumes—*Calcutta 1947* and *Calcutta 1948*—and began comparing the first pages of each. As he compared them he felt a great sadness for what had happened to the country he had known since childhood, and indeed to his own circle of friends, especially those who were English and those who were Muslim.

For no apparent reason he suddenly thought of an extremely unsociable English doctor, a friend of his, who (like him) would escape from parties given in his own house. He would claim a sudden emergency—perhaps a dying patient—and disappear. He would then go to the Bengal Club, where he would sit on a high chair and drink as many whiskies as he could. The doctor's wife, who threw these huge parties, was fairly eccentric herself. She would go around on a bicycle with a large hat, from under which she could see everything that went on in the world without—or so she imagined—being recognized. It was said of her that she once arrived for dinner at Firpo's with some black lace underwear thrown around her shoulders. Apparently, vague as she was, she had thought it was a stole.

Mr Justice Chatterji could not help smiling, but the smile disappeared as he looked at the two pages he had opened for comparison. In microcosm those two pages reflected the passage of an empire and the birth of two countries from the idea—tragic and ignorant—that people of different religions could not live peaceably together in one.

With the red pencil that he used for notations in his law-books, Mr Justice Chatterji marked a small 'x' against those names in the 1947 volume that did not appear in 1948, just one year later. This is what the list looked like when he had done:

CALCUTTA HIGH COURT
1947

CHIEF JUSTICES

	The Hon'ble Sir	Arthur Trevor Harries, Kt., Bar-at-law.
	” ”	Roopendra Kumar Mitter, Kt., M.Sc., M.L. (Actg.).

PUISNE JUDGES

x	The Hon'ble Sir	Nurul Azeem Khundkar, Kt., B.A. (Cantab.), LL.B., Bar-at-law.
x	” ”	Norman George Armstrong Edgley, Kt., M.A., I.C.S., Bar-at-law.
	” Dr.	Bijan Kumar Mukherjee, M.A., D.L.
	” Mr.	Charu Chandra Biswas, C.I.E., M.A., B.L.
x	” ”	Ronald Francis Lodge, B.A. (Cantab.), I.C.S.
x	” ”	Frederick William Gentle, Bar-at-law.
	” ”	Amarendra Nath Sen, Bar-at-law.
	” ”	Thomas James Young Roxburgh, C.I.E., B.A., I.C.S., Bar-at-law.

x	"	"	Abu Saleh Mohamed Akram, B.L.
	"	"	Abraham Lewis Blank, M.A., I.C.S., Bar-at-law.
	"	"	Sudhi Ranjan Das, B.A., LL.B. (Lond.), Bar-at-law.
x	"	"	Ernest Charles Ormond, Bar-at-law.
	"	"	William McCornick Sharpe, D.S.O., B.A., I.C.S.
	"	"	Phani Bhusan Chakravartti, M.A., B.L.
	"	"	John Alfred Clough, Bar-at-law.
x	"	"	Thomas Hobart Ellis, M.A. (Oxon.), I.C.S.
	"	"	Jogendra Narayan Mazumdar, C.I.E., M.A., B.L., Bar-at-law.
x	"	"	Amir-Ud-din Ahmad, M.B.E., M.A., B.L.
x	"	"	Amin Ahmad, Bar-at-law.
	"	"	Kamal Chunder Chunder, B.A. (Cantab.), I.C.S., Bar-at-law.
	"	"	Gopendra Nath Das, M.A., B.L.

There were a few more names at the bottom of the 1948 list, his own included. But half the English judges and all the Muslim judges had gone. There was not a single Muslim judge in the Calcutta High Court in 1948.

For a man who in his friendships and acquaintance looked upon religion and nationality as both significant and irrelevant, the changing composition of the High Court was a cause for sadness. Soon, of course, the British ranks were further depleted. Now only Trevor Harries (still the Chief Justice) and Roxburgh remained.

The appointment of judges had always been a matter of the greatest importance for the British, and indeed (except for a few scandals such as in the Lahore High Court in the forties) the administration of justice under the British had been honest and fairly swift. (Needless to say, there were plenty of repressive laws, but that was a different, if related, matter.) The Chief Justice would sound a man out directly or indirectly if he felt that he was a fit candidate for the bench, and if he indicated that he was interested, would propose his name to the government.

Occasionally, political objections were raised by the government, but in general a political man would not be sounded out in the first place, nor—if he were sounded out by the Chief Justice—would he be keen to accept. He would not want to be stifled in the expression of his views. Besides, if another Quit India agitation came along, he might have to pass a number of judgements that to his own mind would be unconscionable. Sarat Bose, for instance, would not have been offered judgeship by the British, nor would he have accepted if he had been.

After the British left, matters did not greatly change, particularly in Calcutta, which continued to have an Englishman as Chief Justice. Mr Justice Chatterji considered Sir Arthur Trevor Harries to be a good man and a good Chief Justice. He now recalled his own 'interview' with him when, as one of the leading barristers of Calcutta, he had been asked to visit him in his chambers.

As soon as they were both seated, Trevor Harries had said: 'If I may, Mr Chatterji, I'll come straight to the point. I would like to recommend your name for judgeship to the government. Would this be acceptable to you?'

Mr Chatterji had said: 'Chief Justice, this is an honour, but I am afraid I must decline.'

Trevor Harries had been rather taken aback. 'Might I ask why?'

'I hope you do not mind if I am equally direct,' had been Mr Chatterji's reply. 'A junior man was appointed before me some years ago, and his comparative competence could not have been the reason.'

'An Englishman?'

'As it happens. I am not speculating about the reason.'

Trevor Harries had nodded. 'I believe I know whom you are referring to. But that was done by another Chief Justice—and I thought the man was your friend.'

'Friend he is, and I'm not talking about the friendship. But the question is one of principle.'

After a pause, Trevor Harries had continued: 'Well, I, like you, will not speculate about the correctness of that decision. But he was a sick man, and his time was running out.'

'Nevertheless.'

Trevor Harries had smiled. 'Your father made an excellent judge, Mr Chatterji. Just the other day I had occasion to quote a 1933 judgement of his on the question of estoppel.'

'I shall tell him so. He will be most pleased.'

There had been a pause. Mr Chatterji had been about to get up when the Chief Justice, with the slightest suspicion of a sigh, had said:

'Mr Chatterji, I respect you too much to wish to, well, tilt the scales of your judgement in this matter. But I don't mind confessing my disappointment that you wish to decline. I dare say you realize that it is difficult for me to make up the loss of so many good judges at such short notice. Pakistan and England have each claimed several judges of this court. Our workload is increasing steadily, and what with the constitutional work that will be upon us soon, we will need the best new judges we can get. It is in this light that I have asked you to join, and it is in this light that I would like to ask you to reconsider your decision.' He had paused before continuing. 'May I take the liberty of asking you at the end of this coming week if your mind is still unchanged? If so, my regard will remain unchanged, but I will not trouble you further on this point.'

Mr Chatterji had gone home with no intention of changing his mind or of consulting anyone else on the matter. But while talking to his father, he had happened to mention what the Chief Justice had said about the 1933 judgement. 'What did the Chief Justice want to see you about?' his father had asked. And the story had come out.

His father had quoted a line of Sanskrit to him, to the effect that the best ornament for knowledge was humility. He had said nothing at all about duty.

Mrs Chatterji came to know about it because her husband carelessly left a little slip of paper near his bed before he went to sleep, which read: 'CJ Fri 4:45 (?) re J'ship.' When he woke up the next morning he found her quite cross. Again the facts came out. His wife said: 'It'll be much better for your health. No late-night conferences with juniors. A much more balanced life.'

'My health's fine, dear. I thrive on the work. And Orr, Dignam have a pretty good sense of how many cases they should brief me in.'

'Well, I like the thought of your wearing a wig and scarlet robes.'

'I'm afraid we only wear scarlet robes when trying criminal cases on the original side. And no wig. No, there's much less sartorial splendour in it these days.'

'Mr Justice Chatterji. It sounds just the thing.'

'I'm afraid I shall turn into my father.'

'You could do worse.'

How Biswas Babu came to know of it was a complete mystery. But he did. One evening in his chambers Mr Chatterji was dictating an opinion to him when Biswas Babu addressed him unconsciously as 'My Lord'. Mr Chatterji sat up. 'He must have slipped back into the past for a bit,' he thought, 'and have imagined that I'm my father.' But Biswas Babu looked so startled and guilty at his slip that he gave himself away. And, having given himself away, he hastily added, shaking his knees swiftly: 'I am so pleased, although prematurely, Sir, to administer my felici—'

'I'm not taking it, Biswas Babu,' said Mr Chatterji, very sharply, and in Bengali.

So shocked was his clerk that he quite forgot himself. 'Why not, Sir?' he replied, also in Bengali: 'Don't you want to do justice?'

Mr Chatterji, displeased, collected himself and continued to dictate his opinion. But Biswas Babu's words had a slow but profound effect on him. He had not said, 'Don't you want to be a judge?'

What a lawyer did was to fight for his client—his client, right or wrong—with all the intelligence and experience he could summon. What a judge could do was to weigh matters with equity, to decide what was right. He had the power to do justice, and it was a noble power. When he met the Chief Justice at the end of the week, Mr Chatterji told him he would be honoured if his name was submitted to the government. A few months later he was sworn in.

*

He enjoyed his work, though he did not mix a great deal with his brethren. He had a wide circle of friends and acquaintances, and he did not, as some judges did, distance himself from them. He had no ambition to become Chief Justice or to go to the Supreme Court in Delhi. (The Federal Court and appeal to the Privy Council had ceased to exist.)

Apart from everything else, he liked Calcutta too much to uproot himself. He found his uniformed and turbaned servitor irksome and slightly ridiculous, unlike one of his brother judges, who insisted on being trailed by him even when he went to buy fish in the market. But he did not mind being addressed as My Lord or even, by certain barristers, as M'Lud.

Most of all he enjoyed what Biswas Babu, for all his own love of pomp and display, had known would be at the core of his satisfaction: the dispensation of justice within the law. Two cases that he had recently tried illustrated this. One was a case under the Preventive Detention Act of 1950 by which a labour organizer who was Muslim had been detained without being informed of the grounds of his detention except in the broadest terms. One of several such allegations was that he was an agent for Pakistan, although no proof of this was adduced. Another bald and sweeping statement, impossible to rebut, was that he was fomenting public strife. The vagueness and uncertainty of the allegations induced Mr Justice

Chatterji and his colleague on the division bench to set aside the order on the basis of Article 22 Clause 5 of the Constitution.

In another recent case, when the appeal against conviction for conspiracy of one accused had been successful, but his single co-accused had not—possibly because of poverty—filed an appeal against his own conviction, Mr Justice Chatterji and a fellow-judge had themselves issued a Rule on the State to show cause why the conviction and sentence on the co-accused should not also be set aside. This suo motu ruling had led to a great deal of complex jurisdictional wrangling, but finally the court had decided that it was within its inherent jurisdiction to pass a proper order when a manifest injustice was being perpetrated.

Even in the case at present before him, though it gave Mr Justice Chatterji no pleasure to confirm sentences of death, he felt that he was doing what was just. His judgement was clearly thought out and robustly expressed. But he was considerably worried by the fact that in the first draft of his judgement he had named five of the dacoits and missed out the sixth. This was just the kind of potential disaster that the careful housekeeping of Biswas Babu was always saving him from in his lawyering days.

For a moment his mind turned to Biswas Babu. He wondered how he was and what he was doing. The sound of Kuku at the piano wafted through the open door of his study. He remembered what she had said at lunch about shallybhery juishes. Then he had been annoyed, now he was amused. Biswas Babu's written legal English may have been sharp and economical (except for the occasional misplaced article), but his spoken English was a thing of tortuous beauty. And one could hardly expect the high-spirited Kuku not to be alive to its expressive possibilities.

7.38

Biswas Babu, as it happened, was at that very moment with his friend and fellow-clerk, the burra babu of the insurance department of Bentsen Pryce. They had been friends for over twenty years now, and Biswas Babu's adda or den had slowly cemented this relationship. (When Arun had married Meenakshi it was almost as if their families had suddenly found themselves allied.) The burra babu would visit Biswas Babu's house most evenings; here a number of old companions would gather to talk about the world or simply to sit around, drinking tea and reading the newspapers with an occasional comment. Today some of them were thinking of going to a play.

'So it seems that your High Court building has been struck by lightning,' ventured one man.

'No damage, no damage,' said Biswas Babu. 'The main problem is the refugees from East Bengal who have begun to camp in the corridors.' No one here referred to it as East Pakistan.

'The Hindus there are being terrified and driven out. Every day one reads in the *Hindustan Standard* of Hindu girls being kidnapped—'

'Ay, Ma'—this was addressed to Biswas Babu's youngest granddaughter, a girl of six—'tell your mother to send some more tea.'

'One quick war, and Bengal will be united once again.'

This was considered so stupid that no one responded.

For a few minutes there was contented silence.

'Did you read that article where Netaji's air-crash death was contradicted? It appeared two days ago—'

'Well, if he's alive, he's not doing much to prove it.'

'Naturally he has to lie low.'

'Why? The British have gone.'

'Ah—but he has worse enemies among those left behind.'

'Who?'

'Nehru—and all the others,' ended the proponent darkly if lamely.

'I suppose you think Hitler is alive as well?' This elicited a chuckle all around.

'When is your Amit Babu getting married?' asked someone of Biswas Babu after a pause. 'All Calcutta is waiting.'

'Let Calcutta wait,' said Biswas Babu and returned to his newspaper.

'It is your responsibility to do something—"by hooks and by crooks" as they say in English.'

'I have done enough,' said Biswas Babu with stylized weariness. 'He's a good boy, but a dreamer.'

'A good boy—but a dreamer! Oh, let's have that son-in-law joke again,' said someone to Biswas Babu and the burra babu.

'No, no—' they both demurred. But they were easily enough prevailed upon by the others to act it out. Both of them enjoyed acting, and this skit was only a few lines long. They had acted it half a dozen times before, and to the same audience; the adda, normally so torpid, was given to occasional theatricality.

The burra babu walked around the room, examining the produce in a fish market. Suddenly he saw his old friend. 'Ah, ah, Biswas Babu,' he exclaimed joyfully.

'Yes, yes, borro babu—it has been a long time,' said Biswas Babu, shaking out his umbrella.

'Congratulations on your daughter's engagement, Biswas Babu. A good boy?'

Biswas Babu nodded his head vigorously. 'He's a good boy. Very decent. Well, he eats an onion or two sometimes, but that's all.'

The burra babu, clearly shocked, exclaimed: 'What? Does he eat onions every day?'

'Oh no! Not every day. Far from it. Only when he has had a few drinks.'

'But drinking! Surely he doesn't drink often.'

'Oh no!' said Biswas Babu. 'By no means. Only when he's with women of an evening. . . .'

'But women—what!—and does this happen regularly?'

'Oh no!' exclaimed Biswas Babu. 'He can't afford to visit prostitutes so often. His father is a retired pimp, and destitute, and the boy can only sponge off him once in a while.'

The adda greeted this performance with cheers and laughter. It whetted their appetite for the play they would be going to see later in the evening at a local North Calcutta venue—the Star Theatre. The tea soon came in, together with a few delicious lobongo-lotikas and other sweets prepared by Biswas Babu's daughter-in-law; and for a few minutes everyone fell appreciatively silent except for a few tongue-clicks and comments of enjoyment.

7.39

Dipankar sat on the little rug in his room with Cuddles on his lap, and dispensed advice to his troubled siblings.

Whereas no one dared to interrupt Amit while he was working, or for fear that he might be working, on his immortal prose or verse, it was open season on Dipankar's time and energy.

They came in for specific advice, or sometimes just to talk. There was something pleasantly and zanily earnest about Dipankar which was very reassuring.

Although Dipankar was utterly indecisive in his own life—or perhaps for that very reason—he was quite good at throwing out useful suggestions into the lives of others.

Meenakshi dropped in first with a question about whether it was possible to love more than one person—'utterly, desperately, and truly'. Dipankar talked the matter over with her in strictly unspecific terms, and came to the conclusion that it certainly was possible. The ideal, of course, was to love everyone in the universe equally, he said. Meenakshi was far from convinced of this but felt much better for having talked it over.

Kuku came in next with a specific problem. What was she to do with Hans? He couldn't bear Bengali food, he was a worse philistine even than Arun, who refused to eat fish-heads, even the most delicious bits, the eyes. Hans had not taken to fried neem leaves (he found them too bitter, just imagine, said Kuku), and she did not know if she could really love a man who didn't like neem leaves. More importantly, did he really love her? Hans might have to be discarded yet, for all his Schubert and Schmerz.

Dipankar reassured her that she could, and that he did. He mentioned that tastes were tastes, and that, if she recalled, Mrs Rupa Mehra had once thought Kuku herself a barbarian because she had spoken slightingly of the dussehri mango. As for Hans, Dipankar suspected that he was in for an education. Sauerkraut would soon be replaced by the banana flower, and stollen and Sachertorte by lobongo-lotikas and ledikenis; and he would have to adapt, and accept, and appreciate, if he was to remain Kakoli's most-favoured mushroom; for if everyone else was putty in his firmly grasping hands, he was certainly putty in hers.

'And where will I go and live?' asked Kuku, beginning to sniff. 'In that freezing, bombed-out country?' She looked around Dipankar's room, and said, 'You know what's lacking on that wall is a picture of the Sundarbans. I'll paint you one. . . . I hear it rains all the time in Germany, and people spend their whole lives shivering, and if Hans and I quarrel, I can't just walk home like Meenakshi.'

Kakoli sneezed. Cuddles barked. Dipankar blinked and continued.

'Well, Kuku, if I were you—'

'You didn't bless me,' protested Kakoli.

'Oh, sorry, Kuku, bless you.'

'Oh, Cuddles, Cuddles, Cuddles,' said Kuku, 'no one loves us, no one at all, not even Dipankar. No one cares if we get pneumonia and die.'

Bahadur entered. 'A phone call for Baby Memsahib,' he said.

'Oh,' said Kuku, 'I must flee.'

'But you were discussing the direction of your life,' protested Dipankar mildly. 'You don't even know who's called—it couldn't possibly be that important.'

'But it's the phone,' said Kuku and, having delivered herself of this complete and ineluctable explanation, did indeed flee.

Next came Dipankar's mother, not to take, but to give advice.

'Ki korchho tumi, Dipankar? . . .' she began, and continued to upbraid him quietly, while Dipankar continued to smile pacifically. 'Your father is so worried . . . and I also would like you to settle down . . . family business . . . after all, we are not going to live forever . . . responsibility . . . father's getting old . . . look at your brother, only wants to write poetry, and now these novels, thinks he is another Saratchandra . . . you are our only hope . . . then your father and I can rest in peace.'

'But, Mago, we still have some time left to settle the matter,' said Dipankar, who always deferred whatever he could and left the rest undecided.

Mrs Chatterji looked uncertain. When Dipankar was small, whenever Bahadur asked him what he wanted to eat for breakfast, he would just look up and shake his head in one way or another, and Bahadur, understanding intuitively what was required, would turn up with a fried egg or an omelette or whatever, which Dipankar would eat quite happily. The family had been filled with wonderment. Perhaps, Mrs Chatterji now thought, no mental message had ever passed between them at all, and Bahadur merely represented Fate making its offerings to a Dipankar who decided nothing but accepted everything.

'And even among girls, you don't decide,' continued Mrs Chatterji. 'There's Hemangini, and Chitra, and . . . it's as bad as Kuku,' she ended sadly.

Dipankar had rather chiselled features, not like the milder, more rounded, features of the large-eyed Amit, who fitted Mrs Chatterji's Bengali idea of good looks. She always thought of Dipankar as a sort of ugly duckling, was fiercely ready to protect him against accusations of angularity and boniness, and was amazed when women of the younger generation, all these Chitras and Hemanginis, babbled on about how attractive he was.

'None of them is the Ideal, Mago,' said Dipankar. 'I must continue to search for the Ideal. And for Unity.'

'And now you are going to this Pul Mela in Brahmpur. It is so inappropriate for a Brahmo, praying to the Ganga and taking dips.'

'No, Ma, not at all—' said Dipankar seriously. 'Even Keshub Chunder

Sen anointed himself with oil and dipped himself three times in the tank in Dalhousie Square.'

'He did not!' said Mrs Chatterji, shocked by Dipankar's apostasy.

The Brahmos, who believed in an abstract and elevated monotheism, or were supposed to, simply did not go about doing that sort of thing.

'He did, Mago. Well, I'm not sure it was Dalhousie Square,' Dipankar conceded. 'But, on the other hand, I think it was four dips, not three. And the Ganga is so much holier than a stagnant tank. Why, even Rabindranath Tagore said about the Ganga. . . .'

'Oh, Robi Babu!' exclaimed Mrs Chatterji, her face transfigured with muted ecstasy.

The fourth to visit Dipankar's clinic was Tapan.

Cuddles at once jumped out of Dipankar's lap and on to Tapan's. Whenever Tapan's trunk was packed for him to go to school, Cuddles would become almost desperate, would sit on the trunk to prevent its removal, and would be inconsolably ferocious for a week afterwards.

Tapan stroked Cuddles' head and looked at the shiny black triangle formed by his eyes and nose.

'We'll never shoot you, Cuddles,' he promised. 'Your eyes have no whites at all.'

Cuddles wagged his bristly tail in wholehearted approval.

Tapan looked a bit troubled and seemed to want to talk about something, but wasn't very articulate about what he wanted to say. Dipankar let him ramble on for a bit. After a while Tapan noticed a book about famous battles on Dipankar's topmost shelf and asked to borrow it. Dipankar looked at the dusty book in astonishment—it was a remnant of his unenlightened days—and got it down.

'Keep it,' he told Tapan.

'Are you sure, Dada?' asked Tapan gratefully.

'Sure?' asked Dipankar, beginning to wonder whether such a book would really be good for Tapan to keep. 'Well, I'm not really sure. When you've read it, bring it back, and we'll decide what to do with it then . . . or later.'

Finally, just as he was about to begin meditating, Amit wandered by. He had been writing all day and looked tired.

'Are you certain I'm not disturbing you?' he asked.

'No, Dada, not at all.'

'You're quite certain?'

'Yes.'

'Because I wanted to discuss something with you—something that's quite impossible to discuss with Meenakshi or Kuku.'

'I know, Dada. Yes, she's quite nice.'

'Dipankar!'

'Yes; unaffected,' said Dipankar, looking like an umpire indicating a batsman out; 'intelligent,' he continued, like Churchill signalling victory; 'attractive—', he went on, now representing the trident of Shiva; 'Chatterji-compatible,' he murmured, like the Grande Dame emphasizing the four aims of life; 'and Beastly to Bish,' he added finally, in the stance of a benevolent Buddha.

'Beastly to Bish?' asked Amit.

'So Meenakshi told me a little while ago, Dada. Apparently, Arun was quite put out and refuses to introduce her to anyone else. Arun's mother is distraught, Lata is secretly elated, and—oh yes—Meenakshi—who thinks there's nothing wrong with Bish except that he's insufferable—is taking Lata's side. And incidentally, Dada, Biswas Babu, who has heard of her, thinks she is just my type! Did you tell him about her?' asked Dipankar unblinkingly.

'No,' said Amit, frowning. 'I didn't. Perhaps Kuku did—the chatterbox. What a gossip you are, Dipankar, don't you do any work at all? I wish you'd do what Baba says, and get a proper job and handle all these wretched family finances. It would kill both me and my novel if I had to. Anyway, she's not your type in the least, and you know it. Go and find your own Ideal.'

'Anything for you, Dada,' said Dipankar sweetly, and lowered his right hand in gentle blessing.

7.40

Mangoes arrived for Mrs Rupa Mehra from Brahmpur one afternoon, and her eyes gleamed. She had had enough of the langra mango in Calcutta, which (though it was acceptable) did not remind her of her childhood. What she longed for was the delicate, delectable dussehri, and the season for dussehris was, she had thought, over. Savita had sent her a dozen by parcel post a few days earlier, but when the parcel had arrived, apart from three squashed mangoes at the top, there were only stones underneath. Clearly someone in the Post Office had intercepted them. Mrs Rupa Mehra had been as distressed by the wickedness of man as by her own sense of deprivation. She had given up hope of dussehris for this season. And who knows if I'll be alive next year? she thought to herself dramatically—and somewhat unreasonably, since she was still several years short of fifty. But now here was another parcel with two dozen dussehris, ripe but not overripe, and even cool to the touch.

'Who brought them?' Mrs Rupa Mehra asked Hanif. 'The postman?'

'No, Memsahib. A man.'

'What did he look like? Where was he from?'

'He was just a man, Memsahib. But he gave me this letter for you.'

Mrs Rupa Mehra looked at Hanif severely. 'You should have given it to me at once. All right. Bring me a plate and a sharp knife, and wash two mangoes.' Mrs Rupa Mehra pressed and sniffed a few and selected two. 'These two.'

'Yes, Memsahib.'

'And tell Lata to come in from the garden and eat a mango with me at once.'

Lata had been sitting in the garden. It had not been raining, though there was a slight breeze. When she came in, Mrs Rupa Mehra read out the whole of Savita's accompanying letter.

> . . . but I said I could imagine how disappointed you must be feeling, Ma darling, and we ourselves were so sad because we had chosen them so carefully and with so much affection, judging each one to ensure that it would be ripe in six days' time. But then a Bengali gentleman who works in the Registrar's Office told us how to get around the problem. He knows an attendant who works in the air-conditioned bogey of the Brahmpur-Calcutta Mail. We gave him ten rupees to take the mangoes to you, and we hope that they have arrived—safe and cool and complete. Please do tell me if they have arrived in time. If so we might be able to manage another batch before the season is over because we will not have to choose half-ripe mangoes as we had to for the parcel post. But Ma, you must also be very careful not to eat too many because of your blood sugar. Arun should also read this letter, and monitor your intake. . . .

Mrs Rupa Mehra's eyes filled with tears as she read the letter out to her younger daughter. Then she ate a mango with great gusto, and insisted that Lata eat one as well.

'Now we will share another one,' said Mrs Rupa Mehra.

'Ma, your blood sugar—'

'One mango will make no difference.'

'Of course it will, Ma, and so will the next, and so will the next. And don't you want to make them last till the next parcel comes?'

The discussion was cut short by the arrival of Amit and Kuku.

'Where's Meenakshi?' asked Amit.

'She's gone out,' said Mrs Rupa Mehra.

'Not again!' said Amit. 'I had hoped to see her. By the time I heard she had come to see Dipankar, she'd gone. Please tell her I called. Where's she gone?'

'To the Shady Ladies,' said Mrs Rupa Mehra, frowning.

'What a pity,' said Amit. 'But it's nice to see you both.' He turned to Lata and said: 'Kuku was just going off to Presidency College to see an old friend, and I thought that perhaps we might go along together. I remember you wanted to visit that area.'

'Yes!' said Lata, happy that Amit had remembered. 'May I go, Ma? Or do you need me for something this afternoon?'

'That is all right,' said Mrs Rupa Mehra, feeling liberal. 'But you must have some mangoes before you go,' she continued hospitably to Amit and Kuku. 'These have just come from Brahmpur. Savita has sent them. And Pran—it is so good when one's child gets married to such a thoughtful person. And you must also take some home with you,' she added.

When Amit, Kuku and Lata had gone, Mrs Rupa Mehra decided to cut another mango. When Aparna woke up after her nap, she was fed a slice. When Meenakshi came back from the Shady Ladies, having played a few successful games of mah-jongg, the letter from Savita was read out to her, and she was told to eat a mango.

'No, Ma, I really can't—it's not good for my figure—and it will ruin my lipstick. Hello, Aparna darling—no, don't kiss Mummy just yet. Your lips are all sticky.'

Mrs Rupa Mehra was confirmed in her opinion that Meenakshi was extremely odd. To steel yourself against mangoes showed a degree of iciness that was almost inhuman.

'Amit and Kuku enjoyed them.'

'Oh, what a pity I missed meeting them.' Meenakshi's tone implied relief.

'Amit came specially to see you. He's come several times, and you've always been out.'

'I doubt it.'

'What do you mean?' said Mrs Rupa Mehra, who did not enjoy being contradicted, least of all by her daughter-in-law.

'I doubt he came to see me. He very rarely visited us before you came from Brahmpur. He's quite content living in his own dreamworld of characters.'

Mrs Rupa Mehra frowned at Meenakshi but was silent.

'Oh, Ma, you're so slow on the uptake,' continued Meenakshi. 'It's clearly Luts whom he's interested in. I've never seen him behave with any kind of consideration towards a girl before. And it's no bad thing either.'

'No bad thing either,' repeated Aparna, testing out the phrase.

'Be quiet, Aparna,' said her grandmother sharply. Aparna, too astonished to be hurt by a rebuke from this everloving quarter, kept quiet but continued to listen intently.

'That's not true, that is simply not true. And don't give either of them any ideas,' said Mrs Rupa Mehra, shaking her finger at Meenakshi.

'I'll give them no ideas that they don't have already,' was the cool response.

'You are a mischief-maker, Meenakshi, I won't have it,' said Mrs Rupa Mehra.

'My dear Ma,' said Meenakshi, amused. 'Don't fly off the handle. Neither is it mischief, nor have I made it. I'd just accept things as they come.'

'I have no intention of accepting things as they come,' said Mrs Rupa Mehra, the unsavoury vision of sacrificing yet another of her children on the altar of the Chatterjis making her flush with indignation. 'I will take her back to Brahmpur at once.' She stopped. 'No, not to Brahmpur. Somewhere else.'

'And Luts will traipse after you obediently?' said Meenakshi, stretching her long neck.

'Lata is a sensible and a good girl, and she will do as I tell her. She is not wilful and disobedient like girls who think they are very modern. She has been well brought up.'

Meenakshi stretched back her head lazily, and looked first at her nails and then at her watch. 'Oh, I have to be somewhere in ten minutes,' she said. 'Ma, will you look after Aparna?'

Mrs Rupa Mehra silently conveyed her irked consent. Meenakshi knew too well that her mother-in-law would be pleased to look after her only grandchild.

'I'll be back by six thirty,' said Meenakshi. 'Arun said he'd be a little late at the office today.'

But Mrs Rupa Mehra was annoyed, and did not respond. And behind her annoyance a slow panic was beginning to build and take hold of her.

7.41

Amit and Lata were browsing among the innumerable bookstalls of College Street. (Kuku had gone to meet Krishnan at the Coffee House. According to her he needed to be 'appeased', though to her irritation Amit did not ask what she meant by that.)

'One feels so bewildered among all these millions of books,' said Lata, astonished that several hundred yards of a city could actually be given over to nothing but books—books on the pavement, books on makeshift bookshelves out in the street, books in the library and in Presidency College, first-, second-, third- and tenth-hand books, everything from technical monographs on electroplating to the latest Agatha Christie.

'I feel so bewildered among these millions of books, you mean.'

'No, I do,' said Lata.

'What I meant,' said Amit, 'was "I", as opposed to "one". If you meant the general "one", that would be fine. But you meant "I". Far too many people say "one" when they mean "I". I found them doing it all the time in England, and it'll survive here long after they've given up that idiocy.'

Lata reddened but said nothing. Bish, she recalled, referred to himself exclusively and incessantly as 'one'.

'It's like "thrice",' said Amit.

'I see,' said Lata.

'Just imagine if I were to say to you: "One loves you,"' Amit went on. 'Or worse still, "One loves one." Doesn't that sound idiotic?'

'Yes,' Lata admitted with a frown. She felt he was sounding a bit too professional. And the word 'love' reminded her unnecessarily of Kabir.

'That's all I meant,' said Amit.

'I see,' said Lata. 'Or, rather, one sees.'

'I see one does,' said Amit.

'What is it like to write a novel?' asked Lata after a pause. 'Don't you have to forget the "I" or the "one"—?'

'I don't know exactly,' said Amit. 'This is my first novel, and I'm in the process of finding out. At the moment it feels like a banyan tree.'

'I see,' said Lata, though she didn't.

'What I mean is,' continued Amit, 'it sprouts, and grows, and spreads, and drops down branches that become trunks or intertwine with other branches. Sometimes branches die. Sometimes the main trunk dies, and the structure is held up by the supporting trunks. When you go to the Botanical Garden you'll see what I mean. It has its own life—but so do the snakes and birds and bees and lizards and termites that live in it and on it and off it. But then it's also like the Ganges in its upper, middle and lower courses—including its delta—of course.'

'Of course,' said Lata.

'I have the feeling,' said Amit, 'that you're laughing at me.'

'How far have you got so far with writing it?' she said.

'I'm about a third of the way.'

'And aren't I wasting your time?'

'No.'

'It's about the Bengal Famine, isn't it?'

'Yes.'

'Do you have any memory of the famine yourself?'

'I do. I remember it only too well. It was only eight years ago.' He paused. 'I was somewhat active in student politics then. But do you know, we had a dog even then, and fed it well.' He looked distressed.

'Does a writer have to feel strongly about what he writes?' asked Lata.

'I haven't the least idea,' said Amit. 'Sometimes I write best about the things I care about least. But even that's not a consistent rule.'

'So do you just flounder and hope?'

'No, no, not exactly.'

Lata felt that Amit, who had been so open, even expansive, a minute ago, was resisting her questioning now, and she did not press it further.

'I'll send you a book of my poems sometime,' said Amit. 'And you can form your own opinion about how much or how little I feel.'

'Why not now?' asked Lata.

'I need time to think of a suitable inscription,' said Amit. 'Ah, there's Kuku.'

7.42

Kuku had performed her errand of appeasement. Now she wanted to go home as quickly as possible. Unfortunately, it had begun to rain once more, and soon the warm rain was battering down on the roof of the Humber. Rivulets of brown water began running down the sides of the street. A little farther there was no street at all, just a sort of shallow canal, where traffic in the opposite direction created waves that shook the chassis of the car. Ten minutes later the car was trapped in a flash flood. The driver inched forward, trying to keep to the middle of the road, where the camber created a slightly higher level. Then the engine died.

With Kuku and Amit to talk to in the car, Lata did not fret. It was very hot, though, and beads of perspiration formed on her forehead. Amit told her a bit about his college days and how he had begun writing poetry. 'Most of it was terrible, and I burned it,' he said.

'How could you have done that?' asked Lata, amazed that anyone could burn what must have been written with so much feeling. But at least he had burned it and not simply torn it up. That would have been too matter-of-fact. The thought of a fire in the Calcutta climate was odd too. There was no fireplace in the Ballygunge house.

'Where did you burn the poems?' she asked.

'In the washbasin,' interjected Kuku. 'He nearly burned the house down too.'

'It was awful poetry,' said Amit by way of extenuation. 'Embarrassingly bad. Self-indulgent, dishonest.'

> 'Poetry I don't desire
> I will immolate with fire,'

said Kuku.

> 'All my sorrow, all my pain:
> Ashes flowing down the drain,'

continued Amit.

'Aren't there any Chatterjis who don't make flippant couplets?' asked Lata, unaccountably annoyed. Weren't they ever serious? How could they joke about such heartbreaking matters?

'Ma and Baba don't,' said Kuku. 'That's because they've never had Amit as an elder brother. And Dipankar's not quite as skilled as the rest of us. It comes naturally to us, like singing in a raag if you've heard it often enough. People are astonished we can do it, but we're astonished Dipankar can't. Or only once a month or so, when he has his poetic periods. . . .

Rhyming, rhyming so precisely—
Couplets, they are coming nicely,'

gurgled Kakoli, who churned them out with such appalling frequency that they were now called Kakoli-couplets, though Amit had started the trend.

By now most of the motor traffic had come to a halt. A few rickshaws were still moving, the rickshaw-wallahs waist-deep in the flood, their passengers, laden with packages, surveying the watery brown world around them with a kind of alarmed satisfaction.

In due course the water subsided. The driver looked at the engine, examined the ignition wire, which was moist, and wiped it with a piece of cloth. The car still wouldn't start. Then he looked at the carburettor, fiddled a bit here and there, and murmured the names of his favourite goddesses in correct firing sequence. The car began to move.

By the time they got back to Sunny Park it was dark.

'You have taken your own sweet time,' said Mrs Rupa Mehra sharply to Lata. She glared at Amit.

Amit and Lata were both surprised by the hostility of their reception.

'Even Meenakshi has returned before you,' continued Mrs Rupa Mehra. She looked at Amit, and thought: Poet, wastrel! He has never earned an honest rupee in his life. I will not have all my grandchildren speaking Bengali! Suddenly she remembered that the last time Amit had dropped Lata home, she had had flowers in her hair.

Looking at Lata, but presumably addressing both of them—or perhaps all three of them, Kuku included—she continued: 'You have put up my blood pressure and my blood sugar.'

'No, Ma,' said Lata, looking at the fresh mango peels on the plate. 'If your blood sugar has gone up it's because of all those dussehris you've been eating. Now please don't have more than one a day—or at most two.'

'Are you teaching your grandmother to suck eggs?' asked Mrs Rupa Mehra, glowering.

Amit smiled. 'It was my fault, Ma,' he said. 'The streets were flooded not far from the university, and we got caught.'

Mrs Rupa Mehra was in no mood to be friendly. What was he smiling for?

'Is your blood sugar very high?' asked Kakoli quickly.

'Very high,' said Mrs Rupa Mehra with distress and pride. 'I have even been having karela juice, but it has no effect.'

'Then you must go to my homoeopathic doctor,' said Kakoli.

Mrs Rupa Mehra, diverted from her attack, said, 'I already have a homoeopath.'

But Kakoli insisted that her doctor was better than anyone else. 'Doctor Nuruddin.'

'A Mohammedan?' said Mrs Rupa Mehra doubtfully.

'Yes. It happened in Kashmir, when we were on holiday.'

'I am not going to Kashmir,' said Mrs Rupa Mehra decidedly.

'No, he cured me here. His clinic is here, in Calcutta. He cures people of everything—diabetes, gout, skin troubles. I had a friend who had a cyst on his eyelid. He gave him a medicine called thuja, and the cyst dropped right off.'

'Yes,' agreed Amit energetically. 'I sent a friend of mine to a homoeopath, and her brain tumour disappeared, and her broken leg mended, and though she was barren she had twins within three months.'

Both Kuku and Mrs Rupa Mehra glared at him. Lata looked at him with a smile of mixed reproof and approval.

'Amit always makes fun of what he can't understand,' said Kuku. 'He clubs homoeopathy together with astrology. But even our family doctor has slowly become convinced of the effectiveness of homoeopathy. And ever since my terrible problem in Kashmir I am a complete convert. I believe in results,' continued Kuku. 'When something works I believe in it.'

'What problem did you have?' asked Mrs Rupa Mehra eagerly.

'It was the ice-cream in a hotel in Gulmarg.'

'Oh.' Ice-cream was one of Mrs Rupa Mehra's weaknesses too.

'The hotel made its own ice-cream. On the spur of the moment I ate two scoops.'

'And then?'

'Then—then it was terrible.' Kuku's voice reflected her trauma. 'I had an awful throat. I was given some allopathic medicine by the local doctor. It suppressed the symptoms for a day, then they came back again. I couldn't eat, I couldn't sing, I could hardly speak, I couldn't swallow. It was like having thorns in my throat. I had to think before I decided to say something.'

Mrs Rupa Mehra clicked her tongue in sympathy.

'And my sinuses were blocked completely.' Kuku paused, then went on: 'Then I had another dose of medicine. And again it suppressed the condition, but it came back again. I had to be sent to Delhi and flown back to Calcutta. After dose number three, my throat was inflamed, my sinuses and nose were both infected, I was in a terrible state. My aunt, Mrs Ganguly, suggested Dr Nuruddin. "Try him and see," she told my mother. "What's the harm?"'

The suspense, for Mrs Rupa Mehra, was unbearable. Stories involving ailments were as fascinating for her as murder mysteries or romances.

'He took my history, and asked me some strange questions. Then he said: "Take two doses of pulsetilla, and come back to me." I said: "Two doses? Just two doses? Will that be enough? Not a regular course?" He said: "Inshallah, two doses should be enough." And it was. I was cured. The swelling disappeared. My sinuses cleared up completely and the thing never recurred. Allopathic treatment would have required puncturing and draining the sinuses to relieve an endemic complaint—which is what it would have become if I hadn't gone to Dr Nuruddin; and you can stop laughing, Amit.'

Mrs Rupa Mehra was convinced. 'I'll go with you to see him,' she said.

'But you mustn't mind his strange questions,' said Kakoli.

'I can handle myself in all situations,' said Mrs Rupa Mehra.

When they had left, Mrs Rupa Mehra said pointedly to Lata:

'I am very tired of Calcutta, darling, and it is not good for my health. Let us go to Delhi.'

'What on earth for, Ma?' said Lata. 'I'm beginning to have a good time here. And why so suddenly?'

Mrs Rupa Mehra looked closely at her daughter.

'And we have all those mangoes to eat still,' laughed Lata. 'And we have to make sure that Varun studies a little.'

Mrs Rupa Mehra looked severe. 'Tell me—' she began, then stopped. Surely Lata could not be pretending the innocence that was written so plainly on her face. And if she wasn't, why put ideas into her head?

'Yes, Ma?'

'Tell me what you did today.'

This was more in the line of Mrs Rupa Mehra's daily questioning, and Lata was relieved to see her mother behaving more in character. Lata had no intention of being torn away from Calcutta and the Chatterjis. When she thought how unhappy she had been when she had first come here, she felt grateful to that family—and most of all to the comfortable, cynical, considerate Amit—for the way they had absorbed her into their clan—almost as a third sister, she thought.

Meanwhile Mrs Rupa Mehra was also thinking about the Chatterjis, but in less charitable terms. Meenakshi's remarks had made her panic.

I will go to Delhi, by myself if necessary, she was thinking. Kalpana Gaur will have to help me to find a suitable boy at once. Then I will summon Lata. Arun is completely useless. Ever since his marriage he has lost all feeling for his own family. He introduced Lata to this Bishwanath boy, and since then he has done nothing further. He has no sense of responsibility for his sister. I am all alone in the world now. Only my Aparna loves me. Meenakshi was sleeping, and Aparna was with the Toothless Crone. Mrs Rupa Mehra had her granddaughter transferred immediately to her own arms.

7.43

The rain had delayed Arun as well. When he returned home he was in a black temper.

Without more than a grunt apiece for his mother, sister and daughter, he marched straight into the bedroom. 'Damned swine, the whole lot of them,' he announced. 'And the driver too.'

Meenakshi surveyed him from the bed. She yawned:

> 'Arun, darling, why such fury?
> Have a chocolate made by Flury.'

'Oh, stop that moronic Blabberji blather,' shouted Arun, setting down his briefcase and laying his damp coat across the arm of a chair. 'You're my wife. You can at least pretend to be sympathetic.'

'What happened, darling?' said Meenakshi, composing her features into the required emotion. 'Bad day at the office?'

Arun closed his eyes. He sat down on the edge of the bed.

'Tell me,' said Meenakshi, her long, elegant, red-nailed fingers slowly loosening his tie.

Arun sighed. 'This bloody rickshaw-wallah asked me for three rupees to take me across the road to my car. Across the road,' he repeated, shaking his head in disgust and disbelief.

Meenakshi's fingers stopped. 'No!' she exclaimed, genuinely shocked. 'I hope you didn't agree to pay.'

'What could I do?' asked Arun. 'I wasn't going to wade knee-deep through water to get to my car—or risk the car crossing the flooded section of the road and stalling. He could see that—and he was smirking with the pleasure of having a sahib by the balls. "It's your decision," he said. "Three rupees." Three rupees! When normally it would be two annas at the most. One anna would have been a fairer price—it was no more than twenty steps. But he could see there was no other rickshaw in sight and that I was getting wet. Bloody profiteering swine.'

Meenakshi glanced at the mirror from the bed and thought for a moment. 'Tell me,' she said, 'what does Bentsen Pryce do when there's a temporary shortage of, oh, jute in the world market and the price goes up? Don't they put up their prices to whatever level the market will bear? Or is that only a Marwari practice? I know that's what goldsmiths and silversmiths do. And vegetable sellers. I suppose that was what the rickshaw-wallah was doing too. Perhaps I shouldn't have been shocked after all. Or you.'

She had forgotten her intention to be sympathetic. Arun looked at her, injured, but saw, despite himself, the unpleasantly forceful logic of her words.

'Would you like to do my job?' he demanded.

'Oh no, darling,' said Meenakshi, refusing to take offence. 'I couldn't bear to wear a coat and tie. And I wouldn't know how to dictate letters to your charming Miss Christie. . . . Oh, by the way, some mangoes came from Brahmpur today. And a letter from Savita.'

'Oh.'

'And Ma, being Ma, has been glutting away at them without regard for her diabetes.'

Arun shook his head. As if he didn't have troubles enough already. His mother was incorrigible. Tomorrow she'd complain that she wasn't feeling well, and he'd have to take her to the doctor. Mother, sister, daughter, wife: he suddenly felt trapped—a whole bloody household of women. And the feckless Varun to boot.

'Where's Varun?'

'I don't know,' said Meenakshi. 'He hasn't returned, and he hasn't called. I don't think he has, anyway. I've been taking a nap.'

Arun sighed.

'I've been dreaming about you,' lied Meenakshi.

'You have?' asked Arun, mollified. 'Let's—'

'Oh, later, don't you think, darling?' said Meenakshi coolly. 'We have to go out this evening.'

'Isn't there any bloody evening when we don't go out?' asked Arun.

Meenakshi shrugged, as if to say that most of the engagements were not of her making.

'I wish I were a bachelor again.' Arun had said it without meaning to.

Meenakshi's eyes flamed. 'If you want to be like that—' she began.

'No, no, I don't mean it. It's just this bloody stress. And my back's playing up again.'

'I don't find Varun's bachelor life all that admirable,' said Meenakshi.

Nor did Arun. He shook his head again, and sighed. He looked exhausted.

Poor Arun, thought Meenakshi. 'Tea—or a drink, darling?' she said.

'Tea,' said Arun. 'Tea. A nice cup of tea. A drink can wait.'

7.44

Varun had not yet returned because he was busy gambling and smoking in Sajid's house in Park Lane, a street that was seedier than it sounded. Sajid, Jason, Varun and a few other friends were sitting on Sajid's huge bed upstairs, and playing flush: starting from one anna blind, two annas seen. Today, as on a few other occasions, they were joined by Sajid's downstairs tenants, Paul and his sister Hortense. Hortense (referred to by Sajid and his friends among themselves as 'Hot-Ends') was sitting on the lap of her boyfriend (a ship's purser) and playing on his behalf from that position. The stakes had risen to four annas blind, eight annas seen—the maximum they ever allowed themselves. Everyone was jittery, and people were packing in their hands left and right. Eventually only Varun, who was extremely nervous, and Hot-Ends, who was extremely calm, were left.

'Just Varun and Hortense alone together,' said Sajid. 'It'll really hot up now.'

Varun flushed deep red and almost dropped his cards. It was common knowledge among the friends (but not to Hortense's boyfriend the purser) that Paul—who was otherwise unemployed—pimped for his sister whenever her boyfriend was out of town. God knows where he went to get his customers, but he would sometimes come back late in the evening with a businessman in a taxi, and stand, smoking Rhodes Navy Cut, at the foot of the stairs or outside on the steps while Hortense and her client got on with it.

'A royal flush,' said Jason, referring to Varun's expression.

Varun, trembling with nervous tension and glancing at his cards for reassurance, whispered, 'I'll stay in.' He put an eight-anna coin in the kitty, which now contained almost five rupees.

Hot-Ends, without glancing at her cards, or at anyone, and with as blasé an expression as she could manage, wordlessly pushed another eight annas into the pool. Her boyfriend moved his finger up and down the hollow of her throat, and she leaned back.

Varun, his tongue passing nervously over his lips and his eyes glazed with excitement, staked another eight annas. Hot-Ends, looking straight at him this time, and holding his frightened and fascinated glance with her own, said, as huskily as possible: 'Oh you greedy boy! You just want to take advantage of me. Well, I'll give you what you want.' And she put another eight annas into the kitty.

Varun could bear it no longer. Weak with suspense and terrified by what her hand might reveal, he asked for a show. Hot-Ends had a King, Queen and Jack of spades. Varun almost collapsed with relief. He had an Ace, King and Queen of diamonds.

But he looked as shattered as if he had lost. He begged his friends to excuse him and let him go home.

'Not a chance!' said Sajid. 'You can't just make a packet and disappear. You have to fight to keep it.'

And Varun promptly lost all his winnings (and more) over the next few games. Everything I do goes wrong, he thought to himself as he returned home in the tram. I am a useless person—useless—and a disgrace to the family. Thinking of how Hot-Ends had looked at him, he began to get nervous again, and wondered if more trouble was not in store for him if he continued to associate with his Shamshu friends.

7.45

The morning that Mrs Rupa Mehra was about to leave for Delhi, the Mehra family was sitting at the breakfast table. Arun as usual was doing the crossword. After a while he looked at a few other pages.

'You could at least talk to me,' said Mrs Rupa Mehra. 'I am leaving today, and you are hiding behind your newspaper.'

Arun looked up. 'Listen to this, Ma,' he said. 'Just the thing for you.' And he read out an advertisement from the paper in a sarcastic voice:

> 'Diabetes cured in Seven Days. No matter how severe or longstanding, Diabetes can be completely cured by VENUS CHARM, the very latest Scientific Discovery. Some of the main symptoms of this disease are Abnormal thirst and hunger, Excess sugar in urine and Itching etc. In its serious form it causes Carbuncles, Boils, Cataract and other complications. Thousands have escaped from the gallows of death by using VENUS CHARM. The very next day it eradicates sugar and normalises specific gravity. Within 2 or 3 days you will feel more than half cured. No dietary restrictions. Price per phial of 50 tablets 6 rupees 12 annas. Postage free. Available from Venus Research Laboratory (N.H.) Post Box 587. Calcutta.'

Mrs Rupa Mehra had begun weeping silently. 'I hope you never get diabetes,' she said to her elder son. 'Make as much fun of me as you like now, but—'

'But when you are dead and gone—the pyre—the empty chair—yes, yes, we know the rest,' continued Arun rather brutally.

His back had been acting up the previous night, and Meenakshi had not been satisfied with his performance.

'Shut up, Arun Bhai!' said Varun, his face white and twitching with anger. He went to his mother and put his arm around her shoulder.

'Don't speak to me like that,' said Arun, getting up and advancing menacingly towards Varun. '"Shut up"? Did you say "Shut up" to me? Get out at once. Get out!' He was working himself into a fit of rage. 'Get out!' he bellowed once more.

It was unclear whether he wanted Varun out of the room, the house or his life.

'Arun Bhai, really—' protested Lata indignantly.

Varun flinched, and retreated to the other side of the table.

'Oh do sit down, both of you,' said Meenakshi. 'Let's have breakfast in peace.'

Both of them sat down. Arun glared at Varun, Varun glared at his egg.

'And he won't even provide me with a car to get to the station,' continued Mrs Rupa Mehra, reaching into her black bag for a handkerchief. 'I have to depend on the charity of strangers.'

'Really, Ma,' said Lata, putting her arm around her mother and kissing her. 'Amit is hardly a stranger.'

Mrs Rupa Mehra's shoulders became tense.

'You also,' she said to Lata. 'You have no care for my feelings.'

'Ma!' said Lata.

'You will be gallivanting around merrily. Only my darling Aparna will be sorry to see me go.'

'Ma, do be reasonable. Varun and I will be going with you to the homoeopath's and then to the station. And Amit will be here in fifteen minutes with the car. Do you want him to see you in tears?'

'I don't care what he sees or does not see,' said Mrs Rupa Mehra with a snappish edge to her voice.

Amit arrived on time. Mrs Rupa Mehra had washed her face, but her nose was still red with emotion. When she said goodbye to Aparna, both of them began to cry. Luckily Arun had already left for work, so he could not make unhelpful comments from the sidelines.

*

Dr Nuruddin, the homoeopath, was a middle-aged man with a long face, a jovial manner, and rather a drawling voice. He greeted Mrs Rupa Mehra warmly, obtained her general particulars and her medical history, looked at her blood sugar charts, talked for a minute or two about Kakoli Chatterji, stood up, sat down again, and then embarked upon a disconcerting line of questioning.

'You have reached menopause?'

'Yes. But why—'

'Yes?' asked Dr Nuruddin, as of a fractious child.

'Nothing,' said Mrs Rupa Mehra meekly.

'Do you find yourself easily irritable, upset?'

'Doesn't everyone?'

Dr Nuruddin smiled. 'Many people do. Do you, Mrs Mehra?'

'Yes. This morning at breakfast—'

'Tears?'

'Yes.'

'Do you sometimes feel extreme sadness? Abject despair, uncompromising melancholy?'

He pronounced these as one would medical symptoms like itching or intestinal pain. Mrs Rupa Mehra looked at him in perplexity.

'Extreme? How extreme?' she faltered.

'Any answer you can give me will be helpful.'

Mrs Rupa Mehra thought before replying: 'Sometimes I feel very despairing. Whenever I think of my late husband.'

'Are you thinking of him now?'

'Yes.'

'And are you in despair?'

'Not just now,' confessed Mrs Rupa Mehra.

'What are you feeling just now?' asked Dr Nuruddin.

'How peculiar all this is.'

Translated, this meant: 'That you are mad. And so am I, for putting up with these questions.'

Dr Nuruddin touched the eraser on his pencil to the tip of his nose before asking: 'Mrs Mehra, do you think my questions are not pertinent? That they are impertinent?'

'Well—'

'I assure you that they are very pertinent for understanding your condition. In homoeopathy we try to deal with the whole system, we do not merely confine ourselves to the physical side. Now tell me, do you suffer from loss of memory?'

'No. I always remember the names and birthdays of friends, and other important things.'

Dr Nuruddin wrote something down on a small pad. 'Good, good,' he said. 'And dreams?'

'Dreams?'

'Dreams.'

'Yes?' asked Mrs Rupa Mehra in bewilderment.

'What dreams do you have, Mrs Mehra?'

'I don't remember.'

'You don't remember?' he responded with genial scepticism.

'No,' said Mrs Rupa Mehra, gritting her teeth.

'Do you grind your teeth in your sleep?'

'How do I know? I'm sleeping. What does all this have to do with my diabetes?'

Dr Nuruddin continued jovially: 'Do you ever wake up thirsty at night?'

Mrs Rupa Mehra, frowning, replied: 'Yes, quite often. I keep a jug of water by my bedside.'

'Do you feel more tired in the morning or in the evening?'

'In the morning, I think. Until I do my recitations from the Gita. Then I feel stronger.'

'Are you fond of mangoes?'

Mrs Rupa Mehra stared at Dr Nuruddin across the table: 'How do you know?' she demanded.

'It was only a question, Mrs Mehra. Does your urine smell of violets?'

'How dare you?' cried Mrs Rupa Mehra, outraged.

'Mrs Mehra, I am trying to help you,' said Dr Nuruddin, laying his pencil down. 'Will you answer my questions?'

'I will not answer such questions. My train is leaving from Howrah in under an hour. I have to go.'

Dr Nuruddin took down his copy of the *Materia Medica* and opened it to the relevant page. 'You see, Mrs Mehra,' he said, 'I am not conjuring up these symptoms out of my head. But even the strength of your resistance to my questions has been helpful to me in my diagnosis. Now I have only one further question.'

Mrs Rupa Mehra tensed up. 'Yes?' she asked.

'Do the tips of your fingers ever itch?' asked Dr Nuruddin.

'No,' said Mrs Rupa Mehra, and breathed a deep sigh.

Dr Nuruddin stroked the bridge of his nose with his two index fingers for a minute, then wrote out a prescription, and handed it to his dispensing assistant, who began to grind various materials up into a white powder, which he distributed into twenty-one tiny paper packets.

'You will not eat onions or ginger or garlic, and you will take one small packet of powder before each meal. At least half an hour before each meal,' said Dr Nuruddin.

'And this will improve my diabetes?'

'Inshallah.'

'But I thought you would give me those small pills,' protested Mrs Rupa Mehra.

'I prefer powders,' said Dr Nuruddin. 'Come back in seven days, and we will see—'

'I am leaving Calcutta. I won't be back for months.'

Dr Nuruddin, not quite so jovially, said: 'Why didn't you tell me?'

'You didn't ask me. I'm sorry, Doctor.'

'Yes. And where are you going to?'

'To Delhi, and then to Brahmpur. My daughter Savita is expecting,' confided Mrs Rupa Mehra.

'When will you be in Brahmpur?'

'In a week or two.'

'I don't like to prescribe for long periods,' said Dr Nuruddin, 'but there doesn't seem to be much choice.' He spoke to his assistant before continuing:

'I am giving you medicines for two weeks. You must write to me at this address after five days, telling me how you are feeling. And in Brahmpur you must visit Dr Baldev Singh. Here is his address. I will write him a note about you later today. Please pay and collect your medicines at the front. Goodbye, Mrs Mehra.'

'Thank you, Doctor,' said Mrs Rupa Mehra.

'Next,' called Dr Nuruddin cheerfully.

7.46

Mrs Rupa Mehra was unusually quiet on the way to the station. When asked by her children how the appointment with the doctor had gone, she said: 'It was peculiar. You can tell Kuku that.'

'Are you going to follow his prescription?'

'Yes,' said Mrs Rupa Mehra. 'I was not brought up to waste money.' She sounded as if she was irritated by their presence.

Throughout a long traffic jam on Howrah Bridge, while precious minutes ticked by, and the Humber inched its way forward through a raucous, horn-blowing, yelling, deafening throng of buses, trams, taxis, cars, motorcycles, carts, rickshaws, bicycles and—above all—pedestrians, Mrs Rupa Mehra, who would normally have been in a desperate, bangle-clutching panic, hardly seemed to be aware that her train would be leaving in less than fifteen minutes.

Only after the traffic had miraculously got moving and she was ensconced with all her suitcases in her compartment and had had a good chance to look at the other passengers did Mrs Rupa Mehra's natural emotions reassert themselves. Kissing Lata with tears in her eyes she told her that she had to take care of Varun. Kissing Varun with tears in her eyes, she told him that he had to take care of Lata. Amit stood a little apart. Howrah Station with its crowds and smoke and bustle and blare and all-pervasive smell of decaying fish was not his favourite place in the world.

'Really, Amit, it was very nice of you to let us have the car,' said Mrs Rupa Mehra, attempting to be gracious.

'Not at all, Ma, it happened to be free. Kuku, by some miracle, hadn't reserved it.'

'Yes. Kuku,' said Mrs Rupa Mehra, suddenly flustered. Though she was in the habit of telling people that she was invariably called Ma and that she liked it, she was not happy at present to hear herself thus addressed by Amit. She looked at her daughter with alarm. She thought of Lata when she had been as old as Aparna. Who could have thought she would have grown up so quickly?

'Give my best love to your family,' she said to Amit in a voice that carried very little conviction.

Amit was puzzled by what seemed to be—but perhaps he had only imagined it?—an undercurrent of hostility. What, he wondered, had happened at the homoeopath's to upset Lata's mother? Or was she upset with him?

On the way back home, all of them agreed that Mrs Rupa Mehra had been in a most peculiar mood.

Amit said: 'I feel I've done something to upset your mother. I should have brought you back on time that evening.'

Lata said: 'It isn't you. It's me. She wanted me to go with her to Delhi, and I didn't want to go.'

Varun said: 'It's because of me. I know it. She looked so unhappy with me. She can't bear to see me waste my life. I've got to turn over a new leaf. I can't disappoint her again. And when you see me going back to my old ways, Luts, you have to get angry with me. Really angry. Shout at me. Tell me I'm a damn fool and have no leadership qualities. None!'

Lata promised to do so.

Photograph by Aradhana Seth

One of the most celebrated writers of our time, Vikram Seth is the author of three novels—*The Golden Gate* (a novel in verse), *A Suitable Boy* and *An Equal Music*—which are widely regarded as modern classics—and two works of non-fiction. He has also written seven books of poetry, including *All You Who Sleep Tonight* and *Beastly Tales from Here and There.*

'Set in post-independence India, the novel follows for eighteen months or so four linked families in Calcutta, the province of Purva Pradesh and its capital Brahmpur, and the cities—Delhi, Kanpur, Lucknow—trawled by the heroine's mother in her search for a "suitable boy"... But the greatness of the novel, its unassailable truthfulness, owes less to research than to imagination, an instinctive knowledge of the human heart—with all its varieties of kindness and cruelty... As with all the best books, one feels only dismay when the pages on the right of the tome start thinning out.'

—*The Observer*

A Suitable Boy

By the same author

FICTION

The Golden Gate: A Novel in Verse
An Equal Music

POETRY

Mappings
The Humble Administrator's Garden
All You Who Sleep Tonight
Three Chinese Poets (*translations*)
Beastly Tales from Here and There (*fables*)
Arion and the Dolphin (*libretto*)
The Rivered Earth (*libretti and essays*)
Summer Requiem

MEMOIR

Two Lives

NON-FICTION

From Heaven Lake: Travels through Sinkiang and Tibet

A Suitable Boy

{ VOLUME TWO }

VIKRAM
SETH

SPEAKING
TIGER

SPEAKING TIGER BOOKS LLP
125A, Ground Floor, Shahpur Jat,
New Delhi–110002, India

First published by Penguin India 1993
This edition published by Speaking Tiger Books 2023

ISBN: 978-93-5447-487-3

10 9 8 7 6 5 4 3 2 1

Printed at Chaman Enterprises, New Delhi

The author would personally like to thank Jaishree Ram Mohan and her enthusiastic young team at Penguin India for proofreading A Suitable Boy *in 2013, and Ajith Kumar for typesetting it.*

To

Papa and Mama

and

the memory of Amma

A WORD OF THANKS

To these I owe a debt past telling:
My several muses, harsh and kind;
My folks, who stood my sulks and yelling,
And (in the long run) did not mind;
Dead legislators, whose orations
I've filched to mix my own potations;
Indeed, all those whose brains I've pressed,
Unmerciful, because obsessed;
My own dumb soul, which on a pittance
Survived to weave this fictive spell;
And, gentle reader, you as well,
The fountainhead of all remittance.
Buy me before good sense insists
You'll strain your purse and sprain your wrists.

CONTENTS (Volume Two)

ACKNOWLEDGEMENTS

The author and publishers would like to thank the following for permission to quote copyright material:

The Ministry of Human Resources Development, Govt of India for extracts from *Letters to Chief Ministers*, Vol. 2, 1950–1952 by Jawaharlal Nehru, general editor G. Parthasarathi (Jawaharlal Nehru Memorial Fund, distributed by Oxford University Press, 1986)

HarperCollins Publishers Ltd for extracts from *The Koran Interpreted* by A.J. Arberry (George Allen & Unwin Ltd; and Oxford University Press, 1964)

Oxford University Press for an extract from *The Select Nonsense of Sukumar Ray* translated by Sukanta Chaudhuri (Oxford University Press, 1987)

Faber & Faber for an extract from the poem 'Law, Say the Gardeners' published in *W.H. Auden: Collected Poems* edited by Edward Mendelson (Faber & Faber)

Penguin Books Ltd for extracts from *Selected Poems* by Rabindranath Tagore, translated by William Radice (Penguin Books, 1985)

Bantam Books Inc. for extracts from *The Bhagavad-Gita* translated by Barbara Stoler Miller (Bantam Books, 1986)

The Sahitya Akademi for extracts from *Mir Anis* by Ali Jawad Zaidi published in the series 'Makers of Indian Literature' (Sahitya Akademi, 1986)

The Gita Press, Gorakhpur, for extracts from *Sri Ramacharitamanasa* translated into English (Gita Press, 1968)

While every effort has been made to trace copyright holders and obtain permission, this has not been possible in all cases; any omissions brought to our attention will be remedied in future editions.

MEHRAS

DR KISHEN CHAND SETH *m* FIRST WIFE (d) *remarried* PARVATI

CHILDREN including . . . RUPA *m* RAGHUBIR MEHRA (d)

ARUN MEHRA *m* MEENAKSHI (*née* Chatterji) — SAVITA *m* PRAN KAPOOR — VARUN MEHRA — LATA MEHRA

APARNA

KAPOORS

MR TANDON (d) *m* OLD MRS TANDON

MAHESH KAPOOR *m* MRS MAHESH KAPOOR

CHILDREN including . . . KEDARNATH TANDON *m* VEENA — PRAN KAPOOR *m* SAVITA (*née* Mehra) — MAAN KAPOOR

BHASKAR

KHANS

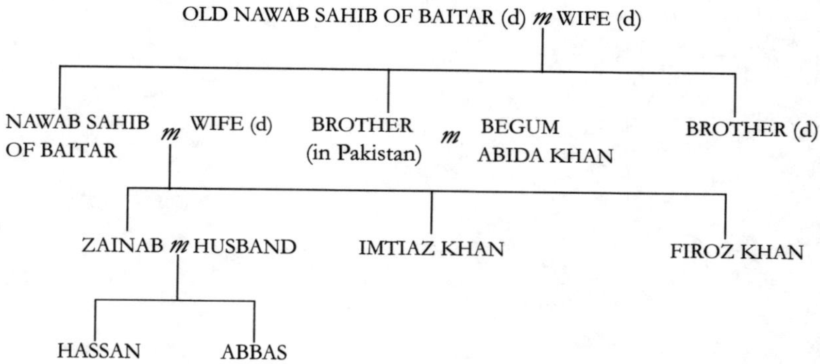

CHATTERJIS

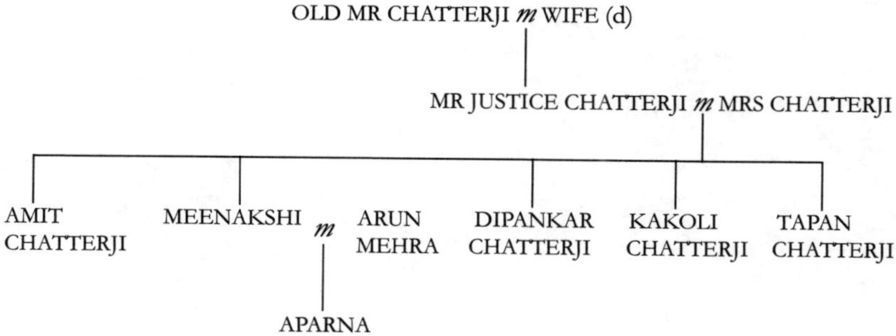

(d)=deceased

The superfluous, that very necessary thing. . . .

VOLTAIRE

The secret of being a bore is to say everything.

VOLTAIRE

Part Eight

8.1

No one saw off Maan and his Urdu teacher Abdur Rasheed at the Brahmpur Railway Station. It was noon. Maan was in such unhappy spirits in fact that even the presence of Pran or Firoz or his more disreputable student companions would not have soothed him much. He felt that he was being exiled, and he was quite right: that was exactly how both his father and Saeeda Bai saw matters. His father's ultimatum to get out of town had been direct, Saeeda Bai's solution had been more artful. One had coerced him and one had cajoled him. Both liked Maan, and both wanted him out of the way.

Maan did not blame Saeeda Bai, or not much; he felt that his absence would be very hard on her, and that by suggesting that he go to Rudhia instead of back to Banaras, she was keeping him as close to herself as, under the circumstances, she could hope to. He was furious with his father, though, who had thrown him out of Brahmpur for hardly any reason at all, had refused to listen to his side of things, and had grunted in a satisfied way when told that he would be going off to his Urdu teacher's village.

'Visit our farm while you're there—I'd like to hear how things are getting on,' was what his father had said. Then, after a pause, he had added, needlessly: 'That is, if you can make the time to travel a few miles. I know what an industrious student you will turn out to be.'

Mrs Mahesh Kapoor had merely hugged her son and told him to come back soon. Sometimes, thought Maan, bridling and frustrated, even his mother's affection was unbearable. It was she who was unshakably set against Saeeda Bai.

'Not before a month is over,' countered Mahesh Kapoor. He was relieved that Maan, despite his chafing, was not going to defy him by remaining in Brahmpur, but annoyed that he himself would have to 'deal with Banaras' in both senses: with the parents of Maan's fiancée, and with Maan's assistant in the cloth business who—and he thanked heaven for medium-sized mercies—was tolerably competent. He had enough on his plate, and Maan was a drain on his time and patience.

The platform was as crowded as ever with passengers and their friends and families and servants, hawkers, railway staff, coolies, vagrants and beggars. Babies wailed and whistles blew. Stray dogs slunk about with punished eyes, monkeys bared aggressive teeth. There was a pervasive railway platform stench. It was a hot day, and the fans were not working in the bogeys. The train sat at the narrow-gauge platform for half an hour after it was due to depart. Maan was stifled by the heat in the second-class compartment, but did not complain. He kept looking up glumly towards his luggage: a deep-blue leather suitcase and several smaller bags.

Rasheed, who, Maan decided, looked rather wolf-like in feature, had loped off to talk to some boys in another carriage. They were students at the Brahmpur madrasa who were going back to their districts for a few days.

Maan began to feel very sleepy. The fans were still not working, and the train showed no sign of starting. He touched the upper part of his ear, where he had placed a small piece of cotton wool containing a drop of Saeeda Bai's rose perfume, and passed his hand slowly across his face. It was wet with perspiration.

To minimize the uncomfortable sensation of sweat trickling down his face, Maan tried to remain as still as he could. The man opposite him was fanning himself with a Hindi newspaper.

The train at last began to move. It passed through the city for a while, then moved into the open countryside. Villages and fields went by, some parched and dusty and fallow, others yellow with wheat or green with other crops. The fans began to whirr and everyone looked relieved.

In some of the fields along the railway track, the wheat harvest was going on. In others it had just taken place, and the dry stubble was glinting in the sun.

Every fifteen minutes or so the train stopped at a small railway station, sometimes in the middle of nowhere, sometimes in a village. Very occasionally it would halt in a small town, the headquarters of a subdivision of the district they were travelling through. A mosque or a temple, a few neem or pipal or banyan trees, a boy driving goats along a dusty dirt track, the sudden turquoise flash of a kingfisher—Maan vaguely registered these. After a while he closed his eyes again, and was overwhelmed by his feeling of separation from the one person whose company he desired. He wanted to see nothing and hear nothing, just to recall the sights and sounds of the house in Pasand Bagh: the delicious perfumes of Saeeda Bai's room, the evening cool, the sound of her voice, the pressure of her hand on his. He began to think even of her parakeet and her watchman with affection.

But even when he closed his eyes to cut out the dry brightness of the afternoon light and the monotonous fields stretching out to the huge visible quadrant of the dusty sky, the sounds of the train bore in on him with amplified volume. The jolting and clicking of the train as it rocked sideways and slightly upwards, the sound of it going over a small bridge or the whooshing of a train rushing past in the opposite direction, the sound of a woman coughing or the crying of a child, even the dropping of a coin or the rustle of a newspaper, all took on an unbearable intensity. He rested his head on his hands, and stayed still.

'Are you all right? Are you feeling all right?' It was Rasheed who was speaking to him.

Maan nodded, and opened his eyes.

He looked at his fellow-passengers, then again at Rasheed. He decided that Rasheed looked too gaunt for someone who was only his own age. He also had a few white hairs.

Well, thought Maan, if I can begin to go bald at twenty-five, why shouldn't he begin to go white?

After a while he asked: 'How's the water at your place?'

'What do you mean?'

'It's fine, isn't it?' said Maan anxiously. He was beginning to wonder what life would be like in the village.

'Oh yes, we pump it up by hand.'

'Don't you have any electricity?'

Rasheed smiled a little sardonically and shook his head.

Maan was silent. The serious practical implications of his exile were beginning to seep in.

They had stopped just beyond a small station. The train tanks were being filled with water from above, and, as the engine steamed out, the sound of water dropping on the roof of the compartment reminded Maan of rain. There would be weeks of unbearable heat until the monsoons.

'Flies!'

It was the man sitting next to Rasheed who had spoken. He looked like a dried-out farmer, about forty years of age. He was rolling some tobacco in his palm with the thumb of his other hand. He rubbed it, then tamped it down, threw off the excess, examined the residue with care, selected out the impurities, took a pinch, licked the inside of his lower lip, and spat out a bit sideways on to the floor.

'Do you speak English?' he said after a while in the local dialect of Hindi. He had noticed Maan's luggage tag.

'Yes,' said Maan.

'Without English you can't do anything,' said the farmer sagely.

Maan wondered what possible use English could be to the farmer.

'What use is English?' said Maan.

'People love English!' said the farmer, with a strange sort of deep-voiced giggle. 'If you talk in English, you are a king. The more people you can mystify, the more people will respect you.' He turned back to his tobacco.

Maan felt a sudden urge to explain himself. As he tried to think of what he should say, he heard the droning of flies getting louder and louder around him. It was too hot to think, and he felt overcome with sleepiness. His head sank on his chest. In a minute he was asleep.

8.2

'Rudhia Junction. It's Rudhia Junction.' Maan woke up to see several passengers getting their luggage out of the train, and several others clambering in. Rudhia, the district town, was the largest town in the district, but not a railway junction in the sense that Brahmpur was, and certainly not in the sense of a great junction like Mughalsarai. Two narrow-gauge lines intersected at Rudhia, that was all. But those who lived there thought that it was the most important centre in Purva Pradesh next to Brahmpur, and the words *Rudhia Jn* on the signs and on the six white-tiled spittoons at the station added to the dignity of the town as much as did the District Court, the Collectorate and other administrative offices, and the steam power house, which was run on coal.

The train stopped at Rudhia a full three minutes before panting on through the afternoon. A sign in front of the stationmaster's office announced: *Our Goal: Security, Safety and Punctuality.* In fact, the train was already an hour and a half late. This was nothing unusual, and most of the passengers, if inconvenienced, did not make things worse by distressing themselves. One and a half hours was nothing.

The train turned a bend, and smoke began to enter the compartment in great gusts. The farmer started struggling with the windows, and Maan and Rasheed gave him a hand.

A large, red-leafed tree in a field caught Maan's attention. 'What's that tree?' he asked, pointing out of the window. 'It looks a bit like a mango with its red leaves, but it isn't a mango.'

'That's a mahua,' said the farmer, before Rasheed could reply. He looked amused, as if he'd had to explain what a cat was.

'Very handsome tree,' said Maan.

'Oh yes. Useful too,' said the farmer.

'In what way?'

'It gets you drunk,' said the farmer with a brown-toothed smile.

'Really?' said Maan, interested. 'Is it the sap?'

But the farmer, delighted with his ignorance, started giggling in his strange, deep way, and volunteered nothing else beyond the word: 'Sap!'

Rasheed leaned forward towards Maan intently and, tapping the steel trunk that rested between them, said:

'It's the flowers. They are very light and fragrant. They would have fallen about a month ago. If you dry them, they last for a year. Ferment them, and they'll give you a liquor.' He sounded slightly disapproving.

'Oh yes?' said Maan, livening up.

But Rasheed continued: 'Cook them, and they'll act as a vegetable. Boil them with milk, and they'll make the milk red and the person who drinks it strong. Mix them with the flour you use to make your rotis with in winter, and you won't feel the cold.'

Maan was impressed.

'Feed them to your cattle,' added the farmer. 'It'll double their energy.'

Maan looked towards Rasheed for verification, not trusting anything that the mocking farmer said.

'Yes, that's true,' said Rasheed.

'What a wonderful tree!' said Maan, delighted. He suddenly became less torpid, and began asking lots of questions. The countryside, which so far had looked entirely monotonous to him, became interesting.

They had just crossed a broad, brown river and entered a jungle. Maan immediately wanted to know if there was any game to be had there, and was pleased to hear that there was fox, jackal, nilgai, wild boar and even the occasional bear. And in the ravines and rocky outcrops not far from here there were wolves, who were sometimes a menace to the local population.

'Actually,' said Rasheed, 'this jungle is part of the Baitar Estate.'

'Ah!' said Maan, delighted. Although he and Pran had been friends with Firoz and Imtiaz from childhood, they had only known them in Brahmpur, and had never visited Baitar Fort or the estate.

'But this is wonderful!' said Maan. 'I know the family well. We must go hunting together.'

Rasheed smiled rather ruefully and said nothing. Perhaps, thought Maan, he was thinking that at this rate he would learn very little Urdu during his stay in the village. But what does that matter? he felt like saying. Instead he said:

'They must have horses at the fort.'

'They do,' said the farmer, with sudden enthusiasm and new respect. 'Many horses. A whole stable. And two jeeps also. And for Moharram they have a tremendous procession and lots of ceremonies. You really know the Nawab Sahib?'

'Well, it's his sons I know,' said Maan.

Rasheed, who was rather tired with the farmer, said quietly: 'This is Mahesh Kapoor's son.'

The farmer's mouth dropped open. This statement was so improbable as to be almost certainly true. But what was he—the son of the great Minister—doing, travelling for all the world like an ordinary citizen in a second-class carriage, and wearing a crumpled kurta-pyjama?

'And I have been joking with you,' he said, shocked by his own temerity.

Maan, whose discomfort he had enjoyed, now enjoyed his discomfort.

'I won't tell my father,' he said.

'He'll take my land away if he hears of it,' said the farmer—who either believed in the exaggerated powers of the Minister of Revenue, or else thought it politic to exaggerate his fear.

'He'll do nothing of the kind,' said Maan. Thinking of his father he felt a sudden spasm of outrage.

'When zamindari is abolished, all these lands will be taken by him,' said the farmer. 'Even the Nawab Sahib's estates. What can a small landowner like me do?'

'I'll tell you what,' said Maan. 'Don't tell me your name. Then you'll be safe.'

The farmer seemed amused by this idea, and repeated it to himself a couple of times.

Suddenly the train started jolting, as if the brake had been applied, and in a short while came to a halt in open countryside.

'This always happens,' said Rasheed with a flicker of irritation.

'What does?' said Maan.

'These schoolboys pulling the chain and stopping the train when it gets close to their village. It's just the boys of this particular locality. By the time the guards get to their carriage, they've disappeared into the sugarcane fields.'

'Can't they do something about it?' said Maan.

'There's no way of controlling them. Either they should simply halt the train here and admit defeat. Or else they should catch one of them somehow, and make an example of him.'

'How?'

'Oh, beat him up soundly,' said Rasheed calmly. 'And lock him up for a few days.'

'But that's very harsh,' said Maan, trying to imagine what it would be like to be locked up for a few days in a cell.

'It's quite effective. We were equally unruly at that age,' continued Rasheed with a brief smile. 'My father beat me up regularly. Once my grandfather—whom you will meet—beat my brother to within an inch of his life—and that was a turning point in his life. He became a wrestler!'

'Your grandfather beat him, not your father?' said Maan.

'My grandfather. He was the one we were most terrified of,' said Rasheed.

'Still?'

'Less so now. He's over seventy. But well into his sixties he was the terror of ten villages. Haven't I mentioned him to you before?'

'You mean he terrorized them?' said Maan, trying to picture this strange patriarch.

'I mean, they all respected him, and came to him to solve their disputes. He's a landowner, a medium-sized landowner, so he has some standing in our community. He is a religious and just man, so people look up to him. And he himself was a wrestler in his youth, so they're afraid of his arm. He used it to beat up any ruffian he could lay his hands on.'

'I suppose I shouldn't gamble or drink while I'm in your village,' said Maan cheerfully.

Rasheed looked very serious. 'No, really, Kapoor Sahib,' he said, quite formally, Maan thought. 'You are my guest, and my family does not know you are coming. For the month you are with me, your behaviour will reflect on me.'

'Oh, don't worry,' Maan said impulsively, 'I won't do anything that will cause you any trouble. I promise.'

Rasheed looked relieved, and Maan realized the rashness of his promise. He had never so far in his life succeeded in behaving himself for a whole month.

8.3

At the small subdivisional town of Salimpur, they dismounted, loaded their bags on the flimsy back of a cycle rickshaw, and got unbalancedly on.

The rickshaw jolted and swerved along the pitted road that led from Salimpur to Rasheed's native village of Debaria. It was evening, and everywhere birds were chattering in the trees. The neem trees rustled in the warm evening breeze. Underneath a small stand of straight, broad-leafed teak trees a donkey, two of its legs tied together, was hobbling painfully forward. On every culvert sat a crowd of children, who shouted at the rickshaw as it went along. There was very little traffic other than the many bullock-carts making their way village-wards from the harvest or a few boys driving cattle down the road.

Since Maan had changed into an orange kurta before getting off the train—the one he had been wearing earlier was drenched with sweat—he presented a colourful spectacle, even in the waning light. As for Rasheed, several people on foot or on bullock-carts greeted him along the way.

'How are you?'

'Very well. And you? Everything all right?'

'Everything all right.'

'How is the harvest?'

'Well—not too good. Back from Brahmpur?'

'Yes.'

'How long will you be staying?'

'A month.'

Throughout the conversation, they would stare not at Rasheed but at Maan, looking him up and down.

The sunset was pink, smoky, and still. The fields stretched out to the dark horizon on either side. There was not a cloud in the sky. Maan began to think once again of Saeeda Bai, and he felt in his bones that it would be impossible for him to live for a whole month without her.

What was he doing anyway in this doltish place so far away from all civilization—among suspicious peasants, illiterate and unelectrified, who knew nothing better than to stare at strangers?

There was a sudden lurch, and Maan, Rasheed, and their luggage were nearly pitched out of the rickshaw.

'What did you do that for?' said Rasheed sharply to the rickshaw-wallah.

'Aré, bhai, there was a hole in the road. I'm not a panther that I can see in the dark,' said the rickshaw-wallah abruptly.

After a while they turned off the road on to an even more inadequate mud track that led to the village, a mile away. This track would clearly become impassable in the rainy season, and the village would virtually be cut off from the world. At the moment it was all the rickshaw-wallah could do to keep his balance. After a while he gave up and asked his passengers to get off.

'I should charge you three rupees for this, not two,' he said.

'One rupee eight annas,' was Rasheed's quiet reply. 'Now get on with it.'

It was completely dark by the time they got to Rasheed's house—or, as he usually called it, his father's house. It appeared to be a moderately large single-storey building made of whitewashed brick. A kerosene lamp was burning on the roof. Rasheed's father was up on the roof, and called out when he heard the sound of the rickshaw—which was bumping along the village lane, guided by the light of Maan's torch.

'Who's that?'

'It's Rasheed, Abba-jaan.'

'Good. We were expecting you.'

'Is everything well here?'

'As well as can be. The harvest is not much good. I'm coming down. Is that someone with you?'

It struck Maan that the voice from the roof sounded like that of a toothless man, more like the voice that he imagined Rasheed's grandfather, not his father, would have.

By the time he came downstairs the man had two kerosene lamps in his hands and a couple of paans in his mouth. He greeted his son with very mild affection. Then the three of them sat on a charpoy out in front of the house under a great neem tree.

'This is Maan Kapoor, Abba-jaan,' said Rasheed.

His father nodded, then said to Maan: 'Are you here on a visit or are you an officer of some kind?'

Maan smiled. 'I'm here on a visit. Your son has been teaching me Urdu in Brahmpur. Now I hope he will continue to teach me in Debaria.'

Maan noticed, by the light of the lamp, that Rasheed's father had large gaps in his teeth. This explained his peculiar voice and the absence of certain consonants. But it made him look sinister even when he was attempting to be welcoming.

Meanwhile another figure emerged out of the dark from across the way to greet Rasheed. He was introduced to Maan, and sat down on another stringed bedstead, which had been laid out in front of the house. He was a man of about twenty, and, therefore, younger than Rasheed, though he was his uncle—his father's younger brother in fact. He was talkative—indeed, very full of himself.

A servant brought out some sherbet in a glass for each of them.

'You've had a long journey,' said Rasheed's father. 'Wash your hands, rinse out your mouth, and drink your sherbet.'

Maan said: 'Is there anywhere. . . .'

'Oh, yes,' said Rasheed's father, 'go behind the cowshed if you want to piss. Is that it?'

'Yes,' said Maan, and went, gripping his torch tightly and stepping into cowdung as he made his way to the other side of the shed. One of the bullocks started lowing at his approach.

When he came back Rasheed poured some water over his hands from a brass pot. In the warm evening the water was wonderfully cool.

So was the sherbet. This was followed quickly by dinner, eaten again by the light of kerosene lamps. Dinner consisted of meat dishes and fairly thick wheat rotis. All four men ate together under the stars and among the insects that whirred all around. They concentrated on eating; conversation was desultory.

'What's this? Pigeon?' asked Maan.

'Yes. We have a pigeon-house up there—or, rather, my grandfather does.' Rasheed pointed into the dark. 'Where is Baba, by the way?' he asked his father.

'He's gone off on one of his tours of inspection of the village,' was the reply. 'Probably also to talk to Vilayat Sahib—to try to convert him back to Islam.'

Everyone laughed except Maan, who did not know the two people involved. He bit into a shami kabab, and began to feel somewhat forlorn.

'He should be back in time for the night prayer,' said Rasheed, who wanted Maan to meet his grandfather.

When someone mentioned Rasheed's wife, Maan sat up. He hadn't known or imagined that Rasheed had a wife. A little later someone mentioned Rasheed's two small daughters and Maan was further astonished.

'Now, we'll lay out some bedding for you,' said Rasheed's father in his brisk but toothless way. 'I sleep on the roof there. In this season, it's good to get what breeze you can.'

'What a good idea,' said Maan. 'I'll do the same.'

There was an awkward silence, then Rasheed said:

'Actually, we should try sleeping under the stars here—outside the house. Our bedding can be laid out here.'

Maan frowned, and was about to ask a question, when Rasheed's father said: 'Good, then, that's settled. I'll send the servant out with the stuff. It's too hot for a mattress. Spread a rug on the charpoy and a sheet or two on top of that. All right, I'll see you tomorrow.'

Later, lying on his bed, looking up at the clear night sky, Maan's thoughts turned towards home. Luckily he was quite sleepy, so thoughts of Saeeda Bai were not likely to keep him up the whole night. Frogs were croaking in a pond somewhere at the edge of the village. A cat yowled. A buffalo snorted in the cattle-shed. A few crickets cried, and the grey-white flash of an owl settled on the branch of a neem tree. Maan took this as a good sign.

'An owl,' he announced to Rasheed, who was lying on the charpoy next to him.

'Oh, yes,' said Rasheed. 'And there's another one.'

Another grey shape flew down on to the branch.

'I'm very fond of owls,' said Maan sleepily.

'Inauspicious birds,' said Rasheed.

'Well, they know they have a friend in me,' said Maan. 'That is why they are watching over my sleep. They will make sure I dream about pleasant things. About beautiful women and so on. Rasheed, you must teach me some ghazals tomorrow. Incidentally, why are you sleeping out here? Shouldn't you be with your wife?'

'My wife is at her father's village,' said Rasheed.

'Ah,' said Maan.

For a while Rasheed said nothing. Then he said, 'Do you know the story of Mahmud of Ghazni and his peace-loving Prime Minister?'

'No.' What that great conqueror and despoiler of cities had to do with what had gone before, Maan could not see. But in that twilight state that precedes sleep, it was not necessary to see.

Rasheed began his story: 'Mahmud of Ghazni said to his vazir: "What are those two owls?"'

'Oh yes?' said Maan. 'Mahmud of Ghazni was lying on a charpoy staring at these owls?'

'Probably not,' said Rasheed. 'Different owls, and probably not on a charpoy. So he, the vazir, said: "One owl has a young boy owl, and one has a young girl owl. They are well matched in every way, and the marriage plans are going ahead. The two owls—fathers-in-law-to-be—are sitting on a branch discussing their children's marriage, especially the all-important question of the dowry." The vazir pauses here. So Mahmud of Ghazni says, "What are they saying?" The vazir replies: "The owl on the boy's side is demanding a thousand deserted villages as a dowry." "Yes? Yes?" says Mahmud of Ghazni, "and what is the other owl saying?" The vazir replies: "The owl on the girl's side is saying: After the latest campaign of Mahmud of Ghazni he can offer five thousand. . . ." Good night. Sleep well.'

'Good night,' said Maan, pleased with the story. However, he remained awake for a minute or two thinking about it. The owls were still on the branch when he fell off to sleep.

The next morning he woke up to the sound of someone saying, with great affection and severity: 'Wake up! Wake up! Won't you say your morning prayers? Oh, Rasheed, go and get some water, your friend has to wash his hands before his prayers.'

An old man, powerful in build and looking like a prophet with his beard, bare-chested and wearing a loosely folded green cotton lungi, was standing over him. Maan guessed that this must be Rasheed's grandfather, or 'Baba' as Rasheed called him. So affectionate and determined was the old man in enforcing piety that Maan hardly had the courage to refuse.

'Well?' said Baba. 'Get up, get up. As it says in the call, prayer is better than sleep.'

'Actually,'—Maan found his voice at last—'I don't go to prayer.'

'You don't read the namaaz?' Baba looked more than injured; he looked shocked. What kind of people was Rasheed bringing home to his village? He felt like pulling the impious young lout out of bed.

'Baba—he's a Hindu,' explained Rasheed, intervening to prevent further embarrassment. 'His name is Maan Kapoor.' He emphasized Maan's surname.

The old man looked at Maan in astonishment. The thought had not occurred to him at all. Then he looked at his grandson and opened his mouth as if to ask him something. But he obviously thought better of it, because the question remained unasked.

There was a pause for a few seconds. Then the old man spoke.

'Oh, he's a Hindu!' he said at last, and turned away from Maan.

8.4

Rasheed explained to Maan a little later where they would have to go for their morning toilet—out in the fields with a brass lota to carry water in. It was the only time of day when it was somewhat cool and when there was a bit of privacy. Maan, feeling quite uncomfortable, rubbed his eyes, filled his lota with water, and followed Rasheed out into the fields.

It was a fine, clear morning. They passed a pond close to the village. A few ducks were swimming among the reeds and a glossy black water buffalo was bathing in it, as deep as its nostrils. A young girl in a pink-and-green salwaar-kameez appeared from a house at the outskirts, saw Maan, gave a shy gasp, and quickly disappeared.

Rasheed was lost in his thoughts. 'It's such a waste,' he said.

'What is?'

'All this.' He pointed in a wide sweep to the countryside around him, taking in the fields, the pond, the village, and another village visible in the distance. Then, since Maan did not ask him why, he continued: 'It is my dream to completely transform. . . .'

Maan began smiling, and lost the thread of what Rasheed was saying. For all Rasheed's knowledge about mahua trees and the finer points of the landscape, Maan felt that he was an impractical visionary. If he had been so exacting with Maan's meems, it would take a millennium for village life to attain the kind of perfection that would satisfy him. Rasheed was now walking very fast, and it was all Maan could do to keep up. Walking on the mud ridges dividing the fields was not easy, especially in rubber chappals. He slipped, and narrowly avoided a twisted ankle. His lota, however, fell, and the water in it splashed and trickled out.

Rasheed, noticing that his companion had fallen behind, turned around, and was alarmed to see him on the ground, rubbing his ankle.

'Why didn't you shout?' he asked. 'Are you all right?'

'Yes,' said Maan. Then, so as not to make a fuss, he added: 'But what were you saying about transforming all this?'

For a moment, Rasheed's rather lean-featured, lupine face carried a worried expression. Then he said: 'That pond, for instance. They could stock it with fish and use it. And there's a large pond, which is part of the common property of the village, like the common grazing ground. But it isn't used for anything. It's an economic waste. Even the water—' He paused, and looked at Maan's spilled lota.

'Here,' he said, about to pour half the water from his lota into Maan's. Then he stopped. 'On second thoughts,' he said, 'I'll pour it later, when we've reached our destination.'

'All right,' said Maan.

Rasheed, remembering that it was his duty to educate Maan and recalling how keen he had been to absorb information yesterday, now began telling him the names of various plants that they passed. But Maan was not in an educable mood this morning, and confined his responses to the occasional repetition of a word to show that his attention had not wandered.

'What's that?' he said suddenly.

They had reached the top of a gentle rise. About half a mile away lay a beautiful blue pool of water with clearly defined mud banks on each side, and a few white buildings on the side farther away from them.

'That's the local school, the madrasa,' said Rasheed matter-of-factly. 'It's actually in the neighbouring village, but all the Muslim children from our village go to it as well.'

'Do they teach mainly Islamic studies there?' asked Maan, who had meant to ask about the pool but had been diverted by Rasheed's reply.

'No—well, yes, some of course. But they begin by taking in little children of five or so, and teach them a bit of everything.' Rasheed paused to survey the landscape, feeling momentarily happy to be back again. He liked Brahmpur because life was less narrow and frustrating there than in the rigid and—in his view—reactionary village, but while in the city he was always rushing around studying or teaching and there was far too much noise everywhere.

He looked for a few seconds at the madrasa where he had been such a difficult pupil that his teachers, at a loss to control him themselves, had regularly reported him to his father—and his grandfather. Then he added: 'It's got a good standard of teaching. Even Vilayat Sahib began his studies here before this fish pond became too small for him. Now that he's such a big name in archaeology, he contributes books to the school library that none of the children can understand. Several of them have been written by himself. He's visiting for the week, but he's very reclusive. Maybe we'll meet him. Well, here we are. Give me your lota.'

They had reached a high field-divider near a small copse of trees. Rasheed shared his water with Maan. Then he squatted down and said: 'Anywhere around here is a good place. Take your time. No one will disturb us.'

Maan was embarrassed, but acted as casually as he could. 'I'll go over there,' he said, and wandered off.

I suppose this is the shape of things to come for the next month, he thought disconsolately. I may as well get used to it. I hope there are no snakes or other unpleasant things around. There isn't very much water either. What if I want to go later in the day? Will I have to walk out here and back in the heat? Better not think about it. And since he was good at avoiding unpleasant thoughts, he turned to other matters.

He began to think how good it would be to swim in the blue pool near the local school. Maan loved swimming, not for the exercise but for the luxury, the tactility of it. In Brahmpur in earlier days, he would go to the lake called Windermere not far from the High Court, and swim in the cordoned-off area reserved for swimmers. He wondered why in the last month he hadn't swum there—or even thought of doing so.

On the way back to the village he said to himself: I must write to Saeeda Bai. Rasheed has got to help me with my letter.

Aloud he said: 'Well, I'm ready for my first Urdu lesson under the neem tree when we get back. If you're not doing anything else, that is.'

'No, I'm not,' said Rasheed, pleased. 'I was afraid that I would have to bring up the subject.'

8.5

While Maan was engaged in his Urdu lesson a crowd of small children gathered around him.

'They find you very interesting,' said Rasheed.

'I can see that,' said Maan. 'Why aren't they at school?'

'Term begins in two weeks' time,' said Rasheed. 'Now go away,' he told them. 'Can't you see that I'm giving a lesson?'

The children could indeed see that he was giving a lesson, and they were fascinated. They were particularly fascinated by an adult who was having a hard time with the alphabet.

They began to imitate Maan under their breath. 'Alif-be-pe-te . . . laam-meem-noon,' they chanted, gathering courage as Maan tried to ignore them.

Maan didn't mind them at all. He suddenly turned on them and roared as fiercely as an angry lion, and they scattered, terrified. Some of them began giggling from a safe distance, and started to approach again, with tentative steps.

'Do you think we should go inside?' said Maan.

Rasheed looked embarrassed. 'Actually, the fact is that we maintain purdah at home. All your bags are inside, of course, for safe custody.'

'Oh!' said Maan, 'of course.' After a while he said, 'Your father must have thought it very odd of me last night to say I'd sleep on the roof.'

'It's not your fault,' said Rasheed. 'I should have warned you. But I take everything about my own home for granted.'

'The Nawab Sahib has purdah in his house in Brahmpur, so I shouldn't have assumed it would be different here,' said Maan.

'It is, though,' said Rasheed. 'The Muslim women of the lower castes need to work in the fields, so they can't maintain purdah. But we Shaikhs and Sayyeds try to. It's simply a matter of honour, of being the big people in the village.'

Just as Maan was about to ask Rasheed if his village was mainly or exclusively Muslim, Rasheed's grandfather came along to look at what they were doing. The old man was still wearing his green lungi, but had added a white vest. With his white beard and somewhat failing eyes, he looked more frail than he did when he had loured over Maan in the morning.

'What are you teaching him, Rasheed?'

'Urdu, Baba.'

'Yes? Good, good.'

To Maan he said:

'How old are you, Kapoor Sahib?'

'Twenty-five.'

'Are you married?'

'No.'

'Why not?'

'Well,' said Maan, 'it hasn't happened yet.'

'There's nothing wrong with you, is there?'

'Oh, no!' said Maan. 'Nothing.'

'Then you should get married. This is the time, when you are young.

Then you won't be an old man when your children are growing up. Look at me. I'm old now, but I wasn't once.'

Maan was tempted to exchange a glance with Rasheed, but sensed that it wasn't the right thing to do.

The old man picked up the exercise book that Maan had been writing on and held it away from his eyes. The whole page was covered with the same two letters. 'Seen, sheen,' said the old man. 'Seen, sheen, seen, sheen, seen, sheen. Enough of this! Teach him something more, Rasheed—this is all very well for children. He'll get bored.'

Rasheed nodded his head but said nothing.

The old man turned back to Maan and said: 'Are you bored yet?'

'Oh no,' said Maan, quickly. 'I've been learning to read. This is just the calligraphy part.'

'That's good,' said Rasheed's grandfather. 'That's very good. Carry on, carry on. I will go over there'—he pointed across the way to a charpoy lying in front of another house—'and read.'

He cleared his throat and spat on to the ground, then walked slowly away. In a few minutes Maan saw him seated cross-legged on the charpoy with his spectacles on, swaying backwards and forwards, reciting from a large book placed in front of him that Maan assumed was the Quran. Since he was only about twenty steps away, the murmur of his recitation merged with the sounds of the children, who were now daring each other to go and touch Maan—'the lion'.

Maan said to Rasheed, 'I've been thinking of writing a letter. Do you think you could write it for me and, well, help me compose it? I can still barely string two words together in this script.'

'Of course,' said Rasheed.

'You really don't mind?' said Maan.

'No, of course not. Why should I?' said Rasheed.

'Actually, it's to Saeeda Bai.'

'I see,' said Rasheed.

'Maybe after dinner?' said Maan. 'I'm not in the mood now with all these kids running around.' He was afraid that they might start chanting 'Saeeda Bai! Saeeda Bai!' at the top of their lungs.

Rasheed didn't say anything for a few moments, then waved away a fly and said: 'The only reason why I'm getting you to write these two letters again and again is that the way you draw the curve is too shallow. It should be more rounded. Like this—' And he drew the letter 'sheen' very slowly.

Maan could sense that Rasheed was not happy, that he in fact disapproved, but he did not know what to do about it. He could not bear to think that he would not hear from Saeeda Bai, and he feared that she might not write to him unless he wrote to her. In fact he wasn't even sure that she had his postal address. Of course 'c/o Abdur Rasheed, village Debaria, tehsil Salimpur, Distt Rudhia, P.P.' would get to him, but Maan was not certain that Saeeda Bai was certain that it would.

Since she could read nothing but Urdu, he would have to get an Urdu scribe to write his letter for him until he himself learned the script sufficiently well to be able to do so. And who other than Rasheed could or would help him by writing it, and—unless Saeeda Bai's hand was exceptionally clear and careful—by reading out her reply to him when it came?

Maan was staring down at the ground in his perplexity when he noticed that a huge crowd of flies had gathered around the spot where Baba had spat. They were ignoring the sherbet that Maan and Rasheed were drinking.

How strange, he thought, and frowned.

'What are you thinking of?' said Rasheed, quite brusquely. 'Once you can read and write the language you'll be free. So do pay attention, Kapoor Sahib.'

'Look at that,' said Maan.

'That's odd. You're not diabetic, are you?' said Rasheed, no longer with sharpness but concern in his voice.

'No,' said Maan, surprised. 'Why? That's where Baba spat just now.'

'Oh, yes, I see,' said Rasheed. 'He is. And the flies gather around his spittle because it's sweet.'

Maan looked over towards the old man, who was shaking his finger at one of the brats.

'But he insists he's in very good general health,' said Rasheed, 'and against all our advice, he still fasts every day during Ramazan. Last year it was in June, and he didn't have a morsel of food or a drop of water from sunrise to sunset. And this year it'll be at almost the same time of year. Long hot days. No one expects it of a man his age. But he won't listen.'

The heat had suddenly begun to get to Maan, but he didn't know what to do about it. He was sitting under the neem tree, which was the coolest place out of doors. If he had been at home, he would have turned on the fan, collapsed on to his bed and stared at the ceiling as the blades went round and round. Here there was nothing to do but suffer. The sweat trickled down his face, and he tried to be grateful that flies didn't settle upon it immediately.

'It's too hot!' said Maan. 'I don't want to live.'

'You should have a bath,' said Rasheed.

'Ah!' said Maan.

Rasheed went on: 'I'll go in and get some soap and tell the fellow to pump the water while you're under the tap. It would have been too cold after dark last night, but now's a good time. . . . Use that tap.' He pointed to the pump directly in front of the house. 'But you should put on your lungi while bathing.'

There was a small, windowless room that jutted forward out of the house and Maan used this to change in. It was not part of the house proper but acted as a sort of shed. It contained spare parts for agricultural machinery and a few ploughs. Some spears and sticks stood in a corner. When Maan entered it there was as much expectation among the children as if an actor had gone backstage to emerge in a brilliant new costume. When he came out they discussed him critically.

'Look at him, he looks so pale.'

'He looks even more bald now.'

'Lion, lion, without a tail!'

All of them became very excited. One odious child of about seven called 'Mr Biscuit' made use of the clamour to aim a stone at a girl. The stone went hurtling through the air and hit her on the back of the head. She started screaming in pain and shock. Baba, jolted out of his recitation, got up from his charpoy and appraised the situation in an instant. Everyone was staring at Mr Biscuit, who was trying to appear nonchalant. Baba caught hold of Mr Biscuit's ear and twisted it.

'Haramzada—bastard—you dare to behave like the animal you are?' cried the old man.

Mr Biscuit began to blubber, and snot ran down from his nostrils. Baba dragged him by the ear to where he had been sitting, and slapped him so hard the boy almost went flying. Then, ignoring him, he sat down to his recitation again. But his concentration had been spoilt.

Mr Biscuit sat stunned on the ground for a few minutes, then got up to perpetrate what further mischief he could. Meanwhile his victim had been taken back home by Rasheed; she was bleeding copiously from the back of her head, and crying her eyes out.

Ignorant and brutal at the age of seven! This, thought Rasheed, is what the village does to you. Anger against his surroundings welled up within him.

Maan had his bath under the scrutiny of the village children. The cool water poured generously out of the spout, pumped by a very vigorous middle-aged man with a friendly, square, deeply furrowed and wrinkled face. He showed no signs of tiring and appeared to enjoy being of service, continuing to pump water even after Maan had finished.

Maan at last was cool and, therefore, at a truce with the world.

8.6

Maan did not eat much at lunch but praised the food a great deal, hoping that some of his praise would get through to the unseen woman or women of the house who had prepared it.

A little after lunch, after they had washed their hands and were resting on the charpoys outside, a couple of visitors arrived at the house. One was Rasheed's maternal uncle.

This man was the elder brother of Rasheed's late mother. He was a huge, kind bear of a man, with a pepper-and-salt stubble. He lived about ten miles away, and Rasheed had once run off and lived with him for a month after he had been beaten at home for half-throttling a fellow-schoolmate to death.

Rasheed got up from the charpoy the instant he saw him. Then he said to Maan—the others were still out of earshot—'The big man is my Mamu. The round one is known as the "guppi" in my mother's village—he blathers on and on and tells ridiculous stories. We're stuck.'

By now the visitors had reached the cattle-shed.

'Ah, Mamu, I didn't know you were coming. How are you?' said Rasheed in warm welcome. And he nodded at the guppi civilly.

'Ah,' said the Bear, and sat down heavily on the charpoy. He was a man of few words.

The man of many words, his friend and travelling companion, also sat down and asked for a glass of water. Rasheed promptly went inside and got some sherbet.

The guppi asked Maan a number of questions and ascertained quickly who, why, what and how he was. He then described to Maan a number of incidents that had occurred on their ten-mile journey. They had seen a snake, 'as thick as my arm' (Rasheed's Mamu frowned in concentration, but did not contradict him); they had almost been blown off their feet by a sudden whirlwind; and the police had shot at them three times at the check-post just outside Salimpur.

Rasheed's Mamu merely mopped his brow and gasped gamely in the heat. Maan leaned forward, amazed by these unlikely adventures.

Rasheed returned, bearing glasses of sherbet. He told them that his father was sleeping. The Bear nodded benevolently.

The talkative one was asking Maan about his love life, and Maan was attempting weakly to fend off the questions.

'People's love lives are not very interesting,' said Maan, sounding unconvincing even to himself.

'How can you say that?' said the guppi. 'Every man's love life is interesting. If he doesn't have one, that's interesting. If he has one, that's interesting. And if he has two, that's twice as interesting.' He laughed delightedly at his sally. Rasheed looked abashed. Baba had gone inside his house already.

Encouraged by the fact that he had not been immediately stifled, as he often was in his own village, the guppi went on:

'But what would you know of love—of true love? You young men have not seen much. You may think that because you live in Brahmpur you have seen the world—or more of the world than we poor yokels see. But some of us yokels have also seen the world—and not just the world of Brahmpur, but of Bombay.'

He paused, impressed by his own words, especially the entrancing word 'Bombay', and looked at his audience with pleasure. Several children had appeared in the last couple of minutes, drawn by the guppi's magic. Whenever the guppi appeared they could be sure of a good story, and probably one that their parents would not want them to hear—involving ghosts or deadly violence or passionate love.

A goat too had appeared, and was standing at the upper end of a cart, trying to graze on the leaves of a branch just overhead. With its crafty yellow eyes it stared at the leaves and strained its neck upwards.

'When I was in Bombay,' the round and reverberant guppi went on, 'long before my fate changed and I had to return to this blessed countryside, I worked in a big shop, a very famous shop run by a mullah, and we would sell carpets to big people, all the very big people of Bombay. They would have so much money, they would take it in wads out of their bags and throw it down on the counter.'

His eyes lit up as if at the memory. The children sat enthralled—or most of them anyway. Mr Biscuit, the seven-year-old horror, was occupied with the goat. Whenever it got near its goal, the leafy branch, Mr Biscuit would tilt the cart downwards, and the poor goat would now try to clamber up to the other end. So far it had not succeeded in eating a single leaf.

'It's a love story, I'm warning you in advance, so if you don't want to listen to it, you can tell me to stop now,' said the guppi in a formulary way. 'Because once I've begun, I can't stop it any more than one can stop the act of love itself.'

Rasheed would have got up and left if he hadn't been so conscious of his duty as a host. But Maan wanted to stay and hear the story.

'Go on, go on,' he said.

Rasheed looked at Maan, as if to say: This man needs no encouragement. If you show any interest at all he'll go on twice as long.

Aloud he said to the guppi: 'Of course, this is an eyewitness account as usual.'

The guppi shot him a glance, at first suspicious, then placatory. He had just been about to say that he had seen the events he was about to recount with his very own eyes.

'I saw these events with my very own eyes,' he said.

The goat started bleating piteously. The guppi shouted at the distracting Mr Biscuit: 'Sit down, or I'll feed you to that goat, your eyes first.'

Mr Biscuit, horrified by such a graphic description of his fate, thought that the guppi must mean business, and sat down on the ground like any ordinary child.

The guppi went on: 'So we'd sell carpets to all the big people, and there were such beautiful women who would come to our shop that our eyes would water with emotion. The mullah in particular had a weakness for beauty, and whenever he saw a beautiful woman walking past our shop or about to enter it he would say: "Oh God! Why have you made such angels? Farishtas have come to earth to haunt us mortals." We would all start laughing. He would get very cross and scold us: "When you're tired of saying Bismillah on your knees you should praise the angels of God."'

The guppi paused for effect.

'Well, one day—this happened before my very eyes—a beautiful woman called Vimla tried to start her car, which was parked near our shop. It wouldn't start, so she got out. She started walking towards our shop. She was beautiful, so beautiful—that we were all entranced. One of us said: "The ground is shaking." The mullah said: "She is so beautiful that if she looks at you, boils will break out all over your body." But then—suddenly—'

The guppi's voice started trembling with the recollection.

'Suddenly—from the other direction—and on the other side of the street—came a young Pathan, so tall and handsome that the mullah started praising God as excitedly as before: "As the Moon leaves the skies, the Sun approaches," and so on.

'They approached each other. Then the young Pathan boy crossed the road towards her—saying, "Please, please—" in an importunate voice and holding out a card that he had whipped out of his pocket. He showed it to her three times. She was reluctant to read it, but finally she took it and bent her head to read it. No sooner had she done this than the young Pathan embraced her like a bear and bit her cheek so hard that the blood streamed down. She screamed!'

The guppi covered his face with his hands to ward off the awful image. Then he rallied and continued:

'The mullah cried, "Quick, quick, lie down, no one has seen anything—no one must get mixed up in this." But a man who was in his underwear on the roof of a nearby hotel saw it and cried, "Toba, toba!" He didn't come down to help but he called the police. Within minutes the streets were sealed off, and there was no way out, no escape at all. Five jeeps rushed towards the Pathan from all directions. The Superintendent of Police was merciless and the policemen used all the force they could, but the Pathan was clinging to the girl so tightly that they could not separate his arms, which were locked around her waist. He had shouldered aside three men before they finally succeeded in knocking him out with the butt of a pistol and separating his hands with a crowbar.'

The guppi paused for further effect before continuing. His audience was spellbound.

'The whole of Bombay was outraged at this gunda-gardi, this hooliganism, and a case was quickly registered against him. Everyone said: "Be strict—or all the girls in Bombay will have their cheeks bitten, and then what will happen?" There was a huge court case. He was put in a cage in court. He rattled the bars with such fury that the courtroom shook. But he was found guilty, and a death sentence was passed. Then the judge said: "Do you want to see anyone before you are hanging breathlessly from the gallows? Do you want one last glimpse of your mother?" The boy said: "No—I've seen enough of her. I've been fed by her breasts and have urinated in her arms when I was a baby—why should I want to see her again?" Everyone was shocked. "Anyone else?" said the judge.

'"Yes," said the doomed man. "Yes. One person, and one person alone: that person, a single sight of whom made me give up all hope of life on earth and made me willing to die—that person who has given me a taste of the world to come, for she has sent me to paradise. I have two things to say to her. She can stand outside the bars, I inside—I will not even touch her—"

'All the big people of Bombay, all the businessmen and ballishtahs stood up in court, turned to stone with the shock of his request. The girl's family started to scream. "Never!" they screamed—"Our daughter will never speak to him." The judge said: "I have said she can—and she must." So she went into the courtroom, and everyone was hissing: "Behayaa—besharam—how shameless can you get in the very face of your own death." But he only held the bars and laughed. It said in the papers also: He laughed.'

The guppi drained his glass of sherbet and held it out to be refilled. Resurrecting the past accurately was a thirsty job. The children stared impatiently as his Adam's apple moved up and down gulp after gulp. With a sigh he continued:

'The young man held the bars of his cage and looked deeply into Vimla's eyes. By God, it was as if he wanted to drink her soul out of her body. But she looked at him with contempt, holding her head up proudly, her once-beautiful cheek scarred and defiled. Finally he found his voice, and said: "I only want to say two things to you. First, no one will marry you now except an old and poor man . . . you have been marked as the one bitten by the Pathan. Second"—and here the young man's voice broke and the tears started streaming down his face—"second, by God I didn't know what happened to me when I did that to you. I lost my senses when I saw you, I never knew what I was doing—forgive me, forgive me! I have had hundreds of offers of marriage. I have refused them all—the most beautiful women. Till I saw you I never knew I had a companion of the soul.

'"I will treat your scar as a mark of beauty and bathe it with my tears and shower kisses on it. I am London-returned and I have thirty-five thousand people in factories working for me and crores of rupees in wealth and I want to give it all to you. God is a witness between us—I never knew what I was doing—but now I am willing to die."

'Hearing this, the girl, who a minute ago could have killed him with her own hands, began to gasp as if she was ill with love, and threw herself towards the judge, begging him to spare the man, saying: "Spare him, spare him—I knew him for a long time, I begged him to bite me—" But the judge had given his sentence and said: "Impossible. Do not lie, or I will put you away." Then in despair she took a knife out of her bag and put it to her throat and said to the whole court—the High Court judge and all the high ballishtahs and sollishtahs and all—"If he is killed, I die. I will write here that I committed suicide because of the sentence you passed."

'So they had to undo the sentence—what could they do? Then she begged that the marriage should take place at the boy's place. The girl was a Punjabi, and there was such enmity towards the Pathan and his family that her parents would have killed her as well as the boy for revenge.'

The guppi paused.

'This is true love,' he said, deeply moved by his narration, and leaned back on the charpoy, spent.

Maan, despite himself, was enthralled. Rasheed looked at him, then at the enraptured children, and closed his eyes in mild contempt for all that had gone on. His large, taciturn Mamu, who hardly appeared to have been listening, patted his friend on the back and said:

'Now Radio Jhutistan takes leave of its listeners.' Then he switched off an imaginary knob near the guppi's ear and clapped his hand over his mouth.

8.7

Maan and Rasheed were walking through the village. It was not very different in appearance from a thousand other villages in Rudhia District: mud walls within which people lived (often together with their cattle), thatched roofs, narrow lanes with no windows facing on to them (the conservative heritage of centuries of conquest and brigandage), the very occasional whitewashed one-storey brick house belonging to a 'big person' in the village. Cows and dogs meandered down the lanes, neem trees raised their heads from inner courtyards or near a village well, the low minarets of a small white mosque stood near the centre of the village close to the five brahmin houses and the bania's shop. Only two families had their own hand-pump: Rasheed's and one other. The rest of the population—about four hundred families in all—obtained their water from one of three wells: the Muslim well, which stood in an open space near a neem tree, the caste-Hindu well, which stood in an open space near a pipal tree, and the outcaste or untouchable well, which stood at the very edge of the village among a dense cluster of mud huts, not far from a tanning pit.

They had almost reached their destination, the grain-parcher's house, when they met Rasheed's younger uncle, who was about to set out for Salimpur. Maan got a better look at him by daylight than he had the previous night. He was a young man of medium height and fairly good looks: dark skin, even features, slightly curly black hair, a moustache. He evidently took care of himself. There was a bit of a swagger to his gait. Though younger than Rasheed, he was very conscious of the fact that he was the uncle and Rasheed the nephew.

'What are you doing walking around in the heat of the afternoon?' he said to Rasheed. 'And why are you dragging your friend around with you? It's hot. He should be resting.'

'He wanted to come,' said Rasheed. 'But what are you doing here yourself?'

'I'm off to Salimpur. There's a dinner there. I thought I'd go early and sort some things out at the Congress Party office there.'

This young man was very energetic and ambitious and had his finger in several pies, including local politics. It was because of these qualities of self-interested leadership that he was called Netaji by most people. Eventually his family had taken to calling him Netaji as well. He didn't like it.

Rasheed was careful not to do so. 'I don't see your motorcycle anywhere,' he said.

'It won't start,' said Netaji plaintively. His second-hand Harley Davidson (war stock originally sold off by the army, it had passed through several hands already) was the pride of his heart.

'That's a pity. So why don't you get your rickshaw to take you there?'

'I've hired it out for the day. Really, this motorcycle is more trouble than it's worth. Since I've got it I've spent more time worrying about it than using it. The village boys, and especially that bastard Moazzam, are always doing things to it. I wouldn't be surprised if they've put water in the fuel tank.'

Like a genie conjured up by his name, Moazzam appeared out of nowhere. He was a boy of about twelve or so, quite strong and compact, and one of the chief troublemakers of the village. He had a very friendly face with hair that bristled up like a porcupine's. Sometimes his face would become dark with some unexpressed thought. He seemed to be beyond anyone's control, especially his parents'. People put him down as eccentric, and hoped that he would sort himself out in a few years. Whereas no one liked Mr Biscuit, Moazzam had his admirers.

'You bastard!' said Netaji as soon as he saw Moazzam. 'What have you done to my motorcycle?'

Moazzam, taken aback by this sudden attack, retreated into a dark expression. Maan looked at him with interest, and Moazzam appeared to wink at him in a fleeting expression of conspiracy.

'Can't you hear me?' said Netaji, advancing towards him.

Moazzam said, in a surly tone: 'I can hear you. I've done nothing to your motorcycle. Why should I care about your wretched motorcycle?'

'I saw you hanging around it this morning with two of your friends.'

'So?'

'Don't ever go near it again. Understand? If I ever see you near it again, I'll run you over.'

Moazzam gave a short laugh.

Netaji wanted to slap Moazzam, but thought better of it. 'Let's leave the swine,' he said dismissively to the others. 'By rights he should have his brain shown to a doctor, but his father is too much of a miser to do so. I must be on my way.'

Moazzam now performed a little dance of rage, and cried to Netaji: 'Swine! Swine yourself! You are the swine. And the miser. You lend money on interest, and you buy rickshaws and won't let anyone use them for free. Look at our great leader, the Netaji of the village! I don't have time for you. Migrate to Salimpur with your motorcycle, I don't care.'

When Netaji, muttering black threats under his breath, had left, Moazzam decided to attach himself to Rasheed and Maan. . . . Now he asked to see Maan's watch.

Maan promptly took it off, and showed it to Moazzam, who, after examining it, put it in his pocket. Rasheed said quite sharply to Moazzam:

'Give the watch to me. Is this the way to behave with guests?'

Moazzam looked puzzled at first, then disgorged the watch. He handed it to Rasheed, who gave it back to Maan.

'Thank you, I'm very grateful,' said Maan to Moazzam.

'Don't be polite to him,' said Rasheed to Maan, as if Moazzam wasn't present, 'or he'll take advantage of you. Keep your things close by if he's around. He's well known for making things disappear by sleight of hand.'

'All right,' said Maan, smiling.

'He's not bad at heart,' Rasheed went on.

'Not bad at heart,' repeated Moazzam absently. His attention, though, was elsewhere. An old man with a stick was walking down the narrow lane towards him. There was an amulet around his wrinkled neck which attracted Moazzam's attention. As they passed each other, he reached out for it.

'Give it to me,' he said.

The old man leaned on his stick and said in a slow and exhausted voice: 'Young man, I have no strength.'

This appeared to please Moazzam, who promptly released the amulet.

A girl of about ten was walking towards them with a goat. Moazzam, who was in an acquisitive mood, made as if to grab for the rope, and said: 'Give it to me!' in the voice of a fierce dacoit.

The girl began to cry.

Rasheed said to Moazzam: 'Do you want to feel the back of this hand? Is this the impression you want to give outsiders?'

Moazzam turned suddenly to Maan and said: 'I'll get you married off. Do you want a Hindu or a Muslim bride?'

'Both,' said Maan with a straight face.

Moazzam took this seriously at first. 'How can you have both?' he said. Then it dawned on him that Maan might be making fun of him, and a hurt look came over his face.

But his high spirits reasserted themselves when a couple of village dogs, seeing Maan, started barking loudly.

Moazzam also started barking with delight—at the dogs. They got more and more agitated and barked louder and louder as he passed.

By now the three were in a small open space in the middle of the village, and they could see a group of about ten people gathered around the grain-parcher's house. Most of them were getting wheat parched, but one or two had brought some rice or gram along.

Maan said to Moazzam: 'Do you want some parched maize?'

Moazzam looked at him in astonishment, then nodded vigorously.

Maan patted his head. His bristly black hair was springy, like the pile of a carpet.

'Good!' he said.

Rasheed introduced Maan to the men at the grain-parcher's. They looked at him suspiciously but were not overtly unfriendly. Most were from this village, one or two from the neighbouring village of Sagal, just beyond the school. After Maan joined them, they confined their conversation mainly to instructions to the parcher-woman. Soon it was Rasheed's turn.

The old parcher-woman divided the maize Rasheed gave her into five equal portions, put one aside for herself as payment, and proceeded to parch the remainder. She heated the grain and a quantity of sand separately—the grain gently, the sand fiercely. Then she poured the sand into the shallow pan containing the warm grain, and stirred it for a couple of minutes. Moazzam looked at the process intently, though he must have seen it a hundred times before.

'Do you want it roasted or popped?' she asked.

'Just roasted,' said Rasheed.

Finally the woman sieved out the sand and returned the parched grain. Moazzam took more than the others, but less than he wanted to.

He ate some on the spot, and stuffed a few handfuls into the deep pockets of his kurta. Then he disappeared as suddenly as he had appeared.

8.8

It was late, and they had reached the far end of the village. Clouds were gathering, and the red sky appeared to be on fire. The evening call to prayer had come faintly to their ears, but Rasheed had decided to complete his round of the village rather than interrupt it with a visit to the mosque.

The inflamed sky loured over the thatched huts, the fields, the spreading green mango and dry, brown-leaved shisham trees in the wasteland to the north of the village. One of the two threshing-grounds of the village was located here, and the tired bullocks were still at work on the spring harvest. Round and round they went on the threshing-floor, round and round. They would continue to do so till late at night.

A light evening breeze blew gently from the north towards the cramped huts of the various untouchables—the washermen, the chamars and the sweepers—that lay on the far outskirts of the village—a breeze that would be stifled by the mud walls and constricted lanes of the village and die before it reached its heart. A few ragged children with brown, sun-bleached, filthy, matted hair played in the dust outside their houses—one dragged a piece of blackened wood, another played with a chipped marble. They were hungry, and they looked thin and ill.

Rasheed visited a few chamar households. One family had continued in its ancestral profession of skinning dead animals and preparing the hides for sale. Most, however, were agricultural labourers, one or two with a bit of land of their own as well. In one house Maan recognized the man with the deeply furrowed face who had pumped water for him with so much willingness while he was having a bath. 'He has worked for our family since he was ten years old,' said Rasheed. 'His name is Kachheru.'

The old man and his wife lived by themselves in a single thatched room which they shared at night with their cow and a large number of insects.

Despite Rasheed's politeness, they treated him with extreme, even fearful, deference. It was only when he agreed to have a cup of tea with them in their hut—agreeing thus on Maan's behalf as well—that they seemed to be a little more at ease.

'What happened to Dharampal's son—your nephew?' asked Rasheed.

'He died a month ago,' said Kachheru shortly.

'All those doctors?'

'No use, except to eat money. Now my brother's in debt with the bania—and my sister-in-law, well, you wouldn't recognize her any more. She's just gone to her father's village. She'll stay there for a month or so—until the rains begin.'

'Why didn't he come to us if he needed money?' said Rasheed, distressed.

'You should ask your father that,' said Kachheru. 'He went to him, I believe, a couple of times. But after that your father became annoyed and told him not to fling good money after bad. But he helped with the funeral.'

'I see. I see. What can one do? God disposes—' Rasheed mumbled a few consolatory words.

After they left, Maan could see that Rasheed was very upset. Neither said anything for a while. Then Rasheed said:

'We are tied to earth by such fine threads. And there is so much injustice—so much—it drives me mad. And if you think this village is bad, it's because you don't know Sagal. There is a poor man there who—God forgive them—has been destroyed and left to die by his own family. And look at that old man and woman,' said Rasheed, pointing out a couple who were sitting outside their hut in rags, begging. 'They have been turned out by their children, all of whom are doing tolerably well.'

Maan looked at them. They were starving and filthy, in a pitiable state. Maan gave them a few annas. They stared at the money.

'They are destitute. They don't have enough to eat, but their children will not help them,' Rasheed went on. 'Each claims it is the other's responsibility, or the responsibility of no one at all.'

'Whom do the children work for?' asked Maan.

'For us,' said Rasheed. 'For us. The great and good of the village.'

'Why don't you tell them that this can't go on?' said Maan. 'That they can't treat their parents this way? Surely you can tell them that they must put their house in order if they want to work for you?'

'Ah, now that is a good question,' said Rasheed. 'But it is a question for my esteemed father and grandfather, not for me,' he added bitterly.

8.9

Maan lay down on his string-bed and stared upwards into what, in contrast with the previous night, was a cloudy sky. No solution appeared to him from either cloud or constellation as to how to get his letter written. Once again he thought of his father with annoyance.

Nearby footsteps made him lean on one elbow and look towards the source of the sound. Rasheed's huge bear-like uncle and his companion the guppi were approaching.

'Salaam aleikum.'

'Wa aleikum salaam,' replied Maan.

'Everything going fine?'

'Thanks to your prayers,' replied Maan. 'And you? Where are you coming from?'

'I went to meet my friends in the other village,' said Rasheed's uncle. 'And my friend came along. Now I am going inside the house, but I will have to leave my friend here with you. You don't mind?'

'Of course not,' lied Maan, who wanted no company, least of all the guppi's. But since he didn't have a room, he didn't have a door.

Rasheed's uncle, noticing a number of charpoys scattered in the outer courtyard, picked up one under each huge arm and put them on their sides along the verandah wall. 'It looks like rain,' he explained. 'And anyway, if they're on their sides, the hens won't come and make a mess of them. Where is Rasheed, by the way?'

'Inside,' said Maan.

Rasheed's uncle belched, stroked his bristly beard of stubble, then went on in a friendly manner: 'You know, he ran away from home and stayed with me a couple of times. He was always very sharp at school, very quarrelsome. It was the same when he went to Banaras for further studies. Religious studies! But since he's been at Brahmpur, there's been a change and he's become a good deal more sober. Or perhaps it began in Banaras.' He thought about the matter for a second. 'It often happens this way,' he said. 'But he doesn't see eye to eye with his people. And there'll be trouble. He sees injustice everywhere; he doesn't pause to understand things in their surroundings. You're his friend—you should talk to him. Well, I'll be going in.'

Left with the guppi, Maan did not know what to say, but he was not faced with the problem for long. The guppi, settling himself comfortably on the other charpoy, said:

'What beauty are you dreaming of?'

Maan was both startled and slightly annoyed.

'You know, I'll show you Bombay,' said the guppi. 'You should come with me.' At the word 'Bombay' excitement once again crept into his voice.

'There are enough beauties there to satisfy all the lovesick young gentlemen of the universe. Tobacco?'

Maan shook his head.

'I have a first-class house there,' continued the guppi. 'It has a fan. A view. There's no heat like this. I'll show you the Irani tea-shops. I'll show you Chowpatty Beach. For four annas of roasted peanuts you can see the world. Munch on them as you walk along and admire the view: the waves, the nymphs, the farishtas, all the beautiful women swimming so shamelessly in the ocean. You can join them. . . .'

Maan shut his eyes but could not shut his ears.

'Actually, it was near Bombay that I saw an amazing event which I will never forget. I'll share it with you if you want,' the guppi continued. He paused for a second and, encountering no resistance, continued with a story which was entirely irrelevant to what had gone before.

'Some Marathi dacoits got on to this train,' said the guppi, beginning calmly enough, but becoming increasingly excited as the tale continued. 'They said nothing, they just got on at a station. The train started to move, and then they stood up—all six of them, bloodthirsty villains—and threatened the people with knives. All the passengers were terrified, and handed their money and jewellery over. The six of them went through the entire compartment, and robbed everyone. Eventually they came to a Pathan.'

'Pathan', like 'Bombay', appeared to act as yeast to the guppi's imagination. He breathed reverently and went on:

'The Pathan—a broad, strong fellow—was travelling with his wife and children, and he had a trunk containing his possessions. Three of the villains were standing around him. "Well—" said one of them. "What are you waiting for?"

'"Waiting?" said the Pathan, as if he did not understand what they were saying.

'"Give me your money," cried one of the Marathi dacoits.

'"I won't," growled the Pathan.

'"What?" yelled the bandit, unable to believe what he was hearing.

'"You've robbed everyone," said the Pathan, remaining seated while the gundas loured over him. "Why rob me as well?"

'"No!" said the dacoits. "Give us your money. Quick."

'The Pathan saw that he couldn't do anything immediately. He played for time. He started fumbling with his key and the lock of his trunk. He bent down as if to open it, judged distances—and suddenly—with one kick here—dharaaam!—he knocked one of them out—then—dhoooosh!—he bashed the other two bandits' heads together, and flung them out of the train; one he actually lifted up by the neck and the crotch and flung out like a sack of wheat. The villain bounced on the next bogey before falling on to the ground.'

The guppi wiped his plump face, which was sweating with excitement and the effort of recall.

'Then the ringleader—who was still in the compartment—pulled out his pistol, and fired. Dhaaaaaaam! . . . The shot went through the Pathan's arm and lodged in the compartment wall. There was blood everywhere. He raised the pistol again to fire. Everyone in the compartment was frozen with fear. Then the Pathan spoke in the voice of a tiger to the passengers: "Bastards! I, one man alone, beat up three of them, and no one raised a hand to help me. I'm saving your money and your wealth for you. Isn't there anyone among you who can hold his hand to stop him from firing again?"

'Then they all came to their senses. They grabbed the bandit's hand and stopped him from killing the Pathan—and they beat him up—dharaaaash! dharaaaash!—till he cried for mercy and wept in pain—and then they thrashed him even more. "Do it properly," said the Pathan, and they did—until he was a mass of blood. And they threw him on to the platform of the next station, a broken pulp. Like a discarded, rotting mango!

'Then the women were all over the Pathan: bandaging his hand, et cetera, et cetera. They treated him as if there was only one man in the whole train. Beautiful women, all filled with admiration.'

The guppi, seeking approval, looked over towards Maan, who was feeling mildly sick.

'Are you feeling all right?' asked the guppi, after a long silence.

'Mmmmh,' said Maan. There was a pause, and he continued: 'Tell me, why do you tell such outrageous stories?'

'But they are all true,' said the guppi. 'Basically true.'

Maan was silent.

'Look at it this way,' continued the guppi. 'If I merely said, "Hello" and you said, "Hello. Where have you come from?" and I said, "From the direction of Baitar. By train"—well, how would the day pass? How would we get through these boiling afternoons and hot nights? So I tell stories—some to keep you cool, some to make you hotter!' The guppi laughed.

But Maan was not listening any longer. He had sat up at the word 'Baitar', as galvanized by it as the guppi had been by 'Bombay'. A wonderful idea had struck him.

He would write to Firoz, that was it. He would write to Firoz and enclose a letter to Saeeda Bai. Firoz wrote excellent Urdu and had none of Rasheed's puritanism. Firoz would translate Maan's letter and send it on to Saeeda Bai. She would be astonished to get his letter: astonished and delighted! And she would write back to him by the next post.

Maan got up from the charpoy and began pacing up and down, composing the letter in his head, adding here and there a couplet or two from Ghalib or Mir—or Dagh—for ornamentation or emphasis. Rasheed could have no objection to mailing a letter to the son of the Nawab of Baitar; Maan would simply hand him the closed envelope.

The guppi, puzzled by Maan's erratic behaviour and disappointed that he had lost his audience, wandered off into the darkness.

Maan sat down once again, leaned against the edge of the verandah, and listened to the hiss of the lantern and the other sounds of the night. Somewhere a baby cried. Somewhere a dog barked, and other dogs joined in. Then all was quiet for a while, except for the drift of a voice or two from the roof, where Rasheed's father spent his summer nights. Sometimes the voices seemed to be raised in argument, sometimes subdued; but Maan could make out nothing of what was being said.

It was a cloudy night, and the papiha or brainfever bird called from time to time from a distant tree, its series of triple notes growing tauter and higher and more intense until it reached a climax and dropped into sudden silence. Maan did not think of the romantic associations of the sound ('pee-kahan? pee-kahan?' Where is my love? Where is my love?). He wanted the bird to be quiet so that he could concentrate on the voice of his own heart.

8.10

That night there was a violent storm. It was a sudden summer thunderstorm of the kind that builds up when the heat is most unbearable. It lashed through the trees and fields, whipped away thatch and even a few tiles from the houses in the village, and drenched the dusty ground. Those who had looked up at the clouds—so often bringers of nothing but the occasional gust of wind—and had decided to sleep outside anyway to avoid the heat, had picked up their charpoys and rushed inside when, without more warning than a heavy drop or two, the clouds had burst over their heads. Then they had gone out again to bring in the cattle tethered outside. Now they all steamed together in the darkness of the huts where most of the villagers lived, the cattle lowing plaintively in the front rooms, the humans talking together in the back.

Kachheru, the chamar who had worked for Rasheed's family since childhood, and whose hut consisted of only a single room, had judged the arrival of the storm to the hour. His buffalo was inside, and safe from the lashing rain. She snorted and urinated from time to time, but these were reassuring sounds.

A little rain came through the roof and fell on Kachheru and his wife, who were lying on the ground. There were many roofs that were flimsier than his, and some that would be blown away in this kind of storm, but Kachheru said sharply:

'Old woman—what use are you if you cannot even save us from the rain?'

His wife said nothing for a while. Then she said: 'We should see how the beggar and his wife are doing. Their hut is on low ground.'

'That is none of our business,' retorted Kachheru.

'On nights like these I think of the night when Tirru was born. I wonder how he's doing in Calcutta. He never writes.'

'Go to sleep, go to sleep,' said Kachheru wearily. He knew the work that lay ahead of him the next morning, and he did not want to waste his hours of sleep in idle and disturbing chatter.

But for a while he lay awake with his own thoughts. The wind howled and ceased and howled again, and water continued to leak in. In the end he got up to improvise some temporary repair to his wife's inefficient thatching.

Outside, the solid world of huts and trees, walls and wells, was now a shapeless, threatening roar of wind, water, moonlight, lightning, clouds and thunder. The land on which the untouchable castes lived was on the northern outskirts of the village. Kachheru was lucky; his own hut, though small, was not on the lowest land; it was in fact on the edge of a low escarpment of earth. But further below him he could see the rain-blurred outlines of huts that would be awash with water and filth by morning.

When he woke up, it was not yet light. He put on his dirty dhoti, and made his way through the slush of the village lanes to Rasheed's father's house. The rain had stopped, but the neem trees were still sprinkling droplets of water on him—and on the sweeper-women who were moving silently from house to house removing the garbage left outside at night by the women of the house. A few pigs grunted their way through the lanes, gobbling up whatever scraps or excrement they could find. All the dogs were silent, though a cock crowed occasionally in the waning darkness.

Gradually it became lighter. By now Kachheru, who had been walking slowly but in a deliberate manner along the slightly drier edges of the slushy lanes, was no longer near the scene of the worst damage, damage that sometimes distressed him as much as it did his wife, but which he had learned to ignore.

Kachheru looked around when he got to Rasheed's father's house. He could not see anyone, but he assumed that Baba at least was awake; he was a stickler for the pre-dawn prayer. A couple of people were sleeping on charpoys on the covered verandah; they must have been sleeping in the courtyard and had probably been caught in the sudden rain. Kachheru passed his hand over his wrinkled face and allowed himself to smile.

Suddenly there was a desperate mixture of quacks and clucks. A duck, king of the courtyard, with its head craned forward aggressively, but with an incongruously pacific expression on its face, was chasing (by turns) a cock, a couple of hens, and a few large chicks across the brick and mud—towards and then away from the cattle-shed, around the neem tree, and across the lane to the house where Baba and his younger son lived.

Kachheru rested on his haunches for a while. Then he went to the water-pump and splashed some water over his bare and muddy feet. A small black goat was butting its head against the shaft of the water-pump. Kachheru scratched its head. Its cynical yellow eyes looked back at him, and it bleated in complaint when he stopped.

Kachheru climbed the four steps to the door of the room where the ploughs were stored. Rasheed's father had three ploughs, two local or desi ones with pointed wooden shares and one mishtan plough with a curved metallic share which Kachheru ignored. He left open the door to the room, and pulled the desi ploughs into the light of the entrance. Then he sat down on his haunches once again and examined the two ploughs. Eventually he placed one on his shoulder and walked across the courtyard to the cattle-shed. The cattle turned their heads at his approach, and he, pleased to see them, said, 'Aaaah! aaaaah!' in a low and comforting tone.

First, he fed all the cattle, mixing a little more grain than usual into the mush of hay and straw and water that was their fare in the hot weather. Even the black water buffaloes—usually sent out to forage for themselves under the supervision of a herdboy—were fed, since it was difficult for them to find enough to graze on in this season. Then he adjusted muzzles and ropes to the necks and noses of the pair of intelligent white bullocks he most liked to work with. He picked up a long stick that was leaning against the wall of the cattle-shed and drove them out gently. Aloud, but so that no one would hear him, he said:

'If it weren't for me, you'd be finished.'

As he was about to yoke the bullocks together he suddenly remembered something. Telling them sternly to remain exactly where they were he went back across the courtyard to the room opposite. He got out a spade and carried it across. The bullocks had not strayed. He praised them, then yoked them, and placed the plough upside down on the yoke, letting them drag it along while he shouldered his spade.

It was expected of Kachheru that whenever there was rain during the dry summer months he would go for the next day or two into his master's fields and plough them while there was still water in the soil. He was to go from field to field, and plough from morning till evening in order to take full advantage of this temporary moisture. It was exhausting labour, and it was not paid for.

Kachheru was one of Rasheed's father's chamars, and was on call at any time he wanted, not just for farming tasks but for any odd jobs—whether it was pumping water for a bath or taking a message to the other end of the village or hauling arhar stalks on to the roof of the house to dry for cooking fuel. Unlike other strangers he was granted the special and very occasional dispensation of entrance into the sanctum of the house, especially if something needed to be lugged on to the roof. After the death of Rasheed's elder brother, it had become necessary to have help in the house for the heavier tasks. But whenever Kachheru was called in, any women at home locked themselves in one of the rooms or slipped out into the vegetable garden at the back, staying as close to the wall of the house as possible.

In return for his services, he was taken care of by the family. This meant that he was given a certain amount of grain at harvest time: not enough, however, to provide for even a basic diet for himself and his wife. He had also been allowed a small plot of land to farm on his own, whenever his time was not required by his master. His master also lent him the use of his plough and bullocks if he felt he could spare them, as well as spades, hoes, and other tools, none of which Kachheru possessed or felt it worthwhile indebting himself to buy in order to till his small plot.

He was overworked, but it was not so much his mind as the exhaustion of his body that told him this. As the years had passed and he had never raised his head in rebellion or rudeness, he was now treated more politely by the family he had served for forty years, ever since he was a boy. They told him what he had to do, but did not shout at him in the voice of insulting command appropriate for the subservient caste to which he belonged. Rasheed's father sometimes called him 'my old one', which pleased Kachheru. He was given a kind of pre-eminence among his chamars, and was asked to supervise them from time to time during the busiest farming seasons.

Yet when his only son Tirru had said that he wanted to get out of Debaria and its caste-ridden, poverty-stricken, unrelievedly back-breaking, hopeless life, Kachheru had not objected. Kachheru's wife had pleaded with her son not to go, but her husband's unspoken support had weighed heavily on the other side.

What future lay for their son in the village? He had no land, he had no money, and it was only at great sacrifice to the family—which had had to forgo the income that the boy would have brought in by herding cattle—that he had been educated to the sixth class at the government primary school a few miles away. Was this in order that he should kill himself working in the burning heat of the fields? Whatever Kachheru thought of his own life, he did not wish it upon his son. Let the boy go to Brahmpur or Calcutta or Bombay or wherever he chose and find work there: any kind of work, whether as a domestic servant or as a factory- or mill-hand.

At first Tirru had sent back money, and had written affectionate letters home in Hindi which Kachheru begged the postman or the bania at the shop—when they had the time—to read out for him. Sometimes he asked them to read them out several times, until they were irritated and puzzled.

Then he would dictate replies which he would beg them to transcribe on a postcard. The boy had returned for the wedding of his two younger sisters, and had even helped with their dowries. But for the last year there had been no letters from Calcutta at all, and several of Kachheru's letters were returned to sender. Not all, though; and so he continued to write a monthly letter to their son's old address. But where he was, what had happened to him, and why he had stopped writing he could not imagine—and feared to. It was as if their son had half-ceased to exist. His wife was distraught. Sometimes she wept to herself in the dark, sometimes she prayed at a small orange-stained niche in a pipal tree where the village deity was said to live and where she had taken her son to be blessed before his departure. Every day she reminded Kachheru of how she had foreseen it all.

Finally one day he suggested to his wife that he would seek his master's permission and financial support (though he knew this meant falling into a bottomless pit of debt) to go to Calcutta to search for their son. But she had fallen weeping on the ground, full of nameless terrors. Kachheru had rarely even been to Salimpur, and never to the district town of Rudhia. Brahmpur, let alone Calcutta, was entirely outside his imagination. She, for her part, had only known two villages, the village into which she had been born and the village into which she had married.

8.11

It was cool, and there was a morning breeze. From the pigeon-house came the sound of unfrantic, heavy cooing. Then a few pigeons began to fly around: some grey ones with black bands, some brownish ones, one or two white ones. Kachheru hummed a bhajan to himself as he walked the bullocks out of the village.

A few poor women and children, mostly of his own caste, had come out with baskets to glean the fields that had been harvested yesterday. Ordinarily by coming out as early as this they would have stolen a march on the birds and small animals that picked the fields bare. But now the gleaners were looking for grains of food in a morass of mud.

It was not unpleasant to be ploughing at this time of day. It was cool, and walking ankle-deep in cool water and mud behind a pair of well-trained and obedient bullocks (Kachheru had trained this pair himself) felt fine. He rarely needed to use his stick; unlike many peasants, he did not enjoy using it at all. The pair responded to his repertory of calls, moving anticlockwise in intersecting circuits around the field, as close to the edge as possible, drawing the plough slowly behind them. Kachheru continued to sing to himself, interrupting his bhajan with 'wo! wo!' or 'taka taka' or other commands, and then picked up the tune not from where he had left off but from where he would have been had he never stopped singing. After the whole of the first field was covered with furrows—a field twice as large as the one he farmed for himself—he was sweating with exertion. The sun had now risen about fifteen degrees in the sky, and it was becoming warm. He let the bullocks rest, and went around the untouched corners of the field, digging up the earth with his spade.

As the morning progressed he stopped singing. A couple of times he lost patience with the bullocks, and gave them a stroke or two with the stick—especially the outer one, who had decided to halt when his fellow did, instead of continuing to wheel around as he had been ordered to.

Kachheru was now working at a steady pace, using with care his finite energy and that of his cattle. It had grown unbearably hot, and the sweat poured down from his forehead into his eyebrows and trickled down from there into his eyes. He wiped it from time to time with the back of his right hand, keeping steady his hold on the plough with the left. By midday he was exhausted. He led the cattle to a ditch, but the water there, though they drank it, was warm. He himself drank from the leather bag that he had filled at the water-pump before setting out.

His wife came out into the fields when the sun was at its height, bringing him rotis, salt, a few chillies, and some lassi to drink. She watched him eat in silence, asked him if he wanted her to do anything else, and returned.

A little later Rasheed's father turned up with an umbrella that he used as a parasol. He squatted on a low ridge of mud that divided one field from another, and said a word or two of encouragement to Kachheru. 'It's true what they say,' he said. 'There's no work as hard as farming.' Kachheru did not answer, but nodded respectfully. He was beginning to feel ill. When Rasheed's father left, the fact of his presence was marked by the red-stained earth where he had spat out his paan-juice.

By now the water in the fields was uncomfortably hot underfoot, and a hot breeze had begun to blow. 'I will have to rest for a while,' he told himself. But he realized the importance of ploughing while the fugitive water was still on the ground, and he did not wish it to be said that he had not done what he knew needed doing.

By the time it was late afternoon his dark face was flushed red. His feet, callused and cracked though they were, felt as if they had been boiled. After a short day's work he usually shouldered the plough himself as he drove the cattle back from the fields. But he had no energy to do so today and gave it to the spent cattle to haul. Hardly a coherent thought formed itself in his mind. The metal of his spade, when it touched his shoulder accidentally, made him wince.

He passed by his own unploughed field with its two mulberry trees and hardly noticed it. Even that small field was not really his own, but it did not strike him to say so—or even think so. His only intention was to place one foot after the other on the path that led back to Debaria. The village lay three-quarters of a mile ahead of him, and it seemed to him that he was walking there through fire.

8.12

Rasheed's father's whitewashed house, while fairly imposing from the outside by the standards of Debaria, contained very few rooms. It basically consisted of a square colonnaded quadrangle open to the sky in the middle. On one side of this quadrangle three quite airless rooms had been constructed by the simple expedient of bricking in the space between the columns. These rooms were occupied by members of the family. There were no other rooms in the house. Cooking was done in a corner of the open colonnade. This saved the women of the household from the smoke of a chimney-less hearth in a closed kitchen—exposure to which in the course of time would have ruined their eyes and lungs.

Other sections of the colonnade contained storage bins and shelves. In the central square was an open space with a lemon tree and a pomegranate tree. Behind the back wall of the quadrangle was a privy for the women and a small vegetable garden. A set of stairs led up to the roof where Rasheed's father held court and ate paan—as he was doing at this moment.

No man could enter the house who was not a close member of the family. Rasheed's maternal or paternal uncles had free access. This was true of the bear-like uncle even after his sister, Rasheed's mother, had died and Rasheed's father had taken a second—and much younger—wife. Since the patriarch, Baba, despite his age and diabetes, didn't mind climbing the stairs, roof conferences were a regular phenomenon. A roof conference was always convened, for instance, when anyone returned from a long absence, in order to sort out family matters.

This evening's was in honour of Rasheed, but before the other men had assembled it had turned quite quickly into an argument—or a series of arguments—between Rasheed and his father. His father had raised his voice on a number of occasions. Rasheed had defended himself, but it would have been almost unthinkable for him to raise his voice in uncontrolled anger. Sometimes he remained silent.

When Rasheed had left Maan outside and entered the courtyard, he had been in an unquiet frame of mind. Maan had not mentioned the letter today, which was good. Rasheed had not liked the thought of disappointing his friend in the matter, but it would have been impossible for him to write the kinds of things that Maan would almost certainly want to dictate. Rasheed did not care for what he saw as the baser human instincts. They made him uncomfortable, at times, even angry. In matters such as these, he preferred to keep his eyes closed. If he suspected that there was anything between Maan and Saeeda Bai—and considering the circumstances of their meetings it was hard to imagine how he could not have known it—he did not wish to dwell on it.

As he walked upstairs to meet his father, he thought about his mother, who had lived in that house until her death two years before. It had seemed unimaginable to him then, as it seemed unimaginable to him now, that after her death his father could have married anyone else. At the age of fifty-five, surely one's appetites became still; and surely the memory of a woman who had devoted her entire life to his service and to the service of his two sons would have stood like a wall between his father and the thought of taking a second wife. But here she was, his stepmother: a pretty woman, not ten years older than himself. And it was she who slept with his father on the roof whenever he decided she should, and who bustled around the house, apparently undaunted by the ghost of the woman who had planted the trees whose fruit she unthinkingly plucked.

What did his father do, Rasheed wondered, other than give in to his appetites? He sat at home and ordered people about, and he ate paan continuously from morning till night, like a chain-smoker. He had ruined his teeth and tongue and throat. His mouth was a mere red slash interrupted by the occasional black tooth. Yet this man with his black, curly, balding hair and thickset, belligerent face was forever provoking and lecturing him—and had done so from Rasheed's infancy to his adulthood.

Rasheed could not remember a time when he had not been lectured to by his father. In school, when he was a small or even adolescent ruffian, he had no doubt deserved it. But later, as he had settled down, and done well in college, he had continued to be a target for his father's dissatisfaction. And everything had got worse since he had lost his elder and favourite son, Rasheed's beloved brother, in a train accident, just a year before the loss of his wife.

'Your place is here, on the land,' his father had told him afterwards. 'I need your help. I am no longer so young. If you want to remain at Brahmpur University, you yourself will have to find the means to do so.' His father was hardly poor, Rasheed thought bitterly. He was apparently young enough to take a young wife. And—Rasheed's mind rebelled at the thought—he was even young enough to want her to give him another child. Late fatherhood was something of a tradition in the family. Baba, after all, had been in his fifties when Netaji was born.

Whenever he thought of his mother, tears came to Rasheed's eyes. She had loved him and his brother almost to excess, and she had been adored in return. His brother had delighted in the pomegranate tree and he in the lemon. Now as he looked around the courtyard, freshened and washed by the rain, he seemed to see everywhere the tangible marks of her love.

The death of her elder son had certainly hastened her own. And before dying she had made Rasheed, heartbroken as he was by his brother's death and her own impending one, promise her something that he had wanted desperately to refuse but did not have the heart or will to: a promise that was no doubt good in itself; but that had tied his life down even before he had begun to taste freedom.

8.13

Rasheed sighed as he walked up the stairs. His father was sitting on a charpoy on the roof, and his stepmother was pressing his feet.

'Adaab arz, Abba-jaan. Adaab arz, Khala,' said Rasheed. He called his stepmother Aunt.

'You have taken your time coming,' said his father curtly.

Rasheed said nothing. His young stepmother looked at him for a second, then turned away. Rasheed had never been impolite to her, but in his presence she always felt conscious of the woman whom she had supplanted, and she felt hurt that he made no attempt to reassure her or show her any affection.

'How is your friend?'

'Fine, Abba. I've left him downstairs—writing a letter, I think.'

'I don't mind him coming, but I would like to have been warned.'

'Yes, Abba. I'll try to do so next time. This came up quite suddenly.'

Rasheed's stepmother got up and said: 'I'll go and make some tea.'

When she had gone, Rasheed said quietly: 'Abba, if you can, please spare me this.'

'Spare you what?' said his father in a sudden fit of temper. He understood just what Rasheed meant, but was unwilling to admit it.

Rasheed at first decided he would say nothing, then reconsidered it. If I don't speak my mind, he thought, will I have to continue to bear the intolerable? 'What I mean, Abba,' he said in a low voice, 'is being criticized in front of her.'

'I will say what I like to you when and where I like,' said his father, chewing his paan and looking out over the edge of the roof. 'Where are the others? Oh, yes—and you can be sure that it is not only I who criticize you and your way of life.'

'My way of life?' said Rasheed, some slight sharpness escaping into his tone of voice. He felt that it hardly suited his father to criticize his way of life.

'On your first evening in the village, you missed both the evening and the night prayer. Today when I went into the fields I wanted you to accompany me—but you were nowhere to be seen. I had something important to show you and discuss with you. Some land. What kind of influence will people think you are under? And you spend your day going around from the house of the washerman to the house of the sweeper, asking about this one's son and that one's nephew, but spending no time with your own family. It is no secret that many people here think that you are a communist.'

Rasheed reflected that this probably meant only that he loathed the poverty and injustice endemic to the village, and that he made no particular secret of it. Visiting poor families was hardly cause for reproach.

'I hope you don't think that what I am doing is wrong,' said Rasheed in a mutedly sarcastic manner.

His father said nothing for a second, then remarked with great asperity: 'Your education in Brahmpur and so on has done a lot for your confidence. You should take advice where you can get it.'

'And what advice would that be?' said Rasheed. 'The advice of the elders of this village that I should make as much money as I can as quickly as I can? Everyone here, as far as I can see, lives entirely for their appetites: for women or drink or food—'

'Enough! You've said enough!' said his father, shouting at him, but losing several of his consonants in the process.

Rasheed did not add '—or paan', as he had been about to do. Instead he kept quiet, resolved not to say anything to his father that he might later regret, no matter how much he was provoked. In the end what Rasheed said was couched in general terms: 'Abba, I feel that one is responsible for others, not only for oneself and one's family.'

'But first of all for one's family.'

'Whatever you say, Abba,' said Rasheed, wondering why he ever returned to Debaria. 'Do you think my marriage, for instance, shows that I don't care for my family? That I didn't care for my mother or my elder brother? I feel I would have been happier—and you as well—if I had been the one who had died.'

His father was silent for a minute. He was thinking of his happy-go-lucky elder son who had been content to live in Debaria and help manage the family land, who had been as strong as a lion, who had taken pride in his place as the son of a local zamindar, and who, rather than seeing everything as a problem, had spread a kind of unconcerned goodwill wherever he had gone. Then he thought of his wife—Rasheed's mother—and he drew in a slow breath.

To Rasheed he said in a gentler voice than before: 'Why do you not leave these schemes of yours—all these educational schemes, historical schemes, socialist schemes, all these schemes of improvement and redistribution, all this, this'—he waved his hand around—'and live here and help us. Do you know what will happen to this land in a year or so when zamindari is abolished? They want to take it away from us. And then all your imaginary poultry farms and high-yielding fish ponds and improved dairy farms with which you intend to benefit the mass of mankind will have to be built in the air, because if all that comes to pass, there certainly won't be enough land to support them. Not in our family, anyway.'

His father might have intended to speak gently, but what had come out of his utterance was inescapable scorn.

'What can I do to prevent it, Abba?' said Rasheed. 'If the land is to be justly taken over it will be taken over.'

'You could do a lot,' his father began hotly. 'For one thing, you could stop using the word "justly" for what is nothing but theft. And for another, you could talk to your friend—'

Rasheed's face became tense. He could not bear the thought of demeaning himself in this way. But he chose an argument that he thought would be more suited to his father's view of the world.

'It would not work,' he said. 'The Revenue Minister is completely unbending. He won't make individual exceptions. In fact he has let it be known that those people who try to use their influence with him or anyone else in the Revenue Department will be the first to be notified under the act.'

'Is that so?' said Rasheed's father thoughtfully. 'Well, we have not been idle ourselves . . . the tehsildar knows us; and the Sub-Divisional Officer is an honest fellow, but lazy . . . let's see.'

'Well, what has been happening, Abba?' asked Rasheed.

'That is what I wanted to speak to you about. . . . I wanted to point out certain fields. . . . We have to make things clear to everyone. . . . As the Minister says, there cannot be exceptions. . . .'

Rasheed frowned. He could not understand what his father was getting at.

'The idea is to move the tenants around,' said his father, cracking a betel nut with a small brass nutcracker. 'Keep them running—this year this field, next year, that. . . .'

'But Kachheru?' said Rasheed, thinking of the small field with the two mulberry trees—Kachheru had not planted a mango tree for fear that such presumption might tempt providence.

'What about Kachheru?' said his father, displaying an anger that he hoped would seal the lid on this uncomfortable subject. 'He will get whatever field I desire to give him. Make an exception for one chamar, and I'll have twenty rebellions. The family is agreed on this.'

'But his trees—?'

'*His* trees?' said Rasheed's father dangerously. 'The trouble is these communist ideas you drink like mother's milk at the university. Let him take one under each arm and clear off if he wants to.'

A sort of sickness gripped Rasheed's heart as he looked at his father. He said softly that he was not feeling well, and asked to be excused. At first his father looked at him intently, then suddenly said, 'Go. And find out what's happening about the tea. Ah, here comes your Mamu.' His brother-in-law's large stubble-bearded face had appeared at the top of the stairs.

'I was telling Rasheed what I thought about his grand idiocies,' said

Rasheed's father with a laugh just before Rasheed walked downstairs and out of sight.

'Oh, yes?' said the Bear mildly. He thought highly of his nephew and did not care for his brother-in-law's attitude towards him.

The Bear knew that Rasheed liked him too, and sometimes wondered at it. After all, he was not an educated man. But what Rasheed admired about him was that he was a man who had attained tolerance and calm without losing his zest. Nor could he ever forget that at his uncle's home he had found a refuge when he had fled from his own.

The Bear's main concern about Rasheed was that he was not looking well. He was too thin, too dark, and too gaunt; and more white had appeared in his hair than should by rights appear in the hair of any young man.

'Rasheed is good,' he said.

He received a grunt in response to this absolute statement.

'The only problem with Rasheed,' added the Bear, 'is that he worries too much about everyone, including you.'

'Oh?' said Rasheed's father, parting his lips and opening his red mouth.

'Not only you, of course,' continued his brother-in-law calmly and with great and expansive definitiveness. 'About his wife. About his children. About the village. About the country. About true religion and false religion. Also about other matters: some important, some less so. Like how one should behave towards one's fellow-man. Like how the world can be fed. Like where the mud goes when you hammer a peg into the ground. And of course the greatest question of all. . . .' The Bear paused and belched.

'What is that?' his brother-in-law could not resist asking.

'Why a goat eats green and shits black,' said the Bear.

8.14

His father's words burning in his ears, Rasheed walked downstairs. He forgot to inquire about the tea. He did not at first know what he should think, let alone do. He felt, above all, ashamed. Kachheru, whom he had known since he was a child, who had carried him on his back, who had stood patiently by the hand-pump while he bathed, who had served the family trustingly and unflaggingly for so many years, ploughing and weeding and fetching and carrying: it was unimaginable that his father should so indifferently have suggested shifting him about from field to field in his old age. He was no longer young; he had aged in their service. A man of settled habits, he had become deeply attached to the small plot that he had tilled for fifteen years. He had made improvements to the field, connecting it by a series of small channels to a larger ditch; he had maintained the raised paths that bordered it; he had planted the mulberry trees for shade and occasional fruit. Strictly speaking, these too may have been the landlord's under the old dispensation, but to speak strictly here was to speak inhumanly. And under the new dispensation that was doubtless soon to come, Kachheru had rights which could not be denied. Everyone knew that he was the tiller of that field. Under the impending zamindari legislation five years of continuous tenancy was enough to establish his right to the land.

That night Rasheed could hardly sleep. He did not want to talk to anyone, not even to Maan. During the night prayer—which he did not avoid—he mouthed the words through habit but his heart remained grounded. When he lay down he felt a painful pressure in his head. After a few hours of restlessness he got up at last and walked through the lanes towards the wastelands at the far northern end of the village. Everything was still. The bullocks had ceased their work on the threshing-ground. The dogs were unperturbed by his presence. The night was starlit and warm. In their cramped thatched huts the poorest of the village slept. They cannot do it, said Rasheed to himself. They cannot do it.

To make sure of this, however, he went the next morning after breakfast to visit the village patwari, the petty government functionary who acted as record-keeper and accountant of the village and who each year painstakingly updated the land records, noting down in detail the ownership and use of every plot. Rasheed estimated that a good third of the land in the village was let out by the landlords; in his own family's case, almost two-thirds of it was. He was confident that in the patwari's thick, cloth-bound ledgers would lie irrefutable proof of Kachheru's continuous tenancy.

The lean old patwari greeted Rasheed politely, with a tired smile. He had heard of Rasheed's social rounds of the village, and felt pleased to have merited a separate visit. Shading his eyes against the sun with his hand, he asked him how his studies were going and how long he planned to stay in the village. And he offered Rasheed some sherbet. It was some time before the patwari realized that the visit was not entirely social, but this did not displease him. His government salary was low, and it was widely accepted that he needed to augment it informally. He expected that Rasheed wished to see how his family's holdings stood. He had no doubt been sent by his grandfather to check the status of their lands. And he was going to be pleased by what he saw.

The patwari went inside to bring out three ledgers, a few field-books, and two large cloth maps, about three feet by five, which covered all the land in the village. He lovingly unrolled one of them upon the wooden seating platform in his small courtyard. He stroked a corner of it gently with the side of his hand. He also fetched his spectacles, which he now placed carefully on his nose.

'Well, Khan Sahib,' he said to Rasheed, 'in a year or two these books, which I have tended as carefully as a garden, will pass into other hands. If the government has its way it will rotate us from village to village every three years. Our lives will not be worth living. And how can some outsider understand the life of the village, its history, the reality of things? Just settling down will take him at least three years.'

Rasheed made sympathetic sounds. He had put down his glass of sherbet and was trying to locate Kachheru's field on the map, which was of fine silk, slightly yellowed.

'And the people of this village have always been very good to this sinful man,' continued the patwari, with a slightly more energetic laugh. 'Ghee, grain, milk, wood . . . even a few rupees now and then—the Khan Sahib's family has been particularly munificent. . . . What are you looking for?'

'Our chamar Kachheru's field.'

The patwari's finger went unerringly to the spot, and came to rest in the air half an inch above it.

'But don't worry, Khan Sahib, it has all been taken care of,' he said.

Rasheed looked at him questioningly.

The patwari was a little surprised that his competence or industry was being called into doubt. He wordlessly rolled up the silken map and unfurled the map of cruder cloth. This, his working map, which he took with him on his recording rounds, was slightly mud-stained, and displayed a denser patchwork of fields, covered with names and numbers and notations of various kinds in black and in red, all in Urdu. For a while he gazed at it, then went to the ledgers and the cracked and battered field-books, opened a few of them to the appropriate pages, consulted them alternately a few times, and with a serious and slightly injured look, nodded at Rasheed. 'See for yourself,' he said.

Rasheed looked at the columns and entries and measurements, landholding numbers and plot numbers and serial numbers, records of land type and land condition and land use; but, as the patwari well suspected, he could make nothing out of the esoteric jumble.

'But—'

'Khan Sahib,' said the mollified patwari, turning his palms upwards in a gesture of openness. 'It would appear from my records that the person who has been cultivating that field and those around it for the last several years has been yourself.'

'What?' cried Rasheed, staring first at the patwari's smiling face, and then at the entry at which his finger was now pointing; again it rested a little above the surface of the page, like the body of a water insect.

'Name of cultivator as given in khatauni register: Abdur Rasheed Khan,' read out the patwari.

'How long has this been the case?' asked Rasheed with difficulty, his mind racing almost too fast for his tongue. He looked painfully agitated and distressed.

Even now the patwari, who was not by any means a stupid man, suspected nothing. He said simply: 'Ever since the land reform legislation became a possible threat, and your esteemed grandfather and father expressed their concern about eventualities, your servant has been diligently safeguarding your family's interests. The lands of the family have been nominally subdivided among the various members, and all of you are down in my records as owner-cultivators. It is the safest way. Large individual landholdings look too suspicious. Of course, you have been away in Brahmpur studying, and these small matters are not of interest to a scholar of history—'

'They are,' said Rasheed grimly. 'How much of our land is let out to tenants?' he asked.

'None,' said the patwari, indicating his ledgers with a casual gesture.

'None?' said Rasheed. 'But everyone knows we have both sharecroppers and rent-paying tenants—'

'Hired employees,' corrected the patwari. 'And in the future they will very wisely be rotated from field to field.'

'But Kachheru, for example'—burst out Rasheed—'everyone knows that he's had that field for years. You yourself understood immediately what I meant by Kachheru's field.'

'It's a manner of speaking,' said the patwari, amused by Rasheed's attempt to play the devil's advocate. 'If I were to refer to Khan Sahib's university, it would not mean that Brahmpur University belonged to you—

or that you had been there for five years.' He gave a short laugh, inviting participation; but when Rasheed did not respond, he continued: 'From my records it appears that, yes, Kachheru, son of Mangalu chamar, did sharecrop the field on occasion, but never for a period of five years without a break. There has always been an interruption—'

'You say the field is now nominally mine?' said Rasheed.

'Yes.'

'I want you to register a change of ownership to Kachheru.'

It was the patwari's turn to look shocked. He looked at Rasheed as if he had taken leave of his senses. He was about to say that the Khan Sahib was, of course, joking, when he realized with a start that he was not.

'Don't worry,' said Rasheed. 'I'll pay you your standard—what should I say?—your standard fee.'

The patwari licked his lips with anxiety.

'But your family? Are they all—'

'Are you questioning my credentials in this matter?'

'Oh no, Khan Sahib, heaven forbid—'

'Our family has discussed this matter at length,' said Rasheed carefully. 'And that is why I am here.' He paused. 'If the mutation of ownership cannot be performed quickly or involves other legal documents, it would be good if the tenancy records for this plot were made to reflect, well, the reality of things. Yes, that is a better method and will cause less disturbance. Make it clear, please, that the chamar has been a continuous tenant.'

The patwari nodded obediently. 'As Huzoor commands,' he said quietly.

Rasheed tried to hide his contempt as he took out some money.

'Here is a little something in advance to express my appreciation. As a student of history, I have been most impressed by the meticulousness of these records. And, as a landlord, I must agree with you that the government's policy of rotating patwaris is a great pity.'

'Some more sherbet, Khan Sahib? Or may I offer you something a little more substantial? Life in the city has worn you down . . . you are looking very thin. . . .'

'No thank you,' said Rasheed. 'I must go. But I will call again in a couple of weeks. That should be sufficient time, shouldn't it?'

'It should,' agreed the patwari.

'Good, then. Khuda haafiz.'

'Khuda haafiz, Khan Sahib,' said the patwari softly. And indeed God would have to protect Rasheed from the trouble he had just plunged himself—and not just himself—into.

Part Nine

9.1

'You're looking very thin, darling,' said Mrs Rupa Mehra to Kalpana Gaur—who was large-boned and vivacious, but less substantial than usual. Mrs Rupa Mehra had just arrived in Delhi in search of a prospective husband for Lata. Since her sons had proven hopeless, she would get Kalpana Gaur, who was 'like a daughter' to her, to deliver the goods.

'Yes, the silly girl has been ill,' said her father, who was impatient with illness. 'God knows how at such a young age she manages to contract all these illnesses. It is some kind of flu this time: flu at the height of summer—very silly. No one goes for walks nowadays. My niece never walked; too lazy. She got appendicitis, had to be operated on, and, naturally, took a long time to recover. When I was in Lahore we would get up every morning at five, and all of us—from my father down to my six-year-old brother—would go walking for an hour. That was how we kept up our health.'

Kalpana Gaur turned to Mrs Rupa Mehra: 'Now you will need tea and rest.' Snuffling a bit, she got busy with the servants and the luggage, and paid off the tonga-wallah. Mrs Rupa Mehra protested, then submitted. 'You must stay with us for a month,' continued Kalpana. 'How can you go travelling in this heat? How is Savita? When is the baby due exactly? And Lata? Arun? Varun? I haven't heard from you in months. We keep reading about the floods in Calcutta, but in Delhi there isn't a cloud in the sky. Everyone is praying that the monsoons will come on time. Let me just tell the servants to get things ready, then you must tell us all your news. Fried tomatoes as usual for breakfast tomorrow? Daddy hasn't been too well, you know. Heart.' She looked indulgently at her father, who frowned back.

'I have been perfectly well,' said the old man dismissively. 'Raghubir was five years younger than me and I'm still going strong. Now you sit down. You must be tired. And give us everyone's news. There's nothing of interest in this.' He indicated the newspaper. 'Just the usual warmongering with Pakistan, flood havoc in Assam, leaders leaving the Congress Party, gas workers on strike in Calcutta . . . and as a result they can't even hold the chemistry practical exams in the university! Oh, but you've just come from Calcutta, so you know all that. And so on and so on. Do you know, if I ran a newspaper with nothing but good news—so-and-so gave birth to a healthy baby, such-and-such a country remained at peace with its neighbour, this river behaved well and that crop refused to be eaten by locusts—I believe people would buy it just to put themselves in good spirits.'

'No, Daddy, they wouldn't.' Kalpana turned her full but pretty face towards Mrs Rupa Mehra. 'Now why didn't you tell us you were coming? We would have come to fetch you from the station.'

'But I did. I sent a telegram.'

'Oh—it'll probably come today. Things have got so bad with the postal service even though they've just put up the rates.'

'It'll take time. They have a reasonable Minister in charge,' said her father. 'The young are always so impatient.'

'Anyway, why didn't you send us a letter?' asked Kalpana.

'I decided to come suddenly. It's Lata,' said Mrs Rupa Mehra in a rush. 'I want you to find her a boy at once. A suitable boy. She is getting involved with unsuitable boys, and I cannot have that.'

Kalpana reflected on her own attachments to unsuitable boys: on an engagement that had broken up because her friend had suddenly changed his mind; on her father's opposition to another. She was still unmarried, which made her rather sad whenever she thought about it. She said: 'Khatri, of course? One or two?'

Mrs Rupa Mehra gave Kalpana a worried smile. 'Two, please. I will stir it myself. Actually, I should have this saccharine but after a journey one can always make an exception. Of course khatri would be best. I think that one's own community creates a sense of comfort. But proper khatris: Seth, Khanna, Kapoor, Mehra—no, not Mehra preferably—'

Kalpana was virtually but not quite out of marriageable range herself; it was perhaps a measure of Mrs Rupa Mehra's desperation that she had decided to entrust such an enterprise to her. Her decision, however, was not unbased on reason. Kalpana knew young people, and Mrs Rupa Mehra knew no one else in Delhi who did. Kalpana was very fond of Lata, who was several years younger than her. And since it was only the khatri community that was to be dredged for prospective candidates, it was not likely that Kalpana herself heaven forbid, should perceive a conflict of interest—especially since she was not a khatri but a brahmin.

'Don't worry, Ma, I don't know any Mehras except you,' said Kalpana

Gaur. She beamed broadly and continued:

'I do know some Khannas and Kapoors in Delhi, though. I'll introduce them to you. Once they see you, they'll know that your daughter's bound to be good-looking.'

'I was much more good-looking before the car accident,' said Mrs Rupa Mehra, stirring her tea and looking through the window—towards a gardenia bush, dry with summer dust.

'Do you have a photograph of Lata? A recent one?'

'Of course.' There was very little that Mrs Rupa Mehra's black bag did not contain. She had a very simple black-and-white photograph of Lata with no jewellery or make-up; there were some flowers—a few phlox—in her hair. There was even a photograph of Lata as a baby, though it was unlikely that this would have impressed the family of a potential groom. 'But first you must get well, darling,' she said to Kalpana. 'I came with no warning at all. You asked me to come at Divali or Christmas but time and tide wait for no man.'

'I'm perfectly well,' said Kalpana Gaur, blowing her nose. 'And this problem will make me better.'

'She's quite right,' said her father. 'Half her illness is laziness. If she isn't careful, she'll die young, like her mother.'

Mrs Rupa Mehra smiled weakly.

'Or your husband,' added Mr Gaur. 'He was a foolish man if ever there was one. Climbing the mountains of Bhutan with a weak heart—and overworking—for whom? For the British and their railways.' He sounded resentful, as he missed his old friend.

Mrs Rupa Mehra reflected that they were everyone's railways, and that what the late Raghubir Mehra was keen on was the work as such and not who his paymasters were. Everyone who was a government servant could be said to have served the British.

'He worked hard, but for the action, not for the fruits of the action. He was a true karma-yogi,' said Mrs Rupa Mehra sadly. The late Raghubir Mehra, though he did work excessively hard, would have been amused at this elevated description of himself.

'Go in and see to the guest room,' said Mr Gaur. 'And make sure that there are flowers in it.'

The days passed pleasantly. When Mr Gaur returned from his general store, they talked of old times. At night, with the jackals howling behind the house, and the scent of gardenias in her room, Mrs Rupa Mehra would think back anxiously on the day's events. She could not summon Lata to Delhi and out of harm's way without having something tangible in hand. So far, for all Kalpana's efforts, she had found no one suitable. She often thought of her husband, who would have allayed her fears—either by getting angry with her or by teasing her and then making up. Before she went to sleep she looked at the photograph of him she kept in her bag, and that night she dreamed of him playing rummy with the children in their saloon car.

In the morning Mrs Rupa Mehra woke up even before the Gaurs to chant in a soft voice her verses from the Bhagavad Gita:

'You grieve for those beyond grief,
and you speak words of insight;
but learned men do not grieve
for the dead or the living.

Never have I not existed
nor you, nor these kings;
and never in the future
shall we cease to exist.

Just as the embodied self
enters childhood, youth, and old age,
so does it enter another body;
this does not confound a steadfast man.

Contacts with matter make us feel
heat and cold, pleasure and pain.
Arjuna, you must learn to endure
fleeting things—they come and go!

When these cannot torment a man,
when suffering and joy are equal
for him and he has courage,
he is fit for immortality.

Nothing of nonbeing comes to be,
nor does being cease to exist;

the boundary between these two
is seen by men who see reality.

Indestructible is this presence
that pervades all this;
no one can destroy
this unchanging reality. . . .'

But it was not the all-pervading essence of reality that clutched at Mrs Rupa Mehra's consciousness but the loved particularities that she had lost or that were losable. What body was her husband in now? If he was born again in human form would she even recognize him if he passed by her in the street? What did it mean when they said of the sacrament of marriage that they would be bound together for seven lives? If they had no memory of who they had been, what use was such knowledge? For all she knew, this last marriage might have been her seventh one. Emotion made her literal; she longed for tangible assurance. The soothing Sanskrit of the small, green, cloth-bound volume passed through her lips, but, while it gave her peace—tears rarely came to her eyes while she was reciting the Gita—it answered none of her questions. And while ancient wisdom so often proved unconsoling, photography, that cruel modern art, helped to ensure that even the image of her husband's face would not grow dim with time.

9.2

Meanwhile, Kalpana tried her best to ferret out likely prospects for Lata. In all she found seven, which was not bad at such short notice. Three were friends or acquaintances, three were friends or acquaintances of friends or acquaintances, and one was the friend of a friend of a friend.

The first, a lively and friendly young man, had been with her at university, and had acted with her in plays. He was rejected by Mrs Rupa Mehra as being too rich. 'You know our circumstances, Kalpana,' said Mrs Rupa Mehra.

'But he is sure not to want a dowry. He's very flush,' said Kalpana.

'They are far too well-to-do,' said Mrs Rupa Mehra with decision. 'There's no point talking about it. Even their normal expectations for the wedding will be too high. We'll have to feed a thousand people. Of those, probably seven hundred will be guests from their side. And we'll have to put them up, and give all the women saris.'

'But he's a good boy,' persisted Kalpana, 'at least look at him.'

Her flu had improved, and she was as energetic as ever.

Mrs Rupa Mehra shook her head. 'If I liked him it would only upset me. He may be good, but he lives with his whole family. Lata will always be compared with the other daughters-in-law—she'll be the poor relation. I won't have it. She won't be happy.'

And so the first prospect was excluded.

The second, whom they went to see, spoke good English and seemed a sober fellow. But he was too tall. He would tower over Lata. He would not do. 'If at first you don't succeed, try, try again,' said Mrs Rupa Mehra to Kalpana, though she herself had begun to feel disheartened.

The third boy was also problematic.

'Too dark, too dark,' said Mrs Rupa Mehra.

'But Meenakshi—' began Kalpana Gaur.

'Don't talk to me about Meenakshi,' said Mrs Rupa Mehra in a tone that brooked no argument.

'Ma, let Lata decide what she thinks of him.'

'I will not have black grandchildren,' said Mrs Rupa Mehra.

'You said exactly that when Arun got married—and see how fond you are of Aparna. And she isn't even dark—'

Mrs Rupa Mehra said: 'Aparna is different.' After a pause she thought of something else. 'The exception proves the rule,' she added.

Kalpana Gaur said: 'Lata isn't all that fair herself.'

'All the more reason,' said Mrs Rupa Mehra. What this meant was unclear; what was clear was that her mind had been made up.

The fourth prospect was the son of a jeweller who had a prosperous shop in Connaught Circus. Within five minutes of their meeting his parents mentioned a dowry of two lakh rupees. Mrs Rupa Mehra stared at Kalpana in astonishment.

When they got out of the house, Kalpana said: 'Honestly, Ma, I didn't know they were like that. I don't even know the boy myself. A friend simply told me that they had a son for whom they were seeking a bride. I'd never have put you through all that if I'd known.'

'If my husband was alive,' said Mrs Rupa Mehra, still smarting, 'he might have been Chairman of the Railway Board, and we'd never have to lower our heads before anyone, certainly not people like these.'

The fifth candidate, though decent enough, could not speak English properly. Try, try again.

The sixth was wanting—harmless, quite pleasant, but slightly deficient. He smiled innocently throughout the interview which Mrs Rupa Mehra conducted with his parents.

Mrs Rupa Mehra, thinking of Robert Bruce and the spider, was convinced that the seventh man would be the one for her daughter.

The seventh, however, had whisky on his breath and his uncertain laugh reminded her uncomfortably of Varun.

Mrs Rupa Mehra was deeply discouraged and, having exhausted her contacts in Delhi, decided that Kanpur, Lucknow, and Banaras (in each of which she or her late husband had relatives) would have to be dredged before she returned to try her luck in Brahmpur (where, however, lurked the undesirable Kabir). But what if Kanpur, Lucknow, and Banaras proved equally fruitless?

By now Kalpana had suffered a relapse and fallen quite seriously ill (though the doctors were puzzled about the diagnosis; she had stopped sneezing, but seemed to be weak and sleepy all the time). Mrs Rupa Mehra decided to spend a few days nursing her before she left Delhi for the rest of her slightly premature Annual Trans-India Rail Pilgrimage.

9.3

One evening, a rather short but energetic young man appeared at the door and was greeted by Mr Gaur.

'Good evening, Mr Gaur—I wonder if you remember me. I'm Haresh Khanna.'

'Oh, yes?' said Mr Gaur.

'I knew Kalpana at St Stephen's. We studied English together.'

'Weren't you the one who went to England to study physics or something? I don't think I've seen you in years.'

'Shoes.'

'Oh. Shoes. I see.'

'Is Kalpana in?'

'Well, yes—but she isn't very well.' Mr Gaur pointed his stick at the tonga, which had a suitcase on it together with a briefcase and a bedding roll. 'Were you thinking of staying here?' he asked, rather alarmed.

'No—no—not at all. My father lives near Neel Darvaza. I've come straight from the station. I work in Cawnpore. I thought I'd drop by and see Kalpana before I went to Baoji's house. But if she isn't well. . . . What is the matter? Nothing serious, I hope?' Haresh smiled, and his eyes disappeared.

Mr Gaur frowned at him for a few seconds, then spoke.

'The doctors can't agree. But she keeps yawning. Health is the most precious possession, young man.' (He had forgotten Haresh's name.) 'Don't forget that.' He paused. 'Well, come in.'

Even though her father had been surprised by his sudden, unannounced arrival, Kalpana, when she entered the drawing room, could not have been more happy than to see Haresh. They had corresponded off and on for a year or so after they left college, but time and distance had taken their toll, and the crush she had had on him had slowly faded. Then had come her unhappy affair and broken engagement. Haresh had heard of this through friends, and he told himself that the next time he was in Delhi he would go over and say hello.

'You!' said Kalpana Gaur, reviving.

'Me!' said Haresh, pleased with his restorative powers.

'You're every bit as good-looking as when I used to admire you during Dr Mathai's lectures on Byron.'

'And you're just as charming as when all of us were laying ourselves and our cloaks under your feet.'

A slight tinge of sadness entered the smile on Kalpana Gaur's face. Since she had been one of the few girls at St Stephen's, she had been in natural demand. She was quite pretty too in those days; indeed, perhaps she still was. But for some reason none of her boyfriends remained boyfriends for long. She had a very decided personality and fairly soon took to telling them what they should do with their lives and studies and work. She began to mother them or perhaps brother them (since she was something of a tomboy)—and this sooner or later took the edge off their romantic excitement. They even began to find her vivacity overpowering, and sooner or later edged away from her—with guilt on their side and pain on hers. This was a great pity, for Kalpana Gaur was a lively, affectionate, and intelligent woman, and deserved some recompense for the help and happiness she gave others.

In Haresh's case, she had never really stood a chance. He was very fond of her at college, but his heart was then—as it was now—with Simran, a Sikh girl, the sweetheart of his adolescence whose family was determined that she should not marry him because he was not a Sikh.

Mutual compliments having been exchanged, Haresh and Kalpana started talking about the old days even before catching up on what had happened to them since they had last written to each other two years ago. Mr Gaur had gone inside; young people, he found, had remarkably little of interest to say.

Suddenly Kalpana Gaur got up. 'Do you remember my good-looking aunt?' She sometimes referred to Mrs Rupa Mehra as her aunt although, strictly speaking, she was nothing of the kind.

'No,' said Haresh. 'I don't think I've ever met her. But I remember you used to talk about her.'

'Well, she's staying with us at the moment.'

'I'd like to meet her,' said Haresh.

Kalpana went to fetch Mrs Rupa Mehra, who had been writing letters in her room.

She was dressed in a brown-and-white cotton sari, slightly crushed—she had been resting half an hour before—and Haresh thought her very fine-looking. His eyes crinkled into a smile as he stood up; Kalpana introduced them.

'Khanna?' said Mrs Rupa Mehra, wheels whirring.

The young man, she noted, was well dressed, in a cream-coloured silk shirt and a pair of fawn trousers. He had a pleasant, squarish face. And he was fairly fair.

Mrs Rupa Mehra for once didn't say much during the ensuing conversation. Although Haresh had been to Brahmpur just a few months ago, it didn't come up, and nor did any common names, so there was no obvious point of entry for her. Anyway, Kalpana Gaur had steered the conversation towards Haresh's recent history, and Mrs Rupa Mehra listened with growing interest. Haresh, for his part, was happy to regale Kalpana with some of his recent achievements and exploits. He was an energetic man, with a great deal of optimism and self-confidence, and was not hindered by too delicate a sense of modesty.

Haresh found his work at the Cawnpore Leather & Footwear Company fascinating, and assumed that everyone else would too. 'I've only been at CLFC a year, but I'm establishing a whole new department—and I've got them orders that they didn't have the know-how or the initiative to get themselves. But there's no future in it, that's the trouble. Ghosh is the top man, and it's all family owned, and I can't aspire to anything really. All of them are Bengalis.'

'Bengali entrepreneurs?' said Kalpana Gaur.

'Sounds odd, doesn't it?' agreed Haresh. 'Ghosh is an impressive man, though. Tall, self-made. He has a construction business that he runs from Bombay. This is only one of his interests.'

Mrs Rupa Mehra nodded in approval. She liked the idea of self-made people.

'Anyway, I'm not a political fellow,' continued Haresh, 'and there's far too much politics among the officers at CLFC. Far too much office politics and not enough work. And three hundred and fifty a month is not much for the kind of work I'm doing. It's just that I had to find the first job I could when I came back from England. I was broke, so I had no choice.' The memory did not appear to disturb him.

Mrs Rupa Mehra looked at Haresh anxiously.

He smiled. His eyes now crinkled up almost completely. He had once been promised ten rupees by his college friends to keep his eyes open when he smiled, and he had not been able to earn it.

Mrs Rupa Mehra couldn't help smiling back.

'So I've come to Delhi not just on work but also to look around.' Haresh passed his hand across his forehead. 'I've brought all my certificates and testimonials and so on, and I have an interview with a firm here. Of course Baoji thinks I should stick with a sure thing, and Umesh Uncle doesn't think much of anything I do, but I'm determined to give it a try. So, Kalpana, do you know of any jobs available in my line? Anyone whom I should see in Delhi? I'll be staying at Neel Darvaza with the family as usual.'

'I don't, but if I hear of anything that might suit you—' began Kalpana. Then, in a sudden flash of inspiration, she said: 'Listen, do you really have your testimonials and so on here?'

'They're in the tonga outside. I came straight from the station.'

'You did?' Kalpana beamed at Haresh.

Haresh threw up his hands in a gesture that could have meant that Kalpana's charm was an irresistible beacon to the weary traveller, or merely that he had decided to get long-deferred social business over with before he got caught up with the family and the world.

'Well, then, let's see them; fetch them.'

'Fetch them?'

'Yes, of course, Haresh. We want to see them even if you don't want to show them.' Kalpana gestured towards Mrs Rupa Mehra, who nodded quite vigorously.

But Haresh was only too willing to show off his certificates. He got his briefcase from the tonga, and brought out all his diplomas from the Midlands College of Technology together with a couple of glowing testimonials, one of them from the Principal himself. Kalpana Gaur read out several of these, and Mrs Rupa Mehra listened with close attention. From time to time Haresh mentioned a relevant fact or two, for example that he had topped the list in the examination for pattern-cutting or had won some medal or other. He was not at all bashful about his achievements.

At the end of it, Mrs Rupa Mehra said to Haresh: 'You should be very proud.'

She would have liked to talk with them further, but she had to go out that evening for dinner and had not yet changed out of her crushed sari. Excusing herself, she got up. As she was about to leave the room, Haresh said: 'Mrs Mehra, it's been a great pleasure to meet you. But are you sure we haven't met before?'

Mrs Rupa Mehra said: 'I never forget a face. I am sure I would have remembered if we had met.' She left the room, looking pleased but slightly preoccupied.

Haresh rubbed his forehead. He felt convinced that he had seen her before, but he couldn't remember where.

9.4

When Mrs Rupa Mehra returned from dinner, she said to Kalpana Gaur:

'Of all the boys we have met, Kalpana, I like that young man the most. Why didn't you introduce me to him before? Was there some, well, particular reason?'

'Well, no, Ma, I didn't even think of him. He just happened to arrive from Kanpur.'

'Oh, yes, Kanpur. Of course.'

'Incidentally, he was much taken by you. He thinks you're very attractive. He said you were "strikingly good-looking".'

'You are a very naughty girl to call me your good-looking aunt.'

'But very truthful.'

'What does your father think of him?'

'My father only met him for a minute. But you really liked him?' continued Kalpana, with a speculative expression.

Mrs Rupa Mehra had indeed liked Haresh. She had liked the fact that he was energetic, that he was independent of his family (though affectionate towards them), and that he clearly took great care with his appearance. Nowadays, many boys looked so scruffy. And one crucial point in Haresh's favour was his name. Being a Khanna, he was bound to be a khatri.

'We must fix up a meeting,' she said. 'Is he—you know—'

'Available?'

'Yes.'

'Well, he was in love with a Sikh girl once,' said Kalpana Gaur quietly. 'I don't know what came of it.'

'Oh. Why didn't you ask him about it when I left? You talked like old friends.'

'I wasn't sure at the time that you were so interested in him,' said Kalpana Gaur, her face reddening a little.

'I am. He might be just the boy for Lata, don't you think? I'll telegram her to come to Delhi immediately. Immediately.' Mrs Rupa Mehra furrowed her forehead. 'Do you know Meenakshi's brother?'

'No. I only met Meenakshi at the wedding—'

'He's causing no end of worry to me.' Mrs Rupa Mehra clicked her tongue.

'Isn't he the poet, Amit Chatterji?' asked Kalpana. 'He's quite famous, you know, Ma.'

'Famous! All he does is sit in his father's house and stare out of the upstairs window. A young man should do a job and earn his living.' Mrs Rupa Mehra enjoyed the poetry of Patience Strong, Wilhelmina Stitch, and various other writers, but that the creation of it involved any activity—or necessary inactivity—she found incomprehensible. 'Lata has been seeing far too much of him.'

'You're not saying that there's a chance—' laughed Kalpana, looking at Mrs Rupa Mehra's expression. 'Well, Ma, at least let him write a couple of poems to Lata.'

'I am not saying anything and I am not speculating,' said Mrs Rupa Mehra, upset by the thought of the developments in Calcutta. 'I am tired now. Why must I run from city to city? I think I must have eaten too much, and I have forgotten to take my homoeopathic medicine.' She got up, turned to speak again, thought better of it, and picked up her big black bag.

'Goodnight, Ma,' said Kalpana. 'I've put a jug of water by your bed. If there's anything you want, please tell me—Ovaltine or Horlicks or anything. And I'll get in touch with Haresh tomorrow.'

'No, darling, you must rest now. It's very late, and you are not very well.'

'Actually, Ma, I'm feeling a lot better than I felt earlier today. Haresh and Lata—Lata and Haresh. Well, no harm trying.'

But the next morning, Kalpana Gaur was not feeling at all well, and spent the day listless and yawning. And the day after, when she sent a message to Neel Darvaza, she found that Haresh Khanna had already returned to Kanpur.

9.5

In the train from Calcutta to Kanpur Lata had plenty of time to wonder about her sudden summons. The telegram from Mrs Rupa Mehra had been cryptic, as the best telegrams are, and had required her to come to Kanpur in two days' time.

It was a day journey, though a long one. Arun had got up early to drop her at Howrah Station. Howrah Bridge was uncrowded. When they got to the station with its familiar smell of smoke, urine and fish, Arun made sure she was well settled in her ladies' compartment.

'What'll you read on the way?'

'*Emma*.'

'Not like our saloons, is it?'

'No,' said Lata with a smile.

'I've telegrammed Brahmpur, so Pran ought to be at the station. Maybe Savita too. Look out for them.'

'All right, Arun Bhai.'

'Now, be good. It won't be the same without you at home. Aparna will be much more difficult.'

'I'll write . . . and, Arun Bhai, when you reply, please type.'

Arun laughed, then yawned.

The train departed on time.

Lata was happy once again to see the green and moist countryside of Bengal, which she loved—with its palms and banana trees, emerald fields of rice and village ponds. After a while, however, the landscape changed into a dry and hilly tract with small ravines over which the train clanked in a different voice.

The land became drier still as they moved westwards into the plains. Dusty fields and poor villages passed by between the telegraph poles and furlong markers. The heat was intense, and Lata's mind began to wander. She would have been happy to stay in Calcutta for the rest of her holidays, but her mother sometimes took it into her head to insist on companionship for her Rail-Pilgrimages—usually when she felt ill or lonely somewhere along the route. She wondered which it was this time.

The other women in her compartment were shy with each other at first, and only talked to those they were travelling with, but as time passed, through the catalysis of a rather charming baby, they established a web of conversation. Young men from their families stopped by to inquire whether everything was all right when the train halted at a station, brought cups of tea in earthenware cups, and replenished the earthenware pitchers with water, for the day was getting even hotter, and the fans functioned only about half the time.

A woman in a burqa, having established which direction was west, rolled out a small prayer-rug and began to pray.

Lata thought of Kabir, and she felt both miserable and—in a curious way that she could not understand—happy. She loved him still—it was pointless to pretend otherwise. Had Calcutta had any effect at all in diminishing what she felt for him? Certainly, his letter had not given her any great hope of the strength of his feelings for her. Was there anything at all to be said for loving and not being loved equally in return? She didn't think so. Why, then, did she smile when she thought of him?

Lata read her *Emma*, and was grateful to be able to. If she had been travelling with her mother, they would have formed the central node in the conversational web, and everyone in the compartment would by now have heard about Bentsen Pryce, Lata's brilliance in her studies, the details of Mrs Rupa Mehra's rheumatism, her false teeth and former beauty, the saloon-sheltered glory of her late husband's inspection tours, the harshness of fate, and the wisdom of acceptance and resignation.

Sootily, fitfully, the train made its way along the great, burning plain of the Ganga.

At Patna a swarm of locusts, a mile long, darkened the sky.

Dust and flies and soot somehow succeeded in entering the compartment even when the glass panes were pulled down.

The Brahmpur telegram could not have arrived, because neither Savita nor Pran was at the platform to meet her. Lata had been looking forward to seeing them, if only for the fifteen minutes that the train stopped at Brahmpur. As the train pulled out of Brahmpur Junction she felt a disproportionate sadness.

As the whistle of the train suddenly wailed out, she caught in the distance a glimpse of the roofs of the university.

Always I am weeping, weeping
In your heart my image keeping

If, for example, he had appeared at the station—say, in the casual clothes he had worn when he had been with her on the boat, smiling with his old friendliness, arguing with a porter about the rate he was charging—suppose he too had been going to Kanpur—or at least as far as Banaras or Allahabad—Lata felt that her heart would have leapt with happiness at the sound of his voice and the sight of his face—and any misunderstanding between them would have vanished in a single puff of steam, a single turn of the wheels.

Lata looked down at her book.

> 'My poor dear Isabella,' said he, fondly taking her hand, and interrupting, for a few moments, her busy labours for some one of her five children—'How long it is, how terribly long since you were here! And how tired you must be after your journey! You must go to bed early, my dear—and I recommend a little gruel to you before you go.—You and I will have a nice basin of gruel together. My dear Emma, suppose we all have a little gruel.'

An egret flew over a field towards a ditch.

A sickly smell of molasses rose from a sugarcane factory.

The train stopped for an hour at a tiny station for no particular reason.

Beggars begged at the barred windows of the compartment.

When the train crossed the Ganga at Banaras, she threw a two-anna coin for luck out of the barred window. It hit a girder, then spun downwards into the river.

At Allahabad the train crossed over to the right bank again, and Lata threw another coin out.

Ganga darshan is so nice.
I have now completed twice.

She told herself that she was in danger of becoming an honorary Chatterji.

She began to hum Raag Sarang, then later drifted into Multani.

She rejected her sandwiches and bought some samosas and tea at the next station.

She hoped her mother was well. She yawned. She put *Emma* aside. She thought once again of Kabir.

She drowsed off for an hour. When she woke she found she had been leaning against the shoulder of an old woman in a white sari, who smiled at her. She had been keeping the flies off Lata's face.

A troop of monkeys were raiding a dusty mango tree in an orchard at dusk, while three men stood below, trying to shoo them off with stones and lathis.

Soon it was night. It was still warm.

In a while the train slowed down once more, and the word 'Cawnpore' greeted her in black on a large yellow sign on the platform. Her mother was there, and her uncle Mr Kakkar, both smiling; but there was a look of strain on her mother's face.

9.6

They went home by car. Kakkar Phupha (as Lata called her father's sister's husband) was a successful accountant with a cheery manner.

When they were alone, Mrs Rupa Mehra told Lata about Haresh: 'a very suitable prospect'.

Lata was speechless for a moment. Then in a tone of disbelief she said: 'You treat me like a child.'

Mrs Rupa Mehra wavered for a few seconds between suppression and placation, then murmured: 'What is the harm, darling? I am not forcing anything on you. And day-after we will be leaving for Lucknow anyway and then back to Brahmpur the day after that.'

Lata looked at her mother, amazed that she should defend herself.

'And it was for this—not because you were unwell or needed my help—that I was summoned from Calcutta.' The tone of Lata's voice was so unloving that Mrs Rupa Mehra's nose reddened. But she pulled herself together and said:

'Darling, I do need your help. Getting you married is not easy. And the boy is of our community.'

'I don't care what community he belongs to. I am not going to see him. I should never have left Calcutta.'

'But he is a khatri—from U.P. originally,' protested her mother.

This cast-iron argument had no effect on Lata. She said:

'Ma, please. I know all your prejudices and I share none of them. You bring me up one way and you act in another.'

To this righteous attack her mother merely murmured: 'You know, Lata, I have nothing against—against Mohammedans as such. It is only your future I am concerned about.' Mrs Rupa Mehra had been expecting an outburst of sorts, and, with an effort, remained emollient.

Lata was silent. O, Kabir, Kabir, she thought.

'Why aren't you eating anything, dear? It's been such a long journey.'

'I'm not hungry.'

'Yes, you are,' insisted Mrs Rupa Mehra.

'Ma, you have brought me here under false pretences,' said Lata, unpacking her suitcase and not looking at her mother. 'You must have known that if you had given your reasons in the telegram I would never have come.'

'Darling, it isn't sensible to add words to a telegram. Telegrams have become terribly expensive these days. Unless of course you send a stock phrase like "Best wishes on a safe and pleasant journey" or "Heartiest Bijoya greetings" or some such thing. And he is such a nice boy. You'll see.'

Lata was so exasperated that a couple of tears squeezed their way into her eyes. She shook her head, even angrier now with herself, her mother, and the unknown Haresh.

'Ma, I hope I am not like you when I am your age,' she said passionately.

Mrs Rupa Mehra's nose immediately reddened again.

'If you don't believe me, at least believe Kalpana. I met him at her house. The boy is Kalpana's friend. He has studied in England and has excellent results. He is good-looking, and he is interested in meeting you. If you are not interested in meeting him, how can I show my face to Kalpana who went through all the trouble of arranging this? Even Mr Gaur approves of him. If you don't believe me, read this letter from her. It's for you.'

'I don't need to read it,' said Lata. 'You can tell me what's in it.'

'How do you know I've read it?' said Mrs Rupa Mehra indignantly. 'Don't you trust your own mother?'

Lata stood the empty suitcase in a corner. 'Ma, there is guilt written all over your face,' she said. 'But I'll read it all the same.'

Kalpana's letter was brief and affectionate. Just as she had told Haresh that Lata was like a sister to her, she now told Lata that Haresh was like a brother to her. Kalpana, it seemed, had written to Haresh. Haresh had written back, saying that he couldn't return to Delhi because he was required at the factory and had taken leave only recently, but that he would be very happy to meet Lata and Mrs Rupa Mehra in Kanpur. He had added that despite his affection for Simran, he had now come to realize that there was no hope for him there. As a result, he was not averse to meeting other girls. At the moment his life consisted of little but work; India was not England, where it was easy to get to know girls on their own.

> As for a dowry [continued Kalpana in her curvaceously looped script], he isn't the kind of man to ask for it, and there is no one to ask for it on his behalf. He is very attached to his father—his foster-father, actually, though he calls him Baoji—but (unlike his foster-brothers) he has established his independence early enough. He ran away from home once when he was fifteen, but you should not hold that against him. If the two of you like each other, you will not have to live with your in-laws. The joint family lives in Neel Darvaza in Delhi, and though I have been there once and like most of them, I know that that environment would not suit you, given the way you have been brought up.
>
> I can tell you honestly, Lata, that I have always liked Haresh. At one time I even had a slight crush on him—we were in the same class at St Stephen's. When my father read his recent letter, he said: 'Well, it is a straightforward reply. At least he makes no bones about his earlier affections.' And certainly, Ma seems set on him. She has been getting more and more worried lately. Perhaps this is the answer to her dreams as well as yours. At any rate, Lata, whatever you do or don't do finally, do meet him, and don't be annoyed with your mother, who has been going frantic trying to ensure your happiness (as she sees it).
>
> Ma will have told you about my health. If I were not myself I would be amused by my own symptoms, which range from yawning to spells of dizziness to hot spots on the soles of my feet. These hot spots are particularly puzzling. Your mother swears by some Doctor Nuruddin in Calcutta, but he sounds like a quack. And anyway, I can't travel. Why don't you visit me after Kanpur and we'll play

> Monopoly, just as we used to as children? It has been so long since I last saw you. My love to you and to Ma. Do pay some attention to her advice; I think that you are very lucky to be her daughter. Please report to me the moment you have something to report. Lying in bed all I can listen to is this painful classical music on the radio, which I know you don't think is painful, and the gup-shup of empty-headed friends. A visit from you would do me good. . . .

Something in the tone of the letter made Lata think of the time at Sophia Convent when, as a schoolgirl, overcome by a sudden impulse, a strange, trance-like state, she had wanted to become a Christian and a nun. She had wanted to convert immediately and Arun had been summoned to Mussourie to talk some sense into her head. He had promptly declared that it was all 'summer moonshine'. It was the first time that Lata had heard the phrase. Though she had been struck by it, she had refused to believe that these religious impulses were moonshine of any kind. She had been determined to go ahead with her resolve. It was in fact a nun at Sophia Convent who had finally sat her down on a bench and talked to her—a green bench some distance away from the school buildings. It had had a view of a slope covered with a well-kept lawn and beautiful flowers; at the foot of the slope was a cemetery in which nuns of the order, many of whom had taught at the school, lay buried. She had said: 'Give yourself a few months, Lata. Wait at least till you leave school. You can always decide a little later. Don't make an immediate commitment. Remember, it will be very hard on your mother, who is a young widow.'

Lata sat on the bed for a while with Kalpana's letter in her hand, trying to avoid looking at her mother's face. Mrs Rupa Mehra arranged her saris in a drawer, deliberately silent. After a minute Lata said:

'All right, Ma. I'll see him.' She did not say anything further. She was angry still, but saw no point in expressing it. When some of the lines of anxiety on her mother's forehead relaxed, she was glad she had left it at that.

9.7

For some time now, Haresh had kept a diary of sorts. These days he usually wrote it at night at a heavy writing desk in the rooms he rented at Elm Villa. He was browsing through it, glancing from time to time at the photograph standing in a silver frame on his desk.

Brahmpur

Lasting here is good, as is the general standard of workmanship. Am having pair of brogues done in Ravidaspur on design of shoes I had brought for Sunil. If my idea works, Brahmpur could become a good source of finished footwear. But quality is the key. Unless an infrastructure of good labour is built up the trade will not advance.

Purchasing of micro-sheets is not a problem: over-supply because of strike. Kedarnath Tandon took me around the market (troubles with labour and suppliers at the moment over local demands) and had lunch with his family. Bhaskar his son is very bright, and his wife is an attractive lady. Veena I think.

Praha people are very difficult to talk to, and are not impressed with my qualifications. The problem, as always, is one of ingress. If I can talk to the top, there is a possibility, otherwise none. They have not even answered my letters seriously.

Sunil in fine form as usual.

Letter to Baoji, Simran, M. and Mme. Poudevigne

Cawnpore

Hot days, and working in the factory is hard. At least in the evening I can rest under the fan at Elm Villa.

I think of Simran all the time, but I know there is little hope. Now her mother has threatened to commit suicide if she marries someone outside her faith. It may be human nature, but I do not want to be at the receiving end of human nature. It is even harder for Simran. No doubt they are trying to get her married off to someone suitable, poor girl.

At work, as usual, supplies are holding things up. I am too short-tempered and impatient. Had row with Rao from the other department. He is a good for nothing man who only knows how to play labour off against each other. He has favourites and is unobjective, and it is to the detriment of the whole organisation. Sometimes he simply takes away one or two people who I need, and then I am short-staffed. Thin lean fellow like Uriah, with a sharp nose. Elsewhere they believe in 'Grow and make the business grow'. In India we believe that the way to rise is to do someone else down.

Today the problem I faced was not nails or soles or stitching thread but sheepskin again. There were quite a few uppers cut which needed lining, also the recent order required sheepskin. After setting the men to work I took Rs. 600/- in suspense a/c and went to the market myself. Buying material is always a training in itself. Maybe I should treat my experience at CLFC as a paid apprenticeship. I felt tired after the day's work. Came home, read a few pages of *The Mayor of Casterbridge* and slept early. No letters.

Watch strap Rs. 12/- (Crocodile skin)

Cawnpore

Very interesting day.

Reached factory in time. It rained. Went about work as usual, there seems no system in the work, one person has to handle so many things.

Saw a shop in market run by a Chinaman, Lee. He has a small shop, I saw a few shoes with striking designs, so entered on impulse, and talked to him. He speaks English and also Hindi in a strange way. Makes shoes himself. I asked him who designed them, and he said he designed them himself as well. I was impressed. His technology of designing is not scientific, but he has a fairly good grasp of proportions and colour-schemes, even though I am colour-blind I could see that. The toe and tongue not lopsided, the type of sole and heel in balance, the total visual impact good. By seeing the quantity of business he did and through the conversation I found out without making him nervous how much he would be likely to make after rent and material and other costs. Lee cannot make much because Praha, Cooper Allen etc. flood the market with cheap shoes of a certain quality and Cawnpore is not a discriminating place for specially designed shoes. I think I could improve his prospects and also help my new department if I could convince Mukherji to take him on for Rs. 250 a month. Of course he will have to speak to Ghosh in Bombay, and that is the rub. If I were in business for myself I would take him on immediately. He would surely not be averse to have a designer's job without all the other troubles he must have.

Got ticket for Delhi and will be leaving tomorrow. A private party is thinking of hiring me, so I should be well prepared. And CLFC wants to get into the Delhi market also. They should first set their own house in order.

Too sleepy to write more.

Delhi

Mukherji agrees about Lee, now it is up to Ghosh.

Was tired, so rested on the train, even though it was a day journey. Freshened up in waiting room, then went to Kalpana. Had a good talk about the old times. She is not well, and has had a sad life, but cheers up everyone around her. Did not talk about S though it was on both our minds. Met her father and her good-looking aunt Mrs Mehra.

Baoji still set upon his farming plans. I tried to dissuade him because he has no experience. But once he decides on something, his mind is difficult to change. I was glad to avoid meeting Umesh Uncle.

Cawnpore

Woke late, reached the factory half an hour late. There was quite a mess and much had to be done. Telegram from Praha, which was not very encouraging, in fact insulting: they offer me Rs. 28 a week—do they think I am a fool? A letter from Simran, one from Jean, and one from Kalpana. Kalpana's letter was rather strange, suggesting engagement with Mrs Mehra's daughter Lata. Jean's letter the usual. Deferred dealing with labour till Monday in order to ascertain the exact position. At least labour knows I am not trying to play anyone off against anyone else. No one else talks to them properly: typical babu attitude. In the evening came home and slept quietly.

There is no place here to spread my wings. What is to be done?

cycle oil Re. 1/4

rent and board etc. to Mrs Mason Rs. 185/-

stamps Re. 1/-

9.8

Before dropping off to sleep, he reread Kalpana's letter, which he looked around for before remembering that he had tucked it in at the back of the diary.

My dear Haresh,

I do not know what sort of reception this letter will get from you. I am writing to you after a very long time, even though we have just met once again. It was so good to see you, and to feel that you have not forgotten me and that my bonds in thee are not entirely determinate. I was not at my best, and I was not prepared for your arrival. But when you left I felt invigorated once again, and in fact mentioned that to my good-looking aunt.

In fact it is at her behest that I am writing this letter—but not only at her behest. I shall be businesslike and precise in whatever I have to say, and I shall expect you to be equally frank in your reply.

The point is that Mrs Mehra has a young daughter Lata—and she was so impressed by you that she wanted to know if there was any possibility of anything being arranged between Lata and you by way of matrimony. Don't be surprised at my writing all this, but I think Lata's marriage is also our responsibility. Her late father and my father were very close friends and thought of each other almost like brothers, so it was natural for my aunt to turn to us for help when she wanted to find a suitable match for her daughters. (The elder one is now happily married.) I showed my aunt all my eligible khatri friends, but because I had lost contact with you and also because you were not in Delhi I did not think of you as a possibility. There may also have been other reservations. But she saw you that evening and was extremely impressed. She thinks it would be a boy of your type who would have made Lata's late father happy.

As for Lata—she is nineteen years old, brilliant at her studies, came first in her Senior Cambridge exams from Sophia Convent, did her Intermediate Arts from Brahmpur University, and has just finished (with excellent marks) her first year B.A. exams in English, also from Brahmpur University. Once she finishes her B.A. next year she is keen to find some work. Her elder brother is working at Bentsen Pryce in Calcutta, her second brother has just finished at Calcutta University and is studying for the IAS. Her elder sister is, as I mentioned, married. Their father died in 1942, and was working with the Railways. He would certainly have been on the Railway Board by now if he had been alive.

She is 5 ft. 5 in. tall, not very fair, but attractive and smart in an Indian sort of way. She looks forward, I think, to a quiet, sober life in the future. I have played with her as a child—she is like my own little sister, and has gone so far as to say: 'If Kalpana thinks well of someone I'm pretty sure I will too.'

I have given you all the particulars. As Byron says, 'Though women are angels, yet wedlock's the devil.' You may hold that view. All I can say is, even if you do not, you are not bound to say 'yes' just because I am saying it. Think it over; if you are interested, just let me know. Of course you must see her and she must see you—and then your reactions and her reactions will count. If you (1) are thinking of getting married (2) have no previous commitments, and (3) are interested in this particular individual, you can come over to Delhi. (I tried to get in touch with you before you left Delhi but was unsuccessful.) If you are not comfortable about staying with your family at Neel Darvaza you can stay with us if you like; your family need not know the purpose of your visit or even that you are here. Lata's mother will be in Delhi for several more days, and tells me that Lata is planning to join her soon. She is a decent girl (if you are interested) and deserves a steady, honest and sincere type like her late father was.

So: the business being over, I should tell you that I am not at all well. I have been confined to bed since yesterday and the doctor does not know what is wrong. I yawn all the time and feel hot spots on the soles of my feet! I'm not allowed to move or talk very much. I'm writing this from bed, hence this terrible writing. I hope I get well soon, especially since Father's leg is also giving him trouble. He is much troubled by the heat as well. He hates ill health and June with an equal passion. All of us are praying that the monsoon is not delayed.

Lastly—if you think I've done anything wrong in writing so frankly to you, you must forgive me. I have presumed upon our friendship in writing to you in this way. If I ought not to have, let's just drop the matter and forget all about it.

I hope to hear from you soon or to see you. A telegram or letter—either would be fine.

Best wishes and everything,
Kalpana

Haresh's eyes closed once or twice as he read through the letter. It would be interesting to meet this girl, he thought. If the mother was anything to go by, she ought to be attractive too. But before he could give the matter his complete consideration, he yawned, and yawned again, and all thoughts whatsoever were displaced by exhaustion. He was asleep in five minutes; it was a pleasant and dreamless sleep.

9.9

'A call for you, Mr Khanna.'

'Just coming, Mrs Mason.'

'It's a lady's voice,' added Mrs Mason helpfully.

'Thank you, Mrs Mason.' Haresh went to the drawing room that her three lodgers used in common. No one else was down, but Mrs Mason was engaged in looking from various angles at a flower vase filled with orange cosmos. She was an Anglo-Indian woman of seventy-five, a widow who lived with her middle-aged, unmarried daughter. She liked to keep tabs on her lodgers.

'Hello. Haresh Khanna.'

'Hello, Haresh, this is Mrs Mehra, you remember, we met at Kalpana's in Delhi—Kalpana Gaur's—and—'

'Yes,' said Haresh with a glance at Mrs Mason, who was standing by the vase in a meditative manner, a finger on her lower lip.

'Do you—er, has Kalpana—'

'Yes, indeed, welcome to Cawnpore. Kalpana telegrammed. I was expecting you. Both of you—'

Mrs Mason cocked her head to one side.

Haresh passed his hand over his forehead.

'I cannot talk right now,' said Haresh. 'I'm a little late for work. When may I come over? I have the address. I'm so sorry I couldn't come to the station to meet you, but I didn't know which train you'd be on.'

'We were on different trains,' said Mrs Rupa Mehra. 'Can you come at eleven o'clock? I am very much looking forward to seeing you again. And so is Lata.'

'So am I,' said Haresh. 'The time suits me very well. I have to buy some sheep—and then I'll come over.' Mrs Mason shifted the vase to another table, then decided that the first one was better.

'Goodbye, Haresh. So we'll see you soon?'

'Yes. Goodbye.'

At the other end of the line Mrs Rupa Mehra turned to Lata and said: 'He sounded very brusque. He didn't even address me by name. And Kalpana says he called me Mrs Mehrotra in his letter to her.' She paused. 'And he wants to buy some sheep. I'm not sure I heard him right.' She paused again. 'But, believe me, he is a very nice boy.'

Haresh kept his bicycle, like his shoes and his comb and his clothes, in excellent condition, but he could not very well cycle down to meet Mrs and Miss Mehra at Mr Kakkar's house. He stopped by the factory and persuaded the factory manager, Mr Mukherji, to lend him one of the two factory cars. There was a big limousine with a grand and impressive driver and a small, rather rickety car with a driver who talked to all his passengers. He liked Haresh because he had no hierarchical airs, and always chatted to him in a friendly way.

Haresh tried for the beauty but ended up with the beast. Well, it's a car anyway, he said to himself.

He bought the sheepskin for the lining, and asked the supplier to ensure that it got to the factory. Then he stopped for a paan, which was something he always enjoyed. He combed his hair once again in the mirror of the car. And he gave the driver strict instructions that he was not to speak to anyone travelling in the car that day (including Haresh) unless he was spoken to.

Mrs Rupa Mehra was waiting for him with increasing nervousness. She had persuaded Mr Kakkar to join them in order to relieve the awkwardness of a first meeting. Mr Kakkar, both as a man and as an accountant, had been held in great respect by the late Raghubir Mehra, and it reassured Mrs Rupa Mehra that he, not she, would be playing nominal host.

She greeted Haresh warmly. Haresh was wearing almost the same clothes as when she had first met him at Kalpana's house in Delhi: a silk shirt and fawn cotton gaberdine trousers. He also had on a pair of brown-and-white co-respondent shoes, which he considered exceptionally smart.

He smiled when he saw Lata seated on the sofa. A nice, quiet girl, he thought.

Lata was wearing a pale pink cotton sari with chikan embroidery from Lucknow. Her hair was in a bun. She wore no jewellery except a pair of plain pearl ear-tops. The first thing Haresh said to her was:

'We've met before, Miss Mehra, haven't we?'

Lata frowned. Her first impression of him was that he was shorter than she had expected. The next—when he opened his mouth to speak—was that he had been chewing paan. This was far from appealing. Perhaps, if he had been wearing kurta-pyjamas, a red-stained mouth would have been appropriate—if not acceptable. Paan did not go at all well with fawn gaberdine and a silk shirt. In fact paan did not go at all well with her idea of a husband. His whole mode of dressing struck her as being flashy. And flashiest of all were the co-respondent shoes. Whom was he trying to impress?

'I don't believe we have, Mr Khanna,' she replied politely. 'But I'm glad we've got the chance to meet.'

Lata had made an immediately favourable impression on Haresh by the simplicity and good taste of her dress. She didn't have any make-up on, yet looked attractive and self-possessed, and her accent was not a heavy Indian accent, he was pleased to note, but light, almost British, because of her convent-school background.

Haresh, on the other hand, had surprised Lata by his accent, which bore traces both of Hindi and of the local Midlands dialect which he had been exposed to in England. Why, both her brothers spoke English better than he did. She could imagine what fun Kakoli and Meenakshi Chatterji might have mocking Haresh's manner of speaking.

Haresh passed his hand over his forehead. Surely he couldn't be mistaken. The same large, beautiful eyes, the same oval face—the eyebrows, the nose, the lips, the same expression of intensity. Well, perhaps he had dreamed it, after all.

Mr Kakkar, a little nervous because of his undefined position as a host, asked him to sit down and offered him tea. For a while no one knew what to talk about, especially since it was quite obvious what the purpose of their meeting was. Politics? No. The weather? No. The morning's news? Haresh had not had time to glance at the papers.

'Did you have a comfortable journey?' he asked.

Mrs Rupa Mehra looked at Lata, and Lata at Mrs Rupa Mehra. Each deferred to the other. Then Mrs Rupa Mehra said:

'Well, go on, Lata, answer the question.'

'I thought Mr Khanna was talking to you, Ma. Yes, thank you, I had a comfortable journey. Perhaps it was a little tiring.'

'Where were you travelling from?'

'From Calcutta.'

'But you must be very tired then. The train arrives very early in the morning.'

'No, I came by the day train, so I've slept in a proper bed and woken up at a reasonable hour,' said Lata. 'Is your tea all right?'

'Yes, thank you, Miss Mehra,' said Haresh, his eyes disappearing in a smile.

The smile was so warm and friendly that despite herself Lata could not help smiling too.

'You should call each other Lata and Haresh,' prompted Mrs Rupa Mehra.

'Perhaps we should leave the young people to talk by themselves,' suggested Mr Kakkar, who had an appointment.

'No, I don't think so,' said Mrs Rupa Mehra firmly. 'They will be very happy to have our company. It is not often that one gets the chance to meet such a fine boy as Haresh.'

Lata winced inwardly at this remark, but Haresh did not seem at all uncomfortable to be thus described.

'Have you ever been to Cawnpore, Miss Mehra?' he asked.

'Lata,' corrected Mrs Rupa Mehra.

'Lata.'

'Just once. Usually I meet Kakkar Phupha when he comes to Brahmpur or Calcutta on work.'

There was a long pause. Much tea was stirred, much tea was sipped.

'How is Kalpana?' asked Haresh finally. 'She didn't seem in the best of health when I saw her, and her letters talk about strange symptoms. I hope the poor girl is all right. She's been through such a lot these last few years.'

It was the right subject to choose. Mrs Rupa Mehra was off and running now. She described Kalpana's symptoms in detail, both from what she had seen, and from what she had read in the letter to Lata. She also talked about the unsuitable boy whom Kalpana had once got herself involved with. He had turned out not to be sincere. She wanted Kalpana to meet a sincere man, a sincere man with good prospects. She valued sincerity as a quality in men. And in women too of course. Didn't Haresh agree?

Haresh agreed. Being a frank and open-hearted fellow, he was about to talk about Simran, but stopped himself.

'Do you have those wonderful certificates with you?' asked Mrs Rupa Mehra suddenly.

'No,' said Haresh, surprised.

'It would be so nice if Lata could read them. Don't you think so, Lata?'

'Yes, Ma,' said Lata, thinking the opposite.

'Tell me, why did you run away from home at fifteen?' said Mrs Rupa Mehra, dropping an extra tablet of saccharine in her tea.

Haresh was startled that Kalpana had mentioned this fact. At his meeting with Lata's mother in Delhi, Kalpana, it seemed to him, had gone out of her way to show him in as favourable a light as possible.

'Mrs Mehra,' said Haresh, 'I believe that a time can come when a young man may have to part company even with those who love him and whom he loves.'

Mrs Rupa Mehra looked rather doubtful, but Lata a little interested. She nodded by way of encouragement, and Haresh continued.

'In this case an engagement was being forced upon me against my will by my father—well, my foster-father—and I could not accept it. I ran away. I had no money. In Mussourie I got a job cleaning a Praha shoe shop—it was my first experience of the shoe business, and not a pleasant one. Eventually I graduated to shop boy. I starved and I froze but I was determined not to go back.'

'Didn't you even write a letter home?' asked Lata.

'No, Miss Mehra, I did not. I was very stubborn.'

Mrs Rupa Mehra frowned at his retreat into the surname.

'What happened in the end?' Lata asked.

'One of my foster-brothers from Neel Darvaza, the one whom I loved most of all, came to Mussourie for a holiday. He saw me in the shop. I pretended I was a customer, but the manager asked me quite sharply why I was gossiping when there was work to do. When my foster-brother realized the truth of the matter, he refused to go back home unless I came with him. You see, his mother had nursed me when my own mother died.'

This last sentence was not exactly an explanation of anything, but made sense to everyone.

'But now I am neither starving nor freezing,' continued Haresh proudly. 'In fact, could I invite you all to my place for lunch, perhaps?' He turned to Mrs Rupa Mehra: 'Kalpana mentioned in her telegram that you are vegetarian.'

Mr Kakkar asked to be excused, but Mrs Rupa Mehra accepted with alacrity on behalf of Lata and herself.

9.10

On the way to Elm Villa, the driver was unusually quiet. The rickety car too behaved well.

'How do you enjoy your job?' asked Mrs Rupa Mehra.

'I enjoy it,' said Haresh. 'You know the department I was telling you about in Delhi? Well, the machinery has all been moved in, and I should begin next week with the new order that I've managed to procure. I'll take you around this afternoon. It's very well organized now that I've taken things in hand.'

'So you plan to live in Kanpur?' said Mrs Rupa Mehra.

'I don't know,' said Haresh. 'I can't advance to the top in CLFC, and I don't want to spend my life in a company where I can't get to the top. I've been trying Bata and James Hawley and Praha and Flex and Cooper Allen and even a job or two in government enterprises. Let's see what happens. I need a godfather to help me get a foot in the door. After that I can stand on my own abilities.'

'My son too thinks the same,' said Mrs Rupa Mehra. 'My elder son, Arun. He is with Bentsen Pryce—and well, Bentsen Pryce is Bentsen Pryce! Sooner or later he is bound to become a director. Maybe even the first Indian director.' She savoured the vision for a few moments. 'His late father would have been so proud of him,' she added. 'He, of course, would have been on the Railway Board by now. Possibly even the Chairman. We would always travel in saloons when he was alive.'

Lata was looking slightly disgusted.

'Here we are. Elm Villa!' said Haresh, rather as if he were announcing the Viceregal Lodge. They got down and went to the drawing room. Mrs Mason was out shopping, and they were alone except for a liveried bearer.

The drawing room was large and light, the liveried bearer extremely deferential. He bowed low and spoke softly. Haresh offered them nimbu pani, and the bearer brought the glasses on a plate, with doilies on the top: finely netted in white, with little glass beads hanging down from the edges. Two coloured prints of Yorkshire (which was where Mrs Mason traced her ancestry to) hung on the wall. The orange cosmos arranged in the vase added an additional touch of brightness to the flower-patterned sofa; it was one of the few flowers of the season that were not white. Haresh had told the cook the previous evening that he might be having guests for lunch, so there had been no need to make any last-minute arrangements.

Mrs Rupa Mehra was impressed by the establishment at Elm Villa. She deferred drinking the nimbu pani for a few minutes after taking her homoeopathic powder. But when she did, she found it satisfactory.

Though the purpose of their meeting was continuously on all three minds, the conversation was easier than before. Haresh talked about England and his teachers, about his plans for improving his position, above all about his work. The order he had procured was much on his mind, and he assumed that Mrs Rupa Mehra and Lata too must be anxiously awaiting the outcome of that project. He talked about his life abroad—without, however, mentioning any of the English girls whom he had had affairs with. On the other hand he could not refrain from mentioning Simran once or twice, and could not entirely conceal his emotion when he did so. Lata did not mind; she was almost indifferent to the proceedings. From time to time her eye would fall on his co-respondent shoes, and she invented a Kakoli-couplet to amuse herself.

Lunch was presided over by Miss Mason, a desperately ugly and lifeless woman of forty-five. Her mother was still out; and the two other lodgers were lunching out as well. In contrast to the drawing room, the dining room was dingy and flowerless (except for a dark still life, which, though it contained roses, did not please Mrs Rupa Mehra). It was full of heavy furniture—two sideboards, an almirah and a huge, heavy table—and at the far end of the room, opposite the still life, hung an oil painting of an English country scene containing cows. Mrs Rupa Mehra immediately thought of their edibility, and was upset. But the meal itself was innocuous, and served on flower-patterned plates with wavy edges.

First there was tomato soup. Then fried fish for everyone except Mrs Rupa Mehra, who had vegetable cutlets. Then there was chicken curry and rice with fried brinjal and mango chutney. (Mrs Rupa Mehra had a vegetable curry.) And finally there was caramel custard. The imperial deference of the liveried servant and the lifelessness of Miss Mason succeeded in freezing most of the conversation.

After lunch Haresh offered to show Mrs Rupa Mehra and Lata his rooms. Mrs Rupa Mehra agreed eagerly. One could learn much from a room. They went upstairs. There was a bedroom, an anteroom, a verandah and a bathroom. Everything was neat, tidy, smart—to Lata it appeared to be in extreme, almost disturbing, order. Even the volumes of Hardy on the small bookshelf were arranged alphabetically. The shoes standing on a shoe rack in a corner of the room were polished to a glacial shine. Lata looked out from the verandah at the garden of Elm Villa, which included a bed of orange cosmos.

Mrs Rupa Mehra, on the other hand—while Haresh was in the bathroom—looked around the room and drew in her breath sharply. A photograph of a smiling, long-haired young woman stood in a silver frame on Haresh's writing table. There were no other photographs in the room, none even of Haresh's family. The girl was fair—Mrs Rupa Mehra could make that out even from the black-and-white picture—and her features were classically beautiful.

She felt that Haresh, before inviting them to Elm Villa, could at least have put the photograph away.

Such a thought, however, would not even have occurred to Haresh. And had Mrs Rupa Mehra by any chance thought fit to talk slightingly about this omission, that would have been the end of matters as far as Haresh went. He would have forgotten about the Mehras' visit in a week.

When Haresh returned after washing his hands, Mrs Rupa Mehra said to him, frowning slightly:

'Let me ask you a question, Haresh. Is there someone else in your life still?'

'Mrs Mehra,' said Haresh, 'I told Kalpana and I am sure she has told you that Simran was and still is very dear to me. But I know that that door is closed to me. I cannot tear her away from her family, and for her family the fact that I am not a Sikh is all that matters. I am now looking for someone with whom I can live a happy married life. You need have no fears on that score. I am very glad that Lata and I have had the chance to get to know each other a little.'

Lata had come back in from the verandah during this exchange. She had overheard his forthright remarks and, without thinking, said to him: 'Haresh, what part will your family play in all this? You have talked very little about them. If—if—you intend to marry someone, will they have any say in the matter?' Her lips were trembling slightly. The thought of talking about such matters in such direct terms embarrassed her painfully. But something about the manner in which Haresh had said, 'I know that that door is closed to me,' had moved her, and so she had spoken.

Haresh, noticing her embarrassment, liked her for it, and smiled; as usual his eyes disappeared. 'No. I will ask for Baoji's blessing, naturally, but not for his consent. He knows that I feel strongly about my engagements.'

After a few moments of silence, Lata said:

'I see you like Hardy.'

'Yes,' said Haresh. 'But not *The Well Beloved*.' Then he looked at his watch and said: 'I have enjoyed this so much that I've lost track of the time. I have to do a bit of work at the factory, but I wonder if you'd like to come and see where I work? I don't want to hide anything from you; the atmosphere there is a little different from Elm Villa. Today I have managed to get the use of the car, so I could either take you there or have you dropped at Mr Kakkar's place. But perhaps you'll want to rest a little. It's a hot day and you must be tired.'

This time it was Lata who said, 'I would like to see the factory. But could I first—?'

Haresh indicated the bathroom.

Before she emerged she looked at the dressing table. Here too everything was neatly and methodically laid out: the Kent combs, the badger-hair shaving brush, the solidified stick of Pinaud deodorant that lent a cool fragrance to the warm day. Lata rubbed a little on the inside of her left wrist, and came out smiling. It was not that she didn't like Haresh. But the thought of their getting married was ridiculous.

9.11

She was no longer smiling a little later in the stench of the tannery. Haresh had to take the new employee Lee around CLFC's own tannery to show him the various kinds of leather (other than sheep, which they bought on the open market) that were available for making shoes. Lee's designs would depend partly on the leather available; and in his turn he could influence the choice of colours that the tannery would supply in the future. Haresh's nose, after a year at CLFC, was somewhat used to its distinctive smell, but Mrs Rupa Mehra felt almost faint, and Lata sniffed her left wrist from time to time, amazed that Lee and Haresh could treat the foul stench almost as if it didn't exist.

Haresh was quick to explain to Lata's mother that the hides were from 'fallen animals', in other words cows that had died a natural death and had not, as in other countries, been slaughtered. He said that they did not accept hides from Muslim slaughterhouses. Mr Lee gave her a reassuring smile, and she looked a little less miserable if not much more enthusiastic.

After a quick visit to the temporary storage godowns where the hides lay piled in salt, they went to the soaking pits. Men with orange rubber gloves were pulling the swollen hides out with grappling-hooks and transferring them to the liming drums where the hair and fat would be removed. As Haresh explained the various processes—de-hairing, de-liming, pickling, chrome tanning and so on—in a voice of enthusiasm, Lata felt a sudden revulsion for his work, and a sense of disquiet about someone who could enjoy this sort of thing. Haresh meanwhile was continuing confidently: 'But once you have it at the wet-blue stage, it's easy enough to see what comes next: fat liquoring, samming, splitting, shaving, dyeing, setting, drying, and then there we are! The leather that we actually think of as leather! All the other processes—glazing, boarding, ironing and so on—are optional, of course.'

Lata looked at the lean, exhausted, bearded man who was squeezing the water out of the wet-blue leather with the help of a roller press, then at Mr Lee, who had gone over to have a word with him.

Mr Lee's Hindi was unusual, and Lata, the rebellion of her nose and eyes notwithstanding, could not help listening to him with interest. He appeared to be knowledgeable not only about shoe design and manufacture but about tanning as well. Soon Haresh had joined them, and they were talking about the reduced volume of hides that went through the tannery during the monsoon weeks, when air-drying was difficult and tunnel-drying had to be resorted to.

Suddenly remembering something, Haresh said, 'Mr Lee, I recall some Chinese tanners from Calcutta telling me that in Chinese there is a word, a special word for ten thousand. Is that so?'

'Oh yes, in proper Peking Chinese it is called "wan".'

'And a wan of wans?'

Mr Lee looked at Haresh in surprise, and, scribbling with the index finger of his right hand on the palm of his left he drew an imaginary character and said something like 'ee'—to rhyme with his own name.

'Ee?' said Haresh.

Mr Lee repeated the word.

'Why do you have such words?' asked Haresh.

Mr Lee smiled sweetly. 'I do not know,' he said. 'Why don't you?'

By now Mrs Rupa Mehra was feeling so weak that she had to ask Haresh to take her out of the tannery.

'Do you want to go to the factory then, where I work?'

'No, Haresh, thank you, that's very sweet of you, but we should go home now. Mr Kakkar will be waiting for us.'

'It will just take twenty minutes, and you can meet Mr Mukherji, my boss. Really, we are doing wonderful work there. And I'll show you the set-up for the new department.'

'Some other time. Actually, I am feeling the heat a little—'

Haresh turned to Lata. Though she was putting on a brave front, her nose was crinkling upwards.

Haresh, suddenly realizing what the matter was, said: 'The smell—the smell. Oh—but you should have told me. I'm sorry—you see, I hardly give it a thought.'

'No, no,' said Lata, a bit ashamed of herself. Somewhere within her had risen an atavistic revulsion against the whole polluting business of hides and carrion and everything associated with leather.

But Haresh was very apologetic. While taking them back to the car he explained that this was a comparatively odourless tannery! Not far away, there was a whole locality with tanneries on both sides of the road, whose wastes and effluents were left in the open to dry or stagnate. At one time there had been a drain that took the stuff to the river, the holy Ganga itself, but there had been objections, and now there was no outlet at all. And people were very funny, said Haresh—they accepted what they had seen since childhood—shavings of leather and other offal strewn all around—they took it all for granted. (Haresh waved his arms to support his contention.) Sometimes he saw cartloads of hides coming in from villages or marketplaces being pulled by buffaloes who were almost dead themselves. 'And of course in a week or two, when the monsoons come, it won't be worth drying these shavings, so they'll just let them lie and rot. And with the heat and the rain—well, you can imagine what the smell is like. It's as bad as the tanning pits on the way to Ravidaspur—in your own city of Brahmpur. There even I had to hold my nose.'

The allusion was lost on Lata and Mrs Rupa Mehra, who would no more have dreamed of going to Ravidaspur than to Orion.

Mrs Rupa Mehra was about to ask Haresh when he had been to Brahmpur when the stench once more overpowered her.

'I'm going to take you back at once,' said Haresh decisively.

He sent a message that he would be back a little late at the factory and summoned the car. On the way back to Mr Kakkar's house he said, a little humbly: 'Well, someone has to make shoes.'

Mrs Rupa Mehra said: 'But you don't work in the tannery, do you, Haresh?'

'Oh, no!' said Haresh. 'Normally I only visit it about once a week. I work in the main factory.'

'Once a week?' said Lata.

Haresh could sense the apprehension behind her words. He was sitting in the front with the driver. Now he turned around and said, in a slightly troubled voice: 'I am proud of the shoes I make. I don't like sitting in an office giving orders and expecting miracles. If this means that I have to stand in a pit and soak a buffalo's hide myself, I'll do it. People who work in managing agencies, for instance, are perfectly happy to deal in commodities but don't like smudging their fingers with anything except ink. If that. And they care less for quality than for profits.'

After a few seconds, in which no one spoke, he added:

'If you have to do something, you should do it without making a fuss. An uncle of mine in Delhi thinks that I have become polluted, that I have lost caste by working with leather. Caste! I think he is a fool, and he thinks that I'm one. I've come close to telling him what I think of him. But I'm sure he knows. People can always tell if you like or dislike them.'

There was another pause. Then Haresh, thrown off a little by his own unexpected profession of faith, said, 'I would like to invite you to dinner. We have very little time to get to know each other. I hope that Mr Kakkar won't mind.'

He had simply assumed that for their part the Mehras wouldn't. Mother and daughter looked at each other in the back seat of the car, neither able to anticipate the other. After five seconds or so, Haresh took their silence for consent.

'Good,' he said. 'I'll come to fetch you at seven thirty. And I will be smelling as sweet as a violet.'

'A violet?' cried Mrs Rupa Mehra in sudden alarm. 'Why a violet?'

'I don't know,' said Haresh. 'A rose, if you like, Mrs Mehra. At any rate, better than wet-blue.'

9.12

Dinner was at the railway restaurant, which provided an excellent five-course meal. Lata was dressed in a pale green chanderi sari with little white flowers and a white border. She wore the same pearl ear-tops as before; they were virtually her only item of jewellery, and since she had not known she was going to be on display she had not bothered to borrow anything from Meenakshi. Mr Kakkar had taken a champa out of a vase and put it in her hair. It was a warm night, and she looked lively and fresh in green and white.

Haresh was wearing an off-white Irish linen suit and a cream tie with brown polka dots. Lata disliked these expensive, over-smart clothes and wondered what Arun would have thought of them. Calcutta tastes were quieter. As for a silk shirt, sure enough, it was there too. Haresh even brought his shirts into the conversation: they were made of the finest silk, the only silk he deigned to have made into shirts—not the silk poplin that was so popular these days, but the kind that had the brand-mark of two horses at the base of the bale. All this meant no more to Lata than did wet-blue, samming and splitting. Luckily Haresh's co-respondent shoes were hidden beneath the table.

The meal was excellent; none of them drank anything alcoholic. The conversation ranged from politics (Haresh thought that Nehru was ruining the country with all his socialist waffle) to English literature (where, with a few misquotations, Haresh asserted that Shakespeare had been written by Shakespeare) to the cinema (Haresh, it seemed, had seen about four films a week while in England).

Lata wondered how he had found the time and energy to do so well in his course and earn a living simultaneously. His accent continued to put her off. She recalled that, by way of overcompensation, he had called daal 'doll' at lunch. And Kanpur 'Cawnpore'. But when she compared his company with that of the polished and covenanted Bishwanath Bhaduri that evening at Firpo's not so long ago, she realized how very much she preferred it. He was lively (even if he repeated himself) and optimistic (even if overconfident of his own abilities), and he appeared to like her.

She reflected that Haresh was not westernized in the proper sense: she sensed that in his manners and style he was a bit half-baked (at least by Calcutta standards), and that consequently he sometimes put on airs. But though he wished to be liked by her, he did not ingratiate himself by attempting to anticipate her opinions before putting forward his own. If anything, he was too certain about the correctness of his views. Nor did he lay on the odious, insincere charm that she had got used to with Arun's young Calcutta friends. Amit, of course, was different; but he was Meenakshi's brother rather than Arun's friend.

Haresh found Mrs Rupa Mehra affectionate as well as good-looking. He had tried to maintain a respectful distance by calling her Mrs Mehra throughout, but she had eventually insisted on him calling her Ma. 'Everyone else does so after five minutes, so you must as well,' she told Haresh. She waxed voluble about her late husband and her coming grandson. She had already forgotten her afternoon's trauma and had appended her future son-in-law to the family.

Over ice-cream, Lata decided she liked his eyes. They were lovely, she thought, and surprisingly so; they were small and lively, did not spoil his good looks, and when he was amused they disappeared completely! It was fascinating. Then, for no accountable reason, she began to dread the thought that after dinner, while driving her back, he would offer to stop for paan—unconscious of how horribly it would jar with the spirit of the evening, the linen, the silverware, the china, how it would undo the threads of her goodwill with the blind torque of distaste, how it would sandwich the entire day with the image of a red mouth stained with betel juice.

Haresh's thoughts were not complicated. He said to himself: This girl is intelligent without arrogance, and attractive without vanity. She does not reveal her thoughts easily, but I like that. And then he thought of Simran, and the old, not entirely appeasable pain came over his heart.

But sometimes, for a few minutes at a time, Haresh forgot about Simran. And, for a few minutes at a time, Lata forgot about Kabir. And sometimes both of them forgot that what they were undergoing amid the clink of cutlery and crockery was a mutual interview that might decide whether or not they would own a common set of those items sometime in the whimsical future.

9.13

The car (with Haresh and driver) picked up Mrs Rupa Mehra and Lata and took them to the railway station early the next morning. They arrived, they thought, just in time. The timing of the Kanpur-Lucknow train, however, had been changed, and they missed it. The bus they attempted to take was full. There was nothing for it but to wait for the 9.42 train. Meanwhile they returned to Elm Villa.

Mrs Rupa Mehra said that nothing like this would have happened in her husband's time. Then the trains ran like clockwork, and changes in train timings were like changes in dynasties: momentous and rare. Now everything was being changed at random: road names, train schedules, prices, mores. Cawnpore and Cashmere were yielding to unfamiliar spellings. It would be Dilli and Kolkota and Mumbai next. And now, shockingly, they were threatening to go metric with the currency—and even with weights and measures.

'Don't worry, Ma,' said Haresh with a smile. 'We've tried to introduce the kilogram since 1870, and it probably won't be brought in for another hundred years.'

'Do you think so?' said Mrs Rupa Mehra, pleased. Seers meant something exact to her, pounds something vague, and kilograms nothing at all.

'Yes,' said Haresh. 'We have no sense of order or logic or discipline. No wonder we let the British rule us. What do you think, Lata?' he added in an artless attempt to draw her in.

But Lata had no opinion handy. She was thinking of other matters. What was foremost on her mind was Haresh's panama hat, which (though he had doffed it) she thought exceptionally stupid. This morning too he had on his Irish linen suit.

They got to the station a little early and sat in the railway cafe. Lata and Mrs Rupa Mehra bought first-class tickets to Lucknow—the journey was a short one and tickets did not need to be reserved in advance. Haresh pressed a cup of Pheasant's cold chocolate—a Dutch concoction—on them. It was delicious, and Lata's face expressed her pleasure. Haresh was so delighted at her innocent enjoyment that he suddenly said, 'May I accompany you to Lucknow? I could stay there with Simran's sister, and come back tomorrow after seeing you off on the train to Brahmpur.' What he had almost said was: I would like to spend a few more hours with you today, even if it means that someone else has to purchase the sheepskin.

Mrs Rupa Mehra did not succeed in dissuading Haresh; he bought a ticket to Lucknow for himself. He made sure that their luggage was loaded safely on and below the berths, that the porter did not swindle them, that they were comfortably seated, that each of them was provided with a magazine, that all was well with them in every way. Throughout the two-hour journey he hardly said a word. He was thinking that contentment consisted of just such moments as these.

Lata on the other hand was thinking that it was very odd that he should have mentioned—as part of his reason for accompanying them to Lucknow—that he planned to stay with Simran's sister. For all the method to his books and brushes, he was an unaccountable man.

When the train steamed into Lucknow Station, Haresh said: 'I would very much like to be of some help to you tomorrow.'

'No, no,' said Mrs Rupa Mehra, almost in a panic. 'The tickets have been reserved already. We don't need any help. They have been reserved by my son—my son in Bentsen Pryce. We'll be travelling very comfortably. You must not come to the station.'

Haresh looked at Lata for a while and was about to ask her something. Then he turned to her mother instead and said: 'May I write to Lata, Mrs Mehra?'

Mrs Mehra was about to agree with enthusiasm, then, checking herself she turned to Lata, and Lata nodded, rather gravely. It would have been too cruel to say no.

'Yes, you may write, of course,' said Mrs Rupa Mehra. 'And you really must call me Ma.'

'Now I'd like to make sure that you get to Mr Sahgal's place safely,' said Haresh. 'I'll get a tonga.'

It was pleasant to be taken care of, and the two women allowed Haresh to fuss competently over them.

In fifteen minutes they had arrived at the Sahgals'. Mrs Sahgal was Mrs Rupa Mehra's first cousin. She was a weak-brained, sweet-natured woman of about forty-five, married to a well-known Lucknow lawyer. 'Who is this gentleman?' she asked of Haresh.

'This is a young man who knew Kalpana Gaur at St Stephen's,' said Mrs Rupa Mehra by way of non-explanatory explanation.

'But he must come in and have tea with us,' said Mrs Sahgal. 'Sahgal Sahib will be so angry if he doesn't.'

Mrs Sahgal's saccharine, foolish life revolved around her husband. No sentence was complete for her without a reference to Mr Sahgal. Some people thought her a saint, some a fool. Mrs Rupa Mehra recalled that her own late husband, usually a good-natured and tolerant man, had thought Mrs Sahgal a doting idiot. He had said this angrily rather than amusedly. The Sahgals' son, who was about seventeen, was mentally deficient. Their daughter, who was Lata's age, was highly intelligent and highly neurotic.

Mr Sahgal was very pleased to see Lata and her mother. He was a sober, wise-looking man with a short-trimmed grey-and-white beard. If an expressionless portrait had been made of him, he would have looked like a judge. Rather than welcoming Haresh, however, he gave him a strange, conspiratorial smirk. Haresh took an instant dislike to him.

'Are you quite sure I can't be of any help to you tomorrow?' he asked.

'Quite sure, Haresh, God bless you,' said Mrs Rupa Mehra.

'Lata?' said Haresh, smiling, but with a trace of uncertainty; perhaps, for once, he was not entirely sure whether he was liked or disliked. Certainly the signals he was receiving were perplexingly mixed. 'You're sure I may write?'

'Yes, that would be nice,' said Lata, as if someone had offered her a piece of toast.

This sounded so lukewarm, even to her, that she added:

'It would really be very nice. It's a good way to get to know each other.'

Haresh was about to say something more, but decided against it.

'Au revoir, then,' he said, smiling. He had taken a few French lessons in England.

'Au revoir,' replied Lata with a laugh.

'Why are you laughing?' asked Haresh. 'Were you laughing at me?'

'Yes,' said Lata honestly. 'I was. Thank you.'

'For what?' asked Haresh.

'For a very enjoyable day.' She glanced once more at his co-respondent shoes. 'I won't forget it.'

'Neither will I,' said Haresh. Then he thought of several things to say but rejected each one.

'You must learn to say shorter goodbyes,' said Lata.

'Do you have any other advice for me?' asked Haresh.

Yes, thought Lata; at least seven pieces. Aloud she said: 'Yes, I do. Keep to the left.'

Grateful for the affectionate banality, Haresh nodded; and his tonga plodded off towards Simran's sister's house.

9.14

Both Lata and Mrs Rupa Mehra were so tired after their Kanpur visit that they went off to sleep soon after lunch. Each had her own room, and Lata welcomed these rare hours of privacy. She knew that the moment they were alone together her mother would begin asking her about what she thought of Haresh.

Before she dropped off to sleep her mother came to her room. The bedrooms were arranged in rows on both sides of a long corridor—as if in a hotel. It was a hot afternoon. Mrs Rupa Mehra had with her her bottle of 4711 Eau de Cologne, one of the objects that had a permanent home in her bag. With this she soaked a corner of one of her rose-embroidered handkerchiefs and dabbed Lata's head affectionately.

'I thought I would say a word to my darling daughter before she fell off to sleep.'

Lata waited for the question.

'Well, Lata?'

'Well, Ma?' Lata smiled. Now that it was a reality rather than an anticipation, the question was not so formidable.

'Don't you think he's suitable?' Mrs Rupa Mehra's voice made it clear that any rejection of Haresh would hurt her to the quick.

'Ma, I've only met him for twenty-four hours!'

'Twenty-six.'

'What do I really know of him, Ma?' said Lata. 'Let's say—it's not negative: he's all right. I've got to know him better.'

This last sentence being ambiguous, Mrs Rupa Mehra wanted an immediate clarification. Lata, smiling to herself said:

'Let me put it like this. He's not rejected. He says he wants to write to me. Let's see what he has to say for himself.'

'You are a very fussy and ungrateful girl,' said her mother. 'You are always thinking of the wrong people.'

Lata said:

'Yes, Ma, you're quite right. I am very fussy and very ungrateful, but at the moment I am also very sleepy.'

'Here. You keep this handkerchief.' And her mother left her to herself.

Lata fell off to sleep almost immediately. The Sunny Park household in Calcutta, the long journey to Kanpur in the heat, the strain of being on display before a marriageable man, the tannery, the tension between her liking and distaste for Haresh, the journey from Kanpur to Lucknow, and her repeated and unbidden thoughts of Kabir, all had exhausted her. She slept well. When she woke up it was four o'clock and teatime. She washed her face, changed, and went to the drawing room.

Her mother, Mr Sahgal, Mrs Sahgal, and their two children were sitting there having tea and samosas. Mrs Rupa Mehra was catching up as usual on her enormous network of acquaintances. Though Mrs Sahgal was, strictly speaking, her cousin, they actually thought of each other as sisters: they had spent a great deal of their childhood together after Rupa's mother's death in the great influenza epidemic.

Mrs Sahgal's wish to please her husband was comic, or perhaps pathetic.

Her eyes were constantly following his. 'Shall I bring that newspaper?' 'Will you have another cup?' 'Do you want me to bring the photograph album?' His eyes had only to rest on some object in the room for her to anticipate his wishes and scurry to fulfil them. He did not treat her with contempt, however; he praised her in measured tones. Sometimes he would stroke his short grey-and-white beard and say: 'You see my luck? With Maya as a wife I have to do nothing! I worship her as a goddess.' His wife would preen with pleasure.

And indeed, there were several photographs of his wife on the wall or in small frames here and there. She was a physically attractive woman (as was her daughter) and Mr Sahgal was something of an amateur photographer. He pointed out one or two to Lata; Lata couldn't help thinking that the poses were a little—she tried to think of a word—'film-starrish'. There were also a couple of pictures of Kiran, the daughter, who was about Lata's age and was studying at Lucknow University. Kiran was tall and pale and quite attractive; but she was abrupt in her movements, and had agitated eyes.

'And now you will be embarking on the journey of life,' said Mr Sahgal to Lata. He leaned forward slightly, and spilt a little tea. His wife rushed to mop it up.

'Mausaji, I don't want to embark on any journey without checking the ticket first,' said Lata, trying to make light of his remark, but annoyed that her mother had presumed to talk about such matters to them.

Mrs Rupa Mehra did not consider her mention of Haresh to be an act of presumption, but, on the contrary, of consideration. Mr and Mrs Sahgal were simply being told that they would not have to trawl their nets through the khatri community of Lucknow for Lata's sake—which they would otherwise certainly have been required to do.

At this point the feeble-minded son, Pushkar, who was a couple of years younger than Lata, began to sing to himself and rock slightly to and fro.

'What is the matter, son?' asked his father gently.

'I want to marry Lata Didi,' said Pushkar.

Mr Sahgal shrugged apologetically towards Mrs Rupa Mehra. 'He is like this sometimes,' he said. 'Come, Pushkar—let us go and make something with your Meccano set.' They left the room.

Lata suddenly felt a peculiar sense of unease, which seemed to reach back to the memory of an earlier visit to Lucknow. But it was so unspecific that she could not recall what had caused it. She felt she needed to be by herself, to get out of the house, to go for a walk.

'I'll take a walk to the old British Residency,' she said. 'It's cooler now, and it's only a few minutes away.'

'But you haven't eaten even one samosa yet,' said Mrs Rupa Mehra.

'Ma, I'm not hungry. But I do want to go for a walk.'

'You can't go by yourself,' said her mother firmly. 'This isn't Brahmpur. Wait till Mausaji comes back, maybe he'll go with you.'

'I'll go with Lata,' said Kiran quickly.

'That's very sweet of you, Kiran,' said Mrs Rupa Mehra. 'But don't dawdle. When girls get together they talk for hours without noticing the time go by.'

'We'll be back by dark,' said Kiran. 'Don't worry, Rupa Masi.'

9.15

There were a few clouds in the eastern sky, greyish, but not rain-bearing. The road to the Residency past the fine red-brick building of the Lucknow Chief Court—now the Lucknow Bench of the Allahabad High Court—was uncrowded. This was where Mr Sahgal practised. Kiran and Lata hardly talked at all, and this suited Lata.

Though Lata had been to Lucknow twice before—once when she was nine, when her father was alive, once when she was about fourteen, after his death—and had stayed each time with the Sahgals, she had never visited the ruined Residency. It was in fact a mere fifteen minutes' walk from the Sahgals' house near Kaiserbagh. What she remembered about her two previous stays were not the historical monuments of Lucknow but the fresh, home-made white butter Mrs Sahgal served; and for some reason she recalled being given a whole bunch of grapes for breakfast. She also remembered how friendly Kiran had been on her first trip, and how unfriendly—even resentful—she had been on the second. By then it was clear that all was not well with her brother, and perhaps she had envied Lata her two brothers, noisy, affectionate, and normal. But you have your father, Lata had thought, and I have lost mine. Why do you dislike me? Lata was glad that Kiran was at last trying to restore the friendship; she only wished that she herself were better placed today to reciprocate.

For today she had no wish at all to talk to Kiran or anyone—least of all to Mrs Rupa Mehra. She wanted to be by herself—to think about her life, and what was happening to it, to her. Or perhaps not even to think about it—to be distracted, rather, by something so far and past and grand that it would limit the scope of her own elations and distresses. She had felt something of that spirit in the Park Street Cemetery that day in the pouring rain. It was that spirit of distance that she was trying to recapture.

The great, shattered, bullet-mottled remains of the Residency rose above them on a hill. The grass at the foot of the hill was brown for lack of rain but green above, where it had been watered. All around, among the broken buildings, were trees and bushes—pipal, jamun, neem, mango, and here and there at least four huge banyan trees. Mynas cried from the rough-barked and smooth-barked palms, a spray of magenta bougainvillaea fell in a massive shower on a lawn. Chameleons and squirrels wandered around among the ruins and obelisks and cannons. Wherever the plaster of the thick walls had crumbled, the thin hard bricks of which it was built were exposed. Plaques and gravestones lay scattered through the sad acres. In the centre of it all, in the main surviving building, was a museum.

'Shall we go to the Museum first?' asked Lata. 'That might close early.'

The question threw Kiran into abrupt anxiety. 'I don't know—I—I don't know. We can do anything now,' she said. 'There's no one to say anything.'

'Let's do that then,' said Lata. They went in.

Kiran was so nervous that she bit—not her nails, but the flesh at the base of her thumb. Lata looked at her in astonishment.

'Are you all right, Kiran?' she asked. 'Shall we go back?'

'No—no,' cried Kiran. 'Don't read that—' she said.

Lata promptly read the plaque that Kiran was pointing at.

SUSANNA PALMER
killed in this room
by a cannon ball on the
1st July 1857
in her nineteenth year

Lata laughed. 'Really, Kiran!' she said.

'Where was her father?' said Kiran. 'Where was he? Why couldn't he protect her?'

Lata sighed. She now wished she had come here alone, but there had been no getting around her mother's insistence that she go nowhere in a strange town unaccompanied.

Since her sympathy appeared to disturb Kiran, Lata tried to ignore her, interesting herself instead in a minutely detailed model of the Residency and the surrounding area during the siege of Lucknow. On one wall hung sepia pictures of battle, of the storming of the batteries, of the billiard room, of an English spy disguising himself to get through the native lines.

There was even a poem by Tennyson, one of Lata's favourite poets. She had, however, never read this particular poem, 'The Relief of Lucknow'. It had seven stanzas, and she read them at first with interest, then with increasing disgust. She wondered what Amit would have thought of them. Each stanza ended with the line:

> And ever upon the topmost roof our banner of England blew!

Occasionally the 'and' was replaced by 'but' or 'that'. Lata could scarcely believe that this was the poet of 'Maud' and 'The Lotos-Eaters'. It was hardly possible, she thought, to be more racially smug than this:

> Handful of men as we were, we were English in heart and in limb,
> Strong with the strength of the race to command, to obey, to endure. . . .
> Now let it speak, and you fire, and the dark pioneer is no more. . . .
> Blessing the wholesome white faces of Havelock's good fusiliers. . . .

And so on and so forth.

She did not consider the fact that if the conquest had taken place the other way around, there would have been equally unspeakable poems, probably in Persian, possibly in Sanskrit, dotting England's green and pleasant land. She felt a great burst of pride for Savita's father-in-law who had played his part in throwing the English out of this country, and she momentarily forgot all about Sophia Convent and *Emma*.

In her indignation she had even forgotten about Kiran, whom she now found staring at the plaque commemorating poor Susanna Palmer. Kiran's body was shaking with sobs, and people were looking at her. Lata put her arm around her shoulder, but did not know what else to do. She drew her out of the building and sat her down on a bench. It was getting dark, and they would have to go home soon.

Kiran resembled her mother in her looks, though there was nothing stupid about her. Tears were now streaming down her face, but she was speechless. Lata tried fumblingly to find out what had upset her. The death of a girl her age almost a century before? The entire atmosphere of the Residency, haunted as it was by desperation? Was there something the matter at home? Near them a boy was standing on the grass, flying an orange-and-purple kite. Sometimes he stared at them.

Twice it seemed to Lata that Kiran was on the verge of a confidence or at least an apology. But since nothing was forthcoming, Lata suggested:

'We should go home now, it's getting late.'

Kiran sighed, got up, and walked down the hill with Lata. Lata started humming a line in Raag Marwa, a raag she loved with a passion. By the time they had got home, Kiran appeared to have recovered. As they got to the house she asked Lata:

'You're going by the evening train tomorrow, aren't you?'

'Yes.'

'I wish I could visit you in Brahmpur. But Savita's house, I hear, is so small, not like my father's luxury hotel.' She spoke the last words bitterly.

'You must come, Kiran. You can easily stay with us for a week—or more. Your term starts fifteen days after ours. And we'll get to know each other better.'

Again Kiran's silence grew almost guilty. She did not even respond aloud to what Lata had said.

Lata was relieved to see her mother again. Mrs Rupa Mehra ticked them off for taking such a long time to return. To Lata's ears the familiar reprimands were like music.

'You must tell me—' Mrs Rupa Mehra began.

'Ma, first we went along the road past the Chief Court, and then we got to the Residency. At the foot of the Residency was an obelisk which commemorated the officers and sepoys who had remained loyal to the British. Three squirrels sat at the base of—'

'Lata!'

'Yes, Ma?'

'You are behaving very badly. All I wanted to know was—'

'Everything.'

Mrs Rupa Mehra frowned, then turned to her cousin.

'Do you have the same trouble with Kiran?' she asked.

'Oh, no,' said Mrs Sahgal. 'Kiran is a very good girl. It is all due to Sahgal Sahib. Sahgal Sahib is always talking to her and giving her advice. There could be no father like him. Even when clients are waiting. . . . But Lata is a good girl too.'

'No,' said Lata, laughing. 'Unfortunately I am a bad girl. Ma, what will you do if I do get married and move away? Whom will you be able to tick off?'

'I will tick you off just the same,' said Mrs Rupa Mehra.

Mr Sahgal had entered meanwhile, and, having heard the last part of the conversation, said in a calm, avuncular voice: 'Lata, you are not a bad girl, I know. I have heard all about your results and we are very proud of you. Sometime soon we must have a long talk about the future.'

Kiran stood up. 'I am going to talk to Pushkar,' she said.

'Sit down,' said Mr Sahgal, in the same calm voice.

Kiran, white-faced, sat down.

Mr Sahgal's eyes wandered around the room.

'Shall I put on the gramophone?' asked his wife.

'Do you have any hobbies?' said Mr Sahgal to Lata.

'Oh, yes,' said Mrs Rupa Mehra. 'She has begun to sing classical music very beautifully. And she is a real bookworm.'

'I enjoy photography,' said Mr Sahgal. 'When I was in England studying law, I began to take an interest in it.'

'The albums?' asked Mrs Sahgal, breathless with the possibility of being of service to him.

'Yes.'

She laid them on the table before him. Mr Sahgal started showing them photographs of his English landladies and their daughters, other girls he had known there, then a few Indian photographs, followed by pages and pages of his wife and daughter, sometimes in poses that Lata found distasteful. In one, Mrs Sahgal had bent forward, and one of her breasts was almost spilling out of her blouse. Mr Sahgal carried on an explanation, gentle and measured, of the art of photography, about composition and exposure, grain and gloss, contrast and depth of field.

Lata glanced at her mother. Mrs Rupa Mehra was looking at the photographs with puzzled interest. Mrs Sahgal's face was flushed with pride. Kiran was sitting rigid, as if she had been taken ill. Again she was biting the base of her thumb in that unusual and disturbing gesture. When she noticed Lata's gaze on her, she looked at her with a mixture of shame and hatred.

After dinner Lata went straight to her room. She felt an acute sense of unease, and was glad they were leaving Lucknow the next day. Her mother, on the other hand, was thinking of postponing their departure, since both Mr and Mrs Sahgal were very keen that they stay on for a few days.

'What is this?' Mrs Sahgal had said at dinner. 'You come for one day, and then you disappear for a year. Is this the way a sister should behave?'

'I want to stay, Maya,' said Mrs Rupa Mehra. 'But Lata's term begins so soon. Otherwise we would have been very happy to stay with you and Sahgal Sahib. Next time we will stay longer.'

Pushkar had held his peace throughout dinner. He could just about feed himself with help from his father. Mr Sahgal had looked very tired by the end of the meal. He had then put Pushkar to bed.

Returning to the drawing room, he had wished everyone goodnight and gone immediately to his room at the near end of the long corridor. His wife's room was opposite his. Then came the guest rooms, and finally, at the far end of the corridor, Pushkar's and Kiran's rooms. Since Pushkar was fond of a huge grandfather clock—a family heirloom—Mr Sahgal had installed it just outside his room. Sometimes Pushkar would sing out the chimes. He had even learned to wind it up himself.

9.16

Lata lay awake for a while. It was the height of summer, so there was only a sheet by way of covering. The fan was on, but there was no need yet for a mosquito net. The chimes on the quarter-hour were soft, but when the clock struck eleven, then midnight, it resounded along the corridor. Lata read a little by the weak light at her bedside, but the events of the last two days swam between her and the pages. Finally she put out the light and closed her eyes, and dreamed, half-awake, of Kabir.

Slow footsteps padded down the carpeted corridor. When they stopped outside her door, she sat up, startled. They were not her mother's footsteps. The door opened, and she saw the silhouette of a man against the dim light in the corridor. It was Mr Sahgal.

Lata turned on the light. Mr Sahgal stood blinking mildly, shaking his head, protecting his eyes with his hand even from the weak light of the bedside lamp. He was dressed in a brown dressing gown tied with a brown rope with tassels. He looked very tired.

Lata looked at him in dismay and astonishment. 'Are you all right, Mausaji?' she asked. 'Are you ill?'

'No, not ill. But I have been working late. That is why—and I saw your light was on. But then you put it off. You are an intelligent girl—a great reader.'

He looked around the room, stroking his short-trimmed beard. He was quite a large man. In a thoughtful voice he said: 'There is no chair here. I must speak to Maya about it.' He sat himself down at the edge of the bed. 'Is everything all right?' he asked Lata. 'Everything is all right, isn't it? The pillows and everything? I remember when you were a little girl you used to like grapes. You were very young. And it is the season for them now. Pushkar also likes grapes. Poor boy.'

Lata tried to pull the sheet closer to cover herself better, but Mr Sahgal was sitting on one corner of it.

'You are very good to Pushkar, Mausaji,' she said, wondering what she could do or what conversation she could make. She could hear and feel her heart beating.

'You see,' said Mr Sahgal in a calm voice, his hands clutching the tassels of the band of his dressing gown, 'living here there is no hope for him. In England they have special schools, special. . . .' He paused, looking at Lata's face and neck. 'That boy, Haresh—he was in England? Maybe he also has photos of his landladies?'

'I don't know,' said Lata, thinking of Mr Sahgal's suggestive photographs and trying to check her rising fear. 'Mausaji, I am very sleepy, I have to go tomorrow—'

'But you are leaving in the evening. We must have our talk now. You see there is no one to talk to in Lucknow. Now in Calcutta—or even Delhi—but I cannot leave Lucknow. My practice, you see.'

'Yes,' said Lata.

'It would also not be good for Kiran. She already sees bad boys, reads bad books. I have to stop these habits. My wife is a saint, she does not see these things.' He was explaining things gently to Lata, and Lata was nodding mechanically.

'My wife is a saint,' he repeated. 'Every morning she does puja for an hour. She will do anything for me. Whatever food I want, she cooks with her own hands. She is like Sita—a perfect wife. If I want her to dance naked for me she will dance. She wants nothing for herself. She only wants Kiran to get married. But I feel that Kiran should complete her education—till then what is wrong with living at home? Once, a boy came to the house—actually to the house. I told him to get out—to get out!' Mr Sahgal no longer looked tired but livid, though his voice was still low. Then he calmed down, and continued in a tone of explanation: 'But who will marry Kiran when sometimes, you know, Pushkar makes such frightening noises. Sometimes

I sense his rage. You don't mind my confiding like this in you? Kiran is a good friend of yours, I know. You must also tell me about yourself, your plans. . . .' He sniffed in an appraising way. 'That is the eau de cologne your mother uses. Kiran never uses eau de cologne. Natural things are best.'

Lata stared at him. Her mouth had become completely dry.

'But I buy saris for her whenever I go to Delhi,' continued Mr Sahgal. 'During the War, society ladies used to wear saris with broad borders; even brocades and tissues. Before she became a widow I once saw your mother wearing her wedding tissue sari. But now all that has gone. Embroidery is considered so vulgar.'

As an afterthought he added:

'Shall I buy you a sari?'

'No—no—' said Lata.

'Georgette drapes better than chiffon, don't you think?'

Lata gave no answer.

'Recently Ajanta pallus have become the craze. The motifs are so—so—imaginative—I saw one with a paisley design, another with a lotus—' Mr Sahgal smiled. 'And now with these short cholis the women show their bare waists at the back as well. Do you think you are a bad girl?'

'A bad girl?' repeated Lata.

'At dinner you said you were a bad girl,' explained her uncle in a kindly, measured way. 'I don't think you are. I think you are a lipstick girl. Are you a lipstick girl?'

With sick horror Lata remembered that he had asked her the same question when they were sitting together in his car five years ago. She had completely buried the memory. She had been fourteen or so at the time, and he had asked her calmly, almost considerately: 'Are you a lipstick girl?'

'A lipstick girl?' Lata had asked, puzzled. At that time she had believed that women who wore lipstick, like those who smoked, were bold and modern and probably beyond the pale. 'I don't think so,' she had said.

'Do you know what a lipstick girl is?' Mr Sahgal had asked with a slow smirk on his face.

'Someone who uses lipstick?' Lata had said.

'On her lips?' asked her uncle slowly.

'Yes, on her lips.'

'No, not on her lips, not on her lips—that is what is known as a lipstick girl.' Mr Sahgal shook his head gently from side to side and smiled, as if enjoying a joke, while looking straight into her bewildered eyes.

Kiran had returned to the car—she had gone to buy something—and they had driven on. But Lata had felt almost ill. Later, she had blamed herself for misunderstanding what her uncle had said. She had never mentioned the incident to her mother or to anyone, and had forgotten it. Now it came back to her and she stared at him.

'I know you are a lipstick girl. Do you want some lipstick?' said Mr Sahgal, moving forward along the bed.

'No—' cried Lata. 'I don't—Mausaji—please stop this—'

'It is so hot—I must take off this dressing gown.'

'No!' Lata wanted to shout, but found she couldn't. 'Don't, please, Mausaji. I—I'll shout—my mother is a light sleeper—go away—go away—Ma—Ma—'

The clock chimed one.

Mr Sahgal's mouth opened. He said nothing for a moment. Then he sighed.

He looked very tired again. 'I thought you were an intelligent girl,' he said in a disappointed voice. 'What are you thinking of? If you had a father to bring you up properly, you would not behave in this way.' He got up. 'I must get a chair for this room, every deluxe hotel should have a chair in every room.' He was about to touch Lata's hair, but perhaps he could sense that she was tense with terror. Instead, in a forgiving voice, he said: 'I know that deep down you are a good girl. Sleep well, God bless you.'

'No!' Lata almost shouted.

When he left, his footsteps padding gently back towards his room, Lata began to tremble. 'Sleep well, God bless you,' is what she remembered her father used to say to her, his 'little monkey'. She switched off the light, then immediately switched it on again. She went to the door, and found that there was no way to lock it. Finally she dragged her suitcase and placed it against the door. There was water in a jug by the bedside lamp, and she drank a glass. Her throat was parched, and her hands trembling. She buried her face in her mother's handkerchief.

She thought of her father. During the school holidays, whenever he came back from work, he would ask her to make tea for him. She adored him, and she adored his memory. He was a jolly man and liked to have his family around him in the evenings. When he had died in Calcutta after a long cardiac illness, she had been at Sophia Convent in Mussourie. The nuns had been very kind. It was not just that she had been excused the test that had been set that day. They had given her an anthology of poetry that was still among the most valued of her possessions. And one nun had said, 'We are so sorry—he was very young to die.' 'Oh no,' Lata had replied. 'He was very old—he was forty-seven years old.' Even then, it had not seemed believable. The term would end in a few months, and she would go home as usual. She had found it difficult to cry.

A month later her mother had come up to Mussourie. Mrs Rupa Mehra had been almost prostrate with grief and had not been able to come up earlier, even to see her daughter. She was dressed in white, and there was no tika on her forehead. That was what had brought things home to Lata, and she had wept.

'He was very old.' Again she heard her uncle's voice saying: 'You were very young.' Lata put off her light once more, and lay in the darkness.

She could not speak to anyone about what had happened. Mrs Sahgal doted on her husband; could she even be aware of what he was like? They had separate rooms: Mr Sahgal often worked late. Mrs Rupa Mehra would hardly have believed Lata. If she had, she would have imagined—or wanted to imagine—that Lata had placed a dramatic construction on innocent events. And even if she had believed Lata entirely, what could she have done? Denounced Maya's husband and destroyed her stupid happiness?

Lata recalled that neither her mother nor Savita had told her even about menstruation before it had suddenly happened to her with no warning while they were on a train. Lata had been twelve. Her father was dead. They were no longer travelling in saloons, but in the intermediate class between second and third. It was the heat of late summer—as now, the monsoons had not yet broken. For some reason she and her mother were travelling alone. She had gone to the toilet when she felt the onset of something uncomfortable—and there, when she saw what it was, she had thought she was bleeding to death. Terrified, she had rushed back to her compartment. Her mother had given her a handkerchief to absorb the flow, but had been very embarrassed. She had told Lata that she must not talk to anybody about it, especially men. Sita and Savitri didn't talk about such things. Lata wondered what she had done to deserve it. Finally, Mrs Rupa Mehra had told her not to get alarmed—that it happened to all women—that it was what made women very special and precious—and that it would happen every month.

'Do you have it?' Lata had asked.

'Yes,' said Mrs Rupa Mehra. 'Previously I used to use soft cloth, but now I use padded napkins, and you must keep a few with you. I have some at the bottom of the suitcase.'

It had been sticky and uncomfortable in the strong heat, but it had to be borne. Nor did it improve over the years. The mess, the backaches, its irregular arrival before exams—Lata felt there was nothing very special or precious about it. When she asked Savita why she hadn't told her about it, Savita said: 'But I thought you knew. I did, before it happened to me.'

The clock down the corridor struck three, and Lata was still awake. Then, once again, she caught her breath with fear. The padded footsteps were coming down the carpeted corridor. She knew they were going to pause at her door. Oh, Ma, Ma—thought Lata.

But the footsteps padded on, softly down the corridor towards the far end, towards Pushkar's and Kiran's rooms. Perhaps Mr Sahgal was going to see that his son was all right. Lata waited for his footsteps to return any minute. She could not sleep. But it was two hours later, a little before five in the morning, that they passed by her room gently, after a momentary pause by her door.

9.17

At breakfast the next morning, Mr Sahgal was absent.

'Sahgal Sahib is not feeling very well. He is tired from working so hard,' said Mrs Sahgal.

Mrs Rupa Mehra shook her head: 'Maya, you must tell him to take it easy. It was overwork that killed my husband. And for what final aim? One must work hard, but enough is really enough. Lata, why aren't you eating your toast? It will get cold. And see, Maya Masi has made that lovely white butter you like so much.'

Mrs Sahgal smiled sweetly at Lata. 'She looks so tired and worried, poor girl. I think she is already in love with H. Now she is spending sleepless nights.' She sighed happily.

Lata buttered her toast in silence.

Without his father to help him, Pushkar was having a hard time with his toast. Kiran, who was looking as sleepy as Lata, went over to give him a hand.

'What does he do when he needs to shave?' asked Mrs Rupa Mehra in a low voice.

'Oh, Sahgal Sahib helps him,' said Mrs Sahgal. 'Or one of the servants does—but Pushkar prefers us to help him. Oh Rupa, I wish you could stay for a few more days. We have so much to talk about. And the girls can get to know each other also.'

'No!' The word was out before Lata could think of what she was saying. She looked frightened and disgusted.

Kiran dropped the knife on Pushkar's plate. Then she rushed out of the room.

'Lata, you must say sorry at once,' said Mrs Rupa Mehra. 'What do you mean by this? Have you no decency?'

Lata was about to tell her mother that all she had meant was that she did not want to stay in the house any longer, and had not meant to hurt Kiran. That, however, would merely exchange one offence for another. So she kept her mouth shut and her head bowed.

'Did you hear me?' Mrs Rupa Mehra's high voice held an edge of anger.

'Yes.'

'Yes what?'

'Yes, Ma, I heard you. I heard you. I heard you.'

Lata got up and went to her room. Mrs Rupa Mehra could hardly believe her eyes.

Pushkar began singing to himself and stuffing the small squares of toast that his sister had cut and buttered for him into his mouth. Mrs Sahgal looked distressed.

'I wish Sahgal Sahib was here. He knows how to deal with the children.'

Mrs Rupa Mehra said: 'Lata is a thoughtless girl sometimes. I am going to have a word with her.' Then she thought that perhaps she was being too harsh. 'Of course, Kanpur was a strain on her. It was on me, too, of course. She does not appreciate the efforts I have made for her. Only He appreciated me.'

'Finish your tea, first, Rupa mine,' said Mrs Sahgal.

A few minutes later, when Mrs Rupa Mehra entered Lata's room, she found her asleep. So soundly was she sleeping that she had to be woken for lunch a few hours later.

At lunch, Mr Sahgal smiled at Lata and said, 'See what I have got for you.' It was a small, flat, square packet wrapped in red paper. The wrapping paper was decorated with holly, bells and other Christmas paraphernalia.

'How lovely!' said Mrs Rupa Mehra, without knowing what it was.

Lata's ears burned with embarrassment and anger.

'I don't want it.'

Mrs Rupa Mehra was too shocked to speak.

'And then we can go to the cinema. There will be time before your train leaves.'

Lata stared at him.

Mrs Rupa Mehra, who had been brought up never to open gifts when they were given but to wait till she was alone, quite forgot herself.

'Open it,' she ordered Lata.

'I don't want it,' said Lata. 'You open it.' She pushed the packet across Something jangled inside.

'Savita would never behave like this,' began her mother. 'And Mausaji has taken the afternoon off just for you—just so that Maya and I can have the time to talk. You don't know how much of an interest he takes in you. He is always saying you are so intelligent, but I am beginning to doubt it. Say thank you.'

'Thank you,' said Lata, feeling dirtied and humiliated.

'And you must tell me all about the film when you come back.'

'I will not go to the film.'

'What?'

'I will not go to the film.'

'Mausaji will be with you, Lata—what are you worried about?' said her mother uncomprehendingly.

Kiran looked at Lata with a bitter glance of jealousy. Mr Sahgal said, 'She is like my own daughter. I will see that she doesn't eat too many ice-creams and other unhealthy things.'

'I will not go!' Lata's voice rose in defiance and panic.

Mrs Rupa Mehra was struggling with the packet. At this cry of rank rebellion, her fingers lost control of themselves. Normally she unpacked every gift with infinite care in order to be able to reuse the paper later. But now the paper ripped open.

'See what you've made me do,' she said to Lata. But then, looking at the contents, she turned to Mr Sahgal, perplexed.

The present was a puzzle, a pink plastic maze with a transparent top. Seven little silver balls were to be jiggled around the square maze so that, with luck, they would eventually come to rest in the central cell.

'She is such a clever girl, I thought I would give her a puzzle. Normally she would be able to do it in five minutes. But on the train everything shakes so much that it will take her an hour,' Mr Sahgal explained in a gentle voice. 'Time passes so slowly sometimes.'

'How thoughtful,' murmured Mrs Rupa Mehra, frowning a little.

Lata lied that she had a headache, and returned to her room. But she did, indeed, feel ill—sick to the pit of her stomach.

9.18

Mr Sahgal's car took them to the station late in the afternoon. He was working, and did not come. Kiran stayed behind with Pushkar. Mrs Sahgal came with them and chattered sweetly and vacuously throughout.

Lata did not say a word.

They were immersed in the crowds on the platform. Suddenly Haresh appeared.

'Hello, Mrs Mehra. Hello, Lata.'

'Haresh? I said you were not to come,' said Mrs Rupa Mehra. 'And I told you to call me Ma,' she added mechanically.

Haresh smiled, pleased to have surprised them.

'My own train back to Cawnpore leaves in fifteen minutes so I thought I would give you a hand. Now where is your coolie?'

He installed them in their compartment cheerfully and efficiently, and made sure that Mrs Rupa Mehra's black handbag was placed where it was both within reach and theft-proof.

Mrs Rupa Mehra looked mortified; it had been a hard decision for her to buy two first-class tickets from Kanpur to Lucknow, but she had felt she had to convey a certain impression to a potential son-in-law. Now he could clearly see that they usually travelled not even by second but by Inter class. And indeed, Haresh was puzzled, though he did not show it. After all this talk by Mrs Rupa Mehra about travelling in saloons and having a son in Bentsen Pryce, he had expected a different style from them.

But what does all that matter? he asked himself. I like the girl.

Lata, who had first seemed glad—relieved, he would have said—to see him, now appeared withdrawn, hardly aware of her own presence, or her mother's, or her aunt's, let alone his.

As the whistle blew, a scene came to Haresh's mind. It was set at about this time of day. It had been warm, so it could not have been many months ago. He had been standing at the platform of a busy station, about to catch a train himself, and his coolie had been about to disappear into the crowd ahead. A middle-aged woman, her back turned partly towards him, had been boarding another train together with a younger woman. This younger woman—he knew now that it had been Lata—had had on her face such a look of intensity and inwardness, perhaps even hurt or anger, that he had caught his breath. There had been a man with them, the young man whom he had met at Sunil Patwardhan's party—that English teacher whose name eluded him. Brahmpur, yes—that was where he had seen them before. He had known it; he had known it, and now it all came back to him. He had not been mistaken, after all. He smiled, his eyes disappearing.

'Brahmpur—a pale blue sari,' he said, almost to himself.

Lata turned to him through the window with a questioning look.

The train began to move.

Haresh shook his head, still smiling. Even if the train had been stationary, he would probably not have explained himself.

He waved as the train pulled out, but neither mother nor daughter waved back. However, being an optimist, Haresh put this down to their anglicized reticence.

A blue sari. That's what it was, he kept thinking to himself.

9.19

Haresh had spent his day in Lucknow at Simran's sister's house. He told her that he had met a woman just yesterday who—since he had no chance of succeeding with Simran—was someone he was thinking seriously about as wife material.

He did not put it exactly like that; but even if he had it would not have been intrinsically offensive. Most marriages he knew had been decided on that basis, and the deciders were usually not even the couple themselves but their elders: fathers or male heads of the concerned families—with the wished-for or unwished-for counsel of dozens of others thrown in. In the case of one of Haresh's distant rural cousins, the go-between had been the village barber; by virtue of his access to most of the houses in the village, this had been the fourth marriage he had been instrumental in arranging that year.

Simran's sister sympathized with Haresh. She knew how long and faithfully Haresh had loved her sister, and she felt that his heart still belonged to her.

Haresh himself would not have thought of this as casually metaphorical.

He and his heart did belong to her. She could do with it and with him what she pleased, and he would still love her. The pleasure in Simran's eyes whenever they met—the sadness underlying that pleasure—the increasing certainty that her parents would not yield, that they would cut her off from themselves—that her mother, emotional woman that she was, might very well even carry out the threat against herself that she now spoke of in every letter to her and every day when she was home—all these had worn Simran down. Her correspondence, erratic even in England (partly because she herself would receive Haresh's letters erratically, whenever the friend to whose address they were sent visited her) became even more so. Sometimes weeks would pass, and Haresh would not hear from her; then he would get three letters in as many days.

Simran's sister knew how hard it would be for her to hear the news that Haresh had decided he might live his life with someone else—or even consider doing so. Simran loved Haresh. Her sister loved him too—even if he was the son of a Lala, which among the Sikhs was something of a term of contempt for Hindus. Her brother too had been part of the conspiracy. When he and Haresh were both seventeen he had been paid to sing ghazals on his friend's behalf under his sister's window: Simran had been annoyed with Haresh for some reason, and Haresh had been trying to appease her. He had had to hire her brother because he himself had, together with a love of music and a belief in its power to move unyielding hearts, a singing voice that even his beloved Simran (who liked his speaking voice well enough) had declared to be tuneless.

'Haresh, have you made up your mind?' said Simran's sister in Punjabi. She was three years older than Simran, and her own marriage had been an arranged one—to a Sikh officer in the army.

'What choice do I have?' replied Haresh. 'I have to think of someone else sooner or later. Time is passing. I am twenty-eight. I'm thinking of her good too—she will refuse everyone whom your parents suggest until she knows that I'm married.'

Haresh's eyes grew moist. Simran's sister patted him on the shoulder.

'When did you make up your mind that this girl might suit you?'

'At Kanpur Station. She was drinking that chocolate drink—you know, Pheasant's.' Haresh, noticing the look on Simran's sister's face, realized she wished to be spared the exact details.

'Have you made any proposal?'

'No. We have agreed to write to each other. Her mother arranged the meeting. They are in Lucknow at the moment, but they didn't seem keen to see me here.'

'Have you written to your father?'

'I'll write to him tonight, when I get back to Kanpur.' Haresh had chosen a train that would enable him to meet Mrs Rupa Mehra and her daughter as if by chance at Lucknow Station.

'Don't write to Simran just yet.'

Haresh said in a hurt voice: 'But why? I'll have to say something sooner or later.'

'If nothing comes out of this you will have hurt her for nothing.'

'She'll wonder if she doesn't hear from me.'

'Write as you always write.'

'How can I do that?' Haresh baulked at the deception.

'Don't say anything that isn't true. Just don't touch on this.'

Haresh thought for a while. 'All right,' he said at last. But he felt that Simran knew him too well not to sense from his letters that something had begun to happen in his life, not just in hers, that could draw the two of them apart.

9.20

The conversation turned after a while to Simran's sister herself. Her young son Monty (only three years old) wanted to join the navy and her husband (who was crazy about the boy) was taking this decision extraordinarily badly. He treated it as a vote of no confidence in himself, and was, it seemed to her, sulking as a result. She herself attributed Monty's preference to the fact that he enjoyed playing with boats in his tub, and had not yet arrived at the model-soldier stage.

Monty, incidentally, had difficulty pronouncing certain words, and just the other day had said (talking in English instead of Punjabi) while splashing around in his favourite element after one brief pre-monsoon shower, that he wanted to go to 'the miggle of the puggle'. This Simran's sister took as being symptomatic of his intrinsic sweetness. She hoped that in years to come he would order his men 'into the heart of backle'. Monty sat through all this with a look of offended dignity. From time to time he tugged at his mother's fingers to get her to stop prattling.

Since he wasn't feeling hungry, Haresh decided to forgo lunch and went to see the twelve o'clock show of a film instead. *Hamlet* was playing at the local cinema hall. He enjoyed it, but Hamlet's indecisiveness irritated him.

He then had a good haircut for a rupee. Finally, he had a paan and went off to the station in order to catch the train back to Kanpur—and, he hoped, to meet Lata and her mother, both of whom he had become quite fond of. That he was successful in this pleased him greatly; that they did not wave to him as the train moved out did not distress him unduly. The coincidence connecting Brahmpur Station and Lucknow Station he took as a propitious sign.

On the two-hour train journey back to Kanpur, Haresh took out a blue writing pad from his portfolio ('H.C. Khanna' was embossed on the top of each page) and a cheap white scribbling pad as well. He looked from one to the other, then to a woman sitting opposite him, then out of the window. It was getting dark. Soon the train lights came on. Finally he decided that it would not do to write a serious letter in a jolting train. He put away the writing pad.

At the top of his scribbling pad, he wrote: 'To Do'. Then he crossed it out and wrote: 'Points to remember'. Then he crossed that out and wrote: 'Action Points'. It occurred to him that he was behaving as stupidly as Hamlet.

After he had listed his correspondence and various work-related items, his thoughts moved to more general matters, and he made a third list, under the heading, 'My Life':

1. Must catch up with news and world affairs.

Haresh felt he had not come off well on this account during his meetings with the Mehras. But his work kept him so busy that sometimes he hardly had time even to glance at the papers.

2. Exercise: at least 15 minutes each morning. How to find the time?
3. Make 1951 the deciding year of my life.
4. Pay off debts to Umesh Uncle in full.
5. Learn to control temper. Must learn to suffer fools, gladly or not.
6. Get brogue scheme with Kedarnath Tandon in Brahmpur working properly.

This he later crossed out and transferred to the work-related list.

7. Moustache?

This he crossed out, and then rewrote together with the question mark.

8. Learn from good people, like Babaram.
9. Finish reading major novels of T.H.
10. Try to keep my diary regularly as before.
11. Make notes of my five best and five worst qualities. Conserve latter and eradicate former.

Haresh read over this last sentence, looked surprised, and corrected it.

9.21

It was late when he got back to Elm Villa. Mrs Mason, however, who sometimes complained when Haresh came late for meals (on the grounds that it would upset the staff), was very welcoming.

'Oh, you look so tired. My daughter has been telling me how busy you have been. And you didn't leave word that you would be gone for more than a day. We prepared lunch for you. And dinner. And lunch again today. But no matter. You're here, back at last, and that's the main thing. It's mutton. A good, hearty roast.'

Haresh was glad to hear it. Mrs Mason was bursting with curiosity, but refrained from asking questions while he ate his dinner. He had eaten nothing since morning.

After dinner Mrs Mason turned to Haresh to speak.

'How is Sophie?' interposed Haresh deftly. Sophie was the Masons' beloved Persian cat, an unfailing subject of animated discourse.

After five minutes of the Sophie saga, Haresh yawned and said, 'Well, goodnight, Mrs Mason. It was very kind of you to keep my dinner warm for me. I think I'll turn in.'

And before Mrs Mason could veer the conversation around to Simran or the two visitors, Haresh had gone to his room.

He was very tired, but he kept awake long enough to write three letters. The rest he was forced to leave unwritten till the next day.

He was about to write to Lata when, sensing Simran's eyes on him, he turned to a shorter and easier letter—a postcard in fact.

It was to Kedarnath Tandon's son Bhaskar.

Dear Bhaskar,

I hope all is well with you. The words you want, according to a Chinese colleague of mine, are wan (to rhyme with 'kaan') and ee (to rhyme with 'knee'). That will give you, in order of powers of ten: one, ten, hundred, thousand, wan, lakh, million, crore, ee, billion. A special word for ten to its own power you will have to invent for yourself. I suggest bhask.

Please give my regards to Dr Durrani, to your parents, and to your grandmother. Also, ask your father to send me the second sample of brogues that I was promised by the man in Ravidaspur. They should have arrived more than a week ago. Perhaps they are already on their way.

Affectionately,
Haresh Chacha.

Next he wrote a short letter of a page and a half to his father, in which he enclosed the small snapshot of Lata he had got off the Mehras. He had wanted to take a photograph of them himself, but they had felt a bit embarrassed, and he had not pressed the matter.

To Lata he wrote a three-page letter on his blue writing pad. Though he had almost been at the point of telling her (or, more strictly, them) over the cold chocolate that he knew that she was the right wife for him, something had held him back. Now he was glad of it. Haresh knew that despite his pragmatism he was highly impulsive. When he had decided to leave home at fifteen it had taken him a minute to decide and ten minutes to leave; it had been months before he had returned. In the market the other day he had almost hired Mr Lee, the designer, on the spot, though he had no real authority to do so; he knew that he was the right man to help design the new orders that he felt sure he could bring in.

So much for decisions that were (or would have been) if not laudable, at least admirable. The money that he once lent a friend of his in Patiala, however, was lent equally impulsively. It had been a good third of his assets, and he now knew that he would never get it back. But the decision that faced him at the present time dealt not with his assets but with himself. If he gave himself away he would not be able to retrieve himself.

He looked at Simran's photograph—nothing would induce him to turn it away even while writing his first letter to Lata. He wondered what she would have said, what advice she would have given him. Her kindness and purity of heart would have led him in the right direction, he knew. She wanted his good as much as he wanted hers.

'Look at it this way, Simran,' he said. 'I am twenty-eight. There is no possibility of anything between us. I will have to settle down one day. If I have to marry I may as well go ahead and do it. They like me. At least I'm confident the mother does; and that makes a change.'

Of the three pages of his letter to Lata, one and a half were about the Praha Shoe Company, the Czech-founded establishment with Indian headquarters in Calcutta and a huge factory at Prahapore fifteen miles away. Haresh wanted his name and copies of his certificates brought to the attention of someone whom Mrs Rupa Mehra had known socially over a period of years and who himself knew someone fairly high up in the company. Haresh saw three advantages in a job with Praha. He would have a better chance of rising to the top in a company that was professionally managed. He would be near Calcutta, which could be considered to be the Mehra home base, and where Lata, he had ascertained, would be spending her Christmas holidays. And finally, he thought his income would surely be larger than the one he was at present living on. The insulting offer of a weekly wage that he had previously received from Praha he was prepared to discount as their badgered response to a persistent series of letters from a man writing to them without any prior introduction. What he needed to do, Haresh believed, was to get the attention of someone at the top.

> This business being over [continued Haresh], let me hope in the usual way that you had a comfortable journey home and that you were missed by all who met you after such a long absence from Brahmpur. [. . .]
>
> I must thank you for your visit to Cawnpore and the nice time we spent together. There was none of that bashfulness or undue modesty and I am convinced that we can be very friendly if nothing else. I quite appreciate your frankness and the way of putting things. I must admit that I have met few English girls who could speak English quite as well as you do. These qualities coupled with your way of dressing and personality make you a person far above the average. I think Kalpana was right in her praise of you. These may all seem flattering remarks but I write as I feel.

I have just today sent your photograph to my foster-father along with my impressions of you formed during our brief hours together. I shall let you know what he has to say.

A couple of final paragraphs about generalities, and the letter was over. Haresh addressed the envelope. As he lay on his bed a few minutes later it struck him that the Mehras would certainly have seen Simran's silver-framed portrait on his writing table. When he had invited them to Elm Villa he had not thought about the photograph at all. It was as much a part of the room as his bed. Between themselves, mother and daughter would doubtless have discussed it—and particularly the fact that he had let it remain there. He wondered what they must have thought, what they could have said. But he was asleep too soon to wonder long.

9.22

One morning, a few days later, Haresh arrived at the factory to find that Rao had assigned Lee to do some trivial work of his own.

'I need Lee,' said Haresh bluntly. 'It's for the HSH order.'

Rao looked at him with distaste down his sharp nose. 'You can have him when I've finished with him,' he said. 'He will be working with me this week.'

Lee, who had witnessed the scene, was very embarrassed. He owed his position to Haresh, and he respected him. He did not respect Rao, but Rao was nominally Haresh's senior in the company structure.

The weekly meeting later that morning in Mukherji's office produced a display of spectacular fireworks.

Mukherji congratulated Haresh heartily for his work in obtaining the HSH order, which had recently been confirmed. The factory would have been in severe difficulties without it.

'But the question of labour should be coordinated with Sen Gupta,' he added.

'Assuredly,' said Sen Gupta. He looked pleased. He was supposed to be in charge of labour and personnel, but there was nothing that this lazy man enjoyed more than chewing his paan and delaying any work that needed desperately to be done. Waiting for Sen Gupta to do anything except stare with his bloodshot eyes at a red-stained file was like waiting for a stupa to disintegrate. Sen Gupta had looked sour when Mukherji had praised Haresh.

'We will have to work a little harder all around, hn? Sen Gupta?' continued the factory manager. 'Now, Khanna,' he continued, turning to Haresh, 'Sen Gupta has been a bit unhappy of late about your interference in labour. Especially the construction job. He feels he could have hired better men more cheaply—and quicker.'

Actually Sen Gupta was hopping mad—and envious.

Quicker! Sen Gupta! was what Haresh was thinking.

'Talking of personnel,' he said aloud, deciding that this was the time to thrash matters out, 'I'd like to have Lee put back to work on the HSH order.' He looked at Rao.

'Back?' said Mukherji, looking from Haresh to Rao.

'Yes. Mr Rao decided to—'

Rao interrupted: 'You will have him back in a week. There is no need to bring it up in this meeting. Mr Mukherji has more important matters to deal with.'

'I need him now. If we fail in this order do you think they'll come back to us cap in hand begging us to make more shoes for them? Can't we get our priorities right? Lee cares about quality. I need him both for design and for the choice of leather.'

'I care for quality too,' said Rao with distaste.

'Tell me another,' said Haresh hotly. 'You steal my workers when I most need them—just two days ago two of my clickers disappeared into your department, because your men did not turn up for work. You can't keep discipline in your area, and you undermine it in mine. Quality is the last thing on your mind.' Haresh turned to Mukherji. 'Why do you let him get away with it? You are the factory manager.'

This was rather too direct, but Haresh's blood was up. 'I cannot work if my men and my designer are pinched,' he added.

'Your designer?' said Sen Gupta, staring redly at Haresh. 'Your designer? You had no authority to hold out a job to Lee. Who were you to hire him?'

'I did not. Mr Mukherji did, with a sanction from Mr Ghosh. I only found him. At least he's a professional.'

'And I am not? Before you were born I had learned how to shave,' said Mr Sen Gupta with hot irrelevance.

'Professional? Look at this place,' said Haresh with barely muted scorn. 'Compare it with Praha or James Hawley or Cooper Allen. How can we hope to keep our customers if we don't fulfil our orders in time? Or if our quality is below par? They make better brogues in the slums of Brahmpur. The way things are run here is just not professional. You need people who know about shoes, not politics. Who work, and don't just set up an adda wherever they are.'

'Unprofessional?' Sen Gupta seized on Haresh's remark and gave it a tiny twist. 'Mr Ghosh will hear of this! You call us unprofessional? You will see, you will see.'

Something about Sen Gupta's bluster and patent envy made Haresh say: 'Yes, it is unprofessional.'

'You heard? You heard?' Sen Gupta looked at Rao and Mukherji, then turned back to Haresh, his red tongue curled a little at the end, his mouth open. 'You are calling us unprofessional?' He pushed his chair not forwards but backwards with rage and puffed out his cheeks. 'You are getting too big for your boots, yes, for your boots.' His red eyes half popped out.

Haresh, having blundered in so far, blundered in a little further. 'Yes, Mr Sen Gupta, that is exactly what I am saying. You are forcing me to be blunt, but it is true, certainly of you. You are unprofessional in every sense—and one of the worst manipulators I have known, not excluding Rao.'

'Surely,' said Mukherji, who was trying to act as peacemaker, but who was wounded by the use of the word that Sen Gupta had inveigled out of Haresh, and which he took in a sense that Haresh had not, at least in the first instance, intended. 'Surely we must improve in any areas where we are deficient. But let us now talk calmly to one another.' He turned to Rao. 'You have been with the firm for many years, even before Mr Ghosh bought it and took it over. You are respected by everyone. Sen Gupta and I are comparative newcomers.' He then said to Haresh: 'And everyone admires the way you have obtained the HSH order.' Finally he said to Sen Gupta: 'Let us leave it at that.' And he added a pacifying word or two in Bengali.

But Sen Gupta turned towards Haresh, unpacifiable: 'You have one success,' he shouted, 'and you want to take over the whole place.' He was yelling and waving his hands about, and Haresh, incensed by this ludicrous display, cut in with disgust:

'I'd run it a good deal better than you, that's for certain. This thing is run like a Bengali fish-market.'

The words were spoken in the heat of the moment, but were unretractable. The unsavoury Rao was furious; and he was not even a Bengali. Sen Gupta was triumphantly indignant. And the simultaneous insult to Bengal and fish did not go down well with Mukherji either.

'You have been working too hard,' he said to Haresh.

That afternoon Haresh was told that Mr Mukherji wanted to see him in his office. Haresh thought it might be something to do with the HSH order, and he brought along a folder containing a week's work and plans to the office. There Mr Mukherji told him that the HSH order would be handled by Rao, not by him.

Haresh looked at him with a helpless sense of injustice. He shook his head as if to get rid of the last sentence he had heard.

'I slogged my guts out to get that order, Mr Mukherji, and you know it. It has changed the fortunes of this factory. You virtually promised it would be handled in my department and under my supervision. I've told my workmen. What will I tell them now?'

'I am sorry.' Mr Mukherji shook his head. 'It was felt that you had a lot on your plate. Let your new department start up slowly and iron out its problems; it will then be ready to undertake a big job like this. HSH will give us other orders. And I am impressed by the possibilities of this other scheme of yours as well. Everything in good time.'

'The new department has no problems,' said Haresh. 'None. It is already running better than the others. And I've been working on the details of fulfilment ever since last week. Look!' He opened the file. Mr Mukherji shook his head.

Haresh went on, anger building up under his voice: 'They won't give us another order if we mess this one up. Give it to Rao and he will butcher the job. I have even worked out how we can fulfil the order almost a fortnight before it is due.'

Mukherji sighed. 'Khanna, you must learn to be calm.'

'I shall go to Ghosh.'

'This instruction has come from Mr Ghosh.'

'It couldn't have,' said Haresh. 'There wouldn't have been time for that.'

Mukherji looked pained. Haresh looked perplexed before continuing: 'Unless Rao himself telephoned Ghosh in Bombay. He must have. Was this Ghosh's idea? I can't believe it came from you.'

'I can't discuss this, Khanna.'

'This won't be the end of the matter. I won't leave it at this.'

'I am sorry.' Mukherji liked Khanna.

Haresh went back to his room. It was a bitter blow. He had banked on the order. He wanted more than anything to get to grips with something substantial that he himself had brought in, to show what he and his new department could do—and, yes, to do something first-rate for the company of which he was an officer. For a while he felt as if his spirit was broken. He conjured up Rao's contempt, Sen Gupta's glee. He would have to break the news to his workers. It was intolerable. And he would not tolerate it.

Disheartened though he was, he refused to sit down and accept that these unfair dealings would form the future pattern of his working life. He had been ill-treated and used. It was true that Ghosh had given him his first job—and that too at short notice—and he was grateful for that. But such swift illogic and injustice shredded his sense of loyalty. It was as if he had rescued a child from a fire, and promptly been thrown into the fire himself as a reward. He would keep this job only as long as he needed to. If on a salary of three hundred and fifty rupees he had concerns about supporting a wife, with a salary of zero he could forget about it. He had heard nothing useful from anyone to whom he had applied for a job. But soon, he hoped very soon, something would come through. Something?—anything. He would take whatever came along.

He closed the door to his office, which he almost always left open, and sat down once more to think.

9.23

It took Haresh ten minutes to decide on immediate action.

He had wanted for some time to explore the possibility of a job at James Hawley. He now decided that he would try to get a job there as soon as he possibly could. He admired the establishment; and it had its headquarters in Kanpur. The James Hawley plant was mechanized and fairly modern. The shoes they produced were of better quality than those that CLFC considered adequate. If Haresh had any god, it was Quality. He also felt in his bones that James Hawley would treat his abilities with more respect and less arbitrariness.

But, as always, ingress was the problem. How could he get a foot in the door—or, to change metaphors, the ear of someone at the top. The Chairman of the Cromarty Group was Sir Neville Maclean; the Managing Director was Sir David Gower; and the manager of its subsidiary James Hawley with its large Kanpur factory (which produced as many as 30,000 pairs of shoes a day) was yet another Englishman. He could not simply march up to the headquarters of the establishment and ask to speak to someone there.

After thinking matters over, he decided he would go to the legendary Pyare Lal Bhalla, who was a fellow-khatri, one of the first khatris to have entered the shoe business. How he entered this business and how he had risen to his present eminence was a story in itself.

Pyare Lal Bhalla came from Lahore. He had originally been a sales agent for hats and children's clothing from England, and had expanded into sportswear and paints and cloth. He was extremely good at what he did, and his business had expanded both through his own efforts and through the recommendation of satisfied principals. One could imagine someone from James Hawley, for instance, on his way out to India being told by a fellow-clubman: 'Well, if you're in Lahore, and you're not happy with your chap in the Punjab, you could do worse than to look up Peary Loll Buller. I don't think he deals in footwear, but he's a first-rate agent, and it might very well be worth his while. And yours too of course. I'll drop him a line to say you might be coming to see him.'

Considering that he was a vegetarian (mushrooms were the closest he approached anything even faintly resembling meat), it was interesting that Pyare Lal Bhalla had quickly agreed to act as agent for the whole of the undivided Punjab for James Hawley & Company. Leather was polluting, and, certainly, many of the animals whose skins continued their post-mortem existence as an additional layer on human feet were not 'fallen'; they had been slaughtered. Bhalla said that he had nothing to do with the killing. He was a mere agent. The line of demarcation was clear. The English did what they did, he did what he did.

Still, he had been stricken with leucoderma, and many people thought that this was the disfiguring mark of the indignant gods, since he had tainted his soul, however indirectly, with the taking of animal life. Others, however, flocked around him, for he was enormously successful and enormously rich. From being sole agent in the Punjab he had became sole agent for the whole of India. He moved to Kanpur, the headquarters of the group of which James Hawley was a part. He dropped many of his other lines of business in order to concentrate on this particular lucrative account. In time he not only sold their shoes, but also told them what would sell best. He suggested that they reduce their output of Gorillas and increase their output of Champions. He virtually determined their product mix. James Hawley flourished because of his acumen, and he because they had grown dependent on him.

During the war, of course, the company had shifted its entire production to military boots. These did not go directly through Bhalla's hands, but James Hawley—out of a combination of fair play and far-sighted interest—continued to pay Bhalla commission. Though this was a smaller percentage, it left him no worse off than before owing to the larger volumes of sales. After the war, again steered by the sales and marketing wizardry of Pyare Lal Bhalla, James Hawley had swung back into civilian lines of production. This too appealed to Haresh, since it was for this sort of production that he had been trained at the Midlands College of Technology.

Not more than an hour after he received the bitter news that the HSH order was to be taken away from him, Haresh bicycled up to the offices of Pyare Lal Bhalla. 'Offices' was perhaps too elevated a word for the warren of small rooms that constituted his residence, his place of business, his showroom and his guest house, all of which occupied the first floor of a congested corner on Meston Road.

Haresh walked up the stairs. He waved a piece of paper at the guard, and muttered, 'James Hawley' and a few words in English. He entered an anteroom, another room with almirahs whose purpose he could not figure out, a storeroom, a room with several clerks seated on the ground at their floor-desks and red ledgers, and finally the audience chamber—for that was its function—of Pyare Lal Bhalla himself. It was a small room, whitewashed rather than painted. The old man, energetic at the age of sixty-five, his face whitened with disease, sat on a great wooden platform covered with a spotless white sheet. He was leaning against a hard, cylindrical cotton bolster. Above him hung a garlanded photograph of his father. There were two benches along the walls contiguous to his platform. Here sat various people: hangers-on, favour-seekers, associates, employees. There were no clerks, no ledgers in this room; Pyare Lal Bhalla was himself the repository of whatever information, experience, and judgement he required for making decisions.

Haresh entered and, lowering his head, immediately put his hands forward as if to touch Pyare Lal Bhalla's knees. The old man raised his own hands over Haresh's head.

'Sit down, son,' said Pyare Lal Bhalla in Punjabi.

Haresh sat down on one of the benches.

'Stand up.'

Haresh stood up.

'Sit down.'

Haresh sat down once more.

Pyare Lal Bhalla looked at him with such intentness that he was almost mesmerized into submission to his orders. Of course, the greater one's need, the greater one's propensity to be mesmerized, and Haresh's need, as he himself saw it, was great.

Besides, Pyare Lal Bhalla expected deference as an elderly man and as a man of substance. Had not his daughter been married to the son—the eldest son—of a first-class gazetted officer—the executive engineer for the Punjab canals—in the finest wedding Lahore had known for years? It was not a question of the Services deigning to acknowledge the existence of Trade. It was an Alliance between them. It announced his arrival in a manner that the endowment of twenty temples would not have. In his usual off-hand manner he had said to the groom's father: 'I am, as you know, a poor man, but I've left word at Verma's and Rankin's, and they'll take measurements for whoever you think appropriate.' Sharkskin achkans, suits of the finest cashmere wool: the groom's father had thought nothing of having fifty sets of clothes made for his family—and the fulfilment of this carte blanche was a drop in the ocean of the wedding expenses that Pyare Lal Bhalla proudly and cannily bore.

'Get up. Show me your hand.'

It was Haresh's fourth tense encounter of the day. He breathed deeply, then put his right hand forward. Pyare Lal Bhalla pressed it in a few places, especially the side of the hand just below the little finger. Then, giving no indication of whether he was satisfied or not, he said:

'Sit down.'

Haresh obediently sat down.

Pyare Lal Bhalla turned his attention to someone else for the next ten minutes.

Reverting to Haresh he said, 'Get up.'

Haresh rose.

'Yes, son? Who are you?'

'I am Haresh Khanna, the son of Amarnath Khanna.'

'Which Amarnath Khanna? The Banaras-wallah? Or the Neel Darvaza-wallah?'

'Neel Darvaza.'

This established a connection of sorts, for Haresh's foster-father was very indirectly related to the executive engineer, Pyare Lal Bhalla's son-in-law.

'Hmm. Speak. What can I do for you?'

Haresh said: 'I'm working in the shoe line. I returned from

Middlehampton last year. From the Midlands College of Technology.'

'Middlehampton. I see. I see.' Pyare Lal Bhalla was obviously somewhat intrigued.

'Go on,' he said after a while.

'I'm working at CLFC. But they make mainly ammunition boots, and my experience is mainly civilian. I have started a new department, though, for civilian—'

'Oh. Ghosh,' interrupted Pyare Lal Bhalla somewhat slightingly. 'He was here the other day. He wanted me to sell some of his lines for him. Yes, yes, he said something about this civilian idea.'

Considering that Ghosh ran one of the biggest construction companies in the country, Pyare Lal Bhalla's dismissive tone might have seemed a little incongruous. The fact, however, was that in the shoe line he was small fry compared to the plump carp of James Hawley.

'You know how things run there,' said Haresh. Having felt too often—but most painfully today—CLFC's inefficiency and arbitrariness, he did not feel that he was in any sense letting down his firm by speaking thus. He had worked his hardest for them. It was they who had let him down.

'Yes. I do. So you have come to me for a job.'

'You honour me, Bhalla Sahib. But actually I have come for a job with James Hawley—which is almost the same thing.'

For a minute or so, while Haresh remained standing, cogs clicked in Pyare Lal Bhalla's business brain. Then he summoned a clerk from the next room and said:

'Write him a letter for Gower and sign it for me.'

Pyare Lal Bhalla then put up his right hand towards Haresh in a combined gesture of assurance, blessing, commiseration and dismissal.

My foot's in the door, thought Haresh, elated.

He took this note and cycled off to the grand four-storey edifice of Cromarty House, the headquarters of the group of which James Hawley was a part. He planned to make an appointment with Sir David Gower, if possible this week or the coming week. It was five thirty, the end of the working day. He entered the imposing portals. When he presented his note at the front office, he was asked to wait. Half an hour passed. Then he was told: 'Kindly continue to wait here, Mr Khanna. Sir David will see you in twenty minutes.'

Still sweaty from bicycling, dressed in nothing better than his silk shirt and fawn trousers—no jacket, not even a tie!—Haresh started at this sudden intimation. But he had no choice except to wait. He didn't even have his precious certificates with him. Luckily, and characteristically, he carried a comb in his pocket, and he used it when he went to the bathroom to freshen up. He passed through his mind what he needed to say to Sir David and the order in which it would be most effective to say it. But when he was escorted up the great, ornamented lift and into the vast office of the Managing Director of the Cromarty Group he forgot his script entirely. Here was a durbar of an entirely different kind from the small whitewashed room in which he had been sitting (and standing) an hour earlier.

The cream-painted walls must have been twenty feet high, and the distance from the door to the massive mahogany table at the end at least forty. As Haresh walked across the deep red carpet towards the grand desk he was aware that behind that desk sat a well-built man—as tall as Ghosh and bulkier—who was looking at him through his spectacles. He sensed that, short as he was, he must look even shorter in these gigantic surroundings. Presumably any interviewee, anyone who was received in this office, was expected to quail with trepidation as he traversed the room under such intent inspection. Though Haresh had stood up and sat down for Pyare Lal Bhalla as unresistingly as a child would before his teacher, he refused to display any nervousness before Gower. Sir David had been kind enough to see him at such short notice; he would have to make allowances for his dress.

'Yes, young man, what can I do for you?' said Sir David Gower, neither getting up nor beckoning Haresh to a chair.

'Quite frankly, Sir David,' said Haresh, 'I am looking for a job. I believe I am qualified for it, and I hope you will give me one.'

Part Ten

10.1

A few days after the storm, there was something of an exodus from the village of Debaria. For a variety of reasons several people left within a few hours for the subdivisional town of Salimpur, the closest railway station for the branch line.

Rasheed left in order to catch the train to go to his wife's village; he planned to get his wife and two children back to Debaria, where they would remain until his studies called him back to Brahmpur.

Maan was to accompany Rasheed. He was not at all keen to do so. To visit the village where Rasheed's wife lived with her father, to travel back without being able to speak a word to her, to see her covered from head to foot in a black burqa, to spend his time imagining what she looked like, to sense Rasheed's discomfort as he attempted to keep two separate two-way conversations going, to exert himself in any way in this terrible heat, none of these struck Maan as being in the least enjoyable. Rasheed, however, had invited him; he had presumably felt that it would be inhospitable not to do so: Maan was, after all, his personal guest before he was his family's. Maan had found it difficult to refuse without a reasonable excuse, and there were none at hand. Besides, to remain in the village was driving him crazy. He was seized with frustration against his life in Debaria and all its discomforts and boredoms.

The Bear and his companion the guppi had completed whatever business they had in Debaria, and were headed somewhere else.

Netaji was going because he had 'some business in the subdivisional courts', but really because he wanted to hobnob with the local administrative functionaries and small-time politicians in Salimpur.

Finally, there was the eminent archaeologist, Vilayat Sahib, of whom Maan had not yet caught a glimpse. He was to return to Brahmpur on his way back to Delhi. Characteristically, he disappeared from Debaria on his own on a bullock-cart before anyone could make the friendly gesture of offering to share their rickshaw with him.

It's as if he didn't exist, thought Maan—as if he's in purdah. I've heard of him but I've never seen him—like the women of the family. I suppose they exist as well. Or perhaps they don't. Perhaps all women are just a rumour. He was beginning to feel immensely restless.

Netaji, very dashing and mustachioed, had insisted that Maan ride into Salimpur on the back of his Harley Davidson. 'Why would you want to ride for an hour in a ramshackle cycle rickshaw in this heat?' he had asked. 'As a Brahmpur-wallah, you're accustomed to luxury, you couldn't be used to having your brains baked. Anyway, I want to talk to you.' Maan had acquiesced, and was now bouncing up and down along the pitted country road on the motorcycle, having his brains vibrated rather than baked.

Rasheed had warned Maan about Netaji and his attempt to extract personal advantage from every possible situation, so Maan was not surprised at the turn their conversation took.

'How are you enjoying yourself? Can you hear me?' asked Netaji.

'Oh, yes,' Maan replied.

'I said, how are you enjoying yourself?'

'Very much. Where did you get this motorcycle?'

'I meant, are you enjoying yourself in our village?'

'Why not?'

'Why not? That means you aren't.'

'No, no—I'm enjoying myself very much.'

'Well, what do you enjoy about it?'

'Er, there's a lot of fresh air in the country,' said Maan.

'Well, I hate it,' shouted Netaji.

'What was that?'

'I hate it. There's nothing to do here. There isn't even any proper politics. That's why if I don't leave the village and visit Salimpur at least twice a week, I fall ill.'

'Ill?' asked Maan.

'Yes, ill. Everyone in the village makes me ill. And the village louts are the worst. That Moazzam for instance, he has no respect for other people's property. . . . You aren't holding on tight. You'll fall off. Hold close to me for balance.'

'All right.'

'I can't even keep my motorcycle safe from them. I have to keep it in an open courtyard, and they damage it out of spite. Now Brahmpur, there's a city!'

'You've been to Brahmpur then?'

'Yes, of course,' said Netaji impatiently. 'You know what I like about Brahmpur?'

'What?' asked Maan.

'You can eat out in hotels.'

'In hotels?' Maan frowned.

'In small hotels.'

'Oh.'

'Now this is a bad patch. Hold on tight. I'll go slow. That way, if we slip, we'll be all right.'

'Fine.'

'Can you hear me?'

'Perfectly.'

'How about the flies?'

'No, you're my shield.'

After a pause, Netaji said, 'You must have a lot of contacts.'

'Contacts?'

'Yes, contacts, contacts, you know what I mean.'

'But—'

'You should use your contacts to help us,' said Netaji bluntly. 'I'm sure you could get me a kerosene dealer's licence. That should be easy enough for the Revenue Minister's son.'

'Actually, all that is under a different ministry,' said Maan, unoffended. 'Civil Supplies, I think.'

'Come on, come on, that doesn't matter. I know how it works.'

'I really can't,' said Maan. 'My father would kill me if I suggested it.'

'No harm in asking. Anyway, your father is very well respected here. . . . Why doesn't he find you a comfortable job?'

'A job . . . er, why do people respect my father here? After all, he'll take away your land, won't he?'

'Well . . .' began Netaji, then stopped. He wondered whether he should confide in Maan that the village record-keeper had cooked the records to suit the family interests. Neither Netaji nor anyone else in the family had so far come to know of Rasheed's visit to the patwari. It was unimaginable that he could have asked him to uncook them on Kachheru's behalf.

'Was that your son who saw us off?' asked Maan.

'Yes. He's just over two, and he's in a bad mood these days.'

'Why?'

'Oh, he's returned from his grandmother's place, where he was spoilt.

Now nothing we do pleases him, and he's acting as contrary as possible.'

'Maybe it's the heat.'

'Maybe,' Netaji agreed. 'Have you ever been in love?'

'What was that?'

'I said, have you ever been in love?'

'Oh yes,' said Maan. 'Tell me, what's that building we just passed?'

In a while they reached Salimpur. They had agreed to meet the others at a cloth and general merchandise shop. But the narrow, crowded streets of Salimpur were completely packed. It was the day of the weekly market. Hawkers, peddlers, vendors of every kind, snake charmers with their torpid cobras, quacks, tinkers, fruit sellers with baskets of mangoes and lichis on their heads, sweetsellers, their barfis and laddus and jalebis encrusted with flies, and a great part of the population not only of Salimpur but of many of the surrounding villages, had managed to squeeze into the centre of the town.

There was a tremendous din. Above the babble of the customers and the shouts of the hawkers came the conflicting sounds of two screeching loudspeakers, one blaring out the current broadcast from All India Radio Brahmpur, the other interspersing its medley of film songs with advertisements for Raahat-e-Rooh or Ease-for-the-Soul Hair Oil.

Electricity! thought Maan, with a sudden leap of joy. Maybe there'll even be a fan around somewhere.

Netaji, with impatient curses and prolonged beeps of his horn, was hardly able to move a hundred yards in fifteen minutes.

'They'll miss their train,' he said of the others, who were coming by rickshaw and were half an hour behind them. But since the train was already three hours late, this was in fact unlikely.

By the time Netaji got to his friend's shop (which, sadly, was not equipped with a fan) he had such a bad headache that, after introducing Maan, he immediately lay down on a bench and closed his eyes. The shopkeeper ordered a few cups of tea. Several other friends had gathered in the shop, which was a sort of den for political and other gossip. One of them was reading an Urdu newspaper, another—the goldsmith from next door—was picking his nose thoroughly and thoughtfully. Soon the Bear and guppi arrived.

Since it was in part a cloth shop, Maan was mildly interested to see how it was run. He noticed that there were no customers.

'Why is there so little business here today?' asked Maan.

'Market day—very little activity in any of the shops,' said the goldsmith. 'Just the occasional yokel from out of town. That's why I've deserted my own. Anyway, I can keep an eye on it from here.'

To the shopkeeper he remarked: 'What is the SDO from Rudhia subdivision doing here in Salimpur today?'

Netaji, who had been lying as still as a corpse, suddenly perked up when he heard 'SDO'. Salimpur had its own SDO, who was in effect administrative prince of this fief. A visit from a Sub-Divisional Officer of a different subdivision was news indeed.

'It must be the archives,' said the shopkeeper. 'I heard someone saying that someone was being sent over from somewhere to look at them.'

'You donkey,' said Netaji, before falling back exhausted on to the bench, 'it's nothing to do with the archives. It has to do with coordinating the process of notification in the various subdivisions once the Zamindari Act comes into force.'

In fact Netaji had no idea why the SDO was in town. But he decided immediately to make it his business to meet him.

A spindly schoolteacher also dropped in for a few minutes, made the sarcastic comment that he did not have the whole day to spend in idle chatter like some people he knew, looked at the prone figure of Netaji with contempt, frowned slightly and quizzically at Maan, and left.

'Where's the guppi?' the Bear asked suddenly. No one knew. He had disappeared. He was found a few minutes later, staring in slack-jawed fascination at a display of bottles and pills that an aged quack doctor had arranged in a semicircle in the middle of the street. A crowd had gathered, and was listening to the quack's patter as he held up a bottle containing an opaque and viscous lime-green liquid:

'And this amazing medicine, truly a panacea, was given to me by Tajuddin, a great baba, and very close to God. He spent twelve years in the jungles of Nagpur, eating nothing—he just chewed leaves for their moisture, and kept a stone against his stomach for food. His muscles rotted, his blood dried, his flesh wasted away. He was mere bone and black skin. Then Allah said to two angels, "Go down and give him my salaams"—'

The guppi, who was staring open-mouthed and listening with absolute conviction to this nonsense, almost had to be dragged away from the scene and back into the shop by the Bear.

10.2

As the tea, paan and newspaper went around, the conversation turned to politics at the state level, especially the recent communal troubles in Brahmpur. The prime object of hatred was the Home Minister, L.N. Agarwal, whose defence of the police firing on the Muslim mob near the Alamgiri Masjid had been widely reported in the newspapers—and who was known to be a strong supporter of the construction—or, as he would have had it, reconstruction—of the Shiva Temple. Rhymed slogans such as the following, which were popular in Brahmpur among the Muslims, had found their way to Salimpur and were repeated with relish:

> Saanp ka zahar, insaan ki khaal:
> Yeh hai L.N. Agarwal!
> The poison of a snake, the skin of a man:
> This is L.N. Agarwal!
>
> Ghar ko loot kar kha gaya maal:
> Home Minister Agarwal!
> He robbed our Home, and devoured our substance:
> Home Minister Agarwal!

This might have been a reference to his 'cold steel' order, under which overzealous policemen had confiscated not merely axes and spears but even household knives, or it might have referred to the fact that L.N. Agarwal, being a member of the Hindu shopkeeping community, was the most important collector of funds for the Congress Party of Purva Pradesh. His origins were also referred to slightingly in the following slogan:

> L.N. Agarwal, wapas jao,
> Baniye ki dukaan chalao!
> L.N. Agarwal, go back,
> Go and run your bania's shop!

The walls, however, might have echoed the uproarious laughter that greeted this final couplet at the expense of the laughers themselves. For it was taking place in a shop, and Maan, being a khatri, was no stranger to trade.

In sharp contrast to L.N. Agarwal, Mahesh Kapoor, though a Hindu, was well known for his tolerance towards other religions—his wife would have said that the only religion he was intolerant towards was his own—and was liked and respected among knowledgeable Muslims. This was why, for example, when Maan and Rasheed first met, Rasheed had been well disposed towards him. He now said to Maan:

'If it were not for people like Nehru at the national level, or your father at the state level, the situation of the Muslims would be even worse than it is.'

Maan, who was not feeling particularly well disposed towards his father, shrugged.

Rasheed wondered why Maan was being so inexpressive. Perhaps, he thought, it was the way he had put it. He had used the words 'the situation of the Muslims' rather than 'our situation' not because he did not feel a part of his community, but because he examined even an issue as close to his heart as this through almost academically balanced categories. It was his constant habit to try to make objective sense of the world, but of late—especially since his rooftop discussion with his father—he felt more and more disgusted by it. He had hated his own deception—or perhaps prevarication—with the patwari, but knew that he had had no alternative. Had the patwari believed that Rasheed's family was not behind him, nothing would have protected Kachheru's right to his land.

'I'll tell you what I think,' said Netaji, sitting up and speaking in as leader-like a voice as his nickname required. 'We must get ourselves together. We have to work together for the good of things. We must get things off their feet. And if the old leaders are discredited, it requires young men—young men like—like we have all around us—who know how to get things done, of course. Doers, not impractical dreamers. Those who know the people, the top people of every subdivision. Now everyone respects my father, he may have known the people who mattered in his day, I don't deny that. But his day is, everyone will agree, now almost over. It is not enough to—'

But what it was not enough to do went unheard. The loudspeaker cart advertising Ease-for-the-Soul Hair Oil, which had been quiescent for a few minutes, now suddenly blared out its ear-splitting melodies from directly outside the shop. The din was so deafening—far worse than it had been in its earlier location—that they had to clap their hands to their ears. Poor Netaji went almost green and clutched his head in agony, and they all poured into the street to suppress the nuisance. But just at that moment Netaji noticed in the crowd a tall figure with an unfamiliar, rather weak-chinned young face under a pith helmet. The SDO from Rudhia—for Netaji with his unerring antennae knew instantly who this must be—looked disdainfully towards the source of the sound before being guided swiftly away by two policemen through the crowd and towards the railway station.

As the three heads (one turban on each side of the sola topi) bobbed through the crowd and disappeared, Netaji clutched at his moustache in panic at losing his quarry. 'To the station, to the station!' he screamed, forgetting his headache, and with such desperate urgency that even the loudspeaker could not stifle his cry. 'The train, the train, you will all miss your train. Grab your bags and run! Hurry! Hurry!'

All this was said with such conviction that no one questioned Netaji's authority or information. Pushing their way through the crowd, sweating and yelling, cursing and being cursed by turns, the convoy arrived at Salimpur Station in ten minutes. There they found that the train was not due for another hour.

The Bear turned with some annoyance towards Netaji. 'Why did you rush us like that?' he asked.

Netaji had been looking up and down the platform anxiously. Now suddenly his face broke into a smile.

The Bear frowned. Cocking his head gently to one side he looked at Netaji and said:

'Well, why?'

'What? What did you say?' asked Netaji. He had just noticed the sola topi at the far end of the platform, near the stationmaster's office.

But the Bear, annoyed, and annoyed that he was annoyed, had turned away.

Netaji, his lust for a new contact aroused, now collared Maan and virtually frog-marched him towards the other end of the platform. Maan was so astonished that he didn't even protest.

With unembarrassed aplomb Netaji went straight up to the young SDO and said:

'SDO Sahib, I am so pleased to meet you. And so honoured. I say this from the bottom of my heart.'

The weak-chinned face under the sola topi looked at him in displeased puzzlement.

'Yes?' he said. 'What can I do for you?' The SDO's Hindi, though tolerable, had a Bengali intonation.

Netaji continued: 'But, SDO Sahib, how can you say that? The question is how I can be of service to you. You are our guest in Salimpur tehsil. I am the son of a zamindar of Debaria village. My name is Tahir Ahmed Khan. The name is known here: Tahir Ahmed Khan. I am a youth organizer for the Congress Party.'

'Good. Glad to meet you,' said the SDO in a voice that was utterly unglad.

Netaji's heart did not sink at this lack of enthusiasm. He now produced his trump card.

'And this is my good friend, Maan Kapoor,' he said with a flourish, nudging Maan forward. Maan looked rather sullen.

'Good,' said the SDO, as unenthusiastically as before. Then a slow frown crossed his face and he said, 'I think I have met you somewhere before.'

'Oh, but this is the son of Mahesh Kapoor, our Revenue Minister!' said Netaji with aggressive obsequiousness.

The SDO looked surprised. Then he frowned again in concentration. 'Ah yes! We met very briefly, I believe, at your father's place about a year ago,' he said in a fairly amiable voice, speaking now in English and, as a result, unintentionally cutting Netaji out of the conversation. 'You have a place near Rudhia too, don't you? Near the town, that is.'

'Yes, my father has a farm there. In fact, coming to think of it, I should be visiting it one of these days,' said Maan, suddenly remembering his father's instructions.

'What are you doing here?' asked the SDO.

'Oh, nothing much, just visiting a friend,' said Maan. Then, after a pause, he added: 'A friend who is standing at the other end of the platform.'

The SDO smiled weakly. 'Well,' he said, 'I'm off to Rudhia later today, and if you want to go to your father's farm and don't mind a very bumpy ride in my jeep, you're most welcome to come with me. I have to do a bit of wolf-hunting myself: an activity, I should add, for which I am utterly untrained and unfit. But because I'm the SDO I have to be seen to be handling the menace myself.'

Maan's eyes lit up. 'Wolf-hunting?' he said. 'Do you really mean that?'

'Yes, indeed,' said the SDO. 'Tomorrow morning is when we go. Are you fond of hunting? Would you care to come along?'

'That would be wonderful,' said Maan with great enthusiasm. 'But I don't have anything except kurta-pyjamas to wear.'

'Oh, I should think we could get you togged up if necessary,' said the SDO. 'Anyway, it's nothing formal—just a beat to try to flush out a few man-eating wolves that have been bothering some villages in my subdivision.'

'Well, I'll speak to my friend,' said Maan. He realized that fortune had delivered him three gifts simultaneously: the chance to do something he loved, the release from a journey he did not wish to make, and a responsible excuse for effecting that release.

He looked at his unexpected benefactor in the friendliest way and said: 'I'll just be back. But I don't think you mentioned your name.'

'I'm very sorry, you're quite right. I am Sandeep Lahiri,' said the SDO, shaking Maan's hand warmly and entirely ignoring the injured and fuming Netaji.

10.3

Rasheed was not unhappy that Maan could not come with him to his wife's village, and was glad to see how enthusiastic Maan was to go to his father's farm.

The SDO was pleased to have company. He and Maan agreed to meet in a couple of hours. After he had finished some work at Salimpur Station—involving a consignment of vaccines for an inoculation programme in the area—Sandeep Lahiri sat down in the stationmaster's office and pulled *Howards End* out of his bag. He was still reading it when Maan found him there. They set out almost immediately.

The jeep ride southwards was as bumpy as Sandeep Lahiri had promised, and very dusty as well. The driver and a policeman sat in front, and Maan and the SDO at the back. They did not talk much.

'It really does work,' said Sandeep at one point, taking off his sola topi and looking at it with appreciation. 'I never believed it until I started work here. I always thought that it was part of the mindless uniform of the pukka sahib.'

At another point he told Maan a few demographic details about his subdivision: what percentage of Muslims, Hindus and so on there were. The details immediately slipped out of Maan's mind.

Sandeep Lahiri had a pleasant, rather tentative way of producing his occasional, well-rounded sentences, and Maan took a liking to him.

This liking increased when, at his bungalow that evening, he became more expansive. Although Maan was a Minister's son, Sandeep made no bones about his dislike of the politicians in his own subdivision and the way they interfered with his work. Since he was the judicial as well as the executive head of his subdivision—separation of powers had not yet been fully realized in Purva Pradesh—he had more work than a human being could be expected to handle. In addition, there were all kinds of emergencies that cropped up: like the wolves or an epidemic or the visit of a political bigwig who insisted on being shepherded around by the SDO himself. Strangely enough, it was not his local MLA who gave Sandeep Lahiri the most trouble but a member of the Legislative Council whose home was in this area and who treated it as his private domain.

This man, Maan learned over a nimbu pani laced with gin, saw the SDO as a competitor to his influence. If the SDO was compliant and consulted him on everything, he was content. If the SDO showed any independence, he tried quickly to bring him to heel.

'The problem is,' said Sandeep Lahiri with a rueful glance at his guest, 'that Jha is an important Congressman—the Chairman of the Legislative Council and a friend of the Chief Minister. Nor does he miss an opportunity to remind me of this. He also reminds me periodically that he is more than twice my age and embodies what he calls "the wisdom of the people". Oh well. In some respects he's quite right, of course. Within eighteen months of appointment we're put in charge of an area of half a million people—handling revenue work and criminal work, quite apart from keeping law and order and managing the general welfare of the subdivision and acting as father and mother of the population. No wonder he feels annoyed whenever he sees me, fresh from my training at Metcalfe House and my six months' field experience in some other district. Another?'

'Please.'

'This bill of your father's is going to make a vast amount of additional work for us, you know,' said Sandeep Lahiri a little later. 'But it's a good thing, I suppose.' He sounded unconvinced. 'Oh, it's almost time for the news.' He went over to his sideboard, on which rested a large radio in a handsome polished wooden cabinet. It had a great many white dials.

He turned it on. A big green valve-light slowly began to glow and the sound of a male voice singing an evening raag gradually filled the room. It was Ustad Majeed Khan. With a grimace of instinctive distaste Sandeep Lahiri turned the volume down.

'Well,' he said to Maan, 'I'm afraid there's no getting around this stuff. It's the price of the news, and I pay it for a minute or two every day. Why can't they put on something listenable, like Mozart or Beethoven?'

Maan, who had heard western classical music perhaps three times in his life, and had not enjoyed the experience, said:

'Oh, I don't know. Most people here wouldn't enjoy it.'

'Do you really think so?' said Sandeep. 'I feel they would. Good music is good music. It's just a question of exposure, I feel. Exposure, and a little bit of guidance.'

Maan looked doubtful.

'Anyway,' said Sandeep Lahiri, 'I'm sure they don't enjoy this awful stuff. What they really want is film songs, which All India Radio will never give them. As for me, if it weren't for the BBC, I don't know what I'd do out here.'

But as if in response to these remarks a series of pips now sounded and a distinctly Indian voice with a distinctly British veneer announced:

'This is All India Radio. . . . The news, read by Mohit Bose.'

10.4

The next morning they drove out for the hunt.

A few cattle were being herded along the road. When they saw the white jeep approach at high speed they scattered in alarm. As the jeep came closer, the driver leaned on the horn for a good twenty seconds, increasing their panic. When it passed them it raised a great cloud of dust. The herdboys coughed in admiration: they recognized the jeep as the SDO's. It was the only motor vehicle on the road, and the driver raced along as if he were absolute king of the highway. Not that the road was a highway exactly: it was a fairly solid dirt road, which might be more difficult to negotiate once the monsoon broke, but was fine for the present.

Sandeep had lent Maan a pair of khaki shorts, a khaki shirt, and a hat. Leaning against the door on Maan's side was the rifle that was kept at the SDO's bungalow. Sandeep had (with distaste) learned to fire it once but was not at all keen to fire it again. Maan could stand in for him.

Maan had gone hunting for nilgai and deer a number of times with friends from Banaras, had hunted wild boar too, and had once, without success, hunted for leopard. He had greatly enjoyed it. He had never hunted wolf before, and was not sure how exactly it would be managed. Presumably there would be beaters. Since Sandeep did not seem to be knowledgeable about matters of technique, Maan asked him about the background to the problem.

'Aren't wolves normally scared of the villagers?' he asked.

'That's what I thought too,' said Sandeep. 'We don't have so many wolves left anyway, and people don't have permission to go around shooting them unless they become a menace. But I've seen children who've been mauled by wolves, and even the remains of children killed and eaten by wolves. It's really terrible. The people of these villages are absolutely terrified. I suppose they are inclined to exaggerate, but the forest officers have confirmed from pug-marks and so on that it's wolves we're talking about, not leopards or hyenas or anything else.'

They were now driving through an area of undulating ground covered with scrub and rocky outcrops. It was getting warmer. The occasional village looked even more barren and destitute than those closer to the town. At one point they stopped and asked the villagers if they had seen the others in their party go past.

'Yes, Sahib,' said one villager, a middle-aged man with white hair, who was awestruck by the fact that the SDO had appeared in their midst. He told them that a jeep and a car had gone past earlier.

'Has there been any problem with wolves in this village?' asked Sandeep.

The villager shook his head from left to right. 'Yes, indeed, Sahib,' he said, his face taut with the memory. 'Bacchan Singh's son was sleeping outside with his mother and a wolf grabbed him and took him off. We chased him with lanterns and sticks, but it was too late. We found the boy's body the next day in a field. It was partly eaten. Sahib, please save us from this menace, you are our mother and father. These days we can neither sleep indoors for the heat nor outside for fear.'

'When did this happen?' asked the SDO sympathetically.

'Last month, Sahib, at the new moon.'

'One day after the new moon,' corrected another villager.

When they got back into the car, Sandeep said nothing more than: 'Very sad, very sad. Sad for the villagers, sad for the wolves.'

'Sad for the wolves?' said Maan, startled.

'Well, you know,' said Sandeep, taking off his sola topi and mopping his forehead, 'though this area looks very bare now, there used to be a lot of forest cover once—sal, mahua and so on—and it supported a lot of small wildlife that the wolves preyed on. But there has been so much logging, first in the War because it was needed, and then, illegally, after the War—often, I'm afraid, with the connivance of the forest officers themselves—and also of the villagers, who want more land for their fields. Anyway, the wolves have been crowded into smaller and smaller areas and have become more and more desperate. The summer's the worst time because everything is dry and there's nothing to eat—hardly any land-crabs or frogs or other small animals. That's when they are driven by hunger to attack the villagers' goats—and when they can't get at the goats, they attack the villagers' children.'

'Can you reafforest any areas?'

'Well, they would have to be areas that aren't used for cultivation. Politically and, well, humanly, anything else isn't possible. I can imagine being flayed alive by the likes of Jha if I even suggested it. But anyway, that's a long-term policy, and what the villagers need is that the terror stop now.'

Suddenly he tapped his driver on the shoulder. The startled man turned his neck around and looked at the SDO questioningly, while continuing to drive full speed ahead.

'Will you stop blaring that horn?' said the SDO in Hindi. Then, after a pause, he took up his conversation with Maan:

'The statistics, you know, are quite appalling. For the last seven years, each summer—from about February to June, when the monsoon breaks—there have been over a dozen kills and about the same number of mauls in an area of about thirty villages. For years officials have kept writing reports and referring and deferring and inferring and talking round and round in circles about what to do: paper solutions for the most part. Occasionally they've tied up a few goats outside the village of the latest victim in the hope that this will somehow solve things. But—' He shrugged his shoulders, frowned and sighed. Maan thought that his weak chin made him look rather grumpy.

'Anyway,' continued Sandeep, 'I felt that this year something practical just had to be done about it. Luckily my DM agreed and helped rope in the police at the district level and so on. They have a couple of good shots, not just with pistols but with rifles. A week ago we learned that a pack of man-eaters was operating in this area and—ah, there they are!' he said, pointing to a tree near an old and now deserted serai—a resting place for travellers—which stood by the side of the road a furlong or so ahead. A jeep and a car were parked underneath the tree, and a large number of people were moving around nearby, many of them local villagers. The SDO's jeep roared up and screeched to a halt, enveloping everyone in a haze of dust.

Although the SDO was the least expert among the gathered officials and the least capable of organizing the task at hand, Maan noticed that everyone insisted on deferring to him, and sought his opinion even when he had none to give. Eventually, in polite exasperation, Sandeep said:

'I do not want to waste any more time in talk. The beaters and hired marksmen, you say, are at the site itself—near the ravine. That's good. However, you'—he indicated the two Forest Department officials, their five helpers, the Inspector, the two crack police shots and the policemen— 'have been here for an hour, waiting, and we have been here for half an hour, talking. We should have coordinated our arrival better, but never mind. Let us not waste further time. It is getting hotter by the minute. Mr Prashant, you say you have drawn up the plans with great care after examining the site for the beat three days ago. Well, please do not reiterate them and ask for my approval of every detail. I accept your plan. Now you tell us where to go, and we will obey you. Imagine that you are the DM himself.'

Mr Prashant, the Forest Officer, looked appalled at the thought, as if Sandeep had made a tasteless joke about God. 'Now, let's go ahead—and kill the killers,' continued Sandeep, almost managing to look fierce.

10.5

The jeeps and car turned off the main road on to a dirt track, leaving the villagers behind. Another village went by, and then there was open countryside: the same scrub and outcrops as before, interspersed with pieces of arable land and the occasional large tree—a flame-of-the-forest, a mahua, or a banyan. The rocks had stored heat over the months, and the landscape began to shimmer in the morning sun. It was about eight thirty and it was already hot. Maan yawned and stretched as the jeep bounced on. He was happy.

The vehicles stopped near a great banyan tree on the bank of a dried stream. There the beaters, armed with lathis and spears, two of them with rudimentary drums strapped across their bodies, sat and chewed tobacco, sang tunelessly, laughed, talked about the two rupees that they would be getting for their morning's work, and asked several times for a re-explanation of Mr Prashant's instructions. They were a mixed bunch in both shape and age, but all of them were eager to be of use and hopeful that they would flush out a man-eating wolf or two. Over the last week the suspected wolves had been sighted on a number of occasions—once as many as four of them together—and had sought escape in the long ravine into which the dry creek ran. This was where they would most likely be hiding. The beaters finally set out across the fields and ridges in the direction of the lower end of the ravine and disappeared into the distance as they trudged along. They would later move forward through the ravine and try to flush the quarry out at the other end.

The jeeps now headed dustily towards the upper end of the ravine. Yet at this upper end—as at the lower end—there were a number of outlets other than the main one, and each exit had to be guarded. The marksmen were distributed at these various exits. Beyond the exits lay rough open land for a couple of hundred yards, and beyond that a patchwork of dry fields and areas of woodland.

Mr Prashant tried to obey Sandeep Lahiri's order that he should forget that he was in the superior, heaven-blessed, twice-born presence of an IAS officer. He donned his cloth cap, nervously twisted it around, and finally mustered the courage to tell people where they should sit and what they should do. Sandeep and Maan were asked to sit at one of the smaller and steeper exits, which a wolf, Mr Prashant thought, would be unlikely to choose because it would too greatly reduce his speed. The police marksmen and hired professional hunters were assigned to different areas, where they sat in the skimpy and sweltering shade of a number of small trees. The long wait for the beat began. There was no stir in the air to provide the least relief.

Sandeep, who found the heat intolerably taxing, did not say much. Maan hummed a little; it was part of a ghazal that he had heard Saeeda Bai sing, but, oddly, it did not bring Saeeda Bai to his mind. He was not even conscious that he was humming. He was in a state of calm excitement, and from time to time he mopped his forehead or took a swig from his water bottle or checked his ammunition. Not that I'll get more than half a dozen shots at most, he told himself. Then he moved his hand along the smooth wood of the rifle, and raised it to his shoulder a few times, aiming in anticipation at the bushes and thickets in the ravine from which a wolf would be most likely to emerge.

More than half an hour passed. The sweat dripped down their faces, and trickled down their bodies. But the air was dry, and it did evaporate; it did not torment them as it would have in the monsoon. A few flies buzzed around, occasionally settling on their faces or their bare arms and legs, and a cicada sitting on a small ber bush in a field chirped shrilly. The faint sound of the drums of the beaters, but not of their shouts, now came to their ears from the distance. Sandeep watched Maan with curiosity, curiosity not at his actions so much as at his expression. Maan had struck him as an easy-going, happy-go-lucky sort of man. But there was something intent and determined in his look now, something that seemed to say, with pleasurable anticipation: A wolf is going to come out there from that thicket, and I will follow it with my rifle until it gets to that spot along the path so that I can be sure of getting a good clear shot sideways on, and I will press the trigger, and the bullet will go true, and it will fall there—dead—and that will be that. A good morning's work.

This was not a bad approximation of Maan's actual thoughts. As for Sandeep's own independent thoughts, the heat had thinned and blurred them. He did not anticipate with any relish the killing of the wolves, but felt that this was the only immediate solution. He only hoped that the menace to the villagers could somehow be diminished or removed. Just last week he had visited the district hospital to see a seven-year-old boy who had been badly mauled by a wolf. The boy was sleeping on a cot in a general ward, and Sandeep had not wanted him woken. But he could not forget the look in the eyes of the boy's parents as they spoke to him—as if somehow he would be able to remove or ameliorate the tragedy that had struck their lives. Apart from severe injuries to his arms and upper body, the boy's neck had been injured, and the doctor had said that he would not be able to walk again.

Sandeep felt restless. He got up to stretch himself and looked down towards the unluxuriant summer vegetation below him in the ravine and the even sparser scrub outside. They could now hear the faint cries and shouts of the beaters in the distance. Maan too appeared lost in his own thoughts.

Suddenly, and far earlier than expected, a wolf, an adult grey wolf, larger than an Alsatian and faster, broke through the main outlet of the gorge where many of the professional marksmen were stationed and bounded over the wasteland and dry fields. It rushed straight for the wood to its left, pursued by a few belated shots.

Maan and Sandeep were not in a position where they could see the wolf clearly, but the shouts and shots that followed it told them that something was going on. Maan caught a brief glimpse of it running across an unploughed, hard-baked field when it swung over to his side at a fair distance and disappeared among the trees, swift and desperate in the face of death.

It's got away! he thought angrily. But the next one won't.

There were shouts of dismay and recrimination for a minute or two, and then everything in the immediate area settled down to silence again. But a brainfever bird had taken up its obsessive triple-cry from somewhere in the wood, and the sound interlaced itself with the cries and drumbeats from the other direction: the beaters were coming swiftly up the ravine now, flushing out whatever was in it in the direction of the hunters. By now Maan could also hear the sounds they made as they whacked the bushes with their lathis and spears.

Suddenly another, smaller grey form bounded out in panic from the ravine, this time towards the steep outlet which Maan was guarding. With an instinctive reflex he swung his rifle towards it and was about to fire—earlier than he had planned to for a good sideways shot—when he muttered to himself, with a shock:

'But it's a fox!'

The fox, not knowing that it had just been spared, and out of its wits with fear, cut across the fields and streaked like lightning into the woods, its black-tipped grey tail stiff and horizontal to the ground. Maan laughed for a second.

But the laugh froze on his face. The beaters could not have been more than a hundred yards away when a huge wolf, grey and rugged, its ears drawn back, and with the hint of an irregularity in its swift bounds, broke cover and rushed up the slope towards the place where Maan and Sandeep were sitting. Maan swung the rifle around, but the wolf presented no large target. Rather, as it bounded towards them, its great grey face with its dark arched eyebrows seeming to stare at them with vengeful savagery, it was an object of gross terror.

All at once it sensed their presence. It swung away from them and leapt down to the path in the ravine where Maan had imagined a wolf might emerge in the first place. Giving himself no chance to think of his own relief and paying not the least attention to the dazed Sandeep, he swung his rifle to follow the wolf to the point where he had earlier judged it would present the best target. It was now in his sights.

But just as he was about to fire, he suddenly saw two marksmen who had not been there before and who had no business to be there, sitting on the low ridge at the far side of the path, directly opposite him, their rifles trained on the wolf, and clearly about to fire as well.

This is mad! thought Maan.

'Don't shoot! Don't shoot!' he shouted.

One of the marksmen shot anyway but missed. The bullet pinged against a rock on the slope two feet away from Maan and ricocheted away.

'Don't shoot! Don't shoot! You crazy fools!' yelled Maan.

The great wolf, having changed its route once, did not do so again.

With the same irregular heavy swiftness it charged out of the ravine and made for the woods, its paws raising a trail of dust until it disappeared for a second behind the low boundary of a rough-surfaced field. The moment they saw it in open countryside some of the marksmen positioned at other exits fired at its diminishing shape. But they had no real chance. The wolf, like the fox and his own earlier fellow, was in the woods in a matter of seconds, safe from this concerted human terror.

The beaters had reached the exit of the ravine, and the beat was over. Not disappointment but a fit of violent anger seized Maan. He unloaded his rifle with trembling hands, then went over to where the errant marksmen were standing and grabbed one of them by his shirt.

The man was taller and possibly stronger than Maan, but he looked apologetic and frightened. Maan released him, then stood before him, saying nothing, merely breathing swiftly and heavily with tension and aggression. Then he spoke. Instead of asking them whether they were hunting humans or wolves, as he had been about to do, he controlled himself somehow and simply said in a semi-feral growl:

'You were placed to guard that route. You were not intended to come over the ridge and hunt in some other place that you decided was more promising. One of us might have been killed. It might have been you.'

The man said nothing. He knew that what he and his companion had just done was inexcusable. He looked at his companion, who shrugged.

Suddenly, Maan felt a wave of disappointment wash over him. He turned away with a shake of the head, and walked back to where his rifle and water bottle were standing. Sandeep and the others had gathered beneath a tree and were discussing the beat. Sandeep was using his sola topi to fan his face. He still looked shaken.

'The real problem,' said someone, 'is that wood there. It's too close to the exit. Otherwise we could get about ten more marksmen and spread them in a very wide arc—there—and there, say—'

'Well, at any rate,' said someone else, 'they've had a bad shock. We'll flush this ravine out again next week. Only two wolves—I'd hoped that there'd be more of them here today.' He pulled a biscuit out of his pocket and munched it.

'Oh, so you think they'll be here next week awaiting your pleasure?'

'We set out too late,' said yet another. 'Early morning's the best time.'

Maan stood apart from them, struggling with a rush of overwhelming feelings—unbearably tense and unbearably slack at the same time.

He took a drink from his water bottle and looked at the rifle from which he had not fired a single shot. He felt exhausted, frustrated, and betrayed by events. He would not join in their pointless post-mortem. And indeed a post-mortem was—in a literal sense—unjustified.

10.6

But later that afternoon Maan heard some good news. One of Sandeep's visitors mentioned that a reliable colleague of his had told him that the Nawab Sahib and his two sons had passed through Rudhia and gone to Baitar with the intention of staying at the Fort for a few days.

Maan's heart leapt up. The lustreless images of his father's farm vanished from his mind. They were replaced by thoughts both of a proper hunt (with horses) on the Baitar Estate and—even more delightfully—of news from Firoz about Saeeda Bai. Ah, thought Maan, the pleasures of the chase! He got his few things together, borrowed a couple of novels from Sandeep—to make his exile in Debaria more bearable—went off to the station, and caught the first possible train along the slow and halting branch line to Baitar.

I wonder if Firoz delivered it personally, he said to himself. He must have! And I shall find out what she said to him when she read his letter—my letter, rather—and discovered that Dagh Sahib, driven desperate by his absence from her and his own inability to communicate, had used the Nawabzada himself as translator, scribe and emissary. And what did she make of my reference to Dagh's lines:

> It is you who wrong me, and then you who ask:
> Dear Sir, please tell me, how do you fare today?

He got off at Baitar Station and hired a rickshaw to the Fort. Since he was dressed in crushed clothes (yet further crumpled from the hot and crowded train journey) and was unshaven, the rickshaw-wallah looked at him and his bag and asked:

'Meeting someone there?'

'Yes,' said Maan, who did not consider his question an impertinence. 'The Nawab Sahib.'

The rickshaw-wallah laughed at Maan's sense of humour. 'Very good, very good,' he said.

After a while he asked:

'What do you think of our town of Baitar?'

Maan said, hardly thinking of his words: 'It's a nice town. Looks like a nice town.'

The rickshaw-wallah said: 'It was a nice town—before the cinema hall was built. Now what with the dancing girls and singing girls on the screen and all that loving and wiggling and so on'—he swerved to avoid a pothole in the road—'it's become an even nicer town.'

The rickshaw-wallah went on: 'Nice from the point of view of decency, nice from the point of view of villainy. Baitar, Baitar, Baitar, Baitar.' He puffed out the words in rhythm to his pedal strokes. 'That—that building with the green signboard—is the hospital, as good as the district hospital in Rudhia. It was established by the present Nawab's father or grandfather. And that is Lal Kothi, which was used as a hunting lodge by the Nawab Sahib's great-grandfather—but is now surrounded by the town. And that'—for, as they rounded a built-up corner of the road they all at once came within sight of a massive, pale yellow building towering on its small hill above a muddle of whitewashed houses—'that is Baitar Fort itself.'

It was a vast and impressive building, and Maan looked at it admiringly.

'But Panditji wants to take it away and give it to the poor people,' said the rickshaw-wallah, 'once zamindari is abolished.'

Needless to say, Pandit Nehru—in distant Delhi, with a few other matters to think of—had no such plan. Nor did the Purva Pradesh Zamindari Abolition Bill—now only a presidential signature away from becoming an act—plan to take over forts or residences or even the self-managed land of the zamindars. But Maan let it go.

'What do you stand to gain from all this?' he asked the rickshaw-wallah.

'I? Nothing! Nothing at all, nothing at all. Not here, anyway. Now if I could get a room, that would be fine. If I could get two, that would be even better; I would rent one out to some other poor fool and live off the sweat of his efforts. Otherwise I will continue to pedal my rickshaw during the day and sleep on it at night.'

'But what do you do during the monsoon?' asked Maan.

'Oh, I find some shelter somewhere—Allah provides, Allah provides, and He will provide as He has always done.'

'Is the Nawab Sahib popular in these parts?' asked Maan.

'Popular? He's the sun and moon put together!' said the rickshaw-wallah. 'And so are the young Nawabzadas, especially Chhoté Sahib. Everyone likes his temperament. And what handsome figures of men. You should see them when they are together: truly a sight to behold. The old Nawab Sahib with one son on either hand. Like the Viceroy and his officers.'

'But if they are so well liked, why do people want to take over their estates?'

'Why not?' said the rickshaw-wallah. 'People want to get land wherever they can. In my village, where my wife and family live, we have worked our land for many years—since my father's uncle's time. But we still have to pay rent to the Nawab Sahib—to his bloodsucker of a munshi. Why should we pay rent? Tell me. We have watered it with our sweat for fifty years, it should be our land, we should own it.'

When they got to the huge, wooden, brass-studded gate in the wall of Baitar Fort, the rickshaw-wallah asked him for twice the normal fare. Maan argued for a minute, since the amount asked was clearly unreasonable; then, feeling bad for the rickshaw-wallah, he took out what he had asked for—plus another four annas—from his kurta pocket and gave it to him.

The rickshaw-wallah went off, well satisfied with his judgement that Maan was slightly crazy. Perhaps he had really imagined he was going to meet the Nawab Sahib. Poor chap, poor chap.

10.7

The porter at the gate took a similar view of things and told Maan to clear off. He had described Maan to the munshi, and the munshi had issued the instructions.

Maan, amazed, wrote a few words on a scrap of paper and said: 'I do not want to talk to any munshi. Now see that the Nawab Sahib or Burré Sahib or Chhoté Sahib gets this. Go and take it in.'

The porter, seeing Maan write something in English, this time asked Maan to follow him, though he did not offer to carry his bag. They entered the inner gate, and walked towards the main building of the Fort: a huge structure, four storeys high, with courtyards on two levels, and turrets at the top.

Maan was left in a courtyard flagged with grey stone; the porter climbed a flight of stairs and disappeared once again. It was late afternoon, and the heat was still intense in this paved and walled oven. Maan looked around him. There was no sign of the porter or Firoz or Imtiaz or anyone. Then he detected a slight movement in one of the windows above. A rustic, middle-aged, well-fleshed face with a grey-and-white walrus moustache was examining him from the upper window.

A minute or two later, the porter returned.

'The munshi asks, what do you want?'

Maan said angrily: 'I told you to give that note to Chhoté Sahib, not the munshi.'

'But the Nawab Sahib and the Nawabzadas are not here.'

'What do you mean, not here? When did they leave?' asked Maan, dismayed.

'They have not been here for a week,' said the porter.

'Well, tell that oaf of a munshi that I am a friend of the Nawabzada's and will be spending the night here.' Maan had raised his voice, and it reverberated around the courtyard.

The munshi scurried down. Though it was hot, he was wearing a bundi over his kurta. He was irritated. It was the end of a long day and he had been looking forward to cycling back into Baitar town, where he lived. Now this unshaven and unfamiliar stranger was demanding to be received at the Fort. What was all this about?

'Yes?' said the munshi, placing his reading glasses in his pocket. He looked Maan up and down and licked a corner of his walrus moustache. 'Of what service can I be to you?' he asked in polite Hindi. But behind his compliant tone and gentle demeanour Maan heard the rapid motion of the cogs of calculation.

'You can get me out of this baking courtyard for a start, and arrange for a room and some hot water for a shave and something to eat,' said Maan. 'I have had a hot and tiring morning hunting, and a hot and tiring train journey, and have been given the run-around for the last half hour by you—and now this man tells me that Firoz has left—or rather, was never here. Well?' For the munshi had made no move to assist him.

'Would Sahib give me a letter of introduction from the Nawab Sahib? Or one of the Nawabzadas?' the munshi said. 'I have not had the pleasure of Sahib's acquaintance, and in the absence of an introduction of some sort, I regret that—'

'You can regret what you like,' said Maan. 'I am Maan Kapoor, a friend of Firoz and Imtiaz. I want to use a bathroom immediately, and I am not going to wait for you to come to your senses.'

Maan's tone of command intimidated the munshi somewhat, but he made no move. He smiled to pacify Maan, but he saw his responsibility clearly. Anyone could come off the street, knowing that the Nawab Sahib and his sons were not there, claim to be a friend of one of them, and, by writing a bit of English and throwing his weight around, insinuate himself into the Fort.

'I am sorry—' he said unctuously. 'I am sorry, but—'

'Now listen,' said Maan. 'Firoz may not have talked about me to you, but he has certainly talked about you to me.' The munshi looked slightly alarmed: the Chhoté Sahib did not like him much. 'And I presume that the Nawab Sahib has mentioned my father's name to you. They are old friends.'

'And who might Sahib's father be?' asked the munshi with solicitous unconcern, expecting to hear at worst the name of some petty landowner.

'Mahesh Kapoor.'

'Mahesh Kapoor!' The munshi's tongue went rapidly to the other side of his moustache. He stared at Maan. It seemed impossible.

'The Minister of Revenue?' he asked, his voice quavering slightly.

'Yes. The Minister of Revenue,' confirmed Maan. 'Now, where is the bathroom?'

The munshi looked quickly from Maan to his bag to the porter and back to Maan. He got no confirmation of anything from anywhere. He thought of asking Maan to produce some proof, any proof, of his identity, not necessarily a letter of introduction—but he knew that this would anger him still further. It was an impossible quandary. This man, judging from his voice and speech, was certainly educated, however sweaty and scruffy he looked. And if it was true that he was the son of the Minister of Revenue, the prime architect of the inexorable bill that was going to dispossess the house of Baitar—and indirectly himself—of its vast holdings of fields and forests and wasteland, he was a very, very important person indeed, and to have slighted him, to have been so unwelcoming to him—it did not bear thinking of. His head began to spin.

When it came to a stop, he bent down with folded hands in a gesture of servility and welcome and, instead of asking the guard or the porter to do so, picked up Maan's bag himself. He started laughing weakly, as if in amazement and embarrassment at his own foolishness. 'But, Huzoor, you should have said so from the beginning. I would have come out of the Fort to meet you. I would have been at the station, waiting with the jeep. Oh, Huzoor, you are welcome, welcome—welcome to the house of your friend. Anything you want, you just ask me. The son of Mahesh Kapoor—the son of Mahesh Kapoor—and I was so awed by Sahib's gracious presence that my senses took leave of me and I did not even offer you a glass of water.' He panted up the first flight of stairs, then handed the bag to the guard.

'Huzoor must stay in the Chhoté Sahib's own room,' continued the munshi with breathless and subservient enthusiasm. 'It is a wonderful room with a fine view of the countryside and the forest where Chhoté Sahib likes to hunt. Huzoor was pleased to mention, was he not, a minute ago, that he went out hunting this morning? I must organize a hunt for him tomorrow morning. Nilgai, deer, wild boar, perhaps even leopard. Is Huzoor amenable to that? There is no shortage of guns—and horses too, if Sahib wishes to ride. And the library is as good as the one in Brahmpur. The Nawab Sahib's father always ordered two of each book; money was no object. And Huzoor must see the town of Baitar: with Huzoor's permission, I will myself arrange a tour of Lal Kothi and the Hospital and the Monuments. Now what may Huzoor's poor munshi fetch him? Something to drink after his journey? I will at once get some almond sherbet with saffron in it. It will cool your head, and give you energy. And Sahib must give me all the clothes he needs washed. There are spare clothes in the guest-rooms, two sets of which I will immediately arrange to have brought up. And I will send Huzoor's personal manservant up in ten minutes with hot water for Huzoor's shave, and to receive the grace of any further commands from Huzoor.'

'Yes. Wonderful,' said Maan. 'Where is the bathroom?'

10.8

In due course, after Maan had washed, shaved, and rested, the young manservant, Waris, who had been assigned to him, showed him around the Fort. This young fellow was an enormous contrast to the old servitor who had seen to Maan's needs in Baitar House in Brahmpur—and certainly to the munshi.

He was in his late twenties, tough, robust, handsome, very hospitable (as a servant trusted by his master has the self-confidence to be), and utterly loyal to the Nawab Sahib and his children, especially to Firoz. He pointed out a fading black-and-white photograph in a small silver frame on a side-table in Firoz's room. This showed the Nawab Sahib posing with his wife (not in purdah for the photograph, clearly), Zainab, Imtiaz and Firoz. Firoz and Imtiaz looked about five years old; Firoz was staring very intently at the camera with his head tilted sideways at an angle of forty-five degrees.

It was odd, thought Maan, that the very first time he was visiting the Fort, it was not Firoz but someone else who was taking him around.

The Fort seemed endless. The overwhelming impression was that of grandeur, the secondary impression that of neglect. They climbed level upon level by flights of steep stairs until they came to the roof with its ramparts and crenellations and its four square towers, each with an empty flagpost on top. It was almost dark. The countryside spread quietly around the Fort in all directions, and the fog of smoke from household fires cast a vagueness over the town of Baitar. Maan wanted to climb one of the towers, but Waris didn't have the keys. He mentioned that an owl lived in the closest tower and had been flying about hooting loudly for the last two nights—and had even made a foray in daylight, sweeping around towards the old zenana sections.

'I'll shoot the haramzada tonight if you want,' volunteered Waris generously. 'I don't want it to disturb your sleep.'

'Oh, no, no, that's not necessary,' said Maan. 'I sleep through anything.'

'That's the library below,' said Waris, pointing downwards through some thick, greenish glass. 'One of the best private libraries, they say, in India. It's two storeys high, and the daylight pours down through this glass. No one's in the Fort now, so we haven't lit it up. But whenever the Nawab Sahib comes here he spends most of his time in the library. He leaves all his estate work to that bastard of a munshi. Now be careful there—that's slippery; it's a depression where the rainwater runs off.'

Maan soon discovered that Waris used the word haramzada—bastard—fairly freely. In fact he used foul language in the friendliest way even when talking to the Nawab's sons. This was part of an easy rusticity which he curbed only when speaking to the Nawab Sahib himself. In his presence, awed, he spoke as little as possible, and kept severe control of his tongue when he did.

Waris usually felt either an instinctive wariness or an instinctive ease when he met new people, and he spoke and behaved with them accordingly. With Maan he felt no need for self-censorship.

'What's wrong with the munshi?' asked Maan, interested that Waris too did not like him.

'He's a thief,' said Waris bluntly. He could not bear the thought that the munshi was absorbing any of the Nawab Sahib's rightful revenues, and it was notorious that he did so all the time, undervaluing produce that he sold, overvaluing purchases that he made, claiming expenses where no work was done, and recording remissions in rent from the peasant tenants where no remissions were made.

'Besides that,' continued Waris, 'he oppresses the people. And besides that, he is a kayasth!'

'What's wrong with being a kayasth?' asked Maan. The kayasths, though Hindus, had been scribes and secretaries to the Muslim courts for centuries, and often wrote better Persian and Urdu than the Muslims themselves.

'Oh,' said Waris, suddenly recalling that Maan was a Hindu himself. 'I'm not against Hindus like you. It's only the kayasths. The munshi's father was the munshi here in the Nawab Sahib's father's time; and he tried to rob the old man blind; except that the old man was not blind.'

'But the present Nawab Sahib?' said Maan.

'He's too good at heart, too charitable, too religious. He never gets really angry with us—and with us the little anger he displays is enough. But when he rebukes the munshi, the munshi grovels for a few minutes and then carries on just as before.'

'How about you? Are you very religious?' said Maan.

'No,' said Waris, surprised. 'Politics is more my line. I keep things in order around these parts. I have a gun—and a gun licence, too. There is a man in this town—a base, pathetic man who was educated by the Nawab Sahib and has eaten his salt—who makes all kinds of trouble for the Nawab Sahib and the Nawabzadas—starting false cases, attempting to prove that the Fort is evacuee property, that the Nawab Sahib is a Pakistani—if this swine becomes MLA here we'll be in trouble. And he is a Congress-wallah and has made it known that he is in the running for the Congress ticket to contest from this constituency. I wish the Nawab Sahib would himself stand as an Independent candidate—or let me stand for him! I'd wipe the ground clean with that bastard.'

Maan was delighted with Waris's sense of loyalty; he clearly felt that the honour and prosperity of the house of Baitar rested entirely on his shoulders.

Maan now descended to the dining room for dinner. What struck him there was not so much the rich carpet or long teak table or carved sideboard, but the oil portraits hanging on the walls: for there were four, two on each of the longer walls.

One was of the Nawab Sahib's dashing great-grandfather, complete with horse, sword and green plume, who had died fighting against the British at Salimpur. The other portrait on the same wall was of his son, who had been permitted his inheritance by the British and who had gone in for more scholarly and philanthropic pursuits. He was not on horseback, merely standing, though in full nawabi regalia. There was a sense of calm, even of withdrawal, in his eyes—as opposed to the attractive arrogance in his father's. On the opposite wall, the elder facing the elder and the younger the younger, hung portraits of Queen Victoria and King Edward VII. Victoria, seated, stared out of the painting with an air of glum plumpness that was emphasized by the tiny round crown on her head. She was wearing a long, dark-blue gown and a cloak trimmed in ermine, and carrying a small sceptre. Her portly, rakish son stood crown-less but not sceptre-less against a dark background; he had on a red tunic with a dark-grey sash, an ermine cloak and velvet gown, and he bristled with braid and tassels. He had a great deal more cheerfulness in his expression but none of his mother's assurance. Maan looked at each of the portraits in turn between courses during his over-spiced and solitary meal.

Later he returned to his room. For some reason the taps and flushes in his bathroom did not work, but there were buckets and brass pots of water sufficient for his needs. After a few days of going out into the fields, or the fairly rudimentary facilities of the SDO's bungalow, the marble-tiled bathroom of Firoz's room, even if he had to pour his own water, was for Maan an extreme luxury. Apart from a tub and shower and two sinks, there was a dusty-seated European-style toilet and an Indian one as well. The former was inscribed in a kind of quatrain as follows:

J B Norton & Sons Ld
Sanitary Engineers
Old Court House Corner
Calcutta

The latter said, more simply:

Norton's Patent
'The Hindu'
Combined Closet
Calcutta

Maan, as he used the latter, wondered whether anyone before him in this erstwhile stronghold of the Muslim League had meditated on this subversive inscription, rebelling perhaps at the thought that this item of their common cultural heritage should have been so arbitrarily ascribed by the British to those of the other and rival religion.

10.9

The next morning Maan met the munshi as he was bicycling in; they exchanged a few words. The munshi was eager to know if everything had been to Maan's satisfaction: the food, the room, the behaviour of Waris. He apologized for Waris's crudity: 'But, Sir, what can we do, they are such yokels hereabouts.' Maan told him that he planned to be taken around town by the yokel, and the munshi licked his moustache in nervous displeasure.

Then he brightened up and informed Maan that he was going to arrange a hunt for him the next day.

Waris packed lunch, offered Maan a choice of hats, and showed him around the sights of the town, telling him all about the improvements that had taken place since the time of the Nawab Sahib's heroic great-grandfather. He shouted roughly at people who stared at the white-shirted, white-trousered sahib. By late afternoon they had returned to the Fort. At the gate the porter spoke sternly to Waris:

'Munshiji said you were to be back by three. There is a shortage of wood in the kitchen. He is very annoyed. He is sitting with the estate tehsildar in the big office room and he says you are to report to him immediately.'

Waris grimaced. He realized he was in some sort of minor trouble. The munshi was always irritable at this time of day; it was like a malarial cycle. Maan, however, said:

'Look, I'll come with you and explain things.'

'No, no, Maan Sahib, why bother? A hornet bites the haramzada's penis at four thirty every day.'

'It's no trouble.'

'You are very good, Maan Sahib. You must not forget me when you go away.'

'Of course I won't. Now let's see what your munshi has to say.'

They entered the hot paved courtyard and walked up the stairs to the large office room. The munshi was sitting not at the big desk in the corner (reserved presumably for the Nawab Sahib) but cross-legged on the floor in front of a small, wooden, brass-inlaid writing desk with a sloping surface. The knuckles of his left hand were pressed into his grey-and-white moustache. He was looking disgustedly at an old woman, very poor by the look of her tattered sari, who was standing before him, her face streaked with tears.

The estate tehsildar was standing behind the munshi and was looking angry and fierce.

'Do you think you can enter the Fort like this under false pretences and then expect us to listen to you?' said the munshi testily. He did not notice Maan and Waris, who were standing just outside the door; they had paused when they heard the sound of his raised voice.

'I had no other way,' faltered the old woman. 'Allah knows I have tried to speak to you—please, Munshiji, listen to my prayers. Our family has served this house for generations—'

The munshi interrupted her: 'Were you serving this house when your son tried to get his tenancy on to the village records? What does he want to do? Take away the land that does not belong to him? If we have taught him a lesson, that is nothing strange.'

'But it is only the truth—the land has been farmed by him—'

'What? Have you come here to argue and to teach me about truth? I know how much truth there is in what you people say.' An abrasiveness now appeared beneath the smoothness of his voice. Nor did he bother to disguise his pleasure in exercising the power of crushing her under his heel.

The old woman started trembling. 'It was a mistake. He should not have done it. But apart from our land, what do we have, Munshiji? We will starve if you take our land away. Your men have beaten him up, he has learned his lesson. Forgive him—and forgive me, who have come to you with folded hands, for having given birth to the miserable boy.'

'Go,' said the munshi. 'I have heard enough. You have your hut. Go and parch grain. Or sell your withered body. And tell your son to plough someone else's fields.'

The woman started weeping helplessly.

'Go,' repeated the munshi. 'Are you deaf as well as stupid?'

'You have no humanity,' said the old woman between sobs. 'A day will come when your deeds will be weighed. On that day, when God says—'

'What?' The munshi had stood up. He stared into the woman's wrinkled face with its tearful and downcast eyes and its bitter mouth. 'What? What was that you said? I was thinking of being lenient, but now I know what it is my duty to do. We cannot have people like you creating trouble on the Nawab Sahib's land after having enjoyed his grace and hospitality for years.' He turned to the estate tehsildar. 'Get the old witch out of here—throw her out of the Fort and tell the men that I want her out of her house in the village by tonight. That will teach her and her ingrate of a son—'

He stopped in mid-sentence and stared, not in real or pretended anger but in unsimulated terror. His mouth closed and opened, he panted almost soundlessly, and his tongue moved towards his moustache.

For Maan, white-faced with rage, his mind a blank of fury, was walking towards him like an automaton, looking neither left nor right, and with murder in his eyes.

The tehsildar, the old woman, the manservant, the munshi himself—no one moved. Maan grabbed hold of the munshi's fat, rough-stubbled neck and started shaking him wordlessly and violently, hardly mindful of the terror in the man's eyes. His own teeth were bared, and he looked terrifying. The munshi gasped and choked—his hands flew up to his neck. The tehsildar stepped forward—but only a step. Suddenly Maan let the munshi go, and he crumpled downwards on to his desk.

No one said anything for a minute. The munshi gasped and coughed. Maan was stunned by what he had just done.

He could not understand why he had reacted in this disproportionate way. He should simply have yelled at the munshi and put the fear of God into him. He shook his head. Waris and the tehsildar each stepped forward now, one towards Maan, one towards the munshi. The old woman's mouth was open in horror, and she was repeating 'Ya Allah! Ya Allah!' softly to herself.

'Sahib! Sahib!' croaked the munshi, finding his voice at last. 'Huzoor knows it was only a joke—a way of—these people—I never intended—a good woman—nothing will happen—her son, his field back—Huzoor must not think—' Tears were rolling down his cheeks.

'I am going,' said Maan, half to himself, half to Waris. 'Get me a rickshaw.' He was sure he had come within an inch of killing the man.

The resilient munshi suddenly leapt forward and almost lunged at Maan's feet, touching them with his hands and his head and lying gasping and prostrate before him. 'No, no, Huzoor—please—please—do not ruin me,' he wept, unmindful of his audience of underlings. 'It was a joke—a joke—a way of making a point—no one means such things, I swear by my father and mother.'

'Ruining you?' said Maan, dazed.

'But your hunt tomorrow—' the munshi gasped out. He realized well enough that he was in double jeopardy. Maan's father was Mahesh Kapoor, and such an incident would not increase his tenderness towards the Baitar Estate. And Maan was Firoz's friend; Firoz was volatile and his father was fond of him and sometimes listened to him; and the munshi feared to think what might happen if the Nawab Sahib, who liked to imagine that an estate could be run painlessly and benevolently, came to hear of the munshi's threats to an old woman.

'Hunt?' said Maan, staring at him.

'And your clothes are still in the wash—'

Maan turned away in disgust. He told Waris to follow him. He went to his room, dumped his belongings in his bag and walked out of the Fort. A rickshaw was summoned to take him to the station. Waris wanted to accompany him, but Maan did not let him come.

Waris's last words to him were: 'I sent a junglefowl to the Nawab Sahib. Could you see if he got it? And give my best to that old fellow, Ghulam Rusool, who used to work here.'

10.10

'So tell me,' said Rasheed to his four-year-old daughter Meher as they sat on a charpoy outside his father-in-law's house, 'what have you learned?'

Meher, who was sitting on her father's lap, rattled off her version of the Urdu alphabet as follows:

'Alif-be-te-se-he-che-dal-bari-ye!'

Rasheed was not pleased. 'That is a very abridged version of the alphabet,' he said. He reflected that during his absence in Brahmpur, Meher's education had very considerably regressed. 'Now, Meher, you must try harder than that. You are a bright girl.'

Though Meher was indeed a bright girl, she did not evince any further interest in the alphabet beyond adding two or three letters to her list.

She was pleased to see her father, but had been very shy with him when he had walked into the house the previous evening after an absence of several months. It had taken all her mother's persuasion and even the bribe of a cream biscuit to make her greet Rasheed. Finally, and very hesitantly, she had said, 'Adaab arz, Chacha-jaan.'

Very softly, her mother had said, 'Not Chacha-jaan. Abba-jaan.' This correction had brought on another attack of shyness. Now, however, Rasheed had re-established himself in her good graces, and she was chatting away with him as if the intervening months had not existed.

'What do they sell in the village shop?' asked Rasheed, hoping that Meher might give a better account of herself in practical affairs than she had with the alphabet.

'Sweets, savouries, soap, oil,' said Meher.

Rasheed was pleased. He bounced her up and down on his knee, and asked for a kiss, which he promptly got.

A short while later, Rasheed's father-in-law emerged from the house where he had been talking to his daughter. He was a tall, gentle man with a well-trimmed white beard, and was known in the village as Haji Sahib in recognition of the fact that he had performed the pilgrimage to Mecca some thirty years earlier.

Seeing his son-in-law and granddaughter still talking away outside the house and making no attempt at activity, he said:

'Abdur Rasheed, the sun is getting higher, and if you must go today, you had better make a move soon.' He paused. 'And be sure that you eat a large spoonful of ghee from that canister at every meal. I make certain that Meher does, and that's why her skin looks so healthy and her eyes shine as bright as diamonds.' Haji Sahib bent down to pick up his granddaughter and hugged her. Meher, who had figured out that she, her baby sister, and her mother would be going to Debaria with their father, clung to her Nana with great affection, and extracted a four-anna coin from his pocket.

'You come too, Nana-jaan,' she insisted.

'What have you found?' said Rasheed. 'Put it back. Bad habit, bad habit,' he said, shaking his head.

But Meher appealed to her Nana, who let her keep her doubtfully gotten gains. He was very sad to see them go, but he went inside to fetch his daughter and the baby.

Rasheed's wife emerged from the house. She was wearing a black burqa with a thin veil across her face, and was holding the baby in her arms. Meher went over to her mother, pulled at her burqa, and asked to hold the baby.

'Not now, Munia is asleep. In a little while,' her mother said in a soft voice.

'Have something to eat. Or at least a glass of sherbet before you go,' said

Haji Sahib, who a few minutes earlier had been pressing them to make haste.

'Haji Sahib, we must go,' said Rasheed. 'We should spend a little time near the town.'

'Then I'll come with you to the railway station,' said Haji Sahib, nodding slowly.

'Please don't trouble yourself,' said Rasheed.

A sudden look of more than ordinary concern, even anxiety, crossed the sober features of the old man.

'Rasheed, I am worried that—' he began, then stopped.

Rasheed, who respected his father-in-law, had unburdened himself to him about his visit to the patwari, but he knew that that was not the source of the old man's concern.

'Please don't worry, Haji Sahib,' said Rasheed, his face also reflecting momentary pain. Then he busied himself with their bags and tins and canisters and they all set off for the road that led past the outskirts of the village. Here there was a small tea-stall where the bus to the town and the railway station stopped. A little crowd of passengers had gathered, together with a larger crowd of those who had come to see them off.

The bus clattered to a halt.

Haji Sahib was in tears as he embraced first his daughter, then his son-in-law. When he took Meher up in his arms, she followed one of his tears with her finger, frowning. The baby slept through all this, even though she was passed from arm to arm.

With a great deal of bustle everyone got on to the bus except for two passengers; a young woman in an orange sari and a little girl of about eight, obviously her daughter.

The woman was embracing a middle-aged woman—presumably her mother, whom she had come to visit, or perhaps her sister—and weeping in a loud voice. They hugged and clutched each other with theatrical abandon, wailing and keening. The younger woman gasped with grief and cried:

'Do you remember the time when I fell down and hurt my knee. . . .'

The other woman wailed: 'You are my only one, my only one. . . .'

The little girl, who was dressed in mauve with one pink ribbon around her single plait, was looking profoundly bored.

'You fed me food—you gave me everything. . . .' continued her mother. 'What will I do without you. . . . Oh God! Oh God!'

This went on for a few minutes despite the desperate honks of the driver's horn. But to drive off without them would have been unthinkable.

The other passengers, though the spectacle had palled and they were now getting impatient, would never have allowed it.

'What is happening?' said Rasheed's wife in a low, troubled voice to Rasheed.

'Nothing, nothing. They are just Hindus.'

Finally, the young woman and her daughter came aboard. She leaned out of the window and continued to wail. With a sneeze and a growl the bus jolted forward. Within seconds, the woman stopped wailing and turned her attention to eating a laddu, which she took out of a packet, broke into two equal hemispheres and shared with her daughter.

10.11

The bus was so ill that it kept collapsing every few minutes. It belonged to a potter who had made a spectacular change of profession—so spectacular in fact that he had got himself ostracized by his local caste-brethren until they found his bus indispensable for getting to the station. The potter drove it and tended it, fed and watered it, diagnosed its sneezes and false death rattles, and coaxed its carcass along the road. Clouds of grey-blue smoke rose from the engine, raw oil leaked from its sump, the smell of burning rubber seared the air whenever it braked, and it punctured or blew a tyre every hour or two. The road, made of vertically laid bricks and little else, was cratered with holes, and the wheels had lost all memory of their shock absorbers. Rasheed felt he was in danger of castration every few minutes. His knees kept knocking the man in front of him because the back boards of the seat were missing.

None of the regular passengers, however, thought that there was any cause for complaint. This was far better and more convenient than a journey of two hours in a bullock-cart. Whenever the bus stopped involuntarily somewhere, the conductor leaned out of the window and looked at the wheels. Another man then jumped out with a pair of pliers and climbed under the bus. Sometimes the bus stopped because the driver wanted to chat to a friend along the route—or simply because he felt like stopping. Nor did the driver have any compunctions about pressing his customers into service. Whenever he needed the bus push-started he would turn around and yell in the powerfully vocalic local dialect:

'Aré, du-char jané utari aauu. Dhakka lagaauu!'

And when the bus was about to move, he would summon them with a battle cry of:

'Aai jao bhaiyya, aai jao. Chalo ho!'

The driver took particular pride in the signs (in standard Hindi) displayed in the bus. Above his seat for instance, it said *Officer Seat* and *Don't talk to the driver when the bus is in motion.* Above the door it said: *Only disembark when the bus has come to a halt.* Along one wall of the bus, the following message was painted in a murderous scarlet: *Do not travel when drunk or with a loaded gun.* But it said nothing about goats, and there were several in the bus.

Halfway to the station, the bus stopped at another small tea-stall, and here a blind man got on. His face was covered with cauliflower-like swellings, and he had a small snub nose. He walked with the help of a stick, and felt his way on to the bus. He could tell which bus it was from a distance by its characteristic sounds. He could also recognize people instantly by their voices, and he liked talking to them. One of his trouser legs was rolled long and the other short. Looking upwards he now sang out in a carefree and untuneful voice:

> 'Oh You Who Give, don't give anyone poverty.
> Give me death, but do not give misfortune.'

He sang this and lyrics of a similar nature while going around the bus collecting small coins and upbraiding the miserly with a volley of relevant couplets. Rasheed, whenever he travelled on this bus, was one of his more generous benefactors, and the beggar recognized his voice immediately. 'What?' he cried. 'You've only spent two nights at your father-in-law's? Shame, shame! You should spend more time with your wife, a young man like you. Or is that baby who is crying your own—and is that your wife with you here? Oh, Wife of Abdur Rasheed, if you are here on this bus, forgive this unfortunate for his insolence and accept his blessing. May you have many more sons, and all with lungs as loud. Give—give—God rewards the generous. . . .' And he moved on through the bus.

Meher's mother blushed furiously beneath her burqa, and then started giggling. After a while she stopped. Then she started sobbing, and Rasheed touched her shoulder gently.

The beggar got off at the last stop, the railway station. 'Peace to you all,' he said. 'And health and safety to all who travel on Indian Railways.'

Rasheed discovered that the train was only a little late, and was disappointed. He had hoped to take a rickshaw and visit his elder brother's grave which was half an hour away in a graveyard outside this small town. For it was at this station that his brother had met with his death by falling under a train three years ago. Before the news had come to his family, the people of the town had arranged for the burial of his crushed remains.

It was now about noon and extremely hot. They had been sitting on the platform for only a few minutes when Rasheed's wife started shivering. Rasheed held her hand and said nothing. Then he said in a low voice: 'I know, I know what you must be feeling. I wanted to visit him too. We'll do it next time we are here. There was no time today. Believe me, there was no time. And with all this luggage—how could we?'

The baby, resting in an improvised crib of a few bags, continued to sleep. Meher too was exhausted and had dozed off. Rasheed looked at them and closed his eyes as well.

His wife said nothing, but moaned softly. Her heart was palpitating swiftly, and she seemed dazed. 'You are thinking of Bhaiyya, aren't you?' he said. She started sobbing again, and trembling uncontrollably. Rasheed felt a sense of pressure building up at the back of his head. He looked at her face, beautiful even through the veil—beautiful perhaps because he knew it was beautiful. He spoke again, holding her hand in his and stroking her forehead:

'Don't cry—don't cry—Meher and the baby will wake up—we'll have left this inauspicious place soon. Why grieve, why grieve, when you can do nothing about it. . . . Look, it could also be the heat. Take your veil off—let the air play a little on your face. . . . We would have had to rush there, and we might have missed the train and have had to spend the night in this miserable town. Next time we'll make time. It is my fault, I should have left the house earlier. But perhaps I could not have borne the grief of it myself. The bus stopped again and again and we got delayed. And now, believe me, Bhabhi, there is no time at all.'

He had addressed her as he used to do in the old days, using the word for sister-in-law. For she had been his brother's wife, and Meher had been his brother's child. He had married her at his mother's dying behest; his mother could not bear that her infant granddaughter should remain fatherless or her daughter-in-law (whom she loved) a widow.

'Take care of her,' she had said to Rasheed. 'She is a good woman and will make you a good wife as well.' Rasheed had promised to do as she had asked, and had kept his difficult and binding promise.

10.12

Most respected Maulana Abdur Rasheed Sahib,

I am taking up my pen to write with much hesitation, and without the knowledge of my sister and guardian. I thought you would want to know how my Arabic was faring in your absence. It is faring well. I am practising every day. At first my sister tried to appoint another teacher for me, an old man who mumbles and coughs and makes no attempt to correct me when I make mistakes. But I was so unhappy that Saeeda Apa discontinued him. You never used to let me get away with any mistakes, and I am afraid I was tearful at times when it seemed I could do nothing right. But you never let me get away with tears either, and did not let me turn to something easier after I had collected myself. I have now come to realize the value of your teaching method, and I miss having to make the effort that I had to when you were here.

Nowadays I spend my time mainly in housework of one kind or another. Apa is in a bad mood these days, I think because her new sarangi player has been playing indifferently. So I am afraid to ask her to let me do something of interest. You advised me not to read novels, but I have so much time on my hands that I find myself turning to them. But I do read the Quran Sharif every day, and copy out a few excerpts. I will now copy out one or two quotations from the surah I am reading, complete with all the special vowel-marks to show you how my Arabic calligraphy is progressing. But I fear it is not progressing at all. In your absence, it is at best standing still.

> Have they not regarded the birds above them
> spreading their wings, and closing them?
> Naught holds them but the All-Merciful. Surely
> He sees everything.

> Say: 'What think you? If in the morning
> your water should have vanished into
> the earth, then who would bring you
> running water?'

The parakeet, who was looking feeble the day before you left, has lately begun to say a few words. Saeeda Apa has taken a fancy to him, I am happy to say.

I hope you will return soon, as I miss seeing you and hearing your criticisms and corrections, and I hope that you are well and in good spirits. I am sending this letter through Bibbo. She will post it; she says this address should be sufficient. I pray that it reaches you.

With many good wishes and renewed respects,

Your student,
Tasneem

Rasheed read this letter slowly, twice, sitting by the side of the lake near the school. He had returned to Debaria to find that Maan had come back a little earlier than expected, and, after inquiries, he had followed him to the lake to make sure he was all right. He appeared to be fine, from the vigorous way he was swimming back from the far end.

Rasheed had been surprised to receive the letter. It had been waiting for him at his father's house. He was interested to see the excerpts, which he recognized instantly from the chapter of the Quran called 'The Kingdom'. How like Tasneem, he thought, to select the most gentle excerpts from a surah that contained terrible descriptions of hellfire and perdition.

Her calligraphy had not deteriorated. If anything it had slightly improved. Her own appraisal of it was both modest and just. There was something in the letter—quite apart from the fact that it had been sent to him behind Saeeda Bai's back—that troubled him, and despite himself he found his thoughts turning to Meher's mother, who was sitting inside his father's house, probably fanning the baby. Poor woman, good-hearted and beautiful though she was, she could barely write her own name. And he once again thought: If I had had any choice, would it ever have been a woman like her whom I would have chosen as my partner and companion through this life?

10.13

Maan laughed a little, then coughed. Rasheed looked at him. He sneezed.

'You should dry your hair,' said Rasheed. 'Don't blame me if you catch a cold. Swimming and then not drying your hair is an absolutely certain way of catching a cold. Summer colds are the worst. Your voice sounds bad too. And you look much darker, more burned by the sun than when I saw you just a few days ago.'

Maan reflected that his voice must have been affected by the dust of the journey. He hadn't actually shouted at anyone, not even at the marksman or the munshi. On his return from Baitar, perhaps to relieve his feelings, he had made straight for the lake near the school, and had swum across and back a few times. When he got out, he saw Rasheed sitting on the bank, reading a letter. Next to him was a small box—of sweets, it appeared.

'It must be all this Urdu you've been teaching me,' Maan said. 'All those guttural letters, ghaaf and khay and so on—my throat can't survive them.'

'You are making excuses,' said Rasheed. 'This is an excuse not to study. In fact you haven't studied more than four hours since you've been here.'

'What are you saying?' said Maan. 'All I do from morning to night is repeat the alphabet forwards and backwards and practise writing Urdu letters in the air. Why, even when I was swimming just now I kept imagining letters: when I swam breaststroke, I was writing qaaf, when I swam backstroke, I was writing noon—'

'Do you want to go up there?' asked Rasheed, with some impatience.

'What do you mean?' said Maan.

'I mean, is there even the slightest truth in what you have been saying?'

'Not the slightest!' laughed Maan.

'So when you go up there, what will you say to God?'

'Oh, well,' said Maan. 'I have topsy-turvy views about all that. Up is down to me, and down is up. In fact, I believe that if there is paradise anywhere, it is here, here on earth. What do you think?'

Rasheed did not much care for flippancy on serious subjects. He did not think paradise was on earth: certainly not in Brahmpur, certainly not here in Debaria, nor in his wife's virtually illiterate village.

'You look worried,' said Maan. 'I hope it isn't anything I said.'

Rasheed thought for a few seconds before answering. 'Actually,' he said, 'it wasn't your answer exactly. I was wondering about Meher's education.'

'Your daughter?' asked Maan.

'Yes. My elder daughter. She's a bright girl—you'll meet her in the evening. But there are no schools like this'—he waved an arm towards the nearby madrasa—'in her mother's village—and she will grow up ignorant unless I do something about it. I try to teach her whenever I'm here, but then I go to Brahmpur for a few months, and the illiterate environment takes over.'

It never struck Rasheed as odd that he loved Meher every bit as much as his own daughter. Perhaps one element of this bond was precisely that Meher had at first been for him purely an object of love, not of responsibility. Even when, a year or so ago, she stopped calling him Chacha and started calling him Abba, some of that sense of the uncle—who would come home and spoil her with presents and affection—remained. With a start, Rasheed recalled that the baby was about as old as Meher had been when her father had died. Perhaps this too had been in her mother's mind when she had lost control of her emotions and broken down at the station.

Rasheed thought of his wife with tenderness, but not with passion, and he felt that she too felt no passion for him, merely a sense of comfort when he was with her. She lived for her children and the memory of her first husband.

This is my life, the only life I will live, thought Rasheed. If only things had been different, we might each have been happy.

At first the very thought of sharing a room with her for an hour had troubled him. Then he grew used to the brief visits he paid to her in the middle of the night when the other men were asleep in the courtyard. But even when fulfilling his obligations as a husband he wondered what she was thinking. Sometimes he imagined that she was close to tears. Had she begun to love him more after the baby had been born? Perhaps. But the women of the zenana in her father's village—her elder brothers' wives—were often quite cruel even when they teased each other, and she would not have been able to express her affection for him openly, even if there had been much to express.

Once more Rasheed began to unfold the letter he had received, then stopped and said to Maan:

'So—how is your father's farm?'

'My father's farm?'

'Yes.'

'Well,' said Maan. 'It should be all right. Not much going on at this time of the year.'

'But haven't you just visited the farm?'

'No. Not exactly.'

'Not exactly?'

'I mean, no. No, I meant to, but—I got caught up in things.'

'So what have you been doing?'

'Losing my temper mainly,' said Maan. 'And trying to kill wolves.'

Rasheed frowned, but did not follow up these interesting possibilities. 'You are being flippant as usual,' he said.

'What are those flowers?' asked Maan, to change the subject.

Rasheed looked across the tank to the far shore.

'The purple ones?'

'Yes. What are they called?'

'Sadabahar—or evergreen,' said Rasheed, 'because it's always spring for them. They never seem to die, and no one can get rid of them. I think they're beautiful—though they often grow in foul places. . . .' He paused. 'Some people call them "behayaa"—or "shameless".' He was lost in meditation for a long while, one thought leading to another.

'Well,' said Maan, 'what were you thinking of?'

'My mother,' said Rasheed. After a pause he continued in a quiet voice: 'I loved her, God protect her spirit. She was an upright woman, and well educated as women go. She loved my brother and me, and only regretted that she never had a daughter. Perhaps that's why—well, anyway, she was the only one who appreciated my wish to educate myself, to make something of myself and do something for this place.' Rasheed said 'this place' with such bitterness that it sounded almost as if he detested it. 'But my love for her has tied my life up in knots. And as for my father—what does he understand of anything outside property and money? I have to be discreet even in what I say at home. I'm always looking up towards the roof and lowering my voice. Baba, for all his piety, understands things—things one might not expect him to. But my father has contempt for everything I revere. And it has become worse lately with the changes in the house.' Maan guessed that Rasheed meant his father's second wife.

But Rasheed was continuing with great bitterness. 'Look all around you,' he said. 'Or look at history. It's always been the same. The old men cling to their power and their beliefs, which admit all their worst vices but exclude the least fault and strangle the smallest innovation of the young. Then, thank God, they die, and can do no more harm. But by then we, the young, are old, and strive to do what little mischief they left undone. This village is the worst,' continued Rasheed, pointing behind the school to the low buildings of Debaria's twin village of Sagal. 'Worse even than ours, and also, of course, more pious. I'll show you one good man in this village—I was on my way to see him when I saw you tempting fate by swimming alone. You'll see the state to which he has been driven by the others—and, I suppose, by the just or unjust anger of God.'

Maan was astonished to hear Rasheed talk in this vein. Rasheed's education before Brahmpur University had been a traditionally religious one, and Maan knew how firmly he believed in God and his Prophet and the Book, the transmitted word of God—even to the extent of refusing to abridge Tasneem's lesson from the Quran when summoned by Saeeda Bai. But Rasheed was not contented with the world that God had made, nor did he understand why it had been arranged in the pathetic way it had. As for the old man, Maan recalled that Rasheed had referred to him briefly during their long walk around the village, but he did not feel particularly eager to be shown assorted samples of village misery.

'Were you always so serious about the state of things?' asked Maan.

'Far from it,' said Rasheed, with a rather twisted smile at the corner of his mouth. 'Far from it. When I was younger, well, I was concerned only with myself and my fists. I've told you about this before, haven't I? I would look around and notice certain things. My grandfather was treated by everyone around him with great respect. People would come from far away to ask him to solve disputes. Sometimes he'd do this with great severity, beating the offenders. This I considered proof of the fact that beating people was a cause of his being honoured. I beat people up too.'

Rasheed paused to look up the slope towards the madrasa, then continued:

'At school I was always hitting the kids. I'd find one by himself, and I'd beat him up. Sometimes I'd come across a boy in the fields or along the road and I'd slap him hard across the face.'

Maan laughed. 'Yes, I remember you telling me that,' he said.

'It's no laughing matter really,' said Rasheed. 'And certainly my parents didn't think so. My mother would beat me very rarely, if at all; well, she did once or twice. But my father—he would beat me regularly.

'Baba, however, who was the real authority in the village, treated me with great love, and his presence would often save me. I was his favourite. He was very regular about his prayers. So I too would always say my prayers even though I did very badly at school. But every so often I would thrash a boy, and his father would report it to Baba. Once Baba told me to sit down and stand up one hundred times while holding my ears as a punishment. Some of my friends were standing around, and I refused to do any such thing. Perhaps I would have got away with it. But my father happened to be passing, and he was so shocked by my insolence towards his father that he hit me across the face very hard. I began crying from shame and pain, and I decided to run away. I ran quite far—till the mango trees beyond the threshing-ground to the north—before they sent someone after me and brought me back.'

Maan was as rapt as if he had been listening to a story by the guppi.

'Was that before the time you ran away to stay with the Bear?' he prompted.

'Yes,' said Rasheed, a bit vexed that Maan appeared to know his story so well.

'Anyway, later,' he continued, 'I began to understand things. I think it happened at the religious training college I went to. It's in Banaras, I'm sure you must have heard of it, it's quite famous, and it has a high academic reputation—though it is a terrible place. Anyway, at first they wouldn't let me in because of my poor school marks from here; but within a year I had come third in my class of sixty boys. I even left off beating people up! And, because of the conditions we had to live in, I became interested in practical politics, and started organizing the boys to protest against the worst abuses at the college! That's probably where I got a taste for reform, though I wasn't a socialist yet. My former associates at school were amazed at me—and probably appalled by the righteous turn I had taken. One of them has become a dacoit. And now when I talk about village improvement and so on, they all think I'm mad. God knows these villages need improvement—and can be improved. But I doubt that God will find time to do it no matter how often people do their namaaz. As for legislation—' Rasheed got up. 'Come. It's getting late, and I have to go for this visit. If I'm not back in Debaria by sunset I'll have to do my namaaz with the elders of this village—hypocrites to a man.' Rasheed clearly viewed Sagal as a sink of iniquity.

'All right,' said Maan, beginning to be curious. 'I suppose it's all right for me to tag along.'

10.14

When they were not far from the old man's place, Rasheed told Maan a little about his background:

'He is about sixty years old and comes from a very wealthy family of many brothers. He himself had many children, but they are all dead now except for the two daughters who take care of him alternately. He's a good man who never did anything wrong in his life—and while his crooked brothers are flourishing with wealth and children, he is in a pitiable condition.' Rasheed paused, then speculated: 'Some say a jinn did this to him. Though they are evil themselves, they often seek the company of good people. Anyway—' Rasheed stopped suddenly. A tall, venerable-looking man passed by him in the narrow lane, and they exchanged greetings, sullen on Rasheed's side.

'That is one of his brothers,' he said to Maan a few moments later, 'one of the brothers who has robbed him of his share of the family's wealth. He is one of the leaders of the community, and when the Imam of the mosque is absent he often leads the congregation in prayer. Even greeting him makes me uncomfortable.'

They now entered a courtyard and came across a strange scene.

Two thin bullocks were tethered to a peg near a feeding trough. A small goat was lying on a charpoy next to a sleeping child, a boy around whose beautiful face a few flies were buzzing. Grass was growing on the wall of the small courtyard; a broom made of twigs was leaning against it in a corner. A pretty eight-year-old girl dressed in red was looking at them. She was holding up the slack wing of a dead crow that stared at them with one opaque grey eye. A bucket, a broken clay drinking pot, a stone board and roller for crushing spices, a few other odds and ends—all these lay scattered around the courtyard as if no one knew what they were for and no one cared.

On the porch of the ramshackle two-room thatched house was a sagging charpoy, and on this lay an old man. Gaunt-featured, with peppery stubble and sunken eyes, he was lying on his side on a dirty, checked-green covering. His body was entirely emaciated and rib-ridden; his hands were like twisted claws, and his spindly legs too were twisted inwards. He looked as if he was ninety years old and near death. But his voice was clear and, when he saw them approach, he said, since he could see their forms only vaguely:

'Who? Who is that?'

'Rasheed,' said Rasheed loudly, knowing that the man was hard of hearing.

'Who?'

'Rasheed.'

'Oh, when did you come?'

'I've just come back from my wife's village.' Rasheed did not wish to say that he had been in Debaria for longer but had not visited until now.

The old man digested this, then said: 'Who is that with you?'

'This is a Babu from Brahmpur,' said Rasheed. 'He comes from a good family.'

Maan did not know what to think of this succinct biography, but reflected that 'Babu' was probably a term of respect in these parts.

The old man leaned forward slightly, then sank back with a sigh.

'How are things in Brahmpur?' he asked.

Rasheed nodded towards Maan.

'Very hot still,' said Maan, not knowing what was expected of him.

'Just turn towards that wall for a moment,' said Rasheed to Maan quietly.

Maan did so without asking why. He turned back, however, before he was told to do so, and caught a brief glimpse of the pretty and fair face of a woman dressed in a yellow sari who hurriedly disappeared behind a square pillar on the porch. In her arms was the child who had been sleeping on the charpoy. Later she joined the conversation from this improvised form of purdah. The little girl in red had dropped her dead crow somewhere and had gone to play with her mother and brother behind the pillar.

'That was his younger daughter,' said Rasheed to Maan.

'Very pretty,' said Maan. Rasheed silenced him with a sharp glance.

'Why don't you sit on the charpoy? Shoo the goat away,' said the woman hospitably.

'All right,' said Rasheed.

From where they were now sitting it was more difficult for Maan to avoid casting a furtive look at her every so often. He did so whenever he was sure Rasheed was not looking. Poor Maan, he had been deprived so long of female company that he felt his heart leap and thud every time he caught the slightest glimpse of her face.

'How is he?' Rasheed asked the woman.

'You can see. The worst is to come. The doctors refuse to treat him. My husband says we should make him comfortable, try to give him what he asks for, that's the extent of it.' She had a happy voice and a lively manner of speech.

They discussed him for a while as if he weren't present.

Then the old man suddenly roused himself to speak. 'Babu!' he said in a loud voice.

Rasheed nodded at Maan again.

'Yes?' said Maan, probably too softly for the man to hear.

'What can I tell you, Babu—I've been ill for twenty-two years—and bedridden for twelve. I am so crippled I can't even sit up. I wish God would take me. I had six children and six daughters too'—Maan was struck by his manner of describing his twelve children—'and only two are left. My wife died three years ago. Never get ill, Babu. It is the worst fate. I eat here, I sleep here, I wash here, I talk here, I pray here, I weep here, I shit and piss here. Why did God do this to me?'

Maan looked at Rasheed. He looked stricken.

'Rasheed!' cried the old man.

'Yes, Phupha-jaan.'

'Her mother'—the old man indicated his daughter with his head—'took care of your father when he was ill. Now he doesn't even visit. It's since your stepmother came. Previously, every time I went past their house—ah, twelve years ago—they insisted that I had to have tea. They visited when I fell ill. Now only you do. I hear Vilayat Sahib was here too. He didn't visit.'

'Vilayat Sahib never visits anyone, Phupha-jaan.'

'What's that you say?'

'Vilayat Sahib never visits anyone.'

'Yes. But your father? Don't take it badly. I'm not criticizing.'

'No, no,' said Rasheed. 'I know. It's not right. I don't say it's right.' He shook his head slowly and looked down. Then he went on: 'I don't take it badly. It's best to say what one thinks. I'm sorry that this is so. But I must listen to it. It's only right.'

'You must visit again before you go back. . . . How do you manage in Brahmpur?'

'I manage very well,' said Rasheed, reassuringly if not accurately. 'I give tuitions, and that covers things comfortably. I am in good shape. I've brought a small gift for you—some sweets.'

'Sweets?'

'Yes. I'll give them to her.'

To the woman Rasheed said: 'They are easy to digest, but don't give him more than one or two at a time.' To the old man he said: 'I must go now, Phupha-jaan.'

'You are a good man.'

'It's easy to earn that title in Sagal,' said Rasheed.

The old man chuckled a little. 'Yes,' he said, finally.

Rasheed got up to go, and Maan followed.

The old man's daughter, with a tender formality in her voice, said: 'What you have done restores our faith in people.'

But as they left the courtyard, Maan heard Rasheed say to himself:

'And what the good people have done to you makes me doubt my faith in God.'

10.15

On the way out of the village of Sagal, they passed a small open area in front of the mosque. Here, standing and talking, was a group of about ten village elders, most of them bearded, including the man who had passed them outside the old man's house. Rasheed recognized two more of the invalid's brothers among the group, but could not see their expressions in the late twilight. They appeared, however, to be looking at him, and their stance was hostile. As he drew nearer, he saw that their expression was no less so. For a few seconds they looked him up and down. Maan, still in his white shirt and trousers, also came under their scrutiny.

'So you've come,' said one in a slightly mocking tone.

'Yes,' said Rasheed, without any warmth, and not even using the customary title of the man who spoke.

'You've taken your time.'

'Well,' said Rasheed, 'some things take time.'

'So you sat talking and exchanging the time of day until it became too late to say the namaaz,' said another, the man who had passed by him a little while ago.

This was indeed true; so involved had Rasheed been that he had not even noticed the evening call to prayer.

'Yes,' he responded angrily. 'That's precisely right.'

He was enraged that he was being baited in this open gathering, not out of any attempt to improve his attendance at prayer but out of sheer mockery and ill will. They're jealous, he thought, because I'm young and have made progress. And they're threatened by my beliefs—they've decided that I'm a communist. And what they hate most of all is my association with that man whose life makes their own a source of shame.

A tall, thickset man glowered at Rasheed. 'And who is this?' he asked, indicating Maan. 'Are you not going to do us the favour of an introduction? Then we will be able to judge what company the Maulana Sahib keeps and benefit from it too.' The orange kurta that Maan had been wearing when he first arrived had given rise to the rumour that he was a Hindu holy man.

'I don't think that is necessary,' said Rasheed. 'He is my friend, that is all. Like should be introduced to like.'

Maan ventured to come forward to stand with Rasheed, but Rasheed with a gesture kept him out of the main line of fire.

'Do you propose to attend the dawn prayer at the mosque at Debaria tomorrow, Maulana Sahib? We understand that you are a late riser and it may involve some sacrifice,' said the thickset man to Rasheed.

'I will attend what prayers I choose to,' said Rasheed hotly.

'So, Maulana Sahib, this is your style,' said someone else.

'Look—' said Rasheed, almost beside himself with anger, 'if any of you want to talk about my style, come any time to my house and we'll talk about it, and we'll see whose style bests the other's. As for whose life is more decent and whose religious beliefs are deeper—society knows and can say. Why society? Even children know about the disreputable lives of many of the punctually pious.' He gestured towards the semicircle of bearded figures. 'If there was any justice, even the courts would ensure—'

'It is not for society or children or courts, but for Him to say,' cried one old man, shaking his finger in Rasheed's face.

'Well, that's a matter for opinion and argument,' retorted Rasheed.

'Iblis knew how to argue before his fall!'

'So did the good angels,' said Rasheed furiously. 'So do others.'

'Are you calling yourself an angel, Maulana Sahib?' sneered the man.

'Are you calling me Iblis?' cried Rasheed.

He suddenly realized that matters had gone far enough, had in fact gone too far. These were his elders, however insulting, reactionary, hypocritical, jealous. He also thought of Maan and how bad a scene like this would look to him—how unfavourable an impression it would convey of his religion.

Once again a pulsing pressure had begun building inside his head. He moved forward—his path had in effect been blocked—and a couple of men moved aside.

'It has become late,' said Rasheed. 'Excuse me. We must go. So, we'll meet again—and then we'll see.' He moved through the broken arc, and Maan followed.

'Perhaps you should say "khuda haafiz",' said a final sarcastic voice.

'Yes, khuda haafiz, God protect you too,' said Rasheed angrily, walking on without turning back.

10.16

Though Debaria and Sagal were separate villages about a mile apart geographically, they could have been a single village for the purposes of rumour. For whatever was said in one was repeated in the other. Whether it was someone from Sagal coming to Debaria to bring some grain to be parched, or someone from Debaria dropping by at the post office at Sagal or the schoolchildren going to study in the common madrasa, or someone visiting someone in the other village or happening to meet him in an adjoining field, the two villages were so indissolubly interlinked through networks of friendship and enmity, ancient ancestry and recent marriage, information and disinformation as to form one single intersecting web of gossip.

Sagal had almost no upper-caste Hindus. Debaria had a few brahmin families, and they too formed a part of this web, for their relations with the better Muslim families like Rasheed's were good, and they would drop by sometimes at each other's houses. They took pride in the fact that feuds within each of the two communities dominated any friction between the communities. This was not the case in some of the surrounding villages, especially where there were memories of violence against Muslims at the time of Partition.

The Football, as one of the brahmin landowners was popularly called, was in fact just on his way to pay a morning visit to Rasheed's father.

Maan was sitting on a charpoy outside the house, playing with Meher. Moazzam was hanging around; he was delighted with Meher, and from time to time passed his hand wonderingly over her head. Mr Biscuit hovered around hungrily.

Rasheed and his father were sitting on another charpoy, talking. A report of Rasheed's altercation with the elders of Sagal had reached his father.

'So you don't think namaaz is important?' he observed.

'It is, it is,' replied Rasheed. 'What can I say? I haven't observed it strictly these last few days—I've had unavoidable responsibilities and duties. And you can't roll out a prayer mat on a bus. Part of it is my own laziness. But if someone had wanted to correct me and explain things to me with sympathy, he would have taken me aside—or spoken to you, Abba—not damaged my honour in a full and open gathering.' He paused, then added with fervour: 'And I believe one's life is more important than any namaaz.'

'What do you mean by that?' said his father sharply. He noticed

Kachheru passing by. 'Ei, Kachheru, go to the bania's shop and get me some supari—I've run out of it for my paan. Yes, yes—I want the usual amount. . . . Ah, the Football is waddling along to pay us a visit; he's probably come because of your Hindu friend. Yes, people's lives are important, but that is no excuse—anyway, no excuse for speaking in that way to the big people of a village. Have you considered my honour when you behave like that? Or your own position in the village?'

Rasheed's eye followed Kachheru for a while. 'All right,' he said, 'please forgive me—the mistake is all mine.'

But ignoring his insincere apology, his father was now greeting his guest with a broad smile, his red mouth wide open: 'Welcome, welcome, Tiwariji.'

'Hello, hello,' said the Football. 'What were father and son discussing so heatedly?'

'Nothing,' said both father and son simultaneously.

'Oh, well. Two or three of us have been thinking of visiting you for some time now, but what with the harvest and so on we couldn't find the time. And then we heard that your guest had gone away for a few days, so we decided to wait till his return.'

'So you've really come to see Kapoor Sahib, not us,' said his host.

The Football shook his head vehemently: 'What are you saying, what are you saying, Khan Sahib? Our friendship goes back for decades. And one gets so little chance to talk to Rasheed either, now that he is improving his mind in Brahmpur most of the year.'

'Anyway,' continued Rasheed's father rather mischievously, 'why don't you have a cup of tea now that you've made such an effort to come. I'll summon Rasheed's friend, and we will talk. Who else is coming, by the way? Rasheed, ask for tea for all of us.'

The Football became agitated. 'No, no—' he said, gesticulating as if he were brushing away a swarm of wasps, 'no tea, no tea.'

'But we will all be having it together, Tiwariji, it is not poisoned. Even Kapoor Sahib will join us.'

'He drinks tea with all of you?' said Tiwari.

'Indeed. He eats with us too.'

The Football was silent while he, so to speak, digested this. After a while he said:

'But I have just had tea, you know, with my breakfast—I've just had tea and also far too much to eat before I left my house. Look at me. I must be careful. Your hospitality knows no bounds. But—'

'You aren't saying, by any chance, Tiwariji, are you, that what we are offering falls below your expectations? Why don't you like to eat with us? Do you think we will pollute you?'

'Oh, no, no, no, it is just that an insect of the gutter like myself does not feel happy when offered the luxuries of a palace. Heh heh heh!' The Football wobbled a little at his witticism, and even Rasheed's father smiled. He decided not to press the point. All of the other brahmins were straightforward about their caste rules, which forbade eating with non-brahmins, but the Football was always evasive.

Mr Biscuit approached their charpoy, attracted by tea and biscuits.

'Clear off, or I'll fry you in ghee,' Moazzam said, his hedgehog-hair bristling. 'He's a glutton,' he explained to Maan.

Mr Biscuit stared at them with a blank gaze.

Meher offered him one of her two biscuits, and he came forward like a zombie to ingest it.

Rasheed was pleased at Meher's generosity, but not at all pleased with Mr Biscuit.

'He does nothing but eat and shit, eat and shit the whole day,' he told Maan. 'That's his entire business in life. He's seven years old, and can hardly read a word. What can one do?—it's the atmosphere of the village. People think he's funny and encourage him.'

As if to prove his other skills, Mr Biscuit, having absorbed the offering, now put his hands to his ears and called out, in a mockery of the muezzin's call to prayer:

'Aaaaaaye Lalla e lalla alala! Halla o halla!'

Moazzam shouted: 'You low creature!' and made as if to slap him, but Maan restrained him.

Moazzam, once again fascinated by Maan's watch, said: 'Look: the two hands are coming together now.'

'Don't give Moazzam your watch,' advised Rasheed. 'I've warned you already. Or your torch. He likes to find out what makes them work, but he doesn't operate very scientifically. I once found him bashing my watch with a brick. He had taken it out of my bag when I wasn't looking. Luckily, the basic machinery still worked. But the glass, needle, spring—all were smashed. It cost me twenty rupees to have it repaired.'

But Moazzam was now counting and tickling Meher's toes—to her great delight. 'Sometimes he says the most interesting and even sensitive things,' said Rasheed. 'He is very puzzling. The trouble is that his parents spoiled him, and did not discipline him at all. Now he just follows his own inclinations. Sometimes he steals money from them or others and goes off into Salimpur. What he does there no one knows. Then he resurfaces after a few days. He's very intelligent, even affectionate. But he'll come to a bad end.'

Moazzam, who had overheard this, laughed and said, a little resentfully: 'I won't. It's you who will come to a bad end. Eight, nine, ten; ten, nine, eight—keep still—seven, six. Give me that charm—you've played with it long enough.'

Noticing a couple of other visitors approaching in the distance, he handed Meher to her great-grandfather, who had emerged from the house, and wandered off to investigate and—if necessary—challenge them.

'Quite a mischievous kid,' said Maan.

'Mischievous?' said Baba. 'He's a rogue—a thief—at the age of twelve!'

Maan smiled.

'He broke the fan of that bicycle-operated winnowing machine there. He's not mischievous, he's a hooligan,' continued Baba, rocking Meher to and fro, very vigorously for an old man.

'Now he's so big,' continued Baba, throwing a dirty look in Moazzam's direction, 'that he has to have fancy food. So he steals—from people's pockets. Every day he steals rice, daal, whatever he can, from his own house and sells it at the bania's shop. Then he's off to Salimpur to eat grapes and pomegranates!'

Maan laughed.

Suddenly Baba thought of something. 'Rasheed!' he said.

'Yes, Baba?'

'Where's that other daughter of yours?'

'Inside, Baba, with her mother. I think she's feeding.'

'She's a weakling. Hardly seems to be a child of my stock. She should be given buffalo's milk to drink. When she smiles she looks like an old woman.'

'Many children do, Baba,' said Rasheed.

'Now this is a healthy child. See how her cheeks glow.'

Two men—also brahmins from the village—now approached the open courtyard, preceded by Moazzam and followed by Kachheru. Baba went forward to greet them, and Rasheed and Maan moved their own charpoy closer to the end of the courtyard where Rasheed's father was sitting with the Football. It was becoming a conference.

To add to the numbers, Netaji also appeared shortly from the direction of Sagal. Qamar, the sardonic schoolteacher who had made a very brief appearance at the shop in Salimpur, was with him. They had just been visiting the madrasa to talk with the teachers.

10.17

Everyone greeted everyone else, though with varying degrees of enthusiasm. Qamar was not delighted to see such an accumulation of brahmins, and greeted them in the most perfunctory manner—although the recent arrivals, Bajpai (complete with his sandalwood-paste caste-mark) and his son Kishor Babu, were very good people. They for their part were not happy to see their fellow-brahmin, the Football, who was a mischief-maker and liked nothing better than to set people off against each other.

Kishor Babu was a shy and gentle soul. He told Maan that he was very pleased to make his acquaintance at last, and took both his hands in his own. After that he tried to pick up Meher, who, however, would not let him and ran off to sit on her grandfather's lap while he examined the betel nuts that Kachheru had brought. Netaji went across the way to fetch another charpoy.

Bajpai had caught hold of Maan's right hand and was examining it carefully. 'One wife. Some wealth,' he said. 'As for the line of wisdom. . . .'

'. . . it seems not to exist.' Maan finished the sentence for him and smiled.

'The line of life is not very favourable,' said Bajpai encouragingly.

Maan laughed.

Qamar meanwhile was looking disgusted at this whole exercise. Here was another example of the pitiful superstition of the Hindus.

Bajpai continued: 'You were four children, only three remain.'

Maan stopped laughing, and his hand tensed.

'Am I right?' said Bajpai.

'Yes,' said Maan.

'Which one passed away?' asked Bajpai, looking at Maan's face intently and kindly.

'No,' said Maan, 'that's what you have to tell me.'

'I believe it was the youngest.'

Maan was relieved. 'I am the youngest,' he said. 'It was the third who died when he was less than a year old.'

'All bogus, all bogus,' said Qamar, with a look of contempt. He was a man of principle and could not abide charlatanism.

'You should not say so, Master Sahib,' said Kishor Babu mildly. 'It is quite scientific. Palmistry—and astrology too. Otherwise why would the stars be where they are?'

'Everything is scientific for you,' said Qamar. 'Even the caste system. Even worshipping the linga and other disgusting things. And singing bhajans to that adulterer, that teaser of women, that thief Krishna.'

If Qamar was spoiling for a quarrel, he did not get what he wanted. Maan looked at him in surprise but did not interfere. He too was interested in what Bajpai and Kishor Babu would say. As for the Football, his small eyes darted swiftly from one side to another.

Kishor Babu now spoke in a slow and considered voice: 'You see, Qamar Bhai, it is like this. It is not these images that we worship. They are only points of concentration. Now tell me, why do you turn towards Mecca when you pray? No one would say that you are worshipping the stone. And with Lord Krishna, we do not think of him in those terms. For us he is the incarnation of Vishnu himself. Why, even I am named after Lord Krishna in a way.'

Qamar snorted. 'Don't tell me,' he said, 'that the ordinary Hindus of Salimpur who do their puja every morning before their four-armed goddesses and their elephant-headed gods are using them as points of concentration. They are worshipping those idols, plain and simple.'

Kishor Babu sighed. 'Ah, the common people!' he said, in a manner that implied that this explained everything. He was a firm believer in the caste system.

Rasheed felt it necessary to intervene on the side of the Hindu minority. 'Anyway, people are good or bad according to what they do, not according to what they worship.'

'Really, Maulana Sahib?' said Qamar sourly. 'So it doesn't matter who or what you worship? What do you think about all this, Kapoor Sahib?' he continued provocatively.

Maan thought for a few seconds but said nothing. He looked over to where Meher and two of her friends were trying to put their arms around the corrugated bark of the neem tree.

'Or don't you have any views on the subject, Kapoor Sahib?' Qamar persisted. Being from outside the village, he could be as abrasive as he wished.

Kishor Babu was now looking quite distressed. Neither Baba nor his sons had so far participated in the theological skirmish. Kishor Babu felt that as his hosts they ought to have intervened to prevent it from getting out of hand. He sensed that Maan did not care at all for Qamar's method of questioning, and feared that he might react strongly.

In the event, Maan did not. Still looking for the most part towards the neem tree and only occasionally glancing at Qamar, Maan said:

'I don't think about these matters. Life is complicated enough without them. But it is clear, Master Sahib, that if you think that I am evading your question, you are not going to give me or anyone else any peace. So I see that you are going to force me to be serious.'

'That is no bad thing,' said Qamar curtly. He had appraised Maan's character quickly and had come to the conclusion that he was a man of very little account.

'What I think is this,' said Maan in the same unusually measured manner as before. 'It is entirely a matter of chance that Kishor Babu was born in a Hindu family and you, Master Sahib, in a Muslim one. I have no doubt that if you had been exchanged after birth, or before birth, or even before conception, you would have been praising Krishanji and he, the Prophet. As for me, Master Sahib, being so little worthy of praise, I don't feel very much like praising anyone—let alone worshipping them.'

'What?' said the Football, rolling belligerently into the conversation and gathering momentum as he spoke: 'Not even holy men like Ramjap Baba? Not even the Holy Ganga at the full moon of the great Pul Mela? Not even the Vedas? Not even God himself?'

'Ah, God,' said Maan. 'God is a big subject—too big for the likes of me. I am sure that He is too big to be concerned about what I think of Him.'

'But don't you ever have the sense of His presence?' asked Kishor Babu, leaning forward in a concerned manner. 'Don't you ever feel that you are in communion with Him?'

'Now that you mention it,' said Maan, 'I feel in direct communion with Him just now. And He is telling me to halt this futile argument and drink my tea before it gets cold.'

Apart from the Football, Qamar and Rasheed, everyone smiled. Rasheed didn't enjoy what he saw as Maan's endemic flippancy. Qamar felt outmanoeuvred by a cheap and irrelevant trick, while the Football was foiled in his attempt to foment trouble. But social harmony had been re-established, and the gathering broke up into smaller groups.

Rasheed's father, the Football, and Bajpai began to discuss what would happen if the zamindari law came into force. It had now received the President's assent but its constitutionality was under challenge in the High Court in Brahmpur. Rasheed, who at present was uncomfortable with that subject, began to talk to Qamar about changes in the curriculum of the madrasa. Kishor Babu, Maan, and Netaji formed a third group—but since Kishor Babu insisted on gently questioning Maan about his views on non-violence while Netaji was eager to ask him about the wolf-hunt, the conversation was a curiously spliced one. Baba went off to amuse himself with his favourite great-granddaughter, whom Moazzam was taking for a piggyback ride from the cattle-shed to the pigeon-house and back.

Kachheru sat against the wall in the shade of the cattle-shed, thinking his own thoughts and looking indulgently at the children playing in the courtyard. He had not listened to any of the discussion. He was not interested. Though pleased to be of service, he was glad that he had not been asked to do anything by anyone for the time it had taken him to smoke two biris.

10.18

The days passed one by one. The heat increased. There was no more rain. The huge sky remained painfully blue for days on end. Once or twice a few clouds did appear over the unending patchwork of plains, but they were small and white, and soon drifted away.

Maan slowly got used to his exile. At first he fretted. The heat tormented him, the vast, flat, low-lying world of the fields disoriented him, and he was bored limp. Godforsaken in this godforsaken place, he was not where he wanted to be at all. He could not imagine he would ever adjust to it. The need for comfort and stimulus, he felt, was an upward-clicking ratchet. And yet, as the days went by, and things moved or did not move according to the volition of the sky or the circulation of the calendar or the wills of other people, he fell in with life around him. The thought struck him that perhaps his father's acceptance of imprisonment had been something like this—except that Maan's days were defined not by morning roll call and lights out, but by the muezzin's call to prayer and the cow-dust hour when the cattle returned lowing through the lanes.

Even his initial outrage against his father had waned; it was too much of an effort being angry for long, and besides, during his stay in the countryside, he had begun to appreciate and even admire the scope of his father's efforts—not that it aroused in him any spirit of emulation.

Being a bit of a layabout, he lay about a bit. Like the lion that the village children had dubbed him when he first arrived, he spent very few hours in active labour, yawned a great deal, and even appeared to luxuriate in his dissatisfied dormancy, which he interrupted off and on by a roar or two and a mild bout of activity—perhaps a swim in the lake by the school, or a walk to a mango grove—for it was the mango season, and Maan was fond of mangoes. Sometimes he lay on his charpoy and read one of the thrillers lent to him by Sandeep Lahiri. Sometimes he looked over his Urdu books. Despite his not very energetic efforts, he was now able to read clearly printed Urdu; and one day Netaji lent him a slim selection of the most famous ghazals of Mir, which, since he knew large parts of them by heart, did not prove too difficult for Maan.

What did people do in the village, anyway? he asked himself. They waited; they sat and talked and cooked and ate and drank and slept. They woke up and went into the fields with their brass pots of water. Perhaps, thought Maan, everyone is essentially a Mr Biscuit. Sometimes they looked upwards at the rainless sky. The sun rose higher, reached its height, sank, and set. After dark, when life used to begin for him in Brahmpur, there was nothing to do. Someone visited; someone left. Things grew. People sat around and argued about this and that and waited for the monsoon.

Maan too sat around and talked, since people enjoyed talking to him. He sat on his charpoy and discussed people, problems, mahua trees, the state of the world, everything and anything. He never doubted that he would be liked or trusted; since he was not suspicious by nature, he did not imagine that others would be suspicious of him. But as an outsider, as a city dweller, as a Hindu, as the son of a politician—and the Minister of Revenue at that—he was open to all kinds of suspicions and rumours—not all of them as fantastic as the one triggered off by his orange kurta. Some people thought that he was staking out the constituency that his father had chosen to fight from in the coming elections, others that he had decided to settle permanently here, having found that city life was not for him, yet others that he was lying low to avoid creditors. But after a while they got used to Maan, saw no harm in his lack of evident purpose, found his opinions pleasantly and humorously unaggressive, and liked the fact that he liked them. As 'lion, lion, without a tail' bathing under the hand-pump, as Maan Chacha dandling a wailing baby, as the source of intriguing objects like a watch and a torch, as the absorbed and incompetent calligrapher who used the wrong Urdu 'Z' in his spelling of simple words, he was fairly quickly accepted and trusted by the children; and the trust and acceptance of their parents followed soon enough. If Maan regretted that he only ever saw the men, he had enough sense not to mention it. Meanwhile he kept out of village feuds and discussions of zamindari or religion. His handling of Qamar and the Football on the subject of God was soon common knowledge throughout the village. Almost everyone approved. Rasheed's family grew to enjoy his company. He even became something of an open-air confessional for them.

The days stretched by, hardly differentiated one from another. When the postman came to the house, he usually greeted Maan's expectant expression with a rueful one. Over the weeks he received two letters: one from Pran, one from his mother. He learned from Pran's letter that Savita was well, that his mother had not been too well, that Bhaskar sent his love and Veena her affectionate admonitions, that the Brahmpur Shoe Mart had woken up, that the English Department was still sound asleep, that Lata had gone to Calcutta, that Mrs Rupa Mehra had gone to Delhi. How distant those worlds appeared, he thought, like the occasional white clouds that fluffed themselves into existence and disappeared miles above him. His father, it seemed, was coming home as late as ever: he was now deep into consultations with the Advocate-General about the legal challenge to the Zamindari Act; he could not spare the time to write, or so his mother explained, but he had asked after Maan's health and about the farm. She insisted that she herself was in good health; occasional minor complaints that Pran might have unnecessarily mentioned she attributed to old age—Maan was not to worry about her. The late onset of the rains had affected the garden, but they were expected soon, and when everything was green again, Maan would be interested to notice two small innovations: a slight unevenness in the side lawn, and a bed of zinnias planted below his window.

Firoz too must be deeply involved in the zamindari case, thought Maan, excusing his friend's silence. As for the one silence that pounded most deeply in his ears, it had hurt him most of all in the days immediately following his own letter, when he could scarcely breathe without thinking of it. Now it too was a dull pain, mediated by the heat and the elastic days. Yet when he lay on the charpoy in the early evening light reading the poems of Mir, especially the one that reminded him of that first evening when he saw her in Prem Nivas, the memory of Saeeda Bai came back to Maan and pierced him with longing and bewilderment.

He could not talk to anyone about this. Rasheed's mildly Cassius-like smile when he saw him lost in tender contemplation of Mir would have turned to patent scorn if he had known whom he wished he were gazing at instead. The one time Rasheed had discussed love in general terms with Maan he had been as intense and definitive and theoretical about it as he was about everything else. It was clear to Maan that he had never experienced it. Maan was often exhausted by Rasheed's earnestness; in this particular case he wished he had never opened the subject.

Rasheed for his part was glad that he had Maan to talk to about his ideas and feelings, but he could not understand Maan's monumental directionlessness. Having got as far as he himself had from a background where higher education had seemed as unattainable as the stars, he believed that will and effort could get him anywhere. He attempted bravely, fervently, and perhaps obsessively, to reconcile everything—family life, learning, calligraphy, personal honour, order, ritual, God, agriculture, history, politics; this world and all the other worlds, in short—into a comprehensible whole. Exacting with himself, he was exacting with others. And it seemed to Maan, who was somewhat in awe of his energy and sense of principle, that he was wearing himself out by feeling so deeply and taking on so insistently all the burdens and responsibilities of mankind.

'By doing nothing—or worse than nothing—I've managed to displease my father,' said Maan to Rasheed as they sat talking under the neem one day. 'And by doing something—or better than something—you've managed to displease yours.'

Rasheed had added in a troubled tone that his father would be much more than displeased if he knew just what he had succeeded in doing. Maan had asked him to explain what he meant, but he had shaken his head, and Maan, though uneasy about the remark, had not followed it up. He was by now used to Rasheed's alternation of secretiveness with sudden, even intimate, confidences. As a matter of fact, when Maan had told him about the munshi and the old woman at Baitar Fort, Rasheed had been on the verge of unburdening himself about his own visit to the patwari. But something had stopped his tongue. After all, no one in this village, not even Kachheru himself, knew about that act of attempted justice; and it was best left so. Besides, the patwari had not been in the village for the past week or two, and Rasheed had not yet received the expected confirmation of his instructions.

Instead Rasheed had said: 'Did you get the woman's name? How do you know the munshi won't want to take his spite out on her?' Maan, shocked by the possible consequences of his own impracticality, had shaken his head.

A couple of times Rasheed did succeed in getting the reluctant Maan to discuss zamindari, but Maan's opinions were characteristically and vexatiously nebulous. He had reacted instinctively, indeed, violently, to suffering and cruelty, but he did not have much of an opinion on the general rights and wrongs of the system. He did not want the legislation on which his father had worked for years to be thrown out by the courts, but neither did he want Firoz and Imtiaz to lose the larger part of their family estate. To Rasheed's specific argument that the larger landlords did not work (or did not have to work) for their living, it was not to be expected that Maan would respond with proletarian indignation.

Rasheed had no qualms about speaking harshly about his own family and their treatment of those who served them. About the Nawab Sahib, though, whom Rasheed had met only once, he spoke no ill to Maan. He had known quite early, as a result of their train journey from Brahmpur, that Maan was a friend of the young Nawabzadas; and he did not wish either to make Maan uncomfortable or to remind himself of past humiliation by describing the treatment he had received when he had gone to Baitar House in search of employment some months ago.

10.19

One evening, when Maan was working on some exercises that Rasheed had set him before going off to the mosque, Rasheed's father interrupted him. He was carrying Meher, who was asleep, in his arms.

Without any preliminaries he said to Maan: 'Now that you're by yourself can I ask you a question? I've been wondering about it for some time.'

'Of course,' Maan replied, setting down his pen.

Rasheed's father sat down.

'Now, let me see,' he began, 'how do I put this? Not being married is considered by my religion and yours to be. . . .' He paused, searching for the word. He had sounded disapproving.

'Adharma? Against correct principles?' suggested Maan.

'Yes, call it adharma,' said Rasheed's father, relieved. 'Well, you're twenty-two, twenty-three. . . .'

'Older.'

'Older? That's bad. You should have got married by now. I believe that a man between the ages of seventeen and thirty-five is in the prime of his life.'

'Ah,' said Maan, nodding in wary agreement. Rasheed's grandfather had brought up the subject at the very beginning of his stay. No doubt Rasheed would be plaguing him next.

'Not that I noticed any falling off in my strength even when I was forty-five,' continued Rasheed's father.

'That's good,' said Maan. 'I know some people who are old at that age.'

'But then, you see,' continued Rasheed's father, 'then came the death of my son, and the death of my wife—and I fell apart.'

Maan remained silent. Kachheru arrived with a lantern, and placed it a little distance away.

Rasheed's father, who had intended to advise Maan, gently swerved off into his own memories: 'My elder son was a wonderful boy. In a hundred villages there was no one like him. He was strong as a lion and over six feet tall—a wrestler and a weight-lifter—he did English exercises. He would lift two maunds of iron easily. And he had a wonderful fresh face; and was always so good-natured and smiling—he greeted people with such great friendliness that he would make their hearts happy. And when he wore the suit I got made for him, he looked so good that people said he should be a Superintendent of Police.'

Maan shook his head sadly. Rasheed's father was telling his story without tears, but not coldly—as if he were recounting with sympathy the story of someone other than himself.

'Well, anyway,' he went on, 'after his accident at the railway station, I don't know what happened to me. I didn't leave the house for months. My strength drained away. I was unconscious for days. He was so young. And then a little later his mother died.'

He looked up towards the house, half-turning away from Maan, and continued:

'This house was ghostly. I don't know what would have happened to me. I was so full of grief and weakness that I wanted to die. There was no one in the house even to offer me water.' He closed his eyes. 'Where is Rasheed?' he asked somewhat coldly, turning back to Maan.

'At the mosque, I think.'

'Ah, yes, well, finally, Baba took me in hand and said I should pull myself together. Our religion says that the izzat, the honour of an unmarried man is half that of a married man. Baba insisted that I should get a second wife.'

'Well, he was speaking from experience,' said Maan with a smile.

'Yes. Well, Rasheed has told you no doubt that Baba had three wives. We two brothers and our sister are all from different wives. He didn't have three wives at the same time, mind you, just one wife at a time. "Marté gae, karté gae." When one died he married another. There's a tradition of remarriage in this family: my grandfather had four wives, my father three and I two.'

'Why not?'

'Why not, indeed,' said Rasheed's father, smiling. 'That's just what I thought eventually—once I'd got over my grief.'

'And was it difficult to find a wife?' asked Maan, intrigued.

'Not really,' said Rasheed's father. 'By the standards of this place we are well off. I was advised to get not a young woman but someone who had been married before—a widow or a woman who had been divorced. So I did get married again—it's been about a year now—to a woman who is fifteen years younger than me—that's not much. She's even related to my wife—of blessed memory—in a distant way. And she handles the house well. My health has improved again. I can walk unaided to my land two miles away. My eyesight is fine, except for seeing things up close. My heart is fine. My teeth, well, my teeth were past treatment anyway. One should be married. No question about it.'

A dog began to bark. Others joined in after a while. Maan tried to veer away from the subject by saying:

'Is she asleep? Can she sleep through all this?'

Rasheed's father looked lovingly down at his granddaughter: 'Yes, she's asleep. She's very fond of me.'

'I noticed that when you came from the fields with the umbrella today she ran after you in the heat.'

Rasheed's father nodded with pride.

'When I ask her if she wants to live in Debaria or Brahmpur she always says Debaria—"because you, Dada-jaan, are here." And once when I went to her mother's village, she left her Nana and ran after me.'

Maan smiled to think of this passionate competitiveness between the two grandfathers. He said: 'Presumably, Rasheed was with you.'

'Well, he may have been. But even if he hadn't been, she would have run after me.'

'In that case she must love you very much,' said Maan, laughing.

'Indeed she does. She was born in this house—which people later began to call ill-fated and inauspicious. But in those dark days she was like a gift of God to me. It was I who pretty much brought her up. In the morning, tea—tea and biscuits! "Dada-jaan", she'd say, "I want tea and biscuits. Cream biscuits"—none of this dry stuff. She'd tell Bittan, a maidservant here, to go and fetch her cream biscuits from my special tin. Her mother would be making the tea in a corner. And she wouldn't eat from her mother's hands. I had to feed her.'

'Well, luckily now there's another child in the house,' said Maan. 'To keep her company.'

'Doubtless,' said Rasheed's father. 'But Meher has decided that I belong to her alone. When she's told that I'm her sister's Dada too, she refuses to believe it.'

Meher shifted in her sleep.

'There has been no child like this in the whole family,' said Rasheed's father definitively.

'She seems to operate on that assumption,' agreed Maan.

Rasheed's father laughed, then continued: 'She has a right to do so. Oh, I remember, there used to be an old man in this village. He had fallen out with his sons, and had come to live with his daughter and son-in-law. Well, he had a pomegranate tree, which for some reason used to bear much better fruit than ours.'

'You have a pomegranate tree?'

'Oh yes, of course, inside. I'll show you some day.'

'How?'

'What do you mean, how?' said Rasheed's father. 'It's my house. . . . Oh, I see what you mean. I'll shunt the women around as you go through. You're a good boy,' he said suddenly. 'Tell me, what do you do?'

'What do I do?'

'Yes.'

'Not much of anything.'

'That's very bad.'

'My father thinks so too,' agreed Maan.

'He's right. He's quite right. No young men want to work these days. It's either studies or staring at the sky.'

'Actually I do have a cloth business in Banaras.'

'Then what are you doing here?' said Rasheed's father. 'You should be making money.'

'Do you think I shouldn't be here?' asked Maan.

'No, no—of course, you are welcome,' said Rasheed's father. 'We are glad you are here as our guest. Though you have chosen a hot and boring time to come. You should visit at the time of Bakr-Id. Then you'll see the village at its most festive. Yes, do that—remember to. . . . Oh, yes, pomegranates. This old man was very lively, and he and Meher made a fine pair. She knew that whenever she went to his house she'd get something. So she was always forcing me to take her there. I remember the first time he gave her a pomegranate. It wasn't ripe. Still, we peeled it with great excitement, and she ate six or seven spoonfuls of the grains and we kept the rest for breakfast!'

An old man walked past. It was the Imam of the Debaria mosque.

'You will drop by tomorrow evening, won't you, Imam Sahib?' asked Rasheed's father in an anxious manner.

'At this time tomorrow—yes. After the prayer,' added the Imam in mild rebuke.

'I wonder where Rasheed is,' said Maan, looking at his unfinished exercises. 'He'll probably be returning any minute.'

'He is probably taking a walk around the village,' said his father in an outburst of quite virulent anger, 'talking to all the low people. That is his style. He should show more sense of discrimination. Tell me, has he taken you to the patwari with him?'

Maan was so taken aback by the tone that he hardly registered the question.

'The patwari. Have you visited the village patwari?' There was a touch of iron in the voice as the question was repeated.

'No,' said Maan, surprised. 'Is something the matter?'

'No,' said Rasheed's father. After a pause he said: 'Please don't mention that I asked you this.'

'If you like,' said Maan readily, but he was still puzzled.

'Well, I've done enough damage to your studies,' said Rasheed's father. 'I'd better not disturb you any further.' And he walked back to the house with Meher in his arms, frowning in the light of the lantern.

10.20

Maan, quite concerned now, fetched the lantern and tried to get back to reading and copying the words that Rasheed had written out for him. But

Rasheed's father was soon back, this time without Meher.

'What's a giggi?' he asked.

'A giggi?'

'You don't know what a giggi is?' The disappointment was palpable.

'No. What is it?' asked Maan.

'I don't know either,' said Rasheed's father in distress.

Maan looked at him, mystified.

'Why do you want to know?' he asked him.

'Oh,' said Rasheed's father. 'I need one—immediately.'

'If you don't know what it is, how do you know you need one?' said Maan.

'It's not for me but for Meher,' said Rasheed's father. 'She woke up and said, "Dada, I want a giggi. Give me a giggi." And now she's crying for it, and I can't find out from her what it is or what it looks like. I'll have to wait till—well, till Rasheed comes back. Maybe he knows. Sorry to have disturbed you again.'

'No, not at all,' said Maan, who hadn't minded this interruption. For a while he couldn't get back to his work. He tried to decide whether a giggi was to be eaten or to be played with or to be ridden on. Finally he picked up his pen again.

Baba, who had returned from the mosque, seeing him sitting by himself in the open courtyard, joined him a minute later. He greeted him, then coughed and spat on the ground.

'What is a young man like you doing wasting your eyes on a book?'

'Well, I'm learning to read and write Urdu.'

'Yes, yes. I remember: seen, sheen . . . seen, sheen. . . . Why bother?' said Baba, and cleared his throat again.

'Why bother?'

'Yes—tell me what is there in Urdu apart from a few sinful poems?'

'Now I've begun it, I should carry it through,' said Maan.

It was the right thing to say. Baba approved of this sentiment, then added: 'Now Arabic, you should learn Arabic. That's the language to learn. Then you can read the Holy Book. You might stop being a kafir.'

'Do you think so?' said Maan cheerfully.

'Oh, most assuredly,' said Baba. He added: 'You aren't taking what I've said badly?'

Maan smiled.

'One of my best friends is a thakur who lives a few villages away,' continued Baba reminiscently. 'In the summer of '47 around the time of Partition, a crowd gathered on the road to Salimpur in order to attack this village because of us Muslims. And Sagal too. I sent an urgent message to my friend, and he and his men went out with lathis and guns, and told the mob that they'd have to reckon with them first. And a good thing too. Otherwise, I'd have died fighting, but I'd have died all right.'

It suddenly struck Maan that he had become a universal confidant.

'Rasheed said that you were the terror of the tehsil,' he told Baba.

Baba nodded his head in vigorous approval. He said emphatically: 'I was strict with people. I turned him'—he pointed in the direction of the roof—'out of the house, naked in the fields, at the age of seven because he would not study.'

Maan tried to imagine what Rasheed's father might have been like as a boy, with a book instead of a paan-pouch in his hand. But Baba was continuing:

'In the time of the English, there was honesty. The government was firm. How can you govern unless you are firm? Now, when the police catch some criminal, the Ministers and MPs and MLAs say, "He's my friend: release him!" And they do.'

'That's too bad,' said Maan.

'The police used to take little bribes then, now they are big ones,' said Baba. 'And the day will come when they will take huge ones. There is no respect for the law. The whole world is being destroyed. These people are selling the country. And now they are trying to take away the land that our forefathers earned with their sweat and blood. Well, no one is going to take away a single bigha of my land, I can tell you that.'

'But if it's the law—' said Maan, thinking of his father.

'Now, you're a sober young man,' said Baba. 'You don't drink or smoke and you are law-abiding and respect our customs. But tell me, if they made a law that you should not pray to Mecca but to Calcutta instead, would you obey it?'

Maan shook his head, trying not to smile at the thought of either eventuality.

'It's the same thing,' said Baba. 'Now Rasheed tells me that your father is a great friend of the Nawab Sahib, who is well respected in this district. What does the Nawab Sahib think of this attempt to grab his land?'

'He does not like it,' said Maan. He had learned by now to state the obvious as blandly as he could.

'And nor would you. I can tell you that things will get worse and worse. As it is, things have begun to fall apart. There's a family of low people in this village who have turned their mother and father out to starve. They eat well enough, but they've turned them out. Independence has come—and now the politicians want to finish the zamindars off—and the country has collapsed. In the old days if someone had done this—dared to turn his mother into a beggar—a mother who had fed him, cleaned him, clothed him—we would have beaten him until his bones and brains were set right. It was our responsibility. Now if we beat people up they'll immediately start a court case, they'll try to lock us up in the police station.'

'Can't you talk to them, convince them?' asked Maan.

Baba shrugged impatiently. 'Of course—but bad characters are improved less by explanations than by the lathi.'

'You must have been a very severe disciplinarian,' said Maan, quite pleased at the traits he would have found intolerable in his own father.

'Oh yes,' agreed Rasheed's grandfather. 'Discipline is the key. You have to work hard at everything you do. You, for instance, should be studying, not wasting your time talking to an old man like me. . . . Tell me, did your father want you to come here?'

'Yes.'

'Why?'

'Well, to learn Urdu—and I suppose to gain some experience of the villages,' improvised Maan.

'Good . . . good. Well, tell him this is a good constituency. He has a good reputation among our community. . . . To study Urdu? Yes, we must protect it . . . it's our heritage. . . . You know, you would make a good politician yourself. You kicked the Football through the goalposts very smoothly. Of course, if you join politics from this place, Netaji would probably assassinate you. . . . Oh, well . . . well, carry on, carry on. . . .'

And he got up and started walking towards his house.

A thought struck Maan.

'You wouldn't happen to know what a giggi is, Baba?' he asked.

Baba stopped. 'A giggi?'

'Yes.'

'No. I've never heard of such a thing. Are you sure you're reading it right?' He walked back and picked up Maan's exercise book. 'I don't have my glasses.'

'Oh, it's Meher who's demanding a giggi,' said Maan.

'But what is it?' asked Baba.

'That's the problem,' said Maan. 'She woke up and wanted a giggi from her grandfather. It must have been part of a dream. No one in the house knows what it means.'

'Hmm,' said Baba, considering the crisis. 'Perhaps I'd better go and help.' He changed his direction and went towards his son's house. 'I am the only one who really understands her.'

10.21

Maan's next visitor was Netaji. It was now quite dark. Netaji, who had been away on mysterious business for some days, wanted to ask Maan about many things: the SDO, the Nawab Sahib's estate at Baitar, the wolf-hunt, and love. But he could see that Maan was quite busy with his Urdu, and decided on love. After all, he had lent Maan the ghazals of Mir.

'Is it all right to sit here?' he asked.

'Fine,' said Maan. He looked up. 'How are things?'

'Oh, all right,' said Netaji. He had by now almost entirely forgiven Maan for his humiliation at the railway station because a number of grander humiliations and successes had occurred since then, and on the whole he was making progress in his plans for world conquest.

'You don't mind me asking you a question?' said Netaji.

'No,' said Maan, 'any question except that one.'

Netaji smiled, and proceeded. 'Tell me, have you ever been in love?'

Maan pretended to be annoyed in order to avoid the question. 'What kind of question is that?' he asked.

Netaji was apologetic. 'You see—I thought life in Brahmpur—in a modern family—' he began.

'So that's what you think of us—' said Maan.

Netaji retreated quickly: 'No, no, I don't—and anyway, why should I mind what your answer is? I only asked out of curiosity.'

'Well, if you've asked such a question,' said Maan, 'you must be prepared to answer it yourself. Have *you* ever been in love?'

Netaji was not at all unwilling to answer. He had given the matter a lot of thought of late. 'Our marriages, you see, are all arranged,' he said to Maan. 'It's always been so. If I had it my way, I'd do it differently. But what's done is done. I'm sure I would have fallen in love otherwise. But now it would only confuse me. How about you?'

'Look, here comes Rasheed,' said Maan. 'Should we ask him to join our discussion?'

Netaji took his leave hurriedly. He had to preserve his nominal position of superiority as Rasheed's uncle. As Rasheed approached, he gave him a peculiar look, and disappeared.

'Who was that?' said Rasheed.

'Netaji. He wanted to talk to me about love.'

Rasheed made an impatient sound.

'Where were you?' said Maan to Rasheed.

'At the bania's shop, talking to a few people—trying to undo some of that ancient Sagal damage.'

'What is there to undo?' said Maan. 'You were very fiery. I was full of admiration. But it seems that for some reason your father is very annoyed with you.'

'There's a great deal to undo,' said Rasheed. 'The latest version of that incident is that I came to blows with the good elders and claimed that the Imam of the Sagal mosque was an incarnation of Satan. I also have a plan to set up a commune on the lands of the madrasa—once I have persuaded you to persuade your father to somehow take it over. But people—at least in Debaria—seem to doubt this part of the story.' Rasheed laughed shortly. 'You have made quite a good impression in the village. Everyone likes you; it amazes me.'

'Looks like you're in trouble, though,' said Maan.

'Perhaps. Perhaps not. How can one argue with ignorance? People know nothing and want to know nothing.'

'Tell me,' said Maan, 'do you know what a giggi is?'

'No,' said Rasheed, frowning.

'Then you're really in worse trouble than you imagine,' said Maan.

'I am?' asked Rasheed, and for a second he looked genuinely worried. 'By the way, how are your exercises going?'

'Tremendously well,' said Maan. 'I've been working on them ever since you left.'

No sooner had Rasheed gone indoors than the postman dropped by on his way home, and handed Maan a letter.

He exchanged a few words with Maan; Maan responded without knowing what he said. He was dazed.

The envelope, a very pale yellow, seemed to be as cool and gentle as moonlight. The Urdu script was fluid, even careless. The postmark said 'Pasand Bagh P.O., Brahmpur'. She had written to him after all.

Desire made him weak as he held the envelope to the light of the lantern. He had to get back to her—at once—no matter what his father—or anyone—said. Whether his exile was officially over made no difference at all.

When he was alone again, Maan opened the envelope. The faint fragrance of her familiar perfume mingled with the night air. He saw immediately that to read this letter—with its almost evasive cursiveness, its casually sprinkled diacritical marks, its compressions—would be far beyond his own rudimentary ability in Urdu. He pieced together the salutation to Dagh Sahib, made out from the physical appearance of the letter that it was laced with poetic couplets, but for the moment could get no further.

If there was no aloneness here in the village, Maan reflected with frustration, there was no privacy either. If Rasheed's father or grandfather were to pass by and his letter happened to be lying open, they would pick it up quite unselfconsciously and read it. And yet to comprehend even part of it, he himself would have to look at it for hours and try to piece it together glyph by glyph.

Maan did not want to have to pore over it for hours. He wanted to know immediately what Saeeda Bai had written to him. But whom should he ask for help? Rasheed? No. Netaji? No. Who would serve as his interpreter?

What had she written? In his mind's eye he saw her right hand with its brilliant rings move from right to left over the pale yellow page. As he did so, he heard a descending scale on the harmonium. He realized with a start that he had never seen her writing anything. The touch of her hands on his face—the touch of her hands on the keyboard—these needed such little conscious interpretation. But here her hands had moved across the page in a pattern of speed and grace, and he had no inkling what it meant of love or indifference, seriousness or playfulness, pleasure or anger, desire or calm.

10.22

Rasheed was indeed in worse trouble than he imagined, but it was the next evening that he found out about it.

When, after an almost sleepless night, Maan had asked him that morning for help with Saeeda Bai's letter, Rasheed had gazed thoughtfully at the envelope for a moment, looked uncomfortable (probably with embarrassment at the request, thought Maan), and, to his great surprise, agreed.

'After dinner,' he had suggested.

Though dinner seemed months away, Maan had nodded gratefully.

But the crisis broke immediately after the evening prayer. Rasheed was summoned to meet five men gathered upstairs on the roof: his grandfather; his father; Netaji; his mother's brother who had arrived that afternoon without his friend the guppi; and the Imam of the mosque.

They were all seated on a large rug in the middle of the roof. Rasheed made his adaabs.

'Sit down, Rasheed,' said his father. No one else said anything beyond responding to the salutations.

Only the Bear appeared to be genuinely welcoming, though he looked profoundly uncomfortable. 'Have a glass of this sherbet, Rasheed,' he said after a while, handing him a glass with a red liquid inside. 'It's made from rhododendrons,' he explained. 'Excellent stuff. When I visited the hills last month. . . .' He tapered off into silence.

'What is this about?' asked Rasheed, looking first at the awkward Bear, then at the Imam. The Imam of the Debaria mosque was a good man, the senior member of the other big landowning family in the village. He usually greeted Rasheed in a warm manner, but Rasheed had noticed a distance in the last couple of days. Perhaps the Sagal incident had upset him as well—or perhaps the rumours that were proliferating had confused one Imam with another. Anyway, whatever his own theological or social errors, it was humiliating to be required to answer charges of rudeness to what looked like an accusatorial committee. And why had the Bear been called to join them from a considerable distance away? Rasheed sipped his sherbet and looked at the others. His father seemed disgusted, his grandfather stern. Netaji was trying to look judicious; he succeeded in looking complacent.

It was Rasheed's father who spoke in his paan-rough voice.

'Abdur Rasheed, how dare you abuse your position as my son and as a member of this family? The patwari came here looking for you two days ago. When he could not find you, he spoke to me, thank God.'

Rasheed's face went white.

He could not speak a word. It was all too clear what had happened. The wretched patwari, who knew perfectly well that it was Rasheed who was supposed to visit him, had decided to find an excuse to talk directly to his family. Suspicious and worried about his instructions, and knowing where the ghee on his roti came from, he had decided to bypass Rasheed himself to seek confirmation. Doubtless he had come during afternoon prayers, when he could be fairly certain that Rasheed would be at the mosque, and completely certain that his father would not.

Rasheed clutched his glass. His lips felt dry. He took a sip of sherbet. This action appeared to infuriate his father further. He pointed his finger at Rasheed's head.

'Don't be impertinent. Answer me. Your hair looks wiser than the mulch it is growing on, but—and keep this well in mind, Rasheed—you are not a child any longer and cannot expect a child's indulgence.'

Baba added: 'Rasheed, this land is not yours to give or take. The patwari has been told to undo your disgraceful instructions. How could you do this? I have trusted you since you were a child. You were never obedient, but you were never underhanded.'

Rasheed's father said: 'In case you are inclined to create further mischief you should know that your name is no longer attached to those lands. And what a patwari writes is difficult for the Supreme Court to undo. Your communist schemes will not work here. We are not so easily taken in by theories and visions as the brilliant students of Brahmpur.'

Rasheed's eyes flashed with anger and resistance. 'You cannot dispossess me like that,' he said. 'The law of our community is clear—' He turned to the Imam, appealing for confirmation.

'I see you have made good use of your years of religious study as well,' said his father bitingly. 'Well, I would advise you, Abdur Rasheed, since you are referring to the law of inheritance, to wait until the auspicious moment when my father and I are both resting in peace near the lake before you avail yourself of it.'

The Imam looked profoundly shocked, and decided to intervene. 'Rasheed,' he said quietly, 'what induced you to go behind your family's back? You know that good order depends on the decent families of the village acting properly.'

Properly! thought Rasheed—what a joke, what a hypocritical joke. It was proper, no doubt, to tear virtual serfs away from the plots they had tilled for years in order to safeguard one's own self-interest. It was becoming increasingly clear that the Imam was present only partly in his capacity as spiritual adviser.

And the Bear? What did he have to do with all this? Rasheed turned his eyes towards him, wordlessly pleading for his support. Surely the Bear must understand and sympathize with his intentions. But the Bear could not hold his gaze.

Rasheed's father read his thoughts. Baring the remnants of his teeth he said: 'Don't look towards your Mamu for encouragement. You cannot go running to him to find shelter any longer. We have discussed the matter thoroughly together—as a family—as a family, Abdur Rasheed. That is why he is here. And he has every right to be involved in this, and to be shocked by your—your behaviour. Some of our land was bought with his sister's dowry. Do you think we will give up so easily what we have worked to develop, to cultivate, to expand for generations? Do you think we don't have enough trouble with the late rains this season to wish a plague of locusts upon our heads as well? If you give one plot of land to one chamar—'

The baby started wailing downstairs. Rasheed's father got up, leaned over the parapet into the courtyard and called out:

'Meher's mother! Can't you stop that child of Rasheed's from making such a racket? Can men not talk together without being disturbed?'

He turned back to say: 'Remember this, Rasheed: our patience is not unending.'

Rasheed, suddenly furious, and hardly thinking of his words, burst out: 'And do you think mine is? Ever since I have come to the village, I have received nothing but taunts and envy. That destitute old man, who was good to you, Abba, in the old days, and whom you now ignore—'

'Don't try to stray from the subject,' said his father sharply. 'Keep your voice low.'

'I am not straying—it is his evil and grasping brothers who waylaid me at their mosque and are now spreading these vile rumours—'

'You see yourself in a very heroic light—'

'If there was justice, they would be dragged to the court in chains and made to expiate their crimes.'

'Courts, now, so you want to bring courts into this, Abdur Rasheed—'

'Yes, I do, if there is no other way. And it will eventually be the courts who will make you too disgorge what for generations you have—'

'Enough!' Baba's voice broke in like a whiplash.

But Rasheed hardly heard him.

'Courts, Abba—' he cried, 'you are complaining about the courts? What do you think this is? This panchayat, this inquisitorial committee of five where you feel you can insult me freely—'

'Enough!' said Baba. He had never before had to raise his voice with Rasheed a second time.

Rasheed was quiet and bowed his head.

Netaji said: 'Rasheed, you must not see us as a court. We are your seniors, your well-wishers, who have gathered together in the absence of strangers to advise you.'

Rasheed kept a tight rein on himself and managed not to say anything. From below the baby began to cry again.

Rasheed got up before his father could, and called towards the courtyard: 'Wife! Wife! See that the child is comfortable.'

'Have you considered them in this matter?' asked his father, indicating with his head towards the courtyard.

Rasheed stared wildly.

'And have you considered Kachheru himself?' added Baba grimly.

'Kachheru—?' said Rasheed. 'He doesn't know about this, Baba. He doesn't know anything about this at all. He didn't ask me to do anything.' He held his hands to his head. Again an intolerable pressure had begun to pound at his temples.

Baba sighed, then, looking above Rasheed's head in the direction of the village, said: 'Well, this affair is bound to get out. That is the problem. There are five of us here. Six. We may all promise not to speak a word, but the word will get spoken somehow. Of course, we understand from our guest, your friend, that you have not involved him in all this, which is good—'

'Maan?' said Rasheed, disbelievingly. 'You've been talking to Maan?'

'—but there is also the patwari, who will hide or reveal whatever suits his convenience. He is a sly man.' Baba paused to consider his next words. 'It will get out, and plenty of people will believe Kachheru put you up to this. We have to set an example. I am afraid you have not made things easier for him.'

'Baba—' protested Rasheed.

But his father cut in, his voice thick with rage: 'You should have thought of all this before. What would have happened to him at worst? We would have rotated him from field to field. He would still have the support of our family, he would still be able to use our cattle and our tools—it is you, it is you who have harmed my old chamar.'

Rasheed covered his face with his hands. The Bear said:

'Well, nothing has yet been decided finally, of course.'

'No,' agreed Baba after a pause. Rasheed was sighing deeply, his chest moving up and down.

Rasheed's father said: 'Instead of being censorious about other people's behaviour, I hope this experience will make you examine your own. We have heard from you no word of apology so far, no admission of wrongdoing. Believe me, if it had not been for your Mamu and the Imam Sahib here, we would not have been so lenient with you. You can still continue to live here whenever you wish. Some land may still be restored to your name in time, depending on whether you show yourself to be worthy of it. But rest assured, if you close the door of trust on this house, the doors of this house will be closed to you. I am not afraid of losing a son. I have lost one already. Now go downstairs. See to your wife and child—children. We have the matter of Kachheru to discuss.'

Rasheed looked around the circle of faces. He saw sympathy in some, but support in none.

He got up, said a low 'Khuda haafiz', and walked down the stairs into the courtyard. For a while he looked at the pomegranate tree, then he went inside. The baby and Meher were asleep. His wife looked deeply worried. He told her he would not be having supper. In a daze he walked out of the house.

Maan, when he saw Rasheed emerge, smiled with relief. 'I heard sounds of people talking, and thought you were never coming down,' he said. He brought out Saeeda Bai's letter from the pocket of his kurta.

For a second, Rasheed thought of unburdening himself to Maan, even of seeking his help. This was the son of the very author of the act that aimed to do justice. But then he turned abruptly away.

'But this—' said Maan, waving the envelope.

'Later, later,' said Rasheed dully, and began to walk away from the house in a northerly direction.

Part Eleven

11.1

At the stroke of ten, from behind the dull scarlet velvet hangings to the right of Courtroom Number One of the High Court of Judicature at Brahmpur, the five white-turbaned, red-liveried, gold-braided ushers of the judges emerged. Everyone rose to his feet. The ushers stood behind the tall-backed chairs of their respective judges and, at a nod from the Chief Justice's usher—who looked even more magnificent than the others owing to the insignia of crossed maces on his chest—pulled them back to give the judges room.

All eyes in the packed courtroom had followed the ushers as they moved towards the bench in what was almost a procession. Normal cases required a single judge or a bench of two, and cases of great importance and complexity might be assigned to three judges. But five judges implied a case of exceptional moment, and here were the heralds of the five in all their resplendent regalia.

And now the judges followed in their black gowns, a sad anticlimax to their ushers. They wore no wigs, and a couple of them appeared to shuffle slightly. They entered in order of seniority: the Chief Justice first, followed by the puisne judges whom he had assigned to this case. The Chief, a small, dry man with almost no hair on his head, stood before the central chair; to his right stood the next seniormost judge, a large, stooping man who fidgeted continually with his right hand; to the Chief's left stood the next seniormost judge of this bench, an Englishman who had served with the judicial service of the ICS and had stayed on after Independence; he was the only Englishman among the nine judges in the High Court at Brahmpur. Finally, at the wings, stood the two juniormost judges.

The Chief Justice did not look at the crowded courtroom—at the famous litigants, the eminent lawyers, the chattering public and the sceptical but excited journalists. He surveyed the table in front of him and his colleagues—the pads of paper, the lace-covered glasses of water laid out on the green baize. He then glanced cautiously to right and left as if checking the traffic on a busy highway, and began a judicious shuffle forward towards the table. As he did so, the other judges followed suit, and the ushers pushed the heavy chairs in, as it were, under the seat of justice.

The Nawab Sahib of Baitar was pleasantly impressed by the grandeur of it all. He recalled the only two other occasions when he had been in the High Court. Once he had gone as a litigant, when his own presence had been indispensable. The case—a property matter—had been up before a single judge. The other occasion was when he had decided to see his son practise. He had known that Firoz would be on his feet before a division bench one afternoon. Just before the case had begun to be argued, the Nawab Sahib had entered the uncrowded courtroom without any of his retainers, and had sat down directly behind Firoz, so that he would not be noticed unless Firoz turned completely around. He had not wished to make him nervous by indicating his presence, and, indeed, Firoz had had no inkling that day that his father was sitting behind him. He had argued well and the Nawab Sahib had been satisfied.

Today, of course, Firoz knew that his father was sitting directly behind him, for it was the constitutional validity of the Zamindari Abolition Act that was under challenge before the bench. If the courts decided for it, it would stand. If not, it would be as if it had never existed.

Two dozen or so writ petitions were to be considered jointly with the main one; these covered roughly the same ground but had a few points of difference. Some petitions were submitted by religious endowments, some by landlords who had been granted lands directly by crown grants, and some by ex-rulers—like the Raja of Marh—who believed that they would be protected by the treaty provisions of the Constitution, even if the lesser fry were fried. Firoz was one of the counsel for two such subsidiary petitions.

'May it please your Lordships—'

The Nawab Sahib's attention—which had wandered somewhat while the Court Reader was reciting the number of the case, the numbers of the main and connected writ petitions, the names of the parties, and the names of counsel appearing in the case—was drawn sharply back to the court. The great G.N. Bannerji was on his feet at the table in the front row that was closest to the aisle. Leaning his long, aged frame against a lectern on the table—upon which were lying both his brief and a small, red cloth-bound notebook—he repeated the opening phrase, then continued with deliberation, glancing up from time to time at the bench, particularly at the Chief Justice:

'May it please your Lordships, I am appearing in this case for all the applicants jointly. Your Lordships, needless to say, will appreciate the gravity of this case. It is probable that no case of similar significance for the people of this state has been fought in this court before, either under the emblem of the Ashoka lion or under the lion and unicorn.' Here G.N. Bannerji glanced slightly to the left of the bench before continuing. 'My Lords, the entire way of life of this state is sought to be altered by the executive of this state through legislation that runs in express and implied contradiction to the Constitution of the country. The act that seeks, in so striking and wholesale a manner, to alter the life of the citizenry of Purva Pradesh is the Purva Pradesh Zamindari Abolition and Land Reform Act of 1951, and it is my contention and that of other counsel for the applicants that this legislation, apart from being patently to the detriment of the people, is unconstitutional, and therefore null and void. Null and void.'

The Advocate-General of Purva Pradesh, the small, plump Mr Shastri, smiled nonchalantly to himself. He had appeared against G.N. Bannerji before. Bannerji liked to repeat significant phrases at the beginning and end of each paragraph of speech. Despite his commanding presence, he had rather a high voice—not unpleasant to listen to, however; more silvery than tinny—and these repetitions were like small shiny nails hammered in twice so that they would imbed themselves properly. This might have been a verbal quirk of his, not something he consciously attempted. But G.N. Bannerji did consciously believe in the value of repetition in general. He would take especial pains to phrase his propositions in three or four different ways which he would then introduce at different points of his argument so that, without insulting the intelligence of the judges, he could be assured that the seeds of his case would take root, even assuming that a few fell upon stony ground. 'It is all very well,' he told his juniors—who in this case included his bespectacled son and grandson—'it is all very well to state something once for our benefit or for the benefit of the other side. We've been steeped in this case for weeks. And Shastri and I have been well briefed by others. But for the bench we must follow the prime rule of advocacy: repeat, repeat, and repeat again. It is a great mistake to overestimate the judges' knowledge of the case even when they have read the affidavits of both sides. And it may even be a mistake to assume they have any detailed knowledge of the law. The Constitution, after all, is barely a year old—and at least one of the judges in this case probably has very little knowledge of what a Constitution is.'

G.N. Bannerji was referring (fairly politely for him) to the juniormost judge on the full bench trying this case, Mr Justice Maheshwari, who had come up through the district judiciary, and who, as it happened, did not possess great intelligence to counter-balance his lack of constitutional experience. G.N. Bannerji did not suffer fools gladly, and he considered Mr Justice Maheshwari, who, at fifty-five, was fifteen years his junior, to be a fool.

Firoz (who had been present for the conference of zamindars' lawyers in G.N. Bannerji's hotel room when the great lawyer had made this remark) had passed it on to the Nawab Sahib. It had not made the Nawab Sahib more optimistic about the result of the case. He had a sense very similar to that of his friend the Minister of Revenue on the other side: less hope of victory than dread of defeat. So much hung on this case that apprehension was the dominant emotion on both sides. The only ones who seemed to be fairly unconcerned—apart from the Raja of Marh, who could not believe in the violation of his inviolate lands—were the lawyers on both sides.

'Sixthly, my Lords,' continued G.N. Bannerji, 'the Zamindari Abolition Act cannot be said to have a public purpose in the strict, or should I say proper, sense of the word. This, my Lords, is a clear requirement of all acts that involve the public taking over of private property according to Article 31 Clause 2 of the Constitution. I shall return to this proposition in due course after I have stated the other grounds under which the impugned act is bad in law.'

G.N. Bannerji continued, after a pause to sip some water, to state his objections to the law, but without adducing detailed reasons at this stage. He found the Zamindari Act unacceptable because it provided derisory compensation and was therefore 'a fraud on the Constitution'; because the compensation offered was, moreover, discriminatory between large and small landowners and thus offended against the provisions of Article 14, which provided for 'the equal protection of the laws'; because it contravened the provisions of Article 19(1) (f) which stated that all citizens had the right 'to acquire, hold and dispose of property'; because, by leaving to junior officers in the administration vast areas for the exercise of discretion in deciding the order of the actual taking over of estates, the legislature had illegitimately delegated its own powers to another authority; and so on and so forth. Having hovered in a hawk-like circuit over the domain of his case for more than an hour, Mr G.N. Bannerji now plunged down on the various weaknesses of the act, attacking them—repeatedly, of course—one by one.

11.2

He had barely begun to do so when the English judge spoke:

'Is there any reason, Mr Bannerji, why you have chosen to deal with the delegation argument first?'

'My Lord?'

'Well, you contend that the impugned act contravenes certain specific provisions of the Constitution. Why not tackle those direct grounds first? There is nothing in the Constitution against delegation. I presume the powers of the legislatures are plenary in their own spheres. They can delegate powers to whomever they choose as long as they do not step beyond the four corners of the Constitution.'

'My Lord, if I may argue the case in my own way—'

Judges retired at sixty, and there was therefore no one on the bench who was not at least ten years G.N. Bannerji's junior.

'Yes, yes, Mr Bannerji. By all means.' The judge mopped his forehead. It was appallingly hot in the courtroom.

'It is precisely my contention, precisely my contention, my Lord, that the authority that the legislature of Purva Pradesh has chosen to delegate to the executive is an abdication of its own powers, and contrary both to the clear intention of the Constitution and to our own statute and constitutional law as laid down in a number of cases, most recently Jatindra Nath Gupta's case. In that case it was decided that a state legislature cannot delegate its legislative functions to any other body or authority, and that case is binding upon us, since it was decided by the Federal Court, the predecessor of the Supreme Court.'

The Chief Justice now spoke, his head still to one side: 'Mr Bannerji, was that case not decided by three judges to two?'

'Nevertheless, my Lord, it was decided. It is, after all, certainly possible that a judgement in the same proportions will issue from this bench too—though I am sure that neither I nor my learned friend opposite would hope for such an eventuality.'

'Yes. Go on, Mr Bannerji,' said the Chief Justice, frowning. It was the last thing he wanted either.

A little while later, the Chief Justice intervened again.

'But The Queen versus Burah, Mr Bannerji? Or Hodge versus The Queen?'

'I was coming to those cases, my Lord, in my own plodding manner.'

What might have been a smile passed across the Chief Justice's face; he was silent.

Half an hour later G.N. Bannerji was in full flow once more:

'But ours, unlike the British but like the American, is a written Constitution expressly declaring the will of the people. And precisely, my Lords, because the same vesting of the different powers of the state among the legislature, the executive and the judiciary exists in the two Constitutions, it is to the rules that have been laid down by the Supreme Court in the United States of America that we must turn for guidance and interpretation.'

'Must, Mr Bannerji?' This was the English judge.

'Should, my Lord.'

'You are not implying that these decisions are binding on us? This question cannot admit of two answers.'

'That, as from your question I have no doubt your Lordship perceives, would be a foolhardy contention. But there are certainly two sides to every question. What I meant was that the American precedents and interpretations, though not binding on us in the strict sense, are our only safe guide through what are for us comparatively uncharted waters. And the rule that has been laid down in America forbidding the delegation of power by any of the separate organs of the state should also be the yardstick for us to apply.'

'Well.' His Lordship sounded unconvinced but susceptible to persuasion.

'The reasons, my Lords, that powers not be delegated, have been succinctly stated by Cooley in *Constitutional Limitations*, Vol. I, page 224.'

The Chief Justice interrupted.

'Just a minute, Mr Bannerji. We do not have this book with us on the bench, and we would like to follow you on the page. This is one danger of crossing the Atlantic for your arguments.'

'Presumably your Lordship means the Pacific.'

There was laughter from both the bench and the courtroom.

'Perhaps I mean both. As you have observed, Mr Bannerji, there are two sides to every question.'

'My Lord, I have had carbon copies made of the relevant pages.'

But the Court Reader promptly produced the book from his table below the rostrum. It was clear that there was only one copy of the volume, however, not five, as there would have been with the Indian and English law reports and authorities.

The Chief Justice said: 'Mr Bannerji, speaking for myself, I prefer the feel of a book in my hands. I hope we have the same edition. Page 224. Yes, it appears we do. My colleagues, however, may avail themselves of the carbon copies you have provided.'

'As your Lordships please. Now, my Lords, Cooley addresses the question in the following words:

> Where the sovereign power of the State has located the authority, there it must remain; and by the constitutional agency alone the laws must be made until the Constitution itself is changed.
>
> The power to whose judgment, wisdom and patriotism this high prerogative has been entrusted cannot relieve itself of the responsibility by choosing other agencies upon which the power shall be devolved, nor can it substitute the judgment, wisdom and patriotism of any other body for those to which alone the people have seen fit to confide this sovereign trust.

'It is this sovereign trust, this sovereign trust, my Lords, that the legislature of Purva Pradesh has delegated to the executive in the Zamindari Abolition Act. Its date of activation; the sequence of the taking over of the estates of the zamindars, these decisions (quite possibly arbitrary, whimsical, even malicious) to be taken in many cases by very junior officials of the administration; the terms of the bonds sought to be offered by way of compensation, and the mix of cash and bonds; and many other points not merely of detail but of substance. My Lords, this is no mere filling in of details, this is improper delegation of authority, and the act, even if there were no other grounds, would be invalid on these grounds alone.'

Small, cheerful Mr Shastri, the Advocate-General, rose smilingly to his feet. His stiff white collar had gone limp with sweat. 'Your Lordships please. A slight cor-rec-tion to my learned friend. Date of vesting is au-to-ma-tic with President's assent. So act is ac-ti-va-ted at once.' Although this was his first interruption, it was offered with undramatic and amiable courtesy. Mr Shastri's English was not elegant (he pronounced 'carte blanche', for instance, as 'ka-thee bi-lan-chee'), nor his manner of advocacy fluent. But he argued superbly if simply from first principles (or, as his irreverent juniors might say, prin-ci-ples), and there were few lawyers in the state, perhaps in the country, who were a match for him.

'I am obliged to my learned friend for his clarification,' said G.N.

Bannerji, leaning forward on the lectern once more. 'I was referring, my Lords, not so much to the date of vesting, which, as my learned friend points out, is immediate, but to the dates of the taking over of the estates.'

'Surely, Mr Bannerji,' said the large judge to the right of the Chief Justice, rubbing his thumb and forefinger together, 'you cannot expect the government to take over all the estates simultaneously? That would be administratively unworkable.'

'My Lord,' said G.N. Bannerji, 'it is not a question of simultaneity but equity. That is what worries me, my Lord. Guidelines could have been laid down in several ways—on the basis of income, for instance, or geography. The present act, however, enables the administration to pick and choose. If, for instance, they decide tomorrow that they do not like some particular zamindar, say the Raja of Marh, because he is too vocal on some issue that goes against the policy or even the interests of the government, they may under the impugned act issue an immediate notification that his estates in Purva Pradesh will be taken over. This is a gateway to tyranny, my Lords, a gateway to nothing less than tyranny.'

The Raja of Marh, who, owing to both heat and sloth, had been drowsing off while leaning further and further forward in his chair, suddenly came back to life on hearing his name. He floundered around in confusion for some time, unable to place himself in his surroundings after his fleshly dreams.

He tugged the gown of a junior lawyer who was seated in front of him.

'What did he say? What is he saying about me?' he demanded.

The lawyer turned around, his hand raised slightly upwards in a gesture of placation. He whispered an explanation. The Raja of Marh stared blankly and uncomprehendingly at him, then, sensing that nothing had been said that harmed his interests, became somnolent once again.

Thus the argument progressed. Those outsiders who had come with the expectation of high or low drama were deeply disappointed. Many of the litigants themselves were mystified by what was going on. They did not know that Bannerji would be on his feet for five days on behalf of the applicants, that this would be followed by five days of Shastri for the state and two final days for Bannerji's rebuttal. They had expected skirmishes and fireworks, the clang of sword on shield. What they were getting instead was an ecumenical but soporific fricassee of Hodge v. The Queen, Jatindra Nath Gupta v. Province of Bihar, and Schechter Poultry Corp. v. United States.

But the lawyers—especially those at the back of the court, who were not involved in the case—loved every minute of it. This, for them, was indeed the clang of sword on shield. They were aware that G.N. Bannerji's manner of constitutional argument, very different in this case from the statute-and-precedent traditions of British and therefore Indian advocacy, had come to be of increasing importance ever since the Government of India Act of 1935 set the frame which the Constitution of India itself would follow fifteen years later. But they had never heard a case argued in such wide-ranging form before, and that too by so distinguished a barrister at such length.

When the court adjourned at one o'clock for lunch, these lawyers streamed out, gowns flapping like bats' wings, and joined the smaller streams of lawyers from other courtrooms. They moved towards the part of the High Court building which was occupied by the Advocates' Association, and headed straight for the urinals, which stank frighteningly in the heat. Then they wandered off in groups to their own chambers, or to the library of the Advocates' Association or to the coffee shop or canteen. Here they sat and discussed with avidity the merits of the case and the mannerisms of eminent senior counsel.

11.3

At the adjournment, the Nawab Sahib walked over to talk to Mahesh Kapoor. Upon discovering that he did not mean to attend the afternoon sitting, he asked him to join him for lunch at Baitar House, and Mahesh Kapoor agreed. Firoz too went over to talk for a few minutes to his father's friend—or his friend's father—before returning to his law-books. This was the most important case he had been associated with in his life, and he was working day and night on the small part of it that he might have to argue—or at least brief his senior in.

The Nawab Sahib looked at him with pride and affection and told him that he would be taking the afternoon off.

'But Abba, G.N. Bannerji will begin his argument on Article 14 today.'

'Now remind me—'

Firoz smiled at his father, but forbore from explaining Article 14.

'But you will be here tomorrow?' he asked.

'Yes, yes, perhaps. In any case, I'll be here when your part comes up,' said the Nawab Sahib, stroking his beard with a look of affectionate amusement in his eyes.

'It's your part too, Abba—lands granted by crown grant.'

'Yes.' The Nawab Sahib sighed. 'Anyway, both I and the man who wants to wrest them away from me have been wearied by all this brilliance, and we're going off for lunch. But tell me, Firoz, why don't they close the courts at this time of year? The heat is dreadful. Doesn't the Patna High Court take its vacation in May and June?'

'Well, I suppose we follow the Calcutta model,' said Firoz. 'But don't ask me why. Well, Abba, I'll be off.'

The two old friends wandered into the corridor, where the heat hit them like a blast, and from there to the Nawab Sahib's car. Mahesh Kapoor instructed his driver to follow them to Baitar House. In the car both studiously avoided discussing the case or its implications, which, in a sense, was a pity because it would have been interesting to know what they would have said. Mahesh Kapoor could not, however, refrain from saying:

'Tell me when Firoz is going to argue. I'll come and listen.'

'I'll do so. That's very friendly of you.' The Nawab Sahib smiled. Although he had not intended it, perhaps his remark would be interpreted as ironic. He was reassured when his friend continued:

'Why—he's like my nephew.' After a pause, Mahesh Kapoor added: 'But isn't Karlekar leading him in the case?'

'Yes, but his brother is very ill, and he may have to go back to Bombay. If that's the case, Firoz will have to argue in his place.'

'Ah.' There was a pause.

'What news of Maan?' asked the Nawab Sahib at last, as they got out at Baitar House. 'We'll eat in the library; we won't be disturbed there.'

Mahesh Kapoor's face darkened.

'If I know him, he's still infatuated with that wretched woman. I wish I'd never asked her to sing at Prem Nivas on Holi. It all came about because of that evening.'

The Nawab Sahib was silent, but he seemed to have stiffened at the words.

'Keep an eye on your son too,' said Mahesh Kapoor with a curt laugh. 'Firoz, I mean.'

The Nawab Sahib looked at his friend, but said nothing. His face had gone white.

'Are you all right?'

'Yes, yes, Kapoor Sahib, I am all right. What were you saying about Firoz?'

'He visits that house too, I've heard. No harm in it if it's a brief thing, it's not as if it's an obsession yet—'

'No!' There was such sharp and unaccountable pain, almost horror, in the Nawab Sahib's voice that Mahesh Kapoor was taken aback. He knew that his friend had turned religious, but he had not imagined he had become such a puritan.

He quickly changed the subject. He talked about a couple of new bills, about how the delimitation of constituencies throughout the country was expected any day now, about the endless troubles in the Congress Party—both at the state level between him and Agarwal, and at the Centre between Nehru and the right wing.

'Why, I, even I, am thinking that this party is no longer a home for me,' said the Minister of Revenue. 'An old teacher—a freedom fighter—came to me the other day and said a number of things that I've been thinking over. Perhaps I should leave the Congress. I believe that if Nehru could be persuaded to leave the party and fight the next elections on his own platform and with a new party, he would win. I would follow him, as would many others.'

But even this startling and momentous confidence provoked no response from the Nawab Sahib. He was equally abstracted at lunch. Indeed, he appeared to have difficulty not only in speaking much but in swallowing his food.

11.4

Two evenings later, all the lawyers for the zamindars and a couple of the clients themselves met in G.N. Bannerji's hotel room. He held these conferences from about six to eight each evening in order to prepare for the next day's arguments. Today, however, there was a dual purpose to the conference. First, the other lawyers were present to help him prepare for the morning session, when he would wind up his opening of the case. Secondly, he too had been requested today to give them advice for their own arguments of the afternoon, when they would be pleading their own particular sections of the case before the bench. G.N. Bannerji was happy to help them, but even more keen to see them go at eight o'clock sharp so that he could enjoy his evening in his standard manner with the person whom the juniors gossiped about as his 'lady-love': a Mrs Chakravarti, whom he had installed in great style (and at the expense of his clients) in a railway saloon on a siding at Brahmpur Junction.

Everyone arrived promptly at six. The local seniors and juniors brought the law-books and a waiter brought cups of tea. G.N. Bannerji complained about the fans in the hotel and about the tea. He was looking forward later to a Scotch or three.

'Sir, I have been waiting to say how fine your argument on public purpose was this afternoon.' This was a local senior lawyer.

The great G.N. Bannerji smiled. 'Yes, you saw how the Chief Justice appreciated the point about the connection between public purpose and public benefit.'

'Justice Maheshwari did not seem to.' This was guaranteed to provoke a response.

'Maheshwari!' The junior member of the bench was dismissed in a single word.

'But, Sir, his comment about the Land Revenue Commission will have to be answered,' piped up one enthusiastic junior.

'What he says is not important. He sits still for two days, then asks two stupid questions, one after another.'

'Quite right, Sir,' said Firoz quietly. 'You addressed the second point at length in yesterday's argument.'

'He's read the whole Ramayana, and still doesn't know whose *father* Sita is!' This twist to the standard witticism provoked laughter, some of it slightly sycophantic.

'Anyway,' continued G.N. Bannerji, 'we should concentrate on the arguments of the Chief Justice and Mr Justice Bailey. They are the best brains on the bench and they will sway the judgement. Is there anything they said that we might deal with?'

Firoz said, a little hesitantly: 'Sir, if I may. It seems to me from Mr Justice Bailey's comments that he is not convinced by your imputation of motives to the state in separating the two payments. You made the point, Sir, that the state had by sleight of hand divided the payment into two parts—the compensation proper and a rehabilitation grant. And that their motive in doing so was to get around the conclusions of the judges of the Patna High Court in the Bihar zamindari case. But would it not in fact be to our advantage to accept the government's contention that the rehabilitation grant and compensation are separate?'

G.N. Bannerji said: 'No, why? Why should we accept their contention?

Anyway, let's see what the Advocate-General has to say. I can reply to all that later.' He turned away.

Firoz ventured on, rather earnestly: 'I mean, Sir, if it could be proved that even an ex-gratia payment like a rehabilitation grant can be thrown out under Article 14.'

G.N. Bannerji's rather pompous grandson cut Firoz off: 'Article 14 was fully argued on the second day.' He was trying to protect his grandfather from what seemed to be a perverse point. To accept the government's contention on such an important point would surely be to throw away their own case.

But G.N. Bannerji silenced his grandson in Bengali with, 'Aachha, choop koré thako!' and turned to Firoz with his finger pointed upwards. 'Say that again,' he said. 'Say that again.'

Firoz repeated his comment, then elaborated it.

G.N. Bannerji considered the point, then wrote something in his red notebook. Turning to Firoz he said, 'Find me whatever American case-law you can on the point, and bring it here to me at eight tomorrow morning.'

Firoz said, 'Yes, Sir.' His eyes were shining with pleasure.

G.N. Bannerji said: 'This is a dangerous weapon to use. It could go badly wrong. I wonder if at this stage—' He went off into his thoughts. 'Bring me the cases anyway, and I will see. Let me see the mood of the court. All right, anything else on Article 14?'

No one spoke.

'Where is Karlekar?'

'Sir, his brother has died and he has had to leave for Bombay. He got the telegram just a few hours ago—while you were on your feet.'

'I see. And who is his junior for the crown grant writs?'

'I am, Sir,' said Firoz.

'You have a momentous day ahead of you, young man. I imagine you will handle it.' Firoz glowed at this unexpected praise, and it was hard for him not to grin.

'Sir, if you have any suggestions—' he said.

'Not really. Just argue that the crown grants conferred absolute rights in perpetuity, and the grantees are therefore not like other intermediaries. But all this is obvious. If I think of something else I'll tell you tomorrow morning when you come here. On second thoughts, come ten minutes earlier.'

'Thank you, Sir.'

The conference continued for an hour and a half. But G.N. Bannerji was becoming restless, and everyone felt that the great lawyer should not be overtaxed when he still had to argue the next day. The questions had not dried up, however, when he took off his spectacles, pointed two fingers upwards and said the single word:

'Aachha.'

It was the signal for people to gather up their papers.

Outside, it was getting dark. On the way out, a couple of juniors, unconscious of the fact that they were still within earshot of G.N. Bannerji's son and grandson, were gossiping about the lawyer from Calcutta.

'Have you seen his lady-love?' asked one.

'Oh, no, no,' said the other.

'I hear she is a real firecracker.'

The other laughed. 'Over seventy, and he has a lady-love!'

'But think of Mrs Bannerji! What must she think? The whole world knows.'

The other shrugged, as if to imply that what a Mrs Bannerji might think was outside either his concern or his imagination.

The son and grandson of the great lawyer heard this exchange though they did not see the shrug. They frowned to themselves, but said nothing to each other, and tacitly allowed the subject to drift away on the evening air.

11.5

The next day G.N. Bannerji wound up the opening for the petitioners, and several other counsel argued for short periods about their own specific points. Firoz too got his chance.

For a few moments before Firoz got to his feet, his mind plunged suddenly into an inexplicable blackness—an emptiness, almost. He could see all his arguments lucidly, but could see no point to anything at all—this case, his career, his father's lands, the scheme of things of which this court and this Constitution were a part, his own existence, even human life itself. The disproportionate strength of the feelings he was undergoing—and the irrelevance of these feelings to the business at hand—bewildered him.

He shuffled his papers for a while, and his mind cleared. But now he was so nervous, so puzzled by the untimely incursion of these thoughts, that at first he had to hide his hands behind the lectern.

He began with the formulary remark: 'My Lords, I adopt the arguments of Mr G.N. Bannerji on all the main points, but would like to add my own arguments with respect to the question of the lands covered by crown grants.' He then argued with great force of logic that these lands fell into a different category from the others, and were protected by contract and proclamation from ever being taken over. The bench listened to him appreciatively; and he defended his contention against their questions as well as he could. His curious uncertainty had disappeared as suddenly as it had arisen.

Mahesh Kapoor had taken time off from his heavy workload to come and hear Firoz. Though he listened with warmth and enjoyment to Firoz's arguments he felt that it would be a disaster if the court accepted them. A fair proportion of the rented land in Purva Pradesh fell under the category of grants given by the crown after the Mutiny in order to establish order once more through the intermediation of powerful local men. Some of these, like the Nawab Sahib's ancestor, had fought against the British; but it had been felt that they and their families could not with safety be antagonized further. The grants were therefore given subject to good behaviour—but to nothing else.

Mahesh Kapoor was also particularly interested in another writ petition, one brought forward by those who had actually ruled their own states under the British, who had signed instruments of accession to the Indian Union after Independence and been granted certain guarantees in the Constitution. One such was the bestial Raja of Marh, whom Mahesh Kapoor would have been only too happy to dispossess completely. Although the state of Marh proper fell in Madhya Bharat, the Raja's ancestors had also been granted land in Purva Pradesh—or Protected Provinces as it was called at the time. His lands in P.P. fell into the category of crown grants, but it was one of the contentions of the Raja's lawyers that his privy purse from the government had been set lower than it otherwise would have been in view of the income that his estates in P.P. were expected to bring in perpetuity. These lands had been allowed to the Raja as personal, rather than State, property, and (they contended) were guaranteed by two articles of the Constitution. One unambiguously declared that the government would pay due regard to any assurances given under the covenants of merger with respect to the personal rights, privileges and dignities of the ex-rulers; and another stated that disputes arising out of such covenants and similar instruments were not justiciable in the courts.

The government lawyers, on the other hand, had insisted in their affidavits that 'personal rights, privileges and dignities' did not include personal property; with regard to personal property the ex-rulers had the status and guarantees of any other citizen. And they too contended that the matter—as they saw it—was not justiciable.

If Mahesh Kapoor had had his way, he would have taken over not only the Raja's personal lands in Purva Pradesh but whatever had been allowed to him as personal land in Madhya Bharat as well—and all his urban property in Brahmpur besides—including the site of the Shiva Temple, which was now under a new spurt of construction on account of the approaching festival of the Pul Mela. This was, alas, not possible; had it been, it would have curbed the Raja's wretched mischief. It would have been a very unwelcome thought to Mahesh Kapoor that this desire of his was in essence not very different from that of the Home Minister L.N. Agarwal when he attempted to take over Baitar House.

The Nawab of Baitar noticed Mahesh Kapoor as he came into court a little into the afternoon session; though they sat on different sides of the aisle, they acknowledged each other with an unspoken salutation.

The Nawab Sahib's heart was full. He had listened with enormous pride and happiness to his son's speech. He could not help thinking once more how Firoz had inherited so many of the finer features of his mother. And she too had sometimes been most nervous when she was most forceful. The attentiveness of the judges to the young man's arguments was savoured even more by his father than by himself for he was too busy parrying their questions to allow himself the pleasure of enjoying them.

Even his senior could not have done better, thought the Nawab Sahib. He wondered what the next day's report in the *Brahmpur Chronicle* would carry of Firoz's arguments. He even somewhat whimsically imagined the great Cicero appearing in the Brahmpur High Court and commending his son's advocacy.

But will it do much good in the end?—this thought struck him again and again in the middle of his happiness. When a government is determined to get its way it usually does so by one means or another. And history is against our class. He looked over to where the Raja and Rajkumar of Marh were sitting. I suppose that if it were merely our class it would not matter, he continued to himself. But it is everyone else besides. He found his thoughts turning not only to his retainers and dependants but to the musicians he used to listen to in his own youth, the poets he used to patronize, and to Saeeda Bai.

And he looked at Firoz with renewed concern.

11.6

Daily the crowds in court lessened until finally hardly anyone other than the press, the lawyers, and a few of the litigants could be seen.

Whether the Nawab Sahib and his class had or did not have history on their side, whether the Law propelled Society or Society the Law, whether the patronage of poetry counter-balanced the torments of the tenantry, such questions of great pitch and moment lay outside the immediate business of the five men in whose hands rested the fate of this case. Their concerns were concentrated on Articles 14, 31(2), and 31(4) of the Constitution of India, and they were grilling the amiable Mr Shastri about his view of these articles and of the statute under challenge.

The Chief Justice was looking through his copy of the Constitution, and scanning for the fourth time the words of Articles 14 and 31.

The other judges (Mr Justice Maheshwari excepted) had been asking some questions of the Advocate-General which the Chief Justice had been following with only half an ear. The Raja of Marh, who seemed to enjoy the atmosphere of the courtroom, was listening with no ear at all. He was present in court, but once more not conscious of the fact. His son, the Rajkumar, did not dare to nudge him awake when he slumped forward.

The questions from the bench spread over the entire field of the immediate argument.

'Mr Advocate-General, what is your response to the argument of Mr Bannerji that the purpose of the Zamindari Act is not a public purpose but the policy of the political party which for the time being is holding office in the state?'

'Could you attempt, Mr Advocate-General, to reconcile these various American authorities? I mean, on the question of public purpose rather than the equal protection of the laws.'

'Mr Advocate-General, are you seriously asking us to believe that "notwithstanding anything in this Constitution" are the controlling words of Article 31 Clause 4 and that any act under the aegis of that article is therefore unchallengable under Article 14 or any other article of that Constitution? Surely it only protects the act from challenge on grounds contained in Article 31 Clause 2.'

'Mr Advocate-General, what about Yick Wo versus Hopkins with respect to Article 14? Or the passage in Willis approved by Justice Fazl Ali in a recent Supreme Court decision as being a correct exposition of the principles underlying Article 14?—"The guarantee of the equal protection of the laws means the protection of equal laws." And so on. Learned counsel for the applicants made much of that, and I do not see how you can counter their contention.'

Several reporters and even lawyers in the courtroom had the strong sense that the case was beginning to go against the government.

The Advocate-General appeared unconscious of this. He continued, unexcitedly, to weigh his words, even his syllables, with such care that he emitted them at only about a third of the rate of G.N. Bannerji.

His answer to the first question was: 'Di-rec-tive Prin-ci-ples, my Lords.' There was a long pause, and then he listed the relevant articles one by one. This was followed by a shorter pause, then the statement: 'Thus your Lordships see it is in Con-sti-tu-tion itself and not party policy merely.'

To the question about reconciling the various American authorities, he merely smiled and said: 'No, my Lords.' It was not for him to attempt to reconcile the irreconcilable, especially since it was not he who was leaning on the American cases for support. Indeed, had not even Dr Cooley said he was 'somewhat at sea' when attempting to determine the meaning of 'public purpose' in the light of conflicting judicial decisions? But why mention that? 'No, my Lords' was enough.

Non-geographically speaking, the Chief Justice had been somewhat on the sidelines during the last few minutes. Now he too entered the fray. Having looked once more at the crucial articles and having doodled a fish on the pad in front of him, he cocked his head to one side and said:

'Now, Mr Advocate-General, I understand that the state contends that the two payments, the flat-scale compensation and the wealth-based, sliding-scale rehabilitation grant, are of an entirely different nature. One is compensation, the other not. Thus they cannot be lumped together, and it cannot be said that the compensation is on a graduated or sliding scale, and it cannot therefore be called discriminatory or unequal against large landlords.'

'Yes, my Lord.'

The Chief Justice waited in vain for elaboration. After a pause he continued:

'And it is further argued by the state that the two payments are different because, for example, different sections of the Zamindari Act relate to these two payments; because there are different officers in charge of their disbursement—Rehabilitation Grant Officers and Compensation Officers and so on.'

'Yes, my Lord.'

'Mr Bannerji's contention for the applicants, on the other hand, was that this distinction is mere sleight of hand, especially since the compensation funds are only about a third of the rehabilitation funds.'

'No, my Lord.'

'No?'

'Not sleight of hand, my Lord.'

'And he says,' continued the Chief Justice, 'that since the distinction was not mentioned in the legislative debates until a late stage, it was introduced by the government after the adverse Patna High Court judgement as a way of fraudulently getting around the constitutional protections.'

'The act is act, my Lord. Debates are debates.'

'And what about the preamble to the act, Mr Advocate-General, which makes no mention of rehabilitation as an objective of the legislation?'

'O-ver-sight, my Lord. The act is act.'

The Chief Justice leaned his head on his other arm. 'Now suppose we were to accept your—that is, the state's—contention that the so-called compensation is all there is by way of real compensation under Article 31 Clause 2, how would you then describe the so-called rehabilitation grant?'

'Ex-gratia payment, my Lord, which state may freely make to anyone in any way it chooses.'

The Chief Justice now leaned his head on both his hands, and examined his prey.

'Would the protection from judicial challenge that Article 32 Clause 4 provides to compensation extend to ex-gratia payments as well? Could the unequal terms—the sliding scale—of this ex-gratia payment not still be challenged under Article 14, which provides for the protection of equal laws?'

Firoz, who had been listening to the argument with the utmost attentiveness, looked at G.N. Bannerji. This was precisely the point he had been veering towards in the conference that evening. The distinguished lawyer had taken off his spectacles and was polishing them very slowly. Finally, he stopped polishing them altogether, and stood completely still, looking—like everyone else in court—at the Advocate-General.

There was silence for a good fifteen seconds.

'Challenge to ex-gratia payment, my Lord?' said Mr Shastri, appearing genially shocked.

'Well,' continued the Chief Justice, frowning, 'it works on a sliding scale to the detriment of the larger zamindars. The smallest ones get ten times the computation based on rent and the largest ones get only one and a half times the computation. Different multiples, ergo unequal treatment, ergo unfair discrimination.'

'My Lords,' protested Mr Shastri, 'ex-gratia payment confers no legal rights. It is pri-vi-lege conferred by the state. Therefore, it is not open to question on ground of un-fair dis-cri-mi-na-tion.' But the Advocate-General was not smiling quite as broadly. This had become almost a one-to-one cross-examination. The other judges did not interpose any questions.

'Now, Mr Advocate-General, in America it has been held by their Supreme Court that their fourteenth amendment—to which our Article 14 happens to correspond in language and spirit—applies not only to liabilities imposed but to privileges conferred as well. So would that not apply to ex-gratia payments?'

'My Lords, American Constitution is short, so gaps are filled by in-ter-pre-ta-tion. Ours is long, so the need is less here.'

The Chief Justice smiled. He looked rather wily now: an old, wise, bald tortoise. The Advocate-General paused. But this time he knew he would have to put forth a less unconvincing and general argument. The two fourteens were too alike. He said:

'My Lords, in India Article 31 Clause 4 protects the act from any challenge whatsoever under the Constitution.'

'Mr Advocate-General, I heard your answer to the query of Mr Justice Bailey on that point. But if this bench does not find that argument convincing and at the same time comes to the conclusion that ex-gratia payments must satisfy the guarantees of Article 14, where does the state stand?'

The Advocate-General said nothing for a while. If self-defeating candour were enjoined on lawyers, his answer would have had to be: 'State does not stand, my Lord, it falls.' Instead he said: 'State would have to consider its position, my Lord.'

'I think the state would do well to consider its position in the light of this possible line of reasoning.'

The tension in court had become so palpable that some of it must have communicated itself into the dreams of the Raja of Marh. He woke up violently. He was in the grip of a paroxysm of anxiety. He stood up and stepped forward into the aisle. He had behaved well during the argument of his own writ petition. Now, when things seemed to be going dangerously for the state on a point that did not refer specifically to him but would have covered him safely as well, he grew desperately agitated.

'It is not right,' he said.

The Chief Justice leaned forward.

'It is not right. We too love our country. Who are they? Who are they? The land—' he expostulated.

The courtroom reacted with shock and amazement. The Rajkumar stood up and took a tentative step towards his father. His father shoved him aside.

The Chief Justice said, rather slowly: 'Your Highness, I cannot hear you.'

The Raja of Marh did not believe this for one instant. 'I will speak louder, Sir,' he announced.

The Chief Justice repeated: 'I cannot hear you, Your Highness. If you have something to say, kindly say it through your counsel. And please be seated in the third row. The first two rows are reserved for the Bar.'

'No, Sir! My land is at stake! My life is at stake!' He glared belligerently upwards, as if he were about to charge the bench.

The Chief Justice looked at his colleagues to either side of him and said to the Court Reader and the ushers in Hindi:

'Remove that man.'

The ushers looked stunned. They had not imagined they would ever have to lay hands on Majesty.

In English, the Chief Justice said to the Reader: 'Call the watch and ward staff.' To the counsel of the Raja of Marh, he said: 'Control your client. Tell him not to test the forbearance of this court. If your client does not leave the court immediately I will commit him for contempt.'

The five magnificent ushers, the Court Reader, and several counsel for the applicants apologetically but bodily moved the Raja of Marh, still spluttering, from Courtroom Number One before he could do further damage to himself, his case, or the dignity of the court. The Rajkumar of Marh, red with shame, followed slowly. He turned around at the door. Every eye in court was following the spasmodic progress of his father. Firoz too was looking at him in contemptuous disbelief. The Rajkumar lowered his eyes and followed his father into the corridor.

11.7

A few days after he had suffered this indignity, the Raja of Marh, feather-turbaned and diamond-buttoned, together with a glittering retinue of retainers, performed a progress to the Pul Mela.

His Highness started out in the morning from the site of the Shiva Temple at Chowk (where he offered obeisance), advanced through the old town of Brahmpur, and arrived at the top of the great earthen ramp which led gently down from the mud cliffs to the sands on the south bank of the Ganga. Every few steps a crier announced the Raja's presence, and rose petals were flung into the air to his greater glory. It was idiotic.

However, it was of a piece with the Raja's conception of himself and his place in the world. He was cross with the world, and especially with the *Brahmpur Chronicle*, which had dwelt lovingly on his ejaculations in and his ejection from the Chief Justice's court. The case had continued for four or five more days before being closed (the judgement was reserved for a later date), and on each day the *Brahmpur Chronicle* had found some occasion to hearken back to the Raja of Marh's unseemly exit.

The procession halted at the top of the ramp under the shade of the great pipal tree, and the Raja looked down. Below him, as far as the eye could see, lay an ocean of tents—khaki, haze-enveloped—spread out along the sands. Instead of the single pontoon bridge across the Ganga there were at present five bridges of boats, effectively cutting off all downriver traffic. But large flotillas of little boats were still plying across the river in order to ferry pilgrims to particularly auspicious bathing spots along sand spits on either side—or simply to provide a swifter and more enjoyable means of crossing the river than facing the crush of people on the improvised and grossly overcrowded bridges.

The grand ramp too was crowded with pilgrims from all over India, many of whom had just arrived by special trains that had been laid on for the Pul Mela traffic. For a few minutes, however, the Raja's retainers forced the crowd back sufficiently to give their master a regal and leisurely view of the scene.

The Raja gazed with reverence at the great brown river, the beautiful and placid Ganga. Its level was still low, and the sands broad. It was mid-June. The monsoons had not yet broken in Brahmpur, and the snow-melt had not yet swollen the river much. In two days it would be the grand bathing day of Ganga Dussehra (when, by popular tradition, the Ganga rose one step along the bathing ghats of Banaras), and four days after that would come the second grand bathing day of the full moon. It was thanks to the grace of Lord Shiva, who had broken the river's fall from heaven by allowing it to flow through his hair that the Ganga had not flooded the earth. It was to Lord Shiva that the Raja was raising the Chandrachur Temple. Tears came to the Raja's eyes as he looked at the holy river and contemplated the virtue of his actions.

The Raja was bound for a specific encampment down below: the tents of the holy man known as Sanaki Baba. This cheerful, middle-aged man was a devotee of Krishna, and spent his time in his praise and in meditation. He was surrounded by attractive disciples and had a great reputation as a source of peaceful energy. The Raja was determined to visit him even before he visited the encampments of the Shaivite holy men. The Raja's anti-Muslim feelings had resolved themselves in pan-Hindu aspirations and ceremonies: he had started his procession from a Shiva temple, it had wound its way through the city named after Brahma, and it would conclude with a visit to a devotee of Krishna, Vishnu's great avatar. The entire Hindu trinity would thus be appeased. Then he would take a dip in the Ganga (immersing one bejewelled toe would be sufficient), and he would have washed away the sins of seven generations, including his own. It was a useful morning's work. The Raja glanced back towards Chowk and stared for a few seconds at the minarets of the mosque. The trident on top of my temple will outsoar you soon enough, he thought, and the martial blood of his ancestors began to boil within him.

But thinking of his ancestors made him think of his descendants, and he looked with perplexed impatience at his son, the Rajkumar, who was trailing in a reluctant way after his father. What a useless fellow he is! thought the Raja. I should get him married off at once. I don't care how many boys he sleeps with as long as he gives me a grandson as well. A few days ago the Raja had taken him to Saeeda Bai's to make a man of him. The Rajkumar had almost run out in terror! The Raja did not know that his son was not unfamiliar with the brothels of the old town, which his university friends sometimes visited. But to be given intimate tutelage by his crass father had been too much for him.

The Raja had instructions from his formidable mother, the Dowager Rani of Marh, to pay more attention to her grandson. Recently he had been doing his best to comply. He had dragged himself and his son to the High Court in order to introduce him to Responsibility, Law and Property. The result had been a fiasco. Procreation and the Life of a Man of the World had not gone much better. Today's lesson was Religion and the Martial Spirit. Even here the Rajkumar had been a wash-out. While the Raja had bellowed 'Har har Mahadeva!' with even greater zest whenever they passed by a mosque, the Rajkumar had lowered his head and mumbled the words even more unwillingly. Finally, there was Ritual and Education. The Raja was determined to fling his son into the Ganga. Since the Rajkumar had only a year to go before finishing his university studies, he should partake—even if a trifle prematurely—of the proper Hindu ritual of graduation—the bath or snaan—in order to become a proper graduate or snaatak. And what better place to become a snaatak than in the Holy Ganga during the sexennial Pul Mela, which was always grander than usual? He would fling him in to the cheers of his retainers. And if the milksop couldn't swim, and had to be dragged spluttering and gasping back to land, that would be hilarious.

'Hurry up, hurry up!' shouted the Raja, as he stumbled down the long ramp to the sands. 'Where is this Sanaki Baba's camp? Where do all these sister-fucking pilgrims come from? Isn't there any organization? Get me my car!'

'Your Highness, the authorities have forbidden all cars except for police and VIPs. We could not get permission,' murmured someone.

'Am I not a VIP?' The Raja's breast swelled with indignation.

'Yes, your Highness. But—'

Finally, among the miles of tents and camps, after they had walked for almost half an hour along makeshift roads of metal plates laid out by army engineers on the sands, they arrived within sight of Sanaki Baba's encampment, and the Raja's retinue moved towards it gratefully. They were only about a hundred yards away.

'At last!' cried the Raja of Marh. The heat was telling on him. He was sweating like a swine. 'Tell the Baba to come out. I want to see him. And I want some sherbet.'

'Your Highness—'

But hardly had the man run ahead with the message than from the other side a police jeep screeched to a halt before the camp, and several people got down and made their way in.

The Raja's eyes popped.

'We were here first. Stop them! I must see the Baba at once,' he cried in an outburst of outrage.

But the jeep people had gone in already.

11.8

When the jeep had first descended to the sands below the Fort, Dipankar Chatterji, who was one of its passengers, had been truly astonished.

The roads on the Pul Mela sands among the tents and encampments were packed with people. Many were carrying rolls of bedding and other possessions with them, including pots and pans for cooking, food supplies, and perhaps a child or two tucked under an arm or clinging on to their back. They carried cloth bags, pails and buckets, sticks, flags, pennants, and garlands of marigolds. Some were panting with heat and exhaustion, others were chatting as if they were on a picnic outing, or singing bhajans and other holy songs because their enthusiasm at finally getting a glimpse of Mother Ganga had removed in an instant the weariness of the journey. Men, women and children, old and young, dark and fair, rich and poor, brahmins and outcastes, Tamils and Kashmiris, saffron-clad sadhus and naked nagas, all jostled together on the roads along the sands. The smells of incense and marijuana and sweat and noonday cooking, the sounds of children crying and loudspeakers blaring and women chanting kirtans and policemen yelling, the sight of the sun glittering on the Ganga and the sand swirling in little eddies wherever the roads were not packed with people, all combined to give Dipankar an overwhelming sense of elation. Here, he felt, he would find something of what he was looking for, or the Something that he was looking for. This was the universe in microcosm; somewhere in its turmoil lay peace.

The jeep struggled, honking, along the sandy, metal-plated routes. At one point the driver appeared to be lost. They came to a crossroads where a young policeman was attempting with difficulty to direct the traffic. The jeep was the only vehicle as such, but great crowds swirled around the policeman, who shouted and flailed his baton in the air to little effect. Mr Maitra, Dipankar's elderly host in Brahmpur, an ex-officer of the Indian Police who had in effect requisitioned the jeep, now took matters into his own hands.

'Stop!' he told the driver in Hindi.

The driver stopped the jeep.

The lone policeman, seeing the jeep, approached it.

'Where is the tent of Sanaki Baba?' asked Mr Maitra in a voice of command.

'There, Sir—two furlongs in that direction—on the left-hand side.'

'Good,' said Mr Maitra. A sudden thought struck him. 'Do you know who Maitra was?'

'Maitra?' said the young policeman.

'R.K. Maitra.'

'Yes,' said the policeman, but it sounded as if he was just saying so to satisfy the whim of his strange questioner.

'Who was he?' demanded Mr Maitra.

'He was our first Indian SP,' replied the policeman.

'I am he!' said Mr Maitra.

The policeman saluted with tremendous smartness. Mr Maitra's face registered delight.

'Let's go!' he said, and they were off again.

Shortly they arrived at Sanaki Baba's camp. As they were about to go in, Dipankar noticed that a flower-flinging procession of some kind was approaching from the other side. He did not pay it much attention, however, and they entered the first tent of the encampment—a large one that acted as a kind of public audience hall.

Rough red and blue rugs were spread on the floor in the tent, and everyone was seated on the ground: men on the left, women on the right. At one end was a long platform covered with white cloth. On this sat a young, thin, bearded man in a white robe; he was giving a sermon in a slow and hoarse voice. Behind him was a photograph of Sanaki Baba, a plump man, fairly bald, very cheerful, naked to the waist with a great deal of curly hair on his chest. A pair of baggy shorts was all he wore. A river—probably the Ganga, but possibly, since he was a devotee of Krishna, the Yamuna—was flowing behind him.

The young man was in mid-sermon when Dipankar and Mr Maitra entered. The policemen accompanying them stayed outside. Mr Maitra was smiling to himself in anticipation of meeting his favourite holy man. He paid no attention to the young man's sermon.

'Listen,' continued the young preacher hoarsely:

'You may have noticed that when it rains it is the useless plants, the grass and weeds and shrubs that flourish.

'They flourish without effort.

'But if you want to grow a worthwhile plant: a rose, a fruit tree, a vine of paan, then you need effort.

'You must water, apply manure, weed it, prune it.

'It is not simple.

'So it is with the world. We are coloured by its colour. We are coloured by its colour without effort. As the world is, so we become.

'We go blindly through the world, as is our nature. It is easy.

'But for knowledge of God, for knowledge of truth, we have to make an effort. . . .'

It was at this point that the Raja of Marh and his retinue entered. The Raja had sent a man a couple of minutes ahead, but he had not been so bold as to interrupt the sermon. The Raja, however, was not a man to be awed by a Chief Justice or a Subsidiary Baba. He caught the young preacher's eye. The young man did namaste, glanced at his watch, and directed a man in a grey khadi kurta to see what the Raja wanted. Mr Maitra thought this an excellent opportunity to get his own arrival announced to Sanaki Baba, who was known to be quite casual about times and places—and sometimes people—and might well not appear for hours. The man in the grey kurta left the tent and went to another, smaller tent deeper in the encampment. Mr Maitra looked impatient, the Raja impatient and highly agitated. Dipankar looked neither impatient nor agitated. He had all the time in the world, and he concentrated again on the sermon. He had come to find an Answer or Answers at the Pul Mela, and a Quest could not be rushed.

The young baba continued in his hoarse, earnest voice:

'What is envy? It is so common. We look at the outside, and we long for things. . . .'

The Raja of Marh was stamping his feet. He was used to giving audiences, not waiting for them. And what had happened to the glass of sherbet he had ordered?

'A flame goes up. Why? Because it yearns for its greater form, which is the sun.

'A clod of mud falls down. Why? Because it yearns for its greater form, the earth.

'The air in a balloon escapes if it can. Why? To join its greater form, the outer air.

'So also the soul in our bodies longs to join the greater world-soul.

'Now we must take God's name:

> Haré Rama, haré Rama, Rama Rama, haré haré.
> Haré Krishna, haré Krishna, Krishna Krishna, haré haré.'

He began chanting slowly and softly. A few of the women joined in, then some more women and some of the men, and soon almost everyone:

> 'Haré Rama, haré Rama, Rama Rama, haré haré.
> Haré Krishna, haré Krishna, Krishna Krishna, haré haré.'

Soon the repetitions had built up to such an extent that the audience, still seated, was swaying from side to side. Small cymbals were clashed, high notes of ecstasy sounded on some of the words. The effect on the singers was hypnotic. Dipankar, feeling he ought to join in, did so out of politeness, but remained unhypnotized. The Raja of Marh glowered. Suddenly the kirtan stopped, and a hymn—a bhajan—began.

> 'Gopala, Gopala, make me yours—
> I am the sinner, you are the merciful one—'

But hardly had this begun than Sanaki Baba, clad only in his shorts, entered the tent, still engaged in conversation with the man in the grey kurta. 'Yes, yes,' Sanaki Baba was saying, his small eyes twinkling, 'you had better go and make arrangements: some pumpkins, some onions, some potatoes. Where will you get carrots in this season? . . . No, no, spread this there. . . . Yes, tell Maitra Sahib . . . and the Professor.'

He disappeared as suddenly as he had come. He had not even noticed the Raja of Marh.

The man in the grey kurta approached Mr Maitra and told him that Sanaki Baba would see them in his tent. Another man, about sixty years old, presumably the Professor, was also asked to join them. The Raja of Marh almost exploded in wrath.

'And what about me?'

'Babaji will see you soon, Raja Sahib. He will make special time for you.'

'I must see him now! I don't care for his special time.'

The man, apparently realizing that the Raja would make mischief unless contained, beckoned to one of Sanaki Baba's closest disciples, a young woman called Pushpa. She was, Dipankar noted with appreciation, very beautiful and serious. He immediately thought of his Search for the Ideal. Surely it could run concurrently with his Quest for an Answer. He noticed Pushpa speak to the Raja and bewitch him into compliance.

Meanwhile the favoured ones entered Sanaki Baba's small tent. Mr Maitra introduced Dipankar to Sanaki Baba.

'His father is a judge of the Calcutta High Court,' said Mr Maitra. 'And he is searching for the Truth.'

Dipankar said nothing but looked at Sanaki Baba's radiant face. A sense of calm had come upon him.

Sanaki Baba appeared impressed. 'Very good, very good,' he said, smiling cheerfully. He turned to the Professor and said: 'And how is your bride?'

The Baba intended this as a compliment to his wife of many years, a woman who usually visited him when her husband came. 'Oh, she's visiting her son-in-law in Bareilly,' said the Professor. 'She's sorry she could not come.'

'These arrangements for my camp are all right,' said Sanaki Baba. 'Only this water problem persists. There is the Ganga, and here—no water!'

The Professor, who appeared to be on the advisory administrative board of the Mela, replied half-unctuously, half-confidently: 'It is all through your kindness and grace, Babaji, that things are basically running so smoothly. I will immediately go and see what can be done in this case.' However, he made no immediate move, and sat staring with adoration at Sanaki Baba.

11.9

Now Sanaki Baba turned to Dipankar and asked:

'Where will you stay during the week of the Pul Mela?'

'He is staying with me here in Brahmpur,' said Mr Maitra.

'And coming such a long distance each day?' said Sanaki Baba. 'No, no, you must stay here in this camp, and go for a bath in the Ganga three times every day. You just follow me!' He laughed. 'You see, I am wearing swimming clothes. It is because I am the swimming champion of the Mela. What a Mela this is. Each year it gets bigger. And every six years it explodes. There are thousands of babas. There is a Ramjap Baba, a Tota Baba, even an Engine-Driver Baba. Who knows the truth? Does anyone? I can see you are searching.' He looked at Dipankar and continued kindly: 'You will find it, but who knows when.' To Mr Maitra he said: 'You can leave him here. He will be good. What did you say your name is—Divyakar?'

'Dipankar, Babaji.'

'Dipankar.' He said the word very lovingly, and Dipankar felt suddenly happy. 'Dipankar, you must speak to me in English, because I must learn it. I speak only a little. Some foreign people have come to listen to my sermons, so I am learning how to preach and meditate in English too.'

Mr Maitra had been containing himself longer than he could bear. Now he burst out: 'Baba, I can get no peace. What shall I do? Tell me a way.'

Sanaki Baba looked at him, smiling, and said: 'I will tell you an unfailing way.'

Mr Maitra said: 'Tell me now.'

Sanaki Baba said: 'It is simple. You will get peace.' He passed his hand backwards—his fingertips scraping the skin—over Mr Maitra's forehead, and asked: 'How does it feel?'

Mr Maitra smiled and said, 'Good.' Then he went on, pettishly: 'I take the name of Rama and tell my beads as you advise. Then I feel calm, but afterwards, thoughts come crowding in.' His heart was on his sleeve and he hardly cared that the Professor was listening. 'My son—he does not want to live in Brahmpur. He took a three-year extension in his job, and I accepted that, but I did not know that he was building a house in Calcutta. He will live there when he retires, not here. Can I live like a pigeon cooped up in Calcutta? He is not the same boy. I am hurt.'

Sanaki Baba looked pleased. 'Did I not tell you that none of your sons would come back? You did not believe me.'

'Yes. What shall I do?'

'What do you need them for? This is the stage of sannyaas, of renunciation.'

'But I get no peace.'

'Sannyaas itself is peace.'

But this did not satisfy Mr Maitra. 'Tell me some method,' he pleaded.

Sanaki Baba soothed him. 'I will, I will,' he said. 'When you come next time.'

'Why not today?'

Sanaki Baba looked around. 'Some other day. Whenever you want to come, come.'

'Will you be here?'

'I will be here until the 20th.'

'How about the 17th? the 18th?'

'It will be very crowded because of the full moon bathing day,' said Sanaki Baba, smiling. 'Come on the morning of the 19th.'

'Morning. What time?'

'19th morning . . . eleven o'clock.'

Mr Maitra beamed with pleasure, having succeeded in getting an exact time for Peace. 'I will come,' he said delightedly.

'Now where will you be going?' asked Sanaki Baba. 'You can leave Divyakar here.'

'I am going to visit Ramjap Baba on the northern shore. I have a jeep, so we'll cross Pontoon Bridge Number Four. Two years ago I visited him and he remembered me—he remembered me from twenty years before. He had a platform in the Ganga then, and you had to wade out to see him.'

'Hiss mammary berry shurp,' said Sanaki Baba to Dipankar in English. 'Old, old, old man. Like a stick.'

'So now, I'll go and visit Sanaki Baba,' said Mr Maitra, getting up.

Sanaki Baba looked nonplussed.

Mr Maitra frowned, and explained again: 'On the other side of the Ganga.'

'But I am Sanaki Baba,' said Sanaki Baba.

'Oh yes,' said Mr Maitra, 'I meant—what's his name?'

'Ramjap Baba.'

'Yes, Ramjap Baba.'

So Mr Maitra left, and after a while the pretty Pushpa showed Dipankar to some straw lying on the sandy ground in one of the tents: this was to be his bed for the next week. The nights were hot, so a single sheet would do.

Pushpa went off to escort the Raja of Marh to Sanaki Baba's tent.

Dipankar sat down and began to read from Sri Aurobindo. But after an hour or so he became restless and decided to follow Sanaki Baba around.

Sanaki Baba appeared to be very practical and caring—happy, bustling, and un-dictatorial. Dipankar looked at him carefully from time to time. His little eyebrows were sometimes knit in thought. He had the neck of a bull, dark curly hairs on his barrel-chest, and a compact paunch. His hair grew only in a forehead tuft and on the sides. His brown oval pate gleamed in the June sunlight. And sometimes, when he listened, his mouth opened in concentration. Whenever he saw Dipankar looking at him, he smiled back.

Dipankar was also very taken with Pushpa and found himself blinking furiously whenever he spoke to her. But whenever she spoke to him it was in a very serious voice, and with a serious frown.

From time to time the Raja of Marh would appear in Sanaki Baba's encampment and roar with rage if Sanaki Baba was not in. Someone had told him of Dipankar's special status, and occasionally during the sermons he would glare at him murderously.

Dipankar felt that the Raja of Marh wanted to be loved, but found it hard to be lovable.

11.10

Dipankar sat in a boat on the Ganga.

An old man, a brahmin, with a caste-mark on his forehead, kept up a loud commentary to the splash of the oars. He compared Brahmpur to Banaras, to the great confluence at Allahabad, to Hardwar, and to Sagar Island where the Ganga met the sea.

'In Allahabad, the meeting of the blue waters of the Yamuna and the brown waters of the Ganga is like the meeting of Rama and Bharat,' said the old man piously.

'But what about the third river of the Triveni which meets them there?' asked Dipankar. 'What would you compare the river Saraswati to?'

The old man looked at Dipankar, annoyed. 'Where are you from?' he asked.

'From Calcutta,' said Dipankar. He had asked the question innocently, and was sorry he had annoyed the man.

'Hmmmh!' snorted the old man.

'And where are you from?' asked Dipankar.

'From Salimpur.'

'Where is that?' asked Dipankar.

'It is in Rudhia District,' said the old man. He was now bending down and examining his disfigured toenails.

'And where is that?' persisted Dipankar.

The old man looked at Dipankar incredulously.

'How far is it from here?' asked Dipankar, seeing that the old man was not going to reply without further prompting.

'It is seven rupees away,' said the old man.

'All right,' yelled the boatman, 'here we are. Now, good people, bathe your fill and pray for the good of all men, including myself.'

But the old man would have none of it. 'This is not the right spot,' he shouted. 'I have been here every year for twenty years and you cannot fool me. It is there.' He pointed to a spot in the middle of the line of boats.

'A policeman without a uniform,' said the boatman in disgust. Reluctantly, he pulled on the oars a few more times, and took the boat to the indicated spot. Here there were quite a number of bathers already. The water was shallow, and it was possible to stand. The splashing and chanting of the bathers merged with the sound of a temple bell. Marigolds and rose petals floated in the muddy water, together with bits of soggy pamphlets, pieces of straw, the indigo-coloured wrapping of matchboxes, and empty packets made of stitched leaves.

The old man stripped down to his lungi, revealing the holy thread that stretched from his left shoulder to his right hip. In an even louder voice than before he exhorted the pilgrims to bathe. 'Hana lo, hana lo,' he shouted, spoonerizing the syllables in his excitement. Dipankar stripped to his underwear and plunged in.

The water did not look clean, but he stood around splashing himself for a minute or two. For some reason, this holiest of all spots did not attract him as much as the spot where the boatman had halted. There he had had the impulse to jump in. The old man, however, was transported with happy excitement. He squatted, ducking himself completely in the water, he cupped it in his hands and drank it, he pronounced 'Hari Om' as deeply and as often as he could. The other pilgrims were equally ecstatic. Men and women alike, they were delighting in the touch of the Ganga as babies delight in the touch of their mothers, and were shouting: 'Ganga Mata ki jai!'

'O Ganga! O Yamuna,' cried the old man, cupping his hands towards the sun and reciting in Sanskrit—

> 'O Ganga! O Yamuna!
> Godavari, Saraswati!
> Narmada, Indus, Kaveri,
> Be manifest in these waters.'

On the way back, he said to Dipankar:

'So you have had your first dip in the Ganga since you've come to Brahmpur!'

'Yes,' said Dipankar, wondering how he could have known that.

'I bathe here every day—five, six times a day,' continued the old man rather boastfully. 'This was only a short dip. I bathe day and night—sometimes for two hours at a time. Mother Ganga washes all your sins away.'

'You must sin a lot,' said Dipankar, some of his Chatterji acerbity rising to the surface.

The old man looked shocked at this sacrilegious humour.

'Don't you all bathe at home?' he asked Dipankar in scathing reproof.

'Yes,' laughed Dipankar. 'But not for two hours at a time.' He thought of Kuku's tub and began smiling. 'And not in the river.'

'Don't say "river",' said the old man sharply. 'Say "Ganga" or "Ganga Mata". It is not just a river.'

Dipankar nodded. He was amazed to notice tears in the old man's eyes.

'From the ice cave of Gaumukh in the glacier to the ocean surrounding Sagar Island, I have travelled along Ganga Mata,' said the old man. 'I could close my eyes and know where I was.'

'Because of the different languages they speak along the route?' asked Dipankar humbly.

'No! Because of the air in my nostrils. The thin piercing air of the glacier, the piny breeze of the gorges, the scent of Hardwar, the stench of Kanpur, the distinct fragrances of Prayag and Banaras . . . and so on down to the humid, salty air of the Sundarbans and Sagar.'

He had closed his eyes and was summoning up his memories. His nostrils opened wider and a look of peace came over his irritable face.

'Next year I will make the return journey,' he said, 'from Sagar in the delta up to the snows of the Himalaya and the great Gaumukh glacier and the open mouth of the ice cave once again, under the great peak of Shivalinga . . . then I will have made a complete circuit, a complete parikrama of the Ganga . . . from ice to salt, from salt to ice. Next year, next year, through ice and salt my spirit will surely be preserved.'

11.11

The following day Dipankar noticed that there were a few perplexed-looking young foreigners in the audience—and wondered what they were making of all this. They probably couldn't understand a word of the sermon or the bhajans. But the beautiful, slightly snub-nosed Pushpa soon came to their rescue.

'Now,' she said in English, 'the idea is simply this: all we are gatting is surrandered to lotus feet of Lord.'

The foreigners nodded vigorously and smiled.

'Now I must mantion there will be maditation in English by Baba himself,' announced Pushpa.

But Sanaki Baba was in no mood for meditation that day. He was chatting away on whatever took his fancy to the Professor and the young preacher, both of whom he had brought up on to the white-sheeted platform. Pushpa looked displeased.

Perhaps sensing this, Sanaki Baba relented, and a very abbreviated meditation session began. He closed his eyes for a couple of minutes and told his audience to do the same. Then he said a long 'Om'. Finally, in a confident, warm and peaceful voice, in atrociously accented English, pausing long between each phrase, he murmured:

'The river of love, the river of bliss, the liver of right. . . .

'Take in environment and supreme being through nostrils. . . .

'Now you will feel anand and alok—blissness and lightness. Feel, do not think. . . .'

Suddenly he got up and began to sing. Someone struck up the rhythm on the tabla, someone else began clashing small cymbals together. Then he began to dance. Seeing Dipankar he said: 'Get up, Divyakar, get up and dance. And you, ladies, get up. Mataji, get up, get up,' he said, dragging a reluctant old woman of sixty to her feet. Soon she was dancing away by herself. Other women began dancing. The foreigners began dancing, and danced with great gusto. Everyone was dancing, each by himself and all together—and smiling with joy and contentment. Even Dipankar, who hated dancing, was dancing to the sound of the cymbals and the tabla and the obsessively chanted name of Krishna, Krishna, Radha's beloved, Krishna.

The cymbals, tabla, and chanting stopped, and the dancing was over as suddenly as it had begun.

Sanaki Baba was smiling benignantly all around and sweating.

Pushpa had some announcements to make, but before she did so, she surveyed the audience and frowned with concentration. For a few seconds she gathered her thoughts. Then she told them rather reprovingly in English: 'You have now dancing and sermon and sankirtan and maditation. And the love. But when you are in offices and factories, then what? Then Babaji is not with you in physical form. Then Babaji is with you, but not in physical form. So you must not become attached to the dancing and the practice. If you get attached, it is no use. You must have the saakshi bhaava, the feeling of witnessing, or else what is the use?'

Clearly Pushpa was not entirely happy. She then announced the time of dinner and mentioned that Sanaki Baba would be speaking to a huge congregation at noon the next day. She provided clear instructions on how to get there.

Dinner was simple but good: curds, vegetables, rice—and rasmalai for dessert. Dipankar managed to sit next to Pushpa. Everything she said seemed to him to be utterly charming and utterly true.

'I used to be in teaching,' she said to him in Hindi. 'I was tied to so many things. But then this came, and Baba said to me, manage it all, and I felt as free as a bird. Young people are not stupid,' she added seriously. 'Most religious sadhus have destroyed religion. They like big funds, big followings, complete control. I am left free by Babaji. I have no boss. Even IAS officers, even Ministers have a boss. Even the Prime Minister has a boss. He must answer to the people.'

Dipankar nodded his head in vigorous assent.

All of a sudden he felt like renouncing everything—Sri Aurobindo, the Chatterji mansion, the possibility of a job in a bank, his hut under the laburnum tree, all the Chatterjis including Cuddles—and being free—free and boss-less as a bird.

'How true,' he said, looking at her wonderingly.

11.12

Postcard 1

Dear Dada,

I am writing to you from a tent near the Ganga, lying on a bed of straw. It's hot here, and noisy, because you can always hear loudspeakers with bhajans and kirtans and other announcements and the whistles of the frequent trains, but I am at peace. I have found my Ideal, Dada. I had a sense on the train coming here that it would be in Brahmpur that I would discover who I truly was and the direction of my individual existence, and I even hoped that I might find my Ideal. But since the only girl I knew in Brahmpur was Lata, I was worried lest it was she who should turn out to be my Ideal. That is partly why I have so far avoided visiting her family, and have deferred meeting Savita and her husband till after the Pul Mela is over. But now I need not worry.

Her name is Pushpa, and she is indeed a flower. But she is a serious person, so our pushpa-lila will consist of throwing ideas and feelings at each other, though I would like to sprinkle her with roses and jasmines. As Robi Babu says:

> . . . for me alone your love has been waiting

Through worlds and ages awake and wandering,
Is this true?
That my voice, eyes, lips have brought you relief,
In a trice, from the cycle of life after life,
Is this true?
That you read on my soft forehead infinite Truth,
My ever-loving friend,
Is this true?

Just looking at her, listening to her is enough for me, though. I think I have gone beyond mere physical attraction. It is the Female Principle that I adore in her.

Postcard 2

A mouse is playing at my feet, and last night I was kept awake by it—and, of course, by my thoughts. But this is all the lila, the play of the Universe, and I have plunged into it with great happiness. I am afraid the first postcard disappeared quickly, so I'm continuing on another one of the two dozen self-addressed postcards that Ma insisted on my taking with me.

Also, you must forgive my handwriting, which is bad. Pushpa has wonderful handwriting. I saw her write my name in the entry book in English, and she put a mystical full moon of a dot above my 'i'.

How are Ma and Baba and Meenakshi and Kuku and Tapan and Cuddles and yourself? I do not miss any of you as yet, and when I think of you, I try to think of you with a disinterested love. I do not even miss my thatched hut where I meditate—or 'maditate', as Pushpa, with her delightful accent and warm smile, puts it. She says we should be free—free as birds—and I have decided to travel after the Mela wherever my spirit takes me in order that I can truly discover the Entirety of

Postcard 3

my own soul and the Being of India. Just wandering around at the Pul Mela has helped me to realize that the Spiritual Source of India is not the Zero or Unity or Duality or even the Trinity, but Infinity itself. If I felt that she might agree, I would ask her to travel with me, but she is a devotee of Sanaki Baba, and has decided to devote her whole life to him.

But I realize I haven't told you who he is. He is the holy man, the baba in whose compound I am staying down here on the sands of the Ganga. Mr Maitra brought me to see him, and Sanaki Baba decided I should stay here. He is a man of great wisdom and sweetness and humour. Mr Maitra told him how unhappy and peace-less he felt, and Sanaki Baba provided him with some relief and told him that he would later explain to him how to meditate. When he left, Babaji turned to me and said: 'Divyakar'—he likes to call me Divyakar sometimes for some reason—'I crash into a table in the darkness, yet it is not the table that has hurt me but the lack of light. So, with old age, all these small things hurt, because the light of meditation is absent.' 'But meditation, Baba,' I said, 'is not easy. You make it sound as if it were easy.' 'Is sleep easy?' he asked. 'Yes,' I replied. 'But not for an insomniac,' he said. 'And meditation is easy, but you must gain that ease again.'

So I have decided to find that ease, and I have also decided that the bank of the Ganga is the place where I will find it.

Yesterday I met an old man in a boat who said that he had gone all

Postcard 4

the way along the Ganga from Gaumukh to Sagar, and it set up a yearning in my heart to do the same. Maybe I will even grow my hair long, renounce everything and take sannyaas. Sanaki Baba was quite interested in the fact that Baba (how confusing all these 'Babas' are) is a High Court Judge, but he said on another occasion during a sermon that even those who live in great mansions turn to dust in the end, in which even donkeys roll. It brought things home to me in every sense. Tapan will take care of Cuddles in my absence, and if not him, someone else will. I remember one of our school songs at Jheel School: Robi Babu's 'Akla Cholo Ré', which sounded absurd to me even then when it was shouted out by 400 voices. But now that I have decided to 'travel alone' myself, it has become a beacon to me, and I hum it all the time (though sometimes Pushpa tells me to stop).

Everything is so much at peace here, there is none of the acrimony that religion sometimes causes, well, such as we saw that evening of the lecture at the Ramakrishna Mission. I have been thinking lately of showing Pushpa my scribblings on various spiritual subjects. If you should meet Hemangini, please tell her to type out my jottings on the Void in triplicate; carbon copies stain one's fingers when one is reading them, and my handwriting is too much to ask Pushpa to read.

Postcard 5

One learns so much here every day, the horizons here are Infinite, and every day they expand. Over the whole of the Mela sands I can imagine the 'Pul' of pipal leaves, like a green rainbow spanning the Ganga from the ramp to the northern sands, carrying souls to the other side, and regenerating our polluted earth with its greenery. And when I bathe in the Ganga, which I do several times a day (don't tell Ila Kaki, she'll have a fit), then I feel a blessing flowing through my bones. Everyone chants, 'Gange cha, Yamune cha aiva', the mantra that Mrs Ganguly taught us to Ma's annoyance, and I too chant it with the best of them!

I remember, Dada, you once told me that the Ganga was a model for your novel, with its tributaries and distributaries and so on, but it now strikes me that the analogy is even more apt than you thought it at the time. For even if you now have to take on the additional burden of handling the family finances—since I won't be able to help you at all—and even if it takes you a few more years to complete your novel, you can still think of the new flow of your life as a Brahmaputra, travelling apparently in a different direction, but which will, by strange courses yet unseen to us, surely merge with the broad Ganga of your imagination. At least I hope so, Dada. Of course I know how much your writing means to you, but what is a novel after all compared to the Quest for the Source?

Postcard 6

Now I have filled up a whole stack of postcards, and I can't decide how to send them. Because if I post them separately at the post office here—they even have a Pul Mela post office! The administrative arrangements are quite amazing—they will arrive in random order, and I am afraid that will cause confusion. As it is, they look confusing with their mixture of Bengali and English, and my handwriting is worse than usual because I have nothing to rest the postcards on except my Sri Aurobindo. And I am afraid of causing you disquiet by the direction I have decided to take, or, rather, have decided I cannot take. Please try to understand, Dada. Perhaps you can take over for a year or two at home, and then maybe I will come back and relieve you. But of course this may not be my final answer because I am learning new things every day. As Sanaki Baba says, 'Divyakar, this is a watershed in your life.' And you have no idea how charming Pushpa is when she says: 'The Vibrations of the true feelings will always reach the Point of Focus.' So perhaps, having written all this, I don't need to send it after all. Anyway, I'll decide about all this later in the day—or maybe it will be decided for me.

Peace and Love to all, and blessings from the Baba. Please reassure Ma that I am well.

Keep smiling!
Dipankar

11.13

Darkness had come over the sands. The city of tents shone with thousands of lights and cooking fires. Dipankar tried to persuade Pushpa to show him a little of the Mela.

'What do I know of all that world?' she insisted. 'This camp of Baba is my world. You go, Dipankar,' she said, almost tenderly. 'Go to the world—to the lights that attract and fascinate.'

This was a dramatic way of putting it, thought Dipankar. Anyway, it was his second night at the Pul Mela, and he wanted to see what it was like. He walked along, pushed here or there by the crowds, or pulled here or there by his curiosity or instinct. He passed a row of stalls—just about to close for the night—where handloom cloth, bangles, trinkets, vermilion powder, flossy candy, sweets, rations, and holy books were being sold. He passed groups of pilgrims lying down on their blankets and clothes or cooking their evening meal before smoky, improvised fires embedded in the sand. He saw a procession of five naked ash-smeared sadhus—carrying their tridents—wandering down to the Ganga to bathe. He joined a large crowd that was watching a religious play about the life of Krishna in a tent close to the handloom stalls. A lively white puppy rushed out at him from nowhere, and snapped playfully at his pyjamas; it wagged its tail and tried to bite his heel. While not vicious like Cuddles, it appeared to be equally persistent. The more Dipankar whirled around to avoid it, the more the puppy seemed to enjoy the game. Finally two sadhus, noticing what was going on, threw clods of sand at the puppy and it ran off.

The night was warm. The moon was a little over half full. Dipankar walked along, not quite knowing where he was going. He did not cross the Ganga, but wandered along the south bank for a long time.

Large areas of the Pul Mela sands were demarcated for various sects or orders of sadhus. Some of these large groups, known as akharas, were famous for their tightly knit, militant organization. It was sadhus from these akharas who formed the most striking part of the traditional procession that took place each year at the Pul Mela on the grand bathing day after the full moon. The various akharas vied with each other for proximity to the Ganga, for precedence in the procession, and in the splendour of their display. They sometimes became violent.

Dipankar chanced to wander through an open gate into the huge covered area that marked one such akhara. He felt a palpable sense of tension. But other people, clearly not sadhus themselves, were wandering in and out, and he decided to remain.

This was the akhara of a Shaivite order. The sadhus sat in groups at dull fires that stretched in a line deep into the smoky recesses of the akhara. Tridents were stuck into the ground beside them, sometimes wound around with garlands of marigolds, sometimes crowned with the small drum associated with Lord Shiva. The sadhus were smoking from clay pipes which they passed around from hand to hand, and the smell of marijuana was thick in the air. As Dipankar wandered deeper and deeper through the akhara, he suddenly stopped short. At the far end of the akhara, in a pall of the thickest smoke, several hundred young men, wearing nothing but short white loin-cloths, their heads shaven, sat around huge iron pots like bees around a row of hives. Dipankar did not know what was going on, but a sense of fear and awe seized him—as if he had come upon a rite of initiation, to view which meant danger to the curious outsider.

And indeed, before he could back away, a naked sadhu, his trident pointed straight at Dipankar's heart, said to him in a low voice:

'Go.'

'But I just—'

'Go.' The naked man pointed the trident towards the part of the akhara from which Dipankar had come.

Dipankar turned and almost ran. His legs seemed to have lost all their strength. Finally, he arrived near the entrance of the akhara. He was coughing—the smoke had caught at his throat. He bent over, and pressed his hands to his stomach.

Suddenly he was pushed to the ground by the thrust of a silver mace. A procession was going past, and he was an obstacle. He looked up to see a dazzling flash of silks and brocades and embroidered shoes. And it was gone.

He was not hurt so much as winded and bewildered. He looked around, still sitting on the rough matting that covered the sandy ground of the akhara. He became aware after a while of a group of five or six sadhus a few feet away. They were sitting around a small ashy fire and smoking ganja. From time to time they looked at him and laughed in high-pitched voices.

'I must go, I must go,' said Dipankar to himself in Bengali, getting up.

'No, no,' said the sadhus in Hindi.

'Yes,' said Dipankar. 'I must go. Om Namah Shivaya,' he added hurriedly.

'Put your right hand forward,' one of them ordered him.

Dipankar, tremblingly, did so.

The sadhu smeared a little ash on his forehead, and placed some in his palm. 'Now eat it,' he commanded.

Dipankar drew back.

'Eat it. Why are you blinking? If I were a tantrik, I would give you the flesh of a dead man to eat. Or worse.'

The other sadhus giggled.

'Eat it,' commanded the sadhu, looking compellingly into his eyes. 'It is the prasad—the grace-offering—of Lord Shiva. It is his vibhuti.'

Dipankar swallowed the horrible powder and made a wry face. The sadhus thought this hilarious, and began to giggle once more.

One asked Dipankar: 'If it rained twelve months each year, why would the streams be dry?'

Another asked: 'If there were a ladder from heaven to earth, why would the earth be populated?'

A third asked: 'If there was a telephone from Gokul to Dwaraka, why would Radha be constantly fretting about Krishna?'

At this they all burst out laughing. Dipankar did not know what to say.

The fourth asked: 'If the Ganga is still flowing from the top-knot of Lord Shiva, what are we doing here in Brahmpur?'

This question made them forget about Dipankar, and he made his way out of the akhara, disturbed and perplexed.

Perhaps, he thought, it is a Question I am looking for, not an Answer.

But outside, the Mela was continuing just as it had been before. The crowds were pouring towards or back from the Ganga, the loudspeakers were announcing the lost and found, the sound of bhajans and shouts was interspersed with the whistles of trains arriving at the Pul Mela Railway Station, and the half moon was only a few degrees higher in the sky.

11.14

'What is so special about Ganga Dussehra?' asked Pran as they walked towards the pontoon bridge along the sand.

Old Mrs Tandon turned to Mrs Mahesh Kapoor. 'Does he really not know?' she asked.

Mrs Mahesh Kapoor said: 'I'm sure I told him once, but all this Angreziyat—this Englishness—has driven everything else out of his mind.'

'Even Bhaskar knows,' said old Mrs Tandon.

'That is because you tell him stories,' said Mrs Mahesh Kapoor.

'And because he listens,' said old Mrs Tandon. 'Most children take no interest.'

'Well,' said Pran with a smile, 'is anyone going to enlighten me? Or is this another case of chicanery disguised as science?'

'Such words,' said his mother, hurt. 'Veena, don't walk so far ahead.'

Veena and Kedarnath stopped and waited for the others to catch up.

'It was the sage Jahnu, child,' said old Mrs Tandon mildly, turning towards him. 'When the Ganga came out of Jahnu's ear and fell to the ground, that day was Ganga Dussehra, and that is why it has been celebrated ever since.'

'But everyone says that it came out of Shiva's hair,' protested Pran.

'That was earlier,' explained old Mrs Tandon. 'Then it flooded Jahnu's sacrificial ground, and he drank it up in his anger. Finally he let it escape through his ear and it came to earth. That is why the Ganga is also called the Jaahnavi, born of Jahnu.' Old Mrs Tandon smiled, imagining both the sage's anger and the eventual happy result.

'And,' she continued, a happy glow on her face, 'three or four days later, on the full-moon night of the month of Jeth, another sage who had been separated from his ashram went across on the pipal-pul, the bridge of pipal leaves. That is why that is the holiest bathing day of the Pul Mela.'

Mrs Mahesh Kapoor begged to differ. This Pul Mela legend, she believed, was pure fiction. Where in the Puranas or the Epics or the Vedas was any such thing mentioned?

'Everyone knows it is true,' said old Mrs Tandon.

They had reached the crowded pontoon bridge, and it was an effort to move, so dense were the crowds.

'But where is it written?' asked Mrs Mahesh Kapoor, gasping a little, but managing to remain emphatic. 'How can we tell that it is a fact? I don't believe it. That is why I never join the superstitious crowds who bathe on Jeth Purnima. It can only bring bad luck.'

Mrs Mahesh Kapoor had very definite views on festivals. She did not even believe in Rakhi, insisting that the festival that truly sanctified the bond between brother and sister was Bhai Duj.

Old Mrs Tandon did not want to quarrel with her samdhin, especially in front of the family, and especially as they were crossing the Ganga, and she left it at that.

11.15

North of the Ganga, across the crowded pontoon bridges, the crowds were sparser. There were fewer tents, and here and there the five of them walked across tracts of unsettled sand. The wind struck up and sand blew towards them as they struggled westward in the direction of the platform of Ramjap Baba.

They were part of a long line of other pilgrims who were bound for the same spot. Veena and the older women covered their faces with the pallus of their saris. Pran and Kedarnath covered their mouths and noses with handkerchiefs. Luckily Pran's asthma did not cause him any immediate trouble, though there could have been no worse conditions imaginable. Finally the long trek took the company to the place where Ramjap Baba's thatched platform, raised high on stilts of wood and bamboo, ornamented with leaves and marigold garlands, and surrounded by a great throng of pilgrims, stood on the gently sloping northern sands about fifty yards from the present bank of the river. Here he would stay even when, in a few weeks, the platform would effectively become an island in the Ganga. He would spend his days doing nothing but reciting the name of God: 'Rama, Rama, Rama, Rama,' almost uninterruptedly throughout his waking hours, and often even in his sleep. This was the source of his popular name.

Because of his austerities and because of what people saw as his basic goodness, he had acquired great merit and power. People walked for miles in the sand, faith written in their eyes, to get a sight of him. They rowed out to him from July to September when the Ganga lapped at the stilts. They had done so for thirty years. Ramjap Baba always came to Brahmpur at the time of the Pul Mela, waited for the water to surround him, and left when it retreated beyond his platform about four months later. It was his own quadrimester or chatur-maas, even though it did not coincide in any strict sense with the traditional four-month sleep of the gods.

What people got from him was difficult to say. Sometimes he spoke to them, sometimes not, sometimes he blessed them, sometimes not. This thin man, as withered as a scarecrow, burned to the colour of dark tanned leather by the sun and the wind, gaunt, exhausted, squatted on his platform, his knees near his ears, his long head faintly visible over the ledge of the parapet. He had a white beard, matted black hair, and sunken eyes that stared almost sightlessly across the sea of people, as if they were so many grains of sand or drops of water.

The crowds of pilgrims—many of whom were clutching copies of the Shri Bhagavad Charit, a yellow-covered edition of which was on sale here—were held back by young volunteers, who were in turn controlled by the gestures of an older man. This man, who in some sense appeared to officiate over the proceedings, had thick spectacles, and looked like an academic. He had in fact been in government service for many years, but had left it in order to serve Ramjap Baba.

One scraggly arm of Ramjap Baba's frail frame rested on the parapet, and with it he blessed the people who were brought forward to receive his blessing. He whispered words to them in a weak voice. Sometimes he just stared ahead. The volunteers were holding the crowds back with difficulty. They were almost hoarse with shouting:

'Get back—get back—please only bring one copy of the book to be touched by Babaji—'

The old holy man touched it exhaustedly with the middle finger of his right hand.

'In order, please—in order—yes, I know you are a student of Brahmpur University with twenty-five companions—please wait your turn—sit down, sit down—get back, Mataji, please get back, don't make things difficult for us—'

Hands outstretched, tears in their eyes, the crowd surged forward. Some wanted to be blessed, some just to have closer darshan of Ramjap Baba, some to give offerings to him: bowls, bags, books, paper, grain, sweets, fruits, money.

'Put the prasad in this shallow basket—put the prasad in this basket,' said the volunteers. What the people had given would be blessed, and having been made sacred would be distributed among them again.

'Why is he so famous?' Pran asked a man standing next to him. He hoped he had not been overheard by his companions.

'I don't know,' said the man. 'But in his place and time he has done many things. He just is.' Then he tried to push himself forward once more.

'They say he takes Rama's name all day. Why does he do so?'

'Wood burns when rubbed and rubbed till it gives you the light you desire.'

While Pran pondered this answer, the thickly bespectacled man who was in charge of things came up to Mrs Mahesh Kapoor and did a very deep namaste.

'You have brought your presence here?' he said in surprise and with deep respect. 'And your husband?' Having been in government service, he knew Mrs Mahesh Kapoor by sight.

'He—well, he was detained by work. May we—?' asked Mrs Mahesh Kapoor shyly.

The man went to the platform, said a few words, and returned.

'Babaji said, it is kind of you to come.'

'But may we go forward?'

'I will ask.'

After a while he returned with three guavas and four bananas, which he gave Mrs Mahesh Kapoor.

'We want to be blessed,' she said.

'Oh, yes, yes, I'll see.'

Eventually they got to the front. They were introduced in turn to the holy man.

'Thank you, thank you—' whispered the haggard face through thin lips.

'Mrs Tandon—'

'Thank you, thank you—'

'Kedarnath Tandon and his wife Veena—'

'Aah?'

'Kedarnath Tandon and his wife.'

'Aah, thank you, thank you, Rama, Rama, Rama, Rama. . . .'

'Babaji, this is Pran Kapoor, son of the Minister of Revenue, Mahesh Kapoor. And this is the Minister's wife.'

The Baba peered at Pran, and repeated tiredly:

'Thank you, thank you.'

He leaned a finger out and touched Pran on the forehead.

But before she could be hurried along, Mrs Mahesh Kapoor, in a beseeching voice, said:

'Baba, the boy is very ill—he has had asthma since he was a child. Now that you have touched him—'

'Thank you, thank you,' said the old wraith. 'Thank you, thank you.'

'Baba, will he be cured?'

The Baba pointed upwards to the sky with the finger that he had used to bless Pran with.

'And Baba, what about his work? I am so worried—'

The Baba leaned forward. The escort tried to plead with Mrs Mahesh Kapoor to give way.

'Work?' The voice was very soft. 'God's work?'

'No, Baba, he is looking for a position. Will he get it?'

'It will depend. Death will make all the difference.' It was almost as if the lips were opening and some other spirit speaking through the skeletal chest.

'A death? Whose, Baba, whose?' asked Mrs Mahesh Kapoor in sudden fear.

'The Lord—your Lord—the Lord of us all—he was—he thought he was—'

The strange, ambiguous words chilled her blood. If it should be her husband! In a panic-stricken voice, Mrs Mahesh Kapoor implored: 'Tell me, Baba, I pray you—will it be a death close to me?'

The Baba seemed to register the terror in the woman's voice; something that may have been compassion passed over the skin-stretched mask of his face. 'Even if so, it would not make a difference to you. . . .' he said. The words appeared to cost him immense effort.

He was talking of her own death. That was what he must mean. She felt it in her bones. Her trembling lips could barely form the next question:

'Are you talking of my death?'

'No. . . .'

Ramjap Baba closed his eyes. Relief and agitation struggled in Mrs Mahesh Kapoor's heart, and she moved forward. Behind her she could hear the voice whispering, 'Thank you, thank you.'

'Thank you, thank you,' it continued to whisper more and more faintly as she, her son, his sister, her husband, and his mother—a chain of love and, consequently, of fear—moved slowly out of the crush on to the open sands.

11.16

Sanaki Baba, his eyes closed, was speaking.

'Om. Om. Om.

'Lord is ocean of the bliss, and I am his drop.

'Lord is ocean of love, and I am part and parcel of it.

'I am part and parcel of Lord.

'Inhale the bivrations through the nostrils.

'Inhale and exhale.

'Om alokam, Om anandam.

'The Lord is in you and you are part of Lord.

'Inhale the environment and divine master.

'Exhale the bad feelings.

'Feel, do not think.

'Do not feel or think.

'This body is not yours . . . this mind is not yours . . . this intellect is not yours.

'Christ, Muhammad, Buddha, Rama, Krishna, Shiva: mantra is anjapa jaap, the Lord is no any name.

'Music is unheard bivrations. Let music open the centres like lovely lotus flower.

'You must not swim, you must flow.

'Or float like lotus flower.

'OK.'

It was over. Sanaki Baba closed his mouth and opened his eyes. Slowly and reluctantly the meditators returned to the world they had left. Outside, the rain poured down. For twenty minutes they had found peace and oneness in a world far from strife and striving. Dipankar felt that everyone who had shared in the meditation must feel a warmth, an affection for all the others. He was all the more shocked by what followed.

The session was barely over when the Professor said: 'Can I ask a question?'

'Why not?' said Sanaki Baba dreamily.

The Professor cleared his throat. 'This question is addressed to Madam,' he said, stressing the word 'Madam' in a manner that implied an open challenge. 'In the inhalation and exhalation that you talked about, is the effect due to oxidation or meditation?'

Someone at the back said: 'Speak in Hindi.' The Professor repeated his question in Hindi.

But it was a curious question, which was either unamenable to any answer—or which could only be answered by a bewildered, 'Both.' For there was no either / or, no necessary contradiction in the two possibilities of oxidation and meditation, whatever they might mean. Clearly the Professor believed that the woman who had usurped too much power and closeness to Babaji needed to be put in her place, and that a question like this would show up both her ignorance and her pretensions.

Pushpa went and stood to the right of Sanaki Baba. He had closed his eyes again, and was smiling beatifically. Indeed, he continued to smile beatifically through the entire exchange that followed.

Everyone's eyes other than Baba's were on Pushpa. She reverted to English and spoke with spirit, and with cold anger:

'Let me make it quite clear that quastions here are not addrassed to "Madam" or anyone else but to the Master. If we give teachings here it is in his voice, and we translate or speak because of his vibrations speaking through us. The "Madam" knows nothing. So quastions should be addrassed to the Master. That is all.'

Dipankar was transfixed by the severity of her response. He looked at the Baba to see what he would say. The Baba's eyes were still closed in a smile, and he did not alter his stance of meditation. Now he opened his eyes and said:

'It is as Pushpa says, and I ask her to speak with my bivrations.'

At the word 'bivrations' there was a flash of lightning outside, followed by a clap of thunder.

The Master had forced Pushpa to answer the question. She covered her face with a cloth from distress and embarrassment.

Then she spoke with anger and sincerity and embattled defensiveness.

Looking straight at the Professor, she said:

'One thing is a must to say, and that is that we are all sadhikas, we are all learning, no matter how aged, and we must only ask the quastion which is ralevant, not any quastion for sake of quastion only, or to hold an examination of "Madam" or Master or anyone. If you are truly troubled by a quastion then you can ask it—if otherwise, then you will not get grace from the guru. So I should make that clear, and now I will answer the quastion. Because I can tell that we will have more quastion and answer sassion, and I must make all that clear from the beginning—'

Here the Professor attempted to interrupt, but she shot him down.

'Let me speak and finish. I am answering Professor Sahib's quastion, whatever spirit it is asked in, then why should the Professor Sahib interrupt? Now I am not a scientist of oxidation . . . oxidation is natural, but it is always there. But what is happening? You may be seeing or hearing, but word or picture as such: what is that? What is effact? It can be different. If you see obscene picture, that will have one effact on you, a strong effact'—she screwed up her nose and closed her eyes in distaste—'and a beautiful picture, different. So, music also. Bhajan music is music, film music also is music, but in one you have certain effact; in other, other. In smell also. It may be burning, but incense burning has wonderful smell, and shoes burning has tarrible smell. Or take prosassions of akharas tomorrow: some are in good spirit, some are fighting. It depends what. And sankirtan also, like this evening: you can have sankirtan with good people, or with bad people.' This was said very pointedly. 'That is why Saint Chaitanya only had sankirtans with good people.

'So let me tell the Professor Sahib, it is not a quastion "Is it maditation? Is it oxidation?" The real quastion is: "What is your dastination? Where do you want to go?"'

Now Sanaki Baba opened his eyes and began to speak. The rain was loud, and his voice was soft, but it was not difficult to hear him. The guru's words were calm and soothing, even as they sought to make distinctions and point out errors. But Pushpa shook her head from left to right as her Master spoke, gleefully smiling as he made his telling points, points which she took to be directed against the 'defeated' Professor. It was all so unloving, possessive and defensive that Dipankar could hardly stand it. The violent revulsion of feeling he was undergoing made him see this beautiful woman in a completely different light. She was gloating over her rival's discomfiture in a way that almost made him sick.

11.17

The wind was now whistling down the alleys of Old Brahmpur and shaking the pipal tree on the ramp with all its force. The pilgrims who were making their way down were wet through by the time they reached the foot of the Fort. Rain was running down the steps of the ghats, merging with the surface of the Ganga, and gouging out channels in the Pul Mela sands. The face of the moon was almost hidden. Above, clouds scurried confusedly across the sky. Below, men and women scurried confusedly around on the ground—trying to protect their belongings; hammering their tent-pegs more firmly into the sand; and tottering through the lashing rain and howling sand-laden wind towards the Ganga to bathe, for the most auspicious bathing time—which would last fifteen hours, until about three the next afternoon—had just begun.

The storm was violent enough to blow a few tents away on the Pul Mela sands, and—in the old town above—to flood a few alleys, shake tiles off some roofs, and even uproot a small pipal tree that stood more than a hundred yards away from the ramp that led down to the sands. But these events were soon magnified by darkness and fear.

'The great pipal tree has come down,' cried someone in dismay. And though it was not true, the rumour spread like the erratic wind itself through the crowds of awestruck pilgrims. They looked at each other and wondered what it all could mean. For if the great pipal tree that stood by the ramp had indeed fallen, what would become of the bridge of leaves, of the Pul Mela itself, or indeed of the very order of things?

11.18

Halfway through the night the storm ceased. The clouds disappeared, the full moon reappeared. The pilgrims bathed in their hundreds of thousands through the night and into the next day.

In the morning the processions of the great akharas began. The sadhus of each order in turn paraded down the main road of the Mela, which ran parallel to the river but a couple of hundred yards up the sands. The display was magnificent: floats, bands, men on horseback, mahants carried on palanquins, banners, flags, drums, whisks, naked nagas bearing fire-tongs or tridents, a huge, barbaric man who yelled holy verses as he brandished a great sword from side to side. Great crowds gathered to gaze at the spectacle and cheer the sadhus on. Hawkers sold flutes, false hair, holy thread, bangles, earrings, balloons, and snacks—peanuts and chana-jor-garam and rapidly melting ice-cream. Policemen on foot—or mounted on horses and in one case on a camel—maintained order. The processions were staggered to avoid confusion—or conflict between one sect of sadhus and another. Since the sadhus were as militant as they were arrogant and competitive, the authorities of the Pul Mela had taken pains to ensure that at least fifteen minutes elapsed between one procession and the next. At the end of their march, the sadhus of each procession took a sharp left turn and made straight for the Ganga, where—to shouts of 'Jai Ganga!' and 'Ganga Maiya ki Jai!'—they took an enthusiastic and rowdy communal dip. Then they returned by another, narrower parallel road to their camps, satisfied that no akhara could be more magnificent or pious than theirs.

The great pipal tree above the broad earthen ramp was, as anyone could now see, intact, and would probably continue to flourish for a few hundred years more. It had not, unlike some lesser trees, been uprooted by the storm. The pilgrims continued to arrive in droves at the Pul Mela Railway Station; they passed by the tree, folded their hands in respect and prayer, and began to make the journey down the ramp to the sands and the Ganga. But today, from time to time, whenever a procession passed along the main Mela route by the foot of the ramp, there was a slight obstruction to the cross-traffic and some congestion on the ramp itself. However, it was all taken in good spirit, especially since the ramp provided to many who stood on it a general view of the processions below—and for those pilgrims who had just arrived on this auspicious day, a first view of the whole tent-covered expanse and the holy river beyond.

Veena Tandon and her friend Priya Goyal, together with a few members of their immediate families, were among the crowds looking downwards from the ramp. Old Mrs Tandon was there, and so was her grandson Bhaskar, who was very eager to see and count and estimate and calculate and enjoy everything. Priya had managed to escape specifically for this holy purpose from her virtual confinement in the joint family home in Old Brahmpur. Her sisters-in-law and mother-in-law had made a fuss, but her husband, in his mild way, had convinced them on religious grounds; in fact, when her friend Veena had come to fetch her, she had persuaded him to come along as well. As for the men of Veena's own family, none of them were present: Kedarnath was out of town on work, Maan was still in

Rudhia, Pran had refused to subject himself to ignorance and superstition yet again, and Mahesh Kapoor had snorted in his most dismissive manner when his daughter brought up the suggestion that he accompany them. Today, in fact, even Mrs Mahesh Kapoor was not with them. She could not bring herself to believe in the scripturally unsanctioned myth of the pipal bridge which was supposed to have spanned the Ganga on this particular day. Jahnu's ear was one thing, the pipal bridge another.

Veena and Priya chatted away like schoolgirls. They discussed their schooldays, their old friends, their families sotto voce whenever Priya's husband appeared not to be listening (including him and his tendency to be more vocal asleep than awake), the sights of the Mela, the most recent antics of the monkeys of Shahi Darvaza. They were dressed up as gaudily as taste permitted, Veena in red and Priya in green. Although Priya planned, like everyone else, to bathe in the Ganga, she wore a thick gold necklace with a design of little buds—for if a daughter-in-law of the Rai Bahadur's house had to be seen out of doors, she could not be seen in unbejewelled nakedness. Her husband, Ram Vilas Goyal, carried Bhaskar on his back to give him a better view. Whenever Bhaskar had any questions, he asked his grandmother to explain things to him, and old Mrs Tandon, though she could not see too well—owing to both her height and her sight—was only too happy to do so. All of them, and everyone around them, was in high spirits. They were surrounded mainly by townspeople and peasants, though here and there a policeman could be seen, or even a sadhu who was not involved in the processions.

It was about ten in the morning, and, despite the previous night's storm, very hot. Some of the pilgrims carried umbrellas to protect themselves from the sun—or possible rain. For the same reason—and because it was a symbol of authority—the more important among the sadhus in the various processions were protected with parasols by their devotees.

The blaring announcements on the loudspeaker continued endlessly, as did the sound of drums and trumpets, and the alternating murmur and roar of the crowd. The processions continued, wave on wave: yellow-clad priests with orange turbans, announced by tubas and conches; a palanquin carrying a sleepy old man who looked like a stuffed partridge, preceded by a red velvet banner announcing that he was *Sri 108 Swami Prabhananda Ji Maharaj, Vedantacharya, M.A.*; semi-nude nagas, with a string tied around their waists and a small white pouch for their genitals; long-haired men carrying silver maces; bands of all kinds, one with black tunics and epaulettes of gold braid blaring tunelessly on clarinets, another (the *Diwana 786* band—obviously Muslim from the lucky number that it had adopted—but why had they been hired for this procession?) with red tunics and piercing oboes. One horse-drawn chariot had a fierce, toothless man on it, who shouted 'Har, har . . .' at the crowd, to evoke the roared response '. . . Mahadeva!' Another mahant, fat and dark and with breasts as plump as a woman's, seated benignly on a man-drawn cart, was flinging marigold flowers at the pilgrims, who scrambled for them where they fell on the moist sand.

By now Veena and her party had got halfway down the broad ramp, which was crowded with pilgrims, almost fifty abreast. They were all being pushed forward continuously by the pressure of the pilgrims behind them who were coming from the town or countryside around, or continuing to arrive on the special Pul Mela shuttle-trains. Since there were deep ditches to either side of the ramp, there was nowhere to go but forward. Unfortunately, the current procession of sadhus that blocked their path was advancing more sluggishly than before, probably owing to some obstruction ahead—or possibly in order to prolong their own enjoyment of their popularity with the spectators. People began to get alarmed. Old Mrs Tandon suggested that they try to go back, but this was clearly impossible. Finally the procession moved on, a welcome gap appeared before the next procession, and the crowds on the ramp surged and stumbled forward across the main route into the mass of spectators who lined the other side of the route. The police managed to restore order, and in a few minutes Bhaskar, from Ram Vilas's shoulders, was able to watch the next procession: several hundred naga ascetics, completely nude, led by six and followed by six huge gold-caparisoned elephants.

Bhaskar and his family were still on the ramp, though now only about twenty feet from its base. They had a closer view of things, and with the release of the people in front of them the crush had eased a little. Bhaskar viewed with absolute astonishment the ash-smeared naked men, decrepit or sturdy, their hair matted, marigold flowers hanging from their ears or around their necks. Their grey penises, flaccid or semi-flaccid, hung down and swung to and fro as they marched past, four to a row, tridents or spears held high in their right hands. He was too astonished to ask his grandmother what all this was about. But a great cheer, almost a roar, rose from the crowd, and several women, young and middle-aged, rushed forward to touch the feet of the nagas, and to gather the dust on which they had trod.

The nagas, however, would not have their formation disturbed. They turned on them fiercely, brandishing their tridents. The police tried to reason with the women, but to no effect. This went on for a while, some women managing to elude the few policemen posted at the foot of the ramp and succeeding in prostrating themselves for an instant before the holy men. Then, suddenly, the procession stopped.

No one knew why. Everyone expected it to start up again in a minute or two. But it did not. The nagas began to get impatient. Once more the pressure on the ramp began to build, as the arriving crowds were pushed forward, and pushed forward others in their turn. The people who were at the base of the ramp now found themselves crushed by the weight of numbers behind them. A man pressed himself into Veena and, indignant, she tried to turn around. But there was no room. It was becoming difficult to breathe. People all around her were beginning to shout. Some yelled at the police to let them through, others shouted up the ramp to find out what was going on. But though the view was wider, the situation was not much clearer to people higher up on the ramp. They could see that the elephants that led the nagas had stopped because the procession in front of them had halted. But why that earlier procession had stopped was impossible to tell. At that distance, processions and spectators merged into one, and nothing was clear. Replies were shouted down the ramp, but in the shouts of the crowd, the sounds of the drums, and the continuous announcements on the loudspeakers, even these were lost.

Completely bewildered, the crowd on the lower reaches of the ramp began to panic. And when in a few minutes those above them saw that the next procession of sadhus had arrived and now formed a continuous barrier below the ramp, with no gap to come, they began to panic as well. The heat, terrible before, was now stifling. The police themselves got swallowed up in the crowd that they were trying to control. And still the tired, heat-battered, but enthusiastic pilgrims kept arriving at the station, and—ignorant of what was happening below—pushed eagerly forward towards the pipal tree and the ramp in order to get to the holy Ganga.

Veena saw Priya clutch the necklace round her neck. Her mouth was open and she was gasping. Bhaskar looked at his mother and grandmother. He could not grasp what was happening, but he was terribly frightened. Ram Vilas, seeing that Priya was being crushed, tried to move towards her, and Bhaskar toppled off his back. Veena managed to get hold of the boy. But old Mrs Tandon was nowhere to be seen—the crowd had swallowed her up in its helpless and irresistible movement. People were screaming now, clutching at each other and stepping on each other, trying to find their husbands and wives, their parents and children, or flailing around for their own survival, desperate to breathe and to avoid being crushed. Some pressed forward into the nagas, who, fearing to be crushed between them and the spectators on the other side, laid into them with their tridents, roaring with anger. People fell, blood pouring from their wounds, on to the ground. At the sight of blood, the crowd reacted with terror, and tried to turn back. But there was nowhere to go.

Some people at the edges of the ramp tried to slip through the bamboo barricades and scramble down to the ditches on either side. But last night's storm had made these steep slopes slippery, and the ditches themselves were filled with water. About a hundred beggars were sheltering by the side of one of the ditches. Many of them were cripples, some were blind. The injured pilgrims, gasping for breath and clawing for a foothold on the slope, now came tumbling down on to them. Some of the beggars were crushed to death, and some tried to flee into the water, which soon turned into a bloodied slush as more of those who were trapped on the ramp sought this, their only route of escape, and fell or slid on to the screaming people below.

At the foot of the ramp, where Veena and her family were trapped, people were maimed or dying. Many of the old and infirm fell to the ground. Some of them, exhausted by the long journey, had little strength to withstand the shock or the pressure of the crowd. A student, unable to move, watched helplessly nearby as his mother was trampled to death and his father's ribs crushed. Many people were literally squeezed to death against each other. Some were suffocated, some succumbed to injuries. Veena saw one old woman, blood pouring out of her mouth, suddenly collapse near her.

There was complete and dreadful chaos.

'Bhaskar—Bhaskar—don't let go of my hand,' cried Veena, clutching him tightly. She had to gasp out every word. But they were thrust to and fro by the great terrified injured mass all around them, and she could feel the weight of someone's body force itself between her hand and his.

'No—no—' she screamed, sobbing with dread. But she felt the small hand slip, palm first, and then digit by digit, out of her own.

11.19

Within fifteen minutes more than a thousand people were dead.

Finally the police managed to communicate with the railway authorities and stop the trains. They set up barriers on the approach routes to the ramp, and cleared the area below and around the ramp. The loudspeakers started telling people to go back, not to enter the Mela grounds, not to watch the processions. They announced that the remaining processions themselves had been cancelled.

It was still not clear what had happened.

Dipankar had been among the spectators on the other side of the main route. He watched with horror the carnage that was taking place less than fifty feet away but—with the nagas between him and the ramp—there was nothing he could do. Anyway, there was nothing he could have done except get killed or injured. He did not recognize anyone on the ramp, so tightly packed was the crowd. It was a hellish scene, like humanity gone mad, each element indistinguishable from the other, all bent on a kind of collective suicide.

He saw one of the younger nagas stab furiously at a man, an old man who had in his terror tried to force his way to safety on the other side of the procession. The man fell, then rose again. Blood was streaming from wounds on his shoulder and back. With horror, Dipankar recognized him as the man whom he had met in the boat, the hardy old pilgrim from Salimpur who had been so insistent upon the correct spot for bathing. The man tried to struggle back, but was flung down by the crowd as it surged forward again. His back and his head were crushed by the trampling feet. When the crowd next surged back at the point of the tridents, the mangled body of the old man remained, like a piece of debris washed up by the tide.

11.20

Meanwhile, a number of VIPs and army officers, who had been watching the great spectacle of the processions from the ramparts of the Brahmpur Fort looked down in disbelief at the scene far below them. The panic began so suddenly, and the whole thing was over so quickly, that the number of motionless bodies lying on the ground when the terrified mob had finally been able to ooze away was unbelievable. What had happened? What arrangements had gone wrong? Who was to blame?

The Fort Commander, without waiting for a formal request, immediately sent troops down to help the police and the Mela officers. They began to clear bodies away, to take the injured to the first-aid centres and the corpses to the Pul Mela Police Station. He also suggested immediately setting up a central control room to deal with the aftermath of the disaster. The temporary telephone exchange that had been set up for the Mela was taken over for this purpose.

Those VIPs who had wanted to bathe on this auspicious day were on a launch in the middle of the Ganga when the captain came up to them in great agitation. The Chief Minister and Home Minister were standing side by side. The captain, holding out a pair of binoculars, said to the Chief Minister: 'Sir—I fear there is some trouble on the ingress ramp. You might wish to take a look for yourself.' S.S. Sharma took the binoculars wordlessly and refocused them. What had looked like a slight perturbation from a distance suddenly came alive to him in all its horrifying actuality. His mouth opened, he closed his eyes in distress, and opened them again to scan the upper reaches of the ramp, then the ditches on either side, the nagas, the embattled police. He handed the binoculars to L.N. Agarwal with the single word: 'Agarwal!'

The Home Minister's first thought was that in the ultimate analysis he might be held responsible for this calamity. Perhaps it is unjust to consider this thought atypically unworthy. Even in the worst calamities of others, some part of our mind, often the one that is quickest to respond, tries to brace itself for the vibration that will reach us from the epicentre. 'But the arrangements were perfect—I went over them with the Mela officer myself—' the Home Minister was about to say, but a second thought stopped him in his tracks.

Priya. Where was Priya? She had planned to go to the Mela today with Mahesh Kapoor's daughter—to watch the procession, to bathe. Surely she was all right. Surely nothing could have happened to her. Torn between love for her and fear of what might have happened, he could not say a word. He handed the binoculars back to the Chief Minister. The Chief Minister was saying something to him, but he could not understand what he was saying. He could not follow the words. He hid his head in his hands.

After a while, the fog in his mind thinned out, and he told himself that there were millions of people at the Mela today, and that the chances, the real chances, of her being one of the unfortunate people caught in the stampede, were very small. But he was still sick with worry for his only child. May nothing have happened to her, he said to himself. O God, may nothing have happened to her.

The Chief Minister continued to look grim, and speak grimly to him. But apart from the sharp tone, the Home Minister caught nothing, understood nothing. After a while he looked at the Ganga. A few rose petals and a coconut were floating on the water near the launch. Pressing his hands together he began to pray to the holy river.

11.21

Because the launch needed a deeper draught than a regular boat, it was difficult to land it on the shallow bank of the Ganga. The captain finally resorted to the expedient of mooring it to a chain of boats, which he in effect commandeered. By the time the launch was moored, more than three-quarters of an hour had passed. The crowds at the main bathing areas on the Brahmpur side had thinned to almost nothing. The news of the disaster had spread swiftly. The bathing posts with their colourful signs—parrot, peacock, bear, scissors, mountain, trident and so on—were almost deserted. A few people, in a restrained, almost fearful way, were still dipping themselves in the river and hurrying away.

The Chief Minister, limping slightly, and the Home Minister, almost trembling with anxiety, accompanied by the few officials who had been with them on the boat, got to the area at the foot of the ramp. The scene was an eerie one. A large stretch of sand was entirely empty of people. There was nothing there: no people, not even bodies—just shoes, slippers, umbrellas, food, pieces of paper, clothes torn to shreds, bags, utensils, belongings of all kinds. Crows were pecking at the food. Here and there one could see patches where the damp sand had been stained darker, but there was nothing to indicate the terrible extent of the calamity.

The Fort Commander presented his compliments. So did the Mela Officer, an ICS man. The press had been fended off after a fashion.

'Where are the dead?' said the Chief Minister. 'You have shifted them rather quickly.'

'At the police station.'

'Which one?'

'The Pul Mela Police Station, Sir.'

The Chief Minister's head was shaking slightly—as it sometimes did when he was tired, but not for that reason now.

'We will go there immediately. Agarwal, this—' The Chief Minister pointed at the scene, then shook his head, and did not continue.

L.N. Agarwal, who could think of nothing but Priya, pulled himself together with an effort. He thought of his great hero, Sardar Vallabhbhai Patel, who had died less than a year ago. It was said that Patel had been in court, at a crucial stage in his defence of a client against a charge of murder, when the news of his wife's death had been brought to him. He had controlled his sorrow and continued with his argument. Only when the court rose did he allow himself to mourn the already dead without risk to the still living. This was a man who knew the meaning of duty, and its precedence over private grief.

> Wherever his faltering mind
> unsteadily wanders,
> he should restrain it
> and bring it under self-control.

The words of Krishna in the Bhagavad Gita came to L.N. Agarwal's mind. But they were followed immediately by Arjuna's more human cry:

> Krishna, the mind is faltering,
> violent, strong, and stubborn;
> I find it as difficult
> to hold as the wind.

On the way to the police station, the Home Minister apprised himself of the situation as well as he could.

'What about the injured?' he asked.

'They have been taken to the first-aid centres, Sir.'

'How many injured are there?'

'I do not know, Sir, but judging from the number of the dead—'

'The facilities are inadequate. The seriously injured must be taken to hospital.'

'Sir.' But the officer knew it was impossible. He decided to risk the Minister's wrath. 'But how, Sir, can we do that when the exit ramp is full of departing pilgrims? We are trying to encourage everyone to leave as soon as possible.'

L.N. Agarwal turned on him caustically. So far he had not uttered one word of recrimination to the officer who had been in charge of the arrangements. He had wanted to ascertain where responsibility lay before he relieved his spleen. But now he said:

'Do you people ever use your brains? I am not thinking of the exit ramp. The ingress ramp is deserted, cordoned off. Use it to get vehicles in and out. It is broad enough. Use the area of the road at the base of the ramp as a car park. And requisition every vehicle within the radius of a mile from the pipal tree.'

'Sir, requisition—?'

'Yes. You heard me. I'll put it in writing in due course. Now give orders so that this is done immediately. And warn the hospitals of what to expect.'

'Yes, Sir.'

'Also get in touch with the university and the law college and the medical college. We will need all the volunteers we can get for the next few days.'

'But they are on vacation, Sir.' Then, catching L.N. Agarwal's look: 'Yes, Sir, I shall see what I can do.' The Mela Officer was about to leave.

'And while you are doing so,' added the Chief Minister, in a milder tone than his colleague, 'get the IG of Police and the Chief Secretary.'

The police station presented a painful sight.

The dead were laid out in rows for identification. There was nowhere to keep them but in the sun. Many of the bodies were horribly distorted, many of the faces crushed. Some of the dead looked merely asleep, but did not brush away the swarms of flies that settled thickly and filthily on their faces and their wounds. The heat was terrible. Sobbing men and women were moving from body to body, looking for their loved ones among the long lines of corpses. Two men were embracing tearfully nearby. They were brothers who had been separated in the crush, and each had come here fearing that the other might be dead. Another man was embracing the body of his dead wife and shaking both her hands almost in anger as if he hoped that this would somehow rouse her to life again.

11.22

'Where is the phone?' said L.N. Agarwal.

'Sir, I will bring it to you,' said a police officer.

'I'll make the call inside,' said L.N. Agarwal.

'But, Sir, here it is already,' said the obliging officer; a telephone on a long lead had been brought out.

The Home Minister called his son-in-law's house. At the news that his daughter and son-in-law had both gone to the Mela—and that they had not been heard from since—he said:

'And the children?'

'They are both at home.'

'Thank God. If you hear from them, you must call me at once at the police station. I will get the message wherever I am. Tell the Rai Bahadur not to worry. No, on second thoughts, if the Rai Bahadur doesn't know what has happened, don't tell him anything at all.' But L.N. Agarwal, who knew how news travelled, was sure that all Brahmpur—indeed, half of India—had probably heard the news of the disaster already.

The Chief Minister nodded at the Home Minister, a note of sympathy entering his voice: 'Ah, Agarwal, I didn't realize—'

L.N. Agarwal's eyes filled with tears, but he said nothing.

After a while he said: 'Has the press been here?'

'Not here, Sir. They were taking photographs of the dead at the site itself.'

'Get them here. Ask them to be cooperative. And get any photographers on the government payrolls here as well. Where are the police photographers? I want all these bodies photographed carefully. Each one of them.'

'But, Sir!'

'These bodies have begun to stink. Soon they will become a source of disease. Let relatives claim their own dead and take them away. The rest must be cremated tomorrow. Arrange a site for cremation on the bank of the Ganga with the help of the Mela authorities. We must have photographs of all the dead who have not yet been identified either by their relatives or by other means of identification.'

The Home Minister walked up and down the lines of the dead, fearing the worst. At the end he said: 'Are there any more dead?'

'Sir, they are still coming in. Mainly from the first-aid centres.'

'And where are the first-aid centres?' L.N. Agarwal still could not control the agitation in his heart.

'Sir, there are several, some quite far away. But the camp for lost and injured children is just over there.'

The Home Minister knew his own grandchildren were safe. He wanted above all to scour the first-aid centres, where the injured were lying, before they began to be dispersed—by his own instructions—through the hospitals of the city. But something struggled in his heart, and he sighed and said: 'Yes, I'll go there first.'

The Chief Minister, S.S. Sharma, had begun to suffer from the heat, and was forced to return. The Home Minister went on to the compound where the children were being temporarily housed. It was chiefly their names that were being announced in the raucous and melancholy messages that the loudspeakers were now broadcasting continuously over the sands. 'Ram Ratan Yadav of Village Makarganj in District Ballia in Uttar Pradesh, a child of about six years old, is waiting for his parents in the lost children compound near the police station. Kindly come to collect him there.' But many children—and the ones here ranged from three months to ten years in age—did not know their names or the names of their villages; and the parents of some of the children, who were whimpering or weeping or just sleeping from shock and exhaustion, were themselves lying stilled in death in the nearby police enclosure.

Women volunteers were feeding the children and giving them what comfort they could. They had compiled lists of those who had been found—incomplete as such lists necessarily were—and transmitted them to the central control room, so that they could be matched with a state-wise list of the missing that was being compiled there. But it was clear to the Home Minister that the foundling children would, like the dead, have to be photographed if they were not claimed soon.

'Take a message to the police station—' he began. And then his heart almost stopped for joy and relief as he heard his daughter's voice say: 'Papa.'

'Priya.' The name, which meant 'beloved' was never truer than now. He looked at her, and began to weep. Then he embraced her and asked, noticing her sad face:

'Where is Vakil Sahib? Is he all right?'

'Yes, Papa, he's over there.' She pointed to the far end of the compound. 'But we can't find Veena's child. That's why we're here.'

'Have you checked at the police station? I didn't look at the children there.'

'Yes, Papa.'

'And?'

'No.'

After a pause she said:

'Do you want to talk to Veena? She and her mother-in-law are frantic with worry. Veena's husband is not even in town.'

'No. No.' L.N. Agarwal, after fearing he had lost his child, could not bear to face someone else in the same anguish.

'Papa—'

'All right. Give me a minute or two.'

In the end he went over to Mahesh Kapoor's daughter, and said what words of comfort and practicality he could. If Bhaskar had not been found so far at the police station the chances were good, etc. . . . But even as he spoke he heard how hollow his words must sound to the mother and the grandmother. He told them that he would go around to the first-aid centres and phone up Bhaskar's grandfather at Prem Nivas if there was any news, either good or bad; they too should phone in periodically to check.

But at none of the first-aid centres was there any sign of the little frog, and as hour followed hour, Veena and old Mrs Tandon, and soon Mr and Mrs Mahesh Kapoor, and Pran and Savita, and of course Priya and Ram Vilas Goyal (who even began to feel themselves responsible for what had happened), sank into a deeper and deeper sense of hopelessness and desperation.

11.23

Mahesh Kapoor, while sympathizing with Priya and reassuring her that she should not be so foolish as to hold herself responsible for what was beyond anyone's control, did not tell her where he placed the responsibility: squarely on her father's shoulders. He was the Home Minister. It had been his duty to ensure that the arrangements were not susceptible to this horrendous eventuality. At least once before, in the firing at Chowk, L.N. Agarwal had shown either lack of personal foresight or unwise confidence in delegating authority to others who lacked it. Mahesh Kapoor, although he usually had very little time for his family, loved his only grandchild greatly, and was distressed beyond measure for his wife and his daughter.

Everyone stayed over at Prem Nivas that night. Kedarnath could not be contacted; he was out of town. Trunk calls were difficult to make, and he was not in Kanpur, where they had thought he might be on business. Maan, who was so fond of Bhaskar, was in Debaria still. Veena and old Mrs Tandon first went home in the flickering hope that Bhaskar might have gone back there. But no one in their neighbourhood had seen Bhaskar. They themselves had no telephone, and to spend the night alone at home would be unbearable. Their rooftop neighbour of the red sari reassured them that she would get in touch with the Minister Sahib's house if they had any news. And so they made their way back to Prem Nivas, Veena in her heart bitterly upbraiding Kedarnath for being, as he so often was, out of Brahmpur.

Like my father when I was born, she thought.

By then Pran and Savita were at Prem Nivas as well. Pran knew he would have to be with his parents and sister, but he was afraid of distressing his wife unduly in her present condition. If her mother or sister had returned from their travels, he would have felt no qualms about leaving her in their care and staying over at Prem Nivas himself. But Mrs Rupa Mehra's last letter had been from Delhi, and she was at this moment either in Kanpur or in Lucknow, far from where she could be of use.

That night the family discussed what could be done. No one could sleep. Mrs Mahesh Kapoor prayed. There was very little that had not already been attempted. All the hospitals of Brahmpur had been searched for Bhaskar, following the conjecture that he had been injured and taken there directly by some helpful person. So had all the police stations—but to no avail.

They were all certain that Bhaskar, intelligent and (usually) self-possessed as he was, would have either gone back home or contacted his grandparents if he had been able to. Had his body been misidentified and taken away for cremation by others? Had he been kidnapped in the confusion? As all the plausible possibilities disappeared one by one in the face of the facts, unlikely imaginings took on a credibility of their own.

No one could sleep that night. As disturbing as their own grief and anxiety was the sound of revelry that echoed through the darkness. For it was the month of Ramazan, the Muslim month of fasting. Because of the purely lunar Muslim calendar, the month of Ramazan had staggered its way back to summer over the last few years. The days were long and hot, and the deprivation great—since strict Muslims were enjoined even from drinking water during the daylight hours. After sunset, the relief therefore was the greater—and the nights were given over to feasting and celebration.

The Nawab Sahib, strict observant though he himself was, had, upon hearing of the calamity at the Pul Mela, forbidden any celebration in his own household. He was even more distressed when he heard that his friend's grandson could not be traced. But such fellow-feeling was not general, or at least not universal, and the sound of Muslim celebration in a town where the news of the disaster had spread like fire, and must be known to everyone, was embittering even to a man like Mahesh Kapoor.

The phone rang from time to time, exciting their hope and fear. But they were messages of sympathy—or intimations from one official source or another that nothing had come up—or else calls that had nothing to do with Bhaskar at all.

11.24

The afternoon before, on the instructions of the Home Minister, a number of cars had been requisitioned in order to ferry the wounded to hospital. One of these cars was the Buick of Dr Kishen Chand Seth.

Dr Seth had decided to see a movie that afternoon, and his car was parked outside a cinema hall, the Rialto. When he emerged, sobbing with sentiment, supported by his hardboiled young wife Parvati, he found two policemen leaning on his car.

Dr Kishen Chand Seth immediately flew into a rage. He raised his cane threateningly, and if Parvati had not restrained him, he would certainly have used it. The policemen, who knew Dr Seth's reputation, were very apologetic.

'We have orders to requisition this car, Sir,' they said.

'You—what?' spluttered Dr Seth. 'Get out, get out, get out of my sight before I—' He was at a loss for words. Nothing seemed severe enough retribution for their gall.

'Because of the Pul Mela—'

'All superstition, all superstition!' said Dr Kishen Chand Seth. 'Let me go at once.' He took out his key.

The Sub-Inspector apologetically took it from his hand in an unexpected and skilful movement. Dr Kishen Chand Seth almost had a heart attack.

'You—you dare—' he gasped. 'Teutonic frightfulness—' he added in English. This was worse than bayoneting babies.

'Sir, there has been a disaster at the Pul Mela, and we—'

'What nonsense! Had there been any such thing, I would certainly have heard of it. I am a doctor—a radiologist. You can't requisition a doctor's car. Let me see your written orders.'

'—we have orders to requisition any vehicle within a mile of the pipal tree.'

'I am just here to see a film, this car is not actually here,' said Dr Kishen Chand Seth, pointing to his Buick. 'Give me my keys back.' He reached out for them.

'Kishy, don't shout, darling,' said Parvati. 'Perhaps there really has been some disaster. We've been seeing a film for the last three hours.'

'I assure you, Sir, there has been,' said the policeman. 'There have been a great many deaths and injuries. I am requisitioning this car on the express instructions of the Home Minister of Purva Pradesh. Only cars of active—non-retired—doctors are exempt. We will take good care of it.'

This last remark was just a soothing formula. Dr Kishen Chand Seth realized immediately that his car would be virtually disabled through misuse and overuse. If what this idiot was saying was true, there would be sand in the engine and blood on the calfskin upholstery by the time he got it back. But had there really been such a disaster? Or was this just another example of post-Independence rot? People were shockingly high-handed these days.

'You!' he shouted at a passer-by.

Taken aback, not accustomed to being addressed in this manner, the man, a respectable clerk in a government department, stopped in his tracks and turned a face of polite, perplexed inquiry towards Dr Kishen Chand Seth.

'Me?'

'Yes, you. Has there been a disaster at the Pul Mela? Hundreds dead?' The last query was pronounced with scornful disbelief.

'Yes, Sahib, there has been,' said the man. 'I heard the rumour, then heard it on the radio. It is certainly true. Even the official estimate is in the hundreds.'

'All right—take it,' said Dr Kishen Chand Seth. 'But mind—no blood on the seats—no blood on the seats. I won't have it. Do you hear me?'

'Yes, Sir. Rest assured that we will return it to you within a week. Your address, Sir?'

'Everyone knows my address,' said Dr Kishen Chand Seth airily. And he stepped out on to the street, waving his cane. He was going to requisition a taxi—or some other car—to take him home.

11.25

L.N. Agarwal was not popular with the students of Brahmpur. He was disliked both for his authoritarian ways and for his manipulativeness on the Executive Council of Brahmpur University. And the pronouncements of most of the political parties on the university campus were virulently anti-Agarwal in tone.

The Home Minister knew this, and his request for student volunteers to help with the aftermath of the disaster was therefore phrased as a request from the Chief Minister. Most of the students were not in Brahmpur, since it was the vacation. But many of those who were there responded. They would almost certainly have responded even if the request had been signed by the Home Minister.

Kabir, being the son of a faculty member, and therefore living close to the university, was one of the first to hear of the appeal. He and his younger brother Hashim went to the central control room that had been set up in the Fort. The sun was about to set over the city of tents. Apart from the lights and cooking fires there were a number of larger fires here and there, where bodies were being cremated. The loudspeakers continued their endless litany of names, and would continue to do so throughout the night.

They were allocated to different first-aid centres. The other volunteers were exhausted, and glad to be relieved. They could get some food and a couple of hours' sleep before they were called back to duty again.

Despite everyone's efforts—the lists, the centres, the stations, the control room—there was more confusion than order. No one knew what to do with the lost women—mostly aged and infirm, penniless and hungry—until the Congress women's committee, impatient with the indecisiveness of the authorities, took them in hand. Few knew where to take the lost or dead or injured in general, few knew where to find them. Unhappy people ran from one end of the hot sands to the other only to be told that the meeting place for pilgrims of their particular state was somewhere else. Injured or dead children were sometimes taken to the compound for lost children, sometimes to the first-aid centres, sometimes to the police enclosure. The instructions on the loudspeaker appeared to change with the person who was temporarily manning it.

After a long night of assisting at the first-aid centre, Kabir was staring blankly ahead of him when he saw Bhaskar being brought in.

He was carried in very tenderly by a fat, melancholy, middle-aged man. Bhaskar appeared to be asleep. Kabir frowned when he saw him and immediately got up. He recognized the boy as his father's mathematical companion.

'I found him on the sand just after the stampede,' explained the man, setting the boy down on the ground where there was a little space. 'He was lying not far from the ramp, so he's lucky not to have got crushed. I took him to our camp, thinking he would wake up soon enough and I could take him home. I'm fond of children, you know. My wife and I don't have any. . . .' He drifted off, then returned to the subject at hand. 'Anyway, he woke up once, but didn't respond to any of my questions. He doesn't even know his name. And then he went off to sleep again, and hasn't woken up since. I haven't been able to feed him anything. I've shaken him, but he doesn't react. He hasn't drunk anything either, you know. But, through the grace of my guru, his pulse is still beating.'

'It's good you brought him here,' said Kabir. 'I think I can trace his parents.'

'Well, you know, I was going to take him to a hospital, but then I happened to be paying attention to that horrible loudspeaker for a minute or two—and it said that those lost children who had been taken under protection by individuals should be kept in the Mela area, otherwise tracing them would be impossible. And so I brought him here.'

'Good. Good,' sighed Kabir.

'Now if there is anything I can do—I am afraid I will be leaving tomorrow morning.' The man passed his hand over Bhaskar's forehead. 'He doesn't have any identification on him so I don't really see how you'll trace him. But stranger things have happened in my life. You are looking for a person, not even knowing who they are, and then you suddenly find them. Well, good-bye.'

'Thank you,' said Kabir, yawning. 'You have done a great deal. Well, yes, you can do one thing more. Would you take this note to an address in the university area?'

'Certainly.'

It had struck Kabir that he might not be able to get through to his father by phone, and that a note to him would be useful. He wrote a few lines—his handwriting was something of a scrawl because of his tiredness—folded it in four, wrote the address on top, and handed it over to the fat man.

'The sooner the better,' he said.

The man nodded and left, humming mournfully to himself.

After he had done his rounds, Kabir picked up the telephone and asked the operator for Dr Durrani's number. The lines were congested, and he was asked to try a little later. Ten minutes later he got through, and his father happened to be at home. Kabir informed him of the situation and asked him to ignore the note he would be getting.

'I know he's your friend, the mini-Gauss, and that his name's Bhaskar. But where does he live?'

His father was at his absent-minded worst.

'Oh, hmm, er—' began Dr Durrani. 'It's very, er, difficult to say. Now what is his last, er, name?'

'I thought that you might know,' said Kabir. He could imagine his father scrunching up his eyes in concentration.

'Now, er, I'm not exactly sure, you see, er, he comes and goes, various people, well, leave him here, and then we talk, and then, er, they come and pick him up. He was here last week—'

'I know—'

'And we were discussing Fermat's conjecture about—'

'Father—'

'Oh, yes, and an, er, interesting variant of the Pergolesi Lemma. Something along the, er, lines of what my young colleague, er, I have an idea—why don't we, er, er, ask him?'

'Ask whom?'

'Yes, Sunil Patwardhan, er, wouldn't he know about the boy? It was his party, I believe. Poor Bhaskar. His, er, parents must be perplexed.'

Whatever this meant, Kabir realized that he would probably get more sense out of this new lead than out of his father. He got in touch with Sunil Patwardhan, who recalled that Bhaskar was Kedarnath Tandon's son and Mahesh Kapoor's grandson. Kabir phoned up Prem Nivas.

Mahesh Kapoor picked up the phone at the second ring.

'Ji?'

'May I speak to the Minister Sahib?' said Kabir in Hindi.

'You are speaking to him.'

'Minister Sahib, I am speaking from the first-aid centre just below the eastern end of the Fort.'

'Yes.' The voice was like a taut spring.

'We have your grandson, Bhaskar, here—'

'Alive?'

'Yes. We have just—'

'Then bring him to Prem Nivas immediately. What are you waiting for?' Mahesh Kapoor's voice cut in.

'Minister Sahib, I apologize, but I am on duty here. You will have to come down yourself.'

'Yes, yes, of course, of course—'

'And I should mention—'

'Yes, yes, go on, go on—'

'It may not be advisable to move him at present. Well, I shall expect you soon.'

'Good. What is your name?'

'Kabir Durrani.'

'Durrani?' Mahesh Kapoor's voice expressed surprise before he told himself that disaster knows no religion. 'Like the mathematician?'

'Yes. I am his elder son.'

'I apologize for my sharpness. We have all been very tense. I will come down immediately. How is he? Why can't he be moved?'

'I think it is best if you see for yourself,' said Kabir. Then, realizing how terrifying these words might sound, he added: 'He does not appear to have any external injury.'

'The eastern end?'

'The eastern end.'

Mahesh Kapoor put down the phone and turned to the family, which had been following every word at his end.

In fifteen minutes Veena had Bhaskar in her arms again. She held him so tight that they seemed to be a single being. The boy was still unconscious, although his face was calm. She touched her forehead to his and whispered his name again and again.

When her father introduced the tired young man at the first-aid centre as Dr Durrani's son, she stretched her hands towards his head and blessed him.

11.26

Dipankar, who had been thinking of death and almost nothing but death since the meaningless disaster of the stampede, said: 'Does it matter, Baba?'

'Yes.' The kind face looked down at the two rosaries, and the small eyes blinked, as if in amusement.

Dipankar had bought these rosaries, one for himself and one—for some reason that he could not explain even to himself—for Amit. He had asked Sanaki Baba to bless them before he left the Mela.

Sanaki Baba had taken them in his cupped hands, and had said: 'What form, what power are you most attracted to? Rama? or Krishna? or Shiva? or Shakti? or Om itself?'

At first, Dipankar had hardly been able to register the question. His mind had reverted to the horror of what he had seen—experienced more than seen. Once more he saw the broken body of the old man a few feet away—the nagas stabbing at him, the crowd crushing him underfoot—the confusion and the madness. Was this what human life was about? Was this why he was here? How pathetic now appeared his hope to understand anything. He was more dismayed and horrified and bewildered than he had ever been.

Sanaki Baba placed his hand on his shoulder. Although he did not repeat his question, his touch brought Dipankar back to the present, back to the triviality, perhaps, of great concepts and great gods.

Now Sanaki Baba was waiting for his answer.

Dipankar thought to himself: Om is too abstract for me; Shakti too mysterious, and I get enough of it in Calcutta; Shiva is too fierce; and Rama too righteous. Krishna is the one for me.

'Krishna,' he said.

The answer seemed to please Sanaki Baba, but he merely repeated the name.

Then he said, taking both Dipankar's hands in his own: 'Now say after me: O God, today—'

'O God, today—'

'— on the bank of the Ganga at Brahmpur—'

'— on the bank of the Ganga at Brahmpur—'

'— on the auspicious occasion of the Pul Mela—'

'— on the occasion of the Pul Mela,' amended Dipankar.

'— on the auspicious occasion of the Pul Mela,' insisted Sanaki Baba.

'— on the auspicious occasion of the Pul Mela—'

'— at the hands of my guru—'

'But are you my guru?' asked Dipankar, suddenly sceptical.

Sanaki Baba laughed. 'At the hands of Sanaki Baba, then,' he said.

'— at the hands of Sanaki Baba—'

'— I take this, the symbol of all your names—'

'— I take this, the symbol of all your names—'

'— by which may all my sorrows be removed.'

'— by which may all my sorrows be removed.'

'Om Krishna, Om Krishna, Om Krishna.' Sanaki Baba began to cough. 'It's the incense,' he said. 'Let's go outside.'

'Now, Divyakar,' said Sanaki Baba, 'I am going to explain how to use this. Om is the seed, the sound. It is shapeless and without form. But if you want a tree, you must have a sprout, and that is why people choose Krishna or Rama. Now you hold the rosary thus—' and he gave one to Dipankar, who imitated his gestures. 'Don't use the second and fifth fingers. Hold it between your thumb and ring finger, and move it bead by bead with your middle finger while you say "Om Krishna". Yes, that's the way. There are 108 beads. When you get to the knot, don't cross it, return and circle the other way. Like waves in the ocean, forwards and backwards.

'Say "Om Krishna" on waking, on putting on your clothes, whenever you think of it. . . . Now I have a question for you.'

'Babaji, I have one for you as well,' said Dipankar, blinking a little.

'My question, however, is a shallow one, and yours a deep one,' said the guru. 'So I will ask mine first. Why did you choose Krishna?'

'I chose him because I admire Rama but I find—'

'Yes, he was after worldly glory too much,' said Sanaki Baba, completing his thought.

'And his treatment of Sita—'

'She was crushed,' said Sanaki Baba. 'He had to choose kingship or Sita and he chose kingship. He had a sad life.'

'Also, his life was one from beginning to end—at least in his character,' said Dipankar. 'But Krishna had so many different stages. And at the end, defeated, when he was in Dwaraka—'

Sanaki Baba was still coughing from the incense.

'Everyone has tragedy,' he said. 'But Krishna had joy. The secret of life is to accept. Accept happiness, accept sorrow; accept success, accept failure; accept fame, accept disgrace; accept doubt, even accept the impression of certainty. Now, when are you leaving?'

'Today.'

'And what was your question?' Sanaki Baba said with gentle seriousness.

'Baba, how do you explain all this?' Dipankar pointed to the distant smoke from a huge funeral pyre, where hundreds of unidentified bodies were being burned. 'Is it all the lila of the universe, the play of God? Are they fortunate because they died on this auspicious spot at this auspicious festival?'

'Mr Maitra is coming tomorrow, isn't he?'

'I think so.'

'When he asked me to give him peace, I told him to return at a later date.'

'I see.' Dipankar could not disguise the disappointment in his voice.

Once again he thought of the old man, crushed to death, who had talked of ice and salt, of completing his journey back to the source of the Ganga the following year. Where would he himself be next year, he wondered. Where would anyone be?

'I did not, however, refuse him an answer,' said Sanaki Baba.

'No, you did not,' sighed Dipankar.

'But do you want an interim answer?'

'Yes,' said Dipankar.

'I think there was a flaw in the administrative arrangements,' replied the guru blandly.

11.27

The newspapers, which had been consistently lauding the 'commendably high standard of the administrative arrangements' came down heavily on both the administration and the police. There were a great many explanations of what had happened. One theory was that a car which supported a float in the procession had overheated and stalled, and that this had started a chain reaction.

Another was that this car belonged not to a procession but to a VIP, and should never have been allowed on the Pul Mela sands in the first place, certainly not on the day of Jeth Purnima. The police, it was alleged, had no interest in pilgrims, only in high dignitaries. And high dignitaries had no interest in the people, only in the appurtenances of office. The Chief Minister had, it was true, made a moving statement to the press in response to the tragedy; but a banquet due to be held that same evening in Government House had not been cancelled. The Governor should at least have made up in discretion what he lacked in compassion.

A third said that the police should have cleared the path far ahead of the processions, and had failed to do so. Because of this lack of foresight the crowd at the bathing spots had been so dense that the sadhus had not been able to move forward. There had been bad coordination, poor communication, and under-staffing. The police had been manned by dictatorial but ineffectual junior officers in charge of groups of policemen from a large number of districts, a motley collection of men whom they did not know well and who were unresponsive to their orders. There had been less than a hundred constables and only two gazetted officers on duty on the bank, and only seven at the crucial juncture at the base of the ramp. The Superintendent of Police of the district had been nowhere in the vicinity of the Pul Mela at all.

A fourth account blamed the slippery condition of the ground after the previous night's storm for the large number of deaths, especially those that had taken place in the ditch on the edge of the ramp.

A fifth said that the administration should—when organizing the Mela in the first place—have used far more of the comparatively empty area on the northern shore of the Ganga for the various camps in order to relieve the predictably dangerous pressure on the southern shore.

A sixth blamed the nagas, and insisted that the criminally violent akharas should be disbanded forthwith or at any rate disallowed from all future Pul Melas.

A seventh blamed the 'faulty and haphazard' training of the volunteers, whose loss of nerve and lack of experience precipitated the stampede.

An eighth blamed the national character.

Wherever the truth lay, if anywhere, everyone insisted on an Inquiry. The *Brahmpur Chronicle* demanded 'the appointment of a committee of experts chaired by a High Court Judge in order to investigate the causes of the ghastly tragedy and to prevent its recurrence'. The Advocates' Association and the District Bar Association criticized the government, in particular the Home Minister, and, in a strongly worded joint resolution, pronounced: 'Speed is of the essence. Let the axe fall where it will.'

A few days later it was announced in a *Gazette Extraordinary* that a Committee of Inquiry with broad terms of reference had been constituted, and that it had been requested to pursue its investigations with all due promptitude.

11.28

The five judges in the zamindari case maintained strict secrecy about their consultations. From the moment that the case was closed and judgement reserved, their taciturnity exceeded even the regular bounds of judicial discretion. They moved around in the same social world as many of those whose lives and properties were bound up in this case, and they were conscious of the weight that even their casual comments were certain to carry. The last thing they wanted was to be in the eye of a storm of speculation.

Even so, speculation was widespread, active, and furiously inconsistent. One of the judges, Mr Justice Maheshwari, unconscious of the low esteem in which he was held by G.N. Bannerji, had greatly praised the eminent lawyer's advocacy to a lady at a tea party. He had made some extremely telling points, the judge confided. The news had spread, and the zamindars began to feel optimistic again. But on the other hand it was the Chief Justice, and not Mr Justice Maheshwari, who would almost certainly write the first draft of the judgement.

And yet it had been the Chief Justice who had given the Advocate-General such a grilling. Shastri had rallied, reconsidered his arguments, and accepted that if he maintained the line that had been so successful in the Bihar case, he might jeopardize his chances in the Purva Pradesh case. Here the judges seemed inclined to make different distinctions. But whether his attempt to double back had been successful was anyone's guess. G.N. Bannerji had, in his final two days of rebuttal, flayed what he called the 'opportunistic drift of my learned friend's rudderless raft, which looks to the current stirring about the bench and changes its course accordingly'. It was the general opinion of those present in court on the final two days that he had destroyed the government's case.

But the Raja of Marh, some of whose lands had been ravaged suddenly one day by a swarm of locusts, saw this as the warning of an unfavourable judgement. Others took note, with more substantial grounds for gloom, of the First Amendment Bill to the Constitution. This bill, which in mid-June received the assent of the President of India Dr Rajendra Prasad (whose father, interestingly, had been the munshi of a zamindar) sought further to protect land reform legislation from challenges under certain articles of the Constitution. Some zamindars believed this to be the final nail in their coffin. Yet others, however, believed that this amendment itself could be challenged—and that the land reform bills it sought to protect could in any case be declared unconstitutional since they infringed other, unprotected, articles—and indeed the spirit of the Constitution itself.

While the zamindars on the one hand and the framers of the act on the other, the tenantry on the one hand and the retainers of the landlords on the other, all underwent these swings of elation and depression, the judges continued to frame their judgement in secret. They assembled in the Chief Justice's chambers shortly after the arguments were over to discuss what shape and direction the judgement should take. There was considerable disagreement over the issues, the line to be taken in arriving at the judgement, and even over the judgement itself. The Chief Justice, however, persuaded the other judges to present a united front. 'Look at that Bihar judgement,' he said. 'Three judges, not essentially in disagreement, each insisting on having his own say, and at—I presume I will not be quoted—at such tedious length. How will the lawyers know what the judgement means? This isn't the House of Lords, and our judgements shouldn't be in the form of individual speeches.' He eventually brought his colleagues around to the idea of a single judgement unless there was strong dissent on a particular point. Rather than entrust any other judge with the first draft of the judgement, he decided to write it himself.

They worked with as much speed as care allowed. The draft judgement did the rounds of the judges in a single circular, gathering comments on separate sheets. 'In view of the argument on page 21 about the non-applicability of implicit concepts wherever specific provision covering a particular matter already exists in the wording of the Constitution, is not the rather lengthy discussion of eminent domain moot?' 'I suggest that on page 16 line 8, we delete the phrase "were tilling their own land" and substitute "were not in fact intermediaries between the agriculturists and the state".' 'I believe we should retain the eminent domain discussion as a second line of defence in case the Supreme Court overrules us on the non-applicability aspect.' And so on. None of the five were unconscious of the heavy burden of responsibility that lay on them in this decision: their judgement would be as momentous as any act of the legislature or executive and would alter the lives of millions.

The judgement—seventy-five pages long—was drawn up, amended, discussed, reamended, examined, approved, finalized. A single copy was typed up by the private secretary of the Chief Justice. Gossip and leakage were as endemic in Brahmpur as in the rest of the country, but no one except these six people got to learn what the judgement—and, most crucially, its final operative paragraph—contained.

11.29

For the last week or so Mahesh Kapoor, like many other senior and junior state politicians, had been shuttling back and forth between Brahmpur and Patna, which was only a few hours away by road or rail. The political aftermath of the Pul Mela and the precarious state of his grandson's health kept him in Brahmpur. But he was pulled towards Patna every second day or so by the momentous events occurring there, events that were likely, in his view, to alter entirely the shape and configuration of the political forces of the country.

These matters came up in a discussion with his wife one morning.

The previous evening he had learned, upon his return from Patna (where several political parties, including the Congress Party, were holding sessions in the mad heat of June), news that would keep him in Brahmpur at least until that afternoon.

'Good,' said Mrs Mahesh Kapoor quietly. 'Then we can go together to visit Bhaskar in hospital.'

'Woman, I will not have time for that,' was Mahesh Kapoor's impatient reply. 'I can't be hanging around hospital wards all day.'

Mrs Mahesh Kapoor said nothing, but that she was upset was obvious to her husband. Bhaskar was no longer unconscious, but he was very far from normal. He had a high temperature, and he could remember nothing of what had happened during the day of the stampede. His memory, even of earlier events, was erratic.

When Kedarnath had returned, he had hardly been able to believe the news. Veena, who had reproached him in his absence, did not have the heart to do so now. They stayed by Bhaskar's bedside day and night. At first heartbreakingly vague even about the identity of his own parents, Bhaskar had slowly begun to identify himself and his surroundings. Numbers still mattered to him however; and he cheered up whenever Dr Durrani visited him. But Dr Durrani did not find these visits particularly interesting, since his nine-year-old colleague had lost some of the acuity of his mathematical insight. Kabir, however, for whom Bhaskar had previously been just an occasional face in his house, had become fond of him. It was in fact he who prodded his absent-minded father into visiting Bhaskar every two or three days.

'What is so important that you can't visit him?' asked Mrs Mahesh Kapoor after a while. Her husband had turned back to the newspaper.

'Yesterday's Cause List,' replied her husband laconically. But Mrs Mahesh Kapoor persisted, and the Minister of Revenue explained, as one would to an idiot, that the Cause List of the Brahmpur High Court contained a bench-by-bench list of the next day's agenda; and that the judgement in the zamindari case would be announced in the Chief Justice's court at ten o'clock that morning.

'And after that?'

'After that? After that—whatever the verdict is—I will have to decide what the next step must be. I'll be closeted with the Advocate-General and Abdus Salaam and God knows who else. And then, when I return to Patna, with the Chief Minister and—why am I explaining all this to you?' He returned pointedly to his newspaper.

'Can't you leave for Patna after seven o'clock? Evening visiting hours are from five to seven.'

Mahesh Kapoor put the newspaper down, and almost yelled: 'Can't a man have peace in his own house? Pran's mother, do you know what is happening in this country? The Congress is threatening to split down the middle, people are defecting left and right to this new party.' He stopped, then continued with increasing emotion: 'Everyone who is decent is leaving. P.C. Ghosh has gone, Prakasam has gone, both Kripalani and his wife have gone. They are accusing us, rightly enough, of "corruption, nepotism, and jobbery". Rafi Sahib, with his usual circus skills, is attending the meetings of both parties—and has got himself elected to the board of this new thing, this KMPP, this Peasants' and Workers' Peoples' Party! And Nehru himself is threatening to resign from the Congress. "We also are tired," he says.' Mahesh Kapoor gave an impatient snort before repeating the last phrase. 'And your own husband feels much the same,' he continued. 'This is not why I spent years of my life in prison. I am sick of the Congress Party, and I too am thinking of leaving it. I have to go to Patna, do you understand, and I have to go to Patna this afternoon. Every hour the shape of things is changing, at every meeting there's some new crisis or other. God knows what is being decided for this state in my absence. Agarwal is in Patna, yes, Agarwal, Agarwal, who should be clearing up the Pul Mela mess, he's in Patna, manoeuvring endlessly, giving as much support to Tandon and as much trouble to Nehru as he possibly can. And you ask me why I won't defer going back to Patna. Bhaskar won't notice my absence, poor boy, and you can explain my reasons to Veena—if you remember one-tenth of them. You take the car. I'll find my own way to court. Now, enough—' And he held up his hand.

Mrs Mahesh Kapoor said nothing further. She would not change; he would not change; he knew that she would not change; she knew that he would not change; and each knew that the other knew this.

She took some fruit with her to the hospital, and he took some files with him to the court. Before departing to visit Bhaskar, she told a servant to prepare and pack some parathas for her husband so that he would have something to eat on the journey to Patna later in the day.

11.30

It was a hot morning, and a scorching wind blew along the exposed corridors of the Brahmpur High Court. By nine thirty, Courtroom Number One was packed solid. Inside the courtroom the physical atmosphere, though stuffy, was not unbearable. The long mats of khas recently suspended over a couple of the windows had been freshly sprinkled with water, converting the hot wind of June into a cooler breeze inside.

As for the emotional atmosphere, it was surcharged with suspense, excitement, and anxiety. Of those who had argued the case, only the local lawyers were present, but it seemed that the Brahmpur Bar, whether connected with the case or not, had decided en masse to attend this historic occasion. The press reporters too were present in force, and were already scribbling away. Swivelling and craning their necks in turn, they tried to catch sight of each famous litigant, each Raja or Nawab or great zamindar, whose fate hung in the balance. Or perhaps it would be more accurate to say that the balance had already tilted, but the curtain that hid the scales was still in place. A few minutes more, and it would be drawn aside.

Mahesh Kapoor entered, talking to the Advocate-General of Purva Pradesh. The reporter for the *Brahmpur Chronicle* could hear only a couple of sentences as they squeezed past him up the side-aisle. 'A trinity is sufficient to run the universe,' said the Advocate-General, his perennial smile a little broader than usual, 'but this case, it appears, needs two extra heads.'

Mahesh Kapoor said: 'There's that bastard Marh and his pederastic son—I'm surprised they have the brazenness to come to this court again. At least they look worried.' Then he shook his head, looking equally worried at the thought of an unfavourable outcome.

The court clock struck ten. The pageant of ushers began. The judges followed in sequence. They looked neither at the government lawyers nor at the advocates for the applicants. It was impossible to make out from their expressions what the judgement might be. The Chief Justice looked to left and right, and the chairs were moved forward. The Court Reader called out the numbers of the several conjoined writ petitions listed 'for pronouncement of judgment'. The Chief Justice looked down at the thick wad of typed pages in front of him, and riffled through them absently. Every eye in court rested on him. He removed the lace doily from the glass in front of him, and took a sip of water.

He turned to the last page of the seventy-five-page judgement, leaned his head to one side, and began reading the operative part of the judgement. He read for less than half a minute, clearly and quickly:

'The Purva Pradesh Zamindari Abolition and Land Reform Act does not contravene any provision of the Constitution and is not invalid. The main application, together with the connected applications, are dismissed. It is our view that parties should bear their own costs, and we order accordingly.'

He signed the judgement and handed it to the judge on his right, the senior puisne judge, who signed and handed it across the Chief Justice to the next-most-senior judge; thus the document ricocheted from side to side until it was handed down to the Court Reader, who stamped it with the seal of the court bearing the legend: 'High Court of Judicature, Brahmpur'. Then the judges rose, for that was the only item of business for which the full bench of five had been constituted. The chair shuffle was reversed, and the judges disappeared behind the dull scarlet curtain to the right, followed by the glittering ushers.

As was the custom of the Brahmpur High Court, all four puisne judges accompanied the Chief Justice to his chambers; then they walked to the chambers of the next-most-senior judge and so on in order. Finally, Mr Justice Maheshwari walked back to his chambers alone. Having thrashed the issues out for weeks in person and on paper no one had been in the mood for further conversation; the black-gowned procession had been almost funereal. As for Mr Justice Maheshwari, he was still puzzled about the document to which he had just affixed his signature, but he was a little closer to understanding Sita's position in the Ramayana.

To say that there was pandemonium in court would be an understatement. As soon as the last judge disappeared from view litigants and lawyers, press and public alike, began cheering and screaming, embracing each other or weeping. Firoz and his father hardly had the chance to look at each other when each was surrounded by a mixed group of lawyers and landlords and journalists—and all coherent speech became impossible. Firoz looked grim.

The Raja of Marh, like everyone else, had risen when the judges rose. But aren't they going to read the judgement? he thought. Have they postponed it? He could not grasp that so much significance could be contained in so few words. But the joy on the government side and the despair and consternation on his own brought home to him the full import of the baleful mantra. His legs gave way; he pitched forward on to the row of chairs in front of him and collapsed on the ground; and darkness came over his eyes.

11.31

Two days later, the Advocate-General of Purva Pradesh, Mr Shastri, carefully perused the full text of the judgement which had been brought out by the High Court printing press. He was pleased that it was unanimous. It was tightly written and clear, and would, he believed, withstand the inevitable appeal to the Supreme Court, especially now that the additional, recently erected wall of the First Amendment stood around it.

The contentions based on delegation of legislation, lack of public purpose and so on, had been dealt with and dismissed.

On the basic question—the one that could easily have gone either way in Mr Shastri's view—the judges had decided thus:

The 'rehabilitation grant' and 'compensation' both together formed the true recompense, the 'actual compensation' for the land taken over. This, according to the judges, put both items beyond constitutional challenge on the grounds either of inadequacy or of discrimination. Had the government's carefully planned contention that the two items were different been upheld, the rehabilitation grant would not have enjoyed the protection afforded under the Constitution to 'compensation', and would therefore have been struck down under its provision for the 'equal protection of the laws'.

As the Advocate-General saw it, the judges had given a violent blow to the government—and thereby moved it out of the path of an unseen but swiftly approaching train. He smiled to himself at the strangeness of it all.

As for the special cases—the Hindu charitable trusts, the waqfs, the crown grantees, the erstwhile rulers and so on—none of their contentions had been upheld. Shastri had only one mild regret, and that had nothing to do with the judgement itself. It was that his rival, G.N. Bannerji, had not been in court to hear the judgement.

But G.N. Bannerji was away in Calcutta, arguing another vastly lucrative if less momentous case, and Mr Shastri reflected that he had probably merely shrugged and poured himself another Scotch when he had heard by telephone or telegram about the result of this one.

11.32

In previous Pul Melas, although the crowds began to thin out after Jeth Purnima, large numbers of pilgrims still remained eleven days later to bathe on the night of Ekadashi, or even fourteen days later at the next 'dark' moon or amavas, which was sacred to Lord Jagannath. Not so this time. The tragedy, apart from the dread it had aroused among the pious, had resulted in a compete dislocation of regular administration on the sands. The health staff, overburdened by the emergency, was forced to neglect its regular tasks. Hygiene suffered, and there were epidemics of gastro-enteritis and diarrhoea, especially on the northern bank. The food-stalls were dismantled in an attempt to discourage the pilgrims from remaining, but those who remained had to eat, and soon profiteering became rife: a seer of puris cost five rupees, a seer of boiled potatoes cost three rupees, and the price of paan trebled.

But soon the pilgrims did disperse entirely. The army engineers removed the electricity poles and the steel plates off the roads, and dismantled the pontoon bridges. River traffic began to move downstream.

In time the Ganga rose with the monsoon rains and covered the sands.

Ramjap Baba remained on his platform, surrounded now on all sides by the Ganga, and continued to recite unceasingly the eternal name of God.

Part Twelve

12.1

Mrs Rupa Mehra and Lata returned from Lucknow to Brahmpur about a week before the Monsoon Term of the university began. Pran was at the station to meet them. It was late at night, and though it was not cold, Pran was coughing.

Mrs Rupa Mehra scolded him for coming.

'Don't be silly, Ma,' said Pran. 'Do you think I'd have sent Mansoor instead?'

'How is Savita?' asked Mrs Rupa Mehra, just as Lata was about to ask the same question.

'Very well,' said Pran. 'But she's getting bigger by the minute—'

'No complications at all?'

'She's fine. She's waiting for you at home.'

'She should be asleep.'

'Well, that's what I told her. But she obviously cares more for her mother and sister than for her husband. She thought you might need a bite to eat when you got home. How was your trip? I hope there was someone to help you at Lucknow Station.'

Lata and her mother exchanged a quick glance.

'Yes,' said Mrs Rupa Mehra in a definitive manner. 'The very nice young man I wrote to you about from Delhi.'

'The shoemaker Haresh Khanna.'

'You shouldn't call him a shoemaker, Pran,' said Mrs Rupa Mehra. 'He will probably turn out to be my second son-in-law, God willing.'

Now it was Pran's turn to give Lata a quick glance. Lata was shaking her head gently from side to side. Pran did not know if she was disavowing the opinion or the certainty of it.

'Lata encouraged him to write to her. That can only mean one thing,' continued Mrs Rupa Mehra.

'On the contrary, Ma,' said Lata, who could hold back no longer. 'It can mean one of several things.' She did not add that she had not encouraged Haresh to write, merely consented to his doing so.

'Well, I agree, he's a good fellow,' said Pran. 'Here's the tonga.' And he got busy telling the coolies how to arrange the luggage.

Lata didn't quite catch Pran's remark, or she would have responded very much as her mother did, which was with great surprise.

'A good fellow? How do you know he is a good fellow?' asked Mrs Rupa Mehra, frowning.

'No mystery,' said Pran, enjoying Mrs Rupa Mehra's perplexity. 'I just happen to have met him, that's all.'

'You mean you know Haresh?' said his mother-in-law.

Pran was coughing and nodding simultaneously. Now both Mrs Rupa Mehra and Lata were looking at him in astonishment.

After his voice returned he said, 'Yes, yes, I know your cobbler.'

'I wish you wouldn't call him that,' said Mrs Rupa Mehra in exasperation. 'He has a degree from England. And I wish you would take care of your health. How can you take care of Savita if you don't?'

'I like him well enough,' said Pran. 'But I can't help thinking of him as a cobbler. When he came to Sunil Patwardhan's party he brought along a pair of brogues he'd made just that morning. Or that he wanted made. Or something like that—' he ended.

'What are you talking about, Pran?' cried Mrs Rupa Mehra. 'I wish you wouldn't speak in riddles. How can you bring along something that you want made? Who is this Sunil Patwardhan, and what brogues are these? And'—she added with a particular air of grievance—'why didn't I know about all this?'

That Mrs Rupa Mehra, whose special business it was to know everyone else's, should not have known that Haresh had met Pran, in all likelihood before she had, irked her greatly.

'Now don't be annoyed with me, Ma, it's not my fault that I didn't tell you. I think things were a bit fraught here at home at the time—or perhaps it just slipped my mind. He was here on business a few months ago, and stayed with a colleague and I happened to meet him. A short man, well-dressed, straightforward, and quite definite in his opinions. Haresh Khanna, yes. I particularly remembered his name because I thought he might be a suitable prospect for Lata.'

'You remember thinking—' began Mrs Rupa Mehra. 'And you did nothing about it?' Here was unbelievable dereliction of duty. Her sons were thoroughly irresponsible in this regard, but she had not believed it of her son-in-law.

'Well—' Pran paused for a while, considering his words, then said:

'Now I don't know how much or how little you know about him, Ma, and it's been a little while since the party, and I can't say that it all comes back to me exactly as I heard it, but it is my understanding from Sunil Patwardhan that there was some girl in his life, some Sikh girl, who—'

'Yes, yes, we know,' Mrs Rupa Mehra cut him off. 'We know perfectly well. But that will not stand in our way.' Mrs Rupa Mehra made it clear by her tone that an armoured corps of Sikh damsels could not come between her and her target.

Pran continued: 'Sunil had some perfectly idiotic couplet about him and this girl. I can't recall it right now. At any rate he gave me to understand that our cobbler was spoken for.'

Mrs Rupa Mehra let the appellation pass. 'Who is this Sunil?' she demanded.

'Don't you know him, Ma?' said Pran. 'Well, I suppose we haven't had him over when you've been here. Savita and I like him a lot. He's very lively, very good at imitations. He'd enjoy meeting you, and I think you'd enjoy meeting him. After a few minutes you'll imagine you're speaking to yourself.'

'But what does he do?' asked Mrs Rupa Mehra. 'What is his work?'

'Oh, sorry, Ma, I see what you mean. He's a lecturer in the Mathematics Department. He works in some of the same areas as Dr Durrani.'

Lata turned her head at the name. A look of tenderness and unhappiness passed over her face. She knew how difficult it would be to avoid Kabir on the campus, and she was uncertain now about whether she wanted to—or would be able to force herself to—avoid him. But after her long silence, what would his feelings towards her be? She feared that she had hurt him, as he had her, and neither thought gave her anything but pain.

'Now you must tell me all the other news about Brahmpur,' said Mrs Rupa Mehra quickly. 'Tell me about this terrible thing we've all been hearing about—at the Pul Mela. This stampede. No one we know was injured, I hope.'

'Well, Ma,' said Pran thoughtfully, unwilling to mention anything about Bhaskar tonight, 'let's talk about the news tomorrow morning. There's lots to tell—the Pul Mela disaster, the zamindari verdict, its effect on my father—oh yes, and on your father's car, the Buick'—here he began coughing—'and, of course, my asthma's been cured by Ramjap Baba, except that the news doesn't seem to have reached my lungs yet. You're both tired, and I admit I feel a bit exhausted myself. Here we are. Ah, darling'—for Savita had come up to the gate—'you really are foolish.' He kissed her forehead.

Savita and Lata kissed. Mrs Rupa Mehra hugged her elder daughter tearfully for a minute, then said: 'My father's car?—'

It was, however, not the time for talk. The tonga was unloaded, hot soup offered and declined, goodnights exchanged. Mrs Rupa Mehra yawned, got ready for bed, removed her false teeth, gave Lata a kiss, said a prayer, and went off to sleep.

Lata stayed awake longer, but—unlike in the tonga—she was thinking of neither Kabir nor Haresh. Even her mother's quiet and regular breathing failed to reassure her. The moment she lay down she remembered where she had spent the previous night. She thought at first that she would not be able to close her eyes. She kept imagining the sound of footsteps outside the door, and her imagination recreated for her the chimes of the grandfather clock that stood at the end of that long corridor, near Pushkar's and Kiran's rooms.

'I thought you were an intelligent girl,' the odious, disappointed, forgiving voice was saying.

But in a while her eyes closed of their own accord, and her mind yielded to a blessed exhaustion.

12.2

Mrs Rupa Mehra and her two daughters had just finished breakfast and had so far had no time to talk about anything of significance when two visitors from Prem Nivas arrived: Mrs Mahesh Kapoor and Veena.

Mrs Rupa Mehra's face lit up at the thought of their kindness and consideration. 'Come in, come in, come in,' she said in Hindi. 'I was just thinking about you, and here you are. You must have breakfast,' she continued, taking over her daughter's house in a manner that was impossible for her in Calcutta under the eye of the gorgon. 'No? Well, tea at least. How is everyone at Prem Nivas? And in Misri Mandi? Why has Kedarnath not come—or his mother? And where is Bhaskar? School hasn't begun yet—or has it? I suppose he is out flying kites with his friends and has forgotten all about his Rupa Nani. Minister Sahib of course is busy, I can imagine, so I don't blame him for not visiting us, but Kedarnath should certainly have come. He doesn't do much in the morning. But tell me all the news. Pran promised to, but far from being able to talk to him, I haven't even seen him this morning. He's gone to attend a meeting of some committee. You should tell him, Savita, not to overexert. And'—turning to Pran's mother—'you should also advise him not to be so active. Your words will carry a lot of weight. A mother's words always do.'

'Who listens to my words?' said Mrs Mahesh Kapoor in her quiet way. 'You know how it is.'

'Yes,' agreed Mrs Rupa Mehra, shaking her head in vehement agreement. 'I know exactly how it is. No one listens to their parents these days. It's a sign of the times.' Lata and Savita glanced at each other. Mrs Rupa Mehra went on: 'Now with my father, no one dares to disobey him. Or he slaps them. He slapped me once even after Arun was born because he said I wasn't handling him properly; Arun was being very difficult, crying for no reason, and it disturbed my father. I began crying of course when he slapped me. And Arun, who was only one at the time, began crying even louder. My husband was on tour at the time.' Her eyes misted over, then cleared up as she remembered something.

'My father's car—the Buick—what has happened to it?' she asked.

'It was requisitioned to help with the casualties at the Pul Mela,' said Veena. 'I think it's been returned; it should have been returned by now. But we haven't followed things up these days, we've been so worried about Bhaskar.'

'Worried? Whatever for?' said Mrs Rupa Mehra.

'What's happened to Bhaskar?' said Lata, simultaneously.

Veena, her mother and Savita were all greatly surprised that Mrs Rupa Mehra hadn't been informed fully by Pran within minutes of her arrival the previous night of Bhaskar's accident and its aftermath. Each filled in the picture with eagerness and distress, and Mrs Rupa Mehra's cries of alarm and sympathy added to the concern, excitement and noise.

If five of us can make the racket we're making, Birbal really did see a miracle under that tree, said Lata to herself, and her thoughts turned temporarily from Bhaskar to Kabir at the very moment that the conversation itself did the same.

Veena Tandon was saying: 'And, really, if it hadn't been for that boy who recognized Bhaskar, God knows what we would ever have done—or who would ever have found him. He was still unconscious when we saw him—and when he came to, he couldn't even remember his own name.' She began to tremble at the thought that an even worse disaster had been so close, so almost unavoidable. Even in her waking hours, even when holding her son's hand by his bedside, she often remembered with frightening distinctness the sense of his fingers slipping out of her grasp. And the return of that hand had depended on so tenuous a chance that there could be no possible explanation for it but the goodness and grace of God.

'Ah, the tea,' said Mrs Rupa Mehra in a rush of tenderness now that she had three young women to mother. 'You must have a cup immediately, Veena, no, you must, even if your hands are trembling. It will do you good instantly. No, Savita, you sit down, it isn't sensible for you in this condition to insist on acting as hostess. What is a mother for, don't you agree?' This last phrase was addressed to Mrs Mahesh Kapoor. 'Lata, darling, give this cup to Veena. Who was this boy who recognized Bhaskar? One of his friends?'

'Oh no,' said Veena, her voice a little steadier. 'He was a young man, a volunteer. We didn't know him, but he knew Bhaskar. He's Kabir Durrani, the son of Dr Durrani, who has been so good to Bhaskar—'

But Mrs Rupa Mehra's own hands, suddenly grown unsteady with shock, spilled the tea that she had just been pouring.

Lata had grown very still upon hearing the name.

What could Kabir have been doing down by the Pul Mela—and as a volunteer—at a Hindu festival?

Mrs Rupa Mehra put down the teapot and looked towards Lata, the original cause of her distress. She was about to say: 'Now look what you've made me do!' when some better instinct prevented her. After all, Veena and Mrs Mahesh Kapoor had no idea about Kabir's interest in Lata. (She preferred to think of it in that direction.)

Instead she said: 'But he's—well, he's—I mean, he must be from his name—what was he doing at the Pul Mela? Surely—'

'I think he was just a volunteer from the university,' said Veena. 'They sent an appeal for volunteers after the disaster, and he went to help. What a decent young man. He refused to leave his duty at the first-aid centre even to oblige a Minister—you know how abrupt Baoji can be on the phone. We had to go down ourselves to see Bhaskar. That was good, because Bhaskar shouldn't have been moved. And though Durrani's son was tired, he spoke to us for quite a long time, reassuring us, telling us how Bhaskar had been brought in, how he did not appear to have any external injury. I was almost beside myself with worry. It makes you think there is God in all of us. He comes quite often to Prem Nivas these days. His father, who knows Bhaskar, often comes along as well. None of us have any idea what they talk about. It makes Bhaskar happy, though, so we just leave them alone with paper and pencil.'

'Prem Nivas?' said Mrs Rupa Mehra. 'Why not Misri Mandi?'

'Well, Rupaji,' said Mrs Mahesh Kapoor. 'I have insisted that Veena stay with us until Bhaskar has quite recovered. It's not good for him to move around too much, the doctor says.' Mrs Mahesh Kapoor had in fact taken the doctor aside and insisted that he say this. 'And for Veena too, it's exhausting enough to take care of Bhaskar without having to run a household. Kedarnath and his mother are staying with us too, naturally. They're both with Bhaskar now. Someone has to be.'

Mrs Mahesh Kapoor made no mention of any additional strain this arrangement imposed on her. Indeed, she did not consider the additional effort of putting four people up in her house to be anything out of the ordinary. The kind of household she ran—had always run—at Prem Nivas involved offering hospitality at all hours to all kinds of people—often strangers, political associates of her husband. If that was an effort she undertook willingly if not gladly, this was one which she undertook both gladly and willingly. She was happy that at a time of crisis like this one, she could be close enough to help. If there had been one silver lining to the dark cloud of Partition, it had been that it had brought her married daughter and her grandson back from Lahore to live in the same town as her. And now, by virtue of another trauma, they were back in Prem Nivas itself.

'He misses his friends, though,' said Veena. 'He wants to go back to our neighbourhood. And once school begins it'll be difficult to keep him away. And then there'll be the rehearsals for the Ramlila—and he insists he wants to be a monkey this time. He's too small to be Hanuman or Nal or Neel or any of the important ones, but certainly he can be part of the army.'

'There'll be plenty of time to catch up with studies,' said Mrs Mahesh Kapoor. 'And the Ramlila is far away. It doesn't take much practice to be a monkey. Health is the main thing. When Pran was ill as a child, he often had to skip his studies. But it hasn't done him any harm.'

Talking of Pran turned Mrs Mahesh Kapoor's thoughts to her younger son, but she had learned not to fret excessively about what it was pointless to fret about. She wished she could curb her anxieties completely. Mahesh Kapoor had insisted that Maan not be informed about the accident that had occurred, for fear that he would instantly return to Brahmpur in order to visit the little frog, and stay on in Brahmpur, entangled in the toils of 'that'. Mahesh Kapoor's spirits had been in turmoil since he had returned from the Congress session at Patna. It was hard enough to decide what he should do in the face of the disastrous turn taken by the affairs of the party and the country. He could do without the presence of Maan, an additional and equally ungovernable thorn in his side—and reputation.

Apropos of nothing that had gone before, Mrs Mahesh Kapoor said, with a slightly embarrassed laugh: 'I sometimes almost feel that Minister Sahib's conversation of late has grown as incomprehensible as Dr Durrani's.'

Everyone was surprised at such a remark, coming as it did from the mild-spirited Mrs Mahesh Kapoor. Veena in particular sensed that only great pressure and anxiety could have wrung such a statement from her. She reproached herself now; in her own anxieties about Bhaskar, she had been unconscious of what her mother must have been undergoing, worried as she must have been by Pran's asthma and Bhaskar's injury, quite apart from Maan's behaviour and her husband's increasing abruptness. She was not looking well herself, but this was probably the least of her worries.

Mrs Rupa Mehra's mind, meanwhile, had swerved on to quite another track as a result of the last comment. 'How did Dr Durrani get to hear of Bhaskar?' she asked.

Veena, whose mind had been far away, said, 'Dr Durrani?' in a puzzled sort of voice.

'Yes, yes, how did Bhaskar and Dr Durrani get together? This dutiful son of his, you say, recognized Bhaskar because of that connection.'

'Oh,' said Veena. 'It began when Kedarnath invited Haresh Khanna to lunch. He's a young man from Kanpur—'

Lata burst out laughing. Mrs Rupa Mehra's face went first white, then pink. This was completely intolerable. Everyone in Brahmpur knew of this Haresh, and she had been the last to hear of it. Why had Haresh not mentioned Kedarnath or Bhaskar or Dr Durrani in his conversation? Why was she, Mrs Rupa Mehra, the last to be informed on a subject closer to her than to anyone else in this room: the acquisition of a son-in-law?

Veena and Mrs Mahesh Kapoor looked astonished by the reactions of both Lata and her mother.

'How long has all this been going on?' demanded Mrs Rupa Mehra with accusation and even resentment in her voice. 'Why does everyone know about everything? Everyone knows this Haresh; everywhere I go it is Haresh, Haresh. And only I am left staring.'

'But you left for Calcutta so soon after he was here that there wasn't any chance to talk to you, Ma,' said Veena. 'Why is it so important?'

When it dawned on Veena and Mrs Mahesh Kapoor from the closeness of the interrogation to which they were being subjected that Haresh was considered to be a 'prospect', they pounced on Mrs Rupa Mehra with a volley of questions of their own, and upbraided her for keeping them in the dark.

Mrs Rupa Mehra, mollified, was soon as eager to divulge as to receive information. She had described Haresh's certificates and qualifications and clothes and looks and had moved on to Lata's reactions to Haresh and his to Lata, when, luckily for Lata's peace of mind, she was interrupted by the arrival of Malati Trivedi.

'Hello, hello,' beamed Malati Trivedi, almost bouncing in. 'I haven't seen you for months, Lata. Namaste, Mrs Mehra—Ma, I mean. And to both of you.' She nodded at Savita and the very visible bulge. 'Hello, Veenaji, how is the music going? How is Ustad Sahib? I turned on the radio the other night and I heard him singing Raag Bageshri. It was so lovely: the lake, the hills, and the raag—all of them merged into one. I felt like dying with pleasure.' With a final namaste to Mrs Mahesh Kapoor, whom she did not recognize, but whom she guessed to be Veena's mother, Malati completed the circle, and sat down. 'I've just come back from Nainital,' she announced happily. 'Where's Pran?'

12.3

Lata looked at Malati as if she were a knight-errant. 'Let's go!' she said to her. 'Let's go for a walk. At once! There are lots of things I want to talk about with you. I've been wanting to get out of the house all morning, but I've been too lazy to do so. And I thought of going to the women's hostel but I didn't know if you were back yet. We ourselves just got back last night.'

Malati obligingly got up again.

'Malati has just come in,' said Mrs Rupa Mehra. 'This is not very hospitable, Lata, or polite either. You must let her have some tea. Then you can go for your walk.'

'That's all right, Ma,' said Malati, smiling. 'I'm not really feeling like tea, and I'll be thirsty when I return. I'll have some then, and we'll catch up on things. Meanwhile Lata and I'll take a walk by the river.'

'Do be careful, Malati, that path down by the banyan trees is very slippery in this weather,' warned Mrs Rupa Mehra.

After going to her room to fetch a couple of things, Lata made good her escape.

'Now what's all this about?' asked Malati as soon as they got out of the door. 'Why did you want to leave?'

Lata lowered her voice for no very good reason.

'They were discussing me and a man whom my mother made me meet in Kanpur just as if I wasn't there, and even Savita didn't object.'

'I'm not sure I would have objected either,' said Malati. 'What were they saying?'

'I'll tell you later,' said Lata. 'I've had enough of myself for a while, and I want to hear something different. What's your news?'

'What sort of news do you want?' asked Malati. 'Intellectual, physical, political, spiritual, or romantic?'

Lata considered the last two, then thought of Malati's comment about the lake, the hills, and a night raag. 'Romantic,' she said.

'That's a bad choice,' said Malati. 'You should get every idea of romance out of your head. But, well—I had a romantic encounter in Nainital. Except, well—' She paused.

'Except what?' asked Lata.

'Except, well, it wasn't really. Anyway, I'll tell you what happened and you decide for yourself.'

'All right.'

'You know my sister, my elder sister, the one who keeps kidnapping us?'

'Yes—I haven't met her, but the one who was married at fifteen to the young zamindar and lives near Bareilly.'

'That's right,' said Malati. 'Near Agra, actually. Anyway, they were having a holiday in Nainital, so I went along as well. And so did my three younger sisters and our cousins and so on. Everyone was given a rupee a day as pocket money, and this was quite enough to fill almost the whole day with one activity or another. I'd had a hard term, and I was eager to get Brahmpur out of my head. Like you, I suppose.' She put her arm around Lata's shoulder.

'At any rate, I would ride in the morning—it's only four annas an hour to hire a horse—and I'd also row, and skate at the rink—I'd sometimes skate twice a day and forget to go home for lunch. The rest of the family were involved in their own activities. Now I bet you can't imagine what happened.'

'You had a fall, and some young gallant at the rink rescued you,' said Lata.

'No,' said Malati. 'I look too self-assured for any Galahads to come chasing after me.'

Lata reflected that this was quite likely. Men did fall for her friend at a rapid rate, it was true, but they would probably fear to pick her up if she fell. Malati's attitude towards most men was that they were beneath her attention.

Malati continued: 'As it happens, I did have a fall or two while skating, but I got up on my own. No, what happened was quite different. I began to notice that a middle-aged man was following me around. Every morning when I was out rowing, I'd see him looking at me from the shore. Sometimes he'd get a boat out himself. He'd even appear at the rink.'

'Horrible!' said Lata, her thoughts immediately turning to her uncle in Lucknow, Mr Sahgal.

'Well, no, not really, Lata, I wasn't disconcerted at first, just puzzled. He didn't come up to me or, well, approach me or anything. But after a while it began to trouble me. So I went up to him.'

'You went up to him?' asked Lata. This was asking for trouble, clearly. 'That was very adventurous.'

'Yes, and I said, "You've been following me around. Is something the matter? Would you like to say something to me?" He said, "Well, I'm on holiday, and I'm staying at such-and-such a hotel in room number so-and-so; would you come and have tea with me this afternoon?" I was surprised, but he looked pleasant and sounded decent, and so I agreed.'

Lata was looking astonished, even shocked. Malati noticed this with pleasure.

'Well,' continued Malati, 'at tea he told me that he had indeed been following me around, and for longer than I had realized. Don't look so thunderstruck, Lata, it's unsettling. Anyway, he told me he had seen me one day when he was out rowing, and, being on holiday with nothing better to do, he had followed me. Having rowed, I hired a horse and went for a ride. Later I skated. I did not seem to care, or so it seemed to him, about eating, about resting, about anything except the activity I was engaged in. He decided that he liked me very much. Don't look so disgusted, it's all true. He had five sons, he said, and he thought that I would make one of them a wonderful match. They lived in Allahabad. If I was ever passing that way, would I agree to meet them? Oh, incidentally, when we were making small talk, it turned out that he had known my family in Meerut many years ago, even before my father's death.'

'And you agreed?' said Lata.

'Yes, I agreed. At least to meet them. No harm in meeting them, Lata; five brothers—perhaps I'll marry them all. Or none. So that was it—that's why he was following me around.' She paused. 'That's my romantic story. At least, I think it's romantic. It's certainly not physical, intellectual, spiritual or political. Now what's been happening to you?'

'But would you marry someone under those circumstances?'

'Why not? I'm sure his sons are quite nice. But I have to have one more affair before I settle down. Five sons! How strange.'

'But you are five sisters, aren't you?'

'I suppose we are,' said Malati. 'Anyway, it seems less strange. I've spent most of my growing-up years among women, and it doesn't seem odd at all. Of course, it's not the same for you. Even though you lost your father, you had brothers. But I had a peculiar sort of feeling when I entered your sister's drawing room just now. As if I was back to an earlier life: six women and no men. But not like the feeling you get in a women's hostel. It was very comforting.'

'But now you're surrounded by men, aren't you Malati?' said Lata. 'Your subject—'

'Oh, yes,' said Malati, 'in class—but what does that matter? It was far worse in Intermediate Science. Sometimes I think that men should simply be lined up against a wall and shot. It's not that I hate them, of course. Now what about you? What has happened about Kabir? How have you dealt with him? And now that you're back, what do you plan to do—short of shooting him and halting an innings?'

12.4

Lata told her friend about what had happened since the painful phone call—it seemed years ago—in which Malati had told her about Kabir and had made it plain (in case Lata could not see this herself—but how could she not?) that the match was impossible. They were walking not far from the spot where Lata had suggested to Kabir that they go away by themselves and ignore the closed-minded closed-hearted world around them. 'Very melodramatic,' commented Lata about her actions that day.

Malati could tell how hurt Lata must have been.

'Very adventurous, rather,' she said reassuringly, thinking, however, that it would have been disastrous if Kabir had agreed to Lata's scheme. 'You're always telling me how bold I am, Lata, but you've outdone me.'

'Have I?' said Lata. 'Well, I haven't spoken or written a word to him since then. I can hardly bear to think of him, though. I thought that by not replying to his letter I could make myself forget him, but it hasn't worked.'

'His letter?' said Malati, surprised. 'Did he write to you in Calcutta?'

'Yes. And now that I've returned to Brahmpur I keep hearing his name. Just last night Pran mentioned his father, and this morning I heard that he himself had helped at the Pul Mela after the stampede. Veena says he helped her recover her son, who was lost. And walking here with you, where we walked together—'

Lata trailed off into silence. 'What's your advice?' she said after a while.

'Well,' said Malati, 'when we go back, perhaps you'll let me read his letter. I need to understand the symptoms before I can make my diagnosis.'

'Here it is,' said Lata, producing the letter. 'I wouldn't let anyone except you read it.'

'Hmm,' said Malati. 'When did—oh, I see, when you went back to your room.' The letter looked well read. Malati sat down on the root of the banyan tree. 'You're sure you don't mind?' she said when she was already halfway through.

After she had read it once, she read it again.

'What are frangrant waters?' she asked.

'Oh, that's a quotation from a guidebook.' Lata cheered up at the memory.

'You know, Lata,' said Malati, folding the letter and handing it back to her, 'I like it, and he seems quite open and good-hearted. But it reads like the letter of a teenage boy who'd rather be talking than writing to his girlfriend.'

Lata considered her friend's remark for a while. Something similar had struck her too, but had not reduced the letter's slow-working effect on her. She reflected that she herself might well be faulted for a lack of maturity. And Malati too. Who, for that matter, was mature? Her elder brother, Arun? Her younger brother, Varun? Her mother? Her eccentric grandfather with his sobs and his stick? And what was the point of being mature anyway? And she thought of her own unbalanced, unsent letter.

'But it's more than the letter, Malati,' she said. 'He's going to be mentioned by Pran's family all the time. And in a few months the cricket season will start and it'll be impossible to avoid reading about him. Or hearing about him. I'm sure I'll be able to pick out his name from fifty yards away.'

'Oh, do stop moaning, Lata, in that feeble way,' said Malati with as much impatience as affection.

'What?' exclaimed Lata, outraged out of her mournfulness. She glared at her friend.

'You need to do something,' said Malati decisively. 'Something outside your studies. Anyway, your final exams are almost a year away, and this is the term when people take things easy.'

'I do sing now, thanks to you.'

'Oh, no,' said Malati, 'that's not what I meant at all. If anything, you should stop singing raags and start singing film songs.'

Lata laughed, thinking of Varun and his gramophone.

'It's a pity this isn't Nainital,' continued Malati.

'You mean, so that I could ride and row and skate?' said Lata.

'Yes,' said Malati.

'The problem is,' said Lata, 'if I row I'll only think of the frangrant waters, and if I ride I'll think of him riding his bicycle. And anyway I can neither ride nor row.'

'Something that is active and takes you out of yourself,' continued Malati, partly to herself. 'Some society—how about a literary society?'

'No,' said Lata with a shake of her head and a smile. Mr Nowrojee's soirées or anything resembling them were too close for comfort.

'A play, then. They're putting on *Twelfth Night*. Get a part in the play. That'll make you laugh at love and life.'

'My mother wouldn't stand for my acting in a play,' said Lata.

'Don't be such a mouse, Lata,' said Malati. 'Of course she'll agree. After all, Pran produced *Julius Caesar* last year and there were a couple of women in it. Not many, not important parts perhaps, but real girl students, not boys dressed up as girls. He was engaged to Savita at the time. Did your mother object? No, she didn't. She didn't see the play, but she was delighted at its success. If she didn't object then, she can't now. Pran will be on your side. And the students in Patna University and in Delhi too have mixed casts now. This is a new age!'

Lata could only imagine what her mother might have to say about the new age.

'Yes!' said Malati with high enthusiasm. 'It's being put up by that philosophy teacher, what's his name—it will come back to me—and auditions are in a week. Female auditions one day, male auditions two days later. Very chaste. Perhaps they'll even rehearse separately. Nothing that a cautious parent could object to. And it's for Annual Day, so that lends it an additional stamp of respectability. You need something like that or you'll just wilt away. Activity—furious, unmeditative activity, in lots of company. Take my word for it, that's what you need. That's how I got over my musician.'

Lata, though she felt that Malati's heartbreaking affair with a married musician was hardly a matter to make light of, was grateful to her for trying to cheer her up. After the unsettling strength of her feelings for Kabir, she could understand better what she had not understood before: why Malati had allowed herself to get involved in something as complicated and hazardous as she had.

'But anyway,' Malati was saying, 'I'm bored with Kabir: I want to hear about all the other men you've met. Who is this Kanpur prospect? And what about Calcutta? And didn't your mother plan to take you to Delhi and Lucknow too? They should have been worth at least one man apiece.'

After Lata had rendered her a full account of her voyage, which turned out not to be a catalogue of men so much as a lively description of events, omitting only the indescribable episode in Lucknow, Malati said:

'It seems to me that the poet and the paan-eater are neck and neck in the matrimonial stakes.'

'The poet?' Lata was dumbfounded.

'Yes, I don't consider his brother Dipankar or the covenanted Bish to be in the running at all.'

'Nor do I,' said Lata, annoyed. 'But nor, I assure you, is Amit. He is a friend. Just as you are. He was the one person whom I felt I could really talk to in Calcutta.'

'Go on,' said Malati. 'This is very interesting. And did he give you a copy of his poems?'

'No, he did not,' said Lata crossly. After a while she reflected that Amit had in fact promised in a vague manner to give her a copy. But if he had really meant to, he could surely have sent one through Dipankar, who had been in Brahmpur and had met Pran and Savita. Lata felt, though, that she was not being quite honest with Malati, and now appended the remark: 'At least he hasn't yet.'

'Well, I'm sorry,' said Malati, uncontritely. 'This is a sensitive point with you.'

'It is not,' said Lata. 'It is not sensitive. It's just irritating. I find it reassuring to think of Amit as a friend, and very unreassuring to think of him in any other way. It's just because you saddled yourself with a musician that you want to saddle me with a poet.'

'Perhaps.'

'Malati, please believe me, you're barking up a non-existent tree.'

'All right,' said Malati. 'Here's an experiment. Close your eyes, and think of Kabir.'

Lata wanted to refuse to go along. But curiosity is a curious thing, and after hesitating for a while she frowned and complied. 'Surely it isn't necessary to close my eyes,' she said.

'No, no, close your eyes,' insisted Malati. 'Now describe what he's wearing—and one or two physical features. Don't open your eyes while you're speaking.'

Lata said: 'He's wearing cricket clothes; a cap; he's smiling—and—this is ridiculous, Malati.'

'Go on.'

'Well, his cap's come off: he's got wavy hair, and broad shoulders, and nice even teeth. Rather a—what do they call it in silly romantic novels?—an aquiline nose. What is the purpose of all this?'

'All right, now think of Haresh.'

'I'm trying,' said Lata. 'All right, I have him in focus now. He's wearing a silk shirt—cream-coloured—and fawn trousers. Oh—and those horrible co-respondent shoes I told you about.'

'Features?'

'He's got small eyes, but they've crinkled up very nicely into a smile—they've almost disappeared.'

'Is he chewing paan?'

'No, thank God. He's drinking a cup of cold chocolate. Pheasant's, he said it was called.'

'And now Amit.'

'All right,' sighed Lata. She tried to picture him, but his features remained vague. After a while she said: 'He refuses to come into focus.'

'Oh,' said Malati, with something like disappointment in her voice. 'But what's he wearing?'

'I don't know,' said Lata. 'How odd. Am I allowed to think instead of imagine?'

'I suppose so,' said Malati.

But try as she might, Lata could not imagine what kind of shirts and trousers and shoes Amit wore.

'Where are you?' asked Malati. 'A house? A street? A park?'

'A cemetery,' said Lata.

'And what are you doing?' said Malati, laughing.

'Talking in the rain. Oh yes, he has an umbrella. Would that count as an item of clothing?'

'All right,' admitted Malati. 'I was wrong. But trees do grow, you know.'

Lata refused to follow up this unprofitable speculation. A little later, as they returned to the house for the promised tea, she said: 'There'll be no avoiding him, Malati. I'm bound to meet him. When he helped out after the disaster, that wasn't the mark of "just a teenage boy". He did that because he felt he had to, not because he meant me to hear about it.'

Malati said: 'What you have got to do is to build up your life without him, intolerable though that may appear at first. Accept the fact that your mother will never accept him. That is an absolute given. You're right, you're bound to bump into him sooner or later, and the one thing that you must make sure of is that you have very little idle time. Yes, a play's just the thing for you. You should act as Olivia.'

'You must think me a fool,' said Lata.

'Well, foolish,' said Malati.

'It's terrible, Malati,' Lata continued. 'I want to meet him more than anything. And I've told my Co-respondent to correspond. He asked at the station, and I couldn't bear to be mean to him when he'd been so helpful to Ma and me.'

'Oh, there's no harm in that,' said Malati. 'So long as you don't either dislike or love him, you can correspond with him. And didn't he make it clear that he was still half in love with someone else?'

'Yes,' said Lata, rather thoughtfully. 'Yes, he did.'

12.5

Two days later Lata got a short note from Kabir asking her whether she was still annoyed with him. Couldn't they meet at the Brahmpur Literary Society on Friday? He would only go if there was a chance of meeting her.

At first Lata thought of asking Malati once again what she should do. Then, partly because Malati could hardly be expected to manage her love-life in every detail, and partly because Malati would probably have told her not to go and to ignore the letter, Lata decided to consult herself and the monkeys.

She took a walk, scattered some peanuts to the monkeys on the cliff, and was the centre of their approving attention for a while. During the Pul Mela the monkeys had been royally feasted, but now it was back to normal lean times; and very few people paused to consider their welfare.

Having performed a generous action, Lata felt she could think more clearly. Kabir had once before waited for her in vain at the Brahmpur Literary Society. He had even had to eat some of Mrs Nowrojee's cake. Lata felt she could not inflict such an experience on him again. She wrote him a short note:

> Dear Kabir,
>
> I have got your note, but will not be going to the Nowrojees' this Friday. I got your letter too when I was in Calcutta. It made me think over and remember everything. I am not annoyed with you in any way; please do not think so. But I feel that there is no purpose at all in our writing or meeting. There would be a lot of pain and very little point.
>
> Lata

After reading over her note three times, and wondering whether to rewrite it without the last sentence, Lata became impatient with herself and posted it as it was.

She did visit Prem Nivas that day, and was relieved to discover that Kabir was not visiting Bhaskar at the time.

A couple of days after the Monsoon Term began, Malati and Lata went to the auditions for *Twelfth Night*. A nervous young philosophy teacher with a lively interest in the theatre was directing the Annual Day play this year. The auditions—it was the day for female auditions—took place not in the university auditorium but in the staff room of the Philosophy Department. It was five o'clock in the afternoon. About fifteen girls were gathered there, chattering nervously in knots, or just looking at Mr Barua with fascinated anxiety. Lata recognized several girls from the English Department, a couple even from her year, but none whom she knew very well. Malati had come along with her in order to ensure that she didn't back out at the last moment. 'I'll audition as well, if you want.'

'But don't you have some of your practicals in the afternoon?' asked

Lata. 'If you get a part and have to rehearse—'

'I won't get a part,' said Malati firmly.

Mr Barua made the girls stand up one by one and read various passages from the play. There were only three female parts and, besides, Mr Barua had not decided definitely that the part of Viola would go to a girl, so the competition was severe. Mr Barua read every role—male or female—other than the one that the auditioner was reading, and he read them so well, discarding entirely the nervousness of his ordinary manner, that many of the girls in the audience, and one or two who were auditioning, started giggling.

Mr Barua first made them read Viola's part beginning: 'Good madam, let me see your face.' Then, depending upon what they made of it, he asked them to read something else, either from Olivia's role or from Maria's, but only in Lata's case from both. Some girls read in a singsong voice or had some other irksome trait of speech; Mr Barua, reverting to his nervous manner, cut them off with: 'Good, thank you, thank you very much, that was good, very good, very good indeed, I have an excellent idea now, well, good, good—' until the girl who was reading got the idea, and (in a couple of cases, tearfully) returned to her chair.

After the auditions, Mr Barua said to Lata, within the hearing of a couple of other girls: 'That was well read, Miss Mehra, I'm surprised I haven't seen you on, well, on stage before.' Overcome by embarrassment he turned to gather his papers.

Lata was delighted with the nervous compliment. Malati told her that she had better prepare Mrs Rupa Mehra for the fact that she was bound to get a part.

'Oh, I'm not bound to get a part at all,' said Lata.

'Make sure that Pran's in the room when you bring up the subject,' said Malati.

Pran, Savita, Mrs Rupa Mehra, and Lata were sitting together after dinner that night when Lata said:

'Pran, what do you think of Mr Barua?'

Pran paused in his reading. 'The philosophy lecturer?'

'Yes—he's doing the Annual Day play this year, and I wanted to know whether you think he'll direct it well.'

'Mm, yes,' said Pran. 'I'd heard he was doing it. *Twelfth Night* or *As You Like It* or something. Makes a good contrast to *Julius Caesar*. He's very good—he's very good as an actor as well, you know,' continued Pran. 'But they say he's rather poor as a lecturer.'

After a moment's pause Lata said: 'It's *Twelfth Night*. I went to the auditions, and it's possible I might get a part in it, so I thought I'd better be forewarned about things.'

Pran, Savita, and Mrs Rupa Mehra all looked up. Mrs Rupa Mehra paused in her sewing and took in her breath sharply.

'Wonderful,' said Pran enthusiastically. 'Well done!'

'Which part?' asked Savita.

'No,' said Mrs Rupa Mehra vehemently, shaking her needle for emphasis. 'My daughter is not going to act in any play. No.' She glared at Lata over the top of her reading glasses.

There was silence all around. After a while Mrs Rupa Mehra added: 'Not at all.'

After a further while, not encountering any response, she went on: 'Boys and girls together—acting!' It was obvious that such a tawdry, immoral thing could not be countenanced.

'Like in *Julius Caesar* last year,' ventured Lata.

'You be quiet,' snapped her mother. 'No one has asked you to speak. Have you ever heard of Savita wanting to act? To act on the stage with hundreds of people staring? And going to those nightly gatherings with boys—'

'Rehearsals,' prompted Pran.

'Yes, yes, rehearsals,' said Mrs Rupa Mehra impatiently. 'It was on the tip of my tongue. I won't have it. Think of the shame. What would your father have said?'

'Now, now, Ma,' said Savita. 'Don't get upset. It's just a play.'

Having invoked her late husband, Mrs Rupa Mehra had reached an emotional climax, and it was possible now to pacify her and even to reason with her. Pran pointed out that the rehearsals would take place during the day except in an emergency. Savita said that she'd read *Twelfth Night* at school, and it was a harmless play; there was nothing scandalous in it.

Savita had read the bowdlerized version that was approved as a school text, but it was very likely that Mr Barua would have to cut out certain passages anyway to avoid causing shock and distress to the parents who attended Annual Day. Mrs Rupa Mehra had not read the play; if she had, she would certainly have thought it unsuitable.

'It is Malati's influence, I know it,' she said.

'Well, Ma, it was Lata's decision to attend the auditions,' said Pran. 'Don't blame Malati for everything.'

'She is too bold, that girl,' said Mrs Rupa Mehra, who was continually struggling between her fondness for Malati and her disapproval of what she saw as her overly forward attitude to life.

'Malati said I needed something to distract me from other things,' said Lata.

It did not take long for her mother to see the justice and weight of this argument. But even while conceding the point, she said, 'If Malati says so, it must be so. Who am I to say anything? I'm just your mother. You'll only value my advice when I'm burning on my pyre. Then you'll know how much I cared for your welfare.' This thought cheered her up.

'Anyway, Ma, there's a good chance that I won't get the part,' said Lata. 'Let's ask the baby,' she added, placing her hand on Savita's stomach.

The litany, 'Olivia, Maria, Viola, nothing,' was recited slowly several times over, and the fourth time around the baby obliged with a sharp kick on the word 'nothing'.

12.6

Two or three days later, however, Lata received a note assigning her the part of Olivia and asking her to attend the first rehearsal on Thursday afternoon at three thirty. She rushed off in high excitement towards the women's hostel, only to meet Malati on the way. Malati had been given the part of Maria. Both of them were equally pleased and astonished.

The first rehearsal was to be merely a reading-through of the play. Again it was not necessary to book the auditorium; a classroom was sufficient. Lata and Malati decided to celebrate by having a preparatory ice-cream at the Blue Danube, and arrived at the classroom in high spirits, just five minutes before the reading was due to begin.

There were about a dozen boys, and only one girl, presumably Viola. She was sitting apart from them, contemplating the empty blackboard.

Also sitting apart from the main knot of actors, and not participating at all in the general air of masculine excitement when the two girls walked in, was Kabir.

At first Lata's heart leapt up when she saw him; then she told Malati to stay where she was. She was going over to talk to him.

His behaviour was too casual to be anything but deliberate. Clearly, he had been expecting her. This was intolerable.

'Who are you?' she said, anger below the low level of her voice.

He was taken aback, both by the tone and by the question. He looked rather guilty.

'Malvolio,' he said, then added: 'Madam.' But he remained seated.

'You never told me you had the least interest in amateur dramatics,' said Lata.

'Nor did you tell me,' was his reply.

'I was not interested until a few days ago, when Malati dragged me to the audition,' said Lata, shortly.

'And my interest dates to about the same time,' said Kabir with an attempt at a smile. 'I heard that you did very well at the auditions.'

Lata could see it all now. Somehow or other he had discovered that she had a good chance of getting a part, and he had decided to attend the auditions for male parts. It was precisely to get away from him that she had undertaken to act in the first place.

'I suppose you instituted the usual inquiries,' said Lata.

'No, I heard about it by chance. I haven't been following you around.'

'And so—'

'Why does there have to be a "so" to it?' said Kabir, innocently. 'I just happen to like the lines of the play.' And he quoted with an easy and unselfconscious air:

> 'There is no woman's sides
> Can bide the beating of so strong a passion
> As love doth give my heart: no woman's heart
> So big to hold so much; they lack retention.
> Alas, their love may be called appetite,—
> No motion of the liver, but the palate,—
> That suffer surfeit, cloyment, and revolt;
> But mine is all as hungry as the sea,
> And can digest as much: make no compare
> Between that love a woman can bear me
> And that I owe Olivia.'

Lata felt her face burning. After a while she said: 'You're reciting someone else's lines, I'm afraid. Those weren't written for you.' She paused, then added: 'But you know them rather too well.'

'I learned them—and a good deal more besides—the night before the auditions,' said Kabir. 'I hardly slept! I was determined to get the part of the Duke. But I had to settle for Malvolio. I hope that doesn't mean anything by way of my fate. I got your note. I keep hoping we'll meet at Prem Nivas or somewhere—'

To her own surprise Lata found herself laughing. 'You're mad, absolutely mad,' she said.

She had turned away, but as she turned back towards him she noticed the last flicker of what was a look of real pain on his face.

'I was only joking,' said Lata.

'Well,' said Kabir, making light of it, 'some are born mad, some achieve madness, and some have madness thrust upon them.'

Lata was tempted to ask him which of the three categories he thought he belonged to. But instead she said: 'So you do know Malvolio's role as well.'

'Oh, those lines,' said Kabir. 'Everyone knows those lines. Just poor Malvolio playing the fool.'

'Why aren't you playing cricket or something else instead?' said Lata.

'What? In the Monsoon Term?'

But Mr Barua, who had arrived a few minutes ago, waved an imaginary baton towards the student who was to play the Duke, and said: 'All right, well, then, now, "If music be . . .", all right? Good.' And the reading began.

As Lata listened, she got drawn into the other world. It was a while before her first entrance. And when she began reading, she lost herself in the language. Soon she became Olivia. She survived her first exchange with Malvolio. Later she laughed with the rest at Malati's rendering of Maria. The girl who played Viola too was excellent, and Lata enjoyed falling in love with her. There was even a slight resemblance between Viola and the boy who was to play her brother. Mr Barua had done his casting well.

From time to time, however, Lata, emerging from the play, remembered where she was. She avoided looking at Kabir as much as she could, and only once did she feel that his eyes were on her. She felt certain that he would wish to talk to her afterwards, and she was glad that Malati and she had both got parts. One passage caused her particular difficulty, and Mr Barua had to coax her through it.

Olivia: Why, how dost thou, man? What is the matter with thee?

Malvolio: Not black in my mind, though yellow in my legs. It did come to his hands, and commands shall be executed. I think we do know the sweet Roman hand.

Mr Barua [puzzled at the pause, and looking at Lata in expectation]: Yes, yes, good?

Olivia: Wilt—

Mr Barua: Wilt? Yes, wilt thou . . . good, excellent, keep on going, Miss Mehra, you're doing very well.

Olivia: Wilt thou—

Mr Barua: Wilt thou? Yes, yes!

Olivia: Wilt thou go to bed, Malvolio?

Mr Barua [holding up one hand to still the guffaws, and waving at the dumbstruck Kabir with his imaginary baton]: How now, Malvolio?

Malvolio: To bed? Ay, sweetheart; and I'll come to thee.

Everyone, other than the two actors and Mr Barua, joined in the laughter that followed. Even Malati. Et tu, thought Lata.

The clown recited, rather than sang, the song at the end of the play, and Lata, catching Malati's eye and avoiding Kabir's, left quickly afterwards. It was not yet dark. But she need not have feared that he would ask her out that evening. It was Thursday, and he had another obligation.

12.7

When Kabir got to his uncle's house, it was dark. He parked his bicycle and knocked. His aunt opened the door. The house, single-storeyed and sprawling, was not well lit. Kabir often remembered playing with his cousins in the large back-garden in his childhood, but for the last several years the house had appeared to him almost to be haunted. It was on Thursday evenings that he usually visited it now.

'How is she today?' he asked his aunt.

His aunt, a thin, rather severe-looking but not unkind woman, frowned. 'For two or three days it was all right. Then again this thing began. Do you want me to be with you?'

'No—no, Mumani, I'd rather be with her alone.'

Kabir entered the room at the back of the house, which for the last five years had been his mother's bedroom. Like the rest of the house, the room was poorly lit, with just a couple of weak bulbs in heavy shades. She was sitting up in a hard-backed armchair, looking out of the window. She had always been a plump woman, but now she had grown fat. Her face was formed of a collection of pouches.

She continued to stare out of the window at the dark shapes of the guava trees at the end of the garden. Kabir came and stood by her. She did not appear to register his presence until she said:

'Close the door, it's cold.'

'I've closed it, Ammi-jaan.'

Kabir did not say that it was not cold at all, that it was July, and that he was sweating after his bicycle ride.

There was a pause. His mother had forgotten about him. He put his hand on her shoulder. She started for a second, then said:

'So it's Thursday night.'

She used the Urdu word for Thursday, 'jumeraat', literally Friday-night. Kabir remembered how, as a boy, he had considered it amusing that Friday-night could itself have a night. His mother used to explain such matters to him in an affectionate, light-hearted way, because his father was far too occupied, voyaging through strange seas of thought alone, to bother much with his children. It was only when they were of an age to talk to him properly that he began to take a fitful interest in them.

'Yes, Thursday night.'

'How is Hashim?' she asked. This was how she usually began.

'Very well, he's doing well in school. He had some very difficult homework, so he couldn't come.'

In fact, Hashim found it hard to bear such meetings, and when Kabir told him it was Thursday evening, he would usually find some reason not to go. Kabir, understanding his feelings only too well, would sometimes not remind him. That was the case this evening.

'And Samia?'

'Still in school in England.'

'She never writes.'

'Sometimes she does, Ammi—but rarely. We too miss her letters.'

It was impossible to tell his mother that her daughter was dead, dead of meningitis, buried a year ago. Surely, he thought, this year-long conspiracy of silence could not have worked. However disturbed people's minds may be, inklings, clues, suggestions, overheard fragments of conversation must work themselves into the mind and lodge themselves into a pattern indicating the truth. Once, indeed, a few months ago, his mother had said: 'Ah, Samia. I won't see her here, but in the other place.' But whatever this meant, it did not prevent her from asking about her daughter subsequently.

Sometimes, within minutes of a conversation or a thought, it would be wiped clean from her mind.

'How is your father? Still asking if two plus two makes four?' For an instant Kabir noticed something of the old amused and amusing light in her eyes, then it was dead.

'Yes.'

'When I was married to him—'

'You still are, Ammi.'

'You're not listening to me. When I—you've made me forget—'

Kabir held her hand. There was no responsive pressure.

'Listen,' his mother said. 'Listen carefully to every word I say. We don't have much time. They want to get me married off to someone else. And they have guards around my room at night. There are several of them. My brother has posted them there.' Her hand became tense in his grasp.

Kabir did not dissuade her. He was thankful they were alone.

'Where?' he asked.

She jerked her head slightly in the direction of the trees.

'Behind the trees?' asked Kabir.

'Yes. Even the children know,' she said. 'They look at me, and they say, toba! toba! One day she will have another baby. The world—'

'Yes, Ammi.'

'The world is a terrible place and people like to be cruel. If this is humanity, I want no part in it. Why are you not paying attention? They play music to tempt me. But, Mashallah, I have my wits about me. It is not for nothing that I am the daughter of an army officer. What do you have there?'

'I brought a few sweets, Ammi. For you.'

'I asked for a brass ring, and you have brought me sweets?' Her voice rose in protest. She was, Kabir thought, much worse than usual. Usually the sweets pacified her and she stuffed them greedily into her mouth. This time, however, she would have none of them. She lost her breath, then continued:

'There is medicine in those sweets. The doctors have put them there. If God had wanted me to have medicine, He would have sent word. Hashim, you do not care—'

'Kabir, Ammi.'

'Kabir came last week, on Thursday.' The voice grew alarmed, wary, as if sensing that this too was part of a trap.

'I—' But now tears came to his eyes, and he could not speak.

His mother appeared to be irritated by this new development, and her hand slipped out of his own, like a dead creature.

'I am Kabir.'

She accepted it. It was irrelevant.

'They want to send me to a doctor, near the Barsaat Mahal. I know what they want.' She looked downwards. Then her head dropped on to her chest, and she was asleep.

Kabir stayed with her for another half hour, but she did not wake up. Finally, he got up and went to the door.

His aunt, seeing his look of distress, said:

'Kabir, son, why don't you eat with us? It will do you good. And it will be good for us to get the chance to talk to you.'

But Kabir wanted to get away on his bicycle, as fast and as far as he could. This was not the mother he had loved and known, but someone stranger than a stranger.

There had been no history of such a condition in the family, nor any specific accident—a fall, a blow—that had caused it. She had been under some emotional strain for about a year after the death of her own mother, but then, that was a grief not unusual in the world. At first she was merely depressed, then she became anxious over trifles and incapable of handling the daily business of life. She had grown suspicious of people: the milkman, the gardener, her relatives, her husband. Dr Durrani, when he could not ignore the problem, sometimes hired people to help her, but her suspicions soon extended to them. Finally, she took it into her head that her husband was working out a detailed plot to harm her, and in order to foil it she tore up sheaves of his valuable and unfinished mathematical papers. It was at this stage that he asked her brother to take her away. The only other alternative was incarceration in an asylum. There was an asylum in Brahmpur, and it was located just beyond the Barsaat Mahal; perhaps it was this that she had been referring to earlier.

When they were children, Kabir, Hashim and Samia had always, and rather proudly, declared their father to be slightly mad. It was clearly his eccentricity—or something aligned with it—that made people respect him so much. But it was their affectionate, amusing and practical mother who had been afflicted with this strange visitation, so causelessly and so incurably. Samia at least, Kabir thought, has been spared the continuing torment of it all.

12.8

The Rajkumar of Marh was in trouble, and was up before Pran. Owing to problems with their landlord, the Rajkumar and his associates had been forced to seek housing in a students' hostel, but they had refused to adapt their style of life to its norms. Now he and two of his friends had been seen by one of the Proctor's assistants in Tarbuz ka Bazaar, just emerging from a brothel. When they were questioned, they had pushed him aside, and one of the boys had said:

'You sister-fucker, what's your business in all this? Are you a commission agent? What are you doing here anyway? Or are you out pimping for your sister as well?' One of them had struck him across the face.

They had refused to give their names, and denied that they were students. 'We're not students, we're the grandfathers of students,' they had asserted.

In mitigation, or perhaps not in mitigation, it could be said that they were drunk at the time.

On the way back, they had sung a popular film song, 'I didn't sigh, I didn't complain—' at the top of their lungs and had disturbed the peace of several neighbourhoods. The Proctor's assistant had followed them at a safe distance. Being overconfident, they had returned to the hostel, where a compliant watchman had let them enter, though it was past midnight. They continued to sing for a while until their fellow-students begged them to shut up.

The Rajkumar woke up the next morning with a bad headache and a premonition of disaster, and disaster came. The watchman, fearful now for his job, had been forced to identify them, and they were hauled up before the warden of the hostel. The warden asked them to leave the hostel immediately and recommended their expulsion. The Proctor, for his part, was generally in favour of severe action. Student rowdyism was getting to be a headache, and if aspirin didn't cure it, decapitation would. He told Pran, who was now on the student welfare committee, which took care of discipline, to handle matters provisionally, as he himself was going to be tied up with arrangements for the students' union elections. Ensuring fair and calm elections was a recurrent problem: students from various political parties (communists, socialists, and—under a different name—the Hindu revivalist RSS) had already started beating each other up with shoes and lathis as a prelude to fighting for votes.

The onus of deciding the fate of others was exactly the sort of thing that Pran fretted a great deal over, and Savita could see how anxious this made him. He couldn't concentrate on his breakfast newspapers. He hadn't been feeling at all well lately—and Savita could sense that the pressure of having to dispense rough justice to these idiotic young men was going to do him no good. He couldn't even work on his lectures on Shakespearian comedy, although he had set some time aside the previous evening.

'I don't see why you have to see them here,' Savita said. 'Ask them to go to the Proctor's office.'

'No, no, darling, that would only alarm them further. I just want to get their side of the story, and they'll be more forthcoming if they're less terrified—if they're sitting with me in a drawing room rather than standing and shuffling in front of a desk. I hope you and Ma don't mind. It'll take half an hour at the most.'

The culprits arrived at eleven o'clock, and Pran offered them tea.

The Rajkumar of Marh was thoroughly ashamed of himself and kept staring at his palms, but his friends, mistaking Pran's kindness for weakness, and knowing that he was popular with students, decided that they were in no danger, and smirked when Pran asked him what they had to say about the charges. They knew that Pran was Maan's brother, and took his sympathy for granted.

'We were minding our own business,' one of them said. 'He should have minded his.'

'He asked you for your names, and you said—' Pran looked down at the papers in his hand. 'Well, you know what you said. I don't need to repeat it. I don't need to quote the regulations of the university to you, either. You seem to know them well enough. According to this, as you approached the hostel you began to sing: "Any student who is seen in an undesirable place shall be liable to immediate expulsion."'

The two main culprits looked at each other with a smile of unbothered complicity.

The Rajkumar, fearing that if he was expelled, his infuriated father would castrate him or worse, mumbled: 'But I didn't even do anything.' It was just his luck that he had decided to go along to be sociable.

One of the other two said, rather contemptuously: 'Yes, that's true, we can vouch for that. He isn't interested in that kind of thing—unlike your brother, who—'

Pran cut the young man off sharply. 'That is not the point. Let us keep non-students out of this. You do not realize, it seems to me, that you will very likely be expelled. A fine is pointless, it will have no effect on you.' He looked from one face to the other, then went on: 'The facts are clear, and your attitude isn't helpful either. Your fathers are having a hard enough time already without being forced to add you to their worries.'

Pran noticed the first look of vulnerability—not of repentance so much as of fear—on their faces. With the impending abolition of zamindari, their fathers had indeed been increasingly impatient with their wastrel sons. Sooner or later their allowances might even be reduced. They had no idea of what to do with themselves other than to have a good time as students, and if this was taken away from them, there was nothing but darkness ahead. They looked at Pran, but he said nothing further for a while. He appeared to be reading the sheaf of papers in front of him.

It's difficult for them, thought Pran. It's sad, all this riotous high living; it's all they know, and it won't last long. They might even have to find work. It's not easy for students these days, whatever their class. Employment's hard to find, the country doesn't seem to be going in any direction, and the example of their elders is pathetic. Images of the Raja of Marh, of Professor Mishra, and of bickering politicians came to his mind. He looked up and said:

'I have to decide what to recommend to the Proctor. I tend to agree with the warden—'

'No, please, Sir—' said one of the students.

The other kept quiet, but gave Pran a beseeching look.

The Rajkumar was now wondering how he would face his grandmother, the Dowager Rani of Marh. Even his father's rage would be easier to bear than the look of disappointment in her eyes.

He began to sniffle.

'We didn't mean to do what we did,' he said. 'We were—'

'Stop,' said Pran. 'And think about what you are saying before you say it.'

'But we were drunk,' said the luckless Rajkumar. 'That's why we behaved like that.'

'So shamefully,' said one of the others in a low voice.

Pran closed his eyes.

All of them reassured him that they would never do anything like this again. They swore it on their fathers' honour, they pledged it in the names of several gods. They began to look repentant, and, indeed, they even began to feel repentant as a result of looking it.

After a while, Pran had had enough, and stood up.

'You'll hear in due course from the authorities,' he told them at the door. The bureaucratic, formulary words sounded strange to him even as he said them. They hesitated, wondering what else they could say in their own defence, then walked off forlornly.

12.9

After telling Savita he would be back for lunch, Pran went to Prem Nivas. It was a warm day, though overcast. By the time he got there he was somewhat out of breath. His mother was in the garden, giving instructions to the mali.

She came forward to welcome him, then stopped. 'Pran, are you all right?' she asked. 'You don't look at all well to me.'

'Yes, Ammaji, I'm fine. Thanks to Ramjap Baba,' he couldn't resist adding.

'You should not make fun of that good man.'

'No, no,' said Pran. 'How is Bhaskar?'

'He's talking quite well, and even walking around. He insists on going back to Misri Mandi. But the air here is so much fresher.' She gestured towards the garden. 'And Savita?'

'She's annoyed that I spend so little time with her. I had to promise to return for lunch. I really don't like all this extra work on the committee, but if I don't do it, someone else will have to.' He paused. 'Other than that, she's very well. Ma fusses over her so much that she's going to want to have a baby every year.'

Mrs Mahesh Kapoor smiled to herself. Then an anxious look appeared on her face, and she said: 'Where has Maan got to, do you know? He isn't in the village, and he isn't on the farm, and no one in Banaras knows where he is. He's just disappeared. He hasn't written for two weeks. I'm very worried about him. All your father says is that he can be in the underworld for all he cares so long as he's not in Brahmpur.'

Pran frowned at this second reference to his brother that morning, then assured his mother that Maan disappearing for two weeks or even ten should not be cause for alarm. He may have decided to go hunting or for a trek in the foothills or for a holiday at Baitar Fort. Firoz might know his whereabouts; he'd be meeting Firoz this afternoon, and he would ask him if he'd heard from his friend.

His mother nodded unhappily. After a while she said:

'Why don't all of you come to Prem Nivas? It'll be good for Savita in the last few days.'

'No, Ammaji, she prefers to be where she's used to living. And now that Baoji's thinking of leaving the Congress Party the house will be full of politicians of every kind trying to persuade him or dissuade him. And you're looking tired too. You take care of everyone, and don't let anyone take care of you. You really look exhausted.'

'Ah, that's old age,' said his mother.

'Why don't you call the mali into the house, where it's cool, and give him his instructions there?'

'Oh no,' said Mrs Mahesh Kapoor. 'That wouldn't work at all. It would have a bad effect on the morale of the flowers.'

12.10

Pran went home, and rested in lieu of lunch. He met Firoz a little later in the Chief Justice's courtroom at the Brahmpur High Court. Firoz was appearing for a student who had a grievance against the university. The student had been one of the brightest chemistry students the university could remember, and was well liked by his teachers. In the April examination, however, at the end of the academic year, he had done something so surprising that it was virtually inexplicable. He had gone to the bathroom in the middle of a paper, and then, seeing a couple of his friends standing just outside the exam hall, had stopped to talk to them for a minute. He claimed that they had talked about the fact that it was too hot to think; and there was no reason to assume that he was not telling the truth. His friends were both philosophy students, and could not possibly have helped him in his exam; in any case, he was by far the best chemistry student of his year.

But he was duly reported. It was clear that he had infringed the stringent rules for the examinations. On the grounds that an exception could not be made for him, his papers were cancelled and he was not allowed to appear for the remaining exams. In effect, he was to lose a year. He had appealed to the Vice-Chancellor to let him appear for the 'compartmental' exams; these exams, normally held in August for students who had failed in a single paper, would enable him to enter the next year if he took them as a set. His appeal had been turned down. In desperation he had turned to the possibility of a legal remedy. Firoz had agreed to be his lawyer.

Pran, being the junior member of the student welfare committee, which had been consulted in the original decision, had been asked by the Proctor to sit in on the hearings. He greeted Firoz with a nod in the courtroom, and said: 'Let's meet outside after this is over.' He was not used to seeing Firoz in a black gown with white bands round his neck, and he was pleasantly impressed even while he thought it looked rather silly.

Firoz had filed a writ petition on the student's behalf, claiming that his rights under the Constitution had been infringed. The Chief Justice made short work of his submission. He told him that hard cases made bad law; that the university could be trusted to act as its own overseeing authority unless the process of such oversight was blatantly unfair, as was not the case here; and that if the student insisted—unwisely, in his view—on recourse to the law, he should have been advised to file a suit with the local magistrate, not to come directly with a writ to the High Court. Writs to the High Court were a newfangled device that had come in under the recent Constitution, and the Chief Justice did not much care for them. He felt they were used far too often simply in order to jump the queue.

He cocked his head to one side, and said, looking down at Firoz: 'I see no reason for a writ at all, young man. Your client should have gone to a munsif magistrate. If he wasn't satisfied with his decision he could have gone to the District Judge on appeal, and then come here on further appeal. You should spend a little time choosing the appropriate forum rather than wasting the time of this court. Writs and suits are two quite different things, young man, two quite different things.'

Outside the court, Firoz was fuming. He had advised his client not to attend the hearing, and he was glad he had. He himself had been shaken by the injustice of it all. And for the Chief Justice to have rebuked him, to have implied that he had not considered the proper forum—that too was intolerable. He had helped argue the zamindari case before this very judge in this very courtroom; the Chief Justice must know that he was not given to flippant arguments and unconsidered recourse. Nor did Firoz like being called 'young man' unless it was imbedded in an approving remark.

Pran, whose heart was on the student's side, sympathized with Firoz. He patted him on his shoulder.

'It's the correct recourse,' said Firoz, loosening the bands around his neck as if they were constraining the flow of blood to his head. 'In a few years writs will be the accepted method in such cases. Suits are just too slow. August would have come and gone by the time we got a hearing.' He paused, and added passionately: 'I hope they're flooded with writs soon.' Then, with a slight smile, he remarked: 'Of course, this old man will have retired by then. He and all his brethren.'

'Oh yes,' said Pran. 'I know what I meant to ask you. Where's Maan?'

'Is he back?' said Firoz with pleasure. 'Is he here?'

'No, I'm asking you. I haven't heard and I thought you might have.'

'Am I your brother's keeper?' said Firoz. 'Well, I suppose, after a fashion, I am,' he went on, gently. 'Or wouldn't mind being. But no, I haven't heard. I thought he might be here by now, what with his nephew and all that. But, as I said, I haven't heard from him. Nothing to worry about, I hope?'

'No, no, nothing. My mother's worried. You know how mothers are.'

Firoz smiled slightly ruefully, rather in the way his mother used to smile. He looked very handsome at that moment.

'Well,' said Pran, changing the subject. 'Are you your own brother's keeper? Why haven't I seen Imtiaz for so many days? Perhaps you can let him take a stroll outside his cage.'

'We hardly see him ourselves, you know. He's out all the time visiting some patient or other. The only way to get his attention is to fall ill.' And here Firoz quoted an Urdu couplet about how the beloved was both the illness and the medicine, not to mention the doctor whose visit made it all worthwhile. Had the Chief Justice been listening he could have been excused for saying, 'I fail to see the relevance of this particular submission.'

'Well, perhaps I'll do just that,' said Pran. 'I've been feeling oddly exhausted lately, with a sort of strain around the heart—'

Firoz laughed. 'One of the best things about genuine illness is that it's a licence for hypochondria.' Then, cocking his head to one side he added: 'The heart and the lungs are two quite different things, young man, two quite different things.'

12.11

The next day Pran was lecturing when he suddenly felt weak and breathless. His mind too began to wander, a most unusual thing for him. His students were puzzled and began to look at one another. Pran continued to speak, leaning on the lectern and staring at the far wall of the classroom.

'Although these plays are permeated with images of the countryside, images of the chase, to the extent that the six words "Will you go hunt, my Lord?" lead you immediately—' Pran paused, then continued: 'lead you immediately to imagine that you are in the world of Shakespearian comedy, there is nevertheless no historical reason to believe that Shakespeare left Stratford for London because—because—' Pran rested his head on the lectern, then looked up. Why was everyone looking at everyone else? And now his eye fell on the first rows, where the girls sat. That was Malati Trivedi sitting there. What was she doing in his lecture? She had not asked for 'permission to attend' in the standard way. He passed his hand over his forehead. He hadn't noticed her when he was taking attendance. But then he never looked up from his ledger when taking attendance. Some of the boys were standing up. So was Malati. They were leading him back to the desk. Now they had sat him down. 'Sir, are you all right?' someone was saying. Malati was taking his pulse. And now there was someone at the door—Professor Mishra and a visitor passing by and looking in. Pran shook his head. As Professor Mishra retreated, Pran heard the words: '. . . fond of amateur dramatics . . . yes, popular with students, but—'

'Please don't crowd around,' said Malati. 'Mr Kapoor needs air.'

The boys, startled at the authority in the voice of this strange girl, stood back a little.

'I'm all right,' said Pran.

'You'd better come with us, Sir,' said Malati.

'I'm all right, Malati,' said Pran impatiently.

But they escorted him to the staff room and sat him down. A couple of his colleagues told the students that they would make sure that Mr Kapoor was all right. After a while things did return to normal for Pran, but he just couldn't understand it. He had not been coughing or breathless. Perhaps it was the heat and humidity, he thought unconvincedly. Perhaps it was just overwork, as Savita insisted.

Malati, meanwhile, had decided to go to Pran's house. When Mrs Rupa Mehra saw her at the door, her face lit up with pleasure. Then she remembered that it was probably Malati who had got Lata into the play, and she frowned. But Malati was looking worried, which was an unusual expression for her, and Mrs Rupa Mehra, in sympathetic concern, had hardly said, 'Is something wrong?' when Malati asked:

'Where's Savita?'

'Inside. Come in. Savita, Malati's here to see you.'

'Hello, Malati,' said Savita, smiling. Then, sensing that something was the matter, she said: 'Are you all right? Is Lata all right?'

Malati sat down, composed herself so as not to discompose Savita unduly, and said:

'I was just attending a lecture by Pran—'

'Why were you attending a lecture by Pran?' Mrs Rupa Mehra could not refrain from asking.

'It was on Shakespearian comedy, Ma,' said Malati. 'I thought it would help me to interpret my role in the play.' Mrs Rupa Mehra's mouth set, but she said nothing further, and Malati continued:

'Now, Savita, don't be alarmed, but he felt a bit faint while giving the lecture, and had to sit down. I had a word with some of the boys later and they said that a couple of days ago something similar had happened, but that it had only lasted a second, and he had insisted on continuing the lecture.'

Mrs Rupa Mehra, too anxious now to rebuke Malati even inwardly for talking so freely to boys, said: 'Where is he? Is he all right?'

Savita said, 'Was he coughing? Breathless?'

'No he wasn't coughing, but he did seem a little breathless. I think he should see a doctor. And perhaps, if he insists on lecturing, he should sit down and lecture.'

'But he's a young man, Malati,' said Savita, placing her hands on her stomach, almost as if to protect the baby from this conversation. 'He won't listen. He overworks, and I can't get him to take his duties less seriously.'

'If he listens to anyone, it'll be to you,' said Malati, getting up and putting her hand on Savita's shoulder. 'I think he's had a bit of a shock; now is probably the best time to talk to him. He has to think of you and the baby too, not only his duties. Now I'll just go back and see that he comes home immediately, and by rickshaw.'

Mrs Rupa Mehra would have marched into the English Department herself to rescue Pran if it hadn't meant leaving Savita behind. Savita for her part was wondering what she could tell her husband that might have greater success than her pleas had had so far. Pran had a stubborn streak and an absurd sense of duty, and might insist on continuing to stand on the strength of them.

12.12

His stubborn streak was being exercised at this very moment. Pran was alone in the staff room with Professor Mishra, who had discovered, though not much to his alarm, that the scene he had happened upon when passing the door of the classroom was not an enactment of Shakespeare, but, rather, real life. He liked to be well informed about things, and he asked the students a few questions. He settled the visitor he had been escorting in the office of the Head of Department, and went off to the staff room.

The bell had just rung, and Pran's colleagues were unsure whether or not to leave Pran to go to their own lectures, when Professor Mishra entered, smiled at them and at Pran, and said: 'Leave the patient to me. I shall cater to his every whim. How are you, dear boy? I have asked the peon to get you some tea.'

Pran nodded gratefully. 'Thank you, Professor Mishra. I don't know what came over me. I'm sure I could have continued to lecture, but my students, you know—'

Professor Mishra placed his vast, pallid arm on Pran's. 'But your students are so protective of you, so protective,' he said. 'That is one of the joys of teaching—contact with one's students. To inspire them in a lecture, to make them think, after forty-five minutes, that the world has changed for them, that it is somehow different from one bell to the next. To open out for them the heart of a poem—ah! Someone said to me the other day that they considered me to be one of those teachers whose lectures students would never forget—a great teacher like Deb or Dustoor or Khaliluddin Ahmed. I was, he said, a presence at the lectern. I was just a moment ago telling Professor Jaikumar of Madras University, whom I was escorting around our department, that it was a compliment I would never forget. Ah, but my dear fellow, I should be talking of your students, not my own. Many of them were intrigued by that charming and extremely competent girl who took charge a little while ago. Who was she? Had you ever seen her before?'

'Malati Trivedi,' said Pran.

'It's none of my business, I know,' continued Professor Mishra, 'but when she asked for permission to attend, what reason did she give? It's always gratifying when one's fame spreads beyond one's own department. I believe I've seen her somewhere before.'

'I can't imagine where,' said Pran. Then he suddenly remembered with a shock that it was probably at the dreadful submersion of Holi.

'I'm sorry, Professor Mishra, I didn't get your question,' said Pran, who was finding it hard to concentrate. The image of Professor Mishra floundering in a tub of pink water was getting the better of him.

'Oh, not to worry, not to worry. Time enough for all that later,' said Professor Mishra, puzzled by Pran's look of anxiety and—what almost appeared to be—amusement. 'Ah, here's the tea.' The subservient peon moved the tray backwards and forwards in deference to his imagined wishes, and Professor Mishra continued: 'But you know, I have been feeling for some time that these duties of yours really are rather onerous. It's difficult to shrug some of them off, of course. University duties, for example. I heard just this morning that the Raja of Marh's son had been to see you yesterday in connection with this unfortunate fracas he got into. Now of course, if anything were done to him, it would outrage the Raja himself, rather an excitable sort of man, wouldn't you say? One makes enemies on a committee such as the one you sit on. But then, the acceptance of power is never without its personal costs, and one must do one's duty. "Stern daughter of the voice of God!" Only, of course, it cannot fail to tell upon one's teaching.'

Pran nodded.

'Departmental duties, of course, are another matter entirely,' continued Professor Mishra. 'I have decided that if you wish to be released from the syllabus committee. . . .' Pran shook his head. Professor Mishra continued: 'Some of my colleagues on the Academic Council have told me frankly that they find your recommendations—our recommendations, I mean—quite untenable. Joyce, you know—a man of most peculiar habits.' He looked at Pran's face and saw that he was making no headway at all.

Pran stirred his tea, and took a sip.

'Professor Mishra,' he said, 'I've been meaning to ask you: has the selection committee been constituted yet?'

'Selection committee?' asked Professor Mishra innocently.

'To decide on the vacant readership.' Savita had been prodding Pran about the subject lately.

'Ah, well,' said Professor Mishra, 'things take time, things take time. The Registrar has been very busy of late. But we have advertised, as you know, and we hope to have all of the applications in soon. I've glanced at a few, and they are strong, very strong. Excellent qualifications, excellent teaching qualifications.'

He paused to give Pran a chance to say something, but Pran remained determinedly silent.

'Well,' said Professor Mishra. 'I don't want to discourage a young man like yourself, but I believe that in a year or two, when your health has settled, and everything else has stabilized—' He smiled sweetly at Pran.

Pran smiled back. After another sip of tea, he said, 'Professor, when do you think the committee will meet?'

'Ah, now, that's difficult to say, very difficult. We aren't like the Patna University, where the Department Head can just get a few people off the Bihar Public Service Commission to sit on the committee, though I must admit I can see advantages to that system. We have this needlessly elaborate system of selecting our committee members: two from a Panel of Experts—and the Chancellor's nominee—and so on. Professor Jaikumar of Madras, who saw your'—he was about to say 'performance' but checked himself—'your distress just now, is on our Panel of Experts. But a time that's convenient for him to come to Brahmpur may not be convenient for someone else on the panel. And now, as you know, the Vice-Chancellor has himself been keeping such indifferent health that he has been talking of retirement. Poor man, he hardly finds time to chair selection committees. Everything takes time. Ah well, ah well, I'm sure you sympathize.' And Professor Mishra stared sadly at his large pale hands.

'With him, with you, or with myself?' asked Pran lightly.

'How acute!' said Professor Mishra. 'I hadn't thought of that. A fertile ambiguity. Well, with all of us, I hope. Sympathy does not run out by being generously bestowed. And yet, there is too little genuine sympathy in the world. People always tell others what they want to hear, not what they feel is truly in the interest of the other person. Now, if I were to advise you, for instance, to withdraw your application for the post of reader—'

'—I wouldn't do it,' completed Pran.

'Your health, my dear boy. I am only thinking of your own health. You are driving yourself too hard. All these articles you've been publishing—' He shook his head in gentle reproof.

'Professor Mishra, my mind is quite made up,' said Pran. 'I would like my name to go ahead. I'll take my chances with the committee. I know that you will be on my side.'

A look of bland ferocity passed over the Professor's face. But when he turned to Pran he was entirely soothing.

'Of course, of course,' he said. 'Some more tea?'

Fortunately, Professor Mishra had left Pran alone by the time Malati came to the door. She told him that Savita was expecting him at home and that he was to go home by the rickshaw that was standing outside.

'But it's just across the campus,' Pran protested. 'Really, Malati, I'm not crippled yet. I walked all the way to Prem Nivas yesterday.'

'Mrs Kapoor's orders, Sir,' said Malati. Pran shrugged, and complied.

When he got home, his mother-in-law was in the kitchen. He told Savita to keep sitting, and put his arms tenderly around her.

'Why are you so stubborn?' she said to him, his tenderness causing her anxiety to flare up again.

'We'll be all right,' whispered Pran. 'We'll all be all right.'

'I'm going to ask for a doctor,' said Savita.

'For yourself, not for me,' said Pran.

'Pran, I am going to insist. If you care for me, you'll take my advice now and then.'

'But my magical masseur is coming tomorrow. He cures both my body and my mind.' Seeing Savita continue to look worried, he said: 'I'll tell you what—if I don't feel fit after his kneading and pummelling, I'll see a doctor. How's that?'

'Better than nothing,' said Savita.

12.13

'This skill is a gift of Lord Shiva—it came to me in a vision—in a dream—suddenly, not by degrees.'

The masseur, Maggu Gopal, a tough, stocky man, was rubbing Pran all over with oil. He was about sixty, had very short-cropped grey hair, and kept up a continuous patter which Pran found very soothing. Pran was lying flat on his stomach on a towel in the verandah, and was wearing only his underwear. The masseur had his sleeves rolled up and was tweaking Pran's rather scraggly neck muscles in a determined manner.

'Ai!' said Pran, wriggling a bit—'that hurts.' He spoke in English, as Maggu Gopal's patter was entirely in English, except for quotations from Hindi. The magical masseur had been recommended to Pran by a friend, and had agreed to come twice a week. He was rather expensive as masseurs went, but he had massaged Pran half a dozen times, and Pran always felt better after his visits.

'If you always move, how you will improve?' asked Maggu Gopal, who was fond of rhyming couplets in his own way.

Pran obeyed and was still.

'I have been masseur in high circles—Chief Minister Sharma, some High Court Judges, two Home Secretaries also, and many Englishmen. And I have a handprint of all these dignitaries. It is all grace of Lord Shiva—you know, the snake God'—he felt that Pran, as a teacher of English, needed such explanations—'the God of Ganga and of the great Chandrachur Temple which is now ascending daily in Chowk.'

Some pummelling later, he said:

'This til oil is very good—it has the warming properties. I have rich clients also—many Marwaris of Calcutta know me. They are not taking care of bodies. But I say the body is like finest vintage car, of which there are no spare parts available in the market. Therefore it needs service and maintenance from competent engineer, namely'—and here he pointed to himself—'Maggu Gopal. And you should not care about expense. Would you give your Swiss watch to the incompetent watchman because he charged cheaply? Some people sometimes call servants, like Ramu or Shamu, to do their massage. They think it is in the oil only.'

He paused, boxed Pran's calves in a businesslike manner, then said:

'Talking of oil, mustard oil is not good—and is internationally prohibited in massage. It stains also. The pores must breathe. Mr Pran, your feet are cold even in this weather. It is weak nervous system. You think too much.'

'Yes, I do,' admitted Pran.

'Too much education is not good,' said Maggu Gopal. 'Ninth standard, non-matric; somehow still I learn the trick.'

He twisted Pran's head violently and looked straight into his eyes.

'You see this boil here on your chin—it is a sign—I will not say a sign, an indication—of constipation—a tendency to constipation. All thinking people—that is, I mean, all those who are thinkers—have this tendency. So you must eat papaya twice a day and take a mild laxative tablet—and have tea without milk, with honey and lemon. And you are too dark—like Lord Shiva—but nothing to be done about it.'

Pran nodded in so far as this was possible. The magical masseur released his head, and went on.

'Thinkers, even if they eat boiled food and light food, will be constipated—their stomachs will not be soft. But your rickshaw-wallahs and servants, even if they eat fried food, will not get it—because they are doing physical labour. Always remember:

> Pair garam, pet naram, sir thanda
> Doctor aaye to maro danda!

This saying I have translated for Englishmen:

> Cold head, soft tummy, warm feet.
> If doctor comes, you may him beat!'

Pran grinned. He was feeling better already. The magical masseur, reacting promptly to his change of mood, asked him why he had been sad.

'But I was not sad,' said Pran.

'No, no, you were sad.'

'Really, Mr Maggu Gopal.'

'Then you are worried.'

'No—no—'

'It is your work life?'

'No.'

'Your married life?'

'No.'

The magical masseur looked doubtful.

'I have had some health problems lately,' admitted Pran.

'Oh, health problems merely?' said the magical masseur. 'That you can leave all to me. Remember, honey is your god. You must substitute honey for sugar always.'

'Because honey has the warming qualities?' suggested Pran.

'Exactly!' said Maggu Gopal. 'Also, dry fruits should be taken in plenty, especially pistachio, which is very warming. But you can take assorted dry fruits also. Agreed?'

'Agreed!' said Pran.

'And take hot bath in tub, and also sun bath: sit in sun and face the sun. Recite the Gayatri Mantra.'

'Ah.'

'But it is also your work, I can see.' Maggu Gopal grabbed Pran's hand with the same painful vigour with which he had twisted his head. He examined it carefully. After a while he said in a solemn tone: 'Your hand is most remarkable. The sky is the limit of your success.'

'Really?' said Pran.

'Really. Consistency! That is the secret of success in any art. In order to obtain proficiency, you must have one goal—one track—consistency.'

'Yes, indeed,' said Pran, thinking, among many other things, of his baby, his wife, his brother, his nephew, his sister, his father, his mother, the department, the English language, the future of the country, the Indian cricket team, and his own health.

'There is a saying of Swami Vivekananda: "Rise! Awake! Stop not—until the goal is achieved!"' The magical masseur smiled assurance on Pran.

'Tell me, Mr Maggu Gopal,' Pran said, turning his head sideways, 'can you tell from my hand if I will have a daughter or a son?'

'Turn over please,' said Maggu Gopal. He examined Pran's right hand again. 'Yes,' he said to himself.

Turning over on to his back had made Pran start to cough, but Maggu Gopal ignored this, so intent was he on gazing at his hand.

'Now you see,' he said, 'you, or rather your missus, will have a daughter.'

'But my missus is sure she will have a son.'

'Mark my words,' said the magical masseur.

'All right,' said Pran, 'but my wife is almost always right.'

'You have a happy married life?' Maggu Gopal inquired.

'You tell me, Mr Maggu Gopal,' said Pran.

Maggu Gopal frowned. 'It is written in your hand that your married life will be a comedy.'

'Oh, good.'

'Yes, yes, you can see—your Mercury is very strong.'

'I suppose I can't escape from destiny,' said Pran.

This word had a magical effect on Maggu Gopal. He drew backward slightly and pointed his finger at Pran's chest. 'Destiny!' he said, and grinned at Pran. 'That is it.' After a pause he continued:

'Behind every successful man is a woman. Behind Mr Napoleon there was Josephine. Not that you have to be married. I do not believe it. In fact I predict that you have had auspicious women in your life before and will continue to after marriage.'

'Really?' said Pran, interested, but rather fearful. 'Will my wife like this? I fear my life may become a comedy of the wrong kind.'

'Oh, no, no,' said the magical masseur reassuringly. 'She will be very tolerant. But the women must be auspicious. If you drink tea made from dirty water you will fall ill. But if you drink tea made from deluxe water it will refresh you.'

Maggu Gopal stared at Pran with some fixity. Seeing that he had got the point, he went on:

'Love is colour-blind. Caste does not matter. It is karma—which means actions according to the vicious of God.'

'The vicious of God?' said Pran, bewildered, before he understood what Maggu Gopal was getting at.

'Yes, yes,' said the magical masseur, pulling Pran's toes one by one until they made clicking and cracking sounds. 'One should not get married just for bringing tea in the morning—or for sex or anything.'

'Ah,' said Pran, with a sudden sense of enlightenment, 'just for living day to day.'

'Today! Yes! Do not live for yesterday or tomorrow.'

'I meant from day to day,' explained Pran.

'Yes, yes, it is all the same. Family life with children is a comedy, both today, yesterday, and tomorrow.'

'And how many children will I have?' asked Pran. He had lately begun to wonder whether he should be bringing a child into the world at all, a terrible world of hatred, intrigue, poverty, and cold war—a world that was unlike even his own unsettled childhood in that the safety of the earth itself was now threatened.

'Ah, exact number is in wife's hand,' said the masseur regretfully. 'But once there is delight in your life through one child, it is like a tonic, a chyavanprash—and then the sky is the limit for offspring.'

'Two or three would be more than enough,' said Pran.

'But you must keep up the massage. To maintain the vital fluids.'

'Oh yes!' agreed Pran.

'It is most essential for all people.'

'But who massages the masseur?' asked Pran.

'I am sixty-three,' said Mr Maggu Gopal, rather affronted. 'I don't need it. Now turn around, please.'

12.14

When Maan returned to Brahmpur, he made straight for Baitar House. It was evening, and Firoz met him. He was delighted to see Maan, but appeared a little awkward, especially when he saw that Maan had brought his bags with him.

'I thought I'd stay here,' said Maan, embracing his friend.

'Not at home?' asked Firoz. 'God, how burnt and wild you look.'

'What a welcome!' said Maan, not at all put out. 'No, here's best—that is, if it's all right with you. Will you have to ask your father? The reason is that I can't bear to deal with my father and everything else at the same time.'

'Of course you're welcome,' said Firoz, smiling at the 'everything else'. 'Good. I'll get Ghulam Rusool to arrange to put your bags in your room—the room you usually stay in.'

'Thanks,' said Maan.

'I hope you'll stay for a while. I didn't mean to sound unwelcoming. I just didn't expect you'd want to stay here rather than at home. I'm glad you're here. Now come in, wash up, and join me for dinner.'

But Maan begged off dinner.

'Oh, sorry,' said Firoz, 'I wasn't thinking. You haven't been home yet.'

'Well,' said Maan. 'I wasn't thinking of going home.'

'Where then?' asked Firoz. 'Oh, I see.'

'Don't sound so disapproving. I can't wait. I'm all keyed up!'

'I am disapproving,' said Firoz seriously. 'You should go home first. Anyway, I made sure your letter got to her,' he went on, with the air of one who does not wish to continue a subject.

'I believe you're interested in Saeeda Bai yourself, and are trying to keep me away,' said Maan, laughing at his own joke.

'No—no—' said Firoz, rather unconvincingly. He didn't want a long discussion about Tasneem, who had cast a light and delicate spell over him.

'Now what's the matter?' said Maan, seeing a complex cast of emotions pass over his friend's face. 'Oh, it's that girl.'

'No, no—' said Firoz, even more unconvincingly.

'Well, it's either the elder sister or the younger—unless it's the maid—Bibbo!' And at the thought of Firoz and Bibbo together Maan burst out laughing. Firoz put his arm around Maan's shoulder and drew him into the house.

'You're not very forthcoming with me,' complained Maan. 'I tell you everything that's in my heart.'

'You tell everyone everything,' said Firoz, smiling.

'Not everything,' said Maan, looking at Firoz.

Firoz coloured slightly. 'No, I suppose not. Anyway, most things. I'm not a very forthcoming person. I tell you as much as I tell anyone. And if I don't tell you more, it's a good thing. It might be disturbing.'

'To me?' said Maan.

'Yes—to you, to me, to us, to Brahmpur, to the universe,' said Firoz evasively. 'I presume you're going to have a bath after the journey?'

'Yes,' said Maan. 'But why are you so keen that I shouldn't go to Saeeda Bai's?'

'Oh,' said Firoz, 'I'm not keen that you shouldn't go there. I was just—what was it you said?—disapproving that you didn't visit your family first. Well, at least your mother. I met Pran the other day and he said that you'd just disappeared—hadn't been heard of or seen for ten days by anyone, not even in the village. And that your mother was very worried. And then I thought that with your nephew and all—'

'What?' said Maan, startled. 'Savita's baby's been born already?'

'No, no, your mathematical nephew—haven't you heard?'

From the expression on Firoz's face Maan could see that the news wasn't good. His mouth opened slightly. 'You mean the little frog?' asked Maan.

'What little frog?'

'Veena's child—Bhaskar.'

'Yes. Well, your only nephew. He was hurt in the stampede at the Pul Mela. You really haven't heard?' he said incredulously.

'But no one wrote to tell me!' said Maan, upset and annoyed. 'And then I went on this trek, and—how is he?'

'He's all right now. Don't look so worried. He really is. But apparently he was concussed, and had amnesia, and it took him some time to become coherent again. Perhaps it was as well that they didn't write. You're very fond of him, aren't you?'

'Yes,' said Maan, agitated with concern for Bhaskar. 'This must be my father's doing. He must have thought I'd come straight back to Brahmpur if I'd heard. Well, I would have—' he began vehemently, then stopped. 'Firoz, you should have written and told me.'

'I didn't think of it,' said Firoz. 'I'm really sorry. I assumed that your family would have told you. I couldn't have imagined that they wouldn't. It isn't as if it was a family secret. All of us knew.'

A sudden, irrelevant thought struck Maan again. 'You're not a secret admirer of Saeeda Bai's, are you?' he asked his friend.

'Oh no,' said Firoz, puzzled. 'Not that I don't admire her.'

'Good,' said Maan, relieved. 'I couldn't compete with a Nawabzada. Oh, er, bad luck about the zamindari case—I heard the news and thought of you. Hmm, will you lend me a walking stick? I feel like twirling something this evening. Oh, and some cologne. And a clean kurta-pyjama. Civilization is hard on those who've reverted to savagery.'

'My clothes won't fit you. Your shoulders are too broad.'

'Imtiaz's would. They did at the Fort.'

'So they would,' said Firoz. 'I'll bring them up to your room. And a half-bottle of whisky.'

'Thanks,' said Maan, ruffling his friend's hair. 'Perhaps civilization isn't so hard after all.'

12.15

While Maan was soaking himself in the delicious sensations of a hot bath, he kept imagining the even more delicious sensations that he was soon to feel in the arms of his beloved. He wrapped himself in the towelled robe that had been provided, and walked into the bedroom.

There, however, more sober thoughts presented themselves. He thought of his nephew, and how hurt he would be if he heard that his Maan Maama had been in town and had not come immediately to see him. Rather glumly Maan decided that he would have to visit Bhaskar first. He poured himself a whisky, drank it quickly, poured another, drank that equally quickly, and took the rest of the half-bottle with him in the pocket of Imtiaz's kurta.

Instead of hiring a tonga, he decided to walk to Prem Nivas, where Firoz had told him Bhaskar would be.

Walking in Pasand Bagh was a pleasure. Maan noticed for the first time in his life that there were even streetlamps on most streets. Just walking on solid roads after the mud and dirt of country tracks was a privilege. He tapped and twirled Firoz's walking stick. After a while, however, he didn't feel much like it. He became rather depressed at the thought of having to face his father again. And his mother too in a way: she would act as a damper on the anticipated excitement of the evening. She would tell him to stay for dinner. She would ask him all about the villages and the state of his health. Maan's steps became slightly slower and more uncertain. Perhaps it was also the whisky taking effect. He had had very little to drink for weeks.

When he came to a fork in the road, not far from his destination, he looked up at the stars for a bit of guidance. Then he tapped his stick on the pavement, and turned first this way, then that. He looked very undecided. Finally, he took the right-hand fork to Saeeda Bai's rather than the road to

Prem Nivas. This cheered him up immediately.

It's much better this way, he decided. If I go home, they'll insist I stay for dinner, and I just can't. And Bhaskar won't really mind. He only cares if I don't give him sums. And how can I give him sums when my mind's distracted? Anyway, he's not well, he shouldn't stay up late, he's probably in bed already. No, it's much better this way. I'll visit him first thing tomorrow. He won't be angry with me.

After a while he said to himself: And besides, Saeeda Bai would never forgive me if she heard I was in Brahmpur and didn't come to see her before anyone else. I can imagine how hard it's been for her while I've been away. This will be a wonderful reunion—she'll be astonished to see me. And at the anticipation of their meeting he felt a pleasant weakness in his limbs.

Soon he was standing not far from the house, under a large neem tree, savouring in advance the delights to come. A thought occurred to him: I haven't brought a gift along with me.

But Maan, not being one to savour anticipations for long, decided after half a minute that he'd waited long enough to collect himself. I'm my own gift, as she is hers! he said cheerfully to himself, and, first tapping and then waving his cane, he walked the remaining distance to the gate.

'Phool Singh!' he greeted the watchman in a loud voice.

'Ah, Kapoor Sahib. It must be months—'

'No, it must be years—' said Maan, getting out a two-rupee note.

The watchman pocketed the note calmly, then said: 'You are in luck. Begum Sahiba has not instructed me about any particular guests this evening. So I think she expects to be alone.'

'Hmm.' Maan frowned. Then he brightened up. 'Well, good,' he said.

The watchman knocked at the door. The buxom Bibbo peered out. Catching a glimpse of Maan, she beamed. She had missed him. He was by far the pleasantest of her mistress's lovers, and the sprucest.

'Ah, Dagh Sahib, welcome, welcome,' she said from the door, loudly enough that he could hear her at the gate. 'Just a minute, I'll go up and inquire.'

'What is there to inquire about?' asked Maan. 'Aren't I welcome here? Do you think I'll bring the village soil of Mother India into the durbar of the Begum Sahiba?' He laughed and Bibbo giggled.

'Yes, yes, you're very welcome,' said Bibbo. 'Begum Sahiba will be delighted. But I should only speak for myself,' she added flirtatiously. 'I won't be a minute.'

She was as good as her word. Soon Maan was traversing the hall, walking up the stairs with the mirror halfway up on the landing (he halted to adjust his white embroidered cap), and then along the upstairs gallery that fringed the hall. Soon he was at the door of Saeeda Bai's room. But there was no sound of voices or of singing or even of the harmonium. When he entered, leaving his shoes outside the door, he noticed that Saeeda Bai was not in the room where she usually entertained. She must be in the bedroom, he thought with a rush of desire. He sat himself down on the sheeted floor, and leaned against a white bolster. Soon afterwards, Saeeda Bai came out from the bedroom. She looked tired but lovely, and enraptured by the sight of Maan.

Maan's heart leapt up when he saw her, and so did he. If she hadn't had a birdcage in her hand he would have embraced her.

But for now the look in her eyes would have to suffice. What an idiotic parakeet, thought Maan.

'Do sit down, Dagh Sahib. How I have pined for this moment.' An appropriate couplet followed.

She waited until Maan was seated before she set down the parakeet, who looked like a proper parrot now, not a ball of pale green fluff. Then she said to the bird:

'You have been very unresponsive, Miya Mitthu, and I can't say I am pleased with you.' To Maan she said, 'Rumour has it, Dagh Sahib, that you have been in town for some days now. Twirling, no doubt, that handsome ivory-headed cane. But the hyacinth that obtained favour yesterday appears withered today to the connoisseur.'

'Begum Sahiba—' protested Maan.

'Even if she has withered away only for lack of the water of life,' continued Saeeda Bai, tilting her head a little to one side, and pulling her sari over her hair in that familiar adjustment that made Maan's heart pound ever since he had seen it that first evening in Prem Nivas.

'Begum Sahiba, I swear—'

'Ah,' said Saeeda Bai, addressing the parakeet, 'why were you away for so long? Even one week was like agony. What are vows to one who is wilting in the desert under a scorching sun?' Suddenly tiring of her metaphor, she said: 'It has been rather hot these last few days. I shall ask for some sherbet for you.' Getting up, she went to the gallery outside the door and, leaning over the rail, clapped her hands: 'Bibbo!'

'Yes, Begum Sahiba?'

'Get us both some almond sherbet. And be sure to mix some saffron in Dagh Sahib's sherbet. He looks so worn out by his pilgrimage to Rudhia. And you have grown rather dark.'

'It was absence from you, Saeeda, that weakened me—' said Maan. 'And it was the laughing-cruel one who exiled me from herself who now blames me for this absence. Could anything be more unjust?'

'Yes—' said Saeeda Bai softly. 'If the heavens had kept us longer apart.'

Since Saeeda Bai's letter to Maan, full of endearments as it was, had urgently enjoined him to remain away from Brahmpur for even longer—for reasons she did not explain—her present answer was hardly fair.

But Maan found it satisfactory; no, more than satisfactory, delightful. Saeeda Bai had as good as confessed that she was longing to take him back in her arms. He made a slight gesture of his head towards the door of the bedroom. But Saeeda Bai had turned to the parakeet.

12.16

'The sherbet first, then conversation, then music, and then we will see whether the saffron has taken effect,' said Saeeda Bai teasingly. 'Or does he need the whisky that is peeping out of his pocket?'

The parakeet looked at Maan. It did not appear to be impressed. When Bibbo entered with the drinks, it cried out her name:

'Bibbo!'

It said this in rather a commanding, somewhat metallic, tone. Bibbo shot the bird a look of annoyance. Maan noticed this; he had been feeling equally irritated by the parakeet, and when he looked at Bibbo in amusement and sympathy, their eyes met for a second. Bibbo, who was a troublemaker and a flirt, held his eyes for a second before turning away.

Saeeda Bai was not amused. 'Stop it, Bibbo, you mischievous girl,' she said.

'Stop what, Saeeda Begum?' asked Bibbo innocently.

'Don't be insolent. I saw you making eyes at Dagh Sahib,' said Saeeda Bai. 'Go to the kitchen at once, and stay there.'

'The accessory is hanged, the principal goes free,' said Bibbo and, having left the tray on the floor near Maan, turned to leave.

'Shameless,' said Saeeda Bai; then, thinking over Bibbo's remark, she turned to Maan with annoyance. 'Dagh Sahib, if the bee finds the bud of an inferior blossom more charming than the opened tulip—'

'Saeeda Begum, you deliberately misunderstand me,' said Maan, sulking a little. 'Every word I say, every look—'

Saeeda Bai did not want him to sulk. 'Drink your sherbet,' she advised him. 'It is not your brains that should be hot.'

Maan tasted his sherbet. It was delicious. Then he frowned, as if he had tasted something bitter.

'What is the matter?' asked Saeeda Bai with concern.

'Something's missing,' said Maan, as if in appraisal of his drink.

'What?' asked Saeeda Bai. 'That Bibbo—she must have forgotten to mix honey in your glass.'

Maan shook his head and frowned. 'I know exactly what's missing,' he said finally.

'Would Dagh Sahib vouchsafe us the solution?'

'Music.'

Saeeda Bai allowed herself a smile. 'All right. Fetch me the harmonium. I am so tired today that I feel that I am at the end of my four days' tenure in the world.'

Instead of asking Maan what he would like to hear, as she usually did, Saeeda Bai began to hum a ghazal to herself, and moved her fingers gently along the keys. After a while she began to sing. Then she stopped, distracted by her thoughts.

'Dagh Sahib, a woman by herself—what place can she find in an ungentle world?'

'That is why she must have someone to protect her,' asserted Maan stoutly.

'There are too many problems for mere admirers to handle. Admirers themselves are sometimes the problem.' She gave a sad laugh. 'House, tax, food, arrangements, this musician loses his hand, that landlord loses his land, this one has to go away for a family wedding, that one fears he can no longer afford his generosity, someone's education must be looked after, a dowry has to be arranged. And a suitable boy must be found. Endless. Endless.'

'You mean, for Tasneem?'

'Yes. Yes. Who would think that there would be people paying court to her? Here, in this house. Yes, it's true. It is for me, her sister, her guardian, to arrange these things. That Ishaq—he has now become Ustad Majeed Khan's disciple, so he moves with his head in the clouds even if his voice is very much of this earth—he visits here, supposedly to see me and pay his respects, but in fact to see her. I've taken to keeping the parakeet in my room. Yet still he contrives to find some excuse or another. And he is not a bad man; but he has no future. His hands are crippled, and his voice untrained. Miya Mitthu can sing better than him. Even my mother's wretched myna could.'

'Are there others?' asked Maan.

'You needn't act so innocent,' said Saeeda Bai, annoyed.

'Saeeda Bai—honestly—' said Maan.

'Not you, not you. Your friend the socialist, who has taken to organizing things in the university in order to be someone in the world.'

This description hardly fitted Firoz. Maan looked puzzled.

'Yes, our young maulvi, her Arabic teacher. Whose hospitality you have partaken of, whose instruction you have imbibed, whose company you have shared for weeks. Do not sell your wares here, Dagh Sahib. There is a market for injured innocence, and it is not to be found between these walls.'

But Maan must have looked completely perplexed. He could not imagine that Rasheed could possibly be paying court to Tasneem. Saeeda Bai continued: 'Yes, yes, it's true. This pious young student, who wouldn't come when summoned into my presence because he was involved with teaching her a passage from the Holy Book, has now taken it into his head that she is in love with him, that she is going mad for his love, and that he owes it to her to marry her. He is a sly and dangerous young wolf.'

'Honestly, Saeeda Begum, this is news to me. I have not seen him for two weeks,' said Maan. He noticed that her pale neck was flushed.

'That is hardly surprising. He returned here two weeks ago. If, as appeared from your protests, you have arrived recently—'

'Recently?' exclaimed Maan. 'I have barely had time to wash my face and hands—'

'Do you mean he never breathed a word of this? That is very unlikely.'

'Indeed not, Saeeda Bai. He is a very earnest soul; he didn't even want to teach me ghazals. Yes, he talked once or twice about socialism and methods for improving the economic status of the village—but love! Why, he is a married man.'

Saeeda Bai smiled. 'Has Dagh Sahib forgotten that men have not forgotten to count to four in our community?' she asked.

'Oh, yes, of course,' said Maan. 'Of course. But—well, you are not pleased—'

'No,' said Saeeda Bai, with a flash of anger. 'I am not pleased.'

'Is Tasneem—'

'No, she is not, she is not, and I will not have her be in love with some village lout—' said Saeeda Begum. 'He wants to marry her for my possessions. Then he will spend them on digging a village ditch. Or planting trees. Trees!'

This did not at all accord with Maan's sense of Rasheed, but he thought better than to contradict Saeeda Bai, who had worked herself into a state of indignation.

'Well, how about a true-hearted admirer for Tasneem?' he suggested by way of diversion.

'It is not for admirers to choose her but to be chosen by me,' said Saeeda Bai Firozabadi.

'May not even a Nawabzada admire her, even if from afar?'

'Whom precisely are you referring to?' asked Saeeda Bai, her eyes flashing dangerously.

'Let me say, a friend,' said Maan, enjoying her unfeigned interest, and admiring the brilliance of her expression—like swordplay at sunset, he thought. How beautiful she looked—and what a wonderful night lay ahead.

But Saeeda Begum got up and went to the gallery. She was biting the inside of her cheek. She clapped her hands again. 'Bibbo!' she shouted. 'Bibbo! Bibbo! That stupid girl must have gone to the kitchen. Ah'—for Bibbo had come running up the stairs at the note of danger in her mistress's voice—'Bibbo, you've decided to grace us with your presence at last? I have been shouting myself hoarse for the last half hour.'

Maan smiled to himself at the charming exaggeration.

'Dagh Sahib is tired, Bibbo. Kindly show him out.' Something caught in her voice.

Maan started. What on earth had got into Saeeda Begum?

He looked at her, but she had averted her face. She had sounded not merely angry but painfully upset.

It must be my fault, he thought. I have said or done something terribly wrong. But what on earth have I done or said? he asked himself. Why should the thought of a Nawabzada paying court to Tasneem worry Saeeda Begum so greatly? After all, Firoz is the very opposite of a village lout.

Saeeda Bai walked past him, picked up the birdcage, and went back to her bedroom, closing the door behind her. Maan was stunned. He looked at Bibbo. She was astonished too. It was her turn to look at him with sympathy.

'Sometimes this happens,' said Bibbo. But in fact it happened very rarely. 'What did you do?' she continued with immense curiosity. Her mistress was normally unshockable. Nothing even the Raja of Marh had done recently—and he had been in a foul mood because of the result of the Zamindari Abolition case—had had this effect.

'Nothing,' said Maan, staring at the closed door. After a minute he said softly, as if speaking to himself: 'But she can't really be serious.' And, he thought to himself, I, for my part, am not going to be brushed off like this. He went to the bedroom door.

'Oh, Dagh Sahib, please, please—' cried Bibbo, horrified. The bedroom, when Saeeda Bai entered it, was sacrosanct.

'Saeeda Begum,' said Maan in a tender and puzzled voice, 'what have I done? Please tell me. Why are you so angry with me? Was it Rasheed—or Firoz—or what?'

There was no answer from inside.

'Please, Kapoor Sahib—' said Bibbo, raising her voice and trying to sound firm.

'Bibbo!' came the parakeet's metallic and commanding voice from the bedroom. Bibbo started giggling.

Maan was now trying to open the door, but the handle wouldn't work. She must have locked it from the inside, he thought angrily. Aloud he said, 'This is an unjust way to treat me, Saeeda Begum—you promise me heaven one minute and you throw me the next minute into hell. I hardly had time to bathe and shave after arriving in Brahmpur, and I came to see you. At least tell me why you are so upset.'

From inside the room came Saeeda Bai's voice: 'Just go away, please, Dagh Sahib, have pity on me. I can't see you today. I can't give you reasons for everything.'

'You didn't give me reasons for keeping me away in your letter, and now that I'm here—'

'Bibbo!' commanded the parakeet. 'Bibbo! Bibbo!'

Maan began to pound on the door. 'Let me in! Talk to me, please—and for God's sake shut that half-witted parakeet up. I know you're feeling bad. How do you think I feel? You've wound me up like a clock, and now—'

'If you ever want to see me again,' said Saeeda Bai from inside, her voice tearful, 'you'll go away now. Or I'll tell Bibbo to call the watchman. You caused me pain involuntarily. I accept it was involuntary. Now you should accept it was pain. Please go away. Come back some other time. Stop it,

Dagh Sahib—for God's sake—if you wish to see me again.'

Maan, in the face of this threat, stopped pounding the door and walked into the gallery, pent up and utterly perplexed. He was so lost that he didn't even say he was going or wish her well. He couldn't understand it at all. This was like a hailstorm falling out of a clear sky. Still, it was clearly no mere coquettishness.

'But what did you do?' persisted Bibbo, a little frightened by her mistress's mood, but enjoying the drama. Poor Dagh Sahib! She had never heard anyone pound on Saeeda Bai's door before. What passion!

'Nothing at all,' said Maan, feeling frustrated and ill-used, and glad of someone's sympathy. 'Nothing at all.' Surely it was not for this that he had exiled himself in the countryside for weeks. She had just a few minutes earlier virtually promised him a night of tenderness and ecstasy, and now—for no reason at all—had decided not merely to default, but to impale him with emotional threats.

'Poor Dagh Sahib,' said Bibbo, looking at his bewildered but attractive face. 'You've forgotten your cane. Here it is.'

'Oh—you're right,' said Maan.

As they walked down the stairs, she contrived to brush, then press against him. She stood on tiptoe and turned her lips to his face. Maan could not refrain from kissing her. He was feeling so frustrated that he would have made immediate and frantically passionate love to anyone, even to Tahmina Bai.

What an understanding girl Bibbo is, thought Maan, as they stood there kissing and embracing for a minute. Intelligent, too. Yes, it isn't fair at all, it isn't fair, and she can see it.

But Bibbo was perhaps not intelligent enough. They were kissing on the landing, and the tall mirror carried their reflection to the gallery. Saeeda Bai's mercurial anger had been followed by mercurial regret at her treatment of Maan. She decided to reassure Maan of her affection for him by bidding him goodbye from the gallery as he walked across the hall. Now she glanced down the stairs to see what was keeping him. What she saw in the mirror made her bite her lower lip to the point where it almost bled.

She stood transfixed. After a bit, Maan came to his senses and disengaged himself. The pretty Bibbo, giggling a little, escorted him across the hall to the door.

When she returned, she crossed the hall and walked up the stairs to clear away the sherbet glasses from Saeeda Bai's outer room. The Begum

Sahiba will probably lie on her bed for an hour, and come out only when she feels hungry, she thought. She giggled a little more at the memory of the kiss. She was still giggling to herself when she got to the gallery. There she saw Saeeda Bai. One look at Saeeda Bai's face, and the giggling stopped.

12.17

The next day Maan visited Bhaskar.

Bhaskar had been bored for a few days. Then he had decided to train himself in the metric system, although it was not yet in use anywhere in India. The advantages of this system over the British one became immediately apparent to him when he started using volume measurements. All sorts of comparisons became obvious when he used the metric system. For instance, if he wanted to compare the volume of Brahmpur Fort with that of Savita's baby-to-be, he could do it instantly, without converting from cubic yards to cubic inches. It wasn't as if that conversion presented great difficulty to Bhaskar; it was just that it was inconvenient and inelegant.

Another delight of the metric system was that Bhaskar could roam with unfettered delight through his beloved powers of ten. But after a few days he had tired of the metric system and its joys. His friend Dr Durrani had not visited him for some time, though Kabir had. Bhaskar liked Kabir well enough, but it was Dr Durrani who always brought new mathematical insights in tow, and without him Bhaskar had had to fend for himself.

Again he was bored, and complained to Mrs Mahesh Kapoor. After a bit of grumbling—he wanted to go back to Misri Mandi, and his grandmother was very reluctant to let him go—he applied to his grandfather instead.

Mahesh Kapoor told Bhaskar with stern affection that he couldn't help him. All such decisions were in his wife's domain.

'But I'm terribly bored,' said Bhaskar. 'And I haven't had a headache in a week. Why must I spend half the day in bed? I want to go to school. I don't like it here in Prem Nivas.'

'What?' said his grandfather. 'Not even with your Nana and Nani here?'

'No,' stated Bhaskar. 'It's all right for a day or two. Besides, you're never actually here.'

'That's true. I have so much work to do—and so many decisions to make. Well, you'll be interested to know that I've decided to leave the Congress Party.'

'Oh,' said Bhaskar, doing his best to sound interested. 'And what does that mean? Will they lose?'

Mahesh Kapoor frowned. The effort and stress that the decision had cost him was not something a child could be expected to understand. Bhaskar, besides, apparently doubted even that two plus two always equalled four, and could not be expected to sympathize greatly when the certainties of his grandfather's life were shifting underfoot. And yet Bhaskar at other times was so certain of his facts and figures, though he may well have arrived at them by erratic frog-leaps of abstract thought. Mahesh Kapoor, who was not awed by anyone else in the family, was perhaps even a little afraid of Bhaskar. A strange boy! He must certainly, thought Mahesh Kapoor, be given every opportunity to develop his rather eerie powers.

'Well, for a start,' said Mahesh Kapoor, 'it means that I will have to decide what constituency I must fight from. The Congress Party is very strong in the city, but that's where my strength lies too. On the other hand, my old constituency in the city has been redrawn, and that will present me with certain problems.'

'What problems?'

'Nothing you would understand,' Mahesh Kapoor told Bhaskar. Then, seeing Bhaskar's intense, even hostile, frown, he continued: 'The caste composition is quite different now. I've been looking over many of the new constituencies that have been delineated by the Election Commissioner, and the population figures—'

'Figures,' breathed Bhaskar.

'Yes, arranged by religion and caste in the 1931 Census. Caste! Caste! You may think it's madness, but you can never ignore it.'

'Can I have a look at these statistics, Nanaji?' said Bhaskar. 'I'll tell you what to do. Just tell me what variables are in your favour—'

'Speak in clear Hindi, idiot, it's impossible to understand what you are saying,' said Mahesh Kapoor to his grandson, still affectionately, but rather irritated by Bhaskar's presumption.

Soon, however, Bhaskar had all the facts and figures he needed to keep him more than happy for at least three days, and he started poring over the constituencies.

12.18

When Maan came to visit, he asked the servant to take him straight to Bhaskar's room. He discovered Bhaskar sitting up in bed. The bed was covered with paper.

'Hello, genius,' said Maan genially.

'Hello,' said Bhaskar, rather abstracted. 'Just a minute.' He stared at a chart for a minute, scribbled down a few numbers with a pencil, and turned towards his uncle.

Maan kissed him, and asked him how he had been.

'Fine, Maan Maama, but everyone makes such a fuss here.'

'How's the head?'

'Head?' said Bhaskar, surprised. 'My head is fine.'

'Well, then, do you want some sums?'

'Not just at the moment,' said Bhaskar. 'My head is full of them.'

Maan could hardly believe this response. It was as if Kumbhkaran had decided to wake up at dawn and go on a diet.

'What are you doing? It looks very serious,' he ventured.

'Very serious indeed,' said Mahesh Kapoor's voice. Maan turned around. His father, mother, and sister had come into the room. Veena hugged Maan tearfully, then sat down on the edge of Bhaskar's bed after moving away a few sheets of paper. Bhaskar didn't object.

'Bhaskar's been complaining that he's bored here. He wants to leave,' said Veena to Maan.

'Oh, I can stay for two or three days more,' said Bhaskar.

'Really?' said Veena, surprised. 'Perhaps I really should have your head examined twice a day.' Maan cheered up at his sister's response. If she could joke in this way, Bhaskar must be all right.

'What's he been up to?' he asked.

Mahesh Kapoor replied laconically: 'He's telling me which constituency I should fight from.'

'Why not from your old one?' asked Maan.

'They've redrawn it.'

'Oh.'

'Besides, I'm going to leave the Congress Party.'

'Oh!' Maan looked at his mother, but she did not say anything. She appeared rather unhappy, though. She was not in favour of her husband's decision, but did not feel she could stop him. He would have to resign as

Minister of Revenue; he would have to move out of the party that was associated in the people's minds with the freedom movement, the party of which he and she had been lifelong members; he would have to find funds from somewhere to compete with the sizeable funds of the state Congress Party, so effectively garnered and dispensed by the Home Minister. Above all, he would have to struggle once again against hard odds, and he was not young.

'Maan, you've grown so thin,' said his mother.

'Thin? Me?' said Maan.

'Yes, and you're so much darker,' she said, sadly. 'Almost like Pran. This village life is not good for you. Now we must take care of you properly. You must tell me what you want at every meal—'

'Yes, well, it's good to see you back, and I hope that things have changed,' said Mahesh Kapoor, pleased but somewhat anxious to see his son.

'Why didn't anyone tell me about Bhaskar?' said Maan.

Both Veena and her mother glanced towards Mahesh Kapoor.

'Well,' said Mahesh Kapoor, 'you must trust us to decide certain things.'

'So if Savita's baby had been born—'

'You're here now, Maan, and that's the main thing,' said his father shortly. 'Where are your things? The servant can't find them. I'll have them sent up to your room. And before you leave for Banaras you must—'

'My things are at Firoz's house. I'm staying there.'

This remark was greeted with an amazed silence.

Mahesh Kapoor looked annoyed, and Maan was not too upset by this. But Mrs Mahesh Kapoor looked hurt, and he felt bad. He began to wonder if, after all, he had done the right thing.

'So this is not your home any more?' she said.

'Of course it is, of course it is, Ammaji, but with so many people staying here—'

'People—really, Maan,' Veena said.

'It's only temporary. I'll move back when I can. I have to talk things over with Firoz as well. My future and so on—'

'Your future lies in Banaras, and no question about it,' said his father impatiently.

His mother, sensing possible trouble, said: 'Well, we will talk about all this after lunch. You can stay for lunch, can't you?' She looked at him tenderly.

'Of course I can, Ammaji,' said Maan, hurt.

'Good. We have alu paratha today.' This was one of Maan's favourite dishes. 'When did you come?'

'I just came. I thought I'd see Bhaskar before anyone else.'

'No, to Brahmpur.'

'Yesterday evening.'

'So why didn't you come and have dinner with us?' asked his mother.

'I was tired.'

'So you had dinner at Baitar House?' asked his father. 'How is the Nawab Sahib?'

Maan flushed but did not answer. This was intolerable. He was glad he was not going to live under the dominating eye of his father.

'So where did you have dinner?' repeated his father.

'I did not have dinner last night. I was not hungry. I nibbled throughout my journey, and by the time I arrived I was not hungry. Not hungry at all.'

'Did you eat well in Rudhia?' asked his mother.

'Yes, Ammaji, I ate well, I ate very well, all the time,' said Maan with a trace of irritation in his voice.

Veena had a good sense of her brother's moods. She remembered him following her all around the house when he was a small boy. He had always been good-humoured unless he was both baulked and perplexed. He had a bad temper, but he was seldom irritable.

Something must have happened to upset or frustrate him recently; she was sure of it. She was about to ask him about it—which would probably only have bothered him further—when Bhaskar, as if waking from a reverie, said: 'Rudhia?'

'What about Rudhia?' asked Maan.

'Which part of Rudhia were you in?' asked Bhaskar.

'The northern part—near Debaria.'

'That is definitely the most favourable constituency among the rural ones,' pronounced Bhaskar. 'Northern Rudhia. Nanaji said that a large proportion of Muslims and jatavs were factors in his favour.'

Mahesh Kapoor shook his head. 'Be quiet,' he told Bhaskar. 'You're nine years old. You don't understand anything about all this.'

'But, Nanaji, really, it's true, it's one of the best!' insisted Bhaskar. 'Why don't you fight from there—you said that the new party would give you any seat you wanted. If you want a rural seat, that's the one to choose. Salimpur-cum-Baitar in Northern Rudhia. I haven't sorted out the urban seats yet.'

'Idiot, you know nothing about politics,' said Mahesh Kapoor. 'I need those papers back.'

'Well, I'm returning to Rudhia at Bakr-Id,' said Maan, siding with Bhaskar. He had cheered up at his father's discomfiture. 'People insist I celebrate with them. I'm very popular! And you can come with me. I'll introduce you to everyone in your future constituency. All the Muslims, all the jatavs.'

Mahesh Kapoor said sharply: 'I know everyone, I don't need to be introduced to them. And it is not my future constituency, let me make that clear. And let me tell you that you are going back to Banaras to settle down, not to Rudhia to make merry at Id.'

12.19

Mahesh Kapoor had not left the party to which he had dedicated his life without pain or regret, and he was still assailed by doubts about his decision. His fear and expectation were that the Congress would not lose. The party was too well entrenched both in office and in the people's consciousness; unless it lost Nehru, how could it fail to win? Dissatisfied though he was with the way things were going, there were other excellent reasons why Mahesh Kapoor should have remained. His brainchild the Zamindari Abolition Act had still to be declared valid by the Supreme Court and to be implemented. And there was the obvious danger that L.N. Agarwal would accumulate yet further power into his hands in the absence of a strong ministerial rival.

Mahesh Kapoor had taken (or been persuaded to take) a calculated gamble to try to prod Nehru out of the Congress Party. Or perhaps it had been not a calculated but a whimsical gamble. Or perhaps not even whimsical but instinctive. For the real gambler behind the scenes was the Minister of Communications in Nehru's own Cabinet in Delhi, the adroit Rafi Ahmad Kidwai, who, leaning on his bed like a genial, white-capped, bespectacled Buddha, had told Mahesh Kapoor (who had come to pay him a friendly visit) that if he didn't jump out now from the drifting boat of the Congress Party, he would never be able to help pull it by its tow-rope back to shore.

It was a far-fetched image, made more dubious by the fact that Rafi Sahib, for all his immense agility of thought and love of fast cars, had never been addicted to swiftness of movement—or, indeed, exercise of any physical kind, let alone jumping, swimming, and tugging. But he was notoriously persuasive. Canny businessmen lost their canniness in his presence and divested themselves of thousands of rupees, which he promptly disbursed to harassed widows, poor students, party politicians, and even his political rivals if they happened to be in need. His likeableness, generosity, and astuteness had cast a spell over many a more hard-headed politician than Mahesh Kapoor.

Rafi Sahib had a taste for a great many things—fountain-pens, mangoes and watches among them—and he also had a taste for jokes; and Mahesh Kapoor, having finally taken the psychological plunge, wondered whether this might not be one of his more zany and disastrous ones. For Nehru had shown no effective sign of leaving the Congress yet, despite the fact that it was his ideological supporters who were bleeding away. Time would tell, however, and timing was the key. Rafi Sahib, who could sit silent and smiling while six conversations swirled all round him, would suddenly latch on to a single sentence of exceptional interest and insight like a chameleon catching a fly. He had a similar instinct for the shifting shoals and currents of politics: the sonar ability to distinguish dolphins from crocodiles even in these murky, silted waters, and an uncanny sense of when to act. Upon Mahesh Kapoor's departure, he had given him a watch—the spring of Mahesh Kapoor's own watch had snapped—and had said: 'I guarantee that Nehru, you and I will fight from the same platform, whatever that may be. At thirteen o'clock on the thirteenth day of the thirteenth month, look at this watch, Kapoor Sahib, and tell me if I was not right.'

12.20

Around the time of the elections to the Brahmpur University Students' Union there was a spurt of political activity both on and off campus. There was a great hodgepodge of issues: cinema concessions on the one hand, and a call for solidarity with primary schoolteachers in their wage bargaining on the other; demands for more employment opportunities together with support for Pandit Nehru's non-aligned foreign policy; amendments to the rigid code of conduct of the university—and insistence that Hindi be used for the civil service examinations. Some parties—or the leaders of some parties, for where parties ended and leaders began was itself a difficult business to fathom—believed that all India's ills would be cured by a return to ancient Hindu traditions. Others insisted that socialism, variously defined or felt, was the cure-all.

There was ferment and fighting. It was the beginning of the academic year, and no one was concentrating on his studies; exams were nine months away. Students chattered in the coffee houses or the delegacy lodges or hostels, gathered in knots outside classes, led small marches, fasted, and beat each other up with sticks and stones. Sometimes they were helped in this by the local parties they were affiliated to, but this was not really necessary. Students had learned how to cause trouble under the British, and there was no reason why hard-earned corporate skills, passed on from batch to batch, should be wasted merely because of the change of dispensation in Delhi and Brahmpur. Besides, the Congress government, by its slow slide into complacency and its inability to solve the country's problems, was unpopular among the students, who by no means valued stability as an end in itself.

The Congress Party expected to win by default, as great, shapeless, centrist lumps often do. It expected to win even though its national leadership was riven by differences, even though Congressmen were leaving their party in droves ever since the meeting in Patna, even though the most prominent local Congressman's name was mud among the students—both as the Treasurer of the university with his manoeuvrings on the Executive Council, and as the lathi-happy Home Minister. The student Congress Party's theme was: 'Give us time. We are the party of Independence, of Jawaharlal Nehru, not really of L.N. Agarwal. Even though things have not improved, they will improve if you continue to place confidence in us. If you change horses now, they assuredly will not.'

But most students were not inclined to vote for the status quo; they had no spouses or children or jobs or income, possible injury to which might counterbalance the excitement of instability. Nor did they trust for the future those who had shown no signs of competence in the past. The country had to beg for food from abroad. The economy, under-planned and over-planned, lurched from crisis to crisis. There were few jobs waiting for the students themselves after graduation.

Their post-Independence romanticism and post-Independence disillusionment formed a volatile mixture. The Congress argument was rejected, and the Socialist Party won the election. Rasheed was on the party slate, and became an office-bearer.

Malati Trivedi, who considered herself an unlikely socialist, but joined in for the enjoyment of it all and because she liked the discussions, and because some friends of hers (including her musician) had been socialists, had no interest whatsoever in office. But she planned to join in the 'victory-cum-protest' march that was planned a week after the elections.

The 'protest' part of the title came from the fact that the Socialist Party—together with any other parties that cared to join in—was going to march in protest against the low pay of primary schoolteachers. There were over ten thousand primary schoolteachers, and it was a disgrace that their salaries were as low as they were, certainly not enough for a decent living, lower in fact than those of village patwaris. The teachers had gone on strike after a number of unsuccessful attempts to get themselves heard. A number of students' federations, including those of the medical and law colleges, had pledged their support to the cause. Education involved them, and it involved the future shape of the university, indeed, the calibre of the citizenry of the country itself. Besides, here was an excellent magnet to which they could attach anything else that came to mind. Some of these federations were interested in stirring up the whole of Brahmpur, not just the university; interestingly enough, one minor hotbed of radicalism was a group of Muslim girls who were still in purdah.

The Home Minister L.N. Agarwal had made it clear that a peaceful procession was one thing, a disorderly surge of rabble another. He would control it with whatever means were available. If a lathi charge was necessary, he would order it.

Since the Chief Minister was in Delhi for a few days, a delegation of ten students (Rasheed among them) went to see the Home Minister, who was in charge in S.S. Sharma's absence. They crowded into his office in the Secretariat. They made brusque demands, as much to impress each other as to hope to persuade him. They did not pay him the respect that he believed was due to their elders, especially those who (unlike them) had suffered blows and ruin and years in jail in order to see their country free. He refused to concede their demands, saying that they should talk either to the Education Minister or to the Chief Minister himself upon his return. Nor did he budge from his stated stance that he would maintain order in the town at any cost.

'Does that mean you will shoot us if we get out of hand?' asked Rasheed with a malignant look.

'I would prefer not to,' said the Home Minister, as if the idea was not entirely unpleasant, 'but, needless to say, it will not come to that.' At any rate, he added to himself, the legislature is not presently in session to take me to task about it.

'This is like the days of the British,' continued Rasheed furiously, staring at the man who had justified the police firing in Chowk, and perhaps seeing embodied in him the image of other arbitrariness and authoritarianism. 'The British used lathis on us, they even shot at us, at us students, during the Quit India movement. Our blood was spilt by the British here in Brahmpur—in Chowk, in Captainganj—'

The rest of the delegation began to buzz rather angrily in response to his oratory.

'Yes, yes,' said the Home Minister, cutting him short. 'I know it. I lived through it. You must have been a boy of twelve then, watching anxiously in the mirror for the first signs of a man's hair. When you say "us students" you don't mean yourselves, it was your predecessors whose blood was spilt. And, I may mention, some of mine. It's easy enough to lubricate your way to office on others' blood. And as for Quit India, this is an Indian government now, and I hope you don't want us to quit India.' He laughed shortly. 'Now if you have anything useful to say, say it. Otherwise go. You may not have your books to read, but I have my files. I know exactly what this march is about. It isn't about the salaries of primary schoolteachers. It is a way of concertedly attacking the Congress government of the state and the country, and trying to spread disaffection and disorder in the town.' He made a dismissive gesture with the back of his hand. 'Stick to your books. That is my advice to you as your true friend—and as the Treasurer of the university—and as the Home Minister—and as the Acting Chief Minister; and it is the advice of your Vice-Chancellor too. And your teachers. And your parents.'

'And God,' added the President of the students' union, who was an atheist.

'Get out,' said the Home Minister in a calm voice.

12.21

But the evening before the day fixed for the march an incident occurred in town that brought the two sides temporarily together on the same side of an issue.

Manorma Talkies, the cinema hall in Nabiganj that was showing *Deedar*, that had indeed been showing *Deedar* continuously to packed or almost packed houses for months, became the scene of what was almost a student riot.

The Brahmpur University ordinances forbade students from going to the second or late-night show, but this was an ordinance that hardly anyone paid any heed to. In particular, those students who lived outside the university hostels flouted it whenever they saw fit. *Deedar* was an immensely popular movie. Its songs were on everyone's lips, and it appealed to old and young alike; it may well have happened that on some evening Dr Kishen Chand Seth and the Rajkumar of Marh sobbed their hearts out to it simultaneously. People saw it several times over. It had an unusually tragic ending, but one which did not make one wish to tear the screen apart or set fire to the theatre.

What caused the trouble was that on this evening the management had given exceptionally strict instructions to the ticket office not to honour student concessions if they got enough ticket-buyers at the full price. It was the early evening show. Two students, one of whom had seen the film before, had been told that the house was full. From past experience they had learned to mistrust the management. When several others who came after them were sold tickets, they began to harangue first the people in the ticket queue—when one woman told them to shut up, they told her the ending of the film—and then began to yell at the employees at the box office. The employees went about their business unperturbed—until the students, one of whom had an umbrella, became desperate enough to smash the glass panes of the doors of the cinema hall. Some of the patrons started shouting and threatening to call the police, but the management was not keen that the police be called. The employees got the projectionist and a few other people together, beat the students up, and threw them out. The mild mêlée was over in a few minutes, and did not disturb too deeply the subsequent mood of the audience.

By the time the first show ended, however, there was a crowd of about four hundred angry students demonstrating threateningly against the illegal actions of the management—and particularly the manhandling of their two fellows. They had driven away from the box office all those who were thinking of buying tickets for the second show or who, having bought their tickets in advance, were seeking to enter the lobby.

It had begun to drizzle, but the students refused to leave. They were angry, and yet they were elated, for here they were, displaying their might in front of the portals of the infamous Manorma Talkies which, because of the continuing success of *Deedar* in attracting customers at the full price, and also because of its hard-headed manager, who cared less for law than profits, had been discriminating against them for months. Refreshed by their vacation, excited by the recent student elections, and indignant at the attack on their pride and their pockets, the students shouted that they would show the management what stuff they were made of, that the cinema hall must 'either learn or burn', and that sticks would teach the employees what passes couldn't. The sorrowful and subdued patrons of the first show began to come out. They were astonished to be faced by a belligerent crowd which condemned their acquiescence in the earlier violence. 'Shame! Shame!' shouted the students. The audience, among them old people and even children, looked perplexedly at them with tear-stained faces.

The scene began to grow ugly. There was no violence, but some of the patrons were not allowed to enter their cars, and hurried away, fearing that if they stayed, their own safety would be threatened. Finally the District Magistrate, the Deputy Superintendent of Police, and the Proctor of the university all arrived on the scene. They tried to ascertain the nature of the problem. All of them felt that the management was to blame but that the students should have taken their complaint through the proper channels. The Proctor even tried to make the point that the students had no right to demonstrate before the second show, but it was clear that when facing four hundred angry students on a rainy night, he could not immediately exercise his normally awesome authority. His voice was drowned out by the shouting. When he perceived that the students would not be pacified or persuaded about the adequacy of the proper channels except by office-bearers of their own union, he tried to seek them out. Two of them, though not Rasheed, happened to be in the crowd. But they made it clear that they would not act unless the Treasurer appeared on their behalf as a representative of the Executive Council in order to show that the Council in general acted to protect, not merely to impose its will on the student body. This was a way of demanding L.N. Agarwal's presence.

The manager, who had gone home just after the students had been thrashed and before the crowd had collected, came hurriedly to the scene when he heard that the police would protect his person from injury but that only he could protect Manorma Talkies. He was abject. He called the students 'my dear dear friends'. He wept when he saw the bruises on the arms and back of one of the students. He talked about his own student days. He offered them all a special showing of *Deedar.* It would not do. 'Our university Treasurer will represent us,' insisted the students' union. 'Only he knows how to restrain us.' As a matter of fact, they themselves were keen that the incident should not turn violent, because it would affect the next day's victory-cum-protest march, and they did not want it to be perceived by the public at large that students demonstrated only for their own trivial privileges and not for the good of society.

L.N. Agarwal, who had told the DSP that he should handle the matter on his own and that he should not ring up the Home Minister for every petty disturbance, was finally persuaded by a phone call from his colleague the Proctor to come to the scene. Most unwillingly, he did so. He found himself utterly out of sympathy with the unruly mob. Students did not realize how privileged they were in comparison to the rest of their countrymen. They chose deliberately to be ignorant of how little they themselves paid for their education, how two-thirds of it was subsidized by the government. They were a cosseted bunch, and he deplored the concessions that they received for what was, after all, mere entertainment. But since the concessions existed, he was forced to tell the manager that he would have to accede to the students' demands.

As a result, the offending employees were dismissed; the manager submitted a letter of apology to the Proctor expressing his regret over the incident and assuring the students of his 'best service at all times'; two hundred rupees was paid to each of the injured students; and the manager agreed to screen a slide of his letter of apology at all the cinema halls of Brahmpur.

The students' union calmed the crowd down. The students melted away. The police retired. And L.N. Agarwal returned to his two rooms in the MLAs' hostel, furious at having had to act on behalf of the rowdy mob. Even when he had emerged from the manager's office, some of the students had jeered him. One went so far as to rhyme his surname with the Hindi word for pimp. For puerility, selfishness and ingratitude, thought the Home Minister, they were hard to beat. And tomorrow again, no doubt, their propensity for violence would come to the fore. Well, the police would be ready if they overstepped the line between propensity and action.

12.22

The next day, L.N. Agarwal's fears or hopes were fulfilled. The march began peacefully when it set out from a primary school. The girls (Malati among them) marched in front so as to foil any police action, and the boys marched behind them. They shouted slogans against the government and in support of the primary schoolteachers, some of whom were marching with them. People looked out at the procession from the windows of their houses, or from the open fronts of their shops, or down from their roofs. Some of them encouraged the students, others complained about the disruption to their business. The primary schools had gone on another day's strike, and many children waved at teachers whom they recognized. The teachers sometimes waved back. It was a clear morning, and only a few puddles remained of the previous night's rain.

A couple of banners protested the action of the university that sought to make membership in the students' union voluntary. Yet others protested growing unemployment. But most of them protested the plight of the primary schoolteachers and expressed their solidarity with them.

When the crowd got to within a hundred yards of the Secretariat, they found their path blocked by a large contingent of policemen armed with lathis. The students stopped. The police advanced until they were within five yards of each other. On the instructions of the DSP an Inspector told the students to either disperse or return. They refused. They had been shouting slogans all the while, but these now became more and more insulting, and embraced not only the government but the police. The police, who were the lackeys of the British, had now become the lackeys of the Congress-wallahs; they should be wearing dhotis, not shorts; and so on.

The policemen became restive. They wanted to get at the loudest slogan-mongers in the crowd. But with a cordon of girls—some wearing burqas—surrounding the boys, it was difficult for them to do anything but brandish their lathis threateningly. The students, for their part, could see that for all L.N. Agarwal's threats, the police were carrying sticks, not firearms, and this made them bolder.

Some of them, recalling the Home Minister's devious behind-the-scenes style, started to bait him personally; apart from rhyming his name with 'dalal' as they had the previous night, they invented a number of new couplets, such as:

'Maananiya Mantri, kya hain aap?
Aadha maanav, aadha saanp.'

Minister, what form do you take?
Half a human, half a snake.

Some challenged his manhood in more direct ways. Rasheed and another office-bearer of the students' union attempted to keep the students calm and their slogans to the purpose, but to little avail. For one thing, some of the protesters belonged to student federations over whom the newly elected Socialist Party students' union had no real control. For another, a certain intoxication had seized hold of the assembly. The high-minded banners now contrasted pathetically with the low-minded mockery.

Finding that the protest that he had helped organize was getting completely out of hand, Rasheed now tried to persuade at least his immediate neighbours to calm down. They did, but others did not follow. Indeed, by then, loud jeers and insults had broken out in several other groups. He tried to shout that this was not what their march or their platform was all about, but found himself becoming a subsidiary butt of their indignation. One young man from the medical college, full of wit and zeal, told him: 'Just now you were All India Radio, now you're a little squirrel squeaking in Agarwal's pocket. First you try to whip us up, then you try to cool us down. We aren't clockwork toys.' And as if to prove his independence of the office-bearers, the boy now made his way through the protective cordon of girls and continued his pejorative peltings, retreating whenever the police advanced. His friends laughed, but Rasheed, frightened now as he looked at the faces of the police, and disgusted by what this principled march had degenerated into, turned away—and, despite the heckling of some other students, turned back. What the boy had said had had enough truth in it to make him feel sick at heart.

It was only small groups that concentrated on the worst kind of unwitty taunt. But these taunts began to antagonize most of the girls and some others in the crowd, including many teachers. They began to leave. L.N. Agarwal, who had been looking down from his office in the Secretariat, noticed with satisfaction that the protective cordon was becoming thinner, and sent a message down that the remaining students should be dispersed. 'Teach them that lessons can be taught outside the classroom as well as inside,' were his words to the DSP who came to him for instructions.

'Yes, Sir,' said the DSP, almost gratefully.

After the insults to the police, the DSP would fulfil his instructions with little regret.

He ordered the Inspectors, Sub-Inspectors and constables to teach the students a good lesson, and this they did with a vengeance. The lathi charge was savage and sudden. Several students were badly beaten. A certain amount of blood mixed with the previous night's rain in the puddles, and stained the surface of the road. Many of the blows were severe. Some young men suffered broken bones: ribs, or legs, or arms which they had lifted in order to protect their heads from injury. The policemen pulled them off the road, sometimes by the feet, their heads bouncing or dragging along the road surface, towards the police vans. They were too incensed to use stretchers.

One boy lay in a van at the point of death, with an injury to the skull. He was the student from the medical college.

12.23

When S.S. Sharma returned that afternoon he found a dangerous situation on his hands. What had begun as a protest march had now upset and unnerved the whole town. Regardless of their political affiliations, the students closed ranks against the brutality, some said criminality, of the police. A vigil began near the medical college, where (once the police realized how serious his injuries were) the student had been unloaded. Several thousand students sat outside the medical college, waiting for news of the boy's health. Needless to say, there were no classes anywhere in the university that day, nor would there be for a while.

The Home Minister, fearing the worst if the boy died, advised the Chief Minister to call out the army, and if necessary to impose martial law. He himself had already imposed a police curfew, which was due to take effect that evening.

S.S. Sharma listened in silence. Then he said: 'Agarwal, why is it that I cannot leave town for two days without you presenting me with some problem? If you are tired of your portfolio, I will give you something else.'

But L.N. Agarwal enjoyed the power that went along with being Home Minister, and he knew that it was not a portfolio that could be given to anyone else, especially now that it was an open secret that Mahesh Kapoor was about to announce his resignation from the Congress Party and the government. He said: 'I have done my best. One cannot run a state by kindness.'

'So you suggest calling out the army?'

'I do, Sharmaji.'

S.S. Sharma looked tired. He said, 'That will be good neither for the army nor for the people of Brahmpur. As for the students, it will inflame them as little else can.' His head began to shake slightly. 'I feel they are like my children. This is a wrong thing we have done.'

L.N. Agarwal smiled somewhat contemptuously at the Chief Minister's sentimentality. But he was relieved to notice the collective 'we'.

'I believe, Sharmaji, that no matter what we do, the students will be inflamed when that student dies.'

'*When*, you say, not *if*? There is no hope for him, then?'

'I don't believe so. But it is difficult to get at facts in this situation. It is true, people exaggerate. Still, it is best to be prepared.' L.N. Agarwal's tone was cold, and not defensive.

The Chief Minister sighed, then continued in his slightly nasal voice: 'Because of this curfew, whatever happens to the student, we will have a problem this evening. What if the students do not disperse? Do you suggest we start firing at them?'

The Home Minister remained silent.

'And when the boy dies, I tell you that the funeral will become uncontrollable. They will want to cremate him by the Ganga, probably near that other unfortunate pyre.'

The Home Minister refused to flinch at this needless reference. When one did one's duty properly, one could face reproof without being inwardly shaken. He had no doubt that the Pul Mela Inquiry Commission, which had begun its sittings a week ago, would absolve him.

'That will be impossible,' he said. 'They will have to do it at a ghat or somewhere else. The sands on this side of the river are already under water.'

S.S. Sharma was about to say something, then thought better of it. Pandit Jawaharlal Nehru, embattled though he was in his own party, had once again asked him to come to the centre to join his Cabinet. It was getting difficult to refuse. But now, with the imminent resignation of Mahesh Kapoor, Sharma's departure would almost certainly result in L.N. Agarwal becoming Chief Minister. And Sharma felt that he could not in conscience hand his state over to this shrewd and rigid man who, for all his intelligence, lacked any human touch. Sharma in his philosophical moments felt like a father towards those in his protection. Sometimes this led to unnecessary conciliation or avoidable compromise, but he believed these were preferable to Agarwal's alternative. Needless to say, a state could not be run on kindness alone. But he dreaded to think of one run on nothing but discipline and fear.

'Agarwal, I am taking over this problem from you. Kindly issue no further instructions in this matter,' said the Chief Minister. 'But do not undo any instructions you have already issued. Let the curfew stand.'

The Chief Minister then looked at his watch, and told his personal assistant to get the Superintendent of the medical college on the telephone. He picked up the day's newspaper, and ignored Agarwal. When the PA got through to the Superintendent, he said: 'The Chief Minister would like to speak to you, Sir,' and handed the phone to the Chief Minister.

'This is Sharma speaking,' said the Chief Minister. 'I wish to come to the medical college immediately. . . . No, no police, no police escort at all. Just one assistant. . . . Yes. . . . I am sorry to hear about the boy. . . . Yes, well, my safety is my concern. I will avoid the students on vigil. . . . What do you mean, impossible? Surely there must be a side gate or something. A private gate to your house? Yes, I'll use that. If you would kindly meet me there. . . . Good, in fifteen minutes then. Do not mention this to anyone, or I will face the kind of reception committee I can do without. . . . No, he won't be with me—no, definitely not.'

Not looking at L.N. Agarwal but at a glass paperweight on his desk, the Chief Minister said: 'I must go to the medical college and see what I can do. I think it best if you don't come with me. If you remain here in my office, I will be able to get in touch with you immediately if there are developments, and my staff will be at your service.'

L.N. Agarwal passed his hand restlessly through the horseshoe of hair around his head.

'I would prefer to come with you,' he said. 'Or at least to give you a police escort.'

'I do not think that would be for the best.'

'You need protection. Those students—'

'Agarwal, you are not Chief Minister yet,' said S.S. Sharma quietly, but with a rather unhappy smile. L.N. Agarwal frowned, but did not say another word.

12.24

When he got to the room where the injured boy was lying, the Chief Minister, hardened though he had been by the deaths and injuries caused by British lathi charges and firings, shook his head for a minute in pity and disbelief. He glanced through the window at the students sitting on the lawn and the road and tried to imagine their feelings of shock and anger. It was as well that they did not know he was in the college. The Superintendent was saying something to him, something about the impossibility of resuming classes. The Chief Minister's attention, however, had wandered to an old man in typical Congress garb, who was sitting quietly in a corner and had not stood up to greet him. He appeared to be lost in his own world, as he himself was.

'And who are you?' asked the Chief Minister.

'I am the father of this unfortunate boy,' said the man.

The Chief Minister bowed his head.

'You must come with me,' he said. 'We can settle the issues later. But you and I have to sort out the immediate problem immediately. In a private room, not with so many people around.'

'I cannot leave this room. My son does not have long to live, I understand.'

The Chief Minister looked around the room and asked everyone to leave except for one doctor. Then he said to the old man:

'I am guilty of letting this happen. I accept the responsibility for it. But I need your help. You see how it is. Only you can save the situation. If you do not, there will be many more unfortunate boys and many more grief-stricken fathers.'

'What can I do?' The old man spoke calmly, as if nothing much mattered to him any more.

'The students are inflamed. When your son dies, they will want to take out a procession. It is bound to be an emotional event, and will get out of hand. If that occurs, and it is almost inevitable, who can answer for what will happen?'

'What do you want me to do?'

'Speak to the students. Tell them to condole with you, tell them to attend the funeral. It will take place wherever you wish it to; I will not allow any police to be present. But please advise them not to take out a procession. That will have an uncontainable effect.'

The old man began to weep. After a while he controlled himself and, looking at his son, whose head was covered almost entirely in bandages, he said in the same calm voice as before: 'I will do as you say.'

Then, to himself, he added: 'So he will have died for nothing?'

The Chief Minister caught the remark, though it was uttered in a low voice. He said: 'Indeed, I will make sure that he will not have. I will try to defuse the situation in my own way. But nothing I do can have the chastening effect of a few words from you. Your act will have prevented more grief than most people can prevent in their lives.'

The Chief Minister returned, as he had come, incognito. Once back in his office he asked L.N. Agarwal to cancel the curfew and to release all the students who had been arrested in the demonstration earlier. 'And send for the President of the students' union,' he added.

Over L.N. Agarwal's protest that it was a march instigated by the union that had been the genesis of this problem in the first place, the Chief Minister met the young man, who seemed less self-assured but more determined than before. He had wanted to bring Rasheed with him—one Hindu, one Muslim, to emphasize the secularism of the socialists—but Rasheed had looked so ill with distress and guilt that he had changed his mind. Now the young man was here alone, face to face with the Chief Minister and the Home Minister, and he was patently nervous.

The Chief Minister said: 'I agree to your terms, but I want the movement to be called off. Are you prepared to do that? Do you have the courage to avoid further bloodshed?'

'The question of membership of the students' unions?' said the young man.

'Yes,' said the Chief Minister. L.N. Agarwal stood tight-lipped nearby, and could not trust himself to utter a word. His silence, he knew, implied consent, and it was a difficult silence to maintain.

'The primary schoolteachers' salaries?'

'We will go into the question, and we will improve the salaries, but we do not know if the extent of the improvement will satisfy you completely. The resources of the state are limited. Still, we will try.'

Thus they went down the list of demands one by one.

'What I can offer,' said the young man, 'is a temporary withdrawal. I have your promise, and you have mine—assuming I can persuade the others. But if the demands are not in fact met, this understanding will no longer hold.'

L.N. Agarwal, disgusted with the proceedings, reflected that the young man thought nothing of the fact that he was parleying on equal terms with the chief executive of the state. And even S.S. Sharma, who normally loved the outward forms of respect and obeisance, had, it appeared, so far forgotten what was due to him as not to mind their absence.

'I understand and agree,' the Chief Minister was saying. L.N. Agarwal looked at S.S. Sharma and thought: You are getting old and weak. You have acceded to unreason in order to buy a temporary peace. But the precedent of this peace will remain to haunt us, your successors. And you may not have bought peace anyway. Still, we will know soon enough about that.

That night the injured student died. The grieving father spoke to those who were holding vigil outside. The next day the body was cremated at the cremation ghat on the Ganga. The students sat on the great steps leading down to the ghat. There was no procession. The dense crowd of mourners was quiet as the flames crackled around the body. The police had been instructed to keep away. There was no violence.

12.25

Dr Kishen Chand Seth had booked two tables in the small bridge room of the Subzipore Club. Noticing his name on the roster for the day, none of the other members had booked either of the two remaining tables. The librarian, who usually made it a point to look at the roster himself (the bridge room was located next door to the library), sighed when he saw the name of the eminent radiologist. There would be little peace for him that afternoon; and, if they continued to play through the film, that evening either.

Dr Kishen Chand Seth was seated facing a tiger skin that was hanging head downwards on the wall. The tiger had been there for as long as anyone could remember, though its connection with bridge was unclear. Prints of Oxford colleges—including one with a pelican perched on a pillar in the quad—hung on the remaining walls. The four green baize-covered bridge tables were arranged squarely in the small square room. Apart from the sixteen hardbacked chairs there were no others. It was a fairly austere room, if one excepted the tiger. Its one large window looked out upon a gravel drive, and beyond that the lawn where members and their guests sat on white cane chairs in the shade of large trees and sipped long drinks; and far beyond that the Ganga.

The seven others constituting Dr Kishen Chand Seth's bridge party were: his wife Parvati, who was wearing an exceptionally tasteless sari with roses printed on it; his relation by marriage, the ex-Minister of Revenue, Mahesh Kapoor, whom Dr Seth seemed to recall he was currently on good terms with; Mr Shastri, the Advocate-General; the Nawab Sahib of Baitar; Professor and Mrs O.P. Mishra; and Dr Durrani. There were six men and two women, and the draw of cards had placed them in such a way that the two women were seated at the same table, though they were not partners. Mrs O.P. Mishra, a frightened but babbling sort of woman, was a good bridge player. Parvati Seth was not a good player, and irritated her husband a great deal by her hesitant and obtuse bidding whenever she happened to be his partner. He very rarely dared to rebuke her, however, and vented his spleen on anyone else who happened to be nearby.

Dr Kishen Chand Seth's idea of an ideal afternoon of bridge was furious, ruthless play combined with continuous conversation; and his idea of entertaining conversation was a series of small shocks and explosions.

When he was most delighted, he actually cackled. And it was a cackle that preceded the following remark:

'Two spades. Hm, hm, hmm, now, Minister—ex-Minister, I should say—you are taking as long to bid as it must have taken you to decide to resign.'

Mahesh Kapoor frowned in concentration. 'What? Pass.'

'Or as long as it took him to frame the Zamindari Act, wouldn't you say, Nawab Sahib? He was always a slow bidder; let's hope he takes his time gobbling up your estates. But there's no reason for you to bid so slowly.'

The Nawab Sahib, somewhat distracted, said, 'Three hearts.'

'But I forget,' said Dr Kishen Chand Seth, turning to the left. 'You won't be doing that any longer. Who will, I wonder. Agarwal? Could he handle both Revenue and Home?'

Mr Mahesh Kapoor sat up a little more stiffly, but said nothing. He held his cards in a slightly tighter grip. He thought for a moment of reminding his host that it had been L.N. Agarwal himself who had issued the order for requisitioning cars. But he held his tongue.

'No, er, no bid,' said Dr Durrani.

Dr Kishen Chand Seth, having seen three of his squibs fizzle out, sent up a fourth. 'It's a portfolio that requires someone responsible, and who else is there in the Cabinet as competent as Agarwal? Now, what shall I bid? What shall I bid? Three spades. Good. But I must say he did a good job teaching those students a lesson. In my day, medical students stuck to their Anatomy and did not make cadavers of themselves. Three spades. Yes, what's your bid, now, Kapoor Sahib?'

Mahesh Kapoor looked across at his partner, and thought of the student who had restored his grandson to him. Dr Durrani seemed to be going through a struggle with himself. 'Well, er, do you, well, consider that the lathi charge was, um, justified?' he asked, scrunching his eyes up. There was as much disapproval in his voice as it was ever capable of holding, which wasn't much. He had expressed only the mildest verbal disapproval when his wife had tried to destroy a large part of his life's work by tearing up his mathematical papers.

'Oh, but I do, I do—' cried Dr Kishen Chand Seth with relish. 'One must be cruel only to be kind. The surgeon's knife; we doctors learn that at an early age. But you are a doctor too, of course. A doctor of a kind. Not yet a professor, but no doubt that will come. You should ask Professor Mishra there what it takes to rise to such a height.'

By such means did Dr Kishen Chand Seth knit the two tables together into a web of distracting conversation. His own game thrived upon the stimulus that this turmoil provided. Most of the others were used to him through acquaintance, and tried not to get provoked. But anyone else who was present and attempting to play in the bridge room at that time would have been tempted to complain to the committee, had Dr Kishen Chand Seth himself not been a member of it. Since he was one of the oldest members of the Subzipore Club and since he believed in terrorizing everyone else before they could complain even mildly about him, his odd behaviour escaped its normal consequences.

When he saw the dummy's hand, Dr Kishen Chand Seth almost had a fit. After he had played the hand, he and the Nawab Sahib were one trick down, and Dr Seth turned roundly on his partner. 'Good heavens, Nawab Sahib, with such a poor hand, how did you go on to bid three hearts? We had no chance of making nine tricks.'

'You could have had hearts.'

Dr Kishen Chand Seth bristled with rage. 'If I had hearts, partner, I would have bid the suit earlier,' he almost shouted. 'If you didn't have spades, you should have shut up—the bidding. This is what happens when you turn your back on your religion and play cards with infidels.'

The Nawab Sahib told himself, as he often had before, that he would never respond to one of Dr Kishen Chand Seth's invitations in the future.

'Now, now, Kishy,' said Parvati mildly, glancing across from the other table.

'Sorry—sorry—' said Dr Kishen Chand Seth. 'I—well—well, whose turn is it to deal? Ah, yes, drinks. What will everyone have to drink?' And he clicked out the small wood and brass extension located immediately to his right in the table; it contained an ashtray and a coaster. 'First the ladies. Gin for the ladies?'

Mrs O.P. Mishra cast a terrified look at her husband. Parvati Seth, catching the look, said, 'Kishy!' rather sharply.

Kishy was brought to heel for the next few minutes. He alternated his concentration between his cards, the tiger, and (once the waiter had brought it in) his whisky. Normally he was restricted to tea and nimbu pani, but he threw such a tantrum if he was not allowed his whisky when playing bridge that Parvati thought it best to husband her strength for more winnable battles. The only problem was that the whisky had unpredictable effects. On some days it made him slightly mellow, on other days more belligerent. It never made him amorous. And rarely did it make him, as it makes some men, sentimental; only movies had that power.

Dr Kishen Chand Seth was looking forward to the movie which was to be screened in the club today: a Charlie Chaplin movie, he recalled. His granddaughter Savita had very much wanted to see it, and despite her husband's and mother's advice, had availed herself of his membership to do so. Pran and Mrs Rupa Mehra, reasonably enough, had insisted on coming along. But Dr Seth could not see them sitting anywhere on the lawn even after an hour had gone by and they were well into the second rubber and thirteenth argument.

'Er, well,' Dr Durrani was remonstrating, 'I can't entirely, you know, agree with you. A fine calculation of probabilities is an essential part—'

'Essential, nothing!' Dr Kishen Chand Seth cut him off. 'Most good bridge play is simply deduction, not a judgement of probabilities. Now I'll give you an example,' he went on. Dr Kishen Chand Seth liked arguing from examples. 'It happened to me just a week ago. A week ago, wasn't it, dear?'

'Yes, dear,' said Parvati. She remembered the game well, because her husband's triumph had spiced their evening conversations throughout the week.

'I was the declarer and I played clubs early in the game. I had five, my dummy had two, and the man on the right ruffed.'

'Woman, Kishy.'

'Yes, yes, woman!' said Dr Kishen Chand Seth, expostulating as much as he dared.

'That meant that the man on my left had to have had six clubs, or, rather, five after this round. Now later in the game it was clear that he could only have space in his hand for two hearts; since he had bid spades, I assumed he must have had at least four spades, and the residue of those had to take up the rest of the place in his hand.'

'Isn't that Rupa, dear?' asked Parvati suddenly, pointing towards the lawn. She had heard the story so often that she had entirely forgotten to treat it with reverence.

This cruel interruption threw her husband completely off his stride. 'Yes, yes, it is Rupa. Let it be Rupa—or anyone else,' he cried, dismissing his daughter from his mind. 'Now, you see, I had the ace, the king, and the jack of hearts. So I played the ace first and then the king. As I had deduced, the queen fell.' He paused to retaste the memory. 'Everyone said that I was a lucky player or that the probabilities were in my favour. But that was not the case at all. Luck—nothing! Probabilities—nothing! I had my eyes open, and, most of all, my brain open. To deduction,' he ended triumphantly. Then, since it sounded like a toast, he took a good gulp of whisky.

Dr Durrani looked unconvinced.

The next table, though often dragged by Dr Seth into the vortex of his own, was much calmer. Mr Shastri, the Advocate-General, was at his genial best, and did his best (in his syllabic manner) to draw out Mrs O.P. Mishra, who played a good game but seemed to be worried that she was doing so; she kept darting glances at her husband opposite. Bridge, where the bidding consisted almost entirely of monosyllabic words, was the ideal game for Mr Shastri. He was happy that he was not sitting at the other table, where he would have been forced by his host into an embarrassing conversation about the taking over of the estates and his estimation of the government's chances when the zamindari case went to the Supreme Court. He sympathized equally with the Nawab Sahib and Mahesh Kapoor. Mahesh Kapoor had exploded twice in the face of Dr Kishen Chand Seth's opinions, and appeared about to do so for the third time. The Nawab Sahib had subsided into icy etiquette; he now refused to contradict even the most outrageous of his host's comments, or to take visible offence at his repeated offers of whisky—indeed, even to repeat what Dr Kishen Chand Seth well knew, that he was a teetotaller. Only Dr Durrani was able to maintain an absent-minded and undisagreeable disagreement, and this exasperated Dr Kishen Chand Seth.

Meanwhile, Professor O.P. Mishra was holding forth for the benefit of Parvati and the Advocate-General:

'Politicians, you know, prefer to appoint mediocrities to important posts not merely because they themselves will look better in comparison or because they are afraid of competition, but also because, you see, a person appointed on merit feels that it is owed to him, while a mediocrity is only too conscious that it is not.'

'I see,' smiled Mr Shastri. 'And it is not so with your pro-fes-sion?'

'Well,' said Professor Mishra, 'there's always the odd case here or there, you know, but in general, in our department at least, one makes every attempt to ensure the pre-eminence of excellence. . . . Simply because someone may, for instance, be the son of an illustrious person ought not, in our eyes—'

'What's that you're saying, Mishra?' cried Dr Seth from the next table. 'Do repeat that—I didn't quite hear you; nor did my friend Kapoor Sahib. . . . '

Dr Seth was never happier than when walking through an emotional minefield—unless it was when he was dragging seven other troops along with him.

Professor Mishra pursed his lips sweetly and said: 'My dear Dr Seth, I have quite forgotten what I was rambling on about—perhaps because I feel so relaxed in these delightful surroundings. Or perhaps it is your excellent whisky that has made my memory as limp as my limbs. But what an amazing mechanism the human body is: who could imagine that one could feed in, say, four arrowroot biscuits and one boiled egg and get an output, say, of three spades—and one trick down?'

Parvati quickly interjected: 'Professor Mishra, a young lecturer was telling us just a few days ago about the pleasures of teaching. What a noble profession it must be.'

'My dear lady,' said Professor Mishra, 'teaching is a thankless task, but one undertakes it because one feels one has a calling, as it were. A couple of years ago I had rather an interesting discussion on the radio about the concept of teaching as a vocation—with a lawyer by the name of Dilip Pandey, in which I said—or was it Deepak Pandey—anyway, I said—'

'Dilip,' said the Advocate-General. 'He is now dead, in fact.'

'Oh, is he? What a pity. Well, I made the point that there are three kinds of teachers: those who are forgotten, those who are remembered and hated, and the third, the lucky ones, and I hope I am one of them, those who are remembered and'—he paused—'forgiven.'

He looked rather pleased with his formulation.

'Oh, you are, you are—' said his wife eagerly.

'What's that?' cried Dr Kishen Chand Seth. 'Speak louder, we can't hear you.' He banged his stick on the floor.

Towards the end of the second rubber, the librarian (having been requested to do so twice already by the users of the library) sent a note to the bridge room. If Parvati had not restrained him, Dr Kishen Chand Seth would have screamed in wrath upon receiving it. As it was, he could neither believe nor stomach the insubordination of the librarian in requesting that the volume of conversation in the bridge room be reduced. He would haul the fellow up before the committee. A useless fellow, who spent most of his time dozing in the stacks, who treated the job as a sinecure, who—

'Yes, dear,' said Parvati. 'Yes, dear, I know. Now we at our table have finished our second rubber, but we're talking quite quietly. Why don't you concentrate on finishing yours, and then we can all go out on to the lawn; the film will begin in about twenty minutes. It's a pity that in the monsoon they screen it indoors. Ah, yes, Pran and Savita are sitting there; eating chips, I suppose. She looks enormous. I think perhaps we'll go and join them immediately, and you can follow.'

'I am afraid we must now be going,' said Professor Mishra, getting up hastily. His wife stood up too.

'Must you go? Can't you join us?' asked Parvati.

'No—no—far too busy these days—there are guests in the house—and I have been saddled with a good deal of unnecessary curriculum revision,' explained Professor Mishra.

Mahesh Kapoor looked at him for a second, then returned to his cards.

'Thank you, thank you,' said the whale, and glided quickly out of sight, followed by his minnow.

'How peculiar,' said Parvati, turning back to the table. 'What do you make of it?' she asked Mr Shastri.

'Force-ful per-son-al-it-y,' was Mr Shastri's opinion. Though it was unrevealing, it was delivered with a smile and conveyed the sense that Mr Shastri had some knowledge of the world, and did not opine where opinion was unnecessary.

Parvati had begun to have second thoughts about letting her husband follow her. For one thing, he might still need to be managed. For another, she did not relish meeting Mrs Rupa Mehra without his support. The reaction of Kishy's daughter to her rose-spangled sari was unpredictable. So Parvati waited for a few more minutes to see if the rubber would end. It did. Her husband was on the winning side. With some glee he was totting up his points for the hand—including an overtrick and a hundred honours. She breathed more freely.

12.26

Out on the lawn, everyone was introduced to everyone else. Savita found herself engaged in a slow and deliberate conversation with Mr Shastri. She found him very interesting. He was telling her about a woman lawyer at the Brahmpur High Court, who was very successful in criminal practice despite the fact that she had had to overcome the reservations of clients, colleagues and judges.

Pran was feeling a bit exhausted, but Savita had insisted on seeing Charlie Chaplin 'once more before I become a mother and see everything differently'; her grandfather's Buick, a little the worse for having been requisitioned, had been sent to fetch them. Lata had gone off to one of those evening rehearsals so dreaded by Mrs Rupa Mehra; the director had said that it was necessary to make up for the rehearsals lost because of the student agitation.

Savita was looking happy and energetic, and eating with great appetite the club speciality: small goli kababs, each with a raisin in the middle. The more she talked to Mr Shastri, the more she thought that it would be very interesting to study law.

Pran walked towards the low wall that separated the Subzipore Club lawn from the sands and the river. He looked over it at the brown water and the few slow boats plying silently along. He was thinking that soon, like his father, he would be a father too, and he was doubtful that he would make a good one. I'll be too worried for my child's own good, he thought. But in a while he reflected that Kedarnath's perpetual air of anxiety had not had a damaging effect on Bhaskar. And, he reflected, thinking with a smile of Maan, one can be too carefree as well. Since he was feeling a little out of breath, he leaned against the wall and watched the others from a few yards away.

Mrs Rupa Mehra had started when she heard Dr Durrani's name. She could hardly believe that her father had known him so well as to invite him for bridge. After all, it had been Dr Kishen Chand Seth to whom she had gone for advice in extremis, and who had told her to get Lata out of Brahmpur as soon as possible in the face of the Durrani threat. Had he deliberately not told her of the acquaintance? Or was it of very recent standing?

Dr Durrani was sitting next to her now, leaning forward slightly in his cane chair, and she was compelled by both politeness and curiosity to swallow her astonishment and talk to him. In response to a question from her, he mentioned that he had two sons.

'Ah, yes,' said Mrs Rupa Mehra, 'one of them rescued Bhaskar at the Pul Mela. What a terrible business. How brave of him. Do have another chip.'

'Yes. Kabir. I fear, though, that the, er, acuity of his, um, um, insight—'

'Whose? Kabir's?'

Dr Durrani looked startled. 'No, er, Bhaskar's.'

'Has suffered?' asked Mrs Rupa Mehra anxiously.

'Er, quite.'

There was a silence; then Mrs Rupa Mehra asked, 'And where is he now?'

'In bed?' asked Dr Durrani, presenting a question in lieu of a reply.

'Isn't it rather early for him to go to bed?' said Mrs Rupa Mehra, puzzled.

'As I, er, understand, his mother and er, grandmother, are quite strict. They tuck him up at, er, seven or so these days. Doctor's orders.'

'Oh,' said Mrs Rupa Mehra. 'We have been talking at cross purposes. I meant, what is your son Kabir doing? Was he involved in these recent student activities?'

'Only after the, er, lamentable, er, injury to that boy. . . .' He shook his head and his eyelids squeezed themselves together. 'No, well, he has other interests. At the moment he is, er, rehearsing in a play . . . er, is something the matter? Dear Mrs Mehra?'

Mrs Rupa Mehra had nearly swallowed some nimbu pani the wrong way.

In order to cover her embarrassment, Dr Durrani tried to pretend that nothing was amiss. He kept on talking—hesitantly, of course—about this and that. When Mrs Rupa Mehra had partially recovered from the shock, she found him discussing the Pergolesi Lemma in a courtly and sympathetic manner.

'It was my paper on that, er, Lemma which my, um, wife nearly destroyed,' he was saying.

'Oh, why?' asked Mrs Rupa Mehra, seizing upon the first two sensible syllables on hand in order to show that she had been following him.

'Ah,' said Professor Durrani. 'Because my wife is, er, mad.'

'Mad?' whispered Mrs Rupa Mehra.

'Yes, er, quite mad. It seems that the film is, er, about to, er, er, commence. Shall we go in?' asked Dr Durrani.

12.27

They entered the dance hall of the club, where, in the cold or rainy seasons, the weekly films were screened. It was much pleasanter in the open air, for the hall was inevitably crowded; but these days there was the risk of a sudden evening shower.

City Lights began, and laughter resounded all around. For Mrs Rupa Mehra, however, this was the laughter of mockery. Too clearly now she saw the deeply laid plot, the scheme whereby Lata, with Malati's connivance, had contrived to act in the same play as Kabir. Lata had not mentioned him once since their return to Brahmpur. When his involvement in the Bhaskar episode had come up in conversation, she had pointedly ignored it. She could well afford to do so, thought Mrs Rupa Mehra indignantly, because she could get all the facts from the protagonist himself in their tête-à-têtes.

That Lata should have acted so furtively with her mother, her mother who loved her and had sacrificed every comfort for the education and happiness of her children, wounded Mrs Rupa Mehra deeply. So this was her reward for being tolerant and understanding. This was what happened if you were a widow, and all alone in the world, with no one to help you control your children for their own good. Her nose had reddened in the darkened hall; and when she thought of her late husband, she started sobbing.

'My wife is, er, mad.' The words started echoing in her head. Who had spoken them? Dr Durrani? A voice in the film? Her own husband Raghubir? Not content with being Muslim, this wretched boy was half-mad as well. Poor Lata, poor, poor Lata. And Mrs Rupa Mehra, out of pity for and anger at her daughter, began to weep noisily and unashamedly.

To her surprise, she saw that people to both left and right of her were sobbing as well. Dr Kishen Chand Seth, for instance, who was sitting next to her, was juddering with grief. When she realized what had brought this about, she glanced sharply up at the small screen. But concentration was impossible. She was not feeling well. She opened her black handbag to get out her eau de cologne.

Someone else who was not feeling at all well was Pran. He could sense, in the crowded and enclosed atmosphere of the slightly musty hall, one of his frightening attacks coming on. He had been feeling a little breathless earlier, but this had improved when he had sat down. Now it was again becoming hard to breathe. He opened his mouth. It was difficult either to expel the stale air or to take in fresh air. He leaned forward, bent over, sat up straight. It was no good. He began to gasp for breath. His chest and neck moved, but to no effect. In a fog of desperation he heard the laughter of the audience, but he had closed his eyes, and could not see the screen.

Pran began to wheeze, and Savita, who had half-turned to him, thinking that his paroxysm was probably one brought on by laughter, and would subside, heard the characteristic danger signal. She held his hand. But Pran had only one thought: how to get oxygen into his lungs. The more he tried, the harder it seemed to be. His efforts became more frantic. He was forced to stand up and bend over. Now other people had turned around, and were beginning to look at the source of the disturbance. Savita spoke in a low voice to the other members of the family, and they all got up to leave. Mrs Rupa Mehra's sobbing for her daughter was converted into a new and more urgent concern for her son-in-law. But Dr Kishen Chand Seth, welded mentally as he was to the joys and woes of *City Lights*, was gnashing his teeth in frustration, and was only restrained from going up in smoke by a warning word from his wife.

Somehow they got to his car, and there Pran collapsed. His struggles to breathe were painful to observe, and Mrs Rupa Mehra tried to prevent her daughter from observing them. The baby was due in two weeks, and she had advised Savita against even the mild excitement of the movie.

Savita held Pran's hand tightly and said to Dr Kishen Chand Seth: 'This is a worse attack than usual, Nanaji. We should go to the hospital.' But Pran managed to gasp out the single word: 'Home.' He felt that once he was there the spasm would subside of its own accord.

They drove back to the house. Pran was put to bed. But the spasm continued. The veins in his neck and forehead stood out. His eyes, even when open, registered very little of the outside world. His chest continued to heave. His coughing, gasping, and wheezing filled the room, and there was a desperate darkness in his mind.

It was now almost an hour since it had begun. Dr Kishen Chand Seth phoned a colleague. Then, despite her mother's dissuasion on the grounds that she should be resting, not distressing herself like this, Savita walked carefully out of the bedroom, picked up the receiver, phoned Baitar House and asked for Imtiaz. By some miracle he was in, though in that vast house it took a little while to summon him to the phone.

'Imtiaz Bhai,' said Savita, 'Pran is having one of his asthma attacks, but it is much worse than usual. Could you come over, please? . . . It's been an hour or more. . . . Yes, I'll remain calm—but please come over . . . please. . . . At the club during the movie. . . . No, your father's still there, but my grandfather is with us, here at home. . . . Yes, yes, I will remain calm, but I'll be calmer once you're here. . . . I can't describe it. It's much worse than usual, and I've seen many of them.'

While she was talking, the young servant, Mansoor, concerned that in her situation she should be standing, had brought a chair for her. Now she sat down, looked at the phone, and sobbed.

After a while, having collected herself, she went back to the bedroom, where everyone was standing around, upset and agitated.

A sound was heard at the front door. 'I'll see who it is,' said Mrs Rupa Mehra.

It was Lata and Malati, back from the rehearsal of *Twelfth Night*.

'Whenever I act or sing,' said Malati, 'I feel I could eat a horse.'

'We're not serving horse today,' said Lata, as the door opened. 'It's one of Ma's fast days. Where is everyone?' she continued, noticing that, despite the car standing outside, the drawing room was empty. 'Ma? Now what are you crying for? I didn't mean to tease you. It was a stupid joke, anyway. . . . Is something the matter? Is anything wrong?'

Part Thirteen

13.1

Maan, Firoz and Imtiaz were over very shortly. Maan tried to cheer Savita up a bit. Firoz said little. Like everyone else, he was distressed to see Pran in such a pitiable state, labouring and panting for breath.

Imtiaz, on the other hand, was not visibly upset by his friend's painful struggles and went about his task of diagnosis swiftly. Parvati Seth was a trained nurse and helped move Pran when necessary. Imtiaz knew that Pran was not in a position to answer questions except occasionally by nodding or shaking his head, so he addressed what questions he could about the background as well as the suddenness of this recent attack to Savita. Malati described fairly clinically the incident in the lecture room a few days earlier. Firoz had already told Imtiaz on the way to the house that Pran had been complaining of exhaustion when he had met him at the High Court a few days earlier—and, of all things, discomfort around his heart.

Mrs Rupa Mehra sat silently in a chair, and Lata stood behind her, an arm on her shoulder. Mrs Rupa Mehra did not say anything to Lata. Concern for Pran had pushed other matters to the side.

Savita looked sometimes at her husband, sometimes at Imtiaz's long, fair, appraising face. There was a small mole on his cheek which drew her attention in particular, though she could not have said why. At the moment Imtiaz was feeling Pran's liver—which seemed an unusual proceeding after an asthmatic attack.

To Dr Kishen Chand Seth he said: 'Status asthmaticus, of course. It should be self-limiting, but if it doesn't go away in a little while I'll administer some adrenaline subcutaneously. If I can, though, I'd prefer to avoid it. I wonder if you could arrange for the ECG machine to be brought in tomorrow?'

At the word 'ECG' not only Dr Seth but everyone else started.

'What do you need that for?' said Dr Seth sharply. There was only one ECG machine in Brahmpur, and it was at the medical college hospital.

'Well, I'd like to take a reading. I would not like Pran to be moved at all, so I wonder if you could arrange for it to be brought here. If I ask for it, they'll just think I'm a young man with newfangled ideas who doesn't know how to treat asthma.'

That was exactly what Dr Kishen Chand Seth himself was thinking. Was Imtiaz implying that he, Dr Seth, had oldfangled ideas? But something in Imtiaz's confident manner of examining the patient had impressed him. He said he would make the necessary arrangements. He knew that institutions with ECG machines guarded them like gold.

Lucknow had a single such machine, and there were none in Banaras at the time. The medical college hospital at Brahmpur was extremely proud and possessive of its recent acquisition. But Dr Seth was a force to be reckoned with there, as elsewhere. The next day the ECG machine was brought in.

Pran, who had stabilized after another traumatic hour of wheezing, and had then collapsed into an exhausted sleep, woke up to find Imtiaz and the machine in his bedroom.

'Where's Savita?' he asked.

'She's resting on the sofa in the other room. Doctor's orders. She's fine.'

'What's that?' Pran asked.

'The ECG machine.'

'It's not very big,' said Pran, rather unimpressed.

'Nor are viruses,' said Imtiaz with a laugh. 'How did you sleep?'

'Fine.' Pran's voice was clear; there was no wheezing.

'How do you feel?'

'A little weak. Really, Imtiaz, what's the purpose of an ECG? That's for the heart, and my problem is my lungs.'

'Why don't you leave that for me to decide. You may well be right, but there's no harm in checking. I suspect that this time a cardiogram may help. I believe that it may not be a simple asthmatic attack.'

Imtiaz knew that he could not lull Pran to peace in a soothing hammock of ignorance, and felt that he should take him into his confidence.

But 'Oh' was all Pran said. He was still sleepy.

After a while, Imtiaz asked him for some other details of his medical history, and added, 'I'm going to ask you to move as little as possible.'

'But my lectures—'

'Out of the question,' said Imtiaz cheerfully.

'And my committees?'

Imtiaz laughed. 'Forget them. Firoz tells me you loathe them anyway.'

Pran lay back on the pillows. 'You always were a bully, Imtiaz,' he said.

'Anyway, it's clear what kind of friend you are. You pop up at Holi, get me into trouble, and then only come to visit me when I'm ill.'

Imtiaz yawned.

'I suppose your excuse is that you work too hard.'

'I do,' said Imtiaz. 'Dr Khan, despite his youth, or perhaps because of it, is one of the most sought-after doctors in Brahmpur. His devotion to his profession is exemplary. And he exacts obedience to his decrees from even the most rebellious of his patients.'

'All right, all right,' said Pran, and submitted to the reading. 'So, when do I expect you next?'

'In a day. Remember, you're not to move out of the house and, preferably, not out of bed.'

'Please, Sir, may I go to the bathroom?'

'Yes.'

'And may I accept visitors?'

'Yes.'

At Imtiaz's next visit, he looked grave. He had examined the ECG reading, and told Pran, without beating about the bush:

'Well, I was right, this time it was not asthma alone, but heart. You have what we like to call "severe right ventricular strain". I am recommending three weeks of complete rest, and I'm going to put you in hospital for a little while. Don't get alarmed. But lectures are out. And committee work and so on.'

'But the baby—'

'Oh, the baby? Are there problems there?'

'Do you mean the baby will be born when I'm in the hospital myself?'

'I suppose that's up to the baby. As far as I am concerned, you are to rest for three weeks, starting now. The baby is none of my concern,' said Imtiaz heartlessly. Then he added: 'You've done what you needed to in the creation of the baby. The rest is up to Savita. If you insist on endangering yourself further, it won't be good for her—or for the baby either.'

Pran accepted the justice of this argument. He closed his eyes, but the moment he did so a wave of nameless anxieties washed over him.

He quickly opened his eyes again, and said: 'Imtiaz, please tell me what this thing is—this ventricular strain you mentioned. Don't tell me I don't need to know. Have I had a heart attack or something?' He recalled Firoz's remark: 'The heart and the lungs are two quite different things, young man, two quite different things,' and, despite himself, began to smile.

Imtiaz looked at him with the same grave expression that seemed so atypical of him, and said: 'Well, I can see that the idea of a heart attack amuses you. It's good you've never had one, and—well—you aren't likely to, exactly. But since you've asked, let me explain things to you as clearly as I can.' He paused, thought a little about how to put it, then continued: 'There's an intimate connection between the heart and the lungs; they share the same cavity, and the right side of the heart supplies stale blood to the lungs for it to freshen, to oxygenate, as we say. So when the lungs don't do their job properly—for instance because of not getting enough air when the air-tubes to the lungs seize up asthmatically—the heart is affected. It tries to supply more blood to the lungs to make up for the bad oxygen exchange, and this causes its own supplying chamber to fill up with blood, to become congested and distended. Do you understand?'

'Yes. You explain things very well,' Pran said sadly.

'Now because of this congestion and distension, the heart loses its efficiency as a pump, and that is what we like to call "congestive cardiac failure". It's got nothing to do with what laymen understand by the term "heart failure". To them that means a heart attack. Well, as I said, you are not in danger of that.'

'Then why must I stay in bed for three weeks? It seems a terribly long time. What will happen to my work?'

'Well, you can do a bit of light work in bed,' said Imtiaz. 'And later, you can go for walks. But cricket is out for a while.'

'Out?'

'I'm afraid so. Now as for medicine. Here are two sets of white tablets. You are to take these three times a day, and these once a day for the first week. Then I'll probably cut down a bit on the digoxin, depending on your pulse rate. But you'll keep on with the aminophylline for a few months. If necessary I might have to give you an injection of penicillin.'

'You sound serious, doctor,' said Pran, attempting to add a touch of lightness to the conversation. This Imtiaz was very different from the one who had helped duck Professor Mishra in the tub.

'I am serious.'

'But if this isn't a heart attack, what danger am I in?'

'If you have congestive heart failure, you will have all the effects of pent up blood in your system. Your liver will become enlarged, so will your feet, your neck veins will become prominent, you will cough, and you will get very breathless, especially on walking or exertion. And it is possible that your brain might become confused as well. I don't want to alarm you—this isn't life-threatening—'

'But you are alarming me,' said Pran, looking at Imtiaz's mole and finding it very irritating. 'What else are you doing? I can't take all this bed rest seriously. I know I'm all right. I'm a, well, I'm a young man. I feel fine. And it's always been the case that when my breathing spasms pass off, I'm as well as ever—as healthy as anyone—every bit as fit. I play cricket. I enjoy trekking—'

'I am afraid,' said Imtiaz, 'that the picture is different now. Formerly you were an asthmatic patient. Now, however, the main problem is with the right side of your heart. You will need rest. You would do well to take my advice seriously.'

Pran looked hurt at the formality with which his friend was addressing him, and did not protest any further. Imtiaz had said that the condition was not immediately life-threatening. Pran knew without asking—both from the seriousness of his friend's demeanour and from his list of possible complications—that it was almost certainly life-shortening in the long run.

When Imtiaz left, Pran tried to face the new fact. But today seemed to be very much like yesterday, and the sudden intrusion of the fact was something that Pran almost felt he could shrug off—like an irrelevant memory or a bad dream. But he was depressed, and found it difficult to conceal this and behave normally with Lata or his mother-in-law or, most of all, with Savita.

13.2

That afternoon Pran was moved to the medical college hospital. Savita had insisted on being able to visit him, so he was given one of the few rooms on the ground floor. About half an hour after he came in, it began to rain heavily, and did not let up for a few hours. Pran found that the rain was the best thing for him in these circumstances. It took him out of himself in a way that even reading would not have been able to do. Besides, Imtiaz had told him that on the first day he should not read or exert himself in any other way at all.

The rain came down. It was a continuing event, and yet it was not stimulating: just the combination that Pran needed. In a short while he found himself dozing off.

He woke up to a mosquito bite on his hand.

It was almost seven o'clock, the end of the visiting hour. He noticed, as he opened his eyes and reached for the spectacles on the nightstand, that apart from Savita there was no one else in the room.

'How are you feeling, darling?' said Savita.

'I've just been bitten by a mosquito,' said Pran.

'Poor darling. Bad mosquitoes.'

'That's the problem with a room on the ground floor.'

'What is?'

'The mosquitoes.'

'We'll close the windows.'

'Too late, they're already in.'

'I'll get them to spray the room with Flit.'

'That spray will knock me out as well; I can't leave the room while they're doing it.'

'That's true.'

'Savita, why don't we ever quarrel?'

'Don't we?'

'No, not really.'

'Well, why should we?' asked Savita.

'I don't know. I feel I'm missing out on something. Now look at Arun and Meenakshi. You tell me they're always having tiffs. Young couples always have tiffs.'

'Well, we can have tiffs about the baby's education.'

'That's too long to wait.'

'Well, about its feeding times. Do go back to sleep, Pran, you're being very tiresome.'

'Who's that card from?'

'Professor Mishra.'

Pran closed his eyes.

'And those flowers?'

'Your mother.'

'She was here—and no one woke me up?'

'No. Imtiaz said you were to rest—and we let you rest.'

'Who else came today? Do you know, I'm feeling rather hungry.'

'Not many people. Today we were supposed to leave you to yourself.'

'Oh.'

'Just to get over things.'

Pran sighed. There was a silence. 'Food?'

'Yes, we've brought some from the house. Imtiaz warned us that the hospital food is horrible.'

'Isn't this the hospital where that boy died—that medical student?'

'Why are you being so morbid, Pran?'

'What's morbid about dying?'

'Well, I wish you wouldn't talk about it.'

'Better to talk about it than to do it,' said Pran.

'Do you want me to have a miscarriage?'

'All right, all right. What's that you're reading?'

'A law-book. Firoz lent it to me.'

'A law-book?'

'Yes. It's interesting.'

'What's the subject?'

'Tort.'

'Are you thinking of studying law?'

'Yes, perhaps. You shouldn't talk so much, Pran, it's not good for you. Shall I read out a bit of the *Brahmpur Chronicle*? The political news?'

'No, no. Tort!' Pran began to laugh a little, then started coughing.

'You see?' said Savita, moving to the bed to prop him up.

'You shouldn't get so worried,' said Pran.

'Worried?' said Savita guiltily.

'I'm not going to die, you know. Why have you suddenly decided to take up a profession?'

'Really, Pran—you seem bent on having that tiff. If I take up law it'll be because Shastri got me interested in it. I want to meet that woman lawyer, Jaya Sood, who practises in the High Court. He told me about her.'

'You're about to have a baby; you shouldn't take up studies immediately,' said Pran. 'And think about what my father would say.'

Mahesh Kapoor, who believed in women's education, did not believe in women working, and made no bones about it.

Savita did not say anything. She folded the *Brahmpur Chronicle* and swatted a mosquito. 'Are you ready for dinner?' she asked Pran.

'I hope you're not here by yourself,' said Pran. 'I'm surprised your mother let you come here unaccompanied. What if you suddenly feel unwell?'

'Only one person is allowed to stay beyond visiting hours. And I threatened to kick up a fuss if it wasn't me. Emotional excitement is very bad for me in my delicate state,' said Savita.

'You are extremely stupid and stubborn,' said Pran tenderly.

'Yes,' said Savita. 'Extremely. But your father's car is waiting downstairs in case it's needed. Incidentally, what does your father think about Nehru's sister, who is a working woman if ever there was one?'

'Ah,' said Pran, preferring not to take up the last remark. 'Fried brinjal. Delicious. Yes, let's hear a bit of the *Brahmpur Chronicle.* No, read me a bit of the *University Regulations*, beginning where that bookmark is. That bit about leave.'

'What does that have to do with your committee?' asked Savita, resting the volume on her stomach.

'Nothing. But I'll have to take leave, you know, for at least three weeks, and I may as well find out what the rules are. I don't want to fall into one of Mishra's traps.'

Savita thought of suggesting that he should forget about the university for a day, but she knew that this was impossible. So she took up the volume and started reading:

> 'The following kinds of leave are permissible:
> (a) Casual leave
> (b) Compensation leave
> (c) Deputation leave
> (d) Duty leave
> (e) Extraordinary leave
> (f) Maternity leave
> (g) Medical leave
> (h) Privilege leave
> (i) Quarantine leave
> (j) Study leave.'

She paused. 'Shall I go on?' she asked, glancing briefly down the page.

'Yes.'

Savita continued: 'Except in urgent cases in which the Vice-Chancellor or the Pro Vice-Chancellor shall take decisions, the power to grant leave in general shall be vested in the Executive Council.'

'No problem there,' said Pran. 'This is an urgent case.'

'But with L.N. Agarwal on the Executive Council—and your father no longer a Minister—'

'What can he do?' said Pran calmly. 'Nothing much. All right—what's next?'

Savita frowned, and read on:

> 'When the day immediately preceding the day on which the leave begins or immediately following the day on which the leave expires is a holiday or a series of holidays or a vacation the person to whom the leave is granted or who is returning from leave may make over charge at the close of the day before or return to duty on the day following such holiday or series of holidays or the vacation provided such early departure or delay in return does not involve the University in extra expenditure. When leave is prefixed or suffixed to such holidays or vacation, the consequential arrangement shall begin or end as the case may be, from the date when the leave begins or expires.'

'What?' said Pran.

'Shall I read it again?' asked Savita, smiling.

'No, no, that's fine. I'm feeling a bit light-headed. Your statutes are going to be as bad as that—or worse, you know. Read something else. Something from the *Brahmpur Chronicle.* No politics—some human interest story—like a child eaten by a hyena. Oh, sorry! Sorry, darling. Like someone winning a lottery—or the "Brahmpur Diary"—that's always soothing. How's the baby?'

'He's sleeping, I think,' said Savita, with a look of concentration.

'He?'

'According to my law-books, "he" includes "she".'

'Books, is it now?' said Pran. 'Oh, well.'

13.3

Mrs Rupa Mehra, torn between solicitude for Pran, concern for Savita, who was due to deliver any day now, and desperate anxiety on behalf of Lata, would have liked nothing better than to have an emotional breakdown. But the press of events would not allow it at present, and she therefore abstained.

When Savita was in the hospital, Mrs Rupa Mehra wanted to be with her. When Lata was at the university—especially when she was at one of her rehearsals—Mrs Rupa Mehra's heart started pounding at the mischief she could be up to. Yet Lata was so busy that her mother hardly got a moment alone with her, let alone the chance for a heart-to-heart talk. At night it was impossible, for when Savita came home to sleep, emotional excitement in the house was the last thing her mother wanted to inflict upon her.

Mrs Rupa Mehra did not know what to do, and neither the Gita nor invocations to her late husband helped her in this exigency. To withdraw Lata from the play at this stage might drive her to God knows what rash action—even outright defiance. She could not avail herself of either Savita's advice or Pran's, since the one was close to birth, and the other—so Mrs Rupa Mehra had convinced herself—to death. She still recited her two chapters from the Gita when she woke up, but the world was too much with her, and the verses were occasionally interrupted by silent starings into space.

Pran, however, had begun to enjoy his stay in hospital. The monsoon weather was too muggy for his liking, but at least the moisture in the air was not too bad for his bronchial tubes. He had managed to rid his room of mosquitoes. He had exchanged the *Brahmpur University Calendar and Regulations* for Agatha Christie. Savita no longer complained that he spent no time with her. He felt like a calm captive, floating along on the currents of the universe. Occasionally the universe would fling someone up near him. If he was asleep, the visitor might wait for a while and then go away. If he was awake, they talked.

This afternoon a whispered and urgent conversation was taking place around him. Lata and Malati had come to visit him after a rehearsal. Finding him asleep, they decided to sit on the sofa and wait. Just a few minutes later, Mrs Rupa Mehra arrived with Savita.

Mrs Rupa Mehra saw the two of them and her eyes narrowed with exasperation.

'So!' she said.

Lata and Malati could not mistake the tone of her voice, but could not understand the cause of it.

'So!' said Mrs Rupa Mehra in a strong whisper, glancing at the sleeping Pran. 'You have come from the rehearsal, I imagine.'

If she thought that this oblique reference to the conspiracy would make the culprits collapse, she was mistaken.

'Yes, Ma,' said Lata.

'It was an excellent rehearsal, Ma—you should see how Lata has opened out,' said Malati. 'You'll really enjoy the play when you come for Annual Day.'

Mrs Rupa Mehra flushed red at the thought of Lata opening out. 'I will certainly see the play, but Lata will not be in it,' said Mrs Rupa Mehra.

'Ma!' said Lata and Malati simultaneously.

'Girls should not be in plays—'

'Ma, we thrashed all this out earlier,' began Lata, with a glance at Savita. 'Let's not wake Pran up.'

'Yes, Ma, that's true,' said Savita. 'You can't withdraw Lata now. You agreed to let her act. It'll be impossible for them to find someone else. She's learned her lines—'

Mrs Rupa Mehra sat down on a chair. 'So you know as well?' she said reproachfully to Savita. 'Children cause one nothing but pain,' she added.

Luckily, Savita did not relate this remark to her present condition. 'Know? Know what?' she said.

'That—that that boy, K'—Mrs Rupa Mehra could not bring herself to take his name—'is acting in the play with Lata. I am ashamed of you, Malati,' she continued, her nose beginning to redden, 'I am ashamed of you. I trusted you. And you have been so devious.' Her voice rose, and Savita put a finger to her lips.

'Ma, please—'

'Yes, yes, it is all very well, when you become a mother you too will find out—' said Mrs Rupa Mehra. 'You will make sacrifices, and then they will break your heart.'

Malati could not help smiling. Mrs Rupa Mehra rounded on her, the prime architect of this plot.

'You may think you are very clever, but I always know what is going on,' said Mrs Rupa Mehra. She did not mention that only a chance conversation had enabled her to discover that Kabir was acting in *Twelfth Night*. 'Yes, you can smile and smile and smile, but it is I who will do the crying.'

'Ma, we had no idea that Kabir would be acting,' said Malati. 'I was trying to keep Lata out of his way.'

'Yes, yes, I know, I know, I know it all,' said Mrs Rupa Mehra in miserable disbelief. She reached into her bag for her embroidered handkerchief.

Pran stirred; Savita went over to stand by his side.

'Ma, let's talk about this later,' said Lata. 'It certainly isn't Malati's fault. And I can't back out now.'

Mrs Rupa Mehra quoted a line from one of her favourite didactic poets to show that nothing was impossible, then said: 'And you have had a letter from Haresh as well. Aren't you ashamed to be even seeing this other boy?'

'How do you know I have had a letter from Haresh?' whispered Lata indignantly.

'I am your mother, that's how I know,' said Mrs Rupa Mehra.

'Well, Ma,' whispered Lata hotly, 'you may trust me or not, but let me tell you that I did not know that Kabir would be in the play, and I am not meeting him afterwards, and there is no plot at all.'

None of this convinced Mrs Rupa Mehra, who—glancing at Savita for a second—had begun to think of the brood of misfits that this unimaginable match could create.

'He is half-mad, do you even know that?' asked Mrs Rupa Mehra.

To her bafflement and shock, this only produced a smile from Lata.

'You are laughing at me?' she said, appalled.

'No, Ma, at him. He's achieving madness quite nicely,' said Lata. Kabir had taken to the part of Malvolio alarmingly well; his initial awkwardness had vanished.

'How can you laugh at this? How can you laugh at this?' said Mrs Rupa Mehra, rising from her chair. 'Two tight slaps will do you some good. Laughing at your own mother.'

'Ma, softly, please,' said Savita.

'I think I'd better go,' said Malati.

'No, you stay there,' said Mrs Rupa Mehra. 'You should hear this too, then you will advise Lata better. I met this boy's father at the Subzipore Club. He told me that his wife was fully mad. And the peculiar way he said it made me think that he was also partly mad.' Mrs Rupa Mehra could not entirely conceal from her voice the triumph of vindication.

'Poor Kabir!' said Lata, appalled.

Kabir's long-forgotten remark about his mother began to make a horrible kind of sense.

But before Mrs Rupa Mehra could reproach Lata further, Pran had woken up. Looking around him, he said: 'What's going on? Hello Ma, hello Lata. Ah, Malati, you've come too—I asked Savita what had happened to you. What's the matter? Something dramatic, I hope. Come on, tell me. I heard someone say someone was mad.'

'Oh, we were discussing the play,' said Lata. 'Malvolio, you know.' It cost her an effort to speak.

'Oh, yes. How's your part going?'

'Fine.'

'And yours, Malati?'

'Fine.'

'Good, good, good. Whether I'm allowed to or not, I'll come and see it. It must be just a month or so away. Wonderful play, *Twelfth Night*—just the thing for Annual Day. How's Barua running the rehearsals?'

'Very well,' said Malati, taking over; she could see that Lata was in no mood to speak. 'He's got real flair. One wouldn't think so, he's so mild-mannered. But from the very first line—'

'Pran is very tired,' said Mrs Rupa Mehra, interrupting this unpleasant description. She wanted to hear nothing positive about the play. In fact she wanted to hear nothing at all from that brazen girl, Malati. 'Pran, you have your dinner now.'

'Yes, excellent idea,' said Pran, rather eagerly for a patient. 'What have you brought for me? This lack of exercise makes me enormously hungry. I seem to live from meal to meal. What's for soup? Oh, vegetable soup,' he said, disappointed. 'Can't I have tomato soup once in a while?'

Once in a while? thought Savita. Pran had had his favourite tomato soup the previous day and the day before, and she had thought that this would make a change.

'Mad! Remember that!' said Mrs Rupa Mehra sotto voce to Lata. 'You remember that when you go gallivanting around having a gala time. Muslim and mad.'

13.4

When Maan came in, he found Pran eating his supper quite happily.

'What's the matter with you now?' he asked.

'Nothing much. Just lungs, heart and liver,' said Pran.

'Yes, Imtiaz said something about your heart. But you don't look like a man with heart failure. Anyway, it doesn't happen to people your age.'

'Well,' said Pran. 'I don't have heart failure yet. At least I don't think I do. What I have is a severe strain.'

'Ventricular,' said Mrs Rupa Mehra.

'Oh. Ah, hello, Ma.' Maan said his hellos all around, and eyed Pran's food with intent. 'Jamuns? Delicious!' he exclaimed, and popped two into his mouth. He spat the seeds into the palm of his hand, placed them on the side of the plate, and took another two. 'You should try them,' he advised Pran.

'So what have you been up to, Maan?' said Savita. 'How's your Urdu?'

'Oh, good, very good. Well, at any rate, I've certainly made progress. I can write a note in Urdu now—and what's more, someone can read it at the other end. And that reminds me, I need to write a note today.' His good-natured face grew perplexed momentarily, then recovered its smile. 'And how are you? Two women in a cast of a dozen men. They must be slobbering all over you. How do you shake them off?'

Mrs Rupa Mehra looked daggers at him.

'We don't,' said Lata. 'We maintain a frigid distance.'

'Very frigid,' agreed Malati. 'We have our reputations to guard.'

'If we aren't careful,' said Lata severely, 'no one will marry us. Or even elope with us.'

Mrs Rupa Mehra had had enough. 'You can make fun,' she exclaimed in exasperation. 'You can make fun—but it's not a laughing matter.'

'You're quite right, Ma,' said Maan. 'Not a laughing matter at all. Why did you allow them—I mean Lata—to act in the first place?'

Mrs Rupa Mehra kept a black silence, and Maan at last realized that this was a sensitive subject.

'Anyway,' he said to Pran, 'I bring for you the affectionate regards of the Nawab Sahib, the love of Firoz, and the concern of Zainab—by way of Firoz. Yes, and that's not all. Imtiaz wants to know if you are having your little white pills. He plans to see you tomorrow morning and count them. And someone else said something else, but I can't remember what it was. Are you really all right, Pran? It's quite upsetting to see you lying in the hospital like this. When's the baby expected? Maybe, if Savita clings to you all the time, the baby'll be born in the same hospital. Perhaps in the same room. How about that? Delicious jamuns.' And Maan popped another two into his mouth.

'You seem very well,' said Savita.

'Except I'm not,' said Maan. 'I fall upon the knives of life, I bleed.'

'Thorns,' said Pran with a grimace.

'Thorns?'

'Thorns.'

'Oh, well, then that's what I fall upon,' said Maan. 'At any rate, I'm miserable.'

'Your lungs are in good shape, though,' said Savita.

'Yes, but my heart isn't. Or my liver,' said Maan, plaintively including both seats of emotion according to the conventions of Urdu poetry. 'The huntress of my heart—'

'Now we must really be going,' said Mrs Rupa Mehra, gathering her daughters chick-like to her side. Malati also took her leave.

'Was it something I said?' asked Maan when he and his brother were left alone.

'Oh, don't worry about it,' said Pran. It had rained again this afternoon, quite heavily, and he had become very philosophical. 'Just sit down and be quiet. Thanks for visiting me.'

'I say, Pran, does she love me still?'

Pran shrugged his shoulders.

'She threw me out of the house the other day. Do you think that's a good sign?'

'Not on the face of it.'

'I suppose you're right,' said Maan. 'But I love her dreadfully. I can't live without her.'

'Like oxygen,' said Pran.

'Oxygen? Yes, I suppose so,' said Maan gloomily. 'Anyway, I'm going to send her a note today. I'm going to threaten to end it all.'

'End what all?' said Pran, not very alarmed. 'Your life?'

'Yes, probably,' said Maan in a doubtful voice. 'Do you think that'll win her back?'

'Well, do you plan to back your threat up with action? To fall upon the knives of life or shoot yourself with the guns of life?'

Maan started. This lapse into practicality was in poor taste. 'No, I don't think so,' he said.

'I don't think so either,' said Pran. 'Anyway, don't. I'll miss you. So will all the people who were in this room. So will all the people whose regards you've brought me. So will Baoji and Ammaji and Veena and Bhaskar. So will your creditors.'

'You're right!' said Maan in a determined manner. He polished off the last two jamuns. 'You're absolutely right. You're a pillar of strength, you know that, Pran? Even when you're lying down. Now I feel I can face everyone and everything. I feel as if I'm a lion.' He roared experimentally.

The door opened, and Mr and Mrs Mahesh Kapoor, Veena, Kedarnath and Bhaskar came in.

The lion subsided, and looked a little shamefaced. He hadn't visited home for two days, and though there was no reproach in his mother's eyes, he felt bad. While she said a few words to Pran, she arranged a fragrant bunch of bela from the garden in a vase that she had brought with her.

And she asked Maan about the Nawab Sahib's family.

Maan hung his head. 'They are all very well, Ammaji,' he said. 'And how is the frog? Recovered enough to be hopping around like this?' He gave Bhaskar a hug, then exchanged a few words with Kedarnath. Veena went over to Pran, put her hand on his forehead, and asked not how he was but how Savita was taking his illness.

Pran shook his head. 'I couldn't have timed it worse,' he said.

'You must take care of yourself,' said Veena.

'Yes,' said Pran. 'Yes, of course.' After a pause he added, 'She wants to study law—in case she becomes a widow and the child an orphan—I mean, fatherless.'

'Don't say such things, Pran,' said his sister sharply.

'Law?' said Mr Mahesh Kapoor equally sharply.

'Oh, I only say them because I don't believe them,' said Pran. 'I'm protected by a mantra.'

Mrs Mahesh Kapoor turned to him and said, 'Pran—Ramjap Baba also said one other thing; he said your chances for a job would be affected by a death. Do not make fun of fate. It is never good. If any of my grown-up children were to die before me, I would want to die myself.'

'What's all this talk of dying?' said her husband, impatient with all this needless emotion. 'This room is full of mosquitoes. One just bit me. Tell Savita she should concentrate on her duties as a mother. All this law will do her no good.'

Mrs Mahesh Kapoor, surprisingly, demurred.

'Unh! What do you understand about anything?' said her husband. Women should have rights. I'm all for giving them property rights. But if they insist on working, they won't be able to spend time on their children, and they'll be brought up neglected. If you had been working, would you have had time to nurse Pran? Would he have been alive today?'

Mrs Mahesh Kapoor said nothing further on the subject. She looked back on Pran's childhood, and thought that what her husband had said was probably true.

'How's the garden, Ammaji?' asked Pran. The scent of the bela blossoms had filled the room.

'The zinnias under Maan's window are out,' said his mother. 'And the malis are laying down the new lawn. Since your father resigned, I've had a little time to spend on it, though we have to pay the malis ourselves now. And I've planted a few new rose bushes. The ground's soft. And the pond herons have been visiting.'

Maan, who had so far been rather subdued and un-leonine, could not resist quoting from Ghalib:

> 'The breeze of the garden of faithfulness has dispersed from my heart,
> And nothing remains to me except unfulfilled desire.'

He lapsed into atypical moroseness.

Veena smiled; Pran laughed; Bhaskar's expression did not change, for his mind was on other things.

But Kedarnath looked more perturbed than usual; Mrs Mahesh Kapoor scanned her younger son's face with fresh anxiety; and the ex-Minister of Revenue told him irritably to shut up.

13.5

Mrs Mahesh Kapoor walked around her garden slowly. It was early morning, cloudy, and comparatively cool. A tall jamun tree, though rooted in the pavement outside, spread its branches over a corner of the garden walk. The purple fruit had indelibly stained the stone path; the pits lay scattered around a corner of her lawn.

Mrs Mahesh Kapoor, like Maan, was very fond of jamuns, and felt that their arrival was more than adequate compensation for the departure of the mango season. The jamun-pickers, who had been given a contract by the horticultural section of the Public Works Department, walked along the street in the early morning, climbing each tree and shaking down with their long lathis the dark, olive-sized, sweetly acerbic fruit. Their women, standing below, collected them on large sheets to sell them in the busy market near Chowk. Every year there would be a tussle about the rights to the fruit that fell on Mrs Mahesh Kapoor's side, and every year it would be peacefully settled. The jamun-pickers would be allowed to enter her garden as long as they gave her a share of the fruit and an undertaking not to trample all over her lawn and flower beds.

The jamun-pickers tried to be careful, but the lawn and flower beds did suffer. Well, thought Mrs Mahesh Kapoor, at least it is the monsoon, and the beauty of the garden at this time of year doesn't really lie in its flowers but in its greenery. She had learned by now not to plant the few bright monsoon flowers—zinnias, balsam, orange cosmos—in the beds that lay close to the jamun trees. And she liked the jamun-pickers, who were cheerful, and without whom she would probably not have benefited even from those branches that did stretch out over her lawn.

Now she walked slowly around the garden of Prem Nivas, thinking of many things, but mainly of Pran. She was dressed in an old sari: a short, nondescript woman who to a stranger might almost have looked like one of the servants. Her husband dressed very well—if, as a Congress MLA, he was compelled to wear homespun cotton it had nevertheless to be of the best quality—and he had often rebuked her for her dowdiness. But since this was only one of many rebukes, just or unjust, she felt that she had neither the energy nor the taste to act on it. It was like her lack of knowledge of English. What could she do about it? Nothing, she had long since decided. If she was stupid, she was stupid; it was God's doing.

The fact that year after year she carried away some of the best prizes in the Rose and Chrysanthemum Show in December as well as in the Annual Flower Show in February never ceased to amaze the more sophisticated inhabitants of Brahmpur. The committee of the Race Club marvelled that her roses displayed a compactness and freshness that theirs could never attain; and the wives of the executives of Burmah Shell or the Praha Shoe Company even deigned, in their anglicized Hindi, to ask her once or twice what it was she put into her lawn that made it so even and springy and green. Mrs Mahesh Kapoor would have been hard-pressed to answer even if she had fully understood their brand of Hindi. She simply stood with gratefully folded hands, accepting their compliments and looking rather foolish, until they gave up. Shaking their heads they decided that she was indeed foolish, but that she—or more probably her head gardener—'had a gift'. Once or twice they had tried to bribe him to leave her by offering him twice his present salary; but the head mali, who was originally from Rudhia, was content to remain at Prem Nivas and see the trees he had planted grow tall and the roses he had pruned bloom brightly. His disagreement with her about the side lawn had been amicably resolved. It had been left slightly uneven, and had become something of a sanctuary for her favourite bird.

The two under-gardeners were in government service, and had been allotted to Mahesh Kapoor in his capacity as Minister of Revenue. They loved the garden at Prem Nivas, and were unhappy that they were to be torn away from it. 'Why did Minister Sahib resign?' they asked sadly.

'You will have to ask Minister Sahib,' said Mrs Mahesh Kapoor, who herself was not happy about his decision, and thought it was an unwise one. Nehru, after all, despite his carping and complaining about his party, was still in Congress. Surely any precipitate action by his followers—such as resignation—was premature. The question was, would it help to force the Prime Minister's hand, and make him leave as well, thus giving birth to a new and possibly more vigorous party? Or would it merely weaken his position in his own party and make things worse than before?

'They will assign us some other house,' said the under-gardeners with tears in their eyes. 'Some other Minister and some other Memsahib. No one will treat us as well as you have.'

'I'm sure they will,' said Mrs Mahesh Kapoor. She was a gentle-hearted and soft-spoken woman, and never raised her voice at her employees. In consequence, and because she often asked about their families, and helped them out in small ways, they loved her.

'What will you do without us, Memsahib?' asked one.

'Can you work for me part-time at Prem Nivas?' she asked. 'That way you won't lose the garden you've worked so hard on.'

'Yes—for an hour or two each morning. The only thing is—'

'Of course, you'll be paid for your work,' said Mrs Mahesh Kapoor, anticipating their awkwardness and making a calculation of her household expenses. 'But I will have to employ someone else full-time. Do you know of anyone?'

'My brother would be a good man,' said one.

'I didn't know you had a brother,' said Mrs Mahesh Kapoor in surprise.

'Not my real brother—my uncle's son.'

'All right. I'll let him work for a month on probation, and Gajraj will tell me how good he is.'

'Thank you, Memsahib. This year we will see that you win First Prize for the best garden.'

This was one prize that had eluded Mrs Mahesh Kapoor, and she thought how pleasant it would be to win it. But, doubting her own abilities, she smiled at their ambition.

'That would be a great feat,' she said.

'And don't worry about Sahib not being a Minister. We'll get you plants from the government nursery at cheap rates. And from other places too.' Good gardeners were adept at filching plants from here and there, or coaxing their fellow-gardeners to part with some of their superfluous seedlings.

'Good,' said Mrs Mahesh Kapoor. 'Tell Gajraj to come here. I want to discuss the layout of things now that I have a bit of time. If Sahib becomes a Minister again, I'll be doing nothing except arranging for cups of tea.'

The malis were rather pleased at this small irreverence. The head mali was summoned, and Mrs Mahesh Kapoor talked to him for a while. The new front lawn was being planted in careful rows, shoot by shoot, and a corner of the lawn was already a mild emerald in colour. The rest was mud, except for the stone path on which they were walking.

Mrs Mahesh Kapoor told him what the others had said about the Flower Show. His opinion was that the reason why they won second and not first prize for the best garden overall was twofold. First, that Mr Justice Bailey (who had won for three years in succession) was bullied by his wife into spending half his income on his garden. They hired a dozen gardeners. Secondly, every bush, shrub or flower in his garden was planted with a particular date in mid-February in mind, the date of the Flower Show. That was when everything was at its most brilliant. Gajraj could arrange something similar if Mrs Mahesh Kapoor desired. But it was clear from his expression that he was sure she did not desire it. And the unevenness of the side lawn this year would not help either.

'No, no—that wouldn't be a garden at all,' said Mrs Mahesh Kapoor. 'Let's plan the winter garden just like we always do—with different flowers blooming at different times, so that it is always a pleasure to sit out. And where that neem tree stood, we should plant a Sita ashok. Now is a good time.' With great regret Mrs Mahesh Kapoor had agreed to have an old neem tree cut down two years ago because of her painful allergy to its blossom; the blankness of the spot had been a continual rebuke to her. But the one outside Maan's window that he used to climb as a boy she had not had the heart to cut down.

Gajraj folded his hands. He was a thin, short man, gaunt of feature, barefooted, and dressed in a plain white dhoti and kurta. He looked dignified, more like the priest of a garden than a gardener. 'Whatever you say, Memsahib,' he said. After a while he added: 'What do you think of the water lilies this year?' He felt they deserved comment, and so far Mrs Mahesh Kapoor had said nothing about them. Her mind had probably been on other matters of late.

'Let's go over and have a look at them again,' she said.

Gajraj, quietly pleased, walked on the muddy lawn beside Mrs Mahesh Kapoor as she negotiated the path slowly, pausing for a second by the pomelo tree. They stopped by the lily pond. The water was turbid, and filled with tadpoles. Mrs Mahesh Kapoor gazed for a minute at the round lily pads and the half-open lilies: pink, red, blue, and white. Three or four bees were buzzing about them.

'No yellow ones this year?' she asked.

'No, Memsahib,' said Gajraj, rather crestfallen.

'They are very beautiful,' said Mrs Mahesh Kapoor, continuing to look at the lilies.

Gajraj's heart leapt up. 'They are better than ever this year,' he ventured. 'Except that the yellow ones have not come out, I don't know why.'

'It doesn't matter,' said Mrs Mahesh Kapoor. 'My children like the bright ones—red and blue. I think it is only you and I who care for the pale yellow lilies. But if they've died, can we get them from somewhere else next year?'

'Memsahib, I don't think you can get them in Brahmpur. It was your Calcutta friend who brought them two years ago.'

Gajraj was referring to a friend of Veena's in fact, a young woman from Shantiniketan who had stayed at Prem Nivas as a guest a couple of times. She had very much enjoyed the garden, and Mrs Mahesh Kapoor found her good company even if her ways were a little surprising. On her second visit, she had brought the yellow lilies with her on the train in a bucket of water.

'A pity,' said Mrs Mahesh Kapoor. 'Anyway, the blue ones are very striking.'

13.6

Out on the muddy surface of the lawn, a few birds—babblers, red-wattled lapwings, and mynas—were walking around, pecking at whatever presented itself. This was the season for earthworms, and the lawn was full of their curled castings.

The sky had grown dark and the sound of distant thunder could be heard.

'Have you seen any snakes this year?' asked Mrs Mahesh Kapoor.

'No,' said Gajraj. 'But Bhaskar said he saw one. A cobra. He shouted for me, but by the time I came, it had disappeared.'

'What?' Mrs Mahesh Kapoor's heart beat more rapidly for a minute. 'When?'

'Just yesterday afternoon.'

'Where did he see this?'

'He was playing on that pile of bricks and rubble over there—standing on it and flying his kite—I told him to be careful, because it was a likely place for snakes, but—'

'Tell him to come out at once. And call Veena Baby as well.'

Veena, though now a mother, was still called Baby by the older servants at Prem Nivas.

'No,' continued Mrs Mahesh Kapoor. 'On second thoughts, I'll go back to the verandah for tea. It looks as if it's about to rain.'

'Veena,' she told her daughter when they came out, 'this boy is like you used to be—very wilful. He was playing on that pile of rubble yesterday, and it is full of snakes.'

'Yes!' said Bhaskar, enthusiastically. 'I saw one yesterday. A cobra.'

'Bhaskar!' said Veena, her blood running cold.

'It didn't threaten me or anything. It was too far away. And by the time I called for Gajraj it wasn't there any more.'

'Why didn't you tell me?' asked his mother.

'I forgot.'

'That's not the sort of thing one forgets,' said Veena. 'Were you intending to play there again today?'

'Well, when Kabir comes we were thinking of flying kites—'

'You are not to play there, do you understand? Neither there nor in any part of the back garden. Do you understand me? Or I won't let you out in the garden at all.'

'But, Mummy—'

'No "but Mummy" or "please Mummy"—you are not to play there. Now go back inside and have your milk.'

'I'm sick of milk,' said Bhaskar. 'I'm nine years old—almost ten. Why should I drink milk forever?' He was not pleased to have been disciplined in front of his grandmother. He also felt that Gajraj, whom he had looked upon as a friend, had betrayed him.

'Milk is good for you. Many boys don't get any milk at all,' said Veena.

'They are lucky,' said Bhaskar. 'I hate the skin that forms on it as it cools. And the glasses here are one-sixth larger than those at home,' he added ungratefully.

'If you drink your milk quickly, nothing will form on it at all,' said his mother unsympathetically. It was very unlike Bhaskar to be so sullen, and she was determined not to encourage it. 'Now, if you disobey me again and behave as if you're six, I'm going to slap you—and Nani won't stop me either.'

There was a roll of thunder, and a few drops of rain pattered down.

Bhaskar withdrew into the house with some dignity. His mother and grandmother smiled at each other.

Neither of them needed to mention that Veena too used to make a great fuss about drinking her milk when she was a child, and that she often gave it to her younger brothers to dispose of.

After a while Mrs Mahesh Kapoor said:

'He looked in good spirits last night despite all that the doctors said. Didn't you think so?'

'Yes, Ammaji, I did.' There was a silence. 'It's a difficult time for them,' Veena continued. 'Why don't you ask Savita, Lata and Ma to stay here in Prem Nivas until the baby's born? We're going to be leaving in a day or two anyway.'

Her mother nodded. 'I asked once before, but Pran thought she wouldn't like it, that she'd feel happier in familiar surroundings.'

Mrs Mahesh Kapoor also reflected that Mrs Rupa Mehra, when she visited Prem Nivas, was liable to mention that she found the rooms exceedingly bare. And this was true. Mahesh Kapoor, though he was of no help in running the house, often exercised his veto on proposed furnishing. It was only on the puja-room and the kitchen that his wife had been able to exercise that loving care that she lavished on the garden.

'And Maan?' said Veena. 'This house feels odd without him. When he's in Brahmpur it is very bad that he isn't staying with his family. We hardly get a chance to meet as it is.'

'No,' said her mother. 'I felt hurt at first, but I think he's right, it's for the best that he stays with his friend. Minister Sahib is going through a hard time, and they would find each other's company difficult, I think.'

This was a mild prediction. Mahesh Kapoor was short with everyone these days. It was not merely the fact that the house was suddenly less full of hangers-on and aspirants of various kinds, company he claimed to despise but in fact now fretted for; it was also the unpredictability of the future that ate at him and made him snap with less than usual cause at whoever happened to be around.

'But apart from his moods, I enjoy this relief,' said Mrs Mahesh Kapoor, completing the arc of her own thoughts aloud. 'In the evening there is time for some bhajans. And I can walk around the garden in the morning now, without feeling that I am ignoring some important political guest.'

By now the clouds had blotted out the sun completely. Gusts of wind were blowing across the garden and turning the silver undersides of the leaves on a nearby poplar tree so violently that it appeared not dark green but silver. But the verandah where they were sitting was protected by a low wall decorated with shallow urns of portulaca and was covered with a corrugated roof, and neither of them felt like moving indoors.

Veena hummed to herself the first few lines of a bhajan, one of her mother's favourites: 'Rise, traveller, the sky is bright'. It came from the anthology used at Gandhi's ashram, and reminded Mrs Mahesh Kapoor of how they would give themselves courage in the most hopeless days of the freedom struggle.

After a few seconds, she too began to hum along, and then to sing the words:

> 'Uth, jaag, musafir, bhor bhaee
> Ab rayn kahan jo sowat hai. . . .'
>
> Rise, traveller, the sky is bright.
> Why do you sleep? It is not night. . . .

Then she laughed. 'Think of the Congress Party in those days. And look at it now.'

Veena smiled. 'But you still get up early,' she said. 'You don't need this bhajan.'

'Yes,' said her mother. 'Old habits die hard. And I need less sleep these days. But I still need the help of that bhajan several times a day.'

She sipped her tea for a while. 'How is your music?' she asked.

'My serious music?' asked Veena.

'Yes,' said her mother with a smile. 'Your serious music. Not bhajans, but what you learn from your Ustad.'

'My mind's not really on it,' said Veena. After a pause she continued: 'Kedarnath's mother has stopped objecting to it. And it's closer from Prem Nivas than from Misri Mandi. But I can't concentrate these days. I can't shut the world out. First it was Kedarnath, then Bhaskar, now Pran; and I hope it isn't Savita next. If only they would all have their troubles simultaneously, it would help: my hair might go white once, but I'd make some real progress the rest of the time.' She paused again. 'But Ustad Sahib is more patient with me than with his other disciples. Or perhaps it's just that he is more content these days, less bitter about life.'

After a while Veena went on: 'I wish I could do something about Priya.'

'Priya Goyal?'

'Yes.'

'What made you think of her?'

'I don't know. I just suddenly thought of her. What was her mother like when she was young?'

'Ah, she was a good woman,' said Mrs Mahesh Kapoor.

'I think,' said Veena, 'the state would be in better shape if you and she ran it rather than Baoji and L.N. Agarwal.'

Instead of ticking Veena off for this subversive remark, Mrs Mahesh Kapoor merely said: 'I don't think so, you know. Two illiterate women—we wouldn't even be able to read a file.'

'At least you would have been generous to each other. Not like men.'

'Oh no,' said her mother sadly. 'You know nothing of the pettiness of women. When brothers agree to split a joint family they sometimes divide lakhs of rupees' worth of property in a few minutes. But the tussle of their wives over the pots and pans in the common kitchen—that nearly causes bloodshed.'

'At any rate,' said Veena, 'Priya and I would run things well. And it would enable her to escape from that wretched house in Shahi Darvaza and from her husband's sister and sisters-in-law. Yes, you're right about women, perhaps. But do you think a woman would have ordered that lathi charge on the students?'

'No, maybe not,' said her mother. 'At any rate, it's pointless thinking about such things. Women will never be called upon to make such decisions.'

'Some day,' said Veena, 'this country will have a woman Prime Minister or a woman President.'

Veena's mother laughed at this forecast. 'Not in the next hundred years,' she said gently, and looked out at the lawn again.

A few plump brown partridges, some big, some small, ran awkwardly across the far end of the lawn and with an immense effort got themselves airborne for a few seconds. They landed on the broad swing that hung down from a branch of the tamarind tree. There the partridges sat while the rain suddenly pelted down.

The gardeners quickly took shelter at the back of the house near the kitchen.

The thunder made a growling noise, and squirrels ran up the tree in alarm. Lightning flashed in sheets all over the sky. The rain came down in torrents, and soon the mud of the lawn had become a thick paste.

The partridges disappeared in the grey barrage; even the swing became indistinct. The sound of the storm on the corrugated roof made speech difficult, and an occasional violent gust of wind drove rain on to the verandah itself.

After a while the door to the house opened, and Bhaskar came out. He sat next to his mother, and the three of them stared at the wall of water.

For about five minutes they looked at the rain in silence, enchanted by the power and the noise of it, and the sight of great trees swaying and shuddering in the wind. Then the rain let up slightly, and speech became possible again.

'It'll be good for the farmers,' said Mrs Mahesh Kapoor. 'There hasn't been enough rain so far this year.'

'But not for the cobblers,' said Veena. Kedarnath had once told her that the small shoemakers, who stretched moistened shoe-uppers on to wooden lasts in order to shape them, sometimes had to wait for a week in this weather till they were dry and could be taken off. Since they lived from hand to mouth, and their capital was tied up in their materials and tools, this was a great hardship.

'Do you like the rain?' Mrs Mahesh Kapoor asked Bhaskar when there was another respite.

'I like flying kites after the rain,' said Bhaskar. 'The air currents are more interesting.'

The rain increased once more, and once again each was lost in private thought.

Bhaskar was thinking of his return in a couple of days to his own house, where there were many more kites in the sky than here, and where he could play once again with his friends. Life here in the 'colonies' was rather limited.

Mrs Mahesh Kapoor thought about her mother, who used to be terrified of storms, and whose final illness had taken a severe turn for the worse in just such a violent storm as this.

And Veena thought of her Bengali friend (she of the yellow water lilies) who, when the monsoon rains first struck after the terrible months of heat, would walk out of the house dressed as she was, humming a Tagore song in welcome, and let the rain streak down her face and her hair, run down her body to her bare feet, and soak her blouse and her sari to the skin.

13.7

Time hung very heavily on Maan's hands. But he realized that he had to make up with Saeeda Bai quickly or he would go crazy with boredom and desire. He therefore wrote his first note in Urdu to her, in which he entreated her to be kind to him, her faithful vassal, her enchanted moth, etc., etc. There were a number of spelling errors, and his script was somewhat unformed, but there was no mistaking the strength of his sentiment. He thought of getting Rasheed's help with some aspects of phrasing, then decided that since Rasheed was out of favour with Saeeda Bai this might merely cause complications. He gave it to the watchman to give her, but did not wait for her response immediately.

He went for a walk to the Barsaat Mahal and stared across the river in the moonlight. Apart from Firoz, no one appeared to be on his side in the world at all. Everyone wanted him to mould himself in one direction or another according to their opinion or will. And even Firoz these days was fairly busy in court, and had only once suggested that they go for polo practice. That too had had to be cancelled at the last moment because of a conference called by his senior in a case.

Something needed to happen soon, thought Maan. He was feeling uncontrollably restless. If Savita had her baby quickly, that would be a good thing. There would be some cheerful activity somewhere. Everyone was going around looking oppressed and careworn these days.

Or if he could persuade his father to explore the option of a rural constituency, they could go on a whirlwind tour of Rudhia District for a few days and perhaps he could forget Saeeda Bai for a bit. His father, being at a loose end himself, had lost a little of his moral authority vis-à-vis Maan, and his company might not be so intolerable; in any case, he had not for the last few days told Maan to settle down. But precisely because he had not come to terms with his own situation, Mahesh Kapoor was exceptionally irritable these days. Perhaps Rudhia was not such a good idea after all.

To add to Maan's woes, he needed money; he had almost none left. Firoz, whom he had approached for a small loan upon his return to Brahmpur, had simply handed over his wallet to Maan and told him to take what he wanted out of it. A few days later, after lunch, without being asked but perhaps in response to a certain hangdog look on Maan's face, he made the same generous gesture. This had helped Maan get by. But he couldn't keep borrowing from his friend. A number of people in Banaras owed him money, some for goods supplied, some because of hard-luck stories which Maan had found difficult to withstand, and Maan felt that now that he was down on his own luck, they would be eager to help him out. He decided to visit Banaras for a couple of days to recoup his funds. It would be easy enough to keep out of the way of one or two of his rather irksome creditors. The problem was that his fiancée's people might well find out that he was in Banaras. Besides, he wasn't sure if this was the best time to visit Banaras at all. He wanted to be on hand to help Savita when the baby was born, since Pran was not able to do so himself in his present condition, and Maan feared that it would be just his luck if the baby was born when he was out of town.

He waited for two whole days for a reply from Saeeda Bai to his note. He had given his address as Baitar House. None came.

Tiring of his own iffing and butting, and being eager for action of some kind, Maan borrowed some more money from Firoz, sent a servant to get his ticket for the next morning's train to Banaras, and prepared to spend a despondent and eventless last evening.

First, he visited the hospital, and instructed Savita to hold off having her baby for at least two days. Savita laughed, and promised to do her best.

Then he had dinner with Firoz. Zainab's husband was present at dinner—he had come alone to Brahmpur for the meeting of some waqf committee or other—and Maan could sense that Firoz was no more than polite to him. Maan could not understand this. Zainab's husband appeared to be a fairly cultivated if rather tremulous man. He kept insisting that he was a peasant at heart, and backing up this assertion with Persian couplets. The Nawab Sahib dined on his own.

Finally, Maan penned another note in Urdu, and gave it to Saeeda Bai's watchman to deliver. Surely Saeeda Bai should tell him what his crime was—and if she couldn't bring herself to forgive him at least she could respond to his letters.

'Please give her this at once—and say that I am going away.' Maan, sensing the drama of this last phrase, sighed deeply.

The watchman knocked at the door, and Bibbo came out.

'Bibbo—' said Maan, gesturing with the ivory-topped cane.

But Bibbo appeared rather scared, and refused to look him in the face. What's the matter with her? thought Maan. She was happy enough to kiss me the last time I was here.

A few minutes later Bibbo came out and said: 'The Begum Sahiba instructs me to admit you.'

'Bibbo!' said Maan, both delighted by his admittance and hurt by the formal, even lifeless, tone of its announcement. He was so pleased that he wanted to hug her, but by turning half away from him when they walked up the stairs, she made it clear that there was no question of that.

'You keep repeating my name, like that parakeet,' said Bibbo. 'All I get for my kindness to people is trouble.'

'But you got a kiss from me last time!' laughed Maan.

Bibbo clearly did not want to be reminded of that. She pouted, Maan thought charmingly.

Saeeda Bai was in a good mood. She, Motu Chand, and an older sarangi player were sitting in her outer chamber, gossiping. Ustad Majeed Khan had recently performed in Banaras, and had been backed up by Ishaq Khan. Ishaq Khan had done well; at all events, he had not shamed his teacher.

'I'm going to Banaras myself,' announced Maan, who had heard the tail end of the conversation.

'And why must the huntsman take himself away from the tame gazelle that, rejoicing, offers itself to his sight?' asked Saeeda Bai, twirling her hand and blinding Maan with a sudden flash of gem-reflected light.

This was an unlikely description of Saeeda Bai, considering how she had avoided him for the last few days. Maan looked at her eyes, but could read nothing there but the most patent sincerity. Instantly he saw that he had misjudged her: she was as delightful as she had always been, and he was an unperceptive dolt.

Saeeda Bai was exceptionally good to him all evening; it almost appeared as if she were wooing him, not he her. She begged him to forgive her lack of courtesy, as she put it, on the earlier occasion. Many things had conspired to upset her that day. Dagh Sahib should excuse the ignorant saki who had, in her excessive nervousness, poured wine over his innocent hands.

She sang for him like one inspired. And then she sent the musicians away.

13.8

The next morning, Maan got to the station just in time to catch the train to Banaras. He was almost puppy-like with happiness. Even the fact that each puff of steam and each circuit of the wheels was taking him further away from Brahmpur did not diminish his pleasure. He smiled to himself from time to time at the memory of the previous evening, with all its endearments and witticisms, all its suspense and fulfilment.

When he got to Banaras, Maan discovered that those who owed him money for goods already received were not delighted to see him. They swore that they had no money at present, that they were moving heaven and earth to pay off their debts, of which his was just one, that the market was moving slowly, that by winter—or next spring at the latest—they envisaged no problem of repayment at all.

Nor did those whose tales of misfortune had led Maan to open his purse now open their purses to him. One young man looked well dressed enough, and appeared to be flourishing. He invited Maan to eat with him in a good restaurant, so that he could explain matters to him at leisure. Maan ended up paying for the meal.

Another man was distantly related to his fiancée's family. He was eager to drag Maan off to meet them, but Maan pleaded that he had to return to Brahmpur by the early afternoon train. He explained that his brother, who was ill and in hospital, was due to become a father any day now. The man appeared surprised at Maan's newfound sense of family obligation, but said nothing further. But Maan, feeling on the defensive, could no longer bring himself to mention the subject of his outstanding loan.

One debtor implied in a circuitous and inoffensive way that now that Mahesh Kapoor had resigned as Minister of Revenue in the neighbouring state, Maan's outstanding loan had stopped preying so frequently or pressingly on his mind.

Maan managed to get back about an eighth of what he had lent, and borrowed about the same amount from various friends and acquaintances. This came to just over two thousand rupees. At first he felt disappointed and disillusioned. But with two thousand rupees in his pocket, and a train ticket back to bliss, he felt that life was pretty good after all.

13.9

Tahmina Bai meanwhile visited Saeeda Bai.

Tahmina Bai's mother had been the madam of the establishment in Tarbuz ka Bazaar where Saeeda Bai and her mother Mohsina Bai had earlier lived.

'What shall we do? What shall we do?' cried Tahmina Bai in high excitement. 'Play chaupar and gossip? Or gossip and play chaupar? Tell your cook to make those delicious kababs, Saeeda. I've brought some biryani—I told Bibbo to take it to the kitchen—now tell me, tell me everything. I have so much to tell you—'

After they had played a few games of chaupar, and exchanged endless gossip, together with some more serious news of the world—such as the effect that the Zamindari Act would have on them, especially on Saeeda Bai, who had a better class of customer; and the education of Tasneem; and the health of Tahmina Bai's mother; and the rising rents and property values, even in Tarbuz ka Bazaar—they turned to the antics of their various clients.

'I'll be Marh,' said Saeeda Bai. 'You be me.'

'No, I'll be Marh,' said Tahmina Bai. 'You be me.' She was giggling away in high delight. She grabbed a flower vase, threw the flowers on to a table, and pretended to drink from it. Soon she was lurching from side to side and grunting. Then she made a lunge for Saeeda Bai, who whipped the pallu of her sari out of reach, ran, screaming 'toba! toba!' to the harmonium, and quickly played a descending scale through two octaves.

Tahmina Bai's eyes grew blurred. As the scale descended, so did she. Soon she was snoring on the carpet. After ten seconds, she heaved her body up, cried 'wah! wah!' and collapsed again, this time squealing and snorting with laughter. Then she leapt up again, upsetting a bowl of fruit, and flung herself on Saeeda Bai, who started moaning in ecstasy. With one hand Tahmina Bai reached for an apple and bit it. Then, at the moment of orgasm, she cried for whisky. And finally she rolled over, belched, and went off to sleep again.

They were almost choking with laughter. The parakeet was squawking in alarm.

'Oh, but his son is even better,' said Tahmina Bai.

'No, no,' said Saeeda Bai, helpless with laughter. 'I can't bear it. Stop, Tahmina, stop, stop—'

But Tahmina Bai had begun enacting the Rajkumar's behaviour on the occasion when he had failed to grace her with his poetry.

Bewildered and protesting, the traumatized Tahmina pulled an imaginary but very drunk friend to his feet. 'No, no,' she cried in a terrified voice, 'no, please, Tahmina Begum—I've already, no, no, I'm not in the mood—come, Maan, let's go.'

Saeeda Bai said: 'What? Did you say Maan?'

Tahmina Bai was having a giggling fit.

'But that's my Dagh Sahib,' continued Saeeda Bai, amazed.

'You mean that that was the Minister's son?' said Tahmina Bai. 'The one whom everyone is gossiping about? Balding at the temples.'

'Yes.'

'He couldn't grace me either.'

'I'm glad to hear it,' said Saeeda Bai.

'Be careful, Saeeda,' said Tahmina Bai affectionately. 'Think of what your mother would say.'

'Oh, it's nothing,' said Saeeda Bai. 'I entertain them; he entertains me. It's like Miya Mitthu here; I'm not a fool.'

And she followed it up with quite a good imitation of Maan making desperate love.

13.10

The first thing Maan did when he got back to Brahmpur was to phone Prem Nivas to find out about Savita. She had been as good as her word. The baby was still inside her, unexposed as yet to the joys and woes of Brahmpur.

It was too late for Maan to visit Pran in hospital; humming to himself, he wandered along to Saeeda Bai's. The watchman looked rather abstracted tonight; he knocked at the door, and held a consultation with Bibbo. Bibbo glanced at Maan, who was standing eagerly at the gate, then turned back to the watchman and shook her head.

But Maan, who had interpreted the negative signal correctly, had leapt over the fence in a flash, and was at the door before she could close it.

'What?' he said, his voice barely controlled. 'The Begum Sahiba said that she would receive me this evening. What has happened?'

'She is indisposed,' said Bibbo, with great emphasis on 'indisposed'. It was clear that Saeeda Bai was nothing of the kind.

'Why are you annoyed with me, Bibbo?' said Maan, helplessly. 'What have I done that all of you should treat me this way?'

'Nothing. But the Begum Sahiba is not receiving anyone today.'

'Has she received anyone already?'

'Dagh Sahib—' said Bibbo, pretending to relent but throwing out a provocative hint instead, 'Dagh Sahib, someone whom I might call Ghalib Sahib is with her. Even among poets there is an order of precedence. This gentleman is a good friend, and she prefers his company to that of all others.'

This was too much for Maan. 'Who is he? Who is he?' he cried, almost beside himself.

Bibbo could simply have told Maan that it was Mr Bilgrami, Saeeda Bai's old admirer whom she found boring but soothing, but she was excited to have evoked such a dramatic response. Besides, she was angry with Maan and felt like giving him a spoonful or two of jealousy as punishment for her own misfortunes. Saeeda Bai had slapped Bibbo very hard several times after the kiss on the staircase, and had threatened to turn her out of the house for her shamelessness. In Bibbo's recollection it was Maan who had initiated the kiss that had got her into all this trouble.

'I can't tell you who he is,' she said, raising her eyebrows slightly. 'Your poetic intuition should tell you.'

Maan grabbed Bibbo by the shoulders and began to shake her. But before he could get her to speak and before the watchman could come to her rescue, she had escaped from his grip and slammed the door in his face.

'Come now, Kapoor Sahib—' said the watchman calmly.

'Who is he?' said Maan.

The watchman slowly shook his head. 'I have no memory for faces,' he said. 'If someone asked me if you had visited this house, I would not remember.'

Stunned by the brazen manner in which the appointment had been broken, and burning with jealousy, Maan somehow made his way back to Baitar House.

Sitting on top of the great stone gate at the entrance to the drive was a monkey. Why it was awake so late was a mystery. It snarled at him as he approached. Maan glared at it.

The monkey leapt down from the gate and rushed at Maan. If Maan had not been away in Banaras over the previous two days, he would have read in the *Brahmpur Chronicle* of a vicious monkey that was loose in the Pasand Bagh area. This monkey had apparently lost her mind when some schoolchildren had stoned her baby to death. She had since been charging at and biting and generally terrifying the local residents. She had attacked seven people so far, usually biting off chunks of flesh from their legs, and Maan was to be the eighth.

She charged at him with fearless malignity. Even though he did not turn and flee, she did not slacken her pace, and when she was close enough, she made a final lunge at his leg. But she had not accounted for Maan's anger. Maan had his cane ready and gave her a blow that stopped her dead.

Into that blow went all his bodily strength and all the power of his jealousy and rage. He raised his stick again, but the monkey was lying on the road, not moving, either stunned or dead.

Maan leaned against the gate for a minute, trembling with anger and nervous shock. Then, feeling suddenly sick at himself, he walked slowly towards the house. Firoz was not in, nor Zainab's husband, and the Nawab Sahib had retired already. But Imtiaz was up reading.

'My dear fellow, you've had a shock. Is everything all right—at the hospital, I mean?'

'I've just killed a monkey, I think. It charged at me. It was sitting on the gate. I need a whisky.'

'Ah, you're a hero,' said Imtiaz, relieved. 'It's a good thing you had that stick on you. I was worried it might be Pran or Savita. The police have been trying to catch her all day. She's bitten quite a few people already. Ice and water? Well, perhaps not such a hero if you've killed her. I'd better get her moved from near the house, or we'll have a religious disturbance on our hands. But did you do anything to upset her?'

'Upset her?' said Maan.

'Yes, you know, did you wave your stick at her or something? Throw a stone perhaps?'

'Nothing,' said Maan with great vehemence. 'She just took one look at me and charged. And I'd done nothing to upset her. Nothing. Nothing at all.'

13.11

Everyone had told Savita that the baby would be a boy; her way of walking, the size of the bulge, and other infallible indications all pointed to a boy.

'Think nice thoughts, read poems,' Mrs Rupa Mehra was continually exhorting her, and this Savita tried to do. She also read a book called *Learning the Law.* Mrs Rupa Mehra advised Savita to listen to music, but this, since she was not particularly musical, she did not do.

The baby kicked from time to time. But sometimes it seemed to sleep for days on end. Lately it had been very quiet.

Mrs Rupa Mehra, while telling Savita to think restful thoughts, often shared her own birth experiences and those of other mothers with her. Some stories were charming, some not. 'You were overdue, you know,' she told Savita fondly. 'And my mother-in-law insisted that I must try her own method of inducing labour. I had to drink a whole glass of castor oil. It's a laxative, you know, and it was supposed to begin my birth pangs. It tasted horrible, but I felt it was my duty, so I had to drink it; it was lying on the sideboard. It was winter, I remember, bitterly cold, the middle of December—'

'It couldn't have been December, Ma, my birthday's in November.'

Mrs Rupa Mehra frowned at this interruption of her reverie, but she quickly saw that the logic of it was irrefutable, and continued calmly:

'November, yes, winter, and I saw it lying on the sideboard, and I drank it in a sudden gulp on the way to lunch. I remember we had parathas for lunch, and so on. I normally didn't eat much, but that day I stuffed myself. But it had no effect. Then came dinner. Then your Daddy came with a pot full of my favourite sweet, rasagullas. I had one, and then I had a second, and the second one was just going down, when it suddenly felt like it had turned into a fist in my stomach! The birth pangs had begun, and I had to run.'

Savita said, 'Ma, I think—'

But Mrs Rupa Mehra continued: 'Our Indian remedies are the best. Now they say that in this season I should eat lots of jamuns, because they are good for diabetes.'

'Ma, I think I'd better finish this chapter,' said Savita.

'Arun was the most painful,' continued Mrs Rupa Mehra. 'You must be prepared, darling; with the first child the pain is so terrible that you want to die, and if I hadn't thought of your Daddy I would have surely died.'

'Ma—'

'Savita, darling, when I'm talking to you you shouldn't be reading that book. Reading about law is not very restful.'

'Ma, let's talk about something else.'

'I am trying to prepare you, darling. Otherwise what is a mother for? I had no mother living to prepare me, and my mother-in-law was not sympathetic. Afterwards she wanted me to be in confinement for more than a month, but my father said this was all superstition and put his foot down, being a doctor himself.'

'Is it really that painful?' said Savita, quite frightened now.

'Yes. Truly unbearable,' said Mrs Rupa Mehra, ignoring all her own admonitions about not scaring or upsetting Savita. 'Worse than any pain I have ever had in my life, especially with Arun. But when the baby is born, it is such a joy to behold—if everything is all right, that is. But with some babies, it is very sad, like Kamini Bua's first child—still, such things happen,' ended Mrs Rupa Mehra philosophically.

'Ma, why don't you read me a poem?' said Savita, trying to get her mother off this latest subject. But when Mrs Rupa Mehra turned to one of her favourites, 'The Blind Boy' by Colley Cibber, Savita regretted her suggestion.

The tears already starting to her eyes, Mrs Rupa Mehra began to read in a tremulous voice:

> 'Oh say, what is that thing called Light,
> That I must ne'er enjoy?
> What are the blessings of the sight?
> Oh, tell your poor blind boy!'

'Ma,' said Savita, 'Daddy was very good to you, wasn't he? Very tender—very loving—'

'Oh, yes,' said Mrs Rupa Mehra, the tears flowing copiously now, 'he was a husband in a million. Now Pran's father would always disappear when Pran's mother gave birth. He couldn't stand childbirth—so when the baby was young and noisy and messy he would try to be away as much as he could. If he had been there, maybe Pran would not have half-drowned in that soapy tub as a baby, and then all this asthma would not have happened—and his heart would have been undamaged.' Mrs Rupa Mehra lowered her voice at the word 'heart'.

'Ma, I'm feeling tired. I think I'll turn in,' said Savita. She insisted on sleeping alone in her bedroom, though Mrs Rupa Mehra had offered to sleep with her in case her labour pains started and she would be too helpless to move or get help.

*

One night at about nine o'clock, while she was reading in bed, Savita suddenly felt a severe pain, and called out aloud. Mrs Rupa Mehra, her ears preternaturally sensitive to Savita's voice these days, came rushing into the room. She had taken out her false teeth already and only had her bra and petticoat on. She asked Savita what the matter was, and whether the pains had begun.

Savita nodded, gripping her stomach, and said she thought so. Mrs

Rupa Mehra promptly shook Lata awake, put on a housecoat, roused the servants, put in her false teeth, and telephoned Prem Nivas for the car to be sent. She could not get through to the obstetrician at his home number. She phoned Baitar House.

Imtiaz answered the phone. 'How often are the contractions taking place?' he asked. 'Who is your obstetrician? Butalia? Good. Have you called him yet? Oh, I see. Leave it to me; he may be at the hospital with another delivery. I'll make sure that they have a private room ready, and are prepared for everything.'

The pains were more frequent now, but irregular. Lata was holding Savita's hand, and sometimes kissing her or stroking her forehead. When the pains were on, Savita closed her eyes. Imtiaz was over in an hour or so. He had had a difficult time tracking down the obstetrician, who had happened to be at a party.

Once she was in the hospital—the medical college hospital—Savita looked around and asked where Pran was. 'Shall I get him?' asked Mrs Rupa Mehra.

'No, no, let him sleep—he shouldn't get out of bed,' said Savita.

'She's quite right,' said Imtiaz firmly. 'It would do him no good at all. There are enough of us here for support and company.'

A nurse informed them that the obstetrician would be coming very soon, and that there was nothing to be alarmed about. 'First births take a long time in general. Twelve hours is quite normal.' Savita's eyes opened wide.

Though she was in great pain, she did not cry out aloud. Dr Butalia, a short Sikh doctor with rather dreamy eyes, arrived, examined her briefly, and again assured her that things were fine.

'Excellent, excellent,' he said with a smile, his eyes fixed on his watch while Savita writhed on the bed. 'Ten minutes—well, good, good.' He then disappeared.

Maan turned up next. The nurse, noting that he was a Mr Kapoor, and that he looked quite dishevelled and concerned, decided that he must be the father, and addressed him in those terms for a few minutes before he corrected her.

'I'm afraid the father is another patient in this hospital,' said Maan. 'I am his brother.'

'Oh, but how awful,' said the nurse. 'Does he know—'

'Not yet.'

'Oh.'

'Yes, he's sleeping, and it's his doctor's orders—and his wife's—that he not move or suffer unnecessary excitement. I'm standing in for him.'

The nurse frowned. 'Now lie quietly,' she advised Savita. 'Lie quietly and think calm thoughts.'

'Yes,' said Savita, tears squeezing themselves out of her eyes.

The night was hot, and despite the fact that the room was on the second floor there were a number of mosquitoes. Mrs Rupa Mehra asked for another bed to be brought in so that she and Lata could take turns to rest. Imtiaz, having made sure that things were in good order, left. Maan sat on a chair in the corridor and went off to sleep.

Savita could not think calm thoughts. She felt as if her body had been taken out of her own control by some terrible, brutal force. She gasped when the pains came, but because her mother had told her that they would be unbearable, and she kept expecting them to get worse, she tried not to cry out aloud, and succeeded. Hour followed hour, and the sweat stood out on her forehead. Lata tried to keep the mosquitoes away from her face.

It was four o'clock, and still dark. In a couple of hours, Pran would be awake. But Imtiaz had made it quite clear that he would not be allowed out of his room. Now Savita began to cry softly to herself, not only because she would be deprived of the comfort of his support, but because she could imagine how anxious he would be for her.

Her mother, thinking she was crying because of the pain, said: 'Now, darling, be brave, it'll all be over soon.'

Savita groaned, and held her mother's hand tightly.

The pain was now very nearly unbearable. Suddenly, she felt the bed wet around her legs, and turned to Mrs Rupa Mehra, flushed with embarrassment and perplexity.

'Ma—'

'What is it, darling?'

'I think—I think the bed is wet.'

Mrs Rupa Mehra woke Maan and sent him to get the nurses on duty.

The bag of waters had broken, and the contractions began coming very fast now, every couple of minutes or so. The nurses took one look at the situation, and wheeled Savita into the labour room. One of them telephoned Dr Butalia.

'Where's my mother?' asked Savita.

'She's outside,' said one rather abrupt nurse.

'Please tell her to come in.'

'Mrs Kapoor, I'm so sorry, we can't do that,' said the other nurse, a large, kind, Anglo-Indian woman. 'The doctor will be here very soon. Hold on to the railing behind your bed if the pain is too bad.'

'I think I can feel the baby—' began Savita.

'Mrs Kapoor, please try to hold on till the doctor arrives.'

'I can't—'

Luckily the doctor appeared almost immediately, and the nurses now both exhorted her to push.

'Hold on to the spring and handle above you.'

'Push, push, push—'

'I can't bear it—I can't bear it—' said Savita, her lips drawn apart in agony.

'Just push—'

'No,' she wept. 'It's horrible. I can't bear it. Give me an anaesthetic. Doctor, please—'

'Push, Mrs Kapoor, you're doing very well,' said the doctor.

Out of a haze of pain, Savita heard one nurse say to the other: 'Is the baby's head coming out first?'

Savita felt a tearing sensation below, then a sudden warm gush. Then more stretching and such pain that she thought she would pass out.

'I can't bear it, oh Ma, I can't bear it any more,' she screamed. 'I never want to have another baby.'

'They all say that,' said the abrupt nurse, 'and they all come back next year. Keep pushing—'

'I won't. I'll never—never—never have another child,' said Savita, who felt herself being stretched beyond endurance, almost torn apart. 'Oh God.'

Suddenly the head slipped out, and she felt a sense of immediate relief.

When, after what seemed a long time, she heard the baby's cry, she opened her eyes, which were still hazy with tears, and looked at the red, wrinkled, black-haired, bawling baby, covered with blood and a sort of greasy film, that the doctor was holding up in his arms.

'It's a girl, Mrs Kapoor,' said the dreamy-eyed doctor. 'With a very powerful voice.'

'A girl?'

'Yes. Quite a large baby. Well done. It was a difficult birth, as such things go.'

Savita lay exhausted for a couple of minutes. The light in the labour room was too bright for her. A baby! she thought.

'Can I hold her?' she asked after a while.

'Just one minute more, and we'll have her cleaned up.'

But the baby was still quite slippery when it—she—came to rest on the cradle of Savita's slack stomach. Savita looked at the top of its head, adoringly and accusingly, then held it gently and closed her eyes with exhaustion once more.

13.12

Pran woke to find himself a father.

'What?' he said in disbelief to Imtiaz.

But seeing his parents sitting there by his bedside, something that would not normally have occurred outside visiting hours, he shook his head and believed it.

'A girl,' added Imtiaz. 'They're upstairs. Maan's there too, quite happy to be mistaken for the father.'

'A girl?' Pran was surprised, perhaps even a little disappointed. 'How is Savita?'

'Fine. I've had a word with the obstetrician. He says the birth was a little difficult, but nothing unusual.'

'Well, let me go to see her and the baby. I suppose she can't move.'

'No, she can't. Not for a couple of days. She has a few stitches. And I'm sorry, Pran, you can't move either. Neither movement nor excitement will conduce to your recovery.' Imtiaz spoke with the slightly severe formality that he found worked best with patients when he wanted to ensure their compliance.

'This is ridiculous, Imtiaz. Be sensible. Please. I suppose you're going to tell me that I can only see photographs of my baby.'

'That's an idea now,' said Imtiaz unable to resist a smile, and rubbing the mole on his cheek. 'But the baby, unlike the mother, is a transportable item, and she can certainly be brought to you here. It's a good thing you aren't infectious, or even that wouldn't have been possible. Butalia guards his babies as if they were something of value.'

'But I must speak to Savita,' said Pran.

'She's doing well, Pran,' said his father reassuringly. 'When I was upstairs she was resting. She's a good girl,' he added irrelevantly.

'Why don't you write her a note?' suggested Imtiaz.

'A note?' said Pran with a short laugh. 'She's not in a different city.' But he asked his mother to give him the pad on the nightstand, and scribbled a few lines:

> Darling,
>
> Imtiaz has forbidden me a sight of you; he claims that walking up a couple of flights of stairs and the excitement of seeing you will undo me. I know that you must be looking as beautiful as ever. I hope you are all right, and I wish I were there to hold your hand and tell you how wonderful our baby is. Because I'm sure she must be wonderful.
>
> I haven't seen her either yet, and this is to request you to relinquish her for a few minutes.
>
> Incidentally, I am fine and, in case you were wondering, had a restful night!
>
> All my love,
> Pran

Imtiaz went off.

'Don't worry that it's a girl, Pran,' said his mother.

'I'm not worried at all,' said Pran. 'I'm just surprised. Everyone kept talking about a boy, so after a while I believed it.'

Mrs Mahesh Kapoor herself was not displeased that she had had a granddaughter, since Bhaskar (though not in the male line) had fulfilled her wish for a grandson.

'Rupa couldn't be pleased, though,' she told her husband.

'Why?' said her husband.

'Two granddaughters and no grandsons.'

'Women should have their brains examined,' was his response, before he returned to the day's newspaper.

'But you always say—'

Mahesh Kapoor held up his hand, and continued reading.

In a short while Mrs Rupa Mehra appeared with the baby.

Pran's eyes filled suddenly with tears. 'Hello, Ma,' he said, reaching out for the baby.

The baby's eyes were open but because of the folds around them, she looked almost as if she was squinting. To Pran she looked extremely raw and wrinkled, but not unattractive. In an unfocused way she too appeared to register Pran.

He held her, not knowing what to do. How did one communicate with a baby? He hummed for a bit. Then he said to his mother-in-law: 'How is Savita? When will she be able to move around?'

'Oh, she's sent a customs note with the parcel,' said Mrs Rupa Mehra, handing Pran a piece of paper.

Pran looked at his mother-in-law, surprised by this sudden flippant touch of wit. He felt that if he had made a joke in the same vein she would have rebuked him.

'Really, Ma!' he said. But Mrs Rupa Mehra was laughing, and tickling the back of the baby's head in a doting manner. Pran rested the note against the baby, and read as follows:

> Dearest P,
>
> Herewith find enclosed one baby, size M, sex F, colour R, to be returned after inspection and approval.
>
> I am very well, and longing to see you, and I have been told that in two or three days I can move around carefully. It's these stitches, which make certain things difficult for me.
>
> The baby has a definite personality and I feel she has taken a liking to me. I hope you are equally lucky. Her nose reminds me of Ma's, but nothing else reminds me of anything in either of our families. She was very slippery when she came out, but now she has been cleaned and talcumed for presentability.
>
> Please don't worry about me, Pran. I am very well, and Ma will be sleeping in my room next to the baby's cot so that I'll be able to rest except for feeding times.
>
> I hope you are all right, my darling, and congratulations. It's difficult to think of myself in my changed status. I know I've had a baby all right, but I can't believe I'm a mother.
>
> Lots of love,
> Savita

Pran rocked his daughter for a while. He smiled at the last sentence. Imtiaz had congratulated him on being a father rather than on having a baby, and he had no difficulty in accepting the fact of his fatherhood.

The baby was asleep in his arms. Pran was amazed at how perfect she was, all of her. Even though she was so small, each vein, each limb and lid and lip, each tiny finger was there—and functioning.

The baby's mouth was open in an unmeaning smile.

Pran saw what Savita meant about the nose. Even though it was very small, he could see that it had the potential of Mrs Rupa Mehra's rather hawk-like nose. He wondered if it would redden in the same way when she cried. At any rate, it couldn't be redder than it was now.

'Isn't she lovely?' asked Mrs Rupa Mehra. 'How proud He would have been to see his second granddaughter.'

Pran rocked the baby a bit more, and touched his nose to hers.

'What do you think of your daughter?' asked Mrs Rupa Mehra.

'She has a nice smile, considering that she's a baby,' said Pran.

As he had thought, Mrs Rupa Mehra did not approve of his flippancy. She told him that if he had given birth to the baby he would have appreciated her more.

'Quite right, Ma, quite right,' said Pran.

He wrote a short note back to Savita, informing her that the baby met with his approval, and reassuring her that slippery people were necessary in the scheme of things. When Mrs Rupa Mehra returned upstairs with the baby, Mr and Mrs Mahesh Kapoor followed, and Pran stared at the ceiling, lost in his thoughts, more happy about the present than worried about the future.

The baby was a little difficult to feed on the first day. At first she didn't want to acknowledge the breast, but once Savita brushed her finger against her cheek she turned around quite swiftly and opened her mouth. This was the opportunity for the nipple to be put to the baby's mouth. The baby's face registered an expression something like surprise. She also had a little difficulty in pulling properly. After that there was no trouble, except that she tended to go to sleep while feeding, and had to be woken up to complete her feed. Sometimes Savita tickled her behind the ears, sometimes on the soles of her feet. The baby was comfortable and contented to the extent that she required a great deal of persuasion to wake up at times.

Grandmother, mother and baby each had a bed in the private room. Lata had to go for classes in the morning, but usually managed to relieve her mother's watch for an hour or two around lunchtime. Sometimes Mrs Rupa Mehra, Savita, and the baby would all be sleeping, with only Lata watching, and an occasional nurse stopping by to ensure that everything was all right. It was a quiet time, and Lata used it to learn her lines. At other times she simply mused. If the baby woke, or needed its nappy changed, she took care of what needed to be done. The baby was content to be rocked by her.

Sometimes, sitting here, with the marked script of *Twelfth Night* open on her lap, Lata substituted the word 'happiness' for 'greatness' in the famous quotation. She wondered what one could do to be born happy, to achieve happiness, or to have it thrust on one. The baby, she thought, had arranged to be born happy; she was placid, and had as good a chance as anyone of happiness in this world, her father's poor health notwithstanding. Pran and Savita, different though their backgrounds were, were a happy couple. They recognized limits and possibilities; their yearnings did not stretch beyond their reach. They loved each other—or, rather, had come to do so. They both assumed, without ever needing to state it—or perhaps without even thinking explicitly about it—that marriage and children were a great good. If Savita was restless—and at the moment in the shaded noon light her sleeping face showed no restlessness but, rather, a peace and pleasure that Lata wondered at—if she was restless, it was because she feared the undoing by forces outside themselves of this great good. She wanted above all to ensure that no matter what happened to her husband, insecurity and unhappiness would not unavoidably thrust themselves on their child. The law-book resting on the table on one side of her bed balanced the baby resting in the cot on the other.

Nowadays, when Mrs Rupa Mehra fussed about Savita or her as-yet-nameless granddaughter, or voiced to Lata her fears about Pran's health or Varun's shiftlessness, Lata was not so impatient as she had earlier been. Her mother appeared to her now as the guardian of the family; and with life and death so near each other here in the hospital, it seemed to Lata that all that provided continuity in the world or protection from it was the family. Calcutta, Delhi, Kanpur, Lucknow—the visits to endless relatives—the Annual Trans-India Rail-Pilgrimages that Arun mocked so relentlessly and the waterworks that vexed him, the sending of cards to third cousins thrice removed on their birthdays, the family gossip at every ritual ceremony from birth to death, and the continual recollection of her husband—that absent but no doubt still benevolently supervising god—all these could be seen as part of the works of a corresponding domestic goddess, whose symbols (false teeth, black bag, scissors and thimble, gold and silver stars) would be remembered with tenderness long after she was gone—as she herself was over-fond of pointing out. She wanted Lata's happiness just as Savita wanted her baby's; and had tried to arrange for it in as determined a manner as she could. Lata no longer resented it.

Thrust so suddenly into the marriage market this year, forced to travel from city to city, Lata had begun to look at marriages (the Sahgals, the

Chatterjis, Arun and Meenakshi, Mr and Mrs Mahesh Kapoor, Pran and Savita) with more than a disinterested eye. But whether it was owing to the hectoring of her mother or her overly copious love or the vision of these different families or Pran's illness or the birth of Savita's baby or all of them combined, Lata felt she had changed. The sleeping Savita was perhaps a more powerful adviser than the voluble Malati.

Lata looked back on her wish to elope with Kabir with a kind of amazement, even as she could not shake off her feelings for him. But where would these feelings lead? A gradual, stable attraction such as Savita's for Pran—was this not the best thing for her, and for the family, and for any children that she might have?

Each day at the rehearsal she feared and hoped that Kabir would come up to her to say something or do something that would begin to unravel once again the unfamiliar, too-solid fabric that she had woven—or that had been woven—around her. But rehearsals passed, and visiting hours came, and matters remained as unspoken and unresolved as ever.

Plenty of people came in to look at the baby: Imtiaz, Firoz, Maan, Bhaskar, old Mrs Tandon, Kedarnath, Veena, the Nawab Sahib himself, Malati, Mr and Mrs Mahesh Kapoor, Mr Shastri (bearing a law-book he had promised Savita), Dr Kishen Chand Seth and Parvati, and many others, including a troop of Rudhia relatives whom Savita did not know. Clearly, the baby had been born not to a couple but to a clan. Dozens of people cooed above her (some acclaiming her looks, others deprecating her sex) and great exception was taken to any proprietary instincts displayed by the mother. Savita, imagining that she had certain special rights to the baby, attempted to protect her from the mist of appreciative droplets that formed a continuous haze around her head for two days. But she gave up at last, and accepted that the Kapoors of Rudhia and Brahmpur had the right to welcome in their own way this freshly minted member of their tribe. She wondered what her brother Arun would have made of the Rudhia relatives. Lata had dispatched a telegram to Calcutta, but so far nothing had been heard from that branch of the Mehras.

13.13

'No, really, Didi—I'm enjoying it. It's no bother at all. I like reading things I don't understand sometimes.'

'You're strange,' said Savita, smiling.

'Yes. Well, as long as I know they do actually make sense.'

'Would you hold her for a while?'

Lata put the book on tort down, went over to Savita, and took over the baby, who smiled at her for a while and then went off to sleep.

She rocked the baby, who appeared to be quite content in her arms.

'Now what's all this, baby?' said Lata. 'What's all this now? Wake up a little and speak to us, speak to your Lata Masi. When I'm awake you go off to sleep, when I'm asleep you wake up, let's do things straight for a change, shall we, this won't do at all, will it, will it now?'

She moved the baby from one arm to the other surprisingly skilfully, cradling her head all the while.

'What do you think about my studying law?' said Savita. 'Do you think I have the temperament for it? Savita Mehra, Government Counsel; Savita Mehra, Senior Advocate; good heavens, I forgot for a moment I'm a Kapoor. Savita Kapoor, Advocate-General; Mrs Justice Savita Kapoor. Will I be called "My lord" or "My lady"?'

'Don't count your chickens before they're hatched,' said Lata, laughing.

'But they might never get hatched,' said Savita. 'I may as well count them now. Ma, you know, doesn't think law is such a bad idea. She feels that if she had had a profession it might have helped.'

'Oh, nothing's going to happen to Pran,' said Lata, smiling at the baby. 'Is it, now? Nothing's going to happen to Papa, nothing, nothing, nothing. He will play his silly, silly April fool jokes for many, many years to come. Do you know, you can actually feel her pulse through her head?'

'How amazing!' said Savita. 'It's going to be very difficult for me to get used to being slim again. When you're pregnant and bulge, you are popular with all the cats on the university campus, and people tell you intimate things about themselves.'

Lata crinkled her nose. 'But what if we don't want to hear intimate things?' she inquired of the baby. 'What if we are quite happy to paddle our own canoe in a pleasant little backwater—and are not interested in the Niagara Falls and the Barsaat Mahal?'

Savita was quiet for a few moments, then she said: 'OK, I'll take her back now. And you can read to me a bit more. What's that book?'

'*Twelfth Night*.'

'No, the other one—the one with the green and white cover.'

'*Contemporary Verse*,' murmured Lata, blushing for some unaccountable reason.

'Oh, read me some of that,' said Savita. 'Ma thinks poetry is good for me. Soothing. Calming.

It was a summer evening,
Old Caspar's work was done.'

Lata took up the recitation:

'And he beside his cottage door
Was sitting in the sun.

There's a skull in that poem somewhere, I remember. Oh yes, and Ma also loves that grisly "Casabianca" with the boy burning on the deck—and "Lord Ullin's Daughter". There has to be some death and heartbreak in it somewhere or it isn't real poetry. I don't know what she'd make of the poetry in this book. All right, what do you want to hear?'

'Open it at random,' suggested Savita. And the book opened to Auden's 'Law, Say the Gardeners'.

'Apt,' said Lata, and began to read. But as she turned the page to the last few lines, and read the poet's similitude between law and love, her face grew pale:

'Like love we don't know where or why
Like love we can't compel or fly
Like love we often weep
Like love we seldom keep.'

She shut the book.

'Strange poem,' she said.

'Yes,' said Savita carefully. 'Let's go back to tort.'

13.14

Meenakshi Mehra arrived in Brahmpur three days after the birth of the baby. She came with her sister Kakoli but without her daughter Aparna.

She was tired of Calcutta and needed a break, and the telegram provided her with an excuse.

She was tired, for a start, of Arun, who was being very boring and covenanted these days, and appeared to have lost interest in anything but premiums on tea to Khurramshahr. She was exhausted with Aparna, who had begun to get on her nerves with her 'Mummy this' and 'Mummy that' and 'Mummy you aren't listening'. She was sick of arguing with the Toothless Crone and Hanif and the part-time mali. She felt she was going mad. Varun would slope and slither guiltily in and out of the house, and every time he went 'heh-heh-heh' in his furtive Shamshu way she would feel like screaming. Even occasional afternoons with Billy and canasta with the Shady Ladies seemed to have lost their savour. It was too too awful. Truly, Calcutta was nothing but tinsel in the mouth.

And then came this telegram informing them that Arun's sister had had a baby. Well, it was nothing less than a godsend. Dipankar had filled postcard after postcard with descriptions of what a beautiful place Brahmpur was, and how nice Savita's in-laws were. They were bound to be hospitable and she would be able to lie under a fan and calm her fraught nerves. Meenakshi felt she needed a holiday, and this was a wonderful opportunity to pounce upon Brahmpur with the intention of helping out. She could give her sister-in-law excellent advice on how to take care of her daughter. She had successfully managed Aparna, and this gave her the authority to manage her niece.

Meenakshi was quite pleased to be an aunt, even if only through her husband's sister. Her own brothers and sister had not provided her with a single nephew or niece. Amit was the most culpable in this regard; he should have got married at least three years ago. In fact, thought Meenakshi, he should make up for his error at once: by marrying Lata.

Here was another reason for going to Brahmpur; she would prepare the ground when she got there. Of course there was no question of mentioning her plan to Amit; he would have hit the roof in so far as he was capable of it. Sometimes she wished he would hit the roof. Surely poets should be more passionate than Amit was. But she could certainly imagine him saying acidly: 'Do your own wooing, Meenakshi darling, and let me do mine.' No, she had better not mention anything to Amit.

Kakoli, however, when she came to visit Sunny Park late one afternoon, was let into the plot, and was delighted. She considered Lata to be quiet but nice, with sudden surprising sparks here and there to leaven things. Amit appeared to like her, but he was incapable of doing anything determined for himself, being content simply to contemplate things and let the years roll on. Kakoli felt that Lata and Amit were well matched but that each needed prodding. She rolled off a Kakoli-couplet to consecrate their match:

> 'Luscious Lata, born to be
> Lady Lata Chatterji.'

She was rewarded by the tinkle of Meenakshi's laughter, and the return of her service:

> 'Luscious Lata, is it hard
> Being wife of famous bard?'

Kakoli, giggling, volleyed the ball low across the net:

> 'Oh, so hard it is in rhyme:
> Loving, doving, all the time.'

And Meenakshi continued the rally:

> 'Kissing, missing, every day,
> Cuddling, muddling all the way.'

Kakoli, suddenly remembering that she had left Cuddles tied up to her bedpost, told Meenakshi she had to go home immediately. 'But why don't both of us go to Brahmpur together?' she suggested. 'To the provinces,' she added airily.

'Why not?' said Meenakshi. 'We could chaperone each other. But wouldn't you miss Hans?'

'We need only go for a week. It'll be good for him to miss me. It'll be well worth the pain of my missing him.'

'And Cuddles? It really is very tiresome of Dipankar not to say when he's coming back. He's been gone for years, and now that he's run out of postcards, we'll never hear from him.'

'It's just typical of him. Well, Amit can be Cuddles' keeper.'

When Mrs Chatterji heard of the trip, she was more concerned with Kakoli missing classes than missing Hans.

'Oh, Ma,' wailed Kakoli, 'don't be such a bore. Weren't you ever young? Didn't you ever want to flee from the chains of life? I have excellent attendance at college, and a week won't make any difference. We can always get a doctor to certify that I've been ill. With a wasting sickness.' She quoted two snowy lines from *Winterreise* about the Inn that represented Death. 'Or malaria,' she continued. 'Look, there's a mosquito.'

'We will do no such thing,' said Mr Justice Chatterji, looking up from his book.

But Kakoli, while conceding this point, wore her parents down on the general question of the Brahmpur jaunt. 'Meenakshi needs me to accompany her. Arun's too busy with work. The family needs us,' she pleaded. 'Babies are so complicated. Every pair of hands helps. And Lata's such a nice girl, her company will improve me. Ask Amit if she isn't nice. And improving.'

'Oh shut up, Kuku, leave me to Keats,' said Amit.

'Kuku, Keats, Kuku, Keats,' said Kakoli, sitting down at the piano. 'What shall I play for you, Amit? La-La-Liebestraum?'

Amit fixed her with a Look.

But Kakoli rippled on:

'Amit lying on his bed,
Dreams of Lata in his head.
Weeping, weeping on his sheets,
Cannot concentrate on Keats.'

'You are by far the stupidest girl I know,' said Amit. 'But why do you advertise your stupidity?'

'Perhaps because I am stupid!' said Kakoli, and giggled at her idiotic answer. 'But don't you like her—a teeeeny weeeeny bit? A soupcon? A little? A tittle?'

Amit got up to go to his room, but not before another Kakoli-couplet had been shot at him.

'Kuku-clock chimes out her name.
Poet fleeing, red with shame.'

'Really, Kuku!' said her mother. 'There are limits.' She turned to her husband. 'You never say anything to her. You never set any limits. You never stop her from doing anything. You always give in. What is a father for?'

'To say no at first,' said Mr Justice Chatterji.

13.15

Most of the Brahmpur news had already got through to Calcutta via the informative letters of Mrs Rupa Mehra. But her last letter had been overtaken by the telegram. So when Meenakshi and Kakoli got to Brahmpur with every intention of plonking themselves and their baggage down at Pran's doorstep, they were shocked to find that he wasn't there at all, but ill in hospital. With Savita in hospital herself, and Lata and her mother fussing about with Pran and Savita, it was clear that Meenakshi and Kuku could not be put up and fussed over in the style to which they were accustomed.

Meenakshi found it hard to believe that the Kapoors had timed their affairs so badly as to have husband and wife bedridden at the same time.

Kakoli was more sympathetic, accepting the fact that baby and bronchii could not confer in advance. 'Why don't we stay at Pran's father's place, what is it called, Prem Nivas?' she asked.

'That's impossible,' responded Meenakshi. 'The mother doesn't even speak English. And they won't have western-style toilets—just those dreadful holes in the ground.'

'Well, what are we to do?'

'Kuku, how about that old dodderer whose address Baba gave us?'

'But who wants to stay with someone who's full of senile reminiscences?'

'Well, where is it?'

'He gave it to you. It must be in your bag,' said Kakoli.

'No, Kuku, he gave it to you,' said Meenakshi.

'I'm quite sure he didn't,' said Kakoli. 'Do check.'

'Well—oh, yes, here it is. Maybe it's on that. Yes, it is: Mr and Mrs Maitra. Let's land on them.'

'Let's see the baby first.'

'What about our luggage?'

So Meenakshi and Kakoli freshened up, changed into a mauve and a red cotton sari respectively, ordered Mateen to provide them with a fortifying breakfast, and set off in a tonga for Civil Lines. Meenakshi was astonished that it was so difficult to hail a taxi in Brahmpur, and shuddered every time the horse farted.

Meenakshi and Kakoli quickly imposed themselves on Mr and Mrs Maitra and then rushed off, waving from the back of the tonga, towards the hospital.

'Well, they claim that they're Chatterji's daughters,' said the old policeman. 'His children seem to be very restless. What was the name of that other boy, their son?'

Mrs Maitra, who was scandalized by the fact that she could see almost four inches of their waists, shook her head and wondered what Calcutta had come to. Her own son's letters did not contain any mention of waistlines.

'When will they be back for lunch?'

'They didn't say.'

'Well, since they are our guests, we should wait for them. But I get so hungry by noon,' said old Mr Maitra. 'And then I have to tell my beads for two hours, and if I begin late, that puts everything out. We'd also better get some more fish.'

'We'll wait till one, and then eat,' said his wife. 'If they can't come, they'll telephone us.'

And so the two considerate old people accommodated themselves to the two young women, who had no intention of eating with them, and to whom the thought of a telephone call would certainly not occur.

*

Mrs Rupa Mehra was transporting the baby from Pran's room to Savita's when she saw the mauve Meenakshi and the crimson Kakoli bearing down upon her along the corridor. She all but dropped the baby.

Meenakshi was wearing those little gold horrors that never failed to upset Mrs Rupa Mehra. And what was Kakoli doing here during term-time? Really, thought Mrs Rupa Mehra, the Chatterjis impose no discipline upon their children. That is why they are all so peculiar.

Aloud she said: 'Oh, Meenakshi, Kakoli, what a lovely surprise. Have you seen the baby yet? No, of course you couldn't have. Just look at her, isn't she sweet? And everyone says she has my nose.'

'How adorable,' said Meenakshi, thinking that the baby looked rather like a red rat, not at all as beautiful as her Aparna had looked a few days after birth.

'And where is my sweetheart?' demanded Mrs Rupa Mehra.

For a second Meenakshi thought Mrs Rupa Mehra was referring to

Arun. Then she realized that it was Aparna whom her mother-in-law was talking about.

'In Calcutta, of course.'

'You didn't bring her with you?' Mrs Rupa Mehra could hardly conceal her amazement at this maternal callousness.

'Oh, Ma, one can't drag the whole world with one when one travels,' said Meenakshi coolly. 'Aparna does get on one's nerves sometimes, and I'd be much less help here if she was with me.'

'You've come to help?' Mrs Rupa Mehra could hardly keep the astonishment and displeasure out of her voice.

'Yes, Ma,' said Kakoli simply.

But Meenakshi elaborated: 'Yes, of course, Ma, darling. What a sweet little thing. Reminds me of a, of a—well, she's unique, she doesn't remind me of anything but herself.' Meenakshi laughed a tinkly laugh. 'Now where is Savita's room?'

'Savita is resting,' said Mrs Rupa Mehra.

'But she'll be so pleased to see us,' said Meenakshi. 'Let's go and see her. It must be feeding time. Six, ten, two, six, ten, as Dr Evans recommended with Aparna. And it's just about ten o'clock now.'

And they descended upon Savita, who was still fairly exhausted, and in quite a lot of pain because her stitches were pulling. She was sitting up in bed, though, and reading a women's magazine rather than a law-book.

Savita was astonished, but pleased to see them. Lata, who had been keeping her company, was very pleased. She enjoyed Meenakshi's attempts to beautify her; and Kuku's flightiness would, she hoped, lighten everyone's mood. Savita had met Kuku only twice since Arun's wedding.

'How did you get here outside visiting hours?' Savita asked, looking rather warrior-like now, with bright lipstick on both her cheeks.

'Oh, Kakoli and I were more than a match for the reception desk,' said Meenakshi. And indeed, the dumbfounded clerk had not known how to prevent these glamorous, waist-bare ladies from breezing past him.

Kakoli had blown him a kiss with casual hauteur. He was still recovering.

13.16

Calcutta and Brahmpur news was exchanged rapidly. Arun was extremely busy with work, Varun showed no signs of studying seriously for the

IAS exams, and there were lots of rows between the brothers, with Arun threatening periodically to throw Varun out of the house. Aparna's vocabulary was increasing apace; a few days ago she had said: 'Daddy, I'm in the doldrums.' Meenakshi suddenly began to miss Aparna. Seeing the baby snuggling up to Savita's breast, she thought of Aparna's own babydom, the lovely feeling of closeness she had experienced when she was suckling her, the sense of 'myness' that she had had towards her before Aparna had grown into a clearly differentiated, and often contrary, individual.

'Why doesn't she have a name-tag?' she asked. 'Dr Evans always insisted on name-tags, in case babies got lost or exchanged by mistake.' Meenakshi's little earrings glinted as she shook her head at the frightful thought.

Mrs Rupa Mehra got irritated. 'I am here to ensure that nothing happens. Mothers should stay with their children. Who can steal the baby when her cot is in this room?'

'Of course, things are much better arranged in Calcutta,' continued Meenakshi. 'In the Irwin Nursing Home, where Aparna was delivered, there's a separate nursery where the babies are kept, and you can only view them through glass—to prevent infection, of course. Here everyone breathes and talks above the baby, and the air is full of germs. She could easily fall ill.'

'Savita is trying to rest,' said Mrs Rupa Mehra severely. 'These are not very restful thoughts, Meenakshi.'

'I agree,' said Kakoli. 'I think things are run splendidly here. In fact, I think it would be rather fun if babies got exchanged. Like in *The Prince and the Gipsy*.' This was a romantic potboiler that Kuku had recently read. 'In fact,' she continued, 'this particular baby looks rather too red and crinkled for my liking. I'd ask for a replacement.' She giggled.

'Kuku,' said Lata, 'how's your singing and piano going? And how is Hans?'

'I think I want to go to the bathroom, Ma—could you help me?' asked Savita.

'Let me help,' said Meenakshi and Kakoli simultaneously.

'Thanks, but Ma and I are used to things,' said Savita with calm authority. It was difficult for her to walk to the bathroom; the stitches made everything more painful. Once she closed the door, she told Mrs Rupa Mehra that she was rather tired, and that Meenakshi and Kakoli should be told to return in the evening at visiting time.

Meenakshi and Kakoli, meanwhile, had been talking to Lata, and had decided that they would come and see that afternoon's rehearsal of *Twelfth Night*.

'I wonder what it must have been like to be married to Shakespeare,' breathed Meenakshi, 'and have him say such wonderful poetic things to one all the time—about love and life—'

'He didn't say much to Anne Hathaway,' said Lata. 'He wasn't there most of the time. And according to Professor Mishra, his sonnets imply that he was interested in other people too—more than one.'

'But who isn't?' said Meenakshi, then suddenly stopped, recalling that Lata was, after all, Arun's sister. 'In any case, I'd forgive Shakespeare anything. It must be so wonderful to be married to a poet. To be his muse, to make him happy. I was just saying so to Amit the other day, but he's so modest, he only said: "I think my wife would have a hell of a time."'

'Which is nonsense, of course,' said Kakoli. 'Amit has a lovely nature. Why, Cuddles bites him less often than anyone else.'

Lata said nothing. Meenakshi and Kuku were being remarkably unsubtle, and their talk about Amit irritated her. She felt fairly sure that Amit could not have acquiesced in this mission. She looked at her watch, and realized that she was almost late for a class.

'See you at three o'clock at the auditorium,' she said. 'Don't you want to see Pran as well?'

'Pran? Oh, yes.'

'He's in room 56. On the ground floor. Where are you staying?'

'With Mr Maitra in Civil Lines. He's a sweet old man, but completely senile. Dipankar stayed with him as well. It's become the Chatterji hostel in Brahmpur.'

'I wish you were staying with us,' said Lata. 'But you see how difficult things are at present.'

'Now, don't worry about us, Lata,' said Kuku kindly. 'Just tell us how to occupy ourselves between now and three o'clock. I think we've had our fill of the baby for the moment.'

'Well, you could go to the Barsaat Mahal,' said Lata. 'I know it's hot at this time of day, but it's as beautiful as they say it is, and much more so than any of the photographs.'

'Oh, monuments!—' said Meenakshi, yawning.

'Isn't there something livelier in Brahmpur?' asked Kakoli.

'Well, there's the Blue Danube café on Nabiganj. And the Red Fox. And the movies, though the English ones are a couple of years out of date. And the bookstores—' Even as she spoke, Lata realized how dreary Brahmpur must seem to the ladies of Calcutta. 'I'm really sorry, I have to run now. My lecture.'

And Kuku was left wondering at Lata's enthusiasm for her studies.

13.17

What with the activity surrounding Pran's illness and the baby's arrival, Lata's own reticence and Malati's protective presence at rehearsals, Lata and Kabir had merely exchanged Shakespeare's lines, and none of their own, for the last few days. Lata longed to tell him how much she sympathized with him about his mother, but did not know how to do so without eliciting an intensity of feeling on both sides that she feared would shake her—and probably him—too painfully. So she said nothing. But Mr Barua noticed that Olivia was kinder to Malvolio than he thought the script merited, and he tried to correct her.

'Now, Miss Mehra, do try that again. "O you are sick of self-love, Malvolio—"'

Lata cleared her throat for a second attempt. 'O you are sick of self-love, Malvolio, and taste with a distempered appetite—'

'No, no, Miss Mehra like this: "O you are sick—" and so on. Slightly sharp, slightly tired. You are irritated by Malvolio. It is he who is mooning over you.'

Lata tried to think of how angry she had been when she saw Kabir at the first rehearsal. She began once more:

'O you are sick of self-love, Malvolio, and taste with a distempered appetite. To be generous, guiltless, and of free disposition, is to take those things for bird-bolts that you deem cannon-bullets—'

'Ah, yes, much better, much better. But you seem rather too annoyed. Tone it down, Miss Mehra, if you would, tone it down a little. That way, when he seems to be really mad later on, even offensive, you'll have an unused range of emotions that you can bring into play. Do you see what I mean?'

'Yes, yes I think I do, Mr Barua.'

Kakoli and Meenakshi had been chatting to Malati for a while, but she suddenly disappeared. 'My cue,' she explained, and bounced into the wings to come on as Maria.

'What do you think, Kuku?' said Meenakshi.

'I think she has a soft spot for that Malvolio chap.'

'Malati assured us she hadn't,' said Meenakshi. 'She even called him a cad. Seemed a strange word to use. A cad.'

'I think he's delicious. He looks so broad-shouldered and soulful. I wish he'd shoot a cannon-bullet at me. Or his bird-bolt.'

'Really, Kuku, you have no decency at all,' said Meenakshi.

'Lata has certainly opened up since she was in Calcutta,' said Kakoli thoughtfully. 'If Amit is to stand a chance, he can't continue to lie low—'

'The early worm catches the bird,' said Meenakshi.

Kakoli giggled.

Mr Barua turned around in annoyance.

'Er, would the two young ladies at the back—'

'But it's so amusing—the lines, I mean—under your direction,' said Kakoli with brazen sweetness. Some of the boys laughed, and Mr Barua turned around, blushing.

But after a few minutes of foolery by Sir Toby, both Kakoli and Meenakshi got bored, and left.

That evening, the two sisters went to the hospital. They spent a few seconds with Pran, whom they found unattractive and negligible—'I knew it the minute I saw him at the wedding,' said Meenakshi—and most of their time upstairs in Savita's room. Meenakshi advised Savita about her feeding times. Savita listened carefully, thinking about other matters. Lots of other people came in, and the room became as crowded as a concert. Meenakshi and Kakoli, pheasants among the Brahmpur pigeons, looked around them with unfeigned contempt, especially at the Rudhia relatives and Mrs Mahesh Kapoor. Some of these people were incapable of speaking English. And the way they dressed!

Mrs Mahesh Kapoor for her part could not believe that these two shamelessly bare-waisted and bold-mouthed girls were the sisters of that nice boy Dipankar, who was so simple in his dress, amiable in his manners, and spiritual in his tastes. She was upset that Maan appeared to be hovering fascinatedly nearby. Kuku was looking at him with liquid eyes. Meenakshi's eyes held a look of come-hither disdain which was as challenging as Kuku's was appealing. Perhaps because she did not understand much English, Mrs Mahesh Kapoor was able more keenly to observe the unobvious undercurrents of hostility and attraction, contempt and admiration, tenderness and indifference that tied together the twenty or so people talking non-stop in this room.

Meenakshi was telling a story, punctuated by her bell-like laugh, about her own pregnancy. 'It had to be Dr Evans, of course. Dr Matthew Evans. Really, if one has to have a baby in Calcutta, there's no other choice. Such a charming man. Absolutely the best gynaecologist in Calcutta. He has such a nice way with his patients.'

'Oh, Meenakshi, you're only saying that because he flirts with his patients shamelessly,' interrupted Kakoli. 'He pats them on their bottoms.'

'Well, he certainly cheers them up,' said Meenakshi. 'That's part of his bedside manner.'

Kakoli giggled. Mrs Rupa Mehra looked at Mr Mahesh Kapoor, who seemed to be going through a paroxysm of self-control.

'Of course he's terribly terribly expensive—his fee for Aparna was 750 rupees. But even Ma, who's so penny-pinching, agrees he was worth every paisa. Don't you, Ma?'

Mrs Rupa Mehra did not agree, but did not say so. When Dr Evans had heard that Meenakshi was in labour, he had merely said, as if sighting the Armada: 'Tell her to hold on. I'm finishing my game of golf.'

Meenakshi was continuing. 'The Irwin Nursing Home is spotless. And there's a nursery too. The mother isn't exhausted by having the baby with her all the time in a cot, yelling and needing its nappy changed. It's just brought to her at feeding times. And they're strict about the number of visitors there.' Meenakshi looked rather pointedly at the riff-raff from Rudhia.

Mrs Rupa Mehra was too embarrassed by Meenakshi's behaviour to say anything.

Mr Mahesh Kapoor said: 'Mrs Mehra, this is very fascinating, but—'

'Do you think so?' said Meenakshi. 'I do think childbirth is so—so ennobling.'

'Ennobling?' said Kuku, astonished.

Savita was beginning to look pale.

'Well, don't you think one shouldn't miss out on the whole thing?' Meenakshi hadn't thought so when she had actually been pregnant.

'I don't know,' said Kakoli. 'I'm not pregnant—yet.'

Maan laughed, and Mr Mahesh Kapoor almost choked.

'Kakoli!' said Mrs Rupa Mehra in a warning voice.

'But not everyone knows when they're pregnant,' continued Kakoli. 'Remember Brigadier Guha's wife in Kashmir? She didn't go through the ennobling experience.'

Meenakshi laughed at the memory.

'What about her?' said Maan.

'Well—' began Meenakshi.

'She was—' began Kakoli simultaneously.

'You tell it,' said Meenakshi.

'No, you tell it,' said Kakoli.

'All right,' said Meenakshi. 'She was playing hockey in Kashmir, where she'd gone for a holiday to celebrate her fortieth birthday. She fell down, and got hurt, and had to return to Calcutta. When she got back, she began to feel shooting pains every few minutes. They called the doctor—'

'Dr Evans,' added Kakoli.

'No, Kuku, Dr Evans came later, this was another one. So she said, "Doctor, what is this?" And he said, "You're going to have a baby. We've got to get you to the nursing home at once."'

'It really caused shock waves in Calcutta society,' said Kakoli to the assembled company. 'When they told her husband he said: "What baby? Bloody nonsense!" He was fifty-five years old.'

'You see,' continued Meenakshi, 'when she stopped having periods, she thought it was her menopause. She couldn't imagine she was going to have a baby.'

Maan, noticing his father's frozen face, began to laugh uncontrollably, and even Meenakshi graced him with a smile. The baby too appeared to be smiling, but it was probably just wind.

13.18

The baby and mother got along very well over the next couple of days. What was most surprising to Savita about the baby was her softness. She was almost unbearably soft, especially the soles of her feet, the inside of her elbows, the back of her neck—here she was even more amazingly, heartbreakingly tender! Sometimes she laid the baby beside her on the bed and looked at her admiringly. The baby appeared satisfied with life; she was quite a hungry baby, but not a noisy one. When she had had her fill, she would look at her mother with half-opened eyes: a snug, smug expression. Savita found that, being right-handed, it was easier to feed her from the left breast. This fact had never struck her before.

She had even begun to consider herself a mother now.

Cushioned by her mother, daughter, and sister in a feminine and loving world, Savita felt the days pass placidly and happily. But from time to time a wave of deep depression swept over her. Once this happened when it was raining outside and a couple of pigeons were cooing on the window ledge. Sometimes she would think of the student who had died in this very hospital a few days ago, and wonder about the world into which she had brought her daughter. Once, when she heard how Maan had dispatched the crazed monkey, she burst into tears. The depth of her sudden sadnesses was unaccountable.

Or perhaps it was not as unaccountable as it seemed to her. With Pran's heart trouble hanging over the family, they would always live under a shadow of uncertainty. Savita began to feel more and more that she had to learn a profession, no matter what Pran's father might say.

Notes passed between Pran and Savita as usual, but most of them these days were about suitable names for the baby. Both agreed that she should be named soon; it was not necessary to wait for her character to develop in order to pick a suitable name.

Everyone made suggestions of one kind or another. Eventually, Pran and Savita decided by correspondence on Maya. Its two simple syllables meant, among other things: the goddess Lakshmi, illusion, fascination, art, the goddess Durga, kindness, and the name of the mother of the Buddha. It also meant: ignorance, delusion, fraud, guile, and hypocrisy; but no one who named their daughter Maya ever paid any attention to these pejorative possibilities.

When Savita announced the baby's name to the family, there was an appreciative murmur from the dozen or so people in the room. Then Mrs Rupa Mehra said:

'You cannot name her Maya, and that is that.'

'Why ever not, Ma?' said Meenakshi. 'It's a very Bengali name, a very nice name.'

'Because it is just impossible,' said Mrs Rupa Mehra. 'Ask Pran's mother,' she added in Hindi.

Veena too, who, like Meenakshi, had just become an aunt by virtue of this baby and felt that she had some rights in the matter, thought the name was a good one. She turned to her mother in surprise.

But Mrs Mahesh Kapoor agreed with Mrs Rupa Mehra.

'No, Rupaji, you are quite right, it won't do.'

'But why, Ammaji?' asked Veena. 'Do you think Maya is inauspicious?'

'It isn't that, Veena. It's just that—as Savita's mother is thinking—you must not name a child after a living relative.'

Savita's aunt in Lucknow was called Maya.

No amount of arguing by the younger generation could budge either of the grandmothers.

'But this is gross superstition,' said Maan.

'Superstition or not, it is our way. You know, Veena, when you were young, Minister Sahib's mother did not even allow me to call you by your name. One should never call the eldest child by her real name, she said, and I had to obey.'

'So what did you call me?' said Veena.

'Bitiya, or Munni, or—I can't remember all the names I called you to get around it. But it was very hard to keep it up. Anyway, I think that is all blind belief. And when my mother-in-law passed away, I dropped it.'

'Well, if you call that blind belief, what do you think this is?' said Veena.

'This has reason to it. How can you scold the child without invoking your aunt? That is very bad. Even if you call her by some other name, it will still be Maya you are scolding in your heart.'

It was no use arguing. The parents were overruled, the name Maya had to be scratched, and the search for a new name began.

Pran, when Maan told him of the veto, took it philosophically.

'Well, I was never a Maya-vadi,' he said. 'I never believed that the whole universe was illusion. Certainly, my cough is real. Like Doctor Johnson, I could refute it thus. So what do the two grandmothers want her to be named?'

'I'm not sure,' said Maan. 'They only agreed on what was not acceptable.'

'This reminds me of my committee work,' said Pran. 'Well, Maan, you'd better rack your brains as well. And why not consult the magical masseur? He's never short of ideas.'

Maan promised to do so.

Sure enough, a few days later, when Savita was fit enough to go home with the baby, she received a card from Mr Maggu Gopal. The picture on the card was one of Lord Shiva complete with his family. In the card Maggu Gopal stated that he had known that Savita would have a daughter despite everyone's opinion to the contrary. He assured her that only the following three names were sufficiently auspicious, given what he had seen of her husband's hand: Parvati, Uma, and Lalita. And he asked whether Pran had replaced sugar with honey 'for all the daily necessaries'. He hoped for

Pran's speedy recovery, and reassured him once more that his married life would be a comedy.

Other cards came in as well, and letters of congratulation, and telegrams, many of them with stock phrase number 6: 'Best congratulations on new arrival'.

A couple of weeks after the baby's birth, it was decided by consensus to name her Uma. Mrs Rupa Mehra sat down with scissors and paste to make a grand congratulatory card to celebrate the baby's arrival. It had taken her a little while to accept the fact that she did not yet have a grandson; and now that she was happy with her granddaughter, she decided to give tangible expression to her pleasure.

Roses, a small, rather malignant-looking cherub, and a baby in a crib were pasted together, and a puppy and three golden stars completed the picture. Under the three stars the three letters of the baby's name were inscribed in red ink and green pencil.

The message inside was a rather prosaically formatted poem in Mrs Rupa Mehra's small and careful hand. She had read it about a year ago in an edifying volume, *The Fragrant Minute for Every Day* by a certain Wilhelmina Stitch—an appropriate name in view of Savita's present condition—and she had copied it out at that time into her small notebook. It was the poem for the 'Twelfth Day'. She was certain that it would draw from Savita's and Pran's eyes the same tears of gratitude and joy that it had drawn from her own. It read as follows:

THE LADY BABY

'A Lady Baby came to-day—' What words are quite so nice to say? They make one smile, they make one pray for Lady Baby's happiness. 'To-day a Lady Baby came.' We have not heard her winsome name, we can address her all the same, as Lady Baby-Come-to-Bless.

When Lady Baby came to earth, her home was filled with joy and mirth. There's not a jewel of half the worth of Lady Baby-to-Caress. We're glad that Lady Baby's here, for at this sunless time of year, there's nought that brings such warmth and cheer as Lady Baby's daintiness.

Hush! Lady Baby's fast asleep, the friendly fire-flames dance and leap and angel's wings above her sweep as on her eyes a kiss they press. 'A Lady Baby!' Lovely phrase, it means she'll have such gentle ways, and grow to goodness all her days—may God this Lady Baby bless!

13.19

Sir David Gower, the Managing Director of the Cromarty Group, looked through his gold-edged, half-moon spectacles at the short but confident young man standing in front of him. He had shown no sign of intimidation, which, in Sir David's experience, was unusual, given the vastness and plushness of his office, the great distance from the door to the desk which he had had to walk under scrutiny, and his own intimidating bulk and glower.

'Do sit down,' he said eventually.

Haresh sat down in the middle chair of the three facing Sir David across his desk.

'I've read Peary Loll Buller's note, and he has had the kindness to call me up as well. I didn't expect you quite so soon, but, well, here you are. You say you want a job. What are your qualifications? And where have you been working?'

'Just across the road, Sir David.'

'You mean at CLFC?'

'Yes. And before that I was at Middlehampton—that's where I studied footwear technology.'

'And why do you want to work with us?'

'I see James Hawley as an excellently run organization, in which a man like myself has a future.'

'In other words, you want to join us to better your own prospects?'

'Put like that, yes.'

'Well, that's no bad thing,' said Sir David in a sort of growl.

He looked at Haresh for a while. Haresh wondered what he was thinking. His glance did not appear to take in his clothing—slightly sweaty for having bicycled over—or his hair, just smoothed and combed back. Nor did it appear to look into his soul. It appeared to concentrate on his forehead.

'And what do you have to offer us?' said the Managing Director after a while.

'Sir, my results in England speak for themselves. And I have, in a short space of time, helped turn around CLFC—in terms both of orders and a sense of direction.'

Sir David raised his eyebrows. 'That is quite a claim,' he said. 'I thought Mukherji was the General Manager. Well, I think you should see John Clayton, our own General Manager.' He picked up the telephone.

'John, ah, you're still here. Good. I'm sending a young man, a Mr'—he glanced down at a piece of paper—'a Mr Khanna, to you. . . . Yes, the one old Peary Loll Buller phoned me about a few minutes ago when you were here. . . . Middlehampton. . . . Well, yes, if you think so. . . . No, I leave it to you.' He put down the phone, and wished Haresh good luck.

'Thank you very much, Sir David.'

'Well, whether we take you on or not depends on what Clayton thinks of you,' said Sir David Gower, and dismissed Haresh from his thoughts.

A letter arrived on Monday morning from James Hawley. It was signed by the General Manager John Clayton, and specified the terms they wished to offer Haresh, which were generous: Rs 325 as salary, and Rs 450 as 'dearness allowance'—an adjustment for inflation over the last few years. That the tail was bigger than the dog struck Haresh as odd but pleasant.

The injustice with which he had been treated by CLFC receded, the crawliness of Rao, the creepiness of Sen Gupta, the decent ineffectuality of Mukherji, the high-handedness of the distant boss Ghosh—and he began to think of his new future, which struck him as glowing. Perhaps some day he would sit on the other side of that huge mahogany desk. And with a job as good as this one, one that was not a cul-de-sac like his job at CLFC, he could embark on married life without any qualms.

Two letters in hand, he went to see Mukherji.

'Mr Mukherji,' he said, once they were both seated, 'I feel I should take you into confidence. I have applied for a job with James Hawley, and they have made me an offer. After last week's events you can imagine how I feel about continuing here. I would like your advice on what I should do.'

'Mr Khanna,' said Mr Mukherji quite unhappily, 'I am sorry to hear this. I assume that you must have applied some time ago.'

'I applied on Friday afternoon, and got the job within the hour.'

Mr Mukherji looked startled. If Haresh said so, however, it must be the truth.

'Here is the letter of appointment.'

The General Manager scanned it, and said, 'I see. Well, you have asked me for my advice. I can only say that I am sorry about the way that that order was taken out of your hands last week. It was not my doing. But I cannot accept your resignation myself—certainly not immediately. The matter will have to go to Bombay.'

'I am sure Mr Ghosh will agree.'

'I am sure he will,' agreed Mr Mukherji, who was his brother-in-law. 'But, well, it has to have his sanction before I can accept it.'

'At any rate,' said Haresh. 'I am tendering my resignation to you now.'

But when Mr Mukherji phoned him to tell him that Haresh was leaving, Mr Ghosh was livid. Haresh was important for the success of his Kanpur factory, and he was not willing to let him go. He was due to go to Delhi to procure a government order for army footwear, and he told Mr Mukherji to hold on to Haresh Khanna until he himself came to Kanpur immediately afterwards.

Upon his arrival he summoned Haresh and tore into him in the presence of Mukherji. His eyes were bulging, and he seemed almost berserk with anger, although he was far from incoherent.

'I gave you your very first job, Mr Khanna, when you arrived in India. And, if you recall, you gave me your assurance at the time that you would stay with us for two years, as long as we wanted you. Well, we do. Looking for another job is an underhand action on your part, and I refuse to let you go.'

Haresh coloured at Ghosh's words and manner. A word like 'underhand' was like a red rag to him. But Ghosh was an older man, and one whose business sense at least he admired. Besides, it was true that he had given him his first job. 'I do recall that conversation, Sir,' he said. 'But you might remember that you gave me certain assurances as well. You said, for one thing, that I should accept three hundred and fifty rupees at the time, because you would increase it once I had proved my worth to the organization. Well, I have certainly proved my worth to you, but you have not kept your side of the understanding.'

'If it is a question of money, there is no problem,' said Ghosh abruptly. 'We can accommodate you—we can match their offer.'

This was news to Haresh—and to Mukherji as well, who looked startled—but the word 'underhand' so rankled against him that he continued: 'I am afraid it is not merely money, Sir, it is the whole style of things.' He paused, then went on: 'James Hawley is a professional organization. I can make my way up that ladder in a way that I cannot in a family organization. I am hoping to get married, and I am sure you will see that I have to look to the future.'

'You are not leaving us,' said Ghosh. 'That is all I have to say.'

'We shall see about that,' said Haresh, very angry himself by Ghosh's high-handedness. 'I have a written offer, and you have my written resignation. I fail to see what you can do about it.' And he stood up, nodded wordlessly to his two superiors, and left.

The moment Haresh left the office, Ghosh phoned John Clayton, whom he had met a number of times in Delhi in a couple of ministries; both had been concerned with procuring government orders for their companies.

Ghosh told Clayton in no uncertain terms that he considered his action in 'pinching' his man to be unethical. He refused to countenance it, and he would not release Haresh. If necessary he would take the matter to court. This was an extremely unfair trade practice, and no way for a reputable British company to behave.

Mr Ghosh was related to various important civil servants and a politician or two—it was partly as a result of this that he had been able to get government orders for CLFC's shoes, which were not of the best quality. He was clearly a man who wielded a great deal of influence. At the moment he was also a very angry man, and he could create problems for James Hawley, indeed for the Cromarty Group as a whole, both in Kanpur and elsewhere.

A couple of days later Haresh got another letter from James Hawley. The crucial sentence read: 'You will have to get clearance from your present employers before we can confirm our offer.' There had been no question in the previous letter of the necessity of any confirmation, and it was clear that James Hawley had buckled under pressure. No doubt Ghosh now believed that Haresh would have no choice but to come to him cap in hand and beg for his old job again. But for Haresh one thing was certain: he would not work one day longer in CLFC. He would rather starve than cringe.

The next day he went to the factory to collect his things and unscrew his brass nameplate from his door. Mukherji happened to pass by as he was doing this, and murmured an offer of help for the future. Haresh shook his head. He spoke to Lee and apologized for the fact that he was leaving so soon after hiring him. He then spoke to the workmen in his department. They were upset and angry at the treatment meted out by Ghosh to a man they had grown to like and respect and whom they had even begun to see—in a curious way—as their champion; certainly they had got more work and more money since he had joined the company, even if he worked them, like himself, very hard. They even offered, astonishingly, to go on strike for him. Haresh could hardly believe this, and was touched almost to the point of tears, but told them that they should do nothing of the sort. 'I would have been leaving in any case,' he said, 'and whether the management behaves nicely or nastily to me makes no difference. I am only sorry that I have to leave you to the incompetence of someone like Rao.' Rao was standing nearby when he said this, but Haresh was past caring.

To take his mind off things, he went to Lucknow for a day to visit Simran's sister. And three days later, seeing nothing further in Kanpur to keep him, and having very little money, he left for Delhi to stay with his family and to see what he might find there. He could not decide whether to write to Lata to tell her the news. He was deeply disheartened; he could see all his prospects of happiness receding into nothingness now that he was unemployed.

But this mood dissolved somewhat after a few days. Kalpana Gaur sympathized with him, his old St Stephen's friends took him up into their jovial company almost as soon as he got to Delhi. And, being basically an optimist—or at any rate having an abundance, perhaps a superabundance, of self-confidence—he refused to believe, even in these hard times, that nothing at all would turn up.

13.20

His own foster-father was understanding, and told him not to be disheartened. But Umesh Uncle, a close friend of the family, who loved to dispense wisdom, told him he had made a big mistake to let pride get in the way of good sense.

'You think you can walk down the street and job offers will drop down on you like ripe mangoes,' he remarked.

Haresh did not say anything. Umesh Uncle always got his goat.

Besides, he thought that his uncle, although he had a Rai Bahadur in front of his name, and an O.B.E. behind it, was an idiot.

Rai Bahadur Umesh Chand Khatri, O.B.E., one of the six brothers of a Punjabi family, was a good-looking man: fair, with delicate features. He was married to the adopted daughter of a very rich and cultured man, who, having no sons, had decided to get a son-in-law to live in the house. Umesh Chand Khatri's only qualifications were his good looks. He managed his father-in-law's estate after a fashion, read perhaps one book a year out of his vast library, and gave him three grandchildren, including two boys.

He had never worked in his life, but felt compelled to tender advice to anyone within earshot. However, when the Second World War broke out, circumstances contrived to give him a fortune. He had access to the Adarsh Condiment Company, and he got government contracts for the manufacture of condiment powder, including curry powder, for the Indian troops. On the basis of this he minted money. He was created a Rai Bahadur 'in recognition of war efforts', became Chairman of the Adarsh Condiment Company, and continued to dispense advice even more insufferably to everyone except Haresh's foster-father, who (being his not very tolerant friend) would tell him periodically to shut up.

Umesh Chand Khatri's grouse against Haresh, whom he loved to needle, was the fact that Haresh was always smartly turned out. Umesh Chand believed that he and his own two sons should be the smartest and most elegant of all his acquaintances. Once, just before he left for England, Haresh had indulged himself by buying a silk handkerchief for thirteen rupees from the Army and Navy Stores in Connaught Place. Umesh Uncle had rebuked him publicly for extravagance.

Now that Haresh was down on his luck, Umesh Uncle said to him:

'So—you think you've done a clever thing—coming back to Delhi to loaf around?'

'I had no choice,' replied Haresh. 'There was no point to my remaining in Kanpur.'

Umesh Uncle laughed shortly. 'You young men are too cocksure, too happy to drop perfectly good jobs. We'll see what happens to all your bravado in two or three months.'

Haresh knew that his money would not last even as long as that. He got annoyed. 'I'll have a job—as good or better than the one I've given up—within a month,' he said—indeed, almost snapped.

'You're a fool,' said Umesh Uncle with genial contempt. 'Jobs are not easy to get.'

His tone and certainty got under Haresh's skin. That afternoon he wrote to several companies and filled in a number of applications, including one for a government job in Indore. He had already applied in vain a number of times to the great Praha Shoe Company. Now he applied once again. Praha, originally a Czech company, and still largely run by Czechs, was one of the biggest shoe manufacturers in the country, and prided itself on the quality of its products. If Haresh could get a decent job at the Praha Shoe factory either in Brahmpur or in Calcutta, he would have achieved two things at once: the reattainment of his self-respect, and proximity to Lata. Umesh Uncle's taunts rang in his ears, as did Ghosh's accusations of underhandedness.

It was a meeting with Mr Mukherji that gave Haresh a contact in the Praha world. Someone told Haresh that his old boss was in town. Haresh went to see him. He had no grudge against Mukherji, who he felt was a decent man, if not a very courageous one. Despite his brother-in-law's obdurate attitude to Haresh, Mukherji felt bad about what had happened. He had previously mentioned to Haresh that Mr Khandelwal—the Chairman of the Praha Shoe Company, and, very remarkably, not a Czech but an Indian—was in town on business. Haresh, who knew no one in the Praha organization, felt that this was a heaven-sent opportunity to try his luck with them—or at least to get an answer to his many requests and letters. He told Mukherji that he would be grateful if he would introduce him to Mr Khandelwal.

Mukherji took Haresh along late one evening to the Imperial Hotel, where Mr Khandelwal always stayed when in Delhi. In fact, Mr Khandelwal always stayed in the Moghul Suite, the fanciest suite of all. He was a relaxed sort of man, of medium height, running both to fat and to the beginning of grey hair. He was dressed in kurta and dhoti. Apparently, he was even more fond of paan than Haresh; he chewed three at a time.

Haresh could not at first believe that this man sitting in a dhoti on the sofa was the legendary Mr Khandelwal. But when he saw how everyone scurried around him, some of them actually trembling while handing him papers which he quickly scanned and commented on, usually in a couple of words, Haresh got a sense both of his acuity and of his undoubted authority. One short, eager Czech, moving around in a most deferential manner, took down notes whenever Mr Khandelwal wanted something done or checked or reported on.

When Mr Khandelwal noticed Mr Mukherji he smiled and welcomed him in Bengali. Despite being a Marwari, Mr Khandelwal, having lived in Calcutta all his life, was fluent in Bengali; in fact he conducted meetings with trade union leaders from the Prahapore factory near Calcutta entirely in Bengali.

'What can I do for you, Mukherji Shaib?' he said, and took a gulp of whisky.

'This young man, who has been working for us, is now looking for a job. He wanted to see if Praha could give him one. He has excellent academic qualifications in footwear technology, and I can vouch for him in all other respects.'

Mr Khandelwal smiled benevolently and, looking now not at Mr Mukherji but at Haresh, exclaimed: 'Why are you being so generous as to give me such a good man?'

Mr Mukherji looked a little shamefaced. He said, quietly: 'He has been hard done by, and I do not have the courage to talk to my brother-in-law about it. I fear, anyway, that it would do no good; his mind is entirely made up.'

'What do you want me to do?' asked Mr Khandelwal of Haresh.

'Sir, I have applied for a job with Praha several times, and have sent several letters, but have not had any proper reply at all. If you were to see that my application is at least considered, I'm sure that my qualifications and work experience will get me a job with the firm.'

'Take his application,' said Mr Khandelwal, and the dapper Czech took it and jotted something down on his pad.

'So—' said Mr Khandelwal, 'you will hear from Praha in less than a week.'

But Haresh, though he did indeed hear within a few days from Praha, was once again offered by the Personnel Office a job at Rs 28 a week: a pittance which succeeded in doing nothing but making him angry.

However, it reassured Umesh Uncle. 'I told you that you would not get a job if you left this one. But you never took my advice; you considered yourself so smart. Look at you now, sponging off others, rather than working, like a man should.'

Haresh controlled himself before replying: 'Thank you for your advice yet again, Umesh Uncle. It is as valuable as it has always been.'

Umesh Uncle, faced by Haresh's sudden meekness, felt that his spirit had been broken, and that he would be an easier recipient for his counsel from then on. 'It's good that you've seen sense at last,' he told him. 'A man should never have too high an opinion of himself.'

Haresh nodded, his thoughts anything but meek.

13.21

When, some weeks previously, Lata had received Haresh's first letter—three pages written in his small, forward-slanting hand on his blue writing pad—she had replied to it in a friendly way. Half of Haresh's letter had been concerned with trying to get a contact at the Praha Shoe Company to present his application to. Mrs Rupa Mehra had mentioned when they had all met in Kanpur that she knew someone who knew someone who might be able to help. In fact, it had turned out to be more difficult than she had imagined, and nothing had come of it. Haresh could not have known at the time that a strange series of events and the sympathy of Mr Mukherji would have got him to meet Mr Khandelwal, the Chairman of Praha, himself.

The other half of the letter had been personal. Lata had read it over a number of times. Unlike Kabir's letter, it had made her smile:

> This business being over [Haresh had written], let me hope in the usual way that you had a comfortable journey home and that you were missed by all who met you after such a long absence from Brahmpur. I hope the town has recovered from the disaster at the Pul Mela.
>
> I must thank you for your visit to Cawnpore and the nice time we spent together. There was none of that bashfulness or undue modesty and I am convinced that we can be very friendly if nothing else. I quite appreciate your frankness and the way of putting things. I must admit that I have met few English girls who could speak English quite as well as you do. These qualities coupled with your way of dressing and personality make you a person far above the average. I think Kalpana was right in her praise of you. These may all seem flattering remarks but I write as I feel.
>
> I have just today sent your photograph to my foster-father along with my impressions of you formed during our brief hours together. I shall let you know what he has to say. . . .

Lata tried to work out what exactly it was about this letter that she liked. Haresh's English was slightly odd. 'In the usual way' and 'the way of putting things', to take just two out of about ten examples in those three short paragraphs, jarred against her sense of the language. And yet the whole was not unpleasing. It was pleasant to be praised by someone who did not seem practised at praising—and who, for all his own abundant self-confidence, clearly admired her.

The more she read the letter, the more she liked it. But she waited a while before replying:

Dear Haresh,

I was very glad to get your letter, as you had indicated at the station that you wanted to write to me. I believe that this is a good way of getting to know each other.

We have not had much luck with the Praha Shoe Company, but the reason for that is that we are not at present in Calcutta and, apart from it being the Head Office of the company, Ma's acquaintance lives there. But Ma has written to him, and let's see what happens. She has also mentioned the matter to Arun, my brother, who lives in Calcutta, and he may be able to help. Let's keep our fingers crossed.

It would be good if you were in Prahapore, for then when I am in Calcutta over the New Year holidays, we could see much more of each other in the ordinary course of things. It was good to meet you in Kanpur. I am very glad I broke journey there. I must thank you again for the trouble you took at Lucknow Station to see us safely into a compartment and to install our luggage there. We had a very comfortable journey back, and Pran—my brother-in-law—was there to greet us at the other end.

I am glad to know that you have written to your foster-father. I shall be keen to know what he thinks and says.

I must admit that it was interesting going around the tannery. I liked your Chinese designer. The way he spoke Hindi was delightful.

I like to see men with ambition like you—you should make good. It is also refreshing to meet a man who doesn't smoke—I can assure you I admire it—because I think it requires a lot of character. I liked you because you were so frank and clear in all your statements—so different from the young men one generally meets in Calcutta, but not only in Calcutta—so polished, so charming, yet so insincere. Your sincerity is refreshing.

You did mention when we met that you had been in Brahmpur very briefly earlier this year, but we got on to other subjects and did not follow this one up. So Ma (and not only Ma, I should admit) was astonished to find that you already know at least two members of our family. Pran mentioned he had met you at a party. In case you don't remember him, he is a thin, tall lecturer in the English Department. It is his address that you have just written to. And then there is Kedarnath Tandon—who is Pran's jijaji—which makes him my jijaji's jijaji, but that is (in the Brahmpur context, and perhaps in your Delhi context too) a fairly close relation. His son Bhaskar has apparently just had a letter from you as well, even shorter than the one you sent me. You will be sorry to hear that he was slightly injured in the Pul Mela stampede, but now appears to be almost fully recovered. Veena mentioned how happy he was to get the postcard and the information it contained.

Brahmpur is unpleasantly hot these days and I am a little concerned for my sister Savita, who is expecting a baby very soon. But Ma is here to take care of things, and there could not be a better or more solicitous husband than Pran.

I have not quite settled back into my studies, but have decided, a little against my wishes but on the advice of a friend, to take a part in *Twelfth Night*, which is our Annual Day play this year. I have the part of Olivia, and am busy learning my lines, which takes up a lot of my time. My friend came to the audition to lend me moral support, but ended up with the part of Maria, which in a way serves her right. Ma, being of the old school, has very mixed feelings about my acting. What do you think?

I look forward to your next letter—do write about yourself. I shall be interested in whatever you have to say.

I'd better say goodbye, for already this letter has grown considerably and I presume you must be yawning by now.

Ma sends you her best wishes, and I wish you all the best,

Lata

There was no mention in Lata's letter of Haresh's opinionatedness, his pronunciation of Kanpur as 'Cawnpore', the stench of the tannery, paan, co-respondent shoes, or the photograph of Simran on his desk. It was not that Lata had forgotten them, but rather that the memory of some of them had grown dimmer, some of them no longer appeared to her in quite such a negative light, and one of them was not something she felt she would ever want to mention—unless it became necessary to do so.

But Haresh brought it up himself in his next letter. He mentioned that one of the things that he had most liked about Lata was her own directness, and that this emboldened him to speak freely, especially since she had asked him to tell her about himself. He talked at some length about how important Simran had been in his life, how he had despaired of finding anyone who could mean anything to him after he had realized that there was no hope for him there, and how she—Lata—had appeared at what was a crucial time for him. He now suggested that she write a note to Simran so that the two of them could get better acquainted. He had already written to Simran about his meeting with her, but because the only photograph that he had of her had been with his foster-father at the time, he was unable to enclose it in his letter to Simran. He wrote:

> . . . I hope you will forgive me for talking about Simran so much but she is a wonderful girl and you two are likely to be good friends. If you should like to write to her, here is her address. You cannot write directly to her as her people might intercept the letter, so address the letter to Miss Pritam Kaura, at the address at the bottom of this letter. I should like you to know me well, specially my past life before you make up your mind, and Simran is part and parcel of it.
>
> Sometimes it seems to me that meeting you is too good to be true. I was at a dead end, I knew not what to do and where to look for company. Poor Simran, she is so placed that she cannot express her feelings, her people are the conservative type—nothing like your mother, even if she has mixed feelings about plays. You came into my life like a brightening influence, like someone for whom I have the desire to become better.
>
> You have used very many compliments with regard to my sincerity—given the circumstances I have lived in, one could not afford to be otherwise. Along with sincerity and frankness there is the worse side of it—just because one cannot hurt someone else one postpones a decision to remove someone's illusions—in the long run one has to suffer for it. When we know each other better and can forgive and forget I shall explain this statement fully. I will give you a hint—perhaps I had better not. Because there are some parts of my life that are far from perfect, and for which you might find it hard to forgive me. Perhaps I have said too much already.
>
> Anyway, I have to thank Kalpana for our chance meeting. But for her we would never have known each other.
>
> Please send me the impression of your foot, because I wish to design something for you—maybe the Chinese man, Mr Lee, can help! Would you like a low sandal for the summer or do you wear the usual High Heels?
>
> Also, I hardly ever see the photograph you gave me because it

does the postal rounds. Please do send me another photograph of yourself, recently taken. I will not send that one around. Today I tried to get a frame for your photograph but failed to get it. I am therefore waiting for your next photograph before I expend the money for a good frame. Do you mind if I keep your photograph on my table? It may tend to keep me more ambitious. As I look at your photograph, just back from my father, I find that smile on the brink very attractive. You certainly have a poise which makes you very attractive to me, but then you must, I am sure, be knowing it yourself—others will have told you all that before me.

My father appears to be in favour of a match.

Remember me to your mother and to Pran, Kedarnath and his wife, and Bhaskar. I find it very hard to think of that boy being hurt in that stampede. I trust he is all right by now.

Affectionately,
Haresh

Lata was unsettled by this letter. Everything from the photograph to the foot impression worried her, and the hints about his past life troubled her too. She could not understand how he could expect her to write to Simran. But because she liked him, she replied as kindly as she could. With Pran's hospitalization, Savita's imminent baby, and the daily rehearsals with Kabir all weighing on her heart, she could manage no more than a couple of pages, and when she reread the letter it appeared to her to be nothing but a linked chain of refusals. She did not encourage him to spill out whatever he was hinting at; indeed she did not mention it at all. She did say that she could not write to Simran until she felt more confident about her feelings (though she was pleased that he had trusted her enough to confide in her about so many things). She was shy about her feet, which she did not think looked very attractive. And as for the photograph:

To tell you the truth, it is real agony for me, being photographed in a studio or by people from a studio. I know it's very silly of me, but I feel dreadful. I think the last photograph that Ma got taken of me—before the one that I gave you—was taken about six years ago, and it wasn't at all good. The one you have was taken in Calcutta this year under compulsion. For the last three years I have been promising to send one in for my old school magazine; really I felt quite ashamed of myself when, just before coming to Kanpur, I met one of my old nuns and she confronted me again about it. At least now I have been able to send her one. But I can't go through that ordeal again. As for the 'smile on the brink' among other things—altogether, I think you flatter me. This is paradoxical, because I think of you as a very sincere and frank sort of person, and surely sincerity and flattery don't go together! Anyway, anything that's ever told me, I have learned to take with a large pinch of salt.

There was a long pause between this letter and Haresh's next one, and Lata felt that her triple refusal must have hurt him too much. She discussed with Malati the question of which of the three refusals had upset Haresh the most, and their discussion of this helped her make light of the matter.

13.22

One day, when Kabir had acted particularly well, Lata told Malati: 'I'm going to tell him afterwards how good I thought his acting was. It's the only way to break the ice.'

Malati said: 'Lata, don't be foolish, it won't be breaking the ice, it'll be releasing the steam. Just leave well enough alone.'

But after the rehearsal was over, when the three of them, among others, were milling around outside the auditorium, Kabir came up to Lata and said: 'Could you give this to Bhaskar? My father thought he might find it interesting.' It was a kite with an unusual shape: a sort of lozenge with streamers behind it.

'Yes, of course,' said Lata, a little uneasily. 'But you know he's no longer at Prem Nivas. He's gone back to his parents' house in Misri Mandi.'

'I hope it's not too much trouble—'

'No, it isn't, Kabir—it isn't at all—we can't thank you enough for what you've done for him.'

Both of them were silent. Malati hung around for a while, thinking that Lata might be grateful if she interposed herself into any intense conversation that Kabir might start. But after a glance or two at Lata, she judged that Lata would be happier if she could talk to him by herself. So she took her leave of both of them—though Kabir had not, in fact, greeted her.

'Why have you been avoiding me?' said Kabir to Lata in a low voice the moment Malati had gone.

Lata shook her head, unable to look at his face. But there was no avoiding a conversation that would not be in the least casual.

'What do you expect?' she said.

'Are you still angry with me—about that?'

'No—I'm getting used to it. Today you acted very well.'

'I don't mean the play,' said Kabir. 'I meant our last real meeting.'

'Oh, that—'

'Yes, that.' He was determined to have it out, it seemed.

'I don't know—so much has happened since then.'

'Nothing has happened except a vacation.'

'I meant, I've thought so much about things—'

'Do you think I haven't?' he said.

'Kabir, please—what I meant was that I've thought about us as well.'

'And no doubt you still think I was unreasonable.' Kabir sounded slightly amused.

Lata looked at his face, then turned away. She didn't say anything.

'Let's take a walk,' said Kabir. 'At least it'll give us something to do in our silences.'

'All right,' said Lata, shaking her head.

They walked along the path that led from the auditorium to the centre of the campus—towards the jacaranda grove, and beyond that, to the cricket nets.

'Do I deserve an answer?' asked Kabir.

'It was I who was unreasonable,' said Lata after a while.

This took the wind out of Kabir's sails. He looked at her in astonishment as she continued:

'You were quite right. I was being unfair and unreasonable and everything else you said. It's not possible—it never was—but not because of time and careers and studies and other practical things.'

'Why then?' said Kabir.

'Because of my family,' said Lata. 'However much they irritate me and constrain me, I can't give them up. I know that now. So much has happened. I can't give up my mother—'

Lata halted, thinking of what effect this last remark might have on Kabir, but decided that she had to explain herself now or never.

'I just see how much she cares about everything and how she would be affected by this,' she said.

'By this!' said Kabir. 'You mean, by you and me.'

'Kabir, do you know of any mixed marriages that have worked out?' said Lata. But even as she said it she thought that perhaps she had gone too far. Kabir had never explicitly mentioned marriage—he wanted to be with her, to be close to her—but marriage? Perhaps he had implied it when he had asked her to wait for a year or two—when he had mentioned his plans for future study, for the Foreign Service, for Cambridge. But now he didn't retreat from the word.

'Do you know of any that haven't?' he said.

'I don't know of any at all in our family,' said Lata.

'Unmixed marriages aren't always ideal either.'

'I know, Kabir; I've heard—' said Lata, miserably, and with such sympathy that Kabir understood that she was referring to his mother.

He stopped, and said:

'Does that also have something to do with it?'

'I can't say—' said Lata. 'I don't know—I'm sure my mother would be affected by that as well.'

'So what you are saying is that my heredity and my religion are insuperable factors—and it doesn't matter if you care for me or not.'

'Don't put it like that, Kabir,' cried Lata. 'That's not how I feel.'

'But it's the basis on which you're acting.'

Lata was unable to reply.

'Don't you care for me?' asked Kabir.

'I do, I do—'

'Then why didn't you write? Why don't you talk to me—'

'Just because of that—' she said, completely overcome.

'Will you always love me? Because I know I will—'

'Oh, please stop, Kabir—I can't take this—' she cried. What she might just as well have said was that she was trying to convince herself as much as him that their feelings were nothing but futile.

He would not allow her to do this, however.

'But why should we stop meeting?' he persisted.

'Meeting? Kabir, you don't see the point. Where would it lead to?'

'Does it have to lead to something?' he said. 'Can't we just spend time together?' After a pause: 'Do you "mistrust my intentions"?'

Lata remembered their kisses in a daze of unhappiness. So intense was the memory that she half mistrusted her own intentions. 'No,' she said, more quietly, 'but wouldn't it all just be miserable?'

She realized that his questions were leading to further questions on her own part and in her own mind, and that every one of these caused a further knot in the huge tangle. Her heart ached for him, but everything told her that it had to come to nothing. She had wanted to tell him that she was writing to someone else, but she could not bring herself to do so now because of the pain she knew it would cause him.

They were passing by the steps outside the examination hall. Kabir looked up at them and frowned. The light was low, and the trees and benches below were casting long shadows on the grass.

'So what do we do?' he said, his mouth set in an attempt at decisiveness.

'I don't know,' said Lata. 'We have to spend some time together now, in a way, at least on stage. At least for another month. We've trapped ourselves into it.'

'Can't you wait for another year?' he said with sudden desperation.

'What will change?' she said despondently, and walked off the path, away from him, towards a bench. She was almost too tired to think—emotionally exhausted, exhausted from watching over the baby, exhausted from the effort of acting—and she sat down on the bench, her head resting on her arms. She was too tired even for tears.

It was the same bench under the gulmohur tree on which she had sat after the exam. He didn't know what to make of this. Should he console her again? Was she even conscious of where she was sitting? She looked so forlorn that he wanted more than anything to put his arms around her. He could sense how close she was to tears.

Both had said what was inevitable, yet Kabir could not feel that they were adversaries. He felt that he had to try and understand her. The pressure of the family, the extended family that enforced a slow and strong acceptance on its members, was something that with his own father and mother he had never had to face. Lata had moved away from him in these last months, and was perhaps already out of reach. If he went up to her now and helped her overcome her unhappiness, could he retrieve some of what was lost? Or would he only burden her with a further and more painful vulnerability?

What was she thinking? He stood there in the late light, looking at her beyond his own long shadow. Her head had not moved from her hands. The strange kite was resting on the bench beside her. She looked weary and unreachable. After a minute or two he walked away sadly.

13.23

Lata sat still for about fifteen minutes, then got up, taking the kite with her. It was almost dark. She had found it hard to think. But now, through her own pain, she began to feel a sympathy for the difficulties of others. She thought of Pran and his anxieties. She reminded herself that it had been a long time since she had written to Varun.

She also thought, strangely enough, of her last letter to Haresh, and how curt she had been on the matter of Simran, which obviously had meant a great deal to him. Poor Haresh—he too had been pursuing an impossible relationship, and here too the difficulty was a similar one.

As for herself, there was another rehearsal tomorrow. Would she face that with more or less trepidation than before? How would it be for Kabir? At least they had talked; she would not be tensely anticipating the terrible moment. Anyway, perhaps it had been less terrible to suffer it than to await it. But how disheartening it had been. Or was it so disheartening after all in the scheme of things?

That evening was a quiet one: her mother, Pran, Savita, the baby, and herself. One of the topics of discussion was Haresh and why he hadn't written yet.

In general, Mrs Rupa Mehra wanted to read every letter that came from Haresh, but Lata only passed on his news and greetings, keeping his agreeable comments to herself, and finding herself unable to share with her mother the more troubling ones.

Haresh had in fact been a little disappointed by Lata's letter, but what had kept him from replying almost immediately was not this disappointment but his sudden status as a workless man. He was very worried about the effect that this news would have on Lata—and even more so on her mother, who, for all the goodwill she bore him, was—he judged—exacting and pragmatic in her criteria for a suitable boy for her daughter.

But when a week had passed, and James Hawley, despite his appeals, had not rectified their injustice, and Delhi too had borne no immediate fruit except Mr Mukherji's promise of a meeting with Mr Khandelwal, he felt he could keep up his silence no longer, and wrote to Lata.

As it happened, Mrs Rupa Mehra had received a letter from Kalpana Gaur the day before Haresh's letter finally arrived, and had come to know that he was out of a job. With Pran, Savita and the baby all back home, there was a great deal to be done, but this latest and somewhat shocking news occupied Mrs Rupa Mehra's mind more than anything else. She talked about it to everyone including Meenakshi and Kakoli, who had dropped by to baby-gaze. She could not understand how Haresh could have dropped his job 'just like that'; her husband had always believed in having two birds in the hand before leaving one in the bush. Mrs Rupa Mehra began to worry about Haresh in more ways than one; and she began to express her reservations to Lata.

'Oh, he's bound to write soon,' said Lata, rather too off-handedly for Mrs Rupa Mehra's taste.

She was proved to be correct the next day, sooner than she herself had expected.

When Mrs Rupa Mehra saw an envelope in Haresh's by now familiar handwriting in the mail, she insisted that Lata open it immediately and read out its contents to her. Lata refused. Kakoli and Meenakshi, delighted to be in on the scene, snatched the letter from the table and began to tease Lata. Lata snatched it back from Kakoli, rushed into her room, and locked the door. She did not emerge for more than an hour. She read the letter, and replied to it without consulting anyone. Mrs Rupa Mehra was extremely annoyed by her daughter's insubordination, and also at Meenakshi and Kakoli.

'Think of Pran,' she said. 'This excitement is not good for his heart.'

Kakoli sang out, so that the sound could be heard on the other side of the locked door:

> 'Sweetest Lata, have a heart!
> Come and kiss me. Don't be tart.'

When she heard no response to this crass creation, she continued:

> 'Let me kiss your hands, my queen:
> Softest pigskin I have seen.'

Mrs Rupa Mehra was about to shout at Kakoli, but the baby began yowling and distracted everyone on that side of the door. Lata continued to read in noisy peace.

Haresh's letter was as straightforward as usual. After mentioning the bad news, he went on to write:

It can be no easy time for you with Pran's illness and by now maybe his baby too, so I feel sorry to burden you with the news I have given above. But I had to write to you today under the very great stress of circumstances. So far I have heard nothing by way of reconsideration from Mr. Clayton of James Hawley, and I am now not quite so hopeful that anything will happen in that direction. It was a fine job fetching Rs. 750/- per month all told, but I have not yet lost hopes entirely. I feel that they will realize the injustice of the whole thing. But perhaps with my resignation from CLFC I have indeed fallen between two stools. Mr. Mukherji, the General Manager, is a fine man but Mr. Ghosh, it seems, is dead set against me.

Yesterday I was with Kalpana for over two hours when you were the only topic of discussion. I do not know how much of my feelings I could hide, for the thought of you was exciting.

Excuse this scribbling pad. I have none other at my disposal at the moment. Kalpana says she has written to your mother about my news, and that I must write to you today—and I have been feeling the same myself.

I have an interview later in the month in Indore (with the State Public Service Commission) for a Small Scale Industry job. And it may be that the Praha matter will work out. At least if I can meet Mr. Khandelwal through the good offices of Mr. Mukherji, I am sure I will get a job interview in Calcutta. There are however a few things that you shall have to decide:

1. Whether you would like me to go to Calcutta via Brahmpur, given so many different factors including your brother-in-law's illness.

2. Whether in my unemployed position you think I am the same as before—i.e. whether you think you could be quite happy in considering me as someone you could care for.

I hope that your mother does not take this too seriously—there are other jobs in the offing I am sure, and it will not take too long to fix up.

Somehow I feel there is a lot of good in my present position—being unemployed gives one a better insight into human character and gives the right value to the right things. I hope Pran is better. Remember me to the family. I shall write again soon.

Yours,
Haresh

13.24

Nothing could have brought out Lata's warmth and tenderness more effectively than this letter. She felt very bad for Haresh, particularly at the thought that there might be a great deal of anxiety behind his brave front. If she had problems, so had he, and far more pressing ones. Yet instead of allowing himself to get depressed by his misfortune, he claimed to see advantages in it. Lata felt a little ashamed of herself for not behaving in a more robust manner in the face of emotional adversity.

She wrote back:

> My dear Haresh,
>
> Your letter came today and I am replying immediately. Yesterday Ma got a letter from Kalpana. Ever since then I have been wanting to write to you, but I felt I couldn't till I had heard the news directly from you. You must believe that it doesn't make any difference to me. Affection doesn't depend on things like jobs. It is unfortunate that you should have missed such a good chance at James Hawley—it really is a very good firm—I should think almost the best. Anyway, don't worry. Everything happens for the best—and, as you say, there is still hope—nothing like going on trying. I feel sure something will emerge.

Here Lata paused and looked out of the bedroom window before continuing. But it was his problems she had to address, not her own, and she continued to write before thoughts could crowd too closely in on her:

> Perhaps, Haresh, you didn't do a very wise thing in not letting your firm know that you were trying elsewhere. Perhaps you should have gone through them. Anyway, let's forget about it—it's all in the past now. The unkindness of people only hurts if we continue to remember it. Now that you are out of a job, perhaps you should try for the best rather than the first that comes your way. Maybe it's worthwhile waiting a little.
>
> You ask if I want you to come to Brahmpur on your way to Calcutta. It would be good to talk to you again. I hope you have not lost your smile. It doesn't sound so from your letter, anyway. You have a very pleasant smile—when you are amused your eyes disappear altogether—and it would be a pity if you lost it.

Here Lata paused again. What on earth am I writing? she asked herself. Is this too much? Then she just shrugged, told herself she wouldn't correct it, and wrote on:

The only problem is that the house is in chaos at the moment, and even if you were to live in a hotel, you would see us at a very confused time. Also, my brother Arun's wife and sister-in-law are here, and though I like them very much, they will not give either of us a moment of peace. And then my afternoons are taken up with rehearsals, which put me in a very confused state. I don't know if I'm myself or one of Shakespeare's creatures. Ma also is in a peculiar mood. All in all, it is not a good time for us to see each other. I hope you do not think that I am trying to put you off.

I am glad that Mr Mukherji has been so kind and understanding. I hope he is successful in helping you.

Pran looks much better for his three weeks in hospital, and the constant presence of the baby—who has been named Uma by the whole family at a sort of board meeting—does him a world of good. He sends his regards to you, as does everyone else here. Ma was worried to get your news from Kalpana, but not exactly in the way you think. She was more worried because she thought I was worried, and she kept telling me not to worry, that everything would be all right. I was only worried because I thought you must be very upset—especially as you hadn't written for a while. So you see it was a sort of vicious circle. I am happy that you haven't lost any of your optimism and are not bitter. I hate people to wear martyred airs—just as I dislike self-pity. It is the cause of too much unhappiness.

Please keep me informed about everything that happens, and write soon. No one else has lost their faith in you, except your Umesh Uncle, who never had it anyway, so you mustn't lose it in yourself.

Affectionately,
Lata

13.25

Lata sent the letter off with Mansoor to be posted at the general post office on his way to the market.

Mrs Rupa Mehra was displeased that she had not been allowed to read either the letter or the response.

'I'll let you read his letter, Ma, if you insist,' said Lata. 'But my reply's gone off so there's no question of reading that.'

Haresh's letter had contained far less of a personal nature than usual, and was therefore showable. Under 'the very great stress of circumstances'—or possibly because of Lata's short response to the subject—Haresh had omitted to bring up the question of Simran again.

Meanwhile, Kakoli had got hold of Mrs Rupa Mehra's card to Pran and Savita, and was enjoying herself, mouthing 'winsome' and 'dainty' to the helpless Lady Baby, and reformulating the lines while kissing Uma on the forehead.

'Hush! Lady Baby's fast asleep, the friendly fire-flames dance and leap and burning her to ash they sweep across the Lady Baby's dress.'

'How horrible!' said Mrs Rupa Mehra.

'A Lady Baby burned today—Her dainty soul has flown away—God's called her back to frisk and play—and that's one Lady Baby less.'

Kakoli giggled. 'Don't worry, Ma, we won't light a fire in Brahmpur in August. It's not a sunless time of year.'

'Meenakshi, you must control your sister.'

'No one can do that, Ma. She's hopeless.'

'You are always saying that with Aparna also.'

'Am I?' said Meenakshi absently. 'Oh, that reminds me, I think I'm pregnant.'

'What?' cried everyone (except the Lady Baby).

'Yes—I've missed my period—it's far too late to be merely delayed. So you may get your grandson after all, Ma.'

'Oh!' said Mrs Rupa Mehra, not knowing what to think. After a pause she added: 'Does Arun know?'

An abstracted look appeared on Meenakshi's face. 'No, not yet,' she said. 'I suppose I'll have to tell him. Should I send him a telegram? No, such things are best done in person. Anyway, I'm tired of Brahmpur. There's no Life here.' She had begun to pine once again for canasta, mah-jongg, the Shady Ladies and the bright lights. About the only lively person in Brahmpur was Maan, and he appeared far too rarely. Mr and Mrs Maitra, her hosts, were too deadly for words. As for the Rudhia riff-raff—words failed her. Besides, Lata appeared to be too immersed in this cobbler and his concerns to be vulnerable to hints about Amit.

'What do you say, Kuku?'

'Say?' said Kuku. 'I'm flabbergasted. When did you know?'

'I meant, about going back to Calcutta.'

'Oh, all right,' said Kakoli obligingly. It wasn't as if she wasn't enjoying herself here. But she missed Cuddles, and Hans, the telephone, the two cooks, the car, and even the family. 'I'm ready to leave whenever you want. But why are you looking so thoughtful?'

It was a look that Meenakshi was to wear off and on for quite a while. When exactly had she managed to get pregnant?

And with whom?

13.26

Haresh was disappointed that he had not been encouraged to stop in Brahmpur on his way to Calcutta or asked to visit Lata's brothers in Calcutta despite the fact that they were surely going to be his future brothers-in-law, but the tone of understanding in Lata's letter gave him great consolation among his uncertainties. The letter from the Praha Shoe Company reiterating their offer to him of a job at Rs 28 a week was such a pathetic response to his application that he couldn't believe that Mr Khandelwal had had anything to do with it. It had probably been passed on to the Personnel Office, they had been forced to respond, and they had done so in their standard, dismissive manner.

Haresh decided that he would go to Calcutta anyway, and he lost no time after his arrival in trying to get Praha to change its corporate mind. He went to Prahapore by train, a journey of less than fifteen miles. It was raining, so his first impression of the grand complex—one of the largest and most efficient in Bengal—took place under gloomy conditions. The endless rows of workers' houses; the offices and cinema; the green palm trees lining the road and the intensely green playing fields; the great, walled factory—the wall itself painted in neat segments advertising the latest lines of Praha footwear; the officers' colony (almost exclusively Czech) hidden behind even higher walls; all these were seen by Haresh through the discomfort and greyness of a hot, wet morning. He was wearing an off-white suit and carrying an umbrella. But the weather and Bengal itself—both of which he found dampening—had seeped a little into his spirits. Memories of Mr Ghosh and Mr Sen Gupta came flooding back as he got a rickshaw from the train station to the Personnel Office. Well, at least I'll have to deal with Czechs here, not Bengalis, thought Haresh.

The Czechs for their part treated all Indians (with one exception) the same, whether they spoke Bengali or not: with contempt. Indians, they had decided from experience, were fond of talking, not working. The Czechs liked nothing better than to work: in order to increase production, quality, sales, profits, and the glory of the Praha Shoe Company. Talking usually put them at a disadvantage; by and large they did not speak or write good English, nor did they have a great deal of culture. It could be said of them that when anyone talked about culture they reached for their awl. People started out young in the Praha Shoe Company, whether in Czechoslovakia or in India; they began on the shop floor; there was no need for the niceties of a university education. The Czechs mistrusted on the one hand what they saw as an Indian glibness with words (union negotiators were the worst), and resented on the other the fact that the British commercial establishment in Calcutta did not treat them, although they were fellow-Europeans, as anything like their equals. The directors and heads of department and even covenanted assistants of the managing agency of Bentsen & Pryce, for example, would not dream of fraternizing with the Czechs of the Praha Shoe Company.

The Czechs had transformed the face of the Indian footwear industry by rolling up their sleeves and creating a great factory and township on what had been virtually a swamp, by following this up with four smaller factories including the one at Brahmpur, and by running a tight network of shops throughout the country, not by hobnobbing over Scotch at the Calcutta Club. The Czech officers, including their Managing Director, had not been born to white collars. For them the Praha Shoe Company was their life and the Praha creed virtually their religion. Their branches and factories and shops spread around the world; and though they had been taken over by the communists in their own homeland, those 'Prahamen' who were abroad at the time or had managed to escape had not been dispossessed of their employment. The Praha Shoe Company was owned and run by Mr Jan Tomin, the eldest and identically named son of its legendary founder, now referred to as 'Old Mr Tomin'. Mr Tomin had made sure that his flock, whether in Canada or England or Nigeria or India, were well taken care of, and they repaid his loyalty to them with a fierce gratitude that verged on feudal fealty. When he decided to retire, this vassalage had been transferred to his son. Whenever Young Mr Tomin visited India from his world headquarters in London (not, alas, Prague any longer), the entire Praha world would be abuzz with excitement. Telephones rang all over Prahapore and urgent messages went back and forth from the head office in Calcutta to announce his god-like progress: 'Mr Tomin has arrived at the airport,' the rumour would go around. 'He is now on the flyover near the Prahapore Station. Mrs Tomin is with him.' 'Mr Tomin is visiting the 416 Department. He praised Mr Bratinka's efforts and showed great interest in the Goodyear Welted shoe line.' 'Mr and Mrs Tomin will be playing tennis this afternoon.' 'Mr Tomin had a swim at the Officers' Club, but thought the water was too warm. The baby too was floated in a rubber tube.'

Mr Tomin's wife was English, with a lovely oval face to contrast with his straightforward, genial, square one. Two years ago, she had given birth to a son, and this son too had been christened Jan, like his father and grandfather before him. This son had been taken along on Mr Tomin's most recent tour of India so that he could survey with infant eyes what would one day all be his.

But the Chairman of the Indian branch of the Praha Shoe Company, who sat in the luxurious head office on Camac Street in Calcutta (far from the sirens and smoke of Prahapore) and who lived in the posh 'Praha Residency' on Theatre Road, a mere five minutes' purr of his Austin Sheerline away, was no stocky Husek or Husak but the cheerful, greying, paan-chewing, Scotch-drinking Marwari, Mr Hiralal Khandelwal, who knew almost nothing (and did not care much more) about the day-to-day manufacture of shoes. How this had come about was an interesting story.

This odd configuration had a history of more than twenty years. Mr Khandelwal had been the solicitor in the family firm of Khandelwal and Company who had handled the legal account of Praha. When one of the grand supremos of Praha had been sent out from Prague in the late twenties to establish the Indian company, Khandelwal had been recommended to him as a capable man. Khandelwal got the company registered and did all the necessary legal spadework, tasks which the Czechs treated with incomprehension and distaste. They wanted to get down to making shoes as quickly and sturdily and excellently as possible.

Mr Khandelwal facilitated whatever needed to be facilitated: the purchase of land, the necessary permissions from the Government of British India, negotiations with labour leaders. But it was in 1939, when the Second World War broke out, that he really came into his own. Since the Germans had occupied Czechoslovakia, Praha's possessions in India were in grave danger of being declared enemy property and confiscated. With his good contacts in government (especially with a powerful group of rising Indian officers in the Indian Civil Service whom he used to wine and dine and to whom—over bridge—he would lose money), Mr Khandelwal was able to retrieve the position of Praha. The powers of the Raj did not declare Praha to be enemy property after all; instead, they gave it massive orders for the manufacture of army boots and other footwear. The Czechs were not merely bewildered but astonished. Mr Khandelwal was promptly taken on to the board of Praha (India), and soon afterwards was made Chairman.

And he was the most shrewd and powerful Chairman that Praha had. One of his great advantages was that labour would eat out of his hands. To them he was a living deity—Khandelwal devta!—the brown man who ruled over the white rulers of Praha. Jawaharlal Nehru had met him, and several Cabinet Ministers knew him, including the Minister for Labour. The previous year there had been a prolonged strike at Prahapore, and a petition against the management had been sent by the workmen to the Prime Minister. Nehru had said to them: 'If you have Hiralal Khandelwal there, why do you need me?' And once the workmen had got him to agree to look into their grievances, Khandelwal had acted as the sole arbitrator between the Czech management and the unions—and that too as the Chairman!

Apart from having met him, Haresh had heard a great deal about the Chairman of Praha from Mr Mukherji, including an interesting snippet or two about his private life. Khandelwal was fond of good living, which definitely included women; and he was married to an attractive singer and ex-courtesan from Bihar—a woman with a formidable temperament.

The fact that it was Khandelwal who had forwarded his application gave Haresh a little courage as he stepped into the outer office of Mr Novak, the head of Personnel at Prahapore. Haresh had on an Irish linen bespoke suit from the best tailors in Middlehampton. His shoes were Saxone, five pounds the pair. He had Trugel in his hair, and he radiated a mild fragrance of expensive soap. Nevertheless, he was told to sit outside in the queue.

Finally, after an hour, he was asked to come in. Novak wore an open shirt and fawn trousers. His coat was hanging across his chair. He was a well-proportioned man, about 5 feet 9 inches in height, and extremely soft-spoken. He was unsmiling and unbending and as hard as nails; it was usually he who dealt with the unions. His eyes were penetrating.

He had Haresh's application before him as he interviewed him. At the end of ten minutes he said:

'Well, I see no reason to change our offer. It is a good one.'

'At twenty-eight rupees a week?'

'Yes.'

'You cannot imagine I can accept an offer like that.'

'That is up to you.'

'My qualifications—my work experience—' said Haresh helplessly, waving a hand at his application.

Mr Novak did not deign to answer. He looked like an old, cold fox.

'Please reconsider your offer, Mr Novak.'

'No.' The voice was soft, and the eyes unsmiling and even—it seemed to Haresh—unflickering.

'I have come here all the way from Delhi. At least give me half a chance. I have been in management on a reasonable monthly salary, and you are asking me to take the weekly wage of a workman—not even a supervisor, a foreman. I am sure you see how unreasonable this offer is.'

'No.'

'The Chairman—'

Mr Novak's voice cut across like a quiet whip:

'The Chairman asked me to consider your application. I did that and sent you a letter. That should have been the end of the matter. You have come here from Delhi for no reason, and I see no reason to change my mind. Good morning, Mr Khanna.'

Haresh got up, fuming, and left. It was still pouring outside. In the train back to Calcutta, he considered what to do. He felt he had been treated like dirt by Novak, and it burned him up. He had hated to plead, and his pleading had not worked.

He was a proud man, but now he had other compulsions. He had to have a job if he was to court Lata. From what he knew of Mrs Rupa Mehra, she would never allow her to marry an unemployed man—and Haresh could anyway not be so irresponsible as to ask Lata to share a hand-to-mouth existence with him. And what would he tell Umesh Uncle when he went back to Delhi? It would be galling beyond endurance to have to put up with his taunts.

So he decided to take the bull by the horns. He stood in the rain that afternoon outside the Praha head office in Camac Street. The next day was sunny, and he did the same. As a result of this reconnaissance he worked out Mr Khandelwal's movements. It became clear that at one o'clock in the afternoon he left the office for lunch.

The third day at lunchtime, as the gates opened to let the Chairman's Austin Sheerline glide out, Haresh stopped the car by standing in front of it. The watchmen ran helter-skelter in confusion and dismay and did not know whether to reason with him or drag him away. Mr Khandelwal, however, looked at him, recognized him, and opened the window.

'Ah,' he said, trying to recall the name.

'Haresh Khanna, Sir—'

'Yes, yes, I remember, Mukherji brought you to see me in Delhi. What happened?'

'Nothing.' Haresh spoke calmly, though he could not bring himself to smile.

'Nothing?' Mr Khandelwal frowned.

'As against an offer of seven hundred and fifty a month with James Hawley, I was offered twenty-eight rupees a week by Mr Novak. It seems that Praha doesn't want qualified people.'

Haresh did not mention that the James Hawley offer had been effectively rescinded, and he was glad that that aspect of the matter had not come up when he and Mukherji had met Khandelwal in Delhi.

'Hmm,' said Mr Khandelwal, 'come and see me the day after tomorrow.'

When Haresh went to see him two days later, Mr Khandelwal had got his file before him. He was brief. He nodded at Haresh and said: 'I have looked over this. Havel will meet you tomorrow for an interview.' Havel was the General Manager at Prahapore.

Mr Khandelwal appeared to have no further questions for Haresh except an inquiry or two about how Mukherji was. 'All right, let us see how things go,' was his parting comment. He did not seem unduly concerned whether Haresh sank or swam.

13.27

But Haresh was nevertheless very encouraged. An interview with Havel meant that the Chairman had forced the Czechs to take his application seriously. The next day, when he boarded the train for the forty-five-minute trip to Prahapore, he was in a fairly confident mood.

The Indian personal assistant to the General Manager told him that Novak would not be attending the interview. Haresh was relieved.

In a few minutes Haresh was ushered into the office of the General

Manager of Prahapore.

Pavel Havel—so named by playfully idiotic parents, who had no conception of how he would be teased at school—was a short man like Haresh, but almost as broad as he was tall.

'Sit, sit, sit—' he said to Haresh.

Haresh sat down.

'Show me your hands,' he said.

Haresh offered Mr Havel his hands, palms upwards.

'Bend your thumb.'

Haresh bent it as much as possible.

Mr Havel laughed in a not unfriendly but rather final way.

'You are not a shoemaker,' he said.

'I am,' said Haresh.

'No, no, no—' Mr Havel laughed. 'Some other line, some other job is best for you. Join some other company. What do you want to do in Praha?'

'I want to sit on the other side of this desk,' said Haresh.

Mr Havel stopped smiling.

'Oh,' he said. 'That high?'

'Eventually,' said Haresh.

'We all start on the shop floor,' explained Mr Havel, feeling sorry for this rather incapable but ambitious young man who would never make a shoemaker. It was perfectly obvious the moment he had tried to bend his thumb. The way shoes were made in Czechoslovakia required bending the thumb. This young man had no more future with Praha than a one-armed man in a wrestling pit. 'Myself, Mr Novak, Mr Janacek, Mr Kurilla, all of us, we all started on the shop floor. If you cannot make shoes,' he continued, 'what hope is there for you in this company?'

'None,' said Haresh.

'So you see—' said Pavel Havel.

'You have not even seen me trying to make a shoe,' said Haresh. 'How would you know what I can or can't do?'

Pavel Havel got slightly irked. He had a great deal of work to do today, and endless empty talk bothered him. Indians always talked big and performed miserably. He looked slightly weary. Gazing out of his window at the bright—too-bright—greenery outside, he wondered if the communists would ever leave Czechoslovakia, and if he and his family would ever get the chance in his lifetime to see his hometown of Bratislava again.

The young man was saying something about being able to make a shoe.

Pavel Havel stared at the lapel of his fancy suit and said rather brutally: 'You will never make a shoe.'

Haresh could not understand Havel's sudden change of tone, but he was not cowed by it. 'I think I can make a shoe right from the design pattern to the finished product,' he said.

'All right,' said Pavel Havel. 'You make a shoe. You make a shoe, and I will give you a foreman's job at eighty rupees a week.' No one had ever started as a foreman at Praha, but Pavel Havel was sure that this was a riskless bet. Paper qualifications were one thing, rigid thumbs and a flaccid national spirit another.

But Haresh was willing to try for something better. He said: 'I have a letter of appointment here from James Hawley offering me a job at seven hundred and fifty rupees. If I make a shoe to your satisfaction, not just an ordinary shoe, but the most difficult one on your production line, will you match their offer?'

Pavel Havel looked at the young man, disconcerted by his confidence, and put a finger to his lips, as if reconsidering his calculated likelihoods. 'No,' he said, slowly. 'That would put you in the managerial grade and cause a revolution at Praha. It is impossible. As it is, if you can make a pair of shoes—of a kind I will choose—if you can make it—you will become a foreman, and that in itself is half a revolution.' Pavel Havel, having suffered from one in Czechoslovakia, did not approve of revolutions.

He phoned Kurilla, the head of the Leather Footwear Division, and asked him to come to his office for a few minutes.

'What do you think, Kurilla?' he said. 'Khanna wants to make a shoe. What should we give him to make?'

'Goodyear Welted,' said Kurilla cruelly.

Pavel Havel smiled broadly. 'Yes, yes, yes,' he said. 'Go and make a pair of Goodyear Welted shoes according to our ready-made pattern.'

This was the most difficult type of shoe to make, and involved over a hundred different operations. Havel frowned, looked at his own thumbs, and dismissed Haresh.

13.28

No poet ever worked harder or more inspiredly to craft a poem than Haresh worked for the next three days on his pair of shoes. He was supplied the materials, and told where the various machines were, and he set to work amid the heat and din of the factory.

He examined and selected fine pieces of upper and lining leather, measured them for thickness, cut, skived, cemented and folded the components, stamped the lining for size and style, fitted the upper and lining components together and carefully stitched them to each other.

He inserted and shaped the counter and toe-puff in the upper, and attached the insole to the last.

Then he mounted the upper to the wooden last and attached it to the insole by toe-lasting, heel-lasting and side-lasting, and checked with satisfaction that the upper was truly down to the last without a wrinkle, that it clung as tightly as a skin.

He stitched a welt all around. He trimmed the surplus material, and bottom-filled the gap with a mixture of cork and adhesive.

He hardly ate. On the way back to Calcutta each night he dreamed of the finished pair of shoes and how they would transform his life.

He cut the sole leather and split it to the correct thickness. He layed it, stitched it through, and attached the heel. Then he trimmed the heel and the sole. He paused for a few minutes before starting this difficult and delicate operation; trimming was like cutting hair—a mistake would be critical and irretrievable. A pair of shoes had to be completely symmetrical, left and right absolutely in proportion to each other. He paused for a few minutes afterwards as well. He knew from experience that after performing a difficult job well he was prone to the kind of relief and overconfidence that led to botching something simple.

After trimming, he fine-scoured the heel, and indented the welt to make it look good. When he had finished, he allowed himself to think that things were going well. He coloured the edges, and hot-waxed and ironed them to make them impermeable to water.

Mr Novak, the cold fox, came around at one stage to see how he was progressing. Haresh was taking his post-trimming breather. Mr Novak nodded but did not greet him, Haresh nodded but did not greet him, and Mr Novak went wordlessly away.

The shoes were now practically ready except that the soles, where stitched, looked a little crude. So Haresh fine-buffed the soles, waxed them and shone them. And lastly he fudged the bottom edges against a hot revolving wheel that hid the ugly stitches under a fine decorative pattern.

That, thought Haresh, carries a lesson for me. If James Hawley hadn't retracted their offer I would still be stuck in the same city. Now perhaps I'll get a job near Calcutta. And in terms of quality, Praha footwear is the best in India.

Appropriately enough, his next operation was to brand-stamp the sole with the name of Praha. He removed the wooden last. He attached the heel (which was attached only temporarily before) with nails. With gold foil he brand-stamped the inside sock with the Praha name and pasted it and cemented it inside the shoe. It was done!

He was halfway to Havel's office when he turned back, shaking his head and smiling at himself.

'What now?' said the man who had been designated to police him while he worked.

'A pair of laces,' said Haresh. 'I must be exhausted.'

The General Manager, the head of Leather, and the head of Personnel gathered together to look at Haresh's pair of shoes, to twist them and turn them, to prod them and peer at them. They spoke in Czech.

'Well,' said Kurilla, 'they're better than anything you or I could make.'

'I've promised him a foreman's job,' said Havel.

'You can't do that,' said Novak. 'Everyone starts on the floor.'

'I've promised him a foreman's job, and he will get one. I don't want to lose a man like this. What do you think Mr K will say?'

Though Khandelwal had appeared indifferent to Haresh's fate, he had in fact (as Haresh was later to learn) been very tough with the Czechs. After looking at Haresh's papers he had said to Havel: 'Show me any other applicants, Czech or Indian, who have the same qualifications.' Havel had not been able to. Even Kurilla, the head of Leather, though he had himself graduated from the Middlehampton College of Technology many years earlier, had not had the distinction, as Haresh had had, of standing first. Mr Khandelwal had then said: 'I forbid you to recruit any person below this man's qualifications until he is first offered a job.' Havel had tried to dissuade Khandelwal from this drastic veto, but had not succeeded. He had tried to persuade Haresh to withdraw, but had not succeeded. He had then set him a task that he had not remotely imagined he could succeed in. But Haresh's shoes were as good as anything he had seen. Pavel Havel, whatever he thought about Indians, would never again speak slightingly about people's thumbs.

The Goodyear Welted shoes were to lie in Havel's office for over a year, and he was to point them out on various occasions to visitors whenever he wanted to discuss fine workmanship.

Haresh was called in.

'Sit, sit, sit,' said Havel.

Haresh sat down.

'Excellent, excellent!' said Havel.

Haresh knew how good his shoes were, but he could not help looking delighted. His eyes disappeared in his smile.

'So I keep my part of the bargain. You get the job. Eighty rupees a week. Starting on Monday. Yes, Kurilla?'

'Yes.'

'Novak?'

Novak nodded, unsmilingly. His right hand was moving over the edge of one of the shoes. 'A good pair,' he said quietly.

'Then good,' said Havel. 'You accept?'

'The salary is too low,' said Haresh. 'Compared both to what I was getting before and what I have been offered.'

'We will put you on probation for six months, and then reconsider the salary. You do not realize, Khanna, how far we go to accommodate you, to make you a Prahaman.'

Haresh said: 'I am grateful. I accept these terms, but there is one thing I will not compromise on. I must live inside the colony and be able to use the Officers' Club.'

He realized that, however momentous in terms of the Praha culture was his direct entry at the supervisory level, he would be fatally disadvantaged in social terms if he was not seen—by Lata and her mother and her much-vaunted Calcutta brother, for example—to be on easy terms with the managers of his company.

'No, no, no—' said Pavel Havel. He looked thoroughly worried.

'Impossible,' said Novak, his eyes boring into Haresh, willing him to give in.

Kurilla did not say anything. He looked at the pair of shoes. He knew that no supervisor—and only one Indian—had been allocated a place among the forty or so houses in the walled compound. But he was glad to see the excellence of the training of his old college vindicated by Haresh. Among his Praha colleagues, most of whom had learned their skills on the job, Kurilla's technical training was often treated as something of a joke.

Haresh too had found out from Havel's Indian assistant that only one Indian had so far gained admittance into the hallowed colony—a manager from the Accounts Department.

He sensed Kurilla's sympathy and Havel's hesitancy. Even the icy Novak had a little earlier—and most uncharacteristically for him—praised his work in three brief syllables. So there appeared to be hope.

'I want above everything else to work for Praha,' said Haresh with feeling. 'You can see how much I care for quality. That is what has drawn me to your company. I have been an officer at the Cawnpore Leather and Footwear Company, and I was offered a manager's, an officer's grade at James Hawley, so my living in the compound would not be so extraordinary. I cannot take the job otherwise. I am sorry. I want to work here so much that I am willing to compromise on salary and on status. Keep me as a foreman, a supervisor, if you wish, and pay me less than I was getting before. But please compromise on this small matter of accommodation.'

There was a confabulation in Czech. The Managing Director was out of the country and could not be consulted. More importantly, the Chairman, who sometimes treated the Czechs as brusquely as they treated Indians, would not be sympathetic to what he would see as their exclusivism. If Haresh refused the job after all this, there would be hell to pay.

Like a litigant listening to legal incomprehensibilities in court, incomprehensibilities that would decide his fortune, Haresh listened to the three men, sensing from their tones and gestures and the occasional word—'colony', 'club', 'Khandelwal', 'Middlehampton', 'Jan Tomin' and so on—that Kurilla had persuaded Havel and that both were now bearing down on Novak. Novak's replies were brief, trenchant, entrenched, consisting only rarely of more than five or six syllables. Then, quite suddenly, Novak made an expressive gesture—he half shrugged, he half threw up his hands. He did not utter a word or even a nod of assent, but there was no further dissent from him either.

Pavel Havel turned to Haresh with a broad smile.

'Welcome—welcome to Praha!' he said, as if he were offering Haresh the keys to the kingdom of heaven.

Haresh beamed with pleasure, as if indeed he were.

And everyone civilly shook hands.

13.29

Arun Mehra and his friend Billy Irani were sitting on the verandah of the Calcutta Club overlooking the lawn. It was lunchtime. The waiter had not yet come around to take his order for a drink. Arun, however, did not wish to press the little brass bell at his white cane table. As a waiter walked past a few yards away, Arun got his attention by patting the top of his left hand with his right.

'Abdar!'

'Yes, Sir.'

'What'll you have, Billy?'

'A gimlet.'

'One gimlet and one Tom Collins.'

'Yes, Sir.'

The drinks came around in due course. Both of them ordered grilled fish for lunch.

They were still on their drinks when Arun, looking around, said: 'That's Khandelwal sitting there by himself—the Praha chap.'

Billy's comment was relaxed: 'These Marwaris—there was a time when membership in this club meant something.'

They had both on several occasions noted with distaste Khandelwal's drinking habits. Being limited at home by the powerful Mrs Khandelwal to one drink in the evening, Khandelwal made it his business to get in as many as possible during the day.

But Arun today found nothing much to object to in Khandelwal's presence, particularly in the fact that he was sitting alone and drinking his fourth Scotch. Mrs Rupa Mehra had written to Arun, ordering him to acquaint himself with Haresh Khanna and to write to her telling her what he thought of him. Haresh apparently had got some job or other in Praha and lived and worked in Prahapore.

It would have been too demeaning for Arun to approach him directly, and he had been wondering how to go about it. But yes, he could certainly mention the matter to the Chairman of Praha and perhaps inveigle a common invitation to tea—on neutral grounds. Here was an excellent opportunity.

Billy was continuing: 'It's remarkable. He no sooner finishes one than another's at his elbow. He never knows when to stop.'

Arun laughed. Then another thought struck him. 'Oh, by the way—Meenakshi's expecting again.'

'Expecting?' Billy was looking slightly blank.

'Yes, you know, old fellow, preggers!'

'Ah, yes, yes, preggers!' Billy Irani nodded his head. Then suddenly a thought struck him, and he began to look bewildered.

'Are you feeling all right, old chap? Another? Abdar—'

The waiter came by. 'Yes, Sir.'

'Another gimlet. Though we were taking the usual precautions. Still, it shows you never can tell. Determined fellows—'

'Fellows?'

'Yes, you know, babies. They want to appear, so they do so without consulting their parents. Meenakshi's been looking worried—but I suppose it's all for the best. Aparna could do with a brother. Or sister, I suppose. I say, Billy, I might have to go over and have a few words with Khandelwal. It's about the new hiring policies of our firm. Praha apparently have been taking on some Indians lately, and I might get a few ideas from him—well, I shouldn't be more than a few minutes. You don't mind, do you?'

'Oh, no, no—not at all.'

'You're looking rather poorly. Is it the sun? We can change tables.'

'No, no—just tired—working too hard, I suppose.'

'Well, take it easy. Doesn't Shireen tick you off? Act as a moderating influence and all that?' Arun smiled as he moved away.

'Shireen?' Billy's handsome face was pale. His mouth was open in rather a fish-like gape. 'Oh, yes, Shireen.'

Arun wondered for a second whether Billy's IQ had sunk to zero, but his mind was soon occupied with other thoughts. He winched up a smile as he approached Mr Khandelwal's table at the far end of the verandah.

'Ah, Mr Khandelwal. Good to see you.'

Mr Khandelwal looked up, half sozzled already, but very genially. This was Arun Mehra, one of a handful of young men in Calcutta who had been accepted into the British commercial establishment—and who with their wives were therefore the leaders of Indian society in Calcutta. Chairman of Praha though he was, he was flattered to be recognized by Arun, to whom he had once been introduced at the races. Khandelwal remembered that the young man had an exceedingly glamorous wife, but he had a bad memory for names, and groped around a bit before Arun, who could not believe that anyone could have forgotten him, said, 'Arun Mehra.'

'Yes, yes, of course—Bentsen Pryce.'

Arun was mollified.

'I wonder if I could have a few words with you, Mr Khandelwal,' he said.

Mr Khandelwal gestured towards a chair and Arun sat down.

'Will you have a drink?' offered Mr Khandelwal, his hand poised above the small brass bell.

'No, thank you, I've had one already.'

In Mr Khandelwal's view that was no good reason not to have another half-dozen. 'What is on your mind?' he asked the younger man.

'Well, as you know, Mr Khandelwal, our firm, and several others like ours, have been recruiting Indians—suitable Indians, of course—for management positions, on a gradual basis. And one hears that you, too, being a big organization, have been thinking of doing the same thing.'

Khandelwal nodded.

'Well,' said Arun. 'In some respects we are in the same predicament. It's rather difficult to get the sort of people we need.'

Khandelwal smiled.

'You may find it difficult,' he said slowly, 'but we find no problem getting qualified people. Only the other day we recruited a man with a good background.' He lapsed into Hindi. 'A good man—he has studied in England, has a fine technical background. They wanted to give him a lower position, but I insisted—' He gestured for another Scotch. 'I can't remember his name, oh yes, Haresh Khanna.'

'From Kanpur?' replied Arun, permitting himself two words in Hindi.

'I don't know,' said Mr Khandelwal. 'Oh yes, from Kanpur. He came to my attention through Mukherji of CLFC. Yes, have you heard of him?'

'It's very curious,' said Arun, to whom none of this was in the least curious. 'But now that you mention the name, Mr Khandelwal, I believe this must be the young man whom my mother talked about a little while ago as a—well, as a prospect for my sister. He's a khatri, and, as you know, so are we—though I'm not in the least a believer in caste and so on. But of course there's no arguing with my mother—she believes in all this khatri-patri business. How interesting; so he works for you?'

'Yes. A good boy. Good technical qualifications.'

Arun shuddered inwardly at the word 'technical'.

'Well, we wouldn't mind his coming over some day to our place,' Arun said. 'But perhaps it might be better if it were not quite so face-to-face, with just him and us. I wonder if perhaps you and Mrs Khandelwal might care to come over for tea one day. We live in Sunny Park, which, as you know, is in Ballygunge: not all that far away from you. I've been thinking of inviting you over for some time anyway; I understand you play an excellent game of bridge.'

Since Mr Khandelwal was a notoriously reckless player—his skill at bridge consisted largely of losing while playing for high stakes (though sometimes in the interests of a larger game)—Arun's remark was pure flattery. But it had its effect.

Mr Khandelwal, although not blind to Arun's charming manipulativeness, was pleased to be flattered. He was a hospitable man—and he had a mansion to display. So, as Arun had hoped and intended that he might when he had tendered his reverse invitation, the Chairman of Praha invited them over instead.

'No, no, you come and join us for tea at our place,' said Mr Khandelwal. 'I'll get this boy over—Khanna. And my wife will be very interested in meeting Mrs Mehra. Please bring her too.'

'That's very kind of you, Mr Khandelwal.'

'Not at all, not at all. Sure you won't have a drink?'

'No, thank you.'

'We can discuss recruiting procedures then.'

'Oh, yes, recruiting,' said Arun. 'Well, which day would suit you?'

'Come any time.' Mr Khandelwal left the matter up in the air. The Khandelwal household ran on very flexible principles. People dropped in and vast formal parties were given, often at the same time. Six large Alsatians joined in the mêlée and terrified the guests. Mrs Khandelwal ruled over Mr Khandelwal with a whip, but he often went astray with drink or women.

'How about next Tuesday?'

'Yes, yes, next Tuesday, any day,' said Mr Khandelwal vaguely.

'At five?'

'Yes, yes, at five, any time.'

'Well, then, at five next Tuesday. I look forward to it,' said Arun, wondering whether Mr Khandelwal would remember this conversation five minutes later.

'Yes, yes, Tuesday, at five,' said Mr Khandelwal, deep in his cups. 'Yes. Abdar—'

13.30

Everyone punched in at the Praha factory gate before the second siren went at eight in the morning; but there was a separate gate for the supervisors and managers, from the foremen upwards. Haresh was shown where he would sit. It was at a table in the open hall next to the conveyor belt. Here he would both supervise and do any office work that was necessary. Only group foremen got cubicles. There was nowhere for him to screw in the brass plate bearing his name that he had removed from his office door at CLFC not very long ago.

But perhaps he would not have been able to use that brass plate anyway. Everything was uniform in Praha and no doubt there was a standard lettering and size to brass plates as to everything else. The Czechs, for example, had brought the metric system with them, and refused to work with anything else, regardless of what had prevailed in the Raj or what now prevailed in Independent India. As for the litany that every Indian schoolchild learned—'three pies to a paisa, four paisas to an anna, sixteen annas to a rupee'—the Czechs treated this as a joke. They had decimalized the rupee for all internal Praha purposes by fiat decades before the government came around to even deciding to do so.

Haresh, who liked order, did not disapprove of this at all. He was happy to be working in a well-organized, well-lit, well-knit environment, and was determined to do his best for the company.

Because he had been started off at the foreman level and granted permission to live in the colony, a number of rumours had begun to do the rounds among the workmen. These were enhanced when he was invited to tea with Mr Khandelwal. The first rumour was that the fair, compact, well-dressed Haresh Khanna was actually a Czech, who for purposes best known to himself had decided to pose as an Indian. The second was that he was Mr Khandelwal's brother-in-law. Haresh did nothing to dispel these rumours, as he found both of them helpful when he wanted to get things done.

Haresh took an hour's leave on the day that he had to go to Calcutta for tea with the Chairman. When he arrived at the huge house on Theatre Road—the 'Praha Residency' as it was popularly known—he was saluted smartly by the guards. The immaculate lawn, the five cars in the drive (including the Austin Sheerline that he had bodily halted a few days before), the palms lining the drive, the grand mansion itself, all impressed him greatly. The only thing that troubled him a little was that one palm tree was slightly out of line.

Mr Khandelwal greeted him in a friendly manner, in Hindi. 'So you have become a Prahaman. Very good.'

'It is because of your kindness—' began Haresh.

'You're quite right,' said Mr Khandelwal, instead of making some self-deprecating rejoinder. 'It was my kindness all right.' He laughed. 'Those crazy Czechs would have got rid of you if they could. Come in, come in. . . . But it was your qualifications that did it. I heard about that pair of shoes.' He laughed again.

Haresh was introduced to Mrs Khandelwal, a strikingly attractive woman in her late thirties, dressed in a gold-and-white sari. A diamond nose-stud and diamond earrings and a charming and lively smile added to the dazzling effect.

Within a few minutes she had sent him off to repair a tap that was not working in the bathroom. 'We must get it going before the other guests arrive,' she said in her most charming manner. 'I hear you are very good with your hands.'

Haresh, slightly puzzled, went to do as he was bid. It was not a test of any kind—either of the Pavel Havel kind or of his vulnerability to her smile. It was simply that when something needed to be done, Mrs Khandelwal expected everyone around her to do it. When she wanted a handyman, she seized upon any man who was handy. All Indian Prahamen had learned that they could be called upon at any time to do the Queen's bidding. Haresh didn't mind; he liked putting things right. He took off his jacket, and wandered through the huge house with a servant until he came to the erring tap. He wondered who these important guests were.

Meanwhile, the guests themselves were on their way. Meenakshi was quite looking forward to it all. After the yawn that was Brahmpur it was good to be back in Calcutta. Aparna had become a little more placid by spending a few days with her grandmother Mrs Chatterji (which is where she had been parked this evening as well); and even the shiftless Varun (who was also out this evening) was a welcome homecoming sight after the Brahmpur baby smells and the Rudhia relatives and the doddering Maitras.

This evening was to be a grand one: tea with the Khandelwals; two cocktail parties to follow (at at least one of which she was bound to meet Billy—what would he say, she wondered, when she laughingly told him her news?); then dinner and dancing. She was curious about the Khandelwals, with their grand house and six dogs and five cars, and she was very interested in meeting the upstart cobbler who had designs on Luts.

The lawns and flowers of the Praha Residency were more than impressive, even for a season when almost nothing bloomed. Mrs Khandelwal, who was an obsessive woman, would have thought nothing of transplanting Kew to Calcutta if it had suited her ends.

Haresh was back in his jacket by the time he was introduced to the tall young gentleman and his elegant wife, both of whom appeared to be appraising him from a height that was not merely literal. The moment he heard his host's words—'Arun Mehra—from Bentsen Pryce'—he realized why. So this was Lata's Calcutta brother.

'Very pleased to meet you,' said Haresh, shaking Arun's hand in perhaps too firm a grip. This was his first real meeting with a brown sahib. They had never been a part of his life. When he had lived for a while in Patiala he had often wondered why people made such a fuss about the young man from Imperial Tobacco or Shell or some other foreign firm who was based in the town or travelling through, not realizing that for a mere trader such a member of the comprador classes was a man important beyond his years; he could dispense and revoke agencies, he could make or break one's fortune. He invariably travelled around in a car with a chauffeur, and a car with a chauffeur in a small town was a great thing.

Arun for his part was thinking: short; a bit brash; something about his manner of dressing that's a bit flashy; has too good an opinion of himself.

But they all sat down to tea, and the opening moves of the conversation were made by the women. Meenakshi noticed that the Rosenthal service in white and gold too perfectly matched her hostess's sari. Typical of these people! she thought. They try too hard.

She looked around the room for something to praise. She couldn't very well praise the heavy furniture, most of which was in rather overdone taste, but there was a Japanese painting that she quite liked: two birds and a bit of calligraphy.

'That's a lovely painting, Mrs Khandelwal,' said Meenakshi. 'Where did you get it?'

'From Japan. Mr Khandelwal went on a trip there—'

'From Indonesia,' said Mr Khandelwal. It had been given to him by a Japanese businessman at a conference in Djakarta that he had attended on behalf of Praha India.

Mrs Khandelwal flashed her eyes at him, and he quailed.

'I know what you got and when,' said Mrs Khandelwal.

'Yes, yes—' said her husband in rather a worried tone.

'Nice furniture!' said Haresh, in the belief that this was the kind of small talk that needed to be made.

Meenakshi looked at him and forbore from comment.

But Mrs Khandelwal gazed at him with her sweetest, most charming expression. He had provided her with an opportunity to say what she had been waiting to say. 'Do you think so?' she asked Haresh. 'It has been done by Kamdar's—Kamdar's of Bombay. Half our rooms are decorated by them.'

Meenakshi looked at the heavy corner settee—in dark, solid wood with dark-blue upholstery. 'If you like this sort of thing, you can always get it in Calcutta,' she said. 'There's the Chowringhee Sales Bureau, for instance, for old-fashioned furniture. And if you want something more modern in style, there's always Mozoomdar. It's a little less'—she paused for a word—'a little less ponderous. But it depends on your taste. These pakoras are delicious,' she added by way of compensation, helping herself to another one.

Her bright laugh tinkled across the china, though there was nothing very obviously humorous in her previous remarks.

'Oh, but I think,' said Mrs Khandelwal, oozing charm, 'I do think that the quality of workmanship and the quality of wood at Kamdar's is unbeatable.'

And the quality of distance, thought Meenakshi. If you lived in Bombay, you'd be importing your furniture from Calcutta. Aloud she said: 'Well, Kamdar's is Kamdar's, of course.'

'Do have some more tea, Mrs Mehra,' said Mrs Khandelwal, pouring it out herself.

She was exquisitely charming, and believed in winning people over—including women. Though she suffered from some insecurity because of her past background, she was never aggressive with them. It was only where sweetness didn't work that she gave vent to fury.

Mr Khandelwal appeared to be getting impatient. After a little while he excused himself to get a breath of fresh air. He came back a minute or two later, smelling of cardamoms and looking happier.

Mrs Khandelwal viewed him with suspicion when he returned, but he looked completely innocent.

Suddenly, without warning, three large Alsatians bounded into the room, barking frenetically. Haresh was bewildered and almost spilled his tea. Arun jumped up. Khandelwal was perplexed; he wondered how they could have got in. Only the two women remained cool. Meenakshi was used to the vicious Cuddles and was fond of dogs. And Mrs Khandelwal turned on them in a low, commanding hiss:

'Sit down! Down, Cassius, down—down—Crystal—down, Jalebi!'

The three dogs sat down in a line, trembling and silent. Each of them knew that if they disobeyed, Mrs Khandelwal would have thought nothing of whipping them unmercifully there and then.

'See—' said Mrs Khandelwal, 'see how sweet he is, my Cassius, look at him, my little pet—how unhappy he looks. He didn't mean to disturb anyone.'

'Well,' said Arun, 'I'm afraid my wife is in rather a—a—well, a delicate state, and these sudden shocks—'

Mrs Khandelwal, horrified, turned on her husband. 'Mr Khandelwal,' she said in a tone of absolute authority, 'do you know what you have done? Do you have any idea?'

'No,' said Mr Khandelwal in fear and trembling.

'You have left the door open. That is how these three beasts have entered. Take them out at once and close the door.'

Having dispatched the dogs and her husband, she turned—dripping concern—towards Meenakshi.

'My poor Mrs Mehra, I cannot apologize enough. Have another pakora. Have two. You must build up your strength.'

'Excellent tea, Mrs Khandelwal,' said Haresh bravely.

'Do have another cup. We get our own blend directly from Darjeeling,' said Mrs Khandelwal.

13.31

There was a pause, and now Haresh decided to beard the lion.

'You must be Lata's brother,' he said to Arun. 'How is Lata?'

'Very well,' said Arun.

'And your mother?'

'Very well, thank you,' said Arun, with some hauteur.

'And the baby?'

'The baby?'

'Your niece.'

'Flourishing, no doubt.'

There was another pause.

'Do you have any children?' asked Haresh of Meenakshi.

'Yes,' said Meenakshi. 'A girl.'

This cobbler, she decided, would make a very poor rival to Amit.

Arun turned to Haresh and said: 'What is it you do exactly, Mr Khanna? I understand you've been taken on by Praha in some sort of position. A managerial position, I presume.'

'Well, not managerial,' said Haresh. 'I am in a supervisory position at the moment, though my previous job was managerial. I decided to take this job because it has more of a future.'

'Supervisory?'

'I am a foreman.'

'Ah! A foreman.'

'Praha usually starts people on the shop floor, not even in supervisory jobs.'

'Hmm.' Arun took another sip of tea.

'James Hawley offered me a managerial job—' began Haresh.

'I could never understand why the Cromarty Group hasn't moved its head office to Calcutta,' said Arun in a distant manner. 'Puzzling that they should wish to remain a provincial concern. Ah well.'

Meenakshi felt that Arun was being too unfriendly. 'You're from Delhi originally, aren't you, Mr Khanna?' she asked.

'Yes, indeed,' said Haresh. 'And I went to St Stephen's College.'

'And then, I understand, you went to England for your education. Was that to Oxford or to Cambridge?'

'I went to the Middlehampton College of Technology.'

There was silence for a few seconds, only interrupted by Mr Khandelwal's return. He was looking even happier. He had an arrangement with the watchman to keep a bottle of whisky and a glass for him at the gate, and he had mastered the art of gulping down a peg in five seconds flat.

Arun continued his conversation with Haresh: 'What plays have you seen recently, Mr Khanna?' Arun named a few that were running in London.

'Plays?'

'Well, since you've come from England, I presume you would have taken the opportunity to visit the theatre.'

'I didn't have much of an occasion to see plays in the Midlands,' said Haresh. 'But I did see a large number of films.'

Arun received this information without comment. 'Well, I expect you visited Stratford; it's not far from Middlehampton.'

'I did,' said Haresh, relieved. This was worse than Novak, Havel and Kurilla put together.

Arun began to talk about the restoration of Anne Hathaway's cottage, and by slow degrees moved from the provinces to post-war reconstruction work in London.

Meenakshi talked about friends of hers who were doing up a mews off Baker Street.

From there the conversation moved to hotels. At the mention of Claridges, Mr Khandelwal, who always booked a suite there whenever he visited London, said:

'Oh, yes, Claridges. I have a good relation with Claridges. The manager always asks me, "Is everything to your satisfaction, Mr Khandelwal?" And I always say, "Yes, it is all to my satisfaction."' He smiled, as if at a private joke.

Mrs Khandelwal looked at him with suppressed anger. She suspected that his trips to London had a carnal as well as a business element to them, and she was right. Sometimes she would phone him up in the middle of the night to ensure that he was where he had said he would be. If he complained, which he rarely dared to do, she would tell him that she had mixed up her time zones.

'What do you like best about London—when you do happen to go there?' asked Arun, turning to Haresh.

'The pubs, of course,' said Haresh. 'No matter where you go you bump into a pub. One of my favourites is that wedge-shaped pub near Trafalgar Square—the Marquis of Anglesey—or is it the Marquis of Granby?'

Mr Khandelwal looked somewhat interested, but Arun, Meenakshi, and Mrs Khandelwal gave a collective shudder. Haresh was behaving like a real bull among the Rosenthal.

'Where do you buy toys for your daughter?' asked Mrs Khandelwal quickly. 'I am always telling Mr Khandelwal to buy toys from England. They make such good gifts. People are always being born in India and I don't know what to give them.'

Arun quickly, and with accuracy and aplomb, gave the names of three toyshops in London, but ended with a hymn to Hamleys:

'I always believe, though, Mrs Khandelwal, that one should go for the tried and tested stores. And really, there still is nothing to compare with Hamleys. Toys from top to bottom—nothing but toys on every floor. And it's done up beautifully at Christmas. It's on Regent Street, not far from Jaeger's—'

'Jaeger's!' said Mr Khandelwal. 'That's where I bought a dozen sweaters last month.'

'When were you last in England, Mr Mehra?' asked Haresh, who was feeling left out of the conversation.

But something appeared to have got stuck in Arun's throat, because he took a handkerchief out of his pocket and began to cough, pointing with his left hand to his Adam's apple.

His hostess was all solicitude. She ordered a glass of water for him. The servant brought in a thick tumbler of water on a stainless steel thali. Seeing Meenakshi's horrified look, Mrs Khandelwal shouted at the servant.

'Is this how you have learned to bring water? I should send you back to the village.' The steel platter contrasted dreadfully with the gold-and-white tea service. Meenakshi looked still more horrified at the public outburst of her hostess.

When Arun had recovered, and the drift of the conversation was about to change, Haresh, feeling that Arun might appreciate his interest in him, repeated his question:

'When was the last time you were in England?'

Arun went red, then collected himself. There was no escape for him. He had to answer the question.

'Well,' he said with as much dignity as he could muster, 'as it happens, it might surprise you to learn that I've never actually had the opportunity to go there—but of course we're going in a few months' time.'

Haresh was startled. He would never have dreamed of asking Arun *whether* he had ever been to England. He felt like laughing, but dared not do so. His eyes, however, disappeared in an expression of amusement. His host and hostess looked startled too.

Meenakshi began to talk quickly about bridge, and how they simply had to have the Khandelwals over sometime. And after a few minutes of polite conversation the Mehras looked at their watches, exchanged glances, thanked their hosts, got up, and left.

13.32

Meenakshi was right. Billy Irani was at the second of the two cocktail parties they went to that evening. Shireen was with him, but Meenakshi managed with some light flirtatious banter to draw him aside in an amusingly public way.

'Do you know, Billy,' she said, softly and laughingly, in a voice that did not carry, and with an expression that indicated that they were making small talk, 'do you know that I'm expecting?'

Billy Irani looked nervous. 'Yes, Arun mentioned it to me.'

'Well?'

'Well—should I congratulate you?'

Meenakshi laughed tinklingly, her eyes cold.

'No, I don't think that's a good idea. You might be congratulating yourself in a few months.'

Poor Billy looked rather haunted.

'But we were careful.' (Except that once, he thought.)

'I've been careful with everyone,' countered Meenakshi.

'Everyone?' Billy looked shocked.

'I mean, with you, and with Arun. All right, let's change the subject, here he comes.'

But Arun, who had spied Patricia Cox and was determined to be gallant to her, walked past them with a nod. Meenakshi was saying:

'—and of course, I understand nothing about these handicaps and so on, but I do like the names, eagles and birdies and so on. They sound so—so—it's all right, he's gone. Now, Billy, when should we meet?'

'We can't meet. Not after this!' Billy sounded horrified. He was, moreover, transfixed by Meenakshi's little pear-like earrings, which he found curiously disconcerting.

'I can't get pregnant twice,' said Meenakshi. 'It's perfectly safe now.'

Billy was looking ill. He glanced quickly across the room at Shireen.

'Really, Meenakshi!'

'Don't "really Meenakshi" me,' said Meenakshi with a sharp edge to her voice. 'We are going to continue as before, Billy, or I won't answer for the consequences.'

'You wouldn't tell him—' gasped Billy.

Meenakshi drew her elegant neck upward and smiled at Billy. She looked tired, perhaps even a little worried. She did not answer his question.

'And the—well—the baby?' said Billy.

'I'll have to think of what to do about that,' said Meenakshi. 'I'd go mad wondering about it otherwise. Not knowing. That's something I might need a little help with too. So, let's say Friday afternoon?'

Billy nodded his head helplessly.

'Friday afternoon, then, that's fixed,' said Meenakshi. 'It really is lovely to see you again. But you're looking a little under the weather, Billy. Eat a raw egg before you come.' And she moved away, blowing him a kiss when she was halfway across the room.

13.33

After dinner and a little dancing ('Don't know how long you'll be able to do this, darling,' said Arun to her), they returned home. Meenakshi turned on the lights, and opened the fridge for a drink of cold water. Arun looked at the thick stack of gramophone records lying on the dining table and growled:

'This is the third time Varun's done this. If he wants to live in this house, he must learn that a house is not a sty. Where is he anyway?'

'He said he'd be out late, darling.'

Arun headed for the bedroom, undoing his tie as he went. He put on the light, and stopped dead.

The place had been ransacked. The long black iron trunk, usually covered with a mattress and a piece of brocade and used as a window seat, was lying open, its lock broken. The sturdy leather attaché case that lay inside the trunk was empty. Its nine-lever lock had been too hard to force, so the top of the thick hide had been slashed and hacked with a knife in a gaping, S-shaped curve. The jewellery boxes inside had been emptied of their contents and were lying scattered here and there on the floor. He looked quickly around the room. Nothing else had been touched, but everything in the attaché case had gone: everything from the jewellery given by both sides of the family to his father's one remaining gold medal. Only the necklace that Meenakshi had worn the previous night and that she hadn't locked away but left on the dressing table had been overlooked; and, of course, whatever she was wearing tonight. Much had been taken that was of great sentimental value. Worst of all—considering that he belonged to the insurance department at Bentsen Pryce and should perhaps have taken the coverage despite the expense of the premium—none of it was insured.

When Arun went back to the drawing room, he looked ashen.

'What's the matter, darling?' asked Meenakshi, moving towards the bedroom.

'Nothing, darling,' said Arun, barring her way. 'Nothing. Sit down. No, in the drawing room.' He could imagine what the scene might do to her, especially in her present state. He shook his head at the image of the hacked attaché case.

'But something is terribly wrong, Arun,' said Meenakshi.

Slowly, and with his arm around her, he told her what had happened.

'Thank God Aparna's with your parents tonight. But where are the servants?'

'I let them off early.'

'We must see if Hanif is asleep in the quarters at the back.'

The bearer-cum-cook was horrified. He had been asleep. He had seen and heard nothing. And he was very afraid that suspicion would fall on him. Clearly there appeared to have been inside knowledge of where the jewellery was kept. Perhaps it was the sweeper, he suggested. He was terrified of what the police would do to him under interrogation.

Arun tried to phone the police, but there was no response on the line.

After a stream of six obscenities, he came to his senses. The last thing he wanted to do was to upset his wife.

'Darling, you wait here,' he said. 'I'll drive over to the police station and inform them.'

But Meenakshi did not want to remain alone in the house, and said that she would go along with Arun. She had begun to tremble slightly. In the car she put her hand on his shoulder while he drove.

'It's all right, darling,' said Arun. 'At least all of us are all right. Don't worry. Try not to think of it. It isn't good for you or the baby.'

13.34

Meenakshi was so upset by the robbery and the loss of her jewellery, which did not include the gold earrings that she had got made but did include her father-in-law's second gold medal, that she needed to recover at her parents' house for a week. Arun was as sympathetic as he could be, and though he knew he would miss her and Aparna, he felt that it would be good for her to be away from the house for a while. Varun returned the next morning after a night with his friends. He grew pale when he heard the news. When Arun told him that if he hadn't been 'drinking around town all night there would have been someone at home to prevent the robbery', his face grew red. Arun too, after all, had been out having a good time. But instead of provoking Arun, who appeared to be at the end of his tether, Varun kept quiet and slunk into his room.

Arun wrote to Mrs Rupa Mehra, telling her about the robbery. He assured her that Meenakshi was well, but was forced to mention that the other medal too had been lost. He could imagine how badly she would take this. He too had loved his father and was upset most particularly about the loss of this medal. But there was nothing to be done except hope that the police would trace the culprit or culprits. They were already interrogating the sweeper-boy: beating him up, to be precise. Arun, when he heard of this, tried to stop them.

'But how else can we find out what happened—how the thieves came to know where you kept the jewellery?' asked the station house officer.

'I don't care. I won't have this,' said Arun, and made sure that they didn't beat him up further. The worst of it was that Arun himself suspected that it was the sweeper-boy who had been in league with the criminals. It was unlikely that it was the Toothless Crone or Hanif. As for the part-time mali or the driver, they never entered the house.

Another matter about which Arun wrote to his mother was his meeting with Haresh. The loss of face he had suffered at the Khandelwals' still made him flush whenever he thought about it. He told Mrs Rupa Mehra precisely what he thought of his prospective brother-in-law: that he was a short, pushy, crass young man with too good an opinion of himself. He had a smattering of the grimy Midlands over a background of the malodorous alleys of Neel Darvaza. Neither St Stephen's nor the culture of London had had much effect on him. He dressed dressily; he lacked the social graces; and his English was oddly unidiomatic for one who had studied it at college and had lived two years in the country. As for mixing in Arun's kind of company (the Calcutta Club and the Tollygunge Racecourse: the elite of Calcutta society, both Indian and European), Arun could not see how it would be possible. Khanna was a foreman—a foreman!—in that Czech shoemaking establishment. Mrs Rupa Mehra could not seriously believe that he was fit material to marry a Mehra of their class and background, or to drag her daughter down with him. Arun added that Meenakshi, by and large, agreed with him.

What he did not add, because he did not know it, was that Meenakshi had other plans for Lata. Now that she was staying with the Chatterjis, she began to work on Amit. Kakoli was a willing accomplice. Both of them liked Lata, and both of them thought that she would be just the right match for their elder brother. She would put up with his quirks, and appreciate his work. She was intelligent and literary; and though Amit could subsist on very little conversation in life (unlike his sisters, or even Dipankar), what conversation he did have could not be fatuous or vacuous—unless, of course, it was with his brothers or sisters, where he was comparatively unbuttoned.

At any rate, Kakoli—who had once told him that she reeeeeally pitied the woman who had to marry him—had decided that she needn't pity Lata, who would be capable both of understanding and of handling her eccentric brother.

Perhaps Meenakshi's plotting was a good thing. Amit, who had liked Lata a great deal, would not have been prodded into action had it not been for his energetic and conniving sisters.

Instead of employing the usual Kakoli-couplets, which had proven to be ineffectual, the two sisters were much more gentle with Amit this time. Meenakshi told him that there was a vague Other on the scene. At first she had thought it was a fellow called Akbar or something who was acting with Lata in *As You Like It*, but the main contender had turned out to be a bumptious cobbler, who was utterly unsuited to Lata; she thus implied that Amit would be rescuing Lata from an unhappy marriage by intervening. Kakoli simply told him that Lata liked him, and that she knew he liked Lata, and that she couldn't see what he was making such a fuss about. Why didn't he send her a love letter and one of his books?

Neither Meenakshi nor Kakoli felt they had much chance of success unless they had appraised Amit's feelings for Lata correctly; but if they had, then they would act as the necessary spurs to action. They did not know much about his time at Oxford and what affairs, if any, he had had there, but they did know that in Calcutta he had rebuffed all the efforts of his female admirers or their mothers to get to know him better. He had remained faithful to Jane Austen. He appeared to be content to lead a life of contemplation. He had a strong, if not very patent, will, and never did anything he didn't want to. As for the law, in which he had earned his degree, in spite of Biswas Babu's exhortations and his father's annoyance, Amit had showed no signs of exerting himself in it at all.

His justification to himself for his idleness went something like this: I need not worry about money; I shall never be in real want. Why earn more than I need? If I take up practising law, apart from boring myself and being irritable to everyone around me, I will achieve nothing of permanent worth. I will be just one among thousands of lawyers. It is better to write one lasting sonnet than to win a hundred spectacular cases. I think I can write at least one lasting sonnet in my life—if I allow myself the scope and time to do so. The less I clog up my life with needless busy-ness, the better I find I write. Therefore I will do as little as possible. I will work on my novel whenever I can, and write a poem whenever inspiration seizes me, and leave it at that.

It was this scheme of his that had been threatened by his father's ultimatum and Dipankar's abscondence. What would happen to his novel if he was saddled with financial drudgery?

Unfortunately, doing as little as possible by way of breadwinning was accompanied in Amit's case by doing as little as possible in his social life as well. He had a few good friends, but they were all abroad—friends from his university days, to whom he wrote and from whom he received short letters, corresponding in style to the desultory conversations he used to have with them. They had been quite different from him in temperament and usually it was they who had befriended him. He was reserved, and found it difficult to make the first move, but was not slow to respond. In Calcutta, however, he had not responded much to anyone. The family had sufficed for society whenever he had needed it. It was because Lata was a member of the clan by marriage that he had felt obliged to make sure she was taken care of at the Chatterji party. Because she was quasi-family he had talked to her almost from the first in an easy and casual manner that normally came to him after months of acquaintance. Later he had grown to like her for herself. That he should have bothered to take her around Calcutta to show her the sights of the city had struck both his sisters and Dipankar as an unusual expenditure of energy. Perhaps Amit too had found his Ideal.

It had stopped there, however. After Lata left Calcutta, they did not correspond. Lata had found Amit kind and comforting; he had taken her out of her sadness into the world of poetry, into the history of the city, and—equally important—into the open air, whether of the cemetery or of College Street. Amit for his part had liked Lata a great deal, but had stopped short of declaring his fondness for her. Though he was a poet and had some insight into human emotion in general, he was far too reticent in his own life for his own happiness. When he was at Oxford, he had been wordlessly attracted to a woman, the sister of one of his friends, and as lively and explosive as a firecracker; only later did he learn that she had liked him too—and had finally in impatience given up on him and attached herself to someone else. 'Wordlessly' meant that he had not said what he had felt for her. He had, however, written a great many words, rhymed and somewhat reasoned, about his feelings, though he had crossed out most of them, published very few of those that were left, and sent or shown her none.

Meenakshi and Kakoli did not know of this affair (or non-affair), though everyone in the family believed that there had to be some explanation for all the unhappy love poems in his first, very successful, volume. Amit was, however, more than capable of fending off in his acid way any sisterly inquiries that approached too closely his sensitive, fertile, lazy core.

His second volume showed a kind of philosophical resignation unusual in a man who was not yet thirty—and who was fairly famous. What on earth, wondered one of his English friends in a letter, was he resigned about? He did not realize that Amit was probably, and perhaps even undiagnosed by himself, lonely. He had no friends—either men or women—in Calcutta; and the fact that this was the fault of his own lack of effort and sociability didn't mitigate his resultant mood: a sort of jocular weariness, and even at times plain if private despondency.

His novel, set in the period of the Bengal famine, took him outside himself into the lives of others. But even here Amit wondered from time to time if he hadn't chosen too black a canvas. The subject was complex and deep—man against man, man against nature, the city against the countryside, the desperate expediencies of war, a foreign government against an unorganized peasantry—perhaps he would have been better off writing social comedy. There was enough material for it in the family around him. And he had a taste for it; he often found himself escaping into light reading—detective stories, the ubiquitous Wodehouse, even comics—from his task of weighty prose.

When Biswas Babu had broached the question of marriage with Amit, he had stated, with his usual vibratory emphasis: 'An arranged marriage with a sober girl, that is the solution.' Amit had said that he would reserve judgement on the matter, though he had felt immediately that nothing would be more repugnant to him; he would rather live a bachelor all his days than under a canopy of feminine sobriety. But after his walk in the cemetery with Lata, when she had not been put off by his whimsical manner and the wild and whirling nature of his words, and had responded to them with surprising liveliness, he had begun to wonder if the fact that she was 'a sober girl' should count so greatly against her. She had shown no awe of him, though he was well known, nor any defensive need to emphasize her own opinions. He remembered her unselfconscious gratitude and pleasure when he had given her a garland of flowers for her hair after the dreadful lecture at the Ramakrishna Mission. Perhaps, he thought, my sisters are right for once. But, well, Lata will be coming to Calcutta at Christmas, and I can show her the great banyan tree at the Botanical Gardens, and we'll see how things work out from there. He felt no sense of urgency about events, only a very mild foreboding about the cobbler, and no concern at all about this Akbar fellow.

13.35

Mournfully, languishingly, Kuku was warbling to her own accompaniment on the piano:

> 'In this house I am so lonely.
> I am loved by Cuddles only.'

'Oh, do shut up, Kuku,' said Amit, putting down his book. 'Must we have this non-stop nonsense? I'm reading this unreadable Proust, and you're making it worse.'

But Kuku felt that it would be a dereliction of inspiration to stop. And a betrayal of Cuddles, who was leashed to the far leg of the piano.

> 'Chatterjis can go to hell,
> I will live in Grand Hotel.
>
> What room number is or where,
> With my Cuddles—I don't care!'

Her left-hand accompaniment livened up, and the rather Schubertian melody gave way to jazz:

> 'I would like room 21:
> With my Cuddles: that is fun!
>
> I would like room 22:
> With my Cuddles: that will do.
>
> I would like room 23:
> With my Cuddles: just for me.
>
> I would like room 24:
> With my Cuddles: . . .'

She played a little, in an extemporaneous manner—trills, broken chords and fragments of uncertain melody—until Amit could bear the suspense no longer, and added: 'To be sure.'

They improvised the rest of the song together:

'I would like room 25:
With my Cuddles: we will thrive.

I would like room 26:
With my Cuddles: please to fix.

I would like room 27:
With my Cuddles: that is heaven.

I would like room 28:
With my Cuddles: that is great.

I would like room 29:
With my Cuddles: that is fine.

I would like room number 30.
"Sorry, no, that room is dirty."'

Both of them laughed with pleasure, and told each other how stupid they were. Cuddles barked hoarsely, but then suddenly grew very excited. His ears pricked up and he strained at the leash.

'Pillow?' said Amit.

'No, he looks pleased.'

The front doorbell rang, and Dipankar walked in.

'Dipankar!'

'Dada! Welcome back.'

'Hello, Kuku, hello, Dada—Oh, Cuddles!'

'He knew you were back even before you rang the bell. Put that bag down.'

'Clever dog. Clever, clever dog.'

'So!'

'So!'

'Look at you—black and gaunt—and why have you shaved your head?' said Kuku, stroking the top of it. 'It feels like a mole.'

'Have you ever stroked a mole, Kuku?' asked Amit.

'Oh, don't be pedantic, Dada, you were so nice a moment ago. The prodigal returns, and—what does "prodigal" mean anyway?'

'What does it matter?' said Amit. 'It's like "lambent", everyone uses it, no one knows what it means. Well, why have you shaved your head? Ma's in for a shock.'

'Because it was so hot—didn't you get my postcards?'

'Oh, yes,' said Kuku, 'but you wrote in one of them that you were going to grow your hair long and that we would never see you again. We loved your postcards, didn't we, Dada? All about the Quest for the Source and the whistles of the pregnant trains.'

'What pregnant trains?'

'That's what it looked like in your handwriting. Welcome back. You must be ravishingly hungry.'

'I am—'

'Bring out the fatted marrow!' said Amit.

'Tell us, have you found another Ideal?' demanded Kuku.

Dipankar blinked.

'Do you worship the Female Principle in her? Or is there more to it than that?' asked Amit.

'Oh, Dada,' said Kuku reproachfully. 'How can you!' She became the Grande Dame of Culture, and pronounced with pontifical languor: 'In our India, like the stupa, the breast nourishes, inflates . . . the breast is not an object of lust to our young men, it is a symbol of fecundity.'

'Well—' said Dipankar.

'We were just floating away on the wings of song, when you came in, Dada,' said Kuku:

> 'Auf Flügeln des Gesanges . . .
> Fort nach den Fluren des Ganges

and now you can keep us firmly on earth—'

'Yes, we need you, Dipankar,' said Amit. 'All of us except you are helium balloons—'

Kuku broke in.

> 'Morning bathing in the Ganga,
> Guaranteed to make you younger,'

she sang. 'Was it really very filthy? Ila Kaki will be furious—'

'Do you mind not interrupting me, Kuku, once I've interrupted you?' said Amit. 'I was saying that you, Dipankar, are the only one who keeps this family sane. Calm down, Cuddles! Now have some lunch and a bath and a rest—Ma's out shopping, but she should be back in an hour. . . . Why didn't you tell us when you were coming? Where have you been? One of your postcards was from Rishikesh! What have you decided about the family business? Won't you handle all that and let me work on my wretched novel? How can I give it up or postpone it when all those characters are howling in my head? When I am pregnant and hungry and full of love and indignation?'

Dipankar smiled. 'I'll have to let my Experiences merge with my Being, Dada, before I can come to an Answer.'

Amit shook his head in exasperation.

'Don't bully him, Dada,' said Kuku. 'He's just come back.'

'I know I'm indecisive,' said Amit, midway between despair and mock-despair, 'but Dipankar really takes the cake. Or, rather, doesn't even know whether to.'

13.36

The Chatterji parliament convened as usual at breakfast; apart from Tapan, who was back in boarding school, everyone was there; Aparna was attended by her ayah; and even old Mr Chatterji had joined them, as he sometimes did after walking his cat.

'Where's Cuddles?' asked Kakoli, looking around.

'Upstairs, in my room,' said Dipankar. 'Because of Pillow.'

'Piddles and Cullow—like the Whalephant,' said Kakoli, referring to her favourite Bengali book, *Abol Tabol*.

'What's that about Pillow?' asked old Mr Chatterji.

'Nothing,' said Mrs Chatterji. 'Dipankar was only saying that Cuddles is afraid of him.'

'Oh, yes?' said the old man, nodding. 'Pillow can hold his own against any dog.'

'Doesn't Cuddles have to go to the vet today?' asked Kakoli.

'Yes,' said Dipankar. 'So I'll need the car.'

Kakoli made a long face. 'But I need it too,' she said. 'Hans's car is out of order.'

'Kuku, you always need the car,' said Dipankar. 'If you're willing to take

Cuddles to the vet yourself, you can have it.'

'I can't do that, it's terribly boring, and he snaps at whoever's holding him.'

'Well, then, take a taxi to meet Hans,' said Amit, who always found this breakfast tussle over the car immensely irritating, and the worst way to begin the day. 'Do stop bickering about it. Pass me the marmalade, please, Kuku.'

'I'm afraid neither of you can have it,' said Mrs Chatterji. 'I am taking Meenakshi to see Dr Evans. She needs a check-up.'

'I don't really, Mago,' said Meenakshi. 'Stop fussing.'

'You've had a very unpleasant shock, darling, and I'm taking no chances,' said her mother.

'Yes, Meenakshi, no harm in having a check-up,' said her father, lowering the *Statesman*.

'Yes,' agreed Aparna, spooning her quarter-boiled egg into her mouth with a great deal of energy. 'No harm.'

'Eat your food, darling,' said Meenakshi to Aparna, a little annoyed.

'The marmalade, Kuku, not the gooseberry jam,' said Amit in a brittle voice. 'Not the gazpacho, not the anchovies, not the sandesh, not the soufflé; the marmalade.'

'What's got into you?' said Kakoli. 'You've been very short-tempered of late. Worse than Cuddles. It must be sexual frustration.'

'Something that you wouldn't know about,' said Amit.

'Kuku! Amit!' said Mrs Chatterji.

'But it's true,' said Kakoli. 'And he's taken to chewing ice cubes, which I've read somewhere is an infallible sign of it.'

'Kuku, I will not have you talking this way at breakfast—with A sitting here.'

Aparna sat up with interest, setting her egg-coated spoon down on the embroidered tablecloth.

'Mago, A doesn't understand the first word we're saying,' said Kakoli.

'Anyway, I'm not,' said Amit.

'I think you must be dreaming about her.'

'Who?' said Mrs Chatterji.

'The heroine of your first book. The White Lady of your sonnets,' said Kakoli, looking at Amit.

'You should talk!' said Amit.

'Foreign woman is so shameless.
Indian also is not blameless,'

murmured Kakoli.

She had tried to eschew couplets, but this one had simply presented itself and rolled off her tongue.

Amit said: 'Marmalade, please, Kuku, my toast is getting cold.'

'Foreign woman is a vulture.
Goes against our ancient culture—'

blurted Kuku blindly. 'It's a good thing you made poetry out of that affair rather than little Chatterjis. Marry someone nice and Indian, Dada; don't follow my example. Have you sent Luts that book yet? She told me you'd promised her one.'

'Less wit. More marmalade,' requested Amit.

Kuku passed it to him at last and he spread it on his toast very carefully, covering every corner. 'She told you that, did she?' asked Amit.

'Oh, yes,' said Kakoli. 'Meenakshi will vouch for me.'

'Oh, yes,' said Meenakshi, looking intently at her tea. 'Everything Kakoli says is true. And we're concerned about you. You're almost thirty now—'

'Don't remind me,' said Amit with dramatic melancholy. 'Just pass me the sugar before I'm thirty-one. What else did she say?'

Rather than invent something entirely implausible and thus risk undoing the effect of her previous statement, Meenakshi wisely refrained.

'Nothing very specific,' she said. 'But with Lata, a small comment goes a long way. And she mentioned you several times.'

'Quite wistfully, I thought,' said Kakoli.

'How is it,' said Amit, 'that Dipankar and I—and Tapan—have turned out to be so honest and decent, and you girls have learned to lie so brazenly? It's amazing that we belong to the same family.'

'How is it,' countered Kakoli, 'that Meenakshi and I, whatever our faults, can make important decisions and make them fast, when you refuse to make them and Dipankar can never decide which one to make?'

'Don't get annoyed, Dada,' said Dipankar, 'they're just trying to bait you.'

'Don't worry,' said Amit. 'They won't succeed. I'm in too good a mood.'

13.37

Late, I admit, but better late than not, /never
A gift to one who can appraise its worth, /need not spare its
This book got ever lot /got /rot /hot /shot /over-shot /sot comes
to you from a word-drunk sot, flaws
A earth hackney bard and bachelor of laws laws.

Amit paused in his scribbling and doodling. He was attempting an inscription for Lata. Now that he had run out of inspiration he began to wonder which of his two books of poems he should send her. Or should he send her both? Perhaps the first one was not such a good idea. The White Lady of his sonnets might give Lata the wrong idea. Besides, the second, though it too contained some love poems, had more of Calcutta in it, more of the places that reminded him of her, and might perhaps remind her of him.

Resolving this problem helped Amit get on with his poem, and by lunchtime he was ready to write his dédicace on the flyleaf of *The Fever Bird*. His scrawled draft was legible only to himself, but what he wrote for Lata was easy enough to read. He wrote it out slowly, using the sterling silver fountain pen which his grandfather had given him on his twenty-first birthday, and he wrote in the comparatively handsome British edition of his poems, of which he had only three copies left.

Late, I admit, but better late than not,
A gift to one who need not spare its flaws,
This book comes to you from a verbal sot,
A babu bard and bachelor of laws.

Lest you should think the man you meet here seems
A lesser cynic than the one you knew,
The truth is that apart from wine and dreams
And children, truth inheres in poems too.

Lies too lie here, and words I do not say
Aloud for fear they savour of despair.
Thus, passionless, I wing my even way
And beat a soundless tattoo on the air.

Love and remembrance, mystery and tears,
A surfeit of pineapples or of bliss,
The swerve of empires and the curve of years,
Accept these in the hand that carves you this.

He signed his name at the bottom, wrote the date, reread the poem while the ink dried, closed the dark-blue-and-gold cover of the book, packed it, sealed it, and had it sent off by registered post to Brahmpur that same afternoon.

13.38

It would have been too much to hope that Mrs Rupa Mehra would not have been at home when the post arrived two days later at Pran's house. She hardly ever went out these days, what with Savita and the baby. Even Dr Kishen Chand Seth, if he wanted to see her, had to come to the university.

When Amit's parcel arrived, Lata was at a rehearsal. Mrs Rupa Mehra signed for it. Since the mail from Calcutta carried nothing but disaster these days, and her curiosity about the contents was unassuageable (especially when she saw the sender's name), she almost opened the parcel herself. Only the fear of being condemned jointly by Lata, Savita and Pran restrained her.

When Lata returned, it was almost dark.

'Where have you been all this time? Why didn't you get back earlier? I've been going mad with anxiety,' said her mother.

'I've been at rehearsal, Ma, you know that. I'm not much later than usual. How's everyone? Baby's sleeping, by the sound of it.'

'This package arrived two hours ago—from Calcutta. Open it at once.' Mrs Rupa Mehra was about to burst.

Lata was going to protest, but then, noticing the anxiety on her mother's face and thinking of her volatility and tearfulness ever since she had received the news about the second medal, she decided that it was not worth asserting her right to privacy if it meant causing her mother further pain. She opened the package.

'It's Amit's book,' she said with pleasure: '*The Fever Bird* by Amit Chatterji. Very handsome—what a beautiful cover.' Mrs Rupa Mehra, forgetting for a second the threat that Amit had once posed, picked up the book and was enchanted. The plain blue-and-gold cover, the paper, which appeared to be far superior to the stock they had seen during the war, the wide margins, the clear, spacious print, the luxury of it all delighted her. She had seen the smaller and shabbier Indian edition of the book in a bookstore once; the poems, which she had glanced through, had not seemed to her to be very edifying, and she had put it down. Mrs Rupa Mehra could not help wishing that the handsome book that she was now holding had been blank: it would have made a wonderful vehicle for the poems and thoughts that she often copied down.

'How lovely. In England they really make such beautiful things,' she said.

She opened the book and began to read the inscription. Her frown grew deeper as she reached the bottom.

'Lata, what does this poem mean?' she asked.

'How can I tell, Ma? You haven't given me a chance to read it myself. Let me have a look at it.'

'But what are all these pineapples doing here?'

'Oh, that's probably Rose Aylmer,' said Lata. 'She ate too many and died.'

'You mean, "A night of memories and sighs"? That Rose Aylmer?'

'Yes, Ma.'

'How painful it must have been!' Mrs Rupa Mehra's nose began to redden in sympathy. Then a sudden alarming thought struck her: 'Lata, this is not a love poem, is it? I can't even understand it, it could be anything. What does he mean by Rose Aylmer? Those Chatterjis are very clever.'

Mrs Rupa Mehra had just had a renewed attack of resentment against the Chatterjis. She attributed the theft of the jewellery to Meenakshi's carelessness. She was always opening the trunk in the presence of the servants, and putting temptation in people's way. Not that Mrs Rupa Mehra wasn't worried about Meenakshi too (who must have been very upset after this shock)—and about her third grandchild, assuredly a grandson this time. In fact, if it hadn't been for Savita's baby, she might well have rushed off to Calcutta, to busy herself with help and commiseration. Besides, there were several things she wanted to check in Calcutta in the wake of Arun's letter, particularly how Haresh was faring—and what exactly it was he was doing. Haresh had said that he was working 'in a supervisory capacity, and living in the European colony at Prahapore'. He had not mentioned that he was a mere foreman.

'I doubt it's a love poem, Ma,' said Lata.

'And he hasn't written "Love" or anything at the bottom, just his name,' said Mrs Rupa Mehra, reassuring herself.

'I like it, but I'll have to reread it,' Lata mused aloud.

'It's too clever for my liking,' said Mrs Rupa Mehra. 'Tattoo and sot and whatnot. These modern poets are like this. And he hasn't even had the politeness to write your name,' she added, further reassured.

'Well, it's on the envelope, and I can't imagine he talks about pineapples to everyone,' said Lata. But she too thought it a little strange.

Later, lying on her bed, she read the poem again at her leisure. She was secretly very pleased to have a poem written for her, but much in it was not immediately clear. When he said that he winged his even and passionless way, did he mean that the temperature of his poems was cool? That he was speaking in the voice of the bird of the title but was not fevered? Or did it mean something private to his imagination? Or anything at all?

After a while, Lata began to read the book, partly for itself, partly as a clue to the inscription. The poems were, by and large, no more unclear than their complexity required; they made grammatical sense, and Lata was grateful for that. And some of them were poems of deep feeling, by no means passionless, though their diction was at times formal. There was an eight-line love poem that she liked, and a longer one, a bit like an ode, about walking alone through the Park Street Cemetery. There was even a humorous one about buying books on College Street. Lata liked most of the poems that she read, and was moved by the fact that when she had been lonely and unoccupied in Calcutta Amit had taken her to places that had meant so much to him and that he was used to visiting alone.

For all their feeling, the tenor of the poems was muted—and sometimes self-deprecating. But the title poem was anything but muted, and the self that it presented appeared to be gripped almost by mania. Lata herself had often been kept awake on summer nights by the papiha, the brainfever bird, and the poem, partly for this reason, disturbed her profoundly.

THE FEVER BIRD

The fever bird sang out last night.
I could not sleep, try as I might.

My brain was split, my spirit raw.
I looked into the garden, saw

The shadow of the amaltas
Shake slightly on the moonlit grass.

Unseen, the bird cried out its grief,
Its lunacy, without relief:

Three notes repeated closer, higher,
Soaring, then sinking down like fire

Only to breathe the night and soar,
As crazed, as desperate, as before.

I shivered in the midnight heat
And smelt the sweat that soaked my sheet.

And now tonight I hear again
The call that skewers through my brain,

The call, the brainsick triple note—
A bone of pain stuck in its throat.

I am so tired I could weep.
Mad bird, for God's sake let me sleep.

Why do you cry like one possessed?
When will you rest? When will you rest?

Why wait each night till all but I
Lie sleeping in the house, then cry?

Why do you scream into my ear
What no one else but I can hear?

Her thoughts a whirl of images and questions, Lata read this poem through five or six times. It was far clearer than most of the poems in the book, clearer certainly than the inscription he had written for her, and yet it was far more mysterious and disturbing. She knew the yellow laburnum, the amaltas tree that stood above Dipankar's meditation hut in the garden at Ballygunge, and she could imagine Amit looking out at its branches at night. (Why, she wondered, had he used the Hindi word for the tree rather than the Bengali—was it just for the sake of the rhyme?) But the Amit she knew—kindly, cynical, cheerful—was even less the Amit of this poem than of the short love poem that she had read and liked.

Did she even like this poem, she wondered. The thought of Amit sweating disturbed her—he was to her a disembodied and comforting spirit, and it was best that he remained that way. By now it had been dark for more than an hour, and Lata could imagine him lying on his bed, hearing the papiha sing its triple note, and tossing restlessly from side to side.

She looked at the personalized inscription again. She wondered why he had used the word 'carve' in the final line. Was it simply to chime—in a slightly overdone manner, she could not help feeling—with the 'swerve' and 'curve' of the previous line? A poem could hardly be carved. But this was probably just poetic licence, like the bird's wings beating a tattoo, or the claim that he was drunk on words.

Then, suddenly, and for no apparent reason at all, for she was not looking out for such a curious feature as this, she realized, with simultaneous delight and dismay, how carved, how personalized the inscription indeed was, and why, after all, he had not written her name above the poem. It went far beyond the reference to pineapples, to the moment in the cemetery that they had shared. She had only to look down the first letters of each of the four lines in each of the four quatrains to realize how inextricably bound she was not merely to the sentiment but to the very structure of Amit's poem.

'Set in post-independence India, the novel follows for eighteen months or so four linked families in Calcutta, the province of Purva Pradesh and its capital Brahmpur, and the cities—Delhi, Kanpur, Lucknow—trawled by the heroine's mother in her search for a "suitable boy"... But the greatness of the novel, its unassailable truthfulness, owes less to research than to imagination, an instinctive knowledge of the human heart—with all its varieties of kindness and cruelty... As with all the best books, one feels only dismay when the pages on the right of the tome start thinning out.'

—*The Observer*

A Suitable Boy

By the same author

FICTION

The Golden Gate: A Novel in Verse
An Equal Music

POETRY

Mappings
The Humble Administrator's Garden
All You Who Sleep Tonight
Three Chinese Poets (*translations*)
Beastly Tales from Here and There (*fables*)
Arion and the Dolphin (*libretto*)
The Rivered Earth (*libretti and essays*)
Summer Requiem

MEMOIR

Two Lives

NON-FICTION

From Heaven Lake: Travels through Sinkiang and Tibet

A Suitable Boy

{ VOLUME THREE }

VIKRAM
SETH

SPEAKING
TIGER

SPEAKING TIGER BOOKS LLP
125A, Ground Floor, Shahpur Jat,
New Delhi–110002, India

First published by Penguin India 1993
This edition published by Speaking Tiger Books 2023

ISBN: 978-93-5447-487-3

10 9 8 7 6 5 4 3 2 1

Printed at Chaman Enterprises, New Delhi

The author would personally like to thank Jaishree Ram Mohan and her enthusiastic young team at Penguin India for proofreading A Suitable Boy *in 2013, and Ajith Kumar for typesetting it.*

To
Papa and Mama
and
the memory of Amma

A WORD OF THANKS

To these I owe a debt past telling:
My several muses, harsh and kind;
My folks, who stood my sulks and yelling,
And (in the long run) did not mind;
Dead legislators, whose orations
I've filched to mix my own potations;
Indeed, all those whose brains I've pressed,
Unmerciful, because obsessed;
My own dumb soul, which on a pittance
Survived to weave this fictive spell;
And, gentle reader, you as well,
The fountainhead of all remittance.
Buy me before good sense insists
You'll strain your purse and sprain your wrists.

CONTENTS (Volume Three)

ACKNOWLEDGEMENTS

The author and publishers would like to thank the following for permission to quote copyright material:

The Ministry of Human Resources Development, Govt of India for extracts from *Letters to Chief Ministers*, Vol. 2, 1950–1952 by Jawaharlal Nehru, general editor G. Parthasarathi (Jawaharlal Nehru Memorial Fund, distributed by Oxford University Press, 1986)

HarperCollins Publishers Ltd for extracts from *The Koran Interpreted* by A.J. Arberry (George Allen & Unwin Ltd; and Oxford University Press, 1964)

Oxford University Press for an extract from *The Select Nonsense of Sukumar Ray* translated by Sukanta Chaudhuri (Oxford University Press, 1987)

Faber & Faber for an extract from the poem 'Law, Say the Gardeners' published in *W.H. Auden: Collected Poems* edited by Edward Mendelson (Faber & Faber)

Penguin Books Ltd for extracts from *Selected Poems* by Rabindranath Tagore, translated by William Radice (Penguin Books, 1985)

Bantam Books Inc. for extracts from *The Bhagavad-Gita* translated by Barbara Stoler Miller (Bantam Books, 1986)

The Sahitya Akademi for extracts from *Mir Anis* by Ali Jawad Zaidi published in the series 'Makers of Indian Literature' (Sahitya Akademi, 1986)

The Gita Press, Gorakhpur, for extracts from *Sri Ramacharitamanasa* translated into English (Gita Press, 1968)

While every effort has been made to trace copyright holders and obtain permission, this has not been possible in all cases; any omissions brought to our attention will be remedied in future editions.

MEHRAS

DR KISHEN CHAND SETH *m* FIRST WIFE (d) *remarried* PARVATI

CHILDREN including . . . RUPA *m* RAGHUBIR MEHRA (d)

ARUN MEHRA *m* MEENAKSHI (*née* Chatterji)

APARNA

SAVITA *m* PRAN KAPOOR

VARUN MEHRA

LATA MEHRA

KAPOORS

MR TANDON (d) *m* OLD MRS TANDON

CHILDREN including . . . KEDARNATH TANDON *m* VEENA

BHASKAR

MAHESH KAPOOR *m* MRS MAHESH KAPOOR

VEENA

PRAN KAPOOR *m* SAVITA (*née* Mehra)

MAAN KAPOOR

KHANS

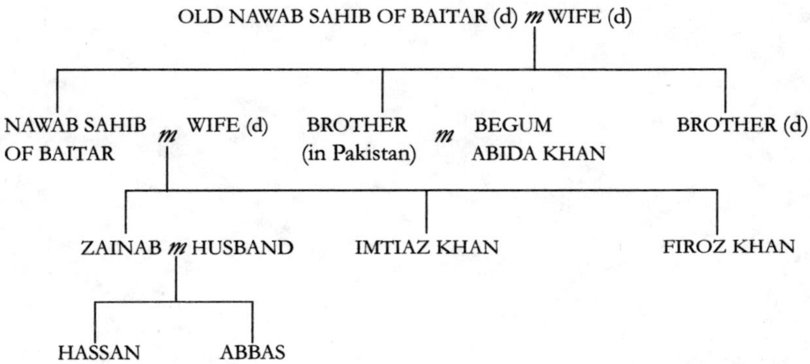

CHATTERJIS

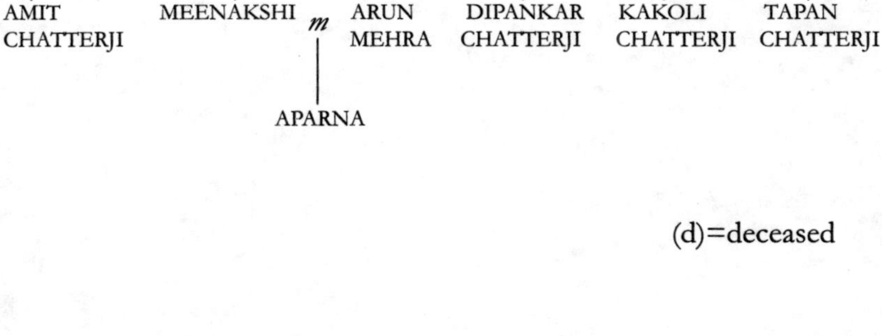

(d)=deceased

The superfluous, that very necessary thing. . . .

VOLTAIRE

The secret of being a bore is to say everything.

VOLTAIRE

Part Fourteen

14.1

Mahesh Kapoor left for his farm in Rudhia in early August in the company of Maan. Now that he was no longer a Minister, he had a little more free time for his own pursuits. Apart from supervising the work on the farm itself—the main activity at present was the transplantation of rice—he had two other purposes in leaving Brahmpur. The first was to see if Maan, who had proved himself uninterested and unsuccessful in working in Banaras, might possibly be happier and more effectively employed in running the farm. The second was to ascertain from where he could best fight a candidate from the Congress Party for an Assembly seat in the coming General Elections—now that he himself had left it and joined the newly formed Peasants' and Workers' Peoples' Party—the KMPP for short. The obvious rural choice was the constituency that contained his farm—which was in the Rudhia subdivision of Rudhia District. As he walked around his fields, his mind turned once more to Delhi and the great figures of the strife-ridden Congress Party vying with each other for power on the national stage.

Rafi Ahmad Kidwai, the wise, wily and playful politician from U.P., who had been responsible for a spate of resignations from the Congress, including Mahesh Kapoor's, was anathema to the Hindu-chauvinist right wing of the party—partly because he was Muslim, partly because he had twice orchestrated opposition to the attempts of Purushottamdas Tandon to become President of the Congress Party. Tandon had been narrowly defeated in 1948, and had narrowly won in 1950—in a dubiously fought battle made more bitter by the knowledge that whoever controlled the Congress Party machine in 1951 would have control over the selection of candidates for the forthcoming General Elections.

Tandon—a barefooted, bearded, austere and rather intolerant man, seven years Nehru's senior and, like him, from Allahabad—now headed the organization of the Congress Party. He had chosen his Working Committee largely from the party bosses of the individual states and their supporters, for in most of the states the party machinery was already in the control of the conservatives. Since Tandon had insisted that the Congress President's choice of his Working Committee should be unfettered, he did not include—and had indeed refused to include—either his defeated opponent Kripalani—or Kidwai, who had planned Kripalani's campaign. Prime Minister Nehru, already upset by Tandon's election, which he rightly interpreted as a victory not only for Tandon but for Sardar Patel, his own great conservative rival, had at first refused to join a Working Committee that excluded Kidwai. But in the interests of unity, because he saw the Congress as the only cohesive force in the localized and divided web of Indian politics, he swallowed his objections and joined it.

Nehru sought to protect his policies as Prime Minister from any possible onslaught by the activist Congress President by proposing party resolutions on each of his main policies, all of which had been overwhelmingly passed by the assembled party. But passing resolutions by acclamation was one thing, controlling the personnel of the party—and the selection of candidates—another. Nehru was left with the uneasy sense that the lip service that was being paid to the policies of his government would change once the right wing got its own slate of MLAs and MPs into Parliament and the state legislatures. Nehru's vast popularity would be used to win the elections, and then he would be left stranded and impotent.

The death of Sardar Patel, a couple of months after Tandon was elected, had left the right wing without its greatest strategist. But Tandon proved to be a formidable opponent in his own right. In the name of discipline and unity he attempted to suppress dissenting groups within the party, such as the Democratic Front established by Kidwai and Kripalani (the so-called K-K Group), which were outspoken in their criticism of his leadership. Stay in the party and support the Working Committee, they were warned, or get out. Unlike his compliant predecessor in the job, Tandon also insisted that the party organization as represented by its President had every right to advise, and indeed control, the policies of the Congress Government headed by Nehru—down to the question of banning hydrogenated cooking oil. And on every important issue his views were diametrically opposed to those of Nehru or his supporters—men such as Kripalani and Kidwai or, closer to Brahmpur, Mahesh Kapoor.

Apart from economic differences, the Nehruites and the Tandonites saw the Muslim question in an entirely different light. Throughout the year there had been a great deal of mutual snarling by India and Pakistan across their borders. It had appeared several times that war might be imminent over the problem of Kashmir. While Nehru saw war as a disastrous possibility for the two poor countries, and attempted to come to some kind of understanding with the Pakistani Prime Minister Liaquat Ali Khan, many embittered members of his party were in favour of war with Pakistan. One member of his Cabinet had resigned, formed his own Hindu revivalist party, and was even talking of conquering Pakistan and reuniting it by force with India. What made things worse was the steady stream of refugees, mainly now from East Pakistan into Bengal, that put an unsupportable burden upon the state. They were fleeing because of ill treatment and insecurity in Pakistan, and several hardliners in India suggested under a theory of reciprocity that for each Hindu migrant from Pakistan a Muslim should be expelled from India. They saw matters in terms of Hindus and Muslims, of collective guilt and collective revenge. So successfully indeed had the two-nation theory—the Muslim League's justification for Partition—taken root in their own minds that they saw Muslim citizens of India as Muslims first and Indians only incidentally; and were willing to visit upon their heads punishment for the actions of their co-religionists in the other country.

Such talk repelled Nehru. The thought of India as a Hindu state with its minorities treated as second-class citizens sickened him. If Pakistan treated its minority citizens barbarically, that was no reason for India to do so. He had, after Partition, personally pleaded with a number of Muslim civil servants to remain in India. He had accepted, if not exactly welcomed, into the Congress fold, a number of leaders who had belonged to the Muslim League, which had virtually ceased to exist in India. He had attempted to reassure Muslims who, because of ill treatment and a sense of insecurity, were still migrating to West Pakistan through Rajasthan and other border states. He had preached against communal enmity in every speech he had given—and Nehru was much given to speeches. He had refused to countenance any of the retaliatory actions urged on him by many of the dispossessed Hindu and Sikh refugees from Pakistan, by the right-wing parties, and by the right wing of his own party. He had tried to soften some of the more draconian decisions of the Custodian-General of Evacuee Property, who had often acted more in the interests of those who hankered after evacuee property than of the evacuees themselves. He had signed a pact with Liaquat Ali Khan which had reduced the likelihood of war with Pakistan. All these actions infuriated people who saw Nehru as a rootless, deracinated Indian, whose sentimental creed was a pro-Muslim secularism, and who was divorced from the majority of his own Hindu citizenry.

The only problem for his critics was that his citizenry loved him and would almost certainly vote for him, as it had done ever since his great tour in the 1930s, when he had travelled around the country, charming and stirring up vast audiences. Mahesh Kapoor knew this—as, indeed, did anyone with the faintest knowledge of the political scene.

While walking around his farm, discussing with his manager irrigation problems in a season when rainfall had been disappointing, Mahesh Kapoor's mind often turned to Delhi and to the momentous events that, he felt, had left him no choice but to leave the party to which he had given his allegiance for thirty years. He, like many others, had hoped that Nehru would come to see how futile were his efforts to maintain his policies in the face of Tandon's activities and would take some firm measure of control; but Nehru, though his own supporters were haemorrhaging away from his party as it drifted into its right-wing orbit, refused to leave the Congress or to take any positive action other than to plead, in meeting after meeting of the All-India Congress Committee, for unity and reconciliation. As he vacillated, his supporters floundered. Eventually, by late summer, a point of crisis had been reached.

In June a special convention of the Congress Party was held in Patna. There, at a parallel convention, the fledgling KMPP was established by several leaders, including Kripalani, who had recently resigned from the Congress, accusing it of 'corruption, nepotism and jobbery'. Kidwai, without actually resigning from the Congress, had been elected to the Executive Committee of the KMPP. This action brought down upon him the wrath of the right-wingers; for how (as one of them wrote to Tandon) could he continue to be a Central Minister of the Congress government and simultaneously belong to the executive of the party that was one of its most vociferous opponents—one which, indeed, hoped to supplant the Congress itself? Kripalani had tendered his resignation as a member of the Congress Party to Tandon, but Kidwai had not. Surely, argued his critics, he had better do so at once.

In early July the Working Committee and then the All-India Congress Committee met once again in Bangalore. Kidwai was asked to explain himself by the Working Committee. He hedged, claimed in his easy-going way that he had no immediate intention of resigning from the Congress, stated that he had tried to get the KMPP session postponed but had failed to do so, and expressed his hope that the Bangalore session of the Congress would make his anomalous position and the atmosphere in general much clearer.

The Bangalore session, however, did no such thing. Nehru, seeing at last that resolutions in his support were not enough, demanded something much more concrete: a complete reconstitution of the two most powerful committees of the Congress—the Working Committee and the Central Election Committee—so as to reduce their domination by the right wing. At this, Tandon offered to resign together with the whole of his Working Committee. Fearing a permanent split in the Congress, Nehru backed down. A few more conciliatory resolutions were passed. Some pulled in one direction, some in another. On the one hand the Congress disapproved of groups within its ranks; on the other, there would be an open door back to the party for those 'seceders' who agreed with the general aims of the Congress. But rather than rejoin the Congress, two hundred more Congressmen resigned and joined the KMPP at Bangalore. The atmosphere remained as murky as ever, and Rafi Ahmad Kidwai decided that the time for vacillation had passed. The battle had to be joined.

He returned to Delhi and wrote a letter to the Prime Minister, resigning both from the Cabinet as Minister of Communications and from the Congress Party. He made it clear that both he and his friend Ajit Prasad Jain, the Minister for Rehabilitation, had resigned because they could not stand Tandon or his policies or his undemocratic method of functioning. They emphasized that they had no quarrel with Nehru himself. Nehru pleaded with them to reconsider their decision, and this they did.

The next day they both announced that they had decided not to resign from the Cabinet after all. They also announced, however, that they would continue to work against the Congress, at any rate against the Congress President and his cohorts, whose views and strategies ran counter to every important resolution or declaration of the party. Their statement explaining their decision was a startling one, coming as it did from two Ministers of the Government:

> Is there a parallel in the world where the executive head, i.e. President of an organisation, is the very antithesis of everything that the organisation stands for? What is there in common between Shri Purushottamdas Tandon and the policies of the Congress—economic, communal, international and refugees? Even at this juncture when our ways parted, we wished and hoped that the working of the Congress would fall in line with its profession.

Tandon and the old guard, goaded by what they perceived as rank disloyalty and indiscipline, demanded that Nehru call his Ministers to heel. There was no way that the dissidents could be allowed to function as Ministers and attempt at the same time to do down their own party. Nehru was forced, sadly, to agree. Jain remained in the Cabinet, agreeing not to issue further provocative statements. Kidwai, unable to agree to such a constraint, offered once more to resign. This time Nehru realized that it would be fruitless to plead with his old colleague and friend, and accepted his resignation.

Nehru was now more isolated in his own party than ever. Together with all the crushing burdens of the Prime Ministership—the food problem, the warmongering on both sides of the border, the Press Bill and the Hindu Code Bill and the endless legislation to be passed through Parliament, the relations between the Centre and the states (which had come to a boil with the declaration of direct Central rule in Punjab), the day-to-day running of the administration, the working out of the First Five-Year Plan, foreign affairs (an area that particularly exercised him), not to mention endless emergencies of one kind or another—Nehru was weighed down by the hard realization that his ideological opponents in his party had, in effect and at last, defeated him. They had elected Tandon, they had forced Nehru's supporters to leave the Congress in droves and form a new opposition party, they had taken over the District Congress Committees and Pradesh Congress Committees and the Working Committee and Central Election Committee, they had forced the resignation of the Minister who, more than any other, was sympathetic to his way of thinking, and they were poised to select their own conservative candidates for the impending General Elections. Nehru's back was to the wall; and he may perhaps have reflected that it was his own indecisiveness that had helped put it there.

14.2

Certainly, Mahesh Kapoor thought so. He was in the habit of unburdening himself to whoever was at hand, and it happened to be Maan with whom he was walking through the fields on a tour of inspection.

'Nehru has finished all of us—and himself in the process.'

Maan, who had been thinking about the wolf-hunt he had enjoyed when he was last in the area, was brought back to earth by the despair in his father's voice.

'Yes, Baoji,' he said, and wondered how to go on from there. After a pause he added, 'Well, I'm sure something will work out. Things have swung so far this way that they have to correct themselves.'

'You are a fool,' said his father shortly. He recalled how annoyed and disappointed S.S. Sharma had been when he and some of his colleagues had said they were resigning from the party. The Chief Minister liked to balance the Agarwal and Kapoor factions of his party against each other, so that he himself had maximum freedom of action; with one wing missing, his craft listed uncomfortably and his own decision-making abilities were necessarily more constrained.

Maan was silent. He began wondering how he could get away to pay a visit to his friend the Sub-Divisional Officer, who had organized the hunt a couple of months earlier.

'That things will swing back into order once they've been displaced is an optimistic and childish conceit,' said his father. 'The toy you should be thinking of is not the swing but the slide,' he continued after a pause. 'Now Nehru cannot control the Congress. And if he cannot control it, I cannot rejoin it—nor Rafi Sahib, nor any of the rest. It's as simple as that.'

'Yes, Baoji,' said Maan, taking a mild swipe at a tall weed with his walking stick, and hoping that he was not going to be treated to a long lecture on the rights and wrongs of various party positions. He was in luck. A man came running across the fields to announce that the jeep of the Sub-Divisional Officer Sandeep Lahiri had been sighted heading towards the farm.

The ex-Minister growled: 'Tell him I'm taking a walk.'

But Sandeep Lahiri appeared a few minutes later, walking gingerly (and without his accompanying policemen) along the little ridges between the fields of emerald-coloured rice. On his head was his sola topi, and there was a nervous smile above his weak chin.

He greeted Mahesh Kapoor with a mere 'Good morning, Sir,' and Maan, whom he had not expected to see, with a hello.

Mahesh Kapoor, who was still used to being addressed by his erstwhile title, looked a little closely at Sandeep Lahiri.

'Yes?' he asked abruptly.

'Quite a pleasant day—'

'Have you simply come to pay your respects?' asked Mahesh Kapoor.

'Oh, no, Sir,' said Sandeep Lahiri, horrified by the thought.

'You have not come to pay your respects?' asked Mahesh Kapoor.

'Well, not not to—but, well, I've come for a little help and advice, Sir. I heard you had just arrived here, and so I thought—'

'Yes, yes—' Mahesh Kapoor was walking on, and Sandeep Lahiri was following him on the narrow divider, rather unsteadily.

Sandeep Lahiri sighed, and plunged into his question. 'It is like this, Sir. The government has authorized us—us SDOs, that is—to collect money from the public—voluntary donations—for a small celebration on Independence Day, which is—well—just a few days away now. Does the Congress Party traditionally have any particular hold on these funds?'

The words 'Congress Party' struck an angry chord in Mahesh Kapoor's breast. 'I have nothing to do with the Congress Party,' he said. 'You are well aware of the fact that I am no longer a Minister.'

'Yes, Sir,' said Sandeep Lahiri. 'But I thought—'

'You had better ask Jha, he virtually runs the District Congress Committee. He can speak for the Congress.'

Jha was the Chairman of the Legislative Council, an old Congressman who had caused Sandeep Lahiri much trouble already, ever since the SDO had arrested his nephew for hooliganism and affray. Jha, whose ego required him to interfere in every decision of the administration, was the cause of half of Sandeep Lahiri's problems.

'But Mr Jha is—' began Sandeep Lahiri.

'Yes, yes, ask Jha. I have nothing to do with it.'

Sandeep Lahiri sighed again, then said:

'On another problem, Sir—'

'Yes?'

'I know that you are no longer Minister of Revenue, and that this is not a direct concern of yours, but, Sir, the increase in the number of evictions of tenants after the Zamindari Act was passed—'

'Who says it is not my concern?' asked Mahesh Kapoor, turning around and nearly bumping into Sandeep Lahiri. 'Tell me who says that?' If there was one subject that cut Mahesh Kapoor to the quick, it was this unspeakable side effect of his pet legislation. Peasants were being evicted from their homes and lands all over the country, wherever Zamindari Abolition Bills were being or had been passed. In almost every case the intention of the zamindar was to show that the land was and always had been under his direct cultivation, and that no one other than him had any rights in it at all.

'But, Sir, you just said—'

'Never mind what I just said. What are you doing about the problem?'

Maan, who had been walking behind Sandeep Lahiri, had also stopped. At first he looked at his father and his friend, and enjoyed their mutual discomfiture. Then, looking upwards at the great cloudy sky that merged with the far horizon, he thought of Baitar and Debaria, and sobered up.

'Sir, the scale of the problem defeats the imagination. I cannot be everywhere at once.'

'Start an agitation,' said Mahesh Kapoor.

Sandeep Lahiri's weak chin dropped. That he, as a civil servant, should start any kind of agitation was unthinkable—and it was amazing that an ex-Minister had suggested it. On the other hand, his sympathy with the evicted peasants, dispossessed and destitute as they were, had forced him to speak to Mahesh Kapoor, who was popularly seen as their champion. It had been his secret hope that Mahesh Kapoor himself might stir things up once he realized the scope of their distress.

'Have you talked to Jha?' asked Mahesh Kapoor.

'Yes, Sir.'

'And what does he say?'

'Sir, it is no secret that Mr Jha and I do not see eye to eye. What distresses me is likely for that very reason to delight him. And since he gets a large part of his funds from the landlords—'

'All right, all right,' said Mahesh Kapoor. 'I'll think about it. I have just arrived here. I have had hardly any time to ascertain things—to talk to my constituents—'

'Your constituents, Sir?' Sandeep Lahiri looked delighted that Mahesh Kapoor should be thinking of fighting from the Rudhia subdivision seat instead of from his regular urban constituency.

'Who can tell, who can tell?' said Mahesh Kapoor in sudden good humour. 'All this is very premature. Now that we are at the house, have some tea.'

Over tea, Sandeep and Maan got a chance to talk. Maan was disappointed to learn that there were no immediate prospects of a hunt. Sandeep had a distaste for hunting, and organized a hunt only when his duties demanded it.

Luckily, from his point of view, they no longer did. With the rains, poor though they were proving to be this year, the natural food chain had revived and the wolf menace had subsided. Some villagers, however, attributed their greater security to the personal intercession of the SDO with the wolves. This, together with his clear goodwill towards the people under his care, his effective on-the-site methods of determining the facts of a case in the course of his judicial duties (even if it meant holding court under a village tree), his fairness in revenue matters, his refusal to countenance those illegal evictions that came to his notice, and his firm hold on law and order in his subdivision, had made Sandeep Lahiri a popular figure in the area. His sola topi was, however, still an object of mockery for some of the younger people.

After a while Sandeep took permission to leave. 'I have an appointment with Mr Jha, Sir, and he is not someone who cares to be kept waiting.'

'About the evictions,' continued the ex-Minister of Revenue, 'I would like to see a list for this area.'

'But, Sir—' began Sandeep Lahiri. He was thinking that he had no such list, and wondering whether he should, ethically speaking, part with it even if he had.

'However inadequate, however incomplete,' said Mahesh Kapoor, and got up to escort the young man to the door before he could mention some new scruple that had occurred to him.

14.3

Sandeep Lahiri's visit to Jha's office was a fiasco.

Jha, as an important political figure, a friend of the Chief Minister, and the Chairman of the Upper House of the state legislature, was used to being consulted by the SDO on all important matters. Lahiri on the other hand saw no need to consult a party leader on matters of routine administration. He had not very long ago been at university, where he had drunk deeply of the general principles of constitutional law, the separation of the party and the state, and liberalism a la Laski. He tried to keep local politicians at arm's length.

A year in his post at Rudhia, however, had convinced him that there was no getting around direct summonses by senior political leaders. When Jha was foaming, he would have to go. He treated such visits as he would the outbreak of local pestilence: as something unforeseeable and unwelcome, but which necessitated his presence. If it was a drain on his time and his nerves, it was part of the penumbra of his job.

It would have been too much to expect the fifty-five-year-old Jha to come to the young man's office, though strictly speaking that was what the proprieties required. But out of a sense of what was due to age rather than to the Congress Party, the SDO went to visit him instead. Sandeep Lahiri was used to Jha's rudeness, so he had come prepared with a sort of silly-ass look that hid what he was really thinking. On one occasion, when Jha had not offered him a seat—apparently because of absent-mindedness, but more probably to impress his underlings of his superiority over the local representative of the state—Lahiri had, equally absent-mindedly, helped himself to one after a few minutes, smiling weakly and benevolently at Jha.

Jha, however, was in a genial mood today. He was smiling broadly, his white Congress cap askew on his huge head.

'You also sit, you also sit,' he told Sandeep. They were alone, and there was no one who needed to be impressed.

'Thank you, Sir,' said Sandeep, relieved.

'Have some tea.'

'Thank you, Sir, I normally would, but I have just had some.'

The conversation circled, then alit.

'I have seen the circular that has been distributed,' said Jha.

'Circular?'

'About the fundraising for Independence Day.'

'Ah, yes,' said Sandeep Lahiri. 'I was wondering if I might ask for your help with that. If you, Sir, respected as you are, were to encourage people to contribute, it would have a considerable effect. We could collect a substantial amount, and put on a good show—distribute sweets, feed the poor and so on. In fact, Sir, I am counting on your help.'

'And I am counting on your help,' said Jha, with a broad smile. 'That is why I have called you.'

'My help?' said Sandeep, smiling helplessly and warily.

'Yes, yes. You see, Congress also has plans for Independence Day, and we will take half the funds you collect, and use them for a separate display—a very good display to help the people and so on, you see. So that is what I expect. The other half you use as you like,' he added generously. 'Naturally, I will encourage people to contribute.'

This was precisely what Sandeep had feared. Though neither the older nor the younger man referred to it now, a couple of Jha's henchmen had made overtures of the kind to Sandeep a few days earlier; the proposal had gone entirely against his grain, and he had told them so. Now he continued to smile in a silly way. But his silence distressed the politician.

'So, then, I will expect half the funds. Good?' he said, a little anxiously.

'We will need the money soon, we will need a couple of days to organize things, and you have not yet begun your collection.'

'Well—' said Sandeep, and threw up his hands in a gesture that implied that if matters were at his discretion, he would have been delighted to give the entire sum he collected to Jha to do with as he pleased, but that, alas, the universe had been cruelly disposed to prevent him from receiving that pleasure.

Jha's face darkened.

'You see, Sir,' said Sandeep, moving his hands around freely in curves of helplessness, 'my hands are tied.'

Jha continued to stare, then exploded.

'What do you mean?' he almost shouted. 'No hands are tied. Congress says that no hands are tied. Congress will untie your hands.'

'Sir, it is like this—' began Sandeep Lahiri.

But Jha did not let him continue. 'You are a servant of the government,' said Jha fiercely, 'and the Congress Party runs the government. You will do as we tell you.' He adjusted the white cap on his head and hitched up his dhoti under the table.

'Mmm,' said Sandeep Lahiri in a non-committal voice, donning a frown as perplexed and silly as his smile.

Realizing that he was making no headway, Jha decided on a conciliatory and persuasive tack. 'Congress Party is the party of Independence,' he said. 'Without Congress there would be no Independence Day.'

'True, true, very true,' said the Sub-Divisional Officer, nodding his head in gratified agreement. 'The party of Gandhi,' he added.

This comment caused geniality to flood back into Jha's ample frame.

'So we understand each other?' he said, eagerly.

'I hope, Sir, that we always will—that no misunderstanding can ever make its way into our relations,' replied Sandeep Lahiri.

'We are two bullocks of one yoke,' said Jha dreamily, thinking of the Congress election symbol. 'Party and Government pulling together.'

'Mmm,' said Sandeep Lahiri, the dangerously silly smile appearing again on his face in order to mask his Laskian doubts.

Jha frowned. 'How much do you think you will collect?' he asked the young man.

'I don't know, Sir, I haven't done this sort of collecting before.'

'Let us say, five hundred rupees. So we will get two hundred and fifty, you will get two hundred and fifty—and everyone will be satisfied.'

'Sir, you see, I am in a difficult position,' said Sandeep Lahiri, biting the bullet.

This time Jha said nothing, simply staring at the presumptuous young fool.

'If I give you some of the money,' continued Sandeep Lahiri, 'the Socialist Party will want some, the KMPP—'

'Yes, yes, I know you have visited Mahesh Kapoor. Did he ask for money?'

'No, Sir—'

'Then what is the problem?'

'But, Sir, to be fair—'

'Fair!' Jha could not mask his contempt for the word.

'To be fair, Sir, we would have to give an equal amount to all these parties—to the Communist Party, to the Bharatiya Jan Sangh, to the Ram Rajya Parishad, to the Hindu Mahasabha, to the Revolutionary Socialist Party—'

'What!' burst out Jha. 'What?' He swallowed. 'What? You are comparing us to the Socialist Party?' He hitched up his dhoti once again.

'Well, Sir—'

'To the Muslim League?'

'Certainly, Sir, why not? The Congress is just one of many parties. In this respect they are all the same.'

Jha, utterly outraged and nonplussed, the image of the Muslim League spinning like a Divali firework through his head, glared at Sandeep Lahiri.

'You equate us with the other parties?' he asked, his voice trembling with anger that was almost certainly unfeigned.

Sandeep Lahiri was silent.

'In that case,' continued Jha, 'I will show you. I will show you what the Congress means. I will make sure that you are not able to raise any funds. Not one paisa will you be able to get. You will see, you will see.'

Sandeep did not say anything.

'Now I have nothing to say,' continued Jha, his right hand gripping a light-blue glass egg that acted as a paperweight. 'But we will see, we will see.'

'Well, yes, Sir, we will see,' said Sandeep, getting up. Jha did not get up from his chair. Turning at the door Sandeep aimed his weak smile at the furious Congressman in a final attempt at goodwill. The Congressman did not smile back.

14.4

Sandeep Lahiri, deciding that there was not much time to spare, and fearing that Jha was quite likely right in his estimate of his fund-gathering abilities, went that afternoon to the marketplace in Rudhia dressed in his khaki shirt and shorts, and with his pith helmet on his head. A small crowd gathered around him because it was not obvious what he was doing there and because, in any case, the visit of the SDO was a notable event.

When a couple of shopkeepers asked him what they could do for him, Sandeep Lahiri said, 'I am collecting funds for the Independence Day celebration, and have been authorized to ask the public for contributions. Would you like to contribute something?'

The shopkeepers looked at each other, and simultaneously, as if by previous consultation, each took out a five-rupee note. Lahiri was known to be an honest man and had used no pressure of any kind, but it was probably best to contribute, they thought, when he asked them to, even if it was to be spent on a government-sponsored event.

'Oh, but that's too much,' said the SDO. 'I think I should set a maximum of one rupee per person. I don't want people to contribute more than they can afford.'

Both shopkeepers, very pleased, pocketed their five-rupee notes and offered him one-rupee coins instead. The SDO looked at the coins, and then absent-mindedly put them in his pocket.

The news spread through the marketplace that the SDO himself was asking for money for Independence Day, that it was going to feed children and the poor, that there was no duress and that he had set a maximum of one rupee for each contribution. This news, together with his personal popularity, worked like magic. As he strolled casually through the lanes of Rudhia, Sandeep—who hated making speeches in his flawed Hindi and felt awkward about the whole business of asking for money—was besieged by smiling contributors, some of whom had heard that Jha was opposed to their SDO's fund-gathering campaign. Sandeep found himself reflecting that in these early years of Independence, local Congressmen had already—through their venality, self-importance and blatant influence-peddling—made themselves quite unpopular, and that the people's sympathy was entirely on his side in any struggle with the politicians. If he had stood for an election against Jha, he would probably, like most young SDOs in their fiefs, have won. Meanwhile, Jha's henchmen, who had come out quickly and in force to try to persuade people to give money for the Congress celebration and not for the government one, ran into a wave of popular resistance. Some people who had already deposited a rupee into Sandeep's kitty decided to contribute once again, and Sandeep could do nothing to stop them.

'No, Sir, this is from my wife, and this is from my son,' said one triple contributor.

When his pockets were full of coins, Sandeep took off his famous sola topi, emptied his pockets into it, and used it as a bowl for further contributions. From time to time he mopped his forehead. Everyone was delighted. Money rained into his hat: some people gave him two annas, some four, some eight, some a rupee. All the urchins of the marketplace formed a processional tail behind him. Some shouted, 'SDO Sahib ki jai!' Others stared at the treasury that was building up in his hat—more coins than they had ever seen in one place—and took bets on how much he would gather.

It was a hot day, and Sandeep paused occasionally for breath on the ledge of a shop.

Maan, who had driven into town, saw the crowd and waded into it to see what the matter was.

'What are you up to?' he asked Sandeep.

Sandeep sighed. 'Enriching myself,' he said.

'I wish I found it so easy to make money,' said Maan. 'You look exhausted. Here, let me help you.' And he took the sola topi from him and started handing it around for contributions.

'I say, you'd better not do that. If Jha hears about it, he won't be pleased,' said Sandeep.

'Bugger Jha,' said Maan.

'No, no, no, here, dear fellow, give it back,' said Sandeep, and Maan gave him his hat back.

After half an hour, when his hat had filled up, and both his pockets were bulging again, Sandeep stopped in order to count the money.

He had gathered an unimaginable eight hundred rupees.

He decided to stop his collection at once, even though there were plenty of people eagerly reaching forward with their coins. He had more than he needed to put on a really excellent show for Independence Day. He made a little speech, thanking the people for their generosity and assuring them that the money would be well used; he masculinized a great many Hindi nouns in the process.

The news spread through the bazaar and reached Jha's ears, which grew red with anger.

'I will show him,' he said aloud, and turned back home. 'I will show him who is the boss in Rudhia.'

14.5

He was still fuming when Mahesh Kapoor came to visit him.

'Oh, Kapoorji, Kapoorji, welcome, welcome to my poor house,' said Jha.

Mahesh Kapoor was short with him. 'Your friend Joshi has been evicting tenants from his land. Tell him to stop. I won't have it.'

Jha, his cap askew, looked shrewdly at Mahesh Kapoor and said, 'I haven't heard anything of the kind. Where has your information come from?'

'Don't worry about that, it's reliable. I don't want this sort of thing taking place on my doorstep. It gives the government a bad name.'

'Why do you care if the government gets a bad name?' said Jha with a broad smile. 'You are no longer part of it. Agarwal and Sharma were talking to me the other day. They were saying that you had joined Kidwai and Kripalani merely to make a K-K-K Group.'

'Are you mocking me?' said Mahesh Kapoor angrily.

'No, no, no, no—how can you say that?'

'Because if you are, let me tell you that I am prepared to fight from this constituency if necessary to make sure that the farmers here are not maltreated by your friends.'

Jha's mouth opened slightly. He could not imagine Mahesh Kapoor fighting from a rural constituency, so closely associated was he in everyone's mind with Old Brahmpur. Mahesh Kapoor had rarely interfered much in the affairs of Rudhia, and Jha resented his new activist role.

'Is this why your son was making speeches in the marketplace today?' Jha said in a surly tone.

'What speeches?' said Mahesh Kapoor.

'With that boy Lahiri, that IAS fellow.'

'What are you talking about?' said Mahesh Kapoor dismissively. 'I'm not interested in all that. All I can tell you is that you'd better get Joshi to lay off—or else I'll get a case registered against him. Whether I'm in the government or not, I don't want the Zamindari Act to become toothless, and if necessary I am prepared to become the local dentist.'

'I have a better suggestion, Maheshji,' said Jha, hitching up his dhoti aggressively. 'If you are so keen on a rural constituency, why not fight from Salimpur-cum-Baitar? Then you can make sure that your friend the Nawab Sahib doesn't evict his tenants, as I understand he is very skilled in doing.'

'Thank you, I will take note of your suggestion,' said Mahesh Kapoor.

'And do tell me when your party, the—what is it called?—it is so difficult to remember these alphabet parties that keep springing up—the KMPP—yes, KMPP—manages to get a hundred votes, Maheshji,' said Jha, who was delighted that he could parley thus with a man who had been so powerful just a few weeks earlier. 'But why have you left us Congress-wallahs bereft of your presence and wisdom? Why have you left the party of Nehru? Chacha Nehru, our great leader—how will he manage without people like you—people of enlightened views? And, more to the point, how will you manage without him? When he comes to ask the people to vote for Congress, do you think they will listen to him or to you?'

'You should be ashamed to take Nehru's name,' said Mahesh Kapoor heatedly. 'You believe in nothing he does, yet you will use him to catch your votes. Jha Sahib, if it were not for Nehru's name, you would be nothing.'

'If. If,' said Jha expansively.

'I have heard enough nonsense,' said Mahesh Kapoor. 'Tell Joshi that I have a list of the tenants he has turned out. How I have got it concerns neither him nor you. He had better reinstate them by Independence Day. That is all I have to say.'

Mahesh Kapoor got up to go. As he was about to leave the room, Joshi, the very man he had been talking about, entered. Joshi looked so worried that he hardly noticed Mahesh Kapoor until he bumped into him. He looked up—he was a small man with a neat white moustache—and said:

'Oh, Kapoor Sahib, Kapoor Sahib, such terrible news.'

'What terrible news?' said Mahesh Kapoor. 'Have your tenants bribed the police before you could get to them yourself?'

'Tenants?' said Joshi blankly.

'Kapoorji has been writing his own Ramayana,' said Jha.

'Ramayana?' said Joshi.

'Must you repeat everything?' said Jha, who was beginning to lose patience with his friend. 'What is this terrible news? I know that this Lahiri fellow has managed to extort a thousand rupees from the people. Is that what you came to tell me? Let me tell you that I will deal with him in my own way.'

'No, no—' Joshi found it difficult to speak, so momentous was the information he was carrying. 'It is just that Nehru—'

His face was wobbling with unhappiness and alarm.

'What?' said Jha.

'Is he dead?' asked Mahesh Kapoor, prepared for the worst.

'No, far worse—resigned—resigned—' gasped Joshi.

'As Prime Minister?' asked Mahesh Kapoor. 'From the Congress? What do you mean "resigned"?'

'From the Congress Working Committee—and from the Central Election Committee,' cried Joshi miserably. 'They say that he is thinking of resigning from the Congress altogether—and joining another party. God knows what will happen. Chaos, chaos.'

Mahesh Kapoor realized immediately that he would have to go back to Brahmpur—and perhaps even to Delhi—for consultations. As he left the room he turned back for one last glance at Jha. Jha's mouth was open, and his hands were clutching the two sides of his white Congress cap. He was entirely incapable of concealing the powerful emotion that had seized him. He was in a state of violent shock.

14.6

Maan had remained behind on the farm when his father had rushed off to Brahmpur in the wake of the news of Nehru's resignation from his party posts. There had been talk of a crisis in the Congress Party for over a year, but there was no doubt now that it was truly upon them. The Prime Minister of the country had virtually declared that he had no confidence in the elected leadership of the party whom he represented in Parliament. And he had chosen to make this declaration just a few days before Independence Day when he, as Prime Minister, would speak to the nation from the ramparts of the Red Fort in Delhi.

Sandeep Lahiri, meanwhile, briefly addressed the assembled population of Rudhia from a podium erected at the edge of the local maidan. He took charge of feeding the poor with the help of various women's organizations in the town. He distributed sweets to children with his own hands—a task he found pleasant but awkward. And he took the salute at the boy scouts' parade and the police parade and hoisted the national flag, which had been filled beforehand with marigold petals, a shower of which fell on him as he looked up in surprise.

Jha was not present. He and his supporters boycotted the whole show. At the end of the ceremonies, after a local band had struck up the National Anthem, and Sandeep Lahiri had shouted 'Jai Hind!' to the cheers of a couple of thousand people, more sweets were distributed. Maan gave him a hand with this, and appeared to be enjoying it a great deal more than Sandeep. The children were finding it difficult not to break ranks and had to be restrained by their flustered teachers. While all this was going on, a postman came up to the SDO, and handed him a telegram. He was about to put it absently into his pocket, when it struck him that it might contain something of importance. But his hand was sticky with jalebis, and he asked Maan, who had managed to avoid that particular hazard, to open it for him and read it out to him.

Maan opened the envelope and read it out. At first the message did not quite register on Sandeep, but then he frowned, and it was not a silly-ass frown but an aggrieved one. Jha had moved fast, it appeared. The telegram had been sent by the Chief Secretary of Purva Pradesh. It informed Shri Sandeep Lahiri, IAS, of his transfer with immediate effect from the post of Sub-Divisional Officer of Rudhia subdivision to a post in the Department of Mines at Brahmpur. He was to relinquish charge as soon as the officer to replace him arrived, on the 16th of August, and to report at Brahmpur the same day.

14.7

One of Sandeep Lahiri's first acts upon arriving in Brahmpur was to request an interview with the Chief Secretary. A couple of months earlier, the Chief Secretary had dropped him a note to say that he had been doing an excellent job in his subdivision, and had especially commended his role in solving—by on-the-spot inquiries in the villages—a large number of land disputes that had appeared for some years to be intractable. He had assured Lahiri of his full support. And now, in effect, he had pulled the rug out from under his feet.

The Chief Secretary, busy though he was, granted him an interview at his house the same evening.

'Now I know what you are going to ask me, young man, and I will be quite frank with you. But I must tell you in advance that there is no question of this order being rescinded.'

'I see, Sir,' said Sandeep, who had grown very fond of Rudhia, and had expected to serve his full term there—or at least to be given the time to apprise his successor of the problems and pitfalls—as well as the pleasures—that he was likely to encounter, and the various schemes that he had set in train which he would be sorry to see fall into neglect.

'You see, orders in your case came directly from the Chief Minister.'

'Did Jha have anything to do with this?' asked Sandeep, frowning

'Jha? Oh, I see—Jha, from Rudhia. I'm afraid I couldn't tell you. It's certainly possible. I'm beginning to think that anything's possible these days. Have you been treading on his toes?'

'I suppose I have, Sir—and he on mine.'

Sandeep filled the Chief Secretary in on the details of their conflict. The Chief Secretary's eyes drifted across his table.

'You do realize that this is a premature promotion, don't you?' he said at last. 'You shouldn't be displeased.'

'Yes, Sir,' said Sandeep. And indeed, the position of Under-Secretary in the Department of Mines, though lowly enough in the hierarchy of the Indian Administrative Service, ranked higher than the post of SDO, with all its freedom of action and its life in the open air. He would in the normal course of things have been transferred to a desk job in Brahmpur six months later.

'Well, then?'

'Did—well, Sir, if I might ask—did you say anything to dissuade the Chief Minister from getting rid of me?'

'Lahiri, I do wish you wouldn't see things in that light. No one has got rid of you, and no one wishes to. You have an excellent career ahead of you. I cannot go into details, but I will tell you that the first thing I did upon receiving the CM's instructions—which, incidentally, did surprise me—was to call for your file. You have an excellent record, with a number of good marks and only one bad mark against you. The only reason that I could think of that the CM wanted you out of Rudhia was that Mahatma Gandhi's birth anniversary is coming around in a couple of months. It appears that your decision in that troublesome matter last year rather annoyed him; I assumed that something had jogged his memory of late, and he thought that your presence in Rudhia might be a provocation. Anyway, it will be no bad thing for you to spend some time in Brahmpur early on in your career,' he continued in a genial tone. 'You'll be spending at least a third of your working life here, and you may as well see how things run in the labyrinths of the state capital. My only specific advice,' continued the Chief Secretary, now rather glumly, 'is that you should not be seen at the bar of the Subzipore Club too often. Sharma, being a true Gandhian, doesn't like people drinking; he makes rather a point of summoning me for some emergency work late in the evening whenever he hears I'm at the club.'

The incident that the Chief Secretary had referred to a little earlier involved the railway colony at Rudhia where the previous year a number of young Anglo-Indian men—the sons of railway employees—had smashed the glass in front of a noticeboard that contained a poster of Mahatma Gandhi, which they had then proceeded to deface. There had been an uproar in response, and the offenders had been arrested, beaten up by the police, and hauled up before Sandeep Lahiri in his magisterial incarnation. Jha had screamed for their trial on the grounds of sedition, or at the very least of having grievously injured the religious sentiments of the population. Sandeep, however, had realized that these were hotheaded but not really ill-meaning young men, who had had no inkling of the possible consequences of their actions. He had waited for them to sober up, and then—after dressing them down and making them apologize in public, had discharged them with a warning. His judgement with respect to the charges sought to be brought against them had been succinct:

> This is quite evidently not a case of sedition: Gandhiji, revere his memory though we do, is not the King-Emperor. Nor is he the head of a religion, so the charge of injuring people's religious sentiments does not hold either. As for the charge of mischief, the smashed glass and defaced portrait do not cost more than eight annas, and de minimis non curat lex. The defendants are discharged with a warning.

Sandeep had been itching for some time to use this Latin tag, and here was the ideal opportunity: the law did not concern itself with trifles, and here was a trifling matter, at least in monetary terms. But his linguistic pleasure was not without cost. The Chief Minister had not been amused, and had instructed the previous Chief Secretary to enter a black mark against him in his character roll. 'Government have considered Mr Lahiri's ill-judged decision in the case of the recent disorder in Rudhia. Government note with regret that he has chosen to make a display of his liberal instincts at the cost of his duty to maintain law and order.'

'Well, Sir,' said Sandeep to the Chief Secretary, 'what would you have done if you had been in my place? Under what provision of the Indian Penal Code could I have chopped off those silly young men's heads, even if I had wished to?'

'Well,' said the Chief Secretary, unwilling to criticize his predecessor. 'I really can't go into all that. Anyway, as you say, it is probably some recent contretemps with Jha that has got you transferred, not that earlier incident. I know what you're thinking: that I should have stood up for you. Well, I have. I made sure that your transfer was not a lateral one, that it involved a promotion. That was the best that I could do. I know when it is useful, and when it is not, to argue with the Chief Minister—who, to give him his due, is an excellent administrator and values good officers. One day, when you are in a position similar to mine—and I don't see why, given your potential, you shouldn't be—you will have to make similar, well, adjustments. Now, can I offer you a drink?'

Sandeep accepted a whisky. The Chief Secretary grew boringly expansive and reminiscent:

'The problem, you see, began in 1937—once you got politicians running things at the provincial level. Sharma was elected Premier, as it was then called, of the Protected Provinces—as our state then was. It became fairly obvious to me early on that other considerations than merit would apply in promotions and transfers. When the lines of power ran from Viceroy to Governor to Commissioner to District Magistrate, things were clear enough. It was when the legislators crawled into every level except the very top that the rot started. Patronage, power bases, agitations, politics, toadying to the elected representatives of the people: all that kind of stuff. One had to do one's own duty of course, but what one saw sometimes dismayed one. Some batsmen could now score a six even if the ball bounced within the boundary. And others were declared out even if they were caught outside the boundary. You see what I mean. Incidentally, Tandon—who's been trying to declare Nehru out by insisting on the rules by which the Congress plays the game—was a fine cricketer—did you know that?—when he was at Allahabad University. I believe he captained the Muir Central College team. Now he goes around bearded and barefoot like a rishi from the Mahabharata, but he was a cricketer once. Cricket has a lot to answer for. Another?'

'No, thanks.'

'There's also the fact that he was the Speaker of the U.P. Legislative Assembly during those years. Rules, rules, and very little flexibility. I always thought it was us bureaucrats who were the sticklers for rules. Well, the country's burning and the politicians are fiddling, not very tunefully at that. It is up to us to keep things going. The iron frame and all that: rusting and buckling, though, I'd have to say. Well, I'm almost at the end of my career, and I can't say I'm sorry. I hope you enjoy your new job, Lahiri—Mines, isn't it? Do let me know how you're getting along.'

'Thank you, Sir,' said Sandeep Lahiri, and got up with a serious expression on his face. He was beginning to understand all too well how things worked. Was this his own future self he had been talking to? He could not hide from himself his dismay and, yes, it would not be too much to say, his disgust, at this new and most unwelcome insight.

14.8

'Sharmaji came here to meet you this morning,' said Mrs Mahesh Kapoor to her husband when he returned to Prem Nivas.

'He came himself?'

'Yes.'

'Did he say anything?'

'What would he say to me?' asked Mrs Mahesh Kapoor.

Her husband clicked his tongue in irritation. 'All right,' he said. 'I'll go and see him.' It was more than civil of the Chief Minister to have come in person to his house, and Mahesh Kapoor had a shrewd idea of what he wanted to discuss. The crisis in the Congress was the talk of the country now, not just of the party. Nehru's resignation from all his party offices had made certain of that.

Mahesh Kapoor called ahead, then visited Sharma at home. Though he had left the Congress, he continued to wear the white cap that had become a natural part of his attire. Sharma was sitting on a white cane chair in the garden, and stood up to greet him as he approached. He should have looked tired, but he did not. It was a warm day, and he had been fanning himself with a newspaper, the headlines of which spoke of the latest moves to conciliate Nehru. He offered his erstwhile colleague a chair and some tea.

'I needn't go around in circles, Kapoor Sahib,' said the Chief Minister. 'I want your help in trying to persuade Nehru to return to the Congress.'

'But he has never left it,' said Mahesh Kapoor with a smile, seeing that the Chief Minister was already thinking two steps ahead.

'I meant, to full participation in the Congress.'

'I sympathize, Sharmaji; these must be troubling times for the Congress Party. But what can I do? I am no longer a member of the party myself. Nor are many of my friends and colleagues.'

'The Congress is your true home,' said Sharma, a little sadly, his head beginning to shake. 'You have given everything for it, you have sacrificed the best years of your life for it. Even now you are sitting in the same position in the Legislative Assembly as before. If that wedge is now labelled the KMPP or something else, I still look upon it with affection. I still consider you my colleagues. There are more idealists there than in those who have remained with me.'

Sharma did not need to state that by this he was referring to the likes of Agarwal. Mahesh Kapoor stirred his tea. He felt great sympathy for the man whose Cabinet he had so recently resigned from. But he hoped that Nehru would leave the Congress and join the party that he himself had joined, and he could not see how Sharma could have imagined that he, of all people, would be keen to dissuade him from doing so. He leaned forward a little and said quietly: 'Sharmaji, I sacrificed those years for my country more than for any party. If the Congress has betrayed its ideals, and forced so many of its old supporters to leave—' He stopped. 'Anyway, I see no immediate danger of Panditji leaving the party.'

'Don't you?' said Sharma.

A couple of letters lay in front of him, and he now handed one of them, the longer one, to Mahesh Kapoor and tapped his finger on a couple of paragraphs at the end. Mahesh Kapoor read slowly, not looking up till he had finished. It was one of Nehru's regular fortnightly letters to his Chief Ministers and was dated August 1—two days after his friend Kidwai, having withdrawn his resignation, had resigned again. The last part of the long letter, which ranged over the entire gamut of foreign and domestic developments, went as follows:

> 24. There has been frequent reference in the press recently to resignations from the Central Cabinet. I confess I have been greatly troubled over this matter, for the two persons concerned have been valuable colleagues who have fully justified their membership of Government. There was no question of a difference of opinion in

regard to governmental policy. Difficulties arose about other matters relating to the National Congress. I do not propose to say anything about this subject here because you will probably soon see some statements in the press which will explain the present position. That position only indirectly affects the Government. Essentially it is a question of the future of the Congress. This is not only of interest to Congressmen but to everybody in India, because the role of the Congress has been great.

25. The next session of Parliament begins on Monday next, August 6th. This is the last session before the elections. It has heavy business before it, some of which is of importance and must be passed during the session. Probably this session will last for about two months.

Yours sincerely,
Jawaharlal Nehru

Mahesh Kapoor, reading the letter in the light of Nehru's resignation less than a week later from the Congress Working Committee and Central Election Committee, could see why Sharma—or anyone else—might think that these resignations were preliminary to Nehru's complete resignation from the Congress. 'Because the role of the Congress has been great' sounded ominously lukewarm.

Sharma had put down his cup and was looking at Mahesh Kapoor. Since the latter made no comment, he said, 'The U.P. Congressmen are going to try to persuade Nehru to withdraw his resignation—or at least to persuade Nehru and Tandon to come to some kind of compromise. I too feel we should send a group to speak to him. I am prepared to go to Delhi myself. But I want you to come with me.'

'I am sorry, Sharmaji,' said Mahesh Kapoor with some annoyance. Sharma might be the great conciliator, but he surely could not imagine that he could persuade him, who was now a member of the opposition, into such a self-defeating position. 'I cannot help you. Panditji respects you, and you will be as persuasive as anyone. For my part, I, like Kidwai and Kripalani and all the others who have left the Congress, hope that Nehru will join us soon. As you say, we have some elements of idealism. Perhaps it is time that politics was based on issues and ideals, and not on the control of party machines.'

Sharma's head began to nod slightly. A peon came out on to the lawn with a message, but he waved him away. For a while he rested his chin on his hands, then said, in his nasal but persuasive manner:

'Maheshji, you must be wondering about my motives, perhaps even about my logic. It may be that I have not made my visualization of the situation clear. I will put before you several pictures. First: Suppose Nehru leaves the Congress. Suppose further that I do not wish to fight him in the forthcoming elections, perhaps because of my respect for him, perhaps because I fear to lose, and—as an old man—care too much about my own self-respect. At any rate, I too resign from the Congress. Or if not from the Congress, from active participation in affairs of state—from the government, from the Chief Ministership. The state will require a new Chief Minister. In the present configuration, unless the ex-Minister of Revenue rejoins the party and persuades those who left with him to rejoin, there will be only one contender for the mantle.'

'You would not permit Agarwal to become Chief Minister,' said Mahesh Kapoor in a hard voice, making no attempt to conceal his resentment and shock. 'You would not deliver the state into his hands.'

Sharma cast an eye around the garden. A cow had got into the radish patch, but he ignored it.

'I am only drawing imaginary scenes,' he said. 'Let me draw a second one. I go to Delhi. I try to talk to Nehru, to persuade him to withdraw his resignations. He, for his part, renews his standard assault on me. He wants me at the Centre, in the Cabinet—a Cabinet now already depleted by resignations. We both know Jawaharlal, we know how persuasive he can be. He will say that more important than the Congress Party is the good of India, the government of the country. He wants good administrators at the Centre, people of stature, people of proven competence. I am only repeating the kind words he has already repeated a score of times to me. So far I have always found some excuse for getting back from Delhi. People say I am ambitious, that I prefer to be King in Brahmpur rather than a baron in Delhi. They may be right. But this time Jawaharlal tells me: "You are asking me to act against my own inclinations for the good of the country, yet you refuse to do the same yourself." It is an unanswerable argument. I go to Delhi as a Cabinet Minister, and L.N. Agarwal takes over as Chief Minister of Purva Pradesh.'

Mahesh Kapoor remained silent. After a while, he said: 'If—if this were the case, and this—this man took over, it would only be for a few months. The people would throw him out in the coming elections.'

'I think you underestimate the Home Minister,' said S.S. Sharma with a smile. 'But now, suppose we leave this bugbear behind and think in broader terms: in terms of the country itself. Do you or I want the kind of battle that will ensue if Nehru leaves the Congress? If you recall the bitterness that was generated in the battle within the Congress Party when Tandon got elected—and it is no secret that I too voted for him rather than Kripalani—can you imagine the bitterness of the battle in the General Elections if Nehru fights on one side and the Congress on the other? Whom will the people turn to? Think how their hearts will be torn, their loyalties divided. The Congress, after all, is the party of Gandhiji, the party of Independence.'

Mahesh Kapoor forbore from remarking that it was the party of a good deal else besides: nepotism, corruption, inefficiency, complacency—and that Gandhiji himself had wanted it dissolved as a political force after Independence. He said: 'Well, if there has to be a battle, it should be fought during these elections. If the Congress uses Nehru to fight its election battles and then turns against him because its right wing has most of the MLAs and MPs in its pocket—that will be far worse. The sooner the matter is fought out, the better. I agree that the two of us should be fighting on the same side. I wish, Sharmaji, that I could persuade you to join my party—and then persuade you to persuade Nehru to do the same.'

The Chief Minister smiled at what he chose to interpret as an attempt at humour by Mahesh Kapoor. Then he picked up the second letter that he had in front of him and said:

'What I am showing you now is not one of Panditji's regular fortnightly letters, but a special letter to the Chief Ministers. It is supposed to be secret. It is dated a couple of days after he wrote to Tandonji submitting his resignation. If you read it you will see why I am so worried about the possibility of divisions in the country at this time.' He handed Mahesh Kapoor the letter, then said: 'I have not shown this to anyone yet, not even to anyone in my Cabinet, though I have told Agarwal to come around to read it because it concerns him as Home Minister. And I will naturally discuss it with the Chief Secretary. It would not be good if the contents of this letter got around.'

He then got up and walked over with the help of his cane to tell his gardener to chase the cow out of the vegetable garden, leaving Mahesh Kapoor to read the letter. Parts of it read as follows:

> New Delhi
> 9 August, 1951
>
> My dear Chief Minister,
>
> The Indo-Pakistan situation shows no signs of improvement. The most that can be said is that it has not grown any worse, but it is bad enough. On the Pakistan side, feverish preparations for war are taking place. . . .
>
> Considering the question logically, I do not consider war likely. But logic does not explain everything and, in any event, we cannot base our activities on pure logic. Logic would not explain the spate of propaganda, full of hatred and falsehood, that issues from Pakistan. . . .

There was a sound of aggrieved if patient lowing from the far end of the garden. Mahesh Kapoor's eyes skimmed rapidly down the letter. Nehru was now talking about the Indian Muslims:

> . . . Sometimes it is said that there might be bad elements among the Muslims who might give trouble. That is quite possible, but I think it highly unlikely that any major trouble will come from that direction. We should be careful of course in regard to strategic areas or vital spots.
>
> I think it is much more likely that trouble may come from Hindu or Sikh communal elements. They would like to take advantage of the occasion to misbehave towards Muslims. If any such thing occurs, it will have very bad consequences and will weaken us. Therefore, this kind of thing must not be allowed to happen. This is of major importance and we must give full protection to our minorities. This means also that we must not permit any propaganda on the part of Hindu or Sikh communal organisations, which is on a par with Pakistan propaganda on the other side. There have been some recent incidents of this where, lacking originality, the Hindu Mahasabha people have tried to imitate the Pakistanis. They did not succeed to any extent. But it is quite possible that if we are unwary and some incidents happen, the communal elements might take advantage of them. I would, therefore, specially request you to keep this in mind. . . .
>
> These are speculations which I am sharing with you. We have

to be prepared for all emergencies and, in a military sense, we are so prepared from now onwards. I still hope and partly believe that there will be no war and I do not wish to do anything on our side which might perhaps tip the balance on the side of war.

Hence my earnest request to you that no public activity that savours of war preparation should be indulged in or encouraged in others, while at the same time our minds must keep prepared.

You will please keep this letter as top secret and not to be shared with others except, perhaps, a very few.

Yours sincerely,
Jawaharlal Nehru

14.9

When Sharma returned from chasing the cow out of the further reaches of the garden, he found Mahesh Kapoor pacing up and down, restless and troubled. 'You see,' said Sharma, homing unerringly into his thoughts, 'you see why we cannot have any unnecessary divisions of opinion in the country at this time, of all times. And also why I am so keen to persuade you to return to the Congress. Agarwal's attitude to the Muslims is well known. As he is the Home Minister, well, I have to leave certain matters in his hands. And the calendar this year makes things worse than ever.'

This last sentence took Mahesh Kapoor by surprise. 'The calendar?' he asked, frowning at Sharma.

'Here—let me show you—' The Chief Minister took a small brown diary out of his kurta pocket. He pointed to the beginning of October. 'The ten days of Moharram and the ten days leading up to Dussehra almost coincide this year. And Gandhi Jayanti falls within the same period.' He closed the diary and laughed humourlessly. 'Rama, Muhammad, and Gandhiji may all have been apostles of peace—but in combination there could be nothing more explosive. And if in addition there is war with Pakistan, and the only cohesive party in India is bitterly divided within itself—I fear to think of what will happen throughout the country between the Hindus and the Muslims. It will be as bad as the Partition riots.'

Mahesh Kapoor did not reply. But he could not deny to himself that he had been deeply affected by the arguments of the Chief Minister. When offered more tea, he accepted, and sat down on a cane chair. After a few minutes he said to his former chief, 'I will think about what you have said.' He was still holding Nehru's letter in his hands. In fact, unconsciously, he had folded it lengthwise two or three times.

It was unfortunate that L.N. Agarwal should have chosen that very moment to visit the Chief Minister. As he walked across the lawn he noticed Mahesh Kapoor. Mahesh Kapoor nodded, but did not get up to greet him. He did not intend to be discourteous, but his thoughts were far away.

'About Panditji's letter—' began L.N. Agarwal.

Sharma reached out for the letter, and Mahesh Kapoor handed it over in an absent manner. Agarwal frowned, obviously displeased that the letter had been shared with Mahesh Kapoor: Sharma appeared to be treating him as if he were still a member of his Cabinet, instead of the renegade that he was.

Perhaps sensing his thoughts, S.S. Sharma began to explain, rather apologetically: 'I was just discussing with Kapoor Sahib the urgency of bringing Panditji back into full participation in the Congress. We cannot do without him, the country cannot do without him, and we must persuade him by any means we can. It is a time to close ranks. Don't you agree?'

A look of disdain slowly formed on L.N. Agarwal's face as he thought about this attitude: dependent, cringing, weak.

'No,' he said at last. 'I do not agree. Tandonji has been democratically elected. He has constituted his own Working Committee, and it has managed very well for several months. Nehru has participated in its meetings; he has no right to try to change its membership now. That is not his prerogative. He claims to be a democrat; let him prove it by doing the right thing. He claims to believe in party discipline; he should abide by it. He claims to believe in unity; let him stand by his beliefs.'

S.S. Sharma closed his eyes. 'That is all very well,' he murmured. 'But if Panditji—'

L.N. Agarwal almost exploded. 'Panditji—Panditji—why should everyone go whimpering and pleading for everything to Nehru? Yes, he is a great leader—but are there no other great leaders in Congress? Does Prasad not exist? Does Pant not exist? Did Patel not exist?' At the thought of Sardar Patel his voice almost choked with emotion. 'Let us see what happens if he leaves us. He doesn't have the least idea how to organize a campaign, how to gather funds, how to select candidates. And he will have no time, as Prime Minister, to storm the country—that is quite obvious. He has too much on his plate as it is, attempting to run it. Let him join Kidwai—he'll get the Muslim vote all right. But we will see what else he gets.'

Mahesh Kapoor got up, nodded curtly to the Chief Minister, and began to walk away. The Chief Minister, distressed and annoyed by Agarwal's explosion, made no attempt to stop him from going; Agarwal and Kapoor in one place did not form a happy combination.

It is like dealing with two refractory children, he thought. But he called out after Mahesh Kapoor:

'Kapoor Sahib, please think about what I have said. We will talk about this again soon. I will come over to Prem Nivas.'

Then he turned to Agarwal and said, with displeased nasality: 'An hour's good work destroyed in a minute. Why are you going out of your way to antagonize him?'

L.N. Agarwal shook his head. 'Everyone is afraid to speak his mind,' he said. He reflected that matters in Purva Pradesh had become much clearer now that the leftists and secularists in Congress did not have Mahesh Kapoor's fine kurta to cling to.

Instead of taking offence at the roughness of this last remark, S.S. Sharma said to him in a calmer voice: 'Here is the letter. Read it through and tell me what steps you think are appropriate. Of course, we are located nowhere near the borders of Pakistan. Still, some measures may be necessary to control the more excitable newspapers—in the case of panic, I mean. Or incitement.'

'Certain processions may need to be controlled as well,' said the Home Minister.

'Let us see, let us see,' said the Chief Minister.

14.10

The uncertainties of the great world were complemented in Brahmpur by the smaller certainties of the calendar. Two days after the flag-hoistings and orations of Independence Day—the most unsettling of the five that India had so far celebrated—came the full moon of the month of Shravan, and the tenderest of all family festivals—when brothers and sisters affirm their bonds to each other.

Mrs Mahesh Kapoor, however, who was normally keen on festivals, did not approve of Rakhi or believe in it. For her it was a typically Punjabi festival. She traced her ancestry back to a part of U.P. where, according to her, at least among khatris, the festival on which brothers and sisters more truly affirmed their bonds was Bhai Duj—located two and a half months from now among the little glut of smaller festivals clustering around the almost moonless skies of Divali. But she was alone in this; neither of her samdhins agreed with her, certainly not old Mrs Tandon, who, having lived in Lahore in the heart of the undivided Punjab, had celebrated Rakhi all her life like all her neighbours, nor Mrs Rupa Mehra, who believed in sentiment at all costs and on every possible occasion. Mrs Rupa Mehra believed in Bhai Duj as well, and sent greetings on that day too to all her brothers—the term included her male cousins—as a sort of confirmatory affirmation.

Mrs Mahesh Kapoor had clear but undogmatic views on various subjects relating to fasts and festivals: she had her own views of the legends underlying the Pul Mela as well. For her daughter, however, living in Lahore with the Tandons had made no difference. Veena had celebrated Rakhi ever since Pran was born. Mrs Mahesh Kapoor, whatever she thought of this festival, did not try to dampen her daughter's enthusiasm for coloured thread and shiny florets when she was a little girl. And when Pran and Maan used to come to their mother as children to show her what their sister had given them, her pleasure was never entirely feigned.

Veena went in the morning to Prem Nivas to tie a rakhi around Pran's wrist. She chose a simple rakhi, a small silver flower of tinsel on a red thread. She fed him a laddu and blessed him, and received in exchange his promise of protection, five rupees and a hug. Although, as Imtiaz had told him, his heart condition was a chronic one, she noticed that he was looking quite a bit better than before; the birth of his daughter, rather than adding to the strain of his life, appeared to have relieved it. Uma was a happy child; and Savita had not got overly or prolongedly depressed in the month following her birth, as her mother had warned her she might. The crisis of Pran's health had given her too much concern, and reading the law too much stimulation, for a lapse into the luxury of depression. Sometimes she felt passionately maternal and tearfully happy.

Veena had brought Bhaskar along.

'Where's my rakhi?' demanded Bhaskar of Savita.

'Your rakhi?'

'Yes. From the baby.'

'You're quite right,' said Savita, smiling and shaking her head at her own thoughtlessness. 'You're quite right. I'll go out and get one at once. Or better still, I'll make one. Ma must have enough material in her bag for a hundred rakhis. And you—I hope you've brought a present for her.'

'Oh, yes,' said Bhaskar, who had cut Uma a bright and multicoloured dodecahedron out of a single sheet of paper. It was to hang above her cot and she could follow it with her eyes as it twirled around. 'I coloured it myself. But I didn't try to use the minimum number of colours,' he added apologetically.

'Oh, that's fine,' said Savita. 'The more colours the better.' And she gave Bhaskar a kiss. When the rakhi was made, she tied it over his right wrist while holding Uma's hand inside her own.

Veena also went to Baitar House, as she went every year, to tie a rakhi around Firoz's wrist, and Imtiaz's. Both were in, since they were expecting her.

'Where is your friend Maan?' she demanded of Firoz.

As he opened his mouth to speak, she popped a sweet in.

'You should know!' said Firoz, his eyes lighting up in a smile. 'He's your brother.'

'You needn't remind me,' said Veena, vexed. 'It's Rakhi, but he's not at home. He has no family feeling. If I'd known he would still be at the farm, I would have sent him the rakhi. He really is very inconsiderate. And now it's too late.'

Meanwhile the Mehra family had duly dispatched their rakhis to Calcutta, and they had arrived well in time. Arun had warned his sisters that anything more elaborate than a single silver thread would be impossible for him to conceal under the sleeve of his suit, and therefore entirely out of the question for him to wear to work at Bentsen Pryce. Varun, almost as if to flaunt a garish taste that could be guaranteed to exasperate his elder brother, always insisted on elaborate rakhis that reached halfway up his bare arm. Savita had not had the chance to meet her brothers this year, and wrote them long and loving letters, rebuking them for being absentee uncles. Lata, busy as she was with *Twelfth Night*, wrote them brief but tender notes. She had a rehearsal on the actual day of Rakhi. Several of the actors were wearing rakhis, and Lata could not help smiling in the course of a conversation between Olivia and Viola when it struck her that if the festival of Rakhi had existed in Elizabethan England, Shakespeare would certainly have made much of it, with Viola perhaps bewailing her shipwrecked brother, imagining his lifeless, threadless, untinselled arm lying outstretched beside his body on some Illyrian beach lit by the full August moon.

14.11

She also thought of Kabir, and of his remark at the concert—so long ago, it seemed—about having had a sister till last year. Lata still did not know for certain what he had meant by the remark, but every interpretation that came to her mind made her feel deeply sorry for him.

As it happened, Kabir was thinking of her that night as well, and talking about her with his younger brother. He had come back home exhausted after the rehearsal, and had hardly eaten any dinner, and Hashim was unhappy to see him look so spent.

Kabir was trying to describe the strangeness of the situation with Lata. They acted together, they spent hours in the same room during rehearsals, but they did not talk to each other. Lata seemed to have turned, thought Kabir, from passionate to ice-cold—he could not believe that this was the same girl who had been with him that morning in the boat—in the grey mist in a grey sweater, and with the light of love in her eyes.

No doubt the boat had been rowing against the current of society, upstream towards the Barsaat Mahal; but surely there was a solution. Should they row harder, or agree to drift downstream? Should they row in a different river or try to change the direction of the river they were in? Should they jump out of the boat and try to swim? Or get a motor or a sail? Or hire a boatman?

'Why don't you simply throw her overboard?' suggested Hashim.

'To the crocodiles?' said Kabir, laughing.

'Yes,' said Hashim. 'She must be a very stupid or unfeeling girl—why does she delight in making you miserable, Bhai-jaan? I don't think you should waste any time on her. It doesn't stand to reason.'

'I know it doesn't. But, as they say, you can't reason someone out of what they've never been reasoned into in the first place.'

'But why her?' said Hashim. 'There are plenty of girls who are crazy about you—Cubs the Cad.'

'I don't know,' said Kabir. 'It mystifies me. Perhaps it was just that first smile in the bookshop—and I'm still feeding on the meaningless memory of it. I don't even think it was me she was smiling at. I don't know. Why was it you whom Saeeda Bai latched on to on Holi evening? I heard all about that.'

Hashim blushed to the roots of his hair. He didn't suggest a solution.

'Or look at Abba and Ammi—was there ever a better-matched couple? And now—'

Hashim nodded. 'I'll come with you this Thursday. I, well, I couldn't come yesterday.'

'Well, good. But, you know, don't force yourself Hashim. . . . I don't know if she notices your absence.'

'But you said she had a sense about—well, about Samia.'

'I think she senses it.'

'Abba pushed her over the edge. He gave her no time, no sympathy, no real companionship.'

'Well Abba is Abba, and it's pointless complaining about who he is.' He yawned. 'I suppose I am tired, after all.'

'Well, goodnight, Bhai-jaan.'

'Goodnight, Hashim.'

14.12

A week after Rakhi came Janamashtami, the day of Krishna's birth. Mrs Rupa Mehra did not celebrate it (she had mixed feelings about Krishna), but Mrs Mahesh Kapoor did. In the garden at Prem Nivas stood the undistinguished, rough-leafed harsingar tree, the tree that Krishna was reputed to have stolen from Indra's heaven for the sake of his wife Rukmini. It was not in bloom yet, and would not be for another two months, but Mrs Mahesh Kapoor stood before the tree for a minute just after dawn, imagining it covered with the fragrant, star-shaped, small white-and-orange flowers that lasted only a single night before falling to the lawn beneath. Then she went inside, and summoned Veena and Bhaskar. They were staying at Prem Nivas for a few days, as was old Mrs Tandon. Kedarnath was away in the south, soliciting the next season's orders at a time when, owing to the moisture in the air, the production of shoes in Brahmpur was slower than usual. Always away, always away, Veena complained to her mother.

Mrs Mahesh Kapoor had chosen a time of day when her husband would not be at home to mock her devotions. She now entered the small room, a mere alcove in the verandah separated by a curtain, that she had set aside for her puja. She placed two small wooden platforms on the floor, on one of which she sat, on one of which she placed a clay lamp, a candle in a low brass stand, a tray, a small bronze bell, a silver bowl half full of water, and a flatter bowl with a small heap of uncooked grains of white rice and some dark-red powder. She sat facing a small ledge above a low cupboard. On this ledge stood a number of bronze statuettes of Shiva and other gods and a beautiful portrait of the infant Krishna playing the flute.

She moistened the red powder, then leaned forward intently and touched it with her finger to the foreheads of the gods, and then, leaning forward once again and closing her eyes, applied some to her own forehead. In a quiet voice she said:

'Veena, matches.'

'I'll get them, Nani,' said Bhaskar.

'You stay here,' said his grandmother, who planned to say a special prayer for him.

Veena came back from the kitchen with a huge box of matches. Her mother lit the lamp and the candle. Noisy people, the endless guests who stayed at Prem Nivas, were walking around talking on the verandah outside, but they did not distract her. She lit the lamp and candle, and placed these two lights on the tray. Ringing the bell with her left hand, she picked up the tray with her right, and described a motion in the air around the portrait of Krishna—not in the form of a circle but something much more irregular, as if she were circumscribing a presence that she saw before her eyes. Then she got up slowly and quite painfully from her confined posture, and did the same for the other gods in the statuettes and calendars scattered around the little room: the statue of Shiva; a picture of Lakshmi and Ganesh together, which included a small mouse nibbling at a laddu; a calendar from 'Paramhans and Co., Chemists and Druggists' of Rama, Sita, Lakshman and Hanuman with the sage Valmiki seated on the ground in front of them writing their story on a scroll; and several others.

She prayed to them, and she asked for comfort from them: nothing for herself, but health for her family, a long life for her husband, blessings on her two grandchildren, and ease to the souls of those no longer here. Her mouth worked silently as she prayed, unselfconscious of the presence of her daughter and her grandson. Throughout she kept the bell lightly ringing.

Finally, the puja was over, and she sat down after putting the things away in the cupboard.

She turned to Veena, and addressed her with the affectionate word for 'son':

'Bété, get Pran on the line, and tell him I want to go with him to the Radhakrishna Temple on the other side of the Ganga.'

This was shrewd. If she had phoned Pran directly, he would have tried to wriggle out of it. Veena, however, who knew he was well enough to go, told him quite firmly that he couldn't upset their mother on Janamashtami. So in a short while all of them—Pran, Veena, Bhaskar, old Mrs Tandon, and Mrs Mahesh Kapoor—were sitting in a boat that was making its way across the water.

'Really, Ammaji,' said Pran, who was not pleased to be dragged from his work, 'if you think of Krishna's character—flirt, adulterer, thief—'

His mother held up her hand. She was not annoyed so much as disturbed by her son's remarks.

'You should not be so proud, son,' she said, looking at him with concern. 'You should humble yourself before God.'

'I may as well humble myself before a stone,' suggested Pran. 'Or . . . or a potato.'

His mother considered his words. After a few more splashes of the boatman's oars, she said in gentle rebuke: 'Don't you even believe in God?'

'No,' said Pran.

His mother was silent.

'But when we die—' she said, and was silent once more.

'Even if everyone I loved were to die,' said Pran, irked for no obvious reason, 'I would not believe.'

'I believe in God,' volunteered Bhaskar suddenly. 'Especially in Rama and Sita and Lakshman and Bharat and Shatrughan.' In his mind there was no clear distinction yet between gods and heroes, and he was hoping to get the part of one of the five swaroops in the Ramlila later this year. If not, he would at least be enrolled in the monkey army and get to fight and have a good time. 'What's that?' he said suddenly, pointing at the water.

The broad, grey-black back of something much larger than a fish had appeared momentarily from beneath the surface of the Ganga, and had sliced back in again.

'What's what?' asked Pran.

'There—that—' said Bhaskar, pointing again. But it had disappeared again.

'I didn't see anything,' said Pran.

'But it was there, it was there, I saw it,' said Bhaskar. 'It was black and shiny, and it had a long face.'

Upon the word, and as if by magic, three large river dolphins with pointed snouts suddenly appeared to the right of the boat and started playing in the water. Bhaskar laughed with delight.

The boatman said, in his Brahmpuri accent: 'There are dolphins here, in this stretch of the water. They don't come out often, but they are here all right. That's what they are, dolphins. No one fishes them, the fishermen protect them and kill the crocodiles in this stretch. That is why there are no crocodiles until that far bend, there beyond the Barsaat Mahal. You are lucky to see them. Remember that at the end of the journey.'

Mrs Mahesh Kapoor smiled and passed him a coin. She remembered the time when the Minister Sahib had lived for a year in Delhi and she had gone on a pilgrimage to the region hallowed by Krishna. There, in the deep water of the Yamuna just below the temple at Gokul, she and the other pilgrims had watched transfixed as the large black river turtles swam lazily to and fro. She thought of them, and of these dolphins, as good creatures, innocent and blessed. It was to protect the innocent, whether man or beast, to cure the recurring ills of the world, and to establish righteousness that Krishna had come down to earth. He had revealed his glory in the Bhagavad Gita on the battlefield of the Mahabharata. Pran's dismissive manner of speaking of him—as if God should be judged by human standards rather than trusted and adored—disturbed and hurt her. What, she asked herself, had happened in one generation that of her three children, only one continued to believe in what their forefathers had believed for hundreds, indeed thousands, of years?

14.13

One morning, a few weeks before Janamashtami, Pandit Jawaharlal Nehru, his mind ostensibly on his files, was thinking back to the time when he was very young, and was unable to keep awake, despite all his mother's blandishments and reproaches, until the midnight hour when Krishna was born in the prison cell. Now, of course, he rarely got to sleep before midnight.

Sleep! It was one of his best-loved words. In Almora Jail he had often been worried by the news he received of his wife Kamala's condition, and his helplessness upset him for a while, but somehow he still managed to sleep soundly in the hill air. On the verge of sleep he often thought what a wonderful and mysterious thing it was. Why should he awake from it? Suppose he did not wake up at all. When he had watched by his father's sickbed, he had mistaken his death for a deep sleep.

He sat at his desk now, his chin resting on his hand, and glanced for a second or two at the photograph of his wife before continuing with his dictation. Thousands of letters every day, a relay of stenographers, endless work in Parliament and in his offices in the South Block and in his office here at home, endless, endless, endless. It was a principle with him never to leave any paper undealt with, any letter unanswered when he went to sleep. And yet he could not help feeling that a sort of vacillation lay hidden in this dispatch. For though he kept up scrupulously with his paperwork, he was too self-analytical not to realize that he avoided coming to terms with less tractable matters—more muddled, more human, more full of bitterness and conflict—like the one that faced him in his own party. It was easier to be indecisive when busy.

He had always been busy except when he was in jail. No, even that was not true: it was in the many jails he had known that he had done most of his reading and almost all of his writing. All three of his books had been written there. Yet it was there too that he had for once had the time to notice what he now had no time to: the bare treetops day by day becoming greener above the high walls of Alipore Jail, the sparrows nesting in the huge barred barn that had housed him in Almora, the glimpse of fresh fields when the warders opened for a second or two the gate of his cell yard in Dehradun.

He got up from his desk and went to the window, from where he had an unimpeded view of the entire garden of Teen Murti House. This used to be the residence of the Commander-in-Chief under the Raj, and it was now his residence as Prime Minister. The garden was green with the monsoons. A little boy of four or five, the child of one of the servants perhaps, was jumping up and down beneath a mango tree, trying to pluck something from a low branch. But surely it was a little late for mangoes?

Kamala, now—he often felt that his imprisonment had been harder on her than on him. They had been married—married off to each other by their parents—very young, and he had only forced himself to make time for her when her illness was beyond cure. His autobiography had been dedicated to her—too late for her to have known. It was only when she was almost lost to him that he had realized how much he loved her. He recalled his own despairing words: 'Surely she was not going to leave me now when I needed her most? Why, we had just begun to know and understand each other really; our joint life was only now properly beginning. We relied so much on each other, we had so much to do together.'

Well—all that had been a long time ago. And if there had been pain and sacrifice and long absence when he had been detained as a guest of the

King, at least the battle lines had been clear. Now, everything was muddied. Old companions had turned political rivals. The purposes for which he had fought were being undermined and perhaps he himself was to blame for letting things slide so long. His supporters were leaving the Congress Party, and it had fallen into the hands of conservatives, many of whom saw India as a Hindu state where others would have to adapt or suffer the consequences.

There was no one to advise him. His father was dead. Gandhiji was dead. Kamala was dead. And the friend whom he might have unburdened himself to, with whom he had celebrated the midnight hour of Independence, was far away. She, so elegant herself, had often teased him about his fastidiousness in dress. He touched the red rose—in this season it came from Kashmir—in the buttonhole of his white cotton achkan, and smiled.

The naked child, having missed several times, had now got a few bricks from near a flower bed, and was painstakingly building himself a little platform. He stood on it and reached out towards the branch, but again without success. Both he and the bricks came tumbling down.

Nehru's smile grew wider.

'Sir?' said the stenographer, his pencil still poised.

'Yes, yes, I'm thinking.'

Huge crowds and loneliness. Prison and Prime Ministership. Intense activity and a longing for nothingness. 'We too are tired.'

He would have to do something, though, and soon. After the elections it would be too late. In a sense this was a sadder battle than he had ever fought before.

A scene from Allahabad more than fifteen years earlier came before his eyes. He had been out of prison for five months or so, and expected any day to be rearrested on some charge or other. He and Kamala had finished tea, Purushottamdas Tandon had just joined them, and they were standing together talking on the verandah. A car had driven up, a police officer had got out, and they had known immediately what it meant. Tandon had shaken his head and smiled wryly, and Nehru had greeted the apologetic policeman with the ironically hospitable comment: 'I have been expecting you for a long time.'

Out on the lawn now, the little boy had piled the bricks on top of each other in a different formation, and was tentatively climbing up again. In an all-or-nothing endeavour, instead of merely reaching out towards the branch, he jumped up to grasp the fruit. But he did not succeed. He fell, hurt himself on the bricks, sat down on the damp grass, and began to cry. Alerted by the sound, the mali emerged, and took in the scene in an instant. Conscious that the Prime Minister was watching from the window of his office, he ran towards the child, shouting angrily, and struck him hard across the face. The child burst into a renewed fit of weeping.

Pandit Nehru, scowling with anger, rushed into the garden, ran up to the mali, and slapped him several times, furious that he should have attacked the child.

'But, Panditji—' said the mali, so thunderstruck that he made no attempt to protect himself. He had only been teaching the trespasser a lesson.

Nehru, still furious, gathered the dirty and terrified little boy into his arms, and, after talking to him gently, put him down. He told the mali to pluck some fruit immediately for the child, and threatened to sack him on the spot.

'Barbarous,' he muttered to himself as he walked back across the lawn, frowning as he realized that his white achkan was now entirely smeared with mud.

14.14

Delhi, August 6, 1951

Dear Mr. President,

I beg to tender my resignation from membership of the Congress Working Committee and the Central Election Board. I shall be grateful if you will be good enough to accept these resignations.

Yours sincerely,
Jawaharlal Nehru

This formal letter of resignation to the President of the Congress Party, Mr Tandon, was accompanied by a letter beginning: 'My dear Purushottamdas,' and ending:

> You will forgive me if by resigning I cause you embarrassment. But the embarrassment has been there anyhow for both of us and others and the best way to deal with it is to remove the cause.
>
> Yours affectionately,
> Jawaharlal Nehru

Mr Tandon replied as soon as he read the letter a couple of days later. In his reply he wrote:

> You have yourself as the leader of the nation appealed to Congressmen and to the country to present a united front to the situation that is facing us both externally and internally. The step that you propose to take, namely, that of resigning from the Working Committee and the Parliamentary Board, goes directly against that appeal for solidarity and is likely to create a schism in the Congress which has greater potentiality for harm to the country than any that the Congress has yet had to face.
>
> I beg of you not to precipitate a crisis at the present juncture and not to press your resignation. I cannot accept it. If you insist on it the only course left to me will be to place it before the Working Committee for consideration. I trust that, in any case, you will attend the meeting of the Working Committee on the 11th instant.
>
> If, to keep you in the Working Committee, it is necessary or desirable that I should resign the presidentship of the Congress I am ready to do so with great pleasure and goodwill.
>
> Yours affectionately,
> Purushottamdas Tandon

Pandit Nehru replied the same day, making rather clearer than before what had been on his mind:

> I have been long distressed at the attitude of some persons which indicated that they wished to drive out others from the Congress who did not fit in with their views or their general outlook. . . .
>
> I feel that the Congress is rapidly drifting away from its moorings and more and more the wrong kind of people, or rather people who have the wrong kind of ideas, are gaining influence in it. The public appeal of the Congress is getting less and less. It may, and probably will, win elections. But, in the process, it may also lose its soul. . . .
>
> I am fully conscious of the consequences of the step I am taking and even the risks involved. But I think these risks have to be taken, for there is no other way out. . . .
>
> I am more conscious than anyone else can be of the critical situation which the country has to face today. I have to deal with it

> from day to day. . . .
>
> There is no reason why you should resign the presidentship of the Congress. This is not a personal matter.
>
> I do not think it would be proper for me to attend the meeting of the Working Committee. My presence will embarrass me as well as others. I think it is better that the questions that arise should be discussed in my absence.

Mr Tandon replied the next day, which was the day before the actual meeting of the Congress Working Committee. He agreed, 'It is no use winning the elections if, as you say, the Congress is "to lose its soul" in the process.' But it was clear from his letter that the two men had very different conceptions of the soul of the Congress. Tandon wrote that he would place Nehru's letter of resignation before the Working Committee the next day. 'But that need not prevent your taking part in some other matters. May I suggest that you come to the meeting though only for a short time and that the matters which concern you may not be discussed in your presence.'

*

Nehru attended the meeting of the Working Committee and explained his letter of resignation; he then withdrew so that the others could discuss it in his absence. The Working Committee, faced with the unimaginable loss of the Prime Minister, attempted to find some way of accommodating him. But all immediate attempts to mediate the conflict failed. One possible means was to reconstitute the Working Committee and appoint new general secretaries of the Congress so that Nehru would feel less 'out of tune' with them. But here Tandon put his foot down. He said he would rather resign than allow the office of the Congress President to become subservient to that of the Prime Minister. Appointing the Working Committee was part of the role of the former; it could not be tampered with at the will of the latter. The Working Committee passed a resolution calling upon Nehru and Tandon to confer to solve the crisis, but could do nothing further.

A few days later, on Independence Day, Maulana Azad resigned from the Congress Working Committee. Just as the resignation from the Congress of the popular Muslim leader Kidwai had stung Nehru into action, the resignation of the scholarly Maulana cemented it. Since it was largely these two leaders at the national level whom the Muslims looked to in their post-Partition uncertainty—Kidwai because of his own great popularity, not only among Muslims but among Hindus, and Azad because of the respect in which he was held and the fact that he had Nehru's ear—it now appeared that the Congress was in danger of losing its Muslim following entirely.

S.S. Sharma made every possible effort to dissuade Nehru from what looked increasingly like a collision course between him and Tandon. In this, Sharma was one of many, for leaders like Pant of U.P. and B.C. Roy of West Bengal had attempted to do the same. When they got to Delhi, however, they found Nehru as vaguely adamant as ever. But this time S.S. Sharma's ego was slightly hurt: Nehru did not suggest that he come to Delhi and join his Cabinet. Presumably he either knew that Sharma would beg off as usual—or he was not pleased with Sharma's attempts to paper over the cracks in the party—or else the invitation had been displaced by other matters of greater urgency that were on his mind.

One of these matters was a meeting of the Members of Parliament from the Congress Party, which he had called in order to explain the events that had led to the drastic rift and his resignation. He asked them for a vote of confidence. Whatever their political complexion (and there were, as Nehru was soon to discover when the bill to reform Hindu law was brought up before Parliament, many diehard conservatives among them), most Congress MPs perceived the dispute largely in terms of a conflict between the mass party and the parliamentary party. They were not enamoured of the thought that the Congress President would try to dictate policy to them through resolutions of the Congress, as he had on several occasions stated that he had the right to do. Besides, they knew that without the national image of Nehru they would have a very difficult time getting themselves re-elected in a few months' time. Whether it was because of the fear that they would lose their soul or their power or the elections, they overwhelmingly passed a motion of confidence in his favour.

Since confidence in Nehru as such had never been at issue, Tandon's supporters resented this action, which smacked of the build-up to a showdown. They were also somewhat surprised by Nehru's most uncharacteristic unwillingness to back down, to understand their point of view, to postpone unpleasantness, to compromise. He was talking now of insisting on a 'change of outlook' and a 'clear-cut verdict'. And rumours had begun to float about of the possibility of Nehru taking on the Congress Presidency together with the Prime Ministership, an onerous—and, in some ways, ominous—combination that he had in the past declared himself against on principle. Indeed, in 1946, he had resigned the Congress Presidency to become the Prime Minister. But now that the main threat to his power came from within the Congress Party itself he had begun to hedge on the issue.

'I definitely think that it is a wrong thing practically and even otherwise, for the Prime Minister to be the Congress President,' he declared at the end of August, just a week before the decisive meeting of the All-India Congress Committee in Delhi. 'But that being the general rule, I cannot say what necessity might compel one to do in special circumstances when a hiatus is created or something like that.'

The typically floppy Nehruvian tail to that sentence could not entirely counter the surprising inflexibility of the body.

14.15

With every passing day, however, it became increasingly clear that the month-long deadlock could not be resolved except by some desperate expedient. Tandon refused to reconstitute the Working Committee at Nehru's dictation, and Nehru rejected anything less if he was to rejoin it.

On the 6th of September, the entire Working Committee dramatically submitted their resignations to Tandon, hoping thereby to retrieve what would otherwise have been, in an open conflict, an irretrievable position for both him and them. The idea was that the much larger body of the All-India Congress Committee (due to meet two days later) should now pass a resolution asking Nehru to withdraw his resignation, expressing confidence in Tandon, and requesting Tandon to reconstitute the Working Committee by election. Nehru and Tandon could then draw up a slate of candidates jointly. Tandon could remain President; he would not have surrendered any presidential prerogatives to the Prime Minister; he would merely have implemented, as he was bound to, a resolution of the AICC.

This should have been, the Working Committee thought, agreeable to both Nehru and Tandon. In fact it was agreeable to neither.

That evening Nehru told a public meeting that he wanted the All-India Congress Committee to make it entirely clear which way the Congress should go and who should hold its reins. He was in a fighting mood.

The next evening Tandon too, at a press conference, refused the face-saving formula proffered by his Working Committee. He said: 'If I am asked by the All-India Congress Committee to reconstitute the Working Committee in consultation with A, B, or C, I would beg the AICC not to press that request but to relieve me.'

He placed the responsibility for the crisis squarely on Nehru's shoulders. Nehru had tendered his resignation over the issue of the reconstitution of the Working Committee; and, by so doing, he had forced its members to tender their own.

Tandon stated that he could not accept these forced resignations. He repudiated any suggestion by Nehru that the Congress Working Committee had failed to implement Congress resolutions. He made a few references to Pandit Nehru as 'my old friend and brother' and added: 'Nehru is not an ordinary member of the Working Committee; he represents the nation more today than any other individual does.' But he reaffirmed the inflexibility of his own stand, which was one based on principle; and he announced that if no acceptable formula could be reached by mediators, he would resign from the Congress Presidency the next day.

And this was what, the next day, with good grace—despite the many personal attacks against him in the press, despite what he saw as the impropriety of Nehru's tactics, and despite the bitterness and length of the battle—he did.

In a noble gesture, which did much to assuage any residual bitterness, he joined the Working Committee under the newly elected Congress President, Jawaharlal Nehru.

It was in effect a coup; and Nehru had won.

Apparently.

14.16

The jeep had hardly arrived at Baitar Fort than Maan and Firoz got horses saddled and rode off to hunt. The oily munshi was all smiles when he saw them, and brusquely ordered Waris to make the necessary preparations. Maan swallowed his gorge with difficulty.

'I'll go with them,' said Waris, who was looking even more rough-hewn than before, perhaps because he appeared not to have shaved for a few days.

'But have a bit of lunch before you disappear,' said the Nawab Sahib.

The two impatient young men refused.

'We've been eating all along the way,' said Firoz. 'We'll be back before dark.'

The Nawab Sahib turned to Mahesh Kapoor and shrugged.

The munshi showed Mahesh Kapoor to his rooms, almost frantic with solicitude. That the great Mahesh Kapoor, who by a stroke of the pen had wiped vast estates off the map of the future, was here in person was a matter of incalculable significance. Perhaps he would be in power again and might threaten to do worse. And the Nawab Sahib had not merely invited him here, but was behaving towards him with great cordiality. The munshi licked the edge of his walrus-like moustache and puffed up the three flights of steep stairs, murmuring platitudes of intense geniality. Mahesh Kapoor said nothing in reply.

'Now, Minister Sahib, I was given instructions that you were to stay in the best suite in the Fort. As you see, it overlooks the mango orchard and then the jungle—there is no sign of disturbance, none of the hubbub of Baitar town, nothing to disturb your contemplation. And there, Minister Sahib, as you can see, are your son and the Nawabzada riding through the orchard. How well your son rides. I had the opportunity of making his acquaintance when he was last at the Fort. What an upright, decent young man. The moment I set eyes on him I knew that he must come from a remarkable family.'

'Who is the third?'

'That, Minister Sahib, is Waris,' said the munshi, who succeeded in conveying by his tone of voice how very little he thought of that bumpkin.

Mahesh Kapoor paid the bumpkin no further attention.

'When is lunch?' he asked, looking at his watch.

'In an hour, Minister Sahib,' said the munshi. 'In an hour. And I will personally send someone up to inform you when it is time. Or perhaps you would care to walk around the grounds? The Nawab Sahib said that you wish to be disturbed as little as possible these next few days—that you wish to think in quiet surroundings. But the garden is very fresh and green in this season—perhaps a little overgrown, that's all—but nowadays, with the new financial stringency—as Huzoor is aware, this is not the most auspicious of times for estates such as ours—but we will make every effort, every effort to ensure that your stay is a happy one, a restful one, Minister Sahib. As Huzoor has no doubt been informed already, Ustad Majeed Khan will be arriving here later this afternoon by train, and will be singing for Huzoor's pleasure both today and tomorrow. The Nawab Sahib was most insistent that you were to be allowed time to yourself for rest and thought, rest and thought.'

Since his effusive prattle had elicited no response, the munshi continued: 'The Nawab Sahib himself is a great believer in rest and thought, Minister Sahib. He spends most of his time in the library when he is here. But if I might suggest to you one or two of the sights of the town that Huzoor would find interesting: the Lal Kothi and, of course, the Hospital, which was founded and expanded by former Nawabs, but which we continue to contribute to, for the betterment of the people. I have already arranged a tour—'

'Later,' said Mahesh Kapoor. He turned his back on the munshi and looked out of the window. The three horsemen appeared sporadically along a forest trail, then grew increasingly difficult to follow.

It was good, thought Mahesh Kapoor, to be here at the estate of his old friend, away from Prem Nivas and the bustle of the house, away from the mild pestering of his wife, the constant incursions of his relatives from Rudhia, the management of the Rudhia farm, away—most of all—from the confused politics of Brahmpur and Delhi. For he was, most atypically, sick of politics for the moment. No doubt he would be able to follow events via the radio or day-old editions of the newspapers, but he would be spared the direct personal turmoil of contact with fellow-politicians and bewildered or importunate constituents. He had no work in the Secretariat any more; he had taken leave from the Legislative Assembly for a few days; and he was not even attending meetings of his new party, one of which was to be held in Madras next week. He was no longer certain that he really belonged in that party even if he still, nominally, belonged to it. In the wake of Nehru's famous victory over the Tandonites in Delhi, Mahesh Kapoor felt the need to reassess his attitude towards the Congress. Like many other secessionists, he was disappointed that Nehru had not split the party and joined him. On the other hand, the Congress no longer appeared to be such a hostile place for those of his views. He was especially interested in seeing what the mercurial Rafi Ahmad Kidwai would do if Nehru asked the seceders to return.

So far, however, Kidwai had acted his usual elusive self, keeping his options open with a series of contradictory statements. He had announced from Bombay that he was delighted by Nehru's victory, but that he saw little prospect of his own return to the Congress fold. 'Realizing now that their election prospects were not bright they have deserted Mr Tandon and sponsored Pandit Nehru's candidature. This is pure opportunism. The future of the country is dark if such opportunism is tolerated,' he said. However, the wily Mr Kidwai added that if certain 'undesirable elements' who were still entrenched in the executives of states such as Uttar Pradesh, Purva Pradesh, Madhya Bharat, and Punjab were to be removed by Pandit Nehru, 'then everything would be all right'. As if to make matters murkier, he mentioned that the KMPP was thinking of an electoral alliance with the Socialist Party, and that then 'the chances of the party succeeding in most of the states are very bright'. (The Socialist Party, for its part, showed no enthusiasm to ally itself with anyone.) A couple of days later Kidwai suggested a purge of 'corrupt elements' in the Congress as a condition for winding up his own party and rejoining the Congress. Kripalani, however, who was the other half of the K-K combine, insisted that there was no question of his deserting the KMPP and rejoining the Congress, no matter what its internal rearrangements.

Kidwai was something of a river dolphin. He enjoyed swimming in silty water and outwitting the crocodiles around him.

Meanwhile, all the other parties were commenting, with various degrees of heat, upon Nehru's reassertion of his power within the Congress. Of the socialist leaders, one denounced the combination of the Congress Presidency with the Prime Ministership as a sign of totalitarianism; one said that this was not a worrying possibility, as Nehru did not have the makings of a dictator; and one simply pointed out that, as a tactical move, the Congress had improved its chances in the General Elections.

On the right, the President of the Hindu Mahasabha inveighed against what he called 'the proclamation of dictatorship'. He added: 'Although this dictatorship has raised Pandit Nehru to the highest pinnacle of glory, it has also got within itself the germs of his fall.'

Mahesh Kapoor attempted to dismiss this confusion of opinion and information from his mind and tried to come to grips with three straightforward questions. Since he was feeling sick of politics, should he simply leave politics and retire? If not, which party was the best place for him—or should he fight as an Independent? And if he decided to remain and fight the next election, what was the best place for him to fight from? He walked up to the roof, where an owl, ensconced in a tower, was startled by his approach; he walked down to the rose garden, where the flowerless bushes edged the fresh green lawn; and he wandered through some of the rooms of the Fort, including the huge Imambara downstairs. Sharma's words to him in another garden came back to haunt his mind. But by the time the anxious munshi had found him and announced that the Nawab Sahib was awaiting him at lunch, he was no nearer a solution.

14.17

The Nawab Sahib had been sitting for the last hour in the huge, vaulted, dust-pervaded library with its green glass skylight, working on his edition of the poems of Mast, some of the documents and manuscripts for which were held here at the Fort. He was deeply saddened by the deterioration of this magnificent room and the poor condition of its holdings. He planned to move all the Mast materials to his library in Brahmpur at the end of this visit, together with some of the other more precious contents of the Baitar Fort library. Given his reduced means, the library at the Fort was becoming impossible for him to maintain—and the dust and confusion and infestation of silverfish grew worse month by month.

This was somewhat on his mind when he greeted his friend in the great, gloomy dining hall decorated with dark portraits of Queen Victoria, King Edward VII and the Nawab Sahib's own ancestors.

'I'll take you to the library after lunch,' said the Nawab Sahib.

'Good,' said Mahesh Kapoor. 'But the last time I entered a library of yours I recall that it resulted in the destruction of one of your books.'

'Well,' said the Nawab Sahib thoughtfully, 'I don't know which is worse: the cerebral seizures of the Raja of Marh or the cancer of the silverfish.'

'You should keep your books in better order,' said Mahesh Kapoor. 'It's one of the finest private libraries in the country. It would be a tragedy if the books were to be damaged.'

'I suppose you might say it is a national treasure,' said the Nawab Sahib with a faint smile.

'Yes,' said Mahesh Kapoor.

'But I doubt that the national purse would open itself to help maintain it.'

'No.'

'And, thanks to plunderers like you, I certainly can't any longer.'

Mahesh Kapoor laughed. 'I was wondering what you were aiming at. Anyway, even if you lose your case in the Supreme Court you'll still be a few thousand times richer than me. And I work for my living, unlike you—you're just decorative.'

The Nawab Sahib helped himself to some biryani. 'You're a useless person,' he countered. 'What does a politician do, in fact, except make trouble for others?'

'Or counter the troubles that other people make,' said Mahesh Kapoor.

Neither he nor the Nawab Sahib needed to mention what he was referring to. Mahesh Kapoor had succeeded, while he was still with the Congress, in getting the Minister for Rehabilitation to bend the ear of the Prime Minister to get the government to grant the Nawab Sahib and Begum Abida Khan certificates entitling them to the permanent retention of their property in Brahmpur. This had been necessary in order to counter an order by the Custodian-General of Evacuee Property issued on the grounds that Begum Abida Khan's husband was a permanent evacuee. Their case was only one of several where similar action had needed to be taken at the governmental level.

'Well,' continued the ex-Minister of Revenue, 'where will you cut back when half your rents disappear? I really do hope that your library won't suffer.'

The Nawab Sahib frowned. 'Kapoor Sahib,' he said, 'I am less concerned about my own house than those who depend on me. The people of Baitar expect me to put on a proper show for our festivals, especially for Moharram. I will have to keep that up in some fashion. I have certain other expenses—the hospital and so on, the monuments, the stables, musicians like Ustad Majeed Khan who expect to be retained by me a couple of times a year, poets who depend on me, various endowments, pensions; God—and my munshi—knows what else. At least my sons don't make vast demands on me; they're educated, they have their own professions, they aren't wastrels, like the sons of others in my position—'

He stopped suddenly, thinking of Maan and Saeeda Bai.

'But tell me,' he continued after the briefest of pauses, 'what, for your part, are you going to do?'

'Me?' said Mahesh Kapoor.

'Why don't you run for the elections from here?'

'After what I've done to you—you want me to run from here?'

'No, really, Kapoor Sahib, you should.'

'That's what my grandson says.'

'Veena's boy?'

'Yes. He's worked out that this constituency is the most favourable for me—among the rural ones.'

The Nawab Sahib smiled at his friend and looked towards the portrait of his great-grandfather. Mahesh Kapoor's remark had made him think of his own grandsons, Hassan and Abbas—who had been named after the brothers of Hussain, the martyr of the festival of Moharram. He thought for a while of Zainab too, and the unhappiness of her marriage. And, fleetingly and regretfully, of his own wife, who lay buried in the cemetery just outside the Fort.

'But why do you think it is such a good idea?' Mahesh Kapoor was asking.

A servant offered the Nawab Sahib some fruit—including sharifas, whose short season had just begun—but the Nawab Sahib refused them. Then he changed his mind, felt three or four sharifas and selected one. He broke the knobbly fruit in half and scooped out the delicious white pulp with a spoon, placing the black seeds (which he transferred from his mouth to the spoon) on the side of his plate. For a minute or two he said nothing. Mahesh Kapoor helped himself to a sharifa as well.

'It is like this, Kapoor Sahib,' said the Nawab Sahib, thoughtfully, putting together the two equal scooped-out halves of his sharifa and then separating them. 'If you look at the population in this constituency, it is about evenly divided between Muslims and Hindus. This is just the kind of place where Hindu communalist parties can whip people into an anti-Muslim panic. They have already begun to do so. And every day there are fresh reasons for Hindus and Muslims to learn to hate each other. If it isn't some idiocy in Pakistan—some threat to Kashmir, some plot, real or imagined, to divert the waters of the Sutlej or to capture Sheikh Abdullah or to impose a tax on Hindus—it is one of our own home-grown brilliances like the dispute over that mosque in Ayodhya which has suddenly flared up again recently after lying quiet for decades—or our own Brahmpur version, which is different—but not so vastly different. Bakr-Id is coming up in a few days; someone is certain to kill a cow somewhere instead of a goat, and there'll be fresh trouble. And, worst of all, Moharram and Dussehra will coincide this year.'

Mahesh Kapoor nodded, and the Nawab Sahib continued. 'I know that this house was one of the strongholds of the Muslim League. I have never held with my father's or my brother's views on the subject, but people do not discriminate in these matters. To men like Agarwal the very name of Baitar is like a red rag—or perhaps a green one—to a bull. Next week he will try to force his Hindi bill through the Legislative Assembly, and Urdu, my language, the language of Mast, the language of most of the Muslims of this province, will be made more useless than ever. Who can protect us and our culture? Only people like you, who know us as we are, who have friends among us, who do not prejudge us because you can judge us from experience.'

Mahesh Kapoor did not say anything, but he was moved by the trust reposed in him by the Nawab Sahib.

The Nawab Sahib frowned, divided his black sharifa pips into two separate piles with his spoon, and went on. 'Perhaps it is worse in this part of the country than elsewhere. This was the heartland of the struggle for Pakistan, this is where much of the bitterness was created, but those of us who have not been able to or have chosen not to leave our homeland are now a smaller minority in a predominantly Hindu territory. No matter what troubles rage around us, I will probably manage to keep my head above water; so will Firoz and Imtiaz and Zainab—those who have means always manage somehow. But most of the ordinary people I talk to are downcast and fearful; they feel beleaguered. They mistrust the majority, and they feel mistrusted by them. I wish you would fight from here, Kapoor Sahib. Quite apart from my support, I hear that your son has made himself popular in the Salimpur area.' The Nawab Sahib allowed himself a smile. 'What do you think?'

'Why don't you stand for election yourself?' asked Mahesh Kapoor. 'Quite frankly, I would rather stand, if I have to, from my old urban constituency of Misri Mandi, redrawn though it has been—or, if it has to be a rural one, from Rudhia West, where my farm is located. Salimpur-cum-Baitar is too unfamiliar. I have no personal standing here—and no personal scores to settle.' Mahesh Kapoor thought for a moment of Jha, then continued: 'It's you who should stand. You would win hands down.'

The Nawab Sahib nodded. 'I have thought about it,' he said slowly. 'But I am not a politician. I have my work—if nothing else, my literary work. I would not enjoy sitting in the Legislative Assembly. I have been there and I have heard the proceedings and, well, I am not suited for that kind of life. And I'm not sure I would win hands down. For a start, the Hindu vote would be a problem for me. And, most importantly, I just couldn't go around Baitar and the villages asking people for votes—at least I could not do that for myself. I would not be able to bring myself to do that.'

He looked up again, rather wearily, at the sword-bearing portrait on the wall before continuing: 'But I am keen that a decent, a suitable man wins from here. Apart from the Hindu Mahasabha and that lot, there is someone here whom I have been good to and who hates me as a result. He plans to try to get the local Congress ticket, and if he becomes the local MLA, he can do me all kinds of harm. I have already decided to nominate a candidate of my own who will fight as an Independent in case this man does get the Congress nomination. But if you stand—whether from this KMPP or from the Congress, or as an Independent—I will make sure that you get my support. And that of my candidate.'

'He must be a very compliant candidate,' said Mahesh Kapoor, smiling. 'Or a self-abnegating one. A rare thing in politics.'

'You met him briefly when we got down from the jeep,' said the Nawab Sahib. 'It's that fellow Waris.'

'Waris!' Mahesh Kapoor laughed out loud. 'That servant of yours, that groom or whatever, the unshaven chap who went off hunting with Firoz and my son?'

'Yes,' said the Nawab Sahib.

'What kind of MLA do you think he would make?'

'Better than the one he'd displace.'

'You mean, better a fool than a knave.'

'Better a yokel, certainly.'

'You're not serious about Waris.'

'Don't underestimate him,' said the Nawab Sahib. 'He may be a bit crude, but he's capable and he's tough. He sees things in black and white, which is a great help when you're electioneering. He would enjoy campaigning, whether for himself or for you. He's popular around these parts. Women think he's dashing. He's absolutely loyal to me and the family, especially to Firoz. He would do anything for us. I really mean that—he keeps threatening to shoot people who have done us harm.' Mahesh Kapoor looked a little alarmed. 'Incidentally, he likes Maan; he took him around the estate when he was here. And the only reason he's unshaven is because he doesn't shave from the sighting of the new moon till Bakr-Id, ten days later. Not that he's all that religious,' added the Nawab Sahib, with a mixture of disapproval and indulgence. 'But if he doesn't have to shave for one reason or another, he feels that he may as well take advantage of the dispensation.'

'Hmm,' said Mahesh Kapoor.

'Think about it.'

'I will. I will think about it. But where I stand from is only one of three questions in my mind.'

'What are the other two?'

'Well—which party?'

'Congress,' said the Nawab Sahib, naming without hesitation the party which had done so much to dispossess him.

'Do you think so?' said Mahesh Kapoor. 'Do you think so?'

The Nawab Sahib nodded, looked at the debris on his plate, then rose. 'And your third question?'

'Whether I should continue in politics at all.'

The Nawab Sahib looked at his old friend in disbelief. 'It's something you ate this morning,' he said. 'Or else a piece of wax in my ear.'

14.18

Waris, meanwhile, was having a fine time away from his standard duties in the Fort and the officious eye of the munshi. He galloped happily along; and although he took with him the gun that he had obtained a licence for, he did not use it, since the hunt was not his prerogative. Maan and Firoz enjoyed the ride as much as the hunting; and there was enough game for them to spot or follow even though they did not actively seek it out. The part of the estate through which they rode was a mixture of firm woodland, rocky soil, and what in this season was sporadic marsh. Early in the afternoon, Maan saw a herd of nilgai splashing through the edge of the marsh at a distance. He aimed, fired, missed, and cursed himself good-naturedly. Later, Firoz got a large spotted deer with magnificent antlers. Waris noted the spot, and when they passed a small hamlet not far away he told one of the local men to get it to the Fort on a cart by the evening.

Apart from deer and wild boar, which they spied only occasionally, there were a great number of monkeys, especially langurs, and a great variety of birds, including peacocks, scattered throughout the forest. They even saw a peacock dancing. Maan was transported with pleasure.

It was a warm day, but there was plenty of shade, and from time to time they rested. Waris noticed how delighted the two young men were in each other's company, and he joined in their banter whenever he felt like it. He had liked Maan from the first, and Firoz's friendship with him cemented his liking.

As for the two young masters, having been cooped up in Brahmpur for a while, they were happy to be out in the open. They were sitting in the shade of a large banyan tree and talking.

'Have you ever eaten peacock?' Waris asked Maan.

'No,' said Maan.

'It's excellent meat,' said Waris.

'Come on, Waris, the Nawab Sahib doesn't like people shooting peacocks on the estate,' said Firoz.

'No, no, by no means,' said Waris. 'But if you shoot one of them by mistake, you may as well eat the bastard. No point in leaving him to the jackals.'

'By mistake!' said Firoz.

'Yes, yes,' said Waris, making an effort at invention or recall. 'Once there was a sudden rustling in the bushes when I was sitting under a tree—just as we are sitting now, and I thought it was a wild boar—so I shot at it, and it was only a peacock. Poor thing. Delicious.'

Firoz frowned. Maan laughed.

'Shall I tell you the next time I do that?' asked Waris. 'You'll like it, Chhoté Sahib, let me tell you. My wife is an excellent cook.'

'Yes, I know,' said Firoz, who had several times eaten junglefowl cooked by her.

'Chhoté Sahib always believes in doing the right thing,' said Waris. 'That's why he is a lawyer.'

'I thought that was a disqualification,' said Maan.

'Soon, if they make him a judge, he will get the zamindari decisions reversed,' asserted Waris.

There was a sudden movement in the bushes not thirty feet away. A large wild boar, its tusks lowered, came charging in their direction, aiming either towards them or past them. Without thinking, Maan lifted his rifle and—hardly taking conscious aim—fired at it when it was just a dozen feet away.

The boar collapsed in its tracks. The three of them got to their feet—at first in fear—and then, standing around it at a safe distance, heard its grunts and squeals and watched it thrash about for a minute or so, while its blood soaked the leaves and mud around it.

'My God—' said Firoz, staring at the beast's huge tusks.

'Not a fucking peacock,' was Waris's comment.

Maan did a little dance. He was looking a little dazed and very pleased with himself.

'Well, what will we do with it?' said Firoz.

'Eat it, of course,' said Maan.

'Don't be an idiot—we can't eat it. We'll give it to—well, someone or other. Waris can tell us which of the servants won't object to eating it.'

They loaded the boar on to Waris's horse. By the time it was evening they were all tired. Maan was resting his rifle in the saddle, holding the reins in his left hand and practising polo strokes with his right. They had come within a few hundred yards of the mango orchard, and were looking forward to a rest before the evening meal. The deer would have preceded them; perhaps it was being prepared at this very moment. It was almost sunset. From the mosque at the Fort they could hear the sound of the evening azaan in the muezzin's fine voice. Firoz, who had been whistling, stopped.

They were almost at the border of the orchard when Maan, who was riding in front, saw a jungle cat on the path—a couple of feet long, lithe and long-legged, with fur that looked to him almost golden, and with sharp, greenish eyes that it turned upon him in an intent and narrow, almost cruel, gaze. The horse, who had not resented the weight of the boar or its scent of death, came to an immediate halt, and Maan again instinctively raised his rifle.

'No—no—don't—' cried Firoz.

The jungle cat bounded away into the tall grass to the right of the path.

Maan turned angrily on Firoz.

'What do you mean—don't? I would have had it.'

'It isn't a tiger or a panther—there's nothing heroic about shooting one. Anyway, my father doesn't like killing what we can't eat—unless, of course, it's an immediate threat.'

'Come on, Firoz, I know you've shot panther before,' said Maan.

'Well, I don't shoot jungle cats. They're too beautiful and harmless. I'm fond of them.'

'What an idiot you are,' said Maan regretfully.

'All of us like jungle cats,' explained Firoz, who didn't want his friend to remain annoyed. 'Once Imtiaz shot one, and Zainab didn't speak to him for days.'

Maan was still shaking his head. Firoz drew alongside him and put his arm around his shoulder. By the time they had crossed the orchard, Maan was mollified.

'Did a cart carrying a deer come this way?' asked Waris of an old man who was walking through the orchard with a stick.

'No, Sahib, I haven't seen any such thing,' said the old man. 'But I've only been here a little while.' He stared at the trussed-up boar, its huge-tusked head hanging across the haunch of Waris's horse.

Waris, pleased to have been called Sahib, grinned and said optimistically: 'It's probably got to the kitchen by now. And we'll be late for the evening prayer. Too bad,' he grinned.

'I need a bath,' said Firoz. 'Have you had our things put in my room?' he asked Waris. 'Maan Sahib is sleeping in my room.'

'Yes, I gave orders just before we left. That's where he slept the last time too,' said Waris. 'But I doubt he'll be able to sleep tonight with that grim fellow gargling away till the early hours. Last time it was the owl.'

'Waris pretends to be thicker than he is,' said Firoz to Maan. 'Ustad Majeed Khan will be singing tonight after dinner.'

'Good,' said Maan.

'When I suggested getting your favourite singer over, my father got annoyed. Not that I was really serious.'

'Well, Veena studies music under Khan Sahib, so we're used to that sort of gargling,' said Maan.

'Here we are,' said Firoz, dismounting and stretching himself.

14.19

The excellent dinner included a roasted haunch of venison. They ate not in the dark-panelled dining room but in the highest of the several open courtyards under a clear sky. Unlike at lunch, the Nawab Sahib was rather quiet throughout dinner; he was thinking about his munshi, who had annoyed him by complaining about the size of the fee that Ustad Majeed Khan now felt he should command. 'What? All this for a song?' was the munshi's view of the matter.

After dinner they adjourned to the Imambara to listen to Ustad Majeed Khan. Since Moharram was still a few weeks away, the Imambara continued to be used as a general meeting hall; indeed, the Nawab Sahib's father had used it as a durbar of sorts except during Moharram itself. Despite the fact that the Nawab Sahib was in general devout—there were, for example, no drinks served at dinner—a number of paintings depicting scenes from the martyrdom of Hussain decorated the walls of the Imambara. These, out of consideration for anyone who followed very strictly the injunctions against representational art, especially with respect to religious depiction, had been covered with white cloth. A few tazias—replicas in various materials of the tomb of Hussain—stood at the far end behind tall white pillars; some

Moharram lances and standards stood in a corner.

Chandeliers glinted down in red and white from the ceiling, but the electric bulbs they contained had not been lit. So that the distant sound of the generator would not disturb them, the hall had been lit by candlelight instead. Ustad Majeed Khan was notoriously temperamental when it came to his art. It was true that he often practised at home in the midst of an appalling domestic racket, the result of his wife's excessive sociability. But when he performed, even the necessity of earning his living at least partly through the diminishing patronage of zamindars and princes would not allow him to compromise with the seriousness of attention he demanded—and the absolute lack of disturbance. If it was true, as it was said, that he sang for himself and God alone, it was equally true that this bond was strengthened by an appreciative audience and strained by a restless one. The Nawab Sahib had not invited any guests from the town of Baitar, largely because he had not found anyone there who appreciated good music. Apart from the musicians there was no one but himself, his friend, and their two sons.

Ustad Majeed Khan was accompanied by his own tabla player; and by Ishaq Khan as an accompanying vocalist, not as a sarangi player. The great musician was now at the stage where he treated Ishaq not as a student or even a nephew but as a son. Ishaq had all the musicality Ustad Majeed Khan could have wished for in a student; and he had, besides, that passionate reverence for his teachers—including his own late father—that had got him into trouble with his Ustad in the first place. Their subsequent reconciliation had astonished them both. The Ustad had seen in it the hand of God. Ishaq did not know what to ascribe it to, but was deeply grateful. Since adaptation to the style of the main performer was instinctive to him as a sarangi player, Ishaq, who had a fine voice, quickly adapted himself to the style of his teacher; and since his teacher's style drew with it a certain bent of mind and a certain manner of creativity, within a few months of his first lessons with Ustad Majeed Khan he was singing with a confidence and ease that first alarmed, and then—despite his own considerable ego—pleased the Ustad. At last he had a disciple worthy of the name; and one, moreover, who more than compensated in the honour he did him for any fleeting dishonour he may have been guilty of in the past.

It was late when they settled down after dinner, and Ustad Majeed Khan immediately, and without tackling any lighter raag to warm up his voice, began to sing Raag Darbari. How appropriate, thought the Nawab Sahib, was the raag to the surroundings, and how his father, whose one sensual vice had been music, would have enjoyed it had he been alive. The regally slow unfolding of the alaap, the wide vibratos on the third and sixth degrees, the stately descents in alternating rises and falls, the richness of the Khan Sahib's voice accompanied from time to time by his young disciple, and the invariant, undazzling, solid beat of the tabla created a structure of majesty and perfection that hypnotized both musicians and audience. Very rarely did any of the listeners even say 'wah! wah!' at some particular brilliance. It was more than two hours and late after midnight when he ended.

'See to the candles, they are guttering,' said the Nawab Sahib quietly to a servant. 'Tonight, Khan Sahib, you have outdone yourself.'

'Through His grace, and yours.'

'Will you rest a little?'

'No, there is life in me still. And the will to sing before this kind of an audience.'

'What will you give us now?'

'What will it be?' said Ustad Majeed Khan, turning to Ishaq. 'It's far too early for Bhatiyar, but I'm in the mood for it, so God will forgive us.'

The Nawab Sahib, who had never heard the master sing with Ishaq before, and had certainly never seen—or even heard of—the Khan Sahib consulting anyone about what he should or should not sing, was astonished, and asked to be introduced to the young singer.

Maan suddenly recalled where he had seen Ishaq Khan.

'We've met before,' he said before he could give himself time to think. 'At Saeeda Begum's, wasn't it? I've been trying to work it out. You were her sarangi player, weren't you?'

There was a sudden and frigid silence. Everyone present except the tabla player looked at Maan with discomfiture or shock. It was as if no one wanted to be reminded at this magical moment of anything from that other world. Whether as patron or employee or lover or acquaintance or fellow-artist or rival, in one sense or another every one of them was tied to Saeeda Bai.

Ustad Majeed Khan got up, as he said, to relieve himself. The Nawab Sahib had bowed his head. Ishaq Khan had started talking in a low voice to the tabla player. Everyone seemed eager to exorcize this unwanted muse.

Ustad Majeed Khan returned and sang Raag Bhatiyar as beautifully as if nothing had happened. Now and then he paused to sip a glass of water. At three o'clock he got up and yawned. As if in response, so did everyone else.

14.20

Later in their room, Maan and Firoz lay in bed, yawning and talking.

'I'm exhausted. What a day,' said Maan.

'It's good I didn't open my emergency bottle of Scotch before dinner, or we'd have been snoring through the Bhatiyar.'

There was a pause.

'What exactly was wrong about my mentioning Saeeda Bai?' asked Maan. 'Everyone froze. So did you.'

'Did I?' said Firoz, leaning on his arm and looking at his friend rather intently.

'Yes.' Firoz was wondering what, if anything, to say in reply, when Maan went on: 'I like that photograph, the one by the window of you and the family—you look just the same now as then.'

'Nonsense,' laughed Firoz. 'I'm five years old in that photograph. And I'm much better-looking now,' he added in a factual sort of way. 'Better-looking than you, in fact.'

Maan explained himself. 'What I meant was that you have the same kind of look, with your head tilted at an angle and that frown.'

'All that that tilt reminds me of is the Chief Justice,' said Firoz. After a while he said: 'Why are you leaving tomorrow? Stay for a few days more.'

Maan shrugged. 'I'd like to. I don't get much time to spend with you. And I really like your Fort. We could go hunting again. The trouble is that I promised some people I know in Debaria that I'd be back for Bakr-Id. And I thought I'd show Baoji the place as well. He's a politician in search of a constituency, so the more he sees of this one the better. Anyway, it's not Bakr-Id so much as Moharram that's important at Baitar, didn't you tell me?'

Firoz yawned again. 'Yes, yes, that's right. Well, but this year I won't be here. I'll be in Brahmpur.'

'Why?'

'Oh, Imtiaz and I take it by turns: Burré Sahib one year, Chhoté Sahib the next. The fact is, we haven't shared a Moharram since we've been eighteen. One of us has to be here, and the other in Brahmpur to take part in the processions there.'

'Don't tell me you beat your breast and flagellate yourself,' said Maan.

'No. But some people do. Some even walk on fire. Come and see it for yourself this year.'

'Perhaps I will,' said Maan. 'Goodnight. Isn't the light switch by your side of the bed?'

'Do you know that even Saeeda Bai closes shop during Moharram?' asked Firoz.

'What?' said Maan in a more wakeful voice. 'How do you know?'

'Everyone knows,' said Firoz. 'She's very devout. Of course, the Raja of Marh will be pretty annoyed. Usually he counts on having a good time around Dussehra.'

Maan's response was a grunt.

Firoz went on: 'But she won't sing for him, and she won't play with him. All she'll consent to sing is marsiyas, laments for the martyrs of the battle of Karbala. Not very titillating.'

'No,' agreed Maan.

'She won't even sing for you,' said Firoz.

'I suppose not,' said Maan, slightly crestfallen and wondering why Firoz was being so unkind.

'Nor for your friend.'

'My friend?' asked Maan.

'The Rajkumar of Marh.'

Maan laughed. 'Oh, him!' he said.

'Yes, him,' said Firoz.

There was something in Firoz's voice that reminded Maan of their younger days.

'Firoz!' laughed Maan, turning towards him. 'All that is over. We were just kids. Don't tell me you're jealous.'

'Well, as you once said, I never tell you anything.'

'Oh?' said Maan, rolling over on his side towards his friend, and taking him in his arms.

'I thought you were sleepy,' said Firoz, smiling to himself in the dark.

'So I am,' said Maan. 'But so what?'

Firoz began to laugh quietly. 'You'll think I've planned all this.'

'Well, perhaps you have,' said Maan. 'But I don't mind,' he added with a small sigh as he passed a hand through Firoz's hair.

14.21

Mahesh Kapoor and Maan borrowed a jeep from the Nawab Sahib and drove off towards Debaria. So full of pits and pools was the dirt road that led off the main road to the village that it was normally impossible to get to it in the monsoon. But they managed somehow, partly because it had not rained too heavily in the past week.

Most of the people they met were very pleased to see Maan; and Mahesh Kapoor—in spite of what the Nawab Sahib had told him—was quite astonished at the popularity of his vagabond son. It struck him with amazement that of the two activities necessary for a politician—the ability to win votes, and the capacity to do something with your mandate after victory—Maan possessed the first in abundant measure, at least in this constituency. The people of Debaria had taken him to their hearts.

Rasheed, of course, was not there, since it was term-time, but his wife and daughters were staying with his father rather than hers for a few days. Meher and the village urchins and the shock-headed Moazzam were all delighted at Maan's arrival. He provided even more entertainment than the various black goats tied up to posts and trees around the village that were due to be sacrificed the next day. Moazzam, who had always been fascinated by Maan's watch, demanded to see it again. Even Mr Biscuit paused in his eating to yell out a triumphant if variant version of the azaan before Baba, furious at his impiety, dealt with him.

The orthodox Baba, who had told Maan to come back for Bakr-Id but had very much doubted that he would, did not actually smile—but it was very apparent that he was glad to see him. He praised him to his father.

'He is a good boy,' said Baba, nodding vigorously at Mahesh Kapoor.

'Yes?' said Mahesh Kapoor.

'Yes, indeed, he is very respectful of our ways. He has won our hearts by his simplicity.'

Simplicity? thought Mahesh Kapoor, but said nothing.

That Mahesh Kapoor, the architect of the Zamindari Abolition Act, had come to the village was a great event in itself, and it was also a matter of great consequence that he had arrived in the Nawab Sahib's jeep. Rasheed's father had no strong views on politics except if something impinged on his interests: any such view was communism. But Baba, who wielded considerable influence in the surrounding villages, respected Mahesh Kapoor for his resignation from the Congress at about the time that Kidwai had resigned. He also identified, as did many people, with the Nawab Sahib.

Now, however, he thought—and said as much to Mahesh Kapoor—that the best thing would be for all men of goodwill to rejoin the Congress. Nehru was firmly back in charge, he felt, and with Nehru, more than with anyone else, people of his community felt safe. When Maan mentioned that his father was considering the option of contesting from Salimpur-cum-Baitar, Baba was encouraging.

'But try to get the Congress ticket. The Muslims will vote for Nehru—and so will the chamars. As for the others, who knows: it will depend on events—and how you run your campaign. The situation is very fluid.'

That was a phrase that Mahesh Kapoor was to hear, read, and use a great deal in the days to come.

The brahmins and banias of the village came separately to see him as he sat on a charpoy under the neem tree outside Rasheed's father's house. The Football was particularly ingratiating. He told Mahesh Kapoor of Baba's methods of foiling the Zamindari Act by forced evictions (omitting his own attempts in the same direction), and offered to act as Mahesh Kapoor's lieutenant in the area should he choose to run from there. Mahesh Kapoor, however, was non-committal in his response. He did not much care for the scheming Football; he realized that there were very few brahmin families in Debaria, none in the twin village of Sagal and not many in the villages around; and it was clear to him that the man who mattered most of all was the ancient and energetic Baba. He disliked what he heard about the evictions, but he tried not to dwell on the sufferings he knew they caused. It was difficult to be someone's guest and prosecutor simultaneously, more particularly if you were hoping to seek their help in the near future.

Baba asked him a number of questions over tea or sherbet.

'How long will you be conferring on us the honour of your presence?'

'I will have to leave this evening.'

'What? Aren't you going to stay for Bakr-Id?'

'I can't. I've promised to be in Salimpur. And if it rains, the jeep will be stuck here, perhaps for days. But Maan will be here for Bakr-Id.' Mahesh Kapoor did not need to mention that if he was sounding out a future fief the subdivisional town of Salimpur, with its concentrated knot of population, was an essential stop, and that his participation there in the Id celebrations would pay rich dividends in the future. Maan had told him that his secular stand was popular in the town.

The one person who had very mixed feelings about Mahesh Kapoor's visit was the young Netaji. When he heard that Mahesh Kapoor was in the village, he rushed back from Salimpur on his Harley Davidson. Netaji, who had recently been put up for election to the District Congress Committee, felt that this was an opportunity for contact-making that was too good to be true. Mahesh Kapoor had a name and a following, and, however thinly such silver was beaten into foil, he hoped that some of it might cover him as well. On the other hand, he was no longer the powerful Minister of Revenue but plain Shri Mahesh Kapoor, MLA, a member no longer of the Congress but of a party of uncertain prospects and unmemorable name that even now seemed riven with disagreement about whether to wind itself up. And the acrobatic Netaji, who had his ear to the ground and his finger to the wind, had concrete proof of Mahesh Kapoor's weakening might and clout. He had heard about Jha's power in Mahesh Kapoor's own tehsil of Rudhia, and had imbibed with particular satisfaction the news of the swift transfer of the arrogant English-speaking SDO who had snubbed him so painfully on the platform of Salimpur Station.

Mahesh Kapoor took a walk around the village in the company of Maan and Baba—as well as Netaji, who forced himself upon them. Mahesh Kapoor appeared to be in an excellent mood; perhaps the respite from Prem Nivas had done him good—or the open air—or Majeed Khan's singing—or simply the fact that he could see political possibilities in this constituency. They were tailed by a motley gang of village children and a small, black, continually bleating goat that one of the children was driving along the muddy path—a glossy-headed goat, with pointed little horns, thick black eyebrows and mild, sceptical yellow eyes. Everywhere Maan was greeted with friendliness and Mahesh Kapoor with respect.

The great monsoon sky over the twin villages—indeed, over much of the Gangetic plain—was overcast, and people were worried that it might rain the next day, on Bakr-Id itself, and spoil the festivities. Mahesh Kapoor for the most part managed to avoid any political talk. All that sort of thing could be left to electioneering time. Now he simply made sure that he was recognized. He did namaste or adaab as was appropriate, drank tea, and made small talk.

'Should I go around Sagal as well?' he asked Baba.

Baba thought for a second. 'No, don't do that. Let the web of gossip do its work.'

Finally, having made his rounds, Mahesh Kapoor drove off, but not before thanking Baba and saying to Maan:

'Perhaps you and Bhaskar are right. At any rate, even if you didn't learn much Urdu, you weren't wasting your time.'

Maan could not remember the last time his father had praised him. He was extremely pleased, and more than a little surprised. A couple of tears came to his eyes!

Mahesh Kapoor pretended not to notice, nodded, looked at the sky, and waved in a general way to the gathered populace as the jeep squelched off.

14.22

Maan slept in the verandah because of the possibility of rain. He woke up late, but did not find Baba louring angrily over him asking him why he hadn't been to morning prayer.

Instead, Baba said: 'So you've got up, I see. Will you be coming to the Idgah?'

'Yes,' said Maan. 'Why not?'

'Then you should get ready quickly,' he said, and patted a fat black goat that was browsing meditatively near the neem tree.

The others in the family had preceded them, and now Baba and Maan walked across the fields from Debaria to Sagal. The Idgah was located in Sagal; it was part of the school near the lake. The sky was still overcast, but there was also an undercast of light that added brilliance to the emerald colour of the transplanted rice. Ducks were swimming in a paddy field, scrabbling for worms and insects. Everything was fresh and refreshing.

All around them, approaching the Idgah from different directions, were men, women and children, all dressed in festive attire—new clothes, or—for those who could not afford them—clothes that were spotlessly clean and freshly pressed. They converged on the school from all the surrounding villages, not merely from Debaria and Sagal. The men were for the most part dressed in white kurta-pyjamas; but some wore lungis, and some allowed themselves coloured kurtas, though of a sober colour. Maan noticed that their headgear varied from white, close-fitting filigreed caps to black, glossy ones. The women and children wore brightly coloured clothes—red, green, yellow, pink, maroon, blue, indigo, purple. Even under the black or dark-blue burqas worn by most of the women Maan could see the hems of their coloured saris or salwaars, and the attractive anklets and chappals on feet patterned with bright red henna and splashed with the inescapable mud of the monsoon.

It was while they were walking along the narrow paths that a man, old, thin and hungry-looking, and dressed in nothing but a dirty dhoti, intercepted Baba and, with his hands folded, said in a desperate voice:

'Khan Sahib, what have I done that you should do this to me and to my family? How can we manage now?'

Baba looked at him, thought for a second, and said: 'Do you want your legs broken? I don't care what you say now. Did you think about this when you went to the kanungo to complain?'

He then kept walking towards Sagal. Maan, however, was so troubled by the man's look—half of hatred born of betrayal, half of supplication—that he stared at his deeply wrinkled face and tried to recall—as he had with the sarangi player—where he had seen him before.

'What's the story behind this, Baba?' he asked.

'Nothing,' said Baba. 'He wanted to get his grasping fingers on my land, that's all.' It was clear from his voice that he wished to dismiss the subject from his mind.

As they approached the school, the sounds of a loudspeaker could be heard repeating the praises of God or else telling the people to get ready for the Id prayers, and not to delay too long at the fair. 'And, ladies, please make yourselves proper; we are about to start; please hurry up, everyone.'

But it was difficult to get the holiday-making crowd to hurry up. Some people, certainly, were performing their ritual ablutions by the edge of the tank; but most of them were milling around the stalls and the improvised market that had formed just outside the school gates along the length of the earthen embankment. Trinkets, bangles, mirrors, balloons—and, best of all, food of all kinds from alu tikkis to chholé to jalebis extruded spluttering into hot tawas, barfis, laddus, flossy pink candy, paan, fruit—everything that Mr Biscuit could have dreamed of in his least constrained imaginings. Indeed, Mr Biscuit was loitering near a stand with half a barfi in his hand. Meher, who had been given some sweets by her grandfather, was sharing them with other children. Moazzam, on the other hand, was busy befriending various vulnerable children—'for their money', as the shaven but mustachioed Netaji pointed out to Maan.

The women and girls disappeared into the school building, from where they would watch and participate in the proceedings, while the men and boys arranged themselves in rows on long rolls of cloth in the compound outside. There were more than a thousand men present. Maan saw among them several of the elders of Sagal who had given Rasheed so much trouble outside the mosque, but he did not see the sick old man whom Rasheed and he had gone to visit—not that in such a large gathering it was possible to be certain about who was not there. He was asked to sit on the edge of the verandah next to two bored policemen of the P.P. Police Constabulary, who lounged about in greenish khaki and surveyed the scene. They were there to see that order was maintained and to act as witnesses in case the Imam's sermon contained anything inflammatory, but their presence was resented, and their manner betrayed that they knew it.

The Imam began the prayers, and the people stood up and knelt down as required with the awesome unanimity of the Islamic service. In the middle of the two snatches of prayers, however, there was a sound of distant thunder. By the time the Imam had begun his sermon, the congregation appeared to be paying more attention to the sky than to his words.

It began to drizzle, and the people started getting restless. Eventually they settled down, but only after the Imam had interrupted his sermon to upbraid them:

'You! Don't you have any patience in the sight of God—on the day we have met to remember the sacrifice of Ibrahim and Ismail? You put up with rain in the fields, and yet on this day you act as if a few drops of water will dissolve you away. Don't you know how those who are doing the pilgrimage this year are suffering on the scorching sands in Arabia? Some of them have even died of heatstroke—and you are in terror of a few drops from the sky. Here I am talking about Ibrahim's willingness to sacrifice his son, and all you are thinking of is keeping dry—you will not even sacrifice a few minutes of your time. You are like the impatient ones who would not come to prayer because the merchants had arrived. In the Surah al-Baqarah, the very surah after which this festival is named, it says:

> Who therefore shrinks from the religion
> of Abraham, except he be foolish-minded?

And later it says:

> We will serve thy God and the God of thy fathers
> Abraham, Ishmael and Isaac, One God;
> to him we surrender.

Is this the quality of your surrender? Stop it, stop it, good people; be still, and do not fidget!

Surely, Abraham was a nation
obedient unto God, a man of pure faith
    and no idolater,
showing thankfulness for His blessings;
He chose him, and He guided him
    to a straight path.
And We gave him in this world good,
and in the world to come he shall be
    among the righteous.
Then We revealed to thee: "Follow thou
the creed of Abraham, a man of pure faith
    and no idolater."'

The Imam got quite carried away with his quotations in Arabic, but after a while he returned to his quieter discourse in Urdu. He talked about the greatness of God and his Prophet, and how everyone should be good and devout in the spirit of Abraham and the other prophets of God.

When it was over, everyone joined in asking for God's blessings, and, after a few minutes, dispersed to their villages, making sure they returned by a different route from the one they had taken to arrive.

'And tomorrow, being Friday, we'll get another sermon,' some of them grumbled. But others thought that the Imam had been at his best.

14.23

As he walked back into the village, Maan bumped into the Football, who drew him aside.

'Where have you been?' asked the Football.

'To the Idgah.'

The Football looked unhappy. 'That is not a place for us,' he said.

'I suppose not,' said Maan indifferently. 'Still, no one made me feel unwelcome.'

'And now, you will watch all this cruel goat business?'

'If I see it, I'll see it,' said Maan, who thought that hunting, after all, was as bloody a business as sacrificing a goat. Besides, he didn't want to get into a false compact of solidarity with the Football, whom he did not greatly care for.

But when he saw the sacrifice, he did not enjoy it.

In some of the houses of Debaria, the master of the house himself performed the sacrifice of the goat or, occasionally, the sheep. (Cow sacrifice had been forbidden in P.P. since British times because of the danger of religious rioting.) But in other houses, a man specially trained as a butcher came around to sacrifice the animal that symbolized God's merciful replacement for Abraham's son. According to popular tradition this was Ishmael, not Isaac, though the Islamic authorities were divided on this matter. The goats of the village seemed to sense that their final hour was at hand, for they set up a fearful and pitiful bleating.

The children, who enjoyed the spectacle, followed the butcher as he made his rounds. Eventually he got to Rasheed's father's house. The plump black goat was made to face west. Baba said a prayer over it while Netaji and the butcher held it down. The butcher then put his foot on its chest, held its mouth, and slit its throat. The goat gurgled, and from the slash in its throat bright red blood and green, half-digested grass poured out.

Maan turned away, and noticed that Mr Biscuit, wearing a garland of marigolds that he must have somehow procured at the fair, was looking at the slaughter with a phlegmatic air.

But everything was proceeding briskly. The head was chopped off. The skin on the legs and underbelly was slit and the entire skin peeled off the fat. The hind legs were broken at the knee, then bound, and the goat was hung from a branch. The stomach was slit, and the entrails, with their blood and filth, were pulled out. The liver and lungs and kidneys were removed, the front legs cut off. Now the goat, which only a few minutes ago had been bleating in alarm and gazing at Maan with its yellow eyes, was just a carcass, to be divided in thirds among the owners, their families, and the poor.

The children looked on, thrilled and enthralled. They especially enjoyed the sacrifice itself and later the spilling out of the grey-pink guts. Now they stared as the front quarters were set aside for the family, and the rest of the body chopped into sections across the ribs and placed on the scales on the verandah to be balanced. Rasheed's father was in charge of the distribution.

The poor children—who got to eat meat very rarely—crowded forward to get their share. Some clustered around the scales and grabbed at the chunks of meat, others tried to but were pushed back; most of the girls sat quietly in one place, and eventually got served. Some of the women, including the wives of the chamars, appeared to be very shy and could hardly bring themselves to come forward to accept the meat. Eventually they carried it off in their hands, or on bits of cloth or paper, praising and thanking the Khan Sahib for his generosity or complaining about their share as they walked to the next house to receive their portion of its sacrifice.

14.24

The previous evening's meal had been hurried because of the preparations for Bakr-Id; but today's late afternoon meal was relaxed. The tastiest dish was one made from the liver, kidneys and tripe of the goat that had just been slaughtered. Then the charpoys were shifted under the neem tree beneath which the goat had earlier been quietly browsing.

Maan, Baba and his two sons, Qamar—the sarcastic schoolteacher from Salimpur—as well as Rasheed's uncle, the Bear, were all present for lunch. The talk turned naturally to Rasheed. The Bear asked Maan how he was doing.

'Actually, I haven't seen him since I returned to Brahmpur,' confessed Maan. 'He has been so busy with his tuitions, I suppose, and I myself with one thing and another—'

It was a feeble excuse, but Maan had not neglected his friend by intention. It was just the way things happened to be in his life.

'I did hear that he was involved in the student Socialist Party,' said Maan. 'With Rasheed, though, there's no fear that he'll neglect his studies.' Maan did not mention Saeeda Bai's remark about Rasheed.

Maan noticed that only the Bear seemed truly concerned about Rasheed. After a while, and long after the conversation had passed on to other matters, he said: 'Everything he does he does too seriously. His hair will be white before he's thirty unless someone teaches him to laugh.'

Everyone was constrained when talking about Rasheed. Maan felt this acutely; but since no one—not even Rasheed himself—had told him how he had disgraced himself, he could not understand it. When Rasheed had read Saeeda Bai's letter to him, Maan, being denied an early return to Brahmpur, had been seized with such restlessness that he had very shortly afterwards set out on a trek. Perhaps it was his own preoccupation that had blinded him to the tension in the family of his friend.

14.25

Netaji planned to hold a party the next night—a feast of meat for which he had another goat handy—in honour of various people of importance in the subdivision: police and petty administration officials and so on. He was trying to persuade Qamar to get the headmaster of his school in Salimpur to come. Qamar not only flatly refused, but made no secret of his contempt for Netaji's transparent attempts to ingratiate himself with the worthy and the influential. Throughout the afternoon Qamar found some way or other of needling Netaji. At one point he turned to Maan with newfound friendliness and said, 'I suppose that when your father was here, he was unable to shake off our Netaji.'

'Well,' said Maan, resisting a smile, 'Baba and he very kindly showed my father around Debaria.'

'I thought it might be something like that,' said Qamar. 'He was having tea with me in Salimpur when he heard from a friend of mine, who had dropped in, that the great Mahesh Kapoor was visiting his own native village. Well, that was the end of tea with me. Netaji knows which cups of tea contain more sugar. He's as smart as the flies on Baba's sputum.'

Netaji, affecting to be above such crude taunts, and still hopeful that he might be able to bag the headmaster, refused to get outwardly annoyed, and Qamar retired, disappointed.

Not long after this late lunch Maan took a rickshaw to Salimpur in order to catch the train back to Baitar. He didn't want to arrive after Firoz had left. Although it was easier for Firoz, given his profession, to get away from Brahmpur than it was for Imtiaz, he might well turn out to have some date in court or some urgent call from a senior for a conference that would cut short his visit.

An attractive young woman with hennaed feet was singing a song to herself in the local accent as the rickshaw passed her. Maan caught just a few lines as he turned around to get a glimpse of her unveiled face:

'O, husband, you can go but get me something from the fair—
Vermilion to overfill the parting in my hair.
Bangles from Firozabad, jaggery to eat—
And sandals made by Praha for my henna-coloured feet.'

She gave Maan a glance that was at once amused and angry as he gazed at her without embarrassment, and the memory of her look kept him in good spirits all the way to Salimpur Station.

14.26

Nehru's coup was not followed by wholesale subservience to his desires.

In Delhi, in Parliament, opposition by MPs from all sections of the House, including his own, forced him to abandon his attempt to pass the Hindu Code Bill. This legislation, very dear to the Prime Minister's heart—and to that of his Law Minister, Dr Ambedkar—aimed to make the laws of marriage, divorce, inheritance and guardianship more rational and just, especially to women.

Nor were the more orthodox Hindu legislators by any means on the defensive in the Legislative Assembly at Brahmpur. L.N. Agarwal had sponsored a bill that would make Hindi the state language from the beginning of the new year, and the Muslim legislators were rising one by one to appeal to him and to the Chief Minister and to the House to protect the status of Urdu. Mahesh Kapoor, who had returned to Brahmpur from the countryside, took no active part in the debate, but Abdus Salaam, his former Parliamentary Secretary, did make a couple of brief interventions.

Begum Abida Khan, of course, was at her oratorical best:

Begum Abida Khan: It is all very well for the honourable Minister to take the name of Gandhiji when espousing the cause of Hindi. I have nothing against Hindi, but why does he not agree to protect the status of Urdu, the second language of this province, and the mother tongue of the Muslims? Does the honourable Minister imagine that the Father of the Nation, who was willing to give his life to protect the minority community, would countenance a bill like the present one which will cause our community and our culture and our very livelihood to die a lingering death? The sudden enforcement of Hindi in the Devanagari script has closed the doors of government service on the Muslims. They cannot compete with those whose language is Hindi. This has created a first-class economic crisis among the Muslims—many of whom depend on the services for their livelihood. All of a sudden they have to face the strange music of the P.P. Official Language Bill. It is a sin to take the name of Gandhiji in this context. I appeal to your humanity, you who have shot us and hunted us down in our houses, do not be the author of further miseries for us.

The Hon'ble the Minister for Home Affairs (Shri L.N. Agarwal): I will ignore, as I am sure the House would wish me to, this last remark, and simply thank the honourable member for her heartfelt advice. If it were equally brain-thought, there might have been grounds for accepting it. The fact of the matter is that duplication of all government work in two languages, two scripts, is utterly impracticable and unworkable. That is all there is to it.

Begum Abida Khan: I will not appeal to the chair against the expressions of the honourable Minister. He is telling the whole world that he thinks that Muslims have no rights and women have no brains. I am hoping to appeal to his better instincts, but what hope do I have? He has been the prime mover in this government policy of stifling Urdu, which has led to the disappearance of many Urdu publications. Why is Urdu receiving this stepmotherly treatment at his hands? Why can the two brother languages not be adopted together? The elder brother has a duty to protect the younger brother, not to torment him.

The Hon'ble the Minister for Home Affairs (Shri L.N. Agarwal): You are asking for a two-language theory now, you will be asking for a two-nation theory tomorrow.

Shri Jainendra Chandla (Socialist Party): I am pained at the twist given to the debate by the honourable Minister. While Begum Abida Khan, whose patriotism nobody can doubt, has only asked that Urdu should not be stifled, the honourable Minister is trying to import the two-nation theory into the debate. I too am dissatisfied with the progress of Hindi. All the work in offices is carried on in English still, despite the many resolutions and regulations. It is English that we should be working to displace, not each other's languages.

Shri Abdus Salaam (Congress): Some of my constituents have brought to my attention the fact that difficulties have been created in the syllabus for Urdu-reading students and that they have thus been deprived of the chance to study Urdu. If a small country like Switzerland can have four official languages, there can be no reason not to treat Urdu as at least a regional language in this state, which is several times as large. Facilities ought to be provided—and not only in name—for the teaching of Urdu in schools.

The Hon'ble the Minister for Home Affairs (Shri L.N. Agarwal): Our resources, unfortunately, are not unlimited. There are many madrasas and religious establishments all over the state where Urdu may be taught. As regards the official language of the state of Purva Pradesh, things must be made abundantly clear, so that there is no confusion, and people do not move on the wrong tracks from childhood, only to discover later that they are at a disadvantage.

Begum Abida Khan: The honourable Minister talks about how things must be made clear. But even the Constitution of India is not clear about the official language. It has stated that English will be replaced at the Centre after fifteen years. But even then it will not happen automatically. A commission will be appointed, which will go into the whole question and report to the government as to what progress Hindi has made and the question of replacing English completely will then be decided on a reasonable basis, not by fiat and prejudice. I wonder, if a foreign language like English can be tolerated in this way, why can Urdu not be tolerated? It is one of the glories of our province—it is the language of its finest poet, Mast. It is the language of Mir, of Ghalib, of Dagh, of Sauda, of Iqbal, of Hindu writers like Premchand and Firaq. Yet even though it has a richer tradition, Urdu does not claim equal status with Hindi. It can be treated like any other regional language. But it must not be dispossessed as is being done.

The Hon'ble the Minister for Home Affairs (Shri L.N. Agarwal): Urdu is not being dispossessed, as the honourable member supposes. Anyone who learns the Devanagari script will find no difficulty in coping.

Begum Abida Khan: Can the honourable Minister tell this House in all heartfelt honesty that there is no real difference between the two languages except one of script?

The Hon'ble the Minister for Home Affairs (Shri L.N. Agarwal): Heartfelt or otherwise, that is what Gandhiji planned: he aimed for Hindustani as the ideal, which would take both languages as its source.

Begum Abida Khan: I am not talking about ideals and about what Gandhiji planned. I am talking about facts and what is happening all around us. Listen to All India Radio and try to understand its news bulletins. Read the Hindi versions of our bills and acts—or if, like me and other Muslims and even many Hindus of this province, you cannot read them, then have them read out to you. You will not understand one word in three. It is all becoming stupidly and stiltedly Sanskritized. Obscure words are being dug out of old religious texts and being reburied in our modern language. It is a plot of the religious fundamentalists who hate anything to do with Islam, even Arabic or Persian words that the common people of Brahmpur have used for hundreds of years.

The Hon'ble the Minister for Home Affairs (Shri L.N. Agarwal): The honourable member has a gift for fantasy that excites my admiration. But she is, as usual, thinking from right to left.

Begum Abida Khan: How dare you speak like that? How dare you? I would like full-fledged Sanskrit to be made the official language of the state—then you too will see! One day it will be full-fledged Sanskrit that you will be forced to read and speak, and it will make you clutch at your hair even harder. Then you too will be made to feel a stranger in your own land. So it will be better if Sanskrit is made the official language. Then both Hindu and Muslim boys will have an equal start and be able to compete on an equal footing.

The debate proceeded in this manner, with importunate waves of protest washing over an adamant sea wall. Finally, closure was moved by a member of the Congress Party and the House rose for the day.

14.27

Just outside the chamber Mahesh Kapoor collared his old Parliamentary Secretary.

'So, you rogue, you're still with the Congress.'

Abdus Salaam turned around, pleased to hear the voice of his ex-Minister.

'We must talk about that,' he said, glancing a little to left and right.

'We haven't talked for a long time, it seems to me—ever since I've been in the opposition.'

'It isn't that, Minister Sahib—'

'Ah, at least you call me by my old title.'

'But of course. It's just that you've been away—in Baitar. Associating with zamindars, I hear,' Abdus Salaam couldn't help adding.

'Didn't you go back home for Id?'

'Yes, that's true. We've both been away, then. And before that I was in Delhi for the AICC meeting. But now we can talk. Let's go to the canteen.'

'And eat those fearful greasy samosas? You young people have stronger stomachs than us.' Mahesh Kapoor appeared, despite everything, to be in a good mood.

Abdus Salaam was in fact quite fond of the greasy samosas that the canteen provided as one of its snacks. 'But where else can we go, Minister

Sahib? Your office, alas—' He smiled regretfully.

Mahesh Kapoor laughed. 'When I left the Cabinet, Sharma should have made you a Minister of State. Then you at least would have had an office of your own. What's the point of remaining a Parliamentary Secretary if there's no one to be secretary to?'

Abdus Salaam too started laughing in a gentle way. He was a scholarly rather than an ambitious man, and he often wondered how he had strayed into politics and why he had remained there. But he had discovered he had a sleepwalker's flair for it.

He thought about Mahesh Kapoor's last remark. 'If nothing else, there's a subject to handle,' he responded. 'The Chief Minister has left me free to manage that.'

'But until the Supreme Court decides the matter there's nothing you can do about it,' said Mahesh Kapoor. 'And even after they've decided whether the First Amendment is valid or not the zamindars' appeal against the High Court judgement about the act itself will have to be decided. And any action is bound to be stayed till then.'

'It's only a question of time; we'll win both cases,' said Abdus Salaam, looking into the vague middle distance as he sometimes did when thinking. 'And by then no doubt you will be Minister of Revenue again—if not something even better. Anything could happen. Sharma could be kicked upwards to the Cabinet in Delhi, and Agarwal could be murdered by one of Begum Abida Khan's glances. And since you would be back in the Congress you would be the obvious choice for Chief Minister.'

'Do you think so?' said Mahesh Kapoor, looking at his protégé piercingly. 'Do you think so? If you are doing nothing better, let's go home for a cup of tea. I like these dreams of yours.'

'Yes, I have been dreaming a lot—and sleeping a lot—these days,' said Abdus Salaam cryptically.

They continued to talk as they strolled along to Prem Nivas.

'Why did you not intervene in the discussion this afternoon, Minister Sahib?' asked Abdus Salaam.

'Why? You know the reason perfectly well. I can't read a word of Hindi, and I don't want attention drawn to the fact. I'm popular enough among the Muslims—it's the Hindu vote that will be my problem.'

'Even if you rejoin the Congress?'

'Even if I rejoin the Congress.'

'Do you plan to?'

'That is what I want to talk over with you.'

'I might be the wrong person to talk to.'

'Why?' asked Mahesh Kapoor. 'Surely you're not thinking of leaving it?'

'That's what I want to talk over with you.'

'Well,' said Mahesh Kapoor thoughtfully, 'this will require several cups of tea.'

Abdus Salaam did not know how to make small talk, so hardly had he sipped his tea than he plunged straight in with a question.

'Do you really think that Nehru is back in the saddle?'

'Do you really doubt it?' countered Mahesh Kapoor.

'In a way I do,' said Abdus Salaam. 'Look at this Hindu Code Bill. It was a great defeat for him.'

'Well,' said Mahesh Kapoor, 'not necessarily. Not if he wins the next election. Then he'll treat it as a mandate. In a way he's made certain of that, because it's now become an election issue.'

'You can't say he intended that. He simply wanted to pass the bill into law.'

'I don't disagree with that,' said Mahesh Kapoor, stirring his cup.

'And he couldn't hold his own MPs, let alone Parliament, together to pass it. Everyone knows what the President of India thinks of the bill. Even if Parliament had passed it, would he have signed it?'

'That is a separate issue,' said Mahesh Kapoor.

'You're right about that,' admitted Abdus Salaam. 'The question in my mind, though, is one of grip and timing. Why place the bill before Parliament when there was so little time to argue it? A few discussions, a filibuster, and it was bound to die.'

Mahesh Kapoor nodded. He was thinking about something else too. It was the fortnight for the performance of shraadh, the rites to appease the spirits of one's dead. Mahesh Kapoor could never be prevailed upon to perform these rites, and this upset Mrs Mahesh Kapoor. And immediately after this fortnight came the nights of the Ramlila leading up to the fiery celebration of Dussehra. This was the great Hindu festive season, and it would continue till Divali. Nehru could not possibly have chosen a worse time, psychologically speaking, to introduce a bill that attempted to upset Hindu law and transform Hindu society.

Abdus Salaam, after waiting for Mahesh Kapoor to speak, continued: 'You saw what happened in the Assembly, you can see how the L.N. Agarwals of this world continue to operate. No matter what happens at the Centre, that is the shape of things to come in the states. At least, so I think. I do not see much changing. The people who have their hands on the party levers—people like Sharma and Agarwal—will not easily let Nehru prise them off. Look at how quickly they're rushing to form their election committees and to start their selection of candidates in the states. Poor Nehru—he is like a rich merchant, who, after crossing the seas, is drowned in a little stream.'

Mahesh Kapoor frowned: 'What on earth are you quoting from?' he asked.

'From a translation of your Mahabharata, Minister Sahib.'

'Well, I wish you wouldn't,' said Mahesh Kapoor, annoyed. 'I get enough of it at home without you—of all people—joining in.'

'I was only making the point, Minister Sahib, that it is the conservatives, and not our liberal Prime Minister, despite his great victory, who are still in control. Or so I think.'

Abdus Salaam did not sound unduly distressed by what doubtless must have distressed him a good deal. If anything, he sounded light-hearted, as if the pleasure of expounding the logic of his scenario sufficiently counterpoised the grimness of the scenario itself.

And, Mahesh Kapoor reflected, marvelling a little at the young man's attitude, things were, if looked at clearly, quite grim. Less than a week after Nehru had defeated Tandon—one of the two crucial resolutions for which had been sponsored by a party boss from West Bengal—the Congress Executive Committee and Election Committee from the state of West Bengal had with miraculous haste begun to deal with the applications for the nomination of candidates. Their purpose was clear: to forestall the effects of any change from the top, and to present the Centre with a fait accompli—a slate of candidates for the General Elections prepared and in place before any possible secessionists could return to the Congress fold and make a bid for candidature. The state Congress bosses had had to be restrained from carrying out their designs by the Calcutta High Court.

In Purva Pradesh too, the State Election Committee of the Congress had been elected with astonishing speed. Under the Congress constitution this had to consist of the President of the State Congress Committee and not more than eight nor less than four other members. If such haste had really been necessary in order to cope with urgent preliminary work, the entrenched powers could have contented themselves with electing a minimum of four members. But by electing all eight and not leaving a single spot vacant for anyone who might later return to the Congress, they had made it clear that, whatever they said in public in deference to Nehru's wishes, they were not serious about wishing the seceders to come back. For it was only through the activities of the Election Committee that Congressmen belonging to various groups could hope to get their due share of candidates—and through them their share of privilege and power.

Mahesh Kapoor could see all this, but he still had faith—or perhaps hope would describe his feeling better—that Nehru would ensure that those who were ideologically close to him would not find themselves displaced and marginalized in the states. This was what he now suggested to Abdus Salaam. Since Nehru faced no one who could pose the least threat to himself in the party, he would surely ensure that the legislatures of the nation would not be filled for the next five years by those who paid no more than lip service to his ideals.

14.28

Abdus Salaam stirred his tea, then murmured, 'Well, from what you have said I can see you are veering towards rejoining the Congress, Minister Sahib.'

Mahesh Kapoor shrugged his shoulders. 'Tell me,' he said, 'why are you so dubious about it? How can you be so sure he won't gain—or regain—a grip on things? He turned the whole party around and seized the reins when no one expected it of him. He may surprise us further.'

'I was at the All-India Congress Committee meeting in Delhi, as you know,' said Abdus Salaam casually, focusing on a spot in the middle distance. 'I saw him seizing the reins at close range. Well, it was quite a sight—do you want a first-hand account?'

'Yes.'

'Well, Minister Sahib, it was the second day. There we were, all of us, in the Constitution Club. Nehru had been elected President the previous day—but of course he had not actually accepted. He said he wanted to sleep over the matter. He asked us to sleep over the matter. Everyone slept over the matter, and the next afternoon we waited for him to speak. He had not accepted, of course, but he was in the chair. Tandon was among the leaders on the dais, but Nehru was in the chair. The previous day he had refused the chair, but today, well, today, perhaps he thought that such extreme delicacy might be misinterpreted. Or perhaps Tandon had put his foot down and refused to sit where he so clearly was not wanted.'

'Tandon,' admitted Mahesh Kapoor, 'was one of the few who refused to go along with the decision to divide the country when the Congress Party voted for Partition. No one says he's not a man of principle.'

'Well,' said Abdus Salaam in passing, 'Pakistan was a good thing.'

Seeing Mahesh Kapoor look shocked, he said: 'For one thing, with the Muslim League wielding so much power in an undivided India neither could you have got rid of princely states like Marh nor forced through the abolition of zamindari. Everyone knows this, yet no one says so. But all this is water under the bridge, history, spilt milk. So there we were, Minister Sahib, looking reverently upwards at the dais, expecting the conqueror to tell us that he would take no nonsense from anybody, that he would make sure that the party apparatus responded to his slightest touch, that the candidates for the elections would all be his men.'

'And women.'

'Yes. And women. Panditji is keen on female representation.'

'Go on, go on, Abdus Salaam, get to the point.'

'Well, instead of getting a commander's battle cry or even a pragmatist's plan, we got a speech about the Unity of the Heart. We should think above divisions, splits, cliques! We must pull along like a team, a family, a battalion. Dear Chacha Nehru, I felt like saying, this is India, Hindustan, Bharat, the country where faction was invented before the zero. If even the heart is divided into four parts can you expect us Indians to divide ourselves into less than four hundred?'

'But what did he say about candidates?' asked Mahesh Kapoor.

Abdus Salaam's answer was not reassuring.

'What would he say, being Jawaharlal? That he just did not know and did not care who belonged to which group. That he entirely agreed with Tandonji that the right way to choose a candidate was to choose a man who did not apply for the slot. Of course, he could see that this might not always be possible in practice. And when he said this, Agarwal, who was sitting near me, visibly relaxed—he relaxed and he smiled. I can tell you, Minister Sahib, I did not feel very reassured by the nature of that smile.'

Mahesh Kapoor nodded and said, 'And then Panditji agreed to accept the Presidency?'

'Not quite,' said Abdus Salaam. 'But he said he had thought about it. Luckily for us, he had been able to obtain some sleep that night. He confided in us that the previous day, when his name had been put up and accepted at once, he did not quite know what to do. Those were his words: "I did not quite know what to do." But now, having slept over it, he told us that he realized that it was not an easy matter for him to escape from this responsibility. Not an easy matter at all.'

'So all of you breathed a sigh of relief.'

'That, Minister Sahib, is correct. But we had breathed too early. A niggling doubt had struck him. A minor doubt, but one that niggled. He had slept, and made up his mind. Or almost, yes, almost made up his mind. But the question was: had we slept and made up our minds again—or at least not changed our minds? And if we had, how could we show him that we meant it? And how could we make him believe it?'

'Well, what did you do?' asked Mahesh Kapoor rather shortly. He found Abdus Salaam's mode of narration far too leisurely for his tastes.

'Well, what could we do? We raised our hands again. But that was not enough. Then some of us raised both our hands. But that would not do either. Panditji wanted no formal show, no revoting with hands or feet. He wanted a demonstration of our "minds and hearts". Only then could he decide whether to accept our request or not.'

Abdus Salaam paused, awaiting a Socratic response, and Mahesh Kapoor, realizing that things would not move without it, supplied it.

'That must have put you in a quandary,' he said.

'It did indeed,' said Abdus Salaam. 'I kept thinking: seize the levers of power; select your candidates. He kept talking about minds and hearts. I noticed Pant and Tandon and Sharma looking at him in perplexity. And L.N. Agarwal kept smiling his twisted little smile to himself.'

'Go on, go on.'

'So then we clapped.'

'But that did not do either?'

'No, Minister Sahib, that did not do either. So then we decided to pass a resolution. But Pandit Nehru would have none of it. We would have shouted "Long live Pandit Nehru!" till we were hoarse, but everyone knew that that would have put him in a temper. He does not care for personality cults. He does not care for flattery—for patent or vociferous flattery. He is a democrat through and through.'

'How was the problem resolved, Salaam? Will you please tell your story, without waiting for me to ask you questions?'

'Well,' said Abdus Salaam, 'there was only one way to resolve it. Exhausted, and unwilling to sleep over anything again, we turned to Nehruji himself. We had racked our brains and thought ourselves thin, and none of our offerings had been acceptable to him. Perhaps he would grace us with a suggestion himself. What would satisfy him that our hearts and minds were with him? At this, our supreme leader looked perplexed. He did not know.'

'He did not know?' Mahesh Kapoor could not help exclaiming.

'He did not know.' Abdus Salaam's face took on one of Nehru's more melancholy expressions. 'But after a few minutes of thought he found his way out of the difficulty. We were all to join him in a patriotic shout of "Jai Hind!" That would show him that our hearts and minds were in the right place.'

'So that was what you did?' said Mahesh Kapoor with rather a rueful smile himself.

'That was what we did. But our first shout was not full-throated enough. Panditji looked unhappy, and we could see the Congress and the country collapsing before our eyes. So we raised another shout, a mighty cry of "Jai Hind!" such as almost caused the Constitution Club to collapse about our ears. And Jawaharlal smiled. He smiled. The sun came out and all was well.'

'And that was that?'

'And that was that.'

14.29

Every year at the time of shraadh, Mrs Rupa Mehra had a struggle with her eldest son, which she, after a fashion, won. Every year, Mrs Mahesh Kapoor had a struggle with her husband, which she lost. And Mrs Tandon had no struggle at all, except with her memories of her husband; for Kedarnath performed his father's rites in full accordance with his duty.

Raghubir Mehra's death had fallen on the second day of a lunar fortnight, and therefore, on the second day of the annual 'fortnight of the ancestors', pandits should have been called to the house of his eldest son to be feasted and given gifts. But the thought of plump, bare-chested, dhoti-clad pandits sitting around in his Sunny Park flat, chanting mantras and gobbling down rice and daal, puris and halwa, curds and kheer, was anathema to Arun. Every year Mrs Rupa Mehra tried to persuade him to perform the rites for his father's spirit. Every year Arun dismissed the whole farrago of superstitious nonsense. Mrs Rupa Mehra next worked upon Varun and sent him the necessary money for the expenses, and Varun agreed—partly because he knew it would bother his brother; partly because of love for his father (though he had a hard time believing, for instance, that the karhi, which was one of his father's favourite foods, and that he was therefore supposed to include in the pandits' feast, would eventually get to him); but mainly because he loved his mother and knew how badly she would suffer if he refused. She could not perform the shraadh herself; it had to be done by a man. And if not by the eldest son, then by the youngest—or, in this case, the younger.

'I will have no such shenanigans in this house, let me tell you that!' said Arun.

'It's for Daddy's spirit,' said Varun, with an attempt at belligerence.

'Daddy's spirit! Utter rubbish. Next we'll have human sacrifice to help you pass your IAS exams.'

'Don't talk like that about Daddy!' cried Varun, livid and cowering. 'Can't you give Ma some mental satisfaction?'

'Mental? Sentimental!' said Arun with a snort.

Varun didn't talk to his brother for days and slunk around the house, glaring balefully; not even Aparna could cheer him up. Every time the phone rang he jumped. Eventually it got on Meenakshi's nerves, and at last even Arun in his native-proof casing began to feel slightly ashamed of himself.

Finally Varun was allowed to feed a single pandit in the garden. He donated the rest of the money to a nearby temple with instructions that it should be used to feed a few poor children. And he wrote to Brahmpur to tell his mother that everything had been performed properly.

Mrs Rupa Mehra read the letter to her samdhin, translating as she went along, with tears in her eyes.

Mrs Mahesh Kapoor listened sadly. Her annual battle was fought not with her sons but with her husband. The shraadh for her own parents was satisfactorily performed each year by her late brother's eldest son. What she wanted now was that the spirits of her father-in-law and mother-in-law should be similarly propitiated. Their son, however, would have nothing to do with it and rebuked her in his usual manner:

'Oh, blessed one, you've been married to me for more than three decades and you have become more ignorant with each passing year.'

Mrs Mahesh Kapoor did not answer back. This encouraged her husband.

'How can you believe in such idiocy? In those grasping pandits and their mumbo jumbo? "So much food I set aside for the cow. So much for the crow. So much for the dog. And the rest I will eat. More! More! More puris, more halwa." Then they belch and hold out their hands for alms: "Give according to your grace and your feelings for the departed one. What? Only five rupees? Is that the extent of your love for them?" I even know of someone who gave snuff to a pandit's wife because his own dead mother liked snuff! Well, I won't disturb my parents' souls with such mockery. All I can say is that I hope no one dares to perform shraadh for me.'

This stung Mrs Mahesh Kapoor into protest. She said: 'If Pran refuses to perform shraadh for you, he will be no son of mine.'

'Pran has too much good sense,' said Mahesh Kapoor. 'And I'm beginning to think that Maan is a sensible boy too. Don't talk just of me—they wouldn't even perform it for you.'

Whether Mahesh Kapoor took delight in baiting and hurting his wife or not, he certainly couldn't stop himself. Mrs Mahesh Kapoor, who could bear much, was almost in tears. Veena was visiting when this argument broke out, and her mother said to her:

'Bété.'

'Yes, Ammaji.'

'If such a thing happens, you will tell Bhaskar that he is to perform shraadh for me. Invest him with the sacred thread if necessary.'

'Sacred thread! Bhaskar will not wear a sacred thread,' said Mahesh Kapoor. 'He'll use it to fly a kite with. Or as Hanuman's tail.' He chuckled rather maliciously at the sacrilege.

'That is for his father to decide,' said Mrs Mahesh Kapoor quietly.

'He is too young anyway.'

'That also is for his father to decide,' said Mrs Mahesh Kapoor. 'Anyway, I'm not dying yet.'

'But you certainly sound determined to die,' said Mahesh Kapoor. 'This time every year we go through the same stupid kind of talk.'

'Of course I am determined to die,' said Mrs Mahesh Kapoor. 'How else can I go through my rebirths and finally end them?' Looking down at her hands she said, 'Do you want to be immortal? I can imagine nothing worse than to be immortal, nothing worse.'

Part Fifteen

15.1

Less than a week after her letter from her younger son, Mrs Rupa Mehra received a letter from her elder son. It was, as always, illegible—and illegible to the extent that it seemed almost to amount to contempt for any possible reader. The news it contained was important, however; and it did no good to Mrs Rupa Mehra's high blood pressure as she tried desperately to decipher bits of it through a forest of random curves and spikes.

The surprising news related mainly to the Chatterji children. Of the two women, Meenakshi and Kakoli, one had lost a foetus and the other had gained a fiancé. Dipankar had returned from the Pul Mela still uncertain, 'but at a higher level'. Young Tapan had written rather an unhappy but unspecific letter home—typical adolescent blues, according to Arun. And Amit had let it drop when he had called around one evening for a drink that he was rather fond of Lata, which, given his extreme reticence, could only mean that he was 'interested' in her. Making sense of the next few squiggles, Mrs Rupa Mehra was shocked to understand that Arun did not think this was such a bad idea. Certainly, according to him, it would take Lata out of the orbit of the entirely unsuitable Haresh. When the idea was put before Varun, he had frowned and said, 'I'm studying,' as if his sister's future mattered not at all to him. But then, Varun was becoming moodier and moodier since his IAS preparations had restrained his Shamshuing. He had behaved most oddly over Daddy's shraadh, attempting to turn the Sunny Park house into a restaurant for fat priests, and even asking them (Meenakshi had overheard him) if shraadh could be performed for a suicide.

With a few remarks about the impending General Elections in England ('At Bentsen Pryce we consider it Hobson's choice: Attlee is puerile and Churchill senile') but none about the Indian elections, with a casual admonition to Mrs Rupa Mehra to mind her blood sugar, and to give his love to his sisters, and to assure everyone that Meenakshi was fine and had suffered no lasting harm, Arun signed off.

Mrs Rupa Mehra sat stunned, her heart beating dangerously fast. She was used to rereading her letters a dozen times, examining for days from every possible angle some remark that someone had made to someone else about something that someone had thought that someone had almost done. So much news—and all so sudden and substantial—was too much to absorb at once. Meenakshi's miscarriage, the Kakoli-Hans nexus, the threat of Amit, the non-mention of Haresh except in an unfavourable passing remark, the disturbing attitude of Varun—Mrs Rupa Mehra did not know whether to laugh or to weep, and immediately asked for a glass of nimbu pani.

And there was no news of her darling Aparna. Presumably she was all right. Mrs Rupa Mehra recalled a remark of hers, now family lore: 'If another baby comes into this house, I will throw it straight into the waste-paper basket.' Precocity appeared to be the fashion among children these days. She hoped that Uma would be as lovable as Aparna, but less trenchant.

Mrs Rupa Mehra was dying to show Savita her brother's letter, but then decided that it would be far better to break the various bits of news to her one by one. It would be less disturbing to Savita, and more informative for herself. Without knowing either Arun's strong opinions or Varun's apparent indifference, where would Savita's own judgement in the matter of Amit lie? So! thought Mrs Rupa Mehra grimly: this must have been behind his gift to Lata of his incomprehensible book of poems.

As for Lata—she had been taking an unnecessary interest in poetry these days, even attending an occasional meeting of the Brahmpur Literary Society. This did not bode well. It was true that she had also been writing to Haresh, but Mrs Rupa Mehra was not privy to the contents of those letters. Lata had become cruelly possessive of her privacy. 'Am I your mother or not?' Mrs Rupa Mehra had asked her once. 'Oh, Ma, please!' had been Lata's heartless reply.

And poor Meenakshi! thought Mrs Rupa Mehra. She must write to her at once. She felt that a creamy cambric was called for, and, her eyes moist with sympathy, she went to get the writing paper from her bag. Meenakshi the cold-hearted medal-melter was replaced for a while with the image of Meenakshi the vulnerable, tender, broken vehicle for Mrs Rupa Mehra's third grandchild, who she felt was bound to have been a boy.

If Mrs Rupa Mehra had known the truth about Meenakshi's pregnancy or her miscarriage, she would doubtless have been less than sympathetic. Meenakshi, terrified that her baby might not be Arun's—and, in milder counterpoint, concerned by what a second pregnancy would do to her figure and social life—had decided to take immediate action. After her doctor—the miracle-working Dr Evans—had refused to help her, she went for advice to her closest friends among the Shady Ladies, swearing them first to secrecy. She was certain that if Arun heard about her attempt to free herself from this unwanted child, he would be as unreasonably angry as he had been when she had liberated herself from one of his father's medals.

How unfortunate, she thought desperately, that neither the jewellery theft nor Khandelwal's dogs had shocked her foetus out of her.

Meenakshi had made herself quite sick with abortifacients, worry, conflicting advice and tortuous gymnastics when one afternoon, to her relief, she had the miscarriage of her dreams. She phoned Billy immediately, her voice unsteady on the line; when he asked anxiously if she was all right, she was able to reassure him. It had been sudden and painless, if alarming and, well, horribly messy. Billy sounded miserable for her sake.

And Arun, for his part, was so tender and protective of her for days afterwards that she began to feel that there might be at least something to be said for the whole sorry business.

15.2

Had wishes been horses, Mrs Rupa Mehra would have been riding at this very moment on the Calcutta Mail, and would soon have been questioning everyone she knew in Calcutta and Prahapore about all they had been doing or thinking or planning or professing. But, quite apart from the cost of the journey, there were compelling reasons for her to remain in Brahmpur. For one thing, baby Uma was still very little, and needed a grandmother's care. Whereas Meenakshi had been by turns possessive of Aparna and perfectly happy to ignore her (treating her mother-in-law as a kind of super-ayah while she traipsed about Calcutta, socializing), Savita shared Uma with Mrs Rupa Mehra (and with Mrs Mahesh Kapoor when she visited) in a natural, daughterly way.

Secondly—and as if there had not been drama enough in the letter she had received from Arun—this evening was the performance of *Twelfth Night*. It was to be held in the university auditorium immediately after the Annual Day ceremonies and tea, and her own Lata would be in it—as would Malati, who was just like a daughter to her. (Mrs Rupa Mehra was well disposed towards Malati these days, seeing in her a chaperone rather than a conniver.) So would that boy K; but thank God, thought Mrs Rupa Mehra, there would be no more rehearsals. And with the university break for Dussehra in just a couple of days, there would be no great possibility of chance meetings on campus either. Mrs Rupa Mehra felt, however, that she must remain in Brahmpur just in case. Only when, for the short Christmas vacation, the whole family—Pran, Savita, Lata, Lady Baby and materfamilias—visited Calcutta would she desert her reconnaissance post.

The hall was packed with students, alumni, teachers, parents and relatives together with smatterings of Brahmpur society, including a few literary lawyers and judges. Mr and Mrs Nowrojee were there, as were the poet Makhijani and the booming Mrs Supriya Joshi. Hema's Taiji was there together with a knot of a dozen giggling girls, most of them her wards. Professor and Mrs Mishra were present. And of the family, Pran of course (since nothing could have kept him away, and he was indeed feeling much better), Savita (Uma had been left with her ayah for the evening), Maan, Bhaskar, Dr Kishen Chand Seth and Parvati.

Mrs Rupa Mehra was in a high state of excitement when the curtain went up to a sudden hush from the audience, and to the strains of a lute that sounded rather like a sitar, the Duke began: 'If music be the food of love, play on—'

She was soon entirely carried away by the magic of the play. And indeed, there was no major mischief, other than some incomprehensible bawdy and buffoonery, in the first half of the play. When Lata came on, Mrs Rupa Mehra could hardly believe that it was her daughter.

Pride swelled in her bosom and tears forced themselves into her eyes. How could Pran and Savita, seated on either side of her, be so indifferent to Lata's appearance?

'Lata! Look, Lata!' she whispered to them.

'Yes, Ma,' said Savita. Pran merely nodded.

When Olivia, in love with Viola, said:

> 'Fate, show thy force. Ourselves we do not owe:
> What is decreed must be; and be this so!'

—Mrs Rupa Mehra nodded her head sadly as she thought philosophically of much that had happened in her own life. How true, she thought, conferring honorary Indian citizenship on Shakespeare.

Malati, meanwhile, had the audience charmed. At Sir Toby's line, 'Here comes the little villain—How now, my nettle of India?' everyone cheered, especially a claque of medical students. And there was another great round of applause at the interval (which Mr Barua had placed in the middle of Act III) for Maria and Sir Toby. Mrs Rupa Mehra had to be restrained from going backstage to congratulate Lata and Malati. Even Kabir-as-Malvolio had so far proven to be innocuous, and she had laughed with the rest of the audience at his gecking and gulling.

Kabir had donned the accent of the officious and unpopular Registrar of the university, and—whether this would prove beneficial for Mr Barua's future or not—it increased the present enjoyment of the students. Dr Kishen Chand Seth, in fact, was Malvolio's only supporter, insisting loudly in the interval that what was being done to him was indefensible.

'Lack of discipline, that is the trouble with the whole country,' he stated vehemently.

Bhaskar was bored with the play. It was nothing like as exciting as the Ramlila, in which he had obtained a role as one of Hanuman's monkey-soldiers. The only interesting part of this play so far had been Malvolio's interpretation of 'M, O, A, I'.

The second half began. Mrs Rupa Mehra nodded and smiled. But she nearly started from her chair when she heard her daughter say to Kabir: 'Wilt thou go to bed, Malvolio?' and she gasped at Malvolio's odious, brazen reply.

'Stop it—stop it at once!' she wanted to shout. 'Is this why I sent you to university? I should never have allowed you to act in this play. Never. If Daddy had seen this he would have been ashamed of you.'

'Ma!' whispered Savita. 'Are you all right?'

'No!' her mother wanted to shout. 'I am not all right. And how can you let your younger sister say such things? Shameless!' Shakespeare's Indian citizenship was immediately withdrawn.

But she said nothing.

Mrs Rupa Mehra's uneasy shufflings, however, were nothing compared to her father's activities in the second half. He and Parvati were seated a few rows away from the rest of the family. He started sobbing uncontrollably at the scene where the disowned sea-captain reproaches Viola, thinking her to be her brother:

'Will you deny me now?
Is't possible that my deserts to you
Can lack persuasion? Do not tempt my misery
Lest that it make me so unsound a man

As to upbraid you with those kindnesses
That I have done for you.'

Loudly sobbed Dr Kishen Chand Seth. Astonished necks swivelled swiftly towards him—but to no effect.

'Let me speak a little. This youth that you see here
I snatched one half out of the jaws of death,
Relieved him with such sanctity of love,—
And to his image, which methought did promise
Most venerable worth, did I devotion.'

By now Dr Kishen Chand Seth was gasping almost asthmatically. He started pounding the floor with his stick to relieve his distress.

Parvati took it from him and said, rather sharply: 'Kishy! This isn't *Deedar*!'—and this brought him heavily back to earth.

But not much later, the distress of Malvolio—cooped up in an inner chamber and driven from bewilderment almost to madness—evoked further distress, and he began to weep to himself as if his heart would break. Several people around him stopped laughing and turned to look at him.

At this, Parvati handed him back his stick and said, 'Kishy, let's go now. Now! At once!'

But Kishy would have none of it. He managed to control himself at last, and sat out the rest of the play, rapt and almost tearless. His daughter, who had no sympathy whatsoever with Malvolio, had grown increasingly reconciled to the play as he made more and more of a fool of himself and finally came to his undignified exit.

Since the play ended with three happy marriages (and even, Indian-movie-style, concluded with the last of four songs), it was a success in the eyes of Mrs Rupa Mehra who had, miraculously and conveniently, forgotten all about Malvolio and the bed. After the curtain calls and the appearance of shy Mr Barua to calls of 'Producer! producer!' she rushed backstage and hugged Lata, and kissed her, make-up and all, saying:

'You are my darling daughter. I am so proud of you. And of Malati too. If only your—'

She stopped, and tears came to her eyes. Then she made an effort to control herself, and said, 'Now get changed quickly, let's go home. It's late, and you must be tired after talking so much.'

She had noticed Malvolio hanging around. He had been chatting to a couple of other actors, but had now turned towards Lata and her mother. It seemed that he wanted to greet her, or at any rate to say something.

'Ma—I can't; I'll join you all later,' said Lata.

'No!' Mrs Rupa Mehra put her foot down. 'You are coming now. You can clean off your make-up at home. Savita and I will help you.'

But whether it was her own newfound thespian confidence or merely a continuation of Olivia's 'smooth, discreet, and stable bearing', Lata simply said, in a quiet voice:

'I am sorry, Ma, there is a party for the cast, and we are going to celebrate. Malati and I have worked on this play for months, and have made friends whom we won't see until after the Dussehra break. And please don't worry, Ma; Mr Barua will make sure I get home safely.'

Mrs Rupa Mehra could not believe her ears.

Now Kabir came up to her and said:

'Mrs Mehra?'

'Yes?' said Mrs Rupa Mehra belligerently, all the more so because Kabir was very obviously good-looking, despite his make-up and curious attire, and Mrs Rupa Mehra in general believed in good looks.

'Mrs Mehra, I thought I would introduce myself,' said Kabir. 'I am Kabir Durrani.'

'Yes, I know,' said Mrs Rupa Mehra rather sharply. 'I have heard about you. I have also met your father. Do you mind if my daughter does not attend the cast party?'

Kabir flushed. 'No, Mrs Mehra, I—'

'I want to attend,' said Lata, giving Kabir a sharp glance. 'This has nothing to do with anyone else.'

Mrs Rupa Mehra was suddenly tempted to give both of them two tight slaps. But instead she glared at Lata, and at Kabir, and even at Malati for good measure, then turned and left without another word.

15.3

'Well there are many possibilities for riots,' said Firoz. 'Shias with Shias, Shias with Sunnis, Hindus with Muslims—'

'And Hindus with Hindus,' added Maan.

'That's something new in Brahmpur,' said Firoz.

'Well, my sister says that the jatavs tried to force themselves on to the local Ramlila Committee this year. They said that at least one of the five swaroops should be selected from among scheduled caste boys. Naturally, no one listened to them at all. But it could spell trouble. I hope you aren't going to participate in too many events yourself. I don't want to have to worry about you.'

'Worry!' laughed Firoz. 'I can't imagine you worrying about me. But it's a nice thought.'

'Oh?' said Maan. 'But don't you have to put yourself in front of some Moharram procession or other—you one year, Imtiaz the next, I thought you said?'

'That's only on the last couple of days. For the most part I just lie low during Moharram. And this year I know where I will spend at least a couple of my evenings.' Firoz sounded deliberately mysterious.

'Where?'

'Somewhere where you, as an unbeliever, will not be admitted; though in the past you have performed your prostrations in that shrine.'

'But I thought she didn't—' began Maan. 'I thought she didn't even allow herself to sing during those ten days.'

'She doesn't,' said Firoz. 'But she has small gatherings at her house where she chants marsiyas and performs soz—it really is something. Not the marsiyas so much—but the soz, from what I hear, is really astonishing.'

Maan knew from his brief incursions into poetry with Rasheed that marsiyas were laments for the martyrs of the battle of Karbala: especially for Hussain, the grandson of the Prophet. But he had no idea what soz was.

'It's a sort of musical wailing,' said Firoz. 'I've only heard it a few times, and never at Saeeda Bai's. It grips the heart.'

The thought of Saeeda Bai weeping and wailing passionately for someone who had died thirteen centuries before was both perplexing and strangely exciting for Maan. 'Why can't I go?' he asked. 'I'll sit quietly and watch—I mean, listen. I attended Bakr-Id, you know, at the village.'

'Because you're a kafir, you idiot. Even Sunnis aren't really welcome at these private gatherings, though they take part in some processions. Saeeda Bai tries to control her audience, from what I've heard, but some of them get carried away with grief and start cursing the first three caliphs because they usurped Ali's right to the caliphate, and this enrages the Sunnis, quite naturally. Sometimes the curses are very graphic.'

'And you'll be attending all this soz stuff. Since when have you become so religious?' asked Maan.

'I'm not,' said Firoz. 'In fact—and you'd better not tell anyone I said this—but I'm not a great fan of Hussain. And Muawiyah, who got him killed, wasn't as dreadful as we make him out to be. After all, the succession was quite a mess before that, with most of the caliphs getting assassinated. Once Muawiyah set things up dynastically, Islam was able to consolidate itself as an empire. If he hadn't, everything would have fallen back into petty tribes bickering with each other and there'd be no Islam to argue about. But if my father heard me say this he'd disown me. And Saeeda Bai would tear me apart with her own lovely soft hands.'

'So why are you going to Saeeda Bai's?' said Maan, somewhat piqued and suspicious. 'Didn't you say you weren't exactly made welcome there when you happened to visit?'

'How can she turn back a mourner during Moharram?'

'And why do you want to go there in the first place?'

'To drink at the fountain of Paradise.'

'Very funny.'

'I mean, to see the young Tasneem.'

'Well, give my love to the parakeet,' said Maan, frowning. He continued to frown when Firoz got up, stood behind his chair, and put his hands on Maan's shoulders.

15.4

'Can you imagine,' said old Mrs Tandon: 'Rama or Bharat or Sita—a chamar!'

Veena looked uncomfortable at such an outright statement of the feelings of the neighbourhood.

'And the sweepers want the Ramlila to continue after Rama's return to Ayodhya and his meeting with Bharat and the coronation. They want all those shameful episodes about Sita put in.'

Maan asked why.

'Oh, you know, they style themselves Valmikis these days, and they say that Valmiki's Ramayana, which goes on and on about all these episodes, is the true text of the Ramayana,' said old Mrs Tandon. 'Just trouble-making.'

Veena said: 'No one disputes the Ramayana. And Sita did have a horrible life after she returned from Lanka. But the Ramlila has always been based on the Ramcharitmanas of Tulsidas, not Valmiki's Ramayana. The worst of all this is that Kedarnath has to do so much of the explaining on both sides and has to shoulder most of the trouble. Because of his contact with the scheduled castes,' she added.

'And I suppose,' said Maan, 'because of his sense of civic duty?'

Veena frowned and nodded, not sure if the irresponsible Maan was being sarcastic at her expense.

'I remember our days in Lahore—none of this could ever have happened,' said old Mrs Tandon with tender nostalgia and a look of shining faith in her eyes. 'The people contributed without being asked, even the Municipal Council provided free lighting, and the effigies we made for Ravana were so frightening that children would hide their faces in their mothers' laps. Our neighbourhood had the best Ramlila in the city. And all the swaroops were brahmin boys,' she added approvingly.

'But that would never do,' said Maan. 'Bhaskar would never have been eligible then.'

'No, he wouldn't,' said old Mrs Tandon thoughtfully. This was the first time she had considered the matter from this angle. 'That would not have been good. Just because we aren't brahmins! But people were old-fashioned then. Some things are changing for the better. Bhaskar must certainly get a part next year. He knows half of them by heart already.'

15.5

Kedarnath had, in this matter of the actor-deities or swaroops, been surprised to find that one of the leaders of the untouchables was the jatav Jagat Ram from Ravidaspur. It was difficult for him to think of Jagat Ram as having anything to do with local agitation, for he was a fairly sober man who had concentrated, by and large, on his work and his large family; and had played no active role in the strike in Misri Mandi. But Jagat Ram had, by virtue of his relative prosperity—if it could be called that—and the fact that he was at least minimally literate, been pressured by his neighbours and fellow-workers into representing them. He did not want to accept; having accepted, though, he did what he could. However, he felt at a disadvantage in two respects. First, it was only by stretching a point that he could claim to have a stake in what went on in Misri Mandi. Secondly, since his livelihood depended on Kedarnath and other local figures, he knew that for the sake of his family he had to tread carefully.

Kedarnath for his part was not unsympathetic in a theoretical sense to the general question of opening up the field of actors. But the Ramlila in his eyes was not a competition or a political act but an enactment of faith by the community. Most of the boys who acted in it had known each other from childhood, and the scenes that were represented had the sanction of hundreds of years of tradition. The Ramlila of Misri Mandi was famous throughout the city. To tack on scenes after the coronation of Rama struck him as being pointlessly offensive—a political invasion of religion, a moralistic invasion of morality. As for some sort of quota system among the swaroops, that would only lead to political conflict and artistic disaster.

Jagat Ram argued that since the brahmin stranglehold over the parts of the heroes had been broken in favour of the other upper castes, it was a logical next step to allow the so-called lower castes and scheduled castes to participate. They contributed to the success of the Ramlila as spectators and even to a small extent as contributors; why not then as actors? Kedarnath responded that it was obviously too late to do anything this year. He would bring up the matter with the Ramlila Committee the following year. But he suggested that the people of Ravidaspur, which was largely a scheduled caste community—and from which the claim largely emanated—should perform a Ramlila of their own as well, so that the demand would not be seen as invasive and mischievous, merely a way of prolonging by other weapons the conflict that had had its first culmination in the disastrous strike earlier in the year.

Nothing was really resolved. Everything was left in uncertainty. And Jagat Ram was not really surprised. This was his first venture into politics, and he had not enjoyed it. His childhood hell in a village, his brutal adolescence in a factory, and the vicious world of competitors and middlemen, poverty and dirt in which he now found himself had served to turn him into something of a philosopher. One did not argue with elephants in a jungle when they were on the rampage, one did not argue with the traffic in Chowk as it hurtled past in murderous confusion. One got out of the way and got one's family out of the way. If possible, one retained what dignity one could. The world was a place of brutality and cruelty and the exclusion of people like him from the rites of religion was almost the least of its barbarities.

The previous year one of the jatavs of his own village, who had spent a couple of years in Brahmpur, had gone back home during the harvest season. After the comparative freedom of the city, he had made the mistake of imagining that he had gained exemption from the generalized loathing of the upper-caste villagers. Perhaps also, being eighteen years old, he had the rashness of youth; at any rate, he cycled around the village singing film songs on a bicycle he had bought from his earnings. One day, feeling thirsty, he had had the brazenness to ask an upper-caste woman who was cooking outside her house for some water to drink. That night he had been set upon by a gang of men, tied to his bicycle, and forced to eat human excreta. His brain and his bicycle had then been smashed to bits. Everyone knew the men who were responsible, yet no one had dared to testify; and the details had been too horrendous for even the newspapers to print.

In the villages, the untouchables were virtually helpless; almost none of them owned that eventual guarantor of dignity and status, land. Few worked it as tenants, and of those tenants fewer still would be able to make use of the paper guarantees of the forthcoming land reforms. In the cities too they were the dregs of society. Even Gandhi, for all his reforming concern, for all his hatred of the concept that any human being was intrinsically so loathsome and polluting as to be untouchable, had believed that people should continue in their hereditarily ordained professions: a cobbler should remain a cobbler, a sweeper a sweeper. 'One born a scavenger must earn his livelihood by being a scavenger, and then do whatever else he likes. For a scavenger is as worthy of his hire as a lawyer or your President. That, according to me, is Hinduism.'

For Jagat Ram, though he would not have said this aloud, this was the most misleading condescension. He knew that there was nothing innately worthy about cleaning lavatories or standing in a foul-smelling tanning pit—and being duty-bound to do so because your parents had. But this was what most Hindus believed, and if beliefs and laws were changing, a few more generations would continue to be crushed under the wheels of the great chariot before it finally ground to a bloodstained halt.

It was with only half a heart that Jagat Ram had argued that the scheduled castes should be allowed to be swaroops in the Ramlila. Perhaps, after all, it was not a question of a logical next step so much as an emotional one. Perhaps, as Nehru's Law Minister Dr Ambedkar, the great, already almost mythical, leader of the untouchables, had asserted, Hinduism had nothing to offer those whom it had cast so pitilessly out of its fold. He had been born a Hindu, Dr Ambedkar had said, but he would not die a Hindu.

Nine months after the murder of Gandhi, the constitutional provision abolishing untouchability was passed by the Constituent Assembly, and its members broke out into loud cheers of 'Victory to Mahatma Gandhi'. However little the measure was to mean in practical as opposed to symbolic terms, Jagat Ram believed that the victory for its formulation lay less with Mahatma Gandhi, who rarely concerned himself with such legalisms, than with quite another—and equally courageous—man.

15.6

On the 2nd of October, which happened to be Gandhiji's birthday, the Kapoor family met at Prem Nivas for lunch. A couple of other guests had dropped in and were invited to join them. One was Sandeep Lahiri, who had come to ask after Maan. The other was a politician from U.P., one of the secessionists from the Congress, who had rejoined, and was attempting to persuade Mahesh Kapoor to do the same.

Maan arrived late. It was a public holiday, and he had spent the morning at the Riding Club playing polo with his friend. He was getting to be quite good at it. He hoped to spend the evening with Saeeda Bai. After all, the Moharram moon had not yet been sighted.

The first thing he did when he saw everyone gathered together was to praise Lata's acting. Lata, feeling herself suddenly the centre of attention, blushed.

'Don't blush,' said Maan. 'No, blush away. I'm not flattering you. You were excellent. Bhaskar, of course, didn't enjoy the play, but that wasn't your fault. I thought it was wonderful. And Malati—she was brilliant too. And the Duke. And Malvolio. And Sir Toby of course.'

Maan had spread his praise too liberally by now for it to make Lata uncomfortable. She laughed and said:

'You've left out the third footman.'

'Quite right,' said Maan. 'And the fourth murderer.'

'Why haven't you come to the Ramlila, Maan Maama?' asked Bhaskar.

'Because it just began yesterday!' said Maan.

'But you've already missed Rama's youth and training,' said Bhaskar.

'Oh, oh, sorry,' said Maan.

'You must come tonight, or I'll be kutti with you.'

'You can't be kutti with your uncle,' said Maan.

'Yes, I can,' said Bhaskar. 'Today is the winning of Sita. The procession will go all the way from Khirkiwalan to Shahi Darvaza. And everyone will be out in the lanes celebrating.'

'Yes, Maan, do—we'll look forward to it,' said Kedarnath. 'And then have dinner with us afterwards.'

'Well, tonight, I—' Maan stopped, sensing that his father's eyes were upon him. 'I'll come when the monkeys first appear in the Ramlila,' he finished lamely, patting Bhaskar on the head. Bhaskar, he decided, was more monkey than frog.

'Let me hold Uma,' said Mrs Mahesh Kapoor, sensing that Savita was tired. She looked at the baby, trying to work out for the thousandth time which features belonged to her, which to her husband, which to Mrs Rupa Mehra and which to the photograph so often pulled out these days for reference, comparison or display from Mrs Rupa Mehra's bag.

Her own husband, meanwhile, was saying to Sandeep Lahiri: 'I understand you got into trouble this time last year over some pictures of Gandhiji?'

'Er, yes,' said Sandeep. 'One picture, actually. But, well, things have sorted themselves out.'

'Sorted themselves out? Hasn't Jha just managed to get rid of you?'

'Well, I've been promoted—'

'Yes, yes, that's what I meant,' said Mahesh Kapoor impatiently. 'But you're very popular with everyone in Rudhia. If you weren't in the IAS, I'd have made you my agent. I'd win the elections easily.'

'Are you thinking of standing from Rudhia?' asked Sandeep.

'I'm not thinking of anything at the moment,' said Mahesh Kapoor. 'Everyone else is doing my thinking for me. My son. And my grandson. And my friend the Nawab Sahib. And my Parliamentary Secretary. And Rafi Sahib. And the Chief Minister. And this most helpful gentleman,' he added, indicating the politician, a short, quiet man who had shared a cell with Mahesh Kapoor many years ago.

'I am only saying: We should all return to the party of Gandhiji,' said the politician. 'To change one's party is not necessarily to change one's principles—or to be unprincipled.'

'Ah, Gandhiji,' said Mahesh Kapoor, not willing to be drawn out. 'He would have been eighty-two today, and a miserable man. He would never have reiterated his wish to live to be a hundred and twenty-five. As for his spirit, we feed it with laddus for one day of the year, and once we've performed his shraadh we forget all about him.'

Suddenly he turned to his wife: 'Why is he taking so long making the phulkas? Must we sit here with our stomachs rumbling till four o'clock? Instead of dandling that baby and making it howl, why don't you get that halfwit cook to feed us?'

Veena said, 'I'll go,' to her mother and went towards the kitchen.

Mrs Mahesh Kapoor once more bowed her head over the baby. She believed that Gandhiji was a saint, more than a saint, a martyr—and she could not bear that anything should be said about him in bitterness. Even now she loved to sing—or to hear sung—the songs from the anthology used in his Ashram. She had just bought three postcards issued by the Posts and Telegraph Department in his memory: one showed him spinning, one showed him with his wife Kasturba, one showed him with a child.

But what her husband said was probably true. Thrust to the sidelines of power at the end of his active life, his message of generosity and reconciliation, it seemed, had been almost forgotten within four years of his death. She felt, however, that he would still have wanted to live. He had lived through times of desperate frustration before, and had borne it with patience. He was a good man, and a man without fear. Surely his fearlessness would have extended into the future.

After lunch, the women went for a walk in the garden. It had been a warmer year than most, but this particular day had been relieved by a little morning rain. The ground was still slightly moist, and the garden fragrant. The pink madhumalati creeper was in bloom near the swing. Mixed with the earth beneath the harsingar tree lay many small white-and-orange flowers that had fallen at dawn; they still held a trace of their fugitive scent. A few gardenias remained on one of two sporadically bearing trees. Mrs Rupa Mehra—who had been singularly quiet during lunch—now held and rocked the baby, who had fallen fast asleep. She sat down on a bench by the harsingar tree. In Uma's left ear was a most delicate vein that branched out into smaller and smaller ones in an exquisite pattern. Mrs Rupa Mehra looked at it for a while, then sighed.

'There is no tree like the harsingar,' she said to Mrs Mahesh Kapoor. 'I wish we had one in our garden.'

Mrs Mahesh Kapoor nodded. A modest, unhandsome tree by day, the harsingar became glorious at night, full of a delicate fragrance, surrounded by enchanted insects. The tiny, six-petalled flowers with their orange hearts wafted down at dawn. And tonight it would again be full, and the flowers would again float down as the sun rose. The tree flowered, but kept nothing for itself.

'No,' agreed Mrs Mahesh Kapoor with a grave smile. 'There is no tree like it at all.' After a pause she added: 'I will have Gajraj plant a seedling in the back garden at Pran's house, next to the lime tree. Then it will always be as old as Uma. And it should flower in two or three years at the most.'

15.7

When Bibbo saw the Nawabzada, she quickly thrust a letter into his hands.

'How in heaven's name did you know I would be coming here tonight? I wasn't invited.'

'No one can be uninvited tonight,' said Bibbo. 'I thought the Nawabzada might be alive to the opportunity.'

Firoz laughed. Bibbo loved intrigue, and it was good for him that she did, because it would have been impossible otherwise for him to communicate with Tasneem. He had seen her only twice, but she fascinated him; and he felt that she must surely feel something for him, for although her letters were gentle and discreet, the very fact that she wrote them without her sister's knowledge required courage.

'And does the Nawabzada have a letter in exchange?' asked Bibbo.

'Indeed, I do; and something else besides,' said Firoz, handing her a letter and a ten-rupee note.

'Oh, but this is unnecessary—'

'Yes, I know how unnecessary it is,' said Firoz. 'Who else is here?' he continued. He spoke in a low voice. He could hear the sound of a lament being chanted upstairs.

Bibbo reeled off a few names including that of Bilgrami Sahib. To Firoz's surprise there were several Sunnis among them.

'Sunnis too?'

'Why not?' said Bibbo. 'Saeeda Begum does not discriminate. Even certain pious women attend—the Nawabzada will admit that that is unusual. And she does not permit any of those mischievous imprecations that mar the atmosphere of most gatherings.'

'If that is the case I would have asked my friend Maan to come along,' said Firoz.

'No, no,' said Bibbo, startled. 'Dagh Sahib is a Hindu; that would never do. Id, yes, but Moharram—how would that be possible? It is a different matter altogether. Outdoor processions are open to everybody, but one must discriminate somewhat for a private gathering.'

'Anyway, he told me to give his love to the parakeet.'

'Oh, that miserable creature—I would like to wring its neck,' said Bibbo. Clearly some recent incident had reduced the bird's lovability in her eyes.

'And Maan—Dagh Sahib, I mean—also wondered—and I too am wondering—about this legend of Saeeda Begum quenching the thirst of travellers in the wilderness of Karbala with her own fair hands.'

'The Nawabzada will be gratified to know that it is not a legend,' said Bibbo, feeling a little annoyed that her mistress's piety was being questioned, but then suddenly giving Firoz a smile as she remembered the ten-rupee note. 'She stands at the corner of Khirkiwalan and Katra Mast on the day the tazias are brought out. Her mother, Mohsina Bai, used to do it, and she never fails to do it herself. Of course, you wouldn't know it was her; she wears a burqa, naturally. But even when she is not well she keeps that post; she is a very devout lady. Some people think one thing precludes another.'

'I do not doubt what you say,' said Firoz seriously. 'I did not mean to give offence.'

Bibbo, delighted with such courtesy from the Nawabzada, said:

'The Nawabzada is about to get a reward for his own religiosity.'

'And what is that?'

'He will see for himself.'

And so Firoz did. Unlike Maan, he did not pause to adjust his cap halfway up the stairs. No sooner had he entered the room where Saeeda Bai—in a dark-blue sari with not a jewel on her face or hands—was holding her session than he saw—or, rather, beheld—Tasneem sitting at the back of the room. She was dressed in a fawn-coloured salwaar-kameez. She looked as beautiful, as delicate as the first time he had seen her. Her eyes were filled with tears. The moment she saw Firoz she lowered them.

Saeeda Bai did not lose a syllable of her marsiya as she saw Firoz enter, though her eyes flashed. Already the listeners were in a high state of excitement. Men and women alike were weeping; some of the women were beating their breasts and lamenting for Hussain. Saeeda Bai's own soul seemed to have entered the marsiya, but one part of it observed the congregation and noted the entrance of the Nawab of Baitar's son. She would have to deal with this trouble later; for the moment she had simply to bear it. But the agitation she felt communicated itself into the force of her indignation against the killer of Imam Hussain:

'And as that accursed mercenary pulled out the bloodied spear
The Prince of Martyrs bowed his head in gratitude to God.
The hell-bent, brutal Shamr unsheathed his dagger and advanced—
The heavens shook, the earth quaked seeing such foul, odious acts.
How can I say how Shamr put the dagger to his throat—
It was as if he trampled on the Holy Book itself!'

'Toba! toba!' 'Ya Allah!' 'Ya Hussain! Ya Hussain!' cried the audience. Some were so choked with grief they could not speak at all, and when the next stanza revealed his sister Zainab's grief—her swooning away—her shock when she reopened her eyes and saw her brother's head, the head of the Holy Prince of Martyrs, raised upon a lance—there was a dreadful silence in the audience, a pause before renewed lamentation. Firoz glanced at Tasneem; her eyes were still cast down, but her lips moved to the famous words that her sister was reciting.

'Anis, thou canst not write of Zainab's lamentations more!
The body of Hussain lay there, unburied, in the sun;
Alas, the Prophet found no peace in his last resting place!
His holy progeny imprisoned and his house burnt down!
How many homes Hussain's death left all ruined, desolate!
The Prophet's progeny, thus never prospered after him.'

Here Saeeda Bai stopped, and looked around the room, her eyes resting for a moment on Firoz, then on Tasneem. After a while she said, casually, to Tasneem: 'Go and feed the parakeet, and tell Bibbo to come here. She likes to be present at the soz-khwani.' Tasneem left the room. Others in the audience began to recover, and talk among themselves.

Firoz's heart fell. His eyes followed Tasneem to the door. He was in a state of volatile distraction. He had never seen her look so beautiful as now, unadorned, her cheeks stained with tears. Lost in contemplation, he hardly noticed when Bilgrami Sahib greeted him.

But Bilgrami Sahib was now telling him about the time he had visited Baitar during the Moharram celebrations—and Firoz's mind was drawn back against his will to the Fort and the Imambara with its red-and-white chandelier and the paintings of Karbala on the wall and the marsiyas chanted under the hundreds of flickering lights.

The Nawab Sahib's great hero was Al-Hur, the officer who had been sent at first to seize Hussain; but who at the end had detached himself with thirty horsemen from the main force of the enemy and had joined the weaker side to face inevitable death. Firoz had tried to argue the point once or twice with his father; but had given it up. His father, whom Firoz suspected of being half in love with noble failure, felt too strongly about the matter.

Saeeda Bai now began singing a short marsiya particularly suited for soz. This contained no introduction, no elaboration of the physical beauty of the hero, no vaunting on the battlefield by the hero of his lineage and prowess and exploits, no long battle scenes, no description of horse or sword, almost nothing but the most moving parts of the story: the scenes of leave-taking from his loved ones, his death, the lamentations of the women and children. At the lamentations Saeeda Bai's voice rose into the air in a strange sobbing wail, intensely musical, intensely beautiful.

Firoz had heard soz before, but it was nothing compared to this. He turned to the spot where Tasneem had been sitting, and noticed the frivolous Bibbo there instead. Her hair was undone, and she was crying her eyes out, beating her breast and leaning forward as if she were about to faint with sorrow. So were many of the women around her. Bilgrami Sahib was sobbing into his handkerchief, which his hands clutched in the gesture of prayer. Saeeda Bai's eyes were closed; even for this supremely controlled artist, her art had passed beyond her own restraint. Her body, like her voice, was shaking with grief and pain. And Firoz, though he did not realize it, was himself weeping uncontrollably.

15.8

'Why did you miss last night?' demanded Bhaskar, who had been promoted tonight to be Angad, a monkey-prince, because the boy playing that part had fallen ill, probably from growling himself hoarse on previous evenings. Bhaskar knew Angad's lines, but unfortunately there was nothing to say today—it was all just running around and fighting.

'I was asleep,' said Maan.

'Asleep! You are like Kumbhkaran,' said Bhaskar. 'You missed the best part of the battle. You missed the building of the bridge to Lanka—it stretched across from the temple to the houses there—and you missed Hanuman going to get the magic herb—and you missed the burning of Lanka.'

'But I'm here now,' said Maan. 'Give your uncle some credit.'

'And this morning, when Daadi was worshipping the weapons and pens and books, where were you?'

'Well, I don't believe in all that,' said Maan, attempting a different tack. 'I don't believe in weapons and shooting and hunting and violence. Did she worship your kites as well?'

'Aré, Maan, shake hands with me,' said a familiar voice out of the crowd. Maan turned around. It was the Rajkumar of Marh, accompanied by the Vakil Sahib's younger brother. Maan was a bit surprised to see the Rajkumar here, at this neighbourhood Ramlila. He would have thought he would be at some great, soulless, official one, trailing his father around. Maan shook hands with him very cordially.

'Have some paan.'

'Thanks,' said Maan, took two, and almost choked. There was a powerful dose of tobacco in the paan. For a minute or two he was literally speechless. He had planned to ask the Rajkumar what he was doing these days without even his studies to occupy him; but by the time he had recovered, young Goyal, who appeared to be very proud to be sporting minor royalty around, had quickly dragged the Rajkumar away to introduce him to someone else.

Maan turned and stared at the effigies. Along the western edge of the square of Shahi Darvaza stood three huge figures—fierce and flammable—of wood, cane, and coloured paper, with red light-bulbs for their eyes. The ten-headed Ravana required twenty bulbs, which flickered more menacingly than those of his lieutenants. He was the embodiment of armed evil: each of his twenty hands carried a weapon—bows made of cane, maces made of silver paper, wooden swords and discuses, bamboo spears, even a mock pistol. To one side of Ravana stood his vile brother Kumbhkaran, fat, vicious, idle and gluttonous; and to his other side stood Meghnad, his courageous and arrogant son who just the previous day had struck Lakshman with a javelin in the breast and almost killed him. Everyone was comparing the effigies with those of earlier years, and excitedly anticipating their conflagration as the climax of the evening: the destruction of evil, the triumph of good.

But before that could happen, the actors playing the parts of these figures had to meet their fates in due order before the public eye.

At seven o'clock the loudspeakers overhead belched forth a sudden cacophony of drumbeats, and the little red-faced monkeys, made up to look fierce and martial with all that art, indigo and zinc oxide could contrive, swarmed out of the temple building in search of the enemy, whom they quickly found and noisily engaged with. Screams were heard, together with pious shouts of 'Jai Siyaram!' and demonic cries of 'Jai Shankar!' Even the vowels in the name of Lord Shiva, the great patron of Ravana, had been extended in a mocking and sinister manner, so that the sound that emerged was more like 'Jai Shenker!' This was followed each time by Ravana's bizarre and grisly laugh that chilled the blood of most of the spectators, even if it made the actor's friends laugh.

Two khaki policemen of the local constabulary wandered along here and there to ensure that the monkey and demon hordes kept to the agreed geographical limits, but since the monkeys and demons were far swifter than the forces of the law, they gave up after a while, stopped at a paan-shop, and demanded free paans instead. Round and round the policemen, in and out of the square, past their own parents who could barely recognize them, and through the lanes ran the monkeys and demons, past the small general store, the two temples, the small mosque, the bakery, the astrologer's house, the public urinal, the electrical junction, and the doorways of the houses; sometimes they were chased into the open courtyards of houses, and chased out again by the Ramlila organizers. Their swords and lances and arrows got stuck in the coloured streamers overhanging the lane, and ripped the overhead banner that read in Hindi: *The Ramlila Welfare Committee heartily welcomes you*. Finally, exhausted, the two armies gathered in the square and glared and growled at each other.

The army of monkeys (with a few bears thrown in) was led by Rama, Lakshman and Hanuman. They had tried to hunt down Ravana, while the twelve-year-old boy playing the beautiful, abducted Sita watched from a balcony above with—so it appeared from his expression—supreme indifference. Ravana, pestered and harried by the monkeys and shot at by his arch-enemy Rama, was on the run and demanded to know where his brother Kumbhkaran had got to—why was he not defending Lanka? When he heard that Kumbhkaran was still sunk in a gluttonous stupor, he demanded that he be woken. The demons and imps did their best, passing food and sweets over the huge, supine form until the scent aroused him from his sleep. He roared, stretched, and gobbled up what was offered to him. Several demons polished off some of the sweets themselves. Then the battle began in earnest.

In the rhyming verse of Tulsidas, which could hardly be heard on the pandit's megaphone above the clamour:

> 'Having feasted on the buffaloes and drunk off the wine, Kumbhkaran roared like a crash of lightning. . . . The moment the mighty monkeys heard this, they rushed forth crying with joy. They plucked up trees and mountains and hurled them against Kumbhkaran, gnashing their teeth all the while. The bears and monkeys threw myriads of mountain-peaks at him each time. But neither did he feel daunted in spirit nor did he stir from his position in spite of the best efforts on the part of the monkeys to push him back, even like an elephant pelted with the fruits of the sun-plant. Thereupon Hanuman struck him with his fist and he fell to the earth, beating his head in great confusion. Rising again, he hit Hanuman back and the latter whirled round and immediately dropped to the ground. . . . The monkey host stampeded; in utter dismay none dared face him.'

Even Bhaskar, who was playing Angad, was knocked down by the mighty Kumbhkaran and lay groaning piteously underneath the pipal tree where he used to play cricket.

Despite the arrows of Rama, the wounded monster was undeterred. 'He burst into a terrible roar and, seizing millions and millions of monkeys, dashed them to the ground like a huge elephant, swearing by his ten-headed brother.' The monkeys cried to Rama in distress; he drew his bow and fired yet more arrows at Kumbhkaran. 'Even as the arrows struck him, the demon rushed forth, burning with rage; the mountains staggered and the earth shook as he ran.' He tore up a rock; but Rama cut off the arm that bore it. He then rushed forward with the rock in his left hand; but the Lord struck off even that arm and it fell to the ground. . . . 'Uttering a most terrible shriek, he rushed on with wide open mouth. The saints and gods in the heavens cried out in their terror, "Alas! Alas!"'

Seeing the distress of the very gods, the All-merciful Rama finally cut off Kumbhkaran's head with another arrow, and let it fall to the ground in front of his horrified brother Ravana. The trunk still ran madly on, until it was cut down. It then fell to the ground, crushing beneath it monkeys, bears, and demons alike.

The crowd yelled and cheered and clapped. Maan cheered with them;

Bhaskar stopped groaning, got up and shouted with joy. Even the subsequent deaths in battle of Meghnad and the arch-enemy himself could not match the delight everyone felt at the death of Kumbhkaran, who was a seasoned actor of many years' standing and had mastered the art of terrifying both antagonists and audience. Finally, when all the actor-demons lay dead in the dust, and 'Jai Shenker!' was heard no more, it was time for the pyromania.

A red carpet of about five thousand small firecrackers was laid out in front of the demon effigies, and lit with a long fuse. The racket was deafening, truly enough to make saints and gods cry out, 'Alas! Alas!' The fire, the sparks, the ash reached the balcony above and made Mrs Mahesh Kapoor wheeze and choke before the unbreathable acrid air was borne away by the wind. Rama fired an arrow at each of Kumbhkaran's arms and they dropped away, manipulated from behind by the prop-man. Again the audience gasped. But instead of striking off his head, the handsome blue figure in his leopard-skin now took a rocket out of his quiver, and aimed it at Kumbhkaran's armless body. The rocket hit the corpse; it lit up in flames, and was consumed in a series of thunderous explosions. Kumbhkaran had been stuffed with fireworks, which now whizzed about him; a green bomb on his nose went off in a fountain of coloured sparks. His huge frame collapsed, the organizers of the Ramlila beat the remnants down to ash, and the crowd cheered Rama on.

After Lakshman had dispatched the effigy of Meghnad, Rama finished off the evil Ravana for the second time in the evening. But to the alarm of the crowd the paper, straw and bamboo with which he had been stuffed refused to burn. There was a sense of alarm now, as if this did not augur well for the forces of good. It was only with the addition of a bit of kerosene that Ravana was finally done away with. And again, with a few strokes of the organizers' lathis and a thorough dousing with pots and pans of water poured down by cheering people from the balconies above, the once-malevolent ten-headed effigy was reduced to ash and charred cane.

Rama, Lakshman, and Hanuman had retired to one side of the square when a rather mocking voice in the crowd reminded them that they had forgotten to rescue Sita after all. Back they hurried over the black-ashed ground, across the scorched-paper residue of five thousand firecrackers. Sita, clad in a yellow sari, and still looking fairly bored with the proceedings, was handed down to them from her balcony without much ceremony and restored to her husband.

Now, with Rama, Lakshman, Sita and Hanuman all together at last, and the forces of evil finally vanquished, the crowd responded enthusiastically to the pandit's prompting:

'Raghupati Shri Ramchandra ji ki—'

'Jai!'

'Bol, Sita Maharani ki—'

'Jai!'

'Lakshman ji ki—'

'Jai!'

'Shri Bajrangbali ki—'

'Jai!'

'Kindly remember, good people,' continued the pandit, 'that the ceremony of Bharat Milaap will take place tomorrow at the time announced on the posters, in Rama's capital of Ayodhya, which for our purposes is the small square near the temple in Misri Mandi. That is where Rama and Lakshman will embrace their long-separated brothers Bharat and Shatrughan—and fall at the feet of their mothers. Please don't forget. It will be a very moving performance and will bring tears to the eyes of all true devotees of Shri Rama. It is the true climax of the Ramlila, even more than the darshan you have had tonight. And please tell everyone who has not had the fortune to be present here to go to Misri Mandi tomorrow night. Now where is the photographer? Mela Ram ji, kindly step forward.'

Photographs were taken, arati was performed several times with lamps and sweets on a silver platter, and each of the good figures, including many of the monkeys and bears, were fed. They looked properly serious now. Some of the rowdier elements of the crowd had already dispersed. But most of the audience remained, and accepted the leftover sweets as a sanctified offering. Even the demons got their share.

15.9

The tazia procession from Baitar House to the city Imambara was a stately business. The Baitar House tazia was famous: it had been made many years before, and was a magnificent affair of silver and crystal. Each year on the ninth day of Moharram it was carried to the city Imambara, where it was displayed overnight and the next morning. Then, on the afternoon of the tenth day, together with all the other replicas of the tomb of the Imam Hussain, it was carried in a grand procession to the 'Karbala', the field outside Brahmpur specially designated for the burial of the tazias. But unlike those made of mere paper and glass, the silver Baitar House tazia (like a few others that were equally precious) was not smashed and buried in an open pit dug for the purpose. It was left on the field for an hour or so, its temporary ornaments of tinsel and kite paper and mica were buried, and the tazia itself was taken back to the house by the servants.

The Baitar House procession this year consisted of Firoz (dressed in a white sherwani), a couple of drummers, six young men (three on each side) carrying the great tazia along on strong wooden poles, some of the house servants who beat their chests rhythmically and cried out the names of the martyrs (but did not use whips or chains), and a couple of constables to represent the forces of law and order. Their route from Pasand Bagh was rather long, so they started out early.

By early evening they had got to the street outside the Imambara which was the meeting place for the various tazia processions of the different guilds and neighbourhoods and great houses. Here stood a tall pole, at least sixty feet high, with a green and black flag fluttering above. Here also stood the statue of a horse, Hussain's brave steed, richly decorated during Moharram with flowers and precious cloth. And here also, just outside the Imambara, near the wayside shrine of a local saint, was a busy fair—where the mourning of the processionists intermingled with the festive excitement of people buying or selling knick-knacks and holy pictures, and children eating all sorts of delicious street food, including sweets, ice-cream and candyfloss—coloured not only pink but also green for Moharram.

Most tazia processions were much less decorous than the one that represented the Nawab Sahib's family: their grief was loud, their drumbeats deafening, their self-flagellations bloody. Nor did they prize decorum above sincerity. The fervour of their feelings was what carried them onwards. Unshod, naked above the waist, their backs a mess of blood from the chains with which they lashed themselves, the men accompanying the tazias panted and moaned as they took the name of Imam Hussain and his brother Hassan repeatedly, rhythmically, in plaintive or agonized lament. Some of the processions that were known to be the most fervent were accompanied by as many as a dozen policemen.

The routes of the tazia processions had been charted out with great care by the organizers and the police together. Hindu areas were to be avoided as far as possible, and in particular the area of the contested temple; low-lying branches of pipal trees were measured in advance against the heights of tazias, so that neither would be damaged; the processionists were enjoined from cursing the caliphs; and timings were matched so that by nightfall all the processions throughout the city would have arrived at the central destination.

Maan met Firoz, as agreed, a little before sunset near the statue of the horse by the Imambara.

'Ah, so you've come, you kafir.' Firoz was looking very handsome in his white sherwani.

'But only to do what all kafirs do,' replied Maan.

'And what is that?'

'Why don't you have your Nawabi walking stick with you?' asked Maan, who had been looking Firoz up and down.

'It wouldn't have been appropriate for the procession,' replied Firoz. 'I'd have been expected to beat myself with it, no doubt. But you haven't answered my question.'

'Oh—what was that?'

'What is it that all kafirs do?'

'Is that a riddle?' asked Maan.

'It is not,' said Firoz. 'You just said that you'd come to do what all kafirs do. And I'm asking you what that is.'

'Oh, to prostrate myself before my idol. You said she'd be here.'

'Well, there she is,' said Firoz, jerking his head lightly in the direction of the nearby crossroads. 'I'm pretty sure.'

A woman dressed in a black burqa was standing at a booth, distributing sherbet to those who passed by in the tazia processions or who milled about the temporary market. They drank, they handed the glasses back, and these were dumped into a bucket of water by another woman in a brown burqa and given a cursory wash before being reused. The stand was very popular, probably because it was known who the lady in black was.

'Quenching the thirst of Karbala,' added Firoz.

'Come,' said Maan.

'No, no, you go along. That other one's Bibbo, by the way, the one in the brown burqa. Not Tasneem.'

'Come with me, Firoz. Please. I really have no business to be here. I'll feel very awkward.'

'Nothing like as awkward as I felt when I went to her gathering last night. No, I'm going to see the tazias lined up. Most of them have arrived already, and each year there's something astonishing to see. Last year there was one in the shape of a double-storeyed peacock with a woman's head—and only half a dome to tell you it was meant to be a tomb. We're becoming Hinduized.'

'Well, if I come with you to see the tazias, will you accompany me to the sherbet-stand?'

'Oh—all right.'

Maan quickly got bored with the tazias, remarkable though they were. Everyone around him appeared to be engaged in heated discussion about which one was the most elegant, the most elaborate, the most expensive. 'I recognize that one,' said Maan with a smile; he had seen it in the Imambara at Baitar House.

'Well, we'll probably use it for another fifty years,' said Firoz. 'I doubt we'll be able to afford to make anything like that again.'

'Come, now, keep your part of the bargain.'

'All right.'

Firoz and Maan walked over to the sherbet-stand.

'It's too unhygienic for words, Maan—you can't drink from those glasses.'

But Maan had gone forward, pushed his way through the crowd and now held his hand out for a glass of sherbet. The woman in black handed it to him, but at the last moment, as her eyes suddenly registered who he was, she was so startled that she spilled the sherbet over his hands.

She took her breath in sharply and said, 'Excuse me, Sir,' in a low voice. 'Let me pour you another glass.'

There was no mistaking her voice. 'No, no, Madam,' protested Maan. 'Please do not trouble yourself. What is left in this glass will more than quench my thirst, however terrible.'

The woman in the brown burqa turned towards him upon hearing his voice. Then the two women turned towards each other. Maan sensed their tension, and he allowed himself a smile.

Bibbo may not have been surprised to see Maan, but Saeeda Bai was both surprised and displeased. As Maan had expected, she thought he had no business to be there; certainly he could not pretend to any lavish fondness for the Shia martyrs. But his smile only succeeded in making her angrier. She contrasted the flippancy of Maan's remark with the terrible thirst of the heroes of Karbala—their tents burning behind them, the river cut off in front of them—and, making no attempt this time to disguise her voice or her indignation, she said to Maan: 'I am running short of supplies. There is a booth half a mile farther on where I would advise you to go when you have finished this glass. It is run by a lady of great piety; the sherbet is sweeter, and you will find the crowd less oppressive.'

And before Maan could respond with an appropriate conciliatory couplet, she had turned to the other thirsty men.

'Well?' said Firoz.

Maan scratched his head. 'No, she wasn't pleased.'

'Well, don't fret; it doesn't suit you. Let's see what the market has to offer.'

Maan looked at his watch. 'No, I can't. I have to go to watch the Bharat Milaap, or I'll lose my standing in the eyes of my nephew. Why don't you come along as well? It's very affecting. Everyone lines the lanes, cheering and weeping and showering flowers on the procession. Rama and company from the left, Bharat and company from the right. And the two brothers embrace in the middle—just outside the city of Ayodhya.'

'Well, I suppose there are enough people to manage without me here,' said Firoz. 'How far is it?'

'Misri Mandi—that's where Ayodhya's located this year. Only a ten-minute walk from here—very close to Veena's house. She'll be pleasantly surprised to see you.'

Firoz laughed. 'That's what you thought Saeeda Bai would be,' he said, as they wandered hand in hand through the bazaar in the direction of Misri Mandi.

15.10

The Bharat Milaap processions began on time. Since Bharat had merely to go to the outskirts of his city to meet his brother, he bided his time until the pandit gave him the signal; but Rama had a long journey to make to the holy capital of Ayodhya—to which he was returning in triumph after many years of exile—and just as it became dark he set out on this journey from a temple situated a good half-mile away from the stage where the brothers were at last to be united.

This stage had been festooned with strings of flowers suspended from the bamboo poles that rose from its four corners; it had been put together by almost the whole neighbourhood with much advice and many marigolds; and several cows that had attempted to eat the marigolds had been shooed off by the monkey army. The cows were normally welcome enough in the neighbourhood—their movements at least were unobstructed—and the poor trusting things must have wondered what had created such a sudden change in their popularity.

Today was a day of pure joy and celebration; for not only were Rama and Lakshman to be reunited with their brothers Bharat and Shatrughan, but it was the day when the people would see their Lord return to them, to rule over them and establish perfect righteousness not only in Ayodhya but in the entire world.

The procession began to wind its way through the narrow lanes of Misri Mandi to the sound of drums and shehnais and a raucous popular band. First came the lights, courtesy of Jawaharlal Light House, the same company that had provided the demons' red eyes the previous evening. The brilliant lights they held above them emitted an intense white glow from what looked like bulbs covered with gauze cloth.

Mahesh Kapoor held his hand against his eyes. He was here partly because his wife wanted him to be, partly because he was more and more coming around to the idea of rejoining the Congress Party and felt he should re-establish his links with his old constituency just in case.

'This light is too bright—I'm going blind—' he said. 'Kedarnath, do something about it. You're one of the organizers, aren't you?'

'Baoji, let's just let them pass. It'll be better later on,' said his son-in-law, who knew that once the procession had begun, there was almost nothing he could do about it. Mrs Mahesh Kapoor had cupped her hands over her ears, but was smiling to herself.

The brass band was deafening. After blaring out a few film songs, they switched to religious melodies. They made a striking sight in their cheap red trousers with white piping and their blue tunics with gold-coloured cotton braid. Every one of their trumpets, trombones and horns was out of tune.

Then came the principal noisemongers, the flat drummers, who had been roasting their instruments carefully over three small fires near the temple to heighten their pitch and crispness. They played as if they had gone mad—in unbelievably swift salvos of unbearable noise. They forced themselves aggressively upon anyone whom they recognized from the Ramlila Committee in a mixture of display and blackmail, compelling them to hand over coins and notes. They thrust their pelvises forward and moved their drums back and forth at a slant from their waists. These were good days for the drummers: they were in demand both by those who celebrated

Dussehra and by those who observed Moharram.

'Where are they from?' asked Mahesh Kapoor.

'What?' asked Kedarnath.

'I said, where are they from?'

'I can't hear you because of these wretched drummers.'

Mahesh Kapoor cupped his hands and shouted into his son-in-law's ears: 'I said, where are they from? Are they Muslim?'

'They're from the market—' shouted Kedarnath, which was a way of admitting that they were.

Even before the swaroops—Rama, Lakshman, and Sita—could appear in their beauty and glory, the master of fireworks—who carried a massive sack on his shoulder—brought out a huge packet, tore off the coloured paper from it, ripped open the cardboard box inside, and rolled out another great red carpet of five thousand firecrackers. As they exploded in series, people drew back from the light and noise, their faces flushed with excitement, their hands clapped over their ears or their fingers inserted into them. The noise was so overwhelming that Mahesh Kapoor decided that even his obligation to be seen in his old constituency was not worth the loss of his hearing and sanity.

'Come,' he shouted to his wife, 'we're going home.'

Mrs Mahesh Kapoor could not hear a word of what he was saying, and kept smiling.

The monkey army, Bhaskar included, was next in the procession, and a great quiver of excitement went through the spectators; the swaroops were to follow shortly. The children started clapping; the old people were the most expectant of all, remembering perhaps the scores of Ramlilas they must have seen enacted in the course of their lives. Some children sat on a low wall along the route, others skilfully scrambled up to the ledges of houses, getting a foothold here or the help of an adult shoulder there. One father, kissing his two-year-old daughter's bare foot, pushed her up on to the flat top of a decorative pillar and held her there to help her get a better view.

And then at last Lord Rama appeared; and Sita, in a yellow sari; and Lakshman, smiling, his quiver glistening with arrows.

The eyes of the spectators filled with tears of joy, and they began showering flowers on the swaroops. The children clambered down from their perches and followed the procession, chanting 'Jai Siyaram' and 'Ramchandra ji ki jai!' and sprinkling rose petals and water from the Ganga on them. And the drummers beat their drums with renewed frenzy.

Mahesh Kapoor, his face flushed with annoyance, seized his wife's hand and pulled her to one side.

'We are leaving,' he shouted directly into her ear. 'Can't you hear me? I have had enough. . . . Veena, your mother and I are leaving.'

Mrs Mahesh Kapoor looked at her husband, astonished, almost disbelieving. Tears filled her eyes when she understood what he had said, what she was to be deprived of. Once she had seen the Bharat Milaap at Nati Imli in Banaras, and she had never forgotten it. The tenderness of the occasion—with the two brothers who had remained in Ayodhya throwing themselves at the feet of their two long-exiled brothers—the throng of spectators, at least a lakh of people—the devotion in everyone's eyes as the small figures came on to the stage—everything came back to her. Whenever she saw the Bharat Milaap here in Brahmpur she thought of that occasion in all its charm and wonder and grace. How simple it was and how wonderful. And it was not merely the tender meeting of long-separated brothers but the first act of Ram Rajya, the rule of Rama when, unlike in these factious, violent, petty times, the four pillars of religion—truth, purity, mercy, and charity—would hold up the edifice of the world.

The words of Tulsidas, long known by heart, came back to her:

> Devoted to duty, the people walked in the path of the Vedas, each according to his own caste and stage of life, and enjoyed perfect happiness, unvexed by fear, or sorrow, or disease.

'Let us at least wait till the procession has reached Ayodhya,' Mrs Mahesh Kapoor pleaded with her husband.

'Stay if you want. I'm going,' snapped Mahesh Kapoor; and, forlornly, she followed. But she decided that tomorrow she would not persuade him to come for Rama's coronation. She would come alone and, not subject to his whims and commands, she would see it from beginning to end. She would not be prised away yet again from a scene that her soul thirsted for.

Meanwhile the procession wound its way through the labyrinthine alleys of Misri Mandi and the contiguous neighbourhoods. Lakshman stepped on one of the burnt-out bulbs from the Jawaharlal Light House, and yelped in pain. Since there was no water to be had immediately, Rama picked up some rose petals that had been strewn in his path and crushed them against the burn. The people sighed at this sign of brotherly solicitude, and the procession moved on. The chief of fireworks now set off a few green-flared rockets that soared into the sky before exploding in a chrysanthemum of sparks. At this, Hanuman rushed forward, waving his tail, as if reminded of his own incendiary activities in Lanka. He was followed by the monkey throng, chattering and shouting with joy; they reached the marigold stage a couple of hundred yards before the three main swaroops. Hanuman, who today was even redder, plumper and jollier than he had been yesterday, leapt on to the stage, hopped, skipped, and danced for a few seconds, then jumped off. Now Bharat understood that Rama and Lakshman were approaching the river Saryu and the city of Ayodhya, and he too began to move towards the stage along the lane from the other side.

15.11

And then suddenly Rama's procession stopped, and the sound of other drums was heard together with cries of terrible grief and lamentation. A group of about twenty men accompanied by drummers was trying to cut across the procession in order to get to the Imambara with their tazia. Some were beating their breasts in sorrow for Imam Hussain; in the hands of others were chains and whips tipped with small knives and razor blades with which they lashed themselves mercilessly in jerky, compulsive motions. They were an hour and a half behind time—their drummers had turned up late, they had got into a scuffle with another tazia procession—and now they were trying to push forward as fast as they could, desperate to get to their destination. It was the ninth night of Moharram. In the distance they could just make out the spire of the Imambara lit up with a string of lights. They moved forward, tears coursing down their cheeks—

'Ya Hassan! Ya Hussain!' 'Ya Hassan! Ya Hussain!' 'Hassan! Hussain!' 'Hassan! Hussain!'

'Bhaskar,' said Veena to her son, who had grabbed her hand—Go home at once. At once. Where's Daadi?—'

'But I want to watch—'

She slapped him once, hard, across his monkey-face. He looked at her unbelievingly, then, crying, backed out of the lane.

Kedarnath had moved forward to talk to the two policemen accompanying the tazia procession. Not caring what her neighbours might think, she went up to him, caught his hands in her own, and said:

'Let's go home.'

'But there's trouble here—I'd better—'

'Bhaskar's ill.'

Kedarnath, torn between two anxieties, nodded.

The two policemen accompanying the tazia-bearers tried to clear a path for them, but this was too much for the people of Misri Mandi, the citizens of the holy city of Ayodhya who had waited so long and devotedly for a sight of Lord Rama.

The policemen realized that what would have been a safe path an hour previously was no longer safe. They ordered, then pleaded with the tazia procession to change its route, to halt, to go back, but to no avail. The desperate mourners thrust forward through the joyous celebrators.

This atrocious and violent interruption—this lunatic mourning that made a mockery of the enactment of Shri Ramachandra ji returning to his home, his brothers, his people, to establish his perfect reign—was not to be borne. The monkeys, who had just been leaping about in uncontrollable joy, angrily threw flowers on to the tazia, shouted and growled aggressively, and then stood threateningly around the intruders who were attempting to force themselves across the path of Rama, Sita and Lakshman.

The actor playing Rama himself moved forward in a motion that was half aggressive, half propitiatory.

A chain lashed out, and he staggered back, to lie gasping in pain against the ledge of a shop. Upon his dark-blue skin a red stain formed and spread.

The crowd went berserk. What all the forces of Ravana had not succeeded in doing these bloodthirsty Muslims had managed to do. It was not a young actor, but God himself who lay wounded there.

Crazed by the sight of the wounded Rama, the man with the fireworks seized a lathi from one of the organizers and led the crowd in a charge against the tazia procession. Within seconds, the tazia, many weeks' work of delicate glass and mica and paper tracery, lay smashed on the ground. Fireworks were thrown on to it and it was set alight. The maddened crowd stamped on it and beat it with lathis until it was charred and splintered. Its horrified defenders lashed out with their knives and chains at these kafirs, leaping about like apes on the very eve of the great martyrdom, who had dared to desecrate the holy image of the tomb.

The sight of the crushed and blackened tazia made them mad.

Both sides now were filled with the lust to kill—what did it matter if they too suffered martyrdom?—to attack pure evil, to defend what was dear to them—what did it matter if they died?—whether to recreate the passion of Karbala or to re-establish Ram Rajya and rid the world of the murderous, cow-slaughtering, God-defiling devils.

'Kill the bastards—finish them off—the spawn of Pakistan—'

'Ya Hassan! Ya Hussain!' It was now a battle cry.

Soon even the crazed cries of the time of Partition—'Allah-u-Akbar' and 'Har har Mahadeva'—were heard above the screams of pain and terror. Knives and spears and axes and lathis had appeared from the neighbouring houses, and Hindus and Muslims hacked at each other's limbs, eyes, faces, guts, throats. Of the two policemen, one was wounded in the back, the other managed to escape. But it was a Hindu neighbourhood and, after a few terrifying minutes of mutual butchery, the Muslims fled down side lanes, most of them small and unfamiliar. Some were hunted down and killed, some escaped and rushed back in the direction from which they had come, some ran forward towards the Imambara by circuitous routes—guided from far off by its illuminated spire and festoons of light. They fled towards the Imambara as one would flee towards a sanctuary—where they would receive protection among those of their own religion and would find hearts that could understand their own fear and hatred and bitterness and grief—for they had seen their friends and relatives killed and wounded—and be inflamed by them in turn.

Soon Muslim mobs would be roaming around other parts of Brahmpur setting fire to Hindu shops and murdering any Hindu they could find. Meanwhile in Misri Mandi, three of the Muslim drummers who had been hired for the Bharat Milaap, who were not even Shias, and who did not care much more for the tazias than they did for the divinity of Rama, lay murdered by the wall of the temple, their drums smashed in, their heads half hacked off, their bodies doused in kerosene and set alight—all, doubtless, to the greater glory of God.

15.12

Maan and Firoz were sauntering along through the dark lane of Katra Mast towards Misri Mandi when Maan stopped suddenly. The sounds he heard approaching them were not those he had expected. They were the sounds neither of a tazia procession—and surely it was too late for a tazia procession—nor the joyful sounds of Bharat Milaap. The sound of drums had stopped on either side—and neither 'Hassan! Hussain!' nor 'Jai Siyaram!' could be heard. Instead he made out the ominous, inchoate sounds of a mob, broken by screams of pain or passion—or shouts of 'Har har Mahadeva'. This aggressive invocation of Shiva would not have sounded out of place yesterday—but today it chilled his blood.

He let go of Firoz's hand and turned him around by the shoulders. 'Run!' he said, his mouth dry with fear. 'Run.' His heart was pounding. Firoz stared at him but did not move.

The crowd was rushing down the lane now. The sounds grew closer. Maan looked around him in desperation. The shops were all closed, their shutters down. There were no side lanes within immediate reach.

'Get back, Firoz—' said Maan, trembling. 'Get back—run! There's nowhere to hide here—'

'What's the matter—isn't it the procession?' Firoz's mouth opened as he registered the terror in Maan's eyes.

'Just listen to me,' Maan gasped—'Do as I say. Run back! Run back towards the Imambara. I'll delay them for a minute or two. That'll be enough. They'll stop me first.'

'I'm not leaving you,' said Firoz.

'Firoz, you fool, this is a Hindu mob. I'm not in danger. But I won't be all right if I come with you. God knows what will be happening there by now. If there's rioting going on, they'll be killing Hindus there.'

'No—'

'Oh God—'

By now the crowd had almost reached them, and it was too late to flee.

Ahead of the pack was a young man, who looked as if he was drunk. His kurta was torn and he was bleeding from a cut along his ribs. He had a bloodstained lathi in his hand, and he made for Maan and Firoz. Behind him—though it was dark and difficult to see—must have been some twenty or thirty men, armed with spears and knives or flaming torches doused in kerosene.

'Mussalmans—kill them also—'

'We're not Mussalmans,' said Maan immediately, not looking at Firoz. He tried to control his voice, but it was high-pitched with terror.

'We can find that out quickly enough,' said the young man nastily. Maan looked at him—he had a lean, clean-shaven face—a handsome face, but one that was full of madness and rage and hatred. Who was he? Who were these people? Maan recognized none of them in the darkness. What had happened? How had the peacefulness of the Bharat Milaap suddenly turned into a riot? And what, he thought, his brain seizing up with fear, what was going to happen?

Suddenly, as if by a miracle, the fog of fear dispersed from his mind.

'No need to find out who we are,' he said in a deeper voice. 'We were frightened because we thought at first you might be Muslims. We couldn't hear what you were shouting.'

'Recite the Gayatri Mantra,' sneered the young man.

Maan promptly recited the few sacred syllables. 'Now go—' he said. 'Don't threaten innocent people. Be on your way. Jai Siyaram! Har har Mahadeva!' He could not keep the rising mockery out of his voice.

The young man hesitated.

Someone in the crowd cried: 'The other's a Muslim. Why would he be dressed like that?'

'Yes, that's certain.'

'Take off his fancy dress.'

Firoz had started trembling again. This encouraged them.

'See if he's circumcised.'

'Kill the cruel, cow-murdering haramzada—cut the sister-fucker's throat.'

'What are you?' said the young man, prodding Firoz in the stomach with his bloodstained lathi. 'Quick—speak—speak, before I use this on your head—'

Firoz flinched and trembled. The blood on the lathi had stained his white sherwani. He did not lack courage normally, but now—in the face of such wild, unreasoning danger—he found he had lost his voice. How could he argue with a mob? He swallowed and said: 'I am what I am. What's that to you?'

Maan was looking desperately around him. He knew there was no time to talk. Suddenly in the erratic, terrifying light of the blazing torches his eyes fell on someone he thought he recognized.

'Nand Kishor!' he shouted. 'What are you doing here in this gang? Aren't you ashamed of yourself? You're supposed to be a teacher.' Nand Kishor, a middle-aged, bespectacled man, looked sullen.

'Shut up—' said the young man to Maan viciously. 'Just because you like circumcised cocks do you think we'll let the Mussalman go?' Again he prodded Firoz and drew another smear of blood down his sherwani.

Maan ignored him and continued to address Nand Kishor. He knew that the time for dialogue was short. It was miraculous that they had been able to speak at all—that they were still alive.

'You teach my nephew Bhaskar. He's part of Hanuman's army. Do you teach him to attack innocent people? Is this the kind of Ram Rajya you want to bring about? We're doing no one any harm. Let us go on our way. Come!' he said to Firoz, grabbing him by the shoulder. 'Come.' He tried to shoulder his way past the mob.

'Not so fast. You can go, you sister-fucking traitor—but you can't,' said the young man.

Maan turned on him and, ignoring his lathi, caught him by the throat in sudden fury.

'You mother-fucker!' he said to him in a low growl that nevertheless carried to every man in the mob. 'Do you know what day this is? This man is my brother, more than my brother, and today in our neighbourhood we were celebrating Bharat Milaap. If you harm one hair of my brother's head—if even one hair of his head is harmed—Lord Rama will seize your filthy soul and send it flaming into hell—and you'll be born in your next life as the filthy krait you are. Go home and lick up your own blood, you sister-fucker, before I break your neck.' He wrenched the young man's lathi from his grasp and pushed him into the crowd.

His face flaming with anger, Maan now walked with Firoz unharmed through the mob, which seemed a little cowed by his words, a little uncertain of its purpose. Before it could think its way out again, Maan, pushing Firoz in front of him, had walked fifty yards and turned a corner.

'Now run!' he said.

He and Firoz ran for their lives. The mob was still dangerous. It was in effect leaderless for a few minutes and uncertain what to do, but it soon regrouped and, feeling cheated of its prey, moved along the alleys to hunt for more.

Maan knew that at all costs they had to avoid the route of the Bharat Milaap procession and still somehow get to his sister's house. Who knew what danger they might have to face on the way, what other mobs or lunatics they might encounter.

'I'll try to get back to the Imambara,' said Firoz.

'It's too late now,' said Maan. 'You're cut off, and you don't know this area. Stay with me now. We're going to my sister's. Her husband's on the Ramlila Committee, no one will attack their house.'

'But I can't. How can I—'

'Shut up!' said Maan, his voice trembling again. 'You've put us through enough danger already. Don't have any more stupid scruples. There's no purdah in our family, thank God. Go through that gate there and don't make a sound.' Then he put his arm around Firoz's shoulder.

He led Firoz through a small washermen's colony, and they emerged in the tiny alley where Kedarnath lived. It was a mere fifty yards from where the stage had been set up for the Bharat Milaap. They could hear the sound of shouting and screaming from close by. Veena's house was in an almost entirely Hindu neighbourhood; no Muslim mobs could range here.

They stared at Firoz as he stumbled into the room in his bloodstained white sherwani—and at Maan, clutching the bloodstained lathi in his hand. Kedarnath stepped forward, the other three shrank back. Old Mrs Tandon clapped her hands to her mouth. 'Hai Ram! Hai Ram!' she gasped in horror.

'Firoz is staying here until we can get him out safely,' said Maan, looking at each of them in turn. 'There's a mob roaming around—and there'll be others. But everyone here is safe. No one will think of attacking this house.'

'But the blood—are you wounded?' asked Veena, turning to Firoz, her eyes distracted with concern.

Maan looked at Firoz's sherwani and his own lathi, and suddenly burst out laughing. 'Yes, this lathi did it, but I didn't—and it's not his blood.'

Firoz greeted his hosts as courteously as his own shock and theirs would allow.

Bhaskar, still tear-faced, seeing the effect of all this on his parents, looked strangely at Maan, who placed the long bamboo staff against the wall, and kissed his nephew on the forehead.

'This is the Nawab Sahib of Baitar's younger son,' said Maan to old Mrs Tandon. She nodded silently. Her mind had turned to the days of Partition in Lahore and her memories and thoughts were those of absolute terror.

15.13

Firoz changed hurriedly out of his long coat into one of Kedarnath's kurta-pyjamas. Veena made them a quick cup of tea with plenty of sugar. After a while, Maan and Firoz climbed up to the roof, to the pots and plants of the small garden. Maan crushed a small tulsi leaf and put it in his mouth.

As they looked around them they saw that fires had already broken out here and there in the city. They could make out several of the main buildings of Brahmpur: the spire of the Imambara still ablaze with light—the lights of the Barsaat Mahal, the dome of the Legislative Assembly, the railway station, and—far beyond the Subzipore Club, the fainter glow of the university. But here and there in the old city it was not lights but fire that lit the sky. The muted din of drums came to them from the direction of the Imambara. And distant shouts, more distinct at times as the breeze changed, reached their ears, together with other sounds that could have been firecrackers, but were more likely the sounds of police firing.

'You saved my life,' said Firoz.

Maan embraced him. He smelt of sweat and fear.

'You should have had a wash before you changed,' he said. 'All that running in your sherwani—thank God you're safe.'

'Maan, I must get back. They'll be worried crazy about me at the house. They'll risk their own lives to look for me. . . .'

Suddenly the lights went out at the Imambara.

Firoz said in quiet dread: 'What could have happened there?'

Maan said: 'Nothing.' He was wondering how Saeeda Bai would have got back to Pasand Bagh. Surely she must have remained in the safe area near the Imambara.

The night was warm, but there was a slight breeze. Neither of them said anything for a while.

A large glow now lit the sky about half a mile to the west. This was the lumberyard of a well-known Hindu trader who lived in a predominantly Muslim neighbourhood. Other fires sprang up around it. The drums were silent now, and the sounds of intermittent firing were very clear. Maan was too exhausted to feel any fear. A numbness and a terrible feeling of isolation and helplessness came over him.

Firoz closed his eyes, as if to shut out the terrible vision of the city in flames. But other fires beset his mind—the fire-acrobats of the Moharram fair; the embers of the trench dug outside the Imambara at Baitar House burning with logs and brushwood for ten days; the candelabra of the Imambara at the Fort blazing and guttering as Ustad Majeed Khan sang Raag Darbari while his father nodded with pleasure.

He suddenly got up, agitated.

Someone shouted from a neighbouring rooftop that curfew had been declared.

'How could it be declared?' asked Maan. 'People couldn't have got home by now.' He added softly, 'Firoz, sit down.'

'I don't know,' shouted the man. 'But it has just been announced on the radio that curfew has been declared and that in an hour police will have orders to shoot on sight. Before then, only if they see actual violence.'

'Yes, that makes sense,' Maan shouted back, wondering what, if anything, made sense any more.

'Who are you? Who's that with you? Kedarnath? Is everyone safe in your family?'

'It's not Kedarnath—it's a friend who came to see the Bharat Milaap. I'm Veena's brother.'

'Well, you'd better not move tonight, if you don't want to get your throat slit by the Muslims—or get shot by the police. What a night. Tonight of all nights.'

'Maan,' said Firoz quietly and urgently, 'can I use your sister's phone?'

'She doesn't have one,' said Maan.

Firoz looked at him with dismay.

'A neighbour's then. I have to get word back to Baitar House. If the news of the curfew is on the radio, my father will hear of it at the Fort in Baitar, and he will be terrified about what's happened here. Imtiaz might try to come back and get a curfew pass. For all I know Murtaza Ali might already be sending out search parties for me, and at a time like this that's crazy. Do you think you might phone from the house of one of Veena's friends?'

'We don't want anyone to know you're here,' said Maan. 'But don't worry, I'll find a way,' he said when he saw the look of sickening anxiety on his friend's face. 'I'll talk to Veena.'

Veena too had memories of Lahore; but her most recent memories were those of losing Bhaskar at the Pul Mela, and she could conceive the Nawab Sahib's agony of mind when he heard that Firoz had not returned home.

'How about trying Priya Agarwal?' said Maan. 'I could go over to her place.'

'Maan, you're not going anywhere,' said his sister. 'Are you mad? It's a five-minute walk through the alleys—this isn't why I tied the rakhi around your wrist.' After a minute's thought she said: 'I'll go to the neighbour whose phone I use in an emergency. It's only two rooftops away. You met her that day—she's a good woman, the only trouble is that she is rabidly anti-Muslim. Let me think. What's the number of Baitar House?'

Maan told her.

Veena came up to the roof with him, crossed over the connected rooftops, and descended the stairs to her neighbour's house.

Veena's large and voluble neighbour, out of her usual friendliness and curiosity, hung around while Veena made the call. The phone, after all, was in her room. Veena told her she was trying to get in touch with her father.

'But I just saw him at the Bharat Milaap, near the temple—'

'He had to go home. The noise was too much for him. And the smoke was not good for my mother either. Or for Pran's lungs—he didn't come. But Maan is here—he's had a lucky escape from a Muslim mob.'

'It must be providence,' said the woman. 'If they had got hold of him—'

The telephone was not a dialling machine; and Veena had to give the Baitar House number to the operator.

'Oh, you're not calling Prem Nivas?' said the woman, who knew that number from Veena's previous calls.

'No. Baoji had to visit friends later this evening.'

When a voice came on the line Veena said: 'I would like to speak to the Sahib.'

An aged voice at the other end said, 'Which Sahib? The Nawab Sahib or the Burré Sahib or the Chhoté Sahib?'

'Anyone,' said Veena.

'But the Nawab Sahib is in Baitar with the Burré Sahib, and Chhoté Sahib has not yet come home from the Imambara.' The aged voice—it was Ghulam Rusool—was halting and agitated. 'They say there has been trouble in town, that you can see fires even from the roof of this house. I must go now. There are arrangements—'

'Please be patient—' said Veena quickly. 'I will speak to anyone—put Sahib's secretary on the line—or anyone responsible. Call someone—anyone—to the line, please. This is Mahesh Kapoor's daughter Veena speaking, and I need to pass on an urgent message.'

There was silence for a few seconds, then the young voice of Murtaza Ali came on the line. He sounded both embarrassed and extremely anxious. He had sensed that perhaps there might be some news of Firoz.

Veena said, choosing her words with extreme care: 'I am Mahesh Kapoor's daughter. This is about Sahib's younger son.'

'The Nawab Sahib's younger son? The Chhoté Sahib?'

'Exactly. There is nothing to worry about. He is unharmed, and quite safe, and staying in Misri Mandi tonight. Please inform Sahib of that in case he should inquire.'

'God is merciful!' came the quiet response.

'He will go home tomorrow when curfew is relaxed. Meanwhile, no search parties should be sent out for him. No one should go to the police station to get a curfew pass—or come here—or talk to anyone about his being here. Just say he is staying with me—with his sister.'

'Thank you, Madam, thank you for calling us—we were just about to set out in an armed party—it would have been terrible—we imagined the worst—'

'I must go now,' said Veena, knowing that the longer she talked the more difficult it would be to maintain a protective ambiguity.

'Yes, yes,' said Murtaza Ali. 'Khuda haafiz.'

'Khuda haafiz,' replied Veena without thinking, and put down the phone.

Her neighbour looked at her strangely.

Unwilling to make further conversation with the curious woman, Veena explained that she had to go back home immediately because Bhaskar had sprained his ankle running about; and Maan and her husband needed to be fed; and old Mrs Tandon, with her memories of Pakistan, was in a panic and would need to be soothed.

15.14

But when she got back to the house, she found her mother-in-law, who was downstairs, almost incoherent with shock. Kedarnath had just gone out into the night, planning, no doubt, to calm down any people he found: to prevent them from harming others and, in case they had not heard about the curfew, themselves.

Veena almost fainted. She leaned against the wall and stared ahead of her. Finally her mother-in-law stopped sobbing and her words began to make more sense.

'He said that in this area there would be no risk from Muslims,' she whispered. 'He wouldn't listen to me. He said that it wasn't Lahore—that he would be back very shortly,' she continued, looking at Veena's face for comfort. '"Very shortly" he said. He said he would be back very shortly.' She broke down once again at the words.

Veena's mouth began to tremble. It was the phrase Kedarnath was fond of using when he went away on his interminable sales trips.

There was no comfort for the old lady to be found in Veena's face. 'Why didn't you stop him? Why didn't Maan stop him?' she cried. She was furious at her husband for this selfish and irresponsible heroism. Did she and Bhaskar and his mother not exist for him?

'Maan was on the roof,' said the old lady.

Now Bhaskar came down the stairs. Something had obviously been troubling him for a while.

'Why did Firoz Maama have so much blood all over him?' he demanded. 'Did Maan Maama beat him up? He said he didn't. But he was holding the lathi.'

'Be quiet, Bhaskar,' said Veena in a desperate voice. 'Go upstairs at once. Go upstairs and back to bed. Everything's all right. I'm here if you need me.' She gave him a hug.

Bhaskar wanted to know exactly what the matter was. 'Nothing,' said Veena. 'I have to prepare some food—don't get in my way.' She knew that if Maan got to know about what had happened he would immediately go out to look for his brother-in-law and would put himself at very grievous risk. Kedarnath at least did know exactly where the Hindu areas ended. But she was tormented with anxiety for him. Before Bhaskar had come down she had been on the verge of going out herself. Now she just waited—the most difficult thing of all.

She quickly heated some food for Maan and Firoz, and took it up, pausing on the stairs in order to appear calm.

Maan smiled when he saw her.

'It's quite warm,' said Maan. 'We'll sleep together on the roof. Just give us a mattress and a light quilt, and we'll be fine. Firoz will need a wash, and I could do with one too. Is something wrong?'

Veena shook her head. 'He almost gets killed, then asks me if something is wrong.'

She took a light quilt out of a trunk, and shook out from its folds the dried neem leaves that she used to preserve winter clothing from pests.

'Sometimes the night flowers on the roof attract insects,' she warned them.

'We'll be fine,' said Firoz. 'I am so grateful to you.'

Veena shook her head. 'Sleep well,' she said.

Kedarnath returned home five minutes before curfew. Veena wept, and refused to speak to him. She buried her face in his scarred hands.

For an hour or so Maan and Firoz remained awake. It felt as if the world was trembling beneath them. The distant sound of gunfire had died down, probably as a result of the imposition of curfew, but the glow from the fires, especially to the west, continued through the night.

15.15

On Sharad Purnima, the brightest night of the year, Pran and Savita hired a boat and went up the Ganga to look at the Barsaat Mahal. Curfew had been lifted that morning. Mrs Rupa Mehra had advised them not to go, but Savita said that no one could set fire to the river.

'And it isn't good for Pran's asthma either,' added Mrs Rupa Mehra, who believed that he should be confined to his bed and his rocking chair, and not overexert himself.

Pran had in fact slowly recovered from the worst of his illness. He was still not able to play cricket, but had built up his strength by walking, at first only around the garden, then a few hundred yards, and finally around campus or along the Ganga. He had avoided the incendiary festivities of Dussehra, and would have to avoid the firecrackers of Divali. But his trouble had not recurred in its acute form, and he had for the most part not allowed it to interfere with his academic work. Some days, when he was feeling weaker, he sat and lectured. His students were protective of him, and even his overworked colleagues on the disciplinary committee tried to relieve him of whatever duties they could.

Tonight, in particular, he felt much better. He reflected on Maan and Firoz's providential escape—and indeed Kedarnath's as well—and was inclined to minimize his own problems.

'Don't worry, Ma,' he reassured his mother-in-law. 'If anything, the river air will do me good. It's still quite warm.'

'Well, it won't be warm on the river. You should take a shawl each. Or a blanket,' grumbled Mrs Rupa Mehra.

After a pause, she said to Lata: 'Why are you looking like that? Do you have a headache?'

'No, Ma, I don't, please let me read.'

She had been thinking: thank God Maan is safe.

'What are you reading?' persisted her mother.

'Ma!'

'Bye, Lata, bye, Ma,' said Pran. 'Keep your knitting needles out of Uma's clutches.'

Mrs Rupa Mehra made a sound that was almost a grunt. She believed that one shouldn't mention such unspeakable dangers. She was knitting booties for the baby in the expectation of colder weather.

Pran and Savita walked down to the river, Pran leading the way with a torch, and helping Savita with a hand where the path was steep. He warned her to watch out for the roots of the banyan tree.

The boatman they hired from near the dhobi-ghat happened to be the same one who had taken Lata and Kabir to see the Barsaat Mahal some months previously at dawn. As usual he demanded an outrageous price. Pran brought it down slightly, but was in no mood for further haggling. He was glad Uma was too small to come with them; he was happy to be alone with Savita if only for an hour or two.

The river was still high, and a pleasant breeze was blowing.

'Ma was right—it is cold—you'd better hold on to me for warmth,' Pran said.

'Aren't you going to recite a ghazal by Mast for me?' asked Savita as she looked out, past the ghats and the Fort towards the vague silhouette of the Barsaat Mahal.

'Sorry, you've married the wrong brother,' said Pran.

'No, I don't think so,' said Savita. She leaned her head against his shoulder. 'What is that thing there with the walls and chimney—beyond the Barsaat Mahal?'

'Hmm—I don't know—perhaps the tannery or the shoe factory,' said Pran. 'But everything looks different from this side, especially at night.'

They were silent for a while.

'What's the latest on that front?' said Pran.

'You mean Haresh?'

'Yes.'

'I don't know. Lata's being secretive. But he does write and she does reply. You're the one who's met him. You said you liked him.'

'Well, it's impossible to judge someone on the basis of a single meeting,' said Pran.

'Oh, so you think so!' said Savita archly, and they both laughed. A thought struck Pran.

'I suppose I too am going to be judged soon enough on the basis of a single meeting,' he said.

'Soon enough!' said Savita.

'Well, things really are going ahead at last—'

'Or so Professor Mishra assures you.'

'No, no—in a month or two at the latest they're going to have their interviews—someone who works in the Registrar's Office mentioned it to one of my father's ex-PAs. So let's see, it's the middle of October now—'

Pran looked across towards the burning ghat. He lost the thread of his thoughts.

'How quiet the city looks,' he said. 'And when you think that Maan and Firoz could have been murdered—'

'Don't.'

'Sorry, darling. Anyway, what were you saying?'

'I've forgotten.'

'Oh, well.'

'I think,' said Savita, 'that you're in danger of becoming complacent.'

'Who—me?' said Pran, surprised rather than affronted. 'Why should I be complacent? A humble university lecturer with a weak heart, who will have to puff his way up the cliff at the end of this boat ride.'

'Well, perhaps not,' said Savita. 'Anyway, what does it feel like to have a wife and child?'

'What does it feel like? It feels wonderful.'

Savita smiled into the darkness. She had fished for a compliment, and landed one.

'This is where you'll get the best view,' said the boatman, driving his long pole deep into the bed of the river. 'I can't go further back into the current. The river's too high.'

'And I suppose it must be quite pleasant to have a husband and child,' added Pran.

'Yes,' said Savita thoughtfully. 'It is.' After a while she said: 'Sad about Meenakshi.'

'Yes. But you've never been very fond of her, have you?'

Savita did not reply.

'Has her miscarriage made you like her more?' said Pran.

'What a question! It has, in a way. Well, let me think about that. I'll know immediately when I see her again.'

'You know,' said Pran, 'I don't look forward to staying with your brother and sister-in-law over the New Year.' He closed his eyes; there was a mild and pleasant breeze on the river.

'I'm not sure there'll even be room for all of us at Sunny Park,' said Savita. 'Ma and Lata can stay with them as usual. And you and I can camp in the garden. Rock-a-bye Baby can hang from the treetop.'

Pran laughed. 'Well, at least the baby doesn't take after your brother, as I feared she might.'

'Which one?'

'Either. But I meant Arun. Well, they'll have to put us up somewhere—I suppose at the Chatterjis. I liked that boy, what's his name—'

'Amit?'

'No, the other one—the holy man who was fond of Scotch.'

'Dipankar.'

'Yes, that's it. . . . At any rate, you'll meet him when we go to Calcutta in December,' said Pran.

'But I've already met him,' Savita pointed out. 'At the Pul Mela, most recently.'

'I meant Haresh. You can appraise him at your leisure.'

'But you were just talking about Dipankar.'

'Was I, dear?'

'Really, Pran, I wish you would keep track of your conversation. It's very confusing. I'm sure this isn't how you lecture.'

'I lecture rather well,' said Pran, 'even if I say so myself. But don't take my word for it. Ask Malati.'

'I have no intention of asking Malati how you lecture. The last time she listened to you, you were so overcome you fainted away.'

The boatman was getting tired of holding his boat steady against the current. 'Do you want to talk or to watch the Barsaat Mahal?' he asked. 'You're paying me good money to come here.'

'Yes, yes, of course,' said Pran vaguely.

'You should have come here three nights ago,' said the boatman—'there were fires burning all along there. Beautiful it looked, and you couldn't smell it here on the Ganga. And the next day lots of corpses at the ghat there. Too many for one ghat to handle. The municipality has been planning another burning ghat for years now but they'll never get down to deciding where.'

'Why?' Pran couldn't resist asking.

'If it's on the Brahmpur side it'll face north like this one. Of course, by rights it should face south, in the direction of Yama. But that would put it on the other shore, and they'd have to ferry the bodies—and the passengers—across.'

'They? You mean you.'

'I suppose so. I wouldn't complain.'

For a while Pran and Savita looked at the Barsaat Mahal, lit in the full light of the full moon. Beautiful by itself, its reflection at night made it look lovelier than ever. The moon shivered gently in the water. The boatman said nothing further.

Another boat passed them. For some reason Pran shuddered.

'What's the matter, darling?'

'Nothing.'

Savita took a small coin out of her purse and put it in Pran's hand.

'Well, what I was thinking was how peaceful it all looks.'

Savita nodded to herself in the darkness. Pran suddenly realized she was crying.

'What's the matter, darling? What have I said?'

'Nothing. I'm so happy. I'm just happy.'

'How strange you are,' said Pran, stroking her hair.

The boatman released his pole and, guided only casually by him, the boat began to move downstream again. Quietly they moved down the calm and sacred river that had come down to earth so that its waters might flow over the ashes of those long dead, and that would continue to flow long after the human race had, through hatred and knowledge, burned itself out.

15.16

For the last few weeks Mahesh Kapoor had been in two minds—two uncertain and troubled minds—about whether to go back to the Congress Party. He, who was so full of definite, often dismissive, opinion, had found himself lost in a dust storm of indecision.

Too many factors were whirling around in his head and each time they came to rest they formed a new configuration.

What the Chief Minister had said to him in his garden; what the Nawab Sahib had said to him at the Fort; the visit to Prem Nivas of the seceder from U.P. who had rejoined the Congress; Baba's advice in Debaria; Nehru's coup; Rafi Sahib's circuitous return to the fold; his own beloved legislation which he wanted to make sure did not merely moulder on the statute-books; irritatingly enough, even his wife's unspoken but palpable view of the whole matter: all these told him to go back to the party that, until his slow but thorough disillusionment, had unquestionably been his home.

Things had doubtless changed greatly since that disillusionment. And yet, when he thought about it deeply, how much had really changed? Could he belong in a party that contained—could he bear to belong to a government that might possibly be run by—the likes of the present Home Minister? The list of Congress candidates that was being drawn up in the state did nothing to dispel his disillusionment. Nor, after his talk with his old Parliamentary Secretary, could he honestly claim to himself that he sensed in Nehru any new surge of decisiveness. Nehru could not even ensure the passage of his favourite bill through Parliament. Compromise and muddle had reigned, and compromise and muddle would reign.

And having once made his break, thought Mahesh Kapoor, would he not be displaying the very indecisiveness he usually condemned by returning? After decades of loyalty to one party, he who believed in principle and firmness would have turned his coat twice in the course of a few months. Kidwai may have returned, but Kripalani had not. Whose had been the more honourable course?

Angry at himself for his own uncharacteristic dithering, Mahesh Kapoor told himself that he had had enough time and enough advice to determine twenty such matters. Whatever he decided, there would be aspects of his decision he would find difficult to live with. He should stop fretting, examine the nub of the matter, and once and for all say Yes or No.

Yet what, if anything, was the nub?

Was it the zamindari legislation? Was it his dread of communal hatred and violence? Was it the real and delicious possibility that he, not Agarwal, might become Chief Minister? Was it the fear that if he remained outside the Congress, he would lose his seat—that he could maintain his purity only in the wilderness? Surely all these things pointed in the same direction. What was really holding him back but uncertainty and pride?

He stared unseeingly out from his small office towards the garden of Prem Nivas.

His wife had his tea sent to him; it went cold.

She came to ask him if he was all right and brought another cup for him herself. She said: 'So you have decided to return to the Congress? That's good.'

He responded with exasperation: 'I have decided nothing. What makes you think I have?'

'After Maan and Firoz nearly—'

'Maan and Firoz have nothing to do with it. I have been thinking this matter over for weeks without coming to any conclusion.' He looked at her in amazement.

She stirred his tea once more and placed it on the table, which was easier to do these days, since it was not covered with files.

Mahesh Kapoor sipped it and said nothing.

After a while he said, 'Leave me alone. I am not going to discuss this matter with you. Your presence is distracting me. I don't know where your far-fetched intuitions come from. But they are more inaccurate and suspect than astrology.'

15.17

Less than a week after the riots in Brahmpur, the Prime Minister of Pakistan, Liaquat Ali Khan, was shot at a public meeting that he was addressing at Rawalpindi. The murderer was done to death on the spot by the crowd.

At the news of his death, all government flags were lowered to half-mast in Brahmpur. The university court convened a meeting to express its condolences. In a city where the memory of rioting was only a week old, this had something of a sobering effect.

The Nawab Sahib was back in Brahmpur when he heard the news. He had known Liaquat Ali well, since both Baitar House and Baitar Fort had been meeting places for Muslim League leaders in his father's time. He looked at some of the old photographs of those conferences and read through some of the old correspondence between his father and Liaquat Ali. He realized—though he did not see what he could do about the fact—that he had begun to live increasingly in the past.

For the Nawab Sahib Partition had been a multiple tragedy: many of those he knew, both Muslim and Hindu, had been killed or injured or scarred by the terror of those days; he had lost two parts of his country; his family had been broken up by migration; Baitar House had come under attack through manipulations of the evacuee property laws; most of the great estate surrounding Baitar Fort was soon to be wrested from him under zamindari laws that would have been almost impossible to pass in a united India; the language of his ancestors and favourite poets was under siege; and he was conscious that even his patriotism was no longer readily accepted by many of his acquaintances. He thanked God that he still had friends like Mahesh Kapoor who understood him; and he thanked God that his son had friends like Mahesh Kapoor's son. But he felt beleaguered and beset by what was happening around him; and he reflected that if this was what he felt, it must be infinitely worse for those of his religion less insulated from the hardships of the world than himself.

I suppose I am getting old, he said to himself and querulousness is a standard symptom of senility. He could not help grieving, though, for the cultivated, level-headed Liaquat Ali, whom he had personally liked. Nor, though he had hated the thought of Pakistan once, could he turn away from it with unconcern now that it actually existed. When the Nawab Sahib thought about Pakistan, it was about West Pakistan. Many of his old friends were there, many of his relatives, many of the places of which he had warm recollections. That Jinnah should have died in the first year of Pakistan's life, and Liaquat Ali early in its fifth was no happy augury for a country that needed, more than anything else, experience in its leadership and moderation in its polity, and appeared now to be bereft of both.

The Nawab Sahib, saddened by things and feeling a stranger in the world, phoned Mahesh Kapoor to invite him over for lunch the next day.

'Please persuade Mrs Mahesh Kapoor to come as well. I will get her food from outside, of course.'

'I can't. The mad woman will be fasting for my health tomorrow. It's Karva Chauth, and she can't eat from sunrise till moonrise. Or drink a drop of water. If she does I'll die.'

'That would be unfortunate, Kapoor Sahib. There has been too much killing and dying of late,' said the Nawab Sahib. 'How is Maan, by the way?' he inquired fondly.

'Much the same. But recently I've stopped telling him three times a day to return to Banaras. There's something to be said for the boy.'

'There's a great deal to be said for the boy,' said the Nawab Sahib.

'Oh, it would have been the same the other way around,' said Mahesh Kapoor. 'Anyway, I've been thinking about my son's advice regarding constituencies. And your advice, of course, as well.'

'And about parties too, I hope.'

There was a long silence on the line.

'Yes, well, I've decided to rejoin the Congress. You're the first to know,' said Mahesh Kapoor.

The Nawab Sahib sounded pleased.

'Fight from Baitar, Kapoor Sahib,' he said. 'Fight from Baitar. You'll win, Inshallah—and with the help of your friends.'

'Let's see, let's see.'

'So you'll come for lunch tomorrow?'

'Yes, yes. What's the occasion?'

'No occasion. Just do me the favour of sitting silently through the meal and hearing me complain about how much better things were in the old days.'

'All right.'

'Give my greetings to Maan's mother,' said the Nawab Sahib. He paused. It would have been more proper to say 'Pran's mother' or even 'Veena's mother'. He stroked his beard, then continued: 'But, Kapoor Sahib, is it a sensible idea for her to fast in her present state of health?'

'Sensible!' was Mahesh Kapoor's response. 'Sensible! My dear Nawab Sahib, you are talking a language that is foreign to her.'

15.18

This language was also presumably foreign to Mrs Rupa Mehra, who stopped knitting the baby's booties on the day of Karva Chauth. Indeed, she locked up her knitting needles together with any sewing and darning needles that were lying about the house. Her reason was simple. Savita was fasting until moonrise for her husband's health and longevity, and touching a needle, even inadvertently, on that day would be disastrous.

One year an unfortunate young woman, famished during her fast, was persuaded by her anxious brothers that the moon had risen when all they had done was to light a fire behind a tree to simulate the moonglow. She had eaten a little before she had realized the trick, and soon enough the news was brought to her of her husband's sudden death. He had been pierced through and through by thousands of needles. By performing many austerities and making many offerings to the goddesses, the young widow had finally extracted their promise that if she kept the fast properly the next year her husband would return to life. Each day for the whole year she removed the needles one by one from her husband's lifeless body. The very last one, however, was removed on the day of Karva Chauth itself by a maidservant just as her master came back to life. Since she was the first woman he saw after opening his eyes, he believed that it was through her pains that he had revived. He had no choice but to discard his wife and marry her. Needles on Karva Chauth were therefore fearfully inauspicious: touch a needle and lose a husband.

What Savita, fortified in logic by law-books and grounded in reality by her baby, thought of all this was not obvious. But she observed Karva Chauth to the letter, even going to the extent of first viewing the rising moon through a sieve.

The Sahib and Memsahib of Calcutta, on the other hand, considered

Karva Chauth a signal idiocy, and were unmoved by Mrs Rupa Mehra's frantic implorations that Meenakshi—even if Brahmo by family—should observe it. 'Really, Arun,' said Meenakshi. 'Your mother does go on about things.'

One by one the Hindu festivals fell, some observed fervently, some lukewarmly, some merely noted, some entirely ignored. On five consecutive days around the end of October came Dhanteras, Hanuman Jayanti, Divali, Annakutam, and Bhai Duj. The day immediately following was observed most religiously by Pran, who kept his ear to the radio for hours: it was the first day of the first Test match of the cricket season, played in Delhi against a visiting English side.

A week later the gods at last awoke from their four months' slumber, having wisely slept through a very boring and slow-scoring draw.

15.19

But though India vs England was humdrum in the extreme, the same could not be said for the University vs Old Brahmpurians match held that Sunday at the university cricket ground.

The university team was not quite as good as it might have been, owing to a couple of injuries. Nor were the Old Brahmpurians a pushover, for their side contained not merely the usual players rustled up from here and there, but also two men who had captained the university in the last ten years or so.

Among the rustled, however, was Maan. Among the uninjured was Kabir. And Pran was one of the umpires.

It was a brilliant, clear, crisp, early November day, and the grass was still fresh and green. The mood was festive, and—with exams and other woes a million miles away—the students were out in force. They cheered and booed and stood around the field talking to the outfielders and generally creating as much excitement off the field as on. A few teachers could be seen among them.

One of these was Dr Durrani; he found cricket curiously fertile. At the moment, unmoved by the fact that his son had just bowled Maan out with a leg-break, he was thinking about the hexadic, octal, decimal and duodecimal systems and attempting to work out their various advantages.

He turned to a colleague:

'Interesting, er, wouldn't you say, Patwardhan, that the number six, which, though "perfect", has a, well, an almost fugitive existence in mathematics—except, er, in geometry, of course, should um, be the—the presiding, one might say, the presiding, um, deity of cricket, wouldn't you say?'

Sunil Patwardhan nodded but would not say. His eyes were glued to the pitch. The next player was no sooner in than out; he had been dispatched on Kabir's next ball: a googly this time. A huge roar of delight rose from the crowd.

'Six balls to an, um, over, don't you see, Patwardhan, six runs to a boundary, a, a lofted boundary, of course, and, um, six stumps on the, er, field!'

The incoming player had hardly had time to pad up. The previous batsman was already back in the pavilion by the time he walked out on to the field, flexing his bat impatiently and aggressively. He was one of the two former captains, and he was damned if he was going to provide Kabir with a hat-trick. In he went and fiercely he glared, in a sweep that encompassed not only the tense but appraising bowler, but also his own batting partner, the opposite stumps, the umpire, and a few innocuous mynas.

Like Arjun aiming his arrow at the eye of the invisible bird, Kabir stared down single-mindedly at the invisible middle stump of his adversary. Straight down the pitch came the ball, but deceptively slowly this time. The batsman tried to play it. He missed; and the dull thump of the ball as it hit his pad was like the sound of muffled doom.

Eleven voices appealed in triumphant delight, and Pran, smiling, raised his finger in the air.

He nodded at Kabir, who was grinning broadly and accepting the congratulations of his teammates.

The cheering of the crowd took more than a minute to die down, and continued sporadically for the rest of Kabir's over. Sunil executed a few swift steps of joy—a sort of kathak jig. He looked at Dr Durrani to see what effect his son's triumph had had on him.

Dr Durrani was frowning in concentration, his eyebrows working up and down.

'Curious, though, isn't it, um, Patwardhan, that the number, er, six should be, um, embodied in one of the most, er, er, beautiful, er, shapes in all nature: I refer, um, needless to say, to the er, benzene ring with its single and, er, double carbon bonds. But is it, er, truly symmetrical, Patwardhan, or, um, asymmetrical? Or asymmetrically symmetrical, perhaps, like those, er, sub-super-operations of the, er, Pergolesi Lemma . . . not really like the, er, rather unsatisfactory petals of an, um, iris. Curious, wouldn't you say . . . ?'

'Most curious,' agreed Sunil.

★

Savita was talking to Firoz:

'Of course, it's different for you, Firoz, I don't mean because you're a man as such, but because, well, you don't have a baby to distract you from your clients. Or perhaps that comes to the same thing. . . . I was talking to Jaya Sood the other day, and she tells me that there are bats—and I don't mean cricket bats!—in the High Court bathroom. When I told her I couldn't bear the thought, she said, "Well, if you're frightened of bats, why are you doing law in the first place?" But, do you know, though I never imagined I would, I actually find law interesting now, really interesting. Not like this awful sleepy game. They haven't made a run for the last ten minutes. . . . Oh no, I've just dropped a stitch, I always feel drowsy in the sun. . . . I simply can't see what Pran sees in it, or why he insists on ignoring all of us for five days with his ear glued to the radio, or being a referee and standing in the sun the whole day, but do you think my protests have any effect? "Standing in the sun is good for me," he insists. . . . Or Maan, for that matter. Before lunch he runs from one wicket to the other seven times, and now after lunch he runs along the edge of the field for a few minutes at the most, and that's that: the whole Sunday's gone! You're very sensible to stick to polo, Firoz—at least that's over in an hour—and you do get some exercise.'

Firoz was thinking about Maan:

My dearest, dearest Maan, you've saved my life all right and I love you dearly, but if you keep nattering to Lata, your captain will forfeit your own.

Maan was talking to Lata:

'No, no, it's all right to talk, no ball ever comes my way. They know what a fantastic player I am, so they've put me here on the boundary where I can't drop any catches or overthrow the ball or anything. And if I go off to sleep, it doesn't matter. Do you know, I think you're looking very beautiful today, no, don't make a face. I've always thought so—green suits you, you know. You just merge with the grass like a . . . a nymph! a peri in paradise. . . . No, no, not at all, I think we're doing tremendously well. All out for 219 isn't bad, after such a poor beginning, and now we've got them at 157 for 7. They've got hopeless people at the bottom of their batting order. I don't think they have a chance. . . . The Old Brahmpurians haven't won in a decade, so it'll be a great victory! The only danger is this wretched Durrani fellow, who's still batting on at . . . what does the scoreboard say? 68. . . . Once we've forked him off the pitch we'll be home and dry. . . .'

Lata was thinking about Kabir:

> O spirit of love! how quick and fresh art thou,
> That notwithstanding thy capacity
> Receiveth as the sea, nought enters there,
> Of what validity and pitch soe'er
> But falls into abatement and low price. . . .

A few mynas were sitting on the field, their faces turned towards the batsmen, and the mild, warm sun shone down on her as the sound of bat on ball continued drowsily—interspersed occasionally by a cheer—through the late afternoon. She broke off a blade of grass, and moved it gently up and down her arm.

Kabir was talking to Pran:

'Thanks; no, the light's fine, Dr Kapoor . . . oh, thank you—well, it was just a fluke this morning. . . .'

Pran was thinking about Savita:

I know our whole Sunday's gone, darling, but next Sunday I'll do whatever you want. I promise. If you wish, I'll hold a huge ball of wool instead, while you knit twenty booties for the baby.

*

Kabir had gone in fourth, higher up than usual in the batting order, but had more than justified himself there. He had noticed Lata in the crowd, but this had the effect, oddly enough, of steadying his nerves—or increasing his determination. His score mounted, mainly through boundaries, not a few of which got past Maan, and it now stood in the nineties.

One by one his partners had dropped away, however, and the fall of wickets told its own story: 140 for 4, 143 for 5, 154 for 6, 154 for 7, 183 for 8, and now 190 for 9. There were 29 runs to score for a tie, 30 for a win, and his new partner was the exceedingly nervous wicket-keeper! Too bad, thought Kabir. He's lived so long behind the stumps that he doesn't know what to do with himself when he's in front of them. Luckily it's the beginning of the over. Still, he'll be out the first ball he faces, poor chap. The whole thing's impossible, but I wonder if I'll at least manage to get my century.

The wicket-keeper, however, played an admirable second fiddle, and Kabir got the strategic singles that enabled him to keep the bowling. When the University stood at 199, with his own score at 98, on the last ball of the last-but-one over—with three minutes to go before end of play—he tried to make his usual single. As he and his partner passed each other, he said: 'We'll draw it yet!'

A cheer had gone up for the anticipated 200 while they were still running. The fielder hurled the ball at Kabir's wicket. It missed by a hair, but hurtled onwards with such force that poor Maan, who had begun, gallantly, to clap, realized too late what was happening. Too late did he run towards it, too late did he try to hurl himself at it as it sped past his extended length to the boundary.

A great cheer rose from the university ranks—but whether for Kabir's fortuitous five off a single ball, or for his century, or for the university's double-century, or for the fact that with sixteen, rather than twenty, runs to win in the last over, they suddenly felt they still had a chance, no one could say.

The captain of the Old Brahmpurians, a major from the cantonment, glared at Maan.

But now, to a background of cheers and jeers and shouts, Kabir faced the final over. He hit a grand cover drive for four, lofted the next ball just over long on for another, and faced the third ball to a complete and petrified silence from spectators of both sides alike.

It was a good-length ball. He hit it towards mid-wicket, but the moment he realized it was only worth a single, he waved his partner urgently back.

They ran two on the next ball.

It was now the last ball but one, with five runs to tie and six to win. No one dared to breathe. No one had the least idea of what Kabir was aiming to do—or the bowler for that matter. Kabir passed his gloved hand through his wavy hair. Pran thought he looked unnaturally calm at the crease.

Perhaps the bowler had succumbed to his tension and frustration, for amazingly enough his next ball was a full-toss. Kabir, with a smile on his face and happiness in his heart, hit it high in the air with all the force he could muster, and watched it as it sailed in a serene parabola towards victory.

High, high, high it rose in the air, carrying with it all the joy and hopes and blessings of the university. A murmur, not yet a cheer, arose all around, and then swelled into a shout of triumph.

But, as Kabir watched, a dreadful thing happened. For Maan, who too had been watching the red grenade ascend and then descend, and whose mouth was open in an expression of trance-like dismay, suddenly found himself at the very edge of the boundary, almost leaning backwards. And, to his considerable amazement, the ball lay in his hands.

The cheer became a sudden silence, then a great collective groan, to be replaced by an amazed shout of victory by the Old Brahmpurians. A finger moved skywards. The bails were taken off. The players stood dazed in the field, shaking hands and shaking heads. And Maan somersaulted five times for sheer joy in the direction of the spectators.

*

What a goof! thought Lata, watching Maan. Perhaps I should elope with him next April 1st.

'How's that? How's that? How's that?' Maan asked Firoz, hugging him, then rushed back to his team to be applauded as the hero of the day.

Firoz noticed Savita raise her eyebrows. He raised his eyebrows back at her; he wondered what she had made of the soporific climax.

'Still awake—just about,' Savita said, smiling at Pran as he came off the field a few minutes later.

A nice fellow—plucky under pressure, thought Pran, watching Kabir detach himself from his friends and walk towards them, his bat under his arm. A pity. . . .

'Fluke of a catch,' murmured Kabir disgustedly, almost under his breath, as he passed Lata on his way back to the pavilion.

15.20

The Hindu festive season was almost over. But for Brahmpur one festival, observed much more devotedly here than almost anywhere in India, that of Kartik Purnima, remained. The full moon of Kartik brings to an end one of the three especially sacred months for bathing; and since Brahmpur lies on the holiest river of all, many pious people observe their daily dip throughout the month, eat their single meal, worship the tulsi plant, and hang lamps suspended from the end of bamboo poles in small baskets to guide departed souls across the sky. As the Puranas say: 'What fruit was obtained in the Perfect Age by doing austerities for one hundred years, all that is obtained by a bath in the Five Rivers during the month of Kartik.'

It is of course also possible that the city of Brahmpur could be said to have a special claim on this festival because of the god whose name the city bears. A seventeenth century commentator on the Mahabharata wrote: 'Brahma's festival is celebrated by all, and is held in autumn when the corn has begun to grow.' Certainly in Pushkar, the greatest living shrine to Brahma in all India (indeed, the only one of any great significance other than Gaya and—possibly—Brahmpur), it is Kartik Purnima that is the time of the great camel fair and the visit of tens of thousands of pilgrims. The image of Brahma in the great temple there is daubed with orange paint and decorated with tinsel by his devotees in the manner of other gods. Perhaps the strong observance of the festival in Brahmpur is a residue of the time when Brahma was worshipped here too, in his own city, as a bhakti god, a god of personal devotion, before he was displaced in this role by Shiva—or by Vishnu in one or other of his incarnations.

A residue is all it is, however, because for most of the year one would not suspect Brahma to be a presence in Brahmpur at all. It is his rivals—or colleagues—of the trinity who hold the limelight. The Pul Mela or the Chandrachur Temple speak of the power of Shiva, whether as the source of the Ganga or as the great sensual ascetic symbolized by the linga. As for Vishnu: the notable presence of numerous Krishna devotees (such as Sanaki Baba) and the fervent celebration (by those like Mrs Mahesh Kapoor) of Janamashtami bear witness to his presence as Krishna; and his presence as Rama is unmistakable not only during Ramnavami early in the year but during the nine nights culminating in Dussehra, when Brahmpur is part of an island of Rama worship in a sea of goddess worship that extends from Bengal to Gujarat.

Why Brahma, the Self-Created or Egg-born, the overseer of sacrifice, the Supreme Creator, the old four-faced god who set in motion the triple world, should have suffered eclipse over the centuries is unclear. At one time even Shiva is shown cringing in the Mahabharata before him; and it is from a common root with Brahma himself that the words not only for 'brahmin' but also for 'brahman', the world-soul, derive. But by the time of the late Puranas, not to mention modern times, his influence had waned to a shadow.

Perhaps it was because—unlike Shiva or Rama or Krishna or Durga or Kali—he was never associated with youth or beauty or terror, those well-springs of personal devotion. Perhaps it was because he was too far above suffering and yearning to satisfy the longing of the heart for an identifiably human ideal or intercessor—one perhaps who had come down to earth to suffer with the rest of mankind in order that righteousness might be established. Perhaps it was because certain myths surrounding him—for instance his creation of mankind by intercourse with his own daughter—were too difficult to accept by a constant following over long ages and changing mores.

Or perhaps it was that, refusing to be turned on and off like a tap by requests for intercession, Brahma at last refused to deliver what was asked of him by millions of upraised hands, and therefore fell out of favour. It is rare for religious feeling to be entirely transcendent, and Hindus as much as anyone else, perhaps more so, are eager for terrestrial, not merely post-terrestrial, blessings. We want specific results, whether to cure a child of disease or to guarantee his IAS results, whether to ensure the birth of a son or to find a suitable match for a daughter. We go to a temple to be blessed by our chosen deity before a journey, and have our account books sanctified by Kali or Saraswati. At Divali, the words 'shubh laabh'—auspicious profit—are seen on the walls of every newly whitewashed shop; while Lakshmi, the presiding goddess, smiles from a poster as she sits on her lotus, serene and beautiful, dispensing gold coins from one of her four arms.

It must be admitted that there are those, mainly Shaivites and Vaishnavites, who claim that Brahmpur has nothing to do with the god Brahma at all—that the name is a corruption of Bahrampur or Brahminpur or Berhampur or some other such name, whether Islamic or Hindu. But for one reason or another these theories may be discarded. The evidence of coins, of inscriptions, of historical records and travellers' accounts from Hsuen Tsang to Al-Biruni, from Babur to Tavernier, not to mention those of British travellers, provide ample evidence of the ancient name of the city.

It should be mentioned in passing that the spelling Brumpore, which the British insisted on imposing on the city, was converted back to its more phonetic transcription when the name of the state itself was changed to

Purva Pradesh under the Protected Provinces (Alteration of Name) Order, 1949, which came into operation a few months before the commencement of the Constitution. The spelling Brumpore was the source, however, of not a few errors by amateur etymologists during the two centuries of its prevalence.

There are even a few misguided souls who assert that the name Brahmpur is a variant of Bhrampur—the city of illusion or error. But the proper response to this hypothesis is that there are always people willing to believe anything, however implausible, merely in order to be contrary.

15.21

'Pran darling, please turn off that light.'

The switch was near the door.

Pran yawned. 'Oh, I'm too sleepy,' was his response.

'But I can't sleep with it on,' said Savita.

'What if I had been sitting in the other room, working late? Wouldn't you have been able to do it yourself?'

'Yes, of course, darling,' yawned Savita, 'but you're closer to the door.'

Pran got out of bed, switched off the light, and staggered back.

'The moment Pran darling appears,' he said, 'a use is found for him.'

'Pran, you're so lovable,' said Savita.

'Of course! Anyone would be who dances attendance. But when Malati Trivedi finds me lovable. . . .'

'As long as you don't find her lovable. . . .'

And they drifted off to sleep.

At two in the morning the phone rang.

The insistent double ring pierced their dreams. Pran woke up with a shock. The baby woke up and started crying. Savita hushed her.

'Good heavens! Who could that be?' cried Savita, startled. 'It'll wake up the whole house—at—what's the time?—I hope it's nothing serious—'

Pran had stumbled out of the room.

'Hello?' he said, picking up the receiver. 'Hello, Pran Kapoor here.'

There was the sound of thick breathing at the other end. Then a voice rasped out:

'Good! This is Marh.'

'Yes?' said Pran, trying to keep his voice low. Savita had got out of bed.

He shook his head to reassure her that it was nothing serious and when she returned to bed he closed the dining room door.

'This is Marh! The Raja of Marh.'

'Yes, yes, I understand. Yes, Your Highness, what can I do for you?'

'You know exactly what you can do for me.'

'I am sorry, Your Highness, but if this is about your son's expulsion, there's nothing I can tell you. You've received a letter from the university—'

'You—you—do you know who I am?'

'Perfectly, Your Highness. Now it is somewhat late—'

'You listen to me, if you don't want something to happen to you—or to someone who matters to you. You rescind that order.'

'Your Highness, I—'

'Just because of some prank—and I know that your brother is just as—my son tells me he turned him upside down and shook the money out of his pockets when he was gambling—you tell your brother—and your land-robbing father—'

'My father?'

'Your whole family needs to be taught a lesson—'

The baby started to cry again. A note of fury appeared in the voice of the Raja of Marh.

'Is that your baby?'

Pran was silent.

'Did you hear me?'

'Your Highness, I would like to forget this conversation. But if you phone me up again at this hour without cause, or if I receive any further threats from you, I will have to report the matter to the police.'

'Without cause?—you expel my son for a prank—'

'Your Highness, this was not some prank. The university authorities made the facts quite clear in their letter to you. Taking part in a communal riot is not a prank. Your son is lucky that he is still alive and out of jail.'

'He must graduate. He must. He has bathed in the Ganga—he is now a snaatak.'

'That was somewhat premature,' Pran said, trying to keep the scorn out of his voice. 'And your distress on that count cannot be expected to outweigh the decision of the committee. Goodnight, Your Highness.'

'Not so quick! You listen to me now—I know you voted to expel him.'

'That is neither here nor there, Your Highness—I saved him from trouble once before, but—'

'It is very much here and there. When my temple is completed—do you know that it will be my son, my son whom you are trying to martyr, who will lead the ceremonies—and that the wrath of Shiva—'

Pran put down the phone. He sat down at the dining table for a minute or two, staring at it and shaking his head.

'Who was that?' asked Savita when he returned to bed.

'Oh, no one, some lunatic who wanted to get his son admitted to the university,' said Pran.

15.22

The Congress Party was hard at work selecting its candidates. Throughout October and November the State Election Committees worked on, while festivals came and went, and disturbances erupted and subsided, and white-and-orange blossoms floated down from their twigs at dawn.

District by district they selected those they believed should be given Congress tickets for the Legislative Assemblies and for Parliament. In Purva Pradesh the well-packed committee guided by L.N. Agarwal did its best to keep the so-called seceders out of the running. They used every ploy imaginable—procedural, technical, and personal—in order to do so. With an average of six applicants for every ticket, there were grounds enough to tilt a decision towards candidates of one's own political persuasion without creating obvious evidence of bias. The board worked hard, and to good effect. It sat for ten hours a day for weeks on end. It balanced caste and local standing, money power and years spent in British jails. Most of all it considered whose faction a particular applicant belonged to and the chances of his (or, rarely, her) electoral success. L.N. Agarwal was well satisfied with the list. So was S.S. Sharma, who was happy to see the popular Mahesh Kapoor back but keen that he should not rejoin with too long a tail of followers.

Finally, with an eye towards the approval of the Prime Minister and the committees in Delhi which would screen their list, the P.P. Election Committee made a token gesture towards the seceders by inviting three of their representatives (among them Mahesh Kapoor) to the last two days of their meetings. When the seceders saw the list prepared by the committee, they were appalled. It contained almost no one from their group. Even sitting MLAs had been dropped as candidates if they belonged to the minority faction. Mahesh Kapoor himself had been deprived of his urban constituency and told that he could not have Rudhia either—it had been promised to a Member of Parliament who was returning to the state to rejoin the Legislative Assembly. If Mahesh Kapoor had not left the Congress (so the committee said) they would not have given his seat away; but by the time he rejoined the party it was too late, and they could do nothing. But instead of forcing him to accept a seat of their choosing, they would be accommodating and allow him a choice of the few seats still unsettled.

The three representatives of the seceders walked out of the meeting in disgust on the morning of the second day. They said that these meetings at the tail-end of the selection process, held in a hostile and partisan spirit when the list was almost complete, had been a waste of time—a farce aimed at duping Delhi into believing that they had been consulted. The election board for its part issued its own statement to the press, stating that it had sought the seceders' opinions earnestly and in a spirit of reconciliation. The board had 'given them every opportunity for cooperation and advice'.

It was not merely the seceders who were disgruntled. For every man or woman selected, there were five others who had had to be rejected, and many of them made haste to smear the names of their rivals before the scrutiny committees that met in Delhi to examine the lists.

The seceders too took their case to Delhi; there the bitterness continued. Nehru, among others, was almost sickened by the naked desire for power, the willingness to injure, and the unconcern for the effect on the party itself, that characterized the process of scrutiny and appeal. The Congress offices in Delhi were besieged by all manner of applicants and supporters who thrust petitions into influential hands and flung mud promiscuously about them. Even old and trusted Congress workers, who had spent years in jail, and had sacrificed everything for their country, now grovelled before junior clerks in the election office in an attempt to get a seat.

Nehru was on the side of the seceders, but the entire business had grown to be so filthy with ego, greed and ambition that his fastidiousness prevented him from championing them properly, from entering the gutter to wrestle with the entrenched powers in the state machines. The seceders grew alarmed and optimistic by turns. Sometimes it appeared to them that Nehru, exhausted by his earlier battle, would be happy to leave politics altogether and retire into his roses and reading. At other times Nehru tilted furiously at the state lists. At one point it appeared that an alternative list presented by the seceders from Purva Pradesh would actually displace the official list submitted by the State Election Committee. But after a talk with S.S. Sharma, Nehru changed his mind once again. Sharma, that wise psychologist, had offered to accept the unwelcome list and even to campaign for it if that was what Nehru wanted, but he begged in that case to be relieved of the office of Chief Minister or any other office in Government. This, as Nehru realized, would never do. Without S.S. Sharma's personal following and his adroitness at coalition-building and campaigning, the Congress Party in Purva Pradesh would be in deep trouble.

So factious and prolonged had been the selection of candidates at every stage that the Congress Party lists were finalized in Delhi just two days before the deadline for the filing of nominations in Purva Pradesh. Jeeps rushed around the countryside, telegraph wires hummed frantically, candidates rushed about in a panic from Delhi to Brahmpur or from Brahmpur to their allotted constituencies. Two of them even missed the deadline, one because his supporters were so keen to smother him with marigold garlands along his route to the station that he missed his train. The other entered the wrong government offices twice before he finally found the correct one and rushed inside, waving his nomination papers. It was two minutes past the deadline of three o'clock. He burst into tears.

But these were merely two constituencies. There were nearly four thousand in the country as a whole. The candidates for these had now been selected, the nominations had been filed, the party symbols chosen, the teeth bared. Already the Prime Minister had paid a few flying visits here and there to speak on behalf of the Congress Party; and soon electioneering in Purva Pradesh too would begin in earnest.

And then finally it would be the voters who mattered, the great washed and unwashed public, sceptical and gullible, endowed with universal adult suffrage, six times as numerous as those permitted to vote in 1946. It was in fact to be the largest election ever held anywhere on earth. It would involve a sixth of its people.

Mahesh Kapoor, having been denied Misri Mandi and Rudhia (West), had managed at least to be selected as the Congress candidate from Salimpur-cum-Baitar. He would never have imagined such an outcome a few months earlier. Now, because of Maan and L.N. Agarwal and the Nawab Sahib and Nehru and Bhaskar and S.S. Sharma and Jha and probably a hundred other known and unknown agents, he was about to fight for his political life and ideals from a constituency where he was a virtual stranger. To say that he was anxious was to put it mildly.

Part Sixteen

16.1

Kabir's face lit up when he saw Malati enter the Blue Danube. He had drunk two cups of coffee already and had ordered a third. Outside the frosted glass the streetlights of Nabiganj glowed brightly but indistinctly, and the shadowy forms of pedestrians wandered past.

'Ah, so you've come.'

'Yes. Of course. I got your note this morning.'

'I haven't chosen a bad time for you?'

'No worse than any other,' said Malati. 'Oh, that sounds bad. What I meant was that life is so hectic I don't know why I don't simply collapse. When I was in Nainital and far away from anyone whom I knew I was quite at peace.'

'I hope you don't mind sitting in a corner? We could change.'

'No, I prefer it.'

'Well, what'll you have?' asked Kabir.

'Oh, just a cup of coffee, nothing more. I have to go to a wedding. That's why I'm so overdressed.'

Malati was wearing a green silk sari with a broad border in a darker green and gold. She was looking ravishing. Her eyes were a deeper green than usual.

'I like what you're wearing,' said Kabir, impressed. 'Green and gold—quite dazzling. And that necklace with those little green things and that paisley pattern.'

'Those little green things are emeralds,' said Malati, laughing a little, indignantly but delightfully.

'Oh, well, you see, I'm not used to this stuff. It looks lovely, though.'

The coffee came. They sipped it and talked to each other about the photographs of the play, which had come out well, about the hill stations they had both been to, about skating and riding, about recent politics and other events, including the religious riots. Malati was surprised how easy Kabir was to talk to, how likable he was, how very handsome. Now that he was no longer Malvolio, it was easier to take him seriously. On the other hand, since he had once been Malvolio, she felt something of a sense of guild solidarity with him.

'Did you know that there's more snow and ice in India than anywhere else in the world other than the poles?'

'Really?' said Malati. 'No I didn't.' She stirred her coffee. 'But I don't know lots of things. Such as, for instance, what this meeting's about.'

Kabir was forced to come to the point.

'It's about Lata.'

'I thought as much.'

'She won't see me, she won't answer my notes. It's as if she hates me.'

'Of course she doesn't, don't be melodramatic,' laughed Malati. 'She likes you, I think,' she said more seriously. 'But you know what the problem is.'

'Well, I can't stop thinking about her,' said Kabir, his spoon going round and round his cup. 'I'm always wondering when she'll meet someone else, just like she met me—whom she'll get to like more than me. Then I won't have any chance at all. I just can't stop thinking of her. And I feel so strangely low, it's no joke. I must have walked around the college grounds five times yesterday, thinking she was here—or she wasn't here—the bench, the slope down to the river, the steps of the exam hall, the cricket field, the auditorium—she's really getting me annoyed. That's why I want you to help me.'

'Me?'

'Yes. I must be crazy to love anyone so much. Not crazy, well. . . .' Kabir looked down, then continued quietly. 'It's difficult to explain, you know, Malati. With her I had a sense of joy—of happiness, which, really, I hadn't had for at least a year. But it lasted for no time at all. She's so cool towards me now. Tell her I'll run away with her if she wants—no, that's ridiculous, tell her—how can she—she's not even religious.' He paused. 'I'll never be able to forget the look on her face when she realized I was Malvolio! She was furious!' He started laughing, then sobered up again. 'So it's all up to you.'

'What can I do?' asked Malati, wanting to pat his head. He seemed in his confusion to believe that she had endless power over Lata, which was quite flattering.

'You can intercede with her on my behalf.'

'But she's just gone to Calcutta with her family.'

'Oh.' Kabir looked thoughtful. 'Calcutta again? Well, write to her then.'

'Why do you love her?' asked Malati, looking at him strangely. In the course of a year, the number of Lata-lovers had shot up from zero to at least three. At this rate it would hit the double digits by next year.

'Why?' Kabir looked at Malati in amazement. 'Why? Because she has six toes. I have no idea why I love her, Malati—anyway, that's irrelevant. Will you help me?'

'All right.'

'All this is having the strangest effect on my batting,' continued Kabir, not even pausing to thank her. 'I'm hitting more sixes, but getting out sooner. But I performed well against the Old Brahmpurians when I knew she was watching. Odd, isn't it?'

'Very odd,' said Malati, trying to restrict her smile to her eyes.

'I'm not exactly an innocent, you know,' said Kabir, a bit piqued at her amusement.

'I should hope not!' said Malati, laughing. 'Good, I'll write to Calcutta. Just remain at the crease.'

16.2

Arun managed to keep his mother's birthday party a secret from her. He had invited a few older ladies for tea—her Calcutta friends with whom she occasionally played rummy—and he had generously forborne from inviting the Chatterjis.

The tip of the tail of the cat was let out of the bag by Varun, however, who, ever since sitting for his IAS exams, had been feeling that he had fulfilled enough of his duty to last a decade. The Winter Season was on, and the beat of galloping hooves was pounding in his ears.

One day he looked up from the racing form and said: 'But I won't be able to go on that day, because that's when your party—oh!'

Mrs Rupa Mehra, who was saying, '3, 6, 10, 3, 6, 20,' looked up from her knitting and said, 'What is that, Varun? . . . You've disturbed my counting. What party?'

'Oh,' said Varun, 'I was talking to myself, Ma. My friends are, you know, well, throwing a party and it will interfere with a race-meeting.' He looked relieved that he had covered up so well.

Mrs Rupa Mehra decided that she wanted to be surprised after all, so she did not follow up the matter. But she was in a state of suppressed excitement for the next few days.

On the morning of her birthday she opened all her cards (a good two-thirds of which were illustrated with roses) and read each one out to Lata and Savita and Pran and Aparna and the baby. (Meenakshi had made good her escape.) Then she complained of eye-strain, and asked Lata to reread them back to her. The one from Parvati read as follows:

> Dearest Rupa,
>
> Your father and I wish you millions of happinesses on the occasion of your birthday, and hope that you are recovering well in Calcutta. Kishy joins me in saying Happy New Year in advance as well.
>
> With fondest affection,
> Parvati Seth

'And what am I supposed to be recovering from?' demanded Mrs Rupa Mehra. 'No, I don't want that one read again.'

In the evening, Arun left work early. He collected the cake that he had ordered from Flury's and a large number of pastries and patties. While waiting at an intersection, he noticed a man selling roses by the dozen. Arun rolled down his window and asked him the price. But the first price the man mentioned was so shocking that Arun yelled at him and began to roll up his window. He continued to glower even though the man was now shaking his head apologetically and pushing the flowers up against the pane.

But now that the car was moving, Arun thought of his mother again, and was almost tempted to tell the driver to halt. But no! it would have been intolerable to go back to the flower seller and haggle with him. He had been absolutely mad angry, and he was still furious.

He thought of a colleague of his father's, about ten years his father's senior, who had recently shot himself out of rage just after his retirement. One evening his drink had been brought upstairs by his old servant, and he had flown into a fury because it had been brought without a tray. He had shouted at the servant, called his wife up, and told her to fire him immediately. This sort of thing had happened often enough in the past, and his wife told the servant to go down. Then she told her husband that she would speak to the servant in the morning, and that he should drink his whisky in the meantime. 'You only care for your servants,' he told her. She went down and, as was her habit, turned on the radio.

A few minutes later, she was startled by the sound of a shot. As she went upstairs, she heard another shot. She found her husband lying in a pool of blood. The first shot, applied immediately to his head, had glanced off and grazed his ear. The second had gone through his throat.

No one else in the Mehra family, when they heard the shocking news, had been able to understand the logic of it, least of all the appalled Mrs Rupa Mehra, who had known the man; but Arun felt that he understood it all too well. Rage did act like this. Sometimes he felt so angry that he wanted to kill himself or someone else, and he cared neither what he said nor what he did.

Once again Arun thought of what his life would have been like had his father been alive. A great deal more carefree than it was today, he thought—with everyone to support financially as he now had to; with Varun to place in a job somehow, since he was bound not to get through the IAS exam; with Lata to get married off to someone suitable before Ma got her married off to this Haresh fellow.

By now he had arrived home. He had the confectionery taken to the kitchen through the back. Then, humming to himself, he greeted his mother once again. Her eyes filled with tears and she hugged him. 'You came back early just for me,' she exclaimed. He noticed that she was wearing her rather nice fawn silk sari, and this puzzled him. But when the guests arrived, she displayed a very satisfying astonishment and delight.

'And I'm not even properly dressed—my sari's all crushed! Oh, Asha Di, how sweet of you to come—how sweet of Arun to have invited you—and I had no idea, none!' she exclaimed.

Asha Di was the mother, as it happened, of one of Arun's old flames, and Meenakshi insisted on telling her how domesticated Arun had become. 'Why, he spends half his evenings on the floor, doing jigsaw puzzles with Aparna.'

A wonderful time was had by all. Mrs Rupa Mehra ate more chocolate cake than her doctor would have advised. Arun told her that he had tried to get her some roses on the way home but had not succeeded.

When the guests had left, Mrs Rupa Mehra began opening her gifts. Arun, meanwhile, with only a word to Meenakshi, drove off in the Austin to try to locate the flower seller again.

But when she opened the gift from Arun and Meenakshi she burst into injured tears. It was a very expensive Japanese lacquer box, which someone had given Meenakshi, and which Meenakshi had once, within earshot of her mother-in-law, described as being 'utterly ugly, but I suppose I can always give it away'.

Mrs Rupa Mehra had retreated from the drawing room and was sitting on her bed in the small bedroom with a hunted expression on her face.

'What's the matter, Ma?' said Varun.

'But the box is beautiful, Ma,' said Savita.

'You can keep the lacquer box, I don't care,' sobbed Mrs Rupa Mehra. 'I don't care whether I have the flowers or not, I know what he was feeling, what love he has for me, you can say anything you like, but I know. You can say anything you like, now you all go away, I want to be by myself.'

They looked at her with incredulity—it was as if Garbo had decided to join the Pul Mela.

'Oh, Ma's just being difficult. Arun treats her much better than he treats me,' said Meenakshi.

'But, Ma—' said Lata.

'You also, go now. I know him, he is like his father. For all his tempers, his tantrums, his blow-ups, his fussiness, he has a big heart. But Meenakshi, for all her style, her thankyous, her goodbyes, her elegant laughter, her lacquer boxes, her Ballygunge Chatterjis, doesn't care for anyone. And least of all for me.'

'That's right, Ma—' said Meenakshi. 'If at first you don't succeed, cry, cry again.'

Impossible! she thought to herself, and walked out of the bedroom.

'But, Ma—' said Savita, turning the box around in her hands.

Mrs Rupa Mehra shook her head.

Slowly, with puzzled looks, her children filed out.

Mrs Rupa Mehra started weeping again and hardly noticed or cared. No one understood her, none of her children, no one, not even Lata. She wanted never to see another birthday. Why had her husband gone and died when she had loved him so much? No one would ever hold her again as a man holds a woman, no one would cheer her up as one cheers up a child, her husband was eight years dead, and soon he would be eighteen years dead, and soon twenty-eight.

She had wanted to have some fun in life when she was young. But her mother had died and she had had to take care of the younger children. Her father had always been impossible. She had had a few happy years of married life, and then Raghubir had died. Life had pressed in on her, a widow with too many encumbrances.

She was seized with anger against her late husband, who used to bring her an armful of red roses every birthday, and against fate, and against God.

Where is there justice in this world, she said, when I have to observe our birthdays and our anniversary each year in loneliness that even my children can't understand? Take me soon from this horrible world, she prayed. Just let me see this stupid Lata married and Varun settled in a job, and my first grandson, and then I can die happily.

16.3

Dipankar stepped out of his hut in the garden after having meditated for an hour or so. He had come to a decision about the next step in his life. This decision was irrevocable unless he changed his mind.

The old gardener and the short, dark, cheerful young fellow who assisted him were at work among the roses. Dipankar stopped to talk to them, and heard disturbing complaints. The driver's ten-year-old son had been at his destruction again; he had lopped the heads off a few of the chrysanthemums that were still blooming against the creeper-covered fence which hid the servants' quarters. Dipankar, for all his non-violence and meditation, felt like cuffing the boy. It was so pointless and idiotic. Speaking to the boy's father had done no good. The driver had merely looked resentful. The fact was that the mother ruled the roost, and let the boy do what he wanted.

Cuddles bounded towards Dipankar, barking hoarsely. Dipankar, though his mind was on other matters, threw him a stick. Back bounded Cuddles, demanding affection: he was a strange dog, murderous and loving by turns. A bedraggled myna tried to dive-bomb Cuddles; Cuddles appeared to take this in his stride.

'Can I take him for a walk, Dada?' said Tapan, who had just come down the steps from the verandah. Tapan was looking, as he had been ever since he had returned for the winter holidays, even more disoriented than he usually did after the long train journey.

'Yes, of course. Keep him out of Pillow's way. . . . What's the matter with you, Tapan? It's been a fortnight since you returned, and you're still looking miserable. I know you haven't been calling Ma and Baba "Ma'am" and "Sir" for the past week—'

Tapan smiled.

'—but you're still keeping out of everyone's way. Come and help me in the garden if you don't know what to do with yourself, but don't just sit in your room reading comics. Ma says she's tried to talk to you but you say that nothing's the matter, that you just want to leave school and never go back again. Well, why? What's wrong with Jheel? I know you've had a few migraines these last few months, and they're very painful, but that could happen anywhere—'

'Nothing,' said Tapan, rubbing his fist on Cuddles' furry white head. 'Bye, Dada. See you at lunch.'

Dipankar yawned. Meditation often had this effect on him. 'So what if you've just got a bad report? Your last term's report wasn't much good either, and you weren't behaving like this. You haven't even spent a day with your Calcutta friends.'

'Baba was very stern when he saw my report.'

Mr Justice Chatterji's gentle reproof carried a great deal of weight with the boys in the family. With Meenakshi and Kuku, it was duck's water.

Dipankar frowned. 'Perhaps you should meditate a bit.'

A look of distaste spread across Tapan's face. 'I'm taking Cuddles for a walk,' he said. 'He looks restless.'

'You're talking to me,' said Dipankar. 'I'm not your Amit Da; you can't fob me off with excuses.'

'Sorry, Dada. Yes.' Tapan tensed.

'Come up to my room.' Dipankar had once been a prefect at Jheel School, and at one level knew how to exercise authority—though now he did it in a sort of dreamy way.

'All right.'

As they walked upstairs Dipankar said:

'And even Bahadur's favourite dishes don't seem to please you. He was saying yesterday that you snapped at him. He's an old servant.'

'I'm sorry.' Tapan really did look unhappy, and now that he was in Dipankar's room, almost trapped.

The room itself contained no chairs, just a bed, a variety of mats (including Buddhist prayer-mats), and a large painting that Kuku had made of the swamps of the Sundarbans. The single bookshelf contained religious books, a few economics textbooks, and a red bamboo flute—which Dipankar, when the mood took him, played very untunefully and fervently.

'Sit down on that mat,' said Dipankar, indicating a square blue cloth mat with a purple and yellow circular design in the middle. 'Now what is it? It's something to do with school, I know, and it isn't the report.'

'It's nothing,' said Tapan, desperately. 'Dada, why can't I leave? I just don't like it there. Why can't I join St Xavier's here in Calcutta, like Amit

Da? He didn't have to go to Jheel.'

'Well, if you want—' shrugged Dipankar.

He reflected that it was only after Amit was well ensconced at St Xavier's that some of Mr Justice Chatterji's colleagues had recommended Jheel School to him—so strongly, in fact, that he had decided to send his second son there. Dipankar had enjoyed it, and had done better than his parents had expected; and Tapan had therefore followed.

'When I told Ma I wanted to leave, she got annoyed and said that I should speak to Baba—and I just can't speak to Baba. He'll ask me for reasons. And there are no reasons. I just hate it, that's all. That's why I get those headaches. Apart from that, I'm not unfit, or anything.'

'Is it that you miss home?' asked Dipankar.

'No—I mean, I don't really—' Tapan shook his head.

'Has someone been trying to bully you?'

'Please let me go, now, Dada. I don't want to talk about it.'

'Well, if I let you go now you'll never tell me. So what is it? Tapan, I want to help you, but you've got to tell me what happened. I promise I won't tell anyone.'

He was distressed to notice that Tapan had started crying; and that now, enraged with himself, he was wiping away his tears and looking resentfully at his elder brother. To cry at thirteen was, he knew, a disgrace. Dipankar put his arm around his shoulder; it was angrily shrugged off. But slowly the story emerged, amid explosive outbursts, long silences, and furious sobs, and it was not a pleasant one, even to Dipankar, who had been to Jheel School years before, and was prepared for quite a lot.

A gang of three senior boys had been bullying Tapan. Their leader was the hockey captain, the seniormost prefect in the house other than the house captain. He was sexually obsessed with Tapan, and made him spend hours every night somersaulting up and down the long verandah as an alternative, he said, to somersaulting naked in his study four times. Tapan knew what he was after and had refused. Sometimes he was made to somersault in assembly because there was an imaginary spot of dust on his shoes, sometimes he had to run around the lake (after which the school was named) for an hour or more till he was near collapse—for no reason other than the prefect's whim. Protest was useless, since insubordination would carry its own penalties. To speak to the house captain was pointless; the solidarity of the barons would have ensured his further torture. To speak to the housemaster, a genial and ineffectual fool with his dogs and his beautiful wife and his pleasant don't-disturb-me life, would have branded Tapan as a sneak—to be shunned and hounded even by those who now sympathized with him. And often enough his peers too could not resist teasing him about his powerful admirer's obsession, and implying that Tapan secretly enjoyed it.

Tapan was physically tough, and was always ready to use his fists or his sharp Chatterji tongue in his own defence; but the combination of major and minor cruelties had worn him down. He felt crushed by their cumulative weight and his own isolation. He had nothing and no one to tell him that he was right except a single Tagore song at assembly, and this made his loneliness even deeper.

Dipankar looked grim as he listened; he knew the system from experience, and realized what pitiful resources a boy of thirteen could summon up against three seventeen-year-olds, invested with the absolute power of a brutal state. But he had no idea of what was to come; and Tapan became almost incoherent as he recounted the worst of it.

One of the nocturnal sports of the prefect's gang was to hunt the civet cats that roamed around under the roof of their house. They would smash their heads in and skin them, then break bounds with the connivance of the night-watchman and sell them for their skin and scent-glands. Because they discovered that Tapan was terrified of the things, they got a particular kick out of forcing him to open trunks in which they were lying dead. He would go berserk, run screaming at the senior boys and hit them with his fists. This they thought was hilarious, especially since they were also able to feel him up at the same time.

In one case they garotted a live civet cat, forced Tapan to watch, heated up an iron bar, and cut its throat from side to side with it. Then they played with its voice-box.

Dipankar stared at his brother, almost paralysed. Tapan was shuddering and gagging in dry heaves.

'Just get me out of there, Dada—I can't spend another term there—I'll jump off the train, I'm telling you—every time the morning bell rings I wish I was dead.'

Dipankar nodded and put his arm around his shoulder. This time it was not shrugged off.

'One day I'll kill him,' said Tapan with such hatred that Dipankar was chilled. 'I'll never forget his name, I'll never forget his face. I'll never forget what he did. Never.'

Dipankar's mind turned back to his own schooldays. There had been plenty of unpleasant incidents, but this psychopathic and persistent sadism left him speechless.

'Why didn't you tell me—why?—that school was like this?' said Tapan, still gasping. His eyes were full of misery and accusation.

Dipankar said: 'But—but school wasn't like that for me—my schooldays weren't unhappy for me on the whole. The food was bad, the omelettes were like lizards' corpses, but—' He stopped, then continued, 'I'm sorry, Tapan. . . . I was in a different house, and, well, times do change. . . . But that housemaster of yours should be sacked immediately. And as for those boys—they should be—'

He controlled himself with an effort, then went on:

'Gangs did terrorize the juniors, even in my time, but this—' He shook his head. 'Do other boys have it just as bad?'

'No—' said Tapan, then corrected himself. 'He picked on another boy earlier, but the boy gave in after a week's treatment, and went to his study.'

Dipankar nodded.

'How long has this been going on?'

'More than a year, but it's been worse since he was made a prefect. These last two terms—'

'Why didn't you tell me before?'

Tapan was silent. Then he burst out passionately:

'Dada, promise me, please promise me you won't tell anyone else.'

'I promise,' said Dipankar. His fists were clenched. 'No, wait; I'll have to tell Amit Da.'

'No!'

Tapan revered Amit, and could not bear that he should hear about his indignities and horrors.

'You've got to leave it to me, Tapan,' said Dipankar. 'We have to be able to convince Ma and Baba to take you out of school without letting them know the details. I can't do that by myself. Amit Da and I together may be able to. I'll tell him, but no one else.' He looked at Tapan with pity, affection, and dismay. 'Is that OK? Just Amit Da? No one else. I promise.'

Tapan nodded and got up, then started crying, and sat down again.

'Do you want to wash your face?'

Tapan nodded, and went off to use the bathroom.

16.4

'I'm writing,' said Amit crossly. 'Go away.' He looked up from his roll-top desk at Dipankar, and looked down again.

'Tell your Muse to go away instead, Dada, and to come back after we've finished.'

Amit frowned. Dipankar was rarely so abrupt. Something must be the matter. But he could feel his inspiration slipping away, and he wasn't pleased.

'Oh, what is it, Dipankar? As if Kuku isn't interruption enough. She came in to tell me something Hans had done that was singularly sweet. I can't even remember what it was now. But she had to tell someone, and you were in your hut. Well, what is it?'

'First, the good news,' said Dipankar tactically. 'I've decided to join a bank. So your Muse can keep visiting you.'

Amit jumped up from his desk and grabbed hold of his hands.

'You're not serious!'

'Yes. When I meditated today it all became clear to me. Crystal clear. It's irrevocable.'

Amit was so relieved that he didn't even ask Dipankar his reasons. In any case, he was sure they would be couched in the form of incomprehensible and capitalized abstractions.

'And how long will it remain irrevocable?'

Dipankar looked hurt.

'Well,' said Amit. 'I'm sorry. And it is very good of you to tell me.' He frowned and capped his pen. 'You're not doing this for me, are you? A sacrifice on the altar of literature?' Amit looked rather sheepishly grateful.

'No,' said Dipankar. 'Not at all.' But this was not entirely true; the effect of his decision on Amit's life had very much entered his thinking. 'But what I want to talk to you about is Tapan. Do you mind?'

'No, now that you've porlocked me already. He doesn't look very happy these days.'

'Oh, so you've noticed?'

Amit, in the throes of his novel, was insensitive to the feelings of his family in proportion to his sensitivity to the feelings of his characters.

'Yes, I have noticed. And Ma says he wants to leave school.'

'Do you know why?'

'No.'

'Well, that's what I want to discuss with you. Do you mind if I shut the door? Kuku—'

'Kuku can gurgle herself through any door; they're no obstacle to Kuku. But do, if you wish.'

Dipankar closed the door and sat down on a chair near the window.

He told Amit what Tapan had told him. Amit listened, nodding his head from time to time, and was sickened. At first he too could hardly speak.

'How long has Tapan had to go through all this?' he asked eventually.

'At least a year.'

'It makes my stomach turn—are you sure he's not—you know—imagining it—some of it? It seems so—'

'He's not imagining anything, Dada.'

'Why didn't he go to the school authorities?'

'It's not a day school, Dada, the boys would have made life worse hell for him—if you can imagine that.'

'This is terrible. This is really terrible. Where is he now? Is he all right?'

'In my room. Or he may have gone for a walk with Cuddles.'

'Is he all right?' repeated Amit.

'Yes,' said Dipankar. 'But he won't be if he has to go back to Jheel in a month.'

'Strange,' said Amit. 'I had no inkling of all this. None at all. Poor Tapan. He's never mentioned anything.'

'Well, Dada—' said Dipankar. 'Is that really his fault? He'd probably think we'd make a couplet out of it. No one ever talks to anyone in our family, we just exchange brilliances.'

Amit nodded.

'Does he want to go to another boarding school?'

'I don't think so. Jheel is as good or as bad as any of them; they all breed conformists or bullies.'

'Well,' said Amit, 'Jheel bred you.'

'I'm talking about a general tendency, Dada, not about invariable effects. But it's up to us to do something. I mean the two of us. Ma will have hysterics if she hears about all this. And Tapan won't be able to face Baba if he thinks he's heard. As for Kuku, she sometimes has good ideas, but it would be idiocy to trust her to be discreet. And Meenakshi's out, obviously: the Mehras would know in a minute, and what Arun's mother knows today the world knows tomorrow. It was difficult enough to get Tapan to speak to me. And I promised him I'd tell only you.'

'And he didn't mind?'

Dipankar hesitated for a fraction of a second. 'No,' he said.

Amit uncapped his pen again, and drew a small circle on the poem he had been writing. 'Won't it be difficult for him to get admission somewhere else at this stage?' he asked, investing the circle with eyes and two large ears.

'Not if you talk to someone at St Xavier's,' replied Dipankar. 'It's your old school, and they're always telling you how proud they are of you.'

'True,' said Amit thoughtfully. 'And I did give a talk and a reading there earlier this year, which I very rarely do. So I suppose I could—but what reason could I give? Not his general health; you said he could swim across that lake and back. His headaches? Well, if they're brought on by travel, perhaps. Anyway, whatever I think of, getting him provisionally into another school would certainly counter one possible objection by Ma. A sort of fait accompli.'

'Well,' said Dipankar quietly, 'as Baba says, no fait is ever accompli until it's accompli.'

Amit thought of Tapan's misery and his own poem went out of his mind.

'I'll go over after lunch,' he said. 'Has the car been kuku'd?'

'I don't know.'

'And how will we convince Ma?' continued Amit, looking worried, almost grim.

'That's the problem,' said Dipankar. His decision to join a bank had made him quite decisive all around for an hour or so, but the effect was wearing off. 'What can he do here in Calcutta that he can't do at a boarding school like Jheel? I suppose he couldn't develop a sudden interest in astronomy, could he, and be unable to live without a roof telescope. The thirst for knowledge, and so on. Then he'd have to live at home and attend a day school.'

Amit smiled. 'I can't see it going down too well with Ma: one poet, one seer, and one astronomer. Sorry, banker-cum-seer.'

'Headaches?'

'Headaches?' asked Amit. 'Oh, I see, his migraines. Yes, well, that'll help, but—let's try thinking not of Tapan, but of Ma. . . .'

After a few minutes, Dipankar suggested: 'How about Bengali culture?'

'Bengali culture?'

'Yes, you know, the Jheel School song book has one paltry song by Tagore, and no provision for teaching Bengali, and—'

'Dipankar, you're a genius.'

'Yes,' Dipankar agreed.

'That's just right. "Tapan is losing his Bengali soul in the swamp of the Great Indian Sensibility." She was complaining about his Bengali just the other day. Certainly it's worth a try. But you know, I'm not sure about letting matters rest here. If this is the state of affairs at Jheel, we ought to complain to the headmaster, and if necessary kick up a wider fuss.'

Dipankar shook his head. 'I'm afraid that if Baba gets involved, that is exactly what is going to happen. And I'm more concerned with Tapan at the moment than with undoing the general brutalities of Jheel. But Dada, do talk to Tapan. And spend a bit of time with him. He admires you.'

Amit accepted the implicit rebuke from his younger brother. 'Well, I'm impressed with us,' he said after a few moments of silence. 'We'd make a very practical team. Movers and Fixers. Wide experience of Law and Economics. Solutions while you wait: Intrepid, Immediate and Irrevocable—'

Dipankar cut him off. 'I'll talk to Ma at teatime, then, Dada. Tapan has had to put up with this for months, he shouldn't have to put up with it for another day. If you and I—and, I hope, Ma—present a united front, and Tapan is so obviously unhappy at Jheel, Baba will give in. Besides, he won't mind having Tapan in Calcutta; he misses him when he's away. He's the only one of his children who isn't a Problem—except for his report card.'

Amit nodded. 'Well, wait for him to reach the age of responsibility before he displays his own variant of irresponsibility. If he's a Chatterji, he will.'

16.5

'But I thought you used to call him Shambhu,' said Mrs Chatterji to her gardener. She was referring to his young helper who had just gone off work at a little after five o'clock.

'Yes,' replied the old man, nodding his head vigorously. 'Memsahib, about the chrysanthemums—'

'But I just heard you call him Tirru when he left,' persisted Mrs Chatterji. 'Is he Shambhu or Tirru? I thought his name was Shambhu.'

'Yes, Memsahib, it is.'

'Well, what is Tirru then?'

'He doesn't use that name now, Memsahib,' continued the gardener candidly. 'He's on the run from the police.'

Mrs Chatterji was astonished.

'The police?'

'Yes, Memsahib. He hasn't done anything. The police just decided to harass him. I think it's to do with his ration card. He may have had to do something illegal to get one, because he's from outside.'

'Isn't he from Bihar or somewhere?' asked Mrs Chatterji.

'Yes, Memsahib. Or Purva Pradesh. Or maybe even Eastern U.P. He seems reluctant to talk about it. But he's a good boy, you can see there's no harm in him.' He pointed with his hoe in the direction of the bed that Tirru had been weeding.

'But why here?'

'He thought a judge's house would be safest, Memsahib.'

Mrs Chatterji was nonplussed by the logic of this. 'But—' she began, then thought better of it. 'What were you saying about the chrysanthemums?'

While the gardener explained the maraudings of the driver's son, Mrs Chatterji continued to nod without listening. How perplexing, she said to herself. I wonder if I should tell my husband. Oh, there's Dipankar. I'll ask him. She waved to him.

Dipankar came over. He was dressed in a kurta-pyjama, and was looking rather serious.

'Something extraordinary has happened, Dipankar,' said his mother. 'I want your advice.'

'And he does it to trees as well, Memsahib,' continued the gardener, seeing his ally approach. 'He broke off all the lichis, then he broke off the guavas, then he broke off all the little jackfruit from the tree at the back. I got really annoyed. Only a gardener can understand the pain of a tree. We sweat for it and see it bear, and then this monster breaks them off with sticks and stones. I showed them to the driver and what did he say? No anger, not even a slap, just "Son, one doesn't do this sort of thing." If my child damaged his big white car,' continued the gardener, nodding forcefully, 'then he'd feel something.'

'Yes, yes, very sad,' said Mrs Chatterji vaguely. 'Dipankar, dear, do you know that that dark young man who helps around the garden is on the run from the police?'

'Oh?' said Dipankar philosophically.

'But aren't you upset?'

'Not yet. Why?'

'Well, we might all be murdered in our—well, in our beds.'

'What's he done?'

'It could be anything. The mali says it's to do with a ration card. But he's not sure. What should I do? Your father will be very upset if he hears that we've been harbouring a fugitive. And, as you know, he's not even from Bengal.'

'Well, he's a good fellow, this Shambhu—'

'Not Shambhu, Tirru. That's what he's called, apparently.'

'Well, we needn't upset Baba—'

'But a High Court Judge—with a wanted criminal working on his chrysanthemums—'

Dipankar looked beyond his hut to the large white chrysanthemums in the far bed—those few that the season and the driver's son had spared. 'I'd advise inaction,' he said. 'Baba will have enough on his plate now that Tapan is leaving Jheel.'

Mrs Chatterji continued: 'Of course, it isn't as if the police are always—what? What did you say?'

'And joining St Xavier's. It's a wise choice. And maybe, then, Ma, he can go on to Shantiniketan.'

'Shantiniketan?' Mrs Chatterji couldn't make out what that holy word had to do with the matter on hand. An image of trees came to her mind—great trees under which she had sat and partaken of the lessons of Gurudeb, her master, the waterer of the garden of the culture of Bengal.

'It's being parted from the soil of Bengal that's been making him so unhappy. He's a divided soul, can't you see, Ma?'

'Well, he certainly has two names,' said Mrs Chatterji, slipping down the wrong fork of the conversation. 'But what's this about Tapan and St Xavier's?'

Dipankar became soulful. His voice filled with a calm sadness, he said: 'It's Tapan I've been talking about, Mago. It's not the lake of Jheel that he needs, it's "your deep ponds, loving and cool as the midnight sky" that he misses. That's why he's been so low. That's why his reports have been so poor. That—and his longing for the songs of Tagore—Kuku and you singing Rabindrasangeet as the evening falls, at the cow-dust hour. . . .' Dipankar spoke with conviction, for he had convinced himself. Now he recited the magic words:

> 'Finally my homesickness grew too great to resist. . . .
>
> I bow, I bow to my beautiful motherland Bengal!
> To your river-banks, to your winds that cool and console;

Your plains, whose dust the sky bends down to kiss;
Your shrouded villages, that are nests of shade and peace;
Your leafy mango-woods, where the herd-boys play;
Your deep ponds, loving and cool as the midnight sky;
Your sweet-hearted women returning home with water;
I tremble in my soul and weep when I call you Mother.'

Mrs Chatterji was repeating the words together with her son. She was deeply moved. Dipankar was deeply moved.

(Not that Calcutta contained any of the above-mentioned features.)

'That is why he weeps,' he concluded simply.

'But he hasn't been weeping,' said Mrs Chatterji. 'Just scowling.'

'It has been to save you and Baba pain that he does not weep in front of you. But, Ma, I swear on my life and soul that he was weeping today.'

'Really, Dipankar,' said Mrs Chatterji, amazed and not entirely pleased at his fervour. Then she thought of Tapan, whose Bengali really had deteriorated since he had been to Jheel; and the thought of his unhappiness overwhelmed her.

'But which school will accept him at this stage?' she asked.

'Oh, that?' said Dipankar, brushing away the insignificant objection. 'I forgot to mention that Amit Da has already got St Xavier's to agree to take him in. All that is needed is his mother's consent. . . . "I tremble in my soul and weep when I call you Mother,"' he murmured to himself again.

At the word 'Mother', Mrs Chatterji, good Brahmo though she was, wiped away a tear.

A thought struck her. 'But Baba?—' she said. She was still overcome by events—in fact she wasn't certain she had comprehended them all. 'This is all so sudden—and the school fees—he really was crying? And it won't disturb his studies?'

'Amit Da has agreed to coach Tapan himself if necessary,' said Dipankar unilaterally. 'And Kuku will teach him one Tagore song a week,' he added. 'And you can improve his Bengali handwriting.'

'And you?' asked his mother.

'I?' said Dipankar. 'I? I will have no time to teach him anything, because I will be working at Grindlays from next month.'

His mother looked at him in amazement, hardly daring to believe what she had heard.

16.6

Seven Chatterjis and seven non-Chatterjis were seated for dinner at the long oval table in the Ballygunge house.

Luckily, Amit and Arun were not too close to each other. Both held strong opinions, Amit on some subjects, Arun on all; and Amit, being at home, would not be as reserved as he might otherwise be. The company, too, was the kind he felt comfortable in: the seven non-Chatterjis were all part of the clan by extension—or about to become so. They were Mrs Rupa Mehra and her four children, together with Pran (who was looking well) and the young German diplomat who was Kakoli's successful suitor. Meenakshi Mehra, when in Ballygunge, was included among the Chatterji count. Old Mr Chatterji had sent a message to say he would not be able to join them.

'It's nothing,' said Tapan, who had just returned from the garden. 'Perhaps he's tired of being tied up. Why don't I set him free? There aren't any other mushrooms around.'

'What? And have him bite Hans again?' said Mrs Chatterji. 'No, Tapan.'

Hans was looking grave and a little bewildered.

'Mushroom?' asked Hans. 'Please, what is a mushroom in this context?'

'You may as well know,' said Amit. 'Since you've been bitten by Cuddles, you are already virtually a blood-brother to us. Or a saliva-brother. A mushroom is a young man who is sweet on Kuku. They spring up everywhere. Some carry flowers, some just moon and mope. You had better be careful when you get married to her. I wouldn't trust any mushrooms, edible or otherwise.'

'No, indeed,' said Hans.

'How is Krishnan, Kuku?' asked Meenakshi, who had been following the conversation only partly.

'He is taking everything very well,' said Kuku. 'He will always have a special place in my heart,' she added defiantly.

Hans was looking even more grave.

'Oh, you needn't worry about that, Hans,' Amit said. 'That doesn't mean much. Kuku's heart is full of specially reserved places.'

'It is not,' said Kuku. 'And you have no right to talk.'

'Me?' said Amit.

'Yes, you. You are completely heartless; Hans takes all this flippant talk about affection very badly. He has a very pure soul.'

Meenakshi, who had had a bit too much to drink, murmured:

'Gentlemen that I allure,
They are always thinking pure.'

Hans blushed.

'Nonsense, Kuku,' said Amit. 'Hans is a strong man and can take anything. You can tell from his handshake.'

Hans flinched.

Mrs Chatterji found it necessary to intervene. 'Hans, you mustn't take what Amit says seriously.'

'Yes,' agreed Amit. 'Only what I write.'

'He gets into these moods when his writing is going badly. Have you had any news from your sister?'

'No, but I am expecting to hear from her any day,' said Hans.

'Do you think we are a typical family, Hans?' said Meenakshi.

Hans considered, then answered diplomatically: 'I would say you are an atypically typical family.'

'Not typically atypical?' suggested Amit.

'He's not always like this,' said Kuku to Lata.

'Isn't he?' asked Lata.

'Oh no—he's much less—'

'Less what?' demanded Amit.

'Less selfish!' said Kuku, annoyed. She had been trying to defend him before Lata. But Amit seemed to be in one of those moods where he cared about no one's feelings.

'If I tried to be more unselfish,' said Amit, 'I would lose all those qualities that make me a net joy-giver.'

Mrs Rupa Mehra looked at Amit, rather astounded.

Amit explained: 'I meant, Ma, that I would become completely sister-pecked and docile, and then my writing would suffer, and since my writing gives pleasure to many more people than I actually meet, there would be a net loss to the universe.'

This struck Mrs Rupa Mehra as astonishingly arrogant. 'Can you use that as a reason to behave badly to those around you?' she asked.

'Oh, yes, I think so,' said Amit, carried away by the force of his argument. 'Certainly, I demand meals at odd hours, and I never answer letters in time. Sometimes, when I'm in the middle of a patch of inspiration, I don't answer them for months.'

To Mrs Rupa Mehra this was sheer villainy. Not to answer letters was unforgivable. If this attitude spread, it would be the end of civilized life as she knew it. She glanced at Lata, who appeared to be enjoying the conversation, though not contributing to it at all.

'I'm sure none of my children would ever do that,' said Mrs Rupa Mehra. 'Even when I am away, my Varun writes to me every week.' She looked pensive.

'I'm sure they wouldn't, Ma,' said Kuku. 'It's just that we've pampered Amit so much that he thinks he can do anything and get away with it.'

'Quite right,' said Amit's father from the other end of the table. 'Savita's just been telling me how fascinating she finds the law and how much she looks forward to practising it. Why have a qualification if you make no use of it?'

Amit fell silent.

'Now Dipankar has settled down at last,' Mr Justice Chatterji added with approval. 'A bank is just the place for him.'

'A river-bank,' Kuku could not refrain from saying. 'With an Ideal to ply him with Scotch and type his ruminations for him.'

'Very amusing,' said Mr Justice Chatterji. He was pleased with Dipankar these days.

'And you, Tapan, you're going to become a doctor, are you?' said Amit with cynical affection.

'I don't think so, Dada,' said Tapan, who looked quite happy.

'Do you think I've made the right decision, Dada?' asked Dipankar uncertainly. He had made up his mind suddenly, having been struck by the insight that one had to be *of* the world before one could get away from it; but he was beginning to have second thoughts.

'Well—' said Amit, thinking of the fate of his novel.

'Well? Do you approve?' said Dipankar, looking with great concentration at the beautiful shell-shaped dish that had contained his baked vegetables.

'Oh, yes,' said Amit. 'But I'm not going to tell you I do.'

'Oh.'

'Because,' continued Amit, 'that would be the surest way of making you feel imposed upon—and then you'll change your mind. But—if this helps—you are certainly blinking less these days.'

'That's true,' said Mr Justice Chatterji with a smile. 'I'm afraid, Hans, you must think we're a very peculiar family.'

'Not so,' said Hans gallantly. 'Not very peculiar.' He and Kakoli exchanged affectionate glances.

'We hope to hear you sing after dinner,' continued Mr Justice Chatterji.

'Ah. Yes. Something from Schubert?'

'Who else is there?' said Kakoli.

'Well—' began Hans.

'For me there can only be Schubert,' said Kakoli giddily. 'Schubert is the only man in my life.'

At the far end of the table, Savita was talking to Varun, who had been looking downcast. As they talked, he cheered up perceptibly.

Meanwhile, Pran and Arun were engaged in a discussion of politics. Arun was lecturing Pran about the future of the country and how India needed a dictatorship. 'None of these stupid politicians,' he continued, unmindful of Pran's feelings. 'We really don't deserve the Westminster model of government. Nor do the British for that matter. We're still an advancing society—as our dhoti-wallahs are fond of telling us.'

'Yes, people are always making advances in our society,' said Meenakshi, rolling her eyes upwards.

Kuku giggled.

Arun glared and said in a low voice: 'Meenakshi, it's impossible to hold a sensible discussion when you're tight.'

Meenakshi was so unused to being ticked off by an Outsider in her parents' home that she did shut up.

After dinner, when everyone had adjourned to the drawing room for coffee, Mrs Chatterji took Amit to one side and said to him: 'Meenakshi and Kuku are right. She's a nice girl, though she doesn't say very much. She could grow on you, I suppose.'

'Mago, you make her sound like a fungus,' said Amit. 'I can see that Kuku and Meenakshi have won you over to their way of thinking. Anyway, I refuse not to talk to her just because you want me to. I'm not Dipankar.'

'Whoever said you were, darling?' said Mrs Chatterji. 'I do wish you had been nicer at dinner, though.'

'Well, anyone I like should be given the chance to see me at my best,' said Amit unrepentantly.

'I don't think that's a very useful way of looking at things, dear.'

'True,' admitted Amit. 'But looking at things in terms of a useful way of looking at things may not be a useful thing either. Why don't you talk to Mrs Mehra for a while? She was rather subdued at dinner. She didn't mention her diabetes once. And I'll talk to her daughter and apologize for my boorishness.'

'Like a good boy.'

'Like a good boy.'

16.7

Amit walked over to Lata, who was chatting to Meenakshi.

'Sometimes he's terribly rude—and for no reason at all,' Meenakshi was saying.

'Talking about me?' said Amit.

'No,' said Lata, 'about my brother, not hers.'

'Ah,' said Amit.

'But the same certainly holds for you,' added Meenakshi. 'You've either been writing something strange or reading something strange. I can tell.'

'Well, you're right, I have. I was going to invite Lata to have a look at some books I promised to lend her but didn't post. Is this a good time, Lata? Or should we look at them some other time?'

'Oh, no, this is a good time,' said Lata. 'But when will they begin singing?'

'I shouldn't think for another fifteen minutes. . . . I'm sorry I was so rude at dinner.'

'Were you?'

'Wasn't I? Didn't you think so? Perhaps I wasn't. I'm not sure now.'

They were walking past the room where Cuddles had been confined, and he let out a growl.

'That dog should have his hypotenuse squared,' said Amit.

'Did he really bite Hans?'

'Oh, yes, quite hard. Harder than he bit Arun. Anyway, everything looks more livid on pale skin. But Hans took it like a man. It's a sort of rite of passage for our in-laws.'

'Oh. Am I within the bitable degrees?'

'I'm not sure. Do you want Cuddles to bite you?'

Upstairs, Lata looked at Amit's room in a new light. This was the room where 'The Fever Bird' had been written, she thought; and where he must have worked out his dedication to her. Papers lay scattered around in far worse disorder than the last time she had visited it. And piles of clothes and books lay on his bed.

'I shivered in the midnight heat,' thought Lata. Aloud she said: 'What sort of view do you get of that amaltas from here?'

Amit opened the window. 'Not a very good view. Dipankar's room is the best for that; it's just above his hut. But enough to see its shadow—'

'—Shake slightly on the moonlit grass.'

'Yes.' Amit didn't normally like his poetry quoted back at him, but with Lata he didn't mind. 'Well, come to the window, sweet is the night-air.'

They stood there together for a while. It was very still, and the shadow of the amaltas did not shake at all. Dark leaves and long, dark, podded beans hung from its branches, but no yellow clusters of flowers.

'Did it take you long to write that poem?'

'No. I wrote it out in a single draft when that damn bird kept me awake. Once, I counted sixteen desperate triplets building upwards to fever pitch. Can you imagine: sixteen. It drove me crazy. And then I polished it over the next few days. I didn't really want to look at it, and kept making excuses. I always do. I hate writing, you know.'

'You—what—?' Lata turned towards him. Amit really puzzled her at times. 'Well, then, why do you write?' she asked.

Amit's face grew troubled. 'It's better than spending my life doing the law like my father and grandfather before me. And the main reason is that I often like my work when it's done—it's just the doing that is so tedious. With a short poem there's the inspiration of course. But with this novel I have to whip myself to my desk—To work, to work, Macbeth doth shirk.'

Lata remembered that Amit had compared the novel to a banyan tree. Now the image seemed somewhat sinister. 'Perhaps you've chosen too dark a topic,' she said.

'Yes. And perhaps too recent.' The Bengal Famine had taken place less than a decade ago, and was a very present memory to anyone who had lived through those times. 'But anyway, I can't go back now,' continued Amit. 'Returning is as tedious as go o'er—I'm two-thirds of the way through. Two-thirds, two-thirds; the fever-birds. Now, those books I promised to show you—' Amit stopped short suddenly. 'You have a nice smile.'

Lata laughed. 'It's a pity I can't see it.'

'Oh no,' said Amit. 'It would be wasted on you. You wouldn't know how to appreciate it—certainly not as much as me.'

'So you're a connoisseur of smiles,' said Lata.

'Far from it,' said Amit, suddenly plunged into a darker mood. 'You know, Kuku's right; I'm too selfish. I haven't asked you a single question about yourself, though I do want to know what's happened since you wrote to thank me for the book. How was your play? And your studies? And singing? And you said you had written a poem "under my influence". Well, where is it?'

'I've brought it along,' said Lata, opening her purse. 'But please don't read it now. It is very despairing, and would only embarrass me. It's only because you're a professional—'

'All right,' nodded Amit. He was completely tongue-tied all of a sudden. He had hoped to make some sort of declaration or indication of his affection to Lata, and he found that he did not know what to say.

'Have you written any poems recently?' asked Lata after a few seconds. They had moved away from the window.

'Here's one,' said Amit, looking through a pile of papers. 'One that does not bare my soul. It's about a family friend—you might even have met him at that party the last time you were in Calcutta. Kuku asked him upstairs to see her painting, and the first two lines suddenly occurred to her. He's rather fat. So she commissioned a poem from the resident poet.'

Lata looked at the poem, which was titled 'Roly Poly':

Roly Poly Mr Kohli
Toiling slowly up the stairs.
Holy souly Mrs Kohli
Tries to catch him unawares.

Finger-wagging, fuming, frowning:
'Why you have not said your prayers?
What means all this upping, downing?
What is magic in the stairs?'

Mr Kohli is Professor,
Always doing complex sums.
Answers mildly to aggressor,
'On the stairs the theory comes.'

'What a nonsense. Stop this summing.
Come and eat. Your food is cold.'
'Just now only I am coming,'
Says her husband, meek as gold.

Lata could not help smiling, though she thought it very silly. 'Is his wife all that fierce?' she asked.

'Oh, no,' said Amit, 'that's just poetic licence. Poets can create wives to suit their convenience. Kuku thinks that only the first stanza has any real force, and she's made up a second stanza of her own, which is much better than mine.'

'Do you remember it?' asked Lata.

'Well—you should ask Kuku to recite it.'

'It seems I won't be able to for a while,' said Lata. 'She's begun playing.'

From below the sound of the piano floated upwards, and Hans's baritone followed.

'We'd better go and join them,' said Amit. 'Toiling slowly down the stairs.'

'All right.'

There was no sound from Cuddles. Music or sleep had soothed him. They entered the drawing room. Mrs Rupa Mehra noted their entrance with a frown.

After a couple of songs, Hans and Kuku bowed, and the audience clapped.

'I forgot to show you the books,' said Amit.

'I forgot about them too,' said Lata.

'Anyway, you're here for a while. I wish you'd arrived on the 24th, as you had planned. I could have taken you to midnight mass at St Paul's Cathedral. It's almost like being back in England—unsettling.'

'My grandfather wasn't too well, so we postponed coming.'

'Well, Lata, are you doing anything tomorrow? I promised to show you the Botanical Gardens. Come see with me—the banyan tree—if you are free—'

'I don't think I'm doing anything—' began Lata.

'Prahapore.' It was Mrs Rupa Mehra's voice, from behind them.

'Ma?' said Lata.

'Prahapore. She is going to Prahapore tomorrow with the whole family,' said Mrs Rupa Mehra, addressing Amit. Then, turning to Lata she said: 'How can you be so thoughtless? Haresh has organized lunch for us at Prahapore, and you are thinking of gallivanting along to the Botanical Gardens.'

'I forgot, Ma—the date just slipped my mind for a moment. I was thinking of something else.'

'Forgot!' said Mrs Rupa Mehra. 'Forgot. You will forget your own name next.'

16.8

Much had happened in Prahapore since Haresh had got his job, indeed since his meeting with Arun and Meenakshi at the Chairman's mansion. He had plunged himself into his work, and become as much a Prahaman in spirit as the Czechs—though there was still not much love lost between them.

He did not mourn for his lost managerial status because he was the kind of man who preferred not to look back, and because in any case there was plenty of work to be done—and, what he liked most of all, battles to be fought, challenges to be overcome. As a foreman he had been put in charge of the Goodyear Welted line, which was the most prestigious line in the factory; Havel and Kurilla and the others knew that he could make this shoe-of-a-hundred-operations from scratch with his own rigid-thumbed hands, and would therefore be able to diagnose most problems in production and quality control.

But Haresh ran into problems almost immediately. He was not disposed to be friendly to Bengalis in general after his experience at CLFC, and now he decided fairly quickly that Bengali workmen were worse than Bengali bosses. Their slogan, which they made no secret of, was, 'Chakri chai, kaaj chai na': We want employment, not work. Their daily production was abysmal compared to what should have been possible, and there was a logic to this. They were attempting to establish a low working norm of about 200 pairs a day so that they could get incentive payments beyond that—or, if nothing else, the leisure to enjoy tea and gossip and samosas and paan and snuff.

They were also afraid, reasonably enough, of overworking themselves out of a job.

Haresh sat at his table near the production line, and bided his time for a few weeks. He noticed that the workmen on the entire line were often standing around idle because some machine or other was not working properly—or so they claimed. As a foreman he had the right to get them to clean the conveyor belt and the machines while they were doing nothing. But after the machines were gleaming, the workmen would saunter past him insolently and stand about in groups, chatting—while Praha and production suffered. It drove Haresh crazy.

Besides, almost all the workmen were Bengali and spoke Bengali, and he didn't understand much of it. He certainly understood when he was being insulted, however, because swear words like 'sala' are common to Hindi and Bengali. Despite his quick temper, he chose not to make an issue of it.

One day he decided that, instead of grinding his teeth with frustration and sending for someone from the machinery department to repair a malfunctioning machine on site or to forklift it out, he would visit the machinery department himself. This was the beginning of what could be called the Battle of the Goodyear Welted Line, and it was fought on many fronts, against several levels of opposition, including that of the Czechs.

The mechanics were pleased to see Haresh. Normally foremen sent them slips asking them to repair their machines. Now a foreman, and that too the famous foreman who had got to live inside the white gates of the Czech compound, was visiting them and chatting to them on terms of equality, and even taking snuff with them. He was prepared to sit on a stool with them and talk and joke and share experiences, and look inside machines without caring if his hands got soiled with grease. And he called them 'Dada' out of respect for their age and abilities.

For once, they got the sense that they were part of the mainstream of production, not a mere auxiliary outfit in a forgotten corner of Praha. Most of the best mechanics were Muslims and spoke Urdu, so Haresh had no language problem. He was well dressed, with a set of working overalls that he had adapted—sleeveless, collarless, extending no lower than the knee—to counter the heat and yet protect the front (if nothing else) of his cream silk shirt—perhaps a foppish appurtenance on the factory floor. But he had no airs of superiority when he talked to them, and this pleased them. Through their pleasure in exchanging the expertise of their trade, Haresh himself got interested in the mechanics of machines: how they worked, how they could be kept in good condition, how he might be able to make small innovations to improve their performance.

The mechanics told him, laughing, that the workmen on his conveyor belt were leading him a dance. Nine times out of ten, there wasn't even anything wrong with the machines.

This did not altogether surprise Haresh. But what could he do about it, he asked them. Because by this time they were friends, they said that they would tell him when something was really wrong—and they would repair his machines first when this was the case.

Now that the machines were out of action for shorter periods, production increased from 180 pairs a day to about 250, but this was still far below the 600 that was possible—or the 400 that Haresh was aiming for—as a realistic norm. Even 400 would have drawn cries of astonishment from his bosses; Haresh was convinced that it was doable, and that he was the man to do it.

The workmen, however, were not at all happy with 250 pairs, and found a new method to stop the conveyor belt. Men were allowed off the belt for five minutes at a time to answer a 'call of nature'. Now they staggered their calls of nature, and went off calmly to the bathroom by organized rotation—so that the conveyor belt was sometimes immobilized for half an hour at a time. By this time, Haresh had worked out who the gang leaders were—they were usually the men doing the most cushy jobs. Despite his short temper, he did not behave in an unfriendly manner towards them, but a line had been clearly drawn, and each side was sizing up the other's strengths. A couple of months after he began his job, when production had plummeted to 160, Haresh decided that the time had come to play his hand.

He called the workmen into conference one morning, and explained to them in a mixture of Hindi and rudimentary Bengali what had been simmering within him for a couple of months.

'I can tell you both from theory and from working with these machines that production should not be less than 400 pairs a day. That is what I would like to see from this line.'

'Oh?' said the man who pasted soles on to shoes—the easiest job on the line—'Do show us, Sir.' And he nudged the operator to his left—a strapping fellow from Bihar who worked on the toughest job, the stitching of the welt to the lasted shoe.

'Yes, do show us, Sir,' said several other workmen, taking their cue from the sole-paster. 'Show us that it can be done.'

'Myself?'

'How else, Sir?'

Haresh fumed for a while, then thought that before any such demonstration, he needed to be certain that the workmen would not try to wriggle out of increasing production. He called together a few of the gang leaders and said:

'What is it that you have against productivity? Are you really afraid that you will be thrown out if you increase production?'

One of them smiled and said: '"Productivity" is a word that management is very fond of. We are not so fond of it. Do you know that before the labour laws came into force last year, Novak would sometimes call people into his office, tell them they were fired and simply tear up their punch-in cards? That was that. And his reason used to be very simple: "We can do the same work with fewer people. We don't need you any more."'

'Don't talk about things that happened long before my time,' said Haresh impatiently. 'Now you have the new labour laws, and you're still deliberately keeping production down.'

'It will take time to build trust,' said the sole-paster philosophically and maddeningly.

'Well, what would induce you to produce more?' asked Haresh.

'Ah.' The man looked at his fellow-operators.

After a great deal of indirect discussion, Haresh came out of the meeting with the sense that if the workmen could get two assurances—that no one would be thrown out and that they would earn considerably more money than they were earning—they would not be averse to increasing production.

He next visited Novak, his old adversary, the fox-like head of Personnel. Would it be possible, he asked, for the workmen on his line to be rewarded with a higher grade—and thus a higher income—if they increased production to 400? Novak looked at him coldly and said, 'Praha cannot up grades for a particular line.'

'Why not?' asked Haresh.

'It would cause resentment among the other ten thousand workers. It cannot be done.'

Haresh had learned about the elaborate, sanctified hierarchy of Praha—it was worse than the civil service: there were eighteen different grades for workmen. But he felt that it could, without unhinging the universe, be given a tiny nudge here and there.

He decided to write a note to Khandelwal explaining his plan and asking for his approval. The plan had four elements. The workers would increase production to at least 400 pairs a day on the Goodyear Welted line. The management would raise the grades of these particular workmen by one level and thereby increase their weekly pay-packet. Beyond the figure of 400 pairs, incentives would be paid in proportion to any extra production. And instead of sacking anyone, a couple of new workmen would be hired at points where it was genuinely difficult to operate at the 400-pair level.

As it happened, about a month earlier, Khandelwal had sent Haresh on a two-day visit to Kanpur to help solve a labour reconciliation matter. An uneconomical depot was to be reduced in size and some workers laid off and though Praha was acting strictly according to the new *Labour Manual*, they had run into trouble; all the workmen had gone on strike. Khandelwal knew that Khanna had been at CLFC and was acquainted with affairs in

Kanpur. He therefore sent him to help sort things out; and he had been pleased with the final result. Haresh had told the workmen who were to be laid off that they should accept Praha's offer. He had said, in effect: 'You idiots, you're getting good money by way of a settlement; take it and start your lives over again. No one is trying to con you.' The CLFC workers, who trusted Haresh and had been sorry to see him go, talked to the workers at the Praha depot; and matters had been settled amicably.

Haresh knew that he had won access to the Chairman's ear, and he decided to use his access immediately. He went to Calcutta one morning (before Khandelwal had had time to get to his whisky at the club) and placed a single sheet of paper in front of him. Khandelwal looked it over, followed the pricings, the costings, the benefits of the scheme, the loss of customers if production did not increase, the necessity of giving the workmen a higher grade. At the end of two minutes he said to Haresh:

'You mean to say you can actually double production?'

Haresh nodded. 'I believe so. Anyway, with your permission, I can try.'

Khandelwal wrote two words across the top of the paper—'Yes. Try.'—and handed it back to Haresh.

16.9

He said nothing to anyone; in particular he avoided the Czechs—especially Novak. Bypassing him—a step for which he was later to pay—he made a surprise move: he went to the union office and met the top union leaders of Prahapore. 'There is a problem in my department,' he said to them, 'and I want your help in solving it.' The Secretary-General of the union, Milon Basu, a man who was corrupt but very intelligent, looked at Haresh suspiciously.

'What do you propose?' he said.

Haresh told him only that he proposed a meeting the next day with his own workmen in the union offices. But it was not necessary to mention the matter to Novak until something had been worked out.

The next day was Saturday, a holiday. The workmen assembled in the union office.

'Gentlemen,' said Haresh, 'I am convinced that you can make 600 pairs a day. It is certainly within the capacity of your machines. I concede that you might need a couple of extra men at crucial points. Now tell me—which man here says that he cannot make 600 pairs?'

The sole-paster, who was the professional speaker, said belligerently: 'Oh, Ram Lakhan cannot do it.' He pointed to the strapping, mustachioed, good-natured Bihari who did the welt-stitching. All the toughest jobs on the conveyor, as well as elsewhere, were performed by Biharis. They stoked the furnaces; they were the policemen on night duty.

Haresh turned to Milon Basu and said: 'I am not asking for the opinion of a professional speaker. The man who has just spoken pastes the sock to the sole—in every other department his norm is 900 pairs a day. All he has to do is cement them and put them in. Let the man who is affected speak. If Ram Lakhan can't make 600 pairs a day, it's for him to speak out now.'

Ram Lakhan laughed and said: 'Sahib, you're talking about 600 pairs. I say that even 400 is impossible.'

Haresh said: 'Anyone else?'

Someone said: 'The capacity of the outsole stitcher isn't high enough.'

Haresh said, 'I have already conceded that. We'll put an extra man there. Anyone else?'

After a few seconds' silence, Haresh said to Ram Lakhan, who towered about a foot above him: 'Well, Ram Lakhan—if I make 400 pairs myself, how many will you make?'

Ram Lakhan shook his head. 'You will never be able to make 400 pairs, Sahib.'

'But if I do?'

'If you do—I'll make 450.'

'And if I make 500?'

'I'll make 550.' There was a recklessness in his answer and, indeed, a kind of intoxication to the challenge. Everyone was quiet.

'And if I make 600?'

'650.'

Haresh put up his hand and said—'All right! It's done! Let's go into the battlefield!' There was no rationality to this exchange, merely a sense of drama, but it had been very impressive, and the issue had in effect been clinched.

'The matter has been decided,' said Haresh. 'On Monday morning I will don my overalls and show you what can be done. But let us talk for the moment of a mere 400. I am prepared to stand and tell you here and now that if our production rises to that level, not a single man will be fired. And the week that you regularly make 400 pairs a day I will fight for all of you to be promoted by one grade. And if this does not happen I am prepared to resign.'

There was a buzz of disbelief. Even Milon Basu thought that Haresh was a real fool. But he did not know of the two reassuring words—'Yes. Try.'—scrawled in the Chairman's hand on the sheet of paper in Haresh's pocket.

16.10

The next Monday, Haresh donned his full overalls, not the natty, abridged ones he usually wore with his cream silk shirt, and told the workmen on his line to pile up the lasted shoes for welt-stitching. Six hundred shoes for an eight-hour day came to about ninety shoes an hour and still left an hour to spare. Each conveyor-rack contained five pairs of shoes. That meant eighteen racks an hour. The workmen gathered around, and those from other lines too could not resist betting on the odds of his succeeding.

Ninety pairs came and went before the hour struck. When it was over, Haresh wiped the sweat from his forehead and said to Ram Lakhan: 'Now I've done it—will you keep your side of the bargain?'

Ram Lakhan looked at the pile of welted shoes and said: 'Sahib, you've done it for an hour. But I have to do it every hour, every day, every week, every year. I will be finished, worn out, if I work at that rate.'

'Well, what do you want me to do to prove you won't?' said Haresh.

'Show me that you can do it for a whole day.'

'All right. But I'm not going to close the production line for a day. We won't stop the conveyor. Everyone will work at the same pace. Is that agreed?'

The conveyor was started up, and the work continued. The operators shook their heads at the unconventionality of it all, but they were amused and worked as hard as they could. Just over 450 pairs were made that day. Haresh was completely exhausted. His hands were trembling from having had to hold each lasted shoe against a needle going in and out of it at high speed. But he had seen people in a factory in England doing this with a single hand, turning the shoe casually around on the machine, and he had known it could be done.

'Well, Ram Lakhan? We have done 450. Now of course you'll make 500?'

'I said so,' said Ram Lakhan, stroking his moustache thoughtfully. 'I won't shift from that stand.'

After a couple of weeks Haresh got an extra man to assist Ram Lakhan with his crucial operation—mainly by handing him the shoes so that he wouldn't have to reach out for them—and the production level reached the final figure of 600.

What in Haresh's mind was the Battle of Goodyear Welted had been won. The Praha standard of production and profit was floating higher—and Haresh's own pennant too had ascended a notch. He was very happy with himself.

16.11

But not everyone was. One consequence of this whole business—and in particular the fact that Haresh had circumvented Novak—was that the Czechs, almost to a man, began to view him with intense suspicion. All kinds of rumours about him began to float around the colony. He had been seen allowing a driver to sit down in his house—to sit down on a chair as an equal. He was a communist at heart. He was a union spy, in fact the secret editor of the union paper *Amader Biplob.* Haresh could sense them cold-shouldering him, but he could do nothing about it. He continued to produce 3,000 pairs a week instead of the earlier 900—and to pour his energy into every task within his direct control, down to the cleaning of his machines. And since he had given his own soul to the organization, he believed that Praha too—maybe in the distant form of Jan Tomin himself—would sooner or later do him justice.

He was in for a rude shock.

One day he went to the Design Centre in order to make a few suggestions that would help streamline the design and production of the shoes under his supervision. He discussed his ideas with the Indian who was the number two in the department. Just then Mr Bratinka, who ran the Design Centre, came in and stared at him.

'What are you doing here?' he said without even an attempt at civility and as if Haresh was trying to pollute his flock with the virus of rebellion.

'What do you mean, Mr Bratinka?' asked Haresh.

'Why are you here without permission?'

'I don't need permission to improve productivity.'

'Get out.'

'Mr Bratinka?'

'GET OUT!'

Mr Bratinka's assistant ventured to suggest that there was some merit in Mr Khanna's suggestions.

'Shut up,' said Mr Bratinka.

Both Bratinka and Haresh were furious. Haresh filed a complaint in the open grievance book that Khandelwal had established for the redress of injuries. And Bratinka reported Haresh to his superiors.

The result was that Haresh was hauled up before the General Manager and a committee of four others: a regular Czech inquisition with all manner of odd allegations other than that he was in the Design Centre without permission.

'Khanna,' said Pavel Havel, 'you have been talking to my driver.'

'Yes, Sir, I have. He came to see me about a matter concerning his son's education.' Pavel Havel's driver was a quiet-spoken, extremely polite man, always spotlessly dressed: Haresh would have said that he was, in every sense that mattered, a gentleman.

'Why did he come to you?'

'I don't know. Perhaps because he thought that as an Indian I might be sympathetic—or would at least understand the difficulties of a young man's career.'

'What is that supposed to mean?' said Kurilla, whose Middlehampton comradeship with Haresh had helped him get his job in the first instance.

'Just what I said. Perhaps he thought I could help him.'

'And it was seen through your windows that he was sitting down.'

'He was,' said Haresh, annoyed. 'He is a decent man, and a much older man than me. As he was standing, I asked him to sit down. He was uncomfortable, but I insisted that he should take a seat. And we discussed the matter. His son has temporary work in the factory on daily wages, and I suggested that in order to improve his prospects he should attend night classes. I lent him a few books. That is all there is to the incident.'

Novak said: 'You think that India is Europe, Mr Khanna? That there is equality between managers and staff? That everyone is at the same level?'

'Mr Novak, I should remind you that I am not a manager. Nor am I a communist, if that is what you are implying. Mr Havel, you know your driver. I am sure you think he is a trustworthy man. Ask him what happened.'

Pavel Havel was looking a little shamefaced, as if he had implied that Haresh was not trustworthy. And what he next said rather proved it.

'Well, there have been rumours of your being the editor of the union newspaper.'

Haresh shook his head in amazement.

'You say you are not?' This was Novak.

'I am not. I don't even think I'm a union member—unless I have become one automatically.'

'You have been inciting the union people to work behind our back.'

'I have not. What do you mean?'

'You visited their offices and held a meeting with them secretly. I did not know of it.'

'It was an open meeting. There was nothing that was done secretly. I am an honest man, Mr Novak, and I do not like these aspersions.'

'How dare you speak like this?' exploded Kurilla. 'How dare you do these things? We are the providers of employment to Indians, and if you do not like this job and the way we run things, you can leave the factory.'

At this, Haresh saw red and said in a trembling voice:

'Mr Kurilla, you provide employment not only to Indians but also to yourselves. As for your second point, I may leave the factory, but I assure you that you will leave India before I do.'

Kurilla almost burst. That a chit of a junior should stand up to the mighty Czech Prahamen was something both incomprehensible and unprecedented. Pavel Havel calmed him down and said to Haresh: 'I think this inquiry is over. We have covered all the points. I will talk to you later.'

A day later he called Haresh to his office and told him to continue as before. He added that he was pleased with his job, especially with respect to production. Perhaps, thought Haresh, he's had a talk with his driver.

Amazingly enough, the Czechs, especially Kurilla, became fairly friendly towards Haresh after this incident. It had, in a way, cleared the air. Now that they believed he was not a communist or an agitator, they were neither panicky nor resentful. They were basically fair-minded men who believed in results, and his tripling of production, once it appeared in the official monthly figures, had the same sort of effect on them as the pair of Goodyear Welted shoes that Haresh had made—and which, as it happened, he had been facing throughout his inquisition in the General Manager's office.

16.12

As Malati was walking out of the university library, en route to a meeting of the Socialist Party, one of her friends—a girl who studied singing at the

Haridas College—got talking with her.

In the course of exchanging gossip, the friend mentioned that Kabir had been seen just a few days earlier at the Red Fox restaurant, in animated and intimate conversation with a girl. The girl who had seen them was entirely reliable, and had said—

But Malati cut her off. 'I'm not interested!' she exclaimed with surprising vehemence. 'I don't have the time to listen. I have to rush to a meeting.' And she turned away, her eyes flashing.

She felt as if she had been personally insulted. Her friend's information was always correct, so there was no point in doubting it. What infuriated Malati most of all was that Kabir must have met this girl at the Red Fox around the time that he was making his protestations of undying love in the Blue Danube. It was enough to put her into a Black Fury.

It confirmed everything she had ever thought about men.

O perfidy.

16.13

On the evening before their meeting, while Lata had been at Ballygunge, Haresh was making last-minute preparations at the Prahapore Officers' Club to entertain his guests the next day. The whole place was festooned with coloured crêpe for the Christmas season.

'So, Khushwant,' said Haresh in Hindi, 'there will be no problem if we are as much as half an hour late? They are coming from Calcutta and something might delay them.'

'No problem at all, Mr Khanna. I have been running the club for five years, and have grown used to adjusting to other people's schedules.' Khushwant had risen from being a bearer to becoming a cook-cum-bearer to becoming the virtual manager of the club.

'The vegetarian dishes will present no difficulty? I know that that is not usual at the club.'

'Please rest assured.'

'And the Christmas pudding with brandy sauce.'

'Yes, yes.'

'Or do you think it should be apple strudel?'

'No, the Christmas pudding is more special.' Khushwant knew how to prepare a variety of Czech desserts as well as dishes.

'No expense is to be spared.'

'Mr Khanna, at eighteen rupees a head instead of seven, there is no need to mention such matters.'

'It's a pity the swimming pool has no water at this time of year.'

Khushwant did not smile, but he thought that it was unlike Mr Khanna to be so concerned about things of this kind. He wondered what this special party was that he was being asked to cater for—at a lunch that would consume two weeks' worth of Mr Khanna's salary in two hours.

Haresh walked home thinking about his next morning's meeting rather than the Goodyear Welted line. It was a two-minute walk to the small flat that he had been provided in the colony. When he got to his room, he sat at his desk for a while. He faced a small, framed photograph; it was the well-travelled picture of Lata that Mrs Rupa Mehra had given him in Kanpur.

He looked at it and smiled, then thought of the other photograph which used to travel with him. It had been left in its silver frame, but put away, lovingly and regretfully, in a drawer. And Haresh, after copying out in his small, slanting hand a few paragraphs and phrases from Simran's letters to him, had sent all her letters back to her. It would not be fair, he felt, to keep them.

The next day just at noon, two cars (the Chatterjis' white Humber which had been kuku'd by Meenakshi for the day, and Arun's little blue Austin) entered the white gates of the Prahapore Officers' Colony and stopped at House 6, Row 3. From the two cars emerged Mrs Rupa Mehra, together with two sons and a son-in-law, and two daughters and a daughter-in-law. The entire Mehra mafia was met and welcomed by Haresh, who took them upstairs to his little three-room flat.

Haresh had made sure that there would be enough beer, Scotch (White Horse, not Black Dog), and gin to keep everyone happy, as well as lots of nimbu pani and other soft drinks. His servant was a boy of about seventeen, who had been briefed that this was a very important occasion; he could not help grinning at the guests as he served them their drinks.

Pran and Varun had a beer, Arun a Scotch, and Meenakshi a Tom Collins. Mrs Rupa Mehra and her two daughters asked for nimbu pani. Haresh spent a lot of time fussing over Mrs Rupa Mehra. He was, most atypically and unlike his first meeting with Lata, quite nervous. Perhaps his meeting with Arun and Meenakshi at the Khandelwals' had given him the sense that they were critical of him. By now he and Lata had exchanged enough letters to make him feel that she was the woman for him. Her most affectionate letter had followed his announcement that he had lost his job; and he had been very moved by this.

Haresh made a few inquiries about Brahmpur and Bhaskar, and told Pran that he was looking very well. How were Veena and Kedarnath and Bhaskar? How was Sunil Patwardhan? He made a little polite conversation with Savita and Varun, whom he had never met before, and tried not to talk to Lata, who he sensed was equally nervous, perhaps even a little withdrawn.

Haresh was very conscious that he was under close family scrutiny, but he was not sure how to handle it. This was no Czech interview where he could talk about brass tacks and production. Some subtlety was required, and Haresh was not given to subtlety.

He talked a little about 'Cawnpore', until Arun said something denigratory about provincial industrial towns. Middlehampton too met with a similar response. Arun's amour propre and his habit of laying down his opinions as statute had clearly recovered from his setback at the Khandelwals'.

Haresh noticed that Lata was looking at his co-respondent shoes with what appeared almost to be distaste. But the moment he looked at her, she turned away a bit guiltily towards his small bookshelf with its maroon-bound set of Hardy novels. Haresh felt a little downcast; he had thought a great deal about what to wear.

But the grand luncheon was still to come, and he was sure that the Mehras would be more than impressed by the spread that Khushwant would lay on, as well as by the great wood-floored hall that constituted almost the entire premises of the Prahapore Officers' Club. Thank God he was not living outside the gates where the other foremen lived. The juxtaposition of those humble quarters with the pink silk handkerchief tucked into Arun's grey suit pocket, with Meenakshi's silvery laugh, with the white Humber parked outside, would have been disastrous.

By the time the party of eight was walking towards the club in the warm winter sunshine, Haresh's general optimism had reasserted itself. He pointed out that beyond the compound walls lay the river Hooghly and that the tall hedge that they were passing bounded the General Manager Havel's house. They walked past a small playground for children and a chapel. The chapel too was festooned for Christmas.

'The Czechs are good chaps at heart,' said Haresh expansively to Arun. 'They believe in results, in being shown rather than told something. I believe they'll even agree to my plan for brogues to be made in Brahmpur—and not by the Praha factory there but by small-scale manufacturers. They're not like the Bengalis, who want to talk everything over the table and do as little work as possible. It is amazing what the Czechs have managed to create—and that too in Bengal.'

Lata listened to Haresh, quite astonished by his bluntness. She had had something of the same opinion about Bengalis, but once their family had become allied to the Chatterjis, she did not make or take such generalizations easily. And didn't Haresh realize that Meenakshi was Bengali? Apparently not, because he was continuing regardless:

'It's hard for them, it must be, to be so far away from home and not be able to go back. They don't even have passports. Just what they call white papers, which makes it difficult for them to travel. They're mostly self-taught, though Kurilla has been to Middlehampton—and a few days ago even Novak was playing the piano at the club.'

But Haresh didn't explain who either of these two gentlemen were; he assumed that everyone else knew them. Lata was reminded of his explanations at the tannery.

By now they had got to the club, and Haresh, proud Prahaman that he had become, was showing them around with a proprietorial air.

He pointed out the pool—which had been drained and repainted a pleasant light blue, and a children's paddling pool nearby, the offices, the palm trees in pots, and the tables where a few Czechs were sitting outside under umbrellas, eating. There was nothing else to point out except the huge hall of the club. Arun, who was used to the subdued elegance of the Calcutta Club, was amazed by Haresh's bumptious self-assurance.

They entered the festooned hall; after the brightness outside, it was rather dark; there were a few groups here and there sitting down to lunch. Along the far wall was their own table for eight, created by joining three small square tables together.

'The hall is used for everything,' said Haresh. 'For dining, for dancing, as a cinema hall, and even for important meetings. When Mr Tomin'—and here Haresh's voice took on a somewhat reverential note—'when Mr Tomin came here last year, he gave a speech from the podium there. But these days it is used for the dance band.'

'Fascinating,' said Arun.

'How wonderful,' breathed Mrs Rupa Mehra.

16.14

Mrs Rupa Mehra was very impressed by all the arrangements. A thick white tablecloth and napkins, several sets of knives and forks, good glasses and crockery, and three flower arrangements consisting of an assortment of sweetpeas.

As soon as Haresh and his party entered, two waiters approached the table, and placed some bread on it, together with three dishes containing curlicues of Anchor butter. The bread had been baked under Khushwant's supervision; he had learned the technique from the Czechs. Varun, who had been walking a little unsteadily, was feeling quite peckish. After a few minutes, when the soup had not yet arrived, he took a slice. It was delicious. He took another.

'Varun, don't eat so much bread,' chided his mother. 'Can't you see how many courses there are?'

'Mm, Ma,' said Varun, his mouth full, and his mind on other things. When more beer was offered to him, he accepted with alacrity.

'How lovely the flower arrangements are,' said Mrs Rupa Mehra. Sweetpeas could never take the place of roses in her heart, but they were a lovely flower. She sniffed the air and took in the delicate colours: pale pink, white, mauve, violet, crimson, maroon, dark pink.

Lata was thinking that the sweetpeas made rather an odd arrangement.

Arun displayed his expertise on the subject of bread. He talked about caraway bread and rye bread and pumpernickel. 'But if you ask me,' he said (though no one had), 'there's nothing like the Indian naan for sheer delicacy.'

Haresh wondered what other kind of naan there was.

After the soup (cream of asparagus) came the first course, which was fried fish. Khushwant made quite a few Czech specialities, but only the simplest and most staple of English dishes. Mrs Rupa Mehra found that she was facing a cheese-covered vegetable bake for the second time in two days.

'Delicious,' she said, smiling at Haresh.

'I didn't know what to ask Khushwant to make for you, Ma; but he thought that this would be a good idea. And he has a treat for the second course, so he says.'

Tears threatened to come to Mrs Rupa Mehra's eyes at the thought of Haresh's kindness and consideration. Over the last few days she felt she had been starved of it. Sunny Park was like a zoo and Arun's explosions had been more frequent as a result. They were all staying together in the same small house, some of them sleeping on mattresses laid out at night in the drawing room. Though the Chatterjis had offered to put the Kapoors up in Ballygunge, Savita had felt that Uma and Aparna should be given the chance to get acquainted with each other. Also, she had quite unwisely wished to recreate the atmosphere of the old days in Darjeeling—or the railway saloons—when the four brothers and sisters had shared the same roof and pleasantly cramped quarters with their father and mother.

Politics was discussed. Results had started coming in from those states that had had early elections. According to Pran, the Congress would make a clean sweep of the elections. Arun did not contest the issue as he had the previous evening. By the end of the fish course politics was exhausted.

The second course was occupied mainly by Haresh impressing the assembled company with various facts of Praha history and production. He mentioned that Pavel Havel had praised him for 'working very hardly'. Although no communist, there was something in Haresh that resembled a cheerfully Stakhanovite Hero of Labour. He told them with pride that he was only the second Indian in the colony, and mentioned the weekly figure of 3,000 pairs to which he had increased production. 'I tripled it,' he added, very happy to share his sense of his own achievement. 'The welt-stitching operation was the real bottleneck.'

A line from Haresh's tour of the tannery had stuck in Lata's mind. 'All the other processes—glazing, boarding, ironing and so on—are optional, of course.' She remembered it again now, and saw in front of her the soaking pits, where thin men with orange rubber gloves were pulling swollen hides out of a dark liquid with grappling hooks. She looked down at the delicious skin of her roast chicken. I can't possibly marry him, she thought.

Mrs Rupa Mehra, on the other hand, had moved several miles forward in the opposite direction, aided by a delicious mushroom vol-au-vent. She had decided not only that Haresh would make an ideal husband for Lata but that Prahapore, with its playground and sweetpeas and protective walls, was the ideal place to bring up her grandsons.

'Lata has been saying how much she has been looking forward to seeing you in your smart new place,' Mrs Rupa Mehra fibbed. 'And now that we have seen it you must come for dinner on New Year's Day to our place in Sunny Park,' she added spontaneously. Arun's eyes opened wide, but he said nothing. 'And you must tell me if there is anything you particularly like to eat. I am so glad it is not Ekadashi today, otherwise I would not be allowed to have the pastry. You must come in the afternoon, that will give you a chance to speak to Lata. Do you like cricket?'

'Yes,' said Haresh, attempting to follow the ball of the conversation. 'But I'm not a good player.' He passed a puzzled hand across his forehead.

'Oh, I'm not talking about playing,' said Mrs Rupa Mehra. 'Arun will take you in the morning to see the Test match. He has got several tickets. Pran also is so fond of cricket,' she continued. 'And then you can come over to the house in the afternoon.' She glanced at Lata, who, for some unknown reason, was looking quite upset.

What can be the matter with the girl? thought Mrs Rupa Mehra, irritated. Moody, that's what she is. She doesn't deserve her good fortune.

Perhaps she did not. At the moment her fortune, Lata couldn't help musing, was somewhat mixed. In immediate terms it consisted of meat curry and rice; Czech sentences floating across from another table followed by a heavy laugh; a Christmas pudding with brandy sauce that Arun took two helpings of and that Mrs Rupa Mehra took three helpings of, her diabetes notwithstanding ('But it's a special day'); coffee; Varun silent and swaying; Meenakshi flirting with Arun and bewildering Haresh with a discussion of the pedigree of Mrs Khandelwal's dogs; suddenly mentioning that her maiden name was Chatterji, to Haresh's consternation—from which he recovered by plunging into talk of Praha; too much, far too much talk of Praha and Messrs Havel, Bratinka, Kurilla, Novak; the sense of a pair of co-respondent shoes lurking invisibly under a thick white tablecloth; the sudden view of a pleasant smile—Haresh's eyes disappearing almost entirely. Amit had said something about a smile—her smile—just the other day—yesterday, was it? Lata's mind wandered off to the Hooghly beyond the wall, the Botanical Gardens on its banks—a banyan tree—boats on the Ganga—another wall near another Praha factory—a field fringed with bamboos and the quiet sound of bat against ball. . . . She suddenly found herself feeling very sleepy.

'Are you all right?' It was Haresh, smiling affectionately.

'Yes, thanks, Haresh,' said Lata unhappily.

'We haven't had the chance to talk.'

'It doesn't matter. We're meeting on New Year's Day.' Lata made an attempt at a smile. She was glad that her latest letters to Haresh had been quite non-committal. She was grateful, in fact, that he had hardly spoken to her at all. What could they talk about? Poetry? Music? Plays? Common friends or acquaintances or members of the family? She was relieved that Prahapore was fifteen miles away from Calcutta.

'That's a lovely salmon-pink sari you're wearing,' Haresh ventured.

Lata began to laugh. Her sari was a pale green. She laughed with pleasure and for the sheer relief of it.

Everyone else was amazed. What on earth had got into Haresh—and what on earth had got into Lata?

'Salmon-pink!' said Lata, happily. 'I suppose just "pink" isn't specific enough.'

'Oh,' said Haresh, suddenly looking uncomfortable. 'It isn't green, is it?'

Varun gave a scornful snort, and Lata kicked him under the table.

'Are you colour-blind?' she asked Haresh with a smile.

'I'm afraid so,' said Haresh. 'But I can see nine out of ten colours accurately.'

'I'll wear pink the next time we meet,' said Lata. 'Then you can praise it without any uncertainty at all.'

Haresh saw the two cars off after lunch. He knew that he would be the topic of conversation for the next fifteen miles. He hoped that each car contained at least one of his supporters. He sensed once again that neither Arun nor Meenakshi wanted to have anything to do with him, but could not see what more he could have done to try to reconcile them to him.

About Lata he felt completely optimistic. He did not know of any rivals. Perhaps the lunch had been too filling, he thought; she had looked a bit sleepy. But it had gone off as well as expected. As for his colour-blindness, she would have had to find out about it sooner or later. He was glad that he had not asked them to come back to his flat for paan—Kalpana Gaur had warned him in a letter that the Mehras did not approve of paan. He had grown to like Lata so much that he wished he had had more time to speak with her. But he knew that it was not she but her family—and especially Ma—who was the target of today's exercise. 'Make 1951 the deciding year of your life,' he had written earlier in the year in one of his Action Points to himself. There were only three days to the new year. He decided to extend his deadline by a week or two, to the time when Lata would return to her studies in Brahmpur.

16.15

Savita had got into the front seat of the Austin; Arun was driving, and she wanted a word with him. Meenakshi sat at the back. The others went back to Calcutta in the Humber.

'Arun Bhai,' said the gentle Savita, 'what did you mean by behaving like that?'

'I don't see what you mean. Don't be a damned fool.'

Savita was the one person in the family who was not daunted by Arun's bullying tactics. There was to be no summary closure of debate.

'Why did you go out of your way to be unpleasant to Haresh?'

'Perhaps you should ask him that question.'

'I don't think he was particularly nasty to you.'

'Well, he certainly said that Praha was a household word in India and that the same couldn't be said for Bentsen Pryce.'

'It's a fact.'

'He had no call to say it even if it is.'

Savita laughed. 'He only said it, Arun Bhai, because you had gone on and on about the Czechs and their crude ways. It was self-defence.'

'I see you are determined to take his side.'

'That's not how I see it. Why couldn't you at least be civil? Don't you have any regard for Ma's feelings—or Lata's?'

'I most certainly do,' said Arun pompously. 'That is precisely why I think this thing should be nipped in the bud. He is simply the wrong sort of man. A shoemaker in the family!'

Arun smiled. When, on the recommendation of a former colleague of his father's, he had been asked to appear for an interview at Bentsen Pryce, they had had the wisdom instantly to perceive that he was the right sort of man. You either were or you weren't, reflected Arun.

'I don't see what's wrong with making shoes,' said Savita mildly. 'We're certainly happy to use them.'

Arun grunted.

'I think I have a bit of a headache,' said Meenakshi.

'Yes, yes,' continued Arun. 'I'm driving as fast as I can, considering I'm being distracted by my passenger. We'll be home soon.'

Savita was quiet for a couple of miles.

'Well, Arun Bhai, what do you have against him that you didn't have against Pran? You didn't have much to say about Pran's accent either when you first met him.'

Arun knew that he was treading on dangerous ground here, and that Savita would take no nonsense about her husband.

'Pran's all right,' conceded Arun. 'He's getting to know the ways of the family.'

'He has always been all right,' said Savita. 'It's just that the family has adjusted itself to him.'

'Have it your way,' said Arun. 'Just let me drive in peace. Or would you like me to pull over and continue this argument? Meenakshi has a headache.'

'Arun Bhai, this is not an argument. I'm sorry, Meenakshi, I have to have things out with him before he starts working on Ma,' said Savita. 'What is it you have against Haresh? That he isn't "one of us"?'

'Well, he certainly isn't,' said Arun. 'He's a dapper little man with co-respondent shoes, a grinning servant and a big head. I have rarely met anyone so arrogant, opinionated or self-satisfied—and with less cause to be.'

Savita merely smiled in reply. This irritated Arun even more than an answer.

'I don't know what you hope to achieve by this discussion,' he said after a few moments of silence.

'I just don't want you to ruin Lata's chances,' said Savita seriously. 'She isn't too certain about things herself, you know, and I want her to make up her own mind, not to have Big Brother deciding everything for her and laying down the law as usual.'

Meenakshi laughed from the back: a silvery, slightly steely laugh.

A huge lorry came towards them from the other side, almost forcing them off the narrow road. Arun swerved and swore.

'Do you mind if we continue this conference at home?' he asked.

'There are hundreds of people at home,' said Savita. 'It will be impossible to make you see sense with all the interruptions. Don't you realize, Arun Bhai, that offers of marriage do not come raining down from the sky every day? Why are you determined to thwart this one?'

'There are certainly others who are interested in Lata—Meenakshi's brother for one.'

'Amit? Do you really mean Amit?'

'Yes, Amit. I do really mean Amit.'

Savita immediately thought that Amit would be most unsuitable, but did not say so. 'Well, let Lata decide for herself,' she said. 'Leave it to her.'

'With Ma fussing around her, she won't be capable of making up her own mind anyway,' said Arun. 'And Ma, as anyone can see, has been well wooed by the foreman. He hardly had a minute for anyone else the whole afternoon. I noticed that he didn't speak much to you, for example.'

'I didn't mind,' said Savita. 'I liked him. And I want you to behave decently on New Year's Day.'

Arun shook his head at the thought of Ma's sudden, unconsulted invitation to Haresh.

'Please let me out at New Market,' said Meenakshi suddenly. 'I'll join you later.'

'But your headache, darling?'

'It's all right. I have to buy a few things. I'll come home in a taxi.'

'Are you sure?'

'Yes.'

'We haven't upset you?'

'No.'

When Meenakshi had got down, Arun turned to Savita:

'You have quite needlessly upset my wife.'

'Oh don't be silly, Arun Bhai—and don't refer to Meenakshi as "my wife". I think she just can't face going home to a dozen people. And I don't blame her. There are too many of us in Sunny Park. Do you think Pran and Uma and I should take up the Chatterjis' invitation?'

'That's another thing. What did he mean by talking about Bengalis in that manner?'

'I don't know,' said Savita. 'But you do it all the time.'

Arun was quiet. Something was troubling him.

'Do you think she got down because she thought we were going to discuss Amit?'

Savita smiled at the thought of such unlikely delicacy on Meenakshi's part but simply said, 'No.'

'Well,' said Arun, still stung by the fact that Savita of all people was being so uncompromising in this matter of Haresh, and feeling a little uncertain as a result, 'you're getting quite a lot of courtroom practice out of me.'

'Yes,' said Savita, refusing to be jollied along. 'Now promise me you're not going to interfere.'

Arun laughed in an indulgent, elder-brotherly manner. 'Well, we all have our opinions—you have yours, and I have mine. And Ma can take whichever she likes. And Lata too, of course. Let's leave it at that, shall we?'

Savita shook her head, but said nothing.

Arun was trying to be winning, but she was not won.

16.16

Meenakshi made straight for the Fairlawn Hotel, where Billy was waiting for her in his room with a mixture of impatience and uncertainty.

'You know, Meenakshi, this thing makes me very anxious,' said Billy. 'I don't like it a bit.'

'I don't believe it makes you anxious,' said Meenakshi. 'Certainly not so anxious that it detracts from your wonderful—'

'—performance?' finished Billy.

'Performance. Just the word. Let's perform. But be nice to me, Billy. I'm sorry I'm late. I've had the most awful time and I have a headache as huge as *Buddenbrooks*.'

'A headache?' Billy was concerned. 'Shall I ask them to get you a couple of aspirin?'

'No, Billy,' said Meenakshi, sitting next to him. 'I think I have a better cure.'

'I thought women were supposed to say, "Not tonight, dear, I have a headache,"' said Billy, helping her with her sari.

'Some women, perhaps,' said Meenakshi. 'Does Shireen say that?'

'I'd rather not discuss Shireen,' said Billy stiffly.

By now Billy was as eager to cure Meenakshi as she was to be cured. About fifteen minutes later, he was lying, panting and pleasantly exhausted, upon her, his head nuzzling her neck. Meenakshi was much sweeter when she was making love than at any other time. She was almost affectionate! He began to withdraw.

'No, Billy, just stay where you are,' said Meenakshi in a sighing voice. 'You feel so nice.' Billy had been at his tenderly athletic best.

'All right,' Billy consented.

After a few minutes though, as he softened, he had to pull out.

'Whoops!' said Billy.

'That was lovely,' said Meenakshi. 'What was the "whoops" for?'

'I'm sorry, Meenakshi—but the thing's slipped off. It's still inside you.'

'But it can't be! I can't feel it.'

'Well, it's not on me, and I could feel it slip off.'

'Don't be ridiculous, Billy,' said Meenakshi sharply. 'It's never happened before—and do you think I wouldn't feel it if it was still there?'

'I don't know about that,' said Billy. 'I think you'd better go and check.' Meenakshi went for a shower, and came out furious.

'How dare you?' she said.

'How dare I what?' responded Billy, looking troubled.

'How dare you let it slip off! I'm not going through all that again,' said Meenakshi, and burst into tears. How horribly, horribly tawdry, she thought.

Poor Billy was very worried by now. He tried to console her by putting his arms around her wet shoulders, but she shook him off angrily. She was trying to work out if today fell within her most vulnerable week. Billy was a real fool.

'Meenakshi, I just can't go on with this sort of thing,' he was saying.

'Oh, do be quiet, and let me think. My headache's come back,' said Meenakshi.

Billy nodded contritely. Meenakshi was putting on her sari again—rather violently.

By the time she had worked out that she was probably safe anyway, she was in no mood to relinquish Billy. She told him so.

'But after Shireen and I are married—' began Billy.

'What does marriage have to do with it?' asked Meenakshi. 'I'm married, aren't I? You enjoy it, I enjoy it; that's all there is to it. Next Thursday, then.'

'But Meenakshi—'

'Don't gape, Billy. It makes you look like a fish. I'm trying to be reasonable.'

'But Meenakshi—'

'I can't stay to discuss all this,' said Meenakshi, putting the finishing touches to her face. 'I'd better be getting home. Poor Arun will be wondering what on earth's happened to me.'

16.17

'Put off the light,' said Mrs Rupa Mehra to Lata as she came out of the bathroom. 'Electricity does not grow on trees.'

Mrs Rupa Mehra was seriously annoyed. It was New Year's Eve and, instead of spending it with her mother as she ought to, Lata was behaving like a Young Person and going out with Arun and Meenakshi for a round of parties. Mischief was afoot, and Mrs Rupa Mehra could sense it.

'Will Amit be going with you?' she demanded of Meenakshi.

'Well, Ma, I hope so—and Kuku and Hans too if we can persuade them,' Meenakshi added as camouflage.

Mrs Rupa Mehra was not deceived. 'Well, then, you will have no objection to Varun going as well,' she asserted. She promptly instructed her younger son to go along with them. 'And do not leave the party for a moment,' she warned him sternly.

Varun was not happy at all with this state of affairs. He had hoped to spend his New Year with Sajid, Jason, Hot-ends and his other Shamshuing and gambling acquaintances. But there was that in Mrs Rupa Mehra's eye which brooked no counter-squeak. 'And I do not want Lata to go off by herself,' said Mrs Rupa Mehra when she got Varun by himself for a moment. 'I do not trust your brother and Meenakshi.'

'Oh, why not?' asked Varun.

'They will be having much too good a time to keep an eye on Lata,' said Mrs Rupa Mehra evasively.

'I suppose I shouldn't have a good time myself,' said Varun with gloomy annoyance.

'No. Not if your sister's future is at stake. What would your father say?'

At the memory of his father Varun felt a sudden sense of resentment of the kind he often had towards Arun. Then, almost immediately, he felt bad about it, and was overcome by a sense of guilt. What kind of son am I? he thought.

Mrs Rupa Mehra and the rump of the family—Pran, Savita, Aparna and Uma—were to go over to Ballygunge that evening to spend New Year's Eve with the senior Chatterjis, including old Mr Chatterji. Dipankar and Tapan would be at home too. It would be a quiet family evening, thought Mrs Rupa Mehra, not like this endless gallivanting that seemed to be the craze these days. Frivolous, that was the word for Meenakshi and Kakoli; and their frivolity was a disgrace in a city as poor as Calcutta—a city moreover where Pandit Nehru had just arrived to talk about the Congress and the freedom struggle and socialism. Mrs Rupa Mehra told Meenakshi exactly what she thought.

Meenakshi's response was a couplet disguised as 'Deck the hall with boughs of holly', of which there had been a good deal too much on the radio recently:

'End the year with fun and frivol.
Fa-la-la-la-la, la-la-la-la!
All the rest is drab and drivel.
Fa-la-la-la-la, la-la-la-la!'

'You are a very irresponsible girl, Meenakshi, I can tell you that,' said Mrs Rupa Mehra. 'How dare you sing to me like that?'

But Mrs Arun Mehra was in too good a mood to be put off by her mother-in-law's ill-temper and, surprisingly and suddenly, gave her a kiss for New Year. Such a sign of affection was rare in Meenakshi, and Mrs Rupa Mehra accepted it with glum grace.

Then Arun, Meenakshi, Varun and Lata whizzed off to enjoy themselves.

They went to several parties, and landed up after eleven o'clock at Bishwanath Bhaduri's, where Meenakshi saw the back of Billy's head.

'Billy!' Meenakshi cooed in a carrying vibrato from halfway across the room.

Billy looked around and his face fell. But Meenakshi traversed the room and managed to detach him as blatantly and flirtatiously as possible from Shireen. When she had got him alone in a corner, she said:

'Billy, I can't make it on Thursday. The Shady Ladies just phoned to say they're having a special meeting.'

Billy's face expressed relief. 'Oh, I'm so sorry,' he said.

'So it will have to be Wednesday.'

'I can't!' pleaded Billy. Then he became annoyed. 'Why did you get me away from my friends?' he said. 'Shireen will begin to suspect me.'

'She will not,' said Meenakshi gaily. 'But it's good your back's turned to her at the moment. If she saw you looking so angry, she certainly would. And indignation doesn't suit you. In fact nothing suits you. Only your birthday suit. Don't blush, Billy, or I shall be forced to kiss you passionately an hour before your New Year kiss is due. Wednesday then. Don't evade your irresponsibilities.'

Billy was horribly unhappy, but he didn't know what to do.

'Did you watch the Test match today?' asked Meenakshi, changing the subject. Poor Billy, he looked so dejected.

'What do you think?' said Billy, cheering up at the memory. India had not done too badly, having managed to get England out for 342 in the first innings.

'So you'll be there tomorrow?' Meenakshi said.

'Oh, yes. I'm looking forward to seeing what Hazare will do with their bowling. The MCC have sent a second-rate team out to India, and I'll be happy to see them taught a lesson. Well, it'll be a pleasant way to spend New Year's Day.'

'Arun has a few tickets,' said Meenakshi. 'I think I'll go and watch the match tomorrow.'

'But you aren't interested in cricket—' protested Billy.

'Ah—there's another woman waving at you,' said Meenakshi. 'You haven't been seeing other women, have you?'

'Meenakshi!' said Billy, so deeply shocked that Meenakshi was forced to believe him.

'Well, I'm glad you're still faithful. Faithfully unfaithful,' said Meenakshi. 'Or unfaithfully faithful. No, it's me she's waving at. Should I deliver you back to Shireen?'

'Yes, please,' said Billy mutedly.

16.18

Varun and Lata were talking to Dr Ila Chattopadhyay in another part of the room. Dr Ila Chattopadhyay enjoyed the company of all sorts of people—and the fact that they were young did not count against them in her view. In fact this was one of her strengths as a teacher of English. Another was her devastating braininess. Dr Ila Chattopadhyay was as crazy and opinionated with her students as with her colleagues. Indeed, she respected her students more than her colleagues. They were, she thought, much more intellectually innocent, and much more intellectually honest.

Lata wondered what she was doing at this party: was she also chaperoning someone? If so, she was performing her duties laxly. At the moment she was entirely absorbed in conversation with Varun.

'No, no,' she was saying, 'don't join the IAS—it's just another one of those Brown Sahib professions, and you'll turn into a variant of your odious brother.'

'But what should I do?' Varun was saying. 'I'm not good for anything.'

'Write a book! Pull a rickshaw! Live! Don't make excuses,' said Dr Ila Chattopadhyay with hectic enthusiasm, shaking her grey hair vigorously. 'Renounce the world like Dipankar. No, he's joined a bank, hasn't he? How did you do in your exams anyway?' she added.

'Terribly!' said Varun.

'I don't think you've done so badly,' said Lata. 'I always think I've done worse than I actually have. It's a Mehra trait.'

'No, I really have done terribly,' said Varun, pulling a morose face and gulping down his whisky. 'I'm sure I've failed. I shall certainly not be called for the interview.'

Dr Ila Chattopadhyay said: 'Don't worry. It could be far worse. A good friend of mine has just had her daughter die of TB.'

Lata looked at Ila Chattopadhyay in amazement. Next she'll say: 'Now don't worry. Just think—it could be far worse. A sister of mine has just had her two-year-old triplets decapitated by her alcoholic husband.'

'You have the most extraordinary expression on your face,' said Amit, who had joined them.

'Oh, Amit! Hello,' said Lata. It was good to see him.

'What were you thinking of?'

'Nothing—nothing at all.'

Dr Ila Chattopadhyay was telling Varun about the idiocy of Calcutta University in making Hindi a compulsory subject at the B.A. level. Amit joined the discussion for a bit. He sensed that Lata's thoughts were still quite far away. He wanted to talk to her a little about her poem. But he was accosted by a woman who said: 'I want to talk to you.'

'Well, here I am,' said Amit.

'My name is Baby,' said the woman, who looked about forty.

'Well, mine is Amit.'

'I know that, I know that, everyone knows that,' said the woman. 'Are you trying to impress me with your modesty?' She was in a quarrelsome mood.

'No,' said Amit.

'I love your books, especially *The Fever Tree.* I think of it all night. I mean *The Fever Bird*. You look smaller than your photographs. You must be very leggy.'

'What do you do?' asked Amit, not knowing what to make of her last few words.

'I like you,' said the lady decisively. 'I know whom I like. Visit me in Bombay. Everyone knows me. Just ask for Baby.'

'All right,' said Amit. He had no plans to go to Bombay.

Bishwanath Bhaduri came over to say hello to Amit. He ignored Lata almost completely. He even ignored the predatory Baby. He was in raptures about some new woman, whom he pointed out: someone who was dressed in black and silver.

'One feels she has such a beautiful soul,' said Bish.

'Repeat that,' said Amit.

Bishwanath Bhaduri drew back. 'One doesn't say such things in order to repeat them,' he said.

'Ah, but one doesn't get to hear such things very often.'

'You'll use it for your novel. One shouldn't, you know.'

'Why shouldn't one?'

'It's just Calcutta chit-chat.'

'It's not chit-chat—it's poetic; very poetic; suspiciously so.'

'You're making fun of me,' said Bishwanath Bhaduri. He looked around. 'One needs a drink,' he murmured.

'One needs to escape,' said Amit quietly to Lata. 'Two need to.'

'I can't. I have a chaperone.'

'Who?'

Lata's eyes indicated Varun. He was talking to a couple of young men, who were clinging to his words.

'I think we can give him the slip,' said Amit. 'I'll show you the lights on Park Street.'

As they walked behind Varun they heard him say: 'Marywallace, of course, for the Gatwick; and Simile for the Hopeful. I have no idea about the Hazra. And for the Beresford Cup it's best to go for My Lady Jean. . . .'

They eluded him with ease and walked down the stairs, laughing.

16.19

Amit hailed a taxi.

'Park Street,' said Amit.

'Why not Bombay?' asked Lata, laughing. 'To meet Baby.'

'She is a thorn in my neck,' said Amit, shaking his knees together rapidly.

'In your neck?'

'As Biswas Babu would say.'

Lata laughed. 'How is he?' she asked. 'Everyone talks about him, but I've never met him.'

'He's been telling me to get married—to produce, he hopes, a fourth generation of Chatterji judge. I suggested that Aparna was half a Chatterji and might easily rise to the bench, given her precocity. He said that that was a different kettle of tea.'

'But his advice ran off your back like duck's water.'

'Exactly so.'

They had been driving along Chowringhee, parts of which were lit up—especially the larger stores, the Grand Hotel, and Firpo's. Now they were at the crossing of Park Street. Here, a large reindeer complete with Santa and sleigh was illuminated by large coloured bulbs. Several people were strolling along the side of Chowringhee adjacent to the Maidan, enjoying the festive atmosphere. As the taxi turned into Park Street, Lata was taken aback by its unaccustomed brilliance. On both sides, multicoloured strings of lights and brightly coloured festoons of crêpe hung from the fronts of shops and restaurants: Flury's, Kwality, Peiping, Magnolia. It was lovely, and Lata turned to Amit with delight and gratitude. When they got to the tall Christmas tree by the petrol pump she said:

'Electricity growing on trees.'

'What was that?' said Amit.

'Oh, that's Ma. "Turn off the lights. Electricity doesn't grow on trees."'

Amit laughed. 'It's very nice to see you again,' he said.

'I feel the same way,' said Lata. 'Mutatis mutandis.'

Amit looked at her in surprise. 'The last time I heard that was at the Inns of Court.'

'Oh,' said Lata, smiling. 'I must have picked it up from Savita. She's always cooing such phrases to the baby.'

'By the way, what were you thinking of when I interrupted you and Varun?' asked Amit.

Lata told him about Dr Ila Chattopadhyay's remark.

Amit nodded, then said: 'About your poem.'

'Yes?' Lata grew tense. What was he going to say about it?

'I sometimes feel that it's a consolation in times of deep grief to know that the world, by and large, does not care.'

Lata was quiet. It was an odd sentiment, though a relevant one. After a while she said: 'Did you like it?'

'Yes,' said Amit. 'As a poem.' He recited a couple of lines.

'The cemetery's on this street, isn't it?' said Lata.

'Yes.'

'Very different from the other end.'

'Very.'

'That was a curious sort of spiral pillar on Rose Aylmer's tomb.'

'Do you want to see it by night?'

'No! It would be strange, seeing all those stars. A night of memories and of sighs.'

'I should have pointed them out to you by day,' said Amit.

'Pointed what out?'

'The stars.'

'By day?'

'Well, yes. I can tell you roughly where the various stars are by day. Why not? They're still in the sky. The sun only blinds us to them. It's midnight. May I?'

And before she could protest, Amit had kissed her.

She was so surprised she didn't know what to say. She was also a bit annoyed.

'Happy New Year,' said Amit.

'Happy New Year,' she answered, hiding her annoyance. She had, after all, conspired to evade her chaperone. 'You didn't plan this, did you?'

'Of course not. Do you want me to deliver you back to Varun? Or should we take a walk by the Victoria Memorial?'

'Neither. I'm feeling tired. I'd like to go to sleep.' After a pause she said: '1952: how new it seems. As if each digit were polished.'

'A leap year.'

'I'd better go back to the party. Varun really will panic if he finds me gone.'

'I'll drop you back home, then go back to the party myself to tell Varun. How's that?'

Lata smiled to think of Varun's expression when he realized his charge had flown.

'All right. Thank you, Amit.'

'You aren't annoyed with me? New Year's licence. I couldn't help it.'

'So long as you don't claim poetic licence the next time.'

Amit laughed, and good relations were restored.

But why don't I feel anything? she asked herself. She did know that Amit was fond of her, but her chief emotion at the kiss was still astonishment.

She was home in a few minutes. Mrs Rupa Mehra had not yet returned. When she did come back half an hour later she found Lata asleep. Lata appeared restless—her head was turning from side to side on her pillow.

She was dreaming—of a kiss—but it was of Kabir that she was dreaming, the one who was absent, the one who above all others she should not meet, the most unsuitable boy of them all.

16.20

1952: the fresh and brilliant digits impressed themselves upon Pran's eye as he opened the morning newspaper. All the past grew veiled by the first of January, and all the future glistened ahead of him, emerging mysteriously from its grubby chrysalis. He thought about his heart and his child and Bhaskar's close brush with death, the mixed gifts of the previous year. And he wondered whether the coming year would bring him his readership—and a new brother-in-law—and possibly even see his father sworn in as the Chief Minister of Purva Pradesh. The last was by no means impossible. As for Maan, surely he would have to settle down sooner or later.

Although no one other than himself and Mrs Rupa Mehra was awake at six o'clock, there was a sudden storm of activity at seven. The time allowed in the two bathrooms was strictly rationed, and everyone was completely ready—and even breakfasted—by eight thirty. The women had decided to spend the day at the Chatterjis'—perhaps they would go on to do a bit of shopping as well. Even Meenakshi, who at first appeared eager to come to the cricket match, decided against it at the last moment.

Amit and Dipankar arrived in the Humber at nine, and Arun, Varun and Pran went off with them to Eden Gardens to watch the third day of the Third Test. Just outside the stadium they met Haresh, as previously arranged, and the six of them made their way to the tier where their seats were located.

It was a wonderful morning. There was a clear blue sky, and dew still glistened on the outfield. Eden Gardens, with its emerald grass and surrounding trees, its huge scoreboard and new Ranji Stadium block, was a magnificent sight. It was packed solid, but luckily one of Arun's English colleagues at Bentsen Pryce, who had bought a bunch of season tickets for his family, was out sightseeing, and had offered his seats to Arun for the day. They were placed just next to the pavilion section, where VIPs and members of the Cricket Association of Bengal sat, and they had a fine view of the field.

India's opening batsmen were still at the crease. Since India had scored 418 and 485 in two previous innings in the series, and since England were all out for 342 in their first innings, there was a good chance that the hosts would be able to make something of the match. The Calcutta crowd—more knowledgeable and appreciative than any other in India—was looking forward to it with eager anticipation.

The chatter, which increased between overs, was reduced, but not quite to silence, every time the bowler came in to bowl. Leadbeater opened the bowling to Roy with a maiden, and Ridgway supported the attack from the other end, bowling to Mankad. Then, for the next over, instead of continuing with Leadbeater, the English skipper Howard brought Statham on.

This provoked a good deal of discussion among the group of six. Everyone started speculating as to why Leadbeater had been brought on for a single over. Amit alone said that it meant nothing at all. Perhaps, because Indian time was several hours ahead of England, Leadbeater had wanted to bowl the first English ball of 1952 and Howard had let him.

'Really, Amit,' said Pran with a laugh. 'Cricket isn't governed by poetical whims of that kind.'

'A pity,' said Amit. 'Reading old reports by Cardus always makes me think that it's just a variant of poetry—in six-line stanzas.'

'I wonder where Billy is,' said Arun in rather a hangover-ish voice. 'Can't see him anywhere.'

'Oh, he's bound to be here,' said Amit. 'I can't imagine him missing a day of a Test.'

'We're off to a rather slow start,' said Dipankar. 'I hope this isn't going to be another awful draw like the last two Tests.'

'I think we're going to teach them a lesson.' This was Haresh's optimistic assessment.

'We might,' said Pran. 'But we should be careful on this wicket. It's a bowler's delight.'

And so it proved to be.

The quick loss of three of the best Indian wickets—including that of the captain—cast a chill on the stadium. When Amarnath—who had hardly had time to pad up—came on to the field to face Tattersall, there was complete silence. Even the women spectators stopped their winter knitting for a second.

He was bowled for a duck in that same fatal over.

The Indian side was collapsing like skittles. If the mayhem continued, India might be all out before lunch. High visions of a victory turned to the dread of an ignominious follow-on.

'Just like us,' said Varun morosely. 'We are a failure as a country. We can always snatch defeat out of the jaws of victory. I'm going to watch the racing in the afternoon,' he added disgustedly. He would have to watch his horses through the palings around the course rather than sit in these forty-rupee season-ticket seats, but at least there was a chance that his horse might win.

'I'm getting up to stretch my legs,' said Amit.

'I'll come with you,' said Haresh, who was annoyed by the poor show that India was putting on. 'Oh—who's that man there—the one in the navy-blue blazer with the maroon scarf—do any of you know? I seem to recognize him from somewhere.'

Pran looked across at the pavilion section and was completely taken aback.

'Oh, Malvolio!' he said, as if he had seen Banquo instead.

'What was that?' said Haresh.

'Nothing. I suddenly remembered something I have to teach next term. Cricket balls, my liege. Something just struck me. No, I—I can't say for sure that I recognize him—I think you'd better ask the Calcutta people.' Pran was not good at deception, but the last thing he wanted to encourage was a meeting between Haresh and Kabir. Any number of complications might ensue, including a visit by Kabir to Sunny Park.

Luckily, no one else recognized him.

'I'm sure I've seen him somewhere,' Haresh persisted. 'I'm bound to remember sometime. Good-looking fellow. You know, the same thing happened to me with Lata. I felt I'd seen her before—and—I'm sure I'm not mistaken. I'll go and say hello.'

Pran could do nothing further. Amit and Haresh wandered over between overs, and Haresh said to Kabir: 'Good morning. Haven't we met somewhere before?'

Kabir looked at them and smiled. He stood up. 'I don't think we have,' he said.

'Perhaps at work—or in Cawnpore?' said Haresh. 'I have the feeling—well, anyway, I'm Haresh Khanna, from Praha.'

'Glad to meet you, Sir.' Kabir shook his hand and smiled. 'Perhaps we've met in Brahmpur, that is if you come to Brahmpur on work.'

Haresh shook his head. 'I don't think so,' he said. 'Are you from Brahmpur?'

'Yes,' said Kabir. 'I'm a student at Brahmpur University. I'm keen on cricket, so I've come down for a while to watch what I can of the Test. A pretty miserable show.'

'Well, it's a dewy wicket,' said Amit in mitigation.

'Dewy wicket my foot,' said Kabir with good-natured combativeness.

'We are always making excuses for ourselves. Roy had no business to cut that ball. And Umrigar did the same. And for Hazare and Amarnath to be bowled neck and crop in the same over—it's really too bad. They send over a team that doesn't include Hutton or Bedser or Compton or Laker or May—and we manage to disgrace ourselves anyway. We've never had a Test victory against the MCC, and if we lose this one, we don't ever deserve to win. I'm beginning to think it's a good thing I'm leaving Calcutta tomorrow morning. Anyway, tomorrow's a rest day.'

'Why, where are you going?' laughed Haresh, who liked the young man's spirit. 'Back to Brahmpur?'

'No—I've got to go to Allahabad for the Inter-'Varsity.'

'Are you on the university team?'

'Yes.' Kabir frowned. 'But I'm sorry, I haven't introduced myself. My name's Kabir. Kabir Durrani.'

'Ah,' said Haresh, his eyes disappearing. 'You're the son of Professor Durrani.'

Kabir looked at Haresh in amazement.

'We met for just a minute,' said Haresh. 'I brought young Bhaskar Tandon over to your house one day to meet your father. In fact, now I come to think of it, you were wearing cricket clothes.'

Kabir said: 'Good heavens. I think I do remember now. I'm terribly sorry. But won't you sit down? These two chairs are free—my friends have gone off to get some coffee.'

Haresh introduced Amit, and they all sat down.

After the next over Kabir turned to Haresh and said: 'I suppose you know what happened to Bhaskar at the Pul Mela?'

'Yes, indeed. I'm glad to hear he's all right now.'

'If he had been here, we wouldn't have needed that fancy Australian-style scoreboard.'

'No,' said Haresh with a smile. 'Pran's nephew,' he said to Amit by way of incomplete explanation.

'I do wish women wouldn't bring their knitting to the match,' said Kabir intolerantly. 'Hazare out. Plain. Umrigar out. Purl. It's like *A Tale of Two Cities*.'

Amit laughed at this pleasant young fellow's analogy, but was forced to come to the defence of his own city. 'Well, apart from our sections of the stadium, where people come to be seen as much as to see, Calcutta's a good place for cricket,' he said. 'In the four-rupee seats the crowd knows its stuff all right. And they start queueing up for day tickets from nine o'clock the previous night.'

Kabir nodded. 'Well, you're right. And it's a lovely stadium. The greenness of the field almost hurts the eyes.'

Haresh thought back for a moment to his mistake about colours, and wondered whether it had done him any harm.

The bowling changed over once again from the Maidan end to the High Court end.

'Whenever I think of the High Court end I feel guilty,' said Amit to Haresh. Making conversation with his rival was one way of sizing him up.

Haresh, who had no sense at all that he had any rival anywhere, answered innocently: 'Why? Have you done anything against the law? Oh, I'm forgetting, your father's a judge.'

'And I'm a lawyer, that's my problem. I should be working, according to him—writing opinions, not poems.'

Kabir half turned towards Amit in astonishment.

'You're not the Amit Chatterji?'

Amit had discovered that coyness made things worse once he was recognized. 'Yes, indeed,' he said. 'The.'

'Why—I'm—how amazing—I like your stuff—a lot of it—I can't say I understand it all.'

'No, nor do I.'

A sudden thought struck Kabir. 'Why don't you come to Brahmpur to read? You have a lot of fans there in the Brahmpur Literary Society. But I hear you never give readings.'

'Well, not never,' said Amit thoughtfully. 'I don't normally—but if I'm asked to come to Brahmpur, and can get leave of absence from my Muse, I might well come. I've often wondered what the town is like: the Barsaat Mahal, you know, and, of course, the Fort—and, well, other objects of beauty and interest. I've never been there before.' He paused. 'Well, would you care to join us there among the season-ticket holders? But I suppose these are better seats.'

'It's not that,' said Kabir. 'It's just that I'm with friends—they've invited me—and it's my last day in town. I'd better not. But I'm very honoured to meet you. And—well—you're sure you wouldn't take it amiss if you were invited to Brahmpur? It wouldn't interfere too much with your writing?'

'No,' said Amit mildly. 'Not Brahmpur. Just write to my publishers. It'll be forwarded to me.'

The game was continuing, a little more steadily than before. It would soon be lunchtime. No more wickets had fallen, which was a blessing, but India was still in perilous straits.

'It's a real pity about Hazare. His form seems to have deserted him after that knock on the head in Bombay,' said Amit.

'Well,' said Kabir, 'you can't blame him entirely. Ridgway's bouncers can be vicious—and he'd scored a century, after all. He was pretty badly stunned. I don't think he should have been forced back out from the pavilion by the Chairman of Selectors. It's demeaning for a skipper to be ordered back—and bad for morale all around.' He went on, almost in a dream: 'I suppose Hazare is indecisive—it took him fifteen minutes to decide whether to bat or to field in the last Test. But, well, I'm discovering that I'm quite indecisive myself, so I sympathize. I've been thinking of visiting someone ever since I arrived in Calcutta, but I can't. I find I just can't. I don't know what kind of bowling I'd have to face,' he added with a rather bitter laugh. 'They say he's lost his nerve, and I think I've lost mine!' Kabir's remarks were not addressed to anyone in particular, but Amit felt—for no very good reason—a strong sense of sympathy for him.

Had Amit identified him as the 'Akbar from *As You Like It*' of Meenakshi's imaginative description, he may not have felt quite so sympathetic.

16.21

Pran did not question either Amit or Haresh about their meeting with Kabir. He waited for one or the other of them to mention that Kabir knew or had heard of either him or Arun; but since neither name had come up in their conversation, there was nothing as such to tell. He breathed a sigh of relief. Clearly Kabir would not be visiting Sunny Park and upsetting well-laid plans.

After a quick lunch of sandwiches and coffee the group of six—still dazed by India's sudden collapse and not optimistic about the afternoon's play—dispersed in cars and taxis. They had to thread their way through huge crowds that had begun to gather on the Maidan to hear Pandit Nehru speak. The Prime Minister—or, in this role, the President of Congress—was on one of his lightning election tours. Just the previous day he had spoken at Kharagpur, Asansol, Burdwan, Chinsurah and Serampore; and just before that he had been canvassing in Assam.

Varun asked to be put down near the smaller—but equally eager—crowds surrounding the racetrack, and started to look around for his friends. After a while he began to wonder whether he shouldn't listen to Nehru's speech instead. But after a brief struggle, My Lady Jean and Windy Wold defeated Freedom Fighter by several lengths. I can always read about it in the newspapers, he told himself.

Haresh had meanwhile gone to visit distant relatives whom his foster-father had told him to look up in Calcutta. So involved had he been with production in Prahapore that he hadn't found the time to do so; but now he had a couple of hours to spare. When he got to his relatives' place he found them all glued to the radio listening to the cricket commentary. They tried to be hospitable, but their minds were clearly elsewhere. Haresh too joined them by the radio.

India was 257 for 6 at close of play. Disgrace at least had been miraculously averted.

Haresh was therefore in a good mood when he arrived at Sunny Park in time for tea. He was introduced to Aparna, whom he tried to humour and who treated him distantly as a result, and to Uma, who gave him an undiscriminating smile which delighted him.

'Are you being polite, Haresh?' asked Savita warmly. 'You're not eating anything at all. Politeness doesn't pay in this family. Pass the pastries, Arun.'

'I must apologize,' said Arun to Haresh. 'I should have mentioned it this morning but it slipped my mind entirely. Meenakshi and I will be out for dinner tonight.'

'Oh,' said Haresh, puzzled. He glanced at Mrs Rupa Mehra. She was looking flushed and upset.

'Yes. Well, we were invited three weeks ago, and couldn't cancel it at the last moment. But Ma and the rest will be here, of course. And Varun will do the honours. Both Meenakshi and I were looking forward to it, needless to say, but when we got home from Prahapore that day, we looked at our diary and—well, there it is.'

'We feel awful,' said Meenakshi gaily. 'Do have a cheese straw.'

'Thank you,' said Haresh, a little dampened. But after a few minutes he bounced back. Lata at least looked pleased to see him. She was indeed wearing a pink sari. Either that or she was very cruel! Today he'd certainly get a chance to talk to her. And Savita, he felt, was kind and warm and encouraging. Perhaps it was no bad thing that Arun wouldn't be there for dinner, though it would be odd to sit down at his table—and that too for the first time—in his host's absence. Haresh could feel muted pulses of antagonism emanating from his direction, and to some extent from the darkly radiant Meenakshi too, and he would not have felt entirely relaxed in their company. But it was certainly an odd response to the hospitality he had offered them.

Varun was looking unusually cheerful. He had won eight rupees at the races.

'Well, we didn't do so badly after all,' said Haresh to him.

'I'm sorry?'

'After this morning, I mean.'

'Oh, yes, cricket. What was the closing score?' asked Varun, who had got up.

'257 for 6,' said Pran, astonished that Varun hadn't been following it.

'Hmm,' said Varun, and went over to the gramophone.

'Don't!' thundered Arun.

'Don't what, Arun Bhai?'

'Don't put on that damn machine. Unless you want me to box your two intoxicated ears.'

Varun recoiled with murderous timidity. Haresh looked startled at the exchange between the brothers. Varun had hardly said a thing that day in Prahapore.

'Aparna likes it,' he said in a resentful tone, not daring to look at Arun. 'And so does Uma.' Unlikely though this was, it was true. Savita, whenever she found that legal Latin did not put Uma to sleep, would sing this song to her while rocking her to and fro.

'I do not care who likes what,' said Arun, his face reddening. 'You will turn it off. And at once.'

'I haven't turned it on in the first place,' said Varun in creeping triumph.

Lata hurriedly asked Haresh the first question that came into her head: 'Have you seen *Deedar*?'

'Oh, yes,' said Haresh. 'Thrice. Once by myself, once with friends in Delhi, and once with Simran's sister in Lucknow.'

There was silence for a few seconds.

'You must have enjoyed the film,' said Lata.

'Yes,' said Haresh. 'I like films. When I was in Middlehampton I sometimes saw two films a day. I didn't see any plays though,' he added rather gratuitously.

'No—I wouldn't have thought so,' said Arun. 'I mean—there's so little opportunity, as you once said. Well, if you'll excuse us, we'll get ready.'

'Yes, yes,' said Mrs Rupa Mehra. 'You get ready. And we have a few things to do. Savita has to put the baby to bed and I have a few New Year's letters to write, and Pran—Pran—'

'—has a book to read?' suggested Pran.

'Yes,' agreed Mrs Rupa Mehra. 'And Haresh and Lata can go into the garden.' She told Hanif to put on the garden light.

16.22

It was not yet quite dark. The two walked around the small garden a couple of times, not knowing quite what to say. Most of the flowers had closed, but white stocks still perfumed one corner near the bench.

'Shall we sit down?' asked Haresh.

'Yes. Why not?'

'Well, it's been such a long time since we met,' said Haresh.

'Don't you count the Prahapore Club?' said Lata.

'Oh, that was for your family. You and I were hardly present.'

'We were all very impressed,' said Lata with a smile. Certainly, Haresh had been very much present, even if she hadn't.

'I hoped you would be,' said Haresh. 'But I'm not sure what your elder brother thinks of all this. Is he avoiding me? This morning he spent half the time looking around for a friend of his, and now he's going out.'

'Oh, he's just being Arun. I'm sorry about the scene just now; that too is typical of him. But he's quite affectionate sometimes. It's just that one never knows when. You'll get used to it.'

The last sentence had slipped out of its own accord. Lata was both puzzled at and displeased with herself. She did like Haresh, but she didn't want to give him any false hopes. Quickly she added: 'Like all his—his colleagues.' But this made things worse; it sounded cruelly distancing and a bit illogical.

'I hope I'm not going to become his colleague!' said Haresh, smiling. He wanted to hold Lata's hand, but sensed that—despite the scent of stocks and Mrs Rupa Mehra's tacit approval of their tête-à-tête—this was not the moment. Haresh was a little bewildered. Had he been with Simran, he would have known what to talk about; in any case they would have been talking in a mixture of Hindi, Punjabi and English. But talking to Lata was different. He did not know what to say. It was much easier to write letters. After a while he said:

'I've been reading one or two Hardys again.' It was better than talking about his Goodyear Welted line or how much the Czechs drank on New Year's Eve.

Lata said: 'Don't you find him a bit pessimistic?' She too was attempting to make conversation. Perhaps they should have kept on writing to each other.

'Well, I am an optimistic person—some people say too optimistic—so it's a good thing for me to read something that is not so optimistic.'

'That's an interesting thought,' said Lata.

Haresh was puzzled. Here they were, sitting on a garden bench in the cool of the evening with the blessing of her mother and his foster-father, and they could hardly piece together a conversation. The Mehras were a complicated family and nothing was what it seemed.

'Well, do I have grounds to be optimistic?' he asked with a smile. He had promised himself to get a clear answer quickly. Lata had said that writing was a good way to get to know each other, and he felt that their correspondence had revealed a great deal. He had perhaps detected a slight cooling off in her last two letters from Brahmpur, but she had promised to spend as much time as she could with him over the vacation. He could understand, however, that she might be nervous about an actual meeting, especially under the critical eye of her elder brother.

Lata said nothing for a while. Then, thinking in a flash over all the time she had spent with Haresh—which seemed to be no more than a succession of meals and train and factories—she said: 'Haresh, I think we should meet and talk a little more before I make up my mind finally. It's the most important decision of my life. I need to be completely sure.'

'Well, I'm sure,' said Haresh in a firm voice. 'I've now seen you in five different places, and my feelings for you have grown with time. I am not very eloquent—'

'It's not that,' said Lata, though she knew that it was at least partly that. What, after all, would they talk about for the rest of their lives?

'Anyway, I'm sure I will improve with your instruction,' said Haresh cheerfully.

'What's the fifth place?' said Lata.

'What fifth place?'

'You said we'd met in five places. Prahapore, Calcutta now, Kanpur, very briefly in Lucknow when you helped us at the station. . . . What's the fifth? It was only my mother you met in Delhi.'

'Brahmpur.'

'But—'

'We didn't meet exactly, but I was at the platform when you were getting on to the Calcutta train. Not this time—a few months ago. You were wearing a blue sari, and you had a very intense and serious expression on your face as if something had—well, a very intense and serious expression.'

'Are you sure it was a blue sari?' said Lata with a smile.

'Yes,' said Haresh, smiling back.

'What were you doing there?' asked Lata wonderingly; her mind was now already back on that platform and what she had been feeling.

'Nothing. Just leaving for Cawnpore. And then, for a few days after we met properly, I kept thinking, "Where have I seen her before?" Like today at the Test match with that young fellow Durrani.'

Lata came out of her dream. 'Durrani?' she said.

'Yes, but I didn't have to wonder long. I discovered where I'd seen him within a few minutes of talking to him. That was in Brahmpur too. I'd taken Bhaskar to meet his father. Everything happens in Brahmpur!'

Lata was silent but looking at him with, he felt, great interest at last.

'Good-looking fellow,' continued Haresh, encouraged. 'Very well informed about cricket. And on the university team. He's leaving tomorrow for the Inter-'Varsity somewhere.'

'At the cricket match?' said Lata. 'You met Kabir?'

'Do you know him?' asked Haresh, frowning a little.

'Yes,' said Lata, controlling her voice. 'We acted in *Twelfth Night* together. How strange. What was he doing in Calcutta? How long has he been here?'

'I don't know,' replied Haresh. 'For the cricket mainly, I suppose. But it seems a pity to have to leave after three days of a Test. Not that this one is likely to end in a win for either side. And he might have come on business too. He did say something about wanting to meet someone but being uncertain about his reception when he met him.'

'Oh,' said Lata. 'Did he meet him eventually?'

'No, I don't think so. Anyway, what were we talking about? Yes, five towns. Brahmpur, Prahapore, Calcutta, Lucknow, Cawnpore.'

'I wish you wouldn't call it Cawnpore,' said Lata with a touch of irritation.

'What should I call it?'

'Kanpur.'

'All right. And if you wish I'll call Calcutta Kolkota.'

Lata didn't answer. The thought that Kabir was still in town, in Calcutta somewhere, but unreachable, and that he would be leaving the next day, made her eyes smart. Here she was, sitting on the same bench where she had read his letter—and with Haresh of all people. Certainly, if her meetings with Haresh were marked by meals, her meetings with Kabir were marked by benches. She felt like both laughing and crying.

'Is something the matter?' said Haresh, a little troubled.

'No, let's go in. It's getting a little chilly. If Arun Bhai has left by now it shouldn't be too difficult to get Varun to put on a few film songs. I feel in the mood for them.'

'I thought you were more fond of classical music.'

'I like everything,' said Lata brightly, 'but at different times. And Varun will offer you a drink.'

Haresh asked for a beer. Varun put on a song from *Deedar*, then left the drawing room; he had instructions from his mother to keep out of the way. Lata's eye fell on the book of Egyptian mythology.

Haresh was more than a little bewildered by her change of mood. It made him feel uneasy. He was being truthful when he wrote in his letters that he had grown to be in love with her. He was sure she too was fond of him. Now she was treating him in a baffling manner.

The record had run its three-minute course. Lata did not get up to change it. The room was quiet. 'I'm tired of Calcutta,' she said light-heartedly. 'It's a good thing I'm going to the Botanical Gardens tomorrow.'

'But I'd set tomorrow aside for you. I planned to spend it with you,' said Haresh.

'You never told me, Haresh.'

'You said—you wrote—that you wanted to spend as much time as possible with me.' Something had changed in their conversation at a certain point. He passed his hand across his forehead and frowned.

'Well, we still have five days before I leave for Brahmpur,' said Lata.

'My leave will be over tomorrow. Cancel your Botanical trip. I insist!' He smiled, and caught her hand.

'Oh, don't be mean—' said Lata.

He released her hand at once. 'I am not mean,' he said.

Lata looked at him. The colour had left his face, and the laugh too had been wiped away. He was suddenly very angry. 'I am not mean,' he repeated.

'No one has ever said that to me before. Don't ever use that word for me again. I—I am going now.' He got up. 'I'll find my way to the station. Please thank your family for me. I can't stay for dinner.'

Lata looked completely stunned, but did not try to stop him. 'Oh, don't be mean!' was an expression that the girls at Sophia Convent must have used twenty times a day to each other. Some of it had survived—especially in certain moods—in her present-day speech. It meant nothing particularly wounding, and she could not imagine for the moment why he was so wounded.

But Haresh, already troubled by something he could not lay his finger on, was stung to the depths of his being. To be called 'mean'—ungenerous, lowly, base—and that too by the woman he loved and for whom he was prepared to do so much—he could tolerate some things, but he would not tolerate that. He was not ungenerous—far less so than her cavalier brother who had had hardly a word of appreciation for his efforts a few days earlier and who did not have the decency to spend an evening with him in order to reciprocate his hospitality. As for being base, his accent might not have their polish nor his diction their elegance, but he came from stock as good as theirs. They could keep their Anglicized veneer. To be labelled 'mean' was something not to be borne. He would have nothing to do with people who held this opinion of him.

16.23

Mrs Rupa Mehra almost had hysterics when she heard that Haresh had gone. 'That was very, very rude of him,' she said, and burst into tears. Then she turned upon her daughter. 'You must have done something to displease him. Otherwise he would never have gone. He would never have gone without saying goodbye.'

It took Savita to calm her down. Then, realizing that Lata looked completely shell-shocked, she sat beside her and held her hand. She was glad that Arun had not been there to fling sawdust into the fire. Slowly she worked out what had happened, and what Haresh might have misconstrued Lata to have meant.

'But if we don't even understand each other when we speak,' said Lata, 'what possible future can we have together?'

'Don't worry about that for the moment,' said Savita. 'Have some soup.'

When all else fails, thought Lata, there is always soup.

'And read something soothing,' added Savita.

'Like a law-book?' There were still tears in her eyes, but she was trying to smile.

'Yes,' said Savita. 'Or—since Sophia Convent is what started this confusion in the first place—why not read your autograph book from school? It's full of old friends and eternal thoughts. I often look through mine when I'm feeling bad. I am quite serious. I'm not merely echoing Ma.'

It was good advice. A hot cup of vegetable soup appeared, and Lata, amused a bit by the idiocy of the suggested remedy, looked through her book. On the small pages of pink and cream and pale blue, in English and (from her aunts, and once from Varun in nationalistic mood) in Hindi, and even in Chinese (an unreadable but beautiful inscription from her classmate Eulalia Wong), the edifying or moving or amusing or facetious lines in their different inks and different hands stirred her memories and diminished her confusion. She had even pasted in a small fragment of a letter from her father, which ended with a rough pencil sketch of four little monkeys, his own 'bandar-log', as he used to call them. More than ever now she missed him. She read her mother's inscription, the first in the book:

> When the world has been unkind, when life's troubles cloud your mind,
> Don't sit down and frown and sigh and moon and mope.
> Take a walk along the square, fill your lungs with God's fresh air,
> Then go whistling back to work and smile and hope.
>
> Remember, Lata darling, that the fate of each man (and woman) rests with himself.
>
> Yours everloving,
> Ma

On the next page a friend had written:

> Lata—
> Love is the star men look up to as they walk along, and marriage is the coal-hole they fall into.
>
> Love and all good wishes,
> Anuradha

Someone else had suggested:

> It is not the Perfect but the Imperfect who have need of Love.

Yet another had written on a page of blue in a hand that sloped slightly backwards:

> Cold words will break a fine heart as winter's first frost does a crystal vase. A false friend is like the shadow on a sun-dial which appears in very fine weather but vanishes at the approach of a cloud.

Fifteen-year-old girls, thought Lata, took a serious view of life.

Savita's own sisterly contribution was:

> Life is merely froth and bubble.
> Two things stand like stone:
> Kindness in another's trouble,
> Courage in our own.

To her own surprise, her eyes became moist again.

I am going to turn into Ma before I'm twenty-five, thought Lata to herself. This quickly stemmed the last of her tears.

The phone rang. It was Amit for Lata.

'So everything's ready for tomorrow,' he said. 'Tapan's coming along with us. He likes the banyan tree. You can tell Ma that I'll take good care of you.'

'Amit, I'm in a terrible mood. I'll be terrible company. Let's go some other time.' Her voice, not yet quite clear, sounded strange even to herself, but Amit did not comment on it.

'That will be for me to decide,' he said. 'Or rather, for both of us. If, when I come to pick you up tomorrow, you decide not to go, I won't force the issue. How's that? Tapan and I will go by ourselves. I've promised him now—and I don't want to disappoint him.'

Lata was wondering what to say when Amit added: 'Oh, I myself have them often enough: breakfast blues, lunchtime lows, dinner doldrums. But if you're a poet, that's your raw material. I suppose that the poem you gave me must have had some such origin.'

'It did not!' said Lata, with some indignation.

'Good, good, you're on your way to recovery,' laughed Amit. 'I can tell.' He rang off.

Lata, still holding the receiver, was left with the thought that some people appeared to understand her far too little and others far too much.

16.24

Dearest Lata,

I have been thinking of you often since you've been away, but you know how busy I always succeed in making myself, even in the holidays. Something, however, has happened which I feel I should write to you about. I have been torturing myself about whether to tell you, but I think the thing to do is simply to go ahead. I was so happy to get your letter and I dread the thought of making you unhappy. Maybe what with the election mail and the Christmas rush this letter will be delayed or will disappear entirely. I don't suppose I'll be sorry.

I'm sorry my thoughts are so scattered. I'm just writing on impulse. I was looking through my papers yesterday and came across the note you wrote to me when I was in Nainital, saying you had found the pressed flower again. I read it twice and suddenly thought of that day in the zoo, and tried to remember why I gave you that flower! I think it unconsciously was a seal to our friendship. It expressed my feelings for you, and I'm glad I can share my joys and sorrows with this wonderful, affectionate person who is so far away from me and yet so close.

Well, Calcutta isn't so far away really, but friends matter all the time, and it's good to know you haven't forgotten me. I was looking at the photographs of the play again while I was sorting things out in my mind, and was thinking how wonderfully you acted. It amazed me at the time and still amazes me—especially from someone who is sometimes so reserved, who doesn't often talk about her fears, fantasies, dreams, anxieties, loves and hates—and whom I would probably never have got to know if it hadn't been for the good luck of sharing the same hospital room—sorry! hostel room.

Well, I've avoided the subject long enough, and I can see your anxious face. The news I have to give you is about K, which—well,

I should just give it and be done with it and I hope you'll find it in your heart to forgive me. I'm just doing the unpleasant duty of a friend.

After you left for Cal, K sent me a note and we met at the Blue Danube. He wanted me to get you to talk to him or write to him. He said all sorts of things about how much he cared for you, sleepless nights, restless wanderings, lovelorn longings, the lot. He spoke very convincingly, and I felt quite sorry for him. But he must be rather practised at that sort of thing, because he was seeing another girl—at the Red Fox—on about the same day. You told me he doesn't have a sister, and anyway, it's clear from my informant, who is completely reliable, that he wasn't behaving in a particularly brotherly way. I was surprised how furious I was to hear of this, but in a way I was glad that this made things quite clear. I made up my mind to fire him up face to face, but found he'd disappeared from town on some university cricket tour, and anyway now I don't think it's worth the stress and bother.

Now, please, Lata, don't let this open up all the old wounds. Just treat it as confirmation of the course of action you've chosen. I'm sure we women make things far worse for ourselves by dwelling endlessly on matters that are best pushed aside. This is my professional opinion too. Some moderate mooning is OK, but please, no perennial pining! He isn't worth it, Lata, and this proves it. If I were you, I would just crush him with the flat of my spoon into mashed potatoes and forget him entirely.

Now for other news.

What with elections coming up, everything is bubbling and swirling around here, and the Socialist Party is mapping out policies and strategies and quackeries and sorceries with the best of them. I attend all the meetings, and canvass and campaign, but I am rather disillusioned. Everyone is involved in pushing himself forward, spouting slogans, making promises, and not bothering about how these promises are to be paid for, let alone implemented. Even sensible people seem to have gone off their heads. One fellow here used to talk a good deal of sense before, but he froths so much and makes such 'big-big eyes' that I'm sure he is quite certifiable now.

And yes, women have been rediscovered: one pleasant side-effect of election fever. 'The time has come when Woman must be restored to the status she occupied in ancient India: we must combine the best of the past and the present, of the West and the East. . . .' Here, however, is our ancient lawbook, the Manusmriti. Take a deep breath:

'Day and night, women must be kept in dependence by the males of their families. In childhood, a woman must be subject to her father, in youth to her husband and in old age to her son; a woman must never be independent because she is innately as impure as falsehood. . . . The Lord created woman as one who is full of sensuality, wrath, dishonesty, malice and bad conduct.' (And, sadly, now, the vote.)

I don't suppose anything is going to bring you back here before the term begins, but I miss you a lot even though, as I said, things are so busy that I find it hard to think even half a thought through.

Love to you, and also to Ma, Pran, Savita and the baby—but you don't have to give them my love if you're afraid they'll start asking you all about my letter. Well, you can give Uma my love anyway.

Malati

P.S. Amongst the inmates of Paradise women will form the minority, and amongst the inmates of Hell a majority. I thought I'd be even-handed, and give you a quotation from the Hadith as well. 'Hit or myth': that, in a nutshell, is the attitude to women in every religion.
P.P.S. Since I'm in the mood for quotations, here is something from a short story in a women's magazine, which describes the symptoms I want you to avoid: 'She became an invalid, a moth-eaten flower. . . . A cloud of despair was roosting on her pale moon of a face. . . . A red and violent anger bubbled out of her. It emanated from the headache hatching in her heart. . . . Like a humbled monarch, bowing its head, the car cringed away, the swirling dust in its wake portraying her emotions.'
P.P.P.S. If you decide to sing him out of your system, I would recommend that you avoid your favourite 'serious' raags like Shri, Lalit, Todi, Marwa, etc., and sing something more melodious like Behag or Kamod or Kedar.
P.P.P.P.S. That's all, dearest Lata. Sleep well.

16.25

Lata did not sleep well. She lay awake for hours, racked with jealousy so intense it almost forced the breath out of her and misery so complete she could not believe it was she who was feeling it. There was no privacy in the house—there was no privacy anywhere—where she could go and be by herself for a week and wash away the image of Kabir that she had, despite herself, stored away with the most treasured of her memories. Malati had said nothing about who this woman was, what she looked like, what they had said, who had seen them. Had they met by chance just as she herself had met him? Was he taking her for dawn jaunts to the Barsaat Mahal? Had he kissed her? No, he couldn't have, he couldn't have kissed her, the thought was unbearable.

Thoughts of what Malati had told her in their discussions about sex came back to torment her.

It was past midnight, but it was impossible to sleep. Quietly, so as not to disturb her mother or the rest of the household, she entered the small garden. There she sat on the bench where in the summer she had sat among the spider lilies and had read his letter. After an hour she found herself shivering from the cold, but she hardly cared.

How could he?—she thought, though she was forced to admit to herself that she had given him precious little encouragement or comfort. And now it was too late. She felt weak and exhausted, and finally went back and lay down on her bed. She slept, but her dreams were not calm. She imagined Kabir was holding her in his arms, was kissing her passionately, was making love to her, and that she was in ecstasy. But suddenly this disturbing ecstasy gave way to terror. For his face was now the deranged face of Mr Sahgal, and he was whispering, almost to himself, as he panted above her: 'You are a good girl, a very good girl. I am so proud of you.'

Part Seventeen

17.1

That Savita had been in Calcutta at all to advise Lata and counter Arun on the question of marriage was something that had not come about automatically. It had been the subject of a family dispute.

In the middle of December Pran had told Savita one morning in bed: 'I think, darling, that we should stay in Brahmpur. Baoji is far too busy with electioneering these days, and he needs all the help he can get.'

Uma was sleeping in her cot. This gave Pran another idea.

'Besides,' he continued, 'is it wise for the baby to go travelling just yet?'

Savita was still sleepy. She just about made sense of what Pran was saying. She thought a little about the repercussions of his suggestion, and said: 'Let's talk about this later.'

Pran, by now quite used to the way she phrased her disagreements, was quiet. After a while Mateen brought in the tea. Savita said: 'And perhaps you think you shouldn't be travelling at this time either?'

'No, perhaps not,' said Pran, pleased that things were going his way. 'And besides, Ammaji is not too well. I'm worried about her. I know you are too, darling.'

Savita nodded. But she felt that Pran had recovered quite rapidly, and was now well enough to travel. Moreover, he needed the holiday and change of scene badly. He should not, she felt, be imposed upon by his demanding father. The baby would be well taken care of in Calcutta. As for Savita's mother-in-law, she was, it was true, not very well, but was nevertheless taking part in election work among the women with the same robustness that had marked her relief work some years previously with the refugees from Punjab.

'So what do you say?' said Pran. 'It's only once in five years, these elections, and I know that Baoji wants me to help him.'

'How about Maan?'

'Well, of course, he'll help.'

'And Veena?'

'You know what her mother-in-law would say.'

They both sipped their tea. The *Brahmpur Chronicle* lay unopened on the bed.

'But how can you help?' asked Savita. 'I'm not going to have you travelling in jeeps and trains to Baitar and Salimpur and other barbaric places, getting all that dust and smoke into your lungs. You'd be asking for a relapse.'

Pran reflected that he probably couldn't visit his father's constituency, but that he could still be of some use to him. He said to Savita: 'I can stay in Brahmpur, darling, and handle things at this end. Besides, I'm a little worried about what Mishra will be doing to spoil my chances here. The selection committee is meeting in a month.'

It was evident that Pran was not keen to go to Calcutta. But he had put forward so many reasons that Savita could not tell whether it was his father or his mother or his baby or himself that he was most concerned about.

'How about me?' said Savita.

'You, darling?' Pran sounded surprised.

'Well, how do you think I will feel if Lata gets engaged to a man whom I haven't even seen?'

Pran paused before replying: 'Well, you got engaged to a man whom Lata hadn't seen.'

'That was quite different,' said Savita, neatly distinguishing the cases. 'Lata isn't my elder sister. I have a responsibility towards her. Arun and Varun aren't the best of advisers.'

Pran thought for a while, then said: 'Well, darling, why don't you go? I'll miss you, of course, but it will only be for a fortnight or so.'

Savita looked at Pran. He did not seem very perturbed at the thought of their separation. She got a little annoyed. 'If I go, the baby goes,' she said. 'And if the baby and I go, you go. And have you forgotten about the Test match?'

So the three of them went to Calcutta with Lata and Mrs Rupa Mehra.

Their departure from Brahmpur was delayed for a couple of days by Dr Kishen Chand Seth falling ill. And their return to Brahmpur was brought forward by a couple of days because of sudden and devastating events. But these events were entirely unforeseeable, and arose neither out of electioneering nor out of anyone's illness nor out of Professor Mishra's manipulations. The events involved Maan; and as a result of them the family was never the same again.

17.2

In the first week of December, Maan was still in Brahmpur. He had no plans whatsoever to go back to Banaras. As far as he was concerned, the entire city—ghats, temples, shop, fiancée, debtors, creditors and all—could have sunk into the Ganga and not a ripple would have been felt downstream. He wandered about Brahmpur quite happily, taking the occasional stroll through the old town to the Barsaat Mahal, passing through Tarbuz ka Bazaar on the way. He met the Rajkumar's university friends for an evening or two of poker. The Rajkumar himself, after his expulsion, had disappeared from Brahmpur for a while and returned to Marh.

Maan appeared erratically at meals at Prem Nivas and Baitar House, and his cheerful presence acted as a tonic on his mother. He visited Veena, Kedarnath and Bhaskar. He spent a little time with Firoz, though not as much as he would have liked: Firoz, after his work in the zamindari case, had had a fair amount of success obtaining briefs. Maan also discussed campaign strategy with his father and with the Nawab Sahib, who had pledged Mahesh Kapoor his support in his candidacy. And he visited Saeeda Bai whenever he could.

In between ghazals one evening Maan said to her:

'I must meet Abdur Rasheed one of these days, Saeeda. But I understand he doesn't come here any more.'

Saeeda Bai looked at Maan thoughtfully, her head slightly to one side. 'He has gone mad,' she stated simply. 'I can't have him here.'

Maan laughed and waited for her to elaborate. She did not.

'What do you mean, mad?' he said at last. 'You told me before that you thought he had an interest in Tasneem, but—surely—'

Saeeda Bai rather dreamily played an ornament on the harmonium, then said:

'He has been sending strange letters to Tasneem, Dagh Sahib, which naturally I don't allow the girl to read. They are offensive.'

Maan could not believe that Rasheed, whom he knew to be an upright man, particularly where it came to women or his sense of duty, could possibly have written letters of an offensive nature to Tasneem. Saeeda Bai, one of whose traits was the habitual exaggeration of nuance, was, to his mind, being over-protective of her sister. He did not say so, however.

'Why do you want to see him anyway?' asked Saeeda Bai.

'I promised his family I would,' said Maan. 'And I also want to talk to him about the elections. My father will be fighting from the constituency that includes his village.'

Now Saeeda Bai became cross. 'Has this entire city lost its senses?' she exclaimed. 'Elections! Elections! Is there nothing else in the world other than paper and boxes?'

Indeed, Brahmpur was talking of very little else. Campaigning had begun; most candidates, after filing their nomination papers, had remained in their constituencies and begun canvassing immediately. Mahesh Kapoor had decided to wait a few weeks in Brahmpur. Since he was Revenue Minister again, he had some work to do.

Maan, by way of apology, said: 'Saeeda, you know I have to help my father with these elections. My elder brother is not well and, besides, he has his teaching. And I know the constituency. But my exile will be short this time.'

Saeeda Bai clapped her hands and called for Bibbo.

Bibbo came running.

'Bibbo, are we on the voting list for Pasand Bagh?' she demanded.

Bibbo did not know, but she thought they were not. 'Should I try to find out?' she asked.

'No. It is not necessary.'

'Whatever you say, Begum Sahiba.'

'Where were you this afternoon? I was looking for you everywhere.'

'I had gone out, Begum Sahiba, to buy some matches.'

'Does it take an hour to buy matches?'

Saeeda Bai was becoming determinedly annoyed.

Bibbo was silent. She could not very well tell Saeeda Bai, who had been in such a flap about Rasheed, that she had surreptitiously been carrying letters to and fro between Firoz and Tasneem.

Saeeda Bai now turned briskly to Maan: 'Why are you lingering here?' she asked him. 'There are no votes to be had in this house.'

'Saeeda Begum—' protested Maan.

Saeeda Bai said sharply to Bibbo: 'What are you gawking at? Didn't you hear me tell you to go?'

Bibbo grinned and left. Suddenly Saeeda Bai got up and went into her room. She returned with three of the letters Rasheed had mailed Tasneem.

'His address is on these,' she said to Maan as she threw them on to the low table. Maan noted the address down in his unformed Urdu script, noticing, however, that Rasheed's writing was very much worse than he remembered it.

'There is something wrong with his head. You will find him a liability in your electoral endeavours,' said Saeeda Bai.

The rest of the evening was not a success. Public life had entered the boudoir, and together with it all Saeeda Bai's fears for Tasneem.

After a while she reverted to a kind of dreaminess again.

'When do you leave?' she asked Maan indifferently.

'In three days, Inshallah,' replied Maan as cheerfully as he could.

'Inshallah,' repeated the parakeet, responding to a phrase he recognized. Maan turned towards it and frowned. He was in no mood for the half-witted bird. A weight had descended on him; Saeeda Bai, it appeared, did not care whether he stayed or left.

'I am tired,' said Saeeda Bai.

'May I visit you on the eve of my departure?'

'No longer did I desire to wander in the garden,' murmured Saeeda Bai to herself, quoting Ghalib.

She was referring to Maan and to the fickleness of men in general, but Maan thought she was referring to herself.

17.3

Maan visited Rasheed's room the next day. It was located in a seedy and crowded part of the old city with narrow, unrepaired lanes and the stench of poor drainage. Rasheed was living alone. He could not afford to keep his family with him in Brahmpur. He cooked for himself whenever he could, he gave his tuitions, he studied, he was involved in some work for the Socialist Party, and he was trying to write a pamphlet—half popular, half scholarly—on the sanction for and meaning of secularism in Islam. He had run his life for months on willpower rather than on a combination of food and affection. When he saw Maan at his door Rasheed looked astonished and worried. Maan noticed with a shock that even more of his hair had gone white. His face was gaunt, but his eyes still held a sort of fire.

'Let us go for a walk,' Rasheed suggested. 'I have a tuition in an hour. There are too many flies here. Curzon Park is on the way. We can sit there and talk.'

In the mild December sunshine they sat in the park under a large, small-leafed ficus. Every time someone passed them, Rasheed would lower his voice. He looked extremely tired, but talked almost without stopping. Early on in the conversation it became apparent to Maan that Rasheed was not going to help his father in any sense. He was going to support the Socialist Party in the Salimpur-cum-Baitar constituency and he was, he said, going to campaign tirelessly for them and against the Congress throughout the university vacation. He talked endlessly about feudalism and superstition and the oppressive structure of society and especially the Nawab Sahib of Baitar's role in the system. He said that the leaders of the Congress Party—and presumably Mahesh Kapoor—were hand in glove with the large landlords, which was why landlords would be compensated for the lands that were to be taken over by the state. 'But the people will not be duped,' he said. 'They understand things only too well.'

So far Rasheed had spoken with great, perhaps slightly exaggerated, conviction, maybe even with excessive animus against the great landowner of the district, who he knew was Maan's friend; but there was nothing particularly odd about his manner of speaking or the logic of it. The word 'duped', however, acted as a kind of fault or fracture in his speech. He suddenly turned to Maan and said pointedly:

'Of course, people who are duped are wiser than you think.'

'Of course,' Maan agreed amiably, though he was rather disappointed. Rasheed, he thought, would have been very helpful to his father in the area around Debaria, and probably even in Salimpur town. If it had not been for Rasheed, he himself would not have known anything about the place.

'To be honest,' said Rasheed, 'I won't deny that I hated you as well as the others when I realized what you were trying to do.'

'Me?' said Maan. He could not see where he came into it, except that he was his father's son. And, anyway, why hatred?

'But I have put all that behind me,' continued Rasheed. 'Nothing is to be gained by hatred. But I must now ask for your help. Since you are partly responsible, you cannot deny me this.'

'What are you talking about?' asked Maan, bewildered. He had sensed, when he visited the village at Bakr-Id, that there was some tension involving Rasheed, but what had he to do with it?

'Please do not pretend ignorance,' said Rasheed. 'You know my family; you have even met Meher's mother—and yet you insisted on these events and these plans. You yourself are associated with the elder sister.'

What Saeeda Bai had said to Maan now clicked in his mind.

'Tasneem?' he asked. 'Are you talking about Saeeda Bai and Tasneem?'

A hard look passed over Rasheed's face—as if Maan had confirmed his own guilt. 'If you know it, what is the need to take her name?' he asked.

'But I don't know it—whatever it is,' protested Maan, amazed by the turn in the conversation.

Rasheed, attempting to be reasonable, said: 'I know that you and Saeeda Bai and others, including important people in the government, are trying to get me married to her. And she has decided on me. The letter she wrote—the looks she has given me—suddenly one day in the middle of her lesson she made a remark which could only mean one thing. I cannot sleep for worry, for three weeks I have hardly slept a wink. I do not want to do this, but I am afraid for her sanity. She will go insane unless I return her love. But even if I undertake this—which I must do on the basis of humanity—even if I undertake this, I must have protection for my own wife and children. You will have to get complete confirmation from Saeeda Begum about this. I will only agree on certain clear conditions.'

'What on earth are you talking about?' said Maan a little sharply. 'I am part of no plot—'

Rasheed cut him off. He was so annoyed that he was trembling. But he tried to get a hold on himself. 'Please do not say that,' he said. 'I cannot accept it when you say this sort of thing to my very face. I know what is what. I have already said I bear no hatred towards you any longer. I have told myself that however mistaken your intentions, you were doing it for my good. But did you never give any thought to my wife and children?'

'I don't know about Saeeda Begum,' said Maan, 'but I doubt she wants Tasneem to marry you. As for myself, this is the first I'm hearing of it.'

A cunning look passed over Rasheed's face. 'Then why did you mention her name a minute ago?'

Maan frowned, trying to think back. 'Saeeda Begum said something about some letters you sent her sister,' he said. 'I wouldn't advise you to write any more. They will only annoy her. And,' he added, getting annoyed himself, but trying to control his temper—for he was, after all, talking to his teacher, young though he was, and one who had, moreover, been his host in the village—'I wish you would not imagine that I am part of some plot.'

'All right,' said Rasheed firmly. 'All right. I won't mention it. When you visited the patwari with my family did I ever criticize you? Let us close the chapter. I won't accuse you, and you will kindly not make these protests, these denials. All right?'

'But of course I will deny it—' said Maan, hardly even wondering where a patwari had entered all this. 'Let me tell you, Rasheed, that you are completely mistaken. I have always had the greatest respect for you, but I can't see where you have got these ideas from. What makes you think that Tasneem is in the least interested in you?'

'I don't know,' said Rasheed speculatively. 'Perhaps it is my looks, or my uprightness, or the fact that I have done so much in life already and will be famous some day. She knows I have helped so many people.' He lowered his voice. 'I did not invite any attentions. I have a religious attitude to life.' He sighed. 'But I know the meaning of duty. I must do what is necessary for her sanity.' He bowed his head in sudden exhaustion and leaned forward.

'I think,' said Maan after a while, patting him on the back in a puzzled manner, 'that you should take better care of yourself—or let your family do so. You should go back to the village as soon as the vacations begin, or even before—and let Meher's mother take care of you. Rest. Sleep. Eat properly. Do not study. And do not exhaust yourself by campaigning for any party.'

Rasheed lifted his head and looked at Maan mockingly. 'So that is what you would like?' he said. 'Then the path will be clear. Then you can farm my field again. Then you can send the police to break my head with a lathi. I may suffer some setbacks, but whatever I put my mind to doing, I do. I understand when things are connected with each other. It is not easy to dupe me, especially if your conscience is uneasy.'

'You are speaking in riddles,' said Maan. 'And I think it is getting late for your tuition. In any case, I don't want to hear anything more on this subject.'

'You must confirm or deny it.'

'What, for God's sake?' cried Maan in exasperation.

'When you visit Saeeda Begum next, tell her that I am willing to spread happiness in her home if she insists on my going ahead with all this, that I will undergo a simple ceremony, but that any children I have in my second marriage cannot usurp the rights of the children I already have. And the marriage with Tasneem must be kept secret, even from the rest of my family. There must be no rumour—she is, after all, the sister of, well—I have my reputation and that of my family. Only those who already know. . . .'

He drifted off.

Maan got up, looking at Rasheed in amazement and shaking his head. He sighed, then leaned against the trunk of the tree, continuing to stare at his former teacher and friend. Then he looked down at the ground and said:

'I am not going back to Saeeda Begum's, nor am I plotting against you. I am not interested in breaking anyone's head. I am leaving for Salimpur tomorrow with my father. You can send your own messages to—to Saeeda

Begum, but I beg you not to. I cannot understand a quarter of what you have been saying. But if you wish, Rasheed, I will accompany you to your village—or to your wife's village—and make sure that you get there safely.'

Rasheed did not move. He pressed his right hand to his forehead.

'Well, what do you say?' asked Maan, concerned and angry. He had planned to go to Saeeda Bai's before leaving. Now he felt obliged to mention to her his meeting with Rasheed and the disturbing turn it had taken. He fervently hoped that nothing harmful would come out of it, and he also hoped that it would not sour the evening of his departure.

'I will sit here,' said Rasheed after a while, 'and think.'

He made the word sound actively ominous.

17.4

Maan had not been following Rasheed's activities. He was troubled by his talk of the patwari, though now he did recall faintly that someone—Rasheed's father or grandfather—had once mentioned something about a patwari to him. He knew that Rasheed had been moved to pity and indignation on behalf of the poorer people in the village; Maan's mind went back to the old man, destitute and dying, whom Rasheed had gone to visit, and because of whom he had taken up cudgels against the elders outside the mosque. But Rasheed was so rigid, expected so much of others and of himself, reacted so much in anger and pride, hammered away so powerfully in every direction he turned to, that—apart from putting other people's backs up—he must have worn himself out completely. Had he suffered from any specific shock that had caused him to crack in this way—to behave so sanely—at least at the beginning—and yet so deludedly? He still gave tuitions; did he still make ends meet? He was looking so poorly. And was he still the exacting, careful teacher, with his insistence on perfect, unbending alifs? What did his students and their families think of him?

And what did Rasheed's own family think? Did they know what had happened to him? If they knew, how could they be indifferent to his pitiable state? When he went to Debaria, Maan decided, he would ask them directly what they knew and tell them what they didn't. And where were Rasheed's wife and children?

Deeply disturbed, he mentioned to Saeeda Bai some of the things that were on his mind. He could not understand how he had obtained either

Rasheed's hatred or his conditional forgiveness. The image of Rasheed and his wild imaginings would haunt Maan for weeks.

Saeeda Bai, for her part, became so concerned about Tasneem's safety that she summoned the watchman and told him that under no circumstances was Tasneem's old Arabic teacher to be admitted to the house. When Maan mentioned Rasheed's belief that there was a plot to marry him against his will to the infatuated Tasneem, Saeeda Bai indignantly and with disgust in her voice read out a part of one of Rasheed's letters, which certainly gave Maan the impression that the overwhelming weight of passion was on Rasheed's side. He had written to Tasneem that he wanted to bury his face in the clouds of her hair and so on and so forth. Even his handwriting, about which he used to be so particular, had regressed to a scrawl under the force of his feelings. The letter, to judge from the excerpt that Saeeda Bai read, was alarming. When he added to this the whole bizarre conception of a plot with all its conditions and ramifications, about which Saeeda Bai had until then been ignorant, Maan could not help sympathizing with her agitation, her inability to concentrate on anything else—on music, on him, on herself. He tried in vain to distract her. So vulnerable did she seem to him that he longed to take her in his arms—but he sensed that hers was a volatile and explosive vulnerability and that he would be hurtfully rebuffed.

'If there is anything I can do at any time,' he told her, 'you have only to send for me. I don't know what to do or what to advise. I will be in Rudhia District, but they will keep track of me at the Nawab Sahib's house.' Maan did not mention Prem Nivas because Saeeda Bai was no longer persona grata there.

Saeeda Bai's face became pale.

'The Nawab Sahib has promised to assist my father's campaign,' Maan explained.

'Poor girl, poor girl,' said Saeeda Bai softly. 'O God, what a world this is. Go now, Dagh Sahib, and may God keep you.'

'Are you sure—'

'Yes.'

'I will not be able to think of anything but you, Saeeda,' said Maan. 'At least give me a smile before I leave.'

Saeeda Bai gave him a smile, but her eyes were still sad. 'Listen, Maan,' she said, addressing him by his name, 'think of many things. Never place your happiness in one person's power. Be just to yourself. And even if I am not invited to sing at Holi in Prem Nivas, come here and I will sing for you.'

'But Holi is more than three months away,' said Maan. 'Why, I will see you in less than three weeks.'

Saeeda Bai nodded. 'Yes, yes,' she said absently. 'That's right, that's quite right.' She shook her head slowly a couple of times and closed her eyes. 'I don't know why I am so tired, Dagh Sahib. I don't even feel like feeding Miya Mitthu. God keep you in safety.'

17.5

The electorate of Salimpur-cum-Baitar consisted of roughly 70,000 people, about half Hindu and half Muslim.

Apart from the two smallish towns included in its name, the constituency encompassed over a hundred villages, including the twin villages of Sagal and Debaria where Rasheed's family lived. It was a single member constituency: only one candidate would be elected to the Legislative Assembly by the voters. Ten candidates in all were standing: six represented parties, and four were Independents. Of the former, one was Mahesh Kapoor, the Minister of Revenue, who was the candidate for the Indian National Congress. Of the latter, one was Waris Mohammad Khan, the candidate who had been put up as a dummy by the Nawab Sahib of Baitar in case his friend did not get the Congress ticket or chose not to stand or bowed out of the race for some reason or other.

Waris was delighted to be a candidate, even though he knew that he would be expected to throw his weight as actively as possible behind Mahesh Kapoor. Just the look of his name on the list of validly nominated candidates outside the office of the Returning Officer made him smile with pride. Khan came just below Kapoor in the list, which was arranged in the order of the English alphabet. Waris thought this significant: the two allies could almost be paired together by a bracket. Though everyone knew what his function in the election was, the fact that he was present on the same list as some of the better-known citizenry of the district—indeed, of the state—gave Waris a certain standing at the Fort. The munshi continued to order him about, but more cagily than before. And when Waris chose not to obey, he had the ready excuse that he was busy with election work.

When Maan and his father arrived at Baitar Fort, Waris reassured them:

'Now, Minister Sahib, Maan Sahib, leave everything in the Baitar area to me. I'll arrange everything—transport, meetings, drums, singers, everything. Just tell the Congress people to send us lots of those Nehru posters, and also a lot of Congress flags. We'll see that they are put up everywhere. And we won't let anyone go to sleep for a month,' he continued happily. 'They won't even be able to hear the azaan for the slogans. Yes. And I've made sure that the water for your bath is hot. Tomorrow morning I've arranged for a tour of some of the villages, and in the evening we return to the town for a meeting. And if Maan Sahib wants to hunt—but I fear there will be no time for that. Votes before nilgai. But first I have to make sure that a good many of our supporters attend the Socialist Party meeting this evening to heckle them properly. Those haramzadas don't even think our Nawab Sahib should get compensation for the land that is going to be snatched from him—just imagine! What an injustice it is already. And now they want to add insult to injury—' Waris suddenly stopped, the realization striking him that he was addressing the very author of the black act. 'What I mean is—' He finished with a grin, and shook his head vigorously, as if shaking the very thought out of his brain. They were, of course, allies now.

'Now I must see to things,' he said, and disappeared for a while.

Maan had a slow and relaxed bath, and came down to find his father waiting for him impatiently. They began to discuss the candidates, the support they could expect from people of different areas or religions or castes, their strategy with regard to women and other particular groups, election expenses and how to cover them, and the faint possibility that Nehru might be induced to give a speech in the constituency during his brief tour of Purva Pradesh in mid-January. What gave Maan a real sense of warmth was the fact that his father was far less dismissive of him than usual. Unlike Maan, he had not lived in this constituency, but Maan had expected that he might simply extrapolate his experiences of the Rudhia farm to this northern subdivision. But Mahesh Kapoor, though he did not believe in caste, and thought little of religion, was more than alive to their electoral implications, and listened with care to Maan's description of the demographic contours of this tricky terrain.

Among the Independent candidates—quite apart from Waris, who was a supporter—there was no one who presented much of a challenge to Mahesh Kapoor. And among the party candidates, because he happened to be the candidate of the Congress Party—anxious though he was about fighting from an unfamiliar constituency—he started out with an immense advantage. The Congress was the party of Independence and the party of Nehru, and it was far better funded, far more widely organized, and far more quickly recognized than the others. Its very flag—saffron, white and green, with a spinning wheel in the middle—resembled the national flag. The Congress Party had a worker or two in almost every village—workers who had been somewhat active in social service during the last few years, and would be very active indeed in electioneering in the coming couple of months.

The other five parties presented a mixed bag.

The Jan Sangh promised to 'advocate the spread and extension of the highest traditions of Bharatiya Sanskriti': a thinly veiled term for Hindu, rather than Indian, culture. It was more than willing to go to war with Pakistan over the issue of Kashmir. It demanded compensation from Pakistan for the property of Hindus who had been forced to migrate to India. And it stood for a United India which included the territory of Pakistan; presumably, it meant a forcibly reunited one.

The Ram Rajya Parishad appeared more peaceable if further removed from reality. It declared that its object was to bring about a state of affairs in the country similar to that of the idyllic age of Rama. Every citizen would be expected to be 'righteous and religious-minded'; artificial foodstuffs such as vanaspati ghee—a kind of hydrogenated vegetable oil—would be banned, as would obscene and vulgar films and the slaughter of cows. The ancient Hindu system of medicine would be 'recognized officially as the national system'. And the Hindu Code Bill would never be passed.

The three parties to the left of the Congress who were fighting from this constituency were the KMPP, the party that Mahesh Kapoor had joined and then left (and whose symbol was a hut); the Socialist Party (whose symbol was a banyan tree); and the Communist Party (whose symbol was a sickle and a few ears of corn). The Scheduled Castes Federation, the party of Dr Ambedkar (who had recently resigned from Nehru's Cabinet on the grounds of irreconcilable differences and the collapse of the Hindu Code Bill), had forged an electoral alliance with the socialists; they had no candidate of their own for this seat. They concentrated mainly on double-member constituencies where at least one member from the scheduled castes was bound by law to be elected to the legislature.

'It would have been good if your mother had been here,' said Mahesh Kapoor. 'It's even more important in this place than in my old constituency—even more of the women here are in purdah.'

'How about the Congress women's groups?' asked Maan.

Mahesh Kapoor clicked his tongue impatiently. 'It's not enough to have Congress women volunteers,' he said. 'What we need is a powerful woman speaker.'

'Ammaji isn't a powerful speaker,' Maan pointed out with a smile. He tried to imagine his mother on a podium and failed. Her speciality was quiet work behind the scenes, mainly in helping people, but sometimes—as in elections—in persuasion.

'No, but she's from the family, and that makes all the difference.'

Maan nodded. 'I think we should try to get Veena out to help,' he said. 'You'll have to talk to old Mrs Tandon, though.'

'The old lady doesn't like my godless ways,' said Mahesh Kapoor to his son. 'We'll have to get your mother to speak to her. You go back next week and tell her. And while you're at it, tell Kedarnath to speak to the jatavs he knows in Ravidaspur to contact the scheduled castes in this area. Caste, caste.' He shook his head. 'Oh yes, and one more thing. For the first few days we should travel around together. Then we can split forces to get more coverage. The Fort has two jeeps. You can go around with Waris and I'll go around with the munshi.'

'When Firoz comes, you should go around with him,' said Maan, who did not care much for the munshi and thought he might well lose his father votes. 'That will make a Hindu-Muslim pair in each jeep.'

'Well, what is keeping him away?' asked Mahesh Kapoor impatiently. 'It would have been much better if he had showed us around Baitar. I can understand why Imtiaz can't leave Brahmpur.'

'He's had a lot of work recently,' said Maan, thinking for a moment of his friend. He had been allotted Firoz's room as usual, high up in the Fort. 'And the Nawab Sahib?' he countered. 'What is his reason for deserting us?'

'He doesn't like elections,' said Mahesh Kapoor shortly. 'In fact, he doesn't like politics at all. And after his father's role in splitting up the country, I don't blame him. Well, he's put everything at our disposal. At least we are mobile. Can you imagine driving my car along these roads? Or going around on bullock-carts?'

'We're perfectly mobile,' said Maan. 'Two jeeps, a pair of bullocks, and a bicycle.' They both laughed. A pair of bullocks was the Congress symbol, and Waris's was a bicycle.

'A pity about your mother,' repeated Mahesh Kapoor.

'There's still a long way to go before the polls,' said Maan optimistically, 'and I'm sure she'll be well enough to give us a hand in a week or two.' He looked forward to the return to Brahmpur that his father had just suggested.

It seemed to him that for almost the first time in his life his father trusted him; indeed, in some ways, depended on him.

Waris entered to announce that they were just on their way to the Socialist Party meeting in town. Did the Minister Sahib or Maan Sahib wish to come along?

Mahesh Kapoor thought that if Waris had organized some heckling it would be inappropriate for him to go. Maan was bound by no such scruples. He wanted to see everything there was to be seen.

17.6

The meeting of the Socialist Party began forty-five minutes late under a huge red-and-green canopy on the playing fields of the government school in Baitar, where most important large meetings in town were held. A few men on the podium were trying to keep the crowd entertained and patient. Several people greeted Waris, and he was delighted to be the centre of a little knot of attention. He went around introducing Maan and greeting people with an adaab or a namaste or a hearty slap on the back. 'This is the man who saved the Nawabzada's life,' he announced so flamboyantly that even the robust Maan was embarrassed.

The socialist procession through the city had got held up somewhere. But now the roll of drums got closer, and soon the candidate was ascending the stage with his entourage. He was a middle-aged teacher who had been a member of the District Board for years. Not only was he known to be a good speaker himself but someone had also spread the false rumour that the great socialist leader Jayaprakash Narayan might possibly be coming to speak in Baitar—so there was a large crowd on the football field. It was seven in the evening, and beginning to get chilly; the almost entirely male audience, townsfolk and villagers alike, had brought shawls and blankets to wrap themselves up in. Cotton durries had been laid out on the ground by the organizers as protection against dust and dew.

Several local luminaries sat on the podium, which was lit in addition by several bright white lights. Behind them on a cloth wall was the huge image of a banyan tree, the socialists' symbol. The speaker, used perhaps to controlling rowdiness in his classroom, had such a powerful voice that the microphone was almost superfluous. In any case it alternately acted up and broke down. From time to time, especially when the candidate got carried away, it set up a vibrating wail. Having been introduced and garlanded, he was soon in the full flow of pure Hindi oratory:

'. . . And that is not all. This Congress government will not spend our taxes on pipes to bring us clean water to drink, but they will spend any amount of money on useless baubles. All of you have walked past that ugly statue of Gandhiji in the town square. I am sorry to say that however much we respect, however much we revere the man whom the statue is supposed to resemble, it is a shameful expense of public money. This great soul is enshrined in our hearts; why do we need to have him direct the traffic in the marketplace? But how can one argue with the government of this state? They would not listen, they had to go ahead. So the government spent this money on a useless statue that is good only for pigeons to defecate upon. If we had spent it instead upon public toilets, our mothers and sisters would not have to defecate in the open. And all this needless expense makes this useless government print more useless money, which in turn increases the prices of all the goods, all the necessities, that we poor people have to buy.' His voice rose in anguish. 'How can we cope? Some of us, like teachers and clerks, have fixed salaries, some of us depend on the mercy of the skies. How can we put up with this backbreaking expense—this inflation that is the true gift of the Congress to the people of this country in the last four years. What will help us take our boat across the river of life in these desperate times of reduced rations, of dwindling supplies of cloth, of the locusts of despair, of corruption and of nepotism? Why, I look at my students and weep—'

'Show us how you weep now! One, two, three, testing!' shouted a voice from the back of the crowd.

'—I will beg my respected and supposedly witty brothers at the back not to interrupt. We know from where they come, from what high nest they swoop down to help in the oppression of the people of this district. . . . I look at my students and weep. And why? Yes, I will tell you, if I may be permitted to by the firecrackers at the back. Because these poor students cannot get work, no matter how good, how decent, how intelligent, how hardworking they are. This is what the Congress has done, this is what it has driven the economy to. Think, my friends, think. Who among us does not know a mother's love? And yet today, that mother who, with tears streaming down her face, looked at her family jewels, her wedding bangles, her very mangalsutra for the last time—those precious things that are dearer to her even than life—and who sold them to support the education of her son—and who saw her son through school, through college, with such high hopes that he would do something worthwhile in life—she now finds that he cannot even get a job as a government clerk without knowing someone or bribing someone. Is this what we threw the British out for? Is this what the people deserve? Such a government that cannot make sure its people are fed, that cannot make sure that its students have jobs, such a government should die of shame, such a government should drown in a handful of water.'

The speaker paused for breath, and the organizers set up a shout:

'The MLA from Baitar, how should he be?'

His supporters in the crowd shouted back in rhyme:

'Ramlal Sinha, one such as he!'

Ramlal Sinha held up his hands in a humble namaste. 'But, my friends, my brothers, my sisters, let me speak further, let me unburden my heart of all the bitterness it has had to swallow these last four years of Congress misrule—I am not a man who likes to use strong language, but I tell you that if we are to prevent a violent revolution in this country, we must throw out the Congress. We must uproot it. This tree whose roots have sunk so deep, which has sucked all the water out of this soil, this tree has become rotten and hollow—and it is our duty—the duty of every one of us, my friends, to uproot this rotten and hollow tree from the soil of Mother India, and to throw it aside—and with it the inauspicious and rapacious owls that have made their dirty nests in it!'

'Get rid of the tree! Don't vote for the tree!' shouted a voice from the back. Maan and Waris looked at each other and laughed, and there was much laughter from the audience too, including the supporters of the Socialist Party. Ramlal Sinha, realizing the blunder in his imagery, thumped the table and shouted: 'This heckling is typical of Congress rowdyism.'

Then, realizing that anger would be counterproductive, he went on in a calm voice: 'Typical, my friends, typical. We fight these elections under this sort of disadvantage and in this sort of shadow. The whole state machinery is in the hands of the Congress Party. The Prime Minister flies around in a plane at state expense. The DMs and SDOs jump to the Congress tune. They hire hecklers to disrupt our meetings. But we must rise above all this and teach them that they can shout themselves hoarse, and we will still not be cowed. This is not some two-anna party they are dealing with, this is the Socialist Party, the party of Jayaprakash Narayan, of Acharya Narendra Deva, of fearless patriots, not venal goons. We will put our ballot papers in the box marked with the symbol of the—of the banyan, the true representation of the Socialist Party. This is the strong tree, the spreading tree, the tree that is neither hollow nor rotten, the tree that is symbolic of the strength and generosity and beauty and glory of this country of ours—the land of Buddha and Gandhi, of Kabir and Nanak, of Akbar and Ashoka, the land of the Himalaya and the Ganga, the land that belongs equally to all of us, Hindus, Muslims, Sikhs, and Christians alike, about which it was truly said, in the undying words of Iqbal,

> Better than all the world is this our Hindustan.
> We are its nightingales, it is our rose garden.'

Ramlal Sinha, overcome by his rhetoric, coughed twice, and drank half a glass of water.

'Does the nightingale have any policies of its own, or does it merely want to smear the Congress statue from on high?' shouted a voice.

Get out of my class! Ramlal Sinha felt like shouting. Instead, he kept calm and said:

'I am delighted that the brainless buffalo from the back has asked that question. It comes very fittingly from one whose symbol ought, more appropriately, to consist of two water buffaloes rather than two bullocks yoked together. Everyone can see how the Minister of Revenue has yoked himself to the biggest landlord in the whole of this district. If there was ever need for proof of collusion between the Congress Party and the zamindars, here it is. See them working together like the two wheels of a bicycle! See the zamindars grow still richer and fatter on the compensation that the government dispenses to them. Why is the Nawab Sahib not here to face the people? Is he afraid of their indignation? Or is he too proud, like those of his class—or too ashamed of the money of the poor, the public largesse that will soon be clinging to his hands? You ask me what are our policies. Let me tell you if you will allow me to. The Socialist Party has given the agrarian problem far more thought than any other party. We are not, like the KMPP, a mere discontented tail of the Congress Party. We are not a doctrinaire tool of foreigners, like the communists. No, good people, we have our own independent views, our own policies.'

As he ticked off his points on his fingers, he winched up his voice in tandem: 'No peasant family will be allowed to possess land more than three times the size of an economic holding. No one who does not personally participate in cultivation will be allowed to possess land. The land will belong to the tiller. No one—not a Nawab, not a Maharaja, not a waqf or a temple trust—will be compensated for more than a hundred acres of appropriated land. The Right to Property in the Constitution will have to go: it is a barrier to just distribution of wealth. To the workers we promise Social Security which will include protection against disability, sickness, unemployment, and old age. To women we guarantee equal pay for equal work, effective universal education, and a civil code that will grant them equal rights.'

'Do you want to take our women out of purdah?' demanded an indignant voice.

'Let me finish; don't shoot your cannon before it's loaded. Listen to what I have to say, then I will happily answer any and all of your questions. To the minorities, let me say: we guarantee full protection, I repeat, full protection for your language, your script and your culture. And we must break our last ties with the British. We cannot remain in the anglophile Nehru's beloved colonialist and imperialist Commonwealth, in the name of whose head, King George, he himself was so often arrested, and whose boots he now desires to lick. Let us finish off with the old ways once and for all. Let us burn to ash once and for all the party of greed and favouritism, the Congress, that has brought the country to the edge of disaster. Take your ghee and sandalwood, my friends, if you can still afford it, or just bring yourselves and your families, and come to the cremation ground on the 30th of January, the day of the poll in this constituency, and let the corpse of the demon party be cremated there once and for all. Jai Hind.'

'Jai Hind!' roared the crowd.

'Baitar ka MLA kaisa ho?' cried someone from the podium.

'Ramlal Sinha jaisa ho!' shouted the crowd.

This antiphonal chant went on for a couple of minutes while the candidate folded his hands respectfully and bowed to the audience.

Maan looked at Waris, but Waris was laughing, and did not appear in the least worried.

'The town is one thing,' said Waris. 'It's in the villages that we will knock them out. Tomorrow our work begins. I will make sure you get a good dinner.'

He slapped Maan on the back.

17.7

Before going to bed, Maan looked at the picture that Firoz kept on his table: the picture of the Nawab Sahib, his wife, and their three children, with Firoz in particular looking very intently at the camera with his head tilted. The owl called out, reminding Maan of the speech he had just heard. He realized with a mild sense of shock that he had forgotten to bring any whisky with him. But nevertheless, in a few minutes, he was fast asleep.

The next day was long and dusty and exhausting. They travelled by jeep along pitted and petering tracks to an endless succession of villages, where Waris introduced them to an endless number of headmen, Congress Party village-level workers, heads of caste 'biradaris' or communities, imams, pandits, and local bigwigs. Mahesh Kapoor's style of speech, in contrast to the political oiliness he detested, was clipped, abrupt, even somewhat arrogant, but quite straightforward; it was not taken amiss by most of those who met him. He gave short talks on various issues, and answered the questions of the villagers who had gathered to hear him. He asked very simply for their vote. Maan, Waris, and he drank innumerable cups of tea and sherbet. Sometimes the women came out, sometimes they stayed in and peeped out from behind the door. But wherever they went, the party was a superb spectacle for the village children. They tailed them in every village, and were even given rides on the jeep to the outskirts of the village when it departed for the next one.

Men of the kurmi caste in particular were very worried about the fact that women would inherit property under Nehru's threatened Hindu Code Bill. These careful agriculturalists did not want their lands to be divided into smaller, entirely uneconomic, holdings. Mahesh Kapoor admitted that he was in favour of the bill, but explained, as well as he could, why he thought it necessary.

Many of the Muslims were worried about the status of their local schools, their language, their religious freedom; they asked about the recent troubles in Brahmpur and, further afield, in Ayodhya. Waris reassured them that in Mahesh Kapoor they had a friend who could both read and write Urdu, who was a personal friend of the Nawab Sahib, and whose son—and here he pointed to Maan with great affection and pride—had actually saved the life of the younger Nawabzada in a religious riot at Moharram.

Some tenant farmers asked about the abolition of zamindari, but very tentatively, since Waris, the Nawab Sahib's man, was present. This caused a great deal of awkwardness all around, but Mahesh Kapoor grasped the nettle and explained people's rights under the new act. 'But this should not be seen as an excuse not to pay rent now,' he said. 'Four separate cases—from Uttar Pradesh, Purva Pradesh, Madhya Bharat and Bihar—are at present before the Supreme Court, and it will decide quite soon whether the new zamindari laws are valid and can be put into effect. Meanwhile, no one is to be evicted forcibly from his land. And there are strict penalties for tampering with land records in order to benefit anyone—landlord or tenant. The Congress government has plans to move the village patwaris around every three years, so that they cannot form deep and profitable roots in one place. Every patwari must know that he will be most severely punished if he allows himself to be bribed into wrongdoing.'

To the totally landless labourers, most of whom were so cowed that they hardly dared to be present, let alone speak, Mahesh Kapoor promised the distribution of surplus unused land where it was possible. But to these most unfortunate people he knew that he could be of little direct assistance—for his Zamindari Abolition Act did not even touch them.

In some places the people were so poor and underfed and ill that they looked like savages in rags. Their huts were in disrepair, their livestock half-dead. In others they were better off and could even afford to hire a schoolteacher and construct a room or two for a small private school.

In a couple of places Mahesh Kapoor was surprised to be asked if it was true that S.S. Sharma was going to be called to Delhi and that he himself was going to be elected the next Chief Minister of Purva Pradesh. He denied the first rumour, and said that even if it were true, the second would not necessarily follow. They could rest assured that he would almost certainly be a Minister, but he was not asking them to vote him in because of that. He wanted them to vote for him simply as their MLA. In this he was entirely sincere, and it went down very well.

By and large, even those villagers who stood to benefit from the abolition of landlordism maintained an attitude of respect for the Nawab Sahib and his wishes. 'Remember,' said Waris, wherever they went, 'the Nawab Sahib is asking for your vote not in my name but in the Minister Sahib's. So put your ballot paper in the box marked with the two bullocks, not in the one marked with a bicycle. And remember to put it inside the box, through the hole in the top. Don't just put it on the top of the box, or the next person who enters the booth will be able to put your ballot paper into any box he chooses. Understand?'

The Congress volunteers and village-level workers, who were very pleased and honoured to see Mahesh Kapoor, and who garlanded him repeatedly, told him which villages they were going to canvass support in and where and when he should try to appear, either with or—and they implied that this was preferable—without Waris. They, being unfettered by a retainer of the Nawab Sahib, were able to play the powerful anti-zamindari card in a much more fiery manner than the author of the Zamindari Abolition Act himself. They walked about in groups of four or five from village to village, with nothing more than a stick, a water bottle, and a handful of dried cereal, gathering potential voters together, singing party, patriotic, or even devotional songs, and dinning into any ears that were willing to listen the great achievements of the Congress Party since its inception. They spent the night in the villages, so that no money was spent out of Mahesh Kapoor's accountable funds. The one thing that disappointed them was that his jeep had not come laden with Congress posters and flags, and they made Mahesh Kapoor promise to provide these in large numbers. They also filled him in on events and issues that were important to particular villages, specific caste structures in various areas, and—as important as anything else—local jokes and references that would go down well.

From time to time Waris would shout out various names, almost at random, in order to stir up the crowd:

'Nawab Sahib—'

'Zindabad!'

'Jawaharlal Nehru—'

'Zindabad!'

'Minister Mahesh Kapoor Sahib—'

'Zindabad!'

'Congress Party—'

'Zindabad!'

'Jai—'

'Hind!'

After a few days of such electioneering in the cold and heat and dust, everyone's voice was painfully hoarse. Finally, after promising to return to the Baitar area in due course, Mahesh Kapoor and his son said goodbye to Waris and, taking a jeep from the Fort with them, made for the Salimpur area. Here their headquarters was the home of a local Congress Party official, and here again they did the rounds of the caste leaders of the small qasbah town: the Hindu and Muslim goldsmiths who were the heads of the jewellery bazaar, the khatri who ran the cloth market, the kurmi who was the spokesman of the vegetable sellers. Netaji, who had inveigled himself on to the local Congress Committee, drove up on his motorcycle, pasted over with Congress flags and symbols, to greet Maan and his father. He embraced Maan like an old friend. One of his first suggestions was that the leaders of the chamars be sent two large tins of locally brewed liquor to sweeten their taste for the Congress. Mahesh Kapoor refused to do any such thing. Netaji looked at Mahesh Kapoor in astonishment, wondering how he had managed to become such a big leader with so little common sense.

That night Mahesh Kapoor confided in his son:

'What country is this that I have had the misfortune to be born into? This election is worse than any previous one. Caste, caste, caste, caste. We should never have extended the franchise. It has made it a hundred times worse.'

Maan said, by way of consolation, that he thought that other things mattered as well, but he could see that his father was deeply disturbed, not by his own chances of winning, which were virtually unassailable, but by the state of the world. He had begun to respect his father more and more as the days passed. Mahesh Kapoor worked as hard and straightforwardly and tactlessly at his campaign as he had worked at the various clauses of the Zamindari Bill. He worked cannily, but with a sense of principle. And this work, besides being much more physically gruelling than the work in the Secretariat, began at dawn and often ended after midnight. Several times he mentioned that he wished that Maan's mother had been there to help him; once or twice he even wondered about her health. But he never complained that circumstances had forced him out of the security of his constituency in Old Brahmpur into a rural district he had hardly even visited, let alone cultivated, before.

17.8

If Mahesh Kapoor had been surprised by Maan's popularity during his Bakr-Id visit, not only he but Maan himself was amazed to discover how popular he now was in the area around Salimpur. While no word had leaked out in Baitar about his attack on the munshi, Maan's stay in Debaria earlier in the year had passed from fact into rumour into a kind of myth, and many exploits of his visit were recounted to him which he found hard to recognize. While in Salimpur he had looked up the spindly and sarcastic schoolteacher Qamar, and had introduced him to his father. Qamar had told Mahesh Kapoor laconically that he could count on his vote. What struck Maan as somewhat odd about this conversation was that neither Mahesh Kapoor nor Maan had asked him for his vote yet. He did not know that Netaji had mentioned rather contemptuously to Qamar Mahesh Kapoor's attitude towards bribing the chamars with liquor, and that Qamar had said forthwith that Mahesh Kapoor, though a Hindu, was the man he would vote for.

Mahesh Kapoor's own very brief visit to Salimpur at Bakr-Id was not forgotten. Although he was an outsider, people felt that he was not merely interested in them for their votes, a fickle migratory bird visible only at election time.

Maan enjoyed meeting people and asking for their votes on his father's behalf. At times he felt quite protective of him. Even when Mahesh Kapoor got annoyed, as he sometimes still did when he was very tired, Maan took it in good part. Perhaps I will become a politician after all, he thought. Certainly, I enjoy it more than most other things I've done. But even if I do manage to become an MLA or MP, what will I do once I get there?

Whenever he felt restless, Maan would take over from the driver and hurtle the colourfully decorated flag-decked jeep at breakneck speed down roads that were meant at best for bullock-carts. This gave him an exhilarating sense of freedom and everyone else a physical and psychological shock. The jeep, which was meant to accommodate two passengers in front and at most four in the back, was often crammed with ten or a dozen people, food, megaphones, posters, and all sorts of other paraphernalia besides. Its horn blew unceasingly and it trailed impressive clouds of dust and glory. Once, when its radiator began to leak, the driver scolded it and mixed some turmeric into the water. This sealed the leak miraculously.

One morning, they drove towards the twin villages of Debaria and Sagal, which were on the agenda for the day. As they approached the village Maan fell into a sudden depression. He had remembered Rasheed on and off during these last few days, and was glad they had been so busy that the memory had not preyed on him even more. But now he thought of what he was going to have to say to Rasheed's family. Perhaps they already knew about him. Certainly, neither Netaji nor Qamar had asked about him. But then, when they had met, there had been very little time to inquire.

Some other questions came to Maan's mind, and instead of humming a ghazal, as he sometimes did when driving, he fell silent. Was Rasheed serious when he had spoken of canvassing for the Socialist Party? What had brought his disturbing rift of delusion about Tasneem to the surface? Again he thought back to the day when they had visited the old and sick man at Sagal. He felt that Rasheed was at heart a good man, not the calculating ogre of Saeeda Bai's fancy.

It was almost the end of the year, and Maan had not seen Saeeda Bai now for two weeks. During the days he was so busy that she did not often enter his mind. But at night, even though he was exhausted, and just before sleep took over, his mind would turn to her. He would think not of her steely tantrums but of her gentleness and softness, of her unhappiness about Tasneem, of the scent of attar of roses, of the taste of Banarasi paan on her lips, of the intoxicating atmosphere of her two rooms. How strange, he thought, that he had never met her anywhere other than in those two rooms—except twice. It had been nine months since Holi evening in Prem Nivas, when he had first quoted Dagh to her in light-spirited public banter. And it seemed ages since he had tasted the sherbet from her hands. Even for one who continued to feel tenderly towards almost all the women he had had affairs with, it was a new experience for Maan to be obsessed by one woman—sexually and emotionally—for so long.

'For God's sake, Maan, drive straight. Do you want to have the election cancelled?' said his father. There was a rule to the effect that if a candidate died before the poll, it would be countermanded and a new election declared.

'Yes, Baoji,' said Maan. 'Sorry.'

In the event, Maan did not have to say much to anyone about Rasheed. Baba, who had met Mahesh Kapoor on the last visit, took over the reins as soon as they arrived in the village.

'So you've rejoined the Congress,' he said to the Minister.

'Yes, I have,' said Mahesh Kapoor. 'It was good advice you gave me.'

Baba was pleased that Mahesh Kapoor had remembered.

'Well,' said Baba, fixing his eyes on the younger man, 'you'll have no problem winning by a large margin in this constituency, even if Nehru doesn't.' He spat a blob of reddish spittle on to the ground.

'Don't you think there's any threat to me at all?' asked Mahesh Kapoor. 'It's true that the Congress is winning hands down in all the states that have had early polls.'

'No threat at all,' said Baba. 'None. The Muslims are behind you and behind the Congress, the scheduled castes are behind the Congress whether they're behind you or not, a few of the upper caste Hindus will go for the Jan Sangh and that other party whose name I forget, but they don't form much of the population. The left is divided into three. And none of the Independents count for much. Do you really want me to take you around these villages?'

'Yes, if you don't mind,' said Mahesh Kapoor. 'If I have it all sewn up anyway, let me at least visit my future flock and find out about their needs.'

'Very well, very well,' said Baba. 'So, Maan, what have you been up to since Bakr-Id?'

'Nothing,' said Maan, wondering where all that time had disappeared.

'You must do something,' said Baba, vaguely but forcefully. 'Something that makes a mark on the world—something that people hear about and talk about.'

'Yes, Baba,' assented Maan.

'I suppose you've met Netaji recently,' snorted the old man, stressing his younger son's title.

Maan nodded.

'In Salimpur. He offered to come with us everywhere and do everything for everyone.'

'But you're not travelling with him?' chuckled Baba.

'Well, no. I think he rubs Baoji up the wrong way.'

'Good, good. Too much dust behind his motorcycle and too much self behind his selflessness.'

Maan laughed.

'The Nawab Sahib's jeep now,' said Baba with approval. 'That's swifter—and sounder.' Baba was pleased at the implicit connection it presented. It would help to keep people in the village in awe of him, and to make it clear to them that the Minister was not above coming to an understanding with certain landlords.

Maan looked across at his father, who was now eating paan and talking to Rasheed's father; he wondered how he would have taken Baba's remark, had he understood its implications.

'Baba—' he said, suddenly. 'Do you know about Rasheed?'

'Yes, yes,' said the old man sternly. 'He's been thrown out. We've forbidden him entrance to the house.' Noticing Maan's appalled look he went on: 'But don't worry. He won't go hungry. His uncle sends him some money every month.'

Maan could say nothing for a while, then burst out: 'But, Baba—his wife? and his children?'

'Oh, they're here. He's lucky we're so fond of Meher—and Meher's mother. He didn't think of them when he disgraced himself. Nor does he think of them now: does he stop to think of the feelings of his wife? She has suffered enough in life already.'

Maan did not quite understand the last part of this remark, but Baba did not give him time to ask for an explanation. He went on: 'In our family we don't marry four women at a time, we do it one by one. One dies, we marry another: we have the decency to wait. But he is talking about another woman now, and he expects his wife to understand. He writes to her saying he wants to marry again, but he wants her agreement first. Obtuse! Marry her, I say, marry her for God's sake, but don't torment your wife by asking for permission. Who this woman is, he doesn't write. We don't even know what family she comes from. He has grown secretive in everything he does. He was never cunning when he was a boy.'

Maan did not try in the face of Baba's indignation to defend Rasheed, about whom he himself had such mixed feelings now; but nor did he mention the wild accusations of conspiracy Rasheed had made against him.

'Baba,' he said, 'if he has trouble of this kind, how could it help to close your doors against him?'

The old man paused, as if uncertain. 'That is not his only offence,' he said, searching Maan's face. 'He has become a complete communist.'

'Socialist.'

'Yes, yes,' said Baba, impatient with such quibbling. 'He wants to take my land away without compensation. What kind of grandson have I produced? The more he studies, the stupider he becomes. If he had stuck to the one Book, his mind would have been more healthy.'

'But, Baba, these are just his views.'

'Just his views? Do you not know how he tried to put them into action?'

Maan shook his head. Baba, seeing no guile in his face, sighed again, more deeply this time, and muttered something under his breath. Looking across at his son, who was still talking to Mahesh Kapoor, he said to Maan:

'Rasheed's father says that you remind him of his elder son.' He mused for a few seconds, then went on: 'I can see you know nothing about this sorry business. I will explain it all later. But now I must take your father round the village. You come as well. We'll talk after dinner.'

'Baba, there may not be time later,' Maan said, knowing Mahesh

Kapoor's impatience to cover as much ground as possible. 'Baoji will want to move on long before dinner.'

Baba ignored this. The tour of the village began. The path was cleared by Moazzam (who clouted anyone younger than himself who dared impede the progress), Mr Biscuit (yelling 'Jai Hind!') and a motley gang of running, shouting village children. 'Lion, lion!' they screamed in simulated terror. Baba and Mahesh Kapoor strode energetically in front, their sons straggled along in the rear. Rasheed's father was friendly enough to Maan, but used his paan as protection against prolonged conversation. Though everyone greeted Maan with affection and friendliness, his mind was on what Baba had said to him and on what he had to say.

'I will not allow you to return to Salimpur tonight,' Baba told Mahesh Kapoor flatly after they had completed the circuit. 'You will eat with us and sleep here. Your son spent a month here, you will have to spend a day.'

Mahesh Kapoor knew when he had met superior force, and consented with good grace.

17.9

After dinner, Baba took Maan aside. There was no privacy in the village itself, especially when such a tremendous event as the visit of a Minister was taking place. Baba got a torch and told Maan to put on something warm. They walked towards the school, talking along the way. Baba told Maan in brief about the incident of the patwari, how the family had got together to warn Rasheed, how he had refused to listen, how he had encouraged some of the chamars and other tenants to take matters up with revenue authorities higher than the patwari, and how his plans had backfired. Anyone who had dared to stray from the path of obedience had been thrown off his land. Rasheed, Baba said, had made troublemakers of some of their most faithful chamars, and he had shown no qualms about instigating this betrayal. The family had had no choice but to cut him off.

'Even Kachheru—do you remember him?' said Baba. 'The man who pumped the water for your bath—'

Alas, Maan remembered all too well now what at Bakr-Id had eluded him, the identity of the man whom Baba had shoved aside on the way to the Idgah.

'It's not easy to find permanent people,' continued Baba sadly. 'The young people find ploughing difficult. Mud, effort, sun. But the older ones have done it since childhood.'

They had by now reached the great tank near the school. On the other side of the water was a small cemetery for the dead of the two villages. The whitewashed tombs stood out at night. Baba said nothing more for a while, and nor did Maan.

Remembering what Rasheed had once said about how generation succeeds generation in working mischief Maan now murmured to himself with a bitter smile: 'The rude forefathers of the hamlet sleep.'

Baba looked at him and frowned. 'I don't understand English,' he said quietly. 'We here are simple people. We do not have any great learning. But Rasheed treats us as if we are ignorant to the core. He writes us letters, threatening us and boasting of his own humanism. Everything has gone—logic, respect, decency; but his pride and his sense of self, lunatically, remain. When I read his letters I weep.' He looked towards the school. 'He had a classmate who became a dacoit. Even he treats his family with more respect.'

After a while he continued, looking past the school towards Sagal. 'He says that we are deluded, that our god is money, that wealth and land is all we are interested in. That sick man whom he visited with you, Rasheed used to tell us we should help him, should support his legal rights, should make him start a court case against his brothers. Such madness, such unrealistic notions—to interfere in the family matters of others and bring about needless strife. Imagine what would have happened if we had taken his advice. The man is dead now but the feud between the villages would have gone on forever.'

Maan said nothing; it was as if his mind was blocked. He hardly even registered the news of this death. His thoughts were still with that work-worn man who with such calm and cheerfulness used to pump water for his bath. Strange to think that even his paltry earnings had been undone by—by what? Perhaps by Maan's own father. The two knew nothing of each other as individuals, but Kachheru was the saddest case of the evil practised under the act, and Mahesh Kapoor was almost directly responsible for his utter devastation, his reduction to the forsaken status of a landless labourer. Linked though they were in this sense of the former's guilt and the latter's despair, if they were to pass each other in the street, thought Maan, neither would know the other.

No doubt the effect of the Zamindari Act would be substantially good, but that would be of no help to Kachheru. Nor, Maan realized, with a seriousness unusual in him, could he do anything about it. To intercede with Baba would be impossible, and to take it up with his father an unthinkable betrayal of trust. To have helped the old woman at the Fort—that was entirely another thing.

And Rasheed? Censorious, pitiable, worn out, torn between family shame and family pride, forced to choose between loyalty and justice, between trust and pity, what must he have been through? Was he too not a victim of the tragedy of the countryside, of the country itself? Maan tried to imagine the pressure and suffering he must have undergone.

But Baba was saying, as if he had read Maan's thoughts: 'You know, the boy is very disturbed. I don't like to think of it. He has almost no friends in the city as far as we can tell, no one to talk to except those communists. Why don't you talk to him and make him see sense? We don't know how it has happened that he has become so strange, so incoherent. Someone said that he got hit on the head during a demonstration. Then we found out that that was not so. But perhaps, as his uncle says, the immediate cause is not important. Sooner or later, what does not bend will snap.'

Maan nodded in the darkness. Whether or not the old man noticed, he continued: 'I am not against the boy. Even now if he mends his ways and repents we will take him back. God is not called the compassionate, the merciful, for nothing. He tells us to forgive those who turn away from evil. But Rasheed—you know—if he changes his mind, he will be as vehement facing south as he was facing north.' He smiled. 'He was my favourite. I had more energy then, when he was ten years old. I would take him to the roof of my pigeon-house, and he would point out all our lands, exactly which bits were ours, and when they came into the family. With pride. And yet this same boy. . . .' The old man was silent. Then, in an almost anguished voice, he said: 'One never knows anyone in this world, one cannot read anyone's heart, one never knows whom to believe and whom to trust.'

A faint call was heard in the distance from Debaria, followed by a closer one from Sagal.

'That is the call to night prayer,' said Baba. 'Let's go back. I shouldn't miss it and I don't want to pray in this Sagal mosque. Come on, get up, get up.'

Maan remembered his first morning in Debaria when he had woken up to find Baba telling him to go to prayer. Then, his excuse had been his religion. Now he said, 'Baba, if it's all right, I'll just sit here for a while. I'll find my own way back.'

'You want to be alone?' asked Baba, his voice betraying his surprise at what was an unusual request, particularly from Maan. 'Here, take the torch. No, no, take it, take it. I only brought it along to guide you. I can cut across these fields blindfolded at midnight at the new moon of Id. Well, I will mention him again in my prayers. May it do him some good.'

Alone Maan sat and looked out over the expanse of water. Into its blackness fell the reflection of the stars. He thought of the Bear, and of how he had done something definite to help Rasheed, and he felt ashamed at his own inaction. Rasheed never rested from his endeavours, thought Maan, shaking his head, whereas he himself did nothing but; or at least would have liked to. He promised himself that when he returned to Brahmpur for a few days' break he would visit him, difficult though the encounter was bound to be. He had been deeply disturbed by his previous meeting, and he did not know if his perplexity had been enhanced or diminished by what Baba had told him.

So much lay beneath the placid surface of things, so much torment and danger. Rasheed was by no means his closest friend, but he had thought he knew him and understood him. Maan was given to trusting and being trusted, but, as Baba said, perhaps one could never read the human heart.

As for Rasheed, Maan felt that for his own sake he had to be made to see the world with all its evil in a more tolerant light. It was not true that one could change everything through effort and vehemence and will. The stars maintained their courses despite his madness, and the village world moved on as before, swerving only very slightly to avoid him.

17.10

Two days later they drove back to Brahmpur for a brief rest. Mrs Mahesh Kapoor greeted them with unaccustomed tears in her eyes. She had helped a little in canvassing among women for local Congress candidates in Brahmpur. Mahesh Kapoor was annoyed when he heard that she had even canvassed in L.N. Agarwal's constituency. Now that Pran, Savita and Uma were in Calcutta, and Veena and Kedarnath were both busy and able only rarely to visit, she had been feeling quite lonely. Nor was she at all well. But she sensed immediately the new warmth of the relationship between her husband and her younger son, and this gave her great joy. She went into the kitchen in a little while to supervise Maan's favourite tahiri herself; and later, after a bath, to do puja and give thanks for their safe return.

Though Mrs Mahesh Kapoor did not have, or have cause to have, a particularly well-developed sense of humour, one object that she had recently added to her puja paraphernalia never failed to make her smile. It was a brass bowl filled with harsingar blossoms and a few harsingar leaves. The bowl rested on a Congress flag made of flimsy paper, and Mrs Mahesh Kapoor looked from one to another with pleasure, admiring the saffron, white and green first of this and then of that as she rang her small brass bell around them—and all the gods—in joint benediction.

The next morning Maan found his mother and sister shelling peas in the courtyard. He had demanded tahiri again, and they were obliging him. He pulled up a morha and joined them. He remembered how as a child he would often sit in the courtyard—on a small morha which was reserved for him—and watch his mother shelling peas while she told him some story or other about the gods and their doings. But now the talk was about more terrestrial matters.

'How is it going, Maan?'

Maan realized that this was probably the first proper news his mother would be getting about the new constituency. If she had asked his father, he would have dismissed her silliness and fobbed her off with a few generalities. Maan gave her as thorough a picture as he could.

At the end of it she said, with a sigh: 'I wish I could have helped.'

'You must take care of yourself, Ammaji,' said Maan, 'and not exert yourself too much. Veena should be the one to help with the women voters. The country air will do her good after the foetid alleys of the old city.'

'I like that!' said Veena. 'That's the last time you're invited to our house. Foetid alleys. And it sounds as if you have a sore throat from all that fresh country air. I know what canvassing among the women is like. Endless shy giggles, and how many children do I have, and why am I not in purdah? You should take Bhaskar along, not me. He's very enthusiastic to go and count all those heads. And he can help with the children's vote,' she added with a laugh.

Maan laughed too. 'All right, I'll take him along. But why can't you give us a hand as well? Does Kedarnath's mother really object so much?' He shelled a pea-pod, and thumbed the peas into his mouth. 'Delicious.'

'Maan,' said Veena reproachfully, with an imperceptible nod towards her mother, 'Pran and Savita are in Calcutta and will be there till the eighth of January. Who is left here in Brahmpur?'

Mrs Mahesh Kapoor said immediately: 'Don't use me as an excuse, Veena.

I can take care of myself. You should help your father get out the vote.'

'Well, maybe in a week or two you can take care of yourself—and Pran will be back. But right now I'm not going. Even Savita's mother didn't leave for Calcutta when her father was unwell. Anyway, everything looks in very good shape in the constituency.'

'Yes, it does,' agreed Maan. 'But the real reason you're not going is that you're too lazy. That is what married life does to people.'

'Lazy!' said Veena, laughing. 'The pot calling the snowflake black,' she added in English. 'And I notice you're eating more than you're shelling,' she continued in Hindi.

'So I am,' said Maan, surprised. 'But they're so fresh and sweet.'

'Have some more, son,' said Mrs Mahesh Kapoor. 'Don't listen to her.'

'Maan should learn to exercise some self-restraint,' said Veena.

'Should I?' asked Maan, popping a few more peas into his mouth. 'I can't resist delicious things.'

'Is that the disease or the diagnosis?' asked his sister.

'I am a changed man,' said Maan. 'Even Baoji's been paying me compliments.'

'I'll believe that when I hear one,' said Veena, popping a few more peas into her brother's mouth.

17.11

That evening Maan strolled along to Saeeda Bai's house. He had had a haircut and a bath. It was a cool evening, so he wore a bundi over his kurta; in a pocket of his bundi was a half-bottle of whisky; and on his head was a starched white cap worked in white.

It was good to be back. The mud roads of the country had their charms, no doubt, but he was a town man. He liked the city—at least this city. And he liked streets—at least this street, the street where Saeeda Bai's house stood—and of that house, he particularly liked Saeeda Bai's two rooms. And of those two rooms, he particularly liked the inner one.

A little after eight o'clock, he arrived at the gate, waved familiarly to the watchman, and was allowed in. Bibbo met him at the door, looked surprised to see him, and walked him up to Saeeda Bai's room. Maan's heart leapt up when he saw that Saeeda Bai was reading from the book that he had given her, the illustrated *Works of Ghalib.* She looked charming, her pale neck and shoulders leaning forward, the book in her hand, a bowl of fruit and a small bowl of water to her left, her harmonium to her right. The room was redolent with attar of roses. Beauty, fragrance, music, food, poetry, and a source of intoxication in his pocket: ah, Maan felt, as their eyes met, this is what happiness means.

She too looked surprised to see him, and Maan began to wonder if the watchman had admitted him by mistake. But she looked down quickly at the book, and idly turned a few pages.

'Come, Dagh Sahib, come, sit down, what time is it?'

'Just after eight, Saeeda Begum, but the year changed some days ago.'

'I was aware of it,' said Saeeda Bai, smiling. 'It will be an interesting year.'

'What makes you say that?' asked Maan. 'Last year was interesting enough for me.' He put out his hand and held hers. Then he kissed her shoulder. Saeeda Bai neither resisted nor responded.

Maan looked hurt. 'Is something the matter?' he said.

'Nothing, Dagh Sahib, that you can help me with. Do you remember what I said the last time we met?'

'I remember something of it,' said Maan—but all he could remember was the sense of the conversation, not the exact words: her fears for Tasneem, her look of vulnerability.

'Anyway,' said Saeeda Bai, changing the subject, 'I do not have much time with you this evening. I am expecting someone in a little while. God knows, I should have been reading the Quran, not Ghalib, but who knows what one will do from one moment to the next.'

'I met Rasheed's family,' said Maan, who was agitated at the thought that he would have no time with her this evening, and wanted to get his unpleasant duty of informing Saeeda Bai over and done with as soon as possible.

'Yes?' said Saeeda Bai almost indifferently.

'They don't know anything, it seems to me, about what is going on in his head,' said Maan. 'Nor do they care. All they are concerned about is that his politics shouldn't cause them any economic loss. That is all. His wife—'

Maan stopped. Saeeda Bai raised her head, and said: 'Yes, yes, I've known that he has one wife already. And you know I know. But I am not interested in all this. Forgive me, I must now ask you to go.'

'Saeeda—but tell me why—'

Saeeda Bai looked down at the book and started turning its pages in a distracted manner.

'A page is torn,' said Maan.

'Yes,' replied Saeeda Bai absently. 'I should have it mended better.'

'Let me do it for you,' said Maan. 'I can have it done. How did it get torn?'

'Dagh Sahib, do you not see what state I am in? I cannot answer questions. I was reading your book when you came in. Why do you not believe that I was thinking of you?'

'Saeeda,' said Maan helplessly. 'I can believe it. But what use is it to me that you should merely think of me when I am not here? I can see that you are distressed by something. But by what? Why don't you tell me? I don't understand it. I can't understand it—and I want to help you. Is there someone else you are seeing?' he said, suddenly sensing that her agitation could be caused by excitement as much as by distress. 'Is that it? Is that it?'

'Dagh Sahib,' said Saeeda Bai in a quiet, exhausted tone. 'This would not matter to you if you had more sakis than one. I told you that the last time.'

'I don't remember what you said the last time,' said Maan, feeling a rush of jealousy. 'Don't tell me how many sakis I should have. You mean everything to me. I don't care about what was said the last time. I want to know why I am being turned away by you this time with so little attempt at courtesy—' He paused, overcome, then looked at her, breathing hard. 'Why did you say this year would be so interesting for you? Why did you say that? What has happened since I've been away?'

Saeeda Bai leaned her head slightly at an angle. 'Oh, that?' she smiled, in a slightly mocking, even self-mocking, manner. 'Fifty-two is the number of a pack of cards. Things are complete. Fate is bound to have shuffled and dealt things in a comprehensive way this year. So far I have lifted the edge of only two cards that have fallen to me, a Queen and a Jack: a Begum and a Ghulam.'

'Of what suit?' asked Maan, shaking his head. Ghulam could mean either a young man or a slave. 'Are they of the same suit or are they antagonistic?'

'Paan, perhaps,' said Saeeda Bai, naming hearts. 'At any rate I can see that they are both red. I can't see any more. But I do not care for this conversation.'

'Nor do I,' said Maan, angrily. 'At least there is no room this year for a joker in the pack.'

Suddenly Saeeda Bai started laughing in a desperate way. Then she covered her face with her hands. 'Now it is up to you to think what you like. Think that I too have gone mad. It is beyond me to say what is the matter.' Even before she uncovered her face Maan could tell that she was crying.

'Saeeda Begum—Saeeda—I am sorry—'

'Do not apologize. This is the easiest part of the night for me. I dread what is to come.'

'Is it the Raja of Marh?' said Maan.

'The Raja of Marh?' said Saeeda Bai softly, her eyes falling on the book. 'Yes, yes, perhaps. Please leave me.' The bowl of fruit was full of apples, pears, oranges, and even some unseasonal, wrinkled grapes. Impulsively she broke off a small bunch and gave them to Maan. 'This will nourish you better than what comes of it,' she said.

Maan put a grape in his mouth without thinking, then suddenly recalled eating peas that morning at Prem Nivas. For some reason, this made him furious. He crushed the rest of the grapes in his hand and dropped them into the bowl of water. His face red, he got up, stepped outside the threshold, put on his jutis, and walked downstairs. There he paused, and covered his face with his hands. Finally he went out and began walking homewards. But he had not gone a hundred yards when he stopped once more. He leaned against a huge tamarind tree and looked back towards Saeeda Bai's house.

17.12

He took the bottle of whisky out of his pocket and began to drink. He felt as if his heart had been crushed. Every night for a fortnight he had thought of her. Every morning when he had woken up, whether at the Fort or in Salimpur, he had lingered for a few minutes in bed, imagining that she was with him. No doubt his dreams too had been of her. And now, after these fifteen days away, she had granted him fifteen minutes of her time, and as good as given him to understand that someone else mattered far more to her than he ever could. But surely not the gross Raja of Marh.

Yet there was so much in her talk that he could not even remotely understand, even though Saeeda Bai at the best of times very rarely spoke except by indirection. If he himself was the slave or the young man whom she was referring to, what then? What did she mean by dread? Who would be coming to the house? Where did the Raja of Marh fit into all this? And what about Rasheed? By now Maan had drunk so much that he hardly cared what he did. He walked halfway back to her house and stood where he could not be observed by the watchman, but could see if anyone went in.

Though it was not late, the street was almost deserted; but then this was a quiet part of town. A car or two and a few bicycles and tongas passed along the road, and now and then a pedestrian walked by. An owl hooted calmly overhead. Maan stood there for half an hour. No car or tonga halted near her house. No one entered and no one left. Occasionally the watchman strolled up and down outside, or knocked the base of his spear hard against the pavement, or stamped his feet against the cold. A variable mist started to descend, obscuring his view from time to time. Maan began to feel that there was no one—no Bilgrami, no Raja, no Rasheed, no mysterious Other—whom Saeeda Bai was to meet. It was simply that she wanted to have nothing further to do with him. She had tired of him. He no longer meant anything to her.

Another pedestrian approached Saeeda Bai's house from the opposite direction, stopped by the gate, and was immediately admitted. Maan's blood ran cold with shock. At first he had been too far away to see him clearly. Then the mist had cleared slightly, and he thought that he recognized Firoz.

Maan stared. The door opened, and the man entered. Was it Firoz? It looked like him from this distance. His bearing was the same as that of his friend. He was carrying a walking stick, but with a young man's air. His gait was that of Firoz. Gripped by disbelief and misery Maan started forward, then stopped. Surely, surely, it could not be Firoz.

And even if it were Firoz, could he not be visiting the younger sister whom he appeared to be so fascinated by? Surely someone else would be visiting Saeeda Bai in due course. But the minutes passed, and no one else stopped by the house. And Maan realized that whoever had entered would never have been admitted to meet Tasneem. It could only be Saeeda Bai whom he was going to see. Again Maan covered his face with his hands.

He had drunk more than half his bottle of whisky. He was unaware of the cold, unaware of what he was doing. He wanted to go to the door again, to enter and to find out who it was who had gone in and for what purpose. It cannot be Firoz, he thought to himself. And yet the man had looked so similar from this distance. The mist, the streetlights, the sudden illumination when the door opened: Maan tried to visualize once again what had happened just a few minutes before. But nothing became clearer.

No one else went in. Nor did anyone come out. After half an hour, Maan could bear it no longer. He walked across the street. When he got to the gate he blurted out to the watchman the first thing that came into his head: 'The Nawabzada asked me to bring his wallet in to him—and to take him a message.'

The watchman was startled, but, hearing Maan mention Firoz's title, he knocked at the door. Maan walked in without waiting for Bibbo to admit him. 'It's urgent,' he explained to the watchman. 'Has the Nawabzada arrived yet?'

'Yes, Kapoor Sahib, he went in some time ago. But can't I—?'

'No. I must deliver this personally,' said Maan.

He walked up the stairs, not glancing at the mirror. If he had, he would have been shocked by the expression on his own face. Perhaps that glance in the mirror would have averted everything that was to happen.

There were no shoes outside the door. Saeeda Bai was alone in her room. She was praying.

'Get up,' said Maan.

She turned towards him and stood up, her face white. 'How dare you?' she began. 'Who let you in? Take your shoes off in my room.'

'Where is he?' said Maan in a low voice.

'Who—' said Saeeda Bai, her voice trembling with anger. 'The parakeet? His cage is covered up, as you can see.'

Maan looked quickly around the room. He noticed Firoz's stick in the corner and was seized by a fit of rage. Without bothering to reply, he opened the bedroom door. There was no one inside.

'Get out!' said Saeeda Bai. 'How dare you think—never come here again—get out, before I call Bibbo—'

'Where is Firoz?'

'He hasn't been here.'

Maan looked at the walking stick. Saeeda Bai's eyes followed his.

'He's gone,' she whispered, agitated and suddenly fearful.

'Why did he come? To meet your sister? Is it your sister he is in love with?'

Suddenly, Saeeda Bai began to laugh as if what he had said was both bizarre and hilarious.

Maan could not stand it. He gripped her by the shoulders and began to shake her. She looked at him, terrified by the expression of fury in his eyes—but she could still not help her grotesque, mocking laughter.

'Why are you laughing? Stop it—stop it—' cried Maan. 'Tell me he came to see your sister—'

'No—' Saeeda Bai gasped out.

'He came to see you about your sister—'

'My sister! My sister!' Saeeda Bai laughed in Maan's face as if he had made some insane joke. 'It is not my *sister* he is in love with—it is not *my* sister he is in love with—' She tried to push Maan violently away. They fell on to the floor and Saeeda Bai screamed as Maan's hands went round her throat. The water in the bowl spilled over. The fruit bowl overturned. Maan noticed none of this. His mind was red with rage. The woman he loved had betrayed him with his friend, and now she was taking delight in mocking his love and his misery.

His hands tightened around her throat. 'I knew it,' he said. 'Tell me where he is. He's still here. Where is he hiding?'

'Dagh Sahib—' gasped Saeeda Bai.

'Where is he?'

'Help—'

'Where is he?'

Saeeda Bai reached with her right hand for the fruit knife, but Maan let go of her throat and wrenched it out of her hand.

They were still on the floor. He stared at the knife.

Saeeda Bai started shrieking for help. From below there was the sound of a door opening, frightened voices, people rushing upstairs. Maan got up. Firoz was the first to reach the door. Bibbo was behind him.

'Maan—' said Firoz, taking in the scene in an instant. Saeeda Bai was resting her head on a pillow and holding her throat with both her hands. She was gasping, and her chest was heaving. Horrible retching sounds were coming from her throat.

Maan looked at Firoz's guilty and agitated face and knew instantly that the worst was true. Again he was seized with blind rage.

'Look here, Maan,' said Firoz, moving gradually towards him. 'What is the matter? Let's talk this over—easy does it—'

Suddenly he lunged forward and tried to disarm Maan. But Maan was too quick for him. Firoz clutched at his stomach. Blood began to stain his waistcoat, and he stumbled on to the floor. He cried out in pain. Blood fell on the white sheet spread on the floor. Maan looked at it like a stupefied ox, then at the knife still in his hands.

For a minute no one said a word. There was no sound apart from Saeeda Bai's attempts to breathe, and Firoz's stifled cries of pain, and Maan's long and bitter sobs.

'Put it down on the table,' said Bibbo quietly.

Maan put the knife down, and knelt by Firoz.

'Leave at once,' said Bibbo.

'But a doctor—'

'Leave at once. We will manage everything. Leave Brahmpur. You have not been to this house this evening. Go.'

'Firoz—'

Firoz nodded.

'Why?' said Maan in a broken voice.

'Go—quick—' said Firoz.

'What have I done to you? What have I done?'

'Quick—'

Maan took one final look around the room and rushed downstairs and out. The watchman was pacing up and down outside the outer gate. He had heard nothing to agitate him. He saw Maan's face and said: 'What is the matter, Sahib?'

Maan did not reply.

'Is something the matter? I heard voices—do they want me?'

'What?' said Maan.

'Do they want me, Sahib? Inside, I mean.'

'Want? No, no—goodnight.'

'Goodnight, Sahib,' said the watchman. He stamped his feet a few times as Maan hurried away into the mist.

17.13

Tasneem appeared at the door of Saeeda Bai's room.

'What is the matter, Apa? Oh my God—' she cried, her eyes taking in the horrible scene: blood, crushed fruit, spilled water, her sister leaning, gasping against the couch, Firoz lying wounded on the floor, the knife on the table.

Firoz saw her and felt that he was about to pass out. Then the true horror of all that had happened that evening swam into his mind.

'I am going,' he said, to no one in particular.

Saeeda Bai was incapable of speaking. Bibbo said: 'The Nawabzada cannot leave like this. He is badly injured. He needs a doctor.'

Firoz got up with an effort. The pain made him gasp. He looked around the room and shuddered. He saw his walking stick.

'Bibbo, give me the stick.'

'The Nawabzada must not—'

'The stick.'

She handed it to him.

'Take care of your mistress. Your mistresses,' he added bitterly.

'Let me help you down the stairs,' said Tasneem.

Firoz stared into her face with a glazed look. 'No,' he said gently.

'You need help,' she said, her lips trembling.

'No!' he cried with sudden vehemence.

Bibbo saw that Firoz was determined to have his way. 'Begum Sahiba—that shawl?' she asked. Saeeda Bai nodded, and Bibbo put a shawl around Firoz's shoulders. She walked downstairs with him to the door. It was still misty outside. Firoz leaned against his stick, hunched forward like an old man. He kept saying to himself: 'I cannot stay here. I cannot stay here.'

Bibbo said to the watchman: 'Go immediately to Dr Bilgrami's. Tell him that the Begum Sahiba and another person have been taken ill.' The watchman stared at Firoz.

'Go. Go quickly, you dolt—' said Bibbo with authority.

The watchman stomped off.

Firoz made to move towards the gate. The night was thick with mist.

'The Nawabzada is in no state to go—please, please wait here—look at the night and at yourself. I have called the doctor. He will be here any minute,' cried Bibbo, holding him back.

'You cannot go—' This time it was Tasneem who had run downstairs to prevent him from leaving. She was standing—for the first time in her life—at the open door, not daring, however, to go further. Had there been no fog she would have been visible from the road.

He was unable to control his tears of pain and shock as he walked along.

Why Maan had stabbed him—what had happened between Maan and Saeeda Bai—he could not even think. But nothing was worse than what had happened before. Saeeda Bai had intercepted one of his letters, and had summoned him. Curtly she had forbidden him to write to Tasneem, to have anything to do with her. When he had protested, she had told him the truth.

'Tasneem is not my sister,' she had said as factually as possible. 'She is yours.'

Firoz had stared at her in horror. 'Yes,' Saeeda Bai had continued. 'She is my daughter, God forgive me.'

Firoz had shaken his head.

'And God forgive your father,' she had continued. 'Now go in peace. I must say my prayers.'

Firoz, speechless with disgust and torn between belief and disbelief, had left her room. Downstairs he told Bibbo he had to see Tasneem.

'No—' said Bibbo. 'No—how can the Nawabzada presume—'

'You have known all along,' he said to her, clutching her arm.

'Known what?' protested Bibbo, shaking him off.

'If you haven't known it, it can't be true,' said Firoz. 'It is a cruel lie. It cannot be true.'

'True? True?' said Bibbo. 'The Nawabzada has taken leave of his senses.'

'I must see Tasneem. I must see her,' Firoz had cried in desperation.

Hearing her name, Tasneem had come out of her room and looked at him. He had gone up to her and stared at her face till tears of embarrassment and misery ran down her cheeks.

'What is the matter? Why is the Nawabzada looking at me in this manner?' she asked Bibbo, turning her face away.

'Go back to your room or your sister will be furious with you,' said Bibbo. Tasneem had turned back.

'I must talk with you,' said Firoz, following Bibbo into another room.

'Then keep your voice low,' said Bibbo curtly. But his questions had been so wild and strange—and so full of guilt and shame—that she had looked at him in real perplexity. 'I can see no resemblance to anyone—to Zainab, to my father—' he had said. She had still been trying to make sense of his words when they had heard the sounds upstairs—of someone falling, and Saeeda Bai crying for help.

The night had become bitterly cold. Firoz stopped, and walked, and stopped again. The mist thinned out here and there, then wound itself around him. The shawl was soaked in blood. His thoughts, his pain, the mist, all dispersed and concentrated about him as if at random. His hands were wet with blood where he had clutched his side. The walking stick slipped in his hand. He did not know if he would be able to get home like this. And if he got home, he thought, how could he bear to look at his father's old and beloved face?

He had hardly walked a hundred yards when he felt that he would not be able to make it. The loss of blood, the physical pain, and the terrible thoughts that oppressed his mind had brought him almost to collapse. A tonga loomed up out of the mist. He raised his stick and tried to hail it, and collapsed on to the pavement.

17.14

It was a quiet night at the Pasand Bagh Police Station, and the station house officer, who was a Sub-Inspector, was yawning, writing up reports, drinking tea, and cracking jokes with his subordinates.

'This is a very subtle one, Hemraj, so listen carefully,' he addressed a writer-constable who was making an entry in the daily diary. 'Two masters each said that their servant was stupider than the other's. So they had a bet. One summoned his servant and said: "Budhu Ram, there's a Buick for sale in a shop on Nabiganj. Here is ten rupees. Go and buy it for me." So Budhu Ram took the ten rupees and went out.'

A couple of the constables burst out laughing, and the Sub-Inspector shut them up. 'I have hardly begun telling you the joke and you idiots start braying. Shut up and listen. . . . So the other master said: "You may think that's stupid, but my servant, Ullu Chand, is even stupider. I'll prove it." He summoned Ullu Chand and said: "Now look here, Ullu Chand, I want you to go to the Subzipore Club and see if I'm there. It's urgent." Ullu Chand immediately went off to do as he was told.'

The constables started laughing uncontrollably. 'See if I'm there—' one said, rolling about. 'See if I'm there.'

'Shut up, shut up,' said the Sub-Inspector. 'I haven't finished.' The constables promptly shut up. The Sub-Inspector cleared his throat. 'On the way, one servant met the other and said—'

A bewildered tonga-wallah entered the room, and mumbled, in obvious distress: 'Daroga Sahib—'

'Oh, shut up, shut up,' said the Sub-Inspector genially. 'So one servant met the other and said: "I say, Ullu Chand, my master is a complete idiot. He gave me ten rupees and told me to buy a Buick. But doesn't he know that today is Sunday and the shops are closed?"'

At this point everyone burst out laughing, including the Sub-Inspector himself. But he hadn't finished yet, and, when the laughter had died down, he continued:

'And the other servant said: "Well, that may be stupid, Budhu Ram, but it's nothing compared to the idiocy of my master. He asked me to find out urgently if he was at the club. But if it was so urgent, why didn't he simply go to the other room and use the telephone?"'

At this the entire room resounded with hoots and shrieks of laughter, and the Sub-Inspector, very pleased, took a loud sip of tea, some of which wet his moustache. 'Yes, what do you want?' he said, noticing the tonga-wallah, who appeared to be trembling.

'Daroga Sahib, there's a body lying on the pavement on Cornwallis Road.'

'It's a bad night. Must be some poor fellow who's succumbed to the cold,' said the Inspector. 'But Cornwallis Road?'

'He's alive,' said the tonga-wallah. 'He tried to hail me, then collapsed. He's covered in blood. I think he's been stabbed. He looks as if he's from a good family. I didn't know whether to leave him or to bring him—to go to the hospital or the police. Please come quickly. Did I do the right thing?'

'You idiot!' cried the Sub-Inspector. 'You've been standing here all this while. Why didn't you speak earlier?' He addressed the others: 'Get some bandages. And you, Hemraj, phone the government doctor at the night clinic. Get the police kit together quickly, and bring a couple of extra torches. And you'—he addressed the tonga-wallah—'come with us and show us where he's lying.'

'Did I do the right thing?' asked the tonga-wallah fearfully.

'Yes, yes, yes—you didn't disturb him, did you?'

'No, Daroga Sahib, I just turned him over to see—to see, well, if he was alive.'

'For God's sake, what is taking you so long?' said the Sub-Inspector impatiently to his subordinates. 'Come on. How far is it from here?'

'Just two minutes away.'

'Then we'll go in your tonga. Hemraj, use the police jeep to get the doctor. Don't fill in more than a line in the daily diary. I'll do the rest later. If he's still alive maybe I'll get an FIR from him rather than from the tonga-wallah. I'm taking Bihari with me. The other Assistant Sub-Inspector will handle the station while I'm gone.'

Within two minutes they had got to Firoz. He was semi-conscious and still bleeding. It was immediately clear to the Sub-Inspector that if his life was to be saved there was no question of first aid and bandages. Time was of the essence. He should be moved to the hospital forthwith.

'Bihari, when the doctor comes, tell him to hurry to the Civil Hospital. We're going there by tonga. Yes, give me the bandages—I'll see what I can do on the way to stop the blood. Oh, yes, follow the blood if you can: keep two torches, I'll take one. I'll take statements from the tonga-wallah and the injured man. Check the walking stick for a hidden blade. See if the weapon's lying around, and so on. His wallet is on him—it doesn't seem as if he's been robbed. But maybe someone tried to rob him and he managed to get away. On Cornwallis Road!' The Sub-Inspector shook his head, licked the right side of his moustache, and wondered what Brahmpur was coming to.

They lifted Firoz into the tonga and got in themselves, and it clopped off into the mist. The Sub-Inspector shone his torch carefully at Firoz's face. Even with the wavering torchlight shining on his pale and distorted features, Firoz's face looked familiar. The Inspector noticed that he was wearing a woman's shawl and frowned. Then he opened his wallet, and saw the name and address on his driving licence; and his frown became one of real concern. He shook his head slowly. This case was going to mean trouble and would have to be handled carefully. As soon as they got to the hospital and put Firoz in the hands of the emergency ward staff the Sub-Inspector telephoned the Superintendent of Police, who himself undertook to inform Baitar House.

17.15

The emergency ward—which had recently been renamed the casualty department—represented a scene of organized chaos. A woman, clutching her stomach, was screaming in pain in a corner. Two men were brought in with head injuries from a lorry accident—they were still alive, but there was no hope for them. A few people had minor cuts of one kind or another, bleeding to a greater or lesser degree.

Two young house surgeons examined Firoz. The Sub-Inspector filled them in on the background: where he had been found, and his name and address.

'This must be Dr Imtiaz Khan's brother,' said one of them. 'Has the police informed him? We would like to have him on hand, especially if permission is needed for an operation. He works at the Prince of Wales College Hospital.'

The Sub-Inspector told them that the SP was getting in touch with Baitar House. Meanwhile, could he speak to the patient? He needed to file a First Information Report.

'Not now, not now,' said the doctors. They checked Firoz's pulse, which was shallow and irregular, his blood pressure, which was low, his respiration, which was rather fast, and the responses of his pupils, which were normal. He was pale and his forehead was clammy. He had lost a lot of blood and appeared to be in shock. He was still speaking a few words, but they were incoherent. The Sub-Inspector, who was an intelligent man, tried to make what sense of them he could. In particular he noted Saeeda Bai's name, the words 'Prem Nivas', and several agitated mentions of a sister or sisters. These might help him to discover what had happened.

He turned to the doctors. 'You mentioned he had a brother. Does he also have a sister?'

'Not that I know,' said one doctor, shortly.

'I believe he does,' said the other. 'But she doesn't live in Brahmpur. He's lost too much blood. Sister, get a drip ready. Normal saline.'

They removed Firoz's shawl and cut away part of his kurta and vest. All his clothes were covered with blood.

The policeman murmured: 'I'll have to get you to write a medical report.'

'I can't find a vein in the arm,' said one of the doctors, ignoring what the Sub-Inspector was saying. 'We'll have to cut down.' They cut a vein in Firoz's ankle, drew out a little blood, and inserted a drip. 'Sister, please take this to the lab for tests, and for grouping and matching. Pretty shawl, that. Dyeing doesn't improve it.'

A few minutes passed. Blood was still seeping from Firoz's wound, and his moments of speech, incoherent as they were, were becoming rarer. He appeared to be sinking into deeper shock.

'There's a little dirt around the wound,' said one of the house surgeons. 'We'd better give him an anti-tetanus shot.' He turned to the policeman. 'Did you recover the weapon? How long was it? Was it rusty at all?'

'We haven't recovered the weapon.'

'Sister, some iodine and cetavalon—please swab the area around the wound.' He turned to his colleague. 'There's blood in the mouth. It's got to be internal injury: stomach possibly, or upper intestine. We can't handle this. Better call the registrar and alert the senior surgeon on duty. And, Sister, please get the lab to hurry up with that blood report, especially the haemoglobin count.'

The senior surgeon, when he came down, took one look at Firoz and at the lab report and said: 'We will have to do an exploratory laparotomy immediately.'

'I need to get an FIR—' said the Sub-Inspector aggressively, nudging his moustache with the back of his fist. The First Information Report was often the most important document in the case, and it was good to have a solid one, preferably from the victim's mouth.

The senior surgeon looked at him in cold incredulity. 'This man is not capable of speech now, nor will he be capable of speech for another twelve hours once he is under anaesthetic. And even after that—assuming he lives—you will not be allowed to examine him for at least twenty-four hours. Get your FIR from whoever found him. Or else wait. And, if you wish, hope.'

The Sub-Inspector was used to the rudeness of doctors, having come into contact—as had most policemen in Brahmpur at one time or other—with Dr Kishen Chand Seth. He took no offence. He knew that doctors and policemen viewed 'cases' in a different light. Besides, he was a realist. He had told the tonga-wallah to wait outside. Now that he knew that Firoz would not be able to speak further, he decided that he would get his First Information Report from the man who had in fact given him his first information.

'Well, thank you, Doctor Sahib, for the advice,' said the Sub-Inspector. 'If the police doctor comes, could he examine the patient for the medical report?'

'We'll do all that ourselves,' said the senior surgeon, unmollified. 'The patient has to be saved, not endlessly examined. Leave the forms here.' He said to the Sister: 'Who is the anaesthetist on duty? Dr Askari? The patient is in shock, so we'd better use atropine for pre-anaesthetic. We'll wheel him into the theatre now. Who did the cut down procedure?'

'I did, Sir,' said one of the house surgeons proudly.

'Untidy job,' said the senior surgeon bluntly. 'Has Dr Khan come yet? Or the Nawab Sahib? We need signatures on those permissions.'

Neither Firoz's brother nor father had arrived yet.

'Well, we can't wait,' said the senior surgeon. And Firoz was wheeled through the corridors of the Civil Hospital into the operating theatre.

The Nawab Sahib and Imtiaz arrived too late to see him being wheeled in. The Nawab Sahib was virtually in a state of shock himself.

'Let me see him,' he said to Imtiaz.

Imtiaz put his arm around his father's shoulder, and said: 'Abba-jaan, that's not possible. He'll be all right, I know. Bhatia is doing the operation. Askari is the anaesthetist. They're both very good.'

'Who would want to do this to Firoz?' said the old man.

Imtiaz shrugged. His face was grim. 'He didn't tell you where he was going this evening, did he?' he asked his father.

'No,' said the Nawab Sahib. After a pause he said, 'But Maan's in town. He might know.'

'All in good time, Abba-jaan. Don't agitate yourself.'

'On Cornwallis Road,' said the Nawab Sahib incredulously. Then he covered his face with his hands and started weeping softly. After a while he said: 'We should tell Zainab.'

'All in good time, Abba-jaan, all in good time. Let's wait till the operation is over and we know how things have gone.'

It was almost midnight. The two of them remained outside the operating theatre. The smell of the hospital began to panic the Nawab Sahib. Occasionally a colleague would walk past and greet Imtiaz or commiserate with him and his father. The news of the attack on Firoz must have got around, because a reporter from the *Brahmpur Chronicle* turned up at just after midnight. Imtiaz was tempted to tell him to buzz off, but decided to answer a few short questions instead. The more publicity Firoz got, he decided, the more likely it was that someone who may have noticed something would come forward with a clue.

At about one o'clock, the doctors emerged from the operating theatre. They looked tired. It was impossible to read Dr Bhatia's expression. But when he saw Imtiaz, he drew a deep breath and said:

'It's good to see you, Dr Khan. I hope it will be all right. He was in severe shock when we operated, but we couldn't wait. And it's a good thing we didn't. We did the usual laparotomy. There was severe laceration of the small intestine, and we had to perform several anastomoses, apart from cleaning out the abdominal cavity. That's why it took us so long.' He turned to the Nawab Sahib. 'Your handsome son is now the proud possessor of a handsome seven-inch scar. I hope he will be all right. I am sorry we couldn't wait for your permission to anaesthetize and operate.'

'May I—' began the Nawab Sahib.

'What about—' said Imtiaz simultaneously.

'What about what?' said Bhatia to Imtiaz.

'What about the danger of sepsis, of peritonitis?'

'Well, let us pray that that has been averted. There was quite a mess inside. But we will keep a close watch. We have given him penicillin. I am sorry, Nawab Sahib, what were you about to say?'

'May I speak to him?' said the old man falteringly. 'I know he will want to speak to me.'

Dr Bhatia smiled. 'Well, he is still under chloroform. If he does say something, you may not be able to make much sense of it. But you might find it interesting. Indeed, people have no idea what interesting things they say under anaesthesia. Your son kept talking about his sister.'

'Imtiaz, you must call Zainab,' said the Nawab Sahib.

'I'll do that at once, Abba. Dr Bhatia, we cannot thank you enough.'

'Not at all, not at all. I only hope they get whoever did this. A single incision, the work of a second, and I don't mind telling you, Dr Khan, if they hadn't brought him to us directly, we would not have been able to save him. Indeed—' He stopped.

'Indeed, what?' said Imtiaz sharply.

'Indeed, it's odd that what one person does in a second can take seven of us—and all this—three hours to undo.'

'What did he say?' said the Nawab Sahib to Imtiaz when Dr Bhatia had taken his leave. 'What did they do to Firoz?'

'Nothing very exciting, Abba,' said Imtiaz, attempting reassurance. 'They cut out the injured parts of his intestinal loops, and joined the healthy parts together again. But we have yards and yards of the stuff, so Firoz won't miss what he's lost.'

In the event, his reply sounded flippant, and far from reassuring to his father.

'So he's all right?' said the Nawab Sahib, searching Imtiaz's face.

Imtiaz paused, then said: 'His chances are good, Abba. There were no complications. The only concern now is infection, and we can deal with that much better now than we could just a few years ago. Don't worry. I am sure he will be well. Inshallah.'

17.16

The Sub-Inspector would have followed up the trail of Firoz's words the next morning if it had not been the case that a trail of his blood led to within a few yards of Saeeda Bai's gate. When informed of this, he decided to act at once. Together with Bihari and another constable, he arrived at Saeeda Bai's door. The watchman, who had been questioned in a threatening manner by the policemen earlier, and who had himself been perplexed and worried by the events of the night, admitted that he had seen both the Nawabzada and Kapoor Sahib from Prem Nivas earlier in the evening, as well as Dr Bilgrami.

'We will need to speak with Saeeda Bai,' said the Sub-Inspector.

'Daroga Sahib, why not wait till morning?' suggested the watchman.

'Did you not hear me?' said the Sub-Inspector, smoothing his moustache like a movie villain.

The watchman knocked and waited. There was no reply. He rapped at the door a few times with the blunt end of his spear. Bibbo emerged, saw the police, shut the door promptly and latched it.

'Let us in at once,' said the Sub-Inspector, 'or we will break down the door. We have questions to ask you about a murder.'

Bibbo opened the door again. Her face was white. 'A murder?' she said.

'Well, an attempt at it. You know what we are talking about. It's pointless to deny it. The Nawab's son might have been dead by now but for our prompt action. For all we know he might be dead anyway. We want to talk with you.'

'I know nothing—'

'He was here this evening, and so was Kapoor.'

'Oh—Dagh Sahib,' said Bibbo, looking daggers at the watchman, who shrugged his shoulders.

'Is Saeeda Bai awake?'

'Saeeda Begum is taking her rest, as any respectable citizen of Brahmpur would be doing at this time of night.'

The Sub-Inspector laughed. 'As any respectable citizen—' Again he laughed, and the constables joined in. 'Wake her up. We have to speak with her here. Unless she would like to come down to the police station.'

Bibbo made a quick decision. She closed the door once again, and disappeared. About five minutes later, during which time the Sub-Inspector asked the watchman a few questions, she came out again.

'Saeeda Begum will see you upstairs. But she has a bad throat, and cannot speak.' Saeeda Bai's room was, as always, in impeccable order, with a clean white sheet laid out on the floor. There was no bowl of fruit, no fruit knife. The three khaki uniforms contrasted absurdly with the scent of attar of roses.

Saeeda Bai had dressed hastily in a green sari. Her throat was wrapped around with a dupatta. Her voice was a croak, and she tried to avoid speaking. Her smile was as charming as ever.

At first she denied that there had been any quarrel. But when the Sub-Inspector said that Firoz had mentioned Prem Nivas, and that his presence at Saeeda Bai's had been corroborated not only by the watchman, who had described his crippled bearing when he had emerged from the house, but also by the physical evidence of an irregular trail of blood, she saw that denial was useless. She agreed that there had been a fight.

'Where did it take place?'

'In this room.'

'Why is there no blood here?'

Saeeda Bai did not answer.

'What was the weapon?'

Saeeda Bai remained silent.

'Answer these questions, please. Or else come down to the police station and make your statement there. In any case, we will ask you to confirm these statements in writing tomorrow.'

'It was a fruit knife.'

'Where is it?'

'He took it with him.'

'Who did? The attacker or the victim?'

'Dagh Sahib,' she managed to croak out. Her hands went to her throat and she looked pleadingly at the policeman.

'What is all this about Prem Nivas?'

Bibbo intervened: 'Please, Sub-Inspector Sahib, Saeeda Begum can hardly speak. She has been singing so much, and the weather has been so bad these last few days, what with the dust and the mist, that her throat is very sore.'

'What is all this about Prem Nivas?' insisted the Sub-Inspector.

Saeeda Bai shook her head.

'That is where Kapoor lives, is it not?'

Saeeda Bai nodded.

'It is the Minister Sahib's house,' added Bibbo.

'And what is all this about a sister?' asked the Sub-Inspector.

Saeeda Bai's body went rigid for a moment, and she began to tremble. Bibbo gave her a sharp and puzzled glance. Saeeda Bai had turned away. Her shoulders were shaking, and she was crying. But she did not say a word.

'What is all this about a sister?' repeated the policeman with a yawn.

Saeeda Bai shook her head.

'Haven't you had enough?' cried Bibbo. 'Haven't you had enough of torturing Saeeda Begum? Why can't this wait till morning? We will complain to the SP about this. Disturbing decent and respectable citizens—'

The Sub-Inspector did not mention that the SP had told him to treat this case like any other, but with greater urgency and dispatch. Nor did he make a sarcastic comment, though it did come to his mind, about decent and respectable citizens stabbing each other in their salons.

But perhaps this specific line of questioning could wait till morning, he thought. Even if matters were not entirely clear, it now was obvious enough to him that Maan Kapoor, the younger son of Mahesh Kapoor, had perpetrated the attack on the Nawabzada. But the Sub-Inspector was in two minds about whether to attempt to arrest him tonight. On the one hand, Prem Nivas, like Baitar House, was one of the great houses of Pasand Bagh, and Mahesh Kapoor one of the great names of the province. For a mere Sub-Inspector to think of rousing that august household in the early hours—and for such a purpose—could be interpreted as the greatest insolence and disrespect. But on the other hand the case was a most serious one. Even if the victim lived, the facts spoke of an attempt at culpable homicide, possibly attempted murder, and certainly grievous hurt.

He had already gone over several levels of authority to telephone the SP earlier in the night. He could not wake him up now to ask him for further instructions. An additional consideration occurred to the Sub-Inspector and determined his course of action. There was, in cases such as these, the danger of the criminal panicking and absconding. He decided to make the arrest at once.

17.17

'Panicking and absconding' was in fact an accurate description of what Maan was doing. He was not at home. It was three o'clock in the morning when the household at Prem Nivas was woken up. Mahesh Kapoor had just come back to town, and was exhausted and irritable. At first he almost threw the police out of his house. But then his indignation turned to disbelief and finally to an appalled concern. He went to call Maan, but did not find him in his room. Mrs Mahesh Kapoor—equally horrified by what had happened to Firoz and fearful for her son—wandered through the house, not knowing what she would do if she found him. Her husband, however, was clear in his mind. He would cooperate with the police. He was surprised that a more senior officer had not come to his house to look for Maan, but the lateness of the hour and the suddenness of events must account for this.

He allowed the policeman to search Maan's room. The bed had not been slept in. There was no sign of anything remotely resembling a weapon.

'Have you found anything to interest you?' asked Mr Mahesh Kapoor.

He kept thinking back to the searches and arrests that he and Prem Nivas had undergone in the time of the British.

The Sub-Inspector looked around as quickly as possible, apologized profusely, and left. 'If Mr Maan Kapoor does return, would Minister Sahib ask him to come to the Pasand Bagh Police Station? It would be better than the police coming here again,' he said. Mahesh Kapoor nodded. He was stunned, but did not appear to be anything but calm and sarcastic.

When they had left, he tried to console his wife with the thought that there had been some mistake. But Mrs Mahesh Kapoor was convinced that something disastrous had indeed happened—and that Maan, somehow, in his impetuousness, had caused it. She wanted to go at once to the Civil Hospital to see how Firoz was, but Mahesh Kapoor said that it would be best to wait till morning. Anyway, in her state of health, it was perhaps best if she did not see Firoz.

'If he comes home, we can't give him up,' she said.

'Don't be stupid,' said Mahesh Kapoor impatiently. Then he shook his head. 'You must go to bed now.'

'I won't be able to sleep.'

'Well, then, pray,' said Mahesh Kapoor impatiently. 'But keep yourself covered up. Your chest sounds bad. I will call a doctor in the morning.'

'Call a lawyer for him, not a doctor for me,' said Mrs Mahesh Kapoor, who was in tears. 'Can't we get him bail?'

'He hasn't been arrested yet,' said Mahesh Kapoor. Then a thought occurred to him. Though it was the middle of the night, he phoned up the middle Bespectacled Bannerji, and asked him about anticipatory bail. The lawyer was irked to be woken up at this amazing hour, but when he recognized Mahesh Kapoor's voice and heard an account of what the police said had happened, he did his best to explain matters.

'The problem, Kapoor Sahib, is that neither attempted murder nor grievous hurt with a dangerous weapon is a bailable offence. Is it, well, feasible, I mean, possible, that the charge might be considered to be ordinary grievous hurt? Or attempted culpable homicide? Those are bailable charges.'

'I see,' said Mahesh Kapoor.

'Or simple hurt?'

'No, I don't think that is possible.'

'You said a Sub-Inspector came to the house. Not even an Inspector. I am astonished.'

'Well, that's who it was.'

'Perhaps you should have a word with the Deputy Superintendent of Police or the SP—to clarify things.'

'Thank you for your explanations and, well, suggestion,' said Mahesh Kapoor disapprovingly. 'I am sorry to have woken you up at this hour.'

There was a pause at the other end. 'Not at all, not at all. Please feel free to call me up at any time.'

When he returned to his room Mahesh Kapoor found his wife praying, and he wished he could have prayed as well. He had always been very fond of his reckless son, but had only realized in these last few weeks how dearly he loved him.

Where are you? he thought, irritated and upset. Don't for God's sake do anything even more stupid than you've already done. At this thought his irritation disappeared, and was replaced with a profound anxiety both for his son and for the son of his friend.

17.18

Maan had disappeared into the mist and reappeared at Brahmpur Railway Station. He knew he had to get out of Brahmpur. He was drunk, and he was not certain why he had to escape. But Firoz had told him to, and Bibbo had told him to. He pictured the scene in his mind. It was terrible. He could not believe what he had done. There had been a knife in his hand. And then his friend had been lying on the ground, wounded and bleeding. Wounded? But Firoz—Firoz—that he and Saeeda Bai—Maan relived the wretchedness of his feelings. What tormented him more than anything was the deception. 'It is not my sister he is in love with'—he thought of the near-hysterical words and realized how much Saeeda Bai must have been obsessed with Firoz. And again he chided himself for having been duped by his own love for her, and his love for his friend. Oh, what a fool I am, he thought. Oh, what a fool. He looked at his own clothes. There was no blood anywhere—not even on his bundi. He looked at his hands.

He bought a ticket to Banaras. He was almost weeping at the counter, and the clerk looked at him strangely.

On the train he offered the remnants of his bottle of whisky to a young man who happened to be awake in the compartment. The man shook his head. Maan looked at the sign near the alarm handle—*To Stop Train Pull Chain*—and began to tremble violently. By the time he got to

Banaras, he had gone off to sleep. The young man woke him up and made sure he got off.

'I'll never forget your kindness—never—' said Maan, as the train steamed off.

Dawn was breaking. He walked along the ghats, singing a bhajan which his mother had taught him when he was ten years old. Then he went to the house where his fiancée lived, and started battering on the door. Those good people got alarmed. When they saw Maan there, they became very angry: they told him to go away and not to make an exhibition of himself. He next went to some people to whom he had lent money. They were not keen to see him at all. 'I've killed my friend,' Maan told them. 'Nonsense,' they replied.

'You'll see—it'll be in all the papers,' Maan said, distraught. 'Please hide me for a few days.'

They thought it a wonderful joke. 'What are you doing in Banaras?' they said. 'Are you here on business?'

'No,' said Maan.

Suddenly he could bear it no longer. He went to the local police station to give himself up.

'I was the man—I—' he said, hardly able to speak coherently.

The policemen humoured him for a while, then grew annoyed, and finally wondered whether there might not be some truth to what he was saying. They tried to telephone Brahmpur but could not get through. Then they sent an urgent telegram. 'Please wait,' they told Maan. 'We'll arrest you if we can.'

'Yes—yes—' said Maan. He was feeling very hungry. All he had had that day was a few cups of tea.

Finally the police got a message back that stated that the younger son of the Nawab Sahib of Baitar had been found seriously wounded on Cornwallis Road in Brahmpur, and that the principal suspect was Maan Kapoor. They looked at Maan as if he was mad, and arrested him. Then, in a few hours, they handcuffed him, and put him on the train back to Brahmpur under the escort of two constables.

'Why must you handcuff me? What have I done?' said Maan.

The station house officer was so tired of Maan, so annoyed with the needless work he had caused him, and so exasperated by his latest and most ludicrous protest that he wanted to beat him up. 'These are the regulations,' he said.

Maan got along better with the constables.

'I suppose you have to be very alert in case I escape,' he said. 'In case I break free and jump from the train.'

The constables laughed good-humouredly. 'You won't escape,' they said.

'How do you know?'

'Oh, you can't,' one of them said. 'We keep the keyholes on top, so that you can't open the handcuffs by striking them on—well, on those window bars, for instance. But if you want to go to the bathroom, you should tell us.'

'We're very careful about our handcuffs,' said the other.

'Yes, we unlock them when they aren't in use. Otherwise the springs can get weak.'

'Can't have that,' said the other constable. 'Why did you give yourself up?' he asked curiously. 'Are you really the son of a Minister?'

Maan shook his head miserably. 'Yes, yes,' he said, and went off to sleep.

He dreamed of a vast and varicose Victoria, like the one in the portrait in the dining room of Baitar Fort. She was removing layer after layer of her regalia and calling to him enticingly. 'I have left something behind,' she was saying. 'I must go back.' The dream was unbearably disturbing. He woke up. Both the constables were asleep, although it was only early evening. When the train approached Brahmpur, they woke up by instinct, and delivered him into the hands of a party from the Pasand Bagh Police Station that was waiting on the platform.

'What will you do?' Maan asked his escorts.

'We'll take the next train back,' they replied.

'Look us up when you are next in Banaras,' one of them said.

Maan smiled at his new escorts, but they were much less inclined to humour him. The mustachioed Sub-Inspector, in particular, appeared very serious. When they got to the police station, he was given a thin grey blanket and put in the lock-up. It was a small, cold, filthy cell—a barred room with nothing but a few pieces of jute on the floor—no straw or mattress or pillow. It stank. In place of a toilet there was a large clay vessel in the corner. The other man in the cell looked tubercular and was drunk. His eyes were red. He stared in a hunted way at the police and, when the door clanged shut, at Maan.

The Sub-Inspector apologized to Maan curtly. 'You will have to stay here tonight,' he said. 'Tomorrow we will decide whether to remand you into judicial custody or not. If we get a proper statement from you we won't need to hold you here much longer.'

Maan sat down on the floor on a piece of jute matting and covered his head with his hands. For a second he imagined the scent of attar of roses, and he began to cry bitterly. More than anything he regretted that the last day had existed. If only he had remained ignorant, he thought. If only he had not known.

17.19

Apart from Firoz, who was still not conscious, there were two people sitting in the room in the ward. One was an Assistant Sub-Inspector, who nodded off because there was nothing for him to take down; the police had insisted on, and the hospital had acquiesced in, his presence. The other was the Nawab Sahib. Imtiaz, because he was a doctor, was not prevented from coming in, and did so from time to time. But it was the Nawab Sahib who kept vigil by the bedside of his son. His servant, Ghulam Rusool, was given a pass so that he could bring the Nawab Sahib his food and a daily change of clothes. At night the Nawab Sahib slept on a couch in the same room; he insisted that it was not a problem for him. Even in winter he was used to sleeping with a single blanket. At the appointed hours, he spread a small rug on the floor and prayed.

On the first day Firoz was not allowed visitors even during visiting hours. Imtiaz did manage to get Zainab into the hospital; she was in purdah. When she saw Firoz—his face pale, his thick curly hair matted to his forehead, the tube of a saline drip stuck in the crook of his right arm (they had moved it from his ankle)—she was so upset that she decided that she would not bring her children to see him until he was better. Nor would it do them any good to see their grandfather so desperate and tearful. But agitated though she was, she was convinced that Firoz would get better. It was the usually optimistic Imtiaz who thought of all the possible complications and was worried.

Whoever came to relieve the policeman on duty usually brought some news for the Nawab Sahib from the police station. By now he knew that Firoz had not been stabbed by a stranger on the street, but that there had been a fight at Saeeda Bai's between Maan and Firoz, and that it was Maan who had nearly killed him. He had not believed this at first. But Maan had been arrested, and had confessed, and there was no question of not believing it now.

Sometimes he would get up and wipe Firoz's forehead with a towel. He would take his name, not so much to wake him as to reassure himself that the name still meant someone living. He remembered Firoz's childhood and thought of his wife, whose features were so like his. Even more than Zainab, Firoz was his link to her. Then he would begin to upbraid himself because he had not prevented Firoz from visiting Saeeda Bai's. He should have known from the experience of his own youth the attraction of places of that kind. But since his wife's death it had grown difficult to speak to his children; his library had more and more taken over his world. Only once had he ordered his secretary not to give Firoz an easy excuse to go to that place. If only, he thought, he had explicitly forbidden Firoz from going there. But what good would it have done? he reflected. In Maan's company he could well have gone regardless—that unthinking young man would have cared as little for the behests of his friend's father as for those of his own.

Now and then, listening to the doctors, and looking at Imtiaz's worried expression as he consulted with them, the Nawab Sahib felt that he was going to lose his son. Then he was overwhelmed with despair, and in bitterness of spirit wished every ill and pain on Maan—even on his family. He wished Maan to suffer as he had made his son suffer. He could not conceive what Firoz could possibly have done to have been stabbed with a knife by the friend who he thought had loved him.

When he prayed, he felt ashamed of these feelings, but he could not control them. That Maan had saved his son's life once seemed to be a fact so hazy, so distant from this present jeopardy, as to be almost irrelevant.

His own connection with Saeeda Bai too had sunk so far back in his consciousness that he did not think of her any more with reference to himself. He did not know where and how she fitted into these events. He felt only the dimmest anxiety in her regard, not the possibility of any revelation of the past. The present provision he made for her and for the daughter who she claimed was his own, this was a duty he accepted as a necessary act of decency, the partial expiation of an old and half-forgotten sin. And it was understood that for her part nothing would ever be said to anyone about what had happened two decades ago between a married man of almost forty and a girl of fifteen. The child who had later been born was never told that she was anything but Saeeda Bai's younger sister; or so the Nawab Sahib had been given to understand. Apart from Saeeda Bai herself only her mother had truly known what had happened, and she was long since dead.

Firoz was now speaking a few words, and, incoherent as they were, for his father they were as miraculous as the words of someone who had returned from the dead. He pulled his chair closer to the bed and held Firoz's left hand. It was reassuringly warm. The policeman too became more alert. 'What is your son saying, Nawab Sahib?' he asked.

'I don't know,' said the Nawab Sahib, smiling. 'But it appears to me to be a good sign.'

'Something about his sister, I think,' said the policeman, his pencil poised over a new page.

'She was here before you took over,' said the Nawab Sahib. 'But, poor girl, she was distressed to see him in this state and did not stay long.'

'Tasneem—' It was Firoz's voice.

The Nawab Sahib heard and flinched. That was her name, the name of Saeeda Bai's daughter. He had spoken it with a terrifying tenderness.

The policeman continued to jot down whatever Firoz said.

The Nawab Sahib looked upwards in sudden fear. A lizard was climbing up the wall in an irregular wriggle, stopping and starting. He stared at it, transfixed.

'Tasneem—'

The Nawab Sahib sighed very slowly, as if the effort of drawing and releasing breath had suddenly become painful. He released Firoz's hand, and unconsciously joined both his own together. Then he let them fall to his side.

He tried, in his fear, to piece the words together. His first feeling was that Firoz had somehow come to learn the truth, or some part of the truth. The thought caused him such pain that he had to lean back in his chair and close his eyes. He had longed for his son to open his eyes and to see him sitting by his side. But now the thought was terrifying. When his eyes open and he finds me sitting here, what will he say to me or I to him?

Then he thought of the policeman's dutiful note-taking. What would happen if ever anyone else pieced together the fragments of the truth? Or if they heard about the past from whoever had told Firoz about it? Things that had long been dead would rear themselves out of the grave; and matters so little known that they had almost lost their sense of existence would become the business of the world at large.

But perhaps no one had said anything at all. Perhaps Firoz did not know anything. The Nawab Sahib reflected that possibly in his own guilt he had merely conjoined a few innocent fragments into a frightening whole.

Perhaps Firoz had merely met the girl at Saeeda Bai's.

'In the name of God, the Merciful, the Compassionate,' he began hurriedly.

> 'Praise belongs to God, the Lord of all Being,
> the All-Merciful, the All-Compassionate,
> the Master of the Day of Doom.
>
> Thee only we serve; to Thee alone we pray for succour.
> Guide us in the straight path—'

The Nawab Sahib stopped. If it was in fact the case that Firoz did not know, that was no cause for relief at all. He would have to know. He would have to be told. The alternative was too terrible to imagine. And it was he who would have to tell him.

17.20

Varun was reading the racing results in the *Statesman* with great interest. Uma, who was in Savita's arms, had grabbed a handful of his hair and was tugging at it, but this did not distract him. Her tongue was poking out between her lips.

'She will be a tell-tale when she grows up,' said Mrs Rupa Mehra. 'A little chugal-khor. Whom will we tell tales on? Whom will we tell tales on? Look at her little tongue.'

'Ow!' said Varun.

'Now, now, Uma,' said Savita in mild reproof. 'I find her very exhausting, Ma. She's so good-natured as a rule, but last night she kept on crying. Then this morning I discovered she was wet. How does one sort out the tantrums from the genuine tears?'

Mrs Rupa Mehra would hear nothing against Uma. 'There are some babies who cry several times in the night until they're two years old. Only their parents have a right to complain.'

Aparna said to her mother: 'I'm not a crybaby, am I?'

'No, darling,' said Meenakshi, flipping through the *Illustrated London News*. 'Now play with the baby, why don't you?'

Meenakshi, whenever she gave the matter any thought, still could not quite figure out how Uma had succeeded in becoming so vigorous, born as she had been in a Brahmpur hospital that was, as Meenakshi saw it, simply seething with septicaemia.

Aparna turned her head down sideways, so that her two eyes were in a vertical line. This amused the baby, and she gave her quite a generous smile. Simultaneously she yanked Varun's hair once more.

'Cracknell's done it again,' murmured Varun to himself. 'Eastern Sea in the King George VI Cup. By just half a length.'

Uma grasped the paper and drew a handful of it towards herself. Varun tried to disengage her clasp. She latched on to one of his fingers.

'Did you bet on the winner?' asked Pran.

'No,' said Varun glumly. 'Need you ask? Everyone else has all the luck. My horse came in fourth, after Orcades and Fair Ray.'

'What peculiar names,' said Lata.

'Orcades is one of the Orient Line boats,' said Meenakshi lazily. 'I am so looking forward to going to England. I shall visit Amit's college at Oxford. And marry a duke.'

Aparna straightened her head. She wondered what a duke was.

Mrs Rupa Mehra did not care for Meenakshi's brand of idiocy. Her hardworking elder son was slaving himself to the bone to support the family, and in his absence his empty-headed wife was making jokes in poor taste. She was a bad influence on Lata.

'You're married already,' Mrs Rupa Mehra pointed out.

'Oh, yes, silly me,' said Meenakshi. She sighed. 'How I wish something exciting would happen. Nothing ever happens anywhere. And I was so looking forward to something happening in 1952.'

'Well, it's a leap year,' said Pran encouragingly.

Varun had reached the end of the racing results and turned to another inside page. Suddenly he exclaimed 'My God!' in such a shocked tone that everyone turned towards him.

'Pran, your brother's been arrested.'

Pran's first instinct was to consider this another joke in dubious taste, but there was something in Varun's voice that made him reach for the paper. Uma tried to grab it on the way, but Savita held her off. As Pran read the few lines dated 'Brahmpur. January 5' his face grew taut.

'What is it?' said Savita, Lata and Mrs Rupa Mehra almost simultaneously. Even Meenakshi raised a languid head in surprise.

Pran shook his head from side to side in agitation. He quickly and silently read about the attack on Firoz—and that he was still in critical condition. The news was worse than he could possibly have imagined. But no telephone call or telegram had come from Brahmpur to inform him or warn him or summon him. Perhaps his father was still campaigning in his constituency. No, thought Pran. He would have heard within hours and rushed back to Brahmpur. Or perhaps he had tried to get through by phone to Calcutta and failed.

'We will have to leave for Brahmpur immediately,' he said to Savita.

'But what on earth has happened, darling?' asked Savita, very alarmed. 'They haven't really arrested Maan? And what for? What does it say?'

Pran read the few lines out aloud, hit his forehead with the palm of his hand and said: 'The idiot—the poor, unthinking, crazy idiot! Poor Ammaji. Baoji has always said—' He stopped. 'Ma, Lata—you should both remain here—'

'Of course not, Pran,' said Lata, very concerned. 'We were due to return in a couple of days anyway. We'll all travel together. How terrible. Poor Maan—I'm sure there's an explanation—he couldn't have done it. There must be—'

Mrs Rupa Mehra, thinking first of Mrs Mahesh Kapoor and then of the Nawab Sahib, felt tears start to her eyes. But tears, she knew, were not helpful, and she controlled herself with an effort.

'We'll go directly to the station,' said Pran, 'and try to get a ticket on the Brahmpur Mail. We only have an hour and a half to pack.'

Uma burst into a happy and meaningless chant. Meenakshi volunteered to hold her while they packed, and to call Arun at the office.

17.21

When Firoz came round from the effect of the anaesthesia, his father was asleep. He was at first uncertain where he was—then he moved, and a stab of terrible pain pierced his side. He noticed the tube in his arm. He turned his head to the right. There was a khaki clad policeman with a notebook beside him, asleep in a chair. The light of a dim lamp fell on his dreaming face.

Firoz bit his lip, and tried to understand this pain, this room, and why he was here. There had been a fight—Maan had had a knife—he had been stabbed. Tasneem came into it somewhere. Someone had covered him with a shawl. His walking stick had been slippery with blood. Then a tonga had reared out of the mist. Everything else was dark.

But the sight of his father's face disturbed him greatly. He could not understand why. There had been something said by someone—what it was he could not for the moment remember—something about his father. His memory of what had happened was like the map of an unexplored continent—the edges were clearer than the core. Yet there was something at that core that he shrank away from even as he approached it. Thinking was an effort, and he kept lapsing into a quiet darkness and emerging once again into the present.

Lying flat on his back he noticed a lizard on the upper reaches of the wall in front of him—one of the permanent denizens of this ward. Firoz found himself wondering what it must be like to be a lizard—what strange surfaces it lived on, where it needed more effort to move in one direction than in another. He was still staring at the lizard, when he heard the policeman say, 'Ah, Sahib, you've woken up.'

'Yes,' Firoz heard himself say. 'I've woken up.'

'Do you feel well enough to make a statement?'

'Statement?' said Firoz.

'Yes,' said the policeman. 'Your assailant has been arrested.'

Firoz looked at the wall. 'I am tired,' he said. 'I think I'll sleep a little longer.'

The Nawab Sahib had woken at the sound of his son's voice. He looked silently at Firoz now, and Firoz at him. The father appeared to be pleading with the son, the son frowning in unhappy concentration. Then he closed his eyes for a while, leaving the Nawab Sahib baffled and disturbed.

'I think he will be able to speak clearly in an hour or so,' said the policeman. 'It is important to get a statement as soon as possible.'

'Please do not disturb him,' said the Nawab Sahib. 'He looks very tired and he needs to rest.'

The Nawab Sahib could not go back to sleep. He got up after a while and paced about the room. Firoz was sound asleep, and did not take anyone's name. After about an hour he woke up again.

'Abba—' he said.

'Yes, son.'

'Abba—there is something—'

His father was silent.

'What is all this?' Firoz said suddenly. 'Did Maan attack me?'

'So it seems. They found you on Cornwallis Road. Do you remember what happened?'

'I am trying to—'

The policeman interrupted: 'Do you remember what happened at Saeeda Bai's?'

Firoz saw his father start at the name, and suddenly he saw the blinding core of what he had been trying to touch, to approach, to remember. He turned towards his father and looked at him with an expression of pain and reproach that pierced him to the heart. The old man could not hold his gaze, and turned away.

17.22

Saeeda Bai had not been idle in the face of calamity. Despite the terror and shock of Maan's attack on her and on Firoz, she—and Bibbo too—had managed, after the initial shock and reaction, to keep their heads. The house had to be protected, and Maan had to be saved from the effect of his own actions. The law might define things as it chose, but Saeeda Bai knew that Maan was not a criminal. And she blamed herself and her own excitability too for his tragic outburst of violence.

For herself, once Dr Bilgrami had examined her, she almost forgot her concern. She knew she would live; what happened to her voice was in God's hands. For Tasneem, however, she felt the clutch of a cold fear. The child she had conceived in terror, had carried in shame, and had borne in pain had been given the name of that paradisal spring which could, if anything could, wash antecedence into non-existence and torment into calm. Yet now again that antecedence and that torment were knocking at the door of the present. Saeeda Bai longed once more for her mother's advice and strong comfort. Mohsina Bai had been a harder, more independent woman than Saeeda; without her courage and persistence Saeeda Bai herself would by now be merely another ageing and impoverished whore from Tarbuz ka Bazaar—and Tasneem a younger version of the same.

That first night, half-expecting a visit from the police or a message from the Nawab Sahib, and sick with fear and pain, she had remained at home, making sure that everything in her room, along the bloodstained stairs, indeed everywhere in the house was as it should be. Sleep, she told herself; sleep; and if you can't sleep, lie in bed and pretend that this is just a night like any other. But she had been seized with restlessness. If it had been possible, she would have got down on her knees and scrubbed clean each drop of blood on the street that led to her door.

As for the man from whose side this blood had flowed, and whose face reminded her not of his mother, whom she had never seen, but most disturbingly of his father, Saeeda Bai felt nothing, a mere coldness, half brother to her daughter though he was. She hardly cared if he lived or died except in so far as it would affect Maan. And yet, when the police had come, she had been terrified into giving testimony that might—she saw it all too clearly now—that might lead her beloved Dagh Sahib to the scaffold.

For Maan, who had almost killed her, her anxiety, her terrified tenderness, knew no limits—but what could she do? And she began now to think as her mother would have thought. Whom did she know? And how well? And whom did they know? And how well? Soon Bilgrami Sahib became the emissary of elliptical communications from Saeeda Bai to a rising Minister of State, to a Joint Secretary in the Home Department, to the kotwal of Brahmpur. And Bilgrami Sahib himself used his own contacts judiciously and persistently in a generous attempt to save his rival—persistently, because he feared for Saeeda Bai's health and spirit if something terrible were to happen to Maan, and judiciously, because he feared that Saeeda Bai, in her attempt to spread the web of her influence too wide, might tempt some contrary spirit to rip it from end to end.

17.23

'Priya, promise me you'll talk to your father.'

This time it had been Veena who had suggested going up on to the roof. She could not bear the looks of satisfaction, distaste, and pity that she had had to face in the Goyal household below. It was a cold afternoon, and they were both wearing shawls. The sky was slate-coloured, except for an area across the Ganga where the sands had been whipped up by the wind into a dirty yellow-brown haze. Veena was crying blindly and pleading with Priya.

'But what good will it do?' said Priya, wiping the tears from her friend's face and her own.

'All the good in the world if it saves Maan.'

'What is your father doing?' asked Priya. 'Hasn't he spoken to anyone?'

'My father,' said Veena bitterly, 'cares more for his image as a man of principle than for his family. I spoke to him; do you think it had any effect? He told me that I should be thinking of my mother, not of Maan. Only now do I realize what a cold man he really is. Maan will be hanged at eight o'clock, and he'll be signing his files at nine. My mother is beside herself. Promise me you'll speak to your father, Priya, promise me. You're his only child, he'll do anything for you.'

'I'll speak to him,' said Priya. 'I promise.'

What Veena did not know—what Priya did not have the heart to tell her—was that she had spoken to her father already, and that the Home Minister had told her that there was nothing he would do to interfere. This was, in his words, an unimportant matter: one ruffian trying to kill another in an infamous establishment. That their fathers were who they were had nothing to do with the business. It touched upon no affairs of state; it provided no excuse for intervention; the local police and magistracy could handle it adequately. He had even gently upbraided his daughter for attempting to use his influence in this manner, and Priya, who was not used to being upbraided by her father, had felt both unhappy and ashamed.

17.24

Mahesh Kapoor was unable to bring himself to do what had been suggested to him over the phone: to try to bring pressure to bear directly or from above on the investigating officer, in this case the Sub-Inspector in charge of the Pasand Bagh Police Station. It went against his grain to do so. Indeed, the just implementation of his own Zamindari Abolition and Land Reforms Act would depend on how far he could prevent landlords from bringing their influence to bear on village record-keepers and local officers. He did not relish the way the politician Jha was undermining the administration near Rudhia town, and he did not see himself as ever being tempted to do the same. So when his wife asked him whether he could not 'talk to someone, even to Agarwal', Mahesh Kapoor told her abruptly to be quiet.

For her the shock and grief of the last two days had been almost unbearable. When she thought of Firoz lying in hospital and Maan in the police lock-up, she could not sleep. Once Firoz had become conscious he had been allowed very few visitors—including his aunt Abida and his sister Zainab. Mrs Mahesh Kapoor had begged her husband to speak to the Nawab Sahib—to express his grief and regret, and to ask if they could visit Firoz.

This he had tried to do. But the Nawab Sahib, being in the hospital, was not available on the phone. And his apologetic, embarrassed, excessively polite secretary Murtaza Ali had made it clear that the Nawab Sahib had indicated from his remarks that a visit by Maan's family at this time would be unwelcome.

The rumour mills, meanwhile, were busy. What was a mere paragraph in the Calcutta papers was the staple of the Brahmpur press and Brahmpur conversation, and would continue to be so for days, despite the alternative attractions of elections and electioneering. The police were still unaware of the connection between Saeeda Bai's establishment and the Nawab Sahib's. They had still not learned of the monthly stipend. But Bibbo had begun to put two and two together, and was unable to resist casting dark and proud hints about Tasneem's ancestry in the strictest (and thus leakiest) confidence to a couple of her closest friends. And a reporter from the Hindi press who was well known for muck-raking had interrogated an old and retired courtesan who had known Saeeda Bai's mother in the days when they had been part of a joint establishment in Tarbuz ka Bazaar. This old woman was induced by money and the promise of more money to describe all she knew about Saeeda Bai's early life. Some of her facts were true, some embroidered, some false, almost all interesting to the journalist. She stated calmly and authoritatively that Saeeda Bai had lost her virginity when she had been raped at the age of fourteen or fifteen by a prominent citizen who had been drunk; it was Saeeda Bai's mother who had told her so. What lent some likelihood to this particular assertion was that the old woman admitted that she did not know who this man was. She had her ideas, that was all.

For every fact or imagined fact that appeared in print, there were ten rumours that hovered about like wasps over a rotting mango. Neither family escaped the whispered voices, the pointed fingers that followed them wherever they went.

Veena, partly to be with her mother at this hard time, and partly to flee from her kindly but insatiable neighbours, moved into Prem Nivas for a few days. That same evening Pran and the Calcutta party returned to Brahmpur.

Within twenty-four hours of his arrest, Maan had been produced before a local magistrate. His father had hired a District Court lawyer to ask for bail or at least a transfer from the lock-up into a proper jail, but the charges that were being investigated did not admit of the former, and the police opposed the latter. The investigating officer, who had been frustrated by his inability to find a weapon and by Maan's lapses of memory about this and other details, had asked that Maan be kept in police custody for a few more days on the grounds that they needed to interrogate him further. The magistrate had allowed the police to keep him for two more days in the lock-up, after which he would be transferred to the comparative decency of the district jail.

Mahesh Kapoor had visited Maan in the police station twice. Maan complained about nothing in his cell—the filth, the discomfort, the cold. He appeared to be so shocked and so remorseful that his father could not find it in his heart to reproach him further for what he had done to himself and to Firoz and to the Nawab Sahib; and indeed to Mahesh Kapoor's own future.

Maan kept asking for information about Firoz—he was in terror that he might die. He asked his father if he had visited him in hospital, and Mahesh Kapoor was forced to admit that he had not been permitted to.

Mahesh Kapoor had told his wife not to visit Maan until he was in jail—the conditions in the police lock-up would, he thought, upset her too much. But finally Mrs Mahesh Kapoor could bear it no longer. She said that if necessary she would go alone. In exasperation her husband finally gave in and asked Pran to take her there.

She saw Maan and wept. Nothing in her life had approached in degradation her experience of these last few days. The police at the door of Prem Nivas, the searches for incriminating evidence, the arrest of someone she loved—these she had known from the time of the British. But she had not been ashamed of the man whom they had hauled off to jail as a political prisoner. Nor had he had to undergo such filth and squalor as this.

As painful as anything to her had been the fact that she had not been granted permission to visit Firoz and expiate with her affection some of the terrible guilt and sadness she felt towards him and his family.

Maan no longer looked like her handsome son but a dirty and unkempt man, one whose looks spoke of shame and desperation.

She hugged him and wept as if her heart would break. Maan wept too.

17.25

In the midst of his regret and repentance, Maan still felt he had to see Saeeda Bai. He could not mention this to his father, and he did not know whom to ask to convey a message to her. Only Firoz, he thought, would have understood. When his mother returned to Prem Nivas by car, Pran remained for a few minutes. Maan asked him to get Saeeda Bai to see him somehow. Pran tried to explain that it was impossible: she would be a material witness in the case, and she would not be allowed to visit him.

Maan seemed hardly to understand his own jeopardy—or the fact that attempted murder or even grievous hurt with a dangerous weapon carried a maximum sentence of life imprisonment. He seemed to believe that it was inexplicably unjust to keep him away from Saeeda Bai. He asked Pran to convey to her his bitter regret and continuing love. He scrawled out a couple of lines in Urdu to that effect. Pran was very unhappy with his mission, but agreed to perform it, and gave the note to the watchman within the hour.

When he returned to Prem Nivas in the late afternoon, he saw his mother lying on a sofa on the verandah. She was facing the garden, which was full of early flowers: pansies, calendulas, gerberas, salvias, cosmos, phlox and a few California poppies. The beds, where they met the lawn, were fringed with sweet alyssum. Bees were buzzing around the first few lemon-scented blossoms on the pomelo tree, and a small, glossy, blue-black sunbird flitted in and out of its branches.

Pran paused for a minute near the pomelo tree and breathed in its scent. It reminded him of his childhood; and he thought sadly of the dramatic changes that had occurred to Veena and himself and Maan since those uncertain but comparatively carefree days. Veena's husband had since become an impoverished refugee from Pakistan, he himself was a cardiac patient, and Maan was lying in jail awaiting a charge-sheet. Then he thought of Bhaskar's miraculous escape and of Uma's birth, of his life with Savita, of his mother's sustaining goodness, of the continuing peace of this garden; and he was swayed a little towards accepting that some good of some kind had been gained or retained.

He walked slowly across the lawn to the verandah. His mother was still lying down on the sofa and looking out at the garden.

'Why are you lying down, Ammaji?' he asked. She would normally have sat up to talk to him. 'Are you feeling tired?'

She sat up immediately.

'Can I get you something?' he asked. He noticed she was trying to say something, but he could not make out what she was saying. Her mouth was open, and had drooped to one side. He understood with difficulty that she wanted tea.

Worried now, he called out for Veena. A servant said she had gone out somewhere with his father in the car. Pran ordered some tea. When it came he gave it to his mother to drink. She began to splutter as she drank it, and he realized that she had had a stroke of some kind.

His first thought was to contact Imtiaz at Baitar House. Then he decided to contact Savita's grandfather. Dr Kishen Chand Seth was not in either. Pran left a message for him saying that his mother was ill, and that Dr Seth should phone Prem Nivas immediately when he returned. He tried a couple of other doctors, but could not get through to anyone. He was about to order a taxi to go to the hospital to find someone when Dr Seth called back. Pran explained what had happened.

'I'll come over,' said Dr Kishen Chand Seth. 'But get Dr Jain—he's the expert at this sort of thing. His telephone number is 873. Tell him I asked him to come immediately.'

When he arrived, Dr Seth said that he thought it was a case of facial paralysis, and made Mrs Mahesh Kapoor lie down flat. 'But this is very far from my speciality,' he added.

At about seven o'clock, Veena and her father returned. Mrs Mahesh Kapoor's voice was slurred but she was making an effort to communicate.

'Is it about Maan?' asked her husband.

She shook her head. In a little while they understood that what she wanted was her dinner.

She tried to drink her soup. Some went down, but she coughed some of it up. They tried to feed her some rice and daal. She took a little into her mouth, chewed it, and asked Veena to give her some more. But it soon became apparent that she was storing it in her mouth and not swallowing it. Very slowly, with sips of water, she was able to take it down.

Dr Jain arrived about half an hour later. He examined her thoroughly, and said: 'This is a serious condition, you see. I am worried that her seventh, tenth and twelfth nerves are affected.'

'Yes, yes—' said Mr Mahesh Kapoor, at the end of his tether. 'What does all this mean?'

'Well, you see,' said Dr Jain, 'these nerves are connected to the main area of the brain. I am worried that the patient's ability to swallow might fail. Or there could be a second stroke. That would be the end. I suggest that the patient should be removed to hospital immediately.'

Mrs Mahesh Kapoor reacted violently to the word 'hospital'. She refused to go. Her speech was slurred and her senses somewhat dulled, but there was no doubt about her will. She gave them to understand that if she was dying, she wanted to die at home. Veena made out the words 'Sundar Kanda'. She wanted her favourite part of the Ramayana to be read out to her.

'Dying!' said her husband, impatiently. 'There is no question of your dying.'

But Mrs Mahesh Kapoor for once defied her husband and did die that night.

17.26

Veena was sleeping in her mother's room when she heard her suddenly cry out in pain. She turned on the light. Mrs Mahesh Kapoor's face was shockingly distorted, and her whole body appeared to be undergoing a violent spasm. Veena ran to fetch her father. He came. Soon the household was roused. Pran and the doctors were called, and Kedarnath's neighbours were asked to tell him to come over immediately. Pran had no doubt of the seriousness of the matter. He told Savita, Lata and Mrs Rupa Mehra that he thought his mother was dying. They came over. Savita brought the baby too, in case her grandmother wanted to see her.

Within half an hour everyone had gathered around. Bhaskar looked on uneasily. He asked his mother if Nani was indeed dying, and she replied tearfully that she thought so, though everything was in God's hands. The doctor said that there was nothing that could be done. Mrs Mahesh Kapoor too, having asked, with incoherent sounds and gestures to have Bhaskar brought close to her, now indicated that she wished to be lowered from her bed on to the ground. At this, all the women began to weep. Mr Mahesh Kapoor, angry, disappointed, and upset, looked at his wife's face, which had grown calm, with irked affection—as if she had deliberately failed him. A small mud lamp was lit and placed in the palm of her hand. Old Mrs Tandon took the name of Rama, and Mrs Rupa Mehra recited from the Gita. A short while afterwards Mrs Mahesh Kapoor struggled to say a word which sounded like 'Maa—'. She could have meant either her mother, who was long dead, or her younger son, whom she could not see among those gathered around her. She closed her eyes. A few tears appeared at the corners of her eyelids, but again her face, so distorted earlier, became calm. A little later, almost at the time she usually woke up, she died.

In the morning a stream of visitors came through the house to pay their last respects. Among them were many of Mahesh Kapoor's colleagues, all of whom, no matter what they thought of him, had had nothing but affection for this decent, kind, and affectionate woman. They had known her as a quiet, bustling wife, untiring and warm in her hospitality, who had compensated with her gentleness for the worst of her husband's acerbity.

Now she lay on the ground on a sheet, her nostrils and mouth lightly plugged with cotton wool, a bandage tying her head to her jaw. She was dressed in red, as she had been at her wedding many years ago, and there was sindoor in the parting of her hair. Incense was burning in a bowl at her feet. All the women, including Savita and Lata, were sitting beside her, and some were weeping, Mrs Rupa Mehra as much as anyone.

S.S. Sharma removed his shoes and entered. His head was trembling slightly. He folded his hands, said a few words of comfort, and went away. Priya comforted Veena. Her father, L.N. Agarwal, took Pran aside, and said:

'When is the cremation?'

'At eleven o'clock at the ghat.'

'What about your younger brother?'

Pran shook his head. His eyes filled with tears.

The Home Minister asked to use the phone, and called the Superintendent of Police. On hearing that Maan was due to be moved from police custody to judicial custody that afternoon, he said:

'Tell them to do it this morning instead, and to take him past the cremation ghat. His brother will go to the police station and join the escort party. There is no danger of the prisoner escaping, so handcuffs will not be necessary. Have the formalities completed by ten o'clock or so.'

The Superintendent said: 'It will be done, Minister Sahib.'

L.N. Agarwal was about to put down the phone, when he thought of something else. He said: 'Also, would you tell the station house officer to make a barber available in case it is necessary—but not to break any news to the young man himself. His brother will do that.'

In the event, when Pran went over to the lock-up to see Maan, he did not have to say a word. When Maan saw his brother's shaven head he knew by some instinct that it was his mother who had died. He burst into horrible, tearless weeping and began to hit his head against the bars of his cell.

The policeman with the keys was bewildered in the face of this display; the Sub-Inspector snatched the keys from him and let Maan out. He fell into Pran's embrace, and kept making these terrible, animal sounds of grief.

After a while, Pran calmed him down by talking continuously and gently to him. He turned to the police officer and said:

'I understand you have got a barber here to shave my brother's head. We should be leaving for the ghat soon.'

The Sub-Inspector was apologetic. A problem had arisen. One of the ticket clerks at the Brahmpur Railway Station was going to be asked to try to pick Maan out at an identification parade in the jail. Under these circumstances, he could not let Maan's head be shaved.

'This is ridiculous,' said Pran, looking at the policeman's moustache and thinking he had a great deal too much hair himself. 'I heard the Home Minister himself say that—'

'I spoke to the SP ten minutes ago,' said the Sub-Inspector. Clearly, for him, the SP was more important than even the PM.

They got to the ghat by eleven. The policemen stood some distance away. The sun was high, the day unseasonably warm. Only the men were there. The cotton wool was removed from the face, the yellow cloth and the flowers were removed from the bier, the body was moved on to two long logs and covered with others.

Her husband performed all the necessary rites under the guidance of a pandit. What the rationalist in him thought of all the ghee and sandalwood and swahas and the demands of the doms who worked at the pyre was not betrayed by his face. The smoke of the pyre was oppressive, but he did not appear to sense it. No breeze blew from the Ganga to disperse it quickly.

Maan stood next to his brother, who almost had to support him. He saw the flames rise and lap over his mother's face—and the smoke cover his father's.

This is my doing, Ammaji, he thought, though no one had said any such thing to him. It is what I did that has led to this. What have I done to Veena and Pran and Baoji? I will never forgive myself and no one in the family will ever forgive me.

17.27

Ash and bones, that was all Mrs Mahesh Kapoor was now, ash and bones, warm still, but soon to cool, and be collected, and sunk in the Ganga at Brahmpur. Why not at Hardwar, as she had wished? Because her husband was a practical man. Because what are bones and ash, what even are flesh and blood and tissue when life has gone? Because it made no difference, the water of the Ganga is the same at Gangotri, at Hardwar, at Prayag, at Banaras, at Brahmpur, even at Sagar to which it was bound from the moment it dropped from the sky. Mrs Mahesh Kapoor was dead, and felt nothing, this ash of hers and sandalwood and common wood could be left to the doms at the cremation ghat to sift for the few pieces of jewellery which had melted with her body and were theirs by right. Fat, ligament, muscle, blood, hair, affection, pity, despair, anxiety, illness: all were no more. She had dispersed. She was the garden at Prem Nivas (soon to be entered into the annual Flower Show), she was Veena's love of music, Pran's asthma, Maan's generosity, the survival of some refugees four years ago, the neem leaves that would preserve quilts stored in the great zinc trunks of Prem Nivas, the moulting feather of some pond heron, a small unrung brass bell, the memory of decency in an indecent time, the temperament of Bhaskar's great-grandchildren. Indeed, for all the Minister of Revenue's impatience with her, she was his regret. And it was right that she should continue to be so, for he should have treated her better while she lived, the poor, ignorant, grieving fool.

17.28

The chautha was held in the afternoon three days later under a small canopy on the lawn of Prem Nivas. The men sat on one side of the aisle, the women on the other. The area under the canopy quickly filled up, and then the aisle itself, and finally people spilled out on to the lawn, some of them as far as the flower beds. Mahesh Kapoor, Pran and Kedarnath received them at the entrance to the garden. Mahesh Kapoor was amazed by how many people had come to attend the chautha of his wife, whom he had always thought of as being a silly, superstitious and limited woman. Refugees she had helped during the days of Partition in the relief camps, their families, all those to whom she had given kindness or shelter from day to day, not merely the Rudhia relatives but a large group of ordinary farmers from Rudhia, many politicians who might well have paid only perfunctory or hypocritical homage if he himself had passed away, and scores of people whom neither he nor Pran recognized, all felt that they had to attend this service in her memory. Many of them folded their hands in respect before the photograph of her that stood, garlanded with marigolds, on a table on the long white-sheeted platform at one end of the shamiana. Some of them tried to utter a few words of condolence before being overcome themselves. When Mahesh Kapoor himself sat down, his heart was even more disturbed than it had been these last four days.

No one from the Nawab Sahib's family came to the chautha. Firoz had taken a turn for the worse. He was suffering from a low infection, and he was being given stronger doses of penicillin to check and suppress it. Imtiaz—aware both of the possibilities and limitations of this comparatively recent form of treatment—was worried sick; and his father, seeing his son's illness as punishment for his own sins, pleaded with God more than five times a day to spare Firoz and take away his own life instead.

Perhaps, too, he could not face the rumours that followed him now wherever he went. Perhaps he could not face the family, friendship with whom had caused him such grief. At any rate, he did not come.

Nor could Maan be present.

The pandit was a large man with a full, oblong face, bushy eyebrows, and a strong voice. He began to recite a few shlokas in Sanskrit, especially from the Isha Upanishad and from the Yajurveda, and to interpret them as a guide to life and to righteous action. God was everywhere, he said, in each piece of the universe; there was no permanent dissolution; this should be accepted. He talked about the deceased and how good and godfearing she had been and how her spirit would remain not only in the memories of those who knew her, but in the very world that surrounded them—in this garden, for instance; in this house.

After a while the pandit told his young assistant to take over.

The assistant sang two devotional songs. For the first one the audience sat silent, but when he began to sing the slow and stately 'Twameva Mata cha Pita twameva'—'You are both mother and father to us'—almost everyone joined in.

The pandit asked people to move forward in order to let people at the back squeeze in under the canopy. Then he asked whether the Sikh singers had arrived. Mrs Mahesh Kapoor had been very fond of their music, and Veena had convinced her father to ask them to sing at the chautha. When the pandit was told that they were on their way, he smoothed his kurta and began a story, which he had told many times before and which went as follows:

There was once a villager who was very poor, so poor that he did not have enough money to pay for his daughter's wedding and had nothing to borrow against. He was in despair. At last someone said: 'Two villages away there is a moneylender who believes in humanity. He will not need any security or property. Your word will be your bond. He lends to people according to their need, and he knows whom to trust.'

The man set out in hope, and reached the moneylender's village by noon. On the outskirts of the village he noticed an old man who was ploughing a field, and a woman, her face covered, who was bringing food out for him, her utensils balanced on her head. He could tell from her gait that she was a young woman and he overheard her say in a young woman's voice: 'Baba, here is some food for you. Eat it, and then please come home. Your son is no more.' The man looked up at the sky and said: 'As God wills.' He then sat down to eat the food.

The villager, puzzled and disturbed by this conversation, tried to make sense of it. He thought to himself: If she were the old man's daughter, why would she cover her face before him? She must be his daughter-in-law. But then he was worried by the identity of the dead man. Surely, if it had been one of her husband's brothers who had died, she would have referred to him as 'jethji' or 'devarji', rather than 'your son'. So it must have been her husband who had died. The calm manner in which both father and wife had accepted his death was unusual, not to say shocking.

At any rate, the villager, considering his own purposes and his own problems, went on to the moneylender's shop. The moneylender asked him what he wanted. The villager told him that he needed some money for his daughter's wedding and had nothing to pledge in exchange.

'That is all right,' said the moneylender, looking at his face. 'How much do you want?'

'A lot,' said the man. 'Two thousand rupees.'

'Fine,' said the moneylender, and asked his accountant to count it out immediately.

While the accountant was counting out the money, the poor villager felt obliged to make some conversation. 'You are a very good man,' he said gratefully, 'but the other people in your village seem peculiar to me.' And he recounted what he had seen and heard.

'Well,' said the moneylender. 'How would the people in your village have reacted to such news?'

'Well, obviously,' said the poor man, 'the whole village would have gone to the family's house to mourn with them. There would have been no question of ploughing your fields, let alone eating anything till the body was disposed of. People would have been wailing and beating their breasts.'

The moneylender turned to the accountant and told him to stop counting out the money. 'It is not safe to lend anything to this man,' he said.

The man, appalled, turned to the moneylender. 'But what have I done?' he asked.

The moneylender replied: 'If you weep and wail so much about returning what has been given to you in trust by God, you will not be happy about returning what is given to you in trust by a mere man.'

While the pandit told this story there was silence. No one knew what to expect, and at the end of it they felt that they had been reproached for their grief. Pran found himself feeling upset rather than consoled: what the pandit had said was perhaps true, he thought, but he wished the Sikh ragis had come earlier.

Still, here they were now, all three of them, dark and full-bearded, their white turbans set off by a blue headband. One of them played the tabla, the other two the harmonium, and all three closed their eyes while they sang songs from Nanak and Kabir.

Pran had heard them before; his mother asked the ragis about once a year to sing at Prem Nivas. But now he thought not of the beauty of their singing or of the words of the saints, but of the last time he had heard tabla and harmonium in Prem Nivas: when Saeeda Bai had sung on the evening of Holi last year. He glanced across to where the women were sitting. Savita and Lata were sitting together, as they had been that other evening as well. Savita's eyes were closed. Lata was looking at Mahesh Kapoor, who seemed once again to have distanced himself from what was going on. She had not seen Kabir, who was sitting far behind her, at the back of the covered area.

Her thoughts had wandered to the life of this woman, Pran's mother, whom she had greatly liked but not much known. Had hers been a full life? Could her marriage be said to have been happy or successful or fulfilled: and if so, what did those words mean? What was at the centre of her marriage: her husband, her children, or the small puja room where every morning she prayed, allowing routine and devotion to create a purpose and imply an order in her daily and annual round? Here sat so many people who were affected by her death, and there sat her husband, the Minister Sahib, transparently fretful about the long proceedings. He was trying to indicate to the pandit that he had had enough, but was unable to catch his eye.

The pandit said: 'I understand that the women would now like to sing some songs.' No one came forward. He was about to speak again, when old Mrs Tandon said: 'Veena, come forward, sit here.' The pandit asked her to sit on the platform where the ragis had been singing, but Veena said, 'No; down here.' She was very simply dressed, as was her friend Priya and another young woman. Veena had on a white cotton sari with a black border. A very thin gold chain, which she kept touching, hung around her neck. Her dark-red tika was smudged. There appeared to be tears on her cheeks, and especially in the dark, puffy rings around her eyes. Her plump face looked sad and strangely placid. She took out a small book, and they began singing. She sang clearly, and from time to time moved her hand slightly in response to the words of the song. Her voice was natural and very affecting. After the first song was over she began, without even a pause, her mother's favourite hymn, 'Uth, jaag, musafir':

'Rise, traveller, the sky is light.
Why do you sleep? It is not night.
The sleeping lose, and sleep in vain.
The waking rise, and rise to gain.

Open your eyelids, you who nod.
O heedless one, pay heed to God.
Is this your way to show your love?
You sleep below, he wakes above.

What you have done, that you must bear.
Where is the joy in sin then, where?
When on your head your sins lie deep,
Why do you clutch your head and weep?

Tomorrow's task, enact today.
Today's at once; do not delay.
When birds have robbed the standing grain
What use to wring your hands in vain?'

Somewhere in the middle of the second stanza she stopped singing—the others continued—and began crying quietly. She tried to stop but couldn't. She started to wipe her tears with the pallu of her sari and then simply wiped them away with her hands. Kedarnath, who was sitting in front, took out his handkerchief and threw it into her lap, but she didn't notice. She slowly looked up, her eyes a little above the crowd, and continued singing. Once or twice she coughed. By the time she was singing the first verse again, her voice was clear; but now it was her irritable father who was in tears.

The song, taken from the hymn-book of Mahatma Gandhi's ashram, brought home to him like nothing else had his unrealized loss. Gandhi was dead, and with him his ideals. That preacher of non-violence whom he had followed and revered had died violently, and now Mahesh Kapoor's own son—more beloved for the danger he was in—was lying in prison for violence of his own. Firoz, whom he had known from childhood, might die. His friendship with the Nawab Sahib, which had stood so much and so long, had shattered under the sudden power of grief and rumour. The Nawab Sahib was not here today, and he had prevented the two of them from visiting Firoz. That visit would have meant much to the dead woman. The lack of it had enhanced her grief and—who knew the workings of sorrow on the brain?—may have hastened her death.

Too late, and perhaps because of the love that everyone else around him so clearly bore her, he began to realize fully what he had lost, indeed, whom he had lost—and how suddenly. There was so much to do, and no one to help him, to advise him quietly, to check his impatience. His son's life and his own future both seemed to him to be in hopeless straits. He wanted to give up and let the world take care of itself. But he could not let Maan go; and politics had been his life.

She would not be there, as she had always been, to help. The birds had robbed the standing grain, and here he was wringing his empty hands. What would she have said to him? Nothing direct, but possibly a few words of circuitous comfort, something that might, a few days or a few weeks later, have taken the edge off his despair. Would she have told him to withdraw from the election? What would she have asked him to do about his son? Which of his several duties—or conceptions of duty—would she have expected him to follow or have anticipated that he would follow, and which would she have wished him to? Even if in the weeks ahead it became clear to him, he did not have those weeks, but only days, and, indeed, very few of those.

17.29

When Maan was admitted to jail after the cremation, he was required to wash himself and his clothing, and he was provided with a cup and a plate. He was examined by the medical officer and weighed. A note was made of the condition of his hair and beard. As an unconvicted prisoner—with no previous convictions either—he was supposed to be kept separate from those undertrial prisoners who had previous convictions. But the district jail was crowded, and he was accommodated in a ward which contained a couple of undertrial prisoners who did know about jail life from experience —and who set out to educate the others about it. Maan they treated as a great curiosity. If he was really a Minister's son—and the one newspaper they were permitted confirmed that indeed he was—what was he doing there? Why had he not managed to get bail on one pretext or another? If the charge being investigated was non-bailable, why had the police not been told to lessen the charge?

If Maan had been in anything resembling his normal state of mind, he would have made friends with a few of his present colleagues. Now he hardly sensed their existence. He could think of no one except those whom he could not see: his mother, and Firoz, and Saeeda Bai. His life, though not easy, was luxury compared to what it had been in the lock-up. He was allowed to receive food and clothes from Prem Nivas; he was allowed to shave his face and to exercise. The jail was comparatively clean. Since he was a 'superior class' prisoner, his cell was equipped with a small table, a bed, and a lamp. They sent him oranges, which he ate in a daze. They sent a quilt of kingfisher blue from Prem Nivas to protect him against the cold. It protected him and it comforted him, while at the same time it reminded him of home—and all that he had destroyed or lost.

Again, as a superior class prisoner, he was shielded from the worst degradations of jail life—the crowded cells and barracks where assorted horrors were perpetrated by the prisoners on one another. The Superintendent of the jail was also aware of whose son he was, and kept an eye on him. He was liberal in permitting him visits.

Pran visited him, and Veena, and his father too before he returned, heartsick, to campaign in his constituency. No one knew what to talk about to Maan. When his father asked him what had happened, Maan started trembling and could say nothing. When Pran said, 'But why, Maan, why?' he stared at him in a hunted manner and turned away.

There were not many safe subjects. Sometimes they talked about cricket. England had just defeated India in the fourth Test match of the series, the first match that had not ended in a draw. But though Pran could spin out cricket talk even in his sleep, Maan began to yawn after a few minutes.

Sometimes they talked about Bhaskar or Pran's baby, but even these conversations took painful turns.

Maan would talk most easily about jail routine. He said that he wanted to work a bit, though it was not compulsory: perhaps in the jail vegetable garden. He asked about the garden in Prem Nivas, but when Veena began to describe it he started weeping.

He yawned a great deal during conversations without knowing why, sometimes when he wasn't even tired.

The lawyer who was sent to visit him by his father often returned frustrated. Maan, when asked anything, said that he had talked about it all with the police and would not go over it again. But this was not true. When the Sub-Inspector and a few other policemen came to the jail to ask him questions, to get him to elaborate on his confession, he insisted that he had nothing more to say to them either. They asked him about the knife. He said he couldn't remember if he had left it at Saeeda Bai's or taken it along with him; he thought the latter. Meanwhile, the case against him grew through a combination of statements and circumstantial evidence.

No one who visited him mentioned Firoz's turn for the worse, but he learned about it from the ward newspaper, the local Hindi paper, *Adarsh*. He also learned, from gossip among the prisoners, about the rumours floating around the Nawab Sahib and Saeeda Bai. He had fits of almost suicidal misery, from the worst of which he was guarded by the ritual of jail life.

Routine took over his days. The *Jail Manual*, to which the Brahmpur District Jail approximately adhered, read as follows:

To perform morning ablutions, etc:	After unlocking up to 7 a.m.
To be on parade in the enclosure:	7 a.m. to 9 a.m.
To be locked up in cell or barracks:	9 a.m. to 10 a.m.
To bathe and take the midday meal:	10 a.m. to 11 a.m.
To be locked up in cell or barracks:	11 a.m. to 3 p.m.
To take exercise, have evening meal, and be searched and locked up:	3 p.m. to locking up.

He was a model prisoner, and never complained about anything. Sometimes he sat at the table in his cell and looked at a piece of paper on which he planned to write a letter to Firoz. But he could never begin it. He took to doodling instead. Having hardly slept in the lock-up, he slept for long hours in his jail cell.

Once he was lined up for an identification parade, but he was not told whether it was to be for himself or for some other prisoner. When he saw that his lawyer was present, he realized it was for himself. But he did not recognize the self-important-looking clerk who walked down the line and paused a little longer when he came to him. And he did not care whether he had been identified or not.

'If he dies, you could well be hanged,' said one experienced prisoner with a sense of humour. 'If that happens we'll all be locked up for the morning, so I'm counting on you to spare us the inconvenience.'

Maan nodded.

Since he was not responding satisfactorily, the prisoner went on: 'After every execution do you know what they do with the ropes?'

Maan shook his head.

'They dress them with beeswax and ghee to keep them smooth.'

'In what proportions?' asked another prisoner.

'Oh, half and half,' said the knowledgeable one. 'And they add a bit of carbolic acid to the mixture to keep off the insects. It would be a pity if white ants or silverfish chewed them away. What do you think?' he asked Maan.

Everyone turned to look at Maan.

Maan, however, had stopped listening. Neither had the man's sense of humour amused him nor had his cruelty upset him.

'And in order to preserve them from rats,' continued the expert, 'they put the five ropes—they have five ropes in this jail, don't ask me why—they put all five ropes in a clay pot, stop up the top, and suspend it from the roof of the storeroom. Think about that. Five Manila ropes, one inch in diameter, each fattened on a diet of ghee and blood slithering about like snakes in a pot, waiting for their next victim—'

He laughed delightedly and looked at Maan.

17.30

Maan may have paid no attention to any distant hazard to his neck, but it was impossible for Saeeda Bai not to be conscious of what had happened to hers. For days afterwards she could hardly speak except in a croak. Her worlds had fallen apart around her: both her own world of nuance and attraction, and her daughter's world of innocence and protection.

For Tasneem was now branded by the rumours. She herself continued to be less than fully aware of them; this was not through lack of intelligence but rather because the outside world had once again been cut off from her. Even Bibbo, whose taste for both intrigue and gossip had caused enough damage already, pitied Tasneem, and did not say anything that could hurt her. But after what had happened in front of Tasneem's eyes to the Nawabzada, the only man whom she had ever felt any deep emotion for, she felt it was safest to withdraw into herself, into her novels and household work. He was in severe danger still; she could tell from the answers that Bibbo gave her that his life was in danger. She could do nothing for him; he was a distant and retreating star. She assumed he had been injured trying to disarm the drunken Maan, but she did not ask what had impelled Maan to become so drunken and murderous. Of the other men who had shown some interest in her, she heard nothing, nor did she wish to hear anything. Ishaq, increasingly influenced by Majeed Khan, retreated from the scandal and neither wrote nor visited. Rasheed wrote another crazy letter to her; but Saeeda Bai tore it up before it reached Tasneem.

More fiercely than ever before, Saeeda Bai tried to protect—and harry—Tasneem. Tender and furious by turns, she once again relived the long torment of having to be a sister to her daughter, of suffering her own strong-willed mother to determine both the course of her own life and the course of the life that Saeeda had been forced, in shame and agony, to relinquish to her.

Saeeda Bai could not now sing, and it seemed to her that she would never again be able to, even if her throat allowed it. The parakeet, however, unmindful of her trauma, burst into a blaze of speech. He took on a sort of grotesque croak in imitation of the mistress of the house. This was one of Saeeda Bai's consolations. The other was Bilgrami Sahib, who not only helped her medically but stood by her through this ordeal of press and police, of fear and distress and pain.

She realized now that she loved Maan.

When his two lines of misspelt Urdu came to her, she wept bitterly, oblivious to the feelings of Bilgrami Sahib, who was at her side. She imagined the guilt and trauma of his imprisonment, and was terrified to think of where it might end. When she heard of the death of his mother, she again wept. She was not the kind of woman who thrives on ill treatment or values those who misprize her, and she could not understand why Maan's attack should have caused her to feel what she did. But perhaps it had merely forced her to realize what she had felt before, but had not known. His note to her said nothing except how sorry he was and how much he loved her still.

When the next instalment of the stipend came from Baitar House, Saeeda Bai, who needed the money, returned it unopened. Bilgrami Sahib, when she told him what she had done, said that he would not have advised it, but that it was well done. For anything she needed now, she should depend on him. She accepted his help. He once again asked her to be his wife and to give up her singing and her profession. Although she did not know if she would ever regain her voice, she refused him once again.

As Bilgrami Sahib had feared, their attempt to bring influence into play had attracted the attention of the Raja of Marh, who quite blatantly began to pay journalists to dig up what dirt they could about the scandal—and particularly to attempt to prevent any subversion of justice by Maan's friends and family. He had also attempted to fund a couple of the Independent candidates who were standing against Mahesh Kapoor in the elections, but this had proved to be a less fruitful investment.

One night the Raja of Marh came with a gang of three guards and virtually forced his way into Saeeda Bai's house. He was delighted by recent events. Mahesh Kapoor, the plunderer of his rightful lands and the derider of his great temple, had been humbled; Maan—whom he saw both as his competitor and as the brother of the man who had expelled his son—was locked safely away; the Nawab Sahib—whose religion and high cultural airs he equally loathed—was stricken with shame and with fear and grief for his son; and Saeeda Bai had been disgraced further before the world and would doubtless abase herself to his, the Raja of Marh's, commands.

'Sing!' he commanded her. 'Sing! I hear your voice has gained a richer tone since your neck was wrung.'

It was fortunate for both him and Saeeda Bai that the watchman had alerted the police. They came in, and he was forced to leave. He did not know, either then or afterwards, how close he had come to becoming that well-washed fruit knife's second victim.

17.31

Firoz lay between life and death for several days. Eventually the Nawab Sahib grew so exhausted that he was ordered home by his elder son.

It was the fear of Firoz's death that finally forced Mahesh Kapoor, that upright and law-abiding man, to speak to the Superintendent of Police.

He knew what he was doing: he did it with his eyes open, and he was ashamed, but he did it. He had lost his wife, he could not bear to lose his son. If Firoz died, and the investigating officer and committal magistrate saw fit, Maan might be tried under Section 302 of the Indian Penal Code—and this thought was so horrific—and to his mind, unjust—that he could not bear it. The SP for his part was a man who knew how many ways bread could be buttered. He said that it was a difficult problem now that matters had been aired so openly in the press, but that he would do what he could. He repeated several times that he had always had the greatest respect for Mahesh Kapoor. Mahesh Kapoor repeated, though the words tore at his sense of his own integrity, that his feelings towards the SP were very similar.

He visited Maan once more in jail. Once again, father and son did not have much to say to each other. He then left for Salimpur for a few days. He did not tell anyone what he had done, and he reproached himself both for having done it and for not having done it earlier.

Maan had begun working in the jail garden, and this did help him somewhat. Even now, he found the visits of his brother and sister painful. Once he asked Pran to send some money anonymously to Rasheed and gave him his address. Once he asked for a few harsingar flowers from the garden of Prem Nivas and Veena had told him that the season was over. For the most part Maan did not know what to say to them. He continued to feel that the shock of his crime had killed their mother, and that they felt the same. But time passed, and exhaustion eased his mind.

Firoz too became better. The advances in medicine of the previous ten years had saved his life, but only just. Had antibiotics not been available in Brahmpur, or had doctors not been sufficiently skilled in their administration, he would surely not have gazed at that lizard again. But despite the wound and the infections, whether he wished to or not, he lived.

A change came over Maan too with the slow recovery of his friend. It was as if he had come out of the valley of the shadow of his own death. If his own danger had caused Saeeda Bai to realize how much she loved him, the danger Firoz had been in had given him a similar insight. He cheered up as soon as Pran told him that Firoz was finally and definitely on the mend. His appetite recovered. He asked for certain kinds of food to be brought from Prem Nivas. He joked about rum chocolates, which a friend had once brought from Calcutta, as a means of smuggling alcohol into jail. He asked for certain visitors: not his immediate family, but people who would bring him a sense of something different: Lata (if she wouldn't mind paying him a visit) and one of his old girlfriends, who was now married. Both came, on consecutive days: one with Pran (after she had overcome Mrs Rupa Mehra's objections), one with her husband (after she had overcome his).

Lata, despite the sad and, in some ways, sinister venue, was pleased to see Maan. It was true that their worlds hardly intersected. It had amazed her that Pran had been able, last April Fool's, to convince her mother of their elopement. But she remembered Maan as she always had—jovial and affectionate—and she was glad to think that he had remembered her. She was not determinedly cheerful, but she could see that talking with her was doing Maan good. They talked about Calcutta, particularly the Chatterjis, and—partly because she wanted to keep him interested—she talked a great deal more freely with him than she normally would have, or than she ordinarily did with Pran. The jail officers sat out of clear hearing, but they looked at them curiously when they burst out laughing. They were not accustomed to that sound in the visiting room.

The next day they heard more of the same. Maan was visited by his old friend Sarla and her husband, who for some reason was called Pigeon by all his friends. Sarla, who had not seen Maan for months, regaled him with a description of a New Year's party that she and Pigeon had been to. It had been organized by Pigeon's friends.

'In order to add a little spice to the gathering,' said Sarla, 'they decided this year to be bold and hire a cabaret dancer—from a cheap hotel in Tarbuz ka Bazaar—one of those hotels that advertises stripteases with a new Salome every week and is constantly being raided by the police.'

'Lower your voice,' laughed Maan.

'Well,' said Sarla, 'she danced, and took off a few of her clothes, and danced some more—and all so suggestively and lasciviously that the women were appalled. The men—well, they had mixed emotions. Pigeon, for instance.'

'No—no,' said Pigeon.

'Pigeon, she sat on your lap, and you didn't stop her.'

'How could I?' said Pigeon.

'Yes, he's right—it isn't easy,' said Maan.

Sarla gave Maan a look, and continued: 'Well, anyway, she then set upon Mala and Gopu, and began to caress Gopu in all kinds of ways. He was quite tipsy, and didn't object. But you know how possessive Mala is of her husband. She pulled him away. But the other woman pulled him back.

Quite shameless. Gopu got scolded badly the next day, and all the wives vowed: Never again.'

Maan burst out laughing, Sarla joined in, and even Pigeon smiled, a little guiltily.

'But you haven't heard the best part,' said Sarla. 'A week later the police raided that Tarbuz ka Bazaar hotel, and it was discovered that the cabaret dancer was a boy! Well, we teased those two unmercifully after that! I can still hardly believe it. He had us all fooled—the voice, the eyes, the gait, the feel of the whole situation—and all along it was a boy!'

'I suspected it all along,' said Pigeon.

'You didn't suspect anything,' said Sarla. 'If you did and still behaved the way you did I'd be even more worried.'

'Well, not all along,' said Pigeon.

'He must have enjoyed himself,' said Sarla. 'Fooling us like that. No wonder he could act so shamelessly. No girl would!'

'Oh no,' said Pigeon sarcastically. 'No girl would. Sarla thinks all women are paragons.'

'Well, compared to men we certainly are,' said Sarla. 'The trouble is, Pigeon, you don't appreciate us. Well, most of you don't. Maan's an exception; he always did. You'd better come out of jail fast and rescue me, Maan. What do you say, Pigeon?'

As their time was up, her husband was spared from having to think of an answer. But for half an hour after they left, Maan kept picturing the scene she had conjured up, and kept laughing to himself in his cell. His fellow-prisoners could not think what had got into him.

17.32

Towards the end of January Maan's case came up for committal proceedings before a magistrate. The question at issue was what charges were to be preferred against him, if any.

Clearly, there would have to be a charge-sheet; no policeman, however dedicated he might be to undo his duty or to misuse his discretion, could easily have spoiled such a case sufficiently to issue a 'final report', which would have stated that there was no case to answer. The Sub-Inspector could perhaps have tried to go around winning over witnesses in such an attempt, but as investigating officer he had done his job well; and he was unhappy enough as it was that his investigation was being interfered with by his superiors. He knew that the matter was still in the public eye, and he also knew who the scapegoat would be if there was any suggestion of interference with the course of justice.

Maan and his lawyer were both present at the committal proceedings.

The Sub-Inspector stood before the committal magistrate and described the events that had led to the investigation, provided a summary of the investigation itself, submitted the documents relevant to the case, stated that the victim was now definitely out of danger, and asserted in conclusion that Maan should be charged with voluntarily causing grievous hurt.

The magistrate was puzzled.

'What about attempted murder?' he said, looking the policeman in the eye, and avoiding Maan's.

'Attempted murder?' said the policeman unhappily, tugging a little at his moustache.

'Or at least attempted culpable homicide,' said the magistrate. 'But from these statements, I am not sure the former charge cannot be made out. Even if there had been grave and sudden provocation, it was not given by the victim. Nor does it appear prima facie that the wound was inflicted by mistake or accident.'

The policeman was silent, but nodded his head.

Maan's lawyer whispered to Maan that he thought they were in trouble.

'And why Section 325 instead of Section 326?' continued the magistrate.

The former section dealt with grievous hurt; when the case came up for trial, the maximum sentence that could be imposed would be seven years; but for the moment Maan could be let out on bail. The latter section also dealt with grievous hurt, but with a dangerous weapon. This was not bailable, and the maximum punishment was life imprisonment.

The Sub-Inspector mumbled something about the weapon not having been discovered.

The magistrate looked at him severely. 'Do you think these injuries'—he looked down at the medical certificate—'these lacerations of the intestine and so on were caused by a stick?'

The Sub-Inspector said nothing.

'I think you should, well, investigate further,' said the magistrate. 'And re-examine your own evidence and the charges that suggest themselves.'

Maan's lawyer stood up to propose that such matters were within the discretion of the investigating officer.

'I am aware of that,' snapped the magistrate, who was disgusted with the proceedings. 'I am not telling him what charge to prefer.' He reflected that if it had not been for the medical certificate, the Sub-Inspector would probably have put forward a charge of simple hurt.

Glancing at Maan, the magistrate noticed that he looked unaffected enough by events. Presumably he was one of those criminals who learned nothing from their crimes.

Maan's lawyer asked that Maan be let out on bail, since the only present charge against him was bailable. The magistrate granted this, but it was clear that he was very annoyed. Part of his annoyance stemmed from the lawyer's reference to 'my client's grievous distress consequent on the demise of his mother'.

Maan's lawyer whispered: 'Thank God you won't be tried by him.'

Maan, who had begun to take an interest in his defence, said: 'Am I free?'

'Yes; for the moment.'

'What will I be charged with?'

'I'm afraid that isn't clear. This magistrate for some reason is after your blood, and is out to—well, to do you grievous hurt.'

The magistrate, however, was not interested in Maan's blood but merely in upholding the law. He would not be a party to the subversion of justice by influential people, and that is what he suspected this to be. He knew of courts where this might be possible, but his was not one of them.

17.33

'No person shall vote at any election if he is confined in a prison, whether under a sentence of imprisonment or transportation or otherwise, or is in the lawful custody of the police.'

The Representation of the People Act, 1951, was quite unambiguous about this, and so it happened that Maan was not able to vote in the great General Elections for which he had fought so hard. He was registered in Pasand Bagh, and elections for the Brahmpur (East) constituency for the Legislative Assembly were held on the 21st of January.

Curiously enough, had he been a resident of Salimpur-cum-Baitar, he would have succeeded in voting; for, owing to a shortage of trained personnel, voting in different constituencies was staggered, and the Legislative Assembly elections there were held on the 30th of January.

The fight now was an extremely harsh one. Waris was as bitter a rival to Mahesh Kapoor as he had been a doughty supporter. Everything had changed; and the Zamindari Act, rumours and scandals, pro- and anti-Congress feeling, religion, nothing was left unexploited in the mauling battle that led up to the polls.

The Nawab Sahib had not stated as such that Waris should fight against Mahesh Kapoor, but it was clear that he did not want him to support him. And Waris, who saw Maan no longer as the saviour but as the attempted murderer of the young Nawabzada, was passionate in his denunciation of him and his father, his clan, his religion, and his party. When the local Congress office belatedly sent a large number of posters and flags to Baitar Fort, he made a bonfire of them.

Waris spoke powerfully because he was so aroused. Already well liked in the area, he now rose on a great wave of popularity. He was the Nawab Sahib's champion, and the champion of his injured son, who even now (so it was convenient to assert) lay at the point of death owing to the treachery of his seeming friend. The Nawab Sahib had to remain in Brahmpur, claimed Waris, but if he could have campaigned, he would have exhorted the people from every podium in the district to throw the betrayer of the salt of his hospitality, the vile Mahesh Kapoor and all he stood for out of the constituency into which he had so recently crawled.

And what did Mahesh Kapoor and the Congress stand for? continued Waris, who had begun to enjoy his role as a political and feudal leader. What had they given the people? The Nawab Sahib and his family had worked for the people for generations, had fought the British in the Mutiny—long before the Congress had even been conceived—had died heroically, had suffered with the people's sufferings, had taken pity on their poverty, had helped them in every way they could. Look at the power station, the hospital, the schools founded by the Nawab Sahib's father and grandfather, said Waris. Look at the religious trusts they had either established or contributed to. Think of the great processions at Moharram—the grand climax of the festivities of the Baitar year—which the Nawab Sahib paid for out of his own pocket as an act of public piety and private charity. And yet Nehru and his ilk were trying to destroy the man who was so well-beloved, and replace him with what? A voracious pack of petty government officials who would eat the very vitals of the people. To those who complained that the zamindars exploited the people he suggested that they compare the state of the peasants on the Baitar estate with those of a certain village just outside, where they were sunk in destitution which aroused not pity so much as horror. There the peasants—especially the landless chamars—were so poor that they sifted the bullocks' droppings on the threshing-floor for residual grain—and washed it and dried it and ate it. And yet many chamars were going to vote blindly for the Congress, the party of the government that had oppressed them for so long. He begged his scheduled caste brothers to see the light and to vote for the bicycle they might aspire to and not for the pair of bullocks, which should only remind them of the degrading scenes they knew so well.

Mahesh Kapoor found himself entirely on the defensive. In any case, his heart lay in Brahmpur now: in a prison cell, in a hospital ward, in the room in Prem Nivas where his wife no longer slept. Increasingly, the fight, which had begun as an irregular ten-pointed star with one huge gleaming point, his own, had polarized into a struggle between two men: the man who tried to project himself as the Nawab Sahib's candidate and the man who realized that his only chance of victory lay in suppressing his individuality and projecting himself as the candidate of Jawaharlal Nehru.

He talked not about himself now but about the Congress Party. But he was heckled at every meeting and asked to explain the actions of his son. Was it true that he had used his influence to try to get him off? What if the young Nawabzada died? Was this a plot to wipe out the leaders of the Muslims one by one? For one who had spent his life fighting for communal amity, such accusations were hard to bear. If he had not been sick at heart, he would have responded as furiously as he usually did in the presence of aggressive stupidity, and this would have done him less good still.

Not once, either by studied implication or in a fit of anger, did he mention the rumours gathering around the Nawab Sahib. Yet now these rumours too began to float around Salimpur and Baitar and the hinterland of the two small towns. They were more damaging morally than those that touched Mahesh Kapoor, even though what they imputed was two decades old; and the Hindu communalist parties tried to use them as well as they could.

But many people, particularly around Baitar, refused to believe these rumours of illegitimacy and rape. And some, who believed them, held that the Nawab Sahib had been punished enough by God through his grief for his son; and that charity suggested that there was a statute of limitations on one's sins.

In practical terms too, Mahesh Kapoor was at his wits' end. He no longer had two jeeps but only one broken-down vehicle provided by the Congress office. His son was no longer with him to provide him with help and support and introductions. His wife, who could have helped him, who could have talked to the shy women of the constituency, was dead. He had hoped at one stage that Jawaharlal Nehru might make time on his whirlwind tour of Purva Pradesh to visit Salimpur, but so certain had his election appeared that he had not pressed his case. And now it seemed that only a visit from Nehru could save him. He telegrammed Delhi and Brahmpur and asked that Nehru's great progress be diverted his way for just a few hours; but he knew that half the Congress candidates in the province were making similar pleas, and that his chances of persuasion were utterly remote.

Veena and Kedarnath came out to help for a few days. Veena felt that her father needed her more than Maan, whom at best she could visit for a few minutes every other day. Her arrival had some effect in the towns, especially in Salimpur. Her homely but lively face, her warm-hearted manner, and the dignity of her sorrow—for her mother, for her brother, for her beleaguered father—affected the hearts of many women. When she spoke, they even attended public meetings. Because of the expansion of the franchise, they now formed half the electorate.

The Congress village-level workers campaigned as hard as they could, but many of them had begun to feel that the tide had turned irreversibly against them, and they were not able to disguise how disheartened they were. They could not even be certain of the scheduled caste vote because the socialists were trumpeting their electoral alliance with Dr Ambedkar's party.

Rasheed had returned to his village to campaign for the socialists. He was disturbed and excitable and he even looked unstable. Every second day he rushed off to Salimpur. But whether he was an asset or a liability to Ramlal Sinha's campaign was difficult to ascertain. He was Muslim, and religious, and that helped; but he had been disowned by almost everyone in his own village of Debaria—from Baba down to Netaji—and he had no particular standing anywhere. The elders of Sagal in particular mocked his pretensions. One joke that was doing the rounds was that 'Abd-ur-Rasheed' or 'The Slave of The Director' thought he had lost the head of his name when he had merely lost his own. Sagal had gone solidly into the Independent camp of Waris Khan.

In Debaria the picture was more complicated. This was partly because there were many more Hindus there: a small knot of brahmins and banias and a large group of jatavs and other scheduled castes. Every party—

the Congress, the KMPP, the socialists, the communists, and the Hindu parties—could hope to garner votes here. Among the Muslims, matters were complicated by Netaji's sporadic presence. He exhorted people to vote for the Congress candidate for Parliament, leaving open the question of the race for the Legislative Assembly; but there was bound to be some spillover in the resulting vote. A villager who placed his parliamentary ballot paper in a green box that carried the symbol of yoked oxen would be very likely to place his other ballot paper in a brown box carrying the same symbol.

When Mahesh Kapoor, after long and dusty hours of campaigning, arrived in Debaria with Kedarnath one evening, Baba met him and greeted him hospitably, but told him plainly that the situation had greatly changed.

'And what about you?' asked Mahesh Kapoor. 'Have you changed? Do you believe that a father should be punished for an offence of his son's?'

Baba said: 'I have never believed that. But I do believe that a father is responsible for the manner in which his son behaves.'

Mahesh Kapoor forbore from remarking that Netaji had not proved a great credit to Baba. The point was irrelevant, and he had no energy to argue. It was perhaps at that moment that he felt most acutely that he had lost the fight.

When he got back to Salimpur late at night, he told his son-in-law that he wished to be alone. The electricity in the room was weak, the bulbs low and flickering. He ate by himself and thought about his life, attempting to dissociate his family life from his public life, and to concentrate on the latter. Now more than ever he felt that he should have dropped out of politics in 1947. The sense of determination he had had when fighting the British had dissipated in the uncertainties and feeblenesses of Independence.

After dinner he looked through his post. He picked up a large envelope containing details of local electoral rolls. Then he picked up another local letter, and was startled to see King George VI's face on the stamp.

For a minute he stared at it, completely disoriented, as if he had seen an omen. Very carefully he placed the envelope down upon the postcard below: a postcard displaying a portrait of Gandhi. He felt as if he had unconsciously trumped his own best card. He stared once again at the stamp.

There was a simple explanation, but it did not occur to him. The Posts and Telegraph Department, under pressure of the great demands of election mail, and concerned about possible shortages, had issued instructions that old stocks of the King George series be put on sale at post offices. That was all. King George VI, from his sick-bed in London, had not visited Mahesh Kapoor in the watches of the night to predict that he would see him again at Philippi.

17.34

The next morning Mahesh Kapoor arose before dawn, and took a walk through the unwoken town. The sky was still starry. A couple of birds had just begun to sing. A few dogs barked. Over the faint voice of the muezzin's call to prayer, a cock crowed. Then again everything was silent except for the occasional birdsong.

> 'Rise, traveller, the sky is light.
> Why do you sleep? It is not night.'

He hummed the tune to himself and felt a renewal, if not of hope, at least of determination.

He looked at the watch that Rafi Sahib had given him, thought of the date, and smiled.

Later that morning, he was about to set out on the election round, when the Sub-Divisional Officer of Salimpur came up to him in a great hurry.

'Sir, the Prime Minister will be coming here tomorrow afternoon. I was instructed by telephone to inform you. He will be speaking at Baitar and at Salimpur.'

'Are you sure?' said Mahesh Kapoor impatiently. 'Are you absolutely sure?' He looked amazed, as if his improvement of mood had of itself brought about an improvement of fortune.

'Yes, indeed, Sir. I am sure.' The SDO looked both excited and extremely anxious. 'I have made no arrangements at all. None at all.'

Within an hour the extraordinary news was all over town, and by midday had percolated into the villages.

Jawaharlal Nehru, amazingly young-looking for his sixty-two years, dressed in an achkan which was already taking on the colour of the dust of the constituency roads, met Mahesh Kapoor and the Congress parliamentary candidate in the Circuit House at Baitar. Mahesh Kapoor could still hardly believe it.

'Kapoor Sahib,' said Nehru, 'they told me I shouldn't come here because it was a lost battle. That made me even more determined to come. Take these things away,' he said irritably to a man standing near him, as he bent his neck and freed himself of seven marigold garlands. 'Then they told me some nonsense about some trouble your son had got himself into. I asked if it had anything to do with you—and it clearly hadn't. People put too much emphasis on the wrong things in this country.'

'I cannot thank you enough, Panditji,' said Mahesh Kapoor with grateful dignity; he was very moved.

'Thank? There is nothing to thank me for. By the way, I am very sorry about Mrs Kapoor. I remember meeting her in Allahabad—but that must have been—what?—five years ago.'

'Eleven.'

'Eleven! What is the matter? Why are they taking so much time to set things up? I'll be late in Salimpur.' He popped a pastille into his mouth. 'Oh, I meant to tell you. I am asking Sharma to come and join my Cabinet. He can't keep refusing me. I know he likes being Chief Minister, but I need a strong team in Delhi too. That is why it is so important that you win here and help to handle things in Purva Pradesh.'

'Panditji,' said Mahesh Kapoor with surprise and pleasure, 'I will do my best.'

'And of course we cannot have reactionary forces winning sensitive seats,' said Nehru, pointing in the general direction of the Fort. 'Where is Bhushan—is that his name? Can't they organize anything?' he continued impatiently. He stepped on to the verandah and shouted for the man from the District Congress Committee who was in charge of logistics. 'How can we expect to run a country if we can't get together a microphone and a platform and a few policemen?' When he heard that the irksome and interminable security arrangements were finally secure, he ran down the steps of the Circuit House two at a time and jumped into the car.

The cavalcade was stopped every hundred yards or so by adoring crowds. When they reached the grounds where he was due to talk, he ran up the steps of the flower-strewn podium before doing namaste to the vast throng gathered below. The people—townsfolk and villagers alike—had been waiting for him with growing anticipation for more than two hours. When they sensed his arrival, even before they saw him, an electric shiver ran through the huge, excited audience, and they shouted:

'Jawaharlal Nehru Zindabad!'

'Jai Hind!'

'Congress Zindabad!'

'Maharaj Jawaharlal ki jai!'

This last was too much for Nehru.

'Sit down, sit down, don't shout!' he shouted.

The crowd laughed delightedly and kept cheering. Nehru got annoyed, jumped down from the podium before anyone could stop him, and started physically pushing people down. 'Hurry up, sit down, we don't have all the time in the world.'

'He gave me a push—a hard push!' said one man proudly to his friends. He was to boast about it ever afterwards.

When he returned to the podium, a Congress bigwig started introducing and seconding someone else on the platform.

'Enough, enough, enough of all this, start the meeting,' said Nehru.

Then someone started talking about Jawaharlal Nehru himself, how flattered, honoured, privileged, blessed they were to have him with them, how he was the Soul of Congress, the Pride of India, the jawahar and lal of the people, their jewel and their darling.

All this got Nehru very angry indeed. 'Come on, don't you have anything better to do?' he said under his breath. He turned to Mahesh Kapoor. 'The more they talk about me, the less use I am to you—or to the Congress—or to the people. Tell them to be quiet.'

Mahesh Kapoor hushed up the speaker, who looked hurt; and Nehru immediately launched into a forty-five-minute speech in Hindi.

He held the crowd spellbound. Whether they understood him or not was hard to say, because he rambled on in an impressionistic manner from idea to idea, and his Hindi was not much good, but they listened to him and stared at him with rapt attention and awe.

His speech went something like this:

> 'Mr Chairman, etc.,—brothers and sisters—we are gathered here at a troubled time, but it is also a time of hope. We do not have Gandhiji with us, so it is even more important that you have confidence in the nation and in yourselves.
>
> The world is also going through a hard time. We have the Korean crisis and the crisis in the Persian Gulf. You have probably heard about the attempt of the British to bully the Egyptians. This will lead to trouble sooner or later. This is bad, and we cannot have it. The world must learn to live in peace.
>
> Here at home also, we must live in peace. As tolerant people we

must be tolerant. We lost our freedom many years ago because we were disunited. We must not let it happen again. Disaster will strike the country if religious bigots and communalists of all descriptions get their way.

We must reform our way of thinking. That is the main thing. The Hindu Code Bill is an important measure which must be passed. The Zamindari Bills of the various states must be implemented. We must look at the world with new eyes.

India is an ancient land of great traditions, but the need of the hour is to wed these traditions to science. It is not enough to win elections, we must win the battle of production. We must have science and more science, production and more production. Every hand has to be on the plough and every shoulder to the wheel. We must harness the forces of our mighty rivers with the help of great dams. These monuments to science and modern thinking will give us water for irrigation and also for electricity. We must have drinking water in the villages and food and shelter and medicine and literacy all around. We must make progress or else we will be left behind. . . .'

Sometimes Nehru was in a reminiscent mood, sometimes he waxed poetic, sometimes he got carried away and scolded the crowd. He was, as they had sensed in their earlier slogans, rather an imperious democrat. But they applauded him, almost regardless of what he said. They cheered when he talked about the size of the Bhakra dam, they cheered when he said that the Americans must not oppress Korea—whatever Korea was. And they cheered most of all when he requested their support, which he did almost as an afterthought. In the eyes of his people, Nehru—the prince and hero of Independence, the heir of Mahatma Gandhi—could do no wrong.

Only in the last ten minutes or so of any speech did he spend time asking for their votes—for the Congress, the party which had brought freedom to the country and which, for all its faults, was the only party that could keep India together; for the Congress parliamentary candidate 'who is a decent man' (Nehru had forgotten his name); and for his old comrade and companion Mahesh Kapoor, who had undertaken such a heavy task for the whole state by framing the crucial zamindari laws. He reminded the audience of certain anachronisms in an age of republicanism who were attempting to misuse feudal loyalties for their own personal ends. Some of them were even standing for election as Independents. One of them, who owned a huge estate, was even using the humble bicycle as his symbol. (This local reference went down well.) But there were many such, and the lesson was a general one. He asked the audience not to swallow the present professions of idealism and humility of such notables, but to contrast these with their ugly past record, a record of oppression of the people and of faithful service to their British overlords who had protected their domains, their rents and their misdeeds. The Congress would have no truck with such feudalists and reactionaries, and it needed the support of the masses to fight them.

When the crowd, carried away with enthusiasm, shouted 'Congress Zindabad!' or, worse still, 'Jawaharlal Nehru Zindabad!' Nehru ticked them off sharply and told them to shout 'Jai Hind!' instead.

And thus his meetings ended, and on he went to the next one, always late, always impatient, a man whose greatness of heart won the hearts of others, and whose meandering pleas for mutual tolerance kept a volatile country, not merely in those early and most dangerous years but throughout his own lifetime, safe at least from the systemic clutch of religious fanaticism.

17.35

The few hours that Jawaharlal Nehru spent in the district had an enormous effect on all the electoral campaigns there, and on none more so than Mahesh Kapoor's. It gave him new hope and it gave the Congress workers new heart. The people too became perceptibly more friendly. If Nehru, who was indeed perceived by the ordinary people as the Soul of Congress and the Pride of India, had put his stamp of approval on his 'old comrade and companion', who were they to doubt his credentials? Had the elections been held the next day instead of two weeks later, Mahesh Kapoor would probably have flown home with a large majority on the hem of Nehru's dusty achkan.

Nehru had also partially drawn the communal sting. For among Muslims throughout the country he was perceived as their true champion and protector. This was the man who at the time of Partition had jumped down from a police jeep in Delhi and rushed unarmed into the midst of fighting mobs in order to save lives, no matter whether the lives were Hindu or Muslim. This was the man whose very dress spoke of nawabi culture, however much he fulminated against Nawabs. Nehru had been to the shrine of the great sufi saint Moinuddin Chishti at Ajmer, and had been honoured with the gift of a gown; he had been to Amarnath, where the Hindu priests had honoured him with puja. The President of India, Rajendra Prasad, would have gone to the latter but not to the former. It gave the frightened minorities heart that the Prime Minister saw no essential difference between the two.

Even Maulana Azad, the most notable leader among the Muslims after Independence, was a moon compared to Nehru's sun; his brightness was largely that of reflection. For it was in Nehru—though he was not a man who was in love with it, and though he did not make the most effectual use of it—that popularity—and national power—was vested.

There were even some—both Hindus and Muslims—who said half-jokingly that he would have made a better leader of the Muslims than Jinnah. Jinnah had no sympathy for them—it was his will that had held them in his sway and led them towards Pakistan. But here was a man who was positively bubbling with sympathy, and who, unembittered by the partition of his country, continued, unlike others, to treat them—as he treated people of all religions or none—with affection and respect. They would have felt a great deal less secure and more fearful if someone else had been ruling in Delhi.

But, as the saying goes, Delhi is far away. And Brahmpur too for that matter—and even the district headquarters of Rudhia. As the days passed, once again local loyalties, local quarrels, local issues, and the local configurations of caste and religion began to reassert themselves. Gossip about Mahesh Kapoor's son and the Nawabzada, about Saeeda Bai and the Nawab Sahib, continued to be exchanged at the small barber's shop in Salimpur—more a pavement stall than a shop—in the vegetable market, over an evening hookah in a village courtyard, and wherever people met and talked.

Many upper-caste Hindus decided that Maan had lost his caste by associating with—and, worse still, falling in love with—that Muslim whore. And with Maan's loss of caste his father had lost his claim on their vote. On the other hand, with the passage of time, many of the poorer Muslims—and most of them were poor—rethought the question of where their interests lay. Though they had a traditional loyalty to the Nawab Sahib, they began to fear what would happen if they elected his man Waris to the Legislative Assembly. What if not only he but other feudal Independents were elected? What if the Congress did not get a clear majority? Would the Zamindari Act—or at least its implementation—not then be at hazard, even if it passed the barrier of the Supreme Court? The danger of permanent tenantry under the cruel control of the munshi and his enforcers held few attractions compared to the possibility of independent ownership, however encumbered, of their own land.

Meanwhile, Kedarnath had some success with the jatavs of Salimpur and the villages around; unlike most upper-caste or even comparatively lower-caste Hindus, he did not refuse to eat with them, and they knew through their relatives or acquaintances in Brahmpur, such as Jagat Ram of Ravidaspur, that he was one of the few footwear traders in Misri Mandi who treated their caste-brethren tolerably well. Nor had Mahesh Kapoor, unlike L.N. Agarwal with his police charge, done anything to dilute their natural affinity for the Congress. Veena for her part continued to go from house to house and village to village with the Congress women's committees to canvass for her father. She was glad of the work, and she was glad that her father was once again immersed in his campaign. It took his mind off matters which would have been too painful to contemplate. Old Mrs Tandon was running Prem Nivas these days, and Bhaskar was staying there. Veena missed him, but there was nothing she could do about it.

The race was now almost a straight contest between Nehru's old comrade-in-arms and the lackey of the reactionary Nawab Sahib; or, equally plausibly, between the father of the villainous Maan and the stout and faithful Waris.

The walls of both Baitar and Salimpur were covered with handbills carrying Nehru's portrait, many defaced with a large green bicycle, whose two wheels covered his two eyes. Waris had been appalled by Nehru's remarks about his master, whom he revered, and he was determined to avenge both that verbal attack and Maan's physical attack on the gallant Firoz. He was not excessively nice about his methods. He would use legitimate means where he could, and anything else where he could not. He coaxed money out of the tight-fisted munshi, he threw feasts and distributed sweets and liquor, he coerced whoever he could and cajoled whoever he could, he promised whatever was necessary, he took the Nawab Sahib's name and God's, certain that he was speaking on their joint behalf and heedless of the possibility of their future disapproval. Maan, whom he had once instinctively liked and who had proved such a false and dangerous friend, was his arch-enemy. But now, after the disruptive magic of the Nehruvian wand, Waris could not be certain that he would defeat his father.

On the day before the election, when it would be too late for any effective refutation, appeared a small handbill in Urdu, printed in the thousands on flimsy pink paper. It carried a black border. It appeared to have no author. There was no printer's name at the bottom. It announced that Firoz had died the previous night, and called upon all faithful people, in his grieving father's name, to cast their vote in such a way as to express their indignation against the author of this great misfortune. The murderer even now walked the streets of Brahmpur, free on bail, free to strangle more helpless Muslim women and slaughter the flower of Muslim manhood. Where could such an abomination occur, such a prostitution of the ideals of justice, than under Congress Raj? It was being said that no matter who or what stood for election as a Congress candidate—even a lamp post or a dog—they would be bound to win. But the people of this constituency should not vote for the shameless lamp post or the foul dog. They should remember that if Mahesh Kapoor got into power, no one's life or honour would be safe.

The fatal flier—for such it was intended to be—appeared, as befitted its flimsiness, to travel on the wind; for by that evening, when all overt electioneering had ceased, it had found its way to almost every village in the constituency. The next day was the vote, and it was too late to suppress or counter the lie.

17.36

'Whose wife are you?' asked Sandeep Lahiri, who was Presiding Officer at one of the many polling stations in Salimpur.

'How can I take his name?' asked the burqa-clad woman in a shocked whisper. 'It is written on that slip of paper which I gave you before you left the room just now.'

Sandeep looked down at the slip of paper, then once more at the voting list. 'Fakhruddin? You are Fakhruddin's wife? From the village Noorpur Khurd?'

'Yes, yes.'

'You have four children, don't you?'

'Yes, yes, yes.'

'Out!' said Sandeep sternly. He had already ascertained that the real woman in question had two children. Strictly speaking, he should have handed the woman over to the police, but he didn't feel her offence merited such stern action. Only once had he had recourse to the police in this election. That had been a few days earlier when a drunken man in Rudhia had threatened a member of his polling party and had tried to tear up a copy of the electoral rolls.

Sandeep enjoyed being away from Brahmpur. His work in the Department of Mines was dull and desk-bound compared to his earlier responsibilities out in the subdivision. This election work—though for the most part also performed at a desk—provided a refreshing respite, and he got to see once again the areas that, for all their backwardness, he had grown to feel such affection for. He looked around the room at a torn map of India and a chart of the Hindi alphabet. The polling station happened to be in a local school.

There were sounds of an argument from the adjoining classroom, where the men's booth was located. Sandeep got up to find out what the matter was and was faced with an unusual sight. A beggar who had no hands was intent on casting his vote, and on doing so unaided by anyone. He refused to be accompanied into the curtained area, insisting that the officer would reveal whom he had voted for. The polling officer was arguing with him, but to no avail, and the flow of voters had halted outside the classroom while voices rose hotly from within. The beggar said that the polling officer should fold his ballot paper for him and put it between his teeth. Then he himself would go behind the curtain and insert it in the box of his choice.

'I can't do that,' said the officer.

'Why not?' insisted the beggar. 'Why should I let you come in with me? How do I know you are not one of the Nawab Sahib's spies? Or the Minister's?' he added hastily.

Sandeep made a quiet gesture to the polling officer, indicating that he should allow the man's request. The beggar performed his electoral duty for both Parliament and the Legislative Assembly. When he emerged for the second time, he gave the officer a contemptuous snort. The officer was quite miffed.

'Wait a second,' said another officer. 'We forgot to mark you with the ink.'

'You'll recognize me if you see me again,' said the beggar.

'Yes, but you might try to vote somewhere else. It's a rule. Everyone has to have their left forefinger marked.'

The beggar snorted again. 'Find my left forefinger,' he said.

The entire polling party appeared to be held at bay by one man. 'I have the answer to that,' Sandeep told his officer with a smile, turned to a page of his instructions, and read out:

> 'Any reference in this rule or in rule 23 to the left fore-finger of an elector shall, in the case where the elector has his left fore-finger missing, be construed as a reference to any other finger of his left hand, and shall, in the case where all the fingers of his left hand are missing, be construed as a reference to the fore-finger or any other finger of his right hand, and shall, in the case where all his fingers of both the hands are missing, be construed as a reference to such extremity of his left or right arm as he possesses.'

He dipped the glass rod into the phial of ink, and smiled weakly at the beggar, who, defeated by the labyrinthine brains of the Raj-trained drafters of the Ministry of Law, held out his left stump with very bad grace.

Polling was fairly brisk. By noon, about three in every ten names on the voting list had been crossed off. After an hour's break for lunch came the second four-hour voting period. By the time the polls closed at five, fifty-five per cent or so of those eligible to vote at that polling station had cast their votes. This represented a very good turnout, Sandeep thought. He knew from his experience of the last few days that—contrary to what he had expected—the urban turnout in most areas was lower than the rural one.

At five o'clock, the school gates were closed, and signed paper slips were given to those already in the queue. When they too had cast their votes, the slits of the ballot boxes were closed with a paper seal, and stamped with a red seal of lac. The polling agents of the various candidates added their own seals. Sandeep made arrangements for the ballot boxes to be locked in the schoolroom overnight and posted a guard over them. The next day these boxes, along with others, were taken under the care of the SDO of Salimpur to the Collectorate at Rudhia, where they were locked up, together with ballot boxes that had begun to arrive from all over the district, in the government treasury.

Because the voting itself had been staggered, the counting of votes too was staggered, with the constituencies that had gone to the polls first being counted first. Some of the polling parties now became counting parties. As a result of this schedule, seven to ten days generally elapsed between the poll and the count in a typical constituency in Purva Pradesh in the General Elections of 1952.

These were days of tormenting anxiety for any candidate who fancied that he or she might have a chance of winning. Certainly, it was so for Waris Khan, though no one would have thought it would be otherwise. But despite his many other anxieties, it was true for Mahesh Kapoor as well.

Part Eighteen

18.1

Lata was not an active participant in the dramatic events of January. She reflected, however, on Meenakshi's prediction, or at least expectation, of excitement in the New Year. Had Brahmpur been Calcutta and Savita's family hers, Meenakshi could not have been entirely disappointed by events: a stabbing, a scandal, a death, a vicious election—and all in a family that was for the most part used to nothing more exciting than strong words between a mother and a daughter—or stronger words between a father and a son.

This was the term that would culminate in her final exams. Each day Lata attended her lectures, her mind only half on what was being said about old novels and older plays. Most of her fellow-students, including Malati, were concentrating on their studies; there were very few extracurricular activities, certainly no plays or anything that required an investment of time. The weekly meetings of the Brahmpur Literary Society continued as before, but Lata had no heart to attend them. Maan had very recently been released from prison on bail, which was a relief but it appeared that the final charge-sheet was going to be more serious than they had come to hope it might.

Lata enjoyed managing Uma, who was a very obliging baby, and whose smiles made her forget that there was a sorrowing or troubled world around her. The baby had inexhaustible energy, and a determined grip on life, her surroundings, and any hair within reach. She had taken to singing and to dictatorially thumping the edge of her wicker cot.

Uma, Lata noticed, had a pacifying effect on Savita and even on Pran. Her father, when he dandled her in his arms, was unconscious for a few moments of his own father—smarting between grief and anger; or his brother, caught equally in the toils of love and the law; or his wife; or his late mother; or his own health and work and ambitions. Pran had learned 'The Lady Baby' by heart, and would declaim it to Uma from time to time. Mrs Rupa Mehra, who had undertaken enormous quantities of winter knitting, would look up, half delighted and half suspicious, whenever Pran began one of his recitations.

Kabir had made no attempt to contact Lata in Calcutta. He did not meet her in Brahmpur either. He saw her at the chautha, and once from a distance on the college campus. She looked quietly unapproachable. With all the recent uproar in the press he could imagine that she, like Pran, would be unable to escape endless expressions of sympathy and curiosity from friends, acquaintances, and strangers.

He reflected unhappily that their meetings had always had a somewhat illogical, incomplete, and insubstantial feel about them. They always met for a very short time, were constantly aware of the risk of discovery, and so, even during the brief while that they were together, seemed extremely awkward with each other. Kabir was straightforward in his conversations with everyone except Lata, and he wondered if she too might not be at her most complex and difficult when she was with him.

He did not expect any longer that she would be thinking much about him. Even if she had not been at the unsettled periphery of so many distractions and distresses, he would not have expected it. He could not know she had heard that he had been in Calcutta and had wanted to meet her. He had no idea of Malati's letter. He too was involved in his studies, and he too had his private sadnesses and consolations. His weekly visit to his mother was an unavoidable sadness—and he found his own solace in whatever interests he could: in playing cricket, for example, or in further news of the Test series with England, the last match of which was still to be played in Madras. Recently, with Mr Nowrojee's active enthusiasm, he had arranged for the poet Amit Chatterji to come to Brahmpur to read and discuss his work at a meeting of the Brahmpur Literary Society. This was due to take place in the first week of February. He hoped, but did not expect, that Lata would be there. He assumed she had heard of Chatterji's work.

At ten past five on the appointed day, there was an air of great excitement at 20 Hastings Road. The stuffed chairs with their flowery prints were all occupied. Glasses of water covered with lace doilies stood on the table from which Mr Nowrojee would introduce the speaker and Amit would recite his poetry. Mrs Nowrojee's rock-like delicacies lurked in a nearby room. The late light fell gently on the translucent skin of Mr Nowrojee, as he looked out with a melancholy tremor at his sundial and wondered why the poet Chatterji had not yet appeared. Kabir was sitting at the back of the room. He was dressed in whites, having just played a friendly match between the History Department and the Eastern India Railway Cricket Club. He had cycled over and was still sweating. The booming poetess, Mrs Supriya Joshi, sniffed the air daintily.

She turned to Mr Makhijani, the patriotic poet.

'I always feel, Mr Makhijani,' she murmured in her resonant voice, 'I always feel—'

'Yes, yes,' said Mr Makhijani fervently. 'That is the ticket. One must feel. Without feeling, wherefrom would the Muse strike?'

Mrs Supriya Joshi continued: 'I always feel that one should approach poetry in a spirit of purity. One must have a freshness of mind, a cleanliness of body. One must lave oneself in sparkling springs—'

'Lave—ah, yes, lave,' said Mr Makhijani.

'Genius may be ninety-nine per cent perspiration, but ninety-nine per cent perspiration is the prerogative of genius.' She looked pleased with her formulation.

Kabir turned to Mrs Supriya Joshi. 'I'm so sorry,' he said. 'I was just playing a match.'

'Oh,' said Mrs Supriya Joshi.

'May I say how very glad I was where I happened to be when you read your remarkable poetry a few months ago.' Kabir beamed at her; she looked smitten. It was not for nothing that he planned to join the diplomatic service. The smell of his sweat had suddenly become aphrodisiac. Indeed, thought Mrs Supriya Joshi, this young man is very good-looking and very courteous.

'Ah—' she whispered. 'Here comes the young master.' Amit had just entered with Lata and Pran. Mr Nowrojee immediately began to talk to Amit earnestly and inaudibly.

Kabir noticed that Lata was looking around for a place to sit in the crowded room. In the gladness and surprise of seeing her, he did not even wonder why she had come in together with Amit.

He stood up. 'There's a place here,' he said.

Lata's mouth opened a little and she took in a quick breath. She glanced at Pran, but his back was turned. Without a word, she joined Kabir, squeezing in between him and Mrs Supriya Joshi, who did not look at all pleased. Far too courteous, she thought.

18.2

Mr Nowrojee, now smiling in wintry relief at the distinguished guest and the distinguished audience which included the Proctor, Mr Sorabjee, as well as the eminent Professor Mishra—removed Amit's doily and his own, and took a sip of water before declaring the meeting open.

He introduced the speaker as 'not the least of those who have merged the vigour of the West with a sensibility distinctly Indian' and then proceeded to treat his audience to a disquisition on the word 'sensibility'. Having touched on several senses of the word 'sensible', he continued to other adjectives: sensitive, sensile, sensate, sensuous and sensual. Mrs Supriya Joshi grew restless. She said to Mr Makhijani:

'Such long long speeches he loves to give.'

Her voice carried, and Mr Nowrojee's cheek, already flushed as a result of his discussion of the last two adjectives, took on a darker tinge of embarrassment.

'But I do not mean to deprive you of the talents of Amit Chatterji with my own poor meanderings,' he stated in a stricken manner, sacrificing the brief history of Indian Poetry in English that he had planned to deliver (it was to have climaxed in a triolet to 'our supreme poetess Toru Dutt'). Mr Nowrojee continued: 'Mr Chatterji will read a selection of his poems and then answer questions about his work.'

Amit began by saying how pleased he was to be in Brahmpur. The invitation had been extended at a cricket match; he noticed that Mr Durrani, who had invited him, was still dressed for cricket.

Lata looked astonished. Amit had told her when he arrived the previous day from Calcutta that he had been invited by the Literary Society, and Lata had simply assumed that it was Mr Nowrojee who had initiated the process. She turned to Kabir and he shrugged. There was a scent of sweat to him that reminded her of the day when she had watched him practising at the nets. He was behaving all too coolly. Was he like this with this other woman? Well, Lata told herself, two could be cool.

Amit for his part, noticing this unconscious and intimate look pass between them, realized that Lata must know Kabir quite well. He lost the thread of his thoughts for a moment, and improvised some guff about the resemblance between cricket and poetry. He then continued to say what he had meant to, which was that it was an honour to be reading in the city associated with the name of the Barsaat Mahal and the Urdu poet Mast. Perhaps it was not widely known that Mast, apart from being a famous writer of ghazals, was also a satirist. What exactly he would have made of the recent elections one could not tell, but he would certainly have made something of the unscrupulous energy with which they had been conducted, nowhere more so than in Purva Pradesh. Amit himself had been inspired to write a short poem after reading the morning's edition of the *Brahmpur Chronicle.* In lieu of 'Vande Mataram' or any such patriotic opening hymn he would lay his poem before this audience as a Victory Hymn to their elected or soon-to-be-elected sovereigns.

He took a sheet of paper out of his pocket and began.

> 'God of pebbles, help us, now the poll is past,
> Not to spurn the small bribes but to snatch the vast,
> To attack the right cause, to defend the wrong,
> To exploit the helpless and protect the strong.
> To our peculations and our victims add.
> Mighty Lord, we pray thee, make us very bad. . . .'

There were three more stanzas, referring among other things to a few local contests that Amit had read about in the newspaper—one of which made both Pran and Lata sit up: it referred in a flippant manner to a landowner and a land-snatcher who had first come together and then bounced apart like billiard balls in the cause of garnering the vote.

Most of the audience enjoyed the poem, especially the local references, and laughed. Mr Makhijani, however, was not amused.

'He is making mockery of our Constitution. He is making mockery,' said the patriotic bard.

Amit went on to read a dozen poems, including 'The Fever Bird', which had so haunted Lata when she first read it. Professor Mishra too thought it very good, listened intently, and nodded his head.

Several of the poems Amit read were not to be found in his books; for the most part they had been written more recently. One, however, about the death of an old aunt of his, which Lata found very moving, had been composed some time before. Amit had kept it aside and rarely read it. Lata noticed that Pran's head was bowed as he listened to this poem, and indeed the whole audience was quite still.

After the reading and applause was over, Amit said that he would be happy to answer any questions.

'Why is it that you do not write in Bengali, your mother tongue?' asked a challenging voice. The young man who spoke appeared to be quite angry.

Amit had been asked this question—and had asked himself this question—many times before. His answer was that his Bengali was not good enough for him to be able to express himself in the manner he could in English. It wasn't a question of choice. Someone who had been trained all his life to play the sitar could not become a sarangi player because his ideology or his conscience told him to. 'Besides,' Amit added, 'we are all accidents of history and must do what we are best at without fretting too much about it. Even Sanskrit came to India from outside.'

Mrs Supriya Joshi, the songbird of free verse, now stood up and said:

'Why do you use rhyming? Moon, June, Moon, June? A poet must be free—free as a bird—a fever bird.' Smiling, she sat down.

Amit said he rhymed because he liked to. He liked the sound, and it helped give pith and memorability to what might otherwise become diffuse. He no more felt chained by it than a musician felt chained by the rules of a raag.

Mrs Supriya Joshi, unconvinced, remarked to Mr Makhijani: 'All is rhyming, chiming, in his poems, like Nowrojee's triolets.'

Professor Mishra asked a question about Amit's influences: did he detect the shadow of Eliot in his writing? He referred to several lines in Amit's poetry, and compared them to lines of his own favourite modern poet.

Amit tried to answer the question as well as he could, but he thought that Eliot was not one of his major influences.

'Have you ever been in love with an English girl?'

Amit sat up sharply, then relaxed. It was a sweet, anxious old lady from the back of the room.

'Well, I—I don't feel I can answer that before an audience,' he said. 'When I asked for questions, I should have added that I would answer any questions so long as they were not too private—or, for that matter, too public. Government policy, for instance, would be out.'

An eager young student, blinking in adoration, and unable to restrain the nervousness in his voice, said: 'Of the 863 lines of poetry in your two published books, thirty-one refer to trees, twenty-two have the word "love" or "loving" in them, and eighteen consist of words of only one syllable. How significant is this?'

Lata noticed Kabir smile; she was smiling herself. Amit attempted to extricate an intelligent question out of what had just been said and talked a little about his themes. 'Does that answer the question?' he asked.

'Oh, yes,' nodded the young man happily.

'Do you believe in the virtue of compression?' asked a determined academic lady.

'Well, yes,' said Amit warily. The lady was rather fat.

'Why, then, is it rumoured that your forthcoming novel—to be set, I understand, in Bengal—is to be so long? More than a thousand pages!' she exclaimed reproachfully, as if he were personally responsible for the nervous exhaustion of some future dissertationist.

'Oh, I don't know how it grew to be so long,' said Amit. 'I'm very undisciplined. But I too hate long books: the better, the worse. If they're bad, they merely make me pant with the effort of holding them up for a few minutes. But if they're good, I turn into a social moron for days, refusing to go out of my room, scowling and growling at interruptions, ignoring weddings and funerals, and making enemies out of friends. I still bear the scars of *Middlemarch*.'

'How about Proust?' asked a distracted-looking lady, who had begun knitting the moment the poems stopped.

Amit was surprised that anyone read Proust in Brahmpur. He had begun to feel rather happy, as if he had breathed in too much oxygen.

'I'm sure I'd love Proust,' he replied, 'if my mind was more like the Sundarbans: meandering, all-absorptive, endlessly, er, sub-reticulated. But as it is, Proust makes me weep, weep, weep with boredom. Weep,' he added. He paused and sighed. 'Weep, weep, weep,' he continued emphatically. 'I weep when I read Proust, and I read very little of him.'

There was a shocked silence: why should anyone feel so strongly about anything? It was broken by Professor Mishra.

'Needless to say, many of the most lasting monuments of literature are rather, well, bulky.' He smiled at Amit. 'Shakespeare is not merely great but grand, as it were.'

'But only as it were,' said Amit. 'He only looks big in bulk. And I have my own way of reducing that bulk,' he confided. 'You may have noticed that in a typical *Collected Shakespeare* all the plays start on the right-hand side. Sometimes, the editors bung a picture in on the left to force them to do so. Well, what I do is to take my pen-knife and slit the whole book up into forty or so fascicles. That way I can roll up *Hamlet* or *Timon*—and slip them into my pocket. And when I'm wandering around—in a cemetery, say—I can take them out and read them. It's easy on the mind and on the wrists. I recommend it to everyone. I read *Cymbeline* in just that way on the train here; and I never would have otherwise.'

Kabir smiled, Lata burst out laughing, Pran was appalled, Mr Makhijani gaped and Mr Nowrojee looked as if he were about to faint dead away.

Amit appeared pleased with the effect.

In the silence that followed, a middle-aged man in a black suit stood up. Mr Nowrojee began to tremble slightly. The man coughed a couple of times.

'I have formulated a conception as the result of your reading,' he announced to Amit. 'It has to do with the atomic age and the place of poetry, and the influence of Bengal. Many things have happened since the War, of course. I have been listening for an hour to the very scintillation of India, that is what I said to myself when I formulated my conception. . . .'

Immensely pleased with himself, he continued in this vein for the oral equivalent of about six paragraphs, punctuated with 'You understand?' Amit nodded, less amiably each time. Some people got up, and Mr Nowrojee in his distress pounded an imaginary gavel on the table.

Finally the man said to Amit: 'Would you care to comment?'

'No thank you,' said Amit. 'But I appreciate your sharing your remarks with us. Any other questions?' he asked, emphasizing the last word.

But there were no more questions. It was time for Mrs Nowrojee's tea and her famous little cakes, the delight of dentists.

18.3

Amit had hoped to talk to Lata a little, but he was mobbed. He had to sign books, he had to eat cake for fear of offending, and the sweet old lady, foiled once, insisted on asking him again whether he had been in love with an English girl. 'Now you can answer, there is no audience now,' she said. Several other people agreed with her. But Amit was spared: Mr Nowrojee, murmuring that his defence of rhyme had been so very heartening and that he himself was an unashamed devotee of rhyme, pressed into Amit's hand the suppressed triolet, and asked Amit to read it and tell him what he thought. 'Now, please be quite honest. Honesty such as yours is so refreshing, and only honesty will do,' said Mr Nowrojee. Amit looked down at the poem in Mr Nowrojee's thin, small, careful, upright handwriting:

A TRIOLET TO THE SONGSTRESS OF BENGAL

Fate snatched away sweet Toru Dutt
At the soft age of twenty-two.

The casuarina tree was cut.
Fate snatched away sweet Toru Dutt.
No bulbuls haunt its branches but
    Her poems still haunt me and you.
Fate snatched away sweet Toru Dutt
    At the soft age of twenty-two.

Meanwhile, Professor Mishra was talking to Pran in another corner of the room. 'My dear boy,' he was saying, 'my commiserations go deeper than words. The sight of your hair, so short still, reminds me of that cruelly abridged life. . . .'

Pran froze.

'You must take care of your health. You must not undertake new challenges at a time of bereavement—and, of course, family anxiety. Your poor brother, your poor brother,' said Professor Mishra. 'Have a cake.'

'Thank you, Professor,' said Pran.

'So you agree?' said Professor Mishra. 'The meeting is too soon, and to subject you to an interview—'

'Agree to what?' said Pran.

'To withdrawing your candidature, of course. Don't worry, dear boy, I will handle all the formalities. As you know, the selection committee is meeting on Thursday. It took so long to arrange a date,' he went on. 'But finally, in the middle of January, I succeeded in fixing one. And now, alas—but you are a young man, and will have many more opportunities for advancement, here in Brahmpur or elsewhere.'

'Thank you for your concern, Professor Mishra, but I believe I will feel well enough to attend,' said Pran. 'That was an interesting question you asked about Eliot,' he added.

Professor Mishra, his pallid face still frozen in disapproval at Pran's unfilial attitude and tempted almost to refer to funeral baked meats, was silent for a while. Then he pulled himself together and said: 'Yes, I gave a paper here a few months ago entitled "Eliot: Whither?" It is a pity you were unable to attend.'

'I didn't hear about it till later,' said Pran. 'I regretted it for weeks afterwards. Do have a cake, Professor Mishra. Your plate is empty now.'

Meanwhile Lata and Kabir were talking.

'So you invited him when you came to Calcutta?' said Lata. 'Did he come up to your expectations?'

'Yes,' said Kabir. 'I enjoy his poetry. But how did you know I went to Calcutta?'

'I have my sources,' said Lata. 'And how do you know Amit?'

'Amit, is it?'

'Mr Chatterji, if you like. How do you know him?'

'I don't—I mean, I didn't,' said Kabir, correcting himself. 'We were introduced by someone.'

'By Haresh Khanna?'

'You really do have your sources,' said Kabir, looking straight into Lata's eyes. 'Perhaps you would care to tell me what I was doing this afternoon.'

'That's easy,' said Lata. 'You were playing cricket.'

Kabir laughed. 'That was too easy,' he said. 'Yesterday afternoon?'

'I don't know,' said Lata. 'I really can't eat this cake,' she added.

'I've put up with some of this cake in the past in the hope of seeing you,' said Kabir. 'But you're worth any amount of chipped enamel.'

Very charming, thought Lata coldly, and did not respond. Kabir's compliment seemed rather too facile.

'So, how do you know Amit—I mean Mr Chatterji?' continued Kabir. His voice had an edge to it.

'What is this, Kabir, an interrogation?'

'No.'

'Well, what is it then?'

'A civil question, which might merit a similar answer,' said Kabir. 'I asked out of interest. Do you want me to withdraw it?'

Lata reflected that the tone of the question had not been civil. It had been jealous. Good!

'No. Let it stand,' she said. 'He's my brother-in-law. I mean,'—and here she flushed—'he's not my own brother-in-law but my brother's.'

'And I imagine you've had plenty of opportunity of meeting him in Calcutta.'

The word Calcutta was like a goad.

'Just what are you trying to get at, Kabir?' said Lata angrily.

'Just that I've been watching him for the last few minutes and during the reading too, and everything he does seems to be aimed at you.'

'Nonsense.'

'Look at him now.'

Lata turned instinctively; and Amit, who had had half an eye on her while he was attempting not too dishonestly to comment on Nowrojee's triolet, gave her a smile. Lata smiled back weakly. Amit, however, was soon obscured by the bulk of Professor Mishra.

'And I suppose you take walks?'

'Sometimes—'

'Reading *Timon* to each other in cemeteries.'

'Not exactly.'

'And I suppose you go up and down the Hooghly on a boat at dawn.'

'Kabir—how dare you, you of all people—'

'And I suppose he writes you letters as well?' continued Kabir, who looked as if he wanted to shake her.

'What if he did?' said Lata. 'What if he does? But he doesn't. It's the other man you met, Haresh, who writes to me—and I write back.'

The colour drained from Kabir's face. He grabbed her right hand and held it tight.

'Let go,' whispered Lata. 'Let me go at once. Or I'll drop this plate.'

'Go ahead,' said Kabir. 'Drop it. It's probably a Nowrojee heirloom.'

'Please—' said Lata, tears starting to her eyes. He was actually hurting her physically, but she was very annoyed about her tears. 'Please don't, Kabir—'

He released her hand.

'Ah, Malvolio's revenge—' said Mr Barua, coming up to them. 'Why have you made Olivia cry?' he asked Kabir.

'I haven't made her cry,' said Kabir. 'No one has an obligation to cry. Any crying of hers is purely voluntary.'

And with that he left.

18.4

Lata, refusing to explain anything to Mr Barua, went to wash her face. She did not return to the room until she felt that it would not be obvious that she had been in tears. But the crowd had thinned, and Pran and Amit were ready to take their leave.

Amit was staying at the home of Mr Maitra, the retired Superintendent of Police; but he was having dinner with Pran, Savita, Mrs Rupa Mehra, Lata, Malati and Maan.

Though Maan, out on bail, was living once again at Prem Nivas, he could not bear to take his meals there. The polls were over, and his father had returned to Brahmpur. He was an angry and grieving man—and wanted Maan with him all the time. He did not know what would happen to his son once a proper charge-sheet was delivered. Everything was collapsing about Mahesh Kapoor's ears. He hoped that he might at least retain his power in politics. But if he did not succeed even in winning his own seat, he knew how drastically this would weaken his following.

He had no immediate activity to lose himself in. Some days he received visitors; on other days, he sat and looked out at the garden, saying nothing. The servants knew that he did not wish to be disturbed. Veena would bring him tea. The counting of the vote for his constituency was due to take place a few days from now; he would go to Rudhia for the day. By the evening of the 6th of February he would know if he had won or lost.

Maan was riding in a tonga to Pran's house for dinner when he saw Malati Trivedi walking along. He greeted her. She said hello, then suddenly looked awkward.

'What's the matter?' said Maan. 'I haven't been convicted yet. And Pran says you're having dinner with us. Get in.'

Malati, feeling ashamed of her hesitancy, did get in, and they rode towards the university together, not saying much for two such outgoing people.

Maan had met three of the Chatterjis—Meenakshi, Kakoli and Dipankar—at various times. He remembered Meenakshi most of all: she had stood out at Pran's wedding—and had made even a hospital room appear a glamorous backdrop for her own dramatic presence. He now looked forward to meeting their brother, whom Lata had mentioned to him during her jail visit. Amit greeted him in a sympathetic and curious manner.

Maan looked worn out and knew it. Sometimes he still couldn't believe where he had been; at other times he couldn't believe that he was, at least for a while, free again.

'We hardly meet these days,' said Lata, who had not been able to concentrate on conversation for the last hour.

Maan began to laugh. 'No, we hardly do,' he said.

Malati could see that something was the matter with Lata. She attributed it to the presence of the Poet. Malati had been keen to examine this contender for Lata's hand. She decided that Amit was not very impressive: he was bent on making small talk. The Cobbler, who (as Malati had been told) had got angry when called mean, had shown far more spirit—even if, she decided, of a rather zany kind.

Malati did not know that Amit, especially after reading his poems or writing a serious one, would often switch into an entirely different mood: cynical and sometimes trivializing. He had been leached of any pretence at profundity. Though no Kuku-couplets flapped away like freed pigeons from his mouth this evening, he began to talk in a light-hearted manner about elected politicians and the way they subverted the system by winning favours for themselves and their families. Mrs Rupa Mehra, who switched off whenever the talk turned to politics, had gone into the other room to put Uma to bed.

'Mr Maitra, with whom I'm staying, has been explaining to me his prescription for Utopia,' said Amit. 'The country should be run by only children—unmarried only children—whose parents are dead. At any rate, he says, all Ministers should be childless.'

Noticing that no one was taking up the subject, Amit continued: 'Otherwise, of course, they're bound to try to get their children out of whatever scrapes they've got themselves into.' He stopped, suddenly realizing what he was saying.

Since everyone was looking at him without speaking, he quickly added: 'Of course, Ila Kaki says it isn't just in politics that this sort of thing happens—academia is just as bad—full of—how does she put it?—"sordid nepotisms and antagonisms". It sounds just like the literary world.'

'Ila?' said Pran.

'Oh, Ila Chattopadhyay,' said Amit, relieved that the points had been switched on the tracks. 'Dr Ila Chattopadhyay.'

'The one who writes about Donne?' asked Pran.

'Yes. Didn't you meet her when you were in Calcutta? Not even at our place? I suppose not. Anyway, she was telling me about a textbook scandal at some university where a professor got a book prescribed as a compulsory textbook when he himself had written it under a pseudonym. She got extremely excited about the whole business.'

'Doesn't she tend to?' asked Lata with a smile.

'Oh, yes,' said Amit, pleased that Lata was at last taking part in the conversation. 'Yes, she does. She's coming to Brahmpur in a few days, as it happens, so you'll have a chance to meet,' he added to Pran. 'I'll tell her to look you up. You'll find her very interesting.'

'The baby's sleeping,' said Mrs Rupa Mehra, returning to the room. 'Very soundly, very sweetly.'

'Well, I thought her book on Donne was very good,' said Pran. 'What's she coming here for?'

'She's sitting on some committee or other—I don't think she mentioned what,' said Amit. 'And I'm not sure, given her erratic ways, that she herself will remember.'

Mrs Rupa Mehra said: 'Yes, she is one of these very intelligent women. Very modern in her views. She was advising Lata against getting married.'

Pran hesitated before saying: 'Was it a selection committee by any chance?'

Amit tried to remember. 'I think so. I'm not sure, but I think that's what it was. Yes, she was talking about the poor calibre of most of the candidates, so it must have been.'

'I don't think I'd better meet her, in that case,' said Pran. 'She'll probably be deciding my fate. I think I'm one of those candidates she was referring to.'

In the straits in which the family now found itself, Pran's possible promotion had become still more important. Even his retention of this house, the conferral of which had been rather ad hoc, could well depend on it.

'Your fate! That sounds very dramatic,' said Amit. 'I should think that with Professor Mishra firmly on your side, Fate would think twice about misbehaving with you.'

Savita leaned forward eagerly. 'What did you say? Professor Mishra?'

'Yes, indeed,' said Amit. 'He spoke most fulsomely about Pran when I told him I was having dinner here.'

'There, darling,' said Savita.

Pran said: 'If I had been born a cockroach, I wouldn't wonder: "What will the selection committee decide?" "What's happening to India?" "Is the cheque in the mail?" "Will I live to see my daughter grow up?" Why on earth am I so concerned about all these things?'

Everyone except Amit looked at Pran with varying degrees of surprise and concern.

'Don't you care what happens to me?' Maan asked suddenly.

'Yes, I do,' said Pran, taking his argument through its paces. 'But I doubt a cockroach would care about what happened to his brother. Or father for that matter.'

'Or mother,' added Maan, getting up immediately to go. He looked as if he could not bear any more such talk.

'Maan,' said Savita, 'don't take it like that. Pran too has been under a lot of strain. And he didn't mean any harm by that remark. Darling, please don't talk like that. It was quite a peculiar thing to say, and it's not like you at all; I'm not surprised Maan's upset.'

Pran, with a look of tired affection, yawned and said: 'I'll try to be careful about what I say. In my own house and with my own family.'

Seeing Savita's expression of hurt he wished he had left the second sentence unsaid. She, after all, succeeded in being careful without appearing constricted, without at all losing her sense of ease. She had never known him in perfect health. Even before the baby had been born, he could sense how much she loved him by the quiet of her footsteps in the room where he was sleeping—by the fact that she might begin to hum and suddenly become quiet. She would never have considered this to be a constraint. Sometimes he used to keep his eyes closed even though he was awake—just for the pleasure of feeling that someone cared for him so much. He supposed she was right: his remark had been a thoughtless one. Perhaps even childish.

Lata was looking at Savita and thinking: Savita was made to be married. She's happy to do all the things a house and a family require, all the small and serious things of life. She's only taken up law because it's been forced upon her by Pran's health. Then the thought struck her that Savita would have loved anyone whom she had married, anyone who was basically a good man, no matter how difficult he was, no matter how different he was from Pran.

18.5

'What were you thinking?' Amit asked Lata after dinner, lingering over his coffee. The other guests were being seen to the door by Pran and Savita, and Mrs Rupa Mehra had gone into her room for a few minutes.

'That I really liked your reading,' said Lata. 'It was very affecting. And I enjoyed the question-and-answer session afterwards. Especially the statistical appendix—and the tearing of the tomes. You should advise Savita to deal as brutally with her law-books.'

'I didn't know you knew young Durrani,' said Amit.

'I didn't know he'd invited you.'

There was a few seconds' pause. Then Amit said: 'I meant, what were you thinking just now?'

'When?' said Lata.

'When you were looking at Pran and Savita. Over the pudding.'

'Oh.'

'Well, what?'

'I can't remember,' said Lata with a smile.

Amit laughed.

'Why are you laughing?' asked Lata.

'I like making you feel uncomfortable, I suppose.'

'Oh. Why?'

'—Or happy—or puzzled—just to see your change of mood. It's such fun. I pity you!'

'Why?' said Lata, startled.

'Because you'll never know what a pleasure it is to be in your company.'

'Do stop talking like that,' said Lata. 'Ma will come in any minute.'

'You're quite right. In that case: will you marry me?'

Lata dropped her cup. It fell on the floor and broke. She looked at the broken pieces—luckily, it had been empty—and then at Amit.

'Quick!' said Amit. 'Before they come running to see what's happened. Say yes.'

Lata had knelt down; she was gathering the bits of the cup together and placing them on the delicately patterned blue-and-gold saucer.

Amit joined her on the floor. Her face was only a few inches away from his, but her mind appeared to be somewhere else. He wanted to kiss her but he sensed that there was no question of it. One by one she picked up the shards of china.

'Was it a family heirloom?' asked Amit.

'What? I'm sorry—' said Lata, snapped out of her trance by the words.

'Well, I suppose I'll have to wait. I was hoping that by springing it on you like that I'd surprise you into agreeing.'

'I wish—' said Lata, putting the last piece of the shattered cup on to the saucer.

'What?' asked Amit.

'I wish I would wake up one day and find I'd been married to someone for six years. Or that I had a wild affair with someone and never got married at all. Like Malati.'

'Don't say that,' said Amit. 'Ma might come in at any moment. Anyway, I wouldn't advise an affair with Malati,' he added.

'Do stop being idiotic, Amit,' said Lata. 'You're so brilliant, do you have to be so stupid as well? I should only take you seriously in black and white.'

'And in sickness and health.'

Lata laughed. 'For better and for worse,' she added. 'Far worse, I suppose.'

Amit's eyes lit up. 'You mean yes?'

'No, I don't,' said Lata. 'I don't mean anything. And nor, I assume, do you. But why are we kneeling here facing each other like Japanese dolls? Get up, get up. Here comes Ma, just as you said.'

18.6

Mrs Rupa Mehra was less sharp with Amit, however, than he had expected, for she was having second thoughts about Haresh.

For fear of having her own judgement called into question, she did not speak her thoughts out aloud. But she was not skilled in dissimulation; and over the next few days, when Amit had left Brahmpur, it was her want of enthusiasm for, rather than her actual criticism of, Haresh that indicated to Lata that all was not at ease in her mind with respect to her former favourite.

That he had been so upset by Lata calling him 'mean' bewildered Mrs Rupa Mehra. On the other hand, it must have been Lata's fault in some way, she decided. What she could not understand was that Haresh had not said goodbye to her, Mrs Rupa Mehra, his self-appointed mother-in-law-to-be. Several days had passed between the altercation and their hurried return to Brahmpur; yet during that time he had not visited or telephoned or written. It was not right; she was hurt; and she did not see why he should have continued to treat her so insensitively. If only he had called, she would have forgiven him immediately and tearfully. Now she was not in a forgiving mood at all.

It also struck her that some of her friends, when she had mentioned that Haresh was involved in the shoe trade, had made remarks such as, 'Well, of course, things have changed nowadays,' and 'Oh! Dear Rupa—but everything is for the best, and Praha is of course Praha.' In the first flush of vicarious romance, such veiled or consolatory comments had not struck home. But now the memory of them caused her to suffer a rush of embarrassment. Who could have predicted that the daughter of the potential Chairman of the Railway Board might be linked to the lowly lineage of leather?

'But such is Fate,' said Mrs Rupa Mehra to herself; and this led to a thought which an advertisement in the next morning's *Brahmpur Chronicle* translated into action. For there she noticed, under the heading 'Astrologer-Royal: Raj Jyotishi', the photograph of a plump and beaming middle-aged man, his hair cut short and parted in the middle. Underneath were the words:

> The greatest Astrologer, Palmist and Tantrik. Pandit Kanti Prasad Chaturvedi, Jyotishtirtha, Tantrikacharya, Examiner, Government Board of Astrological Studies. Highly praised and honoured with unwanted testimonials. Very speedy results.

Very speedily—in fact the same afternoon—Mrs Rupa Mehra made her way to the Astrologer-Royal. He was unhappy that she knew only the place and date of Haresh's birth, not the exact time of day. But he promised to see what he could do. It would require certain extra assumptions, certain extra calculations, and even the use of the adjustment factor of Uranus, which was not standard in Indian astrology; and the use of Uranus was not costless. Mrs Rupa Mehra paid up and he told her to return two days later.

She felt quite guilty about these proceedings. After all, as she had complained to Lata when Mrs Mahesh Kapoor had asked for Savita's horoscope: 'I don't believe in all this matching. If it had been true, my husband and I. . . .' But now she told herself that perhaps the fault lay in the lack of skill of particular astrologers, not in the science itself. And the Astrologer-Royal had been very persuasive. He had explained why her gold wedding ring would 'reinforce and concentrate the power of Jupiter'; he had advised her to wear a garnet because it would control the ecliptic node of Rahu and confer mental peace; he had praised her wisdom, which was patent to him from both her palm and her expression; and a large silver-framed photograph on his desk, facing clientwards, showed him shaking hands with the Governor himself.

When they next met, the Astrologer-Royal said: 'You see, in this man's seventh house, the Jupiter is aspected by Mars. The whole impression is yellow and red, which in combination you may consider to be orange or golden, therefore his wife will be very beautiful. Then you see, the moon is surrounded by lots of planets, that is also a sign of the same thing. But the seventh house has Aries in it, who is very stubborn, and Jupiter, who is strong, which will enhance the stubbornness. So therefore he will marry a beautiful but difficult woman. Is your daughter such a one?'

Mrs Rupa Mehra thought about the matter for a few seconds, then, hoping for better luck elsewhere, said: 'But what about all the other houses?'

'The seventh house is the House of the Wife.'

'But are there no problems at all? In the matching of the two horoscopes, I mean?' His eyes were very piercing, and she was forced to concentrate on the middle parting in his hair.

The Astrologer-Royal looked at her for a few seconds, smiling speculatively, then said: 'Yes, certain problems surely exist. I have examined the totality of the picture, taking into consideration the information of both your daughter and the Prospective. It is quite problematical, I would say. Kindly come and collect the problematical details this evening. I will write them down.'

'And Uranus?' asked Mrs Rupa Mehra. 'What does Uranus say?'

'The effect did not prove to be significant,' said the Astrologer-Royal. 'But of course the calculations had to be made anyway,' he added hastily.

18.7

As they entered the Haridas College of Music together, Malati's friend said: 'Well, there have been no more sightings of the quarry. But if there are, I'll keep you informed.'

'What are you gabbling about?' asked Malati. 'I hope we're not too late.' Ustad Majeed Khan was in an impatient mood these days.

'Oh, you know, the woman he met at the Blue Danube.'

'Who met?'

'Kabir, of course.'

Malati stopped and turned towards her friend:

'But you said the Red Fox.'

Her friend shrugged. 'Did I? I might have. It's quite confusing. But what difference does it make whether you shoot someone in Chowk or in Misri Mandi? . . . What's the matter with you?'

For Malati had seized her friend's arm; her face had gone white.

'What was this woman like? What was she wearing?' she asked.

'Amazing! You didn't want to know anything then, but now—'

'Tell me. Quickly.'

'Well, I wasn't there, but this girl Purnima—I don't think you know her, she's from Patna and she's doing history—it was she who noticed them.

She was sitting a few tables away, though, and you know what it's like with these dimmed lights—'

'But what was she wearing? The woman, I mean, not this wretched girl.'

'Malati, what's the matter with you? It's been weeks—'

'What was she wearing?' asked Malati desperately.

'A green sari. Wait, I'd better make sure I get my colours right this time, or you'll kill me. Yes, Purnima said she was wearing a green sari—and lots of flashy emeralds. And she was tall and quite fair—that's about all—'

'Oh, what have I done—' said Malati. 'Oh, poor fellow—poor Kabir. What a terrible mistake. What have I done, what have I done?'

*

'Malati,' said Ustad Majeed Khan, 'carry the tanpura with respect, with both hands. It isn't the offspring of a cat. What is the matter with you?'

*

'What's the matter with you?' asked Lata, as Malati burst into her room.

'It was me he was with—' said Malati.

'Who?'

'Kabir—that day in the Red Fox, I mean the Blue Danube.'

A pang of literally green-eyed jealousy shot through Lata.

'No—I don't believe it. Not you!'

The cry was so vehement that Malati was taken aback. She almost feared Lata would attack her.

'I don't mean that—I don't mean that at all,' said Malati. 'I mean that he wasn't seeing some other girl. He hasn't been seeing anyone else. I was told the name of the wrong place. I should have waited to hear more. Lata, I blame myself. It's entirely my fault. I can imagine what you've gone through. But please, please don't take my mistake out on him—and on yourself.'

Lata was silent for a minute. Malati expected her to burst into tears of relief or frustration, but no tears came. Then she said: 'I won't. But Malu, don't blame yourself.'

'I do, I do. Poor fellow—he was entirely sincere all along.'

'Don't,' said Lata. 'Don't. Don't. I'm glad Kabir wasn't lying to you—I can't tell you how glad. But I've—well, I've learned something as a result of all this wretchedness—I have, Malu, I really have—about myself—and about, well, the strength of—really, the strangeness of my own feelings for him.'

Her voice seemed to come from a no-man's-land between hope and despair.

18.8

Professor Mishra, frustrated that he had not got Pran to withdraw either his application for the readership or his harebrained schemes of syllabus reform, was grateful nevertheless that things were not going at all well for his father. Opinion in the press was strongly critical of the means deployed by his opponents, but on the question of whether he would win or lose the election, most people were agreed that he had almost certainly lost. Professor Mishra took a lively interest in politics, and almost all his informants told him that he should work on the assumption that Pran's father would not be in a position to wield much power to undo or avenge any injustice done to his son in the matter of the readership.

Professor Mishra was also pleased that he would know this fact for certain by the time the selection committee met. Counting in Mahesh Kapoor's constituency was due to be held on the 6th of February, and the selection committee was to meet on the 7th. He would thus be secure in the knowledge that he could safely stiletto the young lecturer who was proving to be such an obstacle in the smooth running of the department.

At the same time, since one of the prospective candidates, and by no means the worst one, was the nephew of the Chief Minister, Professor Mishra could ingratiate himself further in the eyes of S.S. Sharma by helping him out in this small particular. And Professor Mishra expected that when any committee assignments in the government, particularly—but not necessarily—in the field of education, opened up, the name of the by-then-retired Professor O.P. Mishra would be considered in a not unfavourable light by the reigning powers.

What if S.S. Sharma were called to Delhi, as it was rumoured that Nehru had not merely requested but virtually demanded of him? Professor Mishra reflected that it was not likely that even Nehru would succeed in dislodging so wily a politician as S.S. Sharma from his happy fief. And if he were to go and take charge of a ministry in Delhi, well, plums could fall from Delhi too, not merely from the Secretariat at Brahmpur.

What if S.S. Sharma went to Delhi and Mahesh Kapoor became Chief Minister in Brahmpur? This prospect was horrible, but it was utterly remote. Everything was against it: the scandal surrounding his son, his own recent widowerhood, the fact that his political credibility would be damaged as soon as it was known and published that he had lost his own seat. Nehru liked him, it was true; and was particularly impressed by his work on the Zamindari Act. But Nehru was not a dictator, and the Congress MLAs of Purva Pradesh would elect their own Chief Minister.

That it would be the great, baggy, faction-ridden Congress Party that would continue to run the country and the state was by now entirely clear. Congress, riding high on the popularity of Jawaharlal Nehru, was in the process of winning a landslide across the country. True, the party was garnering less than half the actual vote nationwide. But opposition to Congress was so fragmented and disorganized in most constituencies that it looked—from all the early returns—that Congress would be first-past-the-post in about three-quarters of the parliamentary seats, and in about two-thirds of the seats in the various state legislatures.

That Mahesh Kapoor's candidacy had collapsed for personal and special reasons relating to his constituency and his family, including the great popularity of the man whose agent he was seen to be opposing, would not help him after the elections. If anything, he would be seen to be one of the exceptional electoral failures in a sea of successes. Sympathy for losers counts for little in politics. Mahesh Kapoor would, Professor Mishra devoutly hoped, be finished; and his upstart, Joyce-loving, professor-baiting son would come to realize in due course that he had no future prospects in this department—any more than his younger brother had in civilized society.

And yet—and yet—could anything go wrong in Professor Mishra's plans? The five-person selection committee included himself (as Head of Department); the Vice-Chancellor of the university (who chaired the committee); the Chancellor's nominee (who happened that year to be a distinguished but rather feeble retired professor of history); and two outside experts from the panel of experts approved by the Academic Council. Professor Mishra had looked carefully through the panel and chosen two names, which the Vice-Chancellor had accepted without discussion or demur. 'You know what you are doing,' he had told Professor Mishra encouragingly. Their interests lay in the same direction.

The two experts, who at this moment were travelling from different directions to Brahmpur, were Professor Jaikumar and Dr Ila Chattopadhyay. Professor Jaikumar was a mild-mannered man from Madras, whose specialism was Shelley, and who, unlike that volatile and fiery spirit, believed firmly in the stability of the cosmos and the absence of intra-departmental friction. Professor Mishra had taken him around the department on the day when Pran had had his fortuitous collapse.

Dr Ila Chattopadhyay would present no problem; she was beholden to Professor Mishra. He had sat on the committee that had made her a university reader some years ago, and he had immediately afterwards and on numerous subsequent occasions emphasized to her how instrumental he had been in the process. He had praised her work on Donne with great unctuousness and assiduity. He was certain that she would be compliant. When her train arrived at Brahmpur Station he was there to meet her and escort her to the Brahmpur University guest house.

On the way he tried to veer the conversation prematurely around to the next day's business. But Dr Ila Chattopadhyay did not appear to be at all keen to discuss the various candidates beforehand, which disappointed Professor Mishra. 'Why don't we wait till the interviews?' she suggested.

'Quite so, quite so, dear lady, that is just what I would have suggested myself. But the background—I was sure you would appreciate being informed about—ah, here we are.'

'I am so exhausted,' said Dr Ila Chattopadhyay, looking around. 'What a horrible place.'

There should have been nothing exceptionally horrible about the room to one who had been to such places often before, but it was indeed fairly depressing, Professor Mishra had to agree. The university guest house was a dark series of rooms connected by a corridor. Instead of carpets there was coir matting, and the tables were too low to write at. A bed, two chairs, a few lights that did not work well, a tap that was over-generous with water even when turned off, and a flush that was miserly with it even when tugged violently: these were some of the appurtenances. As if to compensate for this, there was a great deal of dingy and unnecessary lace hanging everywhere: on the windows, on the lampshades, on the backs of the chairs.

'Mrs Mishra and I would be delighted if you would come for dinner to our place,' murmured Professor Mishra. 'The facilities for dining here are, well, adequate at best.'

'I've eaten,' said Dr Ila Chattopadhyay, shaking her head vigorously. 'And I'm really exhausted. I need to take an aspirin and go straight to bed. I'll be on that wretched committee tomorrow, don't worry.'

Professor Mishra went off, rather perturbed by Dr Ila Chattopadhyay's extraordinary attitude.

If it had not been open to misconstruction he would have invited her to stay at his house. When Professor Jaikumar arrived, he did precisely that.

'This is extremely—infinitely kind,' said Professor Jaikumar.

Professor Mishra winced, as he almost invariably did when talking to his colleague. Professor Jaikumar had prefixed a 'y' to both adverbs. The Mask of Yenarchy! thought Professor Mishra.

'Not at all, not at all,' he assured his guest blandly. 'You are the repository of the future stability of our department, and the least we can do is to make you welcome.'

'Yes, welcome, welcome,' said Mrs Mishra meekly and rapidly, doing namaste.

'I am sure you have looked through the candidates' applications and so on,' said Professor Mishra jovially.

Professor Jaikumar looked very slightly surprised. 'Yes, indeed,' he said.

'Well, if I may just indicate a couple of lines of thought that might smoothen the process tomorrow and make everyone's task easier—' began Professor Mishra. 'A sort of foretaste, as it were, of the proceedings. Merely to save time and bother. I know you have to catch the seven o'clock train tomorrow night.'

Professor Jaikumar said nothing. Courtesy and propriety struggled in his breast. Professor Mishra took his silence for acquiescence, and continued. Professor Jaikumar nodded from time to time but continued to say nothing.

'So—' said Professor Mishra finally.

'Thank you, thank you, most helpful,' said Professor Jaikumar. 'Now I am forewarned and forearmed for the interviews.' Professor Mishra flinched at the last word. 'Yes—most helpful,' continued Professor Jaikumar in a non-committal manner. 'Now I must do a little puja.'

'Of course, of course.' Professor Mishra was taken aback by this sudden piety. He hoped it was not a purificatory rite.

18.9

A little before eleven the next morning the committee gathered in the glum-panelled and well-appointed office of the Vice-Chancellor. The Registrar was present too, though not as a participant. A few of the candidates were already waiting in the anteroom outside. After some tea and biscuits and cashew nuts and a little casual social chit-chat, the Vice-Chancellor looked at his watch and nodded at the Registrar. The first candidate was brought in.

Professor Mishra had not been feeling entirely happy about the way preliminary matters were going. Apart from Dr Ila Chattopadhyay, who had continued in her abrupt vein this morning, there was something else that was bothering him. He did not yet know for certain what had happened to Pran's father. He knew that for some reason the counting had not finished by the time of the local news bulletin on the radio the previous evening, for if it had, the name of the winning candidate would have been announced. But that was all he knew, and he had not been able to get in touch with his own informant. He had left instructions at home that he was to be called as soon as any news on the matter was received. Any excuse would do; and if necessary the information could be noted down, sealed in an envelope, and sent in to him. There would be nothing unusual in this. The Vice-Chancellor himself, who was—and took pride in being seen to be—a busy man, was forever interrupting committee meetings by taking telephone calls, and indeed sometimes signing letters that peons brought in.

The interviews went on. The clear February sunlight pouring through the window helped dissipate the grand but dampening atmosphere of the office. The interviewees—thirteen men and two women, all of them lecturers, were, for the most part, treated not as colleagues but as supplicants by the Vice-Chancellor; the nephew of the Chief Minister, on the other hand, was treated with excessive deference by both him and Professor Mishra. Every so often a telephone call would interrupt the proceedings. At one point Dr Ila Chattopadhyay found it necessary to say:

'Vice-Chancellor, can't you take your phone off the hook?'

The Vice-Chancellor looked absolutely amazed.

'My dear lady,' said Professor Mishra.

'We have travelled a very considerable distance to be here,' said Dr Ila Chattopadhyay. 'At least two of us have. These selection committees are a duty, not a pleasure. I haven't seen one decent candidate so far. We are due to go back tonight, but I'm not sure we will be able to at this rate. I do not see why our torment should be further prolonged by these endless interruptions.'

Her outburst had its effect. For the next hour, the Vice-Chancellor told whoever called that he was in the middle of an urgent meeting.

Lunch was served in a room adjoining the Vice-Chancellor's office, and a little academic gossip was exchanged. Professor Mishra begged leave to go home. One of his sons was not very well, he said. Professor Jaikumar looked a little surprised.

Once home, Professor Mishra phoned his informant.

'What is the matter, Badri Nath?' he said impatiently. 'Why have you not got in touch with me?'

'Because of George the Sixth, of course.'

'What are you talking about? George the Sixth is dead. Don't you listen to the news?'

'Well, there you are.' There was a cackle at the other end.

'I can't get any sense out of you, Badri Nath ji. Yes, I have heard you. George the Sixth is dead. I know that. I heard it on the news, and all the flags are at half-mast. But what does that have to do with me?'

'They've stopped the counting.'

'They can't do that!' exclaimed Professor Mishra. This was madness.

'Yes—they can. They began the counting late—I think the DM's jeep broke down—so they didn't finish it by midnight. And at midnight they suspended the counting. All over the country. As a mark of respect.' The thought struck Badri Nath as droll, and he cackled again.

It did not strike Professor Mishra as being in the least droll. The former King-Emperor of India had no business dying at a time like this.

'How far did they get in the counting?' he asked.

'That's what I'm trying to find out,' said Badri Nath.

'Well, find out, please. And tell me the trend.'

'What trend?'

'Can't you at least tell me who's ahead in the race?'

'There's no ahead or behind in this, Mishraji. They don't count the vote polling station by polling station. They count all the boxes of the first candidate first, and then go on down the line.'

'Oh.' Professor Mishra's head had begun to throb.

'Don't worry, though—he's lost. Take it from me. All my sources say so. I guarantee it,' said Badri Nath.

Professor Mishra wanted with all his heart to believe him. But some gnawing little doubt prompted him to say: 'Please call me at four o'clock at the Vice-Chancellor's office. His number is 623. I must know what is happening before we begin our discussion of the candidates.'

'Who would have thought it!' said Badri Nath, laughing. 'The English still run our lives.'

Professor Mishra put down the phone. 'Where is my lunch?' he said coldly to his wife.

'You said that you—' she began, then saw the look on his face. 'I'll just get something ready,' she said.

18.10

Pran's interview was scheduled for the early afternoon. The Vice-Chancellor asked him the usual questions about the relevance of teaching English in India. Professor Jaikumar asked him a careful question about *Scrutiny* and F.R. Leavis. Professor Mishra asked tenderly after his health and fussed about the onerous burdens of academia. The old history professor who was the Chancellor's nominee said nothing at all.

It was with Dr Ila Chattopadhyay that Pran got along really well. She drew him out on the subject of *The Winter's Tale*, one of Pran's favourite plays, and they both got carried away, talking freely of the implausibilities of the plot, the difficulties of imagining, let alone performing, some of the scenes, and the absurd and deeply moving climax. They both thought it should be on every syllabus. They agreed with each other violently and disagreed with each other pleasurably. At one point Dr Chattopadhyay told him outright that he was talking nonsense, and Professor Mishra's troubled face wreathed itself in a smile. But even if she thought that the point Pran had just made was nonsense, it was obviously very stimulating nonsense; her attention was entirely engaged in rebutting it.

Pran's interview—or, rather, his conversation with her—lasted twice as long as the time allotted to him. But, as Dr Chattopadhyay remarked, some of the other candidates had been disposed of in five minutes, and she looked forward to other candidates of Pran's calibre.

By four o'clock the interviews were over, and they broke off for a short tea break. The peon who brought in the tea was not deferential to anyone except the Vice-Chancellor. This irked Professor Mishra, whose afternoon tea was usually sweetened by a little cringing.

'You are looking very pensive, Professor Mishra,' said Professor Jaikumar.

'Pensive?'

'Yes, indeed.'

'Well, I was wondering why it was that Indian academics publish so little. So few of our candidates have worthwhile publications to their name. Dr Chattopadhyay, of course, is a remarkable exception. Many moons ago, my dear lady,'—he turned towards her—'I remember how impressed I was by reading your work on the Metaphysicals. That was long before I sat on the committee which—'

'Well, we're neither of us young now,' interrupted Dr Ila Chattopadhyay, 'and neither of us has published anything of worth in the last ten years. I wonder why that is.'

While Professor Mishra was still recovering from this remark, Professor Jaikumar put forth an explanation which caused him a different kind of pain. 'Our typical young university teacher,' he began, 'is overworked when he is junior—he has to teach yelementary prose and compulsory Yinglish. If he is yinnately conscientious, he has no time for yennything else. By then the fire is out—'

'If it was ever there,' added Dr Ila Chattopadhyay.

'—and the family is growing up, yemoluments are small, and making yends meet is a problem. Luckily,' added Professor Jaikumar, 'my wife was yeconomical in her habits, and I got the opportunity to go to Yingland and that is how I managed to develop my yinterest in Shelley.'

Professor Mishra, his mind distracted by Professor Jaikumar's almost instinctive choice of words beginning with dangerous vowels, said: 'Yes, but I really fail to see why, once we have riper academic experience and more leisure—'

'But by then we have yimportant committees like this one to take up our time,' Professor Jaikumar pointed out. 'And also we may know too much by then and have no yexpress motivation for writing. Writing is yitself discovery. Yexplication is yexploration.' Professor Mishra shuddered inwardly while his colleague continued: 'Ripeness is not all. Perhaps, ripe in years, and thinking he academically now knows yevrything, our university teacher turns from knowledge to religion that goes beyond knowledge—from gyaan to bhakti. Rationality has a very tenuous hold on the Indian psyche.' (He rhymed it with bike.) 'Even the great Shankara, Adi-Shankara, who said in his advaita that the great yinfinite idea was that of Brahman—which needed to be brought down by uncomprehending Man to mere

Ishvara, whom did he pray to? To Durga!' Professor Jaikumar nodded his head around the room and in particular to Dr Ila Chattopadhyay. 'To Durga!'

'Yes, yes,' said Dr Ila Chattopadhyay. 'But I have a train to catch.'

'Well,' said the Vice-Chancellor. 'Let us then make our decision.'

'That shouldn't take us long,' said Dr Ila Chattopadhyay. 'That thin, dark fellow, Prem Khanna, is head and shoulders above everyone else.'

'Pran Kapoor,' Professor Mishra corrected her, pronouncing the syllables with delicate distaste.

'Yes, Prem, Pran, Prem, Pran: I'm always getting things like this wrong. Really, I sometimes wonder what has happened to my brain. But you know whom I mean.'

'Indeed.' Professor Mishra pursed his lips. 'Well, there might be certain difficulties there. Let us look at a few more possibilities—in justice to the other candidates.'

'What difficulties?' said Dr Ila Chattopadhyay bluntly, thinking of the prospect of another night amid lace and coir, and determined not to let this discussion go on at any great length.

'Well, he has had a bereavement recently. His poor mother. He will be in no condition to undertake—'

'Well, he certainly didn't let the thought of his dead mother get in the way of his duelling this afternoon.'

'Yes, when he said that Shakespeare was implausible,' said Professor Mishra, pursing his lips to indicate his sense of how unsound and even sacrilegious Pran's opinions were.

'Nonsense!' said Dr Ila Chattopadhyay, looking quite fierce. 'He said that the plotting of *The Winter's Tale* was implausible. And so it is. But seriously, this question of duty and bereavement is surely none of our concern.'

'Dear lady,' said Professor Mishra in exasperation, 'I am the one who has to run this department. I must see that everyone pulls his weight. Professor Jaikumar will, I am sure, agree that one must not rock the boat.'

'And I suppose that those whom the captain deems unfit for first-class accommodation must be kept firmly, by whatever means necessary, in steerage,' said Dr Ila Chattopadhyay.

She had sensed that Professor Mishra did not like Pran. In the subsequent heated discussion she discovered that he and the Vice-Chancellor had a favourite candidate, one whom she had judged very ordinary, but to whom, she recalled, they had been excessively courteous during the interview.

Assisted by the Vice-Chancellor and with the extremely tacit acquiescence of the Chancellor's nominee, Professor Mishra built up a case for this candidate. Pran was tolerable as an academic, but not very cooperative in the running of the department. He needed to mature. Perhaps, in two years' time, they could consider him again. This other candidate was equally good and a greater asset. Besides, Pran had the strangest views about the syllabus. He thought that Joyce—yes, Joyce—should be thrust down people's throats. His brother was a bad lot and would bring scandal to the name of the department; these might seem to outsiders to be extraneous matters, but one had to observe certain proprieties. And his health was poor; he came late for classes; why, Professor Jaikumar himself had once seen him collapse in mid-lecture. And there had been complaints that he was involved with a certain woman student. In the nature of things, it would be unreasonable to expect concrete evidence for these complaints, but they had to be considered.

'Yes, and I suppose he drinks as well?' said Dr Ila Chattopadhyay. 'I was wondering when the passes-classes-glasses argument was going to come up.'

'Really!' exclaimed the Vice-Chancellor. 'Do you need to cast aspersions on Professor Mishra's motives? You should accept with grace—'

'I will not accept with grace what is a disgrace,' said Dr Ila Chattopadhyay. 'I don't know what is going on but something certainly is, and I am not going to be a part of it.' She had as acute a nose for what she called 'intellectual squalor and academic sordor' as for faulty plumbing.

Professor Mishra was staring at her in outrage. Her treasonous ingratitude to him was beyond belief.

'I think you should discuss matters coolly,' he spluttered.

'Coolly?' cried Dr Ila Chattopadhyay. 'Coolly? If there is one thing I cannot stand, it is rudeness!' Seeing that Professor Mishra had been floored by this remark, she continued: 'And if there is one thing I refuse to deny, it is merit. That young man has merit. He knows his subject. I am sure he makes a very stimulating teacher. And from his folder and the number of committees he is sitting on and the extracurricular activities he is involved in, it does not appear to me that he does not pull his weight in the department or the university. Rather the opposite. He should get the job. Outside panellists like Professor Jaikumar and myself are here as a check on academic—' she was about to say 'rascality' but changed it in mid-flight to 'irresponsibility', before continuing—'I am sorry, I am a very stupid woman, but one thing I have learned is that when it is necessary to speak, one must. If we cannot come to a proper decision and you force your candidate through, I will insist that you put down in your report that the experts disagreed with you—'

Even Professor Jaikumar looked shocked. 'Self-control leads to heaven,' he murmured to himself in Tamil, 'but uncontrolled passion is the road to endless darkness.' No one ever voted on these matters. They were decided by consensus. Voting meant that the matter would have to be put up to the Executive Council of the university for a decision, and no one wanted that. This was rocking the boat with a vengeance. It would mean the end of all stability, all order. Professor Mishra looked at Dr Ila Chattopadhyay as if he would not mind jettisoning her forthwith—and hoped that the water was infested with jellyfish.

'Yif I may speak—' It was Professor Jaikumar, actually interrupting, which was something he almost never did. 'I do not feel a minority report by the outside yexperts is called for. But there should be a proper decision.' He paused. He was a genuinely learned man of deep and unflamboyant probity, and he had been greatly upset by his tête-à-tête with his host the previous evening. He had decided there and then that whoever he selected, it would not be the man who had been so irregularly recommended to him. 'Should we not think of a third candidate?'

'Of course not,' said Dr Ila Chattopadhyay, in whom the zest of battle now raged warmly: 'Why select someone third-rate as a compromise when we have a first-rate man at hand?'

'Certainly, yit is true,' said Professor Jaikumar, 'as yit says in the Tirukural'—and here he paused to translate—'that after assessing that this man can do this task because of this competence he has, and this tool he can use, that task must be assigned to that man. But yit also says: "Yit is a part of wisdom to conform to the ways of the world." But in yet another place yit says—'

The telephone rang. Professor Mishra sprang up. The Vice-Chancellor reached out for the phone. 'Vice-Chancellor here. . . . I'm sorry, I'm in a meeting. . . . Oh, it's for you, Professor Mishra. Were you expecting a call?'

'Er, yes, I asked the doctor to call me—well, yes—Mishra speaking.'

18.11

'You old jackal!' said Badri Nath on the phone. 'I heard all that.'

'Er, yes, Doctor, well, what news?' said Professor Mishra in Hindi.

'Bad.'

Professor Mishra's jaw dropped. Everyone looked at him. The others in the room tried to talk, but it was impossible for them not to listen to his side of the conversation.

'I see. How bad?'

'The counting went alphabetically. It stopped after Kapoor and just before Khan.'

'Then how do you know who—'

'Mahesh Kapoor got 15,575 votes. There aren't enough votes left for Waris Khan to defeat him. Mahesh Kapoor is bound to win.'

Professor Mishra's free hand went to his forehead. Beads of sweat began to form on it.

'What do you mean? How do you know? Could you go a little slowly for me? I'm not used to the terminology.'

'All right, Professor. You will need to ask the Vice-Chancellor for a pen and some paper.' Badri Nath, though obviously unhappy about the result of his inquiries, was nevertheless extracting what little enjoyment he could out of the situation.

'I have them here,' said Professor Mishra. He took a pen and an envelope out of his pocket. 'Please go slowly.'

Badri Nath sighed. 'Why don't you simply accept what I'm saying?' he asked.

Professor Mishra wisely refrained from replying: 'Because you told me this very morning to accept that he'd lost, and now you're telling me to accept that he's won.' He said: 'I'd like to know how you came to this conclusion.'

Badri Nath relented. After another sigh, he said, very slowly and carefully:

'Please listen carefully, Professor. There are 66,918 voters. Given a very high turn-out for this part of the country, say, fifty-five per cent, that would mean a total of 37,000 votes cast in the election. Shall I go on? The first five candidates have been counted. Their total comes to 19,351. That leaves about 18,700 for the last five candidates. Apart from Waris, the other four are bound to get at least 5,000 votes: they include the socialist and the Jan Sangh candidate as well as a fairly popular and well-funded Independent. So what does that leave for Waris Khan, Professor Sahib? Less than 14,000. And Mahesh Kapoor has already got 15,575.' He paused, then continued: 'Too bad. Chacha Nehru's visit turned the tide. Do you want me to repeat the figures?'

'No, no, thank you. When does—when does it resume?'

'When does what resume? You mean the counting?'

'Yes. The treatment.'

'Tomorrow.'

'Thank you. May I call you later this evening?'

'Yes, of course. I'll be in the casualty department,' cackled Badri Nath, and put down the phone.

Professor Mishra sat down heavily in his chair.

'Not bad news, I hope,' said Professor Jaikumar. 'Both your sons looked so well yesterday.'

'No, no—' said Professor Mishra bravely, mopping his forehead. 'We all have our private crosses to bear. But we must press on with our duty. I am so sorry for keeping you all waiting.'

'Not at all,' said Dr Ila Chattopadhyay, thinking that she'd been a bit rough on the poor, pulpy fellow who had, after all, once encouraged her. Really, though, she thought to herself, he can't be allowed to get away with this.

But it now appeared that Professor Mishra was no longer vociferously opposed to Pran. He even found one or two good things to say about him. Dr Ila Chattopadhyay wondered if, in the face of possible minority dissension and scandal, he had merely succumbed to the inevitable—or if perhaps his son's ill health had brought him face to face with his own uncertain soul.

By the end of the meeting, Professor Mishra had regained some of his air of placidity; he was still staggered, however, by the turn of events.

'You have left your telephone numbers behind,' said Professor Jaikumar, handing him his envelope as he walked to the door.

'Oh, yes—' said Professor Mishra. 'Thank you.'

Later, when he was packing hurriedly for his train, Professor Jaikumar was startled to see both Professor Mishra's sons playing about outside, looking as robust as ever.

At the station Professor Jaikumar recalled, apropos of nothing, that telephone numbers in Brahmpur had three, not five, digits.

How peculiar, he said to himself. But he was never to solve either mystery.

Professor Mishra, pleading a previous appointment, had not gone with him to the railway station. Instead, after a few words in private with the Vice-Chancellor, he had walked over to Pran's house. He was resigned to congratulating him.

'My dear boy,' he said, taking both Pran's hands in his. 'It was a close thing, a very close thing. Some of the other candidates were truly excellent, but, well, I believe we have an understanding, you and I, an equation, as it were, and—well, I should not be telling you this until the seal of the envelope containing our decision is broken in the Academic Council—not that your own excellent, er, performance, did not contribute as much to our decision as my own humble words on your behalf—' Professor Mishra sighed before continuing: 'There was opposition. Some people said you were too young, too untried. "The atrocious crime of being a young man . . ." et cetera. But quite apart from the question of merit, at such a sad time for your family one feels a sense of obligation, one feels one has to do one's bit. I am not one who talks of humanity in exaggerated terms, but, well—was it not the great Wordsworth who talked about those "little nameless unremembered acts of kindness and of love"?'

'I believe it was,' said Pran, slowly and wonderingly, as he shook Professor Mishra's pale and perspiring hands.

18.12

Mahesh Kapoor was at the Collectorate at Rudhia when the count for the Salimpur-cum-Baitar election opened. He had got there late, but the District Magistrate had himself been unavoidably delayed: owing to a problem with the ignition, his jeep had broken down. The counting officers, having grouped all the ballot boxes of each candidate together, now began with the first candidate, who was an Independent named Iqbal Ahmad. They emptied one of his ballot boxes on to each of several tables, and—watched carefully by the counting agents of all the candidates—began simultaneously to count his votes.

Secrecy was enjoined on everyone under the canopy, but of course nothing was secret, and news soon leaked out that Iqbal Ahmad was doing as badly as expected. Since the ballot papers in the first General Elections were not stamped by the voter but simply placed in a candidate's box, very few ballot papers were rejected as spoiled. Counting continued briskly, and, had it begun on time, should have been over by midnight. But it was now eleven o'clock, everyone was exhausted, and the Congress candidate's ballot boxes had not yet been completely counted. He was making an unexpectedly good showing: over 14,000 votes, and several more boxes to go.

In some of Mahesh Kapoor's boxes, astonishingly, there was even, in addition to the ballot papers, a little red powder and a few coins. Presumably, some pious peasants, seeing the holy cattle featured on his box, had placed small offerings inside the slot together with their vote.

While the count was continuing under the careful supervision of the District Magistrate and the Sub-Divisional Officer, Mahesh Kapoor walked over to Waris, who was looking very worried, and said: 'Adaab arz, Waris Sahib.'

'Adaab arz,' replied Waris pugnaciously. The 'Sahib' had surely been ironic.

'Is everything all right with Firoz?'

It was said without any rancour, but Waris felt a burning sense of shame; he thought immediately of the pink fliers.

'Why do you ask?' he demanded.

'I wanted to know,' said Mahesh Kapoor sorrowfully. 'I have very little news of him, and I thought you would. I do not see the Nawab Sahib anywhere. Does he plan to come?'

'He is not a candidate,' said Waris bluntly. 'Yes, Firoz is fine.' He turned his eyes downwards, unable to look Mahesh Kapoor in the face.

'I am glad,' said Mahesh Kapoor. He was about to send his good wishes, then thought better of it and turned away.

A little before midnight, the results stood as follows:

1. Iqbal Ahmad	Independent	608
2. Mir Shamsher Ali	Independent	481
3. Mohammed Hussain	KMPP	1,533
4. Shanti Prasad Jha	Ram Rajya Parishad	1,154
5. Mahesh Kapoor	Congress	15,575

At midnight, just after Mahesh Kapoor's boxes had all been counted, the District Magistrate, as Returning Officer, declared the poll temporarily suspended as part of a nationwide mark of respect for King George VI. He had told the candidates and their counting agents a couple of hours earlier that he had orders to this effect, and asked for their patience. The suspense was terrible, especially since Waris Khan came immediately after Mahesh Kapoor alphabetically; but, owing to the timely warning, there were no protests. He got the counted ballots and the uncounted ballot boxes locked up separately under his own seal in the treasury, and announced that they would be unlocked and the count resumed on the 8th of February.

The results so far determined were bound to leak out, and in both Brahmpur and the constituency most people made the same sort of reckoning that Professor Mishra's informant had. Mahesh Kapoor too was optimistic. He stayed on his farm at Rudhia, talking to his farm manager as he walked around the wheat fields.

On the morning of the 8th, he woke up with a sense of freshness and thankfulness, a sense that at least one of his burdens had been lifted off his shoulders.

18.13

The count proceeded once more, and by the time Waris's vote had reached 10,000, it began to appear that the contest would in fact be close. Apparently, in the areas immediately surrounding Baitar town, the voting rate had been far in excess of fifty-five per cent—a figure which, to go by other elections whose results had been announced earlier in the week, was itself very high.

By the time it had reached 14,000 and there were a number of ballot boxes still to be counted, a great sense of unease overtook the Congress camp. The District Magistrate had to tell everyone to be quiet and to let his counting agents proceed; if not, he would have to suspend the count again.

This had some effect, but by the time the vote had reached 15,000 there was a tremendous hubbub. Some of the more feisty Congress workers had started challenging entire ballot boxes. Mahesh Kapoor told them sharply to stop their antics. But his face betrayed his dismay, for by now he feared he would lose. The other side had begun cheering in anticipation of surpassing the magic number. They did not have long to wait.

There were still several of Waris's boxes left to count when the tally reached 15,576. Waris jumped on to a table and shouted for joy. He was raised high on the shoulders of his supporters, and outside the District Headquarters they began to shout to the well-known pattern:

'The MLA from Baitar, who should he be?'

'Waris Khan Sahib, one such as he!'

Waris, delighted to win, delighted to have 'Khan Sahib' appended to his name, and delighted to have avenged the young Nawabzada, was grinning away, having in the flush of victory forgotten his dirty trick with the posters.

He was soon brought literally down to earth by the District Magistrate, who threatened to throw him out of the Collectorate unless his supporters stopped the ruckus. Waris calmed his followers down, and told one or two of them: 'Let's see, let's see, now that I'm an MLA, who gets thrown out of the Collectorate first, him or me.'

Several Congressmen now urged Mahesh Kapoor, who so far had not lodged a complaint or an election petition, to do so immediately—to challenge the election result. It was clear that, even if nowhere else, in the hinterland of Baitar town the false and flimsy posters announcing Firoz's death had had a devastating effect in getting people out of their huts and houses to vote for Waris.

But Mahesh Kapoor, bitter and disillusioned, and not wishing to create further bitterness, refused to lodge an election petition. Waris had got 16,748 votes; the difference was too great to justify even requesting a re-count. After a while he went over to congratulate his rival; he looked shattered, the more so because of his premonition that morning. Waris accepted his congratulations graciously and calmly. Victory had wiped out his sense of shame.

Only after the counting of all the candidates' votes was complete did the District Magistrate officially declare Waris Khan the winner. The radio announced the news in the evening. The final result was as follows:

SALIMPUR-CUM-BAITAR (District Rudhia, Purva Pradesh)
LEGISLATIVE ASSEMBLY ELECTION

No. of seats: 1		
No. of candidates:	total: 10	contesting: 10
No. of electors:		66,918
Total no. of valid votes polled:		40,327
Voting rate:		60.26%

NAME (in English alphabetical order)	PARTY/ INDEPENDENT	VOTES	% OF VOTES
1. Iqbal Ahmad	Independent	608	1.51
2. Mir Shamsher Ali	Independent	481	1.19
3. Mohammed Hussain	KMPP	1,533	3.80
4. Shanti Prasad Jha	Ram Rajya Parishad	1,154	2.86
5. Mahesh Kapoor	Congress	15,575	38.62
6. Waris Mohammad Khan	Independent	16,748	41.53

7. Mahmud Nasir	Communist	774	1.92
8. Madan Mohan Pandey	Independent	1,159	2.87
9. Ramlal Sinha	Socialist	696	1.73
10. Ramratan Srivastava	Jan Sangh	1,599	3.97

Name of successful candidate: Waris Mohammad Khan

18.14

At Baitar Fort that night there was jubilation.

Waris had an immense bonfire built in the grounds, ordered a dozen sheep and a dozen goats to be slaughtered, invited everyone who had helped him or voted for him to come to the feast, and then added that even the bastards who had voted against him were welcome to join in. He was cautious enough not to serve alcohol, but he himself greeted his guests royally drunk, and made a speech—he was by now proficient at speech-making—about the nobility of the house of Baitar, the excellence of the electorate, the glory of God and the wonder of Waris.

About what he planned to do in the State Assembly he was silent; but in his own mind he was certain that he would learn the legislative ropes as quickly as he had mastered the pulling of electoral strings.

The oily munshi sanctioned all the expenses he demanded, had the grand archway of the Fort festooned with flowers, and greeted Waris with folded hands and tears in his eyes. He had always loved Waris, he had always known of the hidden greatness in him, and now at last his prayers for him had been answered. He fell at his feet and begged Waris for his blessings, and Waris, slurred and benevolent, said:

'All right, you sister-fucker, I bless you. Now get up or I'll be sick all over you.'

18.15

Mahesh Kapoor sat in his garden at Prem Nivas one afternoon a few days after the count. He was talking to Abdus Salaam. He looked very weary. The many implications of his loss were coming home to him. He felt that his occupation was gone, the thing that gave his life vigour and direction and the capacity to do good. His wing of the state Congress Party would have to do without his guidance in the legislature. His loss of power affected not only his own pride but would affect his ability to help his son, soon to be charged with he knew not what. The loss of his friendship with the Nawab Sahib was another bitter blow; he felt sad and ashamed of what had happened to Firoz—and to the Nawab Sahib himself. And every moment he spent in Prem Nivas, especially in the garden, could not fail to remind him of the loss of his wife.

He looked at the sheet of paper in his hand; it contained the various figures describing the election he had fought. For a few minutes he succeeded in discussing them with Abdus Salaam with something of his old interest and objectivity. If the KMPP had dissolved itself and rejoined the Congress, as Mahesh Kapoor himself had, their combined votes would have defeated Waris. If his wife had been able to help him, she would have made the quiet difference she always did—a couple of thousand votes, if not more. If the poster about Firoz had not been published, or had been published when it was not too late to refute it with the facts, he would still have won. Whatever other rumours Mahesh Kapoor had come to believe about his friend, he refused to believe that the Nawab Sahib had sanctioned that poster. That was Waris and Waris alone; it had to be.

But every thread of his analysis, objective though he attempted to make it, led him back to his own unhappy situation. After a while he closed his eyes and said nothing.

'Waris is an interesting phenomenon,' said Abdus Salaam. '"I know what is moral and yet I do not have the inclination for it, and I know what is immoral and yet do not have an aversion from it"—as Duryodhana said to Krishna.'

A faint look of exasperation crossed Mahesh Kapoor's face. 'No,' he said, opening his eyes. 'Waris is a different kind of man. He has no sense of evil or immorality as such. I know him. I've been fighting with him and against him. He's the kind who would murder someone over a woman or land or water or a feud—and then give himself up, boasting, "I finished him off!"—and expect everyone to understand.'

'You will remain in politics,' predicted Abdus Salaam.

Mahesh Kapoor laughed shortly. 'Do you think so?' he said. 'I had thought, after my conversation with Jawaharlal, that I might even become Chief Minister. What ambitions! I am not even an MLA. Anyway, I hope you don't let them fob you off with any minor post; you might be a young man, but you've done excellent work and this is your second term. And they'll want two or three Muslims in the Cabinet, no matter whether it's Sharma or Agarwal who is CM.'

'Yes, I suppose that's so,' said Abdus Salaam. 'But I don't think that Agarwal would choose me even at the point of a bayonet.'

'So Sharma is going to Delhi after all?' Mahesh Kapoor noticed a few mynas walking about on the lawn.

'No one knows,' replied Abdus Salaam. 'I don't, anyway. For every rumour, there's an equal and opposite rumour.' He was glad that Mahesh Kapoor was showing at least sporadic interest in the political scene. 'Why don't you go to Delhi for a few days?' he suggested.

'I will stay here,' said Mahesh Kapoor quietly, looking around the garden. Abdus Salaam remembered Maan, and said nothing.

After a while he spoke. 'What happened to your other son and his promotion?' he said.

Mahesh Kapoor shrugged his shoulders. 'He was here this morning with my granddaughter. I asked him. He said he thought things had gone quite well at the interview, that was all.'

Pran, fearing that Professor Mishra might yet be up to something unfathomable, and not daring to believe his report, had decided not to tell anyone—not even Savita—of his supposed selection by the committee. He was afraid of the greater disappointment of his family if the good news turned out to be unfounded. He wished he could have told his father, though. In his black mood it might have done him a little good.

'Well,' said Abdus Salaam. 'You need something good to happen to you now. God brings relief to those who suffer.'

The Arabic word Abdus Salaam naturally used for God reminded Mahesh Kapoor of the use to which religion had been put in his own election battle. Again he closed his eyes and said nothing. He felt sick at heart.

Abdus Salaam uncannily sensed what he was thinking, or so his next remark appeared to indicate. 'Waris's election was determined by prejudice,' he stated. 'You would have felt ashamed to say one word to inflame anyone on the grounds of religion. Waris may at first merely have been a loyal man, but from his use of that poster I would have to say that he became a bad one.'

Mahesh Kapoor sighed again. 'That is a pointless speculation. Anyway, "bad" is too strong a word. He is fond of Firoz, that's all. He's served that family all his life.'

'He will become just as fond of his own position in time,' said Abdus Salaam. 'I will have to face him across the floor of the House soon enough. But what I am curious about is this: how soon will he assert his position against the Nawab Sahib?'

'Well,' said Mahesh Kapoor after a while. 'I don't think he will. But if he does, there's nothing to be done about it. If he's bad, as you say, he's bad.'

Abdus Salaam said: 'Anyway, it is not the prejudices of bad people that are the problem.'

'Ah, and what is the problem then?' said Mahesh Kapoor with a slight smile.

'If only bad people were prejudiced, that would not have such a strong effect. Most people would not wish to imitate them—and so, such prejudices would not have much effect—except in exceptional times. It is the prejudices of good people that are so dangerous.'

'That is too subtle,' said Mahesh Kapoor. 'You should give blame where blame is due. The inflammatory ones are the bad.'

'Ah, but many of the inflammable ones are the otherwise good.'

'I won't argue with you.'

'That is just what I want you to do.'

Mahesh Kapoor made an impatient sound but said nothing.

'The Congress will win seventy per cent of the assembly seats in P.P. You'll soon come back in a by-election,' said Abdus Salaam. 'I suppose people are surprised that you aren't submitting an election petition against the Salimpur result.'

'What people think—' began Mahesh Kapoor, then shook his head.

Abdus Salaam tried one final time to shake his mentor out of his listlessness. He began one of his ruminations, partly because he enjoyed them, mainly because he wanted to strike some spark from the Minister Sahib.

'It is interesting to see how, after just four years of Independence, the Congress has changed so much,' he began. 'Those people who broke their heads fighting for freedom are now breaking each other's. And we have new entrants to the business. If I were a criminal, for example, and I could get into politics profitably and without too much difficulty, I would not say: "I can deal in murder or drugs, but politics is sacred." It would be no more sacred to me than prostitution.'

He looked towards Mahesh Kapoor, who had closed his eyes again. Abdus Salaam went on: 'More and more money is required to fight elections, and politicians will be forced to demand more and more money from businessmen. Then, being corrupt themselves, they won't be able to wipe out corruption in the civil service. They won't even want to. Sooner or later the appointments of judges, election commissioners, the top civil servants and policemen, will be decided by these same corrupt men, and all our institutions will give way. The only hope,' continued Abdus Salaam treasonously, 'is that the Congress will be wiped out two elections from now. . . .'

As at a concert a single false note sung outside the strict scope of a raag can wake up a listener who is apparently asleep, so too Abdus Salaam's last assertion made Mahesh Kapoor open his eyes.

'Abdus Salaam, I am not in a mood to argue with you. Don't make idle statements.'

'Everything I have said is possible. I would say probable.'

'The Congress won't be wiped out.'

'Why not, Minister Sahib? We have got less than fifty per cent of the vote. Next time our opponents will understand electoral arithmetic better and will band together. And Nehru, our vote-catcher, will be dead by then, or retired. He won't last five years more in this job. He will be burned out.'

'Nehru will outlive me, and probably you,' said Mahesh Kapoor.

'Should we take a bet on that?' said Abdus Salaam.

Mahesh Kapoor stirred restlessly. 'Are you trying to get me angry?' he said.

'Just a friendly bet.'

'Now please leave.'

'All right, Minister Sahib. I'll come by again tomorrow at the same time.'

Mahesh Kapoor said nothing.

After a while he looked out at the garden. The kachnar tree was just coming into blossom: the buds looked like long green pods with a slight hint of deep mauve where the flowers would burst forth. Scores of small squirrels were either running around or on the tree, playing with each other. The sunbird, as usual, was flying in and out of the pomelo tree; and from somewhere a barbet was calling insistently. Mahesh Kapoor did not know either the Hindi or the English names of the birds and flowers that surrounded him, but perhaps in his present state of mind he enjoyed the garden more truly for that. It was his only refuge, and a nameless, wordless one, with birdsong its only sound—and it was dominated, when he closed his eyes, by the least intellectualizable sense—that of scent.

When his wife had been alive she had occasionally asked him for his opinion before laying out a new bed or planting a new tree. This had only served to annoy Mahesh Kapoor. 'Do whatever you want,' he had snapped. 'Do I ask you for your opinion on my files?' After a while she had ceased to ask for his advice.

But to Mrs Mahesh Kapoor's great if quiet delight and to the frustration of her various more imposing competitors, who could not understand what she had over them by way of resources or expertise or foreign seeds, the garden at Prem Nivas had won numerous prizes in the Flower Show year after year; and this year would win the First Prize as well, for the first and, needless to say, the last time.

18.16

On the front wall of Pran's house, the yellow jasmine had begun to bloom. Inside, Mrs Rupa Mehra muttered, 'Plain, purl, plain, purl. Where's Lata?'

'She's gone out to buy a book,' said Savita.

'Which book?'

'I don't think she knows yet. A novel, probably.'

'She shouldn't be reading novels but studying for her exams.'

This was, as it happened, what the bookseller was telling Lata at almost the same moment. Luckily for his business, students rarely took his advice.

He reached out for the book with one hand, and extracted wax from his ear with the other.

'I've studied enough, Balwantji,' said Lata. 'I'm tired of my studies. In fact, I'm tired of everything,' she ended dramatically.

'You look just like Nargis when you say that,' said Balwant.

'I am afraid I only have a five-rupee note.'

'Don't worry,' said Balwant. 'Where is your friend Malatiji?' he continued. 'I never see her these days.'

'That's because she's not wasting her time buying novels,' said Lata. 'She's studying hard. I hardly see her myself.'

Kabir entered the shop, looking quite cheerful. He noticed Lata and stopped.

The whole of their last meeting flashed before Lata's eyes—and, immediately afterwards, their first meeting in the bookstore. They looked at each other for a few seconds before Lata broke the silence with a hello.

'Hello,' replied Kabir. 'I see you're on your way out.' Here was another meeting brought about by coincidence, and to be governed, no doubt, by awkwardness.

'Yes,' said Lata. 'I came in to buy a Wodehouse, but I've bought myself a Jane Austen instead.'

'I'd like you to have a coffee with me at the Blue Danube.' It was a statement more than a request.

'I have to get back,' said Lata. 'I told Savita I'd be back in an hour.'

'Savita can wait. I was going to buy a book, but that too can wait.'

'Which book?' asked Lata.

'What does it matter?' replied Kabir. 'I don't know. I was just going to browse. Not in Poetry or Mathematics, though,' he added.

'All right,' said Lata recklessly.

'Good. The cake will be better, at least. Of course, I don't know what excuse you'll make if someone you know walks in.'

'I don't care,' said Lata.

'Good.'

The Blue Danube was just a couple of hundred yards along Nabiganj. They sat down and placed their orders.

Neither spoke. Finally Lata said:

'Good news about the cricket.'

'Excellent.' India had just won the fifth Test match against England in Madras by an innings and eight runs, and no one could quite believe it.

After a while the coffee came. Stirring it slowly, Kabir said: 'Were you serious?'

'About what?'

'You are writing to this man?'

'Yes.'

'How serious is it?'

'Ma wants me to marry him.'

Kabir said nothing, but looked down at his right hand as it kept stirring the coffee.

'Aren't you going to say something?' she asked him.

He shrugged.

'Do you hate me?' asked Lata. 'Don't you care whom I marry?'

'Don't be stupid.' Kabir sounded disgusted with her. 'And please stop those tears. They won't improve your coffee or my appetite.' For again, though she was half unconscious of them, tears had slowly filled Lata's eyes and were falling down her cheeks one by one. She did not try to wipe them away, nor did she take her eyes off Kabir's face. She did not care what the waiters or anyone else thought. Or even he, for that matter.

He continued to stir his coffee with a troubled look.

'I know of two mixed marriages—' he began.

'Ours wouldn't work. No one else will let it work. And now I can't even trust myself.'

'Then why are you sitting here with me?' he said.

'I don't know.'

'And why are you crying?'

Lata said nothing.

'My handkerchief is dirty,' said Kabir. 'If you haven't brought a handkerchief, use that napkin.'

Lata dabbed at her eyes.

'Come on, eat your cake, it'll do you good. I'm the one who's been rejected, and I'm not sobbing my poor little heart out.'

She shook her head. 'Now I must go,' she said. 'Thank you.'

Kabir did not try to dissuade her.

'Don't leave your book behind,' he said. '*Mansfield Park*? I haven't read that one. Tell me if it's any good.'

Neither of them turned around to look at the other as Lata walked towards the door.

18.17

So unsettled was Lata by her meeting with Kabir—but when was she not unsettled by a meeting with him? she wondered—that she took a long walk near the banyan tree. She sat down on the great, twisted root, remembered their first kiss, read some poetry, fed the monkeys, and fell into a reverie.

Walks are my panacea, she thought, bitterly; and my substitute for any decisive action.

The next day, however, she took action of the most decisive kind.

Two letters arrived for Lata by the morning post. She sat on the verandah with its trellis of yellow jasmine and slit open both envelopes. Mrs Rupa Mehra was not at home when they arrived, or she would have recognized the handwriting on the envelopes and demanded to know what news they contained.

The contents of the first envelope consisted of eight lines and a heading, typewritten and unsigned:

A MODEST PROPOSAL

As you've asked for black and white,
May I send these lines to you
In the tacit hope you might
Take my type at least as true.

Let this distance disappear
And our hearts approach from far
Till we come to be as near
As acrostically we are.

Lata began to laugh. The poem was a little trite, but it was skilful and entirely personalized, and it pleased her. She tried to recall exactly what she had said; had she really asked for black and white or merely told Amit that that was all she would believe? And how serious was this 'modest' proposal? After thinking the matter over, she was inclined to believe it was serious; and, as a result, it pleased her somewhat less.

Would she have preferred it to be determinedly sombre and passionate—or not to have been written in the first place? Would a passionate proposal have been in Amit's style at all—or at least in his style with her? Many of his poems were far from light in either sense of the word, but it seemed almost as if he hid that side of himself from her for fear that looking into that dark, pessimistic cynicism might trouble her too greatly and make her shy away.

And yet, what was it he had said about her own poem, the despairing one that she had hesitantly shown him? That he had liked it—but only, he had implied, as a poem. If he disapproved of gloom, what was he doing as a poet? Would he not—at least for his own sake—have been far better off in the practical profession of law? But perhaps he did not disapprove of gloom as such in himself or others, only on the fruitless dwelling on it—which, she had to admit, that poem of hers had been guilty of. Clearly, the unhappiness or unease of Amit's own strongest poems was typical not of his daily behaviour but of certain moments of intensity. Still, Lata felt that high hills rarely rise direct and isolated from the plains, and that there had to be some deeper organic connection between the poet of 'The Fever Bird' and Amit Chatterji as she knew him than he himself encouraged herself or others to believe.

And what would it be like to be married to such a man? Lata got up and paced restlessly about the verandah. How could she consider him seriously—Meenakshi and Kuku's brother, her own friend and guide to Calcutta, the purveyor of pineapples, the castigator of Cuddles? He was just Amit—to convert him into a husband was absurd—the thought of it made Lata smile and shake her head. But again she sat down, and again she read the poem, and she looked out beyond the hedge to the campus, from where the sloped and slated roof of the examination hall was distantly visible. She realized that she had the poem by heart already—as she had his earlier acrostic, and 'The Fever Bird', and other poems besides. Without any attempt on her part to learn them, they had become a part of herself.

18.18

The second letter was from Haresh.

My dearest Lata,

I hope everything is well with you and with the family. I have been so busy with work these last few weeks that I have come home exhausted, and not been in that state of mind in which you deserve to hear from me. But the Goodyear Welted line is going from strength to strength, and I have even persuaded the management to take on a new scheme of mine, by which entire uppers can be made outside and assembled for final manufacture here at Praha. Of course, that would be in other lines, such as brogues. All in all, I think I have already shown them that it was not a mistake to take me on, and that I am not merely someone imposed on them by Mr Khandelwal.

I have some good news to convey. There is talk of promoting me to Group Foreman soon. If so, it will not come a moment too soon, as I find it difficult to keep down my expenses. I am a bit lavish by nature, and it will be good if someone helps me to curb it. If that is so, then it will certainly be true what they say, that two can live cheaper than one.

I have talked to Arun and Meenakshi a few times on the phone, although the line from Prahapore to Calcutta is not as clear as it could be. They have unfortunately been busy with various engagements, but they have promised to make time to come for dinner sometime in the near future.

My own family is well. My doubting Umesh Uncle has been impressed by my obtaining a job like this one so quickly. My foster-mother, who is really like a real mother to me, is also pleased. I remember when I went to England first, she said: 'Son, people go to England to become doctors, engineers, barristers. Why do you need to go all the way to become a cobbler?' I could not help smiling at the time, and even now I smile when I think of it. I am happy, however, that I am not a burden on them, that I am standing on my own two feet, and that my work is useful in its own circle.

You will be glad to know that I have given up eating paan. I was warned by Kalpana that your family does not think it attractive, and, whatever I think about it, I have decided to be accommodating in this respect. I hope you are impressed by all these efforts of mine to Mehra-ise myself.

There is something I have not touched upon in either of my last two letters, and it is good of you not to have mentioned its absence. As you know, I was very upset about a word you used, which I realize in retrospect you did not intend as I took it. I wrote to Kalpana about it that same evening, because I felt the need to unburden myself. For some reason I was also uneasy in general. She ticked me off for my 'thick-skinned sensitivity' (she had a way with words even in college) and told me I should apologize at once and not be truculent. Well, I did not feel sorry, so I did not write it. But now with the passing of the weeks I realise that I was in the wrong.

I am a practical man and I am proud of it—but sometimes I come across situations that I do not know how to handle despite my well-formed opinions, and I find that after all perhaps there is less reason to be proud than I thought. So please accept my apologies, Lata, and forgive me for ending New Year's Day in such an unpleasing manner.

I hope that when we get married—I am hoping that it is *when*, and not *if*—you will tell me, with that lovely quiet smile of yours, whenever I take things amiss that are not badly intended.

Baoji has been asking me about my marriage plans, but on that score I have not been able to reassure him as yet. As soon as you are sure in your mind that I would make you the right husband, please do tell me. I give thanks every day that I should have met you and that you and I should have got to know each other through words and meetings. The feelings I have for you increase every day, and, unlike my shoes, do not take Saturday and Sunday off. Needless to say, I have your framed photograph on my desk before me, and it brings to me tender thoughts of the original.

Apart from what one sometimes reads in the Calcutta papers, I have had a little news of the Kapoor family in the course of some business dealings with Kedarnath, and my deep sympathy goes to all of them. It must be a terrible time for everyone. He says that Veena and Bhaskar are most agitated, but he makes light of his own anxieties. I can also imagine how hard it is for Pran, with his brother's difficulties and the death of his mother coming side by side. It is good that Savita has her baby and her law studies to provide other thoughts, but it could not be easy to concentrate, especially on some subject as hard as law. I do not know what I can do to help in any way, but if there is anything I can do, please tell me. Some things—the latest law-books and so on—are available in Calcutta more easily than in Brahmpur, I think.

I hope you are studying somehow through all this. I am keeping my fingers crossed for you and am very confident, my Lata, that you will come out in flying colours.

My love to Ma, whom I often thank in my mind for bringing you to Kanpur, and to Pran and Savita and the baby. Please tell Kedarnath if you happen to meet him that I will be writing to him very shortly, probably within the week, depending on certain consultations at this end.

With all my love,
Your own,
Haresh

18.19

As Lata read, she smiled to herself from time to time. He had crossed out 'Cawnpore' to write 'Kanpur'. When she came to the end she read it through once more. She was glad to hear about Umesh Uncle and his resolved doubts. She could imagine Haresh's father demanding a similar resolution to his own.

Over the months her world had begun to be populated by the various people Haresh continually mentioned. She even missed Simran; Haresh had probably left her out of this letter for fear of treading on her sensitivities. But Lata realized with a start that, however much she liked Haresh, she was not jealous of Simran.

And who were these people in reality? She thought of Haresh: generous, robust, optimistic, impatient, responsible. There he stood in Prahapore, as solid as a pair of Goodyear Welted shoes, twinkling his eyes affectionately at her from the pages of his letter and telling her as well as he could that he was lonely without her.

But Haresh stood alone: Umesh Uncle, Simran, his foster-father, all these figures whom she felt she knew, could turn out to be entirely different from what she had imagined. And his family of conservative Old Delhi khatris: how could she possibly behave with them as she behaved with Kuku or Dipankar or Mr Justice Chatterji? What would she talk about to the Czechs? But there was something adventurous in losing herself entirely in a world that she did not know with a man whom she trusted and had begun to admire—and who cared for her so deeply and steadily. She thought of a paan-less Haresh, smiling his open smile; she sat him down at a table so that she could not see his co-respondent shoes; she ruffled his hair a bit, and—well, he was quite attractive! She liked him. Perhaps, given time and luck, she could even learn to love him.

18.20

A letter from Arun arrived in the afternoon post and helped clarify her thoughts:

My dear Lata,

You will not mind if I take an elder brother's prerogative to write to you on a matter of great importance to your future and to the future of the family. We are, as such things go, an exceptionally close family, and perhaps as a result of Daddy's death we have been forced even closer together. I, for example, would not have taken on the responsibilities that I have, had Daddy been alive. Varun would probably not have been staying with me, nor would I feel it incumbent on myself to advise him about finding a direction in life, something that left to himself he would, I am afraid, be disinclined to do. Nor would I have the sense that I am, in a manner of speaking, in loco parentis to you.

I imagine you have already guessed the matter I am referring to. Suffice it to say that I have thought about it from every possible angle, and I find myself in disagreement with Ma's judgement on the subject. Hence this letter. Ma has too great a tendency to be swayed by sentiment, and she appears to have taken an irrationally strong liking to Haresh—as well as a strong antipathy—irrational or otherwise—to other people. I experienced something similar in her attitude to my own marriage, which, contrary to her expectations, has turned out to be a happy one based on mutual affection and trust. I believe that as a result I have gained a more objective sense of the choices facing you.

Apart from your temporary infatuation with a certain person in Brahmpur, about which the less said the better, you do not have much experience of the tangled thickets of life, nor have you had the chance to develop criteria for judging the alternatives unguided. It is in this context that I am proffering my advice.

I believe that Haresh has some excellent qualities. He is hardworking, he is in some sense self-made, and he has been educated at—or has at least obtained a degree from—one of the better colleges in India. He is, from all accounts, competent at the trade he has chosen. He has confidence, and he is unafraid to speak his mind. One must give the man his due. That said, however, let me make it clear that I believe that he would not make a suitable addition to our family, and for the following reasons:

1. Despite his having studied English at St Stephen's and having lived in England for two years, his use of the English language leaves a great deal to be desired. This is no trivial point. Conversation between man and wife is the staple of a marriage based on true

understanding. They must be able to communicate, to be, as they say, on the same wave-length. Haresh is simply not on the same wave-length as you—or any of us for that matter. This is not merely a question of his accent, which immediately betrays the fact that English is very far from being his first language; it is a question of his idiom and diction, of his very sense, sometimes, of what is being said. I am glad I was not present at home when that ludicrous fracas about the word 'mean' took place but, as you know, Ma informed me (with many tears and in great detail) about what had occurred the moment Meenakshi and I returned home. If you take the view that Mother knows best, and become engaged to this man, you will continually face painful and absurd situations of this kind.

2. A second, not unrelated, point, is that Haresh does not, and can never aspire to, move in the same social circles as we do. A foreman is not a covenanted assistant, and Praha is simply not Bentsen Pryce. The smell of leather clings rather too closely to the name; the Czechs, who are his bosses, are technicians, sometimes barely literate in English, not graduates from the best universities in England. In a certain sense, by choosing a trade rather than a profession after his graduation from St Stephen's, Haresh has downgraded himself. I hope you do not mind my speaking frankly on a matter of such importance to your future happiness. Society matters, and society is exacting and cruel; you will find yourself excluded from certain circles simply by virtue of being Mrs Khanna.

Nor can Haresh's own background or demeanour counteract the Praha trademark. Unlike say, Meenakshi or Amit, whose father and grandfather have been High Court judges, his family are small people from Old Delhi, and are, to put it bluntly, entirely undistinguished. Certainly, it does him credit that he has brought himself to where he is; but, being a self-made man, he has a tendency to be rather pleased with himself—indeed, a little bumptious. I have noticed that this is often true of short people; he may well have an additional chip on his shoulder as a result of this. I know that Ma thinks of him as a rough diamond. All I can say is that the cut and polish of a stone matter. One does not wear a rough diamond—or one that is chipped—in a wedding ring.

Family, if I may put it plainly, will out. It shows in Haresh's manner of dress, in his liking for snuff and paan, in the fact that, despite his stint in England, he lacks the small social graces. I warned Ma about family background at the time of Savita's engagement to Pran, but she would not listen; and the result, socially speaking, has been the disgraceful connection, through us, of the family of a jailbird to the family of a judge. This is another reason why I feel it is my duty to speak to you before it is too late.

3. Your future family income will in all likelihood not permit you to send your children to the kind of school—for example, St George's or St Sophia's or Jheel or Mayo or Loreto or Doon—that our children—Meenakshi's and mine—will go to. Besides, even if you could afford it, Haresh may have very different views from you about the upbringing of his children or the proportion of the family budget to be devoted to education. With respect to Savita's husband, since he is an academic, I have no concerns on this particular count. But with Haresh I do, and I have to put them to you. I wish the family to remain close, indeed, I feel responsible for the maintenance of this closeness; and differences in the upbringing of our children are bound to draw us apart in time, and to cause you a great deal of heartache besides.

I must ask you to treat this letter as a personal one; to think deeply about it, as befits its contents, but not to show it around the family. Ma would no doubt take it amiss, and, I suppose, so would Savita. As for the subject of this letter, I will only add that he has been pestering us with offers of hospitality; we have been cool to him, and have so far avoided going to Prahapore for another gargantuan lunch. He should, we believe, not presume to be considered part of the family unless he in fact becomes part of it. Needless to say, the choice is yours, and we would welcome your husband, whoever he happened to be, in our private capacity. But it is no use meaning well if you cannot also speak freely, and that is what I have done in this letter.

Rather than add news and small talk, which can wait for another occasion, I will simply end with my love and fondest hopes for your future happiness. Meenakshi, who agrees with me on all points, does the same.

Yours,
Arun Bhai

Lata read the letter through several times, the first time—owing mainly to Arun's wildly erratic handwriting—very slowly; and, as instructed, she pondered its contents deeply. Her first instinct was to have a heart-to-heart talk with Savita, or Malati, or her mother—or with each of them. Then she decided that it would make no difference and would, if anything, only serve to confuse her. This decision was hers to make.

She wrote to Haresh the same evening, accepting with gratitude—and, indeed, warmth—his often repeated offer of marriage.

18.21

'No!' cried Malati, staring at Lata. 'No! I refuse to believe it. Have you posted the letter yet?'

'Yes,' said Lata.

They were sitting in the shadow of the Fort on the Pul Mela sands, looking out over the warm, grey Ganga, which was glinting in the sunlight.

'You are mad—absolutely mad. How could you do it?'

'Don't be like my mother—"O my poor Lata, O my poor Lata!"'

'Was that her reaction? I thought she was keen on Haresh,' said Malati. 'Trust you to do just what Mummy says. But I won't have it, Lata, you can't ruin your life like this.'

'I'm not ruining my life,' said Lata heatedly. 'And yes, that might well be her reaction. She's taken against Haresh for some reason. And Arun's been against him from the beginning. But no, Mummy didn't say. In fact, Mummy doesn't even know. You're the first person I'm telling, and you shouldn't be trying to make me feel miserable.'

'I should. I should. I hope you feel really miserable,' said Malati, her eyes flashing green fire. 'Then perhaps you'll see some sense and undo what you've done. You love Kabir, and you must marry him.'

'There's no must about it. Go and marry him yourself,' said Lata, her cheeks red. 'No—don't! Don't! I'll never forgive you. Please don't talk about Kabir, Malu, please.'

'You're going to regret it bitterly,' said Malati. 'I'm telling you that.'

'Well, that's my look-out,' said Lata, struggling to control herself.

'Why didn't you ask me before you decided?' demanded Malati. 'Whom did you consult? Or did you just make up your silly mind by yourself?'

'I consulted my monkeys,' said Lata calmly.

Malati had the strong urge to slap Lata for making stupid jokes at such a time.

'And a book of poetry,' added Lata.

'Poetry!' said Malati with contempt. 'Poetry has been your complete undoing. You have too good a brain to waste on English literature. No, perhaps you don't, after all.'

'You were the first person to tell me to give him up,' said Lata. 'You told me. Or have you forgotten all that?'

'I changed my mind,' said Malati. 'You know I did. I was wrong, terribly wrong. Look at the danger caused to the world by that sort of attitude—'

'Why do you think I'm giving him up?' asked Lata, turning towards her friend.

'Because he's Muslim.'

Lata didn't answer for a while. Then she said:

'It's not that. It's not just that. There isn't any single reason.'

Malati gave a disgusted snort at this pathetic prevarication.

Lata sighed. 'Malati, I can't describe it—my feelings for him are so confused. I'm not myself when I'm with him. I ask myself who is this—this jealous, obsessed woman who can't get a man out of her head—why should I make myself suffer like this? I know that it'll always be like this if I'm with him.'

'Oh, Lata—don't be blind—' exclaimed Malati. 'It shows how passionately you love him—'

'I don't want to,' cried Lata, 'I don't want to. If that's what passion means, I don't want it. Look at what passion has done to the family. Maan's broken, his mother's dead, his father's in despair. When I thought that Kabir was seeing someone else, what I remember feeling was enough to make me hate passion. Passionately and forever.'

'It's my fault,' said Malati bitterly, shaking her head from side to side. 'I wish to God I'd never written that letter to Calcutta. And you're going to wish the same.'

'It isn't, Malati. And I'm not. Thank God you did.'

Malati looked at Lata with sick unhappiness. 'You just don't realize what you're throwing away, Lata. You're choosing the wrong man. Stay unmarried for a while. Take your time to make up your mind again. Or simply remain unmarried—it's not so tragic.'

Lata was silent. On the side that Malati could not see, she let a handful of sand pass through her fingers.

'What about that other chap?' said Malati. 'That poet, Amit? How has he put himself out of the running?'

Lata smiled at the thought of Amit. 'Well, he wouldn't be my undoing, as you put it, but I don't see myself as his wife at all. We're too alike. His moods veer and oscillate as wildly as mine. Can you imagine the lives of our poor children? And if his mind's on a book I don't know if he'll have any time for me. Sensitive people are usually very insensitive—I should know. As a matter of fact, he's just proposed to me.'

Malati looked shocked and angry.

'You never tell me anything!'

'Everything happened all of a sudden yesterday,' said Lata, fishing Amit's acrostic out of the pocket of her kameez. 'I brought this along, since you usually like to see the documents in the case.'

Malati read it in silence, then said: 'I'd marry anyone who wrote me this.'

'Well, he's still available,' laughed Lata. 'And I won't veto that marriage.' She put her arm around Malati's shoulder before continuing: 'For me, marrying Amit would be madness. Quite apart from everything else, I get more than enough of my brother Arun. To live five minutes away from him would be the ultimate lunacy!'

'You could live somewhere else.'

'Oh no—' said Lata, picturing Amit in his room overlooking the laburnum in bloom. 'He's a poet and a novelist. He wants things laid on for him. Meals, hot water, a running household, a dog, a lawn, a Muse. And why not? After all, he did write "The Fever Bird"! But he won't be able to write if he has to fend for himself away from his family. Anyway, you seem to be happy with anyone but Haresh. Why? Why are you so dead-set against him?'

'Because I see nothing, nothing, nothing at all in common between you two,' said Malati. 'And it's completely obvious you don't love him. Have you thought this thing through, Lata, or are you just making up your mind in a sort of trance? Like that nun business that Ma keeps talking about. Think. Do you like the idea of sharing your possessions with this man? Of making love with him? Does he attract you? Can you cope with the things that irritate you about him—Cawnpore and paan and all that? Please, please, Lata, don't be stupid. Use your brains. What about this Simran woman—doesn't that bother you? And what do you want to do with yourself after your marriage—or are you just content to be a housewife in a walled compound full of Czechs?'

'Do you think I haven't thought about any of this?' said Lata, removing her arm, annoyed once more. 'Or that I haven't tried to visualize what life will be like with him? It'll be interesting, I think. Haresh is practical, he's forceful, he isn't cynical. He gets things done and he helps people without making a fuss about it. He's helped Kedarnath and Veena a great deal.'

'So what? . . . Will he let you teach?'

'Yes, he will.'

'Have you asked him?' pressed Malati.

'No. That's not the best idea,' said Lata. 'But I'm sure of it. I think I know him well enough by now. He hates to see anyone's talent wasted. He encourages them. And he's really concerned about people—about me, about Maan, about Savita and her studies, about Bhaskar—'

'—who, incidentally, is alive today only because of Kabir,' Malati could not resist interposing.

'I don't deny it.' Lata sighed deeply, and looked at the warm sands all around.

For a while neither said anything. Then Malati spoke.

'But what has he done, Lata?' she said quietly. 'What has he done that is wrong—that he should be treated like this? He loves you and he never deserved to be doubted. Is it fair? Just think, is it fair?'

'I don't know,' said Lata slowly, looking over towards the far shore. 'No, it isn't, I suppose. But life isn't always a question of justice, is it? What is that line?—"Use every man after his desert, and who should 'scape whipping?" But it's true the other way around as well. Use every man after his desert and you'll become a complete emotional bankrupt.'

'That's a really mean-spirited view of the world,' said Malati.

'Don't call me mean,' cried Lata passionately.

Malati looked at her in astonishment.

Lata shivered. 'All I meant was, Malati, that when I'm with Kabir, or even away from him but thinking about him, I become utterly useless for anything. I feel I'm out of control—like a boat heading for the rocks—and I don't want to become a wreck.'

'So you're going to instruct yourself not to think of him?'

'If I can,' said Lata, almost to herself.

'What did you say? Speak up,' demanded Malati, wanting to shake her into seeing sense.

'If I can,' said Lata.

'How can you deceive yourself like this?'

Lata was silent.

'Malu, I'm not going to quarrel with you,' she said after a while. 'I care for you as much as I care for any of these men, and I always will. But I'm not going to undo what I've done. I do love Haresh, and—'

'What?' cried Malati, looking at Lata as if she were an imbecile.

'I do.'

'You're full of surprises today,' said Malati, very angry now.

'And, well, you're full of incredulities. But I do. Or I think I do. Thank God it isn't what I feel for Kabir.'

'I don't believe you. You're just making that up.'

'You must. He's grown on me, he really has. I don't find him unattractive. And there's something else—I won't feel I'll be making a fool of myself with him—with regard to, well, with regard to sex.'

Malati stared at her. What a crazy thing to say.

'And with Kabir you will?'

'With Kabir—I just don't know—'

Malati said nothing. She shook her head slowly, not looking at Lata, half lost in her own thoughts.

Lata said: 'Do you know those lines of Clough that go: "There are two different kinds, I believe, of human attraction"?'

Again Malati said nothing but merely shook her head.

'Well, they go something like this:

> There are two different kinds, I believe, of human attraction.
> One that merely excites, unsettles, and makes you uneasy;
> The other that—

Well, I can't remember exactly, but he talks about a calmer, less frantic love, which helps you to grow where you were already growing, "to live where as yet I had languished"—I just read it yesterday, it isn't in my head yet, but it said everything that I couldn't express on my own. Do you understand what I mean? . . . Malati?'

'All I understand,' said Malati, 'is that you can't live on other people's words. You're throwing away the golden casket and the silver one, and you seem to think that you'll be as lucky with the bronze casket as your English literature tells you you'll be. Well, I hope you will, I really hope you will. But you won't be. You won't.'

'You'll grow to like him too, Malu.'

Malati didn't answer.

'You haven't even met him,' continued Lata with a smile. 'And I remember at first you refused to like Pran.'

'I hope you're right.' Malati sounded weary. Her heart was sick for both Lata and Kabir.

'It's more like Nala and Damyanti than Portia and Bassanio,' said Lata, trying to cheer her up. 'Haresh's feet touch the ground, and he has dust and sweat and a shadow. The other two are a bit too God-like and ethereal to be any good for me.'

'So you're at ease,' said Malati, searching her friend's face. 'You're at ease with yourself. And you know exactly what you're going to do. Well, tell me, out of curiosity, before you write him off, are you at least going to drop a line to Kabir?'

Lata's lips began to tremble.

'I'm not at ease—I'm not—' she cried. 'It's not easy—Malu, how can you think it is? I hardly know who I am or what I'm doing—I can't study or even think these days—everything is pressing in on me. I can't bear it when I'm with him, and I can't bear not to see him. How do I know what I may or may not do? I only hope I have the courage to stick to my decision.'

18.22

Maan sat at home or in the garden with his father or visited Pran or Veena. Other than that he did very little. He had been eager to visit Saeeda Bai when he was in jail, but now that he was out of jail, he found that he had inexplicably lost his eagerness to do so. She sent him a note, which he did not reply to. Then she sent him another, more urgent one, upbraiding him for his desertion of her, but to no effect.

Maan was not very fond of reading, but these days he spent whole mornings with the newspapers, reading everything from the international news to the advertisements. Now that Firoz was out of danger he had begun to worry about himself and what was going to happen to him once the charge-sheet was prepared.

Firoz had remained in hospital for about twenty days before the doctors consented to his being moved back to Baitar House. He was physically weak, but on the mend. Imtiaz took charge of him, Zainab stayed on in Brahmpur to nurse him, and the Nawab Sahib watched over him and prayed for his full recovery. For his mind was still clouded and agitated, and he would sometimes cry out in his sleep. These fragments of speech, which would have meant nothing to anyone earlier, could now be fitted into the frame of the rumours by anyone who sat by his bedside.

The Nawab Sahib had turned to religion almost two decades ago partly as the result of his appalled realization of what he had done when he emerged from the worst of his drunken binges, and partly because of the quiet influence of his wife. He had always had a taste for scholarly and analytical pursuits but, being a sensualist, had allowed these to be overlaid by his more urgent needs and pleasures. The change in his life had been sudden; and he had hoped to save his own children from the sins and the repentance that he himself had undergone. The boys knew he did not approve of their drinking, and they never did so in his presence. As for his grandchildren, they would never have been able to imagine him as a young—or even a middle-aged—man. They had known their Nana-jaan throughout their lives as a quiet, pious old man whom only they were permitted to disturb in his library—and who could easily be persuaded to grant them a respite from bedtime by the telling of a ghost story. The Nawab Sahib understood all too well the infidelities of their father and, while his heart went out to his daughter, he was reminded of the suffering he had in his own time inflicted on his own wife. Not that Zainab would have wanted him to speak to her husband. She had needed comfort, but had not expected relief.

The Nawab Sahib now suffered once again, but this time not only from the memory of the past but from the present opinion of the world, and—worst of all—from the sense of what his children must think of him. He did not know what interpretation to place upon the rejection of his continuing financial help to Saeeda Bai. He was more troubled by it than relieved. He did not really think of Tasneem as his daughter, or feel any affection for this unseen being, but he did not want her to suffer. Nor did he wish Saeeda Bai now to feel free to publish to the world whatever it suited her convenience to publish. He begged God to forgive him for the unworthiness of this concern, but he was unable to put it aside.

He had shrunk further into his library in the course of the last month, but every visit to Firoz's bedside and every appearance at meal-time was infinitely painful to him. His children, however, understood this, and continued to be outwardly as respectful towards him as before. Firoz's illness or the acts of the distant past were not to be allowed to split the shell of the family. The grace was said, the meat stew was passed, the kababs served, the permission to rise accepted with routine decorum. Nothing was said or shown to him that might add to his disequilibrium. He had still not heard about the fliers announcing that Firoz had died.

And if I had died, thought Firoz to himself, what would it have mattered to the universe? What have I ever done for anyone? I am a man without attributes, very handsome, very forgettable. Imtiaz is a man of substance, of some use to the world. All that would be left of me is a walking stick, the grief of my family, and terrible danger for my friend.

He had asked to see Maan once or twice, but no one had passed the message on to Prem Nivas. Imtiaz could see no good coming of the meeting, either for his brother or for his father. He knew Maan well enough to realize that the attack had been a sudden one, unpremeditated, almost unintentional. But his father did not see it that way; and Imtiaz wanted to spare him any avoidable shock of emotion, any access of hatred or recrimination. Imtiaz believed that Mrs Mahesh Kapoor's death had indeed been hastened by the sudden and terrible events that had struck their two houses. He would insulate his father from anything similar, and his brother from any agitation about Maan or, through the revival of his memory of that night, about Tasneem.

Tasneem, though she was no doubt his half-sister, meant nothing to Imtiaz at all. Zainab too, though she was curious, realized that wisdom lay in closing the door of interpretation.

Finally, Firoz wrote a note to Maan, which read simply: 'Dear Maan, Please visit me. I'm well enough to see you. Firoz.' He half-suspected his brother of mollycoddling him, and he had had enough of it. He gave the note to Ghulam Rusool, and told him that he was to see that it got to Prem Nivas.

Maan received the note in the late afternoon and did not hesitate. Without telling his father, who was sitting on a bench reading some legislative papers, he walked over to Baitar House. Perhaps this call, rather than a summons from the court of the committal magistrate, was what in his state of idle tension he had been waiting for all along. As he approached the grand main gates, he looked instinctively about him, thinking of the she-monkey who had attacked him here earlier. This time he carried no stick.

A servant asked him to enter. But the Nawab Sahib's secretary, Murtaza Ali, happened to be passing by, and asked him, with stern courtesy, what he imagined he was doing there. He had been given strict orders not to admit anyone from Mahesh Kapoor's family. Maan, whose instinct not very long ago would have been to tell him to go hang himself had been shaken by his jail life into responding to the orders of his social inferiors. He showed him Firoz's note.

Murtaza Ali looked worried but thought quickly. Imtiaz was at the hospital, Zainab was in the zenana, and the Nawab Sahib was at his prayers. The note was unambiguous. He told Ghulam Rusool to take Maan up to see Firoz for a few minutes and asked Maan if he would like something to drink.

Maan would have liked a gallon of whisky to fortify himself. 'No, thank you,' he replied.

Firoz's face lit up when he saw his friend. 'So you've come!' he said. 'I feel I'm in jail here. I've been asking for you for a week, but the Superintendent won't let messages out. I hope you've brought me some whisky.'

Maan started weeping. Firoz looked so pale—really, as if he had just returned from death.

'Have a look at my scar,' Firoz said, trying to lighten the situation. He pushed the bedsheet down and pulled up his kurta.

'Impressive,' said Maan, still in tears. 'Centipede.'

He went to Firoz's bedside, and touched his friend's face.

They talked for a few minutes, each attempting to avoid what might cause the other pain except in such a way as would more probably defuse it.

'You're looking well,' said Maan.

'How poorly you lie,' said Firoz. 'I wouldn't take you on as a client. . . . These days I find I lack concentration. My mind wanders,' he added with a smile. 'It's quite interesting.'

They were silent for a minute. Maan put his forehead to Firoz's and sighed painfully. He did not say how sorry he was for all he had done.

He sat down near Firoz.

'Does it hurt?' he asked.

'Yes, at times.'

'Is everyone at home all right?'

'Yes,' said Firoz. 'How are—how is your father?'

'As well as can be expected,' said Maan.

Firoz did not say how sorry he was about Maan's mother, but shook his head in regret, and Maan understood.

After a while he got up.

'Come again,' said Firoz.

'When? Tomorrow?'

'No—in two or three days.'

'You'll have to send me another note,' said Maan. 'Or I'll be thrown out.'

'Here, give me the old note. I'll revalidate it,' said Firoz with a smile.

As Maan walked home, it struck him that they had avoided talking directly about Saeeda Bai or Tasneem or his experience of prison or the forthcoming case against him, and he was glad.

18.23

That evening, Dr Bilgrami came over to Prem Nivas to have a word with Maan. He told him that Saeeda Bai wished to see him. Dr Bilgrami looked exhausted, and Maan agreed to go with him. The meeting was a painful one.

Saeeda Bai's voice was still not itself, though she had recovered her looks. She reproached Maan for not having visited her since his release from jail. Had he changed so much? she asked with a smile. Had she changed? Had he not received her notes? What had kept him away? She was ill, she was desperate to see him. Her voice broke. She was going mad without him. She impatiently waved Dr Bilgrami away, and turned to Maan with longing and pity. How was he? He looked so thin. What had they done to him?

'Dagh Sahib—what has happened to you? What will happen to you?'

'I don't know.'

He looked around the room. 'The blood?' he asked.

'What blood?' she asked. It had been a month ago.

The room smelt of attar of roses and of Saeeda Bai herself. Sadly and sensuously she leaned back on her cushions against the wall. But Maan thought he saw a scar on her face, and the face itself turned into a portrait of the varicose Victoria.

So shattering had been his mother's death, Firoz's danger, his own disgrace, and his terrible sense of guilt that he had begun to suffer a violent revulsion of feeling against himself and Saeeda Bai. Perhaps he saw her too as a victim. But his greater understanding of events gave him no greater control over his feelings. He had been too deeply scoured by what had occurred, and his present vision of her horrified him. He stared at her face.

I am becoming like Rasheed, he thought. I'm seeing things that don't exist.

He stood up, his face pale. 'I am going,' he said.

'You aren't well,' she said.

'No—no, I'm not,' he said.

Hurt and frustrated by his behaviour, she had been about to rebuke him for his attitude towards her, for what he had done to her household, to her reputation, to Tasneem. But one look at his bewildered face told her it would be no use. He was in another world—beyond the reach of her affections or attractions. She hid her face in her hands.

'Are you all right?' said Maan uncertainly, as if feeling his way to something in the past. 'I am to blame for all that has happened.'

'You don't love me—don't tell me you do—I can see it—' she wept.

'Love—' said Maan. 'Love?' Suddenly he sounded furious.

'And even the shawl that my mother gave me—' said Saeeda Bai.

She was making no sense to him at all.

'Don't let them do anything to you—' she said, refusing to look up, unwilling for once that he should see her tears. Maan looked away.

18.24

On the 29th of February, Maan was brought up before the same magistrate as before. The police had reconsidered their position based on the evidence. Maan had not intended to kill Firoz, but the police now believed that he had intended to cause 'such bodily injury as was sufficient in the ordinary course of nature to cause death'. This was enough to bring him under the hazard of the section dealing with attempted murder. The magistrate was satisfied with the result of the investigation and framed the charges.

> I, Suresh Mathur, Magistrate of the First Class at Brahmpur, hereby charge you, Maan Kapoor, as follows:
>
> That you, on or about the 4th day of January, 1952, at Brahmpur, did an act, to wit, that you did stab with a knife one Nawabzada Firoz Ali Khan of Baitar with such knowledge and under such circumstances, that if by that act you had caused the death of Nawabzada Firoz Ali Khan of Baitar, you would have been guilty of murder and that you caused hurt to the said Nawabzada Firoz Ali Khan of Baitar by the said act, and thereby committed an offence punishable under Section 307 of the Indian Penal Code, and within the cognizance of the Court of Session.
>
> And I hereby direct that you be tried by the said Court on the said charge.

The magistrate also charged Maan with grievous hurt with a deadly weapon. Both these offences carried a possible sentence of imprisonment for life. Neither was bailable, and the magistrate therefore withdrew bail. Maan was recommitted to jail to await trial.

18.25

Also on the 29th of February, Pran's selection as reader in the Department of English at Brahmpur University was confirmed by the Academic Council. But he, and his family, and his father, were sunk in such gloom that this news did not lighten it at all.

Pran, his thoughts dwelling much on death these days, wondered once again about the remark made by Ramjap Baba to his mother at the Pul Mela. If his readership was indeed due to a death, whose death had the Baba meant? Certainly, his mother had died; but just as certainly this could not have influenced the selection committee. Or had Professor Mishra been serious when he had claimed that he had watched out for Pran's interests out of sympathy for his family?

I too am becoming superstitious, thought Pran. It will be my father next. But his father, luckily for his state of mind, had something to occupy him over the next few days other than trying to organize Maan's defence.

18.26

At the beginning of March, Mahesh Kapoor, though defeated in the elections, was asked once again to perform his duties as an MLA. The Legislative Assembly of Purva Pradesh had been elected, but the indirect elections for the Upper House, the Legislative Council, had not yet taken place. The legislature was therefore not complete. Under the Constitution, six months could not be allowed to elapse between sessions of the legislative body, and the old legislature was therefore forced into brief session. Besides, it was budget time; and though propriety demanded that the budget be passed by the new legislature, the financial wheels had to be kept turning somehow. This would be done through a 'vote on account' for the months of April to July, 1952, the first third of the coming financial year. This vote on account had to be passed by the old, soon-to-be-defunct legislature of which Mahesh Kapoor was a part.

In early March, the two Houses of the legislature met in joint session to hear the Governor's address. The discussion following the vote of thanks to the Governor turned into a noisy and angry debate on the Congress government itself: both its policies and the manner in which it had conducted the elections. Many of those who were most vocal were those who had been defeated and whose voice would be heard in this vast round chamber no more—or at least not for the next five years. As the Governor was the constitutional (and largely ceremonial) head of the state, his address had for the most part been written by the Chief Minister S.S. Sharma.

The Governor's address touched briefly on recent events, the achievements of the government, and its future plans. The Congress Party had won three-quarters of the seats in the Lower House, and (because of the system of indirect election) was bound to win a large majority in the Upper House as well. Discussing the elections, the Governor said in passing: 'I am sure that it will be a cause of gratification to you, as it is to me, that almost all my Ministers have been returned to the new Assembly.' At this point many of those in the House turned to look at Mahesh Kapoor.

The Governor also mentioned a 'matter of regret': that the enforcement of the Purva Pradesh Zamindari and Land Reform Act 'is being delayed for reasons which are beyond the control of my government'. This referred to the fact that the constitutionality of the act was still to be decided by the Supreme Court. 'But,' he added, 'I need hardly assure you that no time will be lost in implementing it as soon as it legally becomes possible to do so.'

In the subsequent debate, Begum Abida Khan brought up both these matters. She mentioned in one fiery breath that it was well known that the Government had used unfair methods—including the use of official cars for ministerial travel—to win the elections; and that, despite this abuse, the Minister who was most closely associated in the public mind with robbing the zamindars of their land had very deservedly lost his seat. Begum Abida Khan had won her own seat, but most of the other members of her party had lost, and she was furious.

Her remarks created pandemonium. The Congress benches were indignant at her attempt to rake up the embers of completed legislation. And even L.N. Agarwal, who was secretly pleased that Mahesh Kapoor had not won his election, condemned the means deployed not by the Congress but by 'rank communalists' in that particular race. At this, Begum Abida Khan began talking about attempted murder and 'a heinous plot to extirpate the minority community from the soil of our common province'. And finally the Speaker had to stop her from continuing in this vein by telling her, first, that the case he presumed she was referring to was sub judice, and secondly, that the entire issue was irrelevant to the question of whether the House should vote to thank the Governor for his address.

Mahesh Kapoor sat through all this with head bowed, silent and unresponsive. He had attended because it was his duty to do so. He would rather have been almost anywhere else. Begum Abida Khan, thinking of her nephew lying on what could well have been his deathbed, appealed loudly from the Speaker to God for justice, so that condign punishment would be meted out to the butcher responsible for his grievous injury. Dramatically she pointed a finger at Mahesh Kapoor, and then raised it heavenwards. Mahesh Kapoor closed his eyes and saw the image of Maan in jail; he knew too well that if he had ever had the power or the influence to save his son, he did not have it now.

The vote of thanks passed as overwhelmingly as expected. Various other bits of legislative business were also taken up—such as the announcement of the President's or the Governor's assent to various bills, the resignation of various MLAs who had also been elected as MPs, and the tabling of various ordinances that it had become necessary to promulgate when the legislature had not been in session. The session then broke off for a few days for Holi before going on to the vote on account, which it passed after brief debate.

18.27

Holi was not celebrated at Prem Nivas at all this year, nor at Pran's house. Maan and Imtiaz, high on bhang, helping Professor Mishra into a large tub of pink water; Savita, drenched in colour, laughing and crying and promising revenge; Mrs Mahesh Kapoor making sure that her grandnieces and grandnephews from Rudhia all got their favourite sweets; the bejewelled Saeeda Bai singing ghazals before a charmed audience of men while their wives looked down from the balcony in fascinated disapproval: these must have appeared as scenes of an unreal fantasy to anyone who remembered them.

Pran took some dry pink and green powder and smeared a little on his daughter's forehead, but that was all. It was her first Holi, and he blessed her for her unawareness of all the darkness and sadness that existed in the world.

Lata tried to study, but she was unable to. Her heart was full, as much with Maan and the deep sorrow of his family as with her own forthcoming marriage. Mrs Rupa Mehra, when she heard of Lata's unilateral action in writing to Haresh, was both furious and delighted. Lata had passed on Haresh's message of love for her mother and his words of regret before she had broken the real news. Torn between hugging her daughter to her bosom and giving her at least one tight slap for not having consulted her, Mrs Rupa Mehra burst into tears.

Needless to say, there was no question of the wedding taking place in Prem Nivas. Given Arun's views on Haresh, Lata had refused to get married from Sunny Park either. The Chatterji house at Ballygunge was impossible for several reasons. That only left Dr Kishen Chand Seth's house.

Had Dr Kishen Chand Seth been in Mrs Rupa Mehra's position, he would certainly have slapped Lata. After all, he had slapped Mrs Rupa Mehra when Arun was a year old because he thought she wasn't controlling the baby properly. He had never had any truck with incompetence or insubordination. He now bluntly refused to countenance, let alone assist, the marriage of a granddaughter in which he had not been consulted from the beginning. He told Mrs Rupa Mehra that his house was not a hotel or a dharamshala, and that she would have to look elsewhere.

'And that is that,' he added.

Mrs Rupa Mehra threatened to kill herself.

'Yes, yes, do so,' said her father impatiently. He knew that she loved life too much, especially when she could be justifiably miserable.

'And I will never see you again,' she added. 'Never in all my life. Say goodbye to me,' she sobbed, 'for this is the last time you will see your daughter.' With that she flung herself weeping into his arms.

Dr Kishen Chand Seth staggered back and nearly dropped his stick. Carried away by her emotion and by the greater realism of this threat, he too started sobbing violently, and pounded his stick several times on the floor to give vent to his feelings. Very soon it was all settled.

'I hope Parvati does not mind,' gasped Mrs Rupa Mehra. 'She is so good—so good—'

'If she does, I will get rid of her,' cried Dr Kishen Chand Seth. 'A wife one can divorce—but one's children—never!' These words—which it seemed to him he had heard somewhere before—sent him into a renewed paroxysm of weeping.

When Parvati came back from shopping a few minutes later, holding out a pair of pink high-heeled shoes and saying, 'Kishy darling, look at what I've bought from Lovely,' her husband grinned weakly, terrified to break the news of the inconvenience he had just taken on.

18.28

The Nawab Sahib had heard about Mahesh Kapoor's question to Waris about Firoz's health. He also knew that when the count was over, Mahesh Kapoor had refused a recount. Later he heard from his munshi that he had even refused to lodge an election petition.

'But why would he wish to lodge an election petition? And against whom?' said the Nawab Sahib.

'Against Waris,' said the munshi, and handed him a couple of the fatal pink fliers.

The Nawab Sahib read through one and his face grew pale with anger. The poster had made such shameless and impious use of death that he wondered that God's anger had not fallen on Waris, or on him, or on Firoz, the innocent agency of this outrage. As if he had not sunk deeply enough in the world's opinion, what must Mahesh Kapoor think of him now?

Firoz—whatever he might think of his father—was, by the grace of God, out of danger at last. And Mahesh Kapoor's son was lying in jail in danger of losing his liberty for many years. How strangely the tables had turned, thought the Nawab Sahib, and what small satisfaction Maan's jeopardy and Mahesh Kapoor's grief—both of which in bitterness he had once prayed for—now gave him after all.

That he had not attended Mrs Mahesh Kapoor's chautha made him feel ashamed. Firoz had had an infection at the time and had been in serious danger—but now the Nawab Sahib asked himself whether his son had been in such immediate hazard that he could not have spared half an hour and braved the glances of the world to at least show his face at the service? Poor woman, she had surely died fearing that neither her son nor his might live until the summer, and knowing that Maan at least could not even come to her deathbed. How painful such knowledge must have been; and how little her goodness and generosity had deserved it.

Sometimes he sat in his library and went to sleep from tiredness. Ghulam Rusool would wake him up for lunch or dinner whenever it was necessary to do so. It was becoming warm as well. The coppersmith had begun to sound its short continual call from a fig tree outside. Here in the library, lost in religion or philosophy or the speculations of astronomy, even worlds might seem small, not to speak of personal estates and ambitions, griefs and guilt. Or, lost in his projected edition of Mast's poems, he might have forgotten the uproar of the world around. But the Nawab Sahib discovered that he could read nothing with any concentration. He found himself staring at a page, wondering where he had been for the last hour.

One morning he read in the *Brahmpur Chronicle* about Abida Khan's derisive ad hominem remarks in the House, and how Mahesh Kapoor had not stood up to say a word by way of defence or explanation. He was seized with pain on his friend's behalf. He rang up his sister-in-law.

'Abida, what was the necessity for saying these things I've been reading about?'

Abida laughed. Her brother-in-law was weak and over-scrupulous, and would never make much of a fighter. 'Why, it was my last chance to attack that man face to face,' she said. 'If it wasn't for him, do you think your inheritance and that of your sons would be in such danger? And why talk of inheritance, how about your son's life?'

'Abida, there is a limit to things.'

'Well, when I reach it, I will stop. And if I don't, I will fall over the edge. That is my concern.'

'Abida, have pity—'

'Pity? What pity did that man's son have on Firoz? Or on that helpless woman—' Abida suddenly stopped. Perhaps she felt that she had reached the limit. There was a long pause. Finally she broke it by saying: 'All right, I will accept your advice on this. But I hope that that butcher rots in jail.' She thought of the Nawab Sahib's wife, the only light of her years in the zenana, and she added: 'For many years to come.'

The Nawab Sahib knew that Maan had come to visit Firoz twice at Baitar House before he had again been committed to jail. Murtaza Ali had told him so, and had also told him that Firoz had asked him to come. Now the Nawab Sahib asked himself the question: if Firoz had chosen to forgive his friend, what was the law that it should insist on destroying his life?

That night he was dining alone with Firoz. This was usually very painful: they tried to talk to each other without really speaking of anything. But tonight he turned to his son and said: 'Firoz, what is the evidence against that boy?'

'Evidence, Abba?'

'I mean, from the point of view of the court.'

'He has confessed to the police.'

'Has he confessed before a magistrate?'

Firoz was a little surprised that this legalistic thought should have come to his father rather than to him. 'You're right, Abba,' he said. 'But there's all the other evidence—his flight, his identification, all our statements—mine, and those of the others who were there.' He looked at his father carefully, thinking how hard it must be for him to approach even indirectly the subject of his injury or the other matter behind it. He said after a while: 'When I made my statement, I was very ill; my mind could have been confused, of course. Perhaps it's still confused—I should have thought of all this, not you.'

Neither said anything for a minute. Then Firoz went on: 'If I fell on the knife—stumbled, say—and it was in his hand, he might, since he was drunk, have thought that he had done it—and so might—so might—'

'The others.'

'Yes—the others. That would explain their statements—and his disappearance,' continued Firoz, as if the entire scene was passing once again before his eyes, very clearly, very slowly. But a few seconds of the scene that had been clear before had now begun to blur.

'Enough has happened in Prem Nivas already,' said his father. 'And the same set of facts is open to many interpretations.'

This last remark conjured up different thoughts for each of them.

'Yes, Abba,' said Firoz quietly and gratefully, and with something of a renewal in his heart of his old respect.

18.29

Maan's trial came up in a fortnight before the District and Sessions Judge. Both the Nawab Sahib and Mahesh Kapoor were present in the small courtroom. Firoz was one of the first witnesses. The prosecution lawyer, leading him with quiet confidence through the phrases of the statement he had given to the police, was startled when Firoz said:

'And then I stumbled and fell on to the knife.'

'I am sorry,' said the lawyer. 'What was that you said?'

'I said, I stumbled, and fell on to the knife that he was holding in his hand.'

The government advocate was utterly taken aback. Try as he might, he could not shake Firoz's evidence. He complained to the court that the witness had turned hostile to the state and requested permission to cross-examine him. He put it to Firoz that his evidence was inconsistent with his statement to the police. Firoz replied that he had been ill at the time of his statement, and that his memory had been blurred. It was only after his recovery that it had sharpened and clarified. The prosecutor reminded Firoz that he himself was a lawyer and that he was on oath. Firoz, who was still looking pale, replied with a smile that he was well aware of it, but that even lawyers did not have perfect memories. He had relived the scene many times and he was certain now that he had stumbled against something—he thought it might have been a bolster—and had fallen on to the knife that Maan had just wrested from Saeeda Bai. 'He just stood there. I think he thought he had done it,' added Firoz helpfully, though he was fully aware of the limitations of evidence based on hearsay or the interpretation of the mental state of others.

Maan sat in the dock, staring at his friend, hardly comprehending at first what was happening. A look of disturbed amazement spread slowly across his face.

Saeeda Bai was examined next. She stood in the witness box, her face unseen behind the burqa she was wearing, and spoke in a low voice. She was happy to accept the contention of the defence lawyer that what she had seen was consistent with this interpretation of events. So was Bibbo. The other evidence—Firoz's blood on the shawl, Maan's identification by the railway clerk, the memory of the watchman, and so on—threw no light on the question of what had happened during those two or three vital, almost fatal, seconds. And if Maan had not even stabbed Firoz, if Firoz had simply fallen on the knife held in his hand, the very question of his intention to inflict 'such bodily injury as was sufficient in the ordinary course of nature to cause death' was irrelevant.

The judge saw no reason why a man who had been so badly injured would go out of his way to protect someone who had deliberately inflicted such an injury on him. There was no evidence of collusion among the witnesses, no attempt by the defence to suborn anyone. He was led to the inescapable conclusion that Maan was not guilty.

He acquitted Maan of both charges and ordered him released immediately.

Mahesh Kapoor embraced his son. He too was dumbfounded. He turned towards the courtroom, which was now in uproar, and saw the Nawab Sahib talking to Firoz. Their eyes met for an instant. Mahesh Kapoor's were full of perplexity and gratitude.

The Nawab Sahib shook his head slightly, as if to disown responsibility, and turned again to talk to his son.

18.30

Pran had not been correct in imagining that his father would become superstitious. Mahesh Kapoor did, however, take an unsteady step towards countenancing superstition. In late March, a few days before Ramnavami, he acquiesced in Veena's and old Mrs Tandon's request to hold a reading of the Ramcharitmanas at Prem Nivas for the family and a few friends.

Why he agreed was unclear even to himself. His wife had asked for the reading the previous year and he associated the request with her. She had even asked for a section of the Ramcharitmanas—the section involving Hanuman in Lanka—to be read to her on her deathbed. Perhaps Mahesh Kapoor felt sorry that he had refused her in the past—or perhaps he was simply too exhausted to refuse anyone anything any longer. Or perhaps—though it is unlikely that he would ever have accepted such a reason—perhaps he wished to give thanks to something beneficent and mysterious outside himself that had kept his son safe when he had seemed logically to be doomed and had restored his hope of friendship with the Nawab Sahib when it had appeared to be beyond repair.

Old Mrs Tandon was the only one of the group of three samdhins who attended. Mrs Rupa Mehra was in Calcutta, frantically making wedding purchases. And Mrs Mahesh Kapoor's small brass bell no longer rang in the tiny alcove where she used to perform her puja.

One morning, while the recitation was going on, a white owl walked into the room where the listeners were sitting. It stayed for a few minutes, then slowly walked out again. Everyone was alarmed by the presence of this inauspicious bird in the daytime, and took it as a bad sign. But Veena disagreed. She said that the white owl, being the vehicle of Lakshmi, was a symbol of good luck in Bengal. It might well be an emissary sent from the other world to bring them good fortune and to take back good news.

18.31

When Maan was in jail, his mind had often turned to Rasheed's tormented madness and delusion. They were both outcastes, even if his own delusion had been temporary. The difference between them, Maan had felt, was that he, despite his physical incarceration, had at least preserved the love of his family.

He had asked Pran to send Rasheed some money, not out of a sense of expiation, but because he thought it might be practically useful. He remembered how gaunt and wasted he had looked that day in Curzon Park, and wondered if what his uncle managed to send him together with what Rasheed himself was earning sufficed for rent and food. Maan feared that sooner or later the tuitions too were bound to stop.

When he was out on bail, he did not visit, but sent some more money, again anonymously, by mail. He felt that for him, a man with a violent crime hanging over his head, to visit Rasheed in person might lead to unforeseeable constructions and consequences. In any case, it would not help Rasheed's balance of mind.

When Maan was found innocent and finally set free, his thoughts turned once more to his old teacher and erstwhile friend. But again he was not certain if seeing him was a good idea, so he wrote a letter first. He received no reply.

When a second letter was neither replied to nor returned, Maan decided that at least he had not met with a refusal. He went to Rasheed's address, but Rasheed was not there any longer. He spoke to the landlord and his wife, and told them he was a friend. He sensed that they were not very pleased. He asked them what Rasheed's new address was, and they told him they did not know. When he said that he had written two letters to Rasheed recently and asked them where they were, the man looked at his wife, appeared to come to a decision, fetched them from inside and gave both of them to Maan. They were unopened.

Maan had no idea whether Rasheed had got the money he had sent. He asked the landlord when exactly it was that Rasheed had left, and whether any earlier letters had been received. They replied that he had left some time ago, but he could not get them to be more specific than that. They appeared to be annoyed, but whether at Rasheed or at him, he did not know.

Maan, worried, now asked Pran to trace Rasheed through either the History Department or the Registrar's Office. Neither knew his whereabouts. A clerk in the Registrar's Office mentioned that Rasheed had withdrawn from the university; he had said that he refused to attend lectures when he was needed to campaign for the sake of the country.

Maan next wrote in his rather blunt Urdu script to Baba and Rasheed's father, asking for news and for Rasheed's latest address. Perhaps, Maan suggested, the Bear might know where he was. He got a short and not unsympathetic reply. Baba said that everyone at Debaria was very pleased with his acquittal and sent their respects to his father as well. In addition, the Bear and the guppi had both requested him to send Maan their regards. The guppi had been so impressed by reports of the dramatic scene in court that he was thinking of retiring from his life's vocation in Maan's favour.

As for news of Rasheed, they had none, nor did they have any address. The last they had seen of him was during the campaign, when he had antagonized people still further and harmed his own party with his wild accusations and insults. His wife had been very upset, and now that he had disappeared she was distraught. Meher was fine, except—and here Baba grew a little indignant—her maternal grandfather was trying to claim that she should come and live with her mother and baby sister in his village.

If Maan had any news of Rasheed, Baba said, he should inform them as soon as he could. They would be very grateful. For the moment, sadly, even the Bear had none.

18.32

Saeeda Bai had left the court after her brief appearance, but she knew within half an hour of the verdict that Maan was safe. She gave thanks to God for preserving him. That he was lost to her she had the wisdom or experience to realize, but that his youth would not be spent in imprisonment and misery was a stifling weight off her heart. She saw Maan with all his faults, but could not cut him off from her love.

Perhaps this was the first time in her life that Saeeda Bai herself had loved unrequitedly. Again and again she saw Maan as she had first seen him: the eager Dagh Sahib of that first evening at Prem Nivas, full of liveliness and charm and energy and affection.

Sometimes her mind turned to the Nawab Sahib—and to her mother—and to her own younger self, a mother at fifteen. 'Do not let the bee enter the garden'—she murmured the famous line—'that the moth may not be unjustly killed.' And yet the strange and tenuous links of causation could act beneficently as well. For out of the shame and violation of her youth her beloved Tasneem had been born.

Bibbo rebuked Saeeda Bai for spending so much time these days looking into space. 'At least sing something!' she said. 'Even the parakeet's becoming dumb by example.'

'Do be quiet, Bibbo!' said Saeeda Bai impatiently. And Bibbo, glad to have elicited for once at least some reaction from her mistress, kept up the attack.

'Give thanks for Bilgrami Sahib,' said Bibbo. 'Without him where would all of us be?'

Saeeda Bai clicked her tongue and made a gesture of dismissal.

'Give thanks also to your mightiest admirer, who has spared us his attentions of late,' continued Bibbo.

Saeeda Bai glared. The Raja of Marh had been apparently dormant only because he had been busy with his plans to consecrate his temple with the installation of the ancient Shiva-linga.

'Poor Miya Mitthu,' murmured Bibbo sadly. 'He will forget how to squawk, "Whisky!"'

One day, to stop Bibbo's inane prattling, which was more painful than she intended, Saeeda Bai told her to fetch her harmonium, and let her fingers move up and down the mother-of-pearl keys. But she could not control her thoughts any more than she could in her bedroom, where the framed picture from Maan's book looked down at her from the wall. She called for that book now, and placed it on the harmonium, turning its pages one by one, pausing less at the poems than at the illustrations. She came across the picture of the grief-stricken woman in the cemetery.

I have not visited my mother's grave now for a month, she thought. In my new idiocy as a rejected lover I am neglecting my duties as a daughter. But the more she tried to avoid thinking of herself and the hopelessness of her love for Maan, the more it oppressed her.

And what of Tasneem? she thought. It was worse for her, Saeeda Bai reflected, than for herself. Poor girl, she had become more silent than that godforsaken parakeet. Ishaq, Rasheed, Firoz—three men had come into her life, each more impossible than the last, and in each case she had let her affection grow in silence, and had suffered their sudden absence in silence. She had seen Firoz wounded, her sister almost strangled; she had probably heard, though her strange silence gave no indication of it, of the rumours surrounding herself. What did she think of men now? Or of Saeeda Bai herself if she believed what she heard?

What can I do to help her? thought Saeeda Bai. But there was nothing to be done. To talk to Tasneem about anything that mattered was not within the bounds of possibility.

Though it was evening, and the first few stars had begun to appear in the sky, Saeeda Bai began to hum to herself the lines of Minai's poem announcing the arrival of dawn. It reminded her of the garden in Prem Nivas that carefree evening, and all the grief and pain that had intervened. Tears were in her voice, but not in her eyes. Bibbo came and listened, and Tasneem too walked quietly up from her room to hear what had become so rare. She herself knew the poem by heart, but, entranced by her sister's voice, she did not even murmur the words under her breath:

The meeting has dispersed; the moths
  Bid farewell to the candle-light.
Departure's hour is on the sky.
  Only a few stars mark the night.

What has remained will not remain:
  They too will quickly disappear.
This is the world's way, although we,
  Lost to the world, lie sleeping here.

18.33

Rasheed walked along the parapet of the Barsaat Mahal, his thoughts blurred with hunger and confusion.

Darkness, and the river, and the cool marble wall.

Somewhere where there is nowhere.

It gnaws. They are all around me, the elders of Sagal.

No father, no mother, no child, no wife,

Like a jewel above the water. The parapet, the garden under which a river flows.

No Satan, no God, no Iblis, no Gabriel.

Endless, endless, endless, endless, the waters of the Ganga.

The stars above, below.

> . . . and some were seized by the Cry, and some
> We made the earth to swallow, and some We
> drowned; God would never wrong them, but
> they wronged themselves.

Peace. No prayers. No more prayers.

To sleep is better than to pray.

O my creature, you gave your life too soon. I have made your entry into Paradise unlawful.

A spring in Paradise.

O God, O God.

18.34

Further down the Ganga, with pomp and practicality, other preparations were proceeding.

The great Shiva-linga was about the size that the priest's mantras had said it would be, and in about the same position under the Ganga. But layers of sand and silt covered it. It was some days before it was finally exposed below the murky water, and some days more before it was hoisted up by winches to the first broad step of the cremation ghat above water-level. There it lay beside the Ganga in which it had rested for centuries, at first merely caked with clay and grit, then washed with water and milk and ghee till its black granitic mass glistened in the sun.

People came from far to gaze and to gape, to admire and to worship it. Old women came to do puja: to sing and to recite and to offer flowers and to smear the head of the hereditary pujari with sandalwood paste. It was a propitious combination: the linga of Shiva, and the river that had emerged from his hair.

The Raja of Marh had summoned historians and engineers and astrologers and priests, for preparations now had to be made for the journey of the linga up the grand steps of the cremation ghat, through the dense alleys of Old Brahmpur, into the open space of Chowk, and thence to its place of final, triumphal, reconsecrated rest: the sanctum of the completed temple.

The historians attempted to obtain information about the logistics of other, similar enterprises, such as, for example, the transfer of Ashoka's pillar from near Ambala to Delhi by Firoz Shah—a Buddhist pillar moved by a Muslim king, reflected the Raja of Marh with bifurcated contempt. The engineers worked out that the cylinder of stone, twenty-five feet long, two feet in diameter, and weighing more than six tons, would require two hundred men to haul it safely up the steep steps of the ghat. (The Raja had forbidden the use of winches or pulleys for the unique and dramatic ceremony.) The astrologers calculated an auspicious time, and informed the Raja that if it was not done in a week, he would have to wait for another four months. And the newly appointed priests of the new Chandrachur Temple made plans for auspicious rituals along the route and a vast, festive reception at its destination, so close to where it had stood in the time of Aurangzeb.

The Muslims had tried through the Alamgiri Masjid Hifaazat Committee to obtain an injunction against the installation of the profane monolith behind the western wall, but to no avail. The Raja's title to the land on which the temple stood, now transferred to a trust run by the Linga Rakshak Samiti and dominated by him, was legally clear.

Even among the Hindus, however, there were some who felt that the linga should be left near the cremation ghat—for that was where ten generations of pujaris had prayed to it in sorrow and destitution, and where it would remind worshippers not only of the generative force of Shiva Mahadeva but of his destructive power as well. The hereditary pujari, having prayed to the visible linga in a kind of ecstasy, now claimed that it had already found its proper home. It should be fixed on the low, broad step where it had chanced to rest, and where it had once again been seen and worshipped by the people—and as the Ganga rose or fell with the seasons, it too should appear to sink or rise.

But the Raja of Marh and the Linga Rakshak Samiti would not have it. The pujari had fulfilled his function as an informant. The linga had been found; it had been raised; it would be raised further still. It was not for one ragged, ecstatic pujari to obstruct enterprises of such great moment.

Rounded logs were brought to the site by barge and hauled up the steps of the ghat to form a track of four parallel rollers, ten feet across. A hundred and fifty feet above, where the track turned right from the broad steps into a narrower lane, logs were interlaid to create a gentle guiding curve. From here on, the linga would have to be carried diagonally, and it was necessary to work out an exact and elaborate drill to shift its position.

Long before birdsong on the appointed day, conches began to sound their pompous, plaintive, enchanted calls. The linga was bathed once more, and wrapped first in silk-cotton and then in jute matting. Over the thick brown jute huge ropes were attached, from which branched lesser ropes of varying length. Tens of thousands of marigold flowers were strewn on or stuck into the matting, and it was covered with rose petals. The small drum, the damaru of Shiva, began to sound its high, mesmerizing beat, and the priests kept up a continuous chant that rose for hours through a loudspeaker above the undulating clamour of the crowd.

At noon, in the great heat of the day, the period of greatest austerities, two hundred barefooted, barebacked young initiates of a great Shaivite akhara, five each on either side of the rollers on each of twenty steps, straining forward with the ropes biting into their shoulders, began to move the great linga. The logs creaked, the linga rolled slowly, uncomplainingly upwards, and from the chanting, singing, praying, chattering crowd rose a great gasp of awe.

The doms left their work at the cremation ghat to gaze with wonder at the linga moving slowly away, and the corpses burned on, unattended.

Only the dispossessed pujari and a small group of devotees cried out in distress.

Step by step the linga rolled upwards, pulled in controlled jerks from above. It was even pushed from below by a few men with crowbars. Every so often they inserted wedges beneath it so that the men hauling the linga could rest for a while.

The steep, irregular steps of the ghat burned the soles of their feet, the sun burned down on them from above, and they gasped with effort and from thirst. But their rhythm remained steady, and after an hour the linga had risen seventy feet above the Ganga.

The Raja of Marh, high on the steps, looked downwards with satisfaction and broke out into loud, joyous cries, almost roars, of 'Har har Mahadeva!' He was dressed in full white silken court dress despite the heat, his bulk was thickly beaded with pearls and sweat, and he carried a great golden trident in his right hand.

The young Rajkumar of Marh, an arrogant sneer on his face resembling that of his father, shouted 'Faster! Faster!' in a kind of possession. He thumped the young novitiates on their backs, excited beyond measure by the blood on their shoulders that had begun to ooze out from under the ropes.

The men tried to move faster. Their movement became more ragged.

The ropes on their shoulders, slippery with sweat and blood, had begun to lose some of their purchase.

At the curve where the steps narrowed into a lane, the linga had to be turned sideways. From here on, the Ganga would be seen no more.

On the outer side of the bend, a rope snapped, and a man staggered. The jerk caused a ripple of unequal stresses, and the linga shifted a little. Another rope ripped, and another, and the linga began to jolt. And now a wave of panic smashed through the formation.

'Insert the wedges—insert the wedges!'

'Don't let go—'

'Stay there—wait—don't kill us—'

'Get out—get out—we can't hold it—'

'Stand down—stand down a step—slacken the tension—'

'Pull the rope—'

'Release the ropes—you'll be dragged down—'

'Har har Mahadeva—'

'Run—run for your lives—'

'The wedges—the wedges—'

Another rope snapped, and another, as the linga shifted downwards very slightly, first this way, then that. The cries of the men in front as their bodies were snapped backwards on to the steps were interspersed with the quieter but still more dreadful sounds of the shifting and sliding of the monolith, and the creaking of the rollers beneath. The men below scrambled out of the way. The men above dropped their ropes in a bloodstained tangle, pulled their shocked and injured fellows to one side, and stared down at the orange linga, into the matting of which the marigold flowers had by now been completely crushed. The drumbeat halted. The crowd scattered, screaming in terror. The steps of the ghat below the linga were suddenly deserted, and, far below, the doms too fled from the ghat—as well as the relatives of the burning dead.

The linga protested against the hastily inserted wedges. But for half a minute, if it moved at all, the movement was infinitesimal.

Then it shifted. A wedge gave way. It shifted again and the other wedges slipped and it began slowly to roll down the way it had come.

Down the rollers rolled the great linga, past the next step, and the next, and the next, gathering speed as it rolled. The tree-trunks cracked under the impact of its weight, it veered to left and right, but it kept rolling on, down, down, swifter and swifter towards the Ganga, crushing the pujari who now stood in its downward path with his arms upraised, smashing into the burning pyres of the cremation ghat, and sinking into the water of the Ganga at last, down its submerged stone steps, and on to its muddy bed.

The Shiva-linga rested on the bed of the Ganga once more, the turbid waters passing over it, its bloodstains slowly washed away.

Part Nineteen

19.1

Dearest Kalpana,

This is written in haste because Varun is coming to Delhi at the end of February or so to attend the IAS interview, and we hope you and your father can put him up for a few days. It is like a dream come true, though only one out of five boys interviewed for the civil service is taken in. We can only hope and pray, such things are entirely in His hands. But Varun has squeezed through the first hurdle, since thousands of boys sit the written exams for the IAS and IFS and so few are asked to go to Delhi.

When the letter came intimating Varun of the interview, Arun refused to believe this, and used some strong language at the breakfast table, with Aparna there and the servants, who, I believe, understand every word. He said there must be some mistake, but it was true all right. I was not there, being in Brahmpur around the time of Lata and Haresh's joyful news, but when Varun sent me a letter, I went to the expense of even booking a trunk call through to Calcutta from Pran's house to congratulate my darling boy, and I made Varun tell me all the details and reactions, which he could because Arun and Meenakshi were not at home, they had gone out to a party as is quite usual. He sounded quite surprised, but I told him that in life one only gets what one deserves. Now D.V. he will surprise us in the interview once again. It is all up to you, dearest Kalpana, to make sure that he eats well, and is not nervous and is on his best behaviour and dressed to the nines. Also that he avoids bad company and alcohol, which I am sorry to say he is a little susceptible to. I know you will take care of him, he is so much in need of boosting up.

I am not writing any more news because I am in haste and also have given you the joyous news of Lata and Haresh in the previous letter to which I have yet had no answer or congratulations, but you must be busy, I know, with your father's hip operation. I hope he is now fully recovered. It must be hard for him, he is so impatient with illness, and now he is himself experiencing it. And you must also take care of yourself. Health is truly the most precious possession.

With fondest love to you both,

Yours,
Ma
(Mrs Rupa Mehra)

P.S. Please send me a telegram after the interview is over, otherwise I will not be able to sleep.

*

Varun looked nervously around at his fellow-passengers as the cold, dry, flat countryside around Delhi hurtled past the windows of the train. No one appeared to realize how momentous this journey was for him. Having read the Delhi edition of the *Times of India* from the first page to the last and back again—for who knew what the predatory interviewers might decide to ask him about current affairs?—he stealthily glanced at an advertisement that seemed to leap out at him:

> Dr Dugle. Highly honoured and patronised for his social services (Inland and Overseas) by many eminent persons, Rajas, Maharajas, and chiefs. Dr Dugle. India's leading specialist with international fame in chronic diseases such as nervous debility, premature old age, run down conditions, lack of vigour and vitality, and similar acute diseases. Consultations in complete confidence.

Varun fell gloomily to pondering his innumerable social, intellectual and other inadequacies. Then another ad attracted his attention.

> Dress your hair with the creamed oils of Brylcreem.
> Why creamed oils? Brylcreem is a *creamed* mixture of tonic oils. It is easier to apply, cleaner to use and its *creaminess* gives the right amount of all Brylcreem ingredients each time. Brylcreem gives that smooth soft lustre to the hair which so many women admire.
> Buy Brylcreem today.

Varun felt suddenly miserable. He doubted that even Brylcreem would help women to admire him. He knew he was going to make a fool of himself in the interview, just as in everything else.

*

'The servants will be coming in half an hour,' whispered Kalpana Gaur tenderly, pushing Varun gently out of her bed.

'Oh.'

'And you'd better sleep in your own bed for half an hour, so that they don't wonder.'

Varun looked at her, amazed. She smiled at him in a motherly sort of way, the pale green quilt up around her neck.

'And then you'd better get ready for breakfast and the interview. Today's your big day.'

'Ah.' Varun seemed speechless.

'Now, Varun, don't be tongue-tied, it won't do—at least not today. You have to impress them and charm them. I promised your mother I'd make sure you were well taken care of and that I'd boost your confidence. Do you feel boosted?'

Varun blushed, then smiled weakly. 'Heh, heh,' he laughed anxiously, wondering how he was going to get out of bed without embarrassment. And it was so cold in Delhi compared to Calcutta. The mornings were freezing.

'It's so cold,' he mumbled.

'Do you know,' said Kalpana Gaur, 'I often feel hot spots on my feet which trouble me throughout the night, but last night I didn't feel any at all. You were marvellous, Varun. Now remember, if at any time during the interview you begin to feel anxious, think of last night, and tell yourself: "I am the Iron Frame of India."'

Varun still looked dazed, though not unhappy.

'Use my dressing gown,' suggested Kalpana Gaur.

Varun gave her a grateful and puzzled glance.

A couple of hours later, after breakfast, she examined his appearance critically, patted his pockets, adjusted his striped tie, wiped off the excessive Brylcreem in his hair, and combed it again.

'But—' protested Varun.

'Now I'll make sure you get to the right place at the right time.'

'That's not necessary,' said Varun, not wanting to cause trouble.

'It's on my way to the hospital.'

'Er, give my best to your father when you get there.'

'Of course.'

'Kalpana?'

'Yes, Varun?'

'What happened to that mysterious illness of yours that Ma kept telling us about? It was more than just hot spots, according to her.'

'Oh, that?' Kalpana looked thoughtful. 'It sorted itself out the moment my father had to go to hospital. It made no sense for both of us to be ill.'

The Union Public Service Commission was holding its interviews in a temporary structure in Connaught Place, one which had been set up during the War and had not yet been dismantled. Kalpana Gaur squeezed Varun's hand in the taxi. 'Don't look so dazed,' she said. 'And remember, never say, "I don't know"; always say, "I'm afraid I haven't any idea." You look very presentable, Varun. Much more handsome than your brother.'

Varun glanced at her with a mixture of bewilderment and tenderness, and got out.

In the waiting room, he noticed a couple of candidates who looked like south Indians. They were shivering. They had been even less prepared for the Delhi weather than himself, and it was a particularly cold day. One of them was saying to the other: 'And they say that the Chairman of the UPSC can read you like a book. He can assess you as soon as you enter the door. Every weakness of your personality is laid bare within seconds.'

Varun felt his knees tremble. He went to the bathroom, got out a small bottle that he had managed to secrete on his person, and took two quick swigs. His knees settled down, and he began to think he would conduct himself superbly after all.

'I'm afraid I really have no idea,' he repeated to himself.

'About what?' asked one of his fellow-candidates after a pause.

'I don't know,' said Varun. 'I mean, I'm afraid I really couldn't tell you.'

*

'And then I said "Good morning", and they all nodded, but the Chairman, a sort of bulldog man, said, "Namaste" instead. I was quite shocked for a second, but somehow I got over it.'

'And then?' asked Kalpana eagerly.

'And then he asked me to sit down. It was a roundish table, and I was at one end and the bulldog man was at the other end, he looked at me as if he could read every thought of mine before I had even thought it. Mr Chatterji—no, Mr Bannerji, they called him. And there was a Vice-Chancellor and someone from the Ministry of External Affairs, and—'

'But how did it go?' asked Kalpana. 'Do you think it went well?'

'I don't know. They asked me a question about Prohibition, you see, and I'd just been drinking, so naturally I was nervous—'

'You had just been what?'

'Oh,' said Varun guiltily. 'One or two gulps. Then someone asked me if I liked the odd social drink, and I said, yes. But I could feel my throat become dry, and the bulldog man just kept looking at me and he sniffed slightly and noted something down on a pad. And then he said, Mr Mehra, what if you were posted to a state like Bombay or a district like Kanpur where there was Prohibition, would you feel obliged to refrain from the odd social drink? So I said of course I would. Then someone else on my right said, what if you were visiting friends in Calcutta, and were offered a drink, would you refuse it—as a representative of a dry area? And I could see them staring at me, ten pairs of eyes, and then suddenly I thought, I am the Iron Frame, who are all these people anyway, and I said, No, I saw no reason to, in fact I would drink it with a pleasure enhanced by my previous abstinence—that's what I said. "Enhanced by my previous abstinence."'

Kalpana laughed.

'Yes,' said Varun dubiously. 'It seemed to go down well with them too. I don't think it was I who was answering all those questions, you know. It seemed to be a sort of Arun person who had taken possession of me. Perhaps because I was wearing his tie.'

'What else did they ask?'

'Something about what three books I would take with me to a desert island, and did I know what the initials M.I.T. stood for, and did I think there would be war with Pakistan—and I really can't remember anything, Kalpana, except that the bulldog man had two watches, one on the inside of his wrist and one on the outside. It was all I could do to avoid staring at him. Thank God it's over,' he added morosely. 'It lasted forty-five minutes and it took a year off my life.'

'Did you say forty-five minutes?' said Kalpana Gaur excitedly.

'Yes.'

'I must send a telegram to your mother at once. And I have decided that you must stay in Delhi for another two days. Your being here is very good for me.'

'Really?' said Varun, reddening.

He wondered if it might have been the Brylcreem that had done it.

★

VARUN BOOSTED INTERVIEW CONCLUDED FINGERS CROSSED FATHER MENDING LOVE KALPANA.

Kalpana can always be trusted to do the needful, said Mrs Rupa Mehra happily to herself.

19.2

In Calcutta Mrs Rupa Mehra went around like a whirlwind, buying saris, herding her family into conferences, visiting her son-in-law-to-be twice a week, requisitioning cars (including the Chatterjis' big white Humber) for her shopping and for visits to friends, writing long letters to all her relatives, designing the invitation card, monopolizing the phone in a Kakoli-like manner, and weeping alternately with joy at the prospect of her daughter's marriage, concern for her daughter on her wedding night, and sorrow that the late Raghubir Mehra would not be present.

She looked at a copy of Van de Velde's *Ideal Marriage* in a bookshop on Park Street and, though the contents made her blush, determinedly bought it. 'It's for my daughter,' she informed the sales clerk, who yawned and nodded.

Arun stopped her from adding the design of a rose to the wedding invitation. 'Don't be ridiculous, Ma,' he said. 'What do you think people will think of all that ghich-pich when they receive it? I'll never live it down. Keep the design plain.' He was very aggrieved that Lata, after receiving his egregious letter, had refused to be married from his house, and he was trying to compensate for his loss of authority by a commissarial attempt to take over all the practical arrangements for the wedding—at least those that could be managed at the Calcutta end. But he was up against the powerful personalities of his mother and his grandfather, both of whom had their own ideas about what was required.

Meanwhile, though his view of Haresh had not changed, he bowed—or at least nodded—to the inevitable, and attempted to be gracious. He had lunch once more among the Czechs, and balanced this with a return invitation to Sunny Park.

When Mrs Rupa Mehra asked Haresh about the date for the wedding, he said, beaming with cheerfulness: 'The earlier the better.' But in view of Lata's exams and the fact that his own foster-parents were reluctant to agree to a wedding in the inauspicious last month of the Hindu calendar, the date was set for late, rather than early, April.

Haresh's parents also requested Lata's horoscope in order to ensure that her stars and planets matched those of her husband. They were particularly concerned that Lata should not happen to be a Manglik—a 'Martian' under certain astronomical definitions—because then, for a non-Manglik like Haresh to marry her would certainly result in his early death.

When Haresh passed on this request, Mrs Rupa Mehra got cross. 'If there was any truth in all these horoscopes, there would be no young widows,' she said.

'I agree with you,' said Haresh. 'Well, I'll tell them that no one has ever made a horoscope for Lata.'

But this resulted in a request for Lata's date and time and place of birth. Haresh's parents were going to get her horoscope made themselves.

Haresh went to an astrologer in Calcutta with Lata's place and date of birth, and asked him for a safe time of birth that would ensure that her stars matched his. The astrologer gave him two or three times, one of which Haresh sent on to his parents. Luckily, their astrologer worked on the same principles and calculations as his. Their anxieties were allayed.

Amit, needless to say, was disappointed, but not as much as he might have been. His novel, now that he was free from the worry of handling the Chatterji fortunes, was going well, and many more momentous events were taking place on his pages than in his life. He sank deeper into the novel, and—a little disgusted with himself for doing so—used his disappointment and sadness to portray that of a character who happened to be conveniently on hand.

He wrote a brief note, not in verse, to congratulate Lata, and tried to behave in a sportsmanlike manner. Mrs Rupa Mehra, in any case, did not allow him to behave in any other way. The Chatterji children, like the Chatterji car, were pulled into her orbit. Amit, Kuku, Dipankar and even Tapan (when he had a moment to spare from his homework at St Xavier's) were each assigned various tasks: the making of guest lists, the selection of gifts, the collecting of items that had been ordered from the shops. Perhaps

Lata had known that of the three men courting her, the only one who could be rejected without the loss of his friendship was Amit.

19.3

When Mrs Rupa Mehra told Meenakshi one afternoon to come with her to the jewellers to help her buy, or at least select, a wedding band for Haresh, Meenakshi stretched her neck lazily and said:

'Oh, but Ma, I'm going somewhere this afternoon.'

'But your canasta is tomorrow.'

'Well,' said Meenakshi with a slow and rather feline smile, 'life is not all canasta and rummy.'

'Where are you going?' demanded her mother-in-law.

'Oh, I'm going here and there,' said Meenakshi, adding to Aparna: 'Darling, please release my hair.'

Mrs Rupa Mehra, unaware that she had just been treated to a Kakoli-couplet, became annoyed.

'But these are the jewellers you recommended. I will get much better service if you come with me. If you don't come with me, I'll have to go to Lokkhi Babu's.'

'Oh, no, Ma, you really shouldn't. Go to Jauhri's; they're the ones who made my little gold pears.' Meenakshi stroked her neck just below her ear with the scarlet nail of her middle finger.

This last remark infuriated Mrs Rupa Mehra. 'All right,' she said, 'if that's how much you care about your sister-in-law's wedding, go gallivanting around town. My Varun will come with me.'

When they got to the shop, Mrs Rupa Mehra did not in the event find it difficult to charm Mr Jauhri. Within two minutes he knew all about Bentsen Pryce and the IAS and Haresh's testimonials. When he had reassured her that he could make anything she wished and have it ready for collection in three weeks, she ordered a gold champakali necklace ('It is so pretty with its hollow buds and not too heavy for Lata') and a Jaipur kundan set—a necklace and earrings in glass and gold and enamel.

As Mrs Rupa Mehra chattered on happily about her daughter, Mr Jauhri, who was a sociable man, added his comments and congratulations. When she mentioned her own late husband, who had been in the railways, Mr Jauhri lamented the decline in service. After a while, when everything had been settled satisfactorily, she said that she had to be going. She got out her Mont Blanc pen and wrote down her name and address and telephone number.

Mr Jauhri looked startled.

'Ah,' he said, recognizing the surname and address.

'Yes,' said Mrs Rupa Mehra, 'my daughter-in-law has been here before.'

'Mrs Mehra—was it your husband's medal she gave me to have made into her chain and earrings? Beautiful—just like little pears?'

'Yes,' said Mrs Rupa Mehra, fighting to keep back her tears. 'I will come back in three weeks. Please treat the order as urgent.'

Mr Jauhri said: 'Madam, let me check with my calendar and orders. Maybe I can give them to you in two and a half weeks.' He disappeared into the back of the shop. When he returned he placed a small red box on the counter and opened it.

Inside, sitting on a cushion of white silk, was Raghubir Mehra's gold medal for Engineering.

19.4

Twice that month did Mrs Rupa Mehra shuttle between Calcutta and Brahmpur.

She was so delighted to have the medal restored to her ('The fact is, Madam, I could not bear to melt it down.') that she bought it back instantly, drawing out whatever was necessary from her savings, and trying to economize slightly more on the necessary wedding expenses. She was—for a few days at least—entirely reconciled to Meenakshi and her ways. For if Meenakshi had not given Mr Jauhri this medal, it would have been stolen from the house in Sunny Park with the rest of the jewellery, and, like the Physics medal, would have vanished for good. Meenakshi too, when she got back from wherever it was she had been, looked happy and satisfied and was quite pleasant to her mother-in-law and Varun. When she heard about the medal she was not slow in claiming a perverse credit for events—and her mother-in-law did not object.

When Mrs Rupa Mehra got to Brahmpur she brought the medal with her and showed it triumphantly to everyone in the family, and everyone was delighted with her good fortune.

'You must study hard, Lata, there are so few days left'—Mrs Rupa Mehra cautioned her daughter—'or you will never have your Daddy's academic success. You should not let your wedding and other things distract you.' And with that she put *Ideal Marriage*, carefully wrapped in the bridal colours of red and gold, into her hands.

'This book will teach you everything—about Men,' she said, lowering her voice for some reason. 'Even our Sita and Savitri had to have these experiences.'

'Thank you, Ma,' said Lata, a little apprehensively.

Mrs Rupa Mehra was suddenly embarrassed, and disappeared into the next room with the excuse that she had to phone her father.

Lata promptly unwrapped the package and, forgetting her studies, began to look through the Dutch sexologist's advice. She was as much repelled as fascinated by what he had to offer.

There were numerous graphs describing the man's and the woman's degrees of excitement under different circumstances, for example, coitus interruptus and what the author called 'Ideal Communion'. There were multicoloured, copiously labelled, not very appealing cross-sections of various organs. 'Marriage is a science. (H. de Balzac)' read the epigraph of the book, and Dr Van de Velde evidently took this aphorism seriously not only in his illustrations but also in his taxonomy. He divided what he shyly called his 'Synousiology' into converse and averse types, and further divided these into the habitual or medial attitude, the first attitude of extension, the second attitude of extension (suspensory), the attitudes of flexion (favoured, according to him, by the Chinese), the attitude of equitation (in which Martial described Hector and Andromache), the sedentary attitude, the anterior-lateral attitude, the ventral attitude, the posterior-lateral attitude, the attitude of averse flexion, and the posterior-sedentary attitude. Lata was amazed by the possibilities: she had only thought of one. (Indeed, even Malati had only ever mentioned one.) She wondered what the nuns at St Sophia's would think of a book like this.

A footnote read as follows:

> Arrangements have now been made for the manufacture of Dr Van de Velde's Jellies ('Eugam'): Lubricant, Contraceptive and Proconceptive. They are made by Messrs. Harman Freese, 32 Great Dover Street, London, S.E.1, who are also the makers of the author's other preparations and pessaries ('Gamophile') referred to in 'Fertility and Sterility in Marriage'.

From time to time Dr Van de Velde quoted approvingly the Dutch poet Cats, whose folk wisdom did not emerge well in translation:

> Listen my friend, and know the reason why:
> All beauty lies in the beholder's eye.

But for all that, Lata was glad that her mother had cared enough for her to overcome her own embarrassment and put this book in her hands. She still had a few weeks to prepare herself for Life.

Lata looked thoughtful through most of dinner, glancing at Pran and Savita and wondering whether Savita too had received an *Ideal Marriage* before her wedding There was jelly for pudding, and to Mrs Rupa Mehra's puzzlement—and everyone else's—Lata began to laugh and would not explain why.

19.5

Lata took her final exams as if in a trance: sometimes she got the impression that she was someone other than herself. She felt she had done well, but this was combined with a curious, dislocated feeling—not like the panic of the previous year, but a sense that she was floating above her physical self and looking down on it from a height. Once, after a paper was over, she wandered down from the examination hall and sat on the bench beneath the gulmohur tree. Again the dark-orange flowers lay thick below her feet. Had it only been a year since she had met him?

If you love him so much, can you be happy to leave him miserable?

Where was he? Even if his exams were being held in the same building, he did not stand on the steps afterwards. He did not pass by the bench.

Just after the last paper, there was a concert by Ustad Majeed Khan, to which she went with Malati. Kabir was nowhere to be seen.

Amit had written her a brief note of congratulation, but—after their few moments in the bookshop and the coffee house—Kabir had as good as disappeared.

Whose life am I living? Lata wondered. Was my acceptance just a reaction?

Despite Haresh's encouraging letters and her own cheerful replies, Lata began to feel both uncertain and very lonely.

Sometimes she sat on the banyan root and looked out over the Ganga, recollecting what it was pointless to recollect. Would she have been happy with him? Or he with her? He was so jealous now, so intense, so violent, so unlike the casual cricketer whom she had seen laughing and practising at the nets a year ago. How different he was now from the knight who had rescued her from the gulmohur bench and from Mr Nowrojee's.

And I? she asked herself. How would I have acted in his place? With a jovial attempt at good fellowship? Even now I almost feel it's he who's left me—and I can't bear it.

Two weeks more, she thought, and I will be the Bride of Goodyear Welted.

Oh, Kabir, Kabir—she wept.

I should run away, she thought.

I should run away, she thought, far from Haresh, far from Kabir, far from Arun and Varun and Ma and the whole Chatterji clan, far from Pran and Maan and Hindus and Muslims and passionate love and passionate hatred and all loud noises—just me and Malati and Savita and the baby.

We'll sit on the sand on the other side of the Ganga and go to sleep for a year or two.

19.6

The wedding arrangements proceeded with great verve and much conflict. Mrs Rupa Mehra, Malati, Dr Kishen Chand Seth and Arun each tried to act as major-domo.

Dr Kishen Chand Seth insisted on asking Saeeda Bai to sing at the wedding. 'Who else can one ask,' he said, 'when Saeeda Bai is in Brahmpur? Her throttling has opened her throat, they say.'

It was only when he realized that the entire Prem Nivas contingent would boycott the wedding that he relented. But by then he was off on to something else: the length of the list of invitees. It was too long, he claimed: his garden would be destroyed, his pockets emptied.

Everyone reassured him that they would be careful not to expand their own invitation list, and everyone went ahead and invited everyone they met. As for Dr Kishen Chand Seth, he was the worst offender of all: half the Subzipore Club and half the doctors of Brahmpur were invited, and almost anyone who had ever played bridge with him. 'A wedding is always a time for settling scores,' he explained cryptically.

Arun arrived a few days early and tried to take over the management of events from his grandfather. But Parvati, who apparently realized how good it was for her husband to exhaust himself with excitement, put paid to his attempts at usurpation. She even shouted at Arun in front of the servants, and he retreated before 'that harridan'.

The arrival from Delhi of the baraat—the groom's party—brought its own excitement and complications. Haresh's foster-parents had been satisfied on the score of astrology; his mother, however, insisted on various precautions being taken about the preparation of her food. She would have been horrified to know that at Pran's house, where she ate one day, the cook was a Muslim. His name was therefore converted from Mateen to Matadeen for the duration.

Two of Haresh's foster-brothers and their wives came with the baraat, as did the doubting Umesh Uncle. Their English was terrible and their sense of punctuality so lax as to be almost non-existent, and in general they confirmed Arun's worst fears. Mrs Rupa Mehra, however, gave the women saris and talked to them endlessly.

They approved of Lata.

Haresh was not allowed to meet Lata. He stayed with Sunil Patwardhan, and the St Stephen's contingent gathered around him in the evenings to tease him and enact Scenes from Married Life. The vast Sunil was usually the shrinking bride.

Haresh visited Kedarnath's house in Misri Mandi. He told Veena how sorry he was to hear of Mrs Mahesh Kapoor's death and all the anxieties that the family had had to undergo. Old Mrs Tandon and Bhaskar were happy that he had visited. And Haresh was delighted to be able to mention to Kedarnath that the order for brogues from Prahapore would be coming through within the week, together with a short-term loan for the purchase of materials.

19.7

Haresh also visited Ravidaspur one morning. He took with him some bananas for Jagat Ram's children, the good news about the Praha order, and an invitation to his wedding.

The fruit was a luxury; there were no fruit sellers in Ravidaspur. The barefooted sons of the shoemaker accepted the bananas with suspicious reluctance and ate them with relish, dropping the skins into the drain that ran alongside the house.

The news about the Praha order was met with satisfaction, and the fact that a loan for the purchase of raw materials was to accompany it was greeted with intense relief. Jagat Ram was looking rather subdued, thought Haresh. He had expected elation.

Jagat Ram reacted to Haresh's wedding invitation with visible shock, not so much because Haresh was getting married, and in Brahmpur at that, but because he should have thought of inviting him.

Moved as he was, he had to refuse. The two worlds did not mix. He knew it; it was a fact of life. That a jatav from Ravidaspur should be present as a guest at a wedding at the house of Dr Kishen Chand Seth would cause social distress that he did not wish to be the centre of. It would injure his dignity. Apart from the practical problems of what to wear and what to give, he knew that he would feel no joy and only intense awkwardness at being present on the occasion.

Haresh, reading his mind only partially, said, with brusque tact: 'You're not to bring a gift. I've never been a believer in gifts at weddings. But you must come. We are colleagues. I won't hear of your not coming. And the invitation is also for your wife if you want her to come.'

It was only with the greatest of reluctance that Jagat Ram agreed. The red-and-gold invitation, meanwhile, was being passed by the boys from hand to hand.

'Haven't they left anything for your daughter?' asked Haresh, as the last of the bananas disappeared.

'Oh, her dust has been washed away,' said Jagat Ram quietly.

'What?' said Haresh, shocked.

Jagat Ram shook his head. 'What I mean to say—' he began, and his voice was choked.

'What happened, for heaven's sake?'

'She got an infection. My wife said it was serious, but I thought, children get high fever so quickly, and it comes down just as quickly. And so I delayed. It was the money too; and the doctors here are, well, high-handed with us.'

'Your poor wife—'

'My wife said nothing, she said nothing against me. What she thinks, I don't know.' After a pause he quoted two lines:

'Don't break the thread of love, Raheem has said.
What breaks won't join; if joined, it knots the thread.'

When Haresh commiserated, Jagat Ram merely sucked in his breath through his teeth and shook his head again.

19.8

When Haresh returned to Sunil's, he found his father waiting for him impatiently.

'Where have you been?' he asked Haresh, crinkling his nose. 'It's almost ten. The Registrar will be at Dr Seth's house in a few minutes.'

'Oh!' said Haresh, looking surprised. 'I'd better take a quick shower.'

He had forgotten about the time of the civil ceremony, which Mrs Rupa Mehra had insisted on having on the day before the wedding proper. She felt that she had to protect her daughter from the injustices of the traditional Hindu Law; marriages solemnized before a Registrar were governed by laws that were much fairer to women.

The civil ceremony, however, was such a brief and dry affair that almost no one attached any significance to it, although from the moment it was over, Haresh and Lata were legally man and wife. Only a dozen or so people attended, and Haresh was reproved by his mother for being late.

Lata had alternated between serene optimism and terrifying attacks of uncertainty for the last week. After the civil ceremony was over, she felt calm and almost happy, and fonder of Haresh than before. From time to time he had smiled at her as if he knew exactly when she had most needed reassurance.

19.9

Amit, Kakoli, Dipankar, Meenakshi, Tapan, Aparna, Varun and even Hans had arrived together from Calcutta early that morning and had been present at the civil ceremony. Pran's house was bursting at the seams. Dr Kishen Chand Seth's house too was entirely overrun. Only Prem Nivas, lacking its mistress, remained almost empty.

All manner of known and unknown people wandered in and out of Dr

Kishen Chand's house. Since he had decided to operate on the unusually pacific assumption that anyone whom he didn't recognize must have been asked by someone else, or else must be involved with the lighting or the catering arrangements, he threatened very few people with his stick. Parvati kept an eye on him and made sure that no one came to grief.

It was a hot day. A few birds—mynas, babblers, sparrows, bulbuls, and barbets—were disturbed in their nesting by this constant throng of noisy, busy humans. The beds in the garden had gone to seed; except for a few tobacco flowers, nothing on the ground was in bloom. But the trees—champa, jacaranda, and Sita ashok—were full of white or mauve or red blossom, and bougainvillaea—orange, red, pink, and magenta—fell in great masses over the walls of the house and down the trunks of trees. From time to time, amid the continuous racket of the barbets, the call of a distant brainfever bird sounded high and insistent and clear.

Lata sat in an inner room with the other women for the singing and henna ceremonies. Kuku and Meenakshi, Malati and Savita, Mrs Rupa Mehra, Veena, Hema and her Taiji, all kept themselves entertained and Lata distracted by singing wedding songs, some innocent, some risqué, and dancing to the beat of a dholak while an old woman fitted them all with glass bangles of their choice—from Firozabad, she claimed—and another squeezed bold but delicate patterns of henna on their hands and feet. Lata looked at her hands, covered now with the moist, beautiful tracery, and began to weep.

She wondered how long it would take to set. Savita took out a handkerchief and wiped her tears for her.

Veena quickly began a song about her delicate hands and how she couldn't draw water at the public well. She was her father-in-law's favourite; he had felt sorry for her and had had a well made for her in the garden of the house. She was the favourite of her husband's elder brother; he had given her a gold vessel for the water. She was the favourite of her husband's younger brother; he had given her a silken rope for the bucket. She was the beloved of her husband, and he had hired two water-carriers for her. But her husband's sister and mother were jealous of her, and had secretly gone and covered up the well.

In another song the jealous mother-in-law slept next to the newly married bride so that her husband couldn't visit her at night. Mrs Rupa Mehra enjoyed these songs as much as she always did, probably because it was impossible for her to imagine herself in any such role.

Malati—together with her mother, who had suddenly appeared in

Brahmpur—sang, 'You grind the spices, fat one, and we will eat!'

Kakoli clapped loudly while her henna was still green and moist—and smudged it completely. Her musical contribution was a variant of 'Roly Poly Mr Kohli', which, in the absence of her mother, she sang to the tune of a Tagore song:

'Roly poly Mr Kohli
Walking slowly up the stairs.
Holy souly Mrs Kohli
Comes and takes him unawares.

Mr Kohli, base and lowly,
Stares at choli, dreams of lust,
As the holy Mrs Kohli
With her pallu hides her bust.'

19.10

Before dusk the next day the guests began to gather on the lawn to the sound of the shehnai.

The men of the family stood by the gate and received them. Arun and Varun were dressed in fine, starched, white kurta-pyjamas embroidered with chikan work. Pran was dressed in the white sharkskin sherwani he had worn at his own wedding—though it had been winter then.

Mrs Rupa Mehra's brother had come from Madras as usual, but had arrived too late for the bangle ceremony, which he had been expected to help perform. He knew almost none of the people he was greeting, and only a few of them looked familiar to him, perhaps from the time of Savita's wedding. He greeted everyone decorously as they passed into the garden. Dr Kishen Chand Seth, on the other hand, overheated in the straitjacket of an extremely tight black achkan, got impatient after a while with this endless meeting and greeting, shouted at his son, whom he had not seen for more than a year, loosened a few buttons, and wandered off to supervise something. He had refused to stand in for his late son-in-law in the ceremonies on the grounds that sitting still and listening to priests would destroy both his circulation and his serenity.

Mrs Rupa Mehra was wearing a beige chiffon sari with a beautiful gold border—a gift from her daughter-in-law that had made her entirely forget the incident of the lacquer box. She knew that He wouldn't have wanted her to dress too much like a widow on their younger daughter's wedding day.

The groom's party was fifteen minutes late already. Mrs Rupa Mehra was starving: she was not meant to eat until she had given her daughter away, and she was glad that the astrologers had set the actual time of the wedding for eight o'clock, and not, say, eleven.

'Where are they?' she demanded of Maan, who happened to be standing nearby and was gazing in the direction of the gate.

'I'm sorry, Ma,' said Maan. 'Who do you mean?' He had been looking out for Firoz.

'The baraat, of course.'

'Oh, yes, the baraat—well, they should be coming at any minute. Shouldn't they be here already?'

'Yes,' said Mrs Rupa Mehra, as impatient and anxious as the Boy standing on the Burning Deck. 'Yes, of course they should.'

The baraat was at last sighted, and everyone crowded towards the gate. A large, maroon, flower-adorned Chevrolet drove up. It narrowly avoided scratching Dr Kishen Chand Seth's grey Buick, which was parked somewhat obstructively near the entrance. Haresh stepped out. He was accompanied by his parents and his brothers and was followed by, among others, a motley crowd of his college friends. Arun and Varun escorted him to the verandah. Lata emerged from inside the house, dressed in a red-and-gold sari, and with her eyes lowered, as befitted a bride. They exchanged garlands. Sunil Patwardhan broke into loud cheers, and the photographer clicked away.

They walked across the lawn to the wedding platform, decorated with roses and tuberoses, and sat down facing the young priest from the local Arya Samaj temple. He lit the fire and began the ceremony. Haresh's foster-parents sat near Haresh, Mrs Rupa Mehra sat near Lata, and Arun and Varun sat behind her.

'Sit up straight,' said Arun to Varun.

'I am sitting straight!' retorted Varun Mehra, IAS, angrily. He noticed that Lata's garland had slipped off her left shoulder. He helped rearrange it and glared at his brother.

The guests, unusually for a wedding, were quiet and attentive as the priest went through the rites. Mrs Rupa Mehra was sobbing through her Sanskrit, and Savita was sobbing too, and soon Lata was crying as well. When her mother took her hand, filled it with rose petals and pronounced the words, 'O bridegroom, accept this well-adorned bride called Lata,' Haresh, prompted by the priest, took her hand firmly in his own and repeated the words: 'I thank you, and accept her willingly.'

'Cheer up,' he added in English. 'I hope you won't have to go through this again.' And Lata, whether at that thought or at his tone of voice, did indeed cheer up.

Everything went well. Her brothers poured puffed rice on to her hands and into the fire each time she and Haresh circled it. The knot between their scarves was tied, and bright red sindoor was applied to the parting of Lata's hair with the gold ring that Haresh was to give her. This ring ceremony puzzled the priest (it didn't fit in with his idea of Arya Samaji rituals), but because Mrs Rupa Mehra insisted on it, he went along with it.

One or two children squabbled tearfully over the possession of some rose petals; and an insistent old woman tried without success to get the priest to mention Babé Lalu, the clan deity of the Khannas, in the course of his liturgy; other than that, everything went harmoniously.

But when the people who were gathered together recited the Gayatri Mantra three times before the witnessing fire, Pran, glancing at Maan, noticed that his head was bowed and his lips trembling as he mumbled the words. Like his elder brother, he could not forget the last time that the ancient words had been recited in his presence, and before a different fire.

19.11

It was a warm evening, and there was less silk and more fine cotton than at Savita's wedding. But the jewellery glittered just as gloriously. Meenakshi's little pear-earrings, Veena's navratan and Malati's emeralds glinted across the garden, whispering to each other the stories of their owners.

The younger Chatterjis were out in full force, but there were very few politicians, and no children from Rudhia running wildly around. A couple of executives from the small Praha factory in Brahmpur were present, however, as were some of the middlemen from the Brahmpur Shoe Mart.

Jagat Ram too had come, but not his wife. He stood by himself for a while until Kedarnath noticed him and beckoned him to join them.

When he was introduced to old Mrs Tandon, she was unable to stifle her discomfiture. She looked at him as if he smelt, and gave him a weak namaste.

Jagat Ram said to Kedarnath: 'I have to go now. Would you give this to Haresh Sahib and his bride?' He handed him what looked like a small shoebox covered in brown paper.

'But aren't you going to congratulate him?'

'Well, there's a long line,' said Jagat Ram, tugging a little at his moustache. 'Please congratulate him for me.'

Old Mrs Tandon had turned to Haresh's parents, and was talking to them about Neel Darvaza, which she had visited as a child. She congratulated them and, in the course of the conversation, contrived to mention that Lata was rather too fond of music.

'Oh, good,' said Haresh's foster-father. 'We too are very fond of music.'

Old Mrs Tandon was displeased, and decided to say nothing more.

Malati, meanwhile, was talking to the musicians themselves, a shehnai player who had been known to her own musician-friend, and the tabla player Motu Chand.

Motu, who remembered Malati from the day he had stood in at the Haridas College of Music, asked her about Ustad Majeed Khan and his famous disciple Ishaq, whom, sadly, he very rarely met these days. Malati told him about the concert she had very recently attended, praised Ishaq's musicianship, and mentioned that she had been struck by the indulgence which the arrogant maestro granted to him: he rarely, for instance, broke in with a dominating improvisation of his own when Ishaq was singing. In a world of professional jealousy and rivalry even between teacher and student, they performed with a sense of complementarity that was wonderful to see.

It had begun to be said of Ishaq—and that too within a year of his first strumming the tanpura before his Ustad—that he had the makings of one of the great singers of his time.

'Well,' said Motu Chand, 'things are not the same without him where I work.' He sighed, then, noticing Malati look a bit blank, said: 'Were you not at Prem Nivas at Holi last year?'

'No,' said Malati, realizing from his question that Motu must be Saeeda Bai's tabla player. 'And this year, of course. . . .'

'Of course,' said Motu sadly. 'Terrible, terrible . . . and now with that fellow Rasheed's suicide. . . . He taught Saeeda Bai's, well, sister, you know . . . but he caused so much trouble that they had to get the watchman to beat him up . . . and then we heard later. . . . Well, there's nothing but trouble in the world, nothing but trouble—' He began to hammer at the little wooden cylinders around his tabla to tighten the straps and adjust the pitch. The shehnai player nodded at him.

'This Rasheed you're talking about—' asked Malati, suddenly quite troubled herself. 'He's not the socialist, is he?—the history student—'

'Yes, I think so,' said Motu, flexing his well-padded fingers; and the tabla and shehnai began to play again.

19.12

Maan, dressed in a kurta-pyjama, as suited the weather, was standing a little distance away and heard nothing of this conversation. He looked sad, almost unsociable.

For a moment he wondered where the harsingar tree was, before he realized that he was in a different garden altogether. Firoz came up to him, and they stood there, silent, for a while. A rose petal or two floated down from somewhere. Neither bothered to brush it off. Imtiaz joined them after a while, then the Nawab Sahib and Mahesh Kapoor.

'It's all for the best, on the whole,' said Mahesh Kapoor. 'If I had been an MLA, Agarwal would have had to ask me to join his Cabinet, and I would not have been able to stand it.'

'Well,' said the Nawab Sahib, 'whether things are for the best or not, that's how they are.'

There was a pause. Everyone was friendly enough, but no one knew what to talk about. Every topic seemed closed for one reason or another. There was no mention of law or laws, of doctors or hospitals, of gardens or music, of future plans or past recollections, of politics or religion, of bees or lotuses.

The judges of the Supreme Court had agreed that the Zamindari Acts were constitutional; they were in the process of writing their judgement, which would be announced to the world at large in a few days.

S.S. Sharma had been called to Delhi. The Congress MLAs of Purva Pradesh had elected L.N. Agarwal as Chief Minister. Astoundingly enough, one of his first acts in office had been to send a firm note to the Raja of Marh refusing government or police protection for any further attempts to salvage the linga.

The Banaras people had decided that Maan was no longer a suitable boy; they had informed Mahesh Kapoor of their decision.

All these subjects, and many others, were on everyone's mind—and no one's tongue.

Meenakshi and Kakoli, noticing the notorious Maan, swept up in a shimmer of chiffon, and even Mahesh Kapoor was not unhappy at the diversion they provided. Before they got there, however, Maan—who had just noticed Professor Mishra prowling vastly in the vicinity—had made good his disappearance.

When they heard that Firoz and Imtiaz were twins, Meenakshi and Kakoli were delighted.

'If I have twins,' said Kuku, 'I shall call them Prabodhini and Shayani. Then one can sleep while the other is awake.'

'How very silly, Kuku,' said Meenakshi. 'You'll never get any sleep yourself that way. And they won't ever get to know each other. Tell me, which of you is the elder?'

'I am,' said Imtiaz.

'No, you're not,' said Meenakshi.

'I assure you, Mrs Mehra, I am. Ask my father here.'

'He wouldn't know,' said Meenakshi. 'A very nice man, who gave me a lovely little lacquer box, once told me that, according to the Japanese, the baby who comes out second is the elder, because he proves his courtesy and maturity by allowing his younger brother to emerge first.'

'Mrs Mehra,' said Firoz, laughing, 'I can never thank you enough.'

'Oh, do call me Meenakshi. Charming idea, isn't it? Now if I have twins I shall call them Etah and Etawah! Or Kumbh and Karan. Or Bentsen and Pryce. Or something quite unforgettable. Etawah Mehra—how exquisitely exotic. Where has Aparna got to? And tell me, who are those two foreigners there, talking to Arun and Hans?' She stretched her long neck lazily and pointed with the red-nail-polished finger of a delicately hennaed hand.

'They are from the local Praha factory,' said Mahesh Kapoor.

'Oh, how dreadful!' exclaimed Kuku. 'They're probably discussing the German invasion of Czechoslovakia. Or is it the communists? I must separate them at once. Or at least listen to what they're saying. I'm so desperately bored. Nothing ever happens in Brahmpur. Come, Meenakshi. And we haven't yet given Ma and Luts our heart-deep congratulations. Not that they deserve them. How stupid of her not to marry Amit. Now he'll never marry anyone, I'm sure, and he'll become as grouchy as Cuddles. But of course, they could always have a torrid affair,' she added hopefully.

And in a flash of flesh the Chatterjis of the backless cholis were gone.

19.13

'She's married the wrong man,' said Malati to her mother. 'And it's breaking my heart.'

'Malati,' said her mother, 'everyone must make their own mistakes. Why are you sure it is a mistake?'

'It is, it is, I know it!' said Malati passionately. 'And she'll find out soon enough.' She was determined to get Lata to at least write a letter to Kabir. Surely Haresh, with the simpering Simran in his shady background, would have to accept that as reasonable.

'Malati,' said her mother calmly, 'don't make mischief in someone else's marriage. Get married yourself. What happened to the five boys whose father you met in Nainital?'

But Malati was looking across the crowd at Varun, who was smiling rather weakly and adoringly at Kalpana Gaur.

'Would you like me to marry an IAS officer?' she asked her mother. 'The most sweet and weak-willed and idiotic one I've ever met?'

'I want you to marry someone with character,' said her mother. 'Someone like your father. Someone whom you cannot push around. And that's what you want as well.'

Mrs Rupa Mehra too was staring at Kalpana Gaur and Varun in amazement. Surely not!—surely not!—she thought. Kalpana, who was like a daughter to her: how could she have battened on to her poor son? Could I be imagining things? she wondered. But Varun was so guileless—or, rather, so ineffectual even when he tried to be guileful that the symptoms of his infatuation were unmistakable.

How and when could this have happened?

'Yes, yes, thank you, thank you,' said Mrs Rupa Mehra impatiently to someone who was congratulating her.

What could be done to prevent such a disaster? Kalpana was years older than Varun, and—even if she was like a daughter to her—Mrs Rupa Mehra had no intention of having her as a daughter-in-law.

But now Malati ('that girl who makes nothing but mischief') had gone up to Varun, and was looking deeply, deeply with her peerless green eyes into his. Varun's jaw had dropped slightly and he appeared to be stammering.

Leaving Lata and Haresh to fend for themselves, Mrs Rupa Mehra marched up to Varun.

'Hello, Ma,' said Kalpana Gaur. 'Many congratulations. What a lovely wedding. And I can't help feeling responsible for it, in a way.'

'Yes,' said Mrs Rupa Mehra shortly.

'Hello, Ma,' said Malati. 'Yes, congratulations are in order from me as well.' Receiving no immediate response, she added, without thinking: 'These gulab-jamuns are delicious. You must try one.'

This reference to forbidden sweets annoyed Mrs Rupa Mehra further. She glared at the offending objects for a second or two.

'What is the matter, Malati?' she asked with some asperity. 'You still look a little under the weather—you've been running around so much, I'm not surprised—and, Kalpana, standing in the centre of the crowd is not good for your hot spots; go and sit on that bench there at once, it is much cooler. Now I must have a word with Varun, who is not doing his duties as a host.'

And she took him aside.

'You too will marry a girl I choose,' said Mrs Rupa Mehra firmly to her younger son.

'But—but, Ma—' Varun shifted from foot to foot.

'A suitable girl, that is what I want for you,' said Mrs Rupa Mehra in an admonitory voice. 'That is what your Daddy would have wanted. A suitable girl, and no exceptions.'

While Varun was trying to figure out the implications of that last phrase, Arun joined them, together with Aparna, who held her father's hand in one hand and an ice-cream cone in another.

'Not pistachio, Daadi,' she announced, disappointedly.

'Don't worry, sweetheart,' said Mrs Rupa Mehra, 'we'll get you lots of pistachio ice-cream tomorrow.'

'At the zoo.'

'Yes, at the zoo,' said Mrs Rupa Mehra absently. She frowned. 'Sweetheart, it's too hot to go to the zoo.'

'But you promised,' Aparna pointed out.

'Did I, sweetheart? When?'

'Just now! Just now!'

'Your Daddy will take you,' said Mrs Rupa Mehra.

'Your Varun Chacha will take you,' said Arun.

'And Kalpana Aunty will come with us,' said Varun.

'No,' said Mrs Rupa Mehra, 'I will be talking with her tomorrow about old times and other matters.'

'Why can't Lata Bua come with us?' asked Aparna.

'Because she'll be going to Calcutta tomorrow, with Haresh Phupha,' said Varun.

'Because they're married?'

'Because they're married.'

'Oh. And Bhaskar can come with us, and Tapan Maama.'

'They certainly can. But Tapan says that all he wants to do is to read comics and sleep.'

'And the Lady Baby.'

'Uma's too small to enjoy the zoo,' Varun pointed out. 'And the snakes will frighten her. They might even gobble her up.' He laughed sinisterly and rubbed his stomach, to Aparna's delight.

Uma was at the moment herself the object of enjoyment and admiration. Savita's aunts were cooing over her; they were extremely pleased that, despite their predictions, she had not turned out to be 'as black as her father'. This they said in full hearing of Pran, who laughed. For the colour of Haresh's skin they had nothing but praise; it would cancel out the flaw of Lata's complexion.

With matters of such Mendelian moment did the aunts from Lucknow and Kanpur and Banaras and Madras occupy themselves.

'Lata's baby is bound to be born black,' suggested Pran. 'Things balance out within a family.'

'Chhi, chhi, how can you say such things?' said Mrs Kakkar.

'Pran has babies on the brain,' said Savita.

Pran grinned—rather boyishly, Savita thought.

On the 1st of April this year, he had received a phone call that had sent him beaming back to the breakfast table. Parvati, it appeared, was pregnant. Mrs Rupa Mehra had reacted with horror.

Even when she had recalled the date, she had remained annoyed with Pran. 'How can you joke this year when things are so sad?' she demanded. But in Pran's view one might as well try to be cheerful, however sad the core of things might be. And besides, he felt, it would not be such a terrible thing if Parvati and Kishy had a baby. At present they each dominated the other. A baby would redirect the equation.

'What's wrong with having babies on the brain?' said Pran to the assembly of aunts. 'Veena's expecting, and Bhaskar and Kedarnath seem to be quite happy about it. That's some good news in a sad year. And Uma too will need a brother and a sister sooner or later. Things won't be quite so tight on my new salary.'

'Quite right,' the aunts agreed. 'You can't call it a family unless there are at least three children.'

'Contract and tort permitting, of course,' said Savita. Unhardened by the law she was looking as lovely and soft as ever in a blue-and-silver sari.

'Yes, darling,' said Pran. 'Contract and tort permitting.'

'Our congratulations, Dr Kapoor,' said a strikingly inaudible voice behind him.

Pran found himself pulled into the middle of a little pride of literary lions: Mr Barua, Mr Nowrojee, and Sunil Patwardhan.

'Oh, thank you,' said Pran, 'but I've been married a year and a half now.'

Mr Nowrojee's face registered a fleeting and wintry smile.

'I meant, of course, congratulations on your recent elevation, so'—he smiled sadly—'so very richly deserved. And I have been meaning to tell you for many months now how very much I enjoyed your *Twelfth Night*. But you disappeared so early from Chatterji's reading. I notice he is here this evening—I sent him a sheaf of villanelles a month ago, but have had no response so far; do you think I should trouble him with a reminder?'

'It was Mr Barua who was the producer this year, Mr Nowrojee,' replied Pran. 'Mine was *Julius Caesar*, the year before.'

'Oh, of course, of course, though one often wonders with Shakespeare—as I said to E.M. Forster in—was it—1913?—'

'So, you bastard, you've managed to get Joyce on the syllabus after all,' broke in Sunil Patwardhan. 'An awful decision, an awful decision. I was just talking to Professor Mishra. He sounded stricken.'

'Stick to mathematics, Sunil.'

'I plan to,' said Sunil. 'Have you read Joyce on the sound of cricket bats?' he asked, turning to Mr Barua and Mr Nowrojee: "Pick, pack, pock, puck: like drops of water in a fountain falling softly in the brimming bowl." And that was early Joyce! Shall I do an imitation of Finnegan waking?'

'No,' said Pran. 'Spare us the joy.'

19.14

Food was served at the far end of the garden and the guests roamed around, meeting each other, replenishing their plates, and congratulating the bride and groom and their families. Gifts and envelopes of money piled up near the decorated swing where the two of them were now sitting. One by one Lata met those whom she had not met before.

Kalpana Gaur said: 'I don't know who I am—I don't know if I'm part of the groom's party or the bride's.'

'Yes,' said Haresh, 'it's a problem. A serious problem. The first problem of our married life.'

While Haresh laughed and joked with all his friends, and accepted their boisterous humour and congratulations, Lata said very little.

When Mr Sahgal, her uncle from Lucknow, approached them with a repellent smile, she held Haresh's hand tightly.

'What's the matter?' asked Haresh.

'Nothing,' said Lata.

'But there must be—'

Mr Sahgal was holding out his hand to congratulate Haresh. 'I must congratulate you,' he said. 'I saw from the very beginning that you two would get married—it was meant to be so—it is a match that Lata's father would have approved of. She is a very, very good girl.' Lata had closed her eyes. He looked at her face, at the lipstick on her lips, with a slight sneer, before moving away.

Elsewhere, Dr Durrani, eating kulfi with an absorbed air, was talking to Pran, Kedarnath, Veena and Bhaskar. 'So, er, interesting, as I was saying to your son, this insistence on the number seven . . . seven, um, steps, and seven, er, seven, circles round the fire. Seven er, notes to the scale, speaking in terms of a modulus, of course, and seven days to the, er, week.' He suddenly remembered something and frowned, inching his bushy eyebrows upwards. 'I must apologize, it's Thursday, you see, so my son, my, er, elder son, could not be present. He has to be, er, er, elsewhere—'

The Durrani invitation had been a dreadful mistake in Mrs Rupa Mehra's eyes—and, once extended, was unretractable. 'Do come along—and, of course, bring your family,' Dr Kishen Chand Seth had told him over bridge, but Dr Seth was disappointed that the mad wife and villainous son had not turned up. Dr Durrani himself was so inoffensively vague that he was incapable of locating the groom at his own wedding.

Amit, meanwhile, had been set upon by two elderly women, one of whom was wearing a glorious ruby pendant, like a radiating star, on her breast.

She said: 'That man told us that you're the son of Mr Justice Chatterji.'

'I am,' said Amit with a smile.

'We know your father very well from our Darjeeling days. He would come up every year for the Puja holidays.'

'He still tries to.'

'Yes, but we're not there any longer. You must remember us to him. Now, tell me, are you the clever one?'

'Yes,' said Amit resignedly. 'I'm the clever one.'

This delighted the dazzling lady.

'I knew you when you were that high,' she exclaimed. 'You were very clever, even then, so I'm not surprised you've written all those books.'

'Oh?' said Amit.

Not to be outdone, the other lady asserted that she had known him since he was a bulge.

'But a brainy bulge, no doubt,' said Amit.

'Now, now,' said the lady.

There was a commotion at the gate. A group of five hermaphrodites, hearing that there was a wedding in progress, had turned up, and were singing and dancing and demanding money. So shameless were their gestures that the nearby guests were turning away in shock, but Sunil Patwardhan rushed over with his friends to enjoy the fun. Dr Kishen Chand Seth, brandishing his stick, was trying to drive them away; but they were making lewd remarks about both it and him. They would have to be paid to go away. He offered them twenty rupees, and their leader told him that he wouldn't even service him for that amount. Dr Kishen Chand Seth hopped around in fury, but he could do nothing. They demanded fifty, and they got it.

'It's blackmail,' said Dr Kishen Chand Seth furiously. 'Sheer blackmail.' He had had enough of hosting this wedding. He went inside to lie down and cool his head, and soon fell asleep.

Mrs Rupa Mehra, though she had broken her fast, had not done so with her usual gusto because she had to at the same time accept congratulations, introduce people to each other, watch over Haresh and Lata, keep a wary eye on Varun, and supervise the catering. But she was tearfully happy, and as she looked around her she felt even happier to see Pran talking to Professor Mishra, the Nawab Sahib talking to Mahesh Kapoor, and Maan and Firoz laughing together.

Sunil Patwardhan came up to her.

'Many, many congratulations, Mrs Mehra.'

'Thank you so much, Sunil. I'm so glad you're here. You haven't seen my father anywhere, have you?'

'I'm afraid not—not after that altercation at the gate. . . . Mrs Mehra, I have a small problem. . . . Haresh left his cufflinks at my house, and he told me to put them in the room where he'll be staying tonight.' Sunil fished a pair of cufflinks out of his trouser pockets. 'If you would tell me where I should take them—'

But Mrs Rupa Mehra would not be gulled so easily. She had been warned about Sunil Patwardhan's pranks and practical jokes, and she was not going to allow him to disturb her daughter's night of Ideal Marriage.

'Give them to me,' she said firmly, taking them from him. 'I'll make sure he gets them.' And as a result, Haresh was the richer and Sunil the poorer by one pair of black onyx cufflinks.

19.15

Kabir had not been able to bring himself to come to the wedding. But though it was Thursday night, he had not gone to visit his mother either. Instead he took a walk by the Ganga: upriver past the banyan tree, along the dhobi-ghat, past the Pul Mela sands underneath the Fort, along the waterfront of the old town, following the black water for miles until he came to the Barsaat Mahal.

In the shadow of a wall, he sat down on the sand for an hour, his head in his hands.

Then he got up to walk again, up the tall stairs, across the parapet and to the other side.

After a short while he came to a factory, the walls of which came down to the Ganga and prevented him from going further. But he was too tired anyway. He pressed his head against the wall.

The ceremonies will be over by now, he thought.

He hailed a boatman, and took a boat downriver back to the university and his father's house.

19.16

The morning after the wedding, Haresh suddenly decided over breakfast that since he happened to be in Brahmpur, he should look in on the local Praha factory.

'But you can't just leave me like this,' said Lata, putting down her teacup in astonishment. They were sitting at a small table in the bridal bedroom in her grandfather's house.

'No,' said Haresh. 'I can't. Why don't you come too? You might enjoy it.'

'I think I'll go over to Savita's,' said Lata, and picked up her cup again.

'What's that shoebox?' asked Haresh, and opened it.

Inside was a small, carved wooden cat with a knowing smile on its face. Lata picked it up and examined it with pleasure.

'It's from a cobbler I have to meet later today,' said Haresh.

'I like it,' said Lata.

Haresh kissed her and went off.

Lata walked over to the window after a while and looked out at the bougainvillaea, a little puzzled. This was a strange way to begin her married life. But then she thought about it and decided that it was just as well that Haresh had not spent the day with her wandering around Brahmpur—going to the university, the ghats, the Barsaat Mahal. Since they were going to begin a new life, it was best to begin it elsewhere.

Haresh's family left for Delhi that day, and Arun and Varun and the rest left for Calcutta. And the next day Lata and Haresh were themselves seated in a train bound for Calcutta. Haresh could not take a honeymoon immediately because of the pressure of work, but he promised to take one soon. He was even more considerate to her now than he had been on the journey from Kanpur to Lucknow. Lata smiled and told him to stop fussing over her, but she liked it.

Her mother came to see them off at the railway station, together with Savita and Pran. It was hot and noisy. Mrs Rupa Mehra dabbed first at her forehead and then at her eyes with her cologne-scented handkerchief. Standing on the platform between her two daughters and their husbands, she did not know how she could bear to be without either of them. She was suddenly tempted to go along with Lata and Haresh, but fortunately desisted.

Instead, she made sure that they had enough food for the journey; she had brought extra provisions, just in case they hadn't thought of it themselves, including a large cardboard box marked *Shiv Market: Superb Sweetmeats* and a thermos flask filled with cold coffee.

She hugged Haresh, and clung to Lata as if she would never be seeing her again. In fact she planned to return to Calcutta on the 20th of June—the birthday of a dear friend—and would visit Prahapore the very day of her arrival. She was delighted by the fact that she had yet another home to travel to.

Lata waved from the window as the train pulled out of Brahmpur Junction. Haresh appeared relaxed and happy, and that, she found, made her happy too. Tears came to her eyes at the thought of leaving her mother. She looked at Haresh for a second, and then turned to the view. In a few minutes they would pass into the countryside.

An hour or so later, during a halt at one of the smaller railway stations, she saw a small crowd of monkeys. They became aware of her looking out at them and, anticipating a sympathetic soul, approached her window. She glanced at Haresh: he was taking a nap. It amazed her how he was able to go to sleep for ten or twenty minutes at a time whenever or wherever he wanted to.

She threw them a few biscuits: they gathered around, chattering and insistent. She looked for a moment or two at her hennaed hands, took out a musammi, peeled the thick green skin with care, and began to distribute the segments. The monkeys gobbled them down instantly. The whistle had blown when Lata noticed a rather old monkey, sitting alone almost at the end of the platform.

He was contemplating her carefully and undemandingly.

As the train began to move, Lata quickly reached down into the bag of fruit for another musammi, and threw it in his direction. He moved towards it, but the others, seeing it roll along, began running towards it too; and before she could see what had become of it, the train had steamed out of the station.

Photograph by Aradhana Seth

One of the most celebrated writers of our time, Vikram Seth is the author of three novels—*The Golden Gate* (a novel in verse), *A Suitable Boy* and *An Equal Music*—which are widely regarded as modern classics—and two works of non-fiction. He has also written seven books of poetry, including *All You Who Sleep Tonight* and *Beastly Tales from Here and There.*